JEFFREY ARCHER

JEFFREY ARCHER

KANE AND ABEL

THE PRODIGAL DAUGHTER

NOT A PENNY MORE, NOT A PENNY LESS

A QUIVER FULL OF ARROWS

Kane and Abel first published in Great Britain in 1979
by Hodder and Stoughton Limited
The Prodigal Daughter first published in Great Britain in 1982
by Hodder and Stoughton Limited
Not a Penny More, Not a Penny Less first published in
Great Britain in 1976 by Jonathan Cape Limited
A Quiver Full of Arrows first published in Great Britain in 1980
by Hodder and Stoughton Limited

This edition first published in Great Britain in 1986
by Octopus Books Limited
59 Grosvenor Street
London W1

in collaboration with:

William Heinemann Limited   Martin Secker and Warburg Limited
10 Upper Grosvenor Street   54 Poland Street
London W1   London W1

ISBN 0 86273 300 6

Printed and Bound in Great Britain by
Collins, Glasgow

CONTENTS

KANE
AND
ABEL

Acknowledgements

The author would like to thank the two men who made this book possible. They both wish to remain anonymous, one because he is working on his own autobiography and the other because he is still a public figure in the United States.

To Michael and Jane

BOOK ONE

1

She only stopped screaming when she died. It was then that he started to scream.

The young boy who was hunting rabbits in the forest was not sure whether it had been the woman's last cry or the child's first that alerted him. He turned suddenly, sensing the possible danger, his eyes searching for an animal that was so obviously in pain. He had never known any animal to scream in quite that way before. He edged towards the noise cautiously; the scream had now turned to a whine, but it still did not sound like any animal he knew. He hoped it would be small enough to kill; at least that would make a change from rabbit for dinner.

The young boy moved stealthily towards the river, where the strange noise came from, running from tree to tree, feeling the protection of the bark against his shoulder blades, something to touch. Never stay in the open, his father had taught him. When he reached the edge of the forest, he had a clear line of vision all the way down the valley to the river, and even then it took him some time to realize that the strange cry emanated from no ordinary animal. He continued to creep towards the whining, but he was out in the open on his own now. Then suddenly he saw the woman, with her dress above her waist, her bare legs splayed wide apart. He had never seen a woman like that before. He ran quickly to her side and stared down at her belly, quite frightened to touch. There, lying between the woman's legs, was the body of a small, damp, pink animal. Attached by something that looked like rope. The young hunter dropped his freshly skinned rabbits and collapsed on his knees beside the little creature.

He gazed for a long stunned moment and then turned his eyes towards the woman, immediately regretting the decision. She was already blue with cold; her tired twenty-three-year-old face looked middle-aged to the boy; he did not need to be told that she was dead. He picked up the slippery little body – had you asked him why, and no one ever did, he would have told you that the tiny fingernails clawing the crumpled face had worried him – and then he became aware that mother and child were inseparable because of the slimy rope.

He had watched the birth of a lamb a few days earlier and he tried to remember. Yes, that's what the shepherd had done, but dare he, with a child? The whining had stopped and he sensed that a decision was now urgent. He unsheathed his knife, the one he had skinned the rabbits with, wiped it on his sleeve and hesitating only for a moment, cut the rope close to the child's body. Blood flowed freely from the severed ends. Then what had the shepherd done when the lamb was born? He had tied a knot to stop the blood. Of course, of course; he pulled some grass out of the earth beside him and hastily tied a crude knot in the cord. Then he took the child in his arms. He rose slowly from his knees, leaving behind him three dead rabbits and a dead woman who had given birth to this child. Before finally turning his back on the mother, he put her legs together, and pulled her dress down over her knees. It seemed to be the right thing to do.

'Holy God,' he said aloud, the first thing he always said when he had done something very good or very bad. He wasn't yet sure which this was.

The young hunter then ran towards the cottage where he knew his mother would be cooking supper, waiting only for his rabbits; all else would be prepared. She would be wondering how many he might have caught today; with a family of eight to feed, she needed at least three. Sometimes he managed a duck, a goose or even a pheasant that had strayed from the Baron's estate, on which his father worked. Tonight he had caught a different animal, and when he reached the cottage the young hunter dared not let go of his prize even with one hand, so he kicked at the door with his bare foot until his mother opened it. Silently, he held out his offering to her. She made no immediate move to take the creature from him but stood, one hand on her breast, gazing at the wretched sight.

'Holy God,' she said and crossed herself. The boy stared up at his mother's face for some sign of pleasure or anger. Her eyes were now showing a tenderness that the boy had never seen in them before. He knew then that the thing which he had done must be good.

'Is it a baby, Matka?'

'It's a little boy,' said his mother, nodding her head sorrowfully, 'Where did you find him?'

'Down by the river, Matka,' he said.

'And the mother?'

'Dead.'

She crossed herself again.

'Quickly, run and tell your father what has happened. He will find Urszula Wojnak on the estate and you must take them both to the mother, and then be sure they come back here.'

The young hunter handed over the little boy to his mother, happy enough not to have dropped the slippery creature. Now, free of his quarry, he rubbed his hands on his trousers and ran off to look for his father.

The mother closed the door with her shoulder and called out for her eldest child, a girl, to put the pot on the stove. She sat down on a wooden stool, unbuttoned her bodice and pushed a tired nipple towards the little puckered mouth. Sophia, her youngest daughter, only six months old, would have to go without her supper tonight; come to think of it, so would the whole family.

'And to what purpose?' the woman said out loud, tucking a shawl around her arm and the child together. 'Poor little mite, you'll be dead by morning.'

But she did not repeat those feelings to old Urszula Wojnak when the midwife washed the little body and tended to the twisted umbilical stump late that night. Her husband stood silently by observing the scene.

'When a guest comes into the house, God comes into the house,' declared the woman, quoting the old Polish proverb.

Her husband spat. 'To the cholera with him. We have enough children of our own.'

The woman pretended not to hear him as she stroked the dark, thin hairs on the baby's head.

'What shall we call him?' the woman asked, looking up at her husband. He shrugged. 'Who cares? Let him go to his grave nameless.'

2

18 April 1906   Boston, Massachusetts
The doctor picked up the newborn child by the ankles and slapped its bottom. The infant started to cry.

In Boston, Massachusetts, there is a hospital that caters mainly for those who suffer from the diseases of the rich, and on selected occasions allows itself to deliver the new rich. At the Massachusetts General Hospital the mothers don't scream, and certainly they don't give birth fully dressed. It is not the done thing.

A young man was pacing up and down outside the delivery room; inside, two obstetricians and the family doctor were on duty. This father did not believe in taking risks with his first born. The two obstetricians would be paid a large fee merely to stand by and witness events. One of them, who wore evening clothes under his long white coat, had a dinner party to attend later, but he could not afford to absent himself from this particular birth. The three had earlier drawn straws to decide who should deliver the child, and Doctor MacKenzie, the family GP, had won. A sound, secure name, the father considered, as he paced up and down the corridor. Not that he had any reason to be anxious. Roberts had driven his wife, Anne, to the hospital in the hansom carriage that morning, which she had calculated was the twenty-eighth day of her ninth month. She had started labour soon after breakfast, and he had been assured that delivery would not take place until his bank had closed for the day. The father was a disciplined man and saw no reason why a birth should interrupt his well-ordered life. Nevertheless, he continued to pace. Nurses and young doctors hurried past him, aware of his presence, their voices lowered when they were near him, and raised again only when they were out of his earshot. He didn't notice because everybody had always treated him that way. Most of them had never seen him in person; all of them knew who he was.

If it was a boy, a son, he would probably build the new children's wing that the hospital so badly needed. He had already built a library and a school. The expectant father tried to read the evening paper, looking over the words but not taking in their meaning. He was nervous, even worried. It would never do for them (he looked upon almost everyone as 'them') to realize that it had to be a boy, a boy who would one day take his place as president of the bank. He turned the pages of the *Evening Transcript*. The Boston Red Sox had beaten the New York Highlanders – others would be celebrating. Then he recalled the headline on the front page and returned to it. The worst-ever earthquake in the history of America. Devastation in

San Francisco, at least four hundred people dead – others would be mourning. He hated that. That would take away from the birth of his son. People would remember something else had happened on that day. It never occurred to him, not even for a moment, that it might be a girl. He turned to the financial pages and checked the stock market, down sharply; that damned earthquake had taken one hundred thousand dollars off the value of his own holdings in the bank, but as his personal fortune remained comfortably over sixteen million dollars, it was going to take more than a Californian earthquake to move him. He could now live off the interest from his interest, so the sixteen million capital would always remain intact, ready for his son, still unborn. He continued to pace and pretend to read the *Transcript*.

The obstetrician in evening dress pushed through the swing doors of the delivery room to report the news. He felt he must do something for his large unearned fee and he was the most suitably dressed for the announcement. The two men stared at each other for a moment. The doctor also felt a little nervous, but he wasn't going to show it in front of the father.

'Congratulations, sir, you have a son, a fine-looking little boy.'

What silly remarks people make when a child is born, the father thought; how could he be anything but little? The news hadn't yet dawned on him – a son. He almost thanked God. The obstetrician ventured a question to break the silence.

'Have you decided what you will call him?'

The father answered without hesitation. 'William Lowell Kane.'

3

Long after the excitement of the baby's arrival had passed and the rest of the family had gone to bed, the mother remained awake with the little child in her arms. Helena Koskiewicz believed in life, and she had borne nine children to prove it. Although she had lost three in infancy, she had not let any of them go easily.

Now at thirty-five she knew that her once lusty Jasio would give her no more sons or daughters. God had given her this one; surely he was destined to live. Helena's was a simple faith, which was good, for her destiny was never to afford her more than a simple life. She was grey and thin, not through choice but through little food, hard work, and no spare money. It never occurred to her to complain but the lines on her face would have been more in keeping with a grandmother than a mother in today's world. She had never worn new clothes even once in her life.

Helena squeezed her tired breasts so hard that dull red marks appeared around the nipples. Little drops of milk squirted out. At thirty-five, halfway through life's contract, we all have some useful piece of expertise to pass on and Helena Koskiewicz's was now at a premium.

'Matka's littlest one,' she whispered tenderly to the child, and drew the milky teat across its pursed mouth. The blue eyes opened and tiny drops of sweat broke out on the baby's nose as he tried to suck. Finally the mother slumped unwillingly into a deep sleep.

Jasio Koskiewicz, a heavy, dull man with a full moustache, his only gesture of self-assertion in an otherwise servile existence, discovered his wife and the baby asleep in the rocking chair when he rose at five. He hadn't noticed her absence from their bed that night. He stared down at the bastard who had, thank God, at least stopped wailing. Was it dead? Jasio considered the easiest way out of the dilemma was to get himself to work and not interfere with the intruder; let the woman worry about life and death: his preoccupation was to be on the Baron's estate by first light. He took a few long swallows of goat's milk and wiped his luxuriant moustache on his sleeve. Then he grabbed a hunk of bread with one hand and his traps with the other, slipping noiselessly out of the cottage for fear of waking the woman and getting himself involved. He strode away towards the forest, giving no more thought to the little intruder other than to assume that he had seen him for the last time.

Florentyna, the elder daughter, was next to enter the kitchen, just before the old clock, which for many years had kept its own time, claimed that six a.m. had arrived. It was of no more than ancillary assistance to those who wished to know if it was the hour to get up or go to bed. Among Florentyna's daily duties was the preparation of the breakfast, in itself a minor task involving the simple division of a skin of goat's milk and a lump of rye bread among a family of eight. Nevertheless, it required the wisdom of Solomon to carry out the task in such a way that no one complained about another's portion.

Florentyna struck those who saw her for the first time as a pretty, frail, shabby little thing. It was unfair that for the last three years she had had only one dress to wear, but those who could separate their opinion of the child from that of her surroundings understood why Jasio had fallen in love with her mother. Florentyna's long fair hair shone while her hazel eyes sparkled in defiance against the influence of her birth and diet.

She tiptoed up to the rocking chair and stared down at her mother and the little boy whom she had adored at first sight. She had never in her eight years owned a doll. Actually she had only seen one once, when the family had been invited to a celebration of the feast of St Nicholas at the Baron's castle. Even then she had not actually touched the beautiful object, but now she felt an inexplicable urge to hold this baby in her arms. She bent down and eased the child away from her mother and, staring down into the little blue eyes – such blue eyes – she began to hum. The change of temperature from the warmth of the mother's breast to the cold of the little girl's hands made the baby indignant. He immediately started crying which woke the mother, whose only reaction was of guilt for ever having fallen asleep.

'Holy God, he's still alive,' she said to Florentyna. 'You prepare breakfast for the boys while I try to feed him again.'

Florentyna reluctantly handed the infant back and watched her mother once again pump her aching breasts. The little girl was mesmerized.

'Hurry up, Florcia,' chided her mother, 'the rest of the family must eat as well.'

Florentyna obeyed, and as her brothers arrived from the loft where they all slept, they kissed their mother's hands in greeting and stared at the newcomer in awe. All they knew was that this one had not come from Mother's stomach. Florentyna was too excited to eat her breakfast that morning, so the boys divided her portion among them without a second thought and left their mother's share on the table. No one noticed, as they went about their daily tasks, that their mother hadn't eaten anything since the baby's arrival.

Helena Koskiewicz was pleased that her children had learned so early in life to fend for themselves. They could feed the animals, milk the goats and cows, tend the vegetable garden, and go about their daily tasks without her help or prodding. When Jasio returned home in the evening she suddenly realized that she had not prepared supper for him, but that Florentyna had taken the rabbits from Franck, her brother the hunter, and had already started to cook them. Florentyna was proud to be in charge of the evening meal, a responsibility she was entrusted with only when her mother was unwell, and Helena Koskiewicz rarely allowed herself that luxury. The young hunter had brought home four rabbits and the father six mushrooms and three potatoes: tonight would be a veritable feast.

After dinner, Jasio Koskiewicz sat in his chair by the fire and studied the child properly for the first time. Holding the little baby under the armpits, with his two thumbs supporting the helpless neck, he cast a trapper's eye over the infant. Wrinkled and toothless, the face was redeemed only by the fine, blue, unfocusing eyes. Directing his gaze towards the thin body, something immediately attracted his attention. He scowled and rubbed the delicate chest with his thumbs.

'Have you noticed this, Helena?' said the trapper prodding the baby's ribs. 'The ugly little bastard has only one nipple.'

His wife frowned as she in turn rubbed the skin with her thumb, as though the action would supply the missing organ. Her husband was right: the minute and colourless left nipple was there, but where its mirror image should have appeared on the right-hand side the shallow breast was completely smooth and uniformly pink.

The woman's superstitious tendencies were immediately aroused. 'He has been given to me by God,' she exclaimed. 'See His mark upon him.'

The man thrust the child angrily at her. 'You're a fool, Helena. The child was given to its mother by a man with bad blood.' He spat into the fire, the more precisely to express his opinion of the child's parentage. 'Anyway, I wouldn't bet a potato on the little bastard's survival.'

Jasio Koskiewicz cared even less than a potato that the child should survive. He was not by nature a callous man but the boy was not his, and one more mouth to feed could only compound his problems. But if it was so to be, it was not for him to question the Almighty, and with no more thought of the boy, he fell into a deep sleep by the fire.

.   .   .

As the days passed by, even Jasio Koskiewicz began to believe the child might survive and, had he been a betting man, he would have lost a potato. The eldest son, the hunter, with the help of his younger brothers, made the child a cot out of wood which they had collected from the Baron's forest. Florentyna made his clothes by cutting little pieces off her own dresses and then sewing them together. They would have called him Harlequin if they had known what it meant. In truth, naming him caused more disagreement in the household than any other single problem had done for months; only the father had no opinion to offer. Finally, they agreed on Wladek; the following Sunday, in the chapel on the Baron's great estate, the child was christened Wladek Koskiewicz, the mother thanking God for sparing his life, the father resigning himself to whatever must be.

That evening there was a small feast to celebrate the christening, augmented by the gift of a goose from the Baron's estate. They all ate heartily.

From that day on, Florentyna learned to divide by nine.

4

Anne Kane had slept peacefully through the night. When her son William returned after breakfast in the arms of one of the hospital's nurses, she could not wait to hold him again.

'Now then, Mrs Kane,' said the white-uniformed nurse briskly, 'shall we give baby his breakfast too?'

She sat Anne, who was abruptly aware of her swollen breasts, up in bed and guided the two novices through the procedure. Anne, conscious that to appear embarrassed would be considered unmaternal, gazed fixedly into William's blue eyes, more blue even than his father's, and assimilated her new position, with which it would have been illogical to be other than pleased. At twenty-one, she was not conscious that she lacked anything. Born a Cabot, married into a branch of the Lowell family, and now a first born son to carry on the tradition summarized so succinctly in the card sent to her by an old school friend:

Here's to the city of Boston,
Land of the bean and the cod,
Where Cabots talk only to Lowells,
And Lowells talk only to God.

Anne spent half an hour talking to William but obtained little response. He was then retired for a sleep in the same manner by which he had arrived. Anne nobly resisted the fruit and candy piled by her bedside. She was determined to get back into all her dresses by the summer season and re-assume her rightful place in all the fashionable magazines. Had not the Prince de Garonne said that she was the only beautiful object in Boston? Her long golden hair, fine delicate features, and slim figure had attracted excited admiration in cities she had never even visited. She checked in the mirror: no telltale lines on her face; people would hardly believe that she was the mother of a bouncing boy. Thank God it had been a bouncing boy, thought Anne.

She enjoyed a light lunch and prepared herself for the visitors who would appear during the afternoon, already screened by her private secretary. Those allowed to see her on the first days had to be family or from the very best families; others would be told she was not yet ready to receive them. But as Boston was the last city remaining in America where each knew their place to the finest degree of social prominence, there was unlikely to be any unexpected intruder.

The room which she alone occupied could have easily taken another five beds had it not already been smothered in flowers. A casual passer-by could have been forgiven for mistaking it for a minor horticultural show, if it had not been for the presence of the young mother sitting upright in bed. Anne switched on the electric light, still a novelty for her; Richard and she had waited for the Cabots to have them fitted, which all of Boston had interpreted as an oracular sign that electromagnetic induction was as of that moment socially acceptable.

The first visitor was Anne's mother-in-law, Mrs Thomas Lowell Kane, the head of the family since her husband had died the previous year. In elegant late middle-age, she had perfected the technique of sweeping into a room to her own total satisfaction and to its occupants' undoubted discomfiture. She wore a long chemise dress, which made it impossible to view her ankles; the only man who had ever seen her ankles was now dead. She had always been lean. In her opinion, fat women meant bad food and even worse breeding. She was now the oldest Lowell alive; the oldest Kane, come to that. She therefore expected and was expected to be the first to arrive to view her new grandson. After all, had it not been she who had arranged the meeting between Anne and Richard? Love had seemed of little consequence to Mrs Kane. Wealth, position and prestige she could always come to terms with. Love was all very well, but it rarely proved to be a lasting commodity; the other three were. She kissed her daughter-in-law approvingly on the forehead. Anne touched a button on the wall, and a quiet buzz could be heard. The noise took Mrs Kane by surprise; she could not believe electricity would ever catch on. The nurse reappeared with the heir. Mrs Kane inspected him, sniffed her satisfaction and waved him away.

'Well done, Anne,' the old lady said, as if her daughter-in-law had won a minor gymkhana prize. 'All of us are very proud of you.'

Anne's own mother, Mrs Edward Cabot, arrived a few minutes later. She, like Mrs Kane, had been widowed within recent years and differed so little from her in appearance that those who observed them only from afar tended to get them muddled up. But to do her justice, she took considerably more interest in her new grandson and in her daughter. The inspection moved to the flowers.

'How kind of the Jacksons to remember,' murmured Mrs Cabot.

Mrs Kane adopted a more cursory procedure. Her eyes skimmed over the delicate blooms then settled on the donors' cards. She whispered the soothing names to herself: Adamses, Lawrences, Lodges, Higginsons. Neither grandmother commented on the names they didn't know; they were both past the age of wanting to learn of anything or anyone new. They left together, well pleased: an heir had been born and appeared, on first sight, to be adequate. They both considered that their final family obligation had been successfully, albeit vicariously, performed and that they themselves might now progress to the role of chorus.

They were both wrong.

. . .

Anne and Richard's close friends poured in during the afternoon with gifts and good wishes, the former of gold or silver, the latter in high-pitched Brahmin accents.

When her husband arrived after the close of business, Anne was somewhat overtired. Richard had drunk champagne at lunch for the first time in his life – old Amos Kerbes had insisted and, with the whole Somerset Club looking on, Richard could hardly have refused. He seemed to his wife to be a little less stiff than usual. Solid in his long black frock coat and pinstripe trousers, he stood fully six feet one; his dark hair with its centre parting gleamed in the light of the large electric bulb. Few would have guessed his age correctly as only thirty-three: youth had never been important to him; substance was the only thing that mattered. Once again William Lowell Kane was called for and inspected, as if the father were checking the balance at the end of the banking day. All seemed to be in order. The boy had two legs, two arms, ten fingers, ten toes and Richard could see nothing that might later embarrass him, so William was sent away.

'I wired the headmaster of St Paul's last night. William has been admitted for September, 1918.'

Anne said nothing. Richard had so obviously started planning William's career.

'Well, my dear, are you fully recovered today?' he went on to inquire, never having spent a day in hospital during his thirty-three years.

'Yes – no – I think so,' responded his wife timidly, suppressing a rising tearfulness that she knew would only displease her husband. The answer was not of the sort that Richard could hope to understand. He kissed his wife on the cheek and returned in the hansom carriage to the Red House on Louisburg Square, their family home. With staff, servants, the new baby and his nurse, there would now be nine mouths to feed. Richard did not give the problem a second thought.

William Lowell Kane received the Church's blessing and the names his father had apportioned him before birth at the Protestant Episcopal Church of St Paul's, in the presence of everybody in Boston who mattered and a few who didn't. Ancient Bishop Lawrence officiated, J. P. Morgan and Alan Lloyd, bankers of impeccable standing, along with Milly Preston, Anne's closest friend, were the chosen godparents. His Grace sprinkled the Holy Water on William's head; the boy didn't murmur. He was already learning the Brahmin approach to life. Anne thanked God for the safe birth of her son and Richard thanked God, whom he regarded as an external book-keeper whose function was to record the deeds of the Kane family from generation to generation, that he had a son to whom he could leave his fortune. Still, he thought, perhaps he had better be certain and have a second boy. From his kneeling position he glanced sideways at his wife, well pleased with her.

BOOK TWO

5

Wladek Koskiewicz grew slowly. It became apparent to his foster mother that the boy's health would always be a problem. He caught all the illnesses and diseases that growing children normally catch and many that they don't, and he passed them on indiscriminately to the rest of the Koskiewicz family. Helena treated him as any other of her brood and always vigorously defended him when Jasio began to blame the devil rather than God for Wladek's presence in their tiny cottage. Florentyna, on the other hand, took care of Wladek as if he were her own child. She loved him from the first moment she had set eyes on him with an intensity that grew from a fear that no one would ever want to marry her, the penniless daughter of a trapper. She must, therefore, be childless. Wladek was her child.

The eldest brother, the hunter, who had found Wladek, treated him like a plaything but was too afraid of his father to admit that he liked the frail infant who was growing into a sturdy toddler. In any case, next January the hunter was to leave school and start work on the Baron's estate, and children were a woman's problem, so his father had told him. The three younger brothers, Stefan, Josef and Jan, showed little interest in Wladek and the remaining member of the family, Sophia, was happy enough just to cuddle him.

What neither parent had been prepared for was a character and mind so different from those of their own children. No one could dismiss the physical or intellectual difference. The Koskiewiczes were all tall, large-boned with fair hair and grey eyes. Wladek was short and round, with dark hair and intensely blue eyes. The Koskiewiczes had minimal pretensions to scholarship and were removed from the village school as soon as age or discretion allowed. Wladek, on the other hand, though he was late in walking, spoke at eighteen months. Read at three, but was still unable to dress himself. Wrote at five, but continued to wet his bed. He became the despair of his father and the pride of his mother. His first four years on this earth were memorable only as a continual physical attempt through illness to try to depart from it, and for the sustained efforts of Helena and Florentyna to insure that he did not succeed. He ran around the little wooden cottage barefoot, dressed in the harlequin outfit, a yard or so behind his mother. When Florentyna returned from school, he would transfer his allegiance, never leaving her side until she put him to bed. In her division of the food by nine, Florentyna often sacrificed half of her own share to Wladek or, if he were ill, the entire portion. Wladek wore the clothes she made for him, sang the songs she taught him and shared with her the few toys and presents she had been given.

Because Florentyna was away at school most of the day, Wladek wanted from a young age to go with her. As soon as he was allowed to (holding firmly onto Florentyna's hand until they reached the village school), he walked the eighteen wiorsta, some nine miles, through the woods of moss-covered birches and cypresses and the orchards of lime and cherry to Slonim to begin his education.

Wladek liked school from the first day; it was an escape from the tiny cottage which had until then been his whole world. School also confronted him for the first time in life with the savage implications of the Russian occupation of eastern Poland. He learned that his native Polish was to be spoken only in the privacy of the cottage and that while at school, only Russian was to be used. He sensed in the other children around him a fierce pride in the oppressed mother tongue and culture. He, too, felt that same pride. To his surprise, Wladek found that he was not belittled by Mr Kotowski, his schoolteacher, the way he was at home by his father. Although still the youngest, as at home, it was not long before he rose above all his classmates in everything except height. His tiny stature misled them into continual underestimation of his real abilities: children always imagine biggest is best. By the age of five, Wladek was first in every subject taken by his class except ironwork.

At night, back at the little wooden cottage, while the other children would tend the violets and poplars that bloomed so fragrantly in their spring-time garden, pick berries, chop wood, catch rabbits or make dresses, Wladek read and read, until he was reading the unopened books of his eldest brother and then those of his elder sister. It began to dawn slowly on Helena Koskiewicz that she had taken on more than she had bargained for when the younger hunter had brought home the little animal in place of three rabbits; already Wladek was asking questions she could not answer. She knew soon that she would be quite unable to cope, and she wasn't sure what to do about it. She had an unswerving belief in destiny and so was not surprised when the decision was taken out of her hands.

One evening in the autumn of 1911 came the first turning point in Wladek's life. The family had all finished their plain supper of beetroot soup and meatballs, Jasio Koskiewicz was seated snoring by the fire, Helena was sewing, and the other children were playing. Wladek was sitting at the feet of his mother, reading, when above the noise of Stefan and Josef squabbling over the possession of some newly painted pine cones, they heard a loud knock on the door. They all were silent. A knock was always a surprise to the Koskiewicz family, for the little cottage was eighteen wiorsta from Slonim and over six from the Baron's estate. Visitors were almost unknown, and could be offered only a drink of berry juice and the company of noisy children. The whole family looked towards the door apprehensively. As if it had not happened, they waited for the knock to come again. It did, if anything a little louder. Jasio rose sleepily from his chair, walked to the door and opened it cautiously. When they saw the man standing there, everyone bowed their heads except Wladek, who stared up at the broad, handsome, aristocratic figure in the heavy bearskin coat, whose presence dominated the tiny room and brought fear into the father's eyes. A cordial smile allayed that fear, and the trapper invited the Baron Rosnovski into his home. Nobody spoke. The Baron had never visited them in the past and no one was sure what to say.

Wladek put down his book, rose, and walked towards the stranger, thrusting out his hand before his father could stop him.

'Good evening, sir,' said Wladek.

The Baron took his hand and they stared into each other's eyes. As the Baron released him, Wladek's eyes fell on a magnificent silver band around his wrist with an inscription on it that he could not quite make out.

'You must be Wladek.'

'Yes, sir,' said the boy, neither sounding nor showing surprise that the Baron knew his name.

'It is about you that I have come to see your father,' said the Baron.

Wladek remained before the Baron, staring up at him. The trapper signified to his children by a wave of the arm that they should leave him alone with his master, so two of them curtsied, four bowed and all six retreated silently into the loft. Wladek remained, and no one suggested he should do otherwise.

'Koskiewicz,' began the Baron, still standing, as no one had invited him to sit. The trapper had not offered him a chair for two reasons: first, because he was too shy and second, because he assumed the Baron was there to issue a reprimand. 'I have come to ask a favour.'

'Anything, sir, anything,' said the father, wondering what he could give the Baron that he did not already have a hundred-fold.

The Baron continued. 'My son, Leon, is now six and is being taught privately at the castle by two tutors, one from our native Poland and the other from Germany. They tell me he is a clever boy, but that he lacks competition as he has only himself to beat. Mr Kotowski, the teacher of the village school at Slonim, tells me that Wladek is the only boy capable of providing the competition that Leon so badly needs. I wonder therefore if you would allow your son to leave the village school and to join Leon and his tutors at the castle.'

Wladek continued to stand before the Baron, gazing, while before him there opened a wondrous vision of food and drink, books and teachers wiser by far than Mr Kotowski. He glanced towards his mother. She too, was gazing at the Baron, her face filled with wonder and sorrow. His father turned to his mother, and the instant of silent communication between them seemed an eternity to the child.

The trapper gruffly addressed the Baron's feet. 'We would be honoured, sir.'

The Baron looked interrogatively at Helena Koskiewicz.

'The Blessed Virgin forbid that I should ever stand in my child's way,' she said softly, 'though She alone knows how much it will cost me.'

'But, Madam Koskiewicz, your son can return home regularly to see you.'

'Yes, sir. I expect he will do so, at first.' She was about to add some plea but decided against it.

The Baron smiled. 'Good. It's settled then. Please bring the boy to the castle tomorrow morning by seven o'clock. During the school term Wladek will live with us, and when Christmas comes, he can return to you.'

Wladek burst into tears.

'Quiet, boy,' said the trapper.

'I will not go,' said Wladek firmly, wanting to go.

'Quiet, boy,' said the trapper, this time a little louder.

'Why not?' asked the Baron, with compassion in his voice.

'I will never leave Florcia – never.'

'Florcia?' queried the Baron.

'My eldest daughter, sir,' interjected the trapper. 'Don't concern yourself with her, sir. The boy will do as he is told.'

No one spoke. The Baron considered for a moment. Wladek continued to cry controlled tears.

'How old is the girl?' asked the Baron.

'Fourteen,' replied the trapper.

'Could she work in the kitchens?' asked the Baron, relieved to observe that Helena Koskiewicz was not going to burst into tears, as well.

'Oh yes, Baron,' she replied, 'Florcia can cook and she can sew and she can ...'

'Good, good, then she can come as well. I shall expect to see them both tomorrow morning at seven.'

The Baron walked to the door and looked back and smiled at Wladek, who returned the smile. Wladek had won his first bargain, and accepted his mother's tight embrace while he stared at the closed door and heard her whisper, 'Ah, Matka's littlest one, what will become of you now?'

Wladek couldn't wait to find out.

Helena Koskiewicz packed for Wladek and Florentyna during the night, not that it would have taken long to pack the entire family's possessions. In the morning, the remainder of the family stood in front of the door to watch them both depart for the castle each holding a paper parcel under one arm. Florentyna tall and graceful, kept looking back, crying and waving; but Wladek, short and ungainly, never once looked back. Florentyna held firmly to Wladek's hand for the entire journey to the Baron's castle. Their roles were now reversed; from that day on she was to depend on him.

They were clearly expected by the magnificent man in the embroidered suit of green livery who was summoned by their timid knock on the great oak door. Both children had gazed in admiration at the grey uniforms of the soldiers in the town who guarded the nearby Russian-Polish border, but they had never seen anything so resplendent as this liveried servant, towering above them and evidently of overwhelming importance. There was a thick carpet in the hall and Wladek stared at the green and red patterning, amazed by its beauty, wondering if he should take his shoes off and surprised when he walked across it, his footsteps made no sound. The dazzling being conducted them to their bedrooms in the west wing. Separate bedrooms – would they ever get to sleep? At least there was a connecting door, so they needed never to be too far apart, and in fact for many nights they slept together in one bed.

When they had both unpacked, Florentyna was taken to the kitchen, and Wladek to a playroom in the south wing of the castle to meet the Baron's son, Leon. He was a tall, good-looking boy who was so immediately charming and welcoming to Wladek that he abandoned his prepared pugnacious posture with surprise and relief. Leon had been a lonely child, with no one to play with except his niania, the devoted Lithuanian woman who had breast-fed him and attended to his every need since the premature death of his mother. The stocky boy who had come out of the forest promised companionship. At least in one matter they both knew they had been deemed equals.

Leon immediately offered to show Wladek around the castle, and the tour took the rest of the morning. Wladek remained astounded by its size, the richness of the furniture and fabric, and those carpets in every room. To Leon he admitted only to being agreeably impressed: after all, he had won his place in the castle on merit. The main part of the building is early Gothic, explained the Baron's son, as if Wladek were sure to know what Gothic meant. Wladek nodded. Next Leon took his new friend down into the immense cellars, with line upon line of wine bottles covered in dust and cobwebs. Wladek's favourite room was the vast dining hall, with its massive pillared vaulting and stone-flagged floor. There were animals' heads all around the walls. Leon told him they were bison, bear, elk, boar and wolverine. At the end of the room, resplendent, was the Baron's coat of arms below stag's antlers. The Rosnovski family motto read 'Fortune favours the brave'. After a lunch, which Wladek ate so little of because he couldn't master a knife and fork, he met his two tutors who did not give him the same warm welcome, and in the evening he climbed up onto the longest bed he had ever seen and told Florentyna about his adventures. Her excited eyes never once left his face, nor did she even close her mouth, agape with wonder, especially when she heard about the knife and fork, which Wladek described with the fingers of his right hand held out tight together, those of his left splayed wide apart.

The tutoring started at seven sharp, before breakfast, and continued throughout the day with only short breaks for meals. Initially, Leon was clearly ahead of Wladek, but Wladek wrestled determinedly with his books so that as the weeks passed the gap began to narrow, while friendship and rivalry between the two boys developed simultaneously. The German and Polish tutors found it hard to treat their two pupils, the son of a baron, and the son of a trapper, as equals, although they reluctantly conceded to the Baron when he inquired that Mr Kotowski had made the right academic choice. The tutors' attitude towards Wladek never worried him because by Leon he was always treated as an equal.

The Baron let it be known that he was pleased with the progress the two boys were making and from time to time he would reward Wladek with clothes and toys. Wladek's initial distant and detached admiration for the Baron developed into respect and, when the time came for the boy to return to the little cottage in the forest to rejoin his father and mother for Christmas, he became distressed at the thought of leaving Leon.

His distress was well-founded. Despite the initial happiness he felt at seeing his mother, the short space of three months that he had spent in the Baron's castle had revealed to him deficiencies in his own home of which he had previously been quite unaware. The holiday dragged on. Wladek felt himself stifled by the little cottage with its one room and loft, and dissatisfied by the food dished out in such meagre amounts and then eaten by hand: no one had divided by nine at the castle. After two weeks Wladek longed to return to Leon and the Baron. Every afternoon he would walk the six wiorsta to the castle and sit and stare at the great walls that surrounded the estate.

Florentyna, who had lived only among the kitchen servants, took to returning more easily and could not understand that the cottage would never be
home again for Wladek. The trapper was not sure how to treat the boy, who
was now well-dressed, well-spoken, and talked of things at six that the man
did not begin to understand, nor did he want to. The boy seemed to do
nothing but waste the entire day reading. Whatever would become of him,
the trapper wondered. If he could not swing an axe or trap a hare, how could
he ever hope to earn an honest living? He too prayed that the holiday would
pass quickly.

Helena was proud of Wladek, and at first avoided admitting to herself that
a wedge had been driven between him and the rest of the children. But in
the end it could not be avoided. Playing at soldiers one evening, both Stefan
and Franck, generals on opposing sides, refused to have Wladek in their
armies.

'Why must I always be left out?' cried Wladek. 'I want to learn to fight
too.'

'Because you are not one of us,' declared Stefan. 'You are not really our
brother.'

There was a long silence before Franck continued. 'Ojciec never wanted
you in the first place; only Matka was on your side.'

Wladek stood motionless and cast his eye around the circle of children,
searching for Florentyna.

'What does Franck mean, I am not your brother?' he demanded.

Thus Wladek came to hear of the manner of his birth and to understand why he had been always set apart from his brothers and sisters.
Though his mother's distress at his now total self-containment became
oppressive, Wladek was secretly pleased to discover that he came from
unknown stock, untouched by the meanness of the trapper's blood, containing with it the germ of spirit that would now make all things seem
possible.

When the unhappy holiday eventually came to an end, Wladek returned
to the castle with joy. Leon welcomed him back with open arms; for him,
as isolated by the wealth of his father as Wladek was by the poverty of the
trapper, it had also been a Christmas with little to celebrate. From then on
the two boys grew even closer and soon became inseparable. When the
summer holidays came around, Leon begged his father to allow Wladek to
remain at the castle. The Baron agreed for he too had grown to love Wladek.
Wladek was overjoyed and only entered the trapper's cottage once again in
his life.

.   .   .

When Wladek and Leon had finished their classroom work, they would
spend the remaining hours playing games. Their favourite was chowanego,
a sort of hide and seek; as the castle had seventy-two rooms, the chance of
repetition was small. Wladek's favourite hiding place was in the dungeons
under the castle, in which the only light by which one could be discovered
came through a small stone grille set high in the wall and even then one
needed a candle to find one's way around. Wladek was not sure what
purpose the dungeons served, and none of the servants ever made mention
of them, as they had never been used in anyone's memory.

Wladek was conscious that he was Leon's equal only in the classroom, and was no competition for his friend when they played any game, other than chess. The river Strchara that bordered the estate became an extension to their playground. In spring they fished, in summer they swam, and in winter, when the river was frozen over, they would put on their wooden skates and chase each other across the ice, while Florentyna sat on the river bank anxiously warning them where the surface was thin. But Wladek never heeded her and was always the one who fell in. Leon grew quickly and strong; he ran well, swam well and never seemed to tire or be ill. Wladek became aware for the first time what good-looking and well-built meant, and he knew when he swam, ran, and skated he could never hope to keep up with Leon. Much worse, what Leon called the belly button was, on him, almost unnoticeable, while Wladek's was stumpy and ugly and protruded rudely from the middle of his plump body. Wladek would spend long hours in the quiet of his own room, studying his physique in a mirror, always asking why, and in particular why only one nipple for him when all the boys he had ever seen barechested had the two that the symmetry of the human body appeared to require. Sometimes as he lay in bed unable to sleep, he would finger his naked chest and tears of self-pity would flood onto the pillow. He would finally fall asleep praying that when he awoke in the morning, things would be different. His prayers were not answered.

Wladek put aside each night a time to do physical exercises that could not be witnessed by anyone, not even Florentyna. Through sheer determination he learned to hold himself so that he looked taller. He built up his arms and his legs and hung by the tips of his fingers from a beam in the bedroom in the hope that it would make him grow, but Leon grew taller even while he slept. Wladek was forced to accept the fact that he would always be a head shorter than the Baron's son, and that nothing, nothing was ever going to produce the missing nipple. Wladek's dislike of his own body was unprompted, for Leon never commented on his friend's appearance; his knowledge of other children stopped short at Wladek, whom he adored uncritically.

Baron Rosnovski became increasingly fond of the fierce dark-haired boy who had replaced the younger brother for Leon, so tragically lost when his wife had died in childbirth.

The two boys would dine with him in the great stone-walled hall each evening, while the flickering candles cast ominous shadows from the stuffed animal heads on the wall and the servants came and went noiselessly with the great silver trays and golden plates, bearing geese, hams, crayfish, fine wine and fruits, and sometimes the mazureks that had become Wladek's particular favourites. Afterwards as the darkness fell ever more thickly around the table, the Baron dismissed the waiting servants and would tell the boys stories of Polish history and allowed them a sip of Danzig vodka, in which the tiny gold leaves sparkled bravely in the candlelight. Wladek begged as often as he dared for the story of Tadeusz Kosciuszko.

'A great patriot and hero,' the Baron would apply. 'The very symbol of our struggle for independence, trained in France ...'

'Whose people we admire and love as we have learned to hate all Russians and Austrians,' supplied Wladek, whose pleasure in the tale was enhanced by his word-perfect knowledge of it.

'Who is telling whom the story, Wladek?' The Baron laughed. '. . . And then fought with George Washington in America for liberty and democracy. In 1792 he led the Poles in battle at Dubienka. When our wretched king, Stanislas Augustus, deserted us to join the Russians, Kosciuszko returned to the homeland he loved to throw off the yoke of Tsardom. He won the battle of where, Leon?'

'Raclawice, sir, and then he freed Warsaw.'

'Good, my child. Then, alas, the Russians mustered a great force at Maciejowice and he was finally defeated and taken prisoner. My great-great-great-grandfather fought with Kosciuszko on that day, and later with Dabrowski's legions for the mighty Emperor Napoleon Bonaparte.'

'And for his service to Poland was created the Baron Rosnovski, a title your family will ever bear in remembrance of those great days,' said Wladek, as stoutly as if the title would one day pass to him.

'Those great days will come again,' said the Baron quietly 'I only pray that I may live to see them.'

. . .

At Christmas time, the peasants on the estate would bring their families to the castle for the celebration of the blessed vigil. Throughout Christmas Eve they fasted and the children would look out of the windows for the first star, which was the sign the feast might begin. The Baron would say grace in his fine deep voice: '*Benedicte nobis, Domine Deus, et his donis quae ex liberalitate tua sumpturi sumus,*' and once they had sat down Wladek would be embarrassed by the huge capacity of Jasio Koskiewicz, who addressed himself squarely to every one of the thirteen courses from the barsasz soup through to the cakes and plums, and would as in previous years be sick in the forest on the way home.

After the feast Wladek enjoyed distributing the gifts from the Christmas tree, laden with candles and fruit, to the awe-struck peasant children – a doll for Sophia, a forest knife for Josef, a new dress for Florentyna, the first gift Wladek had ever requested of the Baron.

'It's true,' said Josef to his mother when he received his gift from Wladek, 'he is not our brother, Matka.'

'No,' she replied, 'but he will always be my son.'

. . .

Through the winter and spring of 1914 Wladek grew in strength and learning. Then suddenly, in July, the German tutor left the castle without even saying farewell; neither boy was sure why. They never thought to connect his departure with the assassination in Sarajevo of the Archduke Francis Ferdinand by a student anarchist, described to them by their other tutor in unaccountably solemn tones. The Baron became withdrawn; neither boy was sure why. The younger servants, the children's favourites, began to disappear one by one; neither boy was sure why. As the year passed Leon grew taller, Wladek grew stronger, and both boys became wiser.

One morning in the summer of 1915, a time of fine, lazy days, the Baron set off on the long journey to Warsaw to put, as he described it, his affairs in order. He was away for three and a half weeks, twenty-five days which

Wladek marked off each morning on a calendar in his bedroom; it seemed to him a lifetime. On the day he was due to return, the two boys went down to the railway station at Slonim to await the weekly train with its one carriage and greet the Baron on his arrival. The three of them travelled home in silence.

Wladek thought the great man looked tired and older, another unaccountable circumstance, and during the following week the Baron often conducted with the chief servants a rapid and anxious dialogue, broken off whenever Leon or Wladek entered the room, an uncharacteristic surreptitiousness that made the two boys uneasy and fearful that they were the unwitting cause of it. Wladek despaired that the Baron might send him back to the trapper's cottage - always aware he was a stranger in a stranger's home.

One evening a few days after the Baron had returned he called for the two boys to join him in the great wall. They crept in, fearful of him. Without explanation he told them that they were about to make a long journey. The little conversation, insubstantial as it seemed to Wladek at the time, remained with him for the rest of his life.

'My dear children,' began the Baron in a low, faltering tone, 'the war-mongers of Germany and the Austro-Hungarian empire are at the throat of Warsaw and will soon be upon us.'

Wladek recalled the inexplicable phrase flung out by the Polish tutor at the German tutor during their last tense days together. 'Does that mean that the hour of the submerged peoples of Europe is at last upon us?' he asked.

The Baron regarded Wladek's innocent face tenderly. 'Our national spirit has not perished in one hundred and fifty years of attrition and repression,' he replied. 'It may be that the fate of Poland is as much at stake as that of Serbia, but we are powerless to influence history. We are at the mercy of the three mighty empires that surround us.'

'We are strong, we can fight,' said Leon. 'We have wooden swords and shields. We are not afraid of Germans or Russians.'

'My son, you have only played at war. This battle will not be between children. We will now find a quiet place to live until history has decided our fate and we must leave as soon as possible. I can only pray that this is not the end of your childhood.'

Leon and Wladek were both mystified and irritated by the Baron's words. War sounded like an exciting adventure which they would be sure to miss if they had to leave the castle. The servants took several days to pack the Baron's possessions and Wladek and Leon were informed that they would be departing for their small summer home in the north of Grodno on the following Monday. The two boys continued, largely unsupervised, with their work and play but they could now find no one in the castle with the inclination or time to answer their myriad questions.

On Saturdays, lessons were held in the morning. They were translating Adam Mickiewicz's *Pan Tadeusz* into Latin when they heard the guns. At first, Wladek thought the familiar sounds meant only that another trapper was out shooting on the estate; the boys returned to the poetry. A second volley of shots, much closer, made them look up and then they heard the screaming coming from downstairs. They stared at each other in bewilderment; they feared nothing as they had never experienced anything in their short lives that should have made them fearful. The tutor fled leaving them alone, and then came another shot, this time in the corridor outside their room. The two boys sat motionless, terrified and unbreathing.

Suddenly the door crashed open and a man no older than their tutor, in a grey soldier's uniform and steel helmet, stood towering over them. Leon clung onto Wladek, while Wladek stared at the intruder. The soldier shouted at them in German, demanding to know who they were, but neither boy replied, despite the fact that they had mastered the language, and could speak it as well as their mother tongue. Another soldier appeared behind his companion as the first advanced on the two boys, grabbed them by the necks, not unlike chickens, and pulled them out into the corridor, down the hall to the front of the castle and then into the gardens, where they found Florentyna screaming hysterically as she stared at the grass in front of her. Leon could not bear to look, and buried his head in Wladek's shoulder. Wladek gazed as much in surprise as in horror at a row of dead bodies, mostly servants, being placed face downwards. He was mesmerized by the sight of a moustache in profile agains a pool of blood. It was the trapper. Wladek felt nothing as Florentyna continued screaming.

'Is Papa there?' asked Leon. 'Is Papa there?'

Wladek scanned the line of bodies once again. He thanked God that there was no sign of the Baron Rosnovski. He was about to tell Leon the good news when a soldier came up to them.

'*Wer hat gesprochen?*' he demanded fiercely.

'*Ich,*' said Wladek defiantly.

The soldier raised his rifle and brought the butt crashing down on Wladek's head. He sank to the ground, blood spurting over his face. Where was the Baron, what was happening, why were they being treated like this in their own home? Leon quickly jumped on top of Wladek, trying to protect him from the second blow which the soldier had intended for Wladek's stomach, but as the rifle came crashing down the full force caught the back of Leon's head.

Both boys lay motionless, Wladek because he was still dazed by the blow and the sudden weight of Leon's body on top of him, and Leon because he was dead.

Wladek could hear another soldier berating their tormentor for the action he had taken. They picked up Leon, but Wladek clung onto him. It took two soldiers to prise his friend's body away and dump it unceremoniously with the others, face down on the grass. Wladek's eyes never left the motionless body of his dearest friend until he was finally marched back inside the castle, and, with a handful of dazed survivors, led to the dungeons. Nobody spoke for fear of joining the line of bodies on the grass, until the dungeon doors were bolted and the last murmur of the soldiers had vanished in the distance. Then Wladek said, 'Holy God.' For there in a corner, slumped against the wall, sat the Baron, uninjured but stunned, staring into space, alive only because the conquerors needed someone to be responsible for the prisoners. Wladek went over to him, while the others sat as far away from their master as possible. The two gazed at each other, as they had on the first day they had met. Wladek put his hand out, and as on the first day the

Baron took it. Wladek watched the tears course down the Baron's proud face. Neither spoke. They had both lost the one person they had loved most in the world.

6

William Kane grew very quickly, and was considered an adorable child by all who came in contact with him; in the early years of his life these were generally besotted relatives and doting servants.

The top floor of the Kanes' eighteenth-century house in Louisburg Square on Beacon Hill had been converted into nursery quarters, crammed with toys. A further bedroom and a sitting room were made available for the newly acquired nurse. The floor was far enough away from Richard Kane for him to be unaware of problems such as teething, wet nappies and the irregular and undisciplined cries for more food. First sound, first tooth, first step and first word were all recorded in a family book by William's mother along with the progress in his height and weight. Anne was surprised to find that these statistics differed very little from those of any other child with whom she came into contact on Beacon Hill.

The nurse, an import from England, brought the boy up on a regimen that would have gladdened the heart of a Prussian cavalry officer. William's father would visit him each evening at six o'clock. As he refused to address the child in baby language, he ended up not speaking to him at all; the two merely stared at each other. William would grip his father's index finger, the one with which balance sheets were checked, and hold onto it tightly. Richard would allow himself a smile. At the end of the first year the routine was slightly modified and the boy was allowed to come downstairs to see his father. Richard would sit in his high-backed, maroon leather chair watching his first-born weave his way on all fours in and out of the legs of the furniture reappearing when least expected, which led Richard to observe that the child would undoubtedly become a senator. William took his first steps at thirteen months while clinging onto the tails of his father's topcoat. His first word was 'Dada', which pleased everyone, including Grandmother Kane and Grandmother Cabot, who were regular visitors. They did not actually push the vehicle in which William was perambulated arund Boston, but they did deign to walk a pace behind the nurse in the park on Thursday afternoons, glaring at infants with a less disciplined retinue. While other children fed the ducks in the public gardens, William succeeded in charming the swans in the lagoon of Mr Jack Gardner's extravagant Venetian Palace.

When two years had passed, the grandmothers intimated by hint and innuendo that it was high time for another prodigy, an appropriate sibling for William. Anne obliged them by becoming pregnant and was distressed to find herself feeling and looking progressively off colour as she entered her fourth month.

Doctor MacKenzie ceased to smile as he checked the growing stomach and hopeful mother, and when Anne miscarried at sixteen weeks he was not altogether surprised, but did not allow her to indulge her grief. In his notes he wrote 'pre-eclampsia?' and then told her, 'Anne, my dear, the reason you have not been feeling so well is that your blood pressure was too high, and would probably have become much higher as your pregnancy progressed. I fear doctors haven't found the answer to blood pressure yet, in fact we know very little other than it's a dangerous condition for anyone, particularly for a pregnant woman.'

Anne held back her tears while considering the implications of a future without more children.

'Surely it won't happen in my next pregnancy?' she asked, phrasing her question to dispose the doctor to a favourable answer.

'I should be very surprised if it did not, my dear. I am sorry to have to say this to you, but I would strongly advise you against becoming pregnant again.'

'But I don't mind feeling off-colour for a few months if it means ...'

'I am not talking about feeling off-colour, Anne. I am talking about not taking any unnecessary risks with your life.'

It was a terrible blow for Richard and Anne, who themselves had both been only children, largely as a result of their respective fathers' premature deaths. They had both assumed that they would produce a family appropriate to the commanding size of their house and their responsibilities to the next generation. 'What else is there for a young woman to do?' inquired Grandmother Cabot of Grandmother Kane. No one cared to mention the subject again, and William became the centre of everyone's attention

Richard, who had taken over as the president of Kane and Cabot Bank and Trust Company when his father had died in 1904, had always immersed himself in the work of the bank. The bank, which stood on State Street, a bastion of architectural and fiscal solidity, had offices in New York, London and San Francisco. The last had presented a problem to Richard soon after William's birth when, along with Crocker National Bank, Wells Fargo, and the California Bank, it collapsed to the ground, not financially, but literally, in the great earthquake of 1906. Richard, by nature a cautious man, was comprehensively insured with Lloyd's of London. Gentlemen all, they had paid up to the penny, enabling Richard to rebuild. Nevertheless, Richard spent an uncomfortable year jolting across America on the four-day train journey between Boston and San Francisco, supervising the rebuilding. He opened the new office in Union Square in October 1907, barely in time to turn his attention to other problems arising on the Eastern seaboard. There was a minor run on the New York banks, and many of the smaller establishments were unable to cope with large withdrawals and started going to the wall. J. P. Morgan, the legendary chairman of the mighty bank bearing his name, invited Richard to join a consortium to hold firm during the crisis. Richard agreed, the courageous stand worked, and the problem began to dissipate, but not before Richard had had a few sleepless nights.

William, on the other hand, slept soundly, unaware of earthquakes and collapsing banks. After all, there were swans that must be fed and endless trips to and from Milton, Brookline and Beverly to be shown to his distinguished relatives.

.   .   .

Early in the spring of the following year Richard acquired a new toy in return for a cautious investment of capital in a man called Henry Ford, who was claiming he could produce a motor car for the people. The bank entertained Mr Ford at luncheon, and Richard was coaxed into the acquisition of a Model T for the princely sum of eight hundred and fifty dollars. Henry Ford assured Richard that if only the bank would back him, the cost could eventually fall to three hundred and fifty dollars within a few years and everyone would be buying his cars, thus ensuring a large profit for his backers. Richard did back him, and it was the first time he had placed good money behind someone who wished his product to halve in price.

Richard was initially apprehensive that his motor car, sombrely black though it was, might not be regarded as a serious mode of transport for the chairman of a bank, but he was reassured by the admiring glances from the pavements which the machine attracted. At ten miles an hour it was noisier than a horse but it did have the virtue of leaving no mess in the middle of Mount Vernon Street. His only quarrel with Mr Ford was that the man would not listen to the suggestion that a Model T should be made available in a variety of colours. Mr Ford insisted that every car should be black in order to keep the price down. Anne, more sensitive than her husband to the approbation of polite society, would not drive in the vehicle until the Cabots had acquired one.

William, on the other hand, adored the 'automobile', as the press called it, and immediately assumed that the vehicle had been bought for him to replace his now redundant and unmechanized pram. He also preferred the chauffeur – with his goggles and flat hat – to his nurse. Grandmother Kane and Grandmother Cabot claimed that they would never travel in the dreadful machine and never did, although it should be pointed out that Grandmother Kane travelled to her funeral in a motor car, but was never informed.

During the next two years the bank grew in strength and size, as did William. Americans were once again investing for expansion, and large sums of money found their way to Kane and Cabot's to be reinvested in such projects as the expanding Lowell leather factory in Lowell, Massachusetts. Richard watched the growth of his bank and his son with unsurprised satisfaction. On William's fifth birthday, he took the child out of womens' hands by engaging at four hundred and fifty dollars per annum a private tutor, a Mr Munro, personally selected by Richard from a list of eight applicants who had earlier been screened by his private secretary. Mr Munro was charged to ensure that William was ready to enter St Paul's by the age of twelve. William immediately took to Mr Munro, whom he thought to be very old and very clever. He was, in fact, twenty-three and the possessor of a second-class honours degree in English from the University of Edinburgh.

William quickly learned to read and write with facility but saved his real enthusiasm for figures. His only complaint was that, of the eight lessons taught every weekday, only one was arithmetic. William was quick to point

out to his father that one-eighth of the working day was a small investment
of time for someone who would one day be the president of a bank.

To compensate for his tutor's lack of foresight, William dogged the
footsteps of his accessible relatives with demands for sums to be executed in
his head. Grandmother Cabot, who had never been persuaded that the
division of an integer by four would necessarily produce the same answer
as its multiplication by one quarter, and indeed in her hands the two
operations often did result in two different numbers, found herself speedily
outclassed by her grandson, but Grandmother Kane, with some small
leaning to cleverness, grappled manfully with vulgar fractions, compound
interest and the division of eight cakes among nine children.

'Grandmother,' said William, kindly but firmly, when she had failed
to find the answer to his latest conundrum, 'you can buy me a slide-rule;
then I won't have to bother you.'

She was astonished at her grandson's precocity, but she bought him one
just the same, wondering if he really knew how to use the gadget. It was the
first time in her life that Grandmother Kane had been known to take the
easy way out of any problem.

Richard's problems began to gravitate eastwards. The chairman of his
London branch died at his desk and Richard felt himself required in Lombard Street. He suggested to Anne that she and William should accompany
him to Europe, feeling that the education would not do the boy any harm:
he could visit all the places about which Mr Munro had so often talked.
Anne, who had never been to Europe, was excited by the prospect, and filled
three steamer trunks with elegant and expensive new clothes in which to
confront the Old World. William considered it unfair of his mother not to
allow him to take that equally essential aid to travel, his bicycle.

The Kanes travelled to New York by train to join the *Aquitania* bound for
her voyage to Southampton. Anne was appalled by the sight of the immigrant street peddlers pushing their wares, and she was glad to be safely on
board and resting in her cabin. William, on the other hand, was amazed by
the size of New York; he had, until that moment, always imagined that his
father's bank was the biggest building in America, if not the world. He
wanted to buy a pink and yellow ice cream from a man all dressed in white
and wearing a boater, but his father would not hear of it; in any case,
Richard never carried small change.

William adored the great vessel on sight and quickly became friendly with
the captain, who showed him all the secrets of the Cunard Steamships' prima
donna. Richard and Anne, who naturally sat at the captain's table, felt it
necessary, before the ship had long left America, to apologize for the amount
of the crew's time that their son was occupying.

'Not at all,' replied the white-bearded skipper. 'William and I are already
good friends. I only wish I could answer all his questions about time, speed
and distance. I have to be coached each night by the first engineer in the
hope of first anticipating and then surviving the next day.'

The *Aquitania* sailed into the Solent to dock at Southampton after a six-
day journey. William was reluctant to leave her, and tears would have been
unavoidable had it not been for the magnificent sight of the Rolls-Royce
Silver Ghost, waiting at the quayside complete with a chauffeur, ready to

whisk them off to London. Richard decided on the spur of the moment that he would have the car transported back to New York at the end of the trip, which was the most out-of-character decision he made during the rest of his life. He informed Anne, rather unconvincingly, that he wanted to show the vehicle to Henry Ford.

The Kane family always stayed at the Ritz in Piccadilly when they were in London, which was convenient for Richard's office in the City. Anne used the time while Richard was occupied at the bank to show William the Tower of London, Buckingham Palace and the Changing of the Guard. William thought everything was 'great' except the English accent which he had difficulty in understanding.

'Why don't they talk like us, Mommy?' he demanded, and was surprised to be told that the question was more often put the other way around, as 'they' came first. William's favourite pastime was to watch the soldiers in their bright red uniforms with large shiny brass buttons who kept guard duty outside Buckingham Palace. He tried to engage them in conversation but they stared past him into space and never even blinked.

'Can we take one home?' he asked his mother.

'No, darling, they have to stay here and guard the King.'

'But he's got so many of them, can't I have just one?'

As a 'special treat' – Anne's words – Richard allowed himself an afternoon off to take his wife and son to the West End to see a traditional English pantomime called *Jack and the Beanstalk* playing at the London Hippodrome. William loved Jack and immediately wanted to cut down every tree he laid his eyes on, imagining them all to be sheltering a monster. They had tea after the show at Fortnum and Mason in Piccadilly, and Anne let William have two cream buns and a new-fangled thing called a doughnut. Daily thereafter William had to be escorted back to the tea-room at Fortnum's to consume another 'doughbun', as he called them.

The holiday passed by all too quickly for William and his mother, whereas Richard, satisfied with his progress in Lombard Street and pleased with his newly appointed chairman, began to look forward to the day of their departure. Cables were daily arriving from Boston that made him anxious to be back in his own boardroom. Finally, when one such missive informed him that twenty-five thousand workers at a cotton mill with which his bank had a heavy investment in Lawrence, Massachusetts, had gone out on strike, he was relieved that his planned date of sailing was now only three days away.

William was looking forward to returning and telling Mr Munro all the exciting things he had done in England and to being reunited with his two grandmothers again. He felt sure they had never done anything so exciting as visiting a real live theatre with the general public. Anne was also happy to be going home, although she had enjoyed the trip almost as much as William, for her clothes and beauty had been much admired by the normally undemonstrative North Sea Islanders. As a final treat for William the day before they were due to sail, Anne took him to a tea party in Eaton Square given by the wife of the newly appointed chairman of Richard's London branch. She, too, had a son, Stuart, who was eight – and William had, in the two weeks in which they had been playing together, grown to regard him as an indispensable grown-up friend. The party, however, was rather subdued because Stuart felt unwell and William, in sympathy with his new chum, announced to his mother that he was going to be ill too. Anne and William returned to the Ritz Hotel earlier than they had planned. She was not greatly put out as it gave her a little more time to supervise the packing of the large steamer trunks, although she was convinced William was only putting on an act to please Stuart. When she tucked William up in bed that night, she found that he had been as good as his word and was running a slight fever. She remarked on it to Richard over dinner.

'Probably all the excitement at the thought of going home,' he offered, sounding unconcerned.

'I hope so,' replied Anne. 'I don't want him to be sick on a six-day sea voyage.'

'He'll be just fine by tomorrow,' said Richard, issuing an unheeded directive, but when Anne went to wake William the next morning, she found him covered in little red spots and running a temperature of one hundred and three. The hotel doctor diagnosed measles and was politely insistent that William should on no account be sent on a sea journey, not only for his own good but for the sake of the other passengers. There was nothing for it but to leave him in bed with his stone hot water bottle and wait for the departure of the next ship. Richard was unable to countenance the three-week delay and decided to sail as planned. Reluctantly, Anne allowed the hurried changes of booking to be made. William begged his father to let him accompany him: the twenty-one days before the *Aquitania* was due back in Southampton seemed like an eternity to the child. Richard was adamant, and hired a nurse to attend William and convince him of his poor state of health.

Anne travelled down to Southampton with Richard in the new Rolls-Royce.

'I shall be lonely in London without you, Richard,' she ventured diffidently in their parting moment, risking his disapproval of emotional women.

'Well, my dear, I dare say that I shall be somewhat lonely in Boston without you,' he said, his mind on the striking cotton workers.

Anne returned to London on the train, wondering how she would occupy herself for the next three weeks. William had a better night and in the morning the spots looked less ferocious. Doctor and nurse were unanimous however in their insistence that he should remain in bed. Anne used the extra time to write long letters to the family, while William remained in bed, protesting, but on Thursday morning he got himself up early and went into his mother's room, very much back to his normal self. He climbed into bed next to her and his cold hands immediately woke her up. Anne was relieved to see him so obviously fully recovered. She rang to order breakfast in bed for both of them, an indulgence William's father would never have countenanced.

There was a quiet knock on the door and a man in gold and red livery entered with a large, silver breakfast tray. Eggs, bacon, tomato, toast and marmalade – a veritable feast. William looked at the food ravenously as if he could not remember when he had last eaten a full meal. Anne casually glanced at the morning paper. Richard always read *The Times* when he stayed in London so the management assumed she would require it as well.

'Oh, look,' said William, staring at the photograph on an inside page, 'a picture of Daddy's ship. What's a CA-LA-MITY, Mommy?'

All across the width of the newspaper was a picture of the *Titanic*.

Anne, unmindful of behaving as should a Lowell or a Cabot, burst into frenzied tears, clinging onto her only son. They sat in bed for several minutes, holding onto each other, William wasn't sure why. Anne realized that they had both lost the one person whom they had loved most in the world.

Sir Piers Campbell, young Stuart's father, arrived almost immediately at Suite 107 of the Ritz Hotel. He waited in the lounge while the widow put on a suit, the only dark piece of clothing she possessed. William dressed himself, still not certain what a 'calamity' was. Anne asked Sir Piers to explain the full implications of the news to her son, who only said, 'I wanted to be on the ship with him, but they wouldn't let me go.' He didn't cry because he refused to believe anything could kill his father. He would be among the survivors.

In all Sir Piers' career as a politician, diplomat and now chairman of Kane and Cabot, London, he had never seen such self-containment in one so young. Presence is given to very few, he was heard to remark some years later. It had been given to Richard Kane and had been passed onto his only son.

The lists of survivors, arriving spasmodically from America, were checked and double-checked by Anne. Each confirmed that Richard Lowell Kane was still missing at sea, presumed drowned. After a further week even William almost abandoned hope of his father's survival.

Anne found it hard to board the *Aquitania*, but William was strangely eager to put to sea. Hour after hour, he would sit on the observation deck, scanning the featureless water.

'Tomorrow I will find him,' he promised his mother, at first confidently, and then in a voice that barely disclaimed his own disbelief.

'William, no one can survive for three weeks in the Atlantic.'

'Not even my father?'

'Not even your father.'

'When Anne returned to Boston, both grandmothers were waiting for her at the Red House, mindful of the duty that had been thrust upon them.

The responsibility had been passed back to the grandmothers. Anne passively accepted their proprietory role. Life for her now had little purpose left other than William, whose destiny they now seemed determined to control. William was polite but uncooperative. During the day he sat silently in his lesson with Mr Munro and at night wept into the lap of his mother.

'What he needs is the company of other children,' declared the grandmothers briskly, and they dismissed Mr Munro and the nurse and sent William off to Sayre Academy in the hope that an introduction to the real world and the constant company of other children might bring him back to his old self.

Richard had left the bulk of his estate to William, to remain in the family trust until his twenty-first birthday. There was a codicil added to the will. Richard expected his son to become chairman of Kane and Cabot on merit. It was the only part of his father's testament that inspired William, for the rest was his by birthright. Anne received a capital sum of five hundred thousand dollars and an income for life of one hundred thousand dollars a year after taxes which would cease, if she remarried. She also received the house on Beacon Hill, the summer mansion on the North Shore, the home in Maine, and a small island off Cape Cod, all of which were to pass to William on his mother's death. Both grandmothers received two hundred and fifty thousand dollars, and letters leaving them in no doubt about their responsibility if Richard died before them. The family trust was to be handled by the bank, with William's godparents acting as co-trustees. The income from the trust was to be reinvested each year in conservative enterprises.

It was a full year before the grandmothers came out of mourning, and although Anne was still only twenty-eight, she looked her age for the first time in her life.

The grandmothers, unlike Anne, concealed their grief from William until he finally reproached them for it.

'Don't you miss my father?' he asked, gazing at Grandmother Kane with the blue eyes that brought back memories of her own son.

'Yes, my child, but he would not have wished us to sit around and feel sorry for ourselves.'

'But I want us to always remember him – always,' said William, his voice cracking.

'William, I am going to speak to you for the first time as though you were quite grown up. We will always keep his memory hallowed between us, and you shall play your own part by living up to what your father would have expected of you. You are the head of the family now and the heir to a large fortune. You must, therefore, prepare yourself through work to be fit for the inheritance in the same spirit in which your father worked to increase the inheritance for you.'

William made no reply. He was thus provided with the motive for life which he had lacked before, and he acted upon his grandmother's advice. He learned to live with his sorrow without complaining and from that moment on he threw himself steadfastly into his work at school, satisfied only if Grandmother Kane seemed impressed. At no subject did he fail to excel, and in mathematics he was not only top of his class but far ahead of his years. Anything his father had achieved, he was determined to better. He grew even closer to his mother and became suspicious of anyone who was not family, so that he was often thought of as a solitary child, a loner and, unfairly, as a snob.

The grandmothers decided on William's seventh birthday that the time had come to instruct the boy in the value of money. They therefore allowed him pocket money of one dollar a week, but insisted that he keep an inventory accounting for every cent he had spent. With this in mind, they presented him with a green leather-bound ledger book, at a cost of ninety-five cents, which they deducted from his first week's allowance of one dollar. From the second week the grandmothers divided the dollar every Saturday morning. William invested fifty cents, spent twenty cents, gave ten cents to any charity of his choice, and kept twenty cents in reserve. At the end of each quarter the grandmothers would inspect the ledger and his written report on any transactions. When the first three months had passed, William was well ready to account for himself. He had given one dollar twenty cents to the newly founded Boy Scouts of America, and saved four dollars, which he had asked Grandmother Kane to invest in a savings account at the bank of his godfather, J. P. Morgan. He had spent a further three dollars eight cents for which he did not have to account and had kept a dollar in reserve. The ledger was a source of great satisfaction to the grandmothers: there was no doubt William was the son of Richard Kane.

At school, William made few friends, partly because he was shy of mixing with anyone other than Cabots, Lowells or children from families wealthier than his own. This restricted his choice severely, so he became a somewhat broody child, which worried his mother, who wanted William to lead a more normal existence, and did not in her heart approve of the ledgers or the investment programme. Anne would have preferred William to have a lot of young friends rather than old advisors, to get himself dirty and bruised rather than remain spotless, to collect toads and turtles rather than stocks and company reports; in short to be like any other little boy. But she never had the courage to tell the grandmothers about her misgivings and in any case the grandmothers were not interested in any other little boy.

On his ninth birthday William presented the ledger to his grandmothers for the second annual inspection. The green leather book showed a saving during the two years of more than fifty dollars. He was particularly proud to point out an entry marked B6 to the grandmothers, showing that he had taken his money out of J. P. Morgan's Bank immediately on hearing of the death of the great financier, because he had noted that his own father's bank shares had fallen in value after his death had been announced. He had reinvested the same amount three months later before the public realized the company was bigger than any one man.

The grandmothers were suitably impressed and allowed William to trade in his old bicycle and purchase a new one, after which he still had a capital sum of over one hundred dollars, which his grandmothers had invested for him with the Standard Oil Company of New Jersey. Oil, said William knowingly, can only get more expensive. He kept the ledger meticulously up-to-date until his twenty-first birthday. Had the grandmothers still been alive then, they would have been proud of the final entry in the right-hand column marked 'assets'.

7

Wladek was the only one of those left alive who knew the dungeons well. In his days of hide and seek with Leon he had spent many happy hours in the freedom of the small stone rooms, carefree in the knowledge that he could return to the castle whenever it suited him.

There were in all four dungeons, on two levels. Two of the rooms, a larger and a smaller one, were at ground level. The smaller one was adjacent to the castle wall, which afforded a thin filter of light through a grille set high in the stones. Down five steps there were two more stone rooms in perpetual darkness and with little air. Wladek led the Baron into the small upper dungeon where he remained sitting in a corner, silent and motionless, staring fixedly into space; he then appointed Florentyna to be his personal servant.

As Wladek was the only person who dared to remain in the same room as the Baron, the servants never questioned his authority. Thus, at the age of nine, he took charge of the day-to-day responsibility of his fellow prisoners. And in the dungeon he became their master. He split the remaining twenty-four servants into three groups of eight, trying to keep families together wherever possible. He moved them regularly in a shift system, the first eight hours in the upper dungeons for light, air, food and exercise; the second and most popular shift of eight hours working in the castle for their captors; and the final eight hours given to sleep in one of the lower dungeons. No one except the Baron and Florentyna could be quite sure when Wladek slept, as he was always there at the end of every shift to supervise the servants moving on. Food was distributed every twelve hours. The guards would hand over a skin of goats' milk, black bread, millet and occasionally some nuts which Wladek would divide by twenty-eight, always giving two portions to the Baron without ever letting him know. The new occupants of the dungeons, their placidity rendered into miserable stupefaction by incarceration, found nothing strange in a situation that had put a nine-year-old in control of their lives.

Once Wladek had each shift organized, he would return to the Baron in the smaller dungeon. Initially he expected guidance from him, but the fixed gaze of his master was as implacable and comfortless in its own way as were the eyes of the constant succession of German guards. The Baron had never once spoken from the moment he had been subjected to captivity in his own castle. His beard had grown long and matted on his chest and his strong frame was beginning to dwindle into frailty. The once proud look had been replaced with one of resignation. Wladek could scarcely remember the well-loved voice of his patron, and accustomed himself to the thought that he would never hear it again. After a while, he complied with the Baron's unspoken wishes by remaining silent in his presence.

When he had lived in the safety of the castle, Wladek had never thought of the previous day with so much occupying him from hour to hour. Now he was unable to remember even the previous hour, because nothing ever changed. Hopeless minutes turned into hours, hours into days, and then months that he soon lost track of. Only the arrival of food, darkness or light indicated that another twelve hours had passed, while the intensity of that light, and its eventual giving way to storms, and then ice forming on the dungeon walls, melting only when a new sun appeared, heralded each season in a manner that Wladek could never have learned from a nature study lesson. During the long nights Wladek became even more aware of the stench of death that permeated even the farthest corners of the four dungeons, alleviated occasionally by the morning sunshine, a cool breeze, or the most blessed relief of all, the return of rain.

At the end of one day of unremitting storms, Wladek and Florentyna took advantage of the rain by washing themselves in a puddle of water which formed on the stone floor of the upper dungeon. Neither of them noticed that the Baron's eyes were following Wladek with interest as he removed his tattered shirt and rolled over like a dog in the relatively clean water, continuing to rub himself until white streaks appeared on his body. Suddenly, the Baron spoke.

'Wladek' – the word was barely audible – 'I cannot see you clearly,' he said, the voice cracking. 'Come here.'

Wladek was stupefied by the sound of his patron's voice after so long a silence and didn't even look in the direction. He was immediately sure that it heralded the incipience of the madness which already held two of the older servants in its grip.

'Come here, boy.'

Wladek obeyed fearfully, and stood before the Baron, who narrowed his enfeebled eyes in a gesture of intense concentration as he groped towards the boy. He ran his finger over Wladek's chest and then peered at him incredulously.

'Wladek, can you explain this small deformity?'

'No, sir,' said Wladek, feeling embarrassed. 'It has been with me since birth. My foster-mother used to say it was the mark of God the Father upon me.'

'Stupid woman. It is the mark of your own father,' the Baron said softly, and lapsed into silence for some minutes.

Wladek remained standing in front of him, not moving a muscle.

When at last the Baron spoke again, his voice was brisk. 'Sit down, boy.'

Wladek obeyed immediately. As he sat down, he noticed once again the heavy band of silver, now hanging loosely round the Baron's wrist. A shaft of light through a crack in the wall made the magnificent engraving of the Rosnovski coat of arms glitter in the darkness of the dungeon.

'I do not know how long the Germans intend to keep us locked up here. I thought at first that this war would be over in a matter of weeks. I was wrong, and we must now consider the possibility that it will continue for a very long time. With that thought in mind, we must use our time more constructively as I know my life is nearing an end.'

'No, no,' Wladek began to protest, but the Baron continued as if he had not heard him.

'Yours, my child, has yet to begin. I will, therefore, undertake the continuation of your education.'

The Baron did not speak again that day. It was as if he were considering the implications of his pronouncement. Thus Wladek gained his new tutor and as they neither possessed reading nor writing material he was made to repeat everything the Baron said. He was taught great tracts from the poems of Adam Mickiewicz and Jan Kochanowski and long passages from the *Aeneid*. In that austere classroom Wladek learned geography, mathematics and four languages: Russian, German, French, and English. But his happiest moments were once again when he was taught history. The history of his nation through a hundred years of partition, the disappointed hopes for a united Poland, the further anguish of the Poles at Napoleon's crushing loss to Russia in 1812. He learnt of the brave tales of earlier and happier times, when King Jan Casimir had dedicated Poland to the Blessed Virgin after repulsing the Swedes at Czestochowa, and how the mighty Prince Radziwill, great landowner and lover of hunting, had held his court in the great castle near Warsaw. Wladck's final lesson each day was on the family history of the Rosnovskis. Again and again, he was told – never tiring of the tale – how the Baron's illustrious ancestor who had served in 1794 under General Dabrowski and then in 1809 under Napoleon himself had been rewarded by the great Emperor with land and a barony. He also learned how the Baron's grandfather had sat on the council of Warsaw and his father had played his own part in building the new Poland. Wladek found such happiness when the Baron turned his little dungeon into a classroom.

. . .

The guards at the dungeon door were changed every four hours and conversation between them and the prisoners was '*strengst verboten*'. In snatches and fragments Wladek learned of the progress of the war, of the actions of Hindenburg and Ludendorff, of the rise of revolution in Russia and of her subsequent withdrawal from the war by the Treaty of Brest-Litovsk.

Wladek began to believe that the only escape from the dungeons for the inmates was death. The doors opened nine times during the next two years and Wladek started to wonder if he was destined to spend the rest of his days in that filthy hell-hole, fighting a vain battle against despair, while equipping himself with a mind of useless knowledge that would never know freedom.

The Baron continued to tutor him despite his progressively failing sight and hearing. Wladek had to sit closer and closer to him each day.

Florentyna – his sister, mother and closest friend – engaged in a more physical struggle against the rankness of their prison. Occasionally the guards would provide her with a fresh bucket of sand or straw to cover the soiled floor, and the stench became a little less oppressive for the next few days. Vermin scuttled around in the darkness for any dropped scraps of bread or potato and brought with them disease and still more filth. The sour smell of decomposed human and animal urine and excrement assaulted their nostrils and regularly brought Wladek to a state of sickness and nausea. He longed above all to be clean again, and would sit for hours gazing at the dungeon ceiling, recalling the steaming tubs of hot water and the good, rough soap with which the niania had, so short a distance away and so long a time ago, washed the accretion of a mere day's fun from Leon and himself, with many a muttering and tut-tut for muddy knees or a dirty fingernail.

By the spring of 1918, only fifteen of the twenty-six captives who had been incarcerated with Wladek in the dungeons were still alive. The Baron was always treated by everyone as the master, while Wladek had become his acknowledged steward. Wladek felt saddest for his beloved Florentyna, now twenty. She had long since despaired of life and was convinced that she was going to spend her remaining days in the dungeons. Wladek never admitted in her presence to giving up hope, but although he was only twelve, he too was beginning to wonder if he dared believe in any future.

One evening, early in the autumn, Florentyna came to Wladek's side in the larger dungeon.

'The Baron is calling for you.'

Wladek rose quickly, leaving the allocation of food to a senior servant, and went to the old man. The Baron was in severe pain, and Wladek saw with terribly clarity and – as though for the first time – how illness had eroded whole areas of the Baron's flesh, leaving the green-mottled skin covering a now skeletal face. The Baron asked for water and Florentyna brought it from the half-full mug that balanced from a stick outside the stone grille. When the great man had finished drinking, he spoke slowly and with considerable difficulty.

'You have seen so much of death, Wladek, that one more will make little difference to you. I confess that I no longer fear escaping this world.'

'No, no, it can't be,' cried Wladek, clinging onto the old man for the first time in his life. 'We have so nearly triumphed. Don't give up, Baron. The guards have assured me that the war is coming to an end and then we will soon be released.'

'They have been promising us that for months, Wladek. We cannot believe them any longer, and in any case I fear I have no desire to live in the new world they are creating.' He paused as he listened to the boy crying. The Baron's only thought was to collect the tears as drinking water, and then he remembered that tears were saline and he laughed to himself.

'Call for my butler and first footman, Wladek.'

Wladek obeyed immediately, not knowing why they should be required.

The two servants, woken from a deep sleep, came and stood in front of the Baron. After three years captivity sleep was the easiest commodity to come by. They still wore their embroidered uniforms, but one could no longer tell that they had once been the proud Rosnovski colours of green and gold. They stood silently waiting for their master to speak.

'Are they there, Wladek?' asked the Baron.

'Yes, sir. Can you not see them?' Wladek realized for the first time that the Baron was now completely blind.

'Bring them forward so that I might touch them.'

Wladek brought the two men to him and the Baron touched their faces.

'Sit down,' he commanded. 'Can you both hear me, Ludwik, Alfons?'

'Yes, sir.'

'My name is Baron Rosnovski.'

'We know, sir,' replied the butler innocently.

'Do not interrupt me,' said the Baron. 'I am about to die.'

Death had become so common that the two men made no protest.

'I am unable to make a new will as I have no paper, quill, or ink. Therefore I make my will in your presence and you can act as my two witnesses as recognized by the ancient law of Poland. Do you understand what I am saying?'

'Yes, sir,' the two men replied in unison.

'My first born son, Leon, is dead.' The Baron paused. 'And so I leave my entire estate and possessions to the boy known as Wladek Koskiewicz.'

Wladek had not heard his surname for many years and did not immediately comprehend the significance of the Baron's words.

'And as proof of my resolve,' the Baron continued, 'I give him the family band.'

The old man slowly raised his right arm, removed from his wrist the silver band and held it forward to a speechless Wladek, whom he clasped onto firmly, running his fingers over the boy's chest as if to be sure that it was he. 'My son,' he said, as he placed the silver band on the boy's wrist.

Wladek wept, and lay in the arms of the Baron all night until he could no longer hear his heart, and could feel the fingers stiffening around him. In the morning the Baron's body was removed by the guards and they allowed Wladek to bury him by the side of his son, Leon, in the family churchyard, up against the chapel. As the body was lowered into its shallow grave, dug by Wladek's bare hands, the Baron's tattered shirt fell open. Wladek stared at the dead man's chest.

He had only one nipple.

.   .   .

Thus Wladek Koskiewicz, aged twelve, inherited sixty thousand acres of land, one castle, two manor houses, twenty-seven cottages, and a valuable collection of paintings, furniture and jewelry, while he lived in a small stone room under the earth. From that day on, the captives took him as their rightful master and his empire was four dungeons, his retinue thirteen broken servants and his only love Florentyna.

He returned to what he felt was now an endless routine until long into the winter of 1918. On a mild, dry day there burst upon the prisoners' ears a volley of shots and the sound of a brief struggle. Wladek was sure that the Polish army had come to rescue him and that he would now be able to lay claim to his rightful inheritance. When the German guards deserted the iron door of the dungeons, the inmates remained in terrified silence huddled in the lower rooms. Wladek stood alone at the entrance, twisting the silver band around his wrist, triumphant, waiting for his liberators. Eventually those who had defeated the Germans arrived and spoke in the coarse Slavic tongue, familiar from school days, which he had learned to fear even more than German. Wladek was dragged unceremoniously out into the passage with his retinue. The prisoners waited, then were cursorily inspected and thrown back into the dungeons. The new conquerors were unaware that this twelve-year-old boy was the master of all their eyes beheld. They did not speak his tongue. Their orders were clear and not to be questioned: kill the enemy if they resist the agreement of Brest-Litovsk, which made this section of Poland theirs and send those who do not resist to camp 201 for the rest of their days. The Germans had left meekly to retreat behind their new border while Wladek and his followers waited, hopeful of a new life, ignorant of their impending fate.

After spending two more nights in the dungeons, Wladek resigned himself to believing that they were to be incarcerated for another long spell. The new guards did not speak to him at all, a reminder to him of what life had been like three years before; he began to realize that discipline had at least become lax under the Germans but once again was tight.

On the morning of the third day, much to Wladek's surprise, they were all dragged out onto the grass in front of the castle, fifteen thin filthy bodies. Two of the servants collapsed in the unaccustomed sunlight. Wladek himself found the intense brightness his biggest problem and kept having to shield his eyes from it. The prisoners stood in silence on the grass and waited for the soldiers' next move. The guards made them all strip and ordered them down to the river to wash. Wladek hid the silver band in his clothes and ran down to the water's edge, his legs feeling weak even before he reached the river. He jumped in, gasping for breath at the coldness of the water, although it felt glorious on his skin. The rest of the prisoners followed him, and tried vainly to remove three years of filth.

When Wladek came out of the river exhausted, he noticed that some of the guards were looking strangely at Florentyna as she washed herself in the water. They were laughing and pointing at her. The other women did not seem to arouse the same degree of interest. One of the guards, a large ugly man whose eyes had never left Florentyna for a moment, grabbed her arm as she passed him on her way back up the river bank, and threw her to the ground. He then started to take his clothes off quickly, hungrily, while at the same time folding them neatly on the grass. Wladek stared in disbelief at the man's swollen erect penis and flew at the soldier, who was now holding Florentyna down on the ground, and hit him in the middle of his stomach with his head with all the force he could muster. The man reeled back, and a second soldier jumped up and held Wladek helpless with his hands pinned behind his back. The commotion attracted the attention of the other guards, and they strolled over to watch. Wladek's captor was now laughing, a loud belly laugh with no humour in it. The other soldiers' words only added to Wladek's anguish.

'Enter the great protector,' said the first.

'Come to defend his nation's honour.' The second one.

'Let's at least allow him a ringside view.' The one who was holding him.

More laughter interspersed the remarks that Wladek couldn't always comprehend. He watched the naked soldier advance his hard, well-fed body slowly towards Florentyna, who started screaming. Once again Wladek struggled, trying desperately to free himself from the vice-like grip, but he was helpless in the arms of his guard. The naked man fell clumsily on top of Florentyna and started kissing her and slapping her when she tried to fight or turn away; finally he lunged into her. She let out a scream such as Wladek had never heard before. The guards continued talking and laughing among themselves, some not even watching.

'Goddamn virgin,' said the first soldier as he withdrew himself from her. They all laughed.

'You've just made it a little easier for me,' said the second guard.

More laughter. As Florentyna stared into Wladek's eyes, he began to retch. The soldier holding onto him showed little interest, other than to be sure that none of the boy's vomit soiled his uniform or boots. The first soldier, his penis now covered in blood, ran down to the stream, yelling as he hit the water. The second man undressed, while yet another held Florentyna down. The second guard took a little longer over his pleasure, and seemed to gain considerable satisfaction from hitting Florentyna; when he finally entered her, she screamed again but not quite as loud.

'Come on, Valdi, you've had long enough.'

With that the man came out of her suddenly and joined his companion-at-arms in the stream. Wladek made himself look at Florentyna. She was bruised and bleeding between the legs. The soldier holding him spoke again.

'Come and hold the little bastard, Boris, it's my turn.'

The first soldier came out of the river and took hold of Wladek firmly. Again he tried to hit out, and this made them laugh even louder.

'Now we know the full might of the Polish army.'

The unbearable laughter continued as yet another guard started undressing to take his turn with Florentyna, who now lay indifferent to his charms. When he had finished, and had gone down to the river, the second soldier returned and started putting on his clothes.

'I think she's beginning to enjoy it,' he said, as he sat in the sun watching his companion. The fourth soldier began to advance on Florentyna. When he reached her, he turned her over, forced her legs as wide apart as possible, his large hands moving rapidly over her frail body. The scream when he entered her had now turned into a groan. Wladek counted sixteen soldiers who raped his sister. When the last soldier had finished with her, he swore and then added, 'I think I've made love to a dead woman,' and left her motionless on the grass.

They all laughed even more loudly, as the disgruntled soldier walked down to the river. At last Wladek's guard released him. He ran to Florentyna's side, while the soldiers lay on the grass drinking wine and vodka taken from the Baron's cellar, and eating the bread from the kitchens.

With the help of two of the servants, Wladek carried Florentyna's light body to the edge of the river, weeping as he tried to wash away her blood and bruises. It was useless, for she was black and red all over, insensible to help and unable to speak. When Wladek had done the best he could he covered her body with his jacket and held her in his arms. He kissed her gently on the mouth, the first woman he had ever kissed. She lay in his arms, but he knew she did not recognize him, and as the tears ran down his face onto her bruised body, he felt her go limp. He wept as he carried her dead body up the bank. The guards went silent as they watched him walk towards the chapel. He laid her down on the grass beside the Baron's grave and started digging with his bare hands. When the sinking sun had caused the castle to cast its long shadow over the graveyard, he had finished digging. He buried Florentyna next to Leon and made a little cross with two sticks which he placed at her head. Wladek collapsed on the ground between Leon and Florentyna, and fell asleep, caring not if he ever woke again.

8

William returned to Sayre Academy in September and immediately began to look for competition among those older than himself. Whatever he took up, he was never satisfied unless he excelled in it, and his contemporaries almost always proved too weak an opposition. William began to realize that most of those from backgrounds as privileged as his own lacked any incentive to compete, and that fiercer rivalry was to be found from boys who had, compared with himself, relatively little.

In 1915, a craze for collecting match-box labels hit Sayre Academy. William observed this frenzy for a week with great interest but did not join in. Within a few days, common labels were changing hands at a dime, while rarities commanded as much as fifty cents. William considered the situation and decided to become not a collector, but a dealer.

On the following Saturday, he went to Leavitt and Pearce, one of the largest tobacconists in Boston, and spent the afternoon taking down the names and addresses of all the major match-box manufacturers throughout the world, making a special note of those who were not at war. He invested five dollars in notepaper, envelopes and stamps, and wrote to the chairman or president of every company he had listed. His letter was simple despite having been rewritten seven times.

Dear Mr Chairman or Mr President,
    I am a dedicated collector of match-box labels, but I cannot afford to buy all the matches. My pocket money is only one dollar a week, but I enclose a three-cent stamp for postage to prove that I am serious about my hobby. I am sorry to bother you personally, but yours was the only name I could find to write to.
Your friend,
William Kane (aged 9)
P.S. Yours are one of my favourites.

Within three weeks, William had a fifty-five per cent reply which yielded one hundred and seventy-eight different labels. Nearly all his correspondents also returned the three-cent stamp, as William had anticipated they would.

During the next seven days, William set up a market in labels within the school, always checking what he could sell at even before he had made a purchase. He noticed that some boys showed no interest in the rarity of the match-box label, only in its looks, and with them he made quick exchanges to obtain rare trophies for the more discerning collectors. After a further two weeks of buying and selling he sensed that the market was reaching its zenith and that if he were not careful, with the holidays fast approaching, interest might begin to die off. With much trumpeted advance publicity in the form of a printed handout which cost him a further half cent a sheet, placed on every boy's desk, William announced that he would be holding an auction of his match-box labels, all two hundred and eleven of them. The auction took place in the school washroom during the lunch hour and was better attended than most school hockey games.

The result was that William netted fifty-seven dollars thirty-two cents, a profit of fifty-two dollars thirty-two cents on his original investment. William put twenty-five dollars on deposit with the bank at two and a half per cent, bought himself a camera for eleven dollars, gave five dollars to the Young Men's Christian Association, who had broadened their activities to help the new flood of immigrants, bought his mother some flowers, and put the remaining few dollars into his pocket. The market in match-box labels collapsed even before the school term ended. It was to be the first of many such occasions that William got out at the top of the market. The grandmothers would have been proud of him; it was not unlike the way their husbands had made their fortunes in the panic of 1873.

When the holidays came, William could not resist finding out if it was possible to obtain a better return on his invested capital than the two and a half per cent yielded by his savings account. For the next three months he invested – again through Grandmother Kane – in stocks highly recommended by the *Wall Street Journal*. During the next term at school he lost over half of the money he had made on the match-box labels. It was the only time in his life that he relied on the expertise of the *Wall Street Journal*, or on information available at any street corner.

Angry with his loss of over twenty dollars William decided that it must be recouped during the Easter holidays. On arriving home he worked out which parties and functions his mother expected him to attend, and found he was left with only fourteen free days, just enough time for his new venture. He sold all his remaining *Wall Street Journal* shares, which netted him only twelve dollars. With this money he bought himself a flat piece of wood, two sets of wheels, axles and a piece of rope, at a cost, after some bargaining, of five dollars. He then put on a flat cloth cap and an old suit he had outgrown and went off to the local railroad station. He stood outside the exit, looking hungry and tired, informing selected travellers that the main hotels in Boston were near the railroad station, so that there was no need to take a taxi or the occasional surviving hansom carriage as he, William, could carry their luggage on his moving board for twenty per cent of what the taxis charged; he added that the walk would also do them good. By working six hours a day, he found he could make roughly four dollars.

Five days before the new school term was due to start, he had made back all his original losses and a further ten dollars profit. He then hit a problem. The taxi drivers were starting to get annoyed with him. William assured them that he would retire, aged nine, if each one of them would give him fifty cents to cover the cost of his home-made trolley – they agreed, and he made another eight dollars fifty cents. On the way home to Beacon Hill, William sold his trolley for five dollars to a school friend two years his senior, who was soon to discover that the market had passed its peak; moreover, it rained for every day of the following week.

On the last day of the holidays, William put his money back on deposit in the bank, at two and a half per cent. During the following term this decision caused him no anxiety as he watched his savings rise steadily. The sinking of the *Lusitania* and Wilson's declaration of war against Germany in April 1917 didn't concern William. Nothing and no one could ever beat America, he assured his mother. William even invested ten dollars in Liberty Bonds to back his judgement.

By William's eleventh birthday the credit column of his ledger book showed a profit of four hundred and twelve dollars. He had given his mother a fountain pen and his two grandmothers brooches from a local jewellery shop. The fountain pen was a Parker and the jewellery arrived at his grandmothers' homes in Shreve, Crump and Low boxes, which he had found after much searching in the dustbins behind the famous store. To do the boy justice, he had not wanted to cheat his grandmothers, but he had already learned from his match-box label experience that good packaging sells products. The grandmothers, who noted the missing Shreve, Crump and Low hallmarks still wore their brooches with considerable pride.

The two old ladies continued to follow William's every move and had decided that when he reached the age of twelve, he should proceed as planned to St Paul's School in Concord, New Hampshire. For good measure the boy rewarded them with the top mathematics scholarship, unnecessarily saving the family some three hundred dollars a year. William accepted the scholarship and the grandmothers returned the money for, as they expressed it, 'a less fortunate child'. Anne hated the thought of William leaving her to go away to boarding school, but the grandmothers insisted and, more importantly, she knew it was what Richard would have wanted. She sewed on William's name tapes, marked his boots, checked his clothes, and finally packed his trunk refusing any help from the servants. When the time came for William to go his mother asked him how much pocket money he would like for the new term ahead of him.

'None,' he replied without further comment.

William kissed his mother on the cheek; he had no idea how much she was going to miss him. He marched off down the path, in his first pair of long trousers, his hair cut very short, carrying a small suitcase towards Roberts, the chauffeur. He climbed into the back of the Rolls-Royce and it drove him away. He didn't look back. His mother waved and waved, and later cried. William wanted to cry too, but he knew his father would not have approved.

. . .

The first thing that struck William Kane as strange about his new prep school was that the other boys did not care who he was. The looks of admiration, the silent acknowledgment of his presence were no longer there. One older boy actually asked his name, and what was worse, when told, was not manifestly impressed. Some even called him Bill which he soon corrected with the explanation that no one had ever referred to his father as Dick.

William's new domain was a small room with wooden book-shelves, two tables, two chairs, two beds and a comfortably shabby leather settee. The other chair, table and bed were occupied by a boy from New York called Matthew Lester, whose father was also in banking.

William soon became used to the school routine. Up at seven thirty, wash, breakfast in the main dining room, with the whole school – two hundred and twenty boys munching their way through eggs, bacon and porridge. After breakfast, chapel, three fifty-minute classes before lunch and two after it, followed by a music lesson which William detested because he could not sing a note in tune and he had even less desire to learn to play any musical instrument. Football in the autumn, hockey and squash in the winter, and rowing and tennis in the spring left him with very little free time. As a mathematics scholar, William had special tutorials in the subject three times a week from his housemaster, G. Raglan, Esquire, known to the boys as Grumpy.

During his first year, William proved to be well worthy of his scholarship, among the top few boys in almost every subject, and in a class of his own in mathematics. Only his new friend, Matthew Lester, was any real competition for him, and that was almost certainly because they shared the same room. While establishing himself academically William also acquired a reputation as a financier. Although his first investment in the market had proved disastrous, he did not abandon his belief that to make a significant amount of money, sizeable capital gains on the stock market were essential. He kept a wary eye on the *Wall Street Journal*, company reports and, at the age of twelve, started to experiment with a ghost portfolio of investments. He recorded every one of his ghost purchases and sales, the good and the not-so-good in a newly acquired, different coloured ledger book, and compared his performance at the end of each month against the rest of the market. He did not bother with any of the leading listed stocks, concentrating instead on the more obscure companies, some of which traded only over the counter, so that it was impossible to buy more than a few shares in them at any one time. William expected four things from his investments: a low multiple of earnings, a high growth rate, strong asset backing and a favourable trading outlook. He found few shares which fulfilled all these rigorous criteria, but when he did, they almost invariably showed a profit.

The moment he found that he was regularly beating the Dow-Jones Index with his ghost investment programme, William knew he was ready to invest his own money once again. He started with one hundred dollars and never stopped refining his method. He would always follow profits and cut losses. Once a stock had doubled, he would sell half his holdings but keep the remaining half intact, trading the stock he still held as a bonus. Some of his early finds, such as Eastman Kodak and IBM, went on to become national leaders. He also backed the first mail order company, convinced it was a trend that would catch on.

By the end of his first year he was advising half the school staff and some of the parents. William Kane was happy at school.

.   .   .

Anne Kane had been unhappy and lonely at home with William away at St Paul's and a family circle consisting only of the two grandmothers, now approaching old age. She was miserably conscious that she was past thirty, and that her smooth and youthful prettiness had disappeared without leaving much in its place. She started picking up the threads, severed by Richard's death, with some of her old friends. John and Milly Preston, William's godmother, whom she had known all her life, began inviting her to dinners and the theatre, always including an extra man, trying to make a match for Anne. The Preston's choices were almost always atrocious, and Anne used privately to laugh at Milly's attempts at match-making until one day in January 1919, just after William had returned to school for the winter term, Anne was invited to yet another dinner for four. Milly confessed she had never met her other guest, Henry Osborne, but that they thought he had been at Harvard at the same time as John.

'Actually,' confessed Milly over the phone, 'John doesn't know much about him, darling, except that he is rather good-looking.'

On that score, John's opinion was verified by Anne and Milly. Henry Osborne was warming himself by the fire when Anne arrived and he rose immediately to allow Milly to introduce them. A shade over six feet, with dark eyes, almost black, and straight black hair, he was slim and athletic looking. Anne felt a quick flash of pleasure that she was paired for the evening with this energetic and youthful man, while Milly had to content herself with a husband, who was showing signs of middle-age by comparison with his dashing college contemporary. Henry Osborne's arm was in a sling, almost completely covering his Harvard tie.

'A war wound?' asked Anne sympathetically.

'No, I fell down the stairs the week after I got back from the Western Front,' he said, laughing.

It was one of those dinners, lately so rare for Anne, at which the time at the table slipped by happily and unaccountably. Henry Osborne answered all Anne's inquisitive questions. After leaving Harvard, he had worked for a real estate management firm in Chicago, his home town, but when the war came he couldn't resist having a go at the Germans. He had a fund of splendid stories about Europe and the life he had led there as a young lieutenant preserving the honour of America on the Marne. Milly and John had not seen Anne laugh so much since Richard's death and smiled at one another knowingly when Henry asked if he might drive her home.

'What are you going to do now that you've come back to a land fit for heroes?' asked Anne, as Henry Osborne eased his Stutz out onto Charles Street.

'Haven't really decided,' he replied. 'Luckily, I have a little money of my own, so I don't have to rush into anything. Might even start my own real estate firm right here in Boston. I've always felt at home in the city since my days at Harvard.'

'You won't be returning to Chicago, then?'

'No, there's nothing to take me back there. My parents are both dead, and I was an only child, so I can start afresh anywhere I choose. Where do I turn?'

'Oh, first on the right,' said Anne.

'You live on Beacon Hill?'

'Yes, About a hundred and fifty yards on the right-hand side up Chestnut and it's the red house on the corner of Louisburg Square.'

Henry Osborne parked the car and accompanied Anne to the front door of her home. After saying goodnight, he was gone almost before she had time to thank him. She watched his car glide slowly back down Beacon Hill knowing that she wanted to see him again. She was delighted, though not entirely surprised, when he telephoned her the following morning.

'Boston Symphony Orchestra, Mozart, and that flamboyant new fellow, Mahler, next Monday – can I persuade you?'

Anne was a little taken aback by the extent to which she looked forward to Monday. It seemed so long since a man whom she found attractive had pursued her. Henry Osborne arrived punctually for the outing, they shook hands rather awkwardly, and he accepted a Scotch highball.

'It must be pleasant to live on Louisburg Square. You're a lucky girl.'

'Yes, I suppose so, I've never really given it much thought. I was born and raised on Commonwealth Avenue. If anything, I find this slightly cramped.'

'I think I might buy a house on the Hill myself if I do decide to settle in Boston.'

'They don't come on the market all that often,' said Anne, 'but you may be lucky. Hadn't we better be going? I hate being late for a concert and having to tread on other people's toes to reach my seat.'

Henry glanced at his watch. 'Yes I agree, wouldn't do to miss the conductor's entrance, but you don't have to worry about anyone's feet except mine. We're on the aisle.'

The cascades of sumptuous music made it natural for Henry to take Anne's arm as they walked to the Ritz. The only other person who had done that since Richard's death had been William, and only after considerable persuasion as he considered it sissy. Once again the hours slipped by for Anne: was it the excellent food, or was it Henry's company? This time he made her laugh with his stories of Harvard and cry with recollections of the war. Although she was well aware that he looked younger than herself, he had done so much with his life that she always felt deliciously youthful and inexperienced in his company. She told him about her husband's death, and cried a little more. He took her hand and she spoke of her son with glowing pride and affection. He said he had always wanted a son. Henry scarcely mentioned Chicago or his own home life but Anne felt sure that he must miss his family. When he took her home that night, he stayed for a quick drink and kissed her gently on the cheek as he left. Anne went back over the evening minute by minute before she fell asleep.

They went to the theatre on Tuesday, visited Anne's cottage on Cape Cod on Wednesday, gyrated to the Grizzly Bear and the Temptation Rag on Thursday, shopped for antiques on Friday, and made love on Saturday. After Sunday, they were rarely apart. Milly and John Preston were 'absolutely delighted' that their match-making had at last proved so successful. Milly went around Boston telling everyone that she had been responsible for putting the two of them together.

The announcement during that summer of the engagement came as no surprise to anyone except William. He had disliked Henry intensely from the day that Anne, with a well-founded sense of misgiving, introduced them to each other. Their first conversation took the form of long questions from Henry, trying to prove he wanted to be a friend, and monosyllabic answers from William, showing that he didn't. And he never changed his mind. Anne ascribed her son's resentment to an understandable feeling of jealousy; William had been the centre of her life since Richard's death. Moreover, it was perfectly proper that in William's estimation, no one could possibly take the place of his own father. Anne convinced Henry that given time William would get over his sense of outrage.

Anne Kane became Mrs Henry Osborne in October of that year at the Old North Church just as the golden and red leaves were beginning to fall, a little over ten months after they had met. William feigned illness in order not to attend the wedding and remained firmly at school. The grandmothers did attend, but were unable to hide their disapproval of Anne's remarriage, particularly to someone who appeared to be so much younger than herself. 'It can only end in disaster,' said Grandmother Kane.

The newlyweds sailed for Greece the following day, and did not return to the Red House on the Hill till the second week in December, just in time to welcome William home for the Christmas holidays. William was shocked to find the house had been redecorated, leaving almost no trace of his father.

Over Christmas, William's attitude to his step-father showed no sign of softening despite the present as Henry saw it – bribe as William construed it – of a new bicycle. Henry Osborne accepted this rebuff with surly resignation. It saddened Anne that her splendid new husband made so little effort to win over her son's affection.

William felt ill at ease in his invaded home and would often disappear for long periods during the day. Whenever Anne inquired where he was going, she received little or no response: it certainly was not to the grandmothers. When the Christmas holidays came to an end, William was only too happy to return to school and Henry was not sad to see him go. Only Anne was uneasy about both the men in her life.

9

'Up, boy. Up, boy.'

One of the soldiers was digging his rifle butt into Wladek's ribs. He sat up with a start and looked at the grave of his sister and those of Leon and of the Baron, and he did not shed a single tear as he turned towards the soldier.

'I will live, you will not kill me,' he said in Polish. 'This is my home, and you are on my land.'

The soldier spat on Wladek and pushed him back to the lawn where the servants were waiting, all dressed in what looked like grey pyjamas with numbers on their backs. Wladek was horrified at the sight of them, realizing what was about to happen to him. He was taken by the soldier to the north side of the castle and made to kneel on the ground. He felt a knife scrape across his head as his thick black hair fell onto the grass. With ten bloody strokes, like the shearing of a sheep, the job was completed. Shaven-headed, he was ordered to put on his new uniform, a grey rubaskew shirt and trousers. Wladek managed to keep the silver band well hidden and rejoined his servants at the front of the castle.

While they all stood waiting on the grass – numbers now, not names – Wladek became conscious of a noise in the distance that he had never heard before. His eyes turned towards the menacing sound. Through the great iron gates came a vehicle moving on four wheels, but not drawn by horses or oxen. All the prisoners stared at the moving object in disbelief. When it had come to a halt, the soldiers dragged the reluctant prisoners towards it and made them climb aboard. Then the horseless wagon turned round, moved back down the path and through the iron gates. Nobody dared to speak. Wladek sat at the rear of the truck and stared at his castle until he could no longer see the Gothic turrets.

The horseless wagon somehow drove itself towards Slonim. Wladek would have worried about how the vehicle worked if he had not been even more worried about where it was taking them. He began to recognize the roads from his days at school, but his memory had been dulled by three years in the dungeons, and he could not recall where the road finally led. After only a few miles, the truck came to a stop and they were all pushed out. It was the local railway station. Wladek had only seen it once before in his life, when he and Leon had gone there to welcome the Baron home from his trip to Warsaw. He remembered the guard had saluted them when they first walked onto the platform; this time no guard saluted them. The prisoners were fed on goats' milk, cabbage soup and black bread, Wladek again taking charge, dividing the portions carefully among the remaining fourteen. He sat on a wooden bench, assuming that they were waiting for a train. That night they slept on the ground below the stars, paradise compared with the dungeons. He thanked God for the mild winter.

Morning came and still they waited. Wladek made the servants take some exercise but most collapsed after only a few minutes. He began to make a mental note of the names of those who had survived thus far. Eleven of the men and two of the women, spared from the original twenty-seven in the dungeons. Spared for what? he thought. They spent the rest of the day waiting for a train that never came. Once, a train did arrive, from which more soldiers disembarked, speaking their hateful tongue, but it departed without Wladek's pitiful army. They slept yet another night on the platform.

Wladek lay awake below the stars considering how he might escape, but during the night one of his thirteen made a run for it across the railway track and was shot down by a guard even before he had reached the other side. Wladek gazed at the spot where his compatriot had fallen, frightened to go to his aid for fear he would meet the same fate. The guards left the body on the track in the morning, as a warning to those who might consider a similar course of action.

No one spoke of the incident the next day, although Wladek's eyes rarely left the body of the dead man. It was the Baron's butler, Ludwik – one of the witnesses to the Baron's will, and his heritage – dead.

On the evening of the third day another train chugged into the station, a great steam locomotive pulling open freight cars, the floors strewn with straw and the word 'cattle' painted on the sides. Several cars were already full, full of humans, but from where Wladek could not judge, so hideously did their appearance resemble his own. He and his band were thrown together into one of the cars to begin the journey. After a wait of several more hours the train started to move out of the station, in a direction which Wladek judged, from the setting sun, to be eastward.

To every three carriages there was a guard sitting cross-legged on a roofed car. Throughout the interminable journey an occasional flurry of bullet shots from above demonstrated to Wladek the futility of any further thoughts of escape.

When the train stopped at Minsk, they were given their first proper meal: black bread, water, nuts, and more millet, and then the journey continued. Sometimes they went for three days without seeing another station. Many of the reluctant travellers died of starvation and were thrown overboard from the moving train. And when the train did stop they would often wait for two days to allow another train going west use of the track. These trains which delayed their progress were inevitably full of soldiers, and it became obvious to Wladek that the troop trains had priority over all other transport. Escape was always uppermost in Wladek's mind, but three things prevented him from advancing that ambition. First, no one had yet succeeded; second, there was nothing but miles of wilderness on both sides of the track; and third, those who had survived the dungeons were now totally dependent on him to protect them. It was Wladek who organized their food and drink, and tried to give them all the will to live. He was the youngest and the last one still to believe in life.

At night, it became bitterly cold, often thirty degrees below zero, and they would all lie up against each other in a line on the carriage floor so that each body would keep the person next to him warm. Wladek would recite the *Aeneid* to himself while he tried to snatch some sleep. It was impossible to turn over unless everyone agreed, so Wladek would lie at the end and each hour, as near as he could judge by the changing of the guards, he would slap the side of the carriage, and they would all roll over and face the other way. One after the other, the bodies would turn like falling dominoes. Sometimes a body did not move – because it no longer could – and Wladek would be informed. He in turn would inform the guard and four of them would pick up the body and throw it over the side of the moving train. The guards would pump bullets into the head to be sure it was not someone hoping to escape.

Two hundred miles beyond Minsk, they arrived in the small town of Smolensk, where they received warm cabbage soup and black bread. Wladek was joined in his car by some new prisoners who spoke the same tongue as the guards. Their leader seemed to be about the same age as Wladek. Wladek and his ten remaining companions, nine men and one woman, were immediately suspicious of the new arrivals, and they divided the carriage in half, with the two groups remaining apart for several days.

One night, while Wladek lay awake staring at the stars, trying to get warm, he watched the leader of the Smolenskis crawl towards the end man of his own line with a small piece of rope in his hand. He watched him slip it round the neck of Alfons, the Baron's first footman, who was sleeping. Wladek knew if he moved too quickly, the boy would hear him and escape back to his own half of the carriage and the protection of his comrades, so he crawled slowly on his belly down the line of Polish bodies. Eyes stared at him as he passed, but nobody spoke. When he reached the end of the line, he leaped forward upon the aggressor, immediately waking everyone in the truck. Each faction shrank back to its own end of the carriage, with the exception of Alfons, who lay motionless in front of them.

The Smolenski leader was taller and more agile than Wladek, but it made little difference while the two were fighting on the floor. The struggle lasted for several minutes, with the guards laughing and taking bets as they watched the two gladiators. One guard, who was getting bored by the lack of blood, threw a bayonet into the middle of the car. Both boys scrambled for the shining blade with the Smolenski leader grabbing it first. The Smolenski band cheered their hero as he thrust the bayonet into the side of Wladek's leg, pulled the blood-covered steel back out and lunged again. On the second thrust the blade lodged firmly in the wooden floor of the jolting car next to Wladek's ear. As the Smolenski leader tried to wrench it free, Wladek kicked him in the groin with every ounce of energy he had left, and in throwing his adversary backwards released the bayonet. With a leap, Wladek grabbed the handle and jumped on top of the Smolenski, running the blade right into his mouth. The man gave out a shriek of agony that awoke the entire train. Wladek pulled the blade out, twisting it as he did so, and thrust it back into the Smolenski again and again, long after he had ceased to move. Wladek knelt over him, breathing heavily, and then picked up the body and threw it out of the carriage. He heard the thud as it hit the bank, and the shots that the guards pointlessly aimed after it.

Wladek limped towards Alfons, still lying motionless on the wooden boards, and knelt by his side shaking his lifeless body: his second witness dead. Who would now believe that he, Wladek, was the chosen heir to the Baron's fortune? Was there any purpose left in life? He collapsed to his knees. He picked up the bayonet with both hands, pointing the blade towards his stomach. Immediately a guard jumped down and wrested the weapon away from him.

'Oh no, you don't,' he grunted. 'We need the lively ones like you for the camps. You can't expect us to do all the work.'

Wladek buried his head in his hands, aware for the first time of an aching pain in his bayoneted leg. He had lost his inheritance and traded it to become the leader of a band of penniless Smolenskis.

The whole truck once again became his domain and he now had twenty prisoners to care for. He immediately split them up so that a Pole would always sleep next to a Smolenski, making it impossible for there to be any further warfare between the two groups.

Wladek spent a considerable part of his time learning their strange tongue, not realizing for several days that it was actually Russian, so greatly did it differ from the classical Russian language taught him by the Baron, and then the real significance of the discovery dawned on him for the first time when he realized where the train was heading.

During the day Wladek used to take on two Smolenskis at a time to tutor him, and as soon as they were tired, he would take on two more, and so on until they were all exhausted.

Gradually he became able to converse easily with his new dependents. Some of them were Russian soldiers, exiled after repatriation for the crime of having been captured by the Germans. The rest were White Russians, farmers, miners, labourers, all bitterly hostile to the Revolution.

The train jolted on past terrain more barren than Wladek had ever seen before, and through towns of which he had never heard – Omsk, Novo Sibirsk, Krasnoyarsk – the names rang ominously in his ears. Finally, after three months and more than three thousand miles, they reached Irkutsk, where the railway track came to an abrupt end.

They were hustled off the train, fed, and issued with felt boots, jackets and heavy coats and although fights broke out for the warmest clothing, they still provided little protection from the ever intensifying cold.

Horseless wagons appeared, not unlike the one which had borne Wladek away from his castle, and long chains were thrown out. Then to Wladek's disbelief and horror, the prisoners were cuffed to the chain by one hand, twenty-five pairs side by side on each chain. The trucks pulled the mass of prisoners along while the guards rode on the back. They marched like that for twelve hours, before being given a two-hour rest, and then they marched again. After three days, Wladek thought he would die of cold and exhaustion, but once clear of populated areas they travelled only during the day and rested at night. A mobile field kitchen run by prisoners from the camp supplied turnip soup and bread at first light and then again at night. Wladek learned from these prisoners that conditions at the camp were even worse.

For the first week they were never unshackled from those chains, but later when there could be no thought of escape they were released at night to sleep, digging holes in the snow for warmth. Sometimes on good days they found a forest in which to bed down: luxury began to take strange forms. On and on they marched, past enormous lakes and across frozen rivers, ever northwards, into the face of viciously cold winds and deeper falls of snow. Wladek's injured leg gave him a constant dull pain, soon surpassed in intensity by the agony of frostbitten fingers and ears. There was no sign of life or food in all the expanse of whiteness, and Wladek knew that to attempt an escape at night could only mean slow death by starvation. The old and the sick were starting to die, quietly at night, if they were lucky. The unlucky ones, unable to keep up the pace, were uncuffed from the chains and cast off to be left alone in the endless snow. Those who survived walked on, on, on, always towards the north, until Wladek lost all sense of time and was simply conscious of the inexorable tug of the chain, not even sure when he dug his hole in the snow to sleep at night that he would wake the next morning: those that didn't had dug their own grave.

After a trek of nine hundred miles, those who had survived were met by Ostyaks, nomads of the Russian steppes, in reindeer-drawn sleds. The trucks discharged their cargo and turned back. The prisoners, now chained to the sleds, were led on. A great blizzard forced them to halt for the greater part of two days and Wladek seized the opportunity to communicate with the young Ostyak to whose sled he was chained. Using classical Russian, with a Polish accent, he was understood only very imperfectly but he did discover that the Ostyaks hated the Russians of the south, who treated them almost as badly as they treated their captives. The Ostyaks were not unsympathetic to the sad prisoners with no future, the 'unfortunates' as they called them.

. . .

Nine days later, in the half light of the early Arctic winter night, they reached camp 201. Wladek would never have believed he could have been glad to see such a place: row upon row of wooden huts in the stark open space. The huts, like the prisoners were numbered. Wladek's hut was 33. There was a small black stove in the middle of the room, and, projecting from the walls, tiered wooden bunks on which were hard straw mattresses and one thin blanket. Few of them managed to sleep at all that first night, and the groans and cries that came from hut 33 were often louder than the howls of the wolves outside.

The next morning before the sun rose, they were woken by the sound of a hammer against an iron triangle. There was thick frost on both sides of the window and Wladek thought that he must surely die of the cold. Breakfast in a freezing communal hall lasted for ten minutes and consisted of a bowl of lukewarm gruel, with pieces of rotten fish and a leaf of cabbage floating in it. The newcomers spat the fish bones out on the table while the more seasoned prisoners ate the bones and even the fishes' eyes.

After breakfast, they were allocated tasks. Wladek became a wood chopper. He was taken seven miles through the featureless steppes into a forest and ordered to cut a certain number of trees each day. The guard would leave him and his little group of six to themselves with their food ration, tasteless yellow magara porridge and bread. The guards had no fear of the prisoners attempting to escape, for it was over a thousand miles to the nearest town, even if you knew in which direction to head.

At the end of each day, the guard would return and count the number of logs of wood they had chopped; he informed the prisoners that if they failed to reach the required number, he would stop the group's food for the following day. But when he came back at seven in the evening to collect the reluctant woodsmen, it was already dark, and he could not always see exactly how many new logs they had cut. Wladek taught the others in his team to spend the last part of the afternoon clearing the snow off the wood cut the previous day and lining it up with what they had chopped that day. It was a plan that always worked, and Wladek's group never lost a day's food. Sometimes they managed to return to the camp with a small piece of wood, tied to the inside of their legs, to put in the coal stove at night. Caution was required, for at least one of them was searched every time they left and entered the camp, often having to remove one or both boots, and to stand there in the numbing snow. If they were caught with anything on them it meant three days without food.

As the weeks went by, Wladek's leg started to become very stiff and painful. He longed for the coldest days, when the temperature went down to forty below zero, and outside work was called off, even though the lost day would have to be made up on a free Sunday when they were normally allowed to lie on their bunks all day.

One evening when Wladek had been hauling logs across the waste, his leg began to throb unmercifully. When he looked at the scar caused by the Smolenski, he found that it had become puffy and shiny. That night, he showed the wound to a guard, who ordered him to report to the camp doctor before first light in the morning. Wladek sat up all night with his leg nearly touching the stove, surrounded by wet boots, but the heat was so feeble that it couldn't ease the pain.

The next morning Wladek rose an hour earlier than usual. If you had not seen the doctor before work was due to start, then you missed him until the next day. Wladek couldn't face another day of such intense pain. He reported to the doctor, giving his name and number. Pierre Dubien was a sympathetic old man, bald-headed, with a pronounced stoop, and Wladek thought he looked even older than the Baron. He inspected Wladek's leg without speaking.

'Will the wound be all right, doctor?' asked Wladek.

'You speak Russian?'

'Yes, sir.'

'Although you will always limp, young man, your leg will be good again. But good for what? A life here dragging wood.'

'No, doctor, I intend to escape and get back to Poland,' said Wladek.

The doctor looked sharply at him. 'Keep your voice down, stupid boy.

You must realize by now that escape is impossible. I have been in captivity fifteen years, and not a day has passed that I have not thought of escape. There is no way; no one has ever escaped and lived, and even to talk of it means ten days in the punishment cell, and there they feed you every third day and light the stove only to melt the ice off the walls. If you come out of that place alive, you can consider yourself lucky.'

'I will escape, I will, I will,' said Wladek, staring at the old man.

The doctor looked into Wladek's eyes and smiled. 'My friend, never mention escape again or they may kill you. Go back to work, keep your leg exercised and report to me first thing every morning.'

Wladek returned to the forest and to the chopping of wood, but found that he could not drag the logs more than a few feet, and that the pain was so intense he believed his leg might fall off. When he returned the next morning, the doctor examined the leg more carefully.

'Worse, if anything,' he said. 'How old are you, boy?'

'I think I am thirteen,' said Wladek. 'What year is it?'

'Nineteen hundred and nineteen,' replied the doctor.

'Yes, thirteen. How old are you?' asked Wladek.

The old man looked down into the young boy's blue eyes, surprised by the question.

'Thirty-eight,' he said quietly.

'God help me,' said Wladek.

'You will look like this when you have been a prisoner for fifteen years, my boy,' said the doctor matter of factly.

'Why are you here at all?' said Wladek. 'Why haven't they let you go after all this time?'

'I was taken prisoner in Moscow in 1904, soon after I had qualified as a doctor and I was working in the French Embassy. They said I was a spy and put me in a Moscow jail. I thought that was bad until after the Revolution when they sent me to this hell-hole. Even the French have now forgotten that I exist. Few have been known to complete their sentence at camp Two-O-One so I must die here, like everyone else, and it can't be too soon.'

'No, you must not give up hope, doctor.'

'Hope? I gave up hope for myself a long time ago, perhaps I shall not give it up for you, but always remember never to mention that hope to anyone; there are prisoners here who trade in loose tongues, when their reward can be nothing more than an extra piece of bread or perhaps a blanket. Now Wladek, I am going to put you on kitchen duty for a month and you must continue to report to me every morning. It is the only chance that you have of not losing that leg, and I do not relish being the man who has to cut it off. We don't exactly have the latest surgical instruments here,' he added, staring at a large carving knife.

Wladek shuddered.

Doctor Dubien wrote out Wladek's name on a slip of paper. Next morning, Wladek reported to the kitchens, where he cleaned the plates in freezing water and helped to prepare food that required no refrigeration. After carrying logs all day, he found it a welcome change: extra fish soup, thick black bread with shredded nettles, and the chance to stay inside and keep warm. On one occasion he even shared half an egg with the cook, although neither of them could be sure what fowl had laid it. Wladek's leg mended slowly, leaving him with a pronounced limp. There was little Doctor Dubien could do in the absence of any real medical supplies except keep an eye on his progress. As the days went by, the doctor began to befriend Wladek and even to believe in his youthful hope for the future. They would converse in a different language each morning, but the old man most enjoyed speaking in French, his native tongue.

'In seven days time, Wladek, you will have to return to forest duty; the guards will inspect your leg and I will not be able to keep you in the kitchens any longer. So listen carefully, for I have decided upon a plan for your escape.'

'Together, doctor,' said Wladek. 'Together.'

'No, only you. I am too old for such a long journey, and although I have dreamed about escape for over fifteen years, I would only hold you up. It will be enough for me to know someone else has achieved it, and you are the first person I've ever met who has convinced me that he might succeed.'

Wladek sat on the floor in silence listening to the doctor's plan.

'I have, over the last fifteen years, saved two hundred rubles – you don't exactly get overtime as a Russian prisoner.' Wladek tried to laugh at the camp's oldest joke. 'I keep the money hidden in a drug bottle, four fifty-ruble notes. When the time comes for you to leave, the money must be sewn into your clothes. I will have already done this for you.'

'What clothes?' asked Wladek.

'I have a suit and a shirt I bribed from a guard twelve years ago when I still believed in escape. Not exactly the latest fashion, but they will serve your purpose.'

Fifteen years to scrape together two hundred rubles, a shirt and a suit, and the doctor was willing to sacrifice them to Wladek in a moment. Wladek never again in his life experienced such an act of selflessness.

'Next Thursday will be your only chance,' the doctor continued. 'New prisoners arrive by train at Irkutsk, and the guards always take four people from the kitchen to organize the food truck for the new arrivals. I have already arranged with the senior cook' – he laughed at the word – 'that in exchange for some drugs you will find yourself on the kitchen truck. It was not too hard. No one exactly wants to make the trip there and back – but you will only be making the journey there.'

Wladek was still listening intently.

'When you reach the station, wait until the prisoners' train arrives. Once they are all on the platform, cross the line and get yourself onto the train going to Moscow, which cannot leave until the prisoners' train comes in, as there is only one track outside the station. You must pray that with hundreds of new prisoners milling around the guards will not notice you disappear. From then on you're on your own. Remember if they do spot you, they will shoot you on sight without a second thought. There is only one last thing I can do for you. Fifteen years ago when I was brought here, I drew a map from memory of the route from Moscow to Turkey. It may not be totally accurate any longer, but it should be adequate for your purpose. Be sure to check that the Russians haven't taken over Turkey as well. God knows what they have been up to recently. They may even control France for all I know.'

The doctor walked over to the drug cabinet and took out a large bottle which looked as if it was full of a brown substance. He unscrewed the top and took out an old piece of parchment. The black ink had faded over the years. It was marked October 1904. It showed a route from Moscow to Odessa, and from Odessa to Turkey, seventeen hundred miles to freedom.

'Come to me every morning this week, and we will go over the plan again and again. If you fail, it must not be from lack of preparation.'

Wladek stayed awake each night, gazing at the wolves' sun through the window, rehearsing what he would do in any given situation, preparing himself for every eventuality. In the morning he would go over the plan again and again with the doctor. On the Wednesday evening before Wladek was to try the escape, the doctor folded the map into eight, placed it with the four fifty-ruble notes in a small package and sewed the package into a sleeve of the suit. Wladek took off his clothes, put on the suit and then replaced the prison uniform on top of it. As he put on the uniform again, the doctor's eye caught the Baron's band of silver which Wladek, ever since he had been issued his prison uniform, had always kept above his elbow for fear the guards would spot his only treasure and steal it.

'What's that?' he asked. 'It's quite magnificent.'

'A gift from my father,' said Wladek. 'May I give it to you to show my thanks?' He slipped the band off his wrist and handed it to the doctor.

The doctor stared at the silver band for several moments and bowed his head. 'Never,' he said. 'This can only belong to one person.' He stared silently at the boy. 'Your father must have been a great man.'

The doctor placed the band back on Wladek's wrist and shook him warmly by the hand.

'Good luck, Wladek. I hope we never meet again.'

They embraced and Wladek parted for what he prayed was his last night in the prison hut. He was unable to sleep at all that night for fear one of the guards would discover the suit under his prison clothes. When the morning bell sounded, he was already dressed and he made sure that he was not late reporting to the kitchen. The senior prisoner in the kitchen pushed Wladek forward when the guards came for the truck detail. The team chosen were four in all and Wladek was by far the youngest.

'Why this one?' asked the guard, pointing to Wladek. 'He has been at the camp for less than a year.'

Wladek's heart stopped and he went cold all over. The doctor's plan was going to fail; and there would not be another batch of prisoners coming to the camp for at least three months. By then he would no longer be in the kitchens.

'He's an excellent cook,' said the senior prisoner. 'Trained in the castle of a baron. Only the best for the guards.'

'Ah,' said the guard, greed overcoming suspicion. 'Hurry up, then.'

The four of them ran to the truck, and the convoy started.

The journey was again slow and arduous, but at least he was not walking this time, nor, being summer, was it unbearably cold. Wladek worked hard on preparing the food and, as he had no desire to be noticed, hardly spoke to anyone for the entire journey other than Stanislaw, the chief cook.

When they eventually reached Irkutsk, the drive had taken nearly sixteen days. The train waiting to go to Moscow was already standing in the station. It had been there for several hours, but was unable to continue its journey until the train bringing the new prisoners had arrived. Wladek sat on the side of the platform with the others from the field kitchen, three of them with no interest or purpose in anything around them, dulled by the experience, but one of them intent on every move, studying the train on the other side of the platform carefully. There were several open entrances and Wladek quickly selected the one he would use when his moment came.

'Are you going to try an escape?' asked Stanislaw suddenly.

Wladek began to sweat but did not answer.

Stanislaw stared at him. 'You *are*?'

Still Wladek said nothing.

The old cook stared at the thirteen-year-old boy. He nodded his head up and down in agreement. If he had had a tail, it would have wagged.

'Good luck. I'll make sure they don't realize you're missing for at least two days.'

Stanislaw touched his arm and Wladek caught sight of the prisoners' train in the distance, slowly inching its way towards them. He tensed in anticipation, his heart pounding, his eyes following the movement of every soldier. He waited for the incoming train to come to a halt and watched the tired prisoners pile out onto the platform, hundreds of them, anonymous men with only a past. When the station was a chaos of people and the guards were fully occupied, Wladek ran under the carriage and jumped onto the other train. No one showed any interest as he went into a lavatory at the end of the carriage. He locked himself in and waited and prayed, every moment expecting someone to knock on the door. It seemed a lifetime to Wladek before the train began to move out of the station. It was, in fact, seventeen minutes.

'At last, at last,' he said out loud. He looked through the little window and watched the station growing smaller and smaller in the distance, a mass of new prisoners being hitched up to the chains, ready for the journey to camp 201, the guards laughing as they locked them in. How many would reach the camp alive? How many would be fed to the wolves? How long before they missed him?

Wladek sat in the lavatory for several more minutes, terrified to move, not sure what he ought to do next. Suddenly there was a banging on the door. Wladek thought quickly – the guard, the ticket collector, a soldier – a succession of images flashed through his mind, each one more frightening than the last. He needed to use the lavatory for the first time. The banging persisted.

'Come on, come on,' said a man in coarse Russian.

Wladek had little choice. If it was a soldier, there was no way out, a dwarf could not have squeezed through the little window. If it wasn't a soldier, he would only draw attention to himself by staying there. He took off his prison clothes, made them into as small a bundle as possible, and threw them out of the window. Then he removed a soft hat from the pocket of his suit to cover his shaved head, and opened the door. An agitated man rushed in, pulling down his trousers even before Wladek had left.

Once in the corridor, Wladek felt isolated and terrifyingly conspicuous in his out-of-date suit, an apple placed on a pile of oranges. He immediately went in search of another lavatory. When he found one that was unoccupied, he locked himself in and quickly undid the stitches in his suit, extracting one of the four fifty-ruble notes. He replaced the other three and returned to the corridor. He looked for the most crowded carriage he could find and hid himself in a corner. Some men were playing pitch-and-toss in the middle of the carriage for a few rubles to while away the time. Wladek had always beaten Leon when they had played in the castle, and he would have liked to have joined the contestants, but he feared winning and drawing attention to himself. The game went on for a long time and Wladek began to remember the stratagems. The temptation to risk his two hundred rubles was almost irresistible.

One of the gamblers, who had parted with a considerable amount of his money, retired in disgust and sat down by Wladek, swearing.

'The luck wasn't with you,' said Wladek, wanting to hear the sound of his own voice.

'Ah, it's not luck,' the gambler replied. 'Most days I could beat that lot of peasants, but I have run out of rubles.'

'Do you want to sell your coat?' asked Wladek.

The gambler was one of the few passengers in the carriage wearing a good, old, thick bearskin coat. He stared at the youth.

'Looking at that suit I'd say you couldn't afford it, boy.' Wladek could tell from the man's voice that he hoped he could. 'I would want seventy-five rubles.'

'I'll give you forty,' said Wladek.

'Sixty,' said the gambler.

'Fifty,' said Wladek.

'No. Sixty is the least I'd let it go for; it cost over a hundred,' said the gambler.

'A long time ago,' said Wladek, as he considered the implications of taking extra money from inside the lining of his coat in order to secure the full amount needed. He decided against doing so as it would only draw further attention to himself; he would have to wait for another opportunity. Wladek was not willing to show he could not afford the coat, and he touched the collar of the garment and said, with considerable disdain, 'You paid too much for it, my friend; fifty rubles, not a kopeck more.' Wladek rose as if to leave.

'Wait, wait,' said the gambler. 'I'll let you have it for fifty.'

Wladek took the fifty rubles out of his pocket and the gambler took off his coat and exchanged it for the grimy red note. The coat was far too big for Wladek, nearly touching the ground, but it was exactly what he needed to cover his conspicuous suit. For a few moments, he watched the gambler, back in the game, once again losing. From his new tutor he had learned two things: never to gamble unless the odds are tipped in your favour by superior knowledge or skill, and always to be willing to walk away from a deal when you have reached your limit.

Wladek left the carriage, feeling a little safer under his new-old coat. He started to examine the layout of the train with a little more confidence. The carriages seemed to be in two classes; general ones where passengers stood or sat on the wooden boards and special ones where they could sit on upholstered seats. Wladek found that all the carriages were packed, with but one exception, a sitting carriage with a solitary woman in it. She was middle-aged, as far as Wladek could tell, and dressed a little more smartly with a little more flesh on her bones than most of the other passengers on the train. She wore a dark blue dress and a scarf over her head. She smiled at Wladek as he stood staring at her, and this gesture gave him the confidence to enter the carriage.

'May I sit down?'

'Please do,' said the woman, looking at him carefully.

Wladek did not speak again, but studied the woman and the contents of the carriage. She had a sallow skin covered with tired lines, a little over-weight – the little bit you could be on Russian food. Her short black hair and brown eyes suggested that she once might have been quite attractive. She had two large cloth bags on the rack and a small valise by her side. Despite the danger of his position Wladek was suddenly aware of feeling desperately tired. He was wondering if he dared to sleep when the woman spoke.

'Where are you travelling?'

The question took Wladek by surprise and he tried to think quickly. 'Moscow,' he said, holding his breath.

'So am I,' she replied.

Wladek was already regretting the isolation of the carriage and the information he had given. Don't talk to anyone, the doctor had warned him; remember, trust nobody.

To his relief the woman asked no more questions. As he began to regain his lost confidence, the ticket collector arrived. Wladek started to sweat, despite the temperature being minus twenty degrees. The collector took the woman's ticket, tore it, gave it back to her, and then turned to Wladek.

'Ticket, comrade,' was all he said in a slow, monotonous tone.

Wladek was speechless, and started thumbing around in his coat pocket.

'He's my son,' said the woman firmly.

The ticket collector looked back at the woman, once more at Wladek, and then he bowed to the woman and left the carriage without another word.

Wladek stared at her. 'Thank you,' he breathed, not quite sure what else he could say.

'I watched you come from under the prisoners' train,' the woman remarked quietly. Wladek felt sick. 'But I shall not give you away. I have a young cousin in one of those terrible camps, and all of us fear that one day we might end up there. What do you have on under your coat?'

Wladek weighed the relative merits of dashing out of the carriage and unfastening his coat. If he dashed out of the carriage there was no escape. He unfastened his coat.

'Not as bad as I had feared,' she said. 'What did you do with your prison uniform?'

'Threw it out of the window.'

'Let's hope they don't find it before you reach Moscow.'

Wladek said nothing.

'Do you have anywhere to stay in Moscow?'

He thought again of the doctor's advice to trust nobody, but he had to trust her.

'I have nowhere to go.'

'Then you can stay with me until you find somewhere to live. My husband,' she explained, 'is the station master in Moscow, and this carriage is for government officials only. If you ever make that mistake again, you will be taking the train back to Irkutsk.'

Wladek swallowed. 'Should I leave now?'

'No, not now that the ticket collector has seen you. You will be safe with me for the time being. Do you have any identity papers?'

'No. What are they?'

'Since the Revolution every Russian citizen must have identity papers to show who he is, where he lives and where he works, otherwise he ends up in jail until he can produce them, and as he can never produce them once in jail, he stays there for ever,' she added matter of factly. 'You will have to stick by me once we reach Moscow, and be sure you don't open your mouth.'

'You are being very kind to me,' said Wladek suspiciously.

'Now the Tsar is dead, none of us is safe. I was lucky to be married to the right man,' she added, 'but there is not a citizen in Russia, including government officials, who does not live in constant fear of arrest and the camps. What is your name?'

'Wladek.'

'Good, now you sleep, Wladek, because you look exhausted, the journey is long and you are not safe yet.'

Wladek slept.

When he woke, several hours had passed, and it was now dark outside. He stared at his protectress, and she smiled. Wladek returned her smile, praying that she could be trusted not to tell the officials who he was – or had she already done so? She produced some food from one of her bundles and Wladek ate the offering silently. When they reached the next station, nearly all the passengers got out, some of them permanently, but most to seek what little refreshment was available or to stretch their stiff limbs.

The middle-aged woman rose, looked at Wladek. 'Follow me,' she said.

He stood up and followed her onto the platform. Was he about to be given up? She put out her hand, and he took it as any thirteen-year-old child accompanying his mother would do. She walked towards a lavatory marked for women only. Wladek hesitated. She insisted, and once inside she told Wladek to take off his clothes. He obeyed her unquestioningly as he hadn't anyone since the death of the Baron. While he undressed she turned on the solitary tap, which with reluctance yielded a trickle of cold brownish water. She was disgusted. But to Wladek, it was a vast improvement on the camp water. The woman started to bathe his wounds with a wet rag and attempted hopelessly to wash him. She winced when she saw the scar on his leg. Wladek didn't murmur from the pain that came with each touch, gentle as she tried to be.

'When we get you home, I'll make a better job of those wounds,' she said, 'but that will have to do for now.'

Then she saw the silver band, studied the inscription and looked carefully at Wladek. 'Is that yours?' she asked. 'Who did you steal it from?'

Wladek looked offended. 'I didn't steal it. My father gave it to me before he died.'

She stared at him again, and a different look came into her eyes. Was it fear or respect? She bowed her head. 'Be careful, Wladek, men would kill for such a valuable prize.'

He nodded his agreement and started to dress quickly. They returned to their carriage. A delay of an hour at a station was not unusual and when the train started lurching forward, Wladek was glad to feel the wheels clattering underneath him again. The train took twelve and a half days to reach Moscow. Whenever a new ticket collector appeared, they went through the same routine, Wladek unconvincingly trying to look innocent and young. The woman a convincing mother. The ticket collectors always bowed respectfully to the middle-aged lady, and Wladek began to think that station masters must be very important in Russia.

By the time they completed the one-thousand-mile journey to Moscow, Wladek had put his trust completely in the middle-aged lady and was looking forward to seeing her house. It was early afternoon when the train came to its final halt and despite everything Wladek had been through, he had never visited a big city, let alone the capital of all the Russias. He was terrified, once again tasting the fear of the unknown. So many people all rushing around in different directions. The middle-aged lady sensed his apprehension.

'Follow me, do not speak, and whatever you do don't take your cap off.'

Wladek took her bags down from the rack, pulled his cap over his head – now covered in a black stubble – down to his ears and followed her out onto the platform. A throng of people at the barrier were waiting to go through a tiny exit, which caused a holdup as everyone had to show their identification papers to the guard. As they approached the barrier, Wladek could hear his heart beating like a soldier's drum, but when their turn came the fear was over in a moment. The guard only glanced at the woman's documents.

'Comrade,' he said, and saluted. He looked at Wladek.

'My son,' she explained.

'Of course, comrade.' He saluted again.

Wladek was in Moscow.

Despite the trust he had placed in his new-found companion, his first instinct was to run but as one hundred and fifty rubles was hardly enough to live on, he decided for the time being to stay put. He could always run at some later time. A horse and cart was waiting at the station and took the woman and her new son home. The station master was not there when they arrived, so the woman immediately set about making up the spare bed for Wladek. Then she poured water, heated on a stove, into a large tin tub and told him to get in. It was the first bath he had had in over four years, unless he counted the dip in the stream. She heated some more water and reintroduced him to soap, scrubbing his back, the only part of his body with unbroken skin. The water began to change colour and after twenty minutes, it was black. Once Wladek was dry, the woman put some ointment on his

arms and legs, and bandaged the parts of his body that looked particularly
fierce. She stared at his one nipple. He dressed quickly and then joined her
in the kitchen. She had already prepared a bowl of hot soup and some beans.
Wladek ate the veritable feast hungrily. Neither of them spoke. When he had
finished the meal, she suggested that it might be wise for him to go to bed
and rest.

'I do not want my husband to see you before I have told him why you
are here,' she explained. 'Would you like to stay with us, Wladek, if my
husband agrees?'

Wladek nodded thankfully.

'Then off you go to bed,' she said.

Wladek obeyed and prayed that her husband would allow him to live with
them. He undressed slowly and climbed onto the bed. He was too clean, the
sheets were too clean, the mattress was too soft, and he threw the pillow on
the floor, but he was so tired that he slept despite the comfort of the bed.
He was woken from his deep sleep some hours later by the sound of raised
voices coming from the kitchen. He could not tell how long he had slept.
It was already dark outside as he crept off the bed, walked to the door,
eased it open and listened to the conversation taking place in the kitchen
below.

'You stupid woman.' Wladek heard a piping voice. 'Do you not understand
what would have happened if you had been caught? It would have been you
who would have been sent to the camps.'

'But if you had seen him, Piotr, like a hunted animal.'

'So you decided to turn us into hunted animals,' said the male voice. 'Has
anyone else seen him?'

'No,' said the woman, 'I don't think so.'

'Thank God for that. He must go immediately before anyone knows he's
here, it's our only hope.'

'But go where, Piotr? He is lost, and has no one,' Wladek's protectress
pleaded. 'And I have always wanted a son.'

'I do not care what you want or where he goes, he is not our responsibility
and we must be quickly rid of him.'

'But Piotr, I think he is royal, I think his father was a Baron. He wears
a silver band around his wrist and inscribed on it are the words ...'

'That only makes it worse. You know what our new leaders have decreed.
No tsars, no royalty, no privileges. We would not even have to bother to go
to the camp, the authorities would just shoot us.'

'We have always wanted a son, Piotr. Can we not take this one risk in our
lives?'

'With your life, perhaps, but not mine. I say he must go and go now.'

Wladek did not need to listen to any more of their conversation. Deciding
that the only way he could help his benefactress would be to disappear
without trace into the night, he dressed quickly and stared at the slept-in
bed, hoping it would not be four more years before he saw another one. He
was unlatching the window when the door was flung open and into the room
came the station master, a tiny man, no taller than Wladek, with a large
stomach and an almost bald head covered in long strands of grey hair. He
wore rimless spectacles, which had produced little red semicircles under each

eye. The man carried a paraffin lamp. He stood, staring at Wladek. Wladek
stared defiantly back.

'Come downstairs,' he commanded.

Wladek followed him reluctantly to the kitchen. The woman was sitting
at the table crying.

'Now listen boy,' he said.

'His name is Wladek,' the woman interjected.

'Now listen, boy,' he repeated. 'You are trouble, and I want you out of
here and as far away as possible. I'll tell you what I am going to do to help
you.'

Help? Wladek gazed at him stonily.

'I am going to give you a train ticket. Where do you want to go?'

'Odessa,' said Wladek, ignorant of where it was or how much it would
cost, knowing only that it was the next city on the doctor's map to freedom.

'Odessa, the mother of crime – an appropriate destination,' sneered the
station master. 'You can only be among your own kind and come to harm
there.'

'Then let him stay with us, Piotr. I will take care of him, I will ...'

'No, never. I would rather pay the bastard.'

'But how can he hope to get past the authorities?' the woman pleaded.

'I will have to issue him a working pass for Odessa.' He turned his head
towards Wladek. 'Once you are on that train, boy, if I see or hear of you
again in Moscow, I will have you arrested on sight and thrown into the
nearest jail. You will then be back in that prison camp as fast as the train
can get you there if they don't shoot you first.'

He stared at the clock on the kitchen mantlepiece: five after eleven. He
turned to his wife. 'There is a train that leaves for Odessa at midnight. I will
take him to the station myself. I want to be sure he leaves Moscow. Have
you any baggage, boy?'

Wladek was about to say no, when the woman said, 'Yes, I will go and
fetch it.'

Wladek and the station master stood, staring at each other with mutual
contempt. The woman was away for a long time. The grandfather clock
struck once in her absence. Still neither spoke, and the station master's eyes
never left Wladek. When his wife returned, she was carrying a large brown
paper parcel wrapped up with string. Wladek stared at it and began to
protest, but as their eyes met, he saw such fear in hers that he only just got
out the words, 'Thank you.'

'Eat this,' she said, thrusting her bowl of cold soup towards him.

He obeyed, although his shrunken stomach was now overfull, gulping
down the soup as quickly as possible, not wanting her to be in any more
trouble.

'Animal,' the man said.

Wladek looked at him, hatred in his eyes. He felt pity for the woman,
bound to such a man for life.

'Come, boy, it's time to leave,' the station master said. 'We don't want
you to miss your train, do we?'

Wladek followed the man out of the kitchen. He hesitated as he passed
the woman and touched her hand, feeling the response. Nothing was said;

no words would have been adequate. The station master and the refugee crept through the streets of Moscow, hiding in the shadows, until they reached the station. The station master obtained a one-way ticket to Odessa and gave the little red slip of paper to Wladek.

'My pass?' said Wladek defiantly.

From his inside pocket the man drew out an official looking form, signed it hurriedly, and handed it over furtively to Wladek. The station master's eyes kept looking all around him for any possible danger. Wladek had seen those eyes so many times during the past four years: the eyes of a coward.

'Never let me see or hear of you again,' he said, the voice of a bully.

Wladek had also heard that voice many times before in the last four years. He looked up, wanting to say something, but the station master had already retreated into the shadows of the night where he belonged. He looked at the eyes of the people who hurried past him. The same eyes, the same fear; was anyone in the world free? Wladek gathered the brown paper parcel under his arm, checked his hat, and walked towards the barrier. This time he felt more confident, showing his pass to the guard; he was ushered through without comment. He climbed on board the train. It had been a short visit to Moscow, and he would never see the city again in his life, though he would always remember the kindness of the woman, the station master's wife, Comrade . . . He didn't even know her name.

.   .   .

Wladek stayed in the general class standing carriages for his journey. Odessa looked less distant from Moscow than Irkutsk, about a thumb's length on the doctor's sketch, eight hundred and fifty miles in reality. While Wladek was studying his rudimentary map, he became distracted by another game of pitch-and-toss which was taking place in the carriage. He folded the parchment, replaced it safely in the lining of his suit and began taking a closer interest in the game. He noticed that one of the gamblers was winning consistently, even when the odds were stacked against him. Wladek watched the man more carefully and soon realized that he was cheating.

He moved to the other side of the carriage to make sure he could still spot the man cheating when facing him, but he couldn't. He edged forward and made a place for himself in the circle of gamblers. Every time the cheat had lost twice in a row, Wladek backed him with one ruble, doubling his stake until he won. The cheat was either flattered or considered he would be wise to remain silent about Wladek's luck, because he never once even glanced in his direction. By the time they reached the next station, Wladek had won fourteen rubles, two of which he used to buy himself an apple and a cup of hot soup. He had won enough to last the entire journey to Odessa and, pleased with the thought that he could win even more rubles with his new safe system, he silently thanked the unknown gambler and climbed back onto the train ready to resume the strategy. As his foot touched the top step, he was knocked flying into a corner. His arm was jerked painfully behind his back and his face was pushed hard against the carriage wall. His nose began to bleed and he could feel the point of a knife touching the lobe of his ear.

'Do you hear me, boy?'

'Yes,' said Wladek, petrified.

'If you go back to my carriage again, I take this ear right off, then you won't be able to hear me, will you?'

'No, sir,' said Wladek.

Wladek felt the point of the knife breaking the surface of the skin behind his ear and blood began trickling down his neck.

'Let that be a warning to you, boy.'

A knee suddenly came up into his kidneys with as much force as the gambler could muster. Wladek collapsed to the ground. A hand rummaged into his coat pockets and the recently acquired rubles were removed.

'Mine, I think,' the voice said.

Blood was now coming out of Wladek's nose and from behind his ear. When he summoned up the courage to look up from the corner of the corridor, it was empty, and there was no sign of the gambler. Wladek tried to get to his feet, but his body refused to obey the order from his brain, so he remained slumped in the corner for several minutes. Eventually when he was able to rise, he walked slowly to the other end of the train, as far away from the gambler's carriage as possible, his limp grotesquely exaggerated. He hid in a carriage occupied mostly by women and children, and fell into a deep sleep.

At the next stop, Wladek didn't leave the train. He undid his little parcel and started to investigate. Apples, bread, nuts, two shirts, a pair of trousers and even shoes were contained in that brown-papered treasure trove. What a woman, what a husband.

He ate, he slept, he dreamed. And finally, after six nights and five days, the train chugged into the terminal at Odessa. The same check at the ticket barrier, but the guard hardly gave Wladek a second look. This time his papers were all in order, but now he was on his own. He still had one hundred and fifty rubles in the lining of his suit, and no intention of wasting any of them.

Wladek spent the rest of the day walking around the town trying to familiarize himself with its geography, but he found he was continually distracted by sights he had never seen before: big town houses, shops with windows, hawkers selling their colourful trinkets on the street, gaslights, and even a monkey on a stick. Wladek walked on until he reached the harbour and stopped to stare at the open sea beyond it. Yes, there it was – what the Baron had called an ocean. He gazed into the blue expanse longingly: that way was freedom and escape from Russia. The city must have seen its fair share of fighting: burnt-out houses and squalor were all too evident, grotesque in the mild, flower-scented sea air. Wladek wondered whether the city was still at war. There was no one he could ask. As the sun disappeared behind the high buildings, he began to look for somewhere to spend the night. Wladek took a side road and kept walking. He must have looked a strange sight with his skin coat dragging along the ground and the brown paper parcel under his arm. Nothing looked safe to him until he came across a railway siding in which a solitary old carriage stood in isolation. He stared into it cautiously; darkness and silence: no one was there. He threw his paper parcel into the carriage, raised his tired body up onto the boards, crawled into a corner and lay down to sleep. As his head touched the wooden floor, a body leaped on top of him and two hands were quickly around his throat. He could barely breathe.

'Who are you?' hissed a boy who, in the darkness, sounded no older than himself.

'Wladek Koskiewicz.'

'Where do you come from?'

'Moscow.' Slonim had been on the tip of Wladek's tongue.

'Well, you're not sleeping in my carriage, Muscovite,' said the voice.

'Sorry,' said Wladek. 'I didn't know.'

'Got any money?' His thumbs pressed into Wladek's throat.

'A little,' said Wladek.

'How much?'

'Seven rubles.'

'Hand it over.'

Wladek rummaged in the pocket of his overcoat, while the boy also pushed one hand firmly into it, releasing the pressure on Wladek's throat.

In one movement, Wladek brought up his knee with every ounce of force he could muster into the boy's crotch. His attacker flew back in agony, clutching his testicles. Wladek leaped on him, hitting him in places the boy would never have thought of. The rules had suddenly changed. He was no competition for Wladek; sleeping in a derelict carriage was five-star luxury compared to the dungeons and a Russian labour camp.

Wladek stopped only when his adversary was pinned to the carriage floor, helpless. The boy pleaded with Wladek.

'Go to the far end of the carriage and stay there,' said Wladek. 'If you so much as move a muscle, I'll kill you.'

'Yes, yes,' said the boy, scrambling away.

Wladek heard him hit the far end of the carriage. He sat still and listened for a few moments – no movement – then he lowered his head once more onto the floor, and in moments he was sleeping soundly.

When he awoke, the sun was already shining through the slits between the boards of the carriage. He turned over slowly and studied his adversary of the previous night for the first time. He was lying in a foetal position, still asleep at the other end of the carriage.

'Come here,' commanded Wladek.

The boy woke slowly.

'Come here,' repeated Wladek, a little more loudly.

The boy obeyed immediately. It was the first chance Wladek had had to look at him properly. They were about the same age, but the boy was a clear foot taller with a younger-looking face and scruffy fair hair. His general appearance suggested that talk of soap and water would have been treated as an insult.

'First things first,' said Wladek. 'How does one get something to eat here?'

'Follow me,' said the boy, leaping out of the carriage. Wladek limped after him and followed the boy up the hill into the town where the morning market was being set up. He had not seen so much wholesome food since those magnificent dinners with the Baron. Row upon row of stalls with fruit, vegetables, greens, and even his favourite nuts. The boy could see Wladek was overwhelmed by the sight.

'Now I'll tell you what we do,' the boy said, sounding confident for the first time. 'I will go over to the corner stall and steal an orange, and then make a run for it. You will shout at the top of your voice, "Stop thief". The stallkeeper will chase me and when he does, you move in and fill your pockets. Don't be greedy; enough for one meal. Then you return here. Got it?'

'Yes, I think so,' said Wladek.

'Let's see if you're up to it, Muscovite.' The boy looked at him, snarled, and was gone. Wladek watched him in admiration as he swaggered to the corner of the first market stall, removed an orange from the top of a pyramid, made some short unheard remark to the stallkeeper and started to run slowly. He glanced back at Wladek, who had entirely forgotten to shout 'Stop thief', but the stall owner looked up and immediately began to chase the boy. While everyone's eyes were on Wladek's accomplice, he moved in quickly and managed to take three oranges, an apple and a potato, and put them in the large pockets of his overcoat. When the stallkeeper looked as if he were about to catch his accomplice, the boy lobbed the orange back at him. The man stopped to pick it up and swore at him, waving his fist, complaining vociferously to the other merchants as he returned to his stall.

Wladek was shaking with mirth as he took in the scene when a hand was placed firmly on his shoulder. He turned round in the horror of having been caught.

'Did you get anything, Muscovite, or are you only here as a sightseer?'

Wladek burst out laughing with relief and produced the three oranges, apple and potato. The boy joined in the laughter.

'What's your name?' said Wladek

'Stefan.'

'Let's do it again, Stefan.'

'Hold on, Muscovite, don't you start getting too clever. If we do *my* scheme again, we'll have to go to the other end of the market and wait for at least an hour. You're working with a professional now, but don't imagine you won't get caught occasionally.'

The two boys went quietly through to the other end of the market, Stefan walking with a swagger for which Wladek would have traded the three oranges, apple, potato and his one hundred and fifty rubles. They mingled with the morning shoppers and when Stefan decided the time was right, they repeated the trick twice. Satisfied with the results, they returned to the railway carriage to enjoy their captured spoils; six oranges, five apples, three potatoes, a pear, several varieties of nuts, and the special prize, a melon. In the past, Stefan had never had pockets big enough to hold one. Wladek's greatcoat took care of that.

'Not bad,' said Wladek, as he dug his teeth into a potato.

'Do you eat the skins as well?' asked Stefan, horrified.

'I've been places where the skins are a luxury,' replied Wladek.

Stefan looked at him with admiration.

'Next problem is how do we get some money?' said Wladek.

'You want everything in one day, don't you, o master?' said Stefan. 'Chain gang on the waterfront is the best bet, if you think you're up to some real work, Muscovite.'

'Show me,' said Wladek.

After they had eaten half the fruit and hidden the rest under the straw in the corner of the carriage, Stefan took Wladek down the steps to the harbour and showed him all the ships. Wladek couldn't believe his eyes. He had been told by the Baron of the great ships that crossed the high seas delivering their cargoes to foreign lands, but these were so much bigger than he had ever imagined, and they stood in a line as far as the eye could see.

Stefan interrupted his thoughts. 'See that one over there, the big green one; well, what you have to do is pick up a basket at the bottom of the gangplank, fill it with grain, climb up the ladder and then drop your load in the hold. You get a ruble for every four trips you make. But sure you can count, Muscovite, because the bastard in charge of the gang will swindle you as soon as look at you and pocket the money for himself.'

Stefan and Wladek spent the rest of the afternoon carrying grain up the ladder. They made twenty-six rubles between them. After a dinner of stolen nuts, bread, and an onion they hadn't intended to take, they slept happily in their carriage.

Wladek was the first to wake the next morning and Stefan found him studying his map.

'What's that?' asked Stefan.

'This is a route showing me how to get out of Russia.'

'What do you want to leave Russia for when you can stay here and team up with me?' said Stefan. 'We could be partners.'

'No, I must get to Turkey; there I will be a free man for the first time. Why don't you come with me, Stefan?'

'I could never leave Odessa. This is my home, the railway is where I live and these are the people I have known all my life. It's not good, but it might be worse in the place you call Turkey. But if that's what you want, I will help you to escape because I know how to find out where every ship has come from.'

'How do I discover which ship is going to Turkey?' asked Wladek.

'Easy. We'll get the information from One Tooth Joe at the end of the pier. You'll have to give him a ruble.'

'I'll bet he splits the money with you.'

'Fifty-fifty,' said Stefan. 'You're learning fast, Muscovite.' And with that he leaped out of the carriage.

Wladek followed him as he ran swiftly between the carriages, again conscious of how easily other boys moved, and how he limped. When they reached the end of the pier, Stefan took him into a small room full of dust-covered books and old timetables. Wladek couldn't see anyone there, but then he heard a voice from behind a large pile of books saying. 'What do you want, urchin? I don't have time to waste on you.'

'Some information for my travelling companion, Joe. When is the next luxury cruise to Turkey?'

'Money up front,' said an old man whose head appeared from behind the books, a lined weatherbeaten face wearing a seaman's cap. His black eyes were taking in Wladek.

'Used to be a great sea dog,' said Stefan in a whisper loud enough for Joe to hear.

'None of your cheek, boy. Where is the ruble?'

'My friend carries my purse,' said Stefan. 'Show him the ruble, Wladek.'

Wladek pulled out a coin. Joe bit it with his one remaining tooth, shuffled over to the bookcase and pulled out a large green timetable. Dust flew everywhere. He started coughing as he thumbed through the dirty pages, moving his short, stubby, rope-worn finger down the long columns of names.

'Next Thursday the *Renaska* is coming in to pick up coal, probably will leave on Saturday. If the ship can load quickly enough, she may sail on the Friday night and save the berthing tariffs. She'll dock on berth seventeen.'

'Thanks, One Tooth,' said Stefan. 'I'll see if I can bring along any more of my wealthy associates in the future.'

One Tooth Joe raised his fist cursing, as Stefan and Wladek ran out onto the wharf.

For the next three days the two boys stole food, loaded grain and slept. By the time the Turkish ship arrived on the following Thursday, Stefan had almost convinced Wladek that he should remain in Odessa. But Wladek's fear of the Russians outweighed the attraction of his new life with Stefan.

They stood on the quayside, staring at the new arrival docking at berth 17.

'How will I ever get on the ship?' asked Wladek.

'Simple,' said Stefan. 'We can join the chain gang tomorrow morning. I'll take the place behind you, and when the coal hold is nearly full, you can jump in and hide while I pick up your basket and walk on down the other side.'

'And collect my share of the money, no doubt,' said Wladek.

'Naturally,' said Stefan. 'There must be some financial reward for my superior intelligence or how could a man hope to sustain his belief in free enterprise?'

They joined the chain gang first thing the next morning and hauled coal up and down the gangplank until they were both ready to drop, but it still wasn't enough. The hold wasn't half full by nightfall. The two black boys slept soundly that night. The following morning, they started again and by mid-afternoon, when the hold was nearly full, Stefan kicked Wladek's ankle. 'Next time, Muscovite,' he said.

When they reached the top of the gangway, Wladek threw his coal in, dropped the basket on the deck, jumped over the side of the hold and landed on the coal, while Stefan picked up his basket and continued down the other side of the gangplank whistling.

'Goodbye, my friend,' he said, 'and good luck with the infidel Turks.'

Wladek pressed himself against a corner of the hold and watched the coal come pouring in beside him. The dust was everywhere, in his nose and mouth, in his lungs and eyes. With painful effort he avoided coughing for fear of being heard by one of the ship's crew. Just as he thought that he could no longer bear the air of the hold, and would have to return to Stefan and think of some other way of escape, he saw the doors slide shut above him. He coughed luxuriously.

After a few moments he felt something take a bite at his ankle. His blood went cold, realizing what it had to be. He looked down, trying to work out where it had come from. No sooner had he thrown a piece of coal at the monster and sent him scurrying away than another one came at him, then another and another. The braver ones went for his legs. They seemed to appear from nowhere. Black, large, and hungry. It was the first time in his life that Wladek realized that rats had red eyes. He clambered to the top of the pile of coal and pulled open the hatch. The sunlight came flooding through and the rats disappeared back into their tunnels in the coal. He started to climb out, but the ship was already well clear of the quayside. He fell back into the hold, terrified. If the ship were forced to return and hand Wladek over, he knew it would mean a one-way journey back to camp 201 and the White Russians. He chose to stay with the black rats. As soon as Wladek closed the hatch, they came at him again. As fast as he could throw lumps of coal at the verminous creatures, a new one would appear from another angle. Every few moments Wladek had to open the hatch to let some light in, for light seemed to be the only ally that would frighten the black rodents away.

For two days and three nights Wladek waged a running battle with the rats without ever catching a moment of quiet sleep. When the ship finally reached the port of Constantinople and a deck-hand opened the hold, Wladek was black from his head to his knees with dirt, and red from his knees to his toes with blood. The deck-hand dragged him out. Wladek tried to stand up but collapsed in a heap on the deck.

. . .

When Wladek came to – he knew not where or how much later – he found himself on a bed in a small room with three men in long white coats who were studying him carefully, speaking a tongue he did not know. How many languages were there in the world? He looked at himself, still red and black, and when he tried to sit up, one of the white-coated men, the oldest of the three, with a thin, lined face and a goatee, pushed him back down. He addressed Wladek in the strange tongue. Wladek shook his head. He then tried Russian. Wladek again shook his head – that would be the quickest way back to where he had come. The next language the doctor tried was German, and Wladek realized that his command of the language was greater than his inquisitor's.

'You speak German?'

'Yes.'

'Ah, so you're not Russian, then?'

'No.'

'What were you doing in Russia?'

'Trying to escape.'

'Ah.' He then turned to his companions and seemed to report the conversation in his own tongue. They left the room.

A nurse came in and scrubbed him clean, taking little notice of his cries of anguish. She covered his legs in a thick, brown ointment and left him to sleep again. When Wladek awoke for the second time, he was quite alone. He lay staring at the white ceiling, considering his next move.

Still not sure of which country he was in, he climbed onto the window sill and stared out of the window. He could see a market place, not unlike the one in Odessa, except that the men wore long white robes and had darker skins. They also wore colourful hats that looked like small flower pots upside down, and sandals on their feet. The women were all in black and had even their faces covered except for their black eyes. Wladek watched the strange race in the market place bargaining for their daily food; that was one thing at least that seemed to be international.

He watched the scene for several minutes before he noticed that running down by the side of the building was a red iron ladder stretching all the way to the ground, not unlike the fire escape in his castle in Slonim. His castle. Who would believe him now? He climbed down from the window sill, walked cautiously to the door, opened it and peered into the corridor. Men and women were walking up and down, but none of them showed any interest in him. He closed the door gently, found his belongings in a cupboard in the corner of his room and dressed quickly. His clothes were still black with coal dust and felt gritty on his clean skin. Back to the window sill. The window opened easily. He gripped the fire escape, swung out of the window and started to climb down towards freedom. The first thing that hit him was the heat. He wished he was no longer wearing the heavy overcoat.

Once he touched the ground Wladek tried to run, but his legs were so weak and painful that he could only walk slowly. How he wished he could rid himself of that limp. He did not look back at the hospital until he was lost in the throng of the crowd in the market place.

Wladek stared at the tempting food on the stalls and decided to buy an orange and some nuts. He went to the lining in his suit; surely the money had been under his right arm? Yes it had, but it was no longer there, and far worse, the silver band had also gone. The men in the white coats had stolen his possessions. He considered going back to the hospital to retrieve the lost heirloom and decided against returning until he had had something to eat. Perhaps there was still some money in his pockets. He searched around in the large overcoat pocket and immediately found the three notes and some coins. They were all together with the doctor's map and the silver band. Wladek was overjoyed at the discovery. He slipped the silver band on, and pushed it above his elbow.

Wladek chose the largest orange he could see and a handful of nuts. The stallkeeper said something to him that he could not understand. Wladek felt the easiest way out of the language barrier was to hand over a fifty ruble note. The stallkeeper looked at it, laughed, and threw his arms in the sky

'Allah,' he cried, snatching back the nuts and the orange from Wladek and waving him away with his forefinger. Wladek walked off in despair; a different language meant different money, he supposed. In Russia he had been poor; here he was penniless. He would have to steal an orange; if he were caught, he would throw it back to the stallkeeper. Wladek walked to the other end of the market place in the same way as Stefan had done, but he couldn't imitate the swagger, and he didn't feel the same confidence. He chose the end stall and when he was sure no one was watching, he picked up an orange and started to run. Suddenly there was uproar. It seemed as if half the city were chasing him.

A big man jumped on the limping Wladek and threw him to the ground. Six or seven people seized hold of different parts of his body while a larger group thronged around as he was dragged back to the stall. A policeman awaited them. Notes were taken, and there was a shouted exchange between the stall owner and the policeman, each man's voice rising with each new statement. The policeman then turned to Wladek and shouted at him too, but Wladek could not understand a word. The policeman shrugged his shoulders and marched Wladek off by the ear. People continued to bawl at him. Some of them spat on him. When Wladek reached the police station, he was taken underground and thrown into a tiny cell, already occupied by twenty or thirty criminals; thugs, thieves or he knew not what. Wladek did not speak to them, and they showed no desire to talk to him. He remained with his back to a wall, cowering, quiet, terrified. For at least a day and a night, he was left there with no food or light. The smell of excreta made him vomit until there was nothing left in him. He never thought the day would come when the dungeons in Slonim would seem uncrowded and peaceful.

The next morning Wladek was dragged from the basement by two guards and marched to a hall where he was lined up with several other prisoners. They were all roped to each other around the waist and led from the jail in a long line down into the street. Another large crowd had gathered outside and their loud cheer of welcome made Wladek feel that they had been waiting some time for the prisoners to appear. The crowd followed them all the way to the market place – screaming, clapping and shouting – for what reason Wladek feared even to contemplate. The line came to a halt when they reached the market square. The first prisoner was unleashed from his rope and taken into the centre of the square, which was already crammed with hundreds of people, all shouting at the top of their voices.

Wladek watched the scene in disbelief. When the first prisoner reached the middle of the square, he was knocked to his knees by the guard and then his right hand was strapped to a wooden block by a giant of a man who raised a large sword above his head and brought it down with terrible force, aiming at the prisoner's wrist. He only managed to catch the tips of the fingers. The prisoner screamed with pain as the sword was raised again. This time the sword hit the wrist but still did not finish the job properly and the wrist dangled from the prisoner's arm, blood pouring out onto the sand. The sword was raised for a third time, and for the third time it came down. The prisoner's hand at last fell to the ground. The crowd roared its approval. The prisoner was at last released, and he slumped in a heap, unconscious. He was dragged off by a disinterested guard and left on the edge of the crowd. A weeping woman, his wife, Wladek presumed, hurriedly tied a tourniquet of dirty cloth around the bloody stump. The second prisoner died of shock before the fourth blow was struck. The giant executioner was not interested in death so he continued his task; he was paid to remove hands.

Wladek looked around in terror and would have vomited if there had been anything left in his stomach to bring up. He searched in every direction for help or some means of escape; no one had told him that under Islamic law the punishment for trying to escape would be the loss of a foot. His eyes darted around the mass of faces until he saw a man in the crowd dressed like a European, wearing a dark suit. The man was standing about twenty yards away from Wladek and was watching the spectacle with obvious disgust. But he did not once look in Wladek's direction, nor could he hear his shouts for help in the uproar arising from the crowd every time the sword was brought down. Was he French, German, English or even Polish? Wladek could not tell, but for some reason he was there to witness this macabre spectacle. Wladek stared at him, willing him to look his way. But he did not. Wladek waved his free arm but still could not gain the European's attention. They untied the man two in front of Wladek and dragged him along the ground towards the block. When the sword went up again the crowd cheered, the man in the dark suit turned his eyes away in disgust and Wladek waved frantically at him again.

The man stared at Wladek and then turned to talk to a companion, whom Wladek had not noticed. The guard was now struggling with the prisoner immediately in front of Wladek. He placed the prisoner's hand under the strap; the sword went up and removed the hand in one blow. The crowd seemed disappointed. Wladek stared again at the Europeans. They were now both looking at him. He willed them to move, but they only continued to stare.

The guard came over, threw Wladek's fifty-ruble overcoat to the ground, undid his shirt and rolled up his sleeve. Wladek struggled futilely as he was dragged across the square. He was no match for the guard. When he reached the block, he was kicked in the back of his knees and collapsed to the ground. The strap was fastened over his right wrist, and there was nothing left for him to do but close his eyes as the sword was raised above the executioner's head. He waited in agony for the terrible blow, and then there was a sudden hush in the crowd as the Baron's silver band fell from Wladek's elbow down to his wrist and onto the block. An eerie silence came over the crowd as the heirloom shone brightly in the sunlight. The executioner stopped and put down his sword and studied the silver band. Wladek opened his eyes. He tried to pull it over Wladek's wrist, but he couldn't get it past the leather strap. A man in uniform ran quickly forward and joined the executioner. He too, studied the band and the inscription and then ran to another man, who must have been of higher authority, because he walked more slowly towards Wladek. The sword was resting on the ground and the crowd were now beginning to jeer and hoot. The second officer also tried to pull the silver band off, but could not get it over the block either and he seemed unwilling to undo the strap. He shouted words at Wladek, who did not understand what he was saying and replied in Polish, 'I do not speak your language.'

The officer looked surprised and threw his hands in the air shouting, 'Allah.' That must be the same as 'Holy God' thought Wladek. The officer walked slowly towards the two men in the crowd wearing western suits, arms going in every direction like a disorganized windmill. Wladek prayed to God; in such situations any man prays to any god, be it Allah or the Ave Maria. The Europeans were still staring at Wladek, and Wladek nodded his head up and down frantically. One of the men in the dark suits joined the Turkish officer as he walked back towards the block. The former knelt down by Wladek's side, studied the silver band and then looked carefully at him. Wladek waited. He could converse in five languages and prayed that the gentleman would speak one of them. His heart sank when the European turned to the officer and addressed him in his own tongue. The crowd was now hissing and throwing rotten fruit at the block. The officer was nodding his agreement, while the gentleman stared intently at Wladek.

'Do you speak English?'

Wladek heaved a sigh of relief. 'Yes, sir, not bad. I am Polish citizen.'

'How did you come into possession of that silver band?'

'It belong my father, sir. He die in prison by the Germans in Poland, and I captured and sent to a prison camp in Russia. I escape and come here by ship. I have no eat for days. When stallkeeper no accept my rubles for orange, I take one because I much, much hungry.'

The Englishman rose slowly from his knees, turned to the officer and spoke to him very firmly. The latter, in turn, addressed the executioner who looked doubtful, but when the officer repeated the order a little louder, he bent down and reluctantly undid the leather strap. This time Wladek did vomit.

'Come with me,' said the Englishman. 'And quickly, before they change their minds.'

Still in a daze, Wladek grabbed his coat and followed him. The crowd booed and jeered, throwing things at him as he departed, and the swordsman put the next prisoner's hand on the block and with his first blow only managed to remove a thumb. This seemed to pacify the mob.

The Englishman moved swiftly through the hustling crowd out of the square where he was joined by his companion.

'What's happening, Edward?'

'The boy says he is a Pole and that he escaped from Russia. I told the official in charge that he was English, so now he is our responsibility. Let's get him to the embassy and find out if the boy's story bears any resemblance to the truth.'

Wladek ran between the two men as they hurried on through the bazaar and into the Street of Seven Kings. He could still faintly hear the mob behind him screaming their approval every time the executioner brought down his sword.

The two Englishmen walked over a pebbled courtyard towards a large grey building and beckoned Wladek to follow them. On the door were the welcoming words, British Embassy. Once inside the building Wladek began to feel safe for the first time. He walked a pace behind the two men down a long hall with walls filled with paintings of strangely clad soldiers and sailors. At the far end was a magnificent portrait of an old man in a blue naval uniform liberally adorned with medals. His fine beard reminded Wladek of the Baron. A soldier appeared from nowhere and saluted.

'Take this boy, Corporal Smithers, and see that he gets a bath. Then feed him in the kitchens. When he has eaten and smells a little less like a walking pigsty, bring him to my office.'

'Yes, sir,' said the corporal and saluted.

'Come with me, my lad.' The soldier marched away. Wladek followed him obediently, having to run to keep up with his walking pace. He was taken to the basement of the embassy and left in a little room; this time it had a window. The corporal told him to get undressed and then left him on his own. He returned a few minutes later to find Wladek still sitting on the edge of the bed fully dressed, dazedly twisting the silver band around and around his wrist.

'Hurry up, lad; you're not on a rest cure.'

'Sorry, sir,' Wladek said.

'Don't call me sir, lad. I am Corporal Smithers. You call me corporal.'

'I am Wladek Koskiewicz. You call me Wladek.'

'Don't be funny with me, lad. We've got enough funny people in the British army without you wishing to join their ranks.'

Wladek did not understand what the soldier meant. He undressed quickly.

'Follow me at the double.'

Another marvellous bath with hot water and soap. Wladek thought of his Russian protectress, and of the son he might have become to her but for her husband. A new set of clothes, strange but clean and fresh-smelling. Whose son had they belonged to? The soldier was back at the door.

Corporal Smithers took Wladek to the kitchen and left him with a fat, pink-faced cook, with the warmest face he had seen since leaving Poland. She reminded him of niania. Wladek could not help wondering what would happen to her waistline after a few weeks in camp 201.

'Hello,' she said with a beaming smile. 'What's your name, then?'

Wladek told her.

'Well, laddie, it looks as though you could do with a good British meal inside of you – none of this Turkish muck will suffice. We'll start with some hot soup and beef. You'll need something substantial if you're to face Mr Prendergast.' She laughed. 'Just remember, his bite's not as bad as his bark. Although he is an Englishman, his heart's in the right place.'

'You are not an English, Mrs Cook?' asked Wladek, surprised.

'Good Lord no, laddie, I'm Scottish. There's a world of difference. We hate the English more than the Germans do,' she said, laughing. She set a dish of steaming soup, thick with meat and vegetables, in front of Wladek. He had entirely forgotten that food could smell and taste so appetizing. He ate the meal slowly for fear it might not happen again for a very long time.

The corporal reappeared. 'Have you had enough to eat, my lad?'

'Yes, thank you, Mr Corporal.'

The corporal gave Wladek a suspicious look, but he saw no trace of cheek in the boy's expression. 'Good, then let's be moving. Can't be late on parade for Mr Prendergast.'

The corporal disappeared through the kitchen door, and Wladek stared at the cook. He hated always having to say goodbye to someone he'd just met, especially when they had been so kind.

'Off you go, laddie, if you know what's good for you.'

'Thank you, Mrs Cook,' said Wladek. 'Your food is best I can ever remember.'

The cook smiled at him. He again had to limp hard to catch up with the corporal, whose marching pace still kept Wladek trotting. The soldier came to a brisk halt outside a door that Wladek nearly ran into.

'Look where you're going, my lad, look where you're going.'

The corporal gave a short rap-rap on the door.

'Come,' said a voice.

The corporal opened the door and saluted. 'The Polish boy, sir, as you requested, scrubbed and fed.'

'Thank you, Corporal. Perhaps you would be kind enough to ask Mr Grant to join us.'

Edward Pendergast looked up from his desk. He waved Wladek to a seat without speaking and continued to work at some papers. Wladek sat looking at him and then at the portraits on the wall. More generals and admirals and that old, bearded gentleman again, this time in khaki army uniform. A few minutes later the other Englishman he remembered from the market square came in.

'Thank you for joining us, Harry. Do have a seat, old boy.'

Mr Prendergast turned to Wladek. 'Now, my lad, let's hear your story from the beginning with no exaggerations, only the truth. Do you understand?'

'Yes, sir.'

Wladek started his story with his days in Poland. It took him some time to find the right English words. It was apparent from the looks on the faces of the two Englishmen that they were at first incredulous. They occasionally stopped him and asked questions, nodding to each other at his answers. After an hour of talking Wladek's life history had reached the office of His Britannic Majesty's second consul to Turkey.

'I think, Harry,' said the second consul, 'it is our duty to inform the Polish Delegation immediately and then hand young Koskiewicz over to them as I feel in the circumstances he is undoubtedly their responsibility.'

'Agreed,' said the man called Harry. 'You know, my boy, you had a narrow escape in the market today. The Sher – that is the old Islamic religious law – which provides for cutting off a hand for the theft was officially abandoned in theory years ago. In fact it is a crime under the Ottoman Penal Code to inflict such a punishment. Nevertheless, in practice the barbarians still continue to carry it out.' He shrugged.

'Why not my hand?' asked Wladek, holding onto his wrist.

'I told them they could cut off all the Moslem hands they wanted, but not an Englishman's,' Edward Prendergast interjected.

'Thank God,' said Wladek faintly.

'Edward Prendergast, actually,' he said, smiling for the first time. The second consul continued. 'You can spend the night here, and we will take you to your own delegation tomorrow. The Poles do not actually have an embassy in Constantinople,' he said, slightly disdainfully, 'but my opposite number is a good fellow considering he's a foreigner.' He pressed a button and the corporal reappeared immediately.

'Sir.'

'Corporal, take young Koskiewicz to his room, and in the morning see he is given breakfast and is brought to me at nine sharp.'

'Sir. This way, boy, at the double.'

Wladek was led away by the corporal. He was not even given enough time to thank the two Englishmen who had saved his hand – and perhaps his life. Back in the clean little room, with its clean little bed neatly turned down as if he were an honoured guest, he undressed, threw his pillow on the floor and slept soundly until the morning light shone through the tiny window.

'Rise and shine, lad, sharpish.'

It was the corporal, his uniform immaculately smart and knife-edge pressed, looking as though he had never been to bed. For an instant Wladek, surfacing from sleep, thought himself back in camp 201, as the corporal's banging on the end of the bed frame with his cane resembled the noise he had grown so accustomed to. He fell out of bed and reached for his clothes.

'Wash first, my lad, wash first. We don't want your horrible smells worrying Mr Prendergast so early in the morning, do we?'

Wladek was unsure which part of himself to wash, so unusually clean did he feel himself to be. The corporal was staring at him.

'What's wrong with your leg, lad?'

'Nothing, nothing,' said Wladek, turning himself away from the staring eyes.

'Right. I'll be back in three minutes. Three minutes, do you hear, my lad, be sure you're ready.'

Wladek washed his hands and face quickly and then dressed. He was waiting at the end of the bed in his long bearskin coat when the corporal returned to take him to the second consul. Mr Prendergast welcomed him and seemed to have softened considerably since their first meeting.

'Good morning, Koskiewicz.'

'Good morning, sir.'

'Did you enjoy your breakfast?'

'I no had breakfast, sir.'

'Why not?' said the second consul, looking towards the corporal.

'Overslept, I'm afraid, sir. He would have been late for you.'

'Well, we must see what we can do about that. Corporal, will you ask Mrs Henderson to try and rustle up an apple or something?'

'Yes, sir.'

Wladek and the Second Consul walked slowly along the corridor towards the embassy front door, and across the pebbled courtyard to a waiting car, an Austin, one of the few engine driven vehicles in Turkey and Wladek's first journey in one. He was sorry to be leaving the British embassy. It was the first place in which he had felt safe for years. He wondered if he was ever going to sleep more than one night in the same bed for the rest of his life. The corporal ran down the steps and took the driver's seat. He passed Wladek an apple and some fresh warm bread.

'See there are no crumbs left in the car, lad. The cook sends her compliments.'

The drive through the hot busy streets was conducted at walking pace as the Turks did not believe anything could go faster than a camel, and made no attempt to clear a path for the little Austin. Even with all the windows open Wladek was sweating from the oppressive heat while Mr Prendergast remained quite cool and unperturbed. Wladek hid himself in the back of the car for fear that someone who had witnessed the previous day's events might recognize him and stir the mob to anger again. When the little black Austin came to a halt outside a small decaying building marked 'Konsulat Polski', Wladek felt a twinge of excitement mingled with disappointment.

The three of them climbed out.

'Where's the apple core, boy?' demanded the corporal.

'I eat him.'

The corporal laughed and knocked on the door. A friendly-looking little man with dark hair and firm jaw opened the door to them. He was in shirt sleeves and deeply tanned, obviously by the Turkish sun. He addressed them in Polish. His words were the first Wladek had heard in his native tongue since leaving the labour camp. Wladek answered quickly, explaining his presence. His fellow countryman turned to the British second consul.

'This way, Mr Prendergast,' he said in perfect English. 'It was good of you to bring the boy over personally.'

A few diplomatic niceties were exchanged before Prentergast and the corporal took their leave. Wladek gazed at them, fumbling for an English expression more adequate than 'Thank you.'

Prendergast patted Wladek on the head as he might a cocker spaniel. The corporal closed the door, and winked at Wladek. 'Good luck, my lad; God knows you deserve it.'

The Polish consul introduced himself to Wladek as Pawel Zaleski. Again Wladek was required to recount the story of his life, finding it easier in Polish than he had in English. Pawel Zaleski heard him out in silence, shaking his head sorrowfully.

'My poor child,' he said heavily. 'You have borne more than your share of our country's suffering for one so young. And now what are we to do with you?'

'I must return to Poland and reclaim my castle,' said Wladek.

'Poland,' said Pawel Zaleski. 'Where's that? The area of land where you lived remains in dispute and there is still heavy fighting going on between the Poles and the Russians. General Piludski is doing all he can to protect the territorial integrity of our fatherland. But it would be foolish for any of us to be optimistic. There is little left for you now in Poland. No, your best plan would be to start a new life in England or America.'

'But I don't want to go to England or America. I am Polish.'

'You will always be Polish, Wladek, no one can take that away from you wherever you decided to settle, but you must be realistic about your life – which hasn't even begun.'

Wladek lowered his head in despair. Had he gone through all this only to be told he could never return to his native land? He fought back the tears.

Pawel Zaleski put his arm round the boy's shoulders. 'Never forget that you are one of the lucky ones who escaped and came out of the holocaust alive. You only have to remember your friend, Doctor Dubien, to be aware of what life might have been like.'

Wladek didn't speak.

'Now, you must put all thoughts of the past behind you and think only for the future, Wladek, and perhaps in your lifetime you will see Poland rise again, which is more than I dare hope for.'

Wladek remained silent.

'Well, there's no need to make an immediate decision,' said the consul kindly. 'You can stay here for as long as it takes you to decide on your future.'

10

The future was something that was worrying Anne. The first few months of her marriage were happy, marred only by her anxiety over William's increasing dislike of Henry, and her new husband's seeming inability to start working. Henry was a little touchy on the point, explaining to Anne that he was still disorientated by the war and that he wasn't willing to rush into something he might well have to stick with for the rest of his life. She found this hard to swallow and finally it brought on their first row.

'I don't understand why you haven't opened that real estate business you used to be so keen on, Henry.'

'I can't. The time isn't quite right. The real estate market's not looking that promising at the moment.'

'You've been saying that now for nearly a year; I wonder if it will ever be promising enough for you.'

'Sure it will; truth is, I need a little more capital to help myself set up. Now if you would loan me some of your money, I could get cracking tomorrow.'

'That's impossible, Henry. You know the terms of Richard's will; my allowance was stopped the day we were married, and now I have only the capital left.'

'A little of that would help me on my way, and don't forget that precious boy of yours has well over twenty million in the family trust.'

'You seem to know a lot about William's trust,' said Anne suspiciously.

'Oh, come on, Anne, give me a chance to be your husband. Don't make me feel like a guest in my own home.'

'What's happened to your money, Henry? You always led me to believe that you had enough to start your own business.'

'You've always known I was not in Richard's class financially, and there was a time, Anne, when you claimed it didn't matter. I'd marry you Henry, if you were penniless,' he mocked.

Anne burst into tears, and Henry tried to console her. She spent the rest of the evening in his arms talking the problem over. Anne managed to convince herself she was being unwifely and ungenerous. She had more money than she could possibly need: couldn't she trust a little of it to the man to whom she was so willing to entrust the rest of her life?

Acting upon these thoughts, she agreed to let Henry have one hundred thousand dollars to set up his own real estate firm in Boston. Within a month Henry had found a smart new office in a fashionable part of town, appointed staff, and started work. Soon he was mixing with all the city politicians and real estate men of Boston. They talked of the boom in farm land, and they flattered Henry. Anne didn't care very much for them as social company, but Henry was happy and appeared to be successful at his work.

.   .   .

William, now fourteen, was in his third year at St Paul's, sixth in his class overall and first in mathematics. He had also become a rising figure in the Debating Society. He wrote to his mother once a week, reporting his progress, always addressing his letters to Mrs Richard Kane, refusing to acknowledge that Henry Osborne even existed. Anne wasn't sure whether she should talk to him about it, and each Monday she would carefully extract William's letter from the box to be certain that Henry never saw the envelope. She continued to hope that in time William would come around to liking Henry, but it became clear that that hope was unrealistic when, in one particular letter to his mother, he sought her permission to stay with his friend, Matthew Lester, for the summer holidays. The request came as a painful blow to Anne, but she took the easy way out and fell in with William's plans, which Henry also seemed to favour.

William hated Henry Osborne and nursed the hatred passionately, not sure what he could actually do about it. He was relieved that Henry never visited him at school; he could not have tolerated the other boys seeing his mother with that man. It was bad enough that he had to live with him in Boston.

. . .

For the first time since his mother's marriage, William was anxious for the holidays to come.

The Lesters' Packard chauffeured William and Matthew noiselessly to the summer camp in Vermont. On the journey, Matthew casually asked William what he intended to do when the time came for him to leave St Paul's.

'When I leave I will be top of the class, Class President, and have won the Hamilton Memorial Mathematics Scholarship to Harvard,' replied William without hesitation.

'Why is all that so important?' asked Matthew innocently.

'My father did all three.'

'When you've finished beating your father, I will introduce you to mine.' William smiled.

The two boys had an energetic and enjoyable four weeks in Vermont playing every game from chess to American football. When the month came to an end they travelled to New York to spend the last part of the holiday with the Lester family. They were greeted at the door by a butler who addressed Matthew as sir and a twelve-year-old girl covered in freckles who called him Fatty. It made William laugh because his friend was so thin and it was she who was fat. The little girl smiled and revealed teeth almost totally hidden behind braces.

'You would never believe Susan was my sister, would you?' asked Matthew disdainfully.

'No, I suppose not,' said William, smiling at Susan. 'She's so much better looking than you.'

She adored William from that moment on.

William adored Matthew's father the moment they met; he reminded him in so many ways of his own father and he begged Charles Lester to let him see the great bank of which he was chairman. Charles Lester thought carefully about the request. No child had been allowed to enter the orderly precincts of 17 Broad Street before, not even his own son. He compromised, as bankers often do, and showed the boy around the Wall Street building on a Sunday afternoon.

William was fascinated to see the different offices, the vaults, the foreign exchange dealing room, the board room and the chairman's office. Compared with Kane and Cabot, the Lester bank was considerably more extensive, and William knew from his own small personal investment account, which provided him with a copy of the annual general report, that they had a far larger capital base than Kane and Cabot. William was silent, pensive, as they were driven home in the car.

'Well, William, did you enjoy your visit to my bank?' asked Charles Lester genially.

'Oh, yes, sir,' replied William. 'I certainly did enjoy it.' William paused for a moment and then added, 'I intend to be chairman of your bank one day, Mr Lester.'

Charles Lester laughed, and dined out on the story of how young William Kane had reacted to Lester and Co., which in turn made those who heard it laugh too.

Only William had not meant the remark as a joke. Anne was shocked when Henry came back to her for more money.

'It's as safe as a house,' he assured her. 'Ask Alan Lloyd. As chairman of the bank he can only have your best interests at heart.'

'But two hundred and fifty thousand?' Anne queried.

'A superb opportunity, my dear. Look upon it as an investment that will be worth double that amount within two years.'

After another more prolonged row, Anne gave in once again and life returned to the same smooth routine. When she checked her investment portfolio with the bank, Anne found she was down to one hundred and forty thousand dollars, but Henry seemed to be seeing all the right people and clinching all the right deals. She considered discussing the whole problem with Alan Lloyd at Kane and Cabot, but in the end dismissed the idea; it would have meant displaying distrust in the husband whom she wished the world to respect, and surely Henry would not have made the suggestion at all had he not been sure that the loan would have met with Alan's approval.

Anne also started seeing Doctor MacKenzie again to find out if there was any hope of her having another baby, but he still advised against the idea. With the high blood pressure that had caused her earlier miscarriage, Andrew MacKenzie did not consider thirty-five a good age for Anne to start thinking about being a mother again. Anne raised the idea with the grandmothers, but they agreed wholeheartedly with the views of the good doctor. Neither of them cared for Henry very much, and they cared even less for the thought of an Osborne offspring making claims on the Kane family fortune after they were gone. Anne began to resign herself to the fact that William was going to be her only child. Henry became very angry about what he described as her betrayal, and told Anne that if Richard were still alive, she would have tried again. How different the two men were, she thought, and couldn't account for why she had loved them both. She tried to soothe Henry, praying that his business projects would work out well and keep him fully occupied. He certainly had taken to working very late at the office.

It was on a Monday in October, the weekend after they had celebrated their second wedding anniversary, that Anne started receiving the letters from an unsigned 'friend', informing her that Henry could be seen escorting other women around Boston, and one lady in particular whom the writer didn't care to name. To begin with Anne burned the letters immediately and although they worried her, she never discussed them with Henry, praying that each letter would be the last. She couldn't even summon up the courage to raise the matter with Henry when he asked her for the last hundred and fifty thousand dollars.

'I am going to lose the whole deal if I don't have that money right now, Anne.'

'But it's all I have, Henry. If I give you that amount, I'll be left with nothing.'

'This house alone must be worth over two hundred thousand. You could mortgage it tomorrow.'

'The house belongs to William.'

'William, William, William. It's always William who gets in the way of my success,' shouted Henry as he stormed out.

He returned home after midnight, contrite, and told her he would rather she kept her money and that he went under, for at least they would still have each other. Anne was comforted by his words and later they made love. She signed a cheque for one hundred and fifty thousand dollars the next morning, trying to forget that it would leave her penniless until Henry pulled off the deal he was pursuing. She couldn't help wondering if it was more than a coincidence that Henry had asked for the exact amount that remained of her inheritance.

The next month Anne missed her period.

Doctor Mackenzie was anxious but tried not to show it; the grandmothers were horrified and did; while Henry was delighted and assured Anne that it was the most wonderful thing that had ever happened to him in his whole life, and even agreed to building a new children's wing for the hospital that Richard had planned before he died.

When William heard the news by letter from his mother, he sat deep in thought all evening unable to tell even Matthew what was preoccupying him. The following Saturday morning, having been granted special permission by his housemaster, Grumpy Raglan, he boarded a train to Boston and on arrival withdrew one hundred dollars from his savings account. He then proceeded to the law offices of Cohen, Cohen and Yablons in Jefferson Street. Mr Thomas Cohen, the senior partner, a tall angular man with a dark jowl was somewhat surprised when William was ushered into his office.

'I have never been retained by a sixteen-year-old before,' Mr Cohen began. 'It will be quite a novelty for me –' he hesitated '– Mr Kane.' He found Mr Kane did not run easily off the tongue. 'Especially as your father was not exactly – how shall I put it? – known for his sympathy for my co-religionists.'

'My father,' replied William, 'was a great admirer of the achievements of the Hebrew race and in particular had considerable respect for your firm when you acted on behalf of rivals. I heard him mention your name on several occasions. That's why I have chosen you, Mr Cohen, not you me. That should be reassurance enough.'

Mr Cohen quickly put aside the fact that William was only sixteen. 'Indeed, indeed. I feel I can make an exception for the son of Richard Kane. Now, what can we do for you?'

'I wish you to answer three questions for me, Mr Cohen. One, I want to know if my mother, Mrs Henry Osborne, were to give birth to a child, son or daughter, whether that child would have any legal rights to the Kane family trust. Two, do I have any legal obligations to Mr Henry Osborne because he is married to my mother, and three, at what age can I insist that

Mr Henry Osborne leave my house on Louisburg Square in Boston?'

Thomas Cohen's quill pen sped furiously across the paper in front of him, spattering little blue spots on an already ink-stained desk top.

William placed one hundred dollars on the desk. The lawyer looked taken aback but picked the notes up and counted them.

'Use the money prudently, Mr Cohen. I will need a good lawyer when I leave Harvard.'

'You have already been accepted at Harvard, Mr Kane? My congratulations. I am hoping my son will go there too.'

'No, I have not, but I shall have done so in two years' time. I will return to Boston to see you in one week, Mr Cohen. If I ever hear in my lifetime from anyone other than yourself on this subject, you may consider our relationship at an end. Good day, sir.'

Thomas Cohen would have also said good day, if he could have spluttered the words out before William closed the door behind him.

.   .   .

William returned to the offices of Cohen, Cohen and Yablons seven days later.

'Ah, Mr Kane,' said Thomas Cohen, 'how nice to see you again. Would you care for some coffee?'

'No, thank you.'

'Shall I send someone out for a Coca-Cola?'

William's face was expressionless.

'To business, to business,' said Mr Cohen, slightly embarrassed. 'We have dug around a little on your behalf, Mr Kane, with the help of a very respectable firm of private investigators to assist us with the questions you asked that were not purely academic. I think I can safely say we have the answers to all your questions. You asked if Mr Osborne's offspring by your mother, were there to be any, would have a claim on the Kane estate, or in particular on the trust left to you by your father. No is the simple answer, but of course Mrs Osborne can leave any part of the five hundred thousand dollars bequeathed to her by your father to whom she pleases.'

Mr Cohen looked up.

'However, it may interest you to know, Mr Kane, that your mother has drawn out the entire five hundred thousand from her private account at Kane and Cabot during the last eighteen months, but we have been unable to trace how the money has been used. It is possible she may have decided to deposit the amount in another bank.'

William looked shocked, the first sign of any lack of the self-control that Thomas Cohen had noted.

'There would be no reason for her to do that,' William said. 'The money can only have gone to one person.'

The lawyer remained silent, expecting to hear more, but William steadied himself and added nothing, so Mr Cohen continued.

'The answer to your second question is that you have no personal or legal obligations to Mr Henry Osborne at all. Under the terms of your father's will, your mother is a trustee of the estate along with a Mr Alan Lloyd and a Mrs John Preston, your surviving godparents, until you come of age at twenty-one.'

Thomas Cohen looked up again. William's face showed no expression at all. Cohen had already learned that that meant he should continue.

'And thirdly, Mr Kane, you can never remove Mr Osborne from Beacon Hill as long as he remains married to your mother and continues to reside with her. The property comes into your possession by natural right on her death. Were he still alive then, you could require him to leave. I think you will find that covers all your questions, Mr Kane.'

'Thank you, Mr Cohen,' said William. 'I am obliged for your efficiency and discretion in this matter. Now perhaps you could let me know your professional charges.'

'One hundred dollars doesn't quite cover the work, Mr Kane, but we have faith in your future and . . .'

'I do not wish to be beholden to anyone, Mr Cohen. You must treat me as someone with whom you might never deal again. With that in mind, how much do I owe you?'

Mr Cohen considered the matter for a moment. 'In those circumstances we would have charged you two hundred and twenty dollars, Mr Kane.'

William took six twenty-dollar notes from his inside pocket and handed them over to Cohen. This time, the lawyer did not count them.

'I am grateful to you for your assistance, Mr Cohen, I am sure we shall meet again. Good day, sir.'

'Good day, Mr Kane. May I be permitted to say that I never had the privilege of meeting your distinguished father but having dealt with you, I wish that I had.'

William smiled and softened. 'Thank you, sir.'

. . .

Preparing for the baby kept Anne fully occupied; she found herself easily tired and resting a good deal. Whenever she inquired of Henry how business was going, he always had some plausible answer to hand, enough to reassure her that all was well without supplying her with any actual details.

Then one morning the anonymous letters started coming again. This time they gave more details, the names of the women involved and the places they could be seen with Henry. Anne burned them even before she could commit the names or places to memory. She didn't want to believe that her husband could be unfaithful while she was carrying his child. Someone was jealous and had it in for Henry, and he or she had to be lying.

The letters kept coming, sometimes with new names. Anne continued to destroy them, but now they were beginning to prey on her mind. She wanted to discuss the whole problem with someone, but couldn't think of anybody in whom she could confide. The grandmothers would have been appalled and were, in any case, already prejudiced against Henry. Alan Lloyd at the bank could not be expected to understand as he had never married, and William was far too young. No one seemed suitable. Anne considered consulting a psychiatrist after listening to a lecture given by Sigmund Freud, but a Lowell could never discuss a family problem with a complete stranger.

The matter finally came to a head in a way that even Anne had not been prepared for. One Monday morning, she received three letters, the usual one from William addressed to Mrs Richard Kane, asking if he could once again spend his summer holidays with his friend Matthew Lester in New York.

Another anonymous letter alleging that Henry was having an affair with, with ... Milly Preston, and the third from Alan Lloyd, as chairman of the bank, asking if she would be kind enough to telephone and make an appointment to see him. Anne sat down heavily, feeling breathless and unwell, and forced herself to re-read all three letters. William's letter stung her by its detachment. She hated knowing that he preferred to spend his holidays with Matthew Lester. They had been growing continually further apart since her marriage to Henry. The anonymous letter suggesting that Henry was having an affair with her closest friend was impossible to ignore. Anne couldn't help remembering that it had been Milly who had introduced her to Henry in the first place, and that she was William's godmother. The third letter from Alan Lloyd somehow filled her with even more apprehension. The only other letter she had ever received from Alan was one of condolence on the death of Richard. She feared another could only mean more bad news.

She called the bank. The operator put her straight through.

'Alan, you wanted to see me?'

'Yes, my dear, I would like to have a chat sometime. When would suit you?'

'Is it bad news?' asked Anne.

'Not exactly, but I would rather not say anything over the phone, but there's nothing for you to worry about. Are you free for lunch, by any chance?'

'Yes I am, Alan.'

'Well, let's meet at the Ritz at one o'clock. I look forward to seeing you then, Anne.'

One o'clock, only three hours away. Her mind switched from Alan to William to Henry, but settled on Milly Preston. Could it be true? Anne decided to take a long warm bath and put on a new dress. It didn't help she felt, and was beginning to look, bloated. Her ankles and calves, which had always been so elegant and so slim, were becoming mottled and puffy. It was a little frightening to conjecture how much worse things might become before the baby was born. She sighed at herself in the mirror and did the best she could with her outward appearance.

. . .

'You look very smart, Anne. If I weren't an old bachelor considered well past it, I'd flirt with you shamelessly,' said the silver haired banker, greeting her with a kiss on both cheeks as though he were a French general.

He guided her to his table. It was an unspoken tradition that the table in the corner was always occupied by the chairman of Kane and Cabot, if he were not lunching at the bank. Richard had done so and now it was the turn of Alan Lloyd. It was the first occasion that Anne had sat at that table with anyone. Waiters fluttered around them like starlings, seeming to know exactly when to disappear and reappear without interrupting a private conversation.

'When's the baby due, Anne?'

'Oh, not for another three months.'

'No complications, I hope. I seem to remember ...'

'Well,' admitted Anne, 'the doctor sees me once a week and pulls long faces about my blood pressure, but I'm not too worried.'

'I'm so glad, my dear,' he said and touched her hand gently as an uncle might. 'You do look rather tired, I hope you're not overdoing things.'

Alan Lloyd raised his hand slightly. A waiter materialized at his side, and they both ordered.

'Anne, I want to seek some advice from you.'

Anne was painfully aware of Alan Lloyd's gift for diplomacy. He wasn't having lunch with her for advice. There was no doubt in her mind that he had come to dispense it – kindly.

'Do you have any idea how well Henry's real estate projects are going?'

'No, I don't,' said Anne. 'I never involve myself with Henry's business activities. You'll remember I didn't with Richard's either. Why? Is there any cause for concern?'

'No, no, none of which we at the bank are aware. On the contrary, we know Henry is bidding for a large city contract to build the new hospital complex. I was only inquiring, because he has come to the bank for a loan of five hundred thousand dollars.'

Anne was stunned.

'I see that surprises you,' he said. 'Now, we know from your stock account that you have a little under twenty thousand dollars in reserve, while running a small overdraft of seventeen thousand dollars on your personal account.'

Anne put down her soup spoon, horrified. She had not realized that she was so badly overdrawn. Alan could see her distress.

'That's not what this lunch is about, Anne,' he added quickly. 'The bank is quite happy to lose money on the personal account for the rest of your life. William is making over a million dollars a year on the interest from his trust, so your overdraft is hardly significant, nor indeed is the five hundred thousand Henry is requesting, if it were to receive your backing as William's legal guardian.'

'I didn't realize that I had any authority over William's trust money,' said Anne.

'You don't on the capital sum, but legally the interest earned from his trust can be invested in any project thought to benefit William, and is under the guardianship of yourself, myself and Milly Preston as godparents until William is twenty-one. Now as chairman of William's trust I can put up that five hundred thousand with your backing. Milly has already informed me that she would be quite happy to give her approval so that would give you two votes and my opinion would therefore be invalid.'

'Milly Preston has already given her approval, Alan?'

'Yes. Hasn't she mentioned the matter to you?'

Anne did not reply immediately. 'What is *your* opinion?' she asked finally.

'Well, I haven't seen Henry's accounts, because he only started his company eighteen months ago and he doesn't bank with us, so I have no idea what expenditure is over income for the current year and what return he is predicting for 1923.'

'You realize that during the last eighteen months I've given Henry five hundred thousand of my own money?' said Anne.

'My chief teller informs me any time a large amount of cash is withdrawn from any account. I didn't know that was what you were using the money for, and it was none of my business, Anne. That money was left to you by Richard and is yours to spend as you see fit.

'Now, in the case of the interest from the family trust, that is a different matter. If you decide to withdraw five hundred thousand dollars to invest in Henry's firm, then the bank will have to inspect Henry's books, because the money would be considered as another investment for William's portfolio. Richard did not give the trustees the authority to make loans, only to invest on William's behalf. I have already explained this situation to Henry, and if we were to go ahead and make this investment, the trustees would have to decide what percentage of Henry's company would be an appropriate exchange for the five hundred thousand. William, of course, is always aware what we are doing with his trust income, because we saw no reason not to comply with his request that he receive a quarterly investment programme statement from the bank in the same way as all the trustees do. I have no doubt in my own mind that he will have his own ideas on the subject which he will be fully aware of after he receives the next quarterly report.

'It may amuse you to know, that since William's sixteenth birthday he has been sending me back his own opinions on every investment we make. To begin with I looked on them with the passing interest of a benevolent guardian. Of late, I have been studying them with considerable respect. When William takes his place on the board of Kane and Cabot, this bank may well turn out to be too small for him.

'I've never been asked for advice on Williams' trust before,' said Anne forlornly.

'Well, my dear, you do see the reports that the bank sends you on the first day of every quarter, and it has always been in your power as a trustee to query any of the investments we make on William's behalf.'

Alan Lloyd took a slip of paper from his pocket, and remained silent until the sommelier had finished pouring the Nuits Saint Georges. Once he was out of earshot, Alan continued.

'William has over twenty-one million invested in the bank at four and a half per cent until his twenty-first birthday. We reinvest the interest for him each quarter in stocks and shares. We have never in the past invested in a private company. It may surprise you to hear, Anne, that we now carry out this reinvestment on a fifty-fifty basis: fifty per cent following the bank's advice and fifty per cent following the suggestions put forward by William. At the moment we are a little ahead of him, much to the satisfaction of Tony Simmons, our investment director, whom William has promised a Rolls-Royce in any year that he can beat the boy by over ten per cent.'

'But where would William get hold of the ten thousand dollars for a Rolls-Royce if he lost the bet – when he's not allowed to touch the money in his trust until he is twenty-one?'

'I do not know the answer to that, Anne. What I do know is he would be far too proud to come to us direct and I am certain he would not have made the wager if he could not honour it. Have you by any chance seen his famous ledger book lately?'

'The one given to him by his grandmothers?'

Alan Lloyd nodded.

'No, I haven't seen it since he went away to school. I didn't know it still existed.'

'It still exists and I would,' said the banker, 'give a month's wages to know what the credit column in that ledger book now stands at. I suppose you are aware that he banks that money with Lester's in New York, and not with us? They don't take on private accounts at under ten thousand dollars. I'm also fairly certain they wouldn't make an exception, even for the son of Richard Kane.'

'The son of Richard Kane,' said Anne.

'I'm sorry, I didn't mean to sound rude, Anne.'

'No, no, there is no doubt he is the son of Richard Kane. Do you know he has never asked me for a penny since his twelfth birthday?' She paused. 'I think I should warn you, Alan, that he won't take kindly to being told he has to invest five hundred thousand dollars of his trust money in Henry's company.'

'They don't get on well?' inquired Alan, his eyebrows rising.

'I'm afraid not,' said Anne.

'I'm sorry to hear that. It certainly would make the transaction more complicated if William really stood out against the whole scheme. Although he has no authority over the trust until he is twenty-one, we have already discovered through sources of our own that he is not beyond going to an independent lawyer to find out his legal position.'

'Good God,' said Anne, 'you can't be serious.'

'Oh, yes, quite serious, but there's nothing for you to worry about. To be frank, we at the bank were all rather impressed and once we realized where the inquiry was coming from, we released information we would normally have kept very much to ourselves. For some private reason he obviously didn't want to approach us directly.'

'Good heavens,' said Anne, 'what will he be like when he's thirty?'

'That will depend,' said Alan, 'on whether he is lucky enough to fall in love with someone as lovely as you. That was always Richard's strength.'

'You are an old flatterer, Alan. Can we leave the problem of the five hundred thousand until I have had a chance to discuss it with Henry?'

'Of course, my dear. I told you I had come to seek your advice.'

Alan ordered coffee and took Anne's hand gently in his. 'And do remember to take care of yourself, Anne. You're far more important than the fate of a few thousand dollars.

.   .   .

When Anne returned home from lunch she immediately started to worry about the other two letters she had received that morning. Of one thing she was now certain, after all she had learned about her own son from Alan Lloyd; she would be wise to give in gracefully and let William spend the forthcoming holidays with his friend, Matthew Lester.

Henry and Milly's relationship raised a problem to which she was unable to compose so simple a solution. She sat in the maroon leather chair, Richard's favourite, looking out through the bay window onto a beautiful bed of red and white roses, seeing nothing, only thinking. Anne always took a long time to make a decision, but once she had, she seldom went back on it.

Henry came home earlier than usual that evening, and she couldn't help wondering why. She soon found out.

'I hear you had lunch with Alan Lloyd today,' he said as he entered the room.

'Who told you that, Henry?'

'I have spies everywhere,' he said laughing.

'Yes, Alan invited me to lunch. He wanted to know how I felt about the bank investing five hundred thousand dollars of William's trust money in your company.'

'What did you say?' asked Henry, trying not to sound anxious.

'I told him I wanted to discuss the matter with you first, but why in heaven's name didn't you let me know earlier that you had approached the bank, Henry? I felt such a fool hearing the whole thing from Alan for the first time.'

'I didn't think you took any interest in business, my dear, and I only found out by sheer accident that you, Alan Lloyd and Milly Preston are all trustees, and each have a vote on William's investment income.'

'How did you find out,' asked Anne, 'when I wasn't aware of the situation myself?'

'You don't read the small print, my darling. As a matter of fact, I didn't myself until just recently. Quite by chance Milly Preston told me the details of the trust, and as William's godmother, it seems she is also a trustee. It came as quite a surprise. Now let's see if we can turn the position to our advantage. Milly says she will back me, if you agree.'

The mere sound of Milly's name made Anne feel uneasy.

'I don't think we ought to touch William's money,' she said. 'I've never looked upon the trust as having anything to do with me. I would be much happier leaving well enough alone and just continue letting the bank re-invest the interest as it has always done in the past.'

'Why be satisfied with the bank's investment programme when I am onto such a good thing with this city hospital contract? William would make a lot of money out of my company. Surely Alan went along with that?'

'I'm not certain how he felt. He was his usual discreet self though he certainly said the contract would be an excellent one to win and that you had a good chance of being awarded it.'

'Exactly.'

'But he did want to see your books before he came to any firm conclusions, and he also wondered what had happened to my five hundred thousand.'

'Our five hundred thousand, my darling, is doing very well as you will soon discover. I'll send the books around to Alan tomorrow morning so that he can inspect them for himself. I can assure you that he will be very impessed.'

'I hope so, Henry, for both our sakes,' said Anne. 'Now let's wait and see what opinion he forms; you know how much I have always trusted Alan.'

'But not me,' said Henry.

'Oh, no, Henry, I didn't mean ...'

'I was only teasing. I assumed you would trust your own husband.'

Anne felt the tearfulness that she had always suppressed in front of Richard welling up. For Henry she didn't even try to hold it back.

'I hope I can. I've never had to worry about money before, and it's all too much to cope with just now. The baby always makes me feel so tired and depressed.'

Henry's manner changed quickly to one of solicitude. 'I know, my darling. I don't want you ever to have to bother your head with business matters; I can always handle that side of things. Look, why don't you go to bed early and I'll bring you up some supper on a tray? That will give me a chance to go back to the office and pick up those files I need to show Alan in the morning.'

Anne complied, but once Henry had left, she made no attempt to sleep, tired as she was, but sat up in bed reading Sinclair Lewis. She knew it would take Henry about fifteen minutes to reach his office, so she waited a full twenty and then called his number. The ringing tone continued for almost a minute.

Anne tried a second time twenty minutes later; still no one answered the phone. She kept trying every twenty minutes, but no one ever came on the line. Henry's remark about trust began to echo bitterly in her head.

When Henry eventually returned home after midnight, he appeared apprehensive at finding Anne sitting up in bed. She was still reading Sinclair Lewis.

'You shouldn't have stayed awake for me.'

He gave her a warm kiss. Anne thought she could smell perfume – or was she becoming overly suspicious?

'I had to stay on a little later than I had expected since I couldn't immediately find all the papers Alan would require. Damn silly secretary filed some of them under the wrong headings.'

'It must be lonely sitting there in the office all on your own in the middle of the night,' said Anne.

'Oh, it's not that bad if you have a worthwhile job to do,' said Henry, climbing into bed and settling against Anne's back. 'At least there's one thing to be said for it, you can get a lot more done when the phone isn't continually interrupting you.'

He was asleep in minutes. Anne lay awake, now resolved to carry through the plan she had made that afternoon.

.   .   .

When Henry had left for work after breakfast the next morning – not that Anne was sure where Henry went to work any more – she studied the *Boston Globe* and did a little research among the small advertisements. Then she picked up the phone and made an appointment which took her to the south side of Boston, a few minutes before midday. Anne was shocked by the dinginess of the buildings. She had never previously visited the southern district of the city, and in normal circumstances she could have gone through her entire life without even knowing such places existed.

A small wooden staircase littered with matches, cigarette ends and rubbish created its own paper chase to a door with a frosted glass window on which appeared in large black letters, 'Glen Ricardo', and underneath 'Private Detective (Registered in the Commonwealth of Massachusetts)'. Anne knocked quietly.

'Come right in, the door's open,' shouted a deep, hoarse voice.

Anne entered. The man seated behind the desk, his legs stretched over its surface, glanced up from what might have been a girly magazine. His cigar stub nearly fell out of his mouth when he caught sight of Anne. It was the first time a mink coat had ever walked into his office.

'Good morning' he said, rising quickly. 'My name is Glen Ricardo.' He leant across the desk and offered a hairy, nicotine-stained hand to Anne. She took it, glad that she was wearing gloves. 'Do you have an appointment?' Ricardo asked, not that he cared whether she did or not. He was always available for a consultation with a mink coat.

'Yes, I do.'

'Ah, then you must be Mrs Osborne. Can I take your coat?'

'I prefer to keep it on,' said Anne, unable to see anywhere Ricardo could hang it except on the floor.

'Of course, of course.'

Anne eyed Ricardo covertly as he sat back in his seat and lit a new cigar. She did not care for his light green suit, the motley-coloured tie, or his thickly greased hair. It was only the fact that she doubted if it would be better anywhere else that kept her seated.

'Now what's the problem?' said Ricardo, who was sharpening an already short pencil with a blunt knife. The wooden shavings dropped everywhere except into the wastepaper basket. 'Have you lost your dog, your jewellery, or your husband?'

'First, Mr Ricardo, I want to be assured of your complete discretion,' Anne began.

'Of course, of course, it goes without saying,' replied Ricardo, not looking up from his disappearing pencil.

'Nevertheless, I am saying it,' said Anne.

'Of course, of course.'

Anne thought that if the man said 'of course' once more, she would scream. She drew a deep breath. 'I have been receiving anonymous letters which allege that my husband has been having an affair with a close friend. I want to know who is sending the letters, and if there is any truth in the accusations.'

Anne felt an immense sense of relief at having voiced her fears out loud for the first time. Ricardo looked at her impassively, as if it were not the first time he had heard such fears expressed. He put his hand through his long black hair which, Anne noticed for the first time, matched his finger nails.

'Right,' he began. 'The husband will be easy. Who's responsible for sending the letters will be a lot harder. You've kept the letters, of course?'

'Only the last one,' said Anne.

Glen Ricardo sighed and stretched his hand across the table wearily. Anne reluctantly took the letter out of her bag and then hesitated for a moment.

'I know how you feel, Mrs Osborne, but I can't do the job with one hand tied behind my back.'

'Of course, Mr Ricardo, I'm sorry.'

Anne couldn't believe she had said 'of course'.

Ricardo read the letter through two or three times before speaking. 'Have they all been typed on this sort of paper and sent in this sort of envelope?'

'Yes, I think so,' said Anne. 'As far as I can remember.'

'Well, when the next one comes be sure to –'

'Can you be so certain there will be another one?' interrupted Anne.

'Of course, so be sure to keep it. Now give me all the details about your husband. Do you have a photograph?'

'Yes.' Once again she hesitated.

'I only want to look at the face. Don't want to waste my time chasing the wrong man, do I?' said Ricardo.

Anne opened her bag again and passed him a worn-edged photograph of Henry in a lieutenant's uniform.

'Good-looking man, Mr Osborne,' said the detective. 'When was this photograph taken?'

'About five years ago, I think,' said Anne. 'I didn't know him when he was in the army.'

Ricardo questioned Anne for several minutes on Henry's daily movements. She was surprised to find how little she really knew of Henry's habits, or past.

'Not a lot to go on, Mrs Osborne, but I'll do the best I can. Now, my charges are ten dollars a day plus expenses. I will make a written report for you once a week. Two weeks' payment in advance, please.' His hand came across the desk again, this time more eagerly.

Anne opened her handbag once more and took out two crisp new one hundred-dollar notes and passed them over to Ricardo. He studied the notes carefully as if he wasn't certain which distinguished American should be engraved on them. Benjamin Franklin gazed imperturbably at Ricardo, who obviously had not seen him for some time. Ricardo handed Anne sixty dollars in grubby fives.

'I see you work on Sundays, Mr Ricardo,' said Anne, pleased with her mental arithmetic.

'Of course,' he said. 'Will the same time next week suit you, Mrs Osborne?'

'Of course,' said Anne and left quickly to avoid having to shake hands with the man behind the desk.

. . .

When William read in his quarterly trust report from Kane and Cabot that Henry Osborne – Henry Osborne, he repeated the name out loud to be sure he could believe it – was requesting five hundred thousand dollars for a personal investment, he had a bad day. For the first time in four years at St Paul's he came second in a maths test. Matthew Lester, who beat him, asked if he was feeling well.

That evening, William rang Alan Lloyd at home. The chairman of Kane and Cabot was not altogether surprised to hear from him after Anne's disclosure of the unhappy relationship between her son and Henry.

'William, dear boy, how are you and how are things at St Paul's?'

'All is well this end, thank you, sir, but that's not why I telephoned.'

The tact of an advancing Mack truck, thought Alan. 'No, I didn't imagine it was,' he replied drily. 'What can I do for you?'

'I'd like to see you tomorrow afternoon.'

'On a Sunday, William?'

'Yes, as it's the only day I can get away from school, I'll come to you any time any place.' William made the statement sound as though it were a concession on his part. 'And under no condition is my mother to know of our meeting.'

'Well, William ...' Alan Lloyd began.

William's voice grew firmer. 'I don't have to remind you, sir, that the investment of trust money in my step-father's personal venture, while not actually illegal, could undoubtedly be considered as unethical.'

Alan Lloyd was silent for a few moments, wondering if he should try and placate the boy over the telephone. The boy. He also thought about remonstrating with him, but the time for that had now passed.

'Fine, William. Why don't you join me for a spot of lunch at the Hunt Club, say one o'clock?'

'I'll look forward to seeing you then, sir.' The telephone clicked.

At least the confrontation is to be on my home ground, thought Alan Lloyd with some relief as he replaced the mouthpiece, cursing Mr Bell for inventing the damn machine.

Alan had chosen the Hunt Club because he did not want the meeting to be too private. The first thing William asked when he arrived at the clubhouse was that he should be allowed a round of golf after lunch.

'Delighted, my boy,' said Alan, and reserved the first tee for three o'clock.

He was surprised when William did not discuss Henry Osborne's proposal at all during lunch. Far from it, the boy talked knowledgeably about President Harding's views on tariff reform and the incompetence of Charles G. Dawes as the President's fiscal adviser. Alan began to wonder whether William, having slept on it, had now changed his mind about discussing Henry Osborne's loan, but was going through with the meeting not wishing to admit a change of heart. Well, if that's the way the boy wants to play it, thought Alan, that's fine by me. He looked forward to a quiet afternoon of golf. After an agreeable lunch, and the better part of a bottle of wine – William limited himself to one glass – they changed in the clubhouse and walked to the first tee.

'Do you still have a nine handicap, sir?' asked William.

'Thereabout, my boy. Why?'

'Will ten dollars a hole suit you?'

Alan Lloyd hesitated, remembering that golf was the one game that William played competently. 'Yes, fine.'

Nothing was said at the first hole, which Alan managed in four while William took a five. Alan also won the second and the third quite comfortably, and began to relax a little, rather pleased with his game. By the time they reached the fourth, they were over half a mile from the clubhouse. William waited for Alan to raise his club.

'There are no conditions under which you will loan five hundred thousand dollars of my trust money to any company or person associated with Henry Osborne.'

Alan hit a bad tee shot which went wildly into the rough. Its only virtue was that it put him far enough away from William, who had made a good drive, to give him a few minutes to think about how to address both William and the ball. After Alan Lloyd had played three more shots, they eventually met on the green. Alan conceded the hole.

'William, you know I only have one vote out of three as a trustee and you must also be aware that you have no authority over trust decisions, as you will not control the money in your own right until your twenty-first birthday. You must also realize that we ought not to be discussing this subject at all.'

'I am fully aware of the legal implications, sir, but as both the other trustees are sleeping with Henry Osborne . . .'

Alan Lloyd looked shocked.

'Don't tell me you are the only person in Boston who doesn't know that Milly Preston is having an affair with my step-father?'

Alan Lloyd said nothing.

William continued. 'I want to be certain that I have your vote, and that you intend to do everything in your power to influence my mother against this loan, even if it means going to the extreme of telling her the truth about Milly Preston.'

Alan hit an even worse tee shot. William's went right down the middle of the fairway. Alan chopped the next shot into a bush he had never even realized existed before and swore out loud for the first time in forty-three years. He had got a hiding on that occasion as well.

'That's asking a little too much,' said Alan, as he joined up with William on the fifth green.

'It's nothing compared with what I'd do if I couldn't be sure of your support, sir.'

'I don't think your father would have aproved of threats, William,' said Alan as he watched William's ball sink from fourteen feet.

'The ony thing of which my father would not have approved is Osborne,' retorted William. Alan Lloyd two-putted four feet from the hole.

'In any case, sir, you must be well aware that my father had a clause inserted in the deed that money invested by the trust was a private affair, and the benefactor should never know that the Kane family was personally involved. It was a rule he never broke in his life as a banker. That way he could always be certain there was no conflict of interest between the bank's investments and those of the family trust.'

'Well, your mother obviously feels that the rule can be broken for a member of the family.'

'Henry Osborne is not a member of my family, and when I control the trust it is a rule I, like my father, would never break.'

'You may live to regret taking such a rigid stance, William.'

'I think not, sir.'

'Well, try and consider for a moment the affect such actions might have on your mother,' added Alan.

'My mother has already lost five hundred thousand dollars of her own money, sir. Isn't that enough for one husband? Why do I have to lose five hundred thousand of mine as well?'

'We don't know that to be the case, William. The investment may still yield an excellent return; I haven't had a chance yet to look carefully into Henry's books.'

William winced when Alan Lloyd called his step-father Henry.

'I can assure you, sir, he's blown nearly every penny of my mother's money. To be exact, he has thirty-three thousand, four hundred and twelve dollars of the original sum left. I suggest you take very little notice of Osborne's books and check more thoroughly into his background, past business record and associates. Not to mention the fact that he gambles – heavily.'

From the eighth tee Alan hit his ball into a lake directly in front of them, a lake even novice players managed to clear. He conceded the hole.

'How did you come by your information on Henry?' asked Alan, fairly certain it had been through Thomas Cohen's office.

'I prefer not to say, sir.'

Alan kept his own counsel; he thought he might need that particular ace up his sleeve to play a little later in William's life.

'If all you claim turned out to be accurate, William, naturally I would have to advise your mother against any investment in Henry's firm, and it would be my duty to have the whole thing out in the open with Henry as well.'

'So be it, sir.'

Alan hit a better shot, but felt he wasn't winning.

William continued. 'It may also interest you to know that Osborne needs the five hundred thousand from my trust not for the hospital contract but to clear a long-standing debt in Chicago. I take it that you were not aware of that, sir?'

Alan said nothing; he certainly had not been aware. William won the hole.

When they reached the eighteenth, Alan was eight holes down and was about to complete the worst round he cared to remember. He had a five-foot putt that would at least enable him to halve the final hole with William.

'Do you have any more bombshells for me?' asked Alan.

'Before or after your putt, sir?'

Alan laughed and decided to call his bluff. 'Before the putt, William,' he said, leaning on his club.

'Osborne will not be awarded the hospital contract. It is thought by those who matter that he's been bribing junior officials in the city government. Nothing will be brought out into the open, but to be sure of no repercussions later his company has been removed from the final list. The contract will actually be awarded to Kirkbride and Carter. The last piece of information, sir, is confidential. Even Kirkbride and Carter will not be informed until a week from Thursday, so I'd be obliged if you would keep it to yourself.'

Alan missed his putt. William holed his, walked over to the chairman and shook him warmly by the hand.

'Thank you for the game, sir. I think you'll find you owe me ninety dollars.'

Alan took out his wallet and handed over a hundred-dollar note. 'William, I think the time has come for you to stop calling me "sir". My name, as you well know, is Alan.'

'Thank you, Alan.' William handed him ten dollars.

.   .   .

Alan Lloyd arrived at the bank on Monday morning with a little more to do than he had originally anticipated before the weekend. He put five departmental managers to work immediately on checking out the accuracy of William's allegations. He feared that he already knew what their inquiries would reveal and, because of Anne's position at the bank, he made certain that no one department was aware of what the others were up to. His instructions to each manager were clear: all reports were to be strictly confidential and for the chairman's eyes only. By Wednesday of the same week he had five preliminary reports on his desk. They all seemed to be in agreement with William's judgement although each manager had asked for more time to verify some of the details. Alan decided against worrying Anne until he had some more concrete evidence to go on. The best he felt he could do for the time being was to take advantage of a buffet supper the Osbornes were giving that evening to advise Anne against any immediate decision on the loan.

When Alan arrived at the party, he was shocked to see how tired and drawn Anne looked, which predisposed him to soften his approach even more. When he managed to catch her alone, they only had a few moments together. If only she were not having a baby just at the time all this was happening, he thought.

Anne turned and smiled at him. 'How kind of you to come Alan, when you must be so busy at the bank.'

'I couldn't afford to miss out on one of your parties, my dear, they're still the toast of Boston.'

She smiled. 'I wonder if you ever say the wrong thing.'

'All too frequently. Anne, have you had time to give any more thought to the loan?' He tried to sound casual.

'No, I am afraid I haven't. I've been up to my eyes with other things, Alan. How did Henry's accounts look?'

'Fine, but we only have one year's figures to go on, so I think we ought to bring in our own accountants to check them over. It's normal banking policy to do that with anyone who has been operating for less than three years. I am sure Henry would understand our position and agree.'

'Anne, darling, lovely party,' said a loud voice over Alan's shoulder. He did not recognize the face; presumably one of Henry's politician friends. 'How's the little mother-to-be?' continued the effusive voice.

Alan slipped away, hoping that he had bought some time for the bank. There were a lot of politicians at the party, from City Hall and even a couple from Congress, which made him wonder if William would turn out to be wrong about the big contract. Not that he needed the bank to investigate that: the official announcement from City Hall was due the following week. He said goodbye to his host and hostess, picked up his black overcoat from the cloakroom and left.

'This time next week,' he said aloud, as if to reassure himself as he walked back down Chestnut Street to his own house.

During the party Anne found time to watch Henry whenever he was near Milly Preston. There was certainly no outward sign of anything between them; in fact, Henry spent more of his time with John Preston. Anne began to wonder if she had not misjudged her husband and thought about cancelling her appointment with Glen Ricardo the next day. The party came to an end two hours later than Anne had anticipated; she hoped it meant that everybody had enjoyed themselves.

'Great party, Anne, thanks for inviting us.' It was the loud voice again, leaving last. Anne couldn't remember his name, something to do with City Hall. He disappeared down the drive.

Anne stumbled upstairs, undoing her dress even before she had reached the bedroom, promising herself that she would give no more parties before having the baby in ten weeks' time.

Henry was already undressing. 'Did you get a chance to have a word with Alan, darling?'

'Yes, I did,' replied Anne. 'He said the books look fine, but as the company can only show one year's figures, he must bring his own accountants in to double check; apparently that's normal banking policy.'

'Normal banking policy be damned. Can't you sense William's presence behind all this? He's trying to hold up the loan, Anne.'

'How can you say that? Alan said nothing about William.'

'Didn't he?' said Henry, his voice rising. 'He didn't bother to mention to you that William had lunch with him on Sunday at the golf club while we sat here at home alone?'

'What?' said Anne. 'I don't believe it. William would never come to Boston without seeing me. You must be mistaken, Henry.'

'My dear, half of the city was there, and I don't imagine that William travelled some fifty miles just for a round of golf with Alan Lloyd. Listen, Anne, I need that loan or I'm going to fail to qualify as a bidder for the city contract. Some time – and very soon now – you are going to have to decide whether you trust William or me. I must have the money by a week from tomorrow, only eight days from now, because if I can't show City Hall I'm good for that amount, I'll be disqualified. Disqualified because William didn't approve of your wanting to marry me. Please Anne, will you call Alan tomorrow and tell him to transfer the money?'

His angry voice boomed in Anne's head, making her feel faint and dizzy.

'No, not tomorrow, Henry. Can it wait until Friday? I have a heavy day tomorrow.'

Henry collected himself with an effort and came over to her as she stood naked looking at herself in the mirror. He ran his hand over her bulging stomach. 'I want this little fellow to be given as good a chance as William.'

.   .   .

The next day Anne told herself a hundred times that she would not go to see Glen Ricardo, but a little before noon she found herself hailing a cab. She climbed the creaky wooden stairs, apprehensive of what she might learn. She could still turn back. She hesitated, then knocked quietly on the door.

'Come in.'

She opened the door.

'Ah, Mrs Osborne, how nice to see you again. Do have a seat.'

Anne sat and they stared at each other.

'The news, I am afraid, is not good,' said Glen Ricardo, pushing his hand through his long dark hair.

Anne's heart sank. She felt sick.

'Mr Osborne has not been seen with Mrs Preston or any other woman during the past seven days.'

'But you said the news wasn't good,' said Anne.

'Of course, Mrs Osborne, I assumed you were looking for grounds for divorce. Angry wives don't normally come to me hoping I'll prove their husbands are innocent.'

'No, no,' said Anne, suffused with relief. 'It's the best piece of news I've had in weeks.'

'Oh, good,' said Mr Ricardo, slightly taken aback. 'Let us hope the second week reveals nothing as well.'

'Oh, you can stop the investigation now, Mr Ricardo. I am sure you'll not find anything of any consequence next week.'

'I don't think that would be wise, Mrs Osborne. To make a final judgement on only one week's observation would be, to say the least, premature.'

'All right, if you believe it will prove the point, but I still feel confident that you won't uncover anything new next week.'

'In any case,' continued Glen Ricardo, puffing away at his cigar, which looked bigger and smelled better to Anne than it had the previous week, 'you have already paid for the two weeks.'

'What about the letters?' asked Anne, suddenly remembering them. 'I suppose they must have come from someone jealous of my husband's achievements.'

'Well, as I pointed out to you last week, Mrs Osborne, tracing the sender of anonymous letters is never easy. However, we have been able to locate the shop where the stationery was bought, as the brand was fairly unusual, but for the moment I have nothing further to report on that front. Again, I may have a lead by this time next week. Have you received any more letters in the past few days?'

'No, I haven't.'

'Good, then it all seems to be working out for the best. Let us hope, for your sake, that next week's meeting will be our last.'

'Yes,' said Anne happily, 'let us hope so. Can I settle your expenses next Thursday?'

'Of course, of course.'

Anne had nearly forgotten the phrase, but this time it made her laugh. She decided as she was driven home that Henry must have the five hundred thousand loan and the chance to prove William and Alan wrong. She had still not recovered from the knowledge that William had come to Boston without letting her know; perhaps Henry had been right in his suggestion that William was trying to work behind their backs.

. . .

Henry was delighted when Anne told him that night of her decision on the loan, and he produced the legal documents the following morning for her signature. Anne couldn't help thinking that he must have had the papers prepared for some time, especially as Milly Preston's signature was already on them, or was she being overly suspicious again? She dismissed the thought and signed quickly.

. . .

She was fully prepared for Alan Lloyd when he telephoned the following Monday morning.

'Anne, let me at least hold things over until Thursday. Then we'll know who has been awarded the hospital contract.'

'No, Alan, the decision can't wait. Henry needs the money now. He has to prove to City Hall that he's financially strong enough to fulfil the contract and you already have the signatures of two trustees so the responsibility is no longer yours.'

'The bank could always guarantee Henry's position without actually passing over the money. I'm sure City Hall would find that acceptable. In any case, I haven't had enough time to check over his company's accounts.'

'But you did find enough time to have lunch with William a week ago Sunday, without informing me.'

There was a momentary silence from the other end of the line.

'Anne, I . . .'

'Don't say you didn't have the opportunity. You came to our party on Wednesday, and you could easily have mentioned it to me then. You chose not to, but you did find the time to advise me to postpone judgement on the loan to Henry.'

'Anne, I am sorry. I can understand how that might look and why you are upset, but there really was a reason, believe me. May I come around and explain everything to you?'

'No, Alan, you can't. You're all ganging up against my husband. None of you wants to give him a chance to prove himself. Well, I am going to give him that chance.'

Anne put the telephone down, pleased with herself, feeling she had been loyal to Henry in a way that fully atoned for her ever having doubted him in the first place.

Alan Lloyd rang back, but Anne instructed the maid to say she was out for the rest of the day. When Henry returned home that night, he was delighted to hear how Anne had dealt with Alan.

'It will all turn out for the best, my love, you'll see. On Thursday morning I will be awarded the contract, and you can kiss and make up with Alan; still, you had better keep out of his way until then. In fact, if you like we can have a celebration lunch on Thursday at the Ritz and wave at him from the other side of the room.'

Anne smiled and agreed. She could not help remembering that she was meant to be seeing Ricardo for the last time at twelve o'clock that day. Still, that would be early enough for her to be at the Ritz by one and she could celebrate both triumphs at once.

Alan tried repeatedly to reach Anne, but the maid always had a ready excuse. Since the document had been signed by two trustees, he could not hold up the payment for more than twenty-four hours. The wording was typical of a legal agreement drawn up by Richard Kane; there were no loopholes to crawl out of. When the cheque for five hundred thousand dollars left the bank by special messenger on Tuesday afternoon, Alan sat down and wrote a long letter to William setting out the events that had culminated in the transfer of the money, withholding only the unconfirmed findings of his departmental reports. He sent a copy of the letter to each director of the bank, conscious that although he had behaved with the utmost propriety, he had laid himself open to accusations of concealment.

.   .   .

William received Alan Lloyd's letter at St Paul's on the Thursday morning while having breakfast with Matthew.

. . .

Breakfast on Thursday morning at Beacon Hill was the usual eggs and bacon, hot toast, cold oatmeal, and a pot of steaming coffee. Henry was simultaneously tense and jaunty, snapping at the maid, joking with a junior city official who telephoned to say the name of the company who had been awarded the hospital contract would be posted on the notice board at City Hall around ten o'clock. Anne was almost looking forward to her last meeting with Glen Ricardo. She flicked through *Vogue*, trying not to notice that Henry's hands, clutching the *Boston Globe*, were trembling.

'What are you going to do this morning?' Henry asked, trying to make conversation.

'Oh, nothing much before we have our celebration lunch. Will you be able to build the children's wing in memory of Richard?' Anne asked.

'Not in memory of Richard, my darling. This will be my achievement, so let it be in your honour – "The Mrs Henry Osborne Wing",' he added grandly.

'What a good idea,' Anne said, as she put her magazine down and smiled at him. 'But you mustn't let me drink too much champagne at lunch as I have a full check-up with Doctor MacKenzie this afternoon, and I don't think he would approve of me being drunk only nine weeks before the baby is due. When will you know for certain that the contract is yours?'

'I know now,' Henry said. 'The clerk I just spoke to was a hundred per cent confident, but it will be official at ten o'clock.'

'The first thing you must do then, Henry, is to phone Alan and tell him the good news. I'm beginning to feel quite guilty about the way I treated him last week.'

'No need for you to feel any guilt; he didn't bother to keep you informed of William's actions.'

'No, but he tried to explain later, Henry, and I didn't give him a chance to tell me his side of the story.'

'All right, all right, anything you say. If it'll make you happy, I'll phone him at five past ten, and then you can tell William I've made him another million.'

He looked at his watch. 'I'd better be going. Wish me luck.'

'I thought you didn't need any luck,' said Anne.

'I don't, I don't. It's only an expression. See you at the Ritz at one o'clock.' He kissed her on the forehead. 'By tonight, you'll be able to laugh about Alan, William, contracts, and treat them all as problems of the past, believe me. Goodbye, darling.'

'I hope so, Henry.'

. . .

An uneaten breakfast was laid out in front of Alan Lloyd. He was reading the financial pages of the *Boston Globe*, noting a small paragraph in the right hand column reporting that the city would be announcing at ten o'clock that morning which company had been awarded the five-million-dollar hospital contract.

Alan Lloyd had already decided what course of action he must take if

Henry failed to secure the contract and everything that William had claimed turned out to be accurate. He would do exactly what Richard would have done faced with the same predicament, and act only in the best interests of the bank. The latest departmental reports on Henry's personal finances disturbed Alan Lloyd greatly. Osborne was indeed a heavy gambler and no trace could be found of the trust's five hundred thousand dollars having gone into Henry's company. Alan Lloyd sipped his orange juice and left the rest of his breakfast untouched, apologized to his housekeeper and walked to the bank. It was a pleasant day.

· · ·

'William, are you up to a game of tennis this afternoon?'

Matthew Lester was standing over William as he read the letter from Alan Lloyd for a second time.

'What did you say?'

'Are you going deaf or just becoming a senile adolescent? Do you want me to beat you black and blue on the tennis court this afternoon?'

'No, I won't be here this afternoon, Matthew. I have more important things to attend to.'

'Naturally, old buddy, I forgot that you're off on another of your mysterious trips to the White House. I know President Harding is looking for someone to be his new fiscal advisor, and you're exactly the right man to take the place of that posturing fool, Charles G. Dawes. Tell him you'll accept, subject to his inviting Matthew Lester to be the Administration's next Attorney General.'

There was still no response from William.

'I know the joke was pretty weak, but I thought it worthy of some comment,' said Matthew as he sat down beside William and looked more carefully at his friend. 'It's the eggs, isn't it? Taste as though they've come out of a Russian prisoner-of-war camp.'

'Matthew, I need your help,' said William, as he put Alan's letter back into its envelope.

'You've had a letter from my sister and she thinks you'll do as a temporary replacement for Rudolf Valentino.'

William stood up. 'Quit kidding, Matthew. If your father's bank was being robbed, would you sit around making jokes about it?'

The expression on William's face was unmistakably serious. Matthew's tone changed. 'No, I wouldn't.'

'Right, then let's get out of here, and I'll explain everything.'

· · ·

Anne left Beacon Hill a little after ten to do some shopping before going onto her final meeting with Glen Ricardo. The telephone started to ring as she disappeared down Chestnut Street. The maid answered it, looked out the window and decided that her mistress was too far away to be pursued. If Anne had returned to take the call she would have been informed of City Hall's decision on the hospital contract, whereas instead she selected some silk stockings and tried out a new perfume. She arrived at Glen Ricardo's office a little after twelve, hoping her new perfume might counter the smell of cigar smoke.

'I hope I'm not late, Mr Ricardo,' she began briskly.

'Have a seat, Mrs Osborne.' Ricardo did not look particularly cheerful, but, thought Anne to herself, he never does. Then she noticed that he was not smoking his usual cigar.

Glen Ricardo opened a smart brown file, the only new thing Anne could see in the office, and unclipped some papers.

'Let's start with the anonymous letters, shall we, Mrs Osborne?'

Anne did not like the tone of his voice at all or the word start. 'Yes, all right,' she managed to get out.

'They are being sent by a Mrs Ruby Flowers.'

'Who? Why?' said Anne, impatient for an answer she did not want to hear.

'I suspect one of the reasons must be that Mrs Flowers is at present suing your husband.'

'Well, that explains the whole mystery,' said Anne. 'She must want revenge. How much does she claim Henry owes her?'

'She is not suggesting debt, Mrs Osborne.'

'Well, what is she suggesting then?'

Glen Ricardo pushed himself up from the chair, as if the movement required the full strength of both his arms to raise his tired frame. He walked to the window and looked out over the crowded Boston harbour.

'She is suing for a breach of promise, Mrs Osborne.'

'Oh, no,' said Anne.

'It appears that they were engaged to be married at the time that Mr Osborne met you, when the engagement was suddenly terminated for no apparent reason.'

'Gold digger; she must have wanted Henry's money.'

'No, I don't think so. You see, Mrs Flowers is already well off. Not in your class, of course, but well off all the same. Her late husband owned a soft drink bottling company, and had left her financially secure.'

'Her late husband – how old is she?'

The detective walked back to the table and flicked over a page or two of his file before his thumb started moving down the page. The black nail came to a halt.

'She'll be fifty-three on her next birthday.'

'Oh, my God,' said Anne. 'The poor woman. She must hate me.'

'I dare say she does, Mrs Osborne, but that will not help us. Now I must turn to your husband's other activities.'

The nicotine-stained finger turned over some more pages.

Anne began to feel sick. Why had she come, why hadn't she left well alone last week? She didn't have to know. She didn't want to know. Why didn't she get up and walk away? How she wished Richard was by her side. He would have known exactly how to deal with the whole situation. She found herself unable to move, transfixed by Glen Ricardo and the contents of his smart new file.

'On two occasions last week Mr Osborne spent over three hours alone with Mrs Preston.'

'But that doesn't prove anything,' began Anne desperately, 'I know they were discussing a very important financial document.'

'In a small hotel on La Salle Street.'

Anne didn't interrupt the detective again.

'On both occasions they were seen walking into the hotel holding hands, whispering and laughing. It's not conclusive of course, but we have photographs of them together entering and leaving the hotel.'

'Destroy them,' said Anne quietly.

Glen Ricardo blinked. 'As you wish, Mrs Osborne. I'm afraid there is more. Further inquiries show that Mr Osborne was never at Harvard nor was he an officer in the American armed forces. There was a Henry Osborne at Harvard who was five-foot-five, sandy-haired and came from Alabama. He was killed on the Maine in 1917. We also know that your husband is considerably younger than he claims to be and that his real name is Vittorio Togna, and he has served —'

'I don't want to hear any more,' said Anne, tears flooding down her cheeks. 'I don't want to hear any more.'

'Of course, Mrs Osborne, I understand. I am only sorry that my news is so distressing. In my job sometimes . . .'

Anne fought for a measure of self-control. 'Thank you, Mr Ricardo. I appreciate all you have done. How much do I owe you?'

'Well, you have already paid for the two weeks in advance, and my expenses came to seventy-three dollars.'

Anne passed him a hundred-dollar note and rose from her chair.

'Don't forget your change, Mrs Osborne.'

She shook her head and waved a disinterested hand.

'Are you feeling all right, Mrs Osborne? You look a little pale to me. Can I get you a glass of water or something?'

'I'm fine,' lied Anne.

'Perhaps you would allow me to drive you home?'

'No, thank you, Mr Ricardo, I'll be able to get myself home.' She turned and smiled at him. 'It was kind of you to offer.'

Glen Ricardo closed the door quietly behind his client, walked slowly to the window, bit the end off his last big cigar, spat it out and cursed his job.

*   *   *

Anne paused at the top of the stairs, clinging to the banister, almost fainting. The baby kicked inside her, making her feel nauseous. She found a cab on the corner of the block and huddled in the back, was unable to stop herself sobbing or to think what to do next. As soon as she was dropped at the Red House, she went to her bedroom before any of the staff could see her crying. The telephone was ringing as she entered the room, and she picked it up, more from habit than from any curiosity to know who it might be.

'Could I speak to Mrs Kane, please?'

She recognized Alan's clipped tone at once. Another tired, unhappy voice.

'Hello, Alan. This *is* Anne.'

'Anne, my dear, I was so sorry to learn about this morning's news.'

'How do you know about it, Alan, how can you possibly know? Who told you?'

'City Hall phoned me and gave me the details soon after ten this morning. I tried to call you then, but your maid said that you had already left to do some shopping.'

'Oh, my God,' said Anne. 'I had quite forgotten about the contract.' She sat down heavily, unable to breathe freely.

'Are you all right, Anne?'

'Yes, I'm just fine,' she said, trying unsuccessfully to hide the sobbing in her voice. 'What did City Hall have to say?'

'The hospital contract was awarded to a firm called Kirkbride and Carter. Apparently Henry wasn't even placed in the top three. I've been trying to reach him all morning, but it seems he left his office soon after ten and he hasn't been back since. I don't suppose you know where he is, Anne?'

'No, I haven't any idea.'

'Do you want me to come around, my dear?' he said. 'I could be with you in a few minutes.'

'No, thank you, Alan.' Anne paused to draw a shaky breath. 'Please forgive me for the way I have been treating you these past few days. If Richard were still alive, he would never have forgiven me.'

'Don't be silly, Anne, our friendship has lasted for far too many years for a silly little incident like that to be of any significance.'

The kindness of his voice triggered off a fresh burst of weeping. Anne staggered to her feet.

'I must go, Alan. I can hear someone at the front door; it might be Henry.'

'Take care, Anne, and don't worry about today. As long as I'm chairman, the bank will always support you. Don't hesitate to call if you need me.'

Anne put the telephone down, the noise thudding in her ears. The effort of breathing was stupendous. She sank to the floor and as she did so, the long-forgotten sensation of a vigorous contraction overwhelmed her.

A few moments later the maid knocked quietly on the door. She looked in; William was at her shoulder. He had not entered his mother's bedroom since her marriage to Henry Osborne. The two rushed to Anne's side. She was shaking convulsively, unaware of their presence. Little flecks of foam spattered her upper lip. In a few seconds the attack passed, and she lay moaning quietly.

'Mother,' said William urgently. 'What's the matter?'

Anne opened her eyes and stared wildly at her son. 'Richard. Thank God you've come. I need you.'

'It's William, Mother.'

Her gaze faltered. 'I have no more strength left, Richard. I must pay for my mistakes. Forgive ...'

Her voice trailed off to a groan as another powerful contraction started.

'What's happening?' said William helplessly.

'I think it must be the baby coming,' the maid said, 'although it isn't due for several weeks.'

'Get Dr MacKenzie on the phone immediately,' William said to the maid as he ran to the bedroom door. 'Matthew,' he shouted, 'come up quickly.'

Matthew bounded up the stairs and joined William in the bedroom.

'Help me get my mother down to the car,' he said.

Matthew knelt down. The two boys picked Anne up and carried her gently downstairs and out to the car. She was panting and groaning, and obviously still in immense pain. William ran back to the house and grabbed the phone from the maid while Matthew waited in the car.

'Doctor MacKenzie.'

'Yes, who's this?'

'My name is William Kane; you won't know me, sir.'

'Don't know you, young man? I delivered you. What can I do for you now?'

'I think my mother is in labour. I'll bring her to the hospital immediately. I should be there in a few minutes' time.'

Doctor MacKenzie's tone changed. 'All right, William, don't worry. I'll be here waiting for you and everything will be under control by the time you arrive.'

'Thank you, sir.' William hesitated. 'She seemed to have some sort of fit. Is that normal?'

William's words chilled the doctor. He too hesitated.

'Well, not quite normal. But she'll be all right once she has had the baby. Get here as quickly as you can.'

William put down the phone, ran out of the house and jumped into the Rolls Royce.

He drove the car in fits and starts, never once getting out of first gear and never stopping for anything until they had reached the doctor at the hospital. The two boys carried Anne, and a nurse with a stretcher guided them through to the maternity section. Doctor MacKenzie was standing at the entrance of an operating room, waiting. He took over and asked them both to remain outside.

The two boys sat in silence on the small bench and waited. Frightening cries and screams, unlike any sound they had ever heard anyone make, came from the delivery room; to be succeeded by an even more frightening silence. For the first time in his life William felt totally helpless. The two of them sat there for over an hour, without a word passing between them. Eventually a tired Doctor MacKenzie emerged. The two boys rose, and the doctor looked at Matthew Lester.

'William?' he asked.

'No, sir, I am Matthew Lester; this is William.'

The doctor turned to William and put a hand on his shoulder. 'William, I'm so sorry, your mother died a few minutes ago ... and the child, a little girl, was stillborn.' William's legs gave way and he sank onto the bench. 'We did everything in our power to save them, but it was hopeless.' He shook his head wearily. 'She wouldn't listen to me, she insisted on having the baby. It should never have happened.'

William sat silently, stunned by the whiplash sound of the doctor's words.

'How *could* she die?' he whispered. 'How could you *let* her die?'

The doctor sat down on the bench between the boys. 'She wouldn't listen,' he repeated slowly. 'I warned her repeatedly after her miscarriage not to have another child, but when she married again, she and your step-father never took my warnings seriously. She had high blood pressure during her last pregnancy. It was worrying me during this one, although it was never near danger level. But when you brought her in today, for no apparent reason it had soared up to the level where eclampsia ensues.'

'Eclampsia?'

'Convulsions. Sometimes patients can survive several attacks. Sometimes they simply – stop breathing.'

William drew a shuddering breath and placed his head in his hands.

Matthew Lester guided his friend gently along the corridor. The doctor followed them. Whey they reached the door, he looked at William.

'Her blood pressure went up so suddenly. It's very unusual, and she didn't put up a real fight, almost as if she didn't care. Strange, had something been troubling her lately?'

William raised his tear-streaked face. 'Not some*thing*,' he said with hatred. 'Some*one*.'

. . .

Alan Lloyd was sitting in a corner of the drawing room when the two boys arrived back at the Red House. He rose as they entered.

'William,' he said immediately. 'I blame myself for allowing the loan.'

William stared at him, not taking in what he was saying.

Matthew Lester stepped into the silence. 'I don't think that's important any longer, sir,' he said quietly. 'William's mother has just died in childbirth.'

Alan Lloyd turned ashen, steadied himself by grasping the mantelpiece, and turned away. It was the first time that either of them had seen a grown man weep.

'It's my fault,' said the banker. 'I'll never forgive myself. I didn't tell her everything I knew. I loved her so much that I never wanted her to be distressed.'

His anguish enabled William to be calm.

'It certainly was not your fault, Alan,' he said firmly. 'You did everything you could, I know that, and now it's I who am going to need your help.'

Alan Lloyd braced himself. 'Has Osborne been informed about your mother's death?'

'I neither know nor care.'

'I've been trying to reach him all day about the investment. He left his office soon after ten this morning, and he hasn't been seen since.'

'He'll turn up here sooner or later,' said William grimly.

After Alan Lloyd left, William and Matthew sat alone in the front room most of the night, dozing off and on. At four o'clock in the morning, William counted the chimes of the grandfather clock and thought that he heard a noise in the street. Matthew was staring out of the window down the drive. William walked stiffly over to join him. They both watched Henry Osborne stagger across Louisburg Square with a half-full bottle in his hand. He fumbled with some keys for some time and finally appeared in the doorway, blinking dazedly at the two boys.

'I want Anne, not you. Why aren't you at school? I don't want you,' he said, his voice thick and slurred, trying to push William aside. 'Where's Anne?'

'My mother is dead,' said William quietly.

Henry Osborne looked at him stupidly for a few seconds. The incomprehension of his gaze snapped William's self-control.

'Where were you when she needed a husband?' he shouted.

Still Osborne stood, swaying slightly. 'What about the baby?'

'Stillborn, a little girl.'

Henry Osborne slumped into a chair, drunken tears starting to run down his face. 'She lost my little baby?'

William was nearly incoherent with rage and grief. 'Your baby? Stop thinking about yourself for once,' he shouted. 'You know Doctor MacKenzie advised her against becoming pregnant again.'

'Expert in that as well, are we, like everything else? If you had minded your own fucking business, I could have taken care of my own wife without your interference.'

'And her money, it seems.'

'Money. You tight-fisted little bastard, I bet losing that hurts you more than anything else.'

'Get up,' William said between his teeth.

Henry Osborne pushed himself up, and smashed the bottle across the corner of the chair. Whisky splashed all over the carpet. He swayed towards William with the broken bottle in his raised hand. William stood his ground while Matthew came between them and easily removed the bottle from the drunken man's grasp.

William pushed his friend aside and advanced until his face was only inches away from Henry Osborne's.

'Now, you listen to me and listen carefully. I want you out of this house in one hour. If I ever hear from you again in my life, I shall instigate a full legal investigation into what has happened to my mother's half million dollar investment in your firm, and I shall re-open my research into who you really are and your past life in Chicago. If, on the other hand, I do not hear from you again, ever, I shall consider the ledger balanced and the matter closed. Now get out before I kill you.'

The two boys watched him leave, sobbing, incoherent and furious.

. . .

The next morning William paid a visit to the bank. He was immediately shown into the chairman's office. Alan Lloyd was packing some documents into a briefcase. He looked up, and handed a piece of paper to William without speaking. It was a short letter to all board members tendering his resignation as chairman of the bank.

'Could you ask your secretary to come in?' said William quietly.

'As you wish.'

Alan Lloyd pressed a button on the side of his desk, and a middle-aged, conservatively dressed lady entered the room from a side door.

'Good morning, Mr Kane,' she said when she saw William. 'I was so sorry to learn about your mother.'

'Thank you,' said William. 'Has anyone else seen this letter?'

'No, sir,' said the secretary. 'I was about to type twelve copies for Mr Lloyd to sign.'

'Well, don't type them, and please forget that this draft ever existed. Never mention its existence to anyone, do you understand?'

She stared into those blue eyes of the sixteen-year-old boy. So like his father, she thought. 'Yes, Mr Kane.' She left quietly closing the door. Alan Lloyd looked up.

'Kane and Cabot doesn't need a new chairman at the moment, Alan. You did nothing my father would not have done in the same circumstances.'

'It's not as easy as that,' Alan said.

'It's as easy as that,' said William. 'We can discuss this again when I am twenty-one and not before. Until then I would be obliged if you would run my bank in your usual diplomatic and conservative manner. I want nothing of what has happened to be discussed outside this office. You will destroy any information you have on Henry Osborne and consider the matter closed.'

William tore up the letter of resignation and dropped the pieces of paper into the fire. He put his arm around Alan's shoulders.

'I have no family now, Alan, only you. For God's sake don't desert me.'

. . .

William was driven back to Beacon Hill. On his arrival the butler informed him that Mrs Kane and Mrs Cabot were waiting for him in the drawing room. They both rose as he entered the room. It was the first time that William realized that he was now the head of the Kane family.

. . .

The funeral took place quietly two days later at the Old North Church on Beacon Hill. None but the family and close friends were invited, and the only notable absentee was Henry Osborne. As the mourners departed, they paid their respects to William. The grandmothers stood one pace behind him, like sentinels, watching, approving the calm and dignified way in which he conducted himself. When everyone had left, William accompanied Alan Lloyd to his car.

The chairman was delighted by William's one request of him.

'As you know, Alan, my mother had always intended to build a children's wing to the new hospital, in memory of my father. I would like her wishes carried out.'

11

Wladek stayed at the Polish Delegation in Constantinople for eighteen months, working day and night for Pawel Zaleski, becoming an indispensable aide and close friend. Nothing was too much trouble for him and Zaleski soon began to wonder how he managed before Wladek arrived. He visited the British embassy once a week to eat in the kitchen with Mrs Henderson, the Scottish cook, and, on one occasion, with His Britannic Majesty's second consul himself.

Around them the old Islamic way of life was dissolving, and the Ottoman Empire was beginning to totter. Mustafa Kemal was the name on everyone's lips. The sense of impending change made Wladek restless. His mind returned incessantly to the Baron and all whom he had loved in the castle. The necessity to survive from day to day in Russia had kept them from his mind's eye, but in Turkey they rose up before him, a silent and slow procession. Sometimes, he could see them strong and happy, Leon swimming in the river, Florentyna playing cat's cradle in his bedroom, the Baron's face strong and proud in the evening candlelight, but always each well-remembered, well-loved face would waver and, try as Wladek did to hold them firm, they would change horribly to that last dreadful aspect, Leon dead on top of him, Florentyna bleeding in agony, and the Baron almost blind and broken.

Wladek began to face the fact that he could never return to a land peopled by such ghosts, until he had made something worthwhile of his life. With that single thought in mind he set his heart on going to America, as his countryman Tadeusz Kosciuszko, of whom the Baron had 'told so many enthralling tales, had done so long before him. The United States, described by Pawel Zaleski as the 'New World'. The very name inspired Wladek with a hope for the future and a chance to return to Poland in triumph. It was Pawel Zaleski who put up the money to purchase an immigrant passage for him to the United States. They were difficult to come by, for they were always booked at least a year in advance. It seemed to Wladek as though the whole of Eastern Europe was trying to escape and start afresh in the New World.

In the spring of 1921, Wladek Koskiewicz finally left Constantinople and boarded the SS *Black Arrow*, bound for Ellis Island, New York. He possessed one suitcase, containing all his belongings, and a set of papers issued by Pawel Zaleski.

The Polish consul accompanied him to the wharf, and embraced him affectionately. 'Go with God, my boy.'

The traditional Polish response came naturally from the depths of Wladek's early childhood. 'Remain with God,' he replied.

As he reached the top of the gangplank, Wladek recalled his terrifying journey from Odessa to Constantinople. This time there was no coal in sight, only people, people everywhere, Poles, Lithuanians, Estonians, Ukrainians and others of many racial types unfamiliar to Wladek. He clutched his few belongings and waited in the line, the first of many long waits with which he later associated his entry into the United States.

His papers were sternly scrutinized by a deck officer who was clearly predisposed to the suspicion that Wladek was trying to avoid military service in Turkey, but Pawel Zaleski's documents were impeccable; Wladek invoked a silent blessing on his fellow countryman's head as he watched others being turned back.

Next came a vaccination and a cursory medical examination which, had he not had eighteen months of good food and the chance to recover his health in Constantinople, Wladek would certainly have failed. At last with all the checks over he was allowed below deck into the steerage quarters. There were separate compartments for males, females and married couples. Wladek quickly made his way to the male quarters and found the Polish group occupying a large block of iron berths, each containing four two-tiered bunk beds. Each bunk had a thin straw mattress, a light blanket and no pillow. Having no pillow did not worry Wladek who had never been able to sleep on one since leaving Russia.

Wladek selected a bunk below a boy of roughly his own age and introduced himself.

'I'm Wladek Koskiewicz.'

'I'm Jerzy Nowak from Warsaw,' volunteered the boy in his native Polish, 'and I'm going to make my fortune in America.'

The boy thrust forward his hand.

Wladek and Jerzy spent the time before the ship sailed telling each other of their experiences, both pleased to have someone to share their loneliness with, neither willing to admit their total ignorance of America. Jerzy, it turned out, had lost his parents in the war but had few other claims to attention. He was entranced by Wladek's stories: the son of a baron, brought up in a trapper's cottage, imprisoned by the Germans and the Russians, escaped from Siberia and then from a Turkish executioner thanks to the heavy silver band which Jerzy couldn't take his eyes off. Wladek had packed more in to his fifteen years than Jerzy thought he would manage in a lifetime. Wladek talked all night of the past while Jerzy listened intently, neither wanting to sleep and neither wanting to admit their apprehension of the future.

The following morning the *Black Arrow* sailed. Wladek and Jerzy stood at the rail and watched Constantinople slip away in the blue distance of the Bosphorus. After the calm of the Sea of Marmara the choppiness of the Aegean afflicted them and most of the other passengers with a horrible abruptness. The two washrooms for steerage passengers, with ten basins apiece, six toilets and cold salt water taps were rapidly inundated. After a couple of days the stench of their quarters was nauseating.

Food was served in a large filthy dining hall on long tables; warm soup, potatoes, fish, boiled beef and cabbage, brown or black bread. Wladek had tasted worse food but not since Russia and was glad of the provisions he had brought along with him: sausages, nuts and a little brandy. He and Jerzy shared them huddled in the corner of their berth. It was an unspoken understanding. They ate together, explored the ship together and at night, slept one above the other.

On the third day at sea Jerzy brought a Polish girl to their table for supper. Her name, he informed Wladek casually, was Zaphia. It was the first time in his life that Wladek had ever looked at a woman twice, but he couldn't stop looking at Zaphia. She rekindled memories of Florentyna. The warm grey eyes, the long fair hair that fell onto her shoulders and the soft voice. Wladek found he wanted to touch her. The girl occasionally smiled across at Wladek, who was miserably aware how much better looking Jerzy was than he. He tagged along as Jerzy escorted Zaphia back to the woman's quarters.

Jerzy turned to him afterwards, mildly irritated. 'Can't you find a girl of your own? This one's mine.'

Wladek was not prepared to admit that he had no idea how to set about finding a girl of his own.

'There will be enough time for girls when we reach America,' he said scornfully.

'Why wait for America? I intend to have as many on this ship as possible.'

'How will you go about that?' asked Wladek, intent on the acquisition of knowledge without admitting to his own ignorance.

'We have twelve more days in this awful tub, and I am going to have twelve women,' boasted Jerzy.

'What can you do with twelve women?' asked Wladek.

'Fuck them, what else?'

Wladek looked perplexed.

'Good God,' said Jerzy. 'Don't tell me the man who survived the Germans and escaped from the Russians, killed a man at the age of twelve and narrowly missed having his hand chopped off by a bunch of savage Turks has never had a woman?'

He laughed, and a multilingual chorus from the surrounding bunks told him to 'shut up'.

'Well,' Jerzy continued in a whisper, 'the time has come to broaden your education, because at last I have found something I can teach you.' He peered over the side of his bunk even though he could not see Wladek's face in the dark. 'Zaphia's an understanding girl. I dare say she could be persuaded to expand your education a little. I shall arrange it.'

Wladek didn't reply.

No more was said on the subject, but the next day Zaphia started to pay attention to Wladek. She sat next to him at meals, and they talked for hours of their experiences and hopes. She was an orphan from Pozan, on her way to join her cousins in Chicago. Wladek told Zaphia that he was going to New York and would probably live with Jerzy.

'I hope New York is very near Chicago,' said Zaphia.

'Then you can come and see me when I am the mayor,' said Jerzy expansively.

She sniffed disparagingly. 'You're too Polish, Jerzy. You can't even speak nice English like Wladek.'

'I'll learn,' said Jerzy confidently, 'and I'll start by making my name American. From today I shall be George Novak. Then I'll have no trouble at all. Everyone in the United States will think I'm American. What about you, Wladek Koskiewicz? Nothing much you can do with that name, is there?'

Wladek looked at the newly christened George in silent resentment of his own name. Unable to adopt the title to which he felt himself the rightful heir, he hated Koskiewicz and the continual reminder of his illegitimacy.

'I'll manage,' he said. 'I'll even help you with your English if you like.'

'And I'll help you find a girl.'

Zaphia giggled. 'You needn't bother, he's found one.'

Jerzy, or George, as he now insisted they should call him, retreated after supper each night into one of the tarpaulin-covered lifeboats with a different girl. Wladek longed to know what he did there, even though some of the ladies of George's choice were not merely filthy, as they all were, but would clearly have been unattractive even when scrubbed clean.

One night after supper, when George had disappeared again, Wladek and Zaphia sat out on deck, she put her arms around him and asked him to kiss her. He pressed his mouth stiffly against hers until their teeth touched; he felt horribly unfamiliar with what he was meant to be doing. To his surprise and embarrassment, her tongue parted his lips. After a few moments of apprehension, Wladek found her open mouth intensely exciting and was alarmed to find his penis stiffening. He tried to draw away from her, ashamed, but she did not seem to mind in the least. On the contrary, she began to press her body gently and rhythmically against him and drew his hands down to her buttocks. His swollen penis throbbed against her, giving him almost unbearable pleasure. She disengaged her mouth and whispered in his ear.

'Do you want me to take my clothes off, Wladek?'

He could not bring himself to reply.

She detached herself from him, laughing. 'Well, maybe tomorrow,' she said, getting up from the deck and leaving him.

He stumbled back to his bunk in a daze, determined that the next day he would finish the job Zaphia had started. No sooner had he settled in his berth thinking of how he would go about the task than a large hand grabbed him by the hair and pulled him down from his bunk onto the floor. In an instant his sexual excitement vanished. Two men whom he had never seen before were towering above him. They dragged him to a far corner and threw him up against the wall. A large hand was now clamped firmly on Wladek's mouth while a knife touched his throat.

'Don't breathe,' whispered the man holding the knife, pushing the blade against the skin. 'All we want is the silver band around your wrist.'

The sudden realization that his treasure might be stolen from him was almost as horrifying to Wladek as had been the thought of losing his hand. Before he could think of anything to do, one of the men jerked the band off his wrist. He couldn't see their faces in the dark, and he feared he must have lost the band for ever, when someone leapt onto the back of the man holding the knife. This action gave Wladek the chance to punch the one who was holding him pinned to the ground. The sleepy immigrants around them began to wake and take an interest in what was happening. The two men escaped as quickly as they could, but not before George had managed to stick the knife in the side of one of the assailants.

'Go to the cholera,' shouted Wladek at his retreating back.

'It looks as if I got here just in time,' said George. 'I don't think they'll be back in a hurry.' He stared down at the silver band, lying in the trampled sawdust on the floor. 'It's magnificent,' he said, almost solemnly. 'There will always be men who want to steal such a prize from you.'

Wladek picked the band up and slipped it back onto his wrist.

'Well, you nearly lost the damn thing for good that time,' said George. 'Lucky for you I was a little late getting back tonight.'

'Why were you a little late getting back?' asked Wladek.

'My reputation,' said George boastfully, 'now goes before me. In fact, I found some other idiot in my lifeboat tonight, already with his pants down. I soon got rid of him, though, when I told him he was with a girl I would have had last week but I couldn't be sure she hadn't got the pox. I've never seen anyone get dressed so quickly.'

'What do you do in the boat?' asked Wladek.

'Fuck them silly, you ass, what do you think?' and with that he rolled over and went to sleep.

Wladek stared at the ceiling and, touching the silver band, thought about what George had said, wondering what it would be like to 'fuck' Zaphia.

The next morning they hit a storm, and all the passengers were confined below decks. The stench, intensified by the ship's steam heating system, seemed to permeate Wladek's very marrow.

'And the worst of it is,' groaned George, 'I won't make a round dozen now.'

When the storm abated, nearly all the passengers escaped to the deck. Wladek and George fought their way around the crowded gangways, thankful for the fresh air. Many of the girls smiled at George, but it seemed to Wladek that they didn't notice him at all. He would have thought they couldn't miss him in his fifty-ruble coat. A dark-haired girl, her cheeks made pink by the wind, passed George and smiled at him. He turned to Wladek.

'I'll have her tonight.'

Wladek stared at the girl and studied the way she looked at George.

'Tonight,' said George, as she passed within earshot. She pretended not to hear him and walked away, a little too quickly.

'Turn round, Wladek, and see if she is looking back at me.'

Wladek turned around, 'Yes, she is,' he said, surprised.

'She's mine tonight,' said George. 'Have you had Zaphia yet?'

'No,' said Wladek. 'Tonight.'

'About time, isn't it? You'll never see the girl again once we've reached New York.'

Sure enough, George arrived at supper that night with the dark-haired girl. Without a word being said, Wladek and Zaphia left them, arms round each other's waists, and went onto the deck and strolled around the ship several times. Wladek looked sideways at her pretty young profile. It was going to be now or never, he decided. He led her to a shadowy corner and started to kiss her as she had kissed him, open-mouthed. She moved backwards a little until her shoulders were resting against a bulwark, and Wladek moved with her. She drew his hands slowly down to her breasts. He touched them tentatively, surprised by their softness. She undid a couple of buttons on her blouse and slipped his hand inside. The first feel of the naked flesh was delicious.

'Christ, your hand is cold,' Zaphia said.

Wladek crushed himself against her, his mouth dry, his breath heavy. She parted her legs a little and Wladek thrust clumsily against her through several intervening layers of cloth. She moved in sympathy with him for a couple of minutes and then pushed him away.

'Not here on the deck,' she said. 'Let's find a boat.'

The first three they looked into were occupied, but they finally found an empty one and wriggled under the tarpaulin. In the constricted darkness Zaphia made some adjustments to her clothing that Wladek could not figure out, and pulled him gently on top of her. It took her very little time to bring Wladek to his earlier pitch of excitement through the few remaining layers of cloth between them. He thrust his penis into the yielding softness between her legs and was on the point of orgasm when she again drew her mouth away.

'Undo your trousers,' she whispered.

He felt an idiot but hurriedly undid them, and thrust again, coming immediately, feeling the sticky wetness running down the inside of her thigh. He lay dazed, amazed by the abruptness of the act, suddenly aware that the wooden notches of the boat were digging uncomfortably into his elbows and knees.

'Was that the first time you've made love to a girl?' asked Zaphia, wishing he would move over.

'No, of course not,' said Wladek.

'Do you love me, Wladek?'

'Yes, I do,' he said, 'and as soon as I've settled in New York, I'll come and find you in Chicago.'

'I'd like that, Wladek,' she said as she buttoned up her dress. 'I love you, too.'

'Did you fuck her?' was George's immediate question on Wladek's return.

'Yes.'

'Was it good?'

'Yes,' said Wladek, uncertainly, and then fell asleep.

In the morning, they were woken by a room full of excited passengers, happy in the knowledge that this was their last day on board the *Black Arrow*. Some of them had been up on deck before sunrise, hoping to catch the first sign of land. Wladek packed his few belongings in his new suitcase, put on his only suit, and his cap and then joined Zaphia and George on deck. The three of them stared into the mist that hung over the sea, waiting in silence for their first sight of the United States of America.

'There it is,' shouted a passenger on a deck above them, and cheering went up at the sight of the grey strip of Long Island approaching through the spring morning.

Little tugs bustled up to the side of the *Black Arrow* and guided her between Brooklyn and Staten Island into New York Harbour. The colossal Statue of Liberty regarded them austerely as they gazed in awe at the emerging skyline of Manhattan, great long arms stretching high into the autumn sky.

Finally they moored near the turreted and spired red brick buildings of Ellis Island. The passengers who had private cabins left the ship first. Wladek hadn't noticed them until that day. They must have been on a separate deck with their own dining hall. Their bags were carried for them by porters, and they were greeted by smiling faces at the quayside. Wladek knew that wasn't going to happen to him.

After the favoured few had disembarked, the captain announced over the loudspeaker to the rest of the passengers that they would not be leaving the ship for several hours. A groan of disappointment went up, and Zaphia sat on the deck and burst into tears. Wladek tried to comfort her. Eventually an official came around with coffee, a second with numbered labels which were hung around their necks. Wladek's was B.127; it reminded him of the last time he was a number. What had he let himself in for? Was America like the Russian camps?

In the middle of the afternoon, having been given no food or further information, they were ferried by slow moving barges from the dockside to Ellis Island. There the men were separated from the women and sent off to different sheds. Wladek kissed Zaphia and wouldn't let her go, which held up the line. A nearby official parted them.

'All right, let's get moving,' he said. 'Keep that up and we'll have you two married in no time.'

Wladek lost sight of Zaphia as he was pushed forwards with George. They spent the night in an old, damp shed, unable to sleep as interpreters moved among the crowded rows of bunks, offering curt, but not unkind, assistance to the bewildered immigrants.

In the morning they were sent for medical examinations. The first hurdle was the hardest: Wladek was told to climb a steep flight of stairs. The blue-uniformed doctor made him do it twice, watching his gait carefully. Wladek tried very hard to minimize his limp, and finally the doctor was satisfied. Wladek was made to remove his hat and stiff collar so that his face, eyes, hair, hands and neck could be examined carefully. The man directly behind Wladek had a hare lip; the doctor stopped him immediately, put a chalk cross on his shoulder and sent him to the other end of the shed. After the physical was over, Wladek joined up with George again in another long line outside the Public Examination room where each person seemed to be taking about five minutes. Three hours later when George was ushered into the room Wladek began to wonder what they would ask him.

When George came out, he grinned at Wladek and said, 'Easy, you'll walk right through it.' Wladek could feel the palms of his hands sweating as he stepped forward.

He followed the official into a small, undecorated room. There were two examiners seated and writing furiously on what looked like official papers.

'Do you speak English?' asked the first.

'Yes, sir, I do quite good,' replied Wladek, wishing he had spoken more English on the voyage.

'What is your name?'

'Wladek Koskiewicz, sir.'

The men passed him a big black book. 'Do you know what that is?'

'Yes, sir, the Bible.'

'Do you believe in God?'

'Yes, sir, I do.'

'Put your hand on the Bible, and swear that you will answer our questions truthfully.'

Wladek took the Bible in his left hand, placed his right hand on it and said, 'I promise I tell the truth.'

'What is your nationality?'

'Polish.'

'Who paid for your passage here?'

'I paid from my money that I earn in Polish Consulate in Constantinople.'

One of the officials studied Wladek's papers, nodded and then asked. 'Do you have a home to go to?'

'Yes, sir. I go stay at Mister Peter Novak. He my friend's uncle. He live in New York.'

'Good. Do you have work to go to?'

'Yes, sir. I go work in bakery of Mister Novak.'

'Have you ever been arrested?'

Russia flashed through Wladek's mind. It couldn't count. Turkey – he wasn't going to mention that.

'No, sir, never.'

'Are you an anarchist?'

'No, sir. I hate Communists, they kill my sister.'

'Are you willing to abide by the laws of the United States of America?'

'Yes, sir.'

'Have you any money?'

'Yes, sir.'

'May we see it?'

'Yes, sir.' Wladek placed on the table a bundle of notes and a few coins.

'Thank you,' said the examiner, 'you may put the money back in your pocket.'

The second examiner looked at him. 'What is twenty-one plus twenty-four?'

'Forty-five,' said Wladek, without hesitation.

'How many legs does a cow have?'

Wladek could not believe his ears. 'Four, sir,' he said, wondering if the question was a trick.

'And a horse?'

'Four, sir,' said Wladek still in disbelief.

'Which would you throw overboard if you were out at sea in a small boat which needed to be lightened, bread or money?'

'The money, sir,' said Wladek.

'Good.' The examiner picked up a card marked 'Admitted' and handed it over to Wladek. 'After you have changed your money, show this card to the immigration officer. Tell him your full name and he will give you a registration card. You will then be given an entry certificate. If you do not commit a crime for five years and pass a simple reading and writing examination at the end of that time, you will be permitted to apply for full United States citzenship. Good luck, Wladek.'

'Thank you, sir.'

At the money exchange counter Wladek handed in eighteen months of Turkish savings and the three fifty-ruble notes. He was handed forty-seven dollars twenty cents in exchange for the Turkish money but he was told the rubles were worthless. He could only think of Doctor Dubien and his fifteen years of diligent saving.

The final stop was the immigration officer, who was seated behind a counter at the exit barrier directly under a picture of President Harding. Wladek and George went over to him.

'Full name?' the officer said to George.

'George Novak,' replied Jerzy firmly. The officer wrote the name on a card.

'And your address?' he asked.

'286 Broome Street, New York, New York.'

The officer passed George the card. 'This is your Immigration Certificate, 21871-George Novak. Welcome to the United States, George. I'm Polish too. You'll like it here. Many congratulations and good luck.'

George smiled and shook hands with the officer, stood to one side and waited for Wladek. The officer stared at Wladek in his long bearskin coat. Wladek passed him the card marked 'Admitted'.

'Full name?' asked the officer.

Wladek hesitated.

'What's your name?' repeated the man, a little louder, slightly impatient, wondering if he couldn't speak English.

Wladek couldn't get the words out. How he hated that peasant name.

'For the last time, what's your name?'

George was staring at Wladek. So were others who had joined the queue for the immigration officer. Wladek still didn't speak. The officer suddenly grabbed his wrist, stared closely at the inscription on the silver band, wrote on a card and passed it to Wladek.

'21872-Baron Abel Rosnovski. Welcome to the United States. Many congratulations and good luck, Abel.'

12

William returned to start his last year at St Paul's in September, 1923, and was elected president of the Senior Class, exactly thirty-three years after his father had held the same office. William did not win the election in the usual fashion, by virtue of being the finest athlete or the most popular boy in the school. Matthew Lester, his closest friend, would undoubtedly have won any contest based on those criteria. It was simply that William was the most impressive boy in the school, and for that reason Matthew Lester could not be prevailed upon to run against him. St Paul's entered William's name as their candidate for the Hamilton Memorial Mathematics Scholarship at Harvard, and William worked single-mindedly towards that goal during the autumn term.

When William returned to Beacon Hill for Christmas, he was looking forward to an uninterrupted period in which to get to grips with *Principia Mathematica*. But it was not to be, for there were several invitations to parties and balls awaiting his arrival. To most of them he felt able to return a tactful regret, but one was absolutely inescapable. The grandmothers had arranged a ball, to be held at the Red House on Louisburg Square. William wondered at what age he would find it possible to defend his home against invasion by the two great ladies and decided the time had not yet come. He had few close friends in Boston, but this did not inhibit the grandmothers in their compilation of a formidable guest list.

To mark the occasion they presented William with his first dinner jacket in the latest double-breasted style; he received the gift with some pretence at indifference but later swaggered around his bedroom in the suit, often stopping to stare at himself in the mirror. The next day he put through a long distance call to New York and asked Matthew Lester to join him for the fateful weekend. Matthew's sister wanted to come as well but her mother didn't think it would be suitable.

William was there to meet him off the train.

'Come to think of it,' said Matthew, as the chauffeur drove them back to Beacon Hill, 'isn't it time you got yourself laid, William? There must be some girls in Boston with absolutely no taste.'

'Why, have you had a girl, Matthew?'

'Sure, last winter in New York.'

'What was I doing at the time?'

'Probably touching up on Bertrand Russell.'

'You never told me about it.'

'Nothing much to tell. In any case, you seemed more involved in my father's bank than my budding love life. It all happened at a staff party my father gave to celebrate Washington's birthday. Another first for old wooden teeth. Actually, to put the incident in its proper perspective, I was raped by one of the director's secretaries, a large lady called Cynthia with even larger breasts that wobbled when ...'

'Did you enjoy it?'

'Yes, but I can't believe for one moment that Cynthia did. She was far too drunk to realize I was there at the time. Still. You have to begin somewhere and she was willing to give the boss's son a helping hand.'

The vision of Alan Lloyd's prim, middle-aged secretary flashed across William's mind.

'I don't think my chances of initiation by the chairman's secretary are very good,' he mused.

'You'd be surprised,' said Matthew knowingly. 'The ones that go around with their legs so firmly together are often the ones who can't wait to get them apart. I now accept most invitations, formal or informal, not that dress matters much on these occasions.'

The chauffeur put the car in the garage while the two young men ran up the steps into William's house.

'You've certainly made some changes since I was last here,' said Matthew, admiring the modern cane furniture and new paisley wallpapers. Only the crimson leather chair remained firmly rooted in its usual spot.

'The place needed brightening up a little,' William offered. 'It was like living in the Stone Age. Besides, I didn't want to be reminded of ... Come on, this is no time to hang around discussing interior decoration.'

'When is everybody arriving for this party?'

'Ball, Matthew, the grandmothers insist on calling the event a ball.'

'There is only one thing that can be described as a ball on these occasions.'

'Matthew, one director's secretary does not entitle you to consider yourself a national authority on sex education.'

'Oh, such jealousy, and from one's dearest friend,' Matthew sighed mockingly.

William laughed and looked at his watch. 'The first guest should arrive in a couple of hours. Time for a shower and to change. Did you remember to bring a dinner jacket?'

'Yes, but if I didn't I can always wear my pyjamas. I usually leave one or the other behind, but I've never yet managed to forget both. In fact, it might start a whole new craze if I arrived at the ball in my pyjamas.'

'I can't see my grandmothers enjoying the joke,' said William.

The caterers arrived at six o'clock, twenty-three of them in all, and the grandmothers at seven, regal in long black lace that swept along the floor. William and Matthew joined them in the front room a few minutes before eight.

William was about to remove an inviting red cherry from the top of a magnificent iced cake when he heard Grandmother Kane's voice from behind him.

'Don't touch the food, William, it's not for you.'

He swung round. 'Then who is it for?' he asked, as he kissed her on the cheek.

'Don't be fresh, William, just because you're over six feet doesn't mean I wouldn't spank you.'

Matthew Lester laughed.

'Grandmother, may I introduce my closest friend, Matthew Lester?'

Grandmother Kane subjected him to a careful appraisal through her pince-nez before venturing: 'How do you do, young man?'

'It's an honour to meet you, Mrs Kane. I believe you knew my grandfather.'

'Knew your grandfather? Caleb Longworth Lester? He proposed marriage to me once, over fifty years ago. I turned him down. I told him he drank too much, and that it would lead him to an early grave. I was right, so don't you drink, either of you; remember, alcohol dulls the brain.'

'We hardly get much chance with Prohibition,' remarked Matthew innocently.

'That will end soon enough, I'm afraid,' said Grandmother Kane, sniffing. 'President Coolidge is forgetting his upbringing. He would never have become President if that idiot Harding hadn't foolishly died.'

William laughed. 'Really, Grandmother, your memory is getting selective. You wouldn't hear a word against him during the police strike.'

Mrs Kane did not reply.

The guests began to appear, many of them complete strangers to their host, who was delighted to see Alan Lloyd among the early arrivals.

'You're looking well, my boy,' he said, finding himself looking up at William for the first time in his life.

'You too, Alan. It was kind of you to come.'

'Kind? Have you forgotten that the invitation came from your grandmothers? I am possibly brave enough to refuse one of them, but both ...'

'You too, Alan?' William laughed. 'Can you spare a moment for a private word?' He guided his guest towards a quiet corner. 'I want to change my investment plans slightly and start buying Lester's bank stock whenever it comes onto the market. I'd like to be holding about five per cent of their stock by the time I'm twenty-one.'

'It's not that easy,' said Alan. 'Lester's shares don't come on the market all that often as they are all in private hands, but I'll see what can be done. What is going on in that mind of yours, William?'

'Well, my real aim is ...'

'William.' Grandmother Cabot was bearing down on them at speed. 'Here you are conspiring in a corner with Mr Lloyd and I haven't seen you dance with one young lady yet. What do you imagine we organized this ball for?'

'Quite right,' said Alan Lloyd, rising. 'You come and sit down with me, Mrs Cabot, and I'll kick the boy out into the world. We can rest, watch him dance, and listen to the music.'

'Music? That's not music, Alan. It's nothing more than a loud cacophony of sound with no suggestion of melody.'

'My dear grandmother,' said William, 'that is "Yes, We Have No Bananas", the latest hit song.'

'Then the time has come for me to depart this world,' said Grandmother Cabot, wincing.

'Never,' Alan Lloyd said gallantly.

William danced with a couple of girls whom he had a vague recollection of knowing, but he had to be reminded of their names, and when he spotted Matthew sitting in a corner, he was glad of the excuse to escape the dance floor. He had not noticed the girl sitting next to Matthew until he was right on top of them. When she looked up into William's eyes, he felt his knees give way.

'Do you know Abby Blount?' asked Matthew casually.

'No,' said William, barely restraining himself from straightening his tie.

'This is your host, Mr William Lowell Kane.'

The young lady cast her eyes demurely downwards as he took the seat on the other side of her. Matthew had noted the look William gave Abby and went off in search of some punch.

'How is it I've lived in Boston all my life, and we've never met?' William said.

'We did meet once before. On that occasion, you pushed me into the pond on the Common; we were both three at the time. It's taken me fourteen years to recover.'

'I am sorry,' said William, after a pause during which he searched in vain for more telling repartee.

'What a lovely house you have, William.'

There was a second busy pause. 'Thank you,' said William weakly. He glanced sideways at Abby, trying to look as though he were not studying her. She was slim – oh, so slim – with huge brown eyes, long eyelashes and a profile that captivated William. Abby had bobbed her auburn hair in the style William had hated until that moment.

'Matthew tells me you are going to Harvard next year,' she tried again.

'Yes, I am. I mean, would you like to dance?'

'Thank you,' she said.

The steps that had come to him so easily a few minutes before seemed now to forsake him. He trod on her toes and continually propelled her into other dancers. He apologized, she smiled. He held her a little more closely, and they danced on.

'Do we know that young lady who seems to have been monopolizing William for the last hour?' said Grandmother Cabot suspiciously.

Grandmother Kane picked up her pince-nez and studied the girl accompanying William as he strolled through the open bay windows out onto the lawn.

'Abby Blount,' Grandmother Kane declared.

'Admiral Blount's daughter?' inquired Grandmother Cabot.

'Yes.'

Grandmother Cabot nodded a degree of approval.

William guided Abby Blount towards the far end of the garden and stopped by a large chestnut tree which he had used in the past only for climbing.

'Do you always try to kiss a girl the first time you meet her?' asked Abby.

'To be honest,' said William, 'I've never kissed a girl before.'

Abby laughed. 'I'm very flattered.'

She offered first her pink cheek and then her rosy, pursed lips and then insisted upon returning indoors. The grandmothers observed their early re-entry with some relief.

Later, in William's bedroom, the two boys discussed the evening.

'Not a bad party,' said Matthew. 'Almost worth a trip from New York out here to the provinces, despite your stealing my girl.'

'Do you think she'll help me lost my virginity?' asked William, ignoring Matthew's mock accusation.

'Well, you have three weeks to find out, but I fear you'll discover she hasn't lost hers yet,' said Matthew. 'Such is my expertise in these matters that I'm willing to bet you five dollars she doesn't succumb even to the charms of William Lowell Kane.'

. . .

William planned a careful stratagem. Virginity was one thing, but losing five dollars to Matthew was quite another. He saw Abby Blount nearly every day after that, taking advantage for the first time of owning his own house and car at seventeen. He began to feel he would do better without the discreet but persistent chaperonage of Abby's parents who seemed always to be in the middle distance and he was not perceptibly nearer his goal when the last day of the holidays dawned.

Determined to win his five dollars, William sent Abby a dozen roses early in the day, took her out to an expensive dinner at Joseph's that evening and finally succeeded in coaxing her back into his front room.

'How did you get hold of a bottle of whisky while Prohibition is on?' asked Abby.

'Oh, it's not so hard,' William boasted.

The truth was that he had hidden a bottle of Henry Osborne's bourbon in his bedroom soon after he had left, and was now glad he had not poured it down the drain as had been his original intention.

William poured drinks that made him gasp and brought tears to Abby's eyes.

He sat down beside her and put his arm confidently around her shoulder. She settled in to it.

'Abby, I think you're terribly pretty,' he murmured in a preliminary way at her auburn curls.

She gazed at him earnestly, her brown eyes wide. 'Oh, William,' she breathed. 'And I think you're just wonderful.'

Her doll-like face was irresistible. She allowed herself to be kissed. Thus emboldened, William slipped a tentative hand from her wrist onto her breast, and left it there like a traffic cop halting an advancing stream of automobiles. She became pinkly indignant and pushed his arm down to allow the traffic to move on.

'William, you mustn't do that.'

'Why not?' said William, struggling vainly to retain his grasp of her.

'Because you can't tell where it might end.'

'I've got a fair idea.'

Before he could renew his advances. Abby pushed him away and rose hastily, smoothing her dress.

'I think I ought to be getting home now, William.'

'But you've only just arrived.'

'Mother will want to know what I've been doing.'

'You'll be able to tell her – nothing.'

'And I think it's best it stays that way,' she added.

'But I'm going back tomorrow.' He avoided saying, 'to school'.

'Well, you can write to me, William.'

Unlike Valentino, William knew when he was beaten. He rose, straightened his tie, took Abby by the hand and drove her home.

The following day, back at school, Matthew Lester accepted the proffered five-dollar note with eyebrows raised in mock astonishment.

'Just say one word, Matthew, and I'll chase you right around St Paul's with a baseball bat.'

'I can't think of any words that would truly express my deep feeling of sympathy.'

'Matthew, right around St Paul's.'

. . .

William began to be aware of his housemaster's wife during his last two terms at St Paul's. She was a good-looking woman, a little slack around the stomach and hips perhaps, but she carried her splendid bosom well and the luxuriant dark hair piled on top of her head was no more streaked with grey than was becoming. One Saturday when William had sprained his wrist on the hockey rink, Mrs Raglan bandaged it for him in a cool compress, standing a little closer than was necessary, allowing William's arm to brush against her breast. He enjoyed the sensation. Then on another occasion when he had a fever and was confined to the infirmary for a few days, she brought him all his meals herself and sat on his bed, her body touching his legs through the thin covering, while he ate. He enjoyed that too.

She was rumoured to be Grumpy Raglan's second wife. No one in the house could imagine how Grumpy had managed to secure even one spouse. Mrs Raglan occasionally indicated by the subtlest of sighs and silences that she shared something of their incredulity at her fate.

As part of his duties as house captain, William was required to report to Grumpy Raglan every night at ten thirty when he had completed the lights-out round and was about to go to bed himself. One Monday evening, when he knocked on Grumpy's door as usual, he was surprised to hear Mrs Raglan's voice bidding him to enter. She was lying on the chaise-longue dressed in a loose silk robe of faintly Japanese appearance.

William kept a firm grasp on the cold door knob. 'All the lights are out and I've locked the front door, Mrs Raglan. Goodnight.'

She swung her legs onto the ground, a pale flash of thigh appearing momentarily from under the draped silk.

'You're always in such a hurry, William. You can't wait for your life to start, can you?' She walked over to a side table. 'Why don't you stay and have some hot chocolate? Silly me, I made enough for two, I quite forgot that Mister Raglan won't be back until Saturday.'

There was a definite emphasis on the word 'Saturday'. She carried a steaming cup over to William and looked up at him to see whether the significance of her remarks had registered on him. Satisfied, she passed him the cup, letting her hand touch his. He stirred the hot chocolate assiduously.

'Gerald has gone to a conference,' she continued explaining. It was the first time he had ever heard Grumpy Raglan's first name. 'Do shut the door, William, and come and sit down.'

William hesitated; he shut the door, but he did not want to take Grumpy's chair nor did he want to sit next to Mrs Raglan. He decided Grumpy's chair was the lesser of two evils and moved towards it.

'No, no,' she said, as she patted the seat next to her.

William shuffled over and sat down nervously by her side, staring into his cup for inspiration. Finding none, he gulped the contents down, burning his tongue. He was relieved to see Mrs Raglan getting up. She refilled his cup, ignoring his murmured refusal, and then moved silently across the room, wound up the Victrola and placed the needle on the record.

'Nice and easy does it' were the first words that William heard. He was still looking at the floor, when she returned.

'You wouldn't let a lady dance by herself, would you, William?'

He looked up. Mrs Raglan was swaying slightly in time to the music. 'We're on the road to romance, that's clear to say,' crooned Rudy Vallee. William stood up and put his arm formally round Mrs Raglan. Grumpy could have fitted in between them without any trouble. After a few bars she moved closer to William, and he stared over her right shoulder fixedly to indicate to her that he had not noticed that her left hand had slipped from his shoulder to the small of his back. When the record stopped, William thought it would give him a chance to return to the safety of his hot chocolate, but she turned the record over and was back in his arms before he could move.

'Mrs Raglan, I think I ought to . . .'

'Relax a little, William.'

At last he found the courage to look her in the eyes. He tried to reply, but he couldn't speak. Her hand was now exploring his back, and he felt her thigh move gently into his groin. He tightened his hold around her waist.

'That's better,' she said.

They circled slowly around the room, closely entwined, slower and slower, keeping time with the music as the record gently ran down. When she slipped away and turned out the light, William wanted her to return quickly. He stood there in the dark, not moving, hearing the rustle of silk, and able only to see a silhouette discarding clothes.

The crooner had completed his song, and the needle was scratching at the end of the record by the time she had helped William out of all his clothes and led him back to the chaise-longue. He groped for her in the dark, and his shy novice's fingers encounted several parts of her body that did not feel at all as he had imagined they would. He withdrew them hastily to the comparatively familiar territory of her breast. Her fingers exhibited no such reticence, and he began to feel sensations he would never have dreamed possible. He wanted to moan out loud, but stopped himself, fearing it would sound stupid. Her hands were on his back, pulling him gently on top of her.

William moved around wondering how he would ever enter her without showing his total lack of experience. It was not as easy as he had expected, and he began to get more desperate by the second. Then, once again, her fingers moved across his stomach and guided him expertly. With her help he entered her easily and had an immediate orgasm.

'I'm sorry,' said William, not sure what to do next. He lay silently on top of her for some time before she spoke.

'It will be better tomorrow.'

The sound of the scratching record returned to his ears.

Mrs Raglan remained in William's mind all that endless Tuesday. That night, she sighed. On Wednesday, she panted. On Thursday, she moaned. On Friday she cried out.

On Saturday Grumpy Raglan returned from his conference, by which time William's education was complete.

.   .   .

During the Easter holidays, on Ascension Day to be exact, Abby Blount finally succumbed to William's charms. It cost Matthew five dollars and Abby her virginity. She was, after Mrs Raglan, something of an anti-climax. It was the only event of note that happened during the entire holiday, because Abby went off to Palm Beach with her parents, and William spent most of his time shut away indoors with his books, at home to no one other than the grandmothers and Alan Lloyd. His final examinations were now only a matter of weeks away, and as Grumpy Raglan went to no further conferences, William had no other outside activities.

During their last term, he and Matthew would sit in their study at St Paul's for hours, never speaking unless Matthew had some mathematical problem he was quite unable to solve. When the long awaited examinations finally came, they lasted for only one brutal week. The moment they were over, both boys were sanguine about their results, but as the days went by, and they waited and waited, their confidence began to diminish. The Hamilton Memorial Scholarship to Harvard for mathematics was awarded on a strictly competitive basis and it was open to every schoolboy in America. William had no way of judging how tough his opposition might be. As more time went by and still he heard nothing, William began to assume the worst.

When the telegram arrived, he was out playing baseball with some other sixth formers, killing the last few days of the term before leaving school, those warm summer days when boys are most likely to be expelled for drunkenness, breaking windows or trying to get into bed with one of the master's daughters, if not their wives.

William was declaring in a loud voice to those who cared to listen that he was about to hit his first run ever. The Babe Ruth of St Paul's, declared Matthew. Much laughter greeted this exaggerated claim. When the telegram was handed to him, home runs were suddenly forgotten. He dropped his bat and tore open the little yellow envelope. The pitcher waited, impatient, ball in hand, and so did the outfielders as he read the communication slowly.

'They want you to turn professional,' someone shouted from first base, the arrival of a telegram being an uncommon occurrence during a baseball game. Matthew walked in from the outfield to join William, trying to make out from his friend's face if the news were good or bad. Without changing his expression, William passed the telegram to Matthew, who read it, leaped high into the air with delight, and dropped the piece of paper to the ground to accompany William, racing around the bases on the way to the first home run ever scored without anyone actually hitting the ball. The pitcher watched them, picked the telegram up and read the missive himself and then he threw his ball into the bleachers with gusto. The little piece of yellow paper was then passed eagerly from player to player around the field. The last person to read the message was the second former who, having caused so much happiness but received no thanks, decided the least he deserved was to know the cause of so much excitement.

The telegram was addressed to Mr William Lowell Kane, whom the boy assumed to be the incompetent hitter. It read: 'Congratulations on winning the Hamilton Memorial Mathematics Scholarship to Harvard, full details to follow. Abbot Lawrence Lowell, President.' William never did get his home run as he was sat heavily upon by several fielders before he reached home plate.

Matthew looked on with delight at the success of his closest friend, but he was sad to think that it meant they might now be parted. William felt it too, but said nothing; the two boys had to wait another nine days to learn that Matthew had also been accepted to Harvard.

Yet another telegram arrived, this one from Charles Lester, congratulating his son and inviting the boys to tea at the Plaza Hotel in New York. Both grandmothers sent congratulations to William, but as Grandmother Kane informed Alan Lloyd, somewhat testily, 'the boy has done no less than was expected of him and no more than his father did before him.'

.   .   .

The two young men sauntered down Fifth Avenue on the appointed day with considerable pride. Girls' eyes were drawn to the handsome pair, who affected not to notice. They removed their straw boaters as they entered the front door of the Plaza at three fifty-nine, strolled nonchalantly through the lounge and observed the family group awaiting them in the Palm Court. There, upright in the comfortable chairs sat both grandmothers, Kane and Cabot, flanking another old lady who, William assumed, was the Lester family's equivalent of Grandmother Kane. Mr and Mrs Charles Lester, their daughter Susan (whose eyes never left William), and Alan Lloyd completed the circle leaving two vacant chairs for William and Matthew.

Grandmother Kane summoned the nearest waiter with an imperious eyebrow. 'A fresh pot of tea and some more cakes, please.'

The waiter made haste to the kitchens. 'Pot of tea and some more cakes for table twenty-three,' he shouted above the clatter.

'Coming up,' said a voice from the steamy obscurity.

'A pot of tea and some cream cakes, madam,' the waiter said on his return.

'Your father would have been proud of you today, William,' the older man was saying to the taller of the two youths.

The waiter wondered what it was that the good-looking young man had achieved to elicit such a comment.

William would not have noticed the waiter at all but for the silver band around his wrist. The piece so easily might have come from Tiffany's; the incongruity of it puzzled him.

'William,' said Grandmother Kane. 'Two cakes are quite sufficient; this is not your last meal before you go to Harvard.'

He looked at the old lady with affection and quite forgot the silver band.

13

That night as Abel lay awake in his small room at the Plaza Hotel, thinking about the boy, William, whose father would have been proud of him, he realized for the first time in his life exactly what he wanted to achieve. He wanted to be thought of as an equal by the Williams of this world.

Abel had had quite a struggle on his arrival in New York. He occupied a room that contained only two beds which he was obliged to share with George and two of his cousins. As a result, Abel slept only when one of the beds was free. George's uncle was unable to offer him a job, and after a few anxious weeks during which most of his savings had to be spent on staying alive, Abel searched from Brooklyn to Queens before finding work in a butcher's shop which paid nine dollars for a six and a half day week, and allowed him to sleep above the premises. The shop was in the heart of an almost self-sufficient little Polish community on the lower East Side, and Abel rapidly became impatient with the insularity of his fellow countrymen, many of whom made no effort to learn to speak English.

Abel still saw George and his constant succession of girl friends regularly at weekends, but he spent most of his free evenings during the week at night school learning how to read and write English. He was not ashamed of his slow progress, for he had had very little opportunity to write at all since the age of eight, but within two years he had made himself fluent in his new tongue, showing only the slightest trace of an accent. He now felt ready to move out of the butcher's shop – but to what, and how? Then, while dressing a leg of lamb one morning, he overheard one of the shop's biggest customers, the catering manager of the Plaza Hotel, grumbling to the butcher that he had had to fire a junior waiter for petty theft.

'How can I find a replacement at such short notice?' the manager remonstrated.

The butcher had no solution to offer. Abel did. He put on his only suit, walked forty-seven blocks, and got the job.

Once he had settled in at the Plaza, he enrolled for a night course in English at Columbia University. He worked steadily every night, dictionary open in one hand, pen scratching away in the other; during the mornings, between serving breakfast and setting up the tables for lunch, he would copy out the editorial from the *New York Times*, looking up any word he was uncertain of in his second-hand Webster's.

For the next three years, Abel worked his way through the ranks of the Plaza until he was promoted and became a waiter in the Oak Room, making about twenty-five dollars a week with tips. In his own world, he lacked for nothing.

Abel's instructor at Columbia was so impressed by his diligent progress in English that he advised Abel to enrol in a further night course, which was to be his first step towards a Bachelor of Arts degree. He switched his spare-time reading from English to economics and started copying out the editorials in the *Wall Street Journal* instead of those in the *New York Times*. His new world totally absorbed him, and with the exception of George he lost touch with his Polish friends of the early days.

When Abel served at table in the Oak Room, he would always study the famous among the guests carefully – the Bakers, Loebs, Whitneys, Morgans and Phelps – and try to work out why it was that the rich were different. He read H. L. Mencken, *The American Mercury*, Scott Fitzgerald, Sinclair Lewis and Theodore Dreiser in an endless quest for knowledge. He studied the *New York Times* while the other waiters flipped through the *Mirror*, and he read the *Wall Street Journal* in his hour's break while they dozed. He was not sure where his newly acquired knowledge would lead him, but he never doubted the Baron's maxim that there was no true substitute for a good education.

.   .   .

One Thursday in August 1926 – he remembered the occasion well, because it was the day that Rudolph Valentino died, and many of the ladies shopping on Fifth Avenue wore black – Abel was serving as usual at one of the corner tables. The corner tables were always reserved for top business men who wished to eat in privacy without fear of being overheard by prying ears. He enjoyed serving at that particular table, for it was the era of expanding business, and he often picked up some inside information from the titbits of conversation. After the meal was over, if the host had been from a bank or large holding company, Abel would look up the financial record of the company of the guests at the lunch, and if he felt the meeting had gone particularly well, he would invest one hundred dollars in the smaller company, hoping it would be in line for a takeover or expansion with the help of the larger company. If the host had ordered cigars at the end of the meal, Abel would increase his investment to two hundred dollars. Seven times out of ten, the value of the stock he had selected in this way doubled within six months, the period Abel would allow himself to hold on to the shares. Using this system he lost money only three times during the four years he worked at the Plaza.

What made waiting on the corner table unusual on that particular day was that the guests had ordered cigars even before the meal had started. Later they were joined by more guests who ordered more cigars. Abel looked up the name of the host in the *maître d*'s reservation book. Woolworth. He had seen the name in the financial columns quite recently but he could not immediately place it. The other guest was Charles Lester, a regular patron of the Plaza, whom Abel knew to be a distinguished New York banker. He listened to as much of the conversation as he could while serving the meal. The guests showed absolutely no interest in the attentive waiter. Abel could not discover any specific details of importance, but he gathered that some sort of deal had been closed that morning and would be announced to an unsuspecting public later in the day. Then he remembered. He had seen the name in the *Wall Street Journal*. Woolworth was the man who was going to start the first American five-and-ten-cent stores. Abel was determined to get his five cents worth. While the guests were enjoying their dessert course – most of them chose the strawberry cheese cake (Abel's recommendation) – he took the opportunity to leave the dining room for a few moments to call his broker in Wall Street.

'What are Woolworth's trading at?' he asked.

There was a pause from the other end of the line. 'Two and one-eighth. Quite a lot of movement lately; don't know why though,' came the reply.

'Buy up to the limit of my account until you hear an announcement from the company later today.'

'What will the announcement say?' asked the puzzled broker.

'I am not at liberty to reveal that sort of information over the telephone,' said Abel.

The broker was suitably impressed; Abel's record in the past had led him not to inquire too closely into the source of his client's information.

Abel hurried back to the Oak Room in time to serve the guests coffee. They lingered over it for some time, and Abel returned to the table only as they were preparing to leave. The man who picked up the bill thanked Abel for his attentive service, and turning so that his friends could hear him, said 'Do you want a tip, young man?'

'Thank you, sir,' said Abel.

'Buy Woolworth's shares.'

The guests all laughed. Abel laughed as well, took five dollars from the man and thanked him. He took a further two thousand four hundred and twelve dollars profit on Woolworth's shares during the next six months.

． ． ．

When Abel was granted full citizenship of the United States a few days after his twenty-first birthday, he decided the occasion ought to be celebrated. He invited George and Monika, George's latest love, and a girl called Clara, an ex-love of George's, to the cinema to see John Barrymore in *Don Juan* and then on to Bigo's for dinner. George was still an apprentice in his uncle's bakery at eight dollars a week, and although Abel still looked upon him as his closest friend, he was aware of the growing difference between the penniless George and himself, who now had over eight thousand dollars in the bank and was in his last year at Columbia University studying for his BA in economics. Abel knew where he was going, whereas George had stopped telling everyone he would be the mayor of New York.

The four of them had a memorable evening, mainly because Abel knew exactly what to expect from a good restaurant. His three guests all had a great deal too much to eat, and when the bill was presented, George was aghast to see that it came to more than he earned in a month. Abel paid the bill without a second glance. If you have to pay a bill, make it look as if the amount is of no consequence. If it is, don't go to the restaurant again, but whatever you do, don't comment or look surprised – something else the rich had taught him.

When the party broke up at about two in the morning, George and Monika returned to the lower East Side, while Abel felt he had earned Clara. He smuggled her through the service entrance of the Plaza and up to his room in a laundry lift. She did not require much enticement to end up in

bed, and Abel set about her with haste, mindful that he had some serious
sleeping to do before reporting for breakfast duty. To his satisfaction, he had
completed his task by two-thirty and sank into an uninterrupted sleep until
his alarm rang at six a.m. It left him just time enough to have Clara once
again before he had to get dressed.

Clara sat up in his bed and regarded Abel sullenly as he tied his white
bow tie, and kissed her a perfunctory goodbye.

'Be sure you leave the way you came, or you'll get me into a load of
trouble,' said Abel. 'When will I see you again?'

'You won't,' said Clara stonily.

'Why not?' asked Abel, surprised. 'Something I did?'

'No, something you didn't do.' She jumped out of bed and started to dress
hastily.

'What didn't I do?' said Abel, aggrieved. 'You wanted to go to bed with
me, didn't you?'

She turned around and faced him. 'I thought I did until I realized you
have only one thing in common with Valentino – you're both dead. You may
be the greatest thing the Plaza has seen in a bad year, but in bed I can tell
you, you are nothing.' Fully dressed now, she paused with her hand on the
door handle, composing her parting thrust. 'Tell me, have you ever persuaded any girl to go to bed with you more than once?'

Stunned, Abel stared at the slammed door and spent the rest of the day
worrying about Clara's words. He could think of no one with whom he could
discuss the problem. George would only laugh at him, and the staff at the
Plaza all thought he knew everything. He decided that this problem, like
all the others he had encountered in his life, must be one he could surmount
with knowledge or experience.

After lunch, on his first day, he went to Scribner's bookshop on Fifth
Avenue. They had solved all his economic and linguistic problems, but he
couldn't find anything there that looked as if it might even begin to help his
sexual ones. Their special book on etiquette was useless and *The Nature of
Morals* by W. F. Colbert turned out to be utterly inappropriate.

Abel left the bookshop without making a purchase and spent the rest of
the afternoon in a dingy Broadway cinema, not watching the film, but
thinking only about what Clara had said. The film, a love story with Greta
Garbo that did not reach the kissing stage until the last reel, provided no
more assistance than Scribner's had.

When Abel left the cinema, the sky was already dark and there was a cool
breeze blowing down Broadway. It still surprised Abel that any city could
be as noisy and light by night as it was by day. He started walking uptown
towards Fifty-ninth Street, hoping the fresh air would clear his mind. He
stopped on the corner of Fifty-second to buy an evening paper.

'Looking for a girl?' said a voice from behind the news-stand.

Abel stared at the voice. She was about thirty-five and heavily made up,
wearing the new, fashionable lipstick. Her white silk blouse had a button
undone, and she wore a long black skirt with black stockings and black shoes.

'Only five dollars, worth every penny,' she said, pushing her hip out at
an angle, allowing the slit in her skirt to part and reveal the top of her
stockings.

'Where?' said Abel.

'I have a little place of my own in the next block.'

She turned her head, indicating to Abel which direction she meant, and he could, for the first time, see her face clearly under the street light. She was not unattractive. Abel nodded his agreement, and she took his arm and started walking.

'If the police stop us,' she said, 'you're an old friend and my name's Joyce.'

They walked to the next block and into a squalid little apartment building. Abel was horrified by the dingy room she lived in, with its single bare light bulb, one chair, a wash basin and a crumpled double bed, which had obviously already been used several times that day.

'You live here?' he said incredulously.

'Good God, no, I only use this place for my work.'

'Why do you do this?' asked Abel, wondering if he now wanted to go through with his plan.

'I have two children to bring up and no husband. Can you think of a better reason? Now, do you want me or not.'

'Yes, but not the way you think,' said Abel.

She eyed him warily. 'Not another of those whacky ones, a follower of the Marquis de Sade, are you?'

'Certainly not,' said Abel.

'You're not gonna burn me with cigarettes, then?'

'No, nothing like that,' said Abel, startled. 'I want to be taught properly. I want lessons.'

'Lessons, are you joking? What do you think this is darling, a fucking night school?'

'Something like that,' said Abel and he sat down on the corner of the bed and explained to her how Clara had reacted the night before. 'Do you think you can help?'

The lady of the night studied Abel carefully, wondering if it was April the First.

'Sure,' she said finally, 'but it's going to cost you five dollars a time for a thirty-minute session.'

'More expensive than a BA from Columbia,' said Abel. 'How many lessons will I need?'

'Depends how quick a learner you are, doesn't it?' she said.

'Well let's start right now,' said Abel, taking five dollars out of his inside pocket and handing the money over to her. She put the note in the top of her stocking, a sure sign she never took them off.

'Clothes off, darling,' she said. 'You won't learn much fully dressed.'

When he was stripped, she looked at him critically. 'You're not exactly Douglas Fairbanks, are you? Don't worry about it, it doesn't matter what you look like once the lights are out; it only matters what you can do.'

Abel sat on the edge of the bed while she started telling him about how to treat a lady. She was surprised that Abel really did not want her and was even more surprised when he continued to turn up every day for the next two weeks.

'When will I know I've made it?' Abel inquired.

'You'll know, baby,' replied Joyce. 'If you can make me come, you can make an Egyptian mummy come.'

She taught him first where the sensitive parts of a woman's body were, and then to be patient in his love-making and the signs by which he might know that what he was doing was pleasing. How to use his tongue and lips on every place other than a woman's mouth.

Abel listened carefully to all she said and followed her instructions scrupulously and to begin with, a little bit too mechanically. Despite her assurance that he was improving out of all recognition, he had no real idea if she was telling the truth, until about three weeks and one hundred and ten dollars later, when to his surprise and delight, Joyce suddenly came alive in his arms for the first time. She held his head close to her as he gently licked her nipples. As he stroked her gently between the legs, he found she was wet – for the first time – and after he had entered her she moaned, a sound Abel had never heard before, and found intensely pleasing. She clawed at his back, commanding him not to stop. The moaning continued, sometimes loud, sometimes soft. Finally she cried out sharply, and the hands that had clutched him to her so fiercely relaxed.

When she had caught her breath, she said. 'Baby, you just graduated top of the class.'

Abel hadn't even come.

Abel celebrated the awarding of both his degrees by paying scalpers' price for ringside seats and taking George, Monika and a reluctant Clara to watch Gene Tunney fight Dack Dempsey for the heavyweight championship of the world. That night after the fight, Clara felt it was nothing less than her duty to go to bed with Abel as he had spent so much money on her. By the morning, she was begging him not to leave her.

Abel never asked her out again.

.   .   .

After he had graduated from Columbia, Abel became dissatisfied with his life at the Plaza Hotel, but could not figure out how to secure further advancement. Although he was surrounded by some of the most wealthy and successful men in America, he was unable to approach any of the customers directly, knowing that if he did so, it might well cost him his job and in any case, the customers could not take seriously the aspirations of a waiter. Abel had long ago decided that he wanted to be a head waiter.

One day, Mr and Mrs Ellsworth Statler came to lunch at the Plaza's Edwardian Room, where Abel had been on relief duty for a week. He thought his chance had come. He did everything he could think of to impress the famous hotelier, and the meal went splendidly. As he left, Statler thanked Abel warmly and gave him ten dollars, but that was the end of their association. Abel watched him disappear through the revolving doors of the Plaza, wondering if he was ever going to get a break.

Sammy, the head waiter tapped him on the shoulder: 'What did you get from Mr Statler?'

'Nothing,' said Abel.

'He didn't tip you?' asked Sammy in a disbelieving tone.

'Oh, yes, sure,' said Abel. 'Ten dollars.' He handed the money over to Sammy.

'That's more like it,' said Sammy. 'I was beginning to think you was double-dealing me, Abel. Ten dollars, that's good even for Mr Statler. You must have impressed him.'

'No, I didn't.'

'What do you mean?' asked Sammy.

'It doesn't matter,' said Abel, as he started walking away.

'Wait a moment, Abel, I have a note here for you. The gentleman at table seventeen, a Mr Leroy, wants to speak to you personally.'

'What about, Sammy?'

'How should I know? Probably liked your blue eyes.'

Abel glanced over to number seventeen, strictly for the meek and the unknown, because the table was so badly placed near a swing door into the kitchen. Abel usually tried to avoid serving any of the tables at that end of the room.

'Who is he?' asked Abel. 'What does he want?'

'I don't know,' said Sammy, not bothering to look up. 'I'm not in touch with the life history of every customer the way you are. Give them a good meal, make sure you get yourself a big tip and hope they come again. You may feel it's a simple philosophy but it's sure good enough for me. Maybe they forgot to teach you the basics at Columbia. Now get your butt over there, Abel, and if it's a tip be certain you bring the money straight back to me.'

Abel smiled at Sammy's bald head and went over to seventeen. There were two people seated at the table, a man in a colourful checked jacket, of which Abel did not approve, and an attractive young woman with a mop of blonde, curly hair, which momentarily distracted Abel, who uncharitably assumed she was the checked jacket's New York girlfriend. Abel put on his 'sorry smile', betting himself a dollar that the man was going to make a big fuss about the swing doors and try to get his table changed to impress the stunning blonde. No one liked being near the smell of the kitchens and the continual banging of waiters through the doors, but it was impossible to avoid using the table, when the hotel was already packed with residents and many New Yorkers who used the restaurant as their local eating place, and looked upon visitors as little less than intruders. Why did Sammy always leave the tricky customers for him to deal with? Abel approached the checked jacket cautiously.

'You asked to speak to me, sir?'

'Sure did,' said a Southern accent. 'My name is Davis Leroy, and this is my daughter Melanie.'

Abel's eyes left Mr Leroy momentarily and encountered a pair of eyes as green as any he had ever seen.

'I have been watching you, Abel, for the last five days,' Mr Leroy was saying in his Southern drawl.

If pushed, Abel would have had to admit that he had not noticed Mr Leroy until the last five minutes.

'I have been very impressed by what I've seen, Abel, because you got class, real class, and I am always on the lookout for that. Ellsworth Statler was a fool not to pick you up right away.'

Abel began to take a closer look at Mr Leroy. His purple cheeks and double chin left Abel in no doubt that he had not been told about Prohibition, and the empty plates in front of him accounted for his basketball belly, but neither the name nor the face meant anything to him. At a normal lunchtime, Abel was familiar with the background of anyone sitting at thirty-seven of the thirty-nine tables in the Edwardian Room. That day Mr Leroy was one of the unknown two.

The Southerner was still talking. 'Now, I'm not one of those multi-millionaires who have to sit at your corner table when they stay at the Plaza.'

Abel was impressed. The average customer wasn't supposed to appreciate the relative merits of the various tables.

'But I'm not doing so badly for myself. In fact, my best hotel may well grow to be as impressive as this one some day, Abel.'

'I am sure it will be, sir,' said Abel, playing for time.

Leroy, Leroy, Leroy. The name didn't mean a thing.

'Lemme git to the point, son. The number one hotel in my group needs a new assistant manager, in charge of the restaurants. If you're interested, join me in my room when you come off duty.'

He handed Abel a large embossed card.

'Thank you, sir,' said Abel, looking at it: Davis Leroy. The Richmond Group of Hotels, Dallas. Underneath was inscribed the motto: 'One day a hotel in every state.' The name still meant nothing to Abel.

'I look forward to seeing you,' said the friendly, check-jacketed Texan.

'Thank you, sir,' said Abel. He smiled at Melanie, whose eyes were as coolly green as before and returned to Sammy, still head down, counting his takings.

'Ever heard of the Richmond Group of Hotels, Sammy?'

'Yes, sure, my brother was a junior waiter in one. Must be about eight or nine of them, all over the South, run by a mad Texan, but I can't remember the guy's name. Why you asking?' said Sammy, looking up suspiciously.

'No particular reason,' said Abel.

'There's always a reason with you. Now what did table seventeen want?' said Sammy.

'Grumbling about the noise from the kitchen. Can't say I blame him.'

'What does he expect me to do, put him out on the veranda? Who does the guy think he is, John D. Rockefeller?'

Abel left Sammy to his counting and grumbling and cleared his own tables as quickly as possible. Then he went to his own room and started to check out the Richmond Group. A few calls and he'd learned enough to satisfy his curiosity. The group turned out to be a private company, with eleven hotels in all, the most impressive one a three hundred and forty-two bedroom de luxe establishment in Chicago, the Richmond Continental. Abel decided he had nothing to lose by paying a call on Mr Leroy and Melanie. He checked Mr Leroy's room number – 85 – one of the better smaller rooms. He arrived a little before four o'clock and was disappointed to discover Melanie was no longer with her father.

'Glad you could drop by, Abel. Take a seat.'

It was the first time Abel had sat down as a guest in the more than four years he had worked at the Plaza.

'What are you paid?' said Mr Leroy.

The suddenness of the question took Abel by surprise. 'I take in around twenty-five dollars a week with tips.'

'I'll start you at thirty-five a week.'

'Which hotel are you referring to?' asked Abel.

'If I'm a judge of character, Abel, you got off table duty about three-thirty and took the next thirty minutes finding out which hotel. Am I right?'

Abel was beginning to like the man. 'The Richmond Continental in Chicago?' he ventured.

Davis Leroy laughed. 'I was right, and right about you.'

Abel's mind was working fast. 'How many people are there over the assistant manager on the hotel staff?'

'Only the manager and me. The manager is slow, gentle, and near retirement, and as I have ten other hotels to worry about, I don't think you'll have too much trouble – although I must confess Chicago is my favourite, my first hotel in the North, and with Melanie at school there, I find I spend more time in the Windy City than I ought to. Don't ever make the mistake New Yorkers do of underestimating Chicago. They think Chicago is only a postage stamp on a very large envelope, and they are the envelope.'

Abel smiled.

'The hotel is a little run down at the moment,' Mr Leroy continued, 'and the last assistant manager walked out on me suddenly without an explanation, so I need a good man to take his place and to realize its full potential. Now listen, Abel, I've watched you carefully for the last five days and I know you're that man. Do you think you would be interested in coming to Chicago?'

'Forty dollars and ten per cent of any increased profits, and I'll take the job.'

'What?' said Davis Leroy, flabbergasted. 'None of my managers are paid on a profit basis. The others would raise hell if they ever found out.'

'I'm not going to tell them if you don't,' said Abel.

'Now I know I chose the right man, even if he bargains a damn sight better than a Yankee with six daughters.' He slapped the side of his chair. 'I agree to your terms, Abel.'

'Will you be requiring references, Mr Leroy?'

'References. I know your background and history since you left Europe right through to you getting a degree in economics at Columbia. What do you think I've been doing the last few days? I wouldn't put someone who needed references in as number two in my best hotel. When can you start?'

'A month from today.'

'Good. I look forward to seeing you then, Abel.'

Abel rose from the hotel chair; he felt happier standing. He shook hands with Mr Davis Leroy, the man from table seventeen – the one that was strictly for unknowns.

.   .   .

Leaving New York and the Plaza Hotel, his first real home since the castle near Slonim, turned out to be more of a wrench than Abel had anticipated. Goodbyes to George, Monika, and his few Columbia friends were unexpectedly hard. Sammy and the waiters threw a farewell party for him.

'We haven't heard the last of you, Abel Rosnovski,' Sammy said, and they all agreed.

. . .

The Richmond Continental in Chicago was well-placed on Michigan Avenue, in the heart of the fastest growing city in America. That pleased Abel, who was only too familiar with Ellsworth Statler's maxim that just three things about a hotel really mattered: position, position and position. Abel soon discovered that position was about the only good thing that the Richmond had. Davis Leroy had understated the case when he had said that the hotel was a little run down. Desmond Pacey, the manager, wasn't slow and gentle as Davis Leroy had described him; he was plain lazy and didn't endear himself to Abel by allocating him a tiny room in the staff annex across the road and leaving him out of the main hotel. A quick check on the Richmond's books revealed that the daily occupancy rate was running at less than forty per cent, and that the restaurant was never more than half full, not least of all because the food was so appalling. The staff spoke three or four languages among them, none of which seemed to be English, and there were certainly not any signs of welcome for the stupid Polack from New York. It was not hard to see why the last assistant manager had left in such a hurry. If the Richmond was Davis Leroy's favourite hotel, Abel feared for the other ten in the group, even though his new employer seemed to have a bottomless pot of gold at the end of his Texas rainbow.

The best news that Abel learned during his first days in Chicago was that Melanie Leroy was an only child.

14

William and Matthew started their freshmen year at Harvard in the fall of 1924. Despite his grandmothers' disapproval William accepted the Hamilton Memorial Scholarship and at a cost of two hundred and ninety dollars, treated himself to 'Daisy', the latest Model T Ford, and first real love of his life. He painted Daisy bright yellow, which halved her value and doubled the number of his girlfriends. Calvin Coolidge won a landslide election to return to the White House and the volume on the New York Stock Exchange reached a five-year record of two million, three hundred and thirty-six thousand, one hundred and sixty shares.

Both young men (we can no longer refer to them as children, pronounced Grandmother Cabot) had been looking forward to college. After an energetic summer of tennis and golf, they were ready to get down to more serious pursuits. William started work on the day he arrived in their new room on the 'Gold Coast', a considerable improvement on their small study at St Paul's, while Matthew went in search of the university rowing club. Matthew was elected to captain the freshmen crew, and William left his books every Sunday afternoon to watch his friend from the banks of the Charles

River. He covertly enjoyed Matthew's success but was outwardly scathing.

'Life is not about eight big men pulling unwieldy pieces of misshapen wood through choppy water while one smaller man shouts at them,' declared William haughtily.

'Tell Yale that,' said Matthew.

William, meanwhile, quickly demonstrated to his mathematics professors that he was in his studies what Matthew was in sport – a mile ahead of the field. He also became chairman of the Freshmen Debating Society and talked his great-uncle, President Lowell, into the first university insurance plan, whereby students leaving Harvard would take out a life policy for one thousand dollars each, naming the university as the beneficiary. William estimated that the cost to each participant would be less than a dollar per week and that if forty per cent of the alumni joined the scheme, Harvard would have a guaranteed income of about three million dollars a year from 1950 onwards. The president was impressed and gave the scheme his full support, and a year later he invited William to join the board of the University Fund Raising Committee. William accepted with pride without realizing the appointment was for life. President Lowell informed Grandmother Kane that he had captured one of the best financial brains of his generation, free of charge. Grandmother Kane testily replied to her cousin that, 'everything has its purpose and this will teach William to read the fine print.'

.   .   .

Almost as soon as the sophomore year began, it became time to choose (or to be chosen for) one of the Finals Clubs that dominated the social landscape of the well-to-do at Harvard. William was 'punched' for the Porcellian, the oldest, richest, most exclusive and least ostentatious of such clubs. In the clubhouse on Massachusetts Avenue, which was incongruously situated over a cheap Hayes-Bickford cafeteria, he would sit in a comfortable armchair, considering the four-colour map problem, discussing the repercussions of the Loeb-Leopald trial, and idly watching the street below through the conveniently angled mirror while listening to the large newfangled radio.

During the Christmas holidays, he was persuaded to ski with Matthew in Vermont, and spent a week panting uphill in the footsteps of his fitter friend.

'Tell me, Matthew, what is the point of spending one hour climbing up a hill only to come back down the same hill in a few seconds at considerable risk to life and limb?'

Matthew grunted. 'Sure gives me a bigger kick than graph theory, William. Why don't you admit you're not very good either at the going up or the coming down?'

They both did enough work in their sophomore year to get by, although their interpretations of 'getting by' were wildly different. For the first two months of the summer holidays, they worked as junior management assistants in Charles Lester's bank in New York, Matthew's father having long since given up the battle of trying to keep William away. When the dog days of August arrived, they spent most of their time dashing about the New England countryside in 'Daisy', sailing on the Charles River with as many different girls as possible and attending any house party to which they could get themselves invited. In no time, they were among the accredited personalities of the university, known to the cognoscenti as the Scholar and the Sweat. It was perfectly understood in Boston society that the girl who married William Kane or Matthew Lester would have no fears for her future, but as fast as hopeful mothers appeared with their fresh-faced daughters, Grandmother Kane and Grandmother Cabot despatched them unceremoniously.

. . .

On April 18, 1927, William celebrated his twenty-first birthday by attending the final meeting of the trustees to his estate. Alan Lloyd and Tony Simmons had prepared all the documents for signature.

'Well, William dear,' said Milly Preston as if a great responsibility had been lifted from her shoulders, 'I'm sure you'll be able to do every bit as well as we did.'

'I hope so, Mrs Preston, but if ever I need to lose half a million overnight, I'll know just whom to call.'

Milly Preston went bright red but made no attempt to reply.

The trust now stood at over twenty-eight million dollars, and William had definite plans for the nurture of that money, but he had also set himself the task of making a million dollars in his own right before he left Harvard. It was not a large sum compared with the amount in his trust, but his inherited wealth meant far less to him than the balance in his account at Lester's

That summer, the grandmothers, fearing a fresh outbreak of predatory girls, despatched William and Matthew on the grand tour of Europe, which turned out to be a great success for both of them. Matthew, surmounting all language barriers, found a beautiful girl in every major European capital – love, he assured William, was an international commodity. William secured introductions to a director of most of the major European banks – money, he assured Matthew, was also an international commodity. From London to Berlin to Rome, the two young men left a trail of broken hearts and suitably impressed bankers. When they returned to Harvard in September, they were both ready to hit the books for their final year.

. . .

In the bitter winter of 1927, Grandmother Kane died, aged eighty-five, and William wept for the first time since his mother's death.

'Come on,' said Matthew, after bearing with William's depression for several days. 'She had a good run and waited a long time to find out whether God was a Cabot or a Lowell.'

William missed the shrewd words he had so little appreciated in his grandmother's lifetime, and he arranged a funeral which she would have been proud to attend. Although the great lady arrived at the cemetery in a black Packard hearse ('One of those new-fangled contraptions – over my dead body', but, as it turned out, under it), this unsound mode of transport would have been her only criticism of William's orchestration of her departure. Her death drove William to work with ever more purpose during that final year at Harvard. He dedicated himself to winning the top mathematics prize in her memory. Grandmother Cabot died some six months later, probably, said William, because there was no one left for her to talk to.

. . .

In February 1928, William received a visit from the captain of the Debating Team. There was to be a full-dress debate the following month on the motion 'Socialism or Capitalism for America's Future', and William was naturally asked to represent capitalism.

'And what if I told you I was only willing to speak on behalf of the downtrodden masses?' William inquired of the surprised captain, slightly nettled by the thought that his intellectual views were simply assumed by outsiders because he had inherited a famous name and a prosperous bank.

'Well, I must say, William, we did imagine your own preference would be for, er ...'

'It is, I accept your invitation. I take it that I am at liberty to select my partner?'

'Naturally.'

'Good, then I choose Matthew Lester. May I know who our opponents will be?'

'You will not be informed until the day before, when the posters go up in the yard.'

For the next month Matthew and William turned their breakfast critiques of the newspapers of the left and right, and their nightly discussions about the meaning of life, into strategy sessions for what the campus was beginning to call 'The Great Debate'. William decided that Matthew should lead off.

As the fateful day approached, it became clear that most of the politically aware students, professors, and even some Boston and Cambridge notables would be attending. On the morning before the debate they walked over to the Yard to discover who their opposition would be.

'Leland Crosby and Thaddeus Cohen. Either name ring a bell with you, William? Crosby must be one of the Philadelphia Crosby's, I suppose.'

'Of course he is. "The Red Maniac of Rittenhouse Square", as his own aunt once described him so accurately. He's the most convincing revolutionary on campus. He's loaded, and he spends all his money on the popular radical causes. I can hear his opening now.'

William parodied Crosby's grating tone. '"I know at first hand the rapacity and the utter lack of social conscience of the American monied class." If everyone in the audience hasn't heard that fifty times already, I'd say he'll make a formidable opponent.'

'And Thaddeus Cohen?'

'Never heard of him.'

The following evening, refusing to admit to stage fright, they made their way through the snow and cold wind, heavy overcoats flapping behind them, past the gleaming columns of the recently completed Widener Library – like William's father, the donor's son had gone down on the *Titanic* – to Boylston Hall.

'With weather like this, at least if we take a beating there won't be many to tell the tale,' said Matthew hopefully.

But as they rounded the side of the library, they could see a steady stream of stamping, huffing figures ascending the stairs and filing into the hall. Inside, they were shown to chairs on the podium. William sat still but his eyes picked out the people he knew in the audience: President Lowell, sitting discreetly in the middle row; ancient old Newbury St John, Professor of

Botany; a pair of Brattle Street blue-stockings he recognized from Red House parties; and to his right, a group of Bohemian-looking young men and women, some not even wearing ties, who turned and started to clap as their spokesmen – Crosby and Cohen – walked onto the stage.

Crosby was the more striking of the two, tall and thin almost to the point of caricature, dressed absent-mindedly – or very carefully – in a shaggy tweed suit, but with a stiffly pressed shirt, and dangling a pipe with no apparent connection to his body except at his lower lip. Thaddeus Cohen was shorter and wore rimless glasses and an almost too perfectly-cut, dark worsted suit.

The four speakers shook hands cautiously as the last minute arrangements were made. The bells of Memorial Church, only a hundred feet away, sounded vague and distant as they rang out seven times.

'Mr Leland Crosby, Junior,' said the captain.

Crosby's speech gave William cause for self-congratulation. He had anticipated everything, the strident tone Crosby would take, the overstressed, nearly hysterical points he would make. He recited the incantations of American radicalism – Haymarket, Money Trust, Standard Oil, even Cross of Gold. William didn't think he had made more than an exhibition of himself although he garnered the expected applause from his claque on William's right. When Crosby sat down, he had clearly won no new supporters, and it looked as though he might have lost a few old ones. The comparison with William and Matthew – equally rich, equally socially distinguished, but selfishly refusing martyrdom for the cause of the advancement of social justice – just might be devastating.

Matthew spoke well and to the point, soothing his listeners, the incarnation of liberal toleration. William pumped his friend's hand warmly when he returned to his chair to loud applause.

'It's all over bar the shouting, I think,' he whispered,

But Thaddeus Cohen surprised virtually everyone. He had a pleasant, diffident manner and a sympathetic style. His references and quotations were catholic, pointed and illuminating. Without conveying to the audience the feeling that it was being deliberately impressed, he exuded a moral earnestness which made anything less seem a failure to a rational human being. He was willing to admit the excesses of his own side and the inadequacy of its leaders, but he left the impression that, in spite of its dangers, there was no alternative to socialism if the lot of mankind were ever to be improved.

William was flustered. A surgically logical attack on the political platform of his adversaries would be useless against Cohen's gentle and persuasive presentation. Yet to outdo him as a spokesman of hope and faith in the human spirit would be impossible. William concentrated first on refuting some of Crosby's charges and then countered Cohen's arguments with a declaration of his own faith in the ability of the American system to produce the best results through competition, intellectual and economic. He felt he had played a good defensive game, but no more, and sat down supposing that he had been well beaten by Cohen.

Crosby was his opponents' rebuttal speaker. He began ferociously, sounding as if he now needed to beat Cohen as much as William and Matthew, asking the audience if they could identify an 'enemy of the people' amongst themselves that night. He glared around the room for several long seconds, as members of the audience squirmed in embarrassed silence and his dedicated supporters studied their shoes. Then he leaned forward and roared.

'He stands before you. He has just spoken in your midst. His name is William Lowell Kane.' Gesturing with one hand towards where William sat without looking at him, he thundered: 'His bank owns mines in which the workers die to give its owners an extra million a year in dividends. His bank supports the bloody, corrupt dictatorships of Latin America. Through his bank, the American Congress is bribed into crushing the small farmer. His bank ...'

The tirade went on for several minutes. William sat in stony silence, occasionally jotting down a comment on his yellow legal pad. A few members of the audience had begun shouting 'No.' Crosby's supporters shouted loyally back. The officials began to look nervous.

Crosby's allotted time was nearly up. He raised his fist and said, 'Gentlemen, I submit that not more than two hundred yards from this very room we have the answer to the plight of America. There stands the Widener Library, the greatest private library in the world. Here poor and immigrant scholars come, along with the best educated Americans, to increase the knowledge and prosperity of the world. Why does it exist? Because one rich playboy had the misfortune to set sail sixteen years ago on a pleasure boat called the *Titanic*. I suggest, ladies and gentlemen, that not until the people of America hand each and every member of the ruling class a ticket for his own private cabin on the *Titanic* of capitalism, will the hoarded wealth of this great continent be freed and devoted to the service of liberty, equality and progress.'

As Matthew listened to Crosby's speech, his sentiments changed from exultation that, by this blunder, the victory had been secured for his side, through embarrassment at the behaviour of his adversary, to rage at the reference to the *Titanic*. He had no idea how William would respond to such provocation.

When some measure of silence had been restored, the captain walked to the lectern and said: 'Mr William Lowell Kane.'

William strode to the platform and looked out over the audience. An expectant hush filled the room.

'It is my opinion that the views expressed by Mr Crosby do not merit a response.'

He sat down. There was a moment of surprised silence – and then loud applause.

The captain returned to the platform, but appeared uncertain what to do. A voice from behind him broke the tension.

'If I may, Mr Chairman, I would like to ask Mr Kane if I might use his rebuttal time.' It was Thaddeus Cohen.

William nodded his agreement to the captain.

Cohen walked to the lectern and blinked at the audience disarmingly. 'It has long been true,' he began, 'that the greatest obstacle to the successful democratic socialism in the United States has been the extremism of some of its allies. Nothing could have exemplified this unfortunate fact more clearly than my colleague's speech tonight. The propensity to damage the progressive cause by calling for the physical extermination of those who oppose it might be understandable in a battle-hardened immigrant, a veteran of foreign struggles fiercer than our own. In America it is pathetic and inexcusable. Speaking for myself, I extend my sincere apologies to Mr Kane.'

This time the applause was instantaneous. Virtually the entire audience rose to its feet and clapped continuously.

William walked over to shake hands with Thaddeus Cohen. It was no surprise to either of them that William and Matthew won the vote by a margin of more than one hundred and fifty votes. The evening was over, and the audience filed out into the silent, snow-covered paths, walking in the middle of the street, talking animatedly at the tops of their voices.

William insisted that Thaddeus Cohen should join him and Matthew for a drink. They set off together across Massachusetts Avenue, barely able to see where they were going in the drifting snow, and came to a halt outside a big black door almost directly opposite Boylston Hall. William opened it with his key and the three entered the vestibule.

Before the door shut behind him, Thaddeus Cohen spoke. 'I'm afraid I won't be welcome here.'

William looked startled for a second. 'Nonsense. You're with me.'

Matthew gave his friend a cautionary glance but saw that William was determined.

They went up the stairs and into a large room, comfortably but not luxuriously furnished, in which there were about a dozen young men sitting in armchairs or standing in small knots of two and three. As soon as William appeared in the doorway, the congratulations started.

'You were marvellous, William. That's exactly the way to treat those sort of people.'

'Enter in triumph, Doloki slayer.'

Thaddeus Cohen hung back, still half-shadowed by the doorway, but William had not forgotten him.

'And, gentlemen, may I present my worthy adversary, Mr Thaddeus Cohen.'

Cohen stepped forward hesitantly.

All noise ceased. A number of heads were averted, as if they were looking at the elm trees in the yard, their branches weighed down with new snow.

Finally, there was the crack of a floorboard as one young man left the room by another door. Then there was another departure. Without haste, without apparent agreement, the entire group filed out. The last to leave gave William a long look before he, too, turned on his heel and disappeared.

Matthew gazed at his companions in dismay. Thaddeus Cohen had turned a dull red and stood with his head bowed. William's lips were drawn together in the same tight cold fury that had been apparent when Crosby had made his reference to the *Titanic*.

Matthew touched his friend's arm. 'We'd better go.'

The three trudged off to William's rooms and silently drank some indifferent brandy.

When William woke in the morning, there was an envelope under his door. Inside there was a short note, from the chairman of the Porcellian Club informing him that 'he hoped there would never be a recurrence of last night's, best forgotten, incident.'

By lunchtime the chairman had received two letters of resignation.

. . .

After months of long, studious days, William and Matthew were almost ready – no one ever thinks he is quite ready – for their final examinations. For six days they answered questions and filled up sheets and sheets of the little books, and then they waited, not in vain for they both graduated as expected from Harvard in June of 1928.

A week later it was announced that William was the winner of the President's Mathematics Prize. He wished his father had been alive to witness the presentation ceremony. Matthew managed an honest 'C', which came as a relief to him and no great surprise to anyone else. Neither had any interest in further education, both having elected to join the real world as quickly as possible.

William's bank account in New York edged over the million dollar mark eight days before he left Harvard. It was then that he discussed in greater detail with Matthew his long term plan to gain control of Lester's Bank by merging it with Kane and Cabot.

Matthew was enthusiastic about the idea and confessed, 'That's about the only way I'll ever improve on what my old man will undoubtedly leave me when he dies.'

On graduation day, Alan Lloyd, now in his sixtieth year, came to Harvard. After the graduation ceremony, William took his guest for tea on the square. Alan eyed the tall young man affectionately.

'And what do you intend to do now that you have put Harvard behind you?'

'I'm going to join Charles Lester's bank in New York and gain some experience before I come to Kane and Cabot in a few years' time.'

'But you've been living in Lester's bank since you were twelve years old, William. Why don't you come straight to us now? We would appoint you as a director immediately.'

William said nothing. Alan Lloyd's offer came as a total surprise. With all his ambition, it had never occurred to him, even for a moment, that he might be invited to be a director of the bank before he was twenty-five, the age at which his father had achieved that distinction.

Alan Lloyd waited for his reply. It was not forthcoming. 'Well, I must say, William, it's most unlike you to be rendered speechless by anything.'

'But I never imagined you would invite me to join the board before my twenty-fifth birthday, when my father ...'

'It's true your father was elected when he was twenty-five. However, that's no reason to prohibit you from joining the board before then if the other directors support the idea, and I know that they do. In any case, there are personal reasons why I should like to see you a director as soon as possible. When I retire from the bank in five years' time, we must be sure of electing the right chairman. You will be in a stronger position to influence that decision if you have been working for Kane and Cabot during those five years rather than as a grand functionary at Lester's. Well, my boy, will you join the board?'

It was the second time that day that William wished his father were still alive.

'I should be delighted to accept, sir,' he said.

Alan looked up at William. 'That's the first time you've called me "sir" since we played golf together. I shall have to watch you very carefully.'

William smiled.

'Good,' said Alan Lloyd, 'that's settled then. You'll be a junior director in charge of investments, working directly under Tony Simmons.'

'Can I appoint my own assistant?' asked William.

Alan Lloyd looked at him quizzically. 'Matthew Lester, no doubt?'

'Yes.'

'No. I don't want him doing in our bank what you intended to do in theirs. Thomas Cohen should have taught you that.'

William said nothing but never underestimated Alan again.

Charles Lester laughed when William repeated the conversation word for word to him.

'I'm sorry to hear you won't be coming to us, even as a spy,' he said genially, 'but I have no doubt you'll end up here some day – in one capacity or another.'

BOOK THREE

15

When William started work as a junior director of Kane and Cabot in September 1928, he felt for the first time in his life that he was doing something really worthwhile. He began his career in a small oak-panelled office next to Tony Simmons, the bank's director of finance. From the week that William arrived, he knew without a word being spoken that Tony Simmons was hoping to succeed Alan Lloyd as chairman of the bank.

The bank's entire investment programme was Simmons' responsibility. He quickly delegated to William some aspects of his work; in particular, private investment in small businesses, land, and any other outside entrepreneurial activities in which the bank became involved. Among William's official duties was to make a monthly report on the investments he wished to recommend, at a full meeting of the board. The fourteen board members met once a month in a larger oak-panelled room, dominated at both ends by portraits, one of William's father, the other of his grandfather. William had never known his grandfather, but had always considered he must have been a 'hell of a man' to have married Grandmother Kane. There was ample room left on the walls for his own portrait.

William conducted himself during those early months at the bank with caution, and his fellow board members soon came to respect his judgement and follow his recommendations with rare exceptions. As it turned out, the advice they rejected was among the best that William ever gave. On the first occasion, a Mr Mayer sought a loan from the bank to invest in 'talking pictures' but the board refused to see that the notion had any merit or future. Another time, a Mr Paley came to William with an ambitious plan for United, the radio network. Alan Lloyd, who had about as much respect for telegraphy as for telepathy, would have nothing to do with the scheme. The board supported Alan's views, and Louis B. Mayer later headed MGM and William Paley the company that was to become CBS. William believed in his own judgement and backed both men with money from his trust and, like his father, never informed the recipients of his support.

. . .

One of the more unpleasant aspects of William's day-to-day work was the handling of the liquidations and bankruptcies of clients who had borrowed large sums from the bank and had subsequently found themselves unable to repay their loans. William was not by nature a soft person, as Henry Osborne had learned to his cost, but insisting that old and respected clients liquidate their stocks and even sell their homes did not make for easy sleeping at nights. William soon learned that these clients fell into two distinct categories; those who looked upon bankruptcy as a part of everyday business and those who were appalled by the very word and who would spend the rest of their lives trying to repay every penny they had borrowed.

William found it natural to be tough with the first category but was almost always far more lenient with the second, with the grudging approval of Tony Simmons.

It was during such a case that William broke one of the bank's golden rules and became personally involved with a client. Her name was Katherine Brookes, and her husband, Max Brookes, had borrowed over a million dollars from Kane and Cabot to invest in the Florida land boom of 1925, an investment William would never had backed had he then been working at the bank. Max Brookes had, however, been something of a hero in Massachusetts as one of the new intrepid breed of balloonists and flyers, and a close friend of Charles Lindbergh into the bargain. Brookes' tragic death when the small plane he was piloting, at a height of all ten feet above the ground, hit a tree only a hundred yards after take-off was reported in the press across the length and breadth of America as a national loss.

William, acting for the bank, immediately took over the Brookes estate, which was already insolvent, dissolved it and tried to cut the bank's losses by selling all the land held in Florida except for two acres on which the family home stood. The bank's loss was still over three hundred thousand dollars. Some directors were slightly critical of William's snap decision to sell off the land, a decision with which Tony Simmons had not agreed. William had Simmons' disapproval of his actions entered on the minutes and was in a position to point out some months later, that if they had held onto the land, the bank would have lost most of its original investment of one million. This demonstration of foresight did not endear him to Tony Simmons although it made the rest of the board conscious of William's uncommon perspicacity.

When William had liquidated everything the bank held in Max Brookes' name, he turned his attention to Mrs Brookes, who was under a personal guarantee for her late husband's debts. Although William always tried to secure such a guarantee on any loans granted by the bank, the undertaking of such an obligation was not a course that he ever recommended to friends, however confident they might feel about the venture on which they were about to embark, as failure almost invariably caused great distress to the guarantor.

William wrote a formal letter to Mrs Brookes, suggesting that she make an appointment to discuss the position. He had read the Brookes file conscientiously and knew that she was only twenty-two years old, a daughter of Andrew Higginson, the head of an old and distinguished Boston family, and that she had substantial assets of her own. He did not relish the thought of requiring her to make them over to the bank, but he and Tony Simmons were, for once, in agreement on the line to be taken, so he steeled himself for an unpleasant encounter.

What William had not bargained for was Katherine Brookes herself. In later life, he could always recall in great detail the events of that morning. He had had some harsh words with Tony Simmons about a substantial investment in copper and tin, which he wished to recommend to the board. Industrial demand for the two metals was rising steadily, and William was confident that a world shortage was certain to follow. Tony Simmons could not agree with him, insisting they should invest more cash in the stock market, and the matter was still uppermost in William's mind when his secretary ushered Mrs Brookes into his office. With one tentative smile, she removed copper, tin and all other world shortages from his mind. Before she could sit down, he was around on the other side of his desk, settling her into a chair, simply to assure himself that she would not vanish, like a mirage, on closer inspection. Never had William encountered a woman he considered half as lovely as Katherine Brookes. Her long fair hair fell in loose and wayward curls to her shoulders, and little wisps escaped enchantingly from her hat and clung around her temples. The fact that she was in mourning in no way detracted from the beauty of her slim figure. The fine bone structure ensured that she was a woman who was going to look lovely at every age. Her brown eyes were enormous. They were also, unmistakably, apprehensive of him and what he was about to say.

William strove for his business tone of voice. 'Mrs Brookes, may I say how sorry I was to learn of your husband's death and how much I regret the necessity of asking you to come here today.'

Two lies in a single sentence that would have been the truth five minutes before. He waited to hear her speak.

'Thank you, Mr Kane.' Her voice was soft and had a gentle, low pitch. 'I am aware of my obligations to your bank and I assure you that I will do everything in my power to meet them.'

William said nothing, hoping she would go on speaking. She did not, so he outlined how he had disposed of Max Brookes' estate. She listened with downcast eyes.

'Now, Mrs Brookes, you acted as guarantor for your husband's loan and that brings us to the question of your personal assets.' He consulted his file. 'You have some eighty thousand dollars in investments – your own family money, I believe – and seventeen thousand four hundred and fifty-six dollars in your personal account.'

She looked up. 'Your grasp of my financial position is commendable, Mr Kane. You should add, however, Buckhurst Park, our house in Florida, which was in Max's name, and some quite valuable jewelry of my own. I estimate that all together I am worth the three hundred thousand dollars you still require, and I have made arrangements to realize the full amount as soon as possible.'

There was only the slightest tremor in her voice; William gazed at her in admiration.

'Mrs Brookes, the bank has no intention of relieving you of your every last possession. With your agreement we would like to sell your stocks and bonds. Everything else you mentioned, including the house, we consider should remain in your possession.'

She hesitated. 'I appreciate your generosity, Mr Kane. However, I have no wish to remain under any obligation to your bank or to leave my husband's name under a cloud.' The little tremor again, but quickly suppressed. 'Anyway, I have decided to sell the house in Florida and return to my parents' home as soon as possible.'

William's pulse quickened to hear that she would be coming back to Boston. 'In that case, perhaps we can reach some agreement about the proceeds of the sale,' he said.

'We can do that now,' she said flatly. 'You must have the entire amount.'

William played for another meeting. 'Don't let's make too hasty a decision. I think it might be wise to consult my colleagues and discuss this with you again at a later date.'

She shrugged slightly. 'As you wish. I don't really care about the money either way, and I wouldn't want to put you to any inconvenience.'

William blinked. 'Mrs Brookes, I must confess to have been surprised by your magnanimous attitude. At least allow me the pleasure of taking you to lunch.'

She smiled for the first time, revealing an unsuspected dimple in her right cheek. William gazed at it in delight and did his utmost to provoke its reappearance over a long lunch at the Ritz. By the time he returned to his desk, it was well past three o'clock.

'Long lunch, William,' commented Tony Simmons.

'Yes, the Brookes problem turned out to be trickier than I had expected.'

'It looked fairly straightforward to me when I went over the papers,' said Simmons. 'She isn't complaining about our offer, is she? I thought we were being rather generous in the circumstances.'

'Yes, she thought so too. I had to talk her out of divesting herself of her last dollar to swell our reserves.'

Tony Simmons stared. 'That doesn't sound like the William Kane we all know and love so well. Still, there has never been a better time for the bank to be magnanimous.'

William grimaced. Since the day of his arrival, he and Tony Simmons had been in growing disagreement about where the stock market was heading. The Dow Jones had been moving steadily upward since Herbert Hoover's election to the White House in November 1928. In fact, only ten days later, the New York stock exchange had a record of over six million shares volume in one day. But William was convinced that the upward trend, fuelled by the large influx of money from the automobile industry would result in prices inflating to the point of instability. Tony Simmons, on the other hand, was confident that the boom would continue so that when William advocated caution at board meetings he was invariably overruled. However, with his trust money, he was free to follow his own intuition, and started investing heavily in land, gold, commodities and even in some carefully selected Impressionist paintings, leaving only fifty per cent of his cash in stocks.

When the Federal Reserve Bank of New York put out an edict declaring that they would not re-discount loans to those banks which were releasing money to their customers for the sole purpose of speculation, William considered that the first nail had been driven into the speculator's coffin. He immediately reviewed the bank's lending programme and estimated that Kane and Cabot had over twenty-six million dollars out on such loans. He begged Tony Simmons to call in these amounts, certain that, with such a government regulation in operation, stock prices would inevitably fall in the long term. They nearly had a stand-up fight at the monthly board meeting, and William was voted down by twelve to two.

On 21 March, 1929, Blair and Company announced its consolidation with the Bank of America, the third in a series of bank mergers which seemed to point to a brighter tomorrow, and on 25 March, Tony Simmons sent William a note pointing out to him that the market had broken through to yet another all time record, and proceeded to put more of the bank's money into stocks. By then, William had rearranged his capital so that only twenty-five per cent was in the stock market, a move that had already cost him over two million dollars – and a troubled reprimand from Alan Lloyd.

'I hope to goodness you know what you're doing, William.'

'Alan, I've been beating the stock market since I was fourteen, and I've always done it by bucking the trend.'

But as the market continued to climb through the summer of 1929, even William stopped selling, wondering if Tony Simmons' judgement was, in fact, correct.

As the time for Alan Lloyd's retirement drew nearer, Tony Simmons' clear intent to succeed him as chairman began to take on the look of a *fait accompli*. The prospect troubled William, who considered Simmons' thinking was far too conventional. He was always a yard behind the rest of the market, which is fine during the boom years when things are going well, but can be dangerous for a bank in leaner, more competitive times. A shrewd investor, in William's eyes, did not invariably run with the herd, thundering or otherwise, but worked out in advance in which direction the herd would be turning next. William had already decided that future investment in the stock market still looked risky while Tony Simmons was convinced that America was entering a golden era.

William's other problem was simply that Tony Simmons was only thirty-nine years old and that meant that William could not hope to become chairman of Kane and Cabot for at least another twenty-six years. That hardly fitted into what they had called at Harvard 'one's career pattern'.

.   .   .

Meanwhile, the image of Katherine Brookes remained clearly in his mind. He wrote to her as often as he could about the sale of her stocks and bonds: formal, typewritten letters which elicited no more than formal handwritten responses. She must have thought he was the most conscientious banker in the world. Had she realized her file was becoming as large as any under William's control she might have thought about it – or at least him – more carefully. Early in the autumn she wrote to say she had found a firm buyer for the Florida estate. William wrote to request that she allow him to negotiate the terms of the sale on the bank's behalf, and she agreed.

He travelled down to Florida in early September 1929. Mrs Brookes met him at the station and he was overwhelmed by how much more beautiful she appeared in person than in his memory. The slight wind blew her black dress against her body as she stood waiting on the platform, leaving a profile that ensured that every man except William would look at her a second time. William's eyes never left her.

She was still in mourning and her manner towards him was so reserved and correct that William initially despaired of making any impression on her. He spun out the negotiations with the farmer who was purchasing Buckhurst Park for as long as he could and persuaded Katherine Brookes to accept one-third of the agreed sale price while the bank took two-thirds. Finally, after the legal papers were signed, he could find no more excuses for not returning to Boston. He invited her to dinner at his hotel, resolved to reveal something of his feelings for her. Not for the first time, she took him by surprise. Before he had broached the subject, she asked him, twirling her glass to avoid looking at him, if he would like to stay over at Buckhurst Park for a few days.

'A sort of holiday for us both.' She blushed; William remained silent.

Finally she found the courage to continue 'I know this might sound mad, but you must realize I've been very lonely. The extraordinary thing is that I seem to have enjoyed the last week with you more than any time I can remember.' She blushed again. 'I've expressed that badly, and you'll think the worst of me.'

William's pulse leaped. 'Kate, I have wanted to say something at least as bad as that for the last nine months.'

'Then you'll stay for a few days, William?'

'Yes, Kate, I will.'

That night she installed him in the main guest bedroom at Buckhurst Park. In later life William always looked back on these few days as a golden interlude in his life. He rode with Kate, and she outjumped him. He swam with her, and she outdistanced him. He walked with her and always turned back first and so finally he resorted to playing poker with her and won three and a half million dollars in as many hours of playing.

'Will you take a cheque?' she said grandly.

'You forget I know what you're worth, Mrs Brookes, but I'll make a deal with you. We'll go on playing until you've won it back.'

'It may take a few years,' said Kate.

'I'll wait,' said William.

He found himself telling her of long-buried incidents in his past, things he had barely discussed even with Matthew, his respect for his father, his love for his mother, his blind hatred of Henry Osborne, his ambitions for Kane and Cabot. She, in turn, told him of her childhood in Boston, her schooldays in Virginia, and of her early marriage to Max Brookes.

Five days later when she said goodbye to him at the station, he kissed her for the first time.

'Kate, I'm going to say something very presumptuous. I hope one day you'll feel more for me than you felt for Max.'

'I'm beginning to feel that way already,' she said quietly.

William looked at her steadily. 'Don't stay out of my life for another nine months.'

'I can't – you've sold my house.'

⋅ ⋅ ⋅

On the way back to Boston, feeling more settled and happy than at any time since before his father's death, William drafted a report on the sale of Buckhurst Park, his mind returning continually to Kate and the past five days. Just before the train drew into the South Station, he scribbled a quick note in his neat but illegible handwriting.

Kate, I find I am missing you already. And it's only a few hours. Please write and let me know when you will be coming to Boston. Meanwhile I shall be getting back to the bank's business and find I can put you out of my mind for quite long periods (i.e. 10 ± 5 minutes) at a stretch consecutively.

Love

William

He had just dropped the envelope into the mail box on Charles Street when all thoughts of Kate were driven from his mind by the cry of a newsboy.

'Wall Street collapse.'

William seized a copy of the paper and scanned the lead story rapidly. The market had plummeted overnight; some financiers viewed it as nothing more than a readjustment; William saw it as the beginning of the landslide that he had been predicting for months. He hurried to the bank and went straight to the chairman's office.

'I'm sure the market will steady up in the long run,' said Alan Lloyd soothingly.

'Never,' said William. 'The market is overloaded. Overloaded with small investors who thought they were in for a quick profit and are certain to run for their lives now. Don't you see the balloon is about to burst? I'm going to sell everything. By the end of the year, the bottom will have dropped out of this market, and I did warn you in February, Alan.'

'I still don't agree with you, William, but I'll call a full board meeting for tomorrow, so that we can discuss your views in more detail.'

'Thank you,' said William. He returned to his office and picked up the inter-office phone.

'Alan, I forgot to tell you. I've met the girl I'm going to marry.'

'Does she know yet?' asked Alan.

'No,' said William.

'I see,' said Alan. 'Then your marriage will closely resemble your banking career, William. Anyone directly involved will be informed only after you've made your decision.'

William laughed, picked up the other phone, and immediately placed his own major stock holdings on the market and went into cash. Tony Simmons had just come in, and stood at the open door watching William, thinking he had gone quite mad.

'You could lose your shirt overnight dumping all those shares with the market in its present state.'

'I'll lose a lot more if I hold onto them,' replied William.

The loss he was to make in the following week, over one million dollars, would have staggered a less confident man.

At the board meeting the next day he also lost, by eight votes to six, his proposal to liquidate the bank's stocks; Tony Simmons convinced the board that it would be irresponsible not to hold out for a little longer. The only small victory William notched up was to persuade his fellow directors that the bank should no longer be a buyer.

The market rose a little that day, which gave William the opportunity to sell some more of his own stock. By the end of the week, when the index had risen steadily for four days in a row, William began to wonder if he had been over-reacting, but all his past training and instinct told him that he had made the right decision. Alan Lloyd said nothing; the money William was losing was not his, and he was looking forward to a quiet retirement.

On 22 October the market suffered more heavy losses and William again begged Alan Lloyd to get out while there was still a chance. This time Alan listened and allowed William to place a sell order on some of the bank's major stocks. The following day, the market fell again in an avalanche of selling, and it mattered little what holdings the bank tried to dispose of because there were no longer any buyers. The dumping of stock turned into a stampede, as every small investor in America put in a sell bid to try to get out from under. Such was the panic that the ticker tape could not keep pace with the transactions. Only when the Exchange opened in the morning, after the clerks had worked all night, did traders know for a fact how much they had lost the day before.

Alan Lloyd had a phone conversation with J. P. Morgan, and agreed that Kane and Cabot should join a group of banks who would try to shore up the national collapse in major stocks. William did not disapprove of this policy, on the grounds that if there had to be a group effort, Kane and Cabot should be responsibly involved in the action. And, of course, if it worked, all the banks would be better off. Richard Whitney, the vice-president of the New York Stock Exchange and the representative of the group Morgan had put together, went on the floor of the New York Stock Exchange and purchased thirty million dollars worth of blue-chip stocks the next day. The market began to hold. Twelve million, eight hundred and ninety-four thousand, six hundred and fifty shares were traded that day, and for the next two days the market held steady. Everyone, from President Hoover to the runners in the brokerage house, believed that the worst was behind them.

William had sold nearly all of his private stock and his personal loss was proportionately far smaller than the bank's, which had dropped over three million dollars in four days; even Tony Simmons had taken to following all of William's suggestions. On 29 October, Black Tuesday as the day came to be known, the market fell again. Sixteen million, six hundred and ten thousand and thirty shares were traded. Banks all over the country knew that the truth was that they were now insolvent. If every one of their customers demanded cash – or if they in turn tried to call in all their loans – the whole banking system would collapse around their ears.

A board meeting held on 9 November opened with one minute's silence in memory of John J. Riordan, president of the County Trust, and a director of Kane and Cabot, who had shot himself to death in his own home. It was the eleventh suicide in Boston banking circles in two weeks; the dead man had been a close personal friend of Alan Lloyd's. The chairman went on to announce that Kane and Cabot had themselves lost nearly four million dollars, the Morgan Group had failed in its effort to unite, and it was now expected that every bank should act in in own best interests. Nearly all the bank's small investors had gone under, and most of the larger ones were having impossible cash problems. Angry mobs had already gathered outside banks in New York and the elderly guards had had to be supplemented with Pinkertons. Another week like this, said Alan, and every one of us will be wiped out. He offered his resignation, but the directors would not hear of it. His position was no different from that of any other chairman of a major bank in America. Tony Simmons also offered his resignation, but once again his fellow directors would not consider it. Tony was no longer destined to take Alan Lloyd's place so William kept a magnanimous silence. As a compromise, Simmons was sent to London to take charge of overseas investments. Out of harm's way, thought William, who now found himself appointed Director of Finance, in charge of all the bank's investments. Immediately he invited Matthew Lester to join him as his number two. This time Alan Lloyd didn't even raise an eyebrow.

Matthew agreed to join William early in the New Year, which was as soon as his father could release him. They hadn't been without their own problems. William, therefore, ran the investment department on his own, until Matthew's arrival. The winter of 1929 turned out to be a depressing period for William, as he watched small firms and large firms alike, run by friends he had known all his life, go under. For some time he even wondered if the bank itself could survive.

At Christmas William spent a glorious week in Florida with Kate, helping her pack her belongings in tea chests ready for returning to Boston. 'The ones Kane and Cabot let me keep,' she teased.

William's Christmas presents filled another tea chest and Kate felt quite guilty about his generosity. 'What can a penniless widow hope to give you in return?' she mocked. William responded by bundling her into the remaining tea chest and labelling it 'William's present'.

He returned to Boston in high spirits, and hoped his stay with Kate augured the start of a better year. He settled down into Tony Simmons' old office to read the morning mail, knowing he would have to preside over the usual two or three liquidation meetings scheduled for that week. He asked his secretary whom he was to see first.

'I'm afraid it's another bankruptcy, Mr Kane.'

'Oh, yes, I remember the case,' said William. The name had meant nothing to him. 'I read over the file last night. A most unfortunate affair. What time is he due?'

'At ten o'clock, but the gentleman is already in the lobby waiting for you, sir.'

'Right, said William, 'please send him in. Let's get it over with.'

William opened his file again to remind himself quickly of the salient facts. There was a line drawn through the name of the original client, a Mr Davis Leroy. It had been replaced by that of the morning's visitor, Mr Abel Rosnovski.

William vividly remembered the last conversation he had had with Mr Rosnovski, and was already regretting it.

16

It took Abel about three months to appreciate the full extent of the problems facing the Richmond Continental and why the hotel went on losing so much money. The simple conclusion he came to after twelve weeks of keeping his eyes wide open, while at the same time allowing the rest of the staff to believe that he was half asleep, was that the hotel's profits were being stolen. The Richmond staff was working a collusive system on a scale which even Abel had not previously come across. The system did not, however, take into account a new assistant manager who had, in the past, had to steal bread from the Russians to stay alive. Abel's first problem was not to let anybody know the extent of his discoveries until he had a chance to look into every part of the hotel. It didn't take him long to figure out that each department had perfected its own system for stealing.

Deception started at the front desk where the clerks were registering only eight out of every ten guests and pocketing the cash payments from the remaining two for themselves. The routine they were using was a simple one; anyone who had tried it at the Plaza in New York would have been discovered in a few minutes and fired. The head desk clerk would choose an elderly couple, who had booked in from another state for only one night. He would then discreetly make sure they had no business connections in the city, and simply fail to register them. If they paid cash the following morning, the money was pocketed and, provided they had not signed the register, there was no record of the guests ever having been in the hotel. Abel had long thought that all hotels should automatically have to register every guest. They were already doing so at the Plaza.

In the dining room, the system had been refined. Of course, the cash payments of any casual guest for lunch or dinner were already being taken. Abel had expected that, but it took him a little longer to check through the restaurant bills and establish that the front desk was working with the dining room staff to ensure that there were no restaurant bills for those guests whom they had already chosen not to register. Over and above that there was a steady trail of fictitious breakages and repairs, missing equipment, disappearing food, lost bed linen, and even an occasional mattress had gone astray. After checking every department thoroughly and keeping his ears and eyes open, Abel concluded that over half of the Richmond's staff were involved in the conspiracy, and that no one department had a completely clean record.

When he had first come to the Richmond, Abel had wondered why the manager, Desmond Pacey, hadn't noticed what had been going on under his nose a long time before. He wrongly assumed the reason was that the man was lazy and could not be bothered to follow up complaints. Even Abel was slow to catch onto the fact that the lazy manager was the mastermind behind the entire operation, and the reason it worked so well. Pacey had worked for the Richmond group for over thirty years. There was not a single hotel in the group in which he had not held a senior position at one time or another, which made Abel fearful for the solvency of the other hotels. Moreover, Desmond Pacey was a personal friend of the hotels' owner, Davis Leroy. The Chicago Richmond was losing over thirty thousand dollars a year, a situation Abel knew could be redeemed overnight by firing half the staff, starting with Desmond Pacey. That posed a problem, because Davis Leroy had rarely fired anyone in thirty years. He simply tolerated the problems, hoping that in time they would go away. As far as Abel could see, the Richmond hotel staff went on stealing the hotel blind until they reluctantly retired.

Abel knew that the only way he could reverse the hotel's fortunes was to have a show-down with Davis Leroy, and to that end, early in 1928, he boarded the express train from Illinois Central to St Louis and the Missouri Pacific to Dallas. Under his arm was a two-hundred page report which he had taken three months to compile in his small room in the hotel annex. By the time he had finished reading through the mass of evidence, Davis Leroy sat staring at him in dismay.

'These people are my friends,' were his first words as he closed the dossier. 'Some of them have been with me for thirty years. Hell, there's always been a little fiddling around in the business, but now you tell me they've been robbing me blind behind my back?'

'Some of them, I should think, for all of those thirty years,' said Abel.

'What in hell's name am I going to do about it?' said Leroy.

'I can stop the rot if you remove Desmond Pacey and give me *carte blanche* to sack anyone who has been involved in the thefts, starting tomorrow.'

'Well now, Abel, I wish the problem was as simple as that.'

'The problem is just that simple,' said Abel. 'And if you won't let me deal with the culprits, you can have my resignation as of this minute, because I have no interest in being a part of the most corruptly run hotel in America.'

'Couldn't we just demote Desmond Pacey to assistant manager? Then I could make you manager and the problem would come under your control.'

'Never,' replied Abel. 'Pacey has over two years to go and has a firm hold over the entire Richmond staff, so that by the time I get him in line you'll be dead or bankrupt, or both, as I suspect all of your other hotels are being run in the same cavalier fashion. If you want the trend reversed in Chicago, you'll have to make a firm decision about Pacey right now, or you can go to the wall on your own. Take it or leave it.'

'Us Texans have a reputation for speaking our mind, Abel but we're sure not in your class. Okay, okay, I'll give you the authority. As of this minute congratulations. You're the new manager of the Chicago Richmond. Wait till Al Capone hears you've arrived in Chicago; he'll join me down here in the peace and quiet of the great South-west. Abel, my boy,' continued Leroy, standing up and slapping his new manager on the shoulder, 'don't think I'm ungrateful. You've done a great job in Chicago, and from now on I shall look upon you as my right-hand man. To be honest with you Abel, I have been doing so well on the Stock Exchange I haven't even noticed the losses, so thank God I have one honest friend. Why don't you stay overnight and have a bite to eat?'

'I'd be delighted to join you, Mr Leroy, but I want to spend the night at the Dallas Richmond for personal reasons.'

'You're not going to let anyone off the hook, are you, Abel?'

'Not if I can help it.'

That evening Davis Leroy gave Abel a sumptuous meal and a little too much whisky which he insisted was no more than Southern hospitality. He also admitted to Abel that he was looking for someone to run the Richmond Group so that he could take things a little easier.

'Are you sure you want a dumb Polack?' slurred Abel after one too many drinks.

'Abel, it's me who's been dumb. If you hadn't proved to be so reliable in smoking out those thieves, I might have gone under. But now that I know the truth, we'll lick them together, and I'm going to give you the chance to put the Richmond Group back on the map.'

Abel shakily raised his glass. 'I'll drink to that – and to a long and successful partnership.'

'Go get 'em, boy.'

Abel spent the night at the Dallas Richmond, giving a false name and pointedly telling the desk clerk that he would only be staying one night. In the morning when he observed the hotel's only copy of the receipt for his cash payment disappearing into the wastepaper basket, Abel had his suspicions confirmed. The problem was not Chicago's alone. He decided he would have to get Chicago straightened out first; the rest of the group's finaglings would have to wait until later. He made one call to Davis Leroy to warn him that the disease had spread to the whole group.

Abel travelled back the way he had come. The Mississippi valley lay sullenly alongside the train window, devastated by the floods of the previous year. Abel thought about the devastation he was going to cause when he returned to the Chicago Richmond.

When he arrived, there was no night porter on duty and only one clerk could be found. He decided to let them all have a good night's rest before he bade them farewell. A young bellboy opened the front door for him as he made his way back to the annex.

'Have a good trip, Mr Rosnovski?' he asked.

'Yes, thank you. How have things been here?'

'Oh, very quiet.'

You may find it even quieter this time tomorrow, thought Abel, when you're the only member of the staff left.

Abel unpacked and called room service to order a light meal, which took over an hour to arrive. When he had finished his coffee, he undressed and stood in a cold shower, going over his plan for the following day. He had picked a good time of year for his massacre. It was early February and the hotel had only about a twenty-five per cent occupancy, and Abel was confident that he could run the Richmond with about half its present staff. He climbed into bed, threw the pillow on the floor and slept, like his unsuspecting staff, soundly.

Desmond Pacey, known to every one at the Richmond as Lazy Pacey, was sixty-two years old. He was considerably overweight and it made him rather slow of movement on his short legs. Desmond Pacey had seen seven, or was it eight, assistant managers come and go in the Richmond. Some got greedy and wanted more of his take; some just couldn't understand how it worked. The Polack, he decided, wasn't turning out to be any brighter than the others. He hummed to himself as he walked slowly towards Abel's office for their daily ten o'clock meeting. It was seventeen minutes past ten.

'Sorry to have kept you waiting,' said the manager, not sounding sorry at all.

Abel made no comment.

'I was held up with something at reception, you know how it is.'

Abel knew exactly how it was at reception.

He slowly opened the drawer of the desk in front of him and laid out forty crumpled hotel bills, some of them in four or five pieces, bills that he had recovered from wastepaper baskets and ashtrays, bills for those guests who had paid cash and who had never been registered. He watched the fat little manager trying to work out what they were, upside down.

Desmond Pacey couldn't quite fathom it. Not that he cared that much. Nothing for him to worry about. If the stupid Polack had caught on to the system, he could either take his cut or leave. Pacey was wondering what percentage he would have to give him. Perhaps a nice room in the hotel would keep him quiet for the time being.

'You're fired, Mr Pacey, and I want you off the premises within the hour.'

Desmond Pacey didn't actually take in the words, because he couldn't believe them.

'What was that you said? I don't think I heard you right.'

'You did,' said Abel. 'You're fired.'

'You can't fire me. I'm the manager and I've been with the Richmond Group for over thirty years. If there's any firing to be done, I'll do it. Who in God's name do you think you are?'

'I am the new manager.'

'You're *what?*'

'The new manager,' Abel repeated. 'Mr Leroy appointed me yesterday and I have just fired you, Mr Pacey.'

'What for?'

'For larceny on a grand scale.'

Abel turned the bills around so that the bespectacled man could see them all properly.

'Every one of these guests paid their bill, but not one penny of the money reached the Richmond account, and they all have one thing in common – your signature is on them.'

'You couldn't prove anything in a hundred years.'

'I know,' said Abel. 'You've been running a good system. Well, you can go and run that system somewhere else because your luck's run out here. There is an old Polish saying, Mr Pacey: the pitcher carries water only until the handle breaks. The handle has just broken and you're fired.'

'You don't have the authority to fire me,' said Pacey. Sweat peppered out on his forehead despite the coldness of the February day. 'Davis Leroy is a close personal friend of mine. He's the only man who can fire me. You only came out from New York three months ago. He wouldn't even listen to you once I had spoken to him. I could get you thrown out of this hotel with one phone call.'

'Go ahead,' said Abel.

He picked up the telephone and asked the operator to get Davis Leroy in Dallas. The two men waited, staring at each other. The sweat had now trickled down to the tip of Pacey's nose. For a second Abel wondered if his new employer would hold firm.

'Good morning, Mr Leroy. It's Abel Rosnovski calling from Chicago. I've just fired Desmond Pacey, and he wants a word with you.'

Shakily, Pacey took the telephone. He listened for only a few moments. 'But, Davis, I . . . What could I do . . .? I swear to you it isn't true . . . There must be some mistake.'

Abel heard the line click.

'One hour, Mr Pacey,' said Abel, 'or I'll hand over these bills to the Chicago Police Department.'

'Now wait a moment,' Pacey said. 'Don't act so hasty.' His tone and attitude had changed abruptly. 'We could bring you in on the whole operation, you could make a very steady little income if we ran this hotel together, and no one would be any the wiser. The money would be far more than you're making as assistant manager and we all know Davis can afford the losses . . .'

'I'm not the assistant manager any longer, Mr Pacey. I'm the manager so get out before I throw you out.'

'You fucking Polack,' said the ex-manager, realizing he had played his last card and lost. 'You'd better keep your eyes open because you're going to be brought down to size.'

Pacey left. By lunch he had been joined on the street by the head waiter, head chef, senior housekeeper, chief desk clerk, head porter, and seventeen other members of the Richmond staff whom Abel felt were past redemption. In the afternoon, he called a meeting of the remainder of the employees, explained to them in detail why what he had done had been necessary, and assured them that their jobs were not in any danger.

'But if I can find *one*,' said Abel, 'I repeat, *one* dollar misplaced, the person involved will be sacked without references there and then. Am I understood?'

No one spoke.

Several other members of the staff left the Richmond during the next few weeks when they realized that Abel did not intend to continue Desmond Pacey's system on his own behalf, and they were quickly replaced.

By the end of March, Abel had invited four employees from the Plaza to join him at the Richmond. They had three things in common: they were young, ambitious and honest. Within six months, only thirty-seven of the original staff of one hundred and ten were still employed at the Richmond. At the end of the first year, Abel cracked a large bottle of champagne with Davis Leroy to celebrate the year's figures for the Chicago Richmond. They had shown a profit of three thousand, four hundred and eight-six dollars. Small, but the first profit the hotel had shown in the thirty years of its existence. Abel was projecting a profit of over twenty-five thousand dollars in 1929.

Davis Leroy was mightily impressed. He visited Chicago once a month and began to rely heavily on Abel's judgement. He even came round to the point of admitting that what had been true of the Chicago Richmond might well be true of the other hotels in the group. Abel wanted to see the Chicago hotel running smoothly on its new lines before he considered tackling the others; Leroy agreed but talked of a partnership for Abel if he could do for the others what he had done with Chicago.

They started going to baseball and the races together whenever Davis was in Chicago. On one occasion, when Davis had lost seven hundred dollars without getting close in any of the six races, he threw up his arms in disgust and said, 'Why do I bother with horses, Abel? You're the best bet I've ever made.'

Melanie Leroy always dined with her father on these visits. Cool, pretty, with a slim figure and long legs which attracted many a stare from the hotel guests, she treated Abel with a slight degree of hauteur which gave him no encouragement for the aspirations he had begun to formulate for her, nor did she invite him to substitute 'Melanie' for 'Miss Leroy' until she discovered he was the holder of an economics degree from Columbia and knew more about discounted cash flow than she did herself. After that, she softened a little and came from time to time to dine with Abel alone in the hotel and seek assistance with the work she was doing for her liberal arts degree at the University of Chicago. Emboldened, he occasionally escorted her to concerts and the theatre, and began to feel a proprietorial jealousy whenever she brought other men to dine at the hotel, though she never came with the same escort twice.

So greatly had the hotel cuisine improved under Abel's iron fist that people who had lived in Chicago for thirty years and never realized the place existed were making gastronomic outings every Saturday evening. Abel redecorated the whole hotel for the first time in twenty years and put the staff into smart new green and gold uniforms. One guest, who had stayed at the Richmond for a week every year, actually retreated back out of the front door on arrival, because he thought he had walked into the wrong establishment. When Al Capone booked a dinner party for sixteen in a private room to celebrate his thirtieth birthday, Abel knew he had arrived.

.   .   .

Abel's personal wealth grew during this period, while the stock market flourished. Having left the Plaza with eight thousand dollars, eighteen months before, his brokerage account now stood at over thirty thousand. He was confident that the market would continue to rise, and so he always reinvested his profits. His personal requirements were still fairly modest. He had acquired two new suits and his first pair of brown shoes. He still had his rooms and food provided by the hotel and few out-of-pocket expenses. There seemed to be nothing but a bright future ahead of him. The Continental Trust had handled the Richmond account for over thirty years, so Abel had transferred his own account to them when he first came to Chicago. Every day he would go to the bank and deposit the hotel's previous day's receipts. He was taken by surprise one Friday morning by a message that the manager was asking to see him. He knew his personal account was never overdrawn, so he presumed the meeting must have something to do with the Richmond. The bank could hardly be about to complain that the hotel's account was solvent for the first time in thirty years. A junior clerk guided Abel through a tangle of corridors until he reached a handsome wooden door. A gentle knock and he was ushered in to meet the manager.

'My name is Curtis Fenton,' said the man behind the desk, offering Abel his hand before motioning him into a green leather button seat. He was a neat, rotund man who wore half-moon spectacles and an impeccable white collar and black tie to go with his three piece banker's suit.

'Thank you,' said Abel nervously.

The circumstances brought back to him memories of the past, memories he associated only with the fear of being uncertain what was going to happen next.

'I would have invited you to lunch, Mr Rosnovski –'

Abel's heartbeat steadied a little. He was only too aware that bank managers do not dispense free meals when they have unpleasant messages to deliver.

'– but something has arisen that requires immediate action, and so I hope you won't mind if I discuss the problem with you without delay. I'll come straight to the point, Mr Rosnovski. One of my most respected customers, an elderly lady, Miss Amy Leroy,' – the name made Abel sit up instantly – 'is in possession of twenty-five per cent of the Richmond Group stock. She has offered this holding to her brother, Mr Davis Leroy, several times in the past but he has shown absolutely no interest in purchasing Miss Amy's shares. I can understand Mr Leroy's reasoning. He already owns seventy-five per cent of the company, and I dare say he feels he has no need to worry about the other twenty-five per cent, which incidentally, was a legacy from their late father. However, Miss Amy Leroy is still keen to dispose of her stock as it has never paid a dividend.'

Abel was not surprised to hear that.

'Mr Leroy has indicated that he has no objection to her selling the stock, and she feels that at her age she would rather have a little cash to spend now than wait in the hope that the group may one day prove profitable. With that in mind, Mr Rosnovski, I thought I would apprise you of the situation in case you might know of someone with an interest in the hotel trade and, therefore, in the purchase of my client's shares.'

'How much is Miss Leroy hoping to realize for her stock?' asked Abel.

'Oh, I feel she'd be happy to let them go for as little as sixty-five thousand dollars.'

'Sixty-five thousand dollars is a rather high price for a stock that has never paid a dividend,' said Abel, 'and has no hope of doing so for some years to come.'

'Ah,' said Curtis Fenton, 'but you must remember that the value of the eleven hotels should also be taken into consideration.'

'But control of the company would still remain in the hands of Mr Leroy, which makes Miss Leroy's twenty-five per cent holding nothing but pieces of paper.'

'Come, come, Mr Rosnovski, twenty-five per cent of eleven hotels would be a very valuable holding for only sixty-five thousand dollars.'

'Not while Davis Leroy has overall control. Offer Miss Leroy forty thousand dollars, Mr Fenton, and I may be able to find you someone who is interested.'

'You don't think that person might go a little higher, do you?' Mr Fenton's eyebrows raised on the word 'higher'.

'Not a penny more, Mr Fenton.'

The bank manager brought his fingertips delicately together, pleased with his appraisal of Abel.

'In the circumstances, I can only ask Miss Amy what her attitude would be to such an offer. I will contact you again as soon as she has instructed me.'

After leaving Curtis Fenton's office, Abel's heart was beating as fast as when he had entered. He hurried back to the hotel to double check on his own personal holdings. His brokerage account stood at thirty-three thousand one hundred and twelve dollars, and his personal account at three thousand and eight dollars. Abel then tried to carry out a normal day's work. He found it hard to concentrate for wondering how Miss Amy Leroy would react to the bid and daydreaming about what he would do if he held a twenty-five per cent interest in the Richmond Group.

He hesitated before informing Davis Leroy of his bid, fearful that the genial Texan might view his ambitions as a threat. But after a couple of days during which he considered the matter carefully, he decided the fairest thing to do would be to call Davis Leroy and acquaint him with his intentions.

'I want you to know why I am doing this, Mr Leroy. I believe the Richmond Group has a great future, and you can be sure that I shall work all the harder for you if I know my own money is also involved.' He paused. 'But if you want to take up that twenty-five per cent yourself, I shall naturally understand.'

To his surprise, the escape ladder was not grasped.

'Well, see here, Abel, if you have that much confidence in the group, go ahead, son, and buy Amy out. I'd be proud to have you for a partner. You've earned it. By the way, I'll be up next week for the Red Cubs game. See you then.'

Abel was jubilant. 'Thank you, Davis, you'll never have cause to regret your decision.'

'I'm sure I won't, pardner.'

Abel returned to the bank a week later. This time, it was he who asked to see the manager. Once again he sat in the green leather button chair, and waited for Mr Fenton to speak.

'I am surprised to find,' began Curtis Fenton not looking at all surprised, 'that Miss Leroy will accept the bid of forty thousand dollars for her twenty-five per cent holding in the Richmond Group.' He paused before looking up at Abel. 'As I have now secured her agreement, I must ask if you are in a position to disclose your buyer?'

'Yes,' said Abel confidently. 'I will be the principal.'

'I see, Mr Rosnovski,' again not showing any surprise. 'May I ask how you propose to find the forty thousand dollars?'

'I shall liquidate my stock holdings and release the spare cash in my personal account, which will leave me short of about four thousand dollars. I hoped that you would be willing to loan me that sum, as you are so confident that the Richmond Group stock is undervalued. In any case, the four thousand dollars probably represents nothing more than the bank's commission on the deal.'

Curtis Fenton blinked and frowned. Gentlemen did not make that sort of remark in his office: it stung all the more because Abel had the sum exactly right. 'Will you give me a little more time to consider your proposal, Mr Rosmovski, and then I will come back to you?'

'If you wait long enough, I won't need your loan,' said Abel. 'My other investments will soon be worth the full forty thousand, the way the market is moving at the moment.'

Abel had to wait a further week to be told that Continental Trust was willing to back him. He immediately cleared both his accounts and borrowed a little under four thousand dollars to make up the shortfall on the forty thousand.

.   .   .

Within six months, Abel had paid off his four thousand loan by careful buying and selling of stock from March to August 1929, some of the best days the stock market was ever to know.

By September, both his accounts were slightly ahead again – he even had enough to buy a new Buick – while he was now the owner of twenty-five per cent of the Richmond Group of hotels. Abel was pleased to have acquired such a firm holding in Davis Leroy's empire. It gave him the confidence to pursue his daughter and the other seventy-five per cent.

Early in October, he invited Melanie to a programme of Mozart at the Chicago Symphony Hall. Donning his smartest suit, which only emphasized he was gaining some weight, and wearing his first silk tie, he felt confident as he glanced in the mirror that the evening was to be a success. After the concert was over Abel avoided the Richmond, excellent though its food had become, and took Melanie to The Loop for dinner. He was particularly careful to talk only of economics and politics, two subjects about which he knew she was obliged to accept he was greatly the more knowledgeable. Finally, he asked her back for a drink in his rooms. It was the first time she had seen them, and she was both piqued and surprised by their smartness.

Abel poured the Coca-Cola which she requested, dropped two cubes of ice into the bubbly liquid and gained confidence from the smile he was rewarded with as he passed her the glass. He couldn't help staring at her slim, crossed legs for more than a polite second. He poured himself a bourbon.

'Thank you, Abel, for a wonderful evening.'

He sat down beside her and swirled the drink in his glass reflectively. 'For many years, I heard no music. When I did, Mozart spoke to my heart as no other composer has done.'

'How very middle-European you sound sometimes, Abel.' She pulled the edge of her silk dress, which Abel was sitting on, free. 'Who would have thought a hotel manager would give a damn for Mozart?'

'One of my ancestors, the first Baron Rosnovski,' said Abel, 'once met the maestro, and he became a close friend of the family so I have always felt he was part of my life.'

Melanie's smile was unfathomable. Abel leaned sideways and kissed her cheek just above the ear, where her fair hair was drawn back from her face. She continued the conversation without giving the slightest indication that she had even been aware of his action.

'Frederick Stock captured the mood of the third movement to perfection, wouldn't you say?'

Abel tried the kiss again. This time she turned her face towards him and allowed herself to be kissed on the lips. Then she drew away.

'I think I ought to be getting back to the university.'

'But you've only just arrived,' said Abel, dismayed.

'Yes, I know, but I have to be up early in the morning. I have a heavy day ahead of me.'

Abel kissed her again. She fell back on the couch and Abel tried to move his hand onto her breast. She broke quickly from the kiss and pushed him away.

'I must be going, Abel,' she insisted.

'Oh, come on,' he said, 'you don't have to go yet,' and once again he tried to kiss her.

This time she stopped him by pushing him away more firmly.

'Abel, what do you think you are doing? Because you give me the occasional meal and take me to a concert, doesn't mean you have the right to maul me.'

'But we've been going out together for months,' said Abel. 'I didn't think you would mind.'

'We have not been going out together for months, Abel. I eat with you occasionally in my father's dining room, but you should not construe that to mean we have been going out together for months.'

'I'm sorry,' said Abel. 'The last thing I wanted you to think was that I was mauling you. I only wanted to touch you.'

'I would never allow a man to touch me,' she said, 'unless I was going to marry him.'

'But I want to marry you,' said Abel quietly.

Melanie burst out laughing.

'What's so funny about that?' Abel asked, reddening.

'Don't be silly, Abel, I could never marry you.'

'Why not?' demanded Abel, shocked by the vehemence in her voice.

'It would never do for a Southern lady to marry a first generation Polish immigrant,' she replied, sitting up very straight and pushing her silk dress back into place.

'But I am a Baron,' said Abel, a little haughtily.

Melanie burst out laughing again. 'You don't think anybody believes that, do you Abel? Don't you realize the whole staff laughs behind your back whenever you mention your title?'

He was stunned, and felt sick, his face draining of its red embarrassment. 'They all laugh at me behind my back?' His slight accent sounded more pronounced.

'Yes,' she said. 'Surely you know what your nickname in the hotel is? The Chicago Baron.'

Abel was speechless.

'Now don't be silly and get all self-conscious about it. I think you've done a wonderful job for Daddy, and I know he admires you, but I could never marry you.'

Abel sat quietly. '*I could never marry you*,' he repeated.

'Of course not. Daddy likes you, but he would never agree to having you as a son-in-law.'

'I'm sorry to have offended you,' said Abel.

'You haven't, Abel. I'm flattered. Now let's forget you ever mentioned the subject. Perhaps you would be kind enough to take me home?'

She rose and strode towards the door, while Abel remained seated, still stunned. Somehow he managed to push himself up slowly and help Melanie on with her cloak. He became conscious of his limp as they walked along the corridor together. They went down in the lift and he took her home in a cab: neither spoke. While the taxi waited, he accompanied her to the front gate of her dormitory. He kissed her hand.

'I do hope this doesn't mean we can't still be friends,' said Melanie.

'Of course not.'

'Thank you for taking me to the concert, Abel. I'm sure you'll have no trouble in finding a nice Polish girl to marry you. Goodnight.'

'Goodbye,' said Abel.

.   .   .

Abel did not think there would be any real trouble on the New York Stock market until one of his guests asked if he might settle his hotel bill with stock. Abel held only a small amount of stock himself since nearly all his money was tied up in the Richmond Group, but he took his broker's advice and sold off his remaining shares at a small loss, relieved that the bulk of his savings was secure in bricks and mortar. He had not taken as close an interest in the day-to-day movement of the Dow-Jones as he would have if all his capital had still been in the market.

The hotel did well in the first part of the year, and Abel considered he was set fair to achieve his profit forecast of over twenty-five thousand dollars for 1929, and kept Davis Leroy in constant touch with the way things were turning out. But when the crash came in October the hotel was half empty. Abel placed a call through to Davis Leroy on Black Tuesday. The Texan sounded depressed and preoccupied and would not be drawn into making decisions about the laying off of hotel staff which Abel now considered urgent.

'Stick with it, Abel,' he said. 'I'll come up next week and we'll sort it out together then – or we'll try to.'

Abel did not like the ring of the last phrase. 'What's the problem, Davis? Is it anything I can help with?'

'Not for the time being.'

Abel remained puzzled. 'Why don't you just give me the authority to get on with it, and I can brief you when you come up next week?'

'It's not quite as easy as that, Abel. I didn't want to discuss my problems over the phone, but the bank is giving me a little trouble over my losses in the stock market, and they are threatening to make me sell the hotels if I can't raise enough money to cover my debts.'

Abel went cold.

'Nothing for you to worry about, my boy,' continued Davis, sounding unconvincing. 'I will fill you in on all the details when I come up to Chicago next week. I am sure I can fix up something by then.'

Abel heard the phone click and could feel his whole body sweating. His first reaction was to wonder how he could assist Davis. He put a call through to Curtis Fenton and prised out of him the name of the banker who controlled the Richmond Group, feeling that if he could see him it might make things easier for his friend.

Abel called Davis several times during the next few days to tell him that things were going from bad to worse and that decisions must be made, but he sounded more and more preoccupied and was still unwilling to make any decision. When matters started getting out of control, Abel made a decision. He asked his secretary to get the banker who controlled the Richmond Group on the phone.

'Who are you calling, Mr Rosnovski?' asked a prim-sounding lady.

Abel looked down at the name on the piece of paper in front of him and said it firmly.

'I'll put you through.'

'Good morning,' said an authoritative voice. 'May I help you?'

'I hope so. My name is Abel Rosnovski,' began Abel nervously. 'I am the manager of the Richmond Chicago and wanted to make an appointment to see you and discuss the future of the Richmond Group.'

'I have no authority to deal with anyone except Mr Davis Leroy,' said the clipped accent.

'But I own twenty-five per cent of the Richmond Group,' said Abel.

'Then no doubt someone will explain to you that until you own fifty-one per cent you are in no position to deal with the bank unless you have the authority of Mr Davis Leroy.'

'But he's a close personal friend ...'

'I don't doubt that, Mr Rosnovski.'

'... and I'm trying to help.'

'Has Mr Leroy given you the authority to represent him?'

'No, but ...'

'Then I am sorry. It would be most unprofessional of me to continue this conversation.'

'You couldn't be less helpful, could you?' asked Abel, immediately regretting his words.

'That is no doubt how you see it, Mr Rosnovski. Good day, sir.'

Oh, to hell with you, thought Abel, slamming down the phone, even more worried about what he could do next to help Davis. He didn't have long to find out.

The next evening Abel spotted Melanie in the restaurant, not displaying her usual well-groomed confidence but looking tired and anxious, and he nearly asked her if everything was all right. He decided against approaching her and, as he left the dining room to go to his office, he found Davis Leroy standing alone in the front hall. He had on the checked jacket that he was wearing the first day he had approached Abel at the Plaza.

'Is Melanie in the dining room?'

'Yes,' said Abel. 'I didn't know you were coming into town today, Davis. I'll get the Presidential Suite ready for you immediately.'

'Only for one night, Abel, and I'd like to see you in private later.'

'Certainly.'

Abel didn't like the sound of 'in private'. Had Melanie been complaining to her father; was that why he had not found it possible to get a decision out of Davis during the last few days?

Davis Leroy hurried past him into the dining room while Abel went over to the reception desk to check on whether the suite on floor twelve was available. Half the rooms in the hotel were unoccupied and it came as no surprise that the Presidential Suite was free. Abel booked his employer in and then waited by the reception desk for over an hour. He saw Melanie leave, her face blotched as if she had been crying. Her father followed her out of the dining room a few minutes later.

'Get yourself a bottle of bourbon, Abel – don't tell me we don't have one – and then join me in my suite.'

Abel picked up two bottles of bourbon from his safe and joined Leroy in the Presidential Suite on the twelfth floor, still wondering if Melanie had said anything to her father.

'Open the bottle and pour yourself a very large one, Abel,' Davis Leroy instructed.

Once again Abel felt the fear of the unknown. The palms of his hands began to sweat. Surely he was not going to be fired for wanting to marry the boss's daughter? He and Leroy had been friends for over a year now, close friends. He did not have to wait long to find out what the unknown was.

'Finish your bourbon.'

Abel put the drink down in one gulp, and Davis Leroy swallowed his.

'Abel, I'm wiped out.' He paused, and poured both of them another drink. 'So is half America, come to think of it.'

Abel did not speak, partly because he could not think of what to say. They sat staring at each other for several minutes, then after another glass of bourbon, he managed, 'But you still own eleven hotels.'

'Used to own,' said Davis Leroy. 'Have to put it in the past tense now, Abel. I no longer own any of them; the bank took possession of the freeholds last Thursday.'

'But they belong to you, they have been in your family for two generations,' said Abel.

'They were. They aren't any longer. Now they belong to a bank. There's no reason why you shouldn't know the whole truth, Abel; the same thing's happening to almost everyone in America right now, big or small. About ten years ago I borrowed two million dollars using the hotels as collateral and invested the money right across the board in stocks and bonds, fairly conservatively and in well-established companies. I built the capital up to nearly five million, which was one of the reasons the hotel losses never bothered me too much – they were always tax deducitble against the profit I was making in the market. Today I couldn't give those shares away. We may as well use them as toilet paper in the eleven hotels. For the last three weeks I've been selling as fast as I can, but there are no buyers left. The bank foreclosed on my loan last Thursday.' Abel couldn't help remembering that it was on a Thursday when he spoke to the banker. 'Most people who are affected by the crash have only pieces of paper to cover their loans, but in my case the bank who backed me has the deeds on the eleven hotels as security against their original loan. So when the bottom dropped out, they immediately took possession of them. The bastards have let me know that they intend to sell the group as quickly as possible.'

'That's madness. They'll get nothing for them right now, and if they supported us through this period, together we could show them a good return on their investment.'

'I know *you* could, Abel, but they have my past record to throw back in my face. I went up to their main office to suggest just that. I explained about you and told them I would put all my time into the group if they would give us their backing, but they weren't interested. They fobbed me off with some smooth young puppy who had all the text book answers about cash flows, no capital base and credit restrictions. By God, if I ever get back, I'll screw him personally and then his bank. Right now the best thing we can do is get ourselves uproariously drunk, because I am finished, penniless, bankrupt.'

'Then so am I,' said Abel quietly.

'No, you have a great future ahead of you, son. Anyone who takes over this group couldn't make a move without you.'

'You forget that I own twenty-five per cent of the group.'

Davis Leroy stared at him. It was obvious that that fact had slipped his mind.

'Oh my God, Abel, I hope you didn't put all your money into me.' His voice was becoming thick.

'Every last cent,' said Abel. 'But I don't regret it, Davis. Better to lose with a wise man than win with a fool.' He poured himself another bourbon.

The tears were standing in the corners of Davis Leroy's eyes. 'You know, Abel, you're the best friend a man could ask for. You knock this hotel into shape, you invest your own money, I make you penniless, and you don't even complain, and then for good measure my daughter refuses to marry you.'

'You didn't mind me asking her?' said Abel, less incredulous than he would have been without the bourbon.

'Silly little bitch, doesn't know a good thing when she sees one. She wants to marry some horse-breeding gentleman from the South with three Confederate generals in his family tree or if she does marry a Northerner, his great grandfather has to have come over on *The Mayflower*. If everyone who claims they had a relative on that boat were ever on board together, the whole damn thing would have sunk a thousand times before it reached America. Too bad I don't have another daughter for you, Abel. No one has served me more loyally then you have. I sure would have been proud to have you as a member of the family. You and I would have made a great team, but I still reckon you can beat them all by yourself. You're young, you still have everything ahead of you.'

At twenty-three Abel suddenly felt very old.

'Thank you for your confidence, Davis,' he said, 'and who gives a damn for the stock market anyway? You know, you're the best friend I ever had.' The drink was beginning to talk.

Abel poured himself yet another bourbon and threw it down. Between them they had finished both bottles by early morning. When Davis fell asleep in his chair, Abel managed to stagger down to the tenth floor, undress and collapse onto his own bed. He was awakened from a heavy sleep by a loud banging on the door. His head was going round and round, but the banging went on and on, louder and louder. Somehow he managed to get himself off the bed and grope his way to the door. It was a bellboy.

'Come quickly, Mr Abel, come quickly,' he said as he ran down the hall.

Abel threw on a dressing gown and slippers and staggered down the corridor to join the bellboy, who was holding back the lift door for him.

'Quickly, Mr Abel,' he repeated.

'What's the hurry?' demanded Abel, his head still going around as the lift moved slowly down. Then he recalled the evening's talk. Maybe the bank had come to take possession.

'Someone has jumped out the window.'

Abel sobered up immediately. 'A guest?'

'Yes, I think so,' said the bellboy, 'but I'm not sure.'

The lift came to a stop at the ground floor. Abel thrust back the iron gates and ran out into the street. The police were already there. He wouldn't have recognized the body if it had not been for the checked jacket. A policeman was taking down details. A man in plainclothes came over to Abel.

'You the manager?'

'Yes, I am.'

'Do you have any idea who this man might be?'

'Yes,' said Abel, slurring the word. 'His name is Davis Leroy.'

'Do you know where he's from or how we contact his next of kin?'

Abel averted his eyes away from the broken body and answered automatically.

'He's from Dallas and a Miss Melanie Leroy, his daughter, is his next of kin. She's a student living out on the Chicago University campus.'

'Right, we'll get someone right over to her.'

'No, don't do that. I'll go and see her myself,' said Abel.

'Thank you. It's always better if they don't hear the news from a stranger.'

'What a terrible, unnecessary thing to do,' said Abel, his eyes drawn back to the body of his friend.

'It's the seventh in Chicago today,' said the officer flatly as he closed his little black notebook and strolled over towards the ambulance.

Abel watched the stretcher bearers remove Davis Leroy's body from the pavement. He felt cold, sank to his knees and was violently sick in the gutter. Once again he had lost his closest friend. Maybe if he had drunk less and thought more, he might have saved him. He picked himself up and returned to his room, took a long, cold shower and somehow managed to get himself dressed. He ordered some black coffee and then, reluctantly, went up to the Presidential Suite and unlocked the door. Other than a couple of empty bourbon bottles, there seemed to be no sign of the drama that had been enacted a few minutes earlier. Then he saw the letters on the side table by a bed which had not been slept in. The first was addressed to Melanie, the second to a lawyer in Dallas and the third to Abel. He tore his open but could barely read Davis Leroy's last words.

Dear Abel,

I'm taking the only way out after the bank's decision. There is nothing left for me to live for; I am far too old to start over. I want you to know I believe you're the one person who might make something good come out of this terrible mess.

I have made a new will in which I have left you the other seventy-five per cent of the shares in the Richmond Group. I realize they are worthless, but the stock will secure your position as the legal owner of the group. As you had the guts to buy twenty-five per cent with your own money, you deserve the right to see if you can make some deal with the bank. I've left everything else I own, including the house, to Melanie. Please be the one who tells her. Don't let it be the police. I would have been proud to have you as a son-in-law, partner.

Your friend,
Davis

Abel read the letter again and again and then folded it neatly and put it into his wallet.

He went over to the university campus later that morning and broke the news as gently as he could to Melanie. He sat nervously on the couch, unsure what he could add to the bland statement of death. She took it surprisingly well, almost as if she had known what was going to happen. No tears in front of Abel – perhaps later when he wasn't there. He felt sorry for her for the first time in his life.

Abel returned to the hotel and decided not to have any lunch and asked a waiter to bring him a tomato juice while he went over his mail. There was a letter from Curtis Fenton at the Continental Trust Bank. It was obviously going to be a day for letters. Fenton had received the advice that a Boston bank called Kane and Cabot had taken over the financial responsibility of the Richmond Group. For the time being, business was to continue as usual, until meetings had been arranged with Mr Davis Leroy to discuss the disposal of all the hotels in the group. Abel sat staring at the words, and after a second tomato juice, he drafted a letter to the chairman of Kane and Cabot, a Mr Alan Lloyd. He received a reply some five days later asking Abel to attend a meeting in Boston on 4 January to discuss the liquidation of the group with the director in charge of bankruptcies. The interval would give the bank enough time to sort out the implications of Mr Leroy's sudden and tragic death.

Sudden and tragic death? 'And who caused that death?' said Abel aloud in a fury, suddenly remembering Davis Leroy's own words. 'They fobbed me off with some smooth young puppy ... By God, if I ever get back, I'll screw him personally and then his bank.'

'Don't worry, Davis, I'll finish the job for you,' Abel said out loud.

Abel ran the Richmond hotel during the last weeks of that year with rigid control of his staff and prices and only just managed to keep his head above water. He couldn't help wondering what was happening to the other ten hotels in the group, but he didn't have the time to find out and it was no longer his responsibility anyway.

17

On 4 January 1930 Abel Rosnovski arrived in Boston. He took a taxi from the station to Kane and Cabot and was a few minutes early. He sat in the reception room, which was larger and more ornate than any bedroom in the Chicago Richmond. He started reading the *Wall Street Journal*. 1930 was going to be a better year, the paper was trying to assure him. He doubted it. A prim, middle-aged woman entered the room.

'Mr Kane will see you now, Mr Rosnovski.'

Abel rose and followed her down a long corridor into a small oak-panelled room with a large leather-topped desk, behind which sat a tall, good-looking man who must, Abel thought, have been about the same age as himself. His eyes were as blue as Abel's. There was a picture on the wall behind him of an older man, whom the young man behind the desk greatly resembled. I'll bet that's Dad, thought Abel bitterly. You can be sure he'll survive the collapse; banks always seem to win both ways.

'My name is William Kane,' said the young man, rising and extending his hand. 'Please have a seat, Mr Rosnovski.'

'Thank you,' said Abel.

William stared at the little man in his ill-fitting suit, but also noted the determined eyes.

'Perhaps you will allow me to apprise you of the latest situation as I see it,' continued the blue-eyed young man.

'Of course.'

'Mr Leroy's tragic and premature death ...' William began, hating the pomposity of his words.

Caused by your callousness, thought Abel.

'... seems to have left you with the immediate responsibility of running the group until the bank is in a position to find a buyer for the hotels. Although one hundred per cent of the shares of the group are now in your name, the property, in the form of eleven hotels, which was held as collateral for the late Mr Leroy's loan of two million dollars, is legally in our possession. This leaves you with no responsibility at all, and if you wish to disassociate yourself from the entire operation, we will naturally understand.'

An insulting thing to suggest, thought William, but it has to be said.

The sort of thing a banker would expect a man to do, walk away from something the moment any problem arose, thought Abel.

William Kane continued. 'Until the two million debt to the bank is cleared I fear we must consider the estate of the late Mr Leroy insolvent. We at the bank appreciate your personal involvement with the group, and we have done nothing about disposing of the hotels until we had the opportunity to speak to you in person. We thought it possible you might know of a party interested in the purchase of the property, as the buildings, the land and the business are obviously a valuable asset.'

'But not valuable enough for you to back me,' said Abel. He ran his hand wearily through his thick, dark hair. 'How long will you give me to find a buyer?'

William hesitated for a moment when he saw the silver band around Abel Rosnovski's wrist. He had seen that band somewhere before, but he couldn't think where. 'Thirty days. You must understand that the bank is carrying the day-to-day losses on ten of the eleven hotels. Only the Chicago Richmond is making a small profit.'

'If you would give me the time and backing, Mr Kane, I could turn all the hotels into profitable concerns. I know I could,' said Abel. 'Just give me the chance to prove I can do it, sir.' Abel found the last word sticking in his throat.

'So Mr Leroy assured the bank when he came to see us last autumn,' said William. 'But these are hard times. There's no telling if the hotel trade will pick up, and we are not hoteliers, Mr Rosnovski; we are bankers.'

Abel was beginning to lose his temper with the smoothly dressed banker – 'young': Davis had been right. 'They'll be hard times all right for the hotel staff,' he said. 'What will they do if you sell off the roofs from over their heads? What do you imagine will happen to them?'

'I am afraid they are not our responsibility, Mr Rosnovski. I must act in the bank's best interests.'

'In *your* own best interests, don't you mean, Mr Kane?' said Abel hotly.

The young man flushed. 'That is an unjust remark, Mr Rosnovski, and I would greatly resent it if I did not understand what you are going through.'

'Too bad you didn't wheel out your understanding in time for Davis Leroy,' said Abel. 'He could have used it. You killed him, Mr Kane, just as surely as if you had pushed him out of that window yourself, you and your simon-pure colleagues, sitting here on your backsides while we sweat our guts out to be sure you can take a rake-off when times are good and tread on people when times are bad.'

William, too, was becoming angry. Unlike Abel Rosnovski, he did not show it. 'This line of discussion is getting us nowhere, Mr Rosnovski. I must warn you that if you are unable to find a purchaser for the group within thirty days, I shall have no choice but to put the hotels up for auction on the open market.'

'You'll be advising me to ask another bank for a loan next,' said Abel sarcastically. 'You *know* my record, and you won't back me, so where the hell do you expect me to go from here?'

'I'm afraid I have no idea,' replied William. 'That's entirely up to you. My board's instructions are simply to wind up the account as quickly as possible, and that is what I intend to do. Perhaps you would be kind enough to contact me no later than 4 February, and let me know whether you have had any success in finding a buyer. Good day, Mr Rosnovski.'

William rose from behind the desk, and again offered his hand. This time Abel ignored it and went to the door.

'I thought after our phone conversation, Mr Kane, you might feel embarrassed enough to offer a helping hand. I was wrong. You're just a bastard through and through, so when you go to bed at night, Mr Kane, be sure to think about me. When you wake up in the morning, think about me again, because I'll never cease thinking about my plans for you.'

William stood frowning at the closed door. The silver band still bothered him — where had he seen it before?

His secretary returned. 'What a dreadul little man,' she said.

'No, not really,' replied William. 'He thinks we killed his business partner, and now we are disbanding his company without any thought for his employees, not to mention himself, when he had actually proved to be very capable. Mr Rosnovski was remarkably polite in the circumstances, and I

must confess I was almost sorry the board felt unable to back him.' He looked
up at his secretary.

'Get me Mr Cohen on the phone.'

18

Abel arrived back in Chicago on the morning of the following day, still
preoccupied and furious with his treatment at the hands of William Kane.
He didn't catch exactly what the boy was shouting at the corner news-stand
as he hailed a cab and climbed into the back seat.

'The Richmond Hotel, please.'

'Are you from the newspapers?' asked the cab driver as he moved out onto
State Street.

'No, what made you ask that?' said Abel.

'Oh, only because you asked for the Richmond. All the reporters are there
today.'

Abel couldn't remember any functions scheduled for the Richmond that
would attract the press.

The cab driver continued. 'If you're not a newspaper man, maybe I
should take you to another hotel.'

'Why?' asked Abel, even more puzzled.

'Well, you won't have a very good night's sleep if you're booked in there.
The Richmond has been burned to the ground.'

As the cab turned the corner of the block, Abel was faced head on with
the smouldering shell of the Richmond Hotel. Police cars, fire engines
charred wood and water flooding the street. He stepped out of the cab and
stared at the scorched remains of the flagship of Davis Leroy's group.

The Pole is wise when the damage is done, thought Abel, as he clenched
his fist and started banging on his lame leg. He felt no pain – there was
nothing left to feel.

'You bastards,' he shouted aloud. 'I've been lower than this before, and
I'll still beat every one of you. Germans, Russians, Turks, that bastard Kane,
and now this. Everyone, I'll beat you all. Nobody kills Abel Rosnovski.'

The assistant manager saw Abel gesticulating by the cab and ran over to
him. Abel forced himself to be calm.

'Did all the staff and guests get out of the hotel safely?' he asked.

'Yes, thank God. The hotel was nearly empty, so getting everyone out was
no great problem. There were one or two minor injuries and burns, and they
are being dealt with at the hospital, but there's nothing for you to worry
about.'

'Good, at least that's a relief. Thank God the hotel was well insured, over
a million if I remember. We may yet be able to turn this disaster to our
advantage.'

'Not if what they are suggesting in the late papers is true.'

'What do you mean?' asked Abel.

'I'd rather you read it for yourself, boss,' the assistant manager replied.

Abel walked over to the news-stand and paid the boy two cents for the latest edition of the *Chicago Tribune*. The banner headline told it all.

RICHMOND HOTEL BLAZE – ARSON SUSPECTED

Abel shook his head incredulously and re-read the headline.

'Can anything else happen?' he muttered.

'Got yourself a problem?' the newsboy asked.

'A little one,' said Abel and returned to his assistant manager.

'Who's in charge of the police inquiry?'

'That officer over there leaning on the police car,' said the assistant manager, pointing to a tall, spare man who was going prematurely bald. 'His name is Lieutenant O'Malley.'

'It would be,' said Abel. 'Now you get the staff into the annex, and I'll see them all there at ten o'clock tomorrow morning. If anybody wants me before then, I'll be staying at the Stevens until I get this thing sorted out.'

'Will do, boss.'

Abel walked over to Lieutenant O'Malley and introduced himself.

The tall, thin policeman stooped slightly to shake hands with Abel.

'Ah, the long lost ex-manager has returned to his charred remains.'

'I don't find that funny, officer,' said Abel.

'I'm sorry,' he said. 'It isn't funny. It's been a long night. Let's go and have a drink.'

The policeman took Abel by the elbow and guided him across Michigan Avenue to a café on the corner. Lieutenant O'Malley ordered two milk shakes.

Abel laughed when the white, frothy mixture was put in front of him. Since he had never had a youth, it was his first milk shake.

'I know. It's funny, everybody in this city breaks the law drinking bourbon and beer,' said the detective, 'so someone has to play the game straight. In any case, Prohibition isn't going to last for ever, and then my troubles will begin, because the gangsters are going to discover I really do like milk shakes.'

Abel laughed for a second time.

'Now to your problems, Mr Rosnovski. First I have to tell you, I don't think you have a snowball's chance in hell of picking up the insurance on that hotel. The fire experts have been going over the remains of the building with a fine tooth-comb and they found the place was soaked in kerosene. No attempt to even disguise it. There were traces of the stuff all over the basement. One match and the building must have gone up like a Roman candle.'

'Do you have any idea who is responsible?' asked Abel.

'Let me ask the questions. Do you have any idea who might bear a grudge against the hotel or you personally?'

Abel grunted. 'About fifty people, Lieutenant. I cleared out a real can of worms when I first arrived here. I can give you a list, if you think it might help.'

'I think it might, but the way people are talking out there, I may not need it,' said the lieutenant. 'But if you pick up any definite information, let me know, Mr Rosnovski. You let me know, because I warn you, you have enemies out there.' He pointed into the milling street.

'What do you mean?' asked Abel.

'Someone is saying you did it, because you lost everything in the crash and needed the insurance money.'

Abel leaped off his stool.

'Calm down, calm down. I know you were in Boston all day and, more important, you have a reputation in Chicago for building hotels up, not burning them down. But someone did burn the Richmond down, and you can bet your ass I'm going to find out who. So let's leave it at that for the moment.' He swivelled off his own stool. 'The milk shake's on me, Mr Rosnovski. I'll expect a favour from you sometime in the future.'

He smiled at the girl at the cash desk, admiring her ankles and cursing the new fashion for long skirts. He handed her fifty cents. 'Keep the change, honey.'

'A big thank you,' the girl replied.

'Nobody appreciates me,' said the lieutenant.

Abel laughed for a third time, which he would not have thought possible an hour before.

'By the way,' the lieutenant continued as they reached the door, 'the insurance people are looking for you. I can't remember the name of the guy, but I guess he'll find you. Don't hit him. If he feels you were involved, who can blame him? Keep in touch, Mr Rosnovski. I'll be wanting to talk to you again.'

Abel watched the lieutenant vanish into the crowd of spectators and then walked slowly over to the Stevens Hotel and booked himself in for the night. The desk clerk, who had already checked most of the Richmond's guests in, couldn't suppress a smile at the idea of booking the manager in, too. Once in his room, Abel sat down and wrote a formal letter to Mr William Kane, giving him whatever details of the fire he could supply, and telling him that he intended to use his unexpected freedom to make a round of the other hotels in the group. Abel could see no point in hanging around in Chicago warming himself in the Richmond embers, in the vain hope that someone would come along and bail him out.

After a first class breakfast at the Stevens the next morning – it always made Abel feel good to be in a well-run hotel – he walked over to see Curtis Fenton at the Continental Trust Bank and apprise him of Kane and Cabot's attitude – or to be more accurate of William Kane's attitude. Although Abel thought the request was pointless, he added that he was looking for a buyer for the Richmond Group at two million dollars.

'That fire isn't going to help us, but I'll see what I can do,' said Fenton, sounding far more positive than Abel had expected. 'At the time you bought twenty-five per cent of the group's shares from Miss Leroy I told you that I thought the hotels were a valuable asset and that you'd make a good deal. Despite the crash I see no reason to change my mind about that, Mr Rosnovski. I've watched you running your own hotel for nearly two years now, and I'd back you if the decision were left to me personally, but I fear my bank would never agree to support the Richmond Group. We've seen the financial results for far too long to have any faith in the group's future, and that fire was the last straw, if you'll pardon the expression. Nevertheless, I do have some outside contacts and I'll see if they can do anything to help. You probably have more admirers in this city than you realize, Mr Rosnovski.'

After Lieutenant O'Malley's comments Abel had wondered if he had any friends left in Chicago at all. He thanked Curtis Fenton, returned to the front desk of the bank and asked a teller for five thousand dollars in cash from the hotel account. He spent the rest of the morning in the Richmond annex. He gave every member of his staff two week's wages and told them they could stay on at the annex for at least a month or until they had found new jobs. He then returned to the Stevens, packed the new clothes he'd had to buy as a result of the fire and prepared for a tour of the rest of the Richmond hotels.

He drove the Buick he'd bought just before the stock market crash down south first and started with the St Louis Richmond. The trip around all the hotels in the group took nearly a month and although they were run down and, without exception, losing money, none of them was, in Abel's view, a hopeless case. They all had good locations; some were even the best-placed in the city. Old man Leroy must have been a shrewder man than his son, thought Abel. He checked every hotel insurance policy carefully; no problems there. When he finally reached the Dallas Richmond, he was certain of only one thing: that anyone who managed to buy the group for two million would be making himself a good deal. He wished that he could be given the chance, as he knew exactly what had to be done to make the group profitable.

On his return to Chicago, nearly four weeks later, he checked into the Stevens, where there were several messages awaiting him. Lieutenant O'Malley wished to contact him, so did William Kane, Curtis Fenton, and a Mr Henry Osborne.

Abel started with the law, and after a short phone conversation with O'Malley, agreed to meet him at the café on Michigan Avenue. Abel sat on a high stool, with his back to the counter, staring at the charred shell of the Richmond Hotel, while he waited for the lieutenant. O'Malley was a few minutes late, but he did not bother to apologize as he took the next stool and swivelled around to face Abel.

'Why do we keep meeting like this?' asked Abel.

'You owe me a favour,' said the lietuenant, 'and nobody in Chicago gets away with owing O'Malley a milk shake.'

Abel ordered two, one giant, one regular.

'What did you find out?' asked Abel as he passed the detective two red and white striped straws.

'The boys from the fire department were right, it was arson okay. We've arrested a guy called Desmond Pacey, who turnes out to be the old manager at the Richmond. That was in your time, right?'

'I'm afraid it was,' said Abel.

'Why do you say that?' asked the lieutenant.

'I had Pacey fired for embezzling the hotel's receipts. He said he'd get even with me if it was the last thing he did. I didn't pay any attention. I've had too many threats in my life, Lieutenant, to take any one of them that seriously, especially from a creature like Pacey.'

'Well, I have to tell you that we've taken him seriously, and so have the insurance people, because I'm told they're not paying out one penny until it's proved there was no collusion between you and Pacey over the fire.'

'That's all I need at the moment,' said Abel. 'How can you be so certain it's Pacey?'

'We traced him to the casualty ward at the local hospital, the same day as the fire. A routine check asking the hospital to let us know if anyone had come in that day with severe burns. By chance – which is so often the case in police work since we're not all born to be Sherlock Holmes – a sergeant's wife who had been a waitress at the Richmond told us that he used to be the manager. Even I can put those two and twos together. The guy came clean pretty quick, didn't seem that interested in being caught, only in pulling off what he called his own St Valentine's Day Massacre. Until a few moments ago I wasn't sure what the object of that revenge was, but I sure know now; though I'm not too surprised. So that just about wraps the case up, Mr Rosnovski.'

The lieutenant sucked on his straw until the gurgling sound convinced him he had drained the last drop.

'Have another milk shake?'

'No, I'll give this one a miss. I've got a heavy day ahead of me.' He got down from the stool. 'Good luck, Mr Rosnovski. If you can prove to the insurance boys you had no involvement with Pacey, you'll get your money. I'll do everything I can to help when the case reaches court. Keep in touch.'

Abel watched him disappear through the door. He gave the waitress a dollar and walked out onto the pavement staring into space, a space where the Richmond Hotel had been less than a month ago. Then he turned and strolled back to the Stevens deep in thought.

There was another message from Henry Osborne, still leaving no clue as to who he was. There was only one way to find out. Abel called Osborne, who turned out to be a claims inspector with the Great Western Casualty Insurance Company with whom the hotel had their policy. Abel made an appointment to see the man at noon. He then called William Kane in Boston and gave him a report on the hotels he had visited in the group.

'And may I say again, Mr Kane, that I could turn those hotels' losses into profits if your bank would give me the time and the backing. What I did in Chicago I know I can do for the rest of the group.'

'Possibly you could, Mr Rosnovski, but I fear it will not be with Kane and Cabot's money. May I remind you that you have only five days left in which to find a backer. Good day, sir.'

'Ivy League snob,' said Abel into the deaf telephone. 'I'm not classy enough for your money, am I? Some day, you bastard ...'

The next item on Abel's agenda was the insurance man. Henry Osborne turned out to be a tall good-looking man with dark eyes and a mop of dark hair just turning grey. Abel found his easy manner congenial. Osborne had little to add to Lieutenant O'Malley's story. The Great Western Casualty Insurance Company had no intention of paying any part of the claim, while the police were pressing for a charge of arson against Desmond Pacey, and until it was proved that Abel himself was in no way involved. Henry Osborne seemed to be very understanding about the whole problem.

'Has the Richmond group enough money to rebuild the hotel?' asked Osborne.

'Not a red cent,' said Abel. 'The rest of the group is mortgaged up to the hilt, and the bank is pressing me to sell.'

'Why you?' said Osborne.

Abel explained how he had come to own the group's shares without actually owning the hotels. Henry Osborne was somewhat surprised.

'Surely the bank can see for themselves how well you ran that hotel? Every businessman in Chicago is aware you were the first manager ever to make a profit for Davis Leroy. I know the banks are going through hard times, but even they ought to know when to make an exception for their own good.'

'Not this bank.'

'Continental Trust?' said Osborne. 'I've always found old Curtis Fenton a bit starchy but amenable enough.'

'It's not Continental. The hotels are owned by a Boston bank called Kane and Cabot.'

Henry Osborne went white and sat down.

'Are you all right?' asked Abel.

'Yes, I'm fine.'

'You don't by any chance know Kane and Cabot?'

'Off the record?' said Henry Osborne.

'Sure.'

'Yes, my company had to deal with them once before in the past.' He seemed to be hesitating. 'And we ended up having to take them to court.'

'Why?'

'I can't reveal the details. A messy business. Let's just say one of the directors was not totally honest and open with us.'

'Which one?' asked Abel.

'Which one did you have to deal with?' Osborne inquired.

'A man named William Kane.'

Osborne seemed to hesitate again. 'Be careful,' he said. 'He's the world's meanest son of a bitch. I can give you all the low-down on him if you want it, but that would be strictly between us.'

'I certainly owe him no favours,' said Abel. 'I may well be in touch with you, Mr Osborne. I have a score to settle with young Mr Kane for his treatment of Davis Leroy.'

'Well, you can count on me to help in any way I can if William Kane is involved,' said Henry Osborne, rising from behind his desk. 'But that is strictly between us. And if the court shows that Desmond Pacey burnt the Richmond and no one else was involved, the company will pay up the same day. Then perhaps we can do some more business with all your other hotels.'

'Perhaps,' said Abel.

He walked back to the Stevens and decided to have lunch and find out for himself how well they ran their main dining room. There was another message at the desk for him. A Mr David Maxton wondered if Abel was free to join him for lunch at one.

'David Maxton,' Abel said out loud, and the receptionist looked up. 'Why do I know that name?' he asked the staring girl.

'He owns this hotel, Mr Rosnovski.'

'Ah, yes. Please let Mr Maxton know that I shall be delighted to have lunch with him.' Abel glanced at his watch. 'And would you tell him that I may be a few minutes late?'

'Certainly, sir,' said the girl.

Abel went quickly up to his room and changed into a new white shirt, wondering what David Maxton could possibly want.

The dining room was already packed when Abel arrived. The head waiter showed him to a private table in an alcove where the owner of the Stevens was sitting alone. He rose to greet Abel.

'Abel Rosnovski, sir.'

'Yes, I know you,' said Maxton, 'or, to be more accurate, I know you by reputation. Do sit down and let's order lunch.'

Abel was compelled to admire the Stevens. The food and the service were every bit as good as those at the Plaza. If he were to have the best hotel in Chicago, he knew it would have to be better than this one.

The head waiter reappeared with the menus. Abel studied his carefully, politely declined a first course and selected the beef, the quickest way to tell if a restaurant is dealing with the right butcher. David Maxton did not look at his menu and simply ordered the salmon. The head waiter scurried away.

'You must be wondering why I invited you to join me for lunch, Mr Rosnovski.'

'I assumed,' said Abel, laughing, 'you were going to ask me to take over the Stevens for you.'

'You're absolutely right, Mr Rosnovski.'

It was Maxton's turn to laugh. Abel was speechless. Even the arrival of their waiter wheeling a trolley of the finest beef did not help. The carver waited. Maxton squeezed some lemon over his salmon and continued.

'My manager is due to retire in five months' time after twenty-two years of loyal service and the assistant manager is also due for retirement very soon afterwards, so I'm looking for a new broom.'

'Place looks pretty clean to me,' said Abel.

'I'm always willing to improve, Mr Rosnovski. Never be satisfied with standing still,' said Maxton. 'I've been watching your activities carefully. It wasn't until you took the Richmond over that it could even be classified as a hotel. It was a huge flop house before that. In another two or three years, you would have been a rival to the Stevens if some fool hadn't burned the place down before you were given the chance.'

'Potatoes, sir?'

Abel looked up at a very attractive junior waitress. She smiled at him.

'No, thank you,' he said to her. 'Well, I'm very flattered, Mr Maxton, both by your comments and the offer.'

'I think you'd be happy here, Mr Rosnovski. The Stevens is a well-run hotel, and I would be willing to start you off at fifty dollars a week and two per cent of the profits. You could start as soon as you like.'

'I'll need a few days to think over your generous offer, Mr Maxton,' said Abel, 'but I confess I am very tempted. Nevertheless, I still have a few problems left over from the Richmond.'

'String beans, sir?' The same waitress, and the same smile.

The face looked familiar. Abel felt sure he had seen her somewhere before. Perhaps she had once worked at the Richmond.

'Yes, please.'

He watched her walk away. There was something about her.

'Why don't you stay on at the hotel as my guest for a few days,' Maxton asked, 'and see how we run the place? It may help you make your decision.'

'That won't be necessary, Mr Maxton. After only one day as a guest here I knew how well the hotel is run. My problem is that I own the Richmond Group.'

David Maxton's face registered surprise. 'I had no idea,' he said. 'I assumed old Davis Leroy's daughter would now be the owner.'

'It's a long story,' said Abel, and he explained to Maxton how he had come into the ownership of the group's stock.

'The problem is a simple one, Mr Maxton. What I really want to do is find the two million dollars myself and build that group up into something worthwhile. Something that would even give you a good run for your money.'

'I see,' said Maxton, looking quizzically at his empty plate. A waiter removed it.

'Would you like some coffee?' The same waitress. The same familiar look. It was beginning to worry Abel.

'And you say Curtis Fenton of Continental Trust is looking for a buyer on your behalf?'

'Yes, he has been for nearly a month,' said Abel. 'In fact, I shall know later this afternoon if they've had any success, but I'm not optimistic.'

'Well, that's most interesting. I had no idea the Richmond Group was looking for a buyer. Will you please keep me informed either way?'

'Certainly,' said Abel.

'How much more time is the Boston bank giving you to find the two million?'

'Only a few more days, so it won't be long before I can let you know my decision.'

'Thank you,' said Maxton. 'It's been a pleasure to meet you, Mr Rosnovski. I feel sure I'd enjoy working with you.' He shook Abel warmly by the hand.

'Thank you, sir,' said Abel.

The waitress smiled at him again as he passed her on his way out of the dining room. When Abel reached the head waiter, he stopped and inquired what her name was.

'I'm sorry, sir, we're not allowed to give the names of any of our staff to the customers; it's strictly against company policy. If you have a complaint, perhaps you'd be kind enough to make it to me, sir.'

'No complaint,' said Abel. 'On the contrary, an excellent lunch.'

With a job offer under his belt, Abel felt more confident about facing Curtis Fenton. He was certain the banker would not have found a buyer, but none the less, he strolled over to the Continental Trust with a spring in his heels. He liked the idea of being the manager of the best hotel in Chicago. Perhaps he could make it the best hotel in America. As soon as he arrived at the bank, he was ushered directly into Curtis Fenton's office. The tall, thin banker – did he wear the same suit every day or did he have three identical ones? – offered Abel a seat, and a large smile appeared across his usually solemn face.

'Mr Rosnovski, how good to see you again. If you had come this morning, I would have had no news to give you, but only a few moments ago I received a call from an interested party.'

Abel's heart leaped with surprise and pleasure. He was silent for a few moments and then he said, 'Can you tell me who it is?'

'I'm afraid not. The party concerned has given me strict instructions that he must remain anonymous, as the transaction would be a private investment in some potential conflict with his own business.'

'David Maxton,' Abel murmured under his breath. 'God bless him.'

Curtis Fenton did not respond and continued. 'Well, as I said, Mr Rosnovski, I'm not in a position ...'

'Quite, quite,' said Abel. 'How long do you think it will be before you are in a position to let me know the gentleman's decision one way or the other?'

'I can't be sure at the moment, but I may have more news for you by Monday, so if you happen to be passing by ...'

'Happen to be passing by?' said Abel. 'You're discussing my whole life.'

'Then perhaps we should make a firm appointment for Monday morning.'

As Abel walked down Michigan Avenue on his way back to the Stevens it started to drizzle. He found himself humming 'Singing in the Rain'. He took the lift up to his room and called William Kane to ask for an extension until the following Monday, telling him he hoped to have found a buyer. Kane seemed reluctant but eventually agreed.

'Bastard,' Abel repeated several times as he put the phone back on the hook. 'Just give me a little time, Kane. You'll live to regret killing Davis Leroy.'

Abel sat on the end of his bed, his fingers tapping on the rail, wondering how he could pass the time waiting for Monday. He wandered down into the hotel lobby. There she was again, the waitress who had served him at lunch, now on tea duty in the Tropical Garden. Abel's curiosity got the better of him, and he went over and took a seat at the far side of the room. She came up.

'Good afternoon, sir,' she said. 'Would you like some tea?' The same familiar smile again.

'We know each other, don't we?' said Abel.

'Yes, we do, Wladek.'

Abel cringed at the sound of the name and reddened slightly, remembering how the short fair hair had been long and smooth and the veiled eyes had been so inviting. 'Zaphia, we came to America on the same ship. Of course, you went to Chicago. What are you doing here?'

'I work here, as you can see. Would you like some tea, sir?' Her Polish accent warmed Abel.

'Have dinner with me tonight,' he said.

'I can't, Wladek. We're not allowed to go out with the customers. If we do, we automatically lose our jobs.'

'I'm not a customer,' said Abel. 'I'm an old friend.'

'Who was going to come and visit me in Chicago as soon as he had settled down, and when you did come you didn't even remember I was here,' said Zaphia.

'I know, I know. Forgive me. Zaphia, have dinner with me tonight. Just this once,' said Abel.

'Just this once,' she repeated.

'Meet me at Brundage's at seven o'clock. Would that suit you?'

Zaphia flushed at the name. It was probably the most expensive restaurant in Chicago, and she would have been nervous to be there as a waitress, let alone as a customer.

'No, let's go somewhere less grand, Wladek.'

'Where?' said Abel.

'Do you know The Sausage on the corner of Forty-third?'

'No, I don't,' he admitted, 'but I'll find it. Seven o'clock.'

'Seven o'clock, Wladek. That will be lovely. By the way, do you want any tea?'

'No, I think I'll skip it,' said Abel.

She smiled and walked away. He sat watching her serve tea for several minutes. She was much prettier than he had remembered her being. Perhaps killing time until Monday wasn't going to be so bad after all.

The Sausage brought back all of Abel's worst memories of his first days in America. He sipped a cold ginger beer while he waited for Zaphia and watched with professional disapproval as the waiters slapped the food around. He was unable to decide which looked worse: the service or the food. Zaphia was nearly twenty minutes late by the time she appeared in the doorway, as smart as a band-box in a crisp yellow dress that looked as if it had been recently taken up a few inches to conform with the latest fashion, but still revealed how appealing her formerly slight body had become. Her grey eyes searched the tables for Wladek, and her pink cheeks reddened as she became conscious of other men's eyes upon her.

'Good evening, Wladek,' she said in Polish.

Abel rose and offered her his chair near the fire. 'I am so glad you could make it,' he replied in English.

She looked perplexed for a moment, then, in English, she said, 'I'm sorry I'm late.'

'Oh, I hadn't noticed. Would you like something to drink, Zaphia?'

'No, thank you.'

Neither of them spoke for a moment, and then they both tried to talk at once.

'I'd forgotten how pretty . . .' said Abel.

'How have you . . .' said Zaphia.

She smiled shyly, and Abel wanted to touch her. He remembered so well experiencing the same reaction the first time he had ever seen her, over eight years before.

'How's George?' she asked.

'I haven't seen him for over two years,' replied Abel, suddenly feeling guilty. 'I've been stuck working in a hotel here in Chicago, and then . . .'

'I know,' said Zaphia. 'Somebody burnt the place down.'

'Why didn't you ever come over and say hello?' asked Abel.

'I didn't think you'd remember, Wladek, and I was right.'

'Then how did you ever recognize me?' said Abel. 'I've put on so much weight.'

'The silver band,' she said simply.

Abel looked down at his wrist and laughed. 'I have a lot to thank my band for, and now I can add that it has brought us back together.'

She avoided his eyes. 'What are you doing now that you no longer have a hotel to run?'

'I'm looking for a job,' said Abel, not wanting to intimidate her with the fact that he'd been offered the chance to manage the Stevens.

'There's a big job coming up at the Stevens. My boyfriend told me.'

'Your boyfriend told you?' said Abel, repeating each painful word.

'Yes,' she said, 'the hotel will soon be looking for a new assistant manager. Why don't you apply for the job? I'm sure you'd have a good chance of getting it, Wladek. I always knew you would be a success in America.'

'I might well apply,' Abel said. 'It was kind of you to think of me. Why doesn't your boyfriend apply?'

'Oh, no, he's far too junior to be considered; he's only a waiter in the dining room with me.'

Suddenly Abel wanted to change places with him.

'Shall we have dinner?' he said.

'I'm not used to eating out,' Zaphia said. She gazed at the menu in indecision. Abel, suddenly aware she still could not read English, ordered for them both.

'She ate with relish and was full of praise for the indifferent food. Abel found her uncritical enthusiasm a tonic after the bored sophistication of Melanie. They exchanged the history of their lives in America. Zaphia had started in domestic service and progressed to being a waitress at the Stevens where she had stayed put for six years, Abel told her of all his experiences until finally she glanced at his watch.

'Look at the time, Wladek,' she said, 'it's past eleven and I'm on first breakfast call at six tomorrow.'

Abel had not noticed the four hours pass. He would have happily sat there talking to her for the rest of the night, soothed by her admiration which she confessed so artlessly.

'May I see you again, Zaphia?' he asked, as they walked back to the Stevens arm-in-arm.

'If you want to, Wladek.'

They stopped at the servants' entrance at the back of the hotel.

'This is where I go in,' she said. 'If you were to become the assistant manager, Wladek, you'd be allowed to go in by the front entrance.'

'Would you mind calling me Abel?' he asked her.

'Abel?' she said, as if she were trying the name on like a new glove. 'But your name is Wladek.'

'It was, but it isn't any longer. My name is Abel Rosnovski.'

'Abel's a funny name, but it suits you,' she said. 'Thank you for dinner, Abel. It was lovely to see you again. Goodnight.'

'Goodnight, Zaphia,' he said, and she was gone.

He watched her disappear through the servants' entrance, then he walked slowly around the block and into the hotel by the front entrance. Suddenly

– and not for the first time in his life – he felt very lonely.

Abel spent the weekend thinking about Zaphia and the images associated with her – the stench of the steerage quarters, the confused queues of immigrants on Ellis Island and, above all, their brief but passionate encounter in the lifeboat. He took all his meals in the hotel restaurant to be near her and to study the boyfriend. He came to the conclusion that he must be the young, pimply one. He thought he had pimples, he hoped he had pimples, yes, he did have pimples. He was, regrettably, the best-looking boy among the waiters, pimples notwithstanding.

Abel wanted to take Zaphia out on Saturday, but she was working all day. Nevertheless, he managed to accompany her to church on Sunday morning and listened with mingled nostalgia and exasperation to the Polish priest intoning the unforgotten words of the Mass. It was the first time Abel had been in a church since his days at the castle in Poland. At that time he had yet to see or endure the cruelty which now made it impossible for him to believe in any benevolent deity. His reward for attending church came when Zaphia allowed him to hold her hand as they walked back to the hotel together.

'Have you thought any more about the position at the Stevens?' she inquired.

'I'll know first thing tomorrow morning what their final decision is.'

'Oh, I'm so glad, Abel. I'm sure you would make a very good assistant manager.'

'Thank you,' said Abel, realizing they had been talking at cross purposes.

'Would you like to have supper with my cousins tonight?' Zaphia asked. 'I always spend Sunday evening with them.'

'Yes, I'd like that very much.'

Zaphia's cousins lived right near The Sausage itself, in the heart of the city. They were very impressed when she arrived with a Polish friend who drove a new Buick. The family, as Zaphia called them, consisted of two sisters, Katya and Janina, and Katya's husband, Janek. Abel presented the sisters with a bunch of roses and then sat down and answered, in fluent Polish, all their questions about his future prospects. Zaphia was obviously embarrassed, but Abel knew the same would be required of any new boyfriend in any Polish-American household. He made an effort to play down his progress since his early days in the butcher shop as he was conscious of Janek's envious eyes never leaving him. Katya served a simple Polish meal of pierogi and bigos which Abel would have eaten with a good deal more relish fifteen years earlier. He gave Janek up as a bad job and concentrated on making the sisters approve of him. It looked as though they did. Perhaps they also approved of the pimply youth. No, they couldn't; he wasn't even Polish – or maybe he was – Abel didn't even know his name and had never heard him speak.

On the way back to the Stevens, Zaphia asked, with a flash of coquettishness he remembered, if it was considered safe to drive a motor car and hold a lady's hand at the same time. Abel laughed and put his hand back on the steering wheel for the rest of the drive back to the hotel.

'Will you have time to see me tomorrow?' he asked.

'I hope so, Abel,' she said. 'Perhaps by then you'll be my boss. Good luck anyway.'

He smiled to himself as he watched her go through the back door, wondering how she would feel if she knew the real consequences of tomorrow's decision. He did not move until she disappeared through the service entrance.

'Assistant manager,' he said, laughing out loud as he climbed into bed, wondering what Curtis Fenton's news would bring in the morning, trying to put Zaphia out of his mind as he threw his pillow on the floor.

He woke a few minutes before five the next day. The room was still dark when he called for the early edition of the *Tribune*, and went through the motions of reading the financial section. He was dressed and ready for breakfast when the restaurant opened at seven o'clock. Zaphia was not serving in the main dining room that morning, but the pimply boyfriend was, which Abel took to be a bad omen. After breakfast he returned to his room; had he but known, only five minutes before Zaphia came on duty. He checked his tie in the mirror for the twentieth time and once again looked at his watch. He estimated that if he walked very slowly, he would arrive at the bank as the doors were opening. In fact, he arrived five minutes early and walked once around the block, staring aimlessly into store windows at expensive jewelry and new radios and hand-tailored suits. Would he ever be able to afford clothes like that? he wondered. He arrived back at the bank at four minutes past nine.

'Mr Fenton is not free at the moment. Can you come back in half an hour or would you prefer to wait?' the secretary asked.

'I'll come back,' said Abel, not wishing to appear over-anxious.

It was the longest thirty minutes he could remember since he'd been in Chicago. He had studied every shop window on La Salle Street, even the women's clothes, which made him think happily of Zaphia.

On his return to Continental Trust the secretary informed him, 'Mr Fenton will see you now.'

Abel walked into the bank manager's office, feeling his hands sweating.

'Good morning, Mr Rosnovski. Do have a seat.'

Curtis Fenton took a file out of his desk which Abel could see had 'Confidential' written across the cover.

'Now,' he began, 'I hope you will find my news is to your liking. The principal concerned is willing to go ahead with the purchase of the hotels on what I can only describe as favourable terms.'

'God Almighty,' said Abel.

Curtis Fenton pretended not to hear him and continued. 'In fact, most favourable terms. He will be responsible for putting up the full two million required to clear Mr Leroy's debt while at the same time he will form a new company with you in which the shares will be split sixty per cent to him and forty per cent to you. Your forty per cent is therefore valued at eight hundred thousand dollars, which will be treated as a loan to you by the new company, a loan which will be made for a term not to exceed ten years, at four per cent, which can be paid off from the company profits at the same rate. That is to say, if the company were to make in any one year a profit of one hundred thousand dollars, forty thousand of that profit would be set against your eight hundred thousand debt, plus the four per cent interest. If you clear the loan of eight hundred thousand in under ten years you will be given the one-time option to buy the remaining sixty per cent of the company for a further three million dollars. This would give my client a first-class return on his investment and you the opportunity to own the Richmond Group outright.

'In addition to this, you will receive a salary of three thousand dollars per annum, and your position as president of the group will give you complete day-to-day control of the hotels. You will be asked to refer back to me only on matters concerning finance. I have been entrusted with the task of reporting direct to your principal, and he has asked me to represent his interests on the board of the new Richmond Group. I have been happy to comply with this stipulation. My client does not wish to be involved personally. As I have said before, there might be a conflict of professional interests for him in this transaction, which I am sure you will thoroughly understand. He also insists that you will at no time make any attempt to discover his identity. He will give you fourteen days to consider his terms, on which there can be no negotiation, as he considers, and I must agree with him, that he is striking a more than fair bargain.'

Abel could not speak.

'Pray do say something, Mr Rosnovski.'

'I don't need fourteen days to make a decision,' said Abel finally. 'I accept your client's terms. Please thank him and tell him I will certainly respect his request for anonymity.'

'That's splended,' said Curtis Fenton, permitting himself a wry smile. 'Now, a few small points. The accounts for all the hotels in the group will be placed with Continental Trust affiliates, and the main account will be here in this office under my direct control. I will, in turn, receive one thousand dollars a year as a director of the new company.'

'I'm glad you're going to get something out of the deal,' said Abel.

'I beg your pardon?' said the banker.

'I'll be pleased to be working with you, Mr Fenton.'

'Your principal has also placed two hundred and fifty thousand dollars on deposit with the bank to be used as the day-to-day finance for the running of the hotels during the next few months. This will also be regarded as a loan at four per cent. You are to advise me if this amount turns out to be insufficient for your needs. I consider it would enhance your reputation with my client if you found the two hundred and fifty thousand to be sufficient.'

'I shall bear that in mind,' said Abel, solemnly trying to imitate the banker's locution.

Curtis Fenton opened a desk drawer and produced a large Cuban cigar. 'Do you smoke?'

'Yes,' said Abel, who had never smoked a cigar before in his life.

He coughed himself down La Salle Street all the way back to the Stevens. David Maxton was standing proprietorially in the foyer of the hotel as Abel arrived. Abel stubbed out his half-finished cigar with some relief and walked over to him.

'Mr Rosnovski, you look a happy man this morning.'

'I am, sir, and I am only sorry that I will not be working for you as the manager of this hotel.'

'Then so am I, Mr Rosnovski, but frankly the news doesn't surprise me.'

'Thank you for everything,' said Abel, injecting as much feeling as he could into the little phrase and the look with which he accompanied it.

He left David Maxton and went into the dining room in search of Zaphia, but she had already gone off duty. Abel took the lift to his room, re-lit the cigar, took a cautious puff, and called Kane and Cabot. A secretary put him through to William Kane.

'Mr Kane, I have found it possible to raise the money required for me to take over ownership of the Richmond Group. A Mr Curtis Fenton of Continental Trust will be in touch with you later today to provide you with the details. There will therefore be no necessity to place the hotels for sale on the open market.'

There was a short pause. Abel thought with satisfaction how galling his news must be to William Kane.

'Thank you for keeping me informed, Mr Rosnovski. May I say how delighted I am that you found someone to back you? I wish you every success for the future.'

'Which is more than I wish you, Mr Kane.'

Abel put the phone down, lay on his bed and thought about that future.

'One day,' he promised the ceiling, 'I am going to buy your goddam bank and make you want to jump out of a hotel bedroom on the twelfth floor.' He picked up the phone again and asked the girl on the switchboard to get him Mr Henry Osborne at Great Western Casualty.

19

William put the telephone back on the hook, more amused than annoyed by Abel Rosnovski's pugnacious approach. He was sorry that he had been unable to persuade the bank to support the little Pole who believed so strongly that he could pull the Richmond Group through. He fulfilled his remaining responsibilities by informing the financial committee that Abel Rosnovski had found a backer, preparing the legal documents for the take-over of the hotels, and then finally closing the bank's file on the Richmond Group.

William was delighted when Matthew arrived in Boston a few days later to take up his position as manager of the bank's investment department. Charles Lester made no secret of the fact that any professional expertise gained in a rival establishment could do the boy no harm in his long-term preparation to be chairman of Lester's. William's work load was instantly halved but his time became even more fully occupied. He found himself dragged, protesting in mock horror, onto tennis courts and into swimming pools at every available free moment; only Matthew's suggestion of a ski trip to Vermont brought a determined 'No' from William, but the sudden activity at least served to somewhat alleviate his loneliness and impatience to be with Kate.

Matthew was frankly incredulous. 'I must meet the woman who can make William Kane daydream at a board meeting which is discussing whether the bank should buy more gold.'

'Wait till you see her, Matthew. I think you'll agree she's a better investment than gold.'

'I believe you. I just don't want to be the one to tell Susan. She still thinks you're the only man in the world.'

William laughed. It had never crossed his mind.

.   .   .

The little pile of letters from Kate, which had been growing weekly, lay in the locked drawer of William's bureau in the Red House. He read them over again and again and soon knew them all virtually by heart. At last the one he had been waiting for came, appropriately dated.

Buckhurst Park
14 February 1930

Dearest William,

Finally I have packed up, sold off, given away or otherwise disposed of everything left here and I shall be coming up to Boston in a tea chest on the nineteenth. I am almost frightened at the thought of seeing you again. What if this whole marvellous enchantment bursts like a bubble in the cold of a winter on the Eastern seaboard? Dear God, I hope not. I can't be sure how I would have gotten through these lonely months but for you.

With love,
Kate

The night before Kate was due to arrive, William promised himself that he would not rush her into anything that either of them might later regret. It was impossible for him to assess to what extent her feelings had developed in a transient state of mind engendered by her husband's death, as he told Matthew.

'Stop being so pathetic,' said Matthew. 'You're in love, and you may as well face the fact.'

When he first spotted Kate at the station, William almost abandoned his cautious intentions there and then in the joy of watching that simple smile light up her face. He pushed towards her through the throng of travellers and clasped her so firmly in his arms that she could barely breathe.

'Welcome home, Kate.'

William was about to kiss her when she drew away. He was a little surprised.

'William, I don't think you've met my parents.'

That night William dined with Kate's family and then saw her every day that he could escape from the bank's problems and Matthew's tennis racquet, even if only for a couple of hours. After Matthew had met Kate for the first time, he offered William all his gold shares in exchange for one Kate.

'I never undersell,' replied William.

'Then I insist you tell me,' demanded Matthew, 'where you find someone as valuable as Kate?'

'In the liquidation department, where else?' replied William.

'Turn her into an asset, William, quickly, because if you don't, you can be sure I will.'

. . .

Kane and Cabot's net loss from the 1929 crash came out at over seven million dollars, which turned out to be about average for a bank their size. Many not much smaller banks had gone under, and William found himself conducting a sustained holding operation through 1930 which kept him under constant pressure.

. . .

When Franklin D. Roosevelt was elected President of the United States on a ticket of relief, recovery and reform, William feared that the New Deal would have little to offer Kane and Cabot. Business picked up very slowly, and William found himself planning only tentatively for expansion.

Meanwhile Tony Simmons, still running the London office, had broadened the scope of its activities and made a respectable profit for Kane and Cabot during his first two years. His results looked all the better against those of William, who had barely been able to break even during the same period.

Late in 1932, Alan Lloyd recalled Tony Simmons to Boston to make a full report to the board on the bank's activities in London. No sooner had Simmons reappeared than he announced his intention of running for the chairmanship when Alan Lloyd retired in fifteen months' time. William was completely taken by surprise, for he had dismissed Simmons' chances when he had disappeared to London under a small cloud. It seemed to William unfair that that cloud had been dispelled, not by Simmons' acuity, but simply by dint of the fact that the English economy had some bright spots and was a little less paralysed than American business during the same period.

Tony Simmons returned to London for a further successful year and addressed the first board meeting, after his return, in a blaze of glory, with the announcement that the final third year's figures for the London office would show a profit of over a million dollars, a new record. William had to announce a considerably smaller profit for the same period. The abruptness of Tony Simmons' return to favour left William with only a few months in which to persuade the board that they should support him before his opponent's momentum became unstoppable.

Kate listened for hours to William's problems, occasionally offering an understanding comment, a sympathetic reply or chastizing him for being over dramatic. Matthew, acting as William's eyes and ears, reported that the voting would fall, as far as was ascertainable, fifty-fifty, split between those who considered that William was too young to hold such a responsible post and those who still held Tony Simmons to blame for the extent of the bank's losses in 1929. It seemed that most of the non-executive members of the board, who had not worked directly with William, would be more influenced by the age difference between the two contenders than any of the single factors. Again and again Matthew heard: 'William's time will come.' Once, tentatively, he played the role of Satan the tempter to William: 'With your holdings in the bank, William, you could remove the entire board, replace them with men of your own choosing and get yourself elected chairman.'

William was only too aware of that route to the top, but he had already dismissed such tactics without needing seriously to consider them; he wished to become chairman solely on his own merits. That was after all, the way his father had achieved the position and it was nothing less than Kate would expect of him.

On 2 January 1934 Alan Lloyd circulated to every member the notice of a board meeting that would be held on his sixty-fifth birthday, its sole purpose being to elect his successor. As the day for the crucial vote drew nearer, Matthew found himself carrying the investment department almost single-handed, and Kate found herself feeding them both while they went over the latest state of his campaign again and again. Matthew did not complain once about the extra work load that was placed on him while William spent hours planning his bid to capture the chair. William, conscious that Matthew had nothing to gain by his success, as he would one day take over his father's bank in New York – a far bigger proposition than Kane and Cabot – hoped a time might come when he could offer Matthew the same unselfish support.

It was to come sooner than he imagined.

. . .

When Alan Lloyd's sixty-fifth birthday was celebrated, all seventeen members of the board were present. The meeting was opened by the chairman, who made a farewell speech of only fourteen minutes, which William thought would never come to an end. Tony Simmons was nervously tapping the yellow legal pad in front of him with his pen, occasionally looking up at William. Neither was listening to Alan's speech. At last Alan sat down, to loud applause, or as loud as is appropriate to sixteen Boston bankers. When the clapping died away, Alan Lloyd rose for the last time as chairman of Kane and Cabot.

'And now, gentleman, we must elect my successor. The board is presented with two outstanding candidates, the director of our overseas division, Mr Anthony Simmons, and the director of the American investment department, Mr William Kane. They are both well known to you, gentlemen, and I have no intention of speaking in detail on their respective merits. Instead I have asked each candidate to address the board on how he would see the future of Kane and Cabot were he to be elected chairman.'

William rose first, as had been agreed between the two contestants the night before on the toss of a coin, and addressed the board for twenty minutes, explaining in detail that it would be his ambition to move into new fields where the bank had not previously ventured. In particular he wanted to broaden the bank's base and to get out of a depressed New England, moving close to the centre of banking which he believed was now in New York. He even mentioned the possibility of opening a holding company which might specialize in commercial banking, at which the heads of some of the older board members shook in disbelief. He wanted the bank to consider more expansion, to challenge the new generation of financiers now leading America, and to see Kane and Cabot enter the second half of the twentieth century as one of the largest financial institutions in the United States. When he sat down, he was satisfied by the murmurs of approbation; his speech had, on the whole, been well received by the board.

When Tony Simmons rose he took a far more conservative line: the bank should consolidate its position for the next few years, moving only into carefully selected areas and sticking to the traditional modes of banking that had given Kane and Cabot the reputation they currently enjoyed. He had learnt his lesson during the crash and his main concern, he added – to laughter – was to be certain that Kane and Cabot did enter the second half of the twentieth century at all. Tony spoke prudently and with an authority that William was aware he was too young to match. When Tony sat down, William had no way of knowing in whose favour the board might swing, though he still believed that the majority would be more inclined to opt for expansion rather than standing still.

Alan Lloyd informed the other directors that neither he nor the two contestants intended to vote. The fourteen voting members received their little ballots, which they duly filled in and passed back to Alan who, acting as teller, began to count slowly. William found he could not look up from his doodle-covered pad which also bore the imprint of his sweating hand firmly upon it. When Alan had completed the task of counting, a hush came over the room and he announced six votes for Kane, six votes for Simmons, with two abstentions. Whispered conversation broke out among the board members, and Alan called for order. William took a deep and audible breath in the silence that followed.

Alan Lloyd paused and then said, 'I feel that the appropriate course of action in the circumstances is to have a second vote. If any member who abstained on the first ballot finds himself able to support a candidate on this occasion, that might give one of the contestants an overall majority.'

The little slips were passed out again. William could not bear even to watch the process this time. While members wrote their choices, he listened to the steel-nibbed pens scratching across the voting papers. Once again the ballots were returned to Alan Lloyd. Once again he opened them slowly one by one, and this time he called out the names as he read them.

William Kane.

Anthony Simmons, Anthony Simmons, Anthony Simmons.

Three votes to one for Tony Simmons.

William Kane, William Kane.

Anthony Simmons.

William Kane, William Kane, William Kane. Six to four for William.

Anthony Simmons, Anthony Simmons.

William Kane.

'Seven votes to six in favour of William.

It seemed to William, holding his breath, to take Alan Lloyd a lifetime to open the final voting slip.

'Anthony Simmons,' he declared. 'The vote is seven all, gentlemen.'

William knew that Alan Lloyd would now be obliged to cast the deciding vote, and although he had never told anyone whom he supported for the chair, William had always assumed that if the vote came to a deadlock, Alan would back him against Tony Simmons.

'As the voting has twice resulted in a dead heat, and since I assume that no member of the board is likely to change his mind, I must cast my vote for the candidate whom I feel should succeed me as chairman of Kane and Cabot. I know none of you will envy my position, but I have no alternative except to stand by my own judgement and back the man I feel should be the next chairman of the bank.

'That man is Tony Simmons.'

William could not believe the words he heard and Tony Simmons looked almost as shocked. He rose from his seat opposite William to a round of applause, changed places with Alan Lloyd at the head of the table and addressed Kane and Cabot for the first time as the bank's new chairman. He thanked the board for its support and praised William for never having used his strong financial and familial position to try and influence the vote. He invited William to be vice-chairman of the board and suggested that Matthew Lester should replace Alan Lloyd as a director; both suggestions received unanimous support.

William sat staring at the portrait of his father, acutely conscious of having failed him.

20

Abel stubbed out the Corona for a second time and swore that he would not light another cigar until he had cleared the two million dollars that he needed for complete control of the Richmond Group. This was no time for big cigars, with the Dow-Jones index at its lowest point in history and long soup lines in every major city in America. He gazed at the ceiling and considered his priorities. First, he needed to salvage the best of the staff from the Richmond Chicago.

He climbed off the bed, put on his jacket and went over to the hotel annex, where most of those who had not found employment since the fire were still living. Abel re-employed everyone whom he trusted, giving all those who were willing to leave Chicago work in one of the remaining ten hotels. He made his position very clear that in a period of record unemployment their jobs were secure only as long as the hotels started to show a profit. He believed all the other hotels in the group were being run as dishonestly as the old Chicago Richmond had been; he wanted that changed – and changed quickly. His three assistant managers were each put in charge of one hotel each, the Dallas Richmond, the Cincinnati Richmond and the St Louis Richmond. He appointed new assistant managers for the remaining seven hotels in Houston, Mobile, Charleston, Atlanta, Memphis, New Orleans and Louisville. The original Leroy hotels had all been situated in the South and Mid-West including the Chicago Richmond, the only one Davis Leroy had been responsible for building himself. It took Abel another three weeks to get the old Chicago staff settled into their new hotels.

Abel decided to set up his own headquarters in the Richmond annex and to open a small restaurant on the ground floor. It made sense to be near his backer and his banker rather than to settle in one of the hotels in the South. Moreover, Zaphia was in Chicago, and Abel felt with certainty that given a little time she would drop the pimply youth and fall in love with him. She was the only woman he had ever known with whom he felt self-assured. When Abel was about to leave for New York to recruit more specialized staff, he exacted a promise from her that she would no longer see the pimply boyfriend.

'Still pimply,' said Abel to himself, 'but no longer the boyfriend.'

The night before his departure they slept together for the first time. She was soft, plump, giggly and delicious.

Abel's attentive care and gentle expertise took Zaphia by surprise.

'How many girls have there been since the *Black Arrow*?' she teased.

'None that I really cared about,' he replied.

'Enough of them to forget *me*,' she added.

'I never forgot you,' he said untruthfully, leaning over to kiss her, convinced it was the only way to stop the conversation.

.   .   .

When Abel arrived in New York, the first thing he did was to look up George, whom he found out of work in a garret on East Third Street. He had forgotten what those houses could be like when shared by twenty families. The smell of stale food in every room, toilets that didn't flush and beds that were slept in by three different people every twenty-four hours. The bakery, it seemed, had been closed down, and George's uncle had had to find employment at a large mill on the outskirts of New York which could not take on George as well. George leaped at the chance to join Abel and the Richmond Group – in any capacity.

Abel recruited three new employees: a pastry chef, a comptroller and a head waiter before he and George travelled back to Chicago to set up base in the Richmond annex. Abel was pleased with the outcome of his trip. Most hotels on the East coast had cut their staff to a bare minimum which had made it easy to pick up experienced people, one of them from the Plaza itself.

In early March Abel and George set out for a tour of the remaining hotels in the group. Abel asked Zaphia to join them on the trip, even offering her the chance to work in any of the hotels she chose, but she would not budge from Chicago, the only American territory familiar to her. As a compromise she went to live in Abel's rooms at the Richmond annex while he was away. George, who had acquired middle-class morals along with his American citizenship and Catholic upbringing, urged the advantages of matrimony on Abel, who, lonely in one impersonal hotel room after another, was a ready listener.

It came as no surprise to Abel to find that the other hotels were still being badly, and in some cases dishonestly run, but high national unemployment encouraged most of the staff to welcome his arrival as the saviour of the group's fortunes. Abel did not find it necessary to fire staff in the grand manner he adopted when he had first arrived in Chicago. Most of those who knew of his reputation and feared his methods had already left. Some heads had to fall and they inevitably were attached to the necks of those people who had worked with the Richmond Group for a considerable time and were unable to change their unorthodox ways merely because Davis Leroy was dead. In several cases, Abel found a move of personnel from one hotel to another engendered a new attitude. By the end of his first year as chairman, the Richmond Group was operating with only half the staff they had employed in the past and showed a net loss of only a little over one hundred thousand dollars. The turnover among the senior staff was very low; Abel's confidence in the future of the group was infectious.

Abel set himself the target of breaking even in 1932. He felt the only way he could achieve such a rapid improvement in profitability was to let every manager in the group take the responsibility for his own hotel with a share in the profits, much in the way that Davis Leroy had treated him when he had first come to the Chicago Richmond.

Abel moved from hotel to hotel, never letting up, and never staying in one particular place for more than three weeks at a time. He did not allow anyone, other than the faithful George, his surrogate eyes and ears in Chicago, to know at which hotel he might arrive next. For months he broke this exhausting routine only to visit Zaphia or Curtis Fenton.

After a full assessment of the group's financial position Abel had to make some more unpleasant decisions. The most drastic was to close temporarily the two hotels, in Mobile and Charleston, which were losing so much money that he felt they would become a hopeless drain on the rest of the finances. The staff at the other hotels watched the axe fall and worked even harder. Every time he arrived back at his little office in the Richmond annex in Chicago there would be a clutch of memos demanding immediate attention – burst pipes in washrooms, cockroaches in kitchens, flashes of temperament in dining rooms, and the inevitable dissatisfied customer who was threatening a law suit.

Henry Osborne re-entered Abel's life with a welcome offer of a settlement of $750,000 from Great Western Casualty, who could find no evidence to implicate Abel with Desmond Pacey in the fire at the Chicago Richmond. Lieutenant O'Malley's evidence had proved very helpful on that point. Abel realized he owed him more than a milk shake. Abel was happy to settle at what he considered was a fair price but Osborne suggested to him that he should hold out for a larger amount and give him a percentage of the difference. Abel, whose shortcomings had never included peculation, regarded him somewhat warily after that: if Osborne could so readily be disloyal to his own company, there was little doubt that he would have no qualms about ditching Abel when it suited him.

. . .

In the spring of 1932 Abel was somewhat surprised to receive a friendly letter from Melanie Leroy, more welcoming in tone than she had ever been in person. He was flattered, even excited, and called her to make a date for dinner at the Stevens, a decision he regretted the moment they entered the dining room for there, looking unsophisticated, tired and vulnerable, was Zaphia. Melanie, in contrast, looked ravishing in a long mint green dress which indicated quite clearly what her body would be like if the mint were removed. Her eyes, perhaps taking courage from the dress, seemed greener and more captivating than ever.

'It's wonderful to see you looking so well, Abel,' she remarked as she took her seat in the centre of the dining room, 'and of course, everybody knows how well you are doing with the Richmond Group.'

'The Baron Group,' said Abel.

She flushed slightly. 'I didn't realize you had changed the name.'

'Yes, I changed it last year,' lied Abel. He had in fact decided at that very moment that every hotel in the group would be known as a Baron hotel. He wondered why he had never thought of it before.

'An appropriate name,' said Melanie, smiling.

Zaphia set the mushroom soup in front of Melanie with a little thud that spoke volumes to Abel. Some of the soup nearly ended up on the mint green dress.

'You're not working?' asked Abel, scribbling the words 'Baron Group' on the back of his menu.

'No, not at the moment, but things are looking up a little. A woman with a liberal arts degree in this city has to sit around and wait for every man to be employed before she can hope to find a job.'

'If you ever want to work for the Baron Group,' said Abel, emphasizing the name slightly, 'you only have to let me know.'

'No, no,' said Melanie. 'I'm just fine.'

She quickly changed the subject to music and the theatre. Talking to her was an unaccustomed and pleasant challenge for Abel; she teased him, but with intelligence. She made him feel more confident in her company than he had ever been in the past. The dinner went on until well after eleven, and when everyone had left the dining room, including Zaphia, ominously red-eyed, he drove Melanie home to her flat, and this time she did invite him in for a drink. He sat on the end of a sofa while she poured him a prohibited whisky and put a record on the phonograph.

'I can't stay long,' Abel said. 'Busy day tomorrow.'

'That's what *I'm* supposed to say, Abel. Don't rush away, this evening has been such fun, just like old times.'

She sat down beside him, her dress rising above her knees. Not quite like old times, he thought. Incredible legs. He made no attempt to resist when she edged towards him. In moments he found he was kissing her – or was she kissing him? His hands wandered on to those legs and then to her breasts, and this time she seemed to respond willingly. It was she who eventually led him by the hand to her bedroom, folded back the coverlet neatly, turned around and asked him to unzip her. Abel obliged in nervous disbelief and switched out the light before he undressed. After that it was easy for him to put Joyce's careful tuition into practice. Melanie certainly was not lacking in experience herself; Abel had never enjoyed the act of making love more and fell into a deep contented sleep.

In the morning Melanie made him breakfast and attended to his every need, right up to the moment he had to leave.

'I shall watch the Baron Group with renewed interest,' she told him, 'not that anyone doubts that it's going to be a huge success.'

'Thank you,' said Abel, 'for breakfast and a memorable night.'

'I was hoping we'd be seeing each other again sometime soon,' Melanie added.

'I'd like that,' said Abel.

She kissed him on the cheek as a wife might who was seeing her husband off to work.

'I wonder what kind of woman you'll end up marrying,' she asked innocently as she helped Abel on with his overcoat.

He looked at her and smiled sweetly. 'When I make that decision, Melanie, you can be certain I shall only be influenced by your views.'

'What do you mean? asked Melanie, coyly.

'Simply that I shall heed your advice,' replied Abel, as he reached the front door, 'and be sure to find myself a nice Polish girl who will marry me.'

.   .   .

Abel and Zaphia were married a month later. Zaphia's cousin, Janek, gave her away and George was the best man. The reception was held at the Stevens and the drinking and dancing went on far into the night. By tradition, each man paid a token sum to dance with Zaphia, and George perspired as he battled round the room, photographing the guests in every possible permutation and combination. After a midnight supper of barszcz, pierogi and bigos downed with wine, brandy and Danzig vodka, Abel and Zaphia were allowed to retire to the bridal suite, with many a wink from the men and tears from the women.

Abel was pleasantly surprised to be told by Curtis Fenton the next morning that the bill for his reception at the Stevens had been covered by Mr Maxton and was to be treated as a wedding gift. He used the money he had saved for the reception as a down payment on a little house on Rigg Street.

For the first time in his life he possessed a home of his own.

21

In February of 1934 William decided to take a month's holiday in England before making any firm decision about his future; he even considered resigning from the board, but Matthew convinced him that that was not the course of action his father would have taken in the same circumstances. Matthew appeared to take his friend's defeat even harder than William himself. Twice in the following week he came into the bank with the obvious signs of a hangover and left important work unfinished. William decided to let these incidents pass without comment and invited Matthew to join him and Kate for dinner that night. Matthew declined, claiming that he had a backload of work on which to catch up. William would not have given the refusal a second thought if Matthew had not been dining at the Ritz Carlton that night with an attractive woman whom William could have sworn was married to one of Kane and Cabot's departmental managers. Kate said nothing, except that Matthew did not look very well.

William, preoccupied with his impending departure for Europe, took less notice of his friend's strange behaviour than he might otherwise have done. At the last moment William couldn't face a month in England alone and asked Kate to accompany him. To his surprise and delight she agreed.

William and Kate sailed to England on the *Mauretania* in separate cabins. Once they had settled into the Ritz, in separate rooms, even on separate floors, William reported to the London branch of Kane and Cabot in Lombard Street and fulfilled the ostensible purpose of his trip to England by reviewing the bank's European activities. Morale was high and Tony Simmons had evidently been a well-liked manager; there was little for William to do but murmur his approval.

He and Kate spent a glorious two weeks together in London, Hampshire and Lincolnshire, looking at some land William had acquired a few months previously, over twelve thousand acres in all. The financial return from farming land is never high but, as William explained to Kate, 'It will always be there if things ever go sour again in America.'

A few days before they were due to travel back to the United States, Kate decided she wanted to see Oxford, and William agreed to drive her down early the next morning. He hired a new Morris, a car he had never driven before. In the university city, they spent the day wandering around the colleges: Magdalen, superb against the river; Christchurch, grandiose but cloisterless; and Merton where they just sat on the grass and dreamed.

'Can't sit on the grass, sir,' said the voice of a college porter.

They laughed and walked hand-in-hand like undergraduates by the side of the Cherwell watching eight Matthews straining to push a boat along as fast as possible. William could no longer imagine a life separated in any part from Kate.

They started back for London in mid-afternoon, and when they reached Henley-on-Thames, they stopped to have tea at the Bell Inn overlooking the river. After scones and a large pot of strong English tea (Kate was adventure-some and drank it with only milk, but William added hot water to dilute it), Kate suggested that they should start back before it was too dark to see the countryside, but when William had re-inserted the crank into the Morris, despite strenuous effort he could not get the engine to turn over. Finally he gave up, and since it was getting late, decided that they would have to spend the night in Henley. He returned to the front desk of the Bell Inn and requested two rooms.

'Sorry, sir, I have only one double room left,' said the receptionist.

William hesitated for a moment and then said, 'We'll take it.'

Kate looked somewhat surprised but said nothing; the receptionist looked suspiciously at her.

'Mr and Mrs ... er ...?'

'Mr and Mrs William Kane,' said William firmly. 'We'll be back later.'

'Shall I put your cases in the room, sir?' the hall porter asked.

'We don't have any,' William replied, smiling.

'I see, sir.'

A bewildered Kate followed William up Henley High Street until he came to a halt in front of the parish church.

'May I ask what we're doing, William?' she asked.

'Something I should have done a long time ago, my darling.'

Kate asked no more questions. When they entered the vestry. William found a verger piling up some hymn books.

'Where can I find the vicar?' demanded William.

The verger straightened himself to his full height and regarded him pityingly.

'In the vicarage, I dare say.'

'Where's the vicarage?' asked William, trying again.

'You're an American gentleman, aren't you, sir.'

'Yes,' said William, becoming impatient.

'The vicarage will be next door to the church, won't it?' said the verger.

'I suppose it will,' said William. 'Can you stay here for the next ten minutes?'

'Why should I want to do that, sir?'

William extracted a large, white, five-pound note from his inside pocket and unfolded it. 'Make it fifteen minutes to be on the safe side, please.'

The verger studied the five pounds carefully and said: 'Americans. Yes, sir.'

William left the man with his five-pound note and hurried Kate out of the church. As they passed the main notice board in the porch, he read: 'The Vicar of this Parish is The Reverend Simon Tukesbury, MA (Cantab),' and next to that pronouncement, hanging by one nail, was an appeal notice concerning a new roof for the church. Every penny towards the necessary five hundred pounds will help, declared the notice, not very boldly. William hastened up the path to the vicarage with Kate a few yards behind, and a smiling, pink-cheeked, plump lady answered his sharp knock on the door.

'Mrs Tukesbury?' inquired William.

'Yes.' She smiled.

'May I speak to your husband?'

'He's having his tea at the moment. Would it be possible for you to come back a little later?'

'I'm afraid it's rather urgent,' William insisted.

Kate had caught up with him but said nothing.

'Well, in that case I suppose you'd better come in.'

The vicarage was early sixteenth century and the small stone front room was warmed by a welcoming log fire. The vicar, a tall spare man who was eating wafer-thin cucumber sandwiches, rose to greet them.

'Good afternoon, Mr....?'

'Kane, sir, William Kane.'

'What can I do for you, Mr Kane?'

'Kate and I,' said William, 'want to get married.'

'Oh, how nice,' said Mrs Tukesbury.

'Yes indeed,' said the vicar. 'Are you a member of this parish? I don't seem to remember ...'

'No, sir, I'm an American. I worship at St Paul's in Boston.'

'Massachusetts, I presume, not Lincolnshire,' said the Reverend Tukesbury.

'Yes,' said William, forgetting for a moment that there was a Boston in England.

'Splendid,' said the vicar, his hands raised as if he were about to give a blessing. 'And what date did you have in mind for this union of souls?'

'Now, sir.'

'Now, sir?' said the startled vicar. 'I am not aware of the traditions in the United States that surround the solemn, holy and binding institution of marriage, Mr Kane, though one reads of some very strange incidents involving some of your compatriots from California. I do, however, consider it nothing less than my duty to inform you that those customs have not yet become acceptable in Henley-on-Thames. In England, sir, you must reside for a full calendar month in any parish before you can be married and the banns must be posted on three separate occasions, unless there are very special and extenuating circumstances. Even did such circumstances exist, I would have to seek the bishop's dispensation, and I couldn't do that in under three days,' Mr Tukesbury added, his hands now firmly at his side.

Kate spoke for the first time. 'How much do you still need for the church's new roof?'

'Ah, the roof. Now there is a sad story, but I won't embark upon its history at this moment, early eleventh century you know ...'

'How much do you need?' asked William, tightening his grasp on Kate's hand.

'We are hoping to raise five hundred pounds. We've done commendably well so far; we've reached twenty-seven pounds four shillings and four pence in only seven weeks.'

'No, no dear,' said Mrs Tukesbury. 'You haven't counted the one pound eleven shillings and two pence I made from my "Bring and Buy" sale last week.'

'Indeed I haven't, my dear. How inconsiderate of me to overlook your personal contribution. That will make altogether ...' began the Reverend Tukesbury as he tried to add the figures in his head, raising his eyes towards heaven for inspiration.

William took his wallet from his inside pocket, wrote out a cheque for five hundred pounds and silently proffered it to the Reverend Tukesbury.

'I ... ah, I see there are special circumstances, Mr Kane,' said the surprised vicar. The tone changed. 'Has either of you ever been married before?'

'Yes,' said Kate. 'My husband was killed in a plane crash over four years ago.'

'Oh, how terrible,' said Mrs Tukesbury. 'I am so sorry, I didn't ...'

'Shush, my dear,' said the man of God, now more interested in the church roof than in his wife's sentiments. 'And you, sir?'

'I have never been married before,' said William.

'I shall have to telephone the bishop.' Clutching William's cheque, the Reverend disappeared into the next room.

Mrs Tukesbury invited them to sit down and offered them the plate of cucumber sandwiches. She chatted on, but William and Kate did not hear her words as they sat gazing at each other.

The vicar returned three cucumber sandwiches later.

'It's highly irregular, highly irregular, but the bishop has agreed, on the condition, Mr Kane, that you will confirm everything at the American Embassy tomorrow morning and then with your own bishop at St Paul's in

Boston ... Massachusetts immediately you return home.'

He was still clutching the five-hundred-pound cheque.

'All we need now is two witnesses,' he continued. 'My wife can act as one, and we must hope that the verger is still around, so that he can be the other.'

'He is still around, I assure you,' said William.

'How can you be so certain, Mr Kane?'

'He cost me one per cent.'

'One per cent?' said the Reverend Tukesbury, baffled.

'One per cent of your church roof,' said William.

The vicar ushered William, Kate and his wife down the little path back to the church and blinked at the waiting verger.

'Indeed, I perceive that Mr Sprogget has remained on duty ... He has never done so for me; you obviously have a way with you, Mr Kane.'

Simon Tukesbury put on his vestments and a surplice while the verger stared at the scene in disbelief.

William turned to Kate and kissed her gently. 'I know it's a damn silly question in the circumstances, but will you marry me?'

'Good God,' said the Reverend Tukesbury, who had never blasphemed in the fifty-seven years of his mortal existence. 'You mean you haven't even asked her?'

Fifteen minutes later, Mr and Mrs William Kane left the parish church of Henley-on-Thames, Oxfordshire. Mrs Tukesbury had had to supply the ring at the last moment, which she twitched from a curtain in the vestry. It was a perfect fit. The Reverend Tukesbury had a new roof, and Mr Sprogget a yarn to tell them down at The Green Man where he spent most of his five pounds.

Outside the church the vicar handed William a piece of paper. 'Two shillings and sixpence, please.'

'What for?' asked William.

'Your marriage certificate, Mr Kane.'

'You should have taken up banking, sir,' said William, handing Mr Tukesbury half a crown.

He walked his bride in blissful silence back down the High Street to the Bell Inn. They had a quiet dinner in the fifteenth-century oak-beamed dining room, and went to bed at a few minutes past nine. As they disappeared up the old wooden staircase to their room, the chief receptionist turned to the hall porter and winked. 'If they're married, I'm the King of England.'

William started to hum 'God Save the King'.

The next morning Mr and Mrs Kane had a leisurely breakfast while the car was fixed. (His father would have told him all it needed was a new fan belt.) A young waiter poured them both a coffee.

'Do you like it black or shall I add some milk?' asked William innocently.

An elderly couple smiled benignly at them.

'With milk, please,' said Kate as she reached across and touched William's hand gently.

He smiled back at her, suddenly aware the whole room was now staring at them.

They returned to London in the cool early spring air, travelling through

Henley, over the Thames, and then on up through Berkshire and Middlesex into London.

'Did you notice the look the porter gave you this morning, darling?' asked William.

'Yes, I think perhaps we should have shown him our marriage certificate.'

'No, no, you'd have spoilt his whole image of the wanton American woman. The last thing he wants to tell his wife when he returns home tonight is that we were really married.'

When they arrived back at the Ritz in time for lunch, the desk manager was surprised to find William cancelling Kate's room. He was heard to comment later: 'Young Mr Kane appeared to be such a gentleman. His late and distinguished father would never have behaved in such a way.'

William and Kate took the *Aquitania* back to New York, having first called at the American embassy in Grosvenor Gardens to inform a consul of their new marital status. The consul gave them a long official form to fill out, charged them one pound, and kept them waiting for well over an hour. The American embassy, it seemed, was not in need of a new roof. William wanted to go to Cartier's in Bond Street and buy a gold wedding ring, but Kate would not hear of it – nothing was going to part her from the precious curtain ring.

                              .   .   .

William found it difficult to settle down in Boston under his new chairman. The precepts of the New Deal were passing into law with unprecedented rapidity, and William and Tony Simmons found it impossible to agree on whether the implications for investment would be good or bad. Expansion – on one front at least – became unstoppable when Kate announced soon after their return from England that she was pregnant, news which gave her parents and husband great joy. William tried to modify his working hours to suit his new role as a married man but found himself at his desk increasingly often throughout the hot summer evenings. Kate, cool and happy in her flowered maternity smock, methodically supervised the decoration of the nursery of the Red House. William found for the first time in his life that he could leave his work desk and look forward to going home. If he had work left over he just picked up the papers and took them back to the Red House, a pattern to which he adhered throughout their married life.

While Kate and the baby that was due about Christmas time brought William great happiness at home, Matthew was making him increasingly uneasy at work. He had taken to drinking and coming to the office late with no explanations. As the months passed, William found he could no longer rely on his friend's judgement. At first, he said nothing, hoping it was little more than an odd out-of-character reaction – which might quickly pass – to the repeal of Prohibition. But it wasn't, and the problem went from bad to worse. The last straw came one November morning when Matthew arrived two hours late, obviously suffering from a hangover, and made a simple, unnecessary mistake, selling off an important investment which resulted in a small loss for a client who should have made a handsome profit. William knew the time had come for an unpleasant but necessary head-on confrontation. Matthew admitted his error and apologized regretfully. William was thankful to have the row out of the way and was about to suggest they go to lunch together when his secretary uncharacteristically rushed into his office.

'It's your wife, sir, she's been taken to the hospital.'

'Why?' asked William, puzzled.

'The baby,' said his secretary.

'But it's not due for at least another six weeks,' said William incredulously.

'I know, sir, but Doctor MacKenzie sounded rather anxious, and wanted you to come to the hospital as quickly as possible.'

Matthew, who a moment before had seemed a broken reed, took over and drove William to the hospital. Memories of William's mother's death and her still-born daughter came flooding back to both of them.

'Pray God not Kate,' said Matthew as he drew into the hospital car park.

William did not need to be guided to the Anne Kane Maternity Wing which Kate had officially opened only six months before. He found a nurse standing outside the delivery room who informed him that Doctor MacKenzie was with his wife, and that she had lost a lot of blood. William paced up and down the corridor helplessly, numbly waiting, exactly as he had done years before. The scene was all too familiar. How unimportant being chairman of the bank was compared with losing Kate. When had he last said to her 'I love you'? Matthew sat with William, paced with William, stood with William, but said nothing. There was nothing to be said. William checked his watch each time a nurse ran in or out of the delivery room. Seconds turned into minutes and minutes into hours. Finally Doctor MacKenzie appeared, his forehead shining with little beads of sweat, a surgical mask covering his nose and mouth. William could see no expression on the doctor's face until he removed the white mask, revealing a large smile.

'Congratulations, William, you have a boy, and Kate is just fine.'

'Thank God,' breathed William, clinging onto Matthew.

'Much as I respect the Almighty,' said Doctor Mackenzie, 'I feel I had a little to do with this birth myself.'

William laughed. 'Can I see Kate?'

'No, not right now. I've given her a sedative and she's fallen asleep. She lost rather more blood than was good for her, but she'll be fine by morning. A little weak, perhaps, but well ready to see you. But there's nothing to stop you seeing your son. But don't be surprised by his size; remember he's quite premature.'

The doctor guided William and Matthew down the corridor to a room in which they stared through a pane of glass at a row of six little pink heads in cribs.

'That one,' said Doctor MacKenzie, pointing to the infant that had just arrived.

William stared dubiously at the ugly little face, his vision of a fine, upstanding son receding rapidly.

'Well, I'll say one thing for the little devil,' said Doctor MacKenzie cheerfully, 'he's better looking than you were at that age, and you haven't turned out too badly.'

William laughed out of relief.

'What are you going to call him?'

'Richard Higginson Kane.'

The doctor patted the new father affectionately on the shoulder. 'I hope I live long enough to deliver Richard's first-born.'

William immediately wired the rector of St Paul's, who put the boy down for a place in 1943, and then the new father and Matthew got thoroughly drunk and were both late arriving at the hospital the next morning to see Kate. William took Matthew for another look at young Richard.

'Ugly little bastard,' said Matthew, 'not at all like his beautiful mother.'

'That's what I thought,' said William.

'Spitting image of you, though.'

William returned to Kate's flower-filled room.

'Do you like your son?' Kate asked her husband. 'He's so like you.'

'I'll hit the next person who says that,' William said. 'He's the ugliest little thing I've ever seen.'

'Oh, no,' said Kate in mock indignation, 'he's beautiful.'

'A face only a mother could love,' said William and hugged his wife.

She clung to him, happy in his happiness.

'What would Grandmother Kane have said about our first-born entering the world after less than eight months of marriage? "I don't wish to appear uncharitable, but anyone born in under fifteen months must be considered of dubious parentage; under nine months definitely unacceptable,"' William mimicked. 'By the way, Kate, I forgot to tell you something before they rushed you into the hospital.'

'What was that?'

'I love you.'

Kate and young Richard had to stay in the hospital for nearly three weeks. Not until after Christmas did Kate fully recover her vitality. Richard, on the other hand, grew like an uncontrolled weed, no one having informed him that he was a Kane, and one was not supposed to do that sort of thing. William became the first male Kane to change a nappy and push a perambulator. Kate was very proud of him, and somewhat surprised. William told Matthew that it was high time he found himself a good woman and settled down.

Matthew laughed defensively. 'You're getting positively middle-aged. I shall be looking for grey hairs next.'

One or two had already appeared during the chairmanship battle. Matthew hadn't noticed.

·   ·   ·

William was not able to put a finger on exactly when his relationship with Tony Simmons began to deteriorate badly. Tony would continually veto one policy suggestion after another, and his negative attitude made William seriously consider resignation again. Matthew was not helping matters by returning to his old drinking habits. The period of reform had not lasted more than a few months, and, if anything, he was now drinking more heavily than before and arriving at the bank a few minutes later each morning. William wasn't quite sure how to handle the new situation and found himself continually covering Matthew's work. At the end of each day, William would double-check Matthew's mail and return his unanswered calls.

By the spring of 1936, as investors gained more confidence and depositors returned, William decided the time had come to go tentatively back into the stock market, but Tony vetoed the suggestion in an off-hand, inter-office memorandum to the financial committee. William stormed into Tony's office to ask if his resignation would be welcome.

'Certainly not, William. I merely want you to recognize that it has always been my policy to run this bank in a conservative manner, and that I am not willing to charge headlong back into the market with our investors' money.'

'But we're losing business hand-over-fist to other banks while we sit on the sidelines watching them take advantage of the present situation. Banks which we wouldn't even have considered as rivals ten years ago will soon be overtaking us.'

'Overtaking us in what, William? Not in reputation. Quick profits perhaps, but not reputation.'

'But I'm interested in profits,' said William. 'I consider it a bank's duty to make good returns for its investors, not to mark time in a gentlemanly fashion.'

'I would rather stand still than lose the reputation that this bank built up under your grandfather and father over the better part of half a century.'

'Yes, but both of them were always looking for new opportunities to expand the bank's activities.'

'In good times,' said Tony.

'And in bad,' said William.

'Why are you so upset, William? You still have a free hand in the running of your own department.'

'Like hell I do. You block anything that even suggests enterprise.'

'Let's start being honest with each other, William. One of the reasons I have had to be particularly cautious lately is that Matthew's judgement is no longer reliable.'

'Leave Matthew out of this. It's me you're blocking; I am head of the department.'

'I can't leave Matthew out of it. I wish I could. The final overall responsibility to the board for anyone's actions is mine, and he is the number two man in the bank's most important department.'

'Yes, and therefore my responsibility, because I am the number one man in that department.'

'No, William, it cannot remain your responsibility alone when Matthew comes into the office drunk at eleven o'clock in the morning, no matter how long and close your friendship has been.'

'Don't exaggerate.'

'I am not exaggerating, William. For over a year now this bank has been carrying Matthew Lester, and the only thing that has stopped me mentioning my worries to you before is your close personal relationship with him and his family. I wouldn't be sorry to see him hand in his resignation. A bigger man would have done so long ago, and his friends would have told him so.'

'Never,' said William. 'If he goes, I go.'

'So be it, William,' said Tony. 'My first responsibility is to our investors, not to your old school chums.'

'You'll live to regret that statement, Tony,' said William, as he stormed out of the chairman's office and returned to his own room in a furious temper.

'Where is Mr Lester?' William demanded as he passed his secretary.

'He's not in yet, sir.'

William looked at his watch, exasperated.

'Tell him I'd like to see him the moment he arrives.'

'Yes, sir.'

William paced up and down his office, cursing. Everything Tony Simmons had said about Matthew was accurate, which only made matters worse. He began to think back to when it had all begun, searching for a simple explanation. His thoughts were interrupted by his secretary.

'Mr Lester has just arrived, sir.'

Matthew entered the room looking rather sheepish, displaying all the signs of another hangover. He had aged badly in the past year, and his skin had lost its fine, athletic glow. William hardly recognized him as the man who had been his closest friend for nearly twenty years.

'Matthew, where the hell have you been?'

'I overslept,' Matthew replied, uncharacteristically scratching at his face. 'Rather a late night, I'm afraid.'

'You mean you drank too much.'

'No, I didn't have that much. It was a new girlfriend who kept me awake all night. She was insatiable.'

'When will you stop, Matthew? You've slept with nearly every single woman in Boston.'

'Don't exaggerate, William. There must be one or two left; at least I hope so. And then don't forget all the thousands of married ones.'

'It's not funny, Matthew.'

'Oh, come on, William. Give me a break.'

'Give you a break? I've just had Tony Simmons on my back because of you, and what's more I know he's right. You'll jump into bed with anything wearing a skirt, and worse, you're drinking yourself to death. Your judgement has gone to pieces. Why, Matthew? Tell me why. There must be some simple explanation. Up until a year ago you were one of the most reliable men I have ever met in my life. What is it, Matthew? What am I supposed to say to Tony Simmons?'

'Tell Simmons to go to hell and mind his own business.'

'Matthew, be fair, it *is* his business. We are running a bank, not a bordello, and you came here as a director on my personal recommendation.'

'And now I'm not measuring up to your standards, is that what you're saying?'

'No, I'm not saying that.'

'Then what the hell are you saying?'

'Buckle down and do some work for a few weeks. In no time everyone will have forgotten all about it.'

'Is that all you want?'

'Yes,' said William.

'I shall do as you command, O Master,' said Matthew, and he clicked his heels and walked out of the door.

'Oh, hell,' said William.

That afternoon William wanted to go over a client's portfolio with Matthew but nobody seemed to be able to find him. He had not returned to the office after lunch and was not seen again that day. Even the pleasure of putting young Richard to bed in the evening could not distract William from his worries about Matthew. Richard could already say two and William was trying to make him say three, but he insisted on saying 'tree'.

'If you can't say three, Richard, how can you ever hope to be a banker?' William demanded of his son as Kate entered the nursery.

'Perhaps he'll end up doing something worthwhile,' said Kate.

'What's more worthwhile than banking?' William inquired.

'Well, he might be a musician, or a baseball player, or even President of the United States.'

'Of those three I'd prefer him to be a ball player – it's the only one of your suggestions that pays a decent salary,' said William as he tucked Richard into bed.

Richard's last words before sleeping were, 'Tree, Daddy.' William gave in. It wasn't his day.

'You look exhausted, darling. I hope you haven't forgotten that we're having drinks later with Andrew MacKenzie?'

'Hell, Andrew's party had totally slipped my mind. What time is he expecting us?'

'In about an hour.'

'Well, first I'm going to take a long, hot bath.'

'I thought that was a woman's privilege,' said Kate.

'Tonight I need a little pampering. I've had a nerve-racking day.'

'Tony bothering you again?'

'Yes, but I am afraid this time he's in the right. He's been complaining about Matthew's drinking habits. I was only thankful he didn't mention the womanizing. It's became impossible to take Matthew to any party nowadays without the eldest daughter, not to mention the occasional wife, having to be locked away for their own safety. Will you run my bath?'

William sat in the tub for more than half an hour, and Kate had to drag him out before he fell asleep. Despite her prompting they arrived at the MacKenzie's twenty-five minutes late, only to find that Matthew, already well on the way to being inebriated, was trying to pick up a congressman's wife. William wanted to intervene, but Kate prevented him from doing so.

'Don't say anything,' she whispered.

'I can't stand here and watch him going to pieces in front of my eyes,' said William. 'He's my closest friend. I have to do something.'

But in the end he took Kate's advice and spent an unhappy evening watching Matthew become progressively drunk. Tony Simmons, from the other side of the room, was glancing pointedly at William, who was relieved at Matthew's early departure, even though it was in the company of the only unattached woman left at the party. Once Matthew had gone William started to relax for the first time that day.

'How is little Richard?' Andrew MacKenzie asked.

'He can't say "three",' said William.

'Might turn out to do something civilized after all,' said Doctor MacKenzie.

'Exactly what I thought,' said Kate. 'What a good idea William: he can be a doctor.'

'Pretty safe,' said Andrew. 'Don't know many doctors who can count past two.'

'Except when they send their bills,' said William.

Andrew laughed. 'Will you have another drink, Kate?'

'No thank you, Andrew. It's high time we went home. If we stay any longer, only Tony Simmons and William will be left, and they can both count past two so we would all have to talk banking the rest of the night.'

'Agreed,' said William. 'Thank you for a lovely party, Andrew. By the way, I must apologize for Matthew's behaviour.'

'Why?' said Doctor MacKenzie.

'Oh, come on, Andrew. Not only was he drunk, but there wasn't a woman in the room who felt safe left alone with him.'

'I might well do the same if I were in his predicament,' said Andrew MacKenzie.

'What makes you say that?' said William. 'You can't approve of his habits just because he's single.'

'No, I don't, but I try to understand them and realize I might be a little irresponsible faced with the same problem.'

'What do you mean?' asked Kate.

'My God,' said Doctor MacKenzie. 'He's your closest friend, and he hasn't told you?'

'Told us what?' they said together.

Dr MacKenzie stared at them both, a look of disbelief on his face. 'Come into my study.'

William and Kate followed the doctor into a small room, lined almost wall-to-wall with medical books, interspersed only with occasional, sometimes unframed, photographs of student days at Cornell.

'Please have a seat, Kate,' he said. 'William I make no apology for what I am about to say, because I assumed you knew that Matthew was gravely ill, dying, in fact, of Hodgkin's disease. He has known about his condition for over a year.'

William fell back in his chair, for a moment unable to speak. 'Hodgkin's disease?'

'An almost invariably fatal inflammation and enlargement of the lymph nodes,' said the doctor rather formally.

William shook his head incredulously. 'Why didn't he tell me?'

'You've known each other since you were at school together. My guess is he's far too proud to burden anyone else with his problems. He'd rather die in his own way than let anyone realize what he's going through. I have begged him for the last six months to tell his father, and I have certainly broken my professional promise to him by letting you know, but I can't let you go on blaming him for something over which he has absolutely no control.'

'Thank you, Andrew,' said William. 'How can I have been so blind and so stupid?'

'Don't blame yourself,' said Doctor MacKenzie. 'There's no way you could have known.'

'Is there really no hope?' asked William. 'Are there no clinics, no specialists? Money would be no problem ...'

'Money can't buy everything, William, and I have consulted the three best men in America, and one in Switzerland. I am afraid they are all in agreement with my diagnosis, and medical science hasn't yet discovered a cure for Hodgkin's disease.'

'How long has he got to live?' asked Kate in a whisper.

'Six months at the outside, more likely three.'

'And I thought I had problems,' said William. He held tightly onto Kate's hand as if it were a lifeline. 'We must be going, Andrew. Thank you for telling us.'

'Help him in any way you can,' said the doctor, 'but for God's sake, be understanding. Let him do what he wants to do. It's Matthew's last few months, not yours. And don't ever let him know I told you.'

William drove Kate home in silence. As soon as they reached the Red House, William called the girl Matthew had left the party with.

'Would it be possible to speak to Matthew Lester?'

'He's not here,' said a rather irritable voice. 'He dragged me off to the In and Out Club, but he was already drunk by the time we got there, and I refused to go in that place with him.' Then she hung up.

The In and Out Club. William had a hazy recollection of having seen the sign swinging from an iron bar but he couldn't remember exactly where the place was. He looked it up in the phone book, drove over to the north side of town and eventually, after questioning a passer-by, he found the club. William knocked on the door. A hatch slid back.

'Are you a member?'

'No,' said William firmly, and passed a ten-dollar note through the grill. The hatch slid closed, and the door opened. William walked onto the middle of the dance floor, looking slightly incongruous in his three-piece banker's suit. The dancers, twined around each other, swayed incuriously away from him. William's eyes searched the smoke-filled room for Matthew, but he wasn't there. Finally he thought he recognized one of Matthew's many recent casual girlfriends, whom he felt certain he'd seen coming out of his friend's flat early one morning. She was sitting cross-legged in a corner with a sailor. William went over to her.

'Excuse me, miss,' he said.

She looked up but obviously didn't recognize William.

'The lady's with me, so beat it,' said the sailor.

'Have you see Matthew Lester?'

'Matthew?' said the girl. 'Matthew who?'

'I told you to get lost,' said the sailor, rising to his feet.

'One more word out of you, and I'll knock your block off,' said William.

The sailor had seen anger like that in a man's eyes once before in his life and had nearly lost an eye for his trouble. He sat back down.

'Where is Matthew?'

'I don't know a Matthew, darling.' Now she, too, was frightened.

'Six-feet-two, blond hair, dressed like me, and probably drunk.'

'Oh, you mean Martin. He calls himself Martin here, darling, not Matthew.' She began to relax. 'Now let me see, who did he go off with tonight?'

She turned her head towards the bar and shouted at the bartender. 'Terry, who did Martin go out with?'

The bartender removed a dead cigarette butt from the corner of his mouth. 'Jenny,' he said, and put the unlit cigarette back in place.

'Jenny, that's right,' said the girl. 'Now let me see, she's short sessions. Never lets a man stay for more than half an hour, so they should be back soon.'

'Thank you,' said William.

He waited for almost an hour at the bar sipping a scotch with a lot of water, feeling more and more out of place by the minute. Finally, the bartender, the unlit cigarette still in his mouth, gestured to a girl who was coming through the door.

'That's Jenny,' he said. Matthew was not with her.

The bartender waved for Jenny to join them. A slim, short, dark, not unattractive girl, she winked at William and walked towards him swinging her hips.

'Looking for me, darling? Well, I am available, but I charge ten dollars for half an hour.'

'No, I don't want you,' said William.

'Charming,' said Jenny.

'I'm looking for the man who's been with you, Matthew – I mean Martin.'

'Martin, he was too drunk even to get it up with the help of a crane, darling, but he paid his ten dollars, he always does. A real gentleman.'

'Where is he now?' asked William impatiently.

'I don't know, he gave it up as a bad job and started walking home.'

William ran into the street. The cold air hit him, not that he needed to be awakened. He drove his car slowly away from the club, following the route towards Matthew's flat, looking carefully at each person he passed. Some hurried on when they saw his watchful eyes; others tried to engage him in conversation. When he was passing an all-night café, he caught sight of Matthew through the steam windows, weaving his way through the tables with a cup in his hand. William parked the car, went in and sat down beside him. Matthew had slumped onto the table next to a cup of untouched spilt coffee. He was so drunk that he didn't even recognize William.

'Matthew, it's me,' said William, looking at the crumpled man. The tears started to run down his cheeks.

Matthew looked up and spilled some more of his coffee. 'You're crying, old fellow. Lost your girl, have you?'

'No, my closest friend,' said William.

'Ah, they're much harder to come by.'

'I know,' said William.

'I have a good friend,' said Matthew, slurring his words. 'He's always stood by me until we quarrelled for the first time today. My fault though. You see I've let him down rather badly.'

'No you haven't,' said William.

'How can you know?' said Matthew angrily. 'You're not even fit to know him.'

'Let's go home, Matthew.'

'My name is Martin,' said Matthew.

'I'm sorry, Martin, let's go home.'

'No, I want to stay here. There's this girl who may come by later. I think I'm ready for her now.'

'I have some fine old malt whisky at my house,' said William. 'Why don't you join me?'

'Any women at your place?'

'Yes, plenty of them.'

'You're on, I'll come.'

William hoisted Matthew up and put his arm under his shoulder, guiding him slowly through the café towards the door. It was the first time he'd ever realized how heavy Matthew was. As they passed two policemen sitting at the corner of the counter, William heard one say to the other, 'Goddamn fairies.'

He helped Matthew into the car and drove him back to Beacon Hill. Kate was waiting up for them.

'You should have gone to bed, darling.'

'I couldn't sleep,' she replied.

'I'm afraid he's nearly incoherent.'

'Is this the girl you promised me?' said Matthew.

'Yes, she'll take care of you,' said William, and he and Kate helped him up to the guest room and put him on the bed. Kate started to undress him.

'You must undress as well, darling,' he said. 'I've already paid my ten dollars.'

'When you're in bed,' said Kate lightly.

'Why are you looking so sad, beautiful lady?' said Matthew.

'Because I love you,' said Kate, tears beginning to form in her eyes.

'Don't cry,' said Matthew, 'there's nothing to cry about. I'll manage it this time, you'll see.'

When they had undressed Matthew, William covered him with a sheet and a blanket. Kate turned the light out.

'You promised you'd come to bed with me,' said Matthew, drowsily.

She closed the door quietly.

William slept on a chair outside Matthew's room for fear he might wake up in the night and try to leave. Kate woke him in the morning before taking some breakfast in to Matthew.

'What am I doing here, Kate?' were Matthew's first words.

'You came back with us after Andrew MacKenzie's party last night,' replied Kate rather feebly.

'No, I didn't. I went to the In and Out with that awful girl, Patricia something or other, who refused to come in with me. God, I feel lousy. Can I have a tomato juice? I don't want to be unsociable, but the last thing I need is breakfast.'

'Of course, Matthew.'

William came in. Matthew looked up at him. They stared at each other in silence.

'You know, don't you?' said Matthew finally.

'Yes,' said William, 'and I've been a fool and I hope you'll forgive me.'

'Don't cry, William. I haven't seen you do that since you were twelve, when Covington was beating you up and I had to drag him off you.

Remember? I wonder what Covington is up to now? Probably running a brothel in Tijuana; it's about all he was fit for. Mind you, if Covington is running it, the place will be damned efficient, so lead me to it. Don't cry, William. Grown men don't cry. Nothing can be done. I've seen all the specialists from New York to Los Angeles to Zurich, and there is nothing they can do. Do you mind if I skip the office this morning? I still feel bloody awful. Wake me if I stay too long or if I'm any more trouble, and I'll find my own way home.'

'This is your home,' said William.

Matthew's face changed. 'Will you tell my father, William? I can't face him. You're an only son, too; you understand the problem.'

'Yes, I will,' said William. 'I'll go down to New York tomorrow and tell him if you'll promise to stay with Kate and me. I won't stop you from getting drunk if that's what you wish to do, or from having as many women as you want, but you must stay here.'

'Best offer I've had in weeks, William. Now I think I'll sleep some more. I get so tired nowadays.'

William watched Matthew fall into a deep sleep and removed the half empty glass from his hand. A tomato stain was forming on the sheets.

'Don't die,' he said quietly. 'Please don't die, Matthew. Have you forgotten that you and I are going to run the biggest bank in America?'

. . .

William went to New York the following morning to see Charles Lester. The great man aged visibly at William's news and seemed to shrink into his seat.

'Thank you for coming, William, and telling me personally. I knew something must be wrong when Matthew stopped his monthly visits to see me. I'll come up every weekend. He will want to be with you and Kate, and I'll try not to make it too obvious how hard I took the news. God knows what he's done to deserve this. Since my wife died, I built everything for Matthew, and now there is no one to leave it to. Susan has no interest in the bank.'

'Come to Boston when ever you want to, sir. You'll always be most welcome.'

'Thank you, William, for everything you're doing for Matthew.'

The old man looked up at him. 'I wish your father were alive to see how worthy his son is of the name Kane. If only I could change places with Matthew, and let him live . . .'

'I ought to be getting back to him soon, sir.'

'Yes, of course. Tell him I took the news stoically. Don't tell him anything different.'

'Yes, sir.'

William travelled back to Boston that night to find that Matthew had stayed at home with Kate and started reading America's latest best seller, *Gone With The Wind*, as he sat out on the veranda. He looked up as William came through the French windows.

'How did the old man take it?'

'He cried,' said William.

'The chairman of Lester's bank cried?' said Matthew. 'Never let the shareholders know that.'

Matthew stopped drinking and worked as hard as he could until the last few days. William was amazed by his determination and had continually to make him slow down. He was always on top of his work and would tease William by checking his mail at the end of each day. In the evenings before a large dinner, Matthew would play tennis with William or row against him on the river. 'I'll know I'm dead when I can't beat you,' he mocked. Matthew never entered the hospital, preferring to stay on at the Red House. The weeks went so slowly and yet so quickly for William, waking each morning wondering if Matthew would still be alive.

Matthew died on a Thursday, forty pages still to read of *Gone With The Wind*.

.   .   .

The funeral was held in New York, and William and Kate stayed with Charles Lester. In six months, he had become an old man, and as he stood by the graves of his wife and only son, he told William that he no longer saw any purpose in this life. William said nothing; no words of his could help the grieving father. William and Kate returned to Boston the next day. The Red House seemed strangely empty without Matthew. The past few months had been at once the happiest and unhappiest period in William's life. Death had brought him a closeness, both to Matthew and to Kate, that normal life would never have allowed.

When William returned to the bank after Matthew's death, he found it hard to get back into any sort of normal routine. He would get up and start to head towards Matthew's office for advice or a laugh, or merely to be assured of his existence, but he was no longer there. It was weeks before William could prevent himself from doing this.

Tony Simmons was very understanding, but it didn't help. William lost all interest in banking, even in Kane and Cabot itself, as he went through months of remorse over Matthew's death. He had always taken it for granted that he and Matthew would grow old together and share a common destiny. No one commented that William's work was not up to its usual high standard. Even Kate grew worried by the hours William would spend alone.

Then one morning she awoke to find him sitting on the edge of the bed staring down at her. She blinked up at him. 'Is something wrong, darling?'

'No, I'm just looking at my greatest asset and making sure I don't take it for granted.'

22

By the end of 1932, with America still in the grip of a depression, Abel was becoming a little apprehensive about the future of the Baron Group. Two thousand banks had been closed during the past two years, and more were shutting their doors every week. Nine million people were still unemployed, which had as its only virtue the assurance that Abel could maintain a highly professional staff in his hotels. Still, the Baron Group lost seventy-two thousand dollars during a year in which he had predicted that they would break even, and he began to wonder whether his backer's purse and patience would hold out long enough to allow him the chance to turn things around.

Abel had begun to take an active interest in American politics during Anton Cermak's successful campaign to become mayor of Chicago. Cermak talked Abel into joining the Democratic Party, which had launched a virulent campaign against Prohibition; Abel threw himself wholeheartedly behind Cermak, as Prohibition had proved very damaging to the hotel trade. The fact that Cermak was himself an immigrant, from Czechoslovakia, created an immediate bond between the two men, and Abel was delighted to be chosen as a delegate representative at the Democratic Convention held in Chicago that year where Cermak brought a packed audience to its feet with the words: 'It's true I didn't come over on the *Mayflower*, but I came as soon as I could.'

At the convention Cermak introduced Abel to Franklin D. Roosevelt, who made a lasting impression on him. FDR went on to win the Presidential election easily and he swept Democratic candidates into office all over the country. One of the newly elected aldermen at Chicago City Hall was Henry Osborne. When Anton Cermak was killed a few weeks later in Miami by an assassin's bullet intended for FDR, Abel decided to contribute a considerable amount of time and money to the cause of the Polish Democrats in Chicago.

.   .   .

During 1933 the group lost only twenty-three thousand dollars, and one of the hotels, the St Louis Baron, actually showed a profit. When President Roosevelt had delivered his first fireside chat on 12 March, exhorting his countrymen 'to once again believe in America', Abel's confidence soared and he decided to re-open the two hotels that he had closed the previous year.

Zaphia grew querulous at his long absences in Charleston and Mobile, while he took the two hotels out of mothballs. She had never wanted Abel to be more than the deputy manager of the Stevens, a level at which she felt she could keep pace. The pace was quickening as every month passed, and she became conscious of falling behind Abel's ambitions and feared he was beginning to lose interest in her.

She was also becoming anxious about her childlessness, and started to see doctors who reassured her that there was nothing to prevent her from becoming pregnant. One offered the suggestion that Abel should also be examined, but Zaphia demurred, knowing he would regard the very mention of the subject as a slur on his manhood. Finally, after the subject had become so charged that it was difficult for them to discuss it at all, Zaphia missed her period. She waited hopefully for another month before saying anything to Abel or even seeing the doctor again. He confirmed that she was at last pregnant. To Abel's delight, Zaphia gave birth to a daughter, on New Year's Day, 1934. They named her Florentyna, after Abel's sister. Abel was besotted the moment he set eyes on the child and Zaphia knew from that moment she could no longer be the first love of his life. George and Zaphia's cousin were the child's Kums, and Abel gave a traditional ten-course Polish dinner on the evening of the christening. Many gifts were presented to the child, including a beautiful antique ring from Abel's backer. He returned the gift in kind when the Baron Group made a profit of sixty-three thousand dollars at the end of the year. Only the Mobile Baron was still losing money.

After Florentyna's birth Abel found he was spending much more of his time in Chicago which prompted him to decide that the time had come to build a Baron there. Hotels in the city were booming in the aftermath of the World's Fair. Abel intended to make his new hotel the flagship of the group in memory of Davis Leroy. The company still owned the site of the old Richmond Hotel on Michigan Avenue, and although Abel had had several offers for the land, he had always held out, hoping that one day he would be in a strong enough financial position to rebuild the hotel. The project required capital and Abel decided to use the seven hundred and fifty thousand dollars he had eventually received from Great Western Casualty for the old Chicago Richmond to start construction. As soon as his plans were formulated, he told Curtis Fenton of his intention, with the sole reservation that if David Maxton did not want a rival to the Stevens, Abel was willing to drop the whole project; he felt it was the least he could do in the circumstances. A few days later, Curtis Fenton advised him that his backer was delighted by the idea of 'The Chicago Baron'.

It took Abel twelve months to build the new Baron with a large helping hand from Alderman Henry Osborne, who hurried through the permits required from City Hall in the shortest possible time. The building was opened in 1936 by the mayor of the city, Edward J. Kelly, who, after the death of Anton Cermak, had become the prime organizer of the Democratic machine. In memory of Davis Leroy, the hotel had no twelfth floor – a tradition Abel continued in every new Baron he built.

Both Illinois senators were also in attendance to address the two thousand assembled guests. The Chicago Baron was superb both in design and construction. Abel had wound up spending well over a million dollars on the hotel, and it looked as though every penny had been put to good use. The public rooms were large and sumptuous with high stucco ceilings and decorations in pastel shades of green, pleasant and relaxing; the carpets were thick. The dark green embossed 'B' was discreet but ubiquitous, adorning everything from the flag that fluttered on the top of the forty-two storey building to the neat lapel of the most junior bellhop.

'This hotel already bears the hallmark of success,' said J. Hamilton Lewis, the senior senator from Illinois, 'because, my friends, it is the man, not the building, who will always be known as "The Chicago Baron".' Abel beamed with undisguised pleasure as the two thousand guests roared their approval.

Abel's reply of acknowledgement was well turned and confidently delivered, and it earned him a standing ovation. He was beginning to feel very much at home among big businessmen and senior politicians. Zaphia hovered uncertainly in the background during the lavish celebration: the occasion was a little too much for her. She neither understood nor cared for success on Abel's scale; and even though she could now afford the most expensive clothes, she still looked unfashionable and out-of-place, and she was only too aware that it annoyed Abel. She stood by while Abel chatted with Henry Osborne.

'This must be the high point of your life,' Henry was saying, slapping Abel on the back.

'High point – I've just turned thirty,' said Abel. A camera flashed as he placed an arm round Henry's shoulder. Abel beamed, realizing for the first time how pleasant it was to be treated as a public figure. 'I'm going to put Baron hotels right across the globe,' he said, just loud enough for the reporter to hear. 'I intend to be to America what César Ritz was to Europe. Stick with me, Henry, and you'll enjoy the ride.'

23

At breakfast the next morning, Kate pointed to a small item on page seventeen of the *Globe*, reporting the opening of the Chicago Baron.

William smiled as he read the article. Kane and Cabot had been foolish not to listen when he had advised them to support the Richmond Group. It pleased him that his own judgement on Rosnovski had turned out to be right even though the bank had lost out on the deal. His smile broadened as he read the nickname 'The Chicago Baron'. Then, suddenly, he felt sick. He examined the accompanying photograph more closely, but there was no mistake, and the caption confirmed his first impression: 'Abel Rosnovski, the chairman of the Baron Group talking with Mieczyslaw Szymczak, a governor of the Federal Reserve Board, and Alderman Henry Osborne.'

William dropped the paper onto the breakfast table and thought for a moment. As soon as he arrived at his office, he called Thomas Cohen at Cohen, Cohen and Yablons.

'It's been a long time, Mr Kane,' were Thomas Cohen's first words. 'I was very sorry to learn of the death of your friend, Matthew Lester. How are your wife and your son – Richard – isn't that his name?'

William always admired Thomas Cohen's instant recall of names and relationships.

'Yes, it is. They're both well, thank you, Mr Cohen.'

'Well, what can I do for you this time, Mr Kane?' Thomas also remembered that William could only manage about one sentence of small talk.

'I want to employ, through you, the services of a reliable investigator. I do not wish my name to be associated with this inquiry, but I need another run-down on Henry Osborne. Everything he's done since he left Boston, and in particular whether there is any connection between him and Abel Rosnovski of the Baron Group.'

There was a pause before the lawyer, said, 'Yes.'

'Can you report to me in one week?'

'Two please, Mr Kane, two,' said Mr Cohen.

'Full report on my desk at the bank in two weeks, Mr Cohen?'

'Two weeks, Mr Kane.'

Thomas Cohen was as reliable as ever, and a full report was on William's desk on the fifteenth morning. William read the dossier with care. There appeared to be no formal business connections between Abel Rosnovski and Henry Osborne. Rosnovski, it seemed, found Osborne useful as a political contact, but nothing more. Osborne himself had bounced from job to job since leaving Boston, ending up in the main office of the Great Western Casualty Insurance Company. In all probability, that was how Osborne had come in contact with Abel Rosnovski, as the old Chicago Richmond had always been insured by Great Western. When the hotel burned down, the insurance company had originally refused to pay the claim. A certain Desmond Pacey, the manager, had been sent to prison for ten years, after pleading guilty to arson, and there was some suspicion that Abel Rosnovski might himself have been involved. Nothing was proved, and the insurance company settled later for three-quarters of a million dollars. Osborne, the report went on, is now an alderman and full-time politician at City Hall, and it is common knowledge that he hopes to become a congressman for Chicago. He has recently married a Miss Marie Axton, the daughter of a wealthy drug manufacturer, and as yet they have no children.

William went over the report again to be sure that he had not missed anything, however inconsequential. Although there did not seem to be a great deal to connect the two men, he couldn't help feeling that the association between Abel Rosnovski and Henry Osborne, both of whom hated him, for totally disparate reasons, was potentially dangerous to him. He mailed a cheque to Thomas Cohen and requested that he update the file every quarter, but as the months passed, and the quarterly reports revealed nothing new, he began to stop worrying, thinking perhaps he had over-reacted to the photograph in the *Boston Globe*.

Kate presented her husband with a daughter in the spring of 1937, whom they christened Virginia. William started changing nappies again, and such was his fascination for 'the little lady' that Kate had to rescue the child each night for fear she would never get any sleep. Richard, now two and a half, didn't care too much for the new arrival to begin with, but time and a new wooden soldier on a horse, combined to allay his jealousy.

By the end of the year, William's department at Kane and Cabot had made a handsome profit for the bank. He had emerged from the lethargy that had overcome him on Matthew's death and was fast regaining his reputation as a shrewd investor in the stock market, not least when 'sell 'em short' Smith admitted he had only perfected a technique developed by William Kane of Boston. Even Tony Simmons' direction had become less irksome. Nevertheless, William was secretly worried by the prospect that he could not become chairman of Kane and Cabot until Simmons retired in seventeen years' time, and he began to consider looking around for employment in another bank.

· · ·

William and Kate had taken to visiting Charles Lester in New York about once a month at weekends. The great man had grown very old over the three years since Matthew's death, and rumours in financial circles were that he had lost all interest in his work and was rarely seen at the bank. William was beginning to wonder how much longer the old man would live, and then a few weeks later he died. William travelled down to the funeral in New

York. Everyone seemed to be there including the Vice-President of the United States, John Nance Garner. After the funeral, William and Kate took the train back to Boston, numbly conscious that they had lost their last link with the Lester family.

It was some six months later that William received a communication from Sullivan and Cromwell, the distinguished New York lawyers, asking him if he would be kind enough to attend the reading of the will of the late Charles Lester at their offices in Wall Street. William went to the reading, more from loyalty to the Lester family than from any curiosity to know what Charles Lester had left him. He hoped for a small memento that would remind him of Matthew and join the 'Harvard Oar' that still hung on the wall of the guest room of the Red House. He also looked forward to the opportunity of renewing his acquaintance with many members of the Lester family whom he had come to know in school and college holidays spent with Matthew.

William drove down to New York in his newly acquired Daimler the night before the reading and stayed at the Harvard Club. The will was to be read at ten o'clock the following morning, and William was surprised to find on his arrival in the offices of Sullivan and Cromwell that over fifty people were already present. Many of them glanced up at William as he entered the room, and he greeted several of Matthew's cousins and aunts, looking rather older than he remembered them; he could only conclude that they must be thinking the same about him. His eyes searched for Matthew's sister Susan, but he couldn't see her. At ten o'clock precisely Mr Arthur Cromwell entered the room, accompanied by an assistant carrying a brown leather folder. Everyone fell silent in hopeful expectation. The lawyer began by explaining to the assembled would-be beneficiaries that the contents of the will had not been disclosed until six months after Charles Lester's death at Mr Lester's specific instruction: having no son to whom to leave his fortune he had wanted the dust to settle after his death before his final intentions were made clear.

William looked around the room at the intent faces which were hanging on every syllable issuing from the lawyer's mouth. Arthur Cromwell took nearly an hour to read the will. After reciting the usual bequests to family retainers, charities and Harvard University, Cromwell went on to reveal that Charles Lester had divided his personal fortune among all his relatives, treating them more or less according to their degree of kinship. His daughter, Susan, received the largest share of the estate while the five nephews and three nieces each received an equal portion of the rest. All their money and shares were to be held in trust by the bank until they were thirty. Several other cousins, aunts and distant relations were given immediate cash payments.

William was surprised when Mr Cromwell announced: 'That disposes of all the known assets of the late Charles Lester.'

People began to shuffle around in their seats, as a murmur of nervous conversation broke out. No one wanted to admit that the unfortunate death had made them fortunate.

'That is not, however, the end of Mr Charles Lester's last will and testament,' said the imperturbable lawyer, and everyone sat still again, fearful of some late and unwelcome thunderbolt.

Mr Cromwell went on. 'I shall now continue in Mr Charles Lester's own words: "I have always considered that a bank and its reputation are only as good as the people who serve it. It was well known that I had hoped my son Matthew would succeed me as chairman of Lester's, but his tragic and untimely death has intervened. Until now, I have never divulged my choice of successor for Lester's bank. I therefore wish it to be known that I desire William Lowell Kane, son of one of my dearest friends, the late Richard Lowell Kane, and at present the vice-chairman of Kane and Cabot, be appointed chairman of Lester's Bank and Trust Company following the next full board meeting."'

There was an immediate uproar. Everyone looked around the room for the mysterious Mr William Lowell Kane of whom few but the immediate Lester family had ever heard.

'I have not yet finished,' said Arthur Cromwell quietly.

Silence fell once more, as the members of the audience, anticipating another bombshell, exchanged fearful glances.

The lawyer continued. 'All the above grants and division of shares in Lester's and Company are expressly conditional upon the beneficiaries voting for Mr Kane at the next annual board meeting, and continuing to do so for at least the following five years, unless Mr Kane himself indicates that he does not wish to accept the chairmanship.'

Uproar broke out again. William wished he was a million miles away, not sure whether to be deliriously happy or to concede that he must be the most detested person in that room.

'That concludes the last will and testament of the late Charles Lester,' said Mr Cromwell, but only the front row heard him.

William looked up. Susan Lester was walking towards him. The puppy fat had disappeared while the attractive freckles remained. He smiled, but she walked straight past him without even acknowledging his presence. William frowned.

Ignoring the babble, a tall, grey-haired man wearing a pin-striped suit and a silver tie moved quickly towards William.

'You are William Kane, are you not, sir?'

'Yes, I am,' said William nervously.

'My name is Peter Parfitt,' said the stranger.

'The bank's vice-chairman,' said William.

'Correct, sir,' he said. 'I do not know you, but I do know something of your reputation, and I count myself lucky to have been acquainted with your distinguished father. If Charles Lester thought you were the right man to be chairman of his bank, that's good enough for me.'

William had never been so relieved in his life.

'Where are you staying in New York?' continued Peter Parfitt before William could reply.

'At the Harvard Club.'

'Splendid. May I ask if you are free for dinner tonight by any chance?'

'I had intended to return to Boston this evening,' said William, 'but I expect I shall now have to stay in New York for a few days.'

'Good. Why don't you come to my house for dinner, say about eight o'clock?'

The banker handed William his card with an address embossed in copperplate script. 'I shall enjoy the opportunity of chatting with you in more convivial surroundings.'

'Thank you, sir,' said William, pocketing the card as others began crowding around him. Some stared at him in hostility; others waited to express their congratulations.

When William eventually managed to make his escape and returned to the Harvard Club, the first thing he did was to call Kate and tell her the news.

She said very quietly, 'How happy Matthew would be for you, darling.'

'I know,' said William.

'When are you coming home?'

'God knows. I'm dining tonight with a Mr Peter Parfitt who is a vice-chairman of Lester's. He's being most helpful over the whole affair, which is making life much easier. I'll spend the night here at the club, and then call you sometime tomorrow to let you know how things are working out.'

'All right, darling.'

'All quiet on the Eastern seaboard?'

'Well, Virginia has cut a tooth and seems to think she deserves special attention, Richard was sent to bed early for being rude to Nanny, and we all miss you.'

William laughed. 'I'll call you tomorrow.'

'Yes, please do. By the way, many congratulations. I approve of Charles Lester's judgement even if I'm going to hate living in New York.'

It was the first time William had thought about living in New York.

. . .

William arrived at Peter Parfitt's home on East Sixty-fourth Street at eight o'clock that night and was taken by surprise to find his host had dressed for dinner. William felt slightly embarrassed and ill at ease in his dark banker's suit. He quickly explained to his hostess that he had originally anticipated returning to Boston that evening. Diana Parfitt, who turned out to be Peter's second wife, could not have been more charming to her guest, and she seemed delighted that William was to be the next chairman of Lester's. During an excellent dinner William could not resist asking Peter Parfitt how he thought the rest of the board would react to Charles Lester's wishes.

'They'll all fall in line,' said Parfitt. 'I've spoken to most of them already. There's a full board meeting on Monday morning to confirm your appointment and I can only see one small cloud on the horizon.'

'What's that?' said William, trying not to sound anxious.

'Well, between you and me, the other vice-chairman, Ted Leach, was rather expecting to be appointed chairman himself. In fact, I think I would go as far as saying that he anticipated it. We had all been informed that no nomination could be made until after the will had been read, but Charles Lester's wishes must have come as rather a shock to Ted.'

'Will he put up a fight?' asked William.

'I'm afraid he might, but there's nothing for you to worry about.'

'I don't mind admitting,' said Diana Parfitt, as she studied the rather flat soufflé in front of her, 'that he has never been my favourite man.'

'Now, dear,' said Parfitt reprovingly, 'we mustn't say anything behind Ted's back before Mr Kane has had a chance to judge for himself. There is no doubt in my mind that the board will confirm Mr Kane's appointment at the meeting on Monday, and there's even the possibility that Ted Leach will resign.'

'I don't want anyone to feel they have to resign because of me,' said William.

'A very creditable sentiment,' said Parfitt. 'But don't bother yourself about a puff of wind. I'm confident that the whole matter is well under control. You go quietly back to Boston tomorrow, and I'll keep you informed on the lay of the land.'

'Perhaps it might be wise if I dropped in at the bank in the morning. Won't your fellow officers find it a little curious if I make no attempt to meet any of them?'

'No, I don't think that would be advisable given the circumstances. In fact, I feel it might be wiser for you to stay out of their way until the Monday board meeting is over. They won't want to seem any less independent than necessary, and they may already feel like glorified rubber stamps. Take my advice Bill, you go back to Boston, and I'll call you with the good news before noon on Monday.'

William reluctantly agreed to Peter Parfitt's suggestion and went on to spend a pleasant evening discussing with both of them where he and Kate might stay in New York while they were looking for a permanent home. William was somewhat surprised to find that Peter Parfitt seemed to have no desire to discuss his own views on banking, and he assumed the reason was because of Diana Parfitt's presence. An excellent evening ended with a little too much brandy, and William did not arrive back at the Harvard Club until after one o'clock.

Once William had returned to Boston he made an immediate report to Tony Simmons of what had transpired in New York as he did not want him to hear about the appointment from anyone else. Tony turned out to be surprisingly sanguine about the news.

'I'm sorry to learn that you will be leaving us, William. Lester's may well be two or three times the size of Kane and Cabot, but I shall be unable to replace you, and I hope you'll consider very carefully before accepting the appointment.'

William was surprised and couldn't help showing it. 'Frankly, Tony, I would have thought you'd have been only too glad to see the back of me.'

'William, when will you ever believe that my first interest has always been the bank, and there has never been any doubt in my mind that you are one of the shrewdest investment advisers in America today? If you leave Kane and Cabot now, many of the bank's most important clients will naturally want to follow you.'

'I would never transfer my own money to Lester's,' said William, 'any more than I would expect any of the bank's clients to move with me.'

'Of course you wouldn't solicit them to join you, William, but some of them will want you to continue managing their portfolios. Like your father and Charles Lester, they believe quite rightly that banking is about people and reputations.'

William and Kate spent a tense weekend waiting for Monday and the result of the board meeting in New York. William sat nervously in his office the whole of Monday morning, answering every telephone call personally, but he heard nothing as the morning dragged into the afternoon. He didn't even leave the office for lunch, and Peter Parfitt finally called a little after six.

'I'm afraid there's been some unexpected trouble, Bill,' were his opening words.

William's heart sank.

'Nothing for you to worry about since I still feel I have the situation well under control, but the board wants the right to oppose your nomination with their own candidate. Some of them have produced legal opinions that go as far as saying the relevant clause of the will has no real validity. I've been given the unpleasant task of asking if you would be willing to fight an election against the board's candidate.'

'Who would be the board's candidate?' asked William.

'No names have been mentioned by anyone yet, but I imagine their choice will be Ted Leach. No one else has shown the slightest interest in running against you.'

'I'd like a little time to think about it,' William replied. 'When will the next board meeting be?'

'A week from today,' said Parfitt. 'But don't you go and get yourself all worked up about Ted Leach; I'm still confident that you will win easily, and I'll keep you informed of any further developments as the week goes by.'

'Do you want me to come down to New York, Peter?'

'No, not for the moment. I don't think that would help matters.'

William thanked him and put the phone down. He packed his old leather briefcase and left the office, feeling more than a little depressed. Tony Simmons, carrying a suitcase, caught up with him in the private parking lot.

'I didn't know you were going out of town, Tony.'

'It's only the monthly bankers' dinner in New York. I'll be back by tomorrow afternoon. I think I can safely leave Kane and Cabot for twenty-four hours in the capable hands of the next chairman of Lester's.'

William laughed. 'I may already be the ex-chairman,' he said and explained the latest development. Once again, William was surprised by Tony Simmons' reaction.

'It's true that Ted Leach has always expected to be the next chairman of Lester's,' he mused. 'That's common knowledge in financial circles. But he's a loyal servant of the bank, and I can't believe he would oppose Charles Lester's express wishes.'

'I didn't realize you even knew him,' said William.

'I don't know him all that well,' said Tony. 'He was a class ahead of me at Yale, and now I see him from time to time at these damned bankers' dinners that you'll have to attend when you're a chairman. He's bound to be there tonight. I'll have a word with him if you like.'

'Yes, please do, but be very careful, won't you?' said William.

'My dear William, you've spent nearly ten years of your life telling me I'm far too careful.'

'I'm sorry, Tony. Funny how one's judgement is impaired when one is worrying about one's own problems, however sound the same judgement might be considered when dealing with other peoples'. I'll put myself in your hands and do whatever you advise.'

'Good then, you leave it to me. I'll see what Leach has to say for himself and call you first thing in the morning.'

Tony called from New York a few minutes after midnight and woke William from a deep sleep.

'Have I woken you, William?'

'Yes, who is it?'

'Tony Simmons.'

William switched on the light by the side of the bed and looked at his alarm clock. Ten minutes past twelve.

'Well, you did say you would call first thing in the morning.'

Tony laughed. 'I'm afraid what I have to tell you won't seem quite so funny. The man who is opposing you for chairman of Lester's Bank is Peter Parfitt.'

'*What?*' said William, suddenly awake.

'He's been trying to push the board into supporting him behind your back. Ted Leach, as I expected, is in favour of your appointment as chairman, but the board is now split down the middle.'

'Hell. First, thank you, Tony, and second, what do I do now?'

'If you want to be the next chairman of Lester's, you'd better get down here fast before the members of the board wonder why you're hiding away in Boston.'

'Hiding away?'

'That's what Parfitt has been telling the directors for the past few days.'

'The bastard.'

'Now that you mention the subject, I am unable to vouch for his parentage,' said Tony.

William laughed.

'Come and stay at the Yale Club. Then we can talk the whole thing out first thing in the morning.'

'I'll be there as quickly as I can,' said William.

'I may be asleep when you arrive. It'll be your turn to wake me.'

William put the phone down and looked over at Kate, blissfully oblivious to his new problems. She had slept right through the entire conversation. How he wished he could manage that. A curtain had only to flutter in the breeze, and he was awake. She would probably sleep right through the Second Coming. He scribbled a few lines of explanation to her and put the note on her bedside table, dressed, packed – this time including a dinner jacket – and set off for New York.

The roads were clear and the run in the new Daimler took him only five hours. He drove into New York with cleaners, mailmen, newsboys, and the morning sun, and checked in at the Yale Club as the hall clock chimed once. It was six-fifteen. He unpacked and decided to rest for an hour before waking Tony. The next thing he heard was an instant tapping on his door. Sleepily, he got up to open it only to find Tony Simmons standing outside.

'Nice dressing gown, William,' said Tony, grinning. He was fully dressed.

'I must have fallen asleep. If you wait a minute, I'll be right with you,' said William.

'No, no, I have to catch a train back to Boston. You take a shower and get yourself dressed while we talk.'

William went into the bathroom and left the door open.

'Now your main problem ...' started Tony.

William put his head around the bathroom door. 'I can't hear you while the water's running.'

Tony waited for it to stop. 'Peter Parfitt is your main problem. He assumed he was going to be the next chairman, and that his would be the name that was read out in Charles Lester's will. He's been manoeuvring the directors against you and playing board-room politics ever since. Ted Leach can fill you in on the finer details and would like you to join him for lunch today at the Metropolitan Club. He may bring two or three other board members with him on whom you can rely. The board, by the way, still seems to be split right down the middle.'

William nicked himself with his razor. 'Damn. Which club?'

'Metropolitan, just off Fifth Avenue on East Sixtieth Street.'

'Why there and not somewhere down in Wall Street?'

'William, when you're dealing with the Peter Parfitts of this world, you don't telegraph your intentions. Keep your wits about you, and play the whole thing very coolly. From what Leach tells me, I believe you can still win.'

William came back into the bedroom with a towel round his waist. 'I'll try,' he said, 'to be cool, that is.'

Tony smiled. 'Now, I must get back to Boston. My train leaves Grand Central in ten minutes.' He looked at his watch. 'Damn, six minutes.'

Tony paused at the bedroom door. 'You know, your father never trusted Peter Parfitt. Too smooth, he always used to say. Never anything more, just a little too smooth.' He picked up his suitcase. 'Good luck, William '

'How can I begin to thank you, Tony?'

'You can't. Just put it down to my trying to atone for the lousy way I treated Matthew.'

William watched the door close as he put in his collar stud and then straightened his tie, reflecting on how curious it was that he had spent years working closely with Tony Simmons without ever really getting to know him but that now, in only a few days of personal crisis, he found himself instantly liking and trusting a man he had never before really seen. He went down to the dining room and had a typical club breakfast: a cold boiled egg, one piece of hard toast, butter and English marmalade from someone else's table. The porter handed him a copy of the *Wall Street Journal*, which hinted on an inside page that everything was not running smoothly at Lester's following the nomination of William Kane as their next chairman. At least, the *Journal* did not seem to have any inside information.

William returned to his room and asked the operator for a number in Boston. He was kept waiting for a few minutes before he was put through.

'I do apologize, Mr Kane. I had no idea that you were on the line. May I congratulate you on your appointment as chairman of Lester's. I hope this means that our New York office will be seeing a lot more of you in the future.'

'That may well depend on you, Mr Cohen.'

'I don't think I quite understand,' the lawyer replied.

William explained what had happened over the past few days and read out the relevant section of Charles Lester's will.

Thomas Cohen spent some time taking down each word and then going over his notes carefully.

'Do you think his wishes would stand up in court?' asked William.

'Who knows? I can't think of a precedent for such a situation. A nineteenth-century Member of Parliament once bequeathed his constituency in a will, and no one objected, and the beneficiary went on to become Prime Minister. But that was over a hundred years ago – and in England. Now in this case, if the board decided to contest Mr Lester's will, and you took their decision to court, I wouldn't care to predict which way the judge might jump. Lord Melbourne didn't have to contend with a surrogate of New York County. Nevertheless, a nice legal conundrum, Mr Kane.'

'What do you advise?' said William.

'I am a Jew, Mr Kane. I came to this country on a ship from Germany at the turn of the century, and I have always had to fight hard for anything I've wanted. Do you want to be chairman of Lester's that badly?'

'Yes, Mr Cohen, I do.'

'Then you must listen to an old man who has, over the years, come to view you with great respect, and if I may say so, with some affection, and I'll tell you exactly what I'd do if I were faced with your predicament.'

.   .   .

An hour later William put the phone down, and having some time to kill, he strolled up Park Avenue. Along the way, he passed a site on which a huge building was well into construction. A large, neat billboard announced 'The next Baron Hotel will be in New York. When the Baron has been your host, you'll never want to stay anywhere else.' William smiled for the first time that morning and walked with a lighter step towards the Metropolitan Club.

Ted Leach, a short dapper man with dark brown hair and a lighter moustache, was standing in the foyer of the club, waiting for him. He ushered William into the bar. William admired the Renaissance style of the club, built by Otto Kuhn and Standford White in 1894. J. P. Morgan had founded the club when one of his closest friends was blackballed at the Union League.

'A fairly extravagant gesture even for a very close friend,' Ted Leach suggested, trying to make conversation. 'What will you have to drink, Mr Kane?'

'A dry sherry, please,' said William.

A boy in a smart blue uniform returned a few moments later with a dry sherry and a scotch and water; he hadn't needed to ask Mr Leach for his order.

'To the next chairman of Lester's,' said Ted Leach, raising his glass.

William hesitated.

'Don't drink, Mr Kane. As you know, you should never drink to yourself.'

William laughed, unsure how to reply.

A few minutes later two older men were walking towards them, both tall and confident in the bankers' uniform of grey three-piece suits, stiff collars and dark unpatterned ties. Had they been strolling down Wall Street,

William would not have given them a second glance. In the Metropolitan Club he studied them carefully.

'Mr Alfred Rodgers and Mr Winthrop Davies,' said Ted Leach as he introduced them.

William smiled reservedly, still unsure whose side anyone was on. The two newcomers were studying him equally carefully. No one spoke for a moment.

'Where do we start?' said the one called Rodgers, a monocle falling from his eye as he spoke.

'By going on up to lunch,' said Ted Leach.

The three of them turned around, obviously knowing exactly where they were going. William followed. The dining room on the second floor was vast, with another magnificent high ceiling. The *maître d'* placed them in the window seat, overlooking Central Park, where no one could overhear their conversation.

'Let's order and then talk,' said Ted Leach.

Through the window William could see the Plaza Hotel. Memories of his graduation celebration with the grandmothers and Matthew came flooding back to him – and there was something else he was trying to recall about that tea at the Plaza ...

'Mr Kane, let's put our cards on the table,' said Ted Leach. 'Charles Lester's decision to appoint you as chairman of the bank came as a surprise, not to put too fine a point on it. But if the board ignores his wishes, the bank could be plunged into chaos and that is an outcome none of us needs. He was a shrewd old man, and he will have had his reasons for wanting you as the bank's next chairman, and that's good enough for me.'

William had heard those words before – from Peter Parfitt.

'All three of us,' said Winthrop Davies, taking over, 'owe everything we have to Charles Lester, and we will carry out his wishes if it's the last thing we do as members of the board.'

'It may turn out to be just that,' said Ted Leach, 'if Peter Parfitt does succeed in becoming chairman.'

'I'm sorry, gentlemen,' said William, 'to have caused so much consternation. If my appointment as chairman came as a surprise to you, I can assure you it was nothing less than a bolt from the blue for me. I imagined I would receive some minor personal memento of Matthew's from Charles Lester's will, not the responsibility of running the entire bank.'

'We understand the position you've been placed in, Mr Kane,' said Ted Leach, 'and you must trust us when we say we are here to help you. We are aware that you will find that difficult to believe after the treatment that has been meted out to you by Peter Parfitt and the tactics he has been using behind your back to try and secure the chair for himself.'

'I have to believe you, Mr Leach, because I have no choice but to place myself in your hands and seek your advice as to how you view the current situation.'

'Thank you,' said Leach. 'That situation is clear to me. Peter Parfitt's campaign is well organized, and he now feels he is acting from a position of strength. We, therefore, Mr Kane, must be entirely open with each other if we are to have any chance of beating him. I am assuming, of course, that you have the stomach for such a fight.'

'I wouldn't be here if I didn't, Mr Leach. And now that you have put the position so succinctly, perhaps you will allow me to suggest how we should go about defeating Mr Parfitt.'

'Certainly,' said Ted Leach.

All three men listened intently.

'You are undoubtedly right in saying that Parfitt feels he is now in a strong position because to date he has always been the one on the attack, always knowing what is going to happen next. Might I suggest that the time has come for us to reverse that trend and take up the attack ourselves where and when he least expects it – in his own board room.'

'How do you propose we go about that, Mr Kane?' inquired Winthrop Davies, looking somewhat surprised.

'I'll tell you if you will first permit me to ask you some questions. How many full-time executive directors are there with a vote on the board?'

'Sixteen,' said Ted Leach instantly.

'And with whom does their allegiance lie at this moment?' William asked.

'Not the easiest question to answer, Mr Kane,' Winthrop Davies chipped in. He took a crumpled envelope from his inside pocket and studied the back of it before he continued. 'I think we can count on six sure votes, and Peter Parfitt can be certain of five. It came as a shock for me to discover this morning that Rupert Cork-Smith, who was Charles Lester's closest friend, is unwilling to support you, Mr Kane. Really strange, because I know he doesn't care for Parfitt. I think that may make the voting six apiece.'

'That gives us until Thursday,' added Ted Leach, 'to find out how the other four board members are likely to react to your appointment.'

'Why Thursday?' asked William.

'Day of the next board meeting,' answered Leach, stroking his moustache, which William had noticed he always did when he started to speak. 'And more important, Item One on the agenda is the election of a new chairman.'

'I was told the next meeting would not take place until Monday,' said William in astonishment.

'By whom?' Davies asked.

'Peter Parfitt,' said William.

'His tactics,' Ted Leach commented, 'have not been altogether those of a gentleman.'

'I've learned enough about that gentleman,' William said, placing an ironic stress on the words, 'to make me realize that I shall have to take the battle to him.'

'Easier said than done, Mr Kane. He is very much in the driver's seat at this moment,' said Winthrop Davies, 'and I'm not sure how we go about removing him from it.'

'Switch the traffic lights to red,' replied William. 'Who has the authority to call a board meeting?'

'While the board is without a chairman, either vice-chairman,' said Ted Leach. 'Which in reality means Peter Parfitt or myself.'

'How many board members form a quorum?'

'Nine,' said Davies.

'And if you are one of the two vice-chairmen, Mr Leach, who is the company secretary?'

'I am,' said Alfred Rodgers, who until then had hardly opened his mouth, the exact quality William always looked for in a company secretary.

'How much notice do you have to give to call an emergency board meeting, Mr Rodgers?'

'Every director must be informed at least twenty-four hours beforehand although that has never actually happened except during the crash of twenty-nine. Charles Lester always tried to give at least three days notice.'

'But the bank's rules do allow for an emergency meeting to be held on twenty-four hours notice?' asked William.

'They do, Mr Kane,' Alfred Rodgers affirmed, his monocle now firmly in place and focused on William.

'Excellent, then let's call our own board meeting.'

The three bankers stared at William as if they had not quite heard him clearly.

'Think about it, gentlemen,' William continued. 'Mr Leach, as vice-chairman, calls the board meeting and Mr Rodgers, as company secretary, informs all the directors.'

'When would you want this board meeting to take place?' asked Ted Leach.

'Tomorrow afternoon.' William looked at his watch. 'Three o'clock.'

'Good God, that's cutting it a bit fine,' said Alfred Rodgers. 'I'm not sure ...'

'Cutting it very fine for Peter Parfitt, wouldn't you say?' said William.

'That's true,' said Ted Leach, 'if you know precisely what you have planned for the meeting?'

'You leave the meeting to me. Just be sure that it's correctly convened and that every director is properly informed.'

'I wonder how Peter Parfitt is going to react,' said Ted Leach.

'Don't worry about Parfitt,' said William. 'That's the mistake we've made all along. Let him start to worry about us for a change. As long as he is given the full twenty-four hours notice and he's the last director informed, we have nothing to fear. We don't want him to have any more time than necessary to stage a counter-attack. And gentlemen, do not be surprised by anything I do or say tomorrow. Trust my judgement, and be there to support me.'

'You don't feel we ought to know exactly what you have in mind?'

'No, Mr Leach, you must appear at the meeting as disinterested directors doing no more than carrying out your duty.'

It was beginning to dawn on Ted Leach and his two colleagues why Charles Lester had chosen William Kane to be their next chairman. They left the Metropolitan Club a good deal more confident than when they had arrived, despite their being totally in the dark as to what would actually happen at the board meeting they were about to instigate. William, on the other hand, having carried out the first part of Thomas Cohen's instructions, was now looking forward to pulling off the harder second part.

He spent most of the afternoon and evening in his room at the Yale Club, meticulously considering his tactics for the next day's meeting and taking only a short break to call Kate.

'Where are you, darling?' she said. 'Stealing away in the middle of the night to I know not where.'

'To my mistress in New York,' said William.

'Poor girl,' said Kate. 'She probably doesn't know the half of it. What's her advice on the devious Mr Parfitt?'

'Haven't had time to ask her, we've been so busy doing other things. While I have you on the phone, what's your advice?'

'Do nothing Charles Lester or your father wouldn't have done in the same circumstances,' said Kate, suddenly serious.

'They're probably playing golf together on the eighteenth cloud and taking a side bet watching us the whole time.'

'Whatever you do, William, you won't go far wrong if you do remember they are watching you.'

.   .   .

When dawn broke, William was already awake, having only managed to sleep for short, fitful intervals. He rose a little after six, had a cold shower, went for a long walk through Central Park to clear his head, and returned to the Yale Club for a light breakfast. There was a message waiting for him in the front hall – from his wife. William laughed when he read it for a second time at the line, 'If you're not too busy could you remember to buy Richard a baseball glove.' William picked up the *Wall Street Journal* which was still running the story of trouble in the Lester's board room over the selection of a new chairman. It now had Peter Parfitt's version of the story, hinting that his appointment as chairman would probably be confirmed at Thursday's meeting. William wondered whose version would be reported in tomorrow's paper. Oh, for a look at tomorrow's *Journal* now. He spent the morning double checking the articles of incorporation and by-laws of Lester's Bank. He had no lunch but did find time to visit Schwalts and buy a baseball glove for his son.

At two-thirty William took a cab to the bank on Wall Street and arrived a few minutes before three. The young doorman asked him if he had an appointment to see anyone.

'I'm William Kane.'

'Yes, sir; you'll want the board room.'

Good God, thught William, I can't even remember where it is.

The doorman observed his embarrassment. 'You take the corridor on the left, sir, and then it's the second door on the right.'

'Thank you,' said William, and walked as confidently as he could down the corridor. He had always thought the expression a stomach full of butterflies a stupid one until that moment. He felt his heartbeat was louder than the clock in the front hall; he would not have been surprised to hear himself chiming three o'clock.

Ted Leach was standing alone at the entrance to the board room. 'There's going to be trouble,' were his opening words.

'Good,' said William. 'That's the way Charles Lester would have liked it, and he would have faced the trouble head on.'

William strode into the impressive oak-panelled room and did not need to count heads to be sure that every director was present. This was not going to be one of those board meetings a director could occasionally afford to skip. The conversation stopped the moment William entered the room, and there was an awkward silence as they all stood around and stared at him. William quickly took the chairman's seat at the head of the long mahogany table before Peter Parfitt could realize what was happening.

'Gentlemen, please be seated,' said William, hoping his voice sounded firm.

Ted Leach and some of the other directors took their seats immediately; others were more reluctant. Murmuring started.

William could see that two directors whom he didn't know were about to rise and interrupt him.

'Before anyone else says anything I would, if you will allow me, like to make an opening statement, and then you can decide how you wish to proceed from there. I feel that is the least we can do to comply with the wishes of the late Charles Lester.'

The two men sat down.

'Thank you, gentlemen. To start with, I would like to make it clear to all those present that I have absolutely no desire to be the chairman of this bank—' William paused for effect '— unless it be the wish of the majority of its directors.'

Every eye in the room was now fixed on William.

'I am, gentlemen, at present vice-chairman of Kane and Cabot, and I own fifty-one per cent of their stock. Kane and Cabot was founded by my grandfather, and I think it compares favourably in reputation, though not in size, with Lester's. Were I required to leave Boston and move to New York to become the next chairman of Lester's, in compliance with Charles Lester's wishes, I cannot pretend the move would be an easy one for myself or for my family. However, as it was Charles Lester's wish, that I should do just that – and he was not a man to make such a proposition lightly – I am, gentlemen, bound to take his wishes seriously myself. I would also like to add that his son, Matthew Lester, was my closest friend for over fifteen years, and I consider it a tragedy that it is I, and not he, who is addressing you today as your nominated chairman.'

Some of the directors were nodding their approval.

'Gentlemen, if I am fortunate enough to secure your support today, I will sacrifice everything I have in Boston in order to serve you. I hope it is unnecessary for me to give you a detailed account of my banking experience. I shall assume that any director present who has read Charles Lester's will must have taken the trouble to find out why he considered that I was the right man to succeed him. My own chairman, Anthony Simmons, whom many of you will know, has asked me to stay on at Kane and Cabot.

'I had intended to inform Mr Parfitt yesterday of my final decision, had he taken the trouble to call me and seek out that information. I had the pleasure of dining with Mr and Mrs Parfitt last Friday evening at their home, and on that occasion Mr Parfitt informed me that he had no interest in becoming the next chairman of this bank. My only rival, in his opinion, was Mr Edward Leach, your other vice-chairman. I have since consulted with Mr Leach himself, and he informs me that I have always had his support for the chair. I assumed, therefore, that both vice-chairmen were backing me. After reading the *Wall Street Journal* this morning, not that I have ever trusted their forecasting since the age of eight' – a little laughter – 'I felt I should attend today's meeting to assure myself that I had not lost the support of the two vice-chairmen, and that the *Journal*'s account was inaccurate. Mr Leach called this board meeting, and I must ask him at this juncture if he still supports me to succeed Charles Lester as the bank's next chairman.'

William looked towards Ted Leach, whose head was bowed. The wait for his verdict was palpable. A thumbs-down from him would mean the Parfittians could eat the Christian.

Ted Leach raised his head slowly and said, 'I support Mr Kane unreservedly.'

William looked directly at Peter Parfitt for the first time that day. He was sweating profusely, and when he spoke, he did not take his eyes off the yellow pad in front of him.

'Well, some members of the board,' he began, 'felt I should throw my hat in the ring ...'

'So you have changed your mind about supporting me and complying with Charles Lester's wishes?' interrupted William, allowing a small note of surprise to enter his voice.

Peter Parfitt raised his head a little. 'The problem is not quite that easy, Mr Kane.'

'Yes or no, Mr Parfitt?'

'Yes, I shall stand against you,' said Peter Parfitt suddenly, forcefully.

'Despite telling me last Friday you had no interest in being chairman yourself?'

'I would like to be able to state my own position,' said Parfitt, 'before you assume too much. This is not your board room yet, Mr Kane.'

'Certainly, Mr Parfitt.'

So far, the meeting had gone exactly as William had planned. His own speech had been carefully prepared and delivered, and Peter Parfitt now laboured under the disadvantage of having lost the initiative, to say nothing of having been publicly called a liar.

'Gentlemen,' he began, as if searching for words. 'Well,' he said.

The eyes had turned their gaze from William and now fixed on Parfitt. It gave William the chance to relax and study the faces of the other directors.

'Several members of the board approached me privately after I had dinner with Mr Kane, and I felt that it was no more than my duty to consider their wishes and offer myself for election. I have never at any time wanted to oppose the wishes of Mr Charles Lester, whom I always admired and respected. Naturally, I would have informed Mr Kane of my intention before tomorrow's scheduled board meeting, but I confess to have been taken somewhat by surprise by today's events.'

He drew a deep breath and started again. 'I have served Lester's for twenty-two years, six of them as your vice-chairman. I feel, therefore, that I have the right to be considered for the chair. I would be delighted if Mr Kane were to join the board, but I now find myself unable to back his appointment as chairman. I hope my fellow-directors will find it possible to support someone who has worked for this bank for over twenty years rather than elect an unknown outsider on the whim of a man distraught by the death of his only son. Thank you, gentlemen.'

He sat down.

In the circumstances, William was rather impressed by the speech, but Parfitt did not have the benefit of Mr Cohen's advice on the power of the last word in a close contest. William rose again.

'Gentlemen, Mr Parfitt has pointed out that I am personally unknown to you. I, therefore, want none of you to be in any doubt as to the type of man I am. I am, as I said, the grandson and the son of bankers. I've been a banker all my life and it would be less than honest of me to pretend I would not be delighted to serve as the next chairman of Lester's. If, on the other hand, after all you have heard today, you decide to back Mr Parfitt as chairman, so be it. I shall return to Boston and serve my own bank quite happily. I will, moreover, announce publicly that I have no wish to be the chairman of Lester's, and that will insure you against any claims that you have been derelict in fulfilling the provisions of Charles Lester's will.

'There are, however, no conditions on which I would be willing to serve on your board under Mr Parfitt. I have no intention of being less than frank with you on that point. I come before you, gentlemen, at the grave disadvantage of being, in Mr Parfitt's words, "an unknown outsider". I have however, the advantage of being supported by a man who cannot be present today. A man whom all of you respected and admired, a man not known for yielding to whims or making hasty decisions. I therefore suggest this board wastes no more of its valuable time in deciding whom they wish to serve as the next chairman of Lester's. If any of you have any doubts in your mind about my ability to run this bank, then I can only suggest you vote for Mr Parfitt. I shall not vote in this election myself, gentlemen, and I assume Mr Parfitt will not do so either.'

'You *cannot* vote,' said Peter Parfitt, angrily. 'You are not a member of this board yet. I am, and I shall vote.'

'So be it, Mr Parfitt. No one will ever be able to say you did not have the opportunity to gain every possible vote.'

William waited for the effect of his words to sink in, and as a director who was a stranger to William was about to interrupt, he continued, 'I will ask Mr Rodgers as company secretary to carry out the electoral procedure, and when you have completed your vote, gentlemen, perhaps you could pass the ballot papers back to him.'

Alfred Rodgers' monocle had been popping out periodically during the entire meeting. Nervously, he passed voting slips around to each director. When each had written down the name of the candidate whom he supported, the slips were returned to him.

'Perhaps it might be prudent under the circumstances, Mr Rodgers, if the votes were counted aloud, thus making sure no inadvertent error is made that might lead the directors to require a second ballot.'

'Certainly, Mr Kane.'

'Does that meet with your approval, Mr Parfitt?'

Peter Parfitt nodded his agreement without looking up.

'Thank you. Perhaps you would be kind enough to read the votes out to the board, Mr Rodgers.'

The company secretary opened the first voting slip.

'Parfitt.'

And then the second.

'Parfitt,' he repeated.

The game was now out of William's hands. All the years of waiting for the prize he had told Charles Lester so long ago would be his would be over in the next few seconds.

'Kane. Parfitt. Kane.'

Three votes to two against him; was he going to meet the same fate as he had in his contest with Tony Simmons?

'Kane. Kane. Parfitt.'

Four votes all. He could see that Parfitt was sweating profusely at the other side of the table and he didn't exactly feel relaxed himself.

'Parfitt.'

No expression crossed William's face. Parfitt allowed himself a smile.

Five votes to four.

'Kane. Kane. Kane.'

The smile disappeared.

Just two more, two more, pleaded William, nearly out loud.

'Parfitt. Parfitt.'

The company secretary took a long time opening a voting slip which someone had folded and refolded several times.

'Kane.' Eight votes to seven in William's favour.

The last piece of paper was now being opened. William watched Alfred Rodgers' lips. The company secretary looked up; for that one moment he was the most important man in the room.

'Kane.' Parfitt's head sank into his hands.

'Gentlemen, the tally is nine votes for Mr William Kane, seven votes for Mr Peter Parfitt. I therefore declare Mr William Kane to be the duly elected chairman of Lester's Bank.'

A respectful silence fell over the room and every head except Peter Parfitt's turned towards William and waited for the new chairman's first move.

William exhaled a great rush of air and stood once again, this time to face his board.

'Thank you, gentlemen, for the confidence you have placed in me. It was Charles Lester's wish that I should be your next chairman and I am delighted you have confirmed that wish with your vote. I now intend to serve this bank to the best of my ability, which I shall be unable to do without the wholehearted support of the board. If Mr Parfitt would be kind enough ...'

Peter Parfitt looked up hopefully.

'... to join me in the chairman's office in a few minutes time, I would be much obliged. After I have seen Mr Parfitt, I would like to see Mr Leach. I hope, gentlemen, that tomorrow I shall have the opportunity of meeting all of you individually. The next board meeting will be the monthly one. This meeting is now adjourned.'

The directors began to rise and talk among themselves. William walked quickly into the corridor, avoiding Peter Parfitt's stare. Ted Leach caught up with him and directed him to the chairman's office.

'That was a great risk you took,' said Ted Leach, 'and you only just pulled it off. What would you have done if you'd lost the vote?'

'Gone back to Boston,' said William, sounding unperturbed.

Ted Leach opened the door to the chairman's office for William. The room was almost exactly as he remembered it; perhaps it had seemed a little larger when, as a prep-school boy, he had told Charles Lester that he would one day run the bank. He stared at the portrait of the great man behind his desk and winked at the late chairman. Then he sat down in the big red leather chair, and put his elbows on the mahogany desk. As he took a small, leather-bound book out of his jacket pocket and placed it on the desk in front of him, there was a knock on the door. An old man entered, leaning heavily on a black stick with a silver handle. Ted Leach left them alone.

'My name is Rupert Cork-Smith,' he said, with a hint of an English accent.

William rose to greet him. He was the oldest member of the board. His grey hair, long sideburns and heavy gold watch all came from a past era, but his reputation for probity was legendary in banking circles. No man needed to sign a contract with Rupert Cork-Smith: his word had always been his bond. He looked William firmly in the eye.

'I voted against you, sir, and naturally you can expect my resignation to be on your desk within the hour.'

'Will you have a seat, sir?' said William gently.

'Thank you, sir,' he replied.

'I think you knew my father and grandfather.'

'I had that privilege. Your grandfather and I were at Harvard together, and I still remember with regret your father's tragic death.'

'And Charles Lester?' said William.

'Was my closest friend. The provisions in his will have preyed upon my conscience. It was no secret that my choice would not have been Peter Parfitt. I would have had Ted Leach for chairman, but as I have never abstained from anything in my life, I felt I had to support the candidate who stood against you, as I found myself unable to vote for a man I had never even met.'

'I admire your honesty, Mr Cork-Smith, but now I have a bank to run. I need you at this moment far more than you need me so I, as a younger man, beg you not to resign.'

The old man raised his head and stared into William's eyes. 'I'm not sure it would work, young man. I can't change my attitudes overnight,' said Cork-Smith, both hands resting on his stick.

'Give me six months, sir, and if you still feel the same way I won't put up a fight.'

They both sat in silence before Cork-Smith spoke again. 'Charles Lester was right: you are the son of Richard Kane.'

'Will you continue to serve this bank, sir?'

'I will, young man. There's no fool like an old fool, don't you know.'

Rupert Cork-Smith rose slowly with the aid of his stick. William moved to help him but was waved away.

'Good luck, my boy. You can rely on my total support.'

'Thank you, sir,' said William.

When he opened the door, William saw Peter Parfitt waiting in the corridor. As Rupert Cork-Smith left, the two men did not speak.

Peter Parfitt blustered in. 'Well, I tried and I lost. A man can't do more,' he said laughing. 'No hard feelings, Bill?' He extended his hand.

'There are no hard feelings, Mr Parfitt. As you so rightly say, you tried and you lost, and now you will resign from your post at this bank.'

'I'll do what?' said Parfitt.

'Resign,' said William.

'That's a bit rough, isn't it, Bill? My action wasn't at all personal, I simply felt ...'

'I don't want you in my bank, Mr Parfitt. You'll leave by tonight and never return.'

'And if I say I won't go? I own a good many shares in the bank, and I still have a lot of support on the board, you know, and what's more I could take you to court.'

'Then I would recommend that you read the bank's by-laws, Mr Parfitt, which I spent some considerable time studying only this morning.'

William picked up the small, leather-bound book which was still lying on the desk in front of him and turned a few pages over. Having found a paragraph he had marked that morning, he read aloud: 'The chairman has the right to remove any office holder in whom he has lost confidence.' He looked up. 'I have lost confidence in you, Mr Parfitt, and you will therefore resign, receiving two years' pay. If, on the other hand, you force me to remove you, I shall see that you leave the bank with nothing other than your stock. The choice is yours.'

'Won't you give me a chance?'

'I gave you a chance last Friday night, and you lied and cheated. Not traits I am looking for in my next vice-chairman. Will it be resignation or do I throw you out, Mr Parfitt?'

'Damn you, Kane, I'll resign.'

'Good. Sit down and write the letter now.'

'No, I'll let you have it in the morning in my own good time.' He started walking towards the door.

'Now – or I fire you,' said William.

Peter Parfitt hesitated and then came back and sank heavily into a chair by the side of William's desk. William handed him a piece of the bank's stationery and proffered him a pen. Parfitt took out his own pen and started writing. When he had finished, William picked up the letter and read it through carefully.

'Good day, Mr Parfitt.'

Peter Parfitt left without speaking. Ted Leach came in a few moments later.

'You wanted to see me, Mr Chairman?'

'Yes,' said William. 'I want to appoint you as the bank's overall vice-chairman. Mr Parfitt felt he had to resign.'

'Oh, I'm surprised to hear that, I would have thought ...'

William passed him the letter. Ted Leach read it and then looked at William.

'I shall be delighted to be overall vice-chairman. Thank you for your confidence in me.'

'Good. I will be obliged if you will arrange for me to meet every director during the next two days. I shall start work at eight o'clock tomorrow morning.'

'Yes, Mr Kane.'

'Perhaps you will also be kind enough to give Mr Parfitt's letter of resignation to the company secretary?'

'As you wish, Mr Chairman.'

'My name is William, another mistake Mr Parfitt made.'

'Ted Leach smiled tentatively. 'I'll see you tomorrow morning –' he hesitated '– William.'

When he had left, William sat in Charles Lester's chair and whirled himself around in an uncharacteristic burst of sheer glee till he was dizzy. Then he looked out of the window onto Wall Street, elated by the bustling crowds, enjoying the view of the other great banks and brokerage houses of America. He was part of all that now.

'And who, pray, are you?' said a female voice from behind him.

William swivelled round, and there standing in front of him was a middle-aged woman, primly dressed, looking very irate.

'Perhaps I may ask you the same question,' said William.

'I am the chairman's secretary,' said the woman stiffly.

'And I,' said William, 'am the chairman.'

. . .

During the next few weeks William moved his family to New York where they found a house on East Sixty-eighth Street. Settling in took longer than they had originally anticipated possible. For the first three months William wished, as he tried to extricate himself from Boston in order to carry out his job in New York, that every day had forty-eight hours in it, and he found the umbilical cord was hard to sever completely. Tony Simmons was most helpful, and William began to appreciate why Alan Lloyd had backed him to be chairman of Kane and Cabot, and for the first time was willing to admit Alan had been right.

Kate's life in New York was soon fully occupied. Virginia could already crawl across a room and get into William's study before Kate could turn her head, and Richard wanted a new windbreaker, like every other boy in New York. As the wife of the chairman of a New York bank she regularly had to give cocktail parties and dinners, subtly making sure certain directors and major clients were always given the chance to catch the private ear of William to seek his advice or voice their own opinions. Kate handled all situations with great charm, and William was eternally grateful to the liquidation department of Kane and Cabot for supplying his greatest asset. When she informed William that she was going to have another baby, all he could ask was 'When did I find the time?' Virginia was thrilled by the news, not fully understanding why Mummy was getting so fat, and Richard refused to discuss it.

Within six months the clash with Peter Parfitt was a thing of the past, and William had become the undisputed chairman of Lester's bank and a figure to be reckoned with in New York financial circles. Not many more months had passed before he began to wonder in which direction he should start to set himself a new goal. He had achieved his life's ambition by becoming chairman of Lester's at the age of thirty-three although, unlike Alexander, he felt there were more worlds still to conquer, and he had neither the time nor the inclination to sit down and weep.

Kate gave birth to their third child at the end of William's first year as chairman of Lester's, a second girl, whom they named Lucy. William taught Virginia, who was now walking, how to rock Lucy's cradle; while Richard, now almost five years old and due to enter kindergarten at The Buckley School, used the new arrival as the opportunity to talk his father into a new baseball bat.

In William's first year as chairman of Lester's the bank's profits were slightly up and he was forecasting a considerable improvement in his second year.

Then on 1 September 1939 Hitler marched into Poland.

One of William's first reactions was to think of Abel Rosnovski and his new Baron on Park Avenue, already becoming the toast of New York. Quarterly reports from Thomas Cohen showed that Rosnovski went from strength to strength although his latest ideas for expansion to Europe looked as if they might be in for a slight delay. Cohen continued to find no direct association between Henry Osborne and Abel Rosnovski, but he admitted that it was becoming increasingly difficult to ascertain all the facts he required.

William never thought that America would involve herself in a European war, but nevertheless he kept the London branch of Lester's open to show clearly which side he was on and not for one moment did he consider selling his twelve thousand acres in Hampshire and Lincolnshire. Tony Simmons in Boston, on the other hand, informed William that he intended to close Kane and Cabot's London branch. William used the problems created in London by the war as an excuse to visit his beloved Boston and have a meeting with Tony.

The two chairmen now met on extremely easy and friendly terms since they no longer had any reason to see themselves as rivals. In fact, each had come to use the other as a springboard for new ideas. As Tony had predicted, Kane and Cabot had lost some of its more important clients when William became the chairman of Lester's, but William always kept Tony fully informed whenever an old client expressed a desire to move his account and he never solicited a single one. When they sat down at the corner table of Locke-Ober's for lunch, Tony Simmons lost little time in repeating his intent to close the London branch of Kane and Cabot.

'My first reason is simple,' he said as he sipped the imported burgundy, apparently not giving a moment's thought to the strong likelihood that German boots were about to trample on the grapes in most of the vineyards in France. 'I think the bank will lose money if we don't cut our losses and get out of England.'

'Of course, you will lose a little money,' said William, 'but we must support the British.'

'Why?' asked Tony. 'We're a bank, not a supporter's club.'

'Britain's not a baseball team, Tony; it's a nation of people to whom we owe our entire heritage ...'

'You should take up politics,' said Tony. 'I'm beginning to think your talents are wasted in banking. Nevertheless, I feel there's a far more important reason why we should close the branch. If Hitler marches into Britain the way he has into Poland and France – and I'm sure that is exactly what he intends to do – the bank will be taken over, and we would lose every penny we have in London.'

'Over my dead body,' said William. 'If Hitler puts so much as a foot on British soil, America will enter the war the same day.'

'Never,' said Tony. 'FDR has said, "all aid short of war". And the America Firsters would raise an almighty hue and cry.'

'Never listen to a politician,' said William. 'Especially Roosevelt. When he says "never", that only means not today, or at least not this morning. You only have to remember what Wilson told us in 1916.'

Tony laughed. 'When are you going to run for the Senate, William?'

'Now there is a question to which I can safely answer never.'

'I respect your feelings, William, but I want out.'

'You're the chairman,' replied William. 'If the board backs you, you can close the London branch tomorrow, and I would never use my position to act against a majority decision.'

'Until you join the two banks together, and it becomes your decision.'

'I told you once, Tony, that I would never attempt to do that while you were chairman. It's a promise I intend to honour.'

'But I think we *ought* to merge.'

'What?' said William, spilling his burgundy on the tablecloth, unable to believe what he had just heard. 'Good heavens, Tony, I'll say one thing for you, you're never predictable.'

'I have the best interests of the bank at heart, as always, William. Think about the present situation for a moment. New York is now, more than ever, the centre of US finance, and when England goes under to Hitler, it will be the centre of world finance, so that's where Kane and Cabot needs to be. Moreover, if we merged, we would create a more comprehensive institution because our specialities are complementary. Kane and Cabot has always done a great deal of ship and heavy industry financing while Lester's does very little. Conversely, you do a lot of underwriting, and we hardly touch it. Not to mention the fact that in many cities we have unnecessary duplicating offices.'

'Tony, I agree with everything you've said, but I would still want to stay in Britain.'

'Exactly proving my point, William. Kane and Cabot's London branch would be closed, but we would still keep Lester's. Then, if London goes through a rough passage, it won't matter as much because we would be consolidated and therefore stronger.'

'But how would you feel if I said that while Roosevelt's restrictions on merchant banks will only allow us to work out of one state, a merger could succeed only if we ran the entire operation from New York treating Boston as nothing more than a holding office?'

'I'd back you,' said Tony and added, 'You might even consider going into commercial banking and dropping the straight investment work.'

'No, Tony. FDR has made it impossible for an honest man to do both, and in any case my father believed that you could either serve a small group of rich people or a large group of poor people so Lester's will always remain in traditional merchant banking as long as I'm chairman. But if we did decide to merge the two banks don't you foresee major problems?'

'Very few we couldn't surmount given goodwill on both sides. However, you will have to consider the implications carefully, William, as you would undoubtedly lose overall control of the new bank as a minority shareholder which would always make you vulnerable to a takeover bid.'

'I'd risk that to be chairman of one of the largest financial institutions in America.'

William returned to New York that evening, elated by his discussion and called a board meeting of Lester's to outline Tony Simmons' proposal. When he found that the board approved of a merger in principle, he instructed each manager in the bank to consider the whole plan in greater detail.

The departmental heads took three months before they reported back to the board, and to a man they came to the same conclusion: a merger was no more than common sense, as the two banks were complementary in so many ways. With different offices all over America and branches in Europe, they had a great deal to offer each other. Moreover, the chairman of Lester's had continued to own fifty-one per cent of Kane and Cabot, making the merger simply a marriage of convenience. Some of the directors on Lester's board could not understand why William hadn't thought of the idea before. Ted Leach was of the opinion that Charles Lester must have had it in his mind when he nominated William as his successor.

The details of the merger took nearly a year to negotiate and lawyers were kept at work into the small hours to complete the necessary paper work. In the exchange of shares, William ended up as the largest stockholder with eight per cent of the new company and was appointed the new bank's president and chairman. Tony Simmons remained in Boston as one vice-chairman and Ted Leach in New York as the other. The new merchant bank was renamed Lester, Kane and Company, but was still to be referred to as Lester's.

William decided to hold a press conference in New York to announce the successful merger of the two banks and he chose Monday, 8 December 1941 to inform the financial business world at large. The press conference had to be cancelled, because the morning before the Japanese had launched an attack on Pearl Harbor.

The prepared press release had already been mailed to the newspapers some days before, but the Tuesday morning financial pages understandably allocated the announcement of the merger only a small amount of space. This lack of coverage was no longer foremost in William's mind.

He couldn't quite work out how or when he was going to tell Kate that he intended to enlist. When Kate heard the news she was horrified and immediately tried to talk him out of the decision.

'What do you imagine you can do that a million others can't?' she demanded.

'I'm not sure,' William replied, 'But all I can be certain of is that I must do what my father or grandfather would have done given the same circumstances.'

'They would have undoubtedly done what was in the best interest of the bank.'

'No,' replied William quickly. 'They would have done what was in the best interest of America.'

BOOK FOUR

24

Abel studied the news items on Lester, Kane and Company in the financial section of the *Chicago Tribune*. With all the space devoted to the implications of the Japanese attack on Pearl Harbor, he would have missed the brief article had it not been accompanied by a small out-of-date photograph of William Kane, so out-of-date that Kane looked much as he had when Abel had visited him in Boston over ten years before. Certainly Kane appeared too young in that photograph to live up to the journal's description of him as the brilliant chairman of the newly formed Lester, Kane and Company. The article went on to predict: 'The new bank, a joining of Lester's of New York and Kane and Cabot of Boston, could well become one of the most important financial institutions in America after Mr Kane's decision to merge the two distinguished family banks. As far as the *Trib* could ascertain the shares would be in the hands of about twenty people related to, or closely associated with the two families.'

Abel was delighted by that particular piece of information, realizing that Kane must have lost overall control. He read the news item again. William Kane had obviously risen in the world since they had crossed swords, but then so had he, and he still had an old score to settle with the newly appointed chairman of Lester's.

So handsomely had the Baron Group's fortunes prospered over the decade that Abel had paid back all the loans to his backer and honoured to the letter the original agreement with his backer and had secured one hundred per cent ownership of the company within the required ten-year period.

By the last quarter of 1939, not only had Abel paid off the loan, but the profits for 1940 passed the half million mark. This milestone coincided with the opening of two new Barons, one in Washington, the other in San Francisco.

Though Abel had become a less devoted husband during this period, he could not have been a more doting father. Zaphia, longing for a second child, finally goaded him into seeing his doctor. When he learned that, because of a low sperm count, probably caused by sickness and malnutrition in his days under the Germans and Russians, Florentyna would almost certainly be his only child, he gave up all hope for a son and proceeded to lavish everything on her.

Abel's fame was now spreading across America and even the press had taken to referring to him as 'The Chicago Baron'. He no longer cared about the jokes behind his back. Wladek Koskiewicz had arrived and, more importantly, he was here to stay. By 1941 the profits from his thirteen hotels were just short of one million and, with his new surplus of capital, he decided the time had come for even further expansion.

Then the Japanese attacked Pearl Harbor.

Abel had already been sending considerable sums of money to the British Red Cross for the relief of his countrymen since that dreadful day in September 1939 on which the Nazis had marched into Poland, later to meet the Russians at Brest Litovsk and once again divide his homeland between them. He had waged a fierce battle, both within the Democratic Party and in the press, to push an unwilling America into the war even if now it had to be on the side of the Russians. His efforts so far had been fruitless, but on that December Sunday, with every radio station across the country blaring out the details to an incredulous naton, Abel knew that America must now be committed to the war. On 11 December he listened to President Roosevelt tell the nation that Germany and Italy had officially declared war on the United States. Abel had every intention of joining in, but first he had a private declaration of war he wished to make, and to that end he placed a call to Curtis Fenton at the Continental Trust Bank. Over the years Abel had grown to trust Fenton's judgement and had kept him on the board of the Baron Group when he gained overall control in order to keep a close link between the group and Continental Trust.

Curtis Fenton came on the line, his usual formal and always polite self.

'How much spare cash am I holding in the group's reserve account?' asked Abel.

Curtis Fenton picked out the file marked 'Number 6 Account', remembering the days when he could put all Mr Rosnovski's affairs into one file. He scanned some figures.

'A little under two million dollars,' he said.

'Good,' said Abel. 'I want you to look into a newly formed bank called Lester, Kane and Company. Find out the name of every shareholder, what percentage they control and if there are any conditions under which they would be willing to sell. All this must be done without the knowledge of the bank's chairman, Mr William Kane and without my name ever being mentioned.'

Curtis Fenton held his breath and said nothing. He was glad that Abel Rosnovski could not see his surprised face. Why did Abel Rosnovski want to put money into anything to do with William Kane? Fenton had also read in the *Wall Street Journal* about the merging of the two famous family banks. What with Pearl Harbor and his wife's headache, he too had nearly missed the item. Rosnovski's request jogged his memory – he must send a congratulatory wire to William Kane. He pencilled a note on the bottom of the Baron Group file while listening to Abel's instructions.

'When you have a full rundown I want to be briefed in person, nothing on paper.'

'Yes, Mr Rosnovski.'

I suppose someone knows what's going on between those two, Curtis Fenton added silently to himself, but I'm damned if I do.

Abel continued. 'I'd also like to know in your quarterly reports the details of every official statement issued by Lester's and which companies they are involved with.'

'Certainly, Mr Rosnovski.'

'Thank you, Mr Fenton. By the way, my market research team is advising me to open a new Baron in Montreal.'

'The war doesn't worry you, Mr Rosnovski?'

'Good God, no. If the Germans reach Montreal we can all close down, Continental Trust included. In any case, we beat the bastards last time, and we'll beat them again. The only difference is that this time I'll be able to join the action. Good day, Mr Fenton.'

Will I ever understand what goes on in the mind of Abel Rosnovski, Curtis Fenton wondered, as he hung up the phone. His thoughts switched back to Abel's other request, for the details of Lester's shares. That worried him even more. Although William Kane no longer had any connection with Rosnovski, he feared where this might all end if his client obtained a substantial holding in Lester's. He decided against giving his views to Rosnovski for the time being, supposing the day would come when one of them would explain what they were both up to.

Abel also wondered if he should tell Curtis Fenton why he wanted to buy stock in Lester's but came to the conclusion that the fewer the number of people who knew of his plan, the better.

He put William Kane temporarily out of his mind and asked his secretary to find George, who was now a vice-president of the Baron Group. He had grown along with Abel and was now his most trusted lieutenant. Sitting in his office on the forty-second floor of the Chicago Baron, Abel looked down at Lake Michigan, on what was known as the Gold Coast, but his own thoughts returned to Poland. He wondered if he would ever live to see his castle again, now well inside the Russian borders under Stalin's control. Abel knew he would never settle in Poland, but he still wanted his castle restored to him. The idea of the Germans or Russians occupying his magnificent home once again made him want to ... His thoughts were interrupted by George.

'You wanted to see me, Abel?'

George was the only member of the group who still called the Chicago Baron by his first name.

'Yes, George. Do you think you could keep the hotels ticking along for a few months if I were to take a leave of absence?'

'Sure I can,' said George. 'Why, are you finally going to take that vacation you promised yourself?'

'No,' replied Abel. 'I'm going to war.'

'What?' said George. 'What?' he repeated.

'I'm going to New York tomorrow morning to enlist in the army.'

'You're crazy, you could get yourself killed.'

'That isn't what I had in mind,' replied Abel. 'Killing some Germans is what I plan to do. The bastards didn't get me the first time around and I have no intention of letting them get me now.'

George continued to protest that America could win the war without Abel. Zaphia protested too; she hated the very thought of war and little Florentyna, just turned eight years old, burst into tears. She did not quite know what war meant, but she did understand that Daddy would have to go away for a very long time.

. . .

Despite their protests, Abel took his first plane flight to New York the next day. All of America seemed to be going in different directions and he found the city full of young men in khaki saying their farewells to parents, sweet-hearts and wives, all assuring each other that the war would be over in a few weeks but none of them believing it.

Abel arrived at the New York Baron in time for dinner. The dining room was packed with young people, girls clinging desperately to soldiers, sailors and airmen, while Frank Sinatra crooned to the rhythms of Tommy Dorsey's big band. As Abel watched the young people on the dance floor, he wondered how many of them would ever have a chance to enjoy an evening like this again. He couldn't help remembering Sammy explaining how he had become *maître d'* at the Plaza. The three men senior to him had returned from the Western Front with one leg between them. None of the young people dancing could begin to know what war was really like. He didn't join in the celebration – if that's what it was. He went to his room instead.

In the morning, he dressed in a plain dark suit and went down to the recruiting office in Times Square. He had chosen to enlist in New York because he feared someone might recognize him in Chicago and all he could hope to end up with would be a swivel chair. The office was even more crowded than the dance floor had been the night before, but here no one was clinging onto anyone else. Abel hung around the entire morning in order to fill out one form that would have taken him three minutes in his own office. He couldn't help noticing that all the other recruits looked fitter than he. He then stood in line for two more hours waiting to be interviewed by a recruiting sergeant who asked him what he did for a living.

'Hotel management,' said Abel, and went on to tell the officer of his experiences in the first war. The sergeant stared silently at the five foot seven, one hundred and ninety pound man with an expression of incredulity. If Abel had told him he was the Chicago Baron, the officer would not have doubted his stories of imprisonment and escape, but he chose to keep this information to himself and be treated like any of his fellow countrymen.

'You'll have to take a full physical tomorrow morning,' was all the recruiting sergeant said at the end of Abel's monologue, adding, as though he felt the comment was no less than his duty, 'Thank you for volunteering.'

The next day Abel had to wait several more hours for his physical examination. The doctor in charge was fairly blunt about Abel's general condition. He had been protected from such comments for several years by his position and success. It came as a rude awakening when the doctor classified him 4F.

'You're overweight, your eyes are not too good, your heart is weak, and you limp. Frankly, Rosnovski, you're plain unfit. We can't take soldiers into battle who are likely to have a heart attack even before they find the enemy. That doesn't mean we can't use your talents; there's a lot of paperwork to be done in this war if you are interested.'

Abel wanted to hit him, but he knew that wouldn't help get him into uniform.

'No, thank you … sir,' he said. 'I want to fight the Germans, not send letters to them.'

He returned to the hotel that evening despondent, but Abel decided that he wasn't licked yet. The next day he tried again, going to another recruiting office, but he came back to the Baron with the same result. Admittedly, the second doctor had been a little more polite, but he was every bit as firm about his condition, and once again Abel had ended up with a 4F. It was obvious to Abel that he was not going to be allowed to fight anybody in his present state of health.

The next morning, he found a gymnasium on West Fifty-seventh Street and paid a private instructor to do something about his physical condition. For three months he worked every day on his weight and general fitness. He boxed, wrestled, ran, jumped, skipped, pressed weights and starved. When he was down to one hundred and fifty-five pounds, the instructor assured him he was never going to be much fitter or thinner. Abel returned to the first recruiting office and filled in the same form under the name of Wladek Koskiewicz. Another recruiting sergeant was a lot more hopeful this time, and the medical officer who gave him several tests finally accepted him as a reserve, waiting to be called up.

'But I want to go to war now,' said Abel. 'I want to fight the bastards.'

'We'll be in touch with you, Mr Koskiewicz,' said the sergeant. 'Please keep yourself fit and prepared. You can never be sure when we will need you.'

Abel left, furious as he watched younger, leaner Americans being readily accepted for active service, and as he barged through the door, not sure what his next ploy should be, he walked straight into a tall, gangling man wearing a uniform adorned with stars on the shoulders.

'I'm sorry, sir,' said Abel, looking up and backing away.

'Young man,' said the general.

Abel walked on, not thinking that the officer was addressing him, as no one had called him young man for . . . he didn't want to think for how long, despite the fact that he was still only thirty-five.

The general tried again. 'Young man,' he said a little more loudly.

This time Abel turned around. 'Me, sir?' he asked.

'Yes, you, sir.'

Abel walked over to the general.

'Will you come to my office please, Mr Rosnovski?'

Damn, thought Abel, this man knows who I am, and now nobody's going to let me fight in this war. The general's temporary office turned out to be at the back of the building, a small room with a desk, two wooden chairs, peeling green paint and an open door. Abel would not have allowed a junior member of his staff at a Baron to work in such surroundings.

'Mr Rosnovski,' the general began, exuding energy, 'my name is Mark Clark and I command the US Fifth Army. I'm over from Governors Island for the day on an inspection tour, so literally bumping into you is a pleasant surprise. I have for a long time been an admirer. Your story is one to gladden the heart of any American. Now tell me what you are doing in this recruiting office.'

'What do you think?' said Abel, not thinking. 'I'm sorry, sir,' he corrected himself quickly. 'I didn't mean to be rude, it's only that no one will let me get into this damn war.'

'What do you want to do in this damn war?' asked the general.

'Sign up,' said Abel, 'and fight the Germans.'

'As a foot soldier?' inquired the incredulous general.

'Yes,' said Abel, 'don't you need every man you can get?'

'Naturally,' said the general, 'but I can put your particular talents to a far better use than as a foot soldier.'

'I'll do anything,' said Abel, 'anything.'

'Will you now?' said the general, 'and if I asked you to place your New York hotel at my disposal as army headquarters here, how would you react to that? Because frankly, Mr Rosnovski, that would be of far more use to me than if you managed to kill a dozen Germans personally.'

'The Baron is yours,' said Abel. 'Now will you let me go to war?'

'You know you're mad, don't you?' said General Clark.

'I'm Polish,' said Abel. They both laughed. 'You must understand,' he continued in a more serious tone. 'I was born near Slonim. I saw my home taken over by the Germans, my sister raped by the Russians. I later escaped from a Russian labour camp and was lucky enough to reach America. I'm not mad. This is the only country in the world where you can arrive with nothing and become a millionaire through damned hard work regardless of your background. Now those same bastards want another war. I'm not mad, General. I'm human.'

'Well, if you're so eager to join up, Mr Rosnovski, I could use you, but not in the way you imagine. General Denvers needs someone to take over responsibility as quartermaster for the Fifth Army while they are fighting in the front lines. If you believe Napoleon was right when he said an army marches on its stomach, you could play a vital role. The job carries the rank of major. That is one way in which you could unquestionably help America to win this war. What do you say?'

'I'll do it, General.'

'Thank you, Mr Rosnovski.'

The general pressed a buzzer on his desk and a very young lieutenant came in and saluted smartly.

'Lieutenant, will you take Major Rosnovski to personnel and then bring him back to me?'

'Yes, sir.' The lieutenant turned to Abel. 'Will you come this way, please, Major?'

Abel followed him, turning as he reached the door. 'Thank you, General,' he said.

· · ·

He spent the weekend in Chicago with Zaphia and Florentyna. Zaphia asked him what he wanted her to do with his fifteen suits.

'Hold onto them,' he replied, wondering what she meant. 'I'm not going to get myself killed in this war.'

'I'm sure you're not, Abel,' she replied. 'That wasn't what was worrying me. It's just that now they're all three sizes too large for you.'

Abel laughed and took the suits to the Polish refugee centre. He then returned to New York, went to the Baron, cancelled the advance guest list, and twelve days later handed the building over to the American Fifth Army. The press hailed Abel's decision as a 'selfless gesture', worthy of a man who had been a refugee of the First World War.

It was another three months before Abel was called to active duty, during which time he organized the smooth running of the New York Baron for General Clark and then reported to Fort Benning, to complete an officers' training programme. When he finally did receive his orders to join General Denvers and the Fifth Army, his destination turned out to be somewhere in North Africa. He began to wonder if he would ever get to Germany.

The day before Abel left, he drew up a will, instructing his executors to offer the Baron Group to David Maxton on favourable terms, and dividing the rest of his estate between Zaphia and Florentyna. It was the first time in nearly twenty years that he had contemplated death, not that he was sure how he could get himself killed in the regimental canteen.

As his troop ship sailed out of New York harbour, Abel stared back at the Statue of Liberty. He could well remember how he had felt on seeing the statue for the first time nearly twenty years before. Once the ship had passed the Lady, he did not look at her again, but said out loud, 'Next time I look at you, you French bitch, America will have won this war.'

Abel crossed the Atlantic, taking with him two of his top chefs and five kitchen staff. The ship docked at Algiers on 17 February 1943. He spent almost a year in the heat and the dust and the sand of the desert, making sure that every member of the division was as well fed as possible.

'We eat badly, but we eat a damn sight better than anyone else,' was General Clark's comment.

Abel commandeered the only good hotel in Algiers and turned the building into a headquarters for General Clark. Although Abel could see he was playing a valuable role in the war, he itched to get into a real fight, but majors in charge of catering are rarely sent into the front line.

He wrote to Zaphia and George and watched his beloved daughter Florentyna grow up by photograph. He even received an occasional letter from Curtis Fenton, reporting that the Baron Group was making an even larger profit because every hotel in America was packed because of the continual movement of troops and civilians. Abel was sad not to have been at the opening of the new hotel in Montreal, where George had represented him. It was the first time that he had not been present at the opening of a Baron, but George wrote at reassuring length of the new hotel's great success. Abel began to realize how much he had built up in America and how much he wanted to return to the land he now felt was his home.

He soon became bored with Africa and its mess kits, baked beans, blankets and fly swatters. There had been one or two spirited skirmishes out there in the western desert, or so the men returning from the front assured him, but he never saw any real action, although often when he took the food to the front he would hear the firing, and it made him even angrier. One day to his excitement, General Clark's Fifth Army was ordered to invade Southern Europe.

The Fifth Army landed on the Italian coast in amphibious craft while American aircraft gave them tactical cover. They met considerable resistance, first at Anzio and then at Monte Cassino but the action never involved Abel and he dreaded the end of a war in which he had seen no combat. But he could never devise a plan which would get him into the front lines. His chances were not improved when he was promoted to Lieutenant Colonel and sent to London to await further orders.

.   .   .

With D-Day, the great thrust into Europe began. The Allies marched into France and liberated Paris on 25 August 1944. As Abel paraded with the American and Free French soldiers down the Champs Elysées behind General de Gaulle to a hero's welcome, he studied the still magnificent city and once again decided exactly where he was going to build his first Baron hotel in France.

The Allies moved on through northern France and across the German border in a final drive towards Berlin. Abel was posted to the First Army under General Bradley. Food was coming mainly from England: local supplies were almost non-existent, as each succeeding town at which they arrived had already been ravaged by the retreating German army. When Abel arrived in a new city, it would take him only a few hours to commandeer the entire remaining food supply before other American quartermasters had worked out exactly where to look. British and American officers were always happy to dine with the Ninth Armoured Division and would leave wondering how they had managed to requisition such excellent supplies. On one occasion when General George S. Patton joined General Bradley for dinner, Abel was introduced to the famous general who always led his troops into battle brandishing an ivory-handled revolver.

'The best meal I've had in the whole damn war,' said Patton.

.   .   .

By February 1945, Abel had been in uniform for nearly three years and he knew the war would be over in a matter of months. General Bradley kept sending him congratulaltory notes and meaningless decorations to adorn his ever-expanding uniform, but they didn't help. Abel begged the general to let him fight in just one battle, but Bradley wouldn't hear of it.

Although it was the duty of a junior officer to drive the food trucks up to the front lines and then supervise the meals for the troops, Abel often carried out the responsibility himself. And, as in the running of his hotels, he would never let any of his staff know when or where he next intended to pounce.

It was the continual flow of blanket-covered stretchers into the camp that damp St Patrick's Day that made Abel want to go up to the Front and take a look for himself. When it reached a point where he could no longer bear a one-way traffic of bodies, Abel rounded up his men and personally organized the fourteen food trucks. He took with him one lieutenant, one sergeant, two corporals, and twenty-eight privates.

The drive to the Front, although only twenty miles, was tiresomely slow that morning. Abel took the wheel of the first truck – it made him feel a little like General Patton – through heavy rain and thick mud; he had to pull off the road several times to allow ambulance details the right of way in their return from the Front. Wounded bodies took precedence over empty stomachs. Abel wished that most of them were no more than wounded, but only the occasional nod or wave suggested any sign of life. It became obvious to Abel with each mud-tracked mile that something big was going on near Remagen, and he could feel the beat of his heart quicken. Somehow, he knew this time he was going to be involved.

When he finally reached the command post he could hear the enemy fire in the distance, and he started pounding his leg in anger as he watched stretchers bringing back yet more dead and wounded comrades from he knew not where. Abel was sick of learning nothing about the real war until it was part of history. He suspected that any reader of the *New York Times* was better informed than he was.

Abel brought his convoy to a halt by the side of the field kitchen and jumped out of the truck shielding himself from the heavy rain, feeling ashamed that others only a few miles away were shielding themselves from bullets. He began to supervise the unloading of one hundred gallons of soup, a ton of corned beef, two hundred chickens, half a ton of butter, three tons of potatoes and one hundred and ten pound cans of baked beans – plus the inevitable K rations – in readiness for those going to, or returning from, the front. When Abel arrived in the mess tent he found it full of long tables and empty benches. He left his two chefs to prepare the meal and the orderlies to start peeling one thousand potatoes while he went off in search of the duty officer.

Abel headed straight for Brigadier-General John Leonard's tent to find out what was going on, continually passing stretchers of dead and – worse – nearly dead soldiers, the sight of whom would have made any ordinary man sick but at Remagen had the air of being commonplace. As Abel was about to enter the tent, General Leonard, accompanied by his aide, was rushing out. He conducted a conversation with Abel while continuing to walk.

'What can I do for you, Colonel?'

'I have started preparing the food for your battalion as requested in overnight orders, sir. What . . . ?'

'You needn't bother with the food for now, Colonel. At first light this morning Lieutenant Burrows of the Ninth discovered an undamaged railroad bridge north of Remagen, and I gave orders that it should be crossed immediately and every effort made to establish a bridge head on the east bank of the river. Up to now, the Germans have been successful in blowing up every bridge across the Rhine long before we reached it so we can't hang around waiting for lunch before they demolish this one.'

'Did the Ninth succeed in getting across?' asked a puffing Abel.

'Sure did,' replied the general, 'but they encountered heavy resistance when they reached the forest on the far side of the river. The first platoons were ambushed and God knows how many men we lost. So you had better eat the food yourself, Colonel, because my only interest is getting as many of my men back alive as possible.'

'Is there anything I can do?' asked Abel.

The fighting commander stopped running for a moment and studied the fat colonel. 'How many men have you under your direct command?'

'One lieutenant, one sergeant, two corporals, and twenty-eight privates; thirty-three in all including myself, sir.'

'Good. Report to the field hospital with your men and make yourself useful out there by bringing back as many dead and wounded as you can find.'

'Yes, sir,' said Abel and ran all the way back to the field kitchen where he found his own men sitting in a corner smoking. None of them noticed when he entered the tent.

'Get up, you bunch of lazy bastards. We've got real work to do for a change.'

Thirty-two men snapped to attention.

'Follow me,' shouted Abel, 'on the double.'

He turned and started running again, this time towards the field hospital. A young doctor was briefing sixteen medical corpsmen when Abel and his out of breath, unfit men appeared at the entrance to the tent.

'Can I help you, sir?' asked the doctor.

'No, I hope I can help you,' replied Abel. 'I have thirty-two men here who have been detailed by General Leonard to join your group' – it was the first time they had heard of it.

The doctor stared in amazement at the colonel. 'Yes, sir.'

'Don't call me sir,' said Abel. 'We're here to find out how we can assist *you*.'

'Yes, sir,' the doctor said again.

He handed Abel a carton of Red Cross armbands which the chefs, kitchen orderlies and potato peeler proceeded to put on as they listened to the doctor continue his briefing, giving details of the action in the forest on the far side of the Ludendorff bridge.

'The Ninth has sustained heavy casualties,' he continued. 'Those soldiers with medical expertise will remain in the battle zone, while the rest of you will bring back as many of the wounded as possible to the field hospital.'

Abel was delighted at the opportunity to do something positive for a change. The doctor, now in command of a team of forty-nine men, passed out eighteen stretchers, and each soldier received a full medical pack. He then led his motley band towards the Ludendorff bridge. Abel was only a yard behind him. They started singing as they marched through the mud and rain; they stopped singing when they reached the bridge and were greeted by stretcher after stretcher showing clearly the outline of a body covered only in blankets. They marched silently across the bridge in single file by the side of the railroad track where they could see the results of the German explosion that had failed to destroy its foundations. On up towards the forest and the sound of fire, Abel found he was excited by the thought of being so near the enemy, and horrified by the realization of what that enemy was capable of inflicting on his fellow countrymen. Everywhere he turned he saw, or worse, heard cries of anguish coming from his comrades. Comrades who until that day had wistfully thought the end of the war was near – but not that near.

He watched the young doctor stop again and again and do the best he could for each man. Sometimes he would mercifully kill a man quickly when there was not the slightest hope of trying to patch him up. Abel ran from soldier to soldier organizing the stretchers of those unable to help themselves and guiding the wounded who could still walk back towards the Ludendorff bridge. By the time their group reached the edge of the forest only the doctor, one of the potato peelers and himself were left of the original party; all the others were carrying the dead and wounded back to the camp.

As the three of them marched into the forest they could hear the enemy guns close by. Abel could see the outline of a big gun, hidden in undergrowth and still pointing towards the bridge, but now damaged beyond repair.

Then he heard a volley of bullets that sounded so loud that he realized for the first time that the enemy were only a few hundred yards ahead of him. He quickly crouched down on one knee, expectant, his senses heightened to screaming pitch. Suddenly there was another burst of fire in front of him. He jumped up and ran forward, reluctantly followed by the doctor and the potato peeler. They ran on for another hundred yards, when they came across a beautiful stretch of lush green grass in a hollow covered in a bed of white crocuses, littered with the bodies of American soldiers. Abel and the doctor ran from corpse to corpse. 'It must have been a massacre,' screamed Abel in anger, as he heard the retreating fire. The doctor made no comment: he had screamed three years before.

'Don't worry about the dead,' was all he said. 'Just see if you can find anyone who is still alive.'

'Over here,' shouted Abel as he kneeled down beside a sergeant lying in the German mud. Both his eyes were missing.

'He's dead, Colonel,' said the doctor, not giving the man a second glance. Abel ran to the next body and then the next but it was always the same and only the sight of a severed head placed upright in the mud stopped Abel in his tracks. He kept having to look back at it, like the bust of some Greek god that could no longer move. Abel recited like a child words he had learned at the feet of the Baron: '"Blood and destruction shall be so in use and dreadful objects so familiar that mothers shall but smile when they behold their infants quarter'd with the hands of war." Does nothing change?' said Abel outraged.

'Only the battlefield,' replied the doctor.

When Abel had checked thirty – or was it forty men? – he once again returned to the doctor who was trying to save the life of a captain who but for a closed eye and his mouth was already swathed in blood-soaked bandages. Abel stood over the doctor watching helplessly, studying the captain's shoulder patch – the Ninth Armoured – and remembered General Leonard's words, 'God knows how many men we lost today.'

'Fucking Germans,' said Abel.

'Yes, sir,' said the doctor.

'Is he dead?' asked Abel.

'Might as well be,' replied the doctor mechanically. 'He's losing so much blood it can only be a matter of time.' He looked up. 'There's nothing left for you to do here, Colonel, so why don't you try and get the one survivor back to the field hospital before he dies and let the base commander know that I intend to go forward and need every man he can spare.'

'Right,' said Abel as he helped the doctor carefully lift the captain onto a stretcher. Abel and the potato peeler tramped slowly back towards the camp, the doctor having warned him that any sudden movement to the stretcher could only result in an even greater loss of blood. Abel didn't let the potato peeler rest for one moment during the entire two-mile trek to the base camp. He wanted to give the man a chance to live and then return to the doctor in the forest.

For over an hour they trudged through the mud and the rain, and Abel felt certain the captain had died. When they finally reached the field hospital both men were exhausted, and Abel handed the stretcher over to a medical team.

As the captain was wheeled slowly away he opened his unbandaged eye which focused on Abel. He tried to raise his arm. Abel saluted and could have leapt with joy at the sight of the open eye and the moving hand. How he prayed that man would live.

He ran out of the hospital, eager to return to the forest with his little band of men when he was stopped by the duty officer.

'Colonel,' he said, 'I have been looking for you everywhere. There are over three hundred men who need feeding. Christ, man, where have you been?'

'Doing something worthwhile for a change.'

Abel thought about the young captain as he headed slowly back to the field kitchen.

For both men the war was over.

25

The stretcher bearers took the captain into a tent and laid him gently on an operating table. Captain William Kane could see a nurse looking sadly down at him, but he was unable to hear anything she was saying. He wasn't sure if it was because his head was swathed in bandages or because he was now deaf. He watched her lips move, but learned nothing. He shut his eye and thought. He thought a lot about the past; he thought a little about the future; he thought quickly in case he died. He knew if he lived, there would be a long time for thinking. His mind turned to Kate in New York. She had refused to accept his determination to enlist. He knew she would never understand, and that he would not be able to justify his reasons to her so he had stopped trying. The memory of her desperate face now haunted him. He never really considered death – no man does – and now he wanted only to live and return to his old life.

William had left Lester's under the joint control of Ted Leach and Tony Simmons until he returned . . . until he returned. He had given no instructions for them to follow if he did not return. Both of them had begged him not to go. Two more men who couldn't understand. When he signed up a few days later, he couldn't face the children. Richard, aged ten, had found his own way to the station; he had held back the tears until his father told him he could not go along with him to fight the Germans.

They sent him first to an Officers' Candidate School in Vermont. Last time he had seen Vermont, he had been skiing with Matthew, slowly up the hills and quickly down. Now the journey was slow both ways. The course lasted for three months and made him fit again for the first time since he had left Harvard.

His first assignment was in a London full of Yanks, where he acted as a liaison officer between the Americans and the British. He was billeted at the Dorchester, which the British War Office had taken over and seconded for use by the American army. William had read somewhere that Abel Rosnovski had done the same thing with the Baron in New York and he had thoroughly approved at the time. The blackouts, the doodle-bugs, and the air raid warnings all made him believe that he was involved in a war, but he felt strangely detached from what was going on only a few hundred miles from Hyde Park Corner. Throughout his life he had taken the initiative, and had never been an onlooker. Moving between Eisenhower's staff head-quarters in St James and Churchill's War Operations room in Storey's Gate wasn't William's idea of initiative. It didn't look as if he was going to meet a German face-to-face for the entire duration of the war unless Hitler invaded Trafalgar Square.

When part of the First Army was posted to Scotland for training exercises with the Black Watch, William was sent along as an observer and told to report back with his findings. The long, slow journey to Scotland and back in a train that never stopped stopping made him realize that he was fast becoming a glorified messenger boy and he was beginning to wonder why he had ever signed up. Scotland, William found, was different. There at least they had the air of preparing for war and when he returned to London, he put in a request for an immediate transfer to join the First Army. His colonel, who never believed in keeping a man who wanted to see action behind a desk, released him.

Three days later William returned to Scotland to join his new regiment and begin his training with the American troops at Inveraray for the invasion they all knew had to come soon. Training was hard and intense. Nights spent in the Scottish hills fighting mock battles with the Black Watch made more than a slight contrast to evenings at the Dorchester writing reports.

Three months later they were parachuted into northern France to join Omar N. Bradley's army, moving across Europe. The scent of victory was in the air and William wanted to be the first soldier in Berlin.

The First Army advanced towards the Rhine, determined to cross any bridge they could find. Captain Kane received orders that morning that his division was to advance over the Ludendorff bridge and engage the enemy a mile north-east of Remagen in a forest on the far side of the river. He stood on the crest of a hill and watched the Ninth Division cross the bridge, expecting it to be blown sky high at any moment.

His colonel led his own division in behind them. He followed with the hundred and twenty men under his command, most of them, like William, going into action for the first time. No more exercises with wily Scots pretending to kill him, with blank cartridges and then a meal together afterwards. Germans, with real bullets, death – and perhaps no afterwards.

When William reached the edge of the forest, he and his men met with no resistance, so they decided to press further on into the woods. The going was slow and dull and William was beginning to think the Ninth must have done such a thorough job that his division would only have to follow them through, when from nowhere they were suddenly ambushed by a hail of bullets and mortars. Everything seemed to be coming at them at once. William's men went down, trying to protect themselves among the trees, but he lost over half of the platoon in a matter of seconds. The battle, if that's what it could be called, had lasted for less than a minute, and he hadn't even seen a German. William crouched in the wet undergrowth for a few more seconds and then saw, to his horror, the next Division coming through the forest. He ran from his shelter behind a tree to warn them of the ambush. The first bullet hit him in the head, and, as he sank to his knees in the German mud and continued to wave a frantic warning to his advancing comrades, the second hit him in the neck and a third in the chest. He lay still in the mud and waited to die, not having even seen the enemy – a dirty, unheroic death.

The next thing William knew, he was being carried on a stretcher, but he couldn't hear or see anything and he wondered if it was night or whether he was blind.

It seemed a long journey. When his eye opened, it focused on a short fat colonel limping out of a tent. There was something familiar about him, but he couldn't think what. The stretcher bearers took him into the operating tent and placed him on the table. He tried to fight off sleep for fear it might be death. He slept.

William woke. He was conscious of two people trying to move him. They were turning him over as gently as they could, and then they stuck a needle into him. William dreamed of seeing Kate, and then his mother, and then Matthew playing with his son Richard. He slept.

.   .   .

He woke. He knew they had moved him to another bed; slight hope replaced the thought of inevitable death. He lay motionless, his one eye fixed on the canvas roof of the tent, unable to move his head. A nurse came over to study a chart and then him. He slept.

.   .   .

He woke. How much time had passed? Another nurse. This time he could see a little more and – joy, oh joy – he could move his head, if only with great pain. He lay awake as long as he possibly could; he wanted to live. He slept.

He woke. Four doctors were studying him, deciding what? He could not hear them and so learnt nothing.

They moved him once again. This time he was able to watch them put him in an army ambulance. The doors closed behind him, the engine started, and the ambulance began to move over rough ground while a new nurse sat by his side holding him steady. The journey felt like an hour, but he no longer could be sure of time. The ambulance reached smoother ground and then came to a halt. Once again they moved him. This time they were walking on a flat surface and then up some stairs into a dark room. They waited again and then the room began to move, another car perhaps. The room took off. The nurse stuck another needle into him, and he remembered nothing until he felt a plane landing and taxiing to a halt. They moved him yet again. Another ambulance, another nurse, another smell, another city. New York, or at least America, he thought, no other smell like that in the world. The new ambulance took him over another smooth surface, continually stopping and starting, until it finally arrived at where it wanted to be. They carried him out once again and up some more steps into a small white-walled room. They placed him in a comfortable bed. He felt his head touch the pillow, and when next he woke, thought he was totally alone. Then his eye focused and he saw Kate standing in front of him. He tried to lift his hand and touch her, to speak, but no words came. She smiled, but he knew she could not see his smile, and when he woke again Kate was still there but wearing a different dress. Or had she come and gone many times? She smiled again. How long had it been? He tried to move his head a little, and saw his son Richard, so tall, so good-looking. He wanted to see his daughters, but couldn't move his head any further. They moved into his line of vision, Virginia – she couldn't be that old, and Lucy, it wasn't possible. Where had the years gone? He slept.

He woke. No one was there, but now he could move his head. Some bandages had been removed and he could see more clearly; he tried to say something, but no words came. He slept.

He woke. Less bandages than before. Kate was there again, her fair hair longer, now falling to her shoulders, her soft brown eyes and unforgettable smile, looking beautiful, so beautiful. He said her name. She smiled. He slept.

He woke. Even fewer bandages than before. This time his son spoke. Richard said, 'Hello, Daddy.'

He heard him and replied, 'Hello, Richard,' but didn't recognize the sound of his own voice. The nurse helped him to sit up ready to greet his family. He thanked her. A doctor touched his shoulder.

'The worst is over, Mr Kane. You'll soon be well, and then you can return home.'

He smiled as Kate came into the room, followed by Virginia and Lucy. So many questions to ask them. Where should he begin? There were gaps in his memory that demanded satisfaction. Kate told him that he had nearly died. He knew that but had not realized that over a year had passed since his division had been ambushed in the forest at Remagen.

Where had the months of being unaware gone, life lost resembling death? Richard was almost twelve, already hoping to go to Harvard, Virginia was nine, and Lucy nearly seven. Their dresses seemed rather short. He would have to get to know them all over again.

Kate was somehow more beautiful than William even rememberemd her. She told William how she never learned to face the fact that he might have died, how well Richard was doing at Buckley and how Virginia and Lucy needed a father. She braced herself to tell him of the scars on his face and chest that would never heal and thanked God that the doctors felt certain there would be nothing wrong with his mind and his sight would be restored. Now all she wanted to do was help him recover. Kate slowly, William quickly.

Each member of the family played their part in the process. First sound, then sight, then speech. Richard helped his father to walk, until he no longer needed the crutches. Lucy helped him with his food, until he could feed himself once more and Virginia read Mark Twain to him. William was not sure if the reading was for her benefit or his, they both enjoyed it so much. And then at last, after Christmas had passed, they allowed him to return to his own home.

Once William was back in East Sixty-eighth Street, he recovered more quickly, and his doctors were predicting that he would be able to return to work at the bank within six months. A little scarred, but very much alive, he was allowed to see visitors.

The first was Ted Leach, somewhat taken aback at William's appearance. Something else he would have to learn to live with for the time being. From Ted Leach, William learned news that brought him satisfaction. Lester's had progressed in his absence and his colleagues looked forward to welcoming him back as their chairman. A visit from Tony Simmons brought him news that made him sad. Alan Lloyd and Rupert Cork-Smith had both died. He would miss their prudent wisdom. And then Thomas Cohen called to say how glad he was to learn of his recovery and to prove, as if it were still necessary, that time had moved on by informing William he was now semi-retired and had turned over many of his clients to his son Thaddeus who had opened an office in New York. William remarked on both of them being named after apostles. Thomas Cohen laughed and expressed the hope that Mr Kane would continue to use the firm. William assured him he would.

'By the way, I do have one piece of information you ought to know about.'

William listened to the old lawyer in silence and became angry, very angry.

BOOK FIVE

26

General Alfred Jodl signed the unconditional surrender at Rheims on 7 May 1945 as Abel arrived back into a New York preparing for victory celebrations and an end to the war. Once again, the streets were filled with young people in uniform, but this time their faces showed elation, not fear. Abel was saddened by the sight of so many men with one leg, one arm, blind or badly scarred. For them the war would never be over, whatever piece of paper had been signed four thousand miles away.

When Abel walked into the Baron in his colonel's uniform, no one recognized him. Why should they? When they had last seen him in civilian clothes two years before, there were no lines on his still youthful face. The face they now saw was older than its thirty-nine years and the deep, worn ridges on his forehead showed that the war had left its mark on him. He took the lift to his forty-second floor office, and a security guard told him firmly he was on the wrong floor.

'Where's George Novak?' asked Abel.

'He's in Chicago, Colonel,' the guard replied.

'Well, get him on the phone,' said Abel.

'Who shall I say is calling him?'

'Abel Rosnovski.'

The guard moved quickly.

George's familiar voice crackled down the line with welcome. At once Abel realized just how good it felt to be back home. He decided not to stay in New York that night but to fly the eight hundred miles on to Chicago. He took with him George's up-to-date reports to study on the plane. He read every detail of the Baron Group's progress during the war, and it became obvious that George had done well in keeping the group on an even keel during Abel's absence. His cautious stewardship left Abel with no complaints; the profits were still high because so many staff had been called up to fight in the war, while the hotels had remained full because of the continual movement of personnel across America. Abel decided that he would have to start employing new staff immediately, before other hotels picked up the best of those returning from the Front.

When he arrived at Midway Airport, Terminal 11C, George was standing by the gate waiting to greet him. He'd hardly changed, a little more weight, a little less hair perhaps, and within an hour of swapping stories and bringing each other up to date on the past three years, it was almost as though Abel had never been away. Abel would always be thankful to the *Black Arrow* for the introduction to his senior vice-president.

George, however, was uncharitable about Abel's limp which seemed more pronounced since he'd gone off to the war.

'The Hopalong Cassidy of the hotel business,' he said mockingly. 'Now you don't have a leg to stand on.'

'Only a Pole would make such a dumb crack,' replied Abel.

George stared at Abel, looking slightly hurt, as a puppy does when scolded by its master.

'Thank God I had a dumb Polack to take care of everything while I was away looking for Germans,' Abel added reassuringly.

Abel couldn't resist checking once around the Chicago Baron before he drove home. The veneer of luxury had worn rather thin during the wartime shortages. He could see several things that needed renovation, but they would have to wait, because now all he wanted to do was see his wife and daughter. That was when the first shock came. In George he had seen little change in three years, but Florentyna was now eleven and had blossomed into a beautiful young girl, while Zaphia, although only thirty-eight, had become plump, dowdy and distinctly middle-aged.

To begin with, the two of them were not sure quite how to treat one another, and after only a few weeks Abel began to realize that their relationship was never going to be the same again. Zaphia made little effort to excite Abel or take any pride in his achievements. It saddened Abel to observe her lack of interest and he tried to get her involved in his life once again but she did not respond to any of his suggestions. She only seemed contented when staying at home and having as little to do with the Baron Group as possible. He resigned himself to the fact that she could never change and wondered ho long he could remain faithful to her. While he was enchanted with Florentyna, Zaphia, without her looks and with her figure gone, left him cold. When they slept together he avoided making love, and, on the rare occasions when they did, he thought of other women. Soon he began to find any excuse to be away from Chicago and Zaphia's despondent and silently accusing face.

He began by making long trips to his other hotels, taking Florentyna along with him during her school holidays. He spent the first six months after his return to America visiting every hotel in the Baron Group in the same way he had done when he had taken over the company after Davis Leroy's death. Within the year, they were all back to the high standard he expected of them, but Abel wanted to move forward again. He informed Curtis Fenton at the group's next quarterly meeting that his market research team was now advising him to build a hotel in Mexico and another in Brazil, and they were also searching for new lands on which to erect a Baron.

'The Mexico City Baron and the Rio de Janeiro Baron,' said Abel. He liked the ring of those names.

'Well, you have adequate funds to cover the building costs,' said Curtis Fenton. 'The cash has certainly been accumulating in your absence. You could build a Baron almost anywhere you choose. Heaven knows where you'll stop, Mr Rosnovski.'

'One day, Mr Fenton, I'll put a Baron in Warsaw, and then I'll think about stopping,' replied Abel. 'I may have licked the Germans, but I still have a little score to settle with the Russians.'

Curtis Fenton laughed. Only later that evening when he repeated the story to his wife did he decide that Abel Rosnovski had meant exactly what he had said ... a Baron in Warsaw.

'Now where do I stand with Kane's bank?'

The sudden change in Abel's tone bothered Curtis Fenton. It worried him that Abel Rosnovski still clearly held Kane responsible for Davis Leroy's premature death. He opened the special file and started reading.

'Lester, Kane and Company's shares are divided among fourteen members of the Lester family and six past and present employees while Mr Kane himself is the largest stockholder, holding eight per cent.'

'Are any of the Lester family willing to sell their shares?' inquired Abel.

'Perhaps if we can offer the right price. Miss Susan Lester, the late Charles Lester's daughter, has given us reason to believe she might consider parting with her shares, and Mr Peter Parfitt, a former vice-chairman of Lester's, has also showed some interest in our approaches.'

'What percentage do they both hold?'

'Susan Lester holds six per cent. While Peter Parfitt has only two per cent.'

'How much do they want for their shares?'

Curtis Fenton looked down at his file again while Abel glanced at Lester's latest annual report. His eyes came to a halt on Article Seven.

'Miss Susan Lester wants two million dollars for her six per cent and Mr Parfitt one million dollars for his two per cent.'

'Mr Parfitt is greedy,' said Abel. 'We will therefore wait until he is hungry. Buy Miss Susan Lester's shares immediately without revealing whom you represent and keep me briefed on any change of heart by Mr Parfitt.'

Curtis Fenton coughed.

'Is something bothering you, Mr Fenton?' asked Abel.

Curtis Fenton hesitated. 'No, nothing,' he said unconvincingly.

'From now on I am putting someone in overall charge of the account whom you will know or certainly know of – Henry Osborne.'

'Congressman Osborne?' asked Curtis Fenton.

'Yes – are you acquainted with him?'

'Only by reputation,' said Fenton, with a faint note of disapproval, his head bowed.

Abel ignored the implied comment. He was only too aware of Henry's reputation, but while he had the ability to cut out all the middle men of bureaucracy and could ensure quick political decisions, he considered the risk was worthwhile. Not to mention the bond of common loathing of Kane. 'I'm also inviting Mr Osborne to be a director of the Baron Group with special responsibility for the Kane account. This information must, as always, be treated in the strictest confidence.'

'As you wish,' said Fenton unhappily, wondering if he should express his personal misgivings to Abel Rosnovski.

'Brief me as soon as you have closed the deal with Miss Susan Lester.'

'Yes, Mr Rosnovski,' said Curtis Fenton without raising his head.

Abel returned to the Baron for lunch, where Henry Osborne was waiting to join him.

'Congressman,' said Abel as they met in the foyer.

'Baron,' said Henry, and they laughed and went, arm-in-arm into the dining room and sat at the corner table.

Abel chastised a waiter for serving at table when a button was missing from his tunic.

'How's your wife, Abel?'

'Swell. And yours Henry?'

'Just great.'

They were both lying.

'Any news to report?'

'Yes. That concession you needed in Atlanta has been taken care of,' said Henry in a conspiratorial voice. 'The necessary documents will be pushed through some time in the next few days. You'll be able to start building the Atlanta Baron round the first of the month.'

'We're not doing anything too illegal, are we?'

'Nothing your competitors aren't up to – that I can promise you, Abel.' Henry Osborne laughed.

'I'm glad to hear that, Henry. I don't want any trouble with the law.'

'No, no,' said Henry. 'Only you and I know all the facts.'

'Good,' said Abel. 'You've made yourself very useful to me over the years, Henry, and I have a little reward for your past services. How would you like to become a director of the Baron Group?'

'I'd be flattered, Abel.'

'Don't give me that. You know you've been invaluable with these state and city permits. I'd never have had the time to deal with all those politicians and bureaucrats. In any case, Henry, they prefer to deal with a Harvard man even if he doesn't so much open doors, as simply kick them down.'

'You've been very generous in return, Abel.'

'It's no more than you have earned. Now, I want you to take on an even bigger job which is close to my heart. This exercise will also require complete secrecy, but it shouldn't take too much of your time and it will give us a little revenge on our mutual friend from Boston, Mr William Kane.'

The *maître d'hotel* arrived with two large rump steaks, medium rare, Henry listened intently as Abel unfolded his plans for William Kane.

A few days later on 8 May 1946, Abel travelled to New York to celebrate the first anniversary of V-E day. He had laid on a dinner for over a thousand Polish veterans at the Baron Hotel and had invited General Kazimierz Sosnkowski, commander-in-chief of the Polish Forces in France after 1943, to be the guest of honour. Abel had looked forward impatiently to the event for weeks and took Florentyna with him to New York while leaving Zaphia behind in Chicago.

On the night of the celebration, the banqueting room of the New York Baron looked magnificent, each of the one hundred and twenty tables decorated with the stars and stripes of America and the white and red of the Polish national flag. Huge photographs of Eisenhower, Patton, Bradley, Hodges, Paderewski and Sikorski festooned the walls. Abel sat at the centre of the head table with the general on his right and Florentyna on his left.

When General Sosnkowski rose to address the gathering, he announced that Lieutenant Colonel Rosnovski had been made a life president of the Polish Veterans' Society, in acknowledgement of the personal sacrifices he had made for the Polish-American cause, and in particular for his generous gift of the New York Baron throughout the entire duration of the war.

Someone who had drunk a little too much shouted from the back of the room.

'Those of us who survived the Germans had to survive Abel's food as well.'

The thousand veterans laughed and cheered, toasted Abel in Danzig vodka and then fell silent as the general talked of the plight of post-war Poland, in the grip of Stalinist Russia, urging his fellow expatriates to be tireless in their campaign to secure the ultimate sovereignty of their native land. Abel wanted to believe that Poland would one day be free again and that he might even live to see his castle restored to him, but doubted if that was realistic after Stalin's success at the Yalta agreement.

The general went on to remind the guests that Polish-Americans had, per capita, sacrificed more lives and given more money for the war than any other single ethnic group in the United States. '. . . How many Americans would believe that Poland lost six million of her countrymen while Czechoslovakia only lost one hundred thousand. Some observers declare we were stupid not to surrender when we must have known we were beaten. How could a nation that staged a cavalry charge against the might of the Nazi tanks ever believe they were beaten and my friends I tell you we are not beaten now.' Every Pole in the room applauded the general loudly.

Abel felt sad to think that most Americans would still laugh at the thought of the Polish war effort – or, funnier still, a Polish war hero. The general then waited for complete silence to tell an intent audience the story of how Abel had led a band of men to recover troops who had been killed or wounded at the battle of Remagen. When the general had finished his speech and sat down, the veterans stood and cheered the two men resoundingly. Florentyna felt very proud of her father.

Abel was surprised when the story hit the papers the next morning, as Polish achievements were rarely reported in any medium other than *Dziennik Zwiazkiwy*. He doubted that the press would have bothered on this occasion had he not been the Chicago Baron. Abel basked in his new-found glory as an un-sung American hero and spent most of the day having his photograph taken and giving interviews to newsmen.

By the evening Abel felt a sense of anti-climax. The general had flown on to Los Angeles and another function, Florentyna had returned to school in Lake Forest, George was in Chicago, and Henry Osborne in Washington. The hotel seemed rather large and empty, and he felt no desire to return to Zaphia in Chicago.

He decided to have an early dinner and go over the weekly reports from the other hotels in the group before returning to the penthouse adjoining his office. He seldom ate alone in his private suite as he welcomed the opportunity of being served in one of the dining rooms whenever possible; it was one of the sure ways to keep in constant touch with hotel life. The more hotels he acquired and built, the more he feared losing touch with his staff on the ground.

He took the lift downstairs and stopped at the reception desk to ask how many people were booked into the hotel that night, but he was distracted by a striking woman signing a registration form. He could have sworn he recognized the profile, but it was difficult to be certain from the side. Mid-thirties, he thought. When she had finished writing, she turned and looked at him.

'Abel,' she said. 'How marvellous to see you.'

'Good God, Melanie. I hardly recognized you.'

'No one could fail to recognize you, Abel.'

'I didn't know you were in New York.'

'Only overnight. I'm here on some business for my magazine.'

'You're a journalist?' asked Abel with a hint of disbelief.

'No, I'm the economic advisor to a group of magazines whose head-quarters are in Dallas, and they've sent me to New York on a market research project.'

'Sounds very impressive.'

'I can assure you it isn't,' said Melanie, 'but it keeps me out of mischief.'

'Are you free for dinner, by any chance?'

'What a nice idea. Abel, but I need a bath and a change of clothes if you don't mind waiting?'

'Sure, I can wait. I'll meet you in the main dining room whenever you're ready. Come to my table, say in about an hour.'

She smiled in agreement and followed a bellhop to the lift. He noticed her perfume as she passed him.

Abel spent the hour checking the dining room to be sure that his table had fresh flowers, and the kitchen to select the dishes he would order for Melanie. Finally, by lack of anything better to do, he was compelled to sit down. He found himself glancing at his watch and looking at the dining room door every few moments to see if Melanie would walk in. She took a little over an hour but it turned out to be worth the wait. When at last she appeared at the doorway, in a long clinging dress that shimmered and sparkled in the dining room lights in an unmistakably expensive way, she looked ravishing. The *maître d'* ushered her to Abel's table. He rose to greet her as a waiter opened a bottle of vintage Krug and poured them both a glass.

'Welcome, Melanie,' said Abel as he raised his goblet. 'It's good to see you in the Baron.'

'It's good to see the Baron,' she replied, 'especially on his day of celebration.'

'What do you mean?' asked Abel.

'I read all about your big dinner in the *New York Post* tonight, how you risked your own life to save those who had been wounded at Remagen. It kept me glued to the page all the way over here from the station. They made you sound like a cross between Audie Murphy and the Unknown Soldier.'

'It's all exaggerated,' said Abel.

'I've never known you to be modest about anything before, Abel, so I can only believe every word must be true.'

He poured her a second glass of champagne.

'The truth is, I've always been a little frightened of you, Melanie.'

'The Baron is frightened of someone? I don't believe it.'

'Well, I'm no Southern gentleman, as you once made very clear, my dear.'

'And you have never stopped reminding me.' She smiled, teasingly. 'Did you marry your nice Polish girl?'

'Yes, I did.'

'How did that work out?'

'Not so well. She's now fat and forty and no longer has any appeal for me.'

'You'll be telling me next that she doesn't understand you,' said Melanie, the tone of her voice betraying her pleasure at his reply.

'And did you find yourself a husband?' asked Abel.

'Oh, yes,' replied Melanie. 'I married a real Southern gentleman with all the right credentials.'

'Many congratulations,' said Abel.

'I divorced him last year ... with a large settlement.'

'Oh, I'm sorry,' said Abel, sounding pleased. 'More champagne?'

'Are you by any chance trying to seduce me, Abel?'

'Not before you've finished your soup, Melanie. Even first-generation Polish immigrants have some standards, although I must admit it's my turn to do the seducing.'

'Then I must warn you, Abel, I haven't slept with another man since my divorce came through. No lack of offers, but no one's been quite right. Too many groping hands and not enough affection.'

After smoked salmon, young lamb, crème brûlée and a pre-war Mouton Rothschild, they had both thoroughly reviewed their lives since their last meeting.

'Coffee in the penthouse, Melanie?'

'Do I have any choice, after such an excellent meal?' she inquired.

Abel laughed and escorted her out of the dining room and into the lift. She was teetering very slightly on her high heels as she entered. Abel touched the button marked 'forty-two'. Melanie looked up at the numbers as they ticked by.

'Why no twelfth floor?' she asked innocently. Abel could not find the words to reply.

'The last time I had coffee in your room ...' Melanie tried again.

'Don't remind me,' said Abel, remembering his own vulnerability. As they stepped out of the lift on the forty-second floor, the bellhop opened the door of his suite.

'Good God,' said Melanie, as her eyes swept round the inside of the penthouse for the first time. 'I must say, Abel, you've learned how to adjust to the style of a multi-millionaire. I've never seen anything more extravagant in my life.'

A knock at the door stopped Abel as he was about to reach out for her. A young waiter appeared with a pot of coffee and a bottle of Rémy Martin.

'Thank you Mike,' said Abel. 'That will be all for tonight.'

'Will it?' She smiled.

The waiter would have turned red if he hadn't been black and left quickly.

Abel poured her coffee and brandy. She sipped slowly, sitting cross-legged on the floor. Abel would have sat cross-legged as well, but he couldn't quite manage the position, so instead he lay down beside her. She stroked his hair, and tentatively he began to move his hand up her leg. God, how well he remembered those legs. As they kissed for the first time, Melanie kicked a shoe off and knocked her coffee all over the Persian carpet.

'Oh, hell,' she said. 'I've ruined your beautiful carpet.'

'Forget it,' said Abel, as he pulled her back into his arms and started to unzip her dress. Melanie unbuttoned his shirt, and Abel tried to get it off while he was still kissing her, but his cufflinks stopped him, so he helped her out of her dress instead. Her figure had lost none of its beauty and was exactly as he remembered it, except that it was enticingly fuller. Those firm breasts and long graceful legs. He gave up the one-handed battle with the cufflinks and released her from his grasp to undress himself, aware what an abrupt physical contrast he must have appeared compared to her beautiful body. He hoped all he had read about women being fascinated by powerful men was true. She didn't seem to grimace as she once had at the sight of him. Gently, he caressed her breasts and began to part her legs. The Persian carpet was proving better than any bed. It was her turn to try to undress completely while they were kissing. She too gave up and finally took off everything except for – at Abel's request – her garter belt and nylon stockings.

When he heard her moan, he was aware how long it had been since he had experienced such ecstasy – and then – how quickly the sensation was past. Neither of them spoke for several moments, both breathing heavily.

Then Abel chuckled.

'What are you laughing at?' Melanie inquired.

'Nothing,' said Abel, recalling Dr Johnson's observation about the position being ridiculous and the pleasure momentary.

Abel rolled over, and Melanie rested her head on his shoulder. Abel was surprised to find that he no longer wanted to be near Melanie, and as he lay there wondering how to get rid of her without actually being rude, she said, 'I'm afraid I can't stay all night, Abel, I have an early appointment tomorrow and I must get *some* sleep. I don't want to look as if I spent the night on your Persian carpet.'

'Must you go?' said Abel, sounding desperate, but not too desperate.

'I'm sorry, darling, yes.' She stood up and walked to the bathroom.

Abel watched her dress, and helped her with her zipper. How much easier the garment was to fasten at leisure than it had been to unfasten in haste. He kissed her gallantly on the hand as she left.

'I hope we'll see each other again soon,' he said, lying.

'I hope so, too,' she said, aware that he did not mean it.

He closed the door behind her and walked over to the phone by his bed.

'Which room was Miss Melanie Leroy booked into?' he asked.

There was a moment's pause; he could hear the flicking of the registration cards.

Abel tapped impatiently on the table.

'There's no one registered under that name, sir,' came the eventual reply. 'We have a Mrs Melanie Seaton from Dallas, Texas, who arrived this evening, sir, and checks out tomorrow morning?'

'Yes, that will be the lady,' said Abel. 'See that her bill is charged to me.'

'Yes, sir.'

Abel replaced the phone and took a long cold shower before preparing for bed. He felt relaxed as he walked over to the fire to turn out the lamp that had illuminated his first adulterous act and noticed that the large coffee stain had now dried on his Persian carpet.

'Silly bitch,' he said out loud and switched off the light.

.   .   .

After that night, Abel found that several more coffee stains appeared on the Persian carpet during the next few months, some caused by waitresses, some by other nocturnal visitors, as he and Zaphia grew further apart. What he hadn't anticipated was that she would hire a private detective to check on him and then sue for divorce. Divorce was almost unknown in Abel's circle of Polish friends, separation or desertion being far more common. Abel even tried to talk Zaphia out of her desired course, only too aware it would do nothing to enhance his standing in the Polish community, and certain it would not advance any social or political ambitions he had started to hanker after. But Zaphia was determined to carry the divorce proceedings to their bitter conclusion. Abel was surprised to find that the woman who had been so unsophisticated in his triumph was, to use George's words, a little demon in her revenge.

When Abel consulted his own lawyer, he found out for the second time just how many waitresses and non-paying guests there had been during the last year. He gave in and the only thing he fought for was the custody of Florentyna, now thirteen, and the first true love of his life. Zaphia agreed after a long struggle, accepting a settlement of five hundred thousand dollars, the deed to the house in Chicago, and the right to see Florentyna on the last weekend in every month.

Abel moved his headquarters and permanent home to New York and George dubbed him the Chicago Baron-in-exile, as he roamed America north and south building new hotels, only returning to Chicago when he had to see Curtis Fenton.

27

The letter lay open on a table by William's chair in the living room. He sat in his dressing gown reading it for the third time, trying to figure out why Abel Rosnovski would want to buy so heavily into Lester's Bank, and why he had appointed Henry Osborne as a director of the Baron Group. William felt he could no longer take the risk of guessing and picked up the phone.

The new Mr Cohen turned out to be a younger version of his father. When he arrived at East 68th Street, he had no need to introduce himself; the hair was beginning to go grey and thin in exactly the same places and the round body was encased in an exactly similar suit. Perhaps, it was in fact the same suit. William stared at him, but not simply because he looked so like his father.

'You don't remember me, Mr Kane,' said the lawyer.

'Good God,' said William. 'The great debate at Harvard. Nineteen twenty...' 'Twenty-eight. You won the debate and sacrificed your membership of the Porcellian.'

William burst out laughing. 'Maybe we'll do better on the same team, if your brand of socialism will allow you to act for an unabashed capitalist.'

He rose to shake hands with Thaddeus Cohen. For a moment, they both might have been undergraduates again.

William smiled. 'You never did get that drink at the Porcellian. What would you like?'

Thaddeus Cohen declined the offer. 'I don't drink,' he said, blinking in the same disarming way that William recalled so well. '... and I'm afraid I'm now an unabashed capitalist, too.'

He turned out to have his father's head on his shoulders mentally as well as physically, and had clearly briefed himself on the Rosnovski-Osborne file to the finest detail before he faced William. William explained exactly what he now required.

'An immediate report and a further updated one every three months as in the past. Secrecy is still of paramount importance,' he said, 'but I want every fact you can lay your hands on. Why is Abel Rosnovski buying the bank's shares? Does he still feel I am responsible for Davis Leroy's death? Is he continuing his battle with Kane and Cabot even now that they are part of Lester's? What role does Henry Osborne play in all of this? Would a meeting between myself and Rosnovski help, especially if I tell him that it was the bank, not I, who refused to support the Richmond Group?'

Thaddeus Cohen's pen was scratching away as furiously as his father's had before him.

'All these questions must be answered as quickly as possible so that I can decide if it's necessary to brief my board.'

Thaddeus Cohen gave his father's shy smile as he shut his briefcase. 'I'm sorry that you should be troubled in this way while you are still convalescing. I'll be back to you as soon as I can ascertain the facts.' He paused at the door. 'I admire greatly what you did at Remagen.'

William recovered his sense of well-being and vigour rapidly in the following months, and the scars on his face and chest faded into relative insignificance. At night Kate would sit up with him until he fell asleep and whisper, 'Thank God you were spared.' The terrible headaches and periods of amnesia grew to be things of the past, and the strength returned to his right arm. Kate would not allow him to return to work until they had taken a long and relaxing cruise in the West Indies. William relaxed with Kate more than at any time since their two weeks together in London. She revelled in the fact that there were no banks on the ship for him to do business with, although she feared if they stayed on board another week William would have acquired the floating vessel as one of Lester's latest assets, reorganizing the crew, routes, timings and even the way they sailed 'the boat', as William insisted on calling the great liner. He was tanned and restless once the ship docked in New York Harbour, and Kate could not dissuade him from returning immediately to the bank.

He soon became deeply involved again in Lester's problems. A new breed of men, toughened by war, enterprising and fast-moving, seemed to be running America's modern banks, under the watchful eye of President Truman, the man who had won a surprise victory for a second term in the White House after the world had been informed that Dewey was certain to win the election. As if not satisfied with their prediction, the *Chicago Tribune* went on to announce that Dewey had actually won the election, but it was

Harry S. Truman who remained in the White House. William knew very little about the diminutive ex-senator from Missouri, except what he read in the newspapers, and as a staunch Republican, he hoped that his party would find the right man to lead them into the 1952 campaign.

The first report came in from Thaddeus Cohen; Abel Rosnovski was still looking for shares in Lester's bank and had approached all the other benefactors of the will but only one agreement had been concluded. Susan Lester had refused to see William's lawyer when he approached her, so he was unable to discover why she had sold her six per cent. All he could ascertain was that she had no financial reason for doing so. 'Hell hath no fury,' mumbled William.

The document was admirably comprehensive.

Henry Osborne, it seemed, had been appointed a director of the Baron Group in May of 1947, with special responsibility for the Lester's account. More importantly, Abel Rosnovski secured Susan Lester's shares without it being possible to trace the acquisition back to either him or to Osborne. Rosnovski now owned six per cent of Lester's Bank and appeared to be willing to pay at least another $750,000 to obtain Peter Parfitt's two per cent. William was only too aware of the actions Abel Rosnovski could carry out once he was in possession of eight per cent. Even more worrying to William was the fact that the growth rate of Lester's compared unfavourably with that of the Baron Group, which was already catching up its main rivals, the Hilton and the Sheraton Groups. William began to wonder if it would now be wise to brief his board of directors on this newly obtained information, and even whether he ought not to contact Abel Rosnovski direct. After some sleepless nights, he turned to Kate for advice.

'Do nothing,' was Kate's reaction, 'until you can be absolutely certain that his intentions are as disruptive as you fear. The whole affair may turn out to be a tempest in a teapot.'

'With Henry Osborne as his hatchet man you can be sure that the tempest will pour far beyond the teacup: nothing can be totally innocent. I don't have to sit around and wait to find out what he is planning for me.'

'He might have changed, William. It must be twenty years since you've had any personal dealings with him.'

'Al Capone might have changed, if he had been allowed to complete his jail sentence. We'll never know for certain, but I would not be willing to put a bet on it.'

Kate added nothing more, but William let himself be persuaded by her and did little except to keep a close eye on Thaddeus Cohen's quarterly reports and hope that Kate's intuition would turn out to be right.

28

The Baron Group profited greatly from the post-war explosion in the American economy. Not since the twenties had it been so easy to make so much money so quickly – and by the early fifties, people were beginning to believe that this time it was going to last. But Abel was not content with financial success alone; as he grew older, he began to worry about Poland's place in the post-war world and to feel that his success did not allow him to be a bystander four thousand miles away. What had Pawel Zaleski, the Polish consul in Turkey said? 'Perhaps in your lifetime you will see Poland rise again.' Abel did everything he could to influence and persuade the United States Congress to take a more militant attitude towards Russian control of its Eastern European satellites. It seemed to Abel, as he watched one puppet socialist government after another come into being, that he had risked his life for nothing. He began to lobby Washington politicians, brief journalists and organize dinners in Chicago and New York and other centres of the Polish-American community, unil the Polish cause itself became synonymous with the Chicago Baron.

Dr Teodor Szymanowski, formerly professor of history at the university of Cracow, wrote a glowing editorial about Abel's 'Fight To Be Recognized' in the journal *Freedom*, which prompted Abel to contact him and see what else he could do to help. The professor was now an old man, and when Abel was ushered into his study, he was surprised by the frailty of his appearance, knowing the vigour of his opinions. He greeted Abel warmly and poured him a Danzig vodka. 'Baron Rosnovski,' he said, handing him the glass, 'I have long admired the way you work on and on for our cause and although we make such little headway, you never seem to lose faith.'

'Why should I? I have always believed anything is possible in America.'

'But I fear, Baron, the very men you are now trying to influence are the same ones who had allowed these things to take place. They will never do anything positive to free our people.'

'I do not understand what you mean, Professor,' said Abel. 'Why will they not help us?'

The professor leaned his back in his chair. 'You are surely aware, Baron, that the American armies were given specific orders to slow down their advance east to allow the Russians to take as much of central Europe as they could lay their hands on. Patton could have been in Berlin long before the Russians but Eisenhower told him to hold back. It was our leaders in Washington – the same men you are trying to persuade to put American guns and troops back into Europe – who gave those orders to Eisenhower.'

'But they couldn't have known then what the USSR would eventually become. The Russians were then our allies. I accept that we were too weak and conciliatory with them in 1945, but it was not the Americans who directly betrayed the Polish people.'

Before Szymanowski spoke, he leaned back again and closed his eyes wearily.

'I wish you could have known my brother, Baron Rosnovski. I had word only last week that he died six months ago, in a Soviet camp not unlike the one from which you escaped.'

Abel moved forward as if to offer sympathy, but Szymanowski raised his hand.

'No, don't say anything. You have known the camps yourself. You would be the first to realize that sympathy is no longer important. We must change the world, Baron, while others sleep.' Szymanowski paused. 'My brother was sent to Russia by the Americans.'

Abel looked at him in astonishment.

'By the Americans? How is that possible? If your brother was captured in Poland by Russian troops . . .'

'My brother was never taken prisoner in Poland. He was liberated from a German war camp near Frankfurt. The Americans kept him in a DP camp for a month and then they handed him over to the Russians.'

'It can't be true. Why would they do that?'

'The Russians wanted all Slavs repatriated. Repatriated so that they could then be exterminated or enslaved. The ones that Hitler didn't get, Stalin did. And I can prove my brother was in the American Sector for over a month.'

'But,' Abel began, 'was he an exception or were there many others like him?'

'He was no exception: there were many others,' said Szymanowski without apparent emotion. 'Hundreds of thousands. Perhaps as many as a million. I don't think we will ever know the true figures. It's most unlikely the American authorities ever kept careful records of Operation Kee Chanl.'

'Operation Kee Chanl? Why don't people ever mention this? Surely if others realized that we, the Americans, had been sending liberated prisoners back to die in Russia, they would be horrified.'

'There is no proof, no known documentation of Operation Kee Chanl. Mark Clark, God bless him, disobeyed his orders and a few of the prisoners were warned in advance by some kindly disposed G.I.s, and they managed to escape before the Americans could send them to the camps. But they are now lying low and would never admit as much. One of the unlucky ones was my brother. Anyway, it's too late now.'

'But the American people must be told. I'll form a committee, print pamphlets, make speeches. Surely Congress will listen to us if we tell them the truth.'

'Baron Rosnovski, I think this one is too big even for you.'

Abel rose from his seat.

'No, no, I do not underestimate you, my friend. But you do not yet understand the mentality of world leaders. America agreed to hand over those poor devils because Stalin demanded as much. I am sure they never thought that there would be trials, labour camps and executions to follow. But now, as we approach the fifties, no one is going to admit they were indirectly responsible? No, they will never do that. Not for a hundred years. And then, all but a few historians will have forgotten that Poland lost more lives in the war than any other single nation on earth, including Germany.'

'I had hoped the one conclusion you might come to was that you must play a more direct role in politics.'

'I have already been considering the idea but cannot decide what form it should take.'

'I have my own views on that subject, Baron, so keep in touch.'

The old man raised himself slowly to his feet and embraced Abel. 'In the meantime do what you can for our cause, but don't be surprised when you meet closed doors.'

The moment Abel returned to The Baron, he picked up the phone and told the hotel operator to get him Senator Douglas' office. Paul Douglas was Illinois' liberal Democratic senator, elected with the help of the Chicago machine, and he had always been helpful and responsive to any of Abel's past requests, mindful of the fact that his constituency contained the largest Polish community in the country. His assistant, Adam Tomaszewicz always dealt with his Polish constituents.

'Hello, Adam. It's Abel Rosnovski. I have something very disturbing to discuss with the senator. Could you arrange an early meeting with him?'

'I'm afraid he's out of town today, Mr Rosnovski. I know he'll be glad to speak with you as soon as he returns on Thursday. I'll ask him to call you direct. Can I tell him what it's all about?'

'Yes. As a Pole you will be interested. I've heard reports from reliable sources that the US authorities in Germany assisted in the return of displaced Polish citizens to territories occupied by the Soviet Union, and that many of these Polish citizens were then sent on to Russian labour camps and have never been heard of since.'

There was a moment's silence from the other end of the line.

'I'll brief the senator on his return, Mr Rosnovski,' said Adam Tomaszewicz. 'Thank you for calling.'

The senator did not get in touch with Abel on Thursday. Nor did he try on Friday or over the weekend. On Monday morning, Abel put through another call to his office. Again, Adam Tomaszewicz answered the telephone.

'Oh, yes, Mr Rosnovski.' Abel could almost hear him blushing. 'The senator did leave a message for you. He's been very busy, you know, what with all the emergency bills that have to be acted on before Congress recesses. He asked me to let you know that he'll call back just as soon as he has a spare moment.'

'Did you give him my message?'

'Yes, of course. He asked me to assure you that he felt certain the rumour you heard was nothing more than a piece of anti-American propaganda. He added that he'd been told personally by one of the Joint Chiefs that American troops had orders not to release any of the DPs under their supervision.'

Tomaszewicz sounded as if he was reading a carefully prepared statement, and Abel sensed that he had encountered the first of those closed doors. Senator Douglas had never evaded him in the past.

Abel put down the phone and dialed the number of another senator who did make news and didn't evade sitting in judgement on anybody.

Senator Joseph McCarthy's office came on the line asking who was calling. 'I'll try and find the senator,' said a young voice when she heard who it was and his reason for wanting to speak to her boss. McCarthy was approaching the peak of his power, and Abel realized he would be lucky to have more than a few moments on the phone with him.

'Mr Rosenevski,' were McCarthy's first words.

Abel wondered if he had mangled his name on purpose, or if it was a bad connection. 'What is it you wanted to discuss with me and no one else, this matter of grave urgency?' the senator asked. Abel hesitated; actually speaking to McCarthy directly had slightly taken him aback.

'Your secrets are safe with me,' he heard the senator say, sensing his hesitation.

'If you say so,' said Abel and paused for a moment to collect his thoughts. 'You, Senator, have been a forthright spokesman for those of us who would like to see the Eastern European nations freed from the yoke of communism.'

'So I have. So I have. And I'm glad to see you appreciate the fact, Mr Rosenevski.'

This time Abel was sure he had mispronounced his name on purpose, but resolved not to comment on it.

'As for Eastern Europe,' the senator continued, 'you must realize that only after the traitors have been driven from within our own government can any real action be taken to free your captive country.'

'That is exactly what I want to speak to you about, Senator. You have had a brilliant success in exposing treachery within our own government. But to date, one of the communists' greatest crimes has as yet gone unpublicized.'

'Just what great crime did you have in mind, Mr Rosenevski? I have found so many since I came to Washington.'

'I am referring' – Abel drew himself up a little straighter in his chair – 'to the forced repatriation of thousands of displaced Polish citizens by the American authorities after the war ended. Innocent enemies of communism who were sent back to Poland, and then on to the USSR, to be enslaved and sometimes murdered.'

Abel waited for a response, but none was forthcoming. He heard a click and wondered if someone else was listening to the conversation.

'Now, Rosenevski, listen to me, you simpleton. You dare to phone me to say that Americans – loyal United States soldiers – sent thousands of Poles back to Russia and nobody heard a word about it? Are you asking me to believe that? Even a Polack couldn't be that stupid. And I wonder what kind of person accepts a lie like that without any proof? Do you want me also to believe that American soldiers are disloyal? Is that what you want? Tell me, Rosenevski, tell me what it is with you people? Are you too stupid to recognize communist propaganda even when it hits you right in the face? Do you have to waste the time of an overworked United States senator because of a rumour cooked up by the *Pravda* slime to create unrest in America's immigrant communities?'

Abel sat motionless, stunned by the outburst. Before half of his tirade was over, Abel felt that any counter-argument was going to be pointless. He waited for the histrionic speech to come to an end, and was glad the senator couldn't see his startled face.

'Senator, I'm sure you're right and I'm sorry to have wasted your time,' Abel said quietly. 'I hadn't thought of it in quite that light before.'

'Well, it just goes to show how tricky those commie bastards can be,' said McCarthy, his tone softening. 'You have to keep an eye on them all the time. Anyway, I hope you're more alert now to the continual danger the American people face.'

'I am indeed, Senator. Thank you once again for taking the trouble to speak to me personally. Goodbye, Senator.'

'Goodbye, Rosenovski.'

Abel heard the phone click and realized it was the same sound as a closing door.

29

William became aware of feeling older when Kate teased him about his greying hair, hairs which he used to be able to count and now no longer could, and Richard started to bring girls home whom he found attractive. William almost always approved of Richard's choice of young ladies, as he called them, perhaps because they were all rather like Kate who, he considered, was more beautiful in middle-age than she had ever been. His daughters, Virginia and Lucy, now also becoming young ladies, brought him great happiness as they grew in the image of their mother. Virginia was becoming quite an artist and the kitchen and children's bedrooms were always covered in her latest works of genius, as Richard described them mockingly. Virginia's revenge came the day Richard started cello lessons when even the servants were heard to murmur unsavoury comments whenever the bow came in contact with the strings. Lucy adored them both and considered Virginia with uncritical prejudice the new Picasso and Richard the new Casals. William began to wonder what the future would hold for all three of them when he was no longer around. In Kate's eyes all three children advanced satisfactorily. Richard, now at St Paul's, had improved enough at the cello to be chosen to play in a school concert, while Virginia was painting well enough for one of her pictures to be hung in the front room. But it became obvious to all the family that Lucy was going to be the beauty when, aged only eleven, she started receiving little love notes from boys who until then had only shown an interest in baseball.

In 1951, Richard was accepted at Harvard and although he did not win the top mathematics scholarship, Kate was quick to point out to William that he had played baseball and the cello for St Paul's, two accomplishments William had never so much as attempted to master. William was secretly proud of Richard's achievements but mumbled to Kate something about not knowing many bankers who played baseball or the cello.

Banking was moving into an expansionist period as Americans began to believe in a lasting peace. William soon found himself overworked, and for a short time, the threat of Abel Rosnovski and the problems associated with him had to be pushed into the background.

The flow of quarterly reports from Thaddeus Cohen indicated that Rosnovski had embarked on a course which he had no intention of abandoning – through a third party he had let every stockholder other than William know of his interest in Lester's shares. William wondered if that course was heading towards a direct confrontation between himself and the Pole. He began to feel that the time was fast approaching when he would have to inform the Lester's board of Rosnovski's actions and perhaps even to offer his resignation if the bank looked to be under siege, a move that would result in a complete victory for Abel Rosnovski, which was the one reason William did not seriously contemplate such a move. He decided that if he had to fight for his life, fight he would, and if one of the two had to go under, he would do everything in his power to ensure that it wasn't William Kane.

The problem of what to do about Abel Rosnovski's investment programme was finally taken out of William's hands.

Early in 1951, the bank had been invited to represent one of America's new airline companies, Interstate Airways, when the Federal Aviation Agency granted them a franchise for flights between the East and West coasts. The airline approached Lester's bank when they needed to raise the thirty million dollars to provide them with the financial backing required by governmental regulations.

William considered the airline and the whole project to be well worth supporting, and he spent virtually his entire time setting up a public offering to raise the necessary thirty million. The bank, acting as the sponsor for the project, put all their resources behind the new venture. The project became William's biggest since he had returned to Lester's, and he realized that his personal reputation was at stake when he went to the market for the thirty million dollars. In July, when the details of the offering were announced, the stock was snapped up in a matter of days. William received lavish praise from all quarters for the way he had handled the project and carried it through to such a successful conclusion. He could not have been happier about the outcome himself, until he read in Thaddeus Cohen's next report that ten per cent of the airline's stock had been obtained by one of Abel Rosnovski's dummy corporations.

William knew then that the time had come to acquaint Ted Leach and Tony Simmons with his worst fears. He asked Tony to come to New York where he called both of the vice-chairmen to his office and related to them the saga of Abel Rosnovski and Henry Osborne.

'Why didn't you let us know about all this before?' was Tony Simmons' first reaction.

'I dealt with a hundred companies like the Richmond Group when I was at Kane and Cabot, Tony, and I couldn't know at the time that he was that serious about revenge. I was only finally convinced of his obsession when Rosnovski purchased ten per cent of Interstate Airways.'

'I suppose it's possible you may be over-reacting,' said Ted Leach. 'Of one thing I am certain: it would be unwise to inform the rest of the board of this information. The last thing we want a few days after launching a new company is a panic on our hands.'

'That's for sure,' said Tony Simmons. 'Why don't you see this fellow Rosnovski and have it out with him?'

'I expect that's exactly what he'd like me to do,' replied William. 'It would leave him in no doubt that the bank feels it's under siege.'

'Don't you think his attitude might change if you told him how hard you tried to talk the bank into backing the Richmond Group, but they wouldn't support you and ...'

'I've no reason to believe he doesn't know that already,' said William. 'He seems to know everything else.'

'Well what do you feel the bank should do about Rosnovski?' asked Ted Leach. 'We certainly can't stop him from purchasing our stock if he can find a willing seller. If we went in for buying our own stock, far from stopping him, we would play right into his hands by raising the value of his holding and jeopardizing our own financial position. I think you can be certain he would enjoy watching us sweat that one out. We are about the perfect size to be taken on by Harry Truman, and there's nothing the Democrats would enjoy more than a banking scandal with an election in the offing.'

'I realize there's little I can do about it,' said William, 'but I had to let you know what Rosnovski was up to in case he springs another surprise on us.'

'I suppose there's still an outside chance,' said Tony Simmons, 'that the whole thing is innocent, and he simply respects your talent as an investor.'

'How can you say that, Tony, when you know my stepfather is involved? Do you think Rosnovski employed Henry Osborne to further my career in banking? You obviously don't understand Rosnovski as I do. I've watched him operating now for over twenty years. He's not used to losing; he simply goes on throwing the dice until he wins. I couldn't know him much better if he was one of my own family. He will ...'

'Now don't become paranoid, William, I expect ...'

'Don't become paranoid you say, Tony. Remember the power our Articles of Incorporation give to anyone who gets his hands on eight per cent of the bank's stock. An article I had originally inserted to protect myself from being removed. The man already has six per cent and if that's not a bad enough prospect for the future, remember that Rosnovski could wipe out Interstate Airways overnight just by placing his entire stock on the market at once.'

'But he would gain nothing from that,' said Ted Leach. 'On the contrary, he would stand to lose a great deal of money.'

'Believe me, you don't understand how Abel Rosnovski's mind works,' said William. 'He has the courage of a lion, and the loss would mean nothing to him. I'm fast becoming convinced his only interest is in getting even with me. Yes, of course he'd lose money on those shares if he dumped them, but he always has his hotels to fall back on. There are twenty-one of them now, you know, and he must realize that if Interstate stock collapses overnight, we will also be knocked backwards. As bankers, our credibility depends on the fickle confidence of the public, confidence Abel Rosnovski can now shatter as and when it suits him.'

'Calm down William,' said Tony Simmons. 'It hasn't come to that yet.

Now we know what Rosnovski is up to, we can keep a closer watch on his activities and counter them as and when we need to. The first thing we must be sure of is that no one else sells their shares in Lester's before first offering them to you. The bank is always going to support any action you take. My own feeling is still that you should speak to Rosnovski personally and have it out in the open with him. At least that way we will know how serious his intentions are, and we can prepare ourselves accordingly.'

'Is that also your opinion, Ted?' asked William.

'Yes, it is. I agree with Tony. I think you should contact the man directly. It can only be in the bank's interests to discover how innocent or otherwise his intentions really are.'

William sat silently for a few moments. 'If you both feel that way, I'll give it a try,' he eventually said. 'I must add that I don't agree with you, but I may be too personally involved to make a dispassionate judgement. Give me a few days to think about how I should best approach him, and I'll let you know the outcome.'

After the two vice-chairmen had left his office, William sat alone, thinking about the action he had agreed to take, certain there could be little hope of success with Abel Rosnovski if Henry Osborne was involved.

. . .

Four days later, William sat alone in his office, having given instructions that he was not to be interrupted under any circumstances. He knew that Abel Rosnovski was also sitting in his office in the New York Baron: he had had a man posted at the hotel all morning whose only task had been to report the moment Rosnovski showed up. The waiting man had phoned; Abel Rosnovski had arrived that morning at eight twenty-seven, had gone straight up to his office on the forty-second floor and had not been seen since. William picked up his telephone and asked the operator to get him the Baron Hotel.

'New York Baron.'

'Mr Rosnovski, please,' said William nervously. He was put through to a secretary.

'Mr Rosnovski, please,' he repeated. This time his voice was a little steadier.

'May I ask who is calling?' she said.

'My name is William Kane.'

There was a long silence – or did it simply seem long to William?

'I'm not sure if he's in, Mr Kane. I'll find out for you.'

Another long silence.

'Mr Kane?'

'Mr Rosnovski?'

'What can I do for you, Mr Kane?' asked a very calm lightly accented voice.

Although William had prepared his opening remarks carefully, he was aware that he sounded anxious.

'I'm a little worried about your holdings in Lester's Bank, Mr Rosnovski,' he said, 'and indeed in the strong position you have built up in one of the companies we represent. I thought perhaps the time had come for us to meet and discuss your full intentions. There is also a private matter I should like to make known to you.'

Another long silence. Had he been cut off?

'There are no conditions which would ever make a meeting with you possible, Kane. I know enough about you already without wanting to hear your excuses about the past. You keep your eyes open all the time, and you'll find out only too clearly what my intentions are, and they differ greatly from those you will find in the Book of Genesis, Mr Kane. One day you're going to want to jump out of the twelfth floor window of one of my hotels, because you'll be in deep trouble with Lester's Bank over your own holdings. I only need two more per cent to invoke Article Seven, and we both know what that means, don't we? Then perhaps you'll appreciate for the first time what it felt like for Davis Leroy, wondering for months what the bank might do with his life. Now you can sit and wonder for years what I am going to do with yours once I obtain that eight per cent.'

Abel Rosnovski's words chilled William, but somehow he forced himself to carry on calmly, while at the same time banging his fist angrily on the table. 'I can understand how you feel, Mr Rosnovski, but I still think it would be wise for us to get together and talk this whole thing out. There are one or two aspects of the affair I know you can't be aware of.'

'Like the way you swindled Henry Osborne out of five hundred thousand dollars, Mr Kane?'

William was momentarily speechless and wanted to explode, but once again managed to control his temper.

'No, Mr Rosnovski, what I want to talk to you about has nothing to do with Mr Osborne. It's a personal matter and it involves only you. However, I most emphatically assure you that I have never swindled Henry Osborne out of one red cent.'

'That's not Henry's version. He says you were responsible for the death of your own mother, to make sure that you didn't have to honour a debt to him. After your treatment of Davis Leroy, I find that only too easy to believe.'

William had never had to fight harder to control his emotions, and it took him several seconds to muster a reply. 'May I suggest we clear this whole misunderstanding up once and for all by meeting at a neutral place of your choice where no one would recognize us?'

'There's only one place left where no one would recognize you, Mr Kane.'

'Where's that?' asked William.

'Heaven,' said Abel, and placed the phone back on the hook.

.   .   .

'Get me Henry Osborne at once,' he said to his secretary.

He drummed his fingers on the desk while the girl took nearly fifteen minutes to find Congressman Osborne who, it turned out, had been showing some of his constituents around the Capitol building.

'Abel, is that you?'

'Yes, Henry, I thought you'd want to be the first to hear that Kane knows everything, so now the battle is out in the open.'

'What do you mean, he knows everything? Do you think he knows I'm involved?' asked Henry anxiously.

'He sure does, and he also seems to be aware of the special company accounts, my holdings in Lester's Bank and Interstate Airways.'

'How could he possibly know everything in such detail? Only you and I know about the special accounts.'

'And Curtis Fenton,' said Abel, interrupting him.

'Right. But he would never inform Kane.'

'He must have. There's no one else. Don't forget that Kane dealt directly with Curtis Fenton when I brought the Richmond Group from his bank. I suppose they must have maintained some sort of contact all along.'

'Jesus.'

'You sound worried, Henry.'

'If William Kane knows everything, it's a different ball game. I'm warning you, Abel, he's not in the habit of losing.'

'Nor am I,' replied Abel. 'And William Kane doesn't frighten me; not while I'm holding all the aces in my hand. What is our latest holding in Kane's stock?'

'Off the top of my head, you own six per cent of Lester's Bank, and ten per cent of Interstate Airways, and odd bits of other companies they're involved with. You only need another two per cent of Lester's to invoke Article Seven and Peter Parfitt is still biting.'

'Excellent,' said Abel. 'I don't see how the situation could be better. Continue talking to Parfitt, remembering that I'm in no hurry while Kane can't even approach him. For the time being we'll let Kane wonder what we're up to. And be sure you do nothing until I return from Europe. After my phone conversation with Mr Kane this morning, I can assure you that, to use a gentleman's expression, he's perspiring but I'll let you into a secret, Henry. I'm not sweating. He can go on that way because I have no intention of making a move until I'm good and ready.'

'Fine,' said Henry. 'I'll keep you informed if anything comes up at this end that we should worry about.'

'You must get it through your head, Henry, there's nothing for *us* to worry about. We have your friend, Mr Kane, by the balls, and I know intend to squeeze them very slowly.'

'I shall enjoy watching that,' said Henry, sounding a little happier.

'Sometimes I think you hate Kane more than I do.'

Henry laughed nervously. 'Have a good trip to Europe.'

Abel put the phone back on the hook and sat staring into space as he considered his next move, his fingers still tapping noisily on the desk. His secretary came in.

'Get Mr Curtis Fenton at the Continental Trust Bank,' he said, without looking at her. His fingers continued to tap. His eyes continued to stare. A few moments later the phone rang.

'Fenton?'

'Good morning, Mr Rosnovski, how are you?'

'I want you to close all my accounts with your bank.'

There was no reply from the other end.

'Did you hear me, Fenton?'

'Yes,' said the stupefied banker. 'May I ask why, Mr Rosnovski?'

'Because Judas never was my favourite apostle, Fenton, that's why. As of this moment, you are no longer on the board of the Baron Group. You will shortly receive written instructions confirming this conversation and telling you to which bank the accounts should be transferred.'

'But I don't understand why, Mr Rosnovski. What have I done ...?'

Abel hung up as his daughter walked into the office.

'That didn't sound very pleasant, Daddy.'

'It wasn't meant to be pleasant, but it's nothing to concern yourself with, darling,' said Abel, his tone changing immediately. 'Did you manage to find all the clothes you need for Europe?'

'Yes, thank you, Daddy, but I'm not absolutely sure what they're wearing in London and Paris. I can only hope that I've got it right. I don't want to stick out like a sore thumb.'

'You'll stick out all right, my darling, by being the most beautiful thing the British have seen in years. They'll know your clothes didn't come out of a ration book with your natural flair and sense of colour. Those young Europeans will be falling all over themselves to get alongside you, but I'll be there to stop them. Now let's go and have some lunch and discuss what we are going to do while we're in London.'

. . .

Ten days later, after Florentyna had spent a long weekend with her mother – Abel never inquired after her – the two of them flew from New York's Idlewild Airport to London's Heathrow. The flight in a Boeing 377 took nearly fourteen hours, and although they had private berths, when they arrived at Claridges in Brook Street, the only thing they both wanted to do was have another long sleep.

Abel was making the trip to Europe for three reasons: first to confirm building contracts for new Baron hotels in London, Paris and possibly Rome; second, to give Florentyna her first view of Europe before she went to Radcliffe to study modern languages; and third, and most important to him, to revisit his castle in Poland to see if there was even an outside chance of proving his ownership

London turned out to be a success for both of them. Abel's advisors had found a site on Hyde Park corner, and he instructed solicitors to proceed immediately with all the negotiations for the land and the permits that would be needed before England's capital could boast a Baron. Florentyna found the austerity of post-war London forbidding after the excess of her own home, but the Londoners seemed to be undaunted by their war-damaged city, still believing themselves to be a world power. She was invited to lunches, dinners and balls, and her father was proved right about her taste in clothes and the reaction of young European men. She returned each night with sparkling eyes and stories of new conquests made – and forgotten by the following morning. She couldn't make up her mind whether she wanted to marry an Etonian from the Grenadier Guards who saluted her all the time or a member of the House of Lords who was in waiting to the King. She wasn't quite sure what 'in waiting' meant, but he certainly knew exactly how to treat a lady.

In Paris, the pace never slackened and because they both spoke good French, they both managed as well with the Parisians as they had with the English. Abel was normally bored by the end of the second week of any holiday, and would start counting the days until he could return home to work. But not while he had Florentyna as his companion. She had, since his separation from Zaphia, become the centre of his life and the sole heir to his fortune.

When the time came for Abel to leave Paris, neither of them wanted to go, so they stayed on a few more days claiming as an excuse that Abel was still negotiating to buy a famous but now run-down hotel on the Boulevard Raspail. He did not inform the owner, a Monsieur Neuffe, who looked, if it were possible, even more run-down than the hotel, that he planned to demolish the building and start again from scratch. When Monsieur Neuffe signed the papers a few days later, Abel ordered the building razed to the ground while he and Florentyna, with no more excuses left for remaining in Paris, departed reluctantly for Rome.

After the friendliness of the British and the gaiety of the French capital, the sullen and dilapidated Eternal City immediately dampened their spirits, for the Romans felt they had nothing behind them. In London, they had strolled through the magnificent Royal parks together, admired historic buildings, and Florentyna had danced until the small hours. In Paris, they had been to the Opéra, lunched on the banks of the Seine, and taken a boat down the river past Nôtre Dame and on to supper in the Latin Quarter. In Rome, Abel found only an overpowering sense of financial instability and decided that he would have to shelve his plans to build a Baron in the Italian capital. Florentyna sensed her father's anxiety to see once again his castle in Poland, so she suggested they leave Italy a day early.

Abel had found bureaucracy more reluctant to grant a visa for Florentyna and himself to enter an Iron Curtain country than it had been to issue a permit to build a new five-hundred-room hotel in London. A less persistent visitor would probably have given up, but with the appropriate visas firmly stamped in their passports, Abel and Florentyna set off in a hired car for Slonim. The two travellers were kept waiting for hours at the Polish border, helped along only by the fact that Abel was fluent in the language. Had the border guards known why his Polish was so good, they would doubtless have taken an entirely different attitude to allowing him to return. Abel changed five hundred dollars into zlotys – that at least seemed to please the Poles – and motored on. The nearer they came to Slonim, the more Florentyna was aware of how much the journey meant to her father.

'Daddy, I can never remember you being so excited about anything.'

'This is where I was born,' Abel explained. 'After such a long time in America, where things change every day, it's almost unreal to be back where it looks as if nothing has changed since I left.'

They drove on towards Slonim, Abel's senses heightened in anticipation, while horrified and angry at the devastation of the once trim countryside and small, neat cottages. Across a time span of nearly forty years he heard his childish voice ask the Baron whether the hour of the submerged peoples of Europe had arrived and would he be able to play his part, and tears came to his eyes to think how short that hour had been, and what a little part he had played.

When they rounded the final corner before approaching the Baron's estate and saw the great iron gates that led to the castle, Abel laughed aloud in excitement as he brought the car to a halt.

'It's all just as I remember it. Nothing's changed. Come on, let's start by visiting the cottage where I spent the first five years of my life – I don't expect anyone is living there now – and then we'll go and see my castle.'

Florentyna followed her father as he marched confidently down a small track into the forest of moss-covered birches and oaks, which was not going to change in a hundred years. After they had walked for about twenty minutes, the two of them came out into a small clearing, and there in front of them was the trapper's cottage. Abel stood and stared. He had forgotten how tiny his first home was: could nine people really have lived there? The thatched roof was now in disrepair, and the building left the impression of being uninhabited with its eroded stone and broken windows. The once tidy vegetable garden was indistinguishable in the matted undergrowth.

Had the cottage been deserted? Florentyna took her father by the arm and led him slowly to the front door. Abel stood there, motionless, so Florentyna knocked gently. They waited in silence. Florentyna knocked again, this time a little more loudly, and they heard someone moving within.

'All right, all right,' said a querulous voice in Polish, and a few moments later, the door inched open. They were being studied by an old woman, bent and thin, dressed entirely in black. Wisps of untidy snow-white hair escaped from her handkerchief and her grey eyes looked vacantly at the visitors.

'It's not possible,' said Abel softly in English.

'What do you want?' asked the old woman suspiciously.

She had no teeth and the line of her nose, mouth and chin formed a perfect concave arc.

Abel answered in Polish, 'May we come in and talk to you?'

Her eyes looked from one to the other fearfully. 'Old Helena hasn't done anything wrong,' she said in a whine.

'I know,' said Abel gently. 'I have brought good news for you.'

With some reluctance, she allowed them to enter the bare, cold room but she didn't offer them a seat. The room hadn't changed: two chairs, one table and the memory that until he had left the cottage, he hadn't known what a carpet was. Florentyna shuddered.

'I can't get the fire going,' wheezed the old woman, prodding the grate with her stick. The faintly glowing log refused to rekindle, and she scrabbled ineffectually in her pocket. 'I need paper.' She looked at Abel, showing a spark of interest for the first time. 'Do you have any paper?'

Abel looked at her steadily. 'Don't you remember me?' he said.

'No, I don't know you.'

'You do, Helena. My name is ... Wladek.'

'You knew my little Wladek?'

'I am Wladek.'

'Oh, no,' she said with sad and distant finality. 'He was too good for me, the mark of God was upon him. The Baron took him away to be an angel, yes, he took away Matka's littlest one ...'

Her old voice cracked and died away. She sat down, but the ancient, lined hands were busy in her lap.

'I have returned,' said Abel, more insistently, but the old woman paid him no attention, and her old voice quavered on as though she were quite alone in the room.

'They killed my husband, my Jasio, and all my lovely children were taken to the camps, except little Sophia. I hid her, and they went away.' Her voice was even and resigned.

'What happened to little Sophia?' asked Abel.

'The Russians took her away in the other war,' she said dully.

Abel shuddered.

The old woman roused herself from her memories. 'What do you want? Why are you asking me these questions?' she demanded.

'I wanted you to meet my daughter, Florentyna.'

'I had a daughter called Florentyna once, but now there's only me.'

'But I . . .' began Abel, starting to unbutton his shirt.

Florentyna stopped him. 'We know,' she said, smiling at the old lady.

'How can you possibly know? It was all so long before you were even born.'

'They told us in the village,' said Florentyna.

'Have you any paper with you?' the old lady asked, 'I need paper for the fire.'

Abel looked at Florentyna helplessly. 'No,' he replied, 'I'm sorry, we didn't bring any with us.'

'What do you want?' reiterated the old woman, once again hostile.

'Nothing,' said Abel, now resigned to the fact that she would not remember him. 'We just wanted to say hello.' He took out his wallet, removed all the new zloty notes he had acquired at the border and handed them over to her.

'Thank you, thank you,' she said as she took each note, her old eyes watering with pleasure.

Abel bent over to kiss his foster-mother, but she backed away.

Florentyna took her father's arm and led Abel out of the cottage and back down the forest track in the direction of their car.

The old woman watched from her window until she was sure they were out of sight. Then she took the new bank notes, crumpled each one into a ball and placed them all carefully in the grate. They kindled immediately. She placed twigs and small logs on top of the blazing zlotys and sat slowly down by her fire, the best in weeks, rubbing her hands together at the comfort of the warmth.

Abel did not speak on the walk back to the car until the iron gates were once again in sight. Then he promised Florentyna, trying his best to forget the little cottage, 'You are about to see the most beautiful castle in the world.'

'You must stop exaggerating, Daddy.'

'In the world,' Abel repeated quietly.

Florentyna laughed. 'I'll let you know how it compares with Versailles.'

They climbed back into the car and Abel drove through the gates, remembering the vehicles he had been in when he last passed through them, and up the mile-long drive to the castle. Memories came flooding back to him. Happy days as a child with the Baron and Leon, unhappy days of his life when he was taken away from his beloved castle by the Russians, imagining he would never see the building again. But now he, Wladek Koskiewicz, was returning, returning in triumph to reclaim what was his.

The car bumped up the winding road and both remained silent in anticipation as they rounded the final bend to the first sight of Baron Rosnovski's home. Abel brought the car to a halt and gazed at his castle. Neither of them spoke, but simply stared in disbelief at the devastation of the bombed-out remains of his dream.

He and Florentyna climbed slowly out of the car. Still neither spoke. Florentyna held her father's hand very, very tightly as the tears rolled down his cheeks. Only one wall remained precariously standing in a semblance of its former glory; the rest was nothing more than a neglected pile of rubble and red stone. He could not bear to tell her of the great halls, the wings, the kitchens, the bedrooms. Abel walked over to the three mounds, now smooth with thick green grass, that were the graves of the Baron and his son Leon and the other of beloved Florentyna. He paused at each one and could not help but think that Leon and Florentyna could still be alive today. He knelt at their heads, the dreadful visions of their final moments returning to him vividly. His daughter stood by his side, her hand resting on his shoulder, saying nothing. A long time passed before Abel rose slowly and then they tramped over the ruins together. Stone slabs marked the places where once magnificent rooms had been filled with laughter. Abel still said nothing. Holding hands, they reached the dungeons. There Abel sat down on the floor of the damp little room near the grille, or the half of the grille that was still left. He twisted the silver band round and round.

'This is where your father spent four years of his life.'

'It can't be possible,' said Florentyna, who did not sit down.

'It's better now than it was then,' said Abel. 'At least now there is fresh air, birds, the sun and a feeling of freedom. Then there was nothing, only darkness, death, the stench of death, and worst of all, the hope of death.'

'Come on, Daddy, let's leave. Staying here can only make you feel worse.'

Florentyna led her reluctant father to the car and drove him slowly down the long avenue. Abel didn't look back towards the ruined castle as they passed for the last time through its iron gates.

On the journey back to Warsaw he hardly spoke and Florentyna abandoned her attempts at vivacity. When her father said 'There is now only one thing left that I must achieve in this life,' Florentyna wondered what he could mean but did not press him to explain. She did, however, manage to coax him into spending another weekend in London on the return journey, which she convinced herself would cheer her father up a little and perhaps even help him to forget the memory of his demented old foster-mother and the remains of his castle in Poland.

They flew to London the next day. Abel was glad to be back in a country where he could communicate quickly with America. Once they had booked into Claridges, Florentyna went off to reunite with old friends and make new ones. Abel spent his time reading all the papers he could lay his hands on, in the hope of bringing himself up to date with what had happened in America while he had been abroad. He didn't like to feel things *could* happen while he was away; it reminded him only too clearly that the world could get along very well without him.

A little item on an inside page of Saturday's *Times* caught his eye. Things had happened while he was away. A Vickers Viscount of Interstate Airways had crashed immediately after take-off at the Mexico City airport the previous morning. The seventeen passengers and crew had all been killed. The Mexican authorities had been quick to place the blame on Interstate's bad servicing of their aircraft. Abel picked up the phone and asked the girl for the overseas operator.

Saturday, he's probably back in Chicago, thought Abel. He thumbed through his little phone book to find the home number.

'There'll be a delay of about thirty minutes,' said a precise, not unattractive, English voice.

'Thank you,' said Abel, and he lay down on the bed with the phone by his side, thinking. It rang twenty minutes later.

'Your overseas call is on the line, sir,' said the same precise voice.

'Abel, is that you? Where are you?'

'Sure is, Henry. I'm in London.'

'Are you through?' said the girl, who was back on the line.

'I haven't even started,' said Abel.

'I'm sorry, sir. I mean are you speaking to America?'

'Oh yes, sure. Thank you. Jesus, Henry, they speak a different language over here.'

Henry Osborne laughed.

'Now listen. Did you read that item in the press about an Interstate Airways' Vickers Viscount crashing at the Mexico City airport?'

'Yes, I did,' said Henry, 'but there's nothing for you to worry about. The plane was properly insured and the company is completely covered, so they incurred no loss and the stock has remained steady.'

'The insurance is the last thing I'm interested in,' said Abel. 'This could be our best chance yet for a little trial run to discover just how strong Mr Kane's constitution is.'

'I don't think I understand, Abel. What do you mean?'

'Listen carefully, and I'll explain exactly what I want you to do when the Stock Exchange opens on Monday morning. I'll be back in New York by Tuesday to orchestrate the final crescendo myself.'

Henry Osborne listened attentively to Abel Rosnovski's instructions. Twenty minutes later, Abel replaced the phone on the hook.

He was through.

30

William realized he could expect more trouble from Abel Rosnovski the morning that Curtis Fenton phoned to let him know that the Chicago Baron was closing all the group's bank accounts with Continental Trust and was accusing Fenton himself of disloyalty and unethical conduct.

'I thought I did the correct thing in writing to you about Mr Rosnovski's acquisitions in Lester's,' said the banker unhappily, 'and it has ended with me losing one of my biggest customers. I don't know what my board of directors will say.'

William formulated an inadequate apology, and calmed Fenton down a little by promising him he would speak to his superiors. He was, however, more preoccupied with wondering what Abel Rosnovski's next move would be.

Nearly a month later, he found out. He was going through the bank's Monday morning mail when a call came through from his broker, telling him that someone had placed a million dollars worth of Interstate Airways' stock on the market. William had to make the instant decision that his personal trust should pick up the shares, and he issued an immediate buy order for them. At two o'clock that afternoon, another million dollars worth was put on the market. Before William had a chance to pick them up, the price had started falling. By the time the New York Stock Exchange closed at three o'clock, the price of Interstate Airways had fallen by a third.

At ten minutes past ten the next morning, William received a call from his now agitated broker. Another million dollars worth of shares had been placed on the market at the opening bell. The broker reported that the latest dumping had had an avalanche effect: Interstate sell orders were coming onto the floor from every quarter, the bottom had fallen out, and the stock was now trading at only a few cents a share. Only twenty-four hours previously, Interstate had been quoted at four and a half.

William instructed Alfred Rodgers, the company secretary, to call a board meeting for the following Monday. He needed the time to confirm who was responsible for the dumping. By Wednesday, he had abandoned any attempt at shoring up Interstate by buying all the shares that came on the market himself. At the close of business that day, the Securities and Exchange Commission announced that they would be conducting an inquiry into all Interstate transactions. William knew that Lester's board would now have to decide whether to support the airline for the three to six months it would take the SEC to complete their investigation or whether to let the company go under. The alternatives looked extremely damaging, both to William's pocket and to the bank's reputation.

It came as no surprise to William to discover from Thaddeus Cohen the next day that the company that had dumped the original three million dollars worth of Interstate shares was one of those fronting for Abel Rosnovski, Guaranty Investment Corporation by name. A corporation spokesman had issued a plausible little press release explaining their reasons for selling, they had been concerned for the future of the Company after the Mexican government's responsible statement about Interstate Airways' inadequate servicing facilities.

'Responsible statement,' said William, outraged. 'The Mexican government hasn't made a responsible statement since they claimed Speedy Gonzales would win the one hundred metres at the Helsinki Olympics.'

The media made the most of Guaranty Investment's press release, and on Friday, the Federal Aviation Agency grounded the airline until it could conduct an in-depth investigation of its servicing facilities.

William was confident Interstate had nothing to fear from such an inspection, but the action proved disastrous for the short-term passenger bookings.

No aviation company can afford to leave aircraft on the ground; they can only make money when they are in the air.

To compound William's problems, other major companies represented by Lester's were reconsidering future commitments. The press had been quick to point out that Lester's was Interstate Airways' underwriters. Surprisingly, Interstate's shares began to pick up again late Friday afternoon, and it did not take William long to guess why, a guess that was later confirmed by Thaddeus Cohen: the buyer was Abel Rosnovski. He had sold his Interstate shares at the top and was now buying them back in small amounts while they were at the bottom. William shook his head in begrudging admiration. Rosnovski was making a small fortune for himself while bankrupting William both in reputation and financial terms.

William worked out that although the Baron Group must have risked over three million dollars, they might well end up making a huge profit. Moreover, it was evident that Rosnovski was unconcerned about a temporary loss, which he could in any case use as a tax write-off; his only interest was in the total destruction of Lester's reputation.

When the board met on Monday, William explained the entire history of his clash with Rosnovski and offered his resignation. It was not accepted, nor was a vote taken, but there were murmurings, and William knew that if Rosnovski attacked again, his colleagues might not take the same tolerant attitude a second time.

The board went on to consider whether they should continue the support for Interstate Airways. Tony Simmons convinced them that the FAA's inquiry would come out in the bank's favour, and that Interstate would in time recover all their money. Tony had to admit to William after the meeting that their decision could only help Rosnovski in the long run, but the bank had no choice if it wished to protect its reputation.

He proved right on both counts. When the SEC finally published its findings, they declared Lester's 'reproach-proof' although they had some stern words for Guaranty Investment Corporation. When the market started trading in Interstate shares that morning, William was surprised to find the stock rising steadily. It was soon back up to its original four and a half.

Thaddeus Cohen informed William that the principal purchaser was once again Abel Rosnovski.

'That's all I need at the moment,' said William. 'Not only does he make a large profit on the whole transaction, but now he can repeat the same exercise again whenever the time suits him.'

'In fact,' said Thaddeus Cohen, 'that is exactly what you do need.'

'Whatever do you mean, Thaddeus?' said William 'I've never known you speak in riddles.'

'Mr Abel Rosnovski has made his first error in judgement, because he's breaking the law and now it's your turn to go after him. He probably doesn't even realize that what he was involved in was illegal, because he was doing it for all the wrong reasons.'

'What are you talking about?' asked William.

'Simple,' said Thaddeus Cohen. 'Because of your obsession with Rosnovski – and his with you – it seems that both of you have overlooked the obvious: if you sell shares with the sole intention of causing the market to drop in order to pick up those same shares at the bottom and therefore be certain of a profit, you're breaking Rule 10b-5 of the Securities and Exchange Commission and you are committing the crime of fraud. There's no doubt in my mind that making a quick profit was not Mr Rosnovski's original intention; in fact, we know very well he only wanted to embarrass you personally. But who is going to believe Rosnovski if he gives as an explanation that he dumped the stock because he thought the company was unreliable, when he has bought all the same shares back when they reached rock bottom? Answer: nobody – and certainly not the SEC. I'll have a full written report sent around to you by tomorrow, William, explaining the legal implications.'

'Thank you,' said William, jubilant over the news.

Thaddeus Cohen's report was on William's desk at nine the next morning and after William had read over the contents very carefully, he called another board meeting. The directors agreed with the course of action William wanted to take. Thaddeus Cohen was instructed to draft a carefully written press release to be issued that evening. The *Wall Street Journal* ran a piece on their front page the following morning.

Mr William Kane, the chairman of Lester's Bank has reason to believe that the sell orders placed by Guaranty Investment Corporation in November 1952 on Interstate Airways shares, a company underwritten by Lester's Bank, were issued for the sole purpose of making an illegal profit.

It has been established that Guaranty Investment Corporation was reponsible for placing a million dollars worth of Interstate stock on the market when the exchange opened on Monday, 12 May 1952. A further million dollars worth was on the market six hours later. A third million dollars worth was placed on a sell order by Guaranty Investment Corporation when the exchange reopened on Tuesday, 13 May 1952. This caused the stock to fall to a record low. After an SEC inquiry showed there had been no illegal dealing within either Lester's Bank or Interstate Airways, the market picked up again with the stock trading at the depressed price. Guaranty Investment was quickly back in the market to purchase the shares at as low a price as possible. They continued to buy until they had replaced the three million dollars worth of stock they had originally released onto the market.

The chairman and directors of Lester's Bank have sent a copy of all the relevant documents to the Fraud Division of the Securities and Exchange Commission, and have asked them to proceed with a full inquiry.

The story below the statement gave SEC Rule 10b-5 in full and commented that this was exactly the sort of test case that President Truman had been looking for; a cartoon below the article showed Harry S. Truman catching a businessman with his hands in the cookie jar.

William smiled as he read through the item, confident that that would be the last he would hear of Abel Rosnovski.

. . .

Abel Rosnovski frowned and said nothing as Henry Osborne read the statement over to him. Abel looked up, his fingers tapping in irritation on the desk.

'The boys in Washington,' said Osborne, 'are determined to get to the bottom of this one.'

'But Henry, you know very well I didn't sell Interstate shares to make a quick killing on the stock market,' said Abel. 'The profit I made was of no interest to me at all.'

'I know that,' said Henry, 'but you try and convince the Senate Finance Committee that the Chicago Baron had no interest in financial gain, that all he really wanted to do was settle a personal grudge against one William Kane, and they'll laugh you right out of court – or out of the Senate, to be more exact.'

'Damn,' said Abel. 'Now what the hell do I do?'

'Well, first you'll have to lie very low until this has had time to blow over. Start praying that some bigger scandal comes along for Truman to get himself worked up about, or that the politicians become so involved in the election that they haven't time to press for an inquiry. With luck, a new administration may even drop the whole thing. Whatever you do, Abel, don't buy any more shares that are connected with Lester's Bank, or the least you're going to end up with is a very large fine. Leave me to swing what I can with the Democrats in Washington.'

'Remind Harry Truman's office that I gave fifty thousand dollars to his campaign fund during the last election and I intend to do the same for Adlai.'

'I've already done that,' said Henry. 'In fact I would advise you to give fifty thousand to the Republicans as well.'

'They're making a mountain out of a molehill,' said Abel. 'A molehill that Kane will turn into a mountain if we give him the chance.' His fingers continued to tap on the table.

31

Thaddeus Cohen's next quarterly report revealed that Abel Rosnovski had stopped buying or selling stock in any of Lester's companies. It seemed he was now concentrating all his energy on building more hotels in Europe. Cohen's opinion was that Rosnovski was lying low, until a decision had been made by the SEC on the Interstate affair.

Representatives of the SEC had visited William at the bank on several occasions. He had spoken to them with complete frankness, but they never revealed how their inquiries were progressing. The SEC finally finished their investigation and thanked William for his cooperation. He heard nothing more from them.

As the Presidential election grew nearer and Truman seemed to be concentrating his own efforts on the dissolution on the Du Pont industrial combine, William began to fear that Abel Rosnovski might have been let off the hook. He couldn't help feeling that Henry Osborne must have been able to pull a few strings in Congress. He remembered that Cohen had once underlined a note about a fifty thousand dollar donation from the Baron Group to Harry Truman's campaign fund and was surprised to read in Cohen's latest report that Rosnovski had repeated the donation for Adlai Stevenson, the Democrats' choice for President, along with another fifty thousand for the Eisenhower campaign fund. Cohen had underlined the item again.

William, who had never considered supporting anyone for public office who was not a Republican, wanted General Eisenhower, the candidate who had emerged on the first ballot at the convention in Chicago, to defeat Adlai Stevenson, although he was aware that a Republican administration was less likely to press for a share manipulation inquiry than the Democrats.

When General Dwight D. Eisenhower – it appeared that the nation did like Ike – was elected as the thirty-fourth President of the United States on 4 November 1952, William assumed that Abel Rosnovski had escaped any charge and could only hope that the experience would persuade him to leave Lester's affairs well enough alone in the future. The one small compensation to come out of the election for William was that Congressman Henry Osborne lost his Congressional seat to a Republican candidate. The Eisenhower jacket had turned out to have coat-tails, and Osborne's rival had clung to them. Thaddeus Cohen was inclined to think that Henry Osborne no longer exerted quite the same influence over Abel Rosnovski that he had in the past. The rumour in Chicago was that, since divorcing his rich wife, Osborne owed large sums of money to Rosnovski and was gambling heavily again.

William was happier and more relaxed than he had been for some time and looked forward to joining the prosperous and peaceful era that Eisenhower had promised in his Inauguration speech.

As the first years of the new President's administration went by, William began to put Rosnovski's threats at the back of his mind and to think of them as a thing of the past. He informed Thaddeus Cohen that he believed they had heard the last of Abel Rosnovski. The lawyer made no comment. He wasn't asked to.

William put all his efforts into building Lester's, both in size and reputation, increasingly aware that he was now doing it as much for his son as for himself. Some of his staff at the bank had already started referring to him as the 'old man'.

'It had to happen,' said Kate.

'Then why hasn't it happened to you?' replied William.

Kate looked up at William and smiled. 'Now I know the secret of how you have closed so many deals with vain men.'

William laughed. 'And one beautiful woman,' he added.

With Richard's twenty-first birthday only a year away, William revised the provisions of his will. He set aside five million dollars for Kate and two million for each of the girls, and left the rest of the family fortune to Richard, noting ruefully the bite that would go in estate tax. He also left one million dollars to Harvard.

Richard had been making good use of his four years at Harvard. At the start of his senior year, not only did he look set for a *Summa Cum Laude*, but he was also playing the cello in the university orchestra, and was a pitcher with the varsity baseball team, which even William had to admire. As Kate liked rhetorically to ask, how many students spent Saturday afternoon playing baseball for Harvard against Yale and Sunday evening playing the cello in the Lowell concert hall for the university string quartet?

The final year passed quickly and when Richard left Harvard, armed with a Bachelor of Arts degree in mathematics, a cello and a baseball bat, all he required before reporting to the business school on the other side of the Charles River was a good holiday. He flew to Barbados with a girl called Mary Bigelow of whose existence Richard's parents were blissfully unaware. Miss Bigelow had studied music, among other things, at Vasser, and when they returned two months later almost the same colour as the natives, Richard took her home to meet his parents. William approved of Miss Bigelow; after all, she was Alan Lloyd's great niece.

Richard returned to the Harvard Business School on 1 October 1955 to start his graduate work. He took up residence in the Red House, threw out all William's cane furniture and removed the paisley wallpaper that Matthew Lester had once found so modern, and installed a wall-to-wall carpet in the living room, an oak table in the dining room, a dishwasher in the kitchen and, more than occasionally, Miss Bigelow in the bedroom.

32

Abel returned from a trip to Istanbul in October 1952, immediately upon hearing the news of David Maxton's fatal heart attack. He attended the funeral in Chicago with George and Florentyna and later told Mrs Maxton that she could be a guest at any Baron in the world whenever she so pleased for the rest of her life. She could not understand why Abel had made such a generous gesture.

When Abel returned to New York the next day, he was delighted to find on the desk of his forty-second floor office a report from Henry Osborne indicating that the heat was now off. In Henry's opinion, the new Eisenhower administration was unlikely to pursue an inquiry into the Interstate Airways fiasco, especially as the stock had now held steady for nearly a year. There had, therefore, been no further incidents to renew any interest in the scandal. Eisenhower's Vice-President, Richard M. Nixon, seemed more involved in chasing the spectral communists whom Joe McCarthy missed.

Abel spent the next two years concentrating on building his hotels in Europe. He opened the Paris Baron in 1953 and the London Baron at the end of 1954. Barons were also in various stages of development for Brussels, Rome, Amsterdam, Geneva, Bonn, Edinburgh, Cannes and Stockholm in a ten-year expansion programme.

Abel became so overworked that he had little time to consider William Kane's continued prosperity. He had not made any attempt to buy shares in Lester's Bank or its subsidiary companies, although he held onto those he already possessed in the hope that another opportunity might be forthcoming to deal a blow againt William Kane from which he would not recover so easily. The next time, Abel promised himself, he'd make sure he didn't unwittingly break the law.

During Abel's increasingly frequent absences abroad George ran the Baron Group and Abel was hoping that Florentyna would join the board as soon as she left Radcliffe in June of 1955. He had already decided that she should take over responsibility for all the shops in the hotels and consolidate their buying, as they were fast becoming an empire in themselves.

Florentyna was very excited by the prospect but was insistent that she wanted some outside experience before joining her father's group. She did not consider her natural gifts for design, colour, and organization were any substitute for experience. Abel suggested that she train in Switzerland under Monsieur Maurice at the famed *École Hôtelière* in Lausanne. Florentyna baulked at the idea, explaining that she wanted to work for two years in a New York store before she would consider taking over the shops. She was determined to be worth employing, '. . . and not just as my father's daughter,' she informed him. Abel thoroughly approved.

'A New York store, that's done easily enough,' he said. 'I'll ring up Walter Hoving at Tiffany's and you can start at the top.'

'No,' said Florentyna, revealing that she'd inherited her father's streak of stubbornness. 'What's the equivalent of a junior waiter at the Plaza Hotel?'

'A sales girl at a department store,' said Abel, laughing.

'Then that's exactly what I'm going to be,' she said.

Abel stopped laughing. 'Are you serious? With a degree from Radcliffe and all the experience and knowledge you've gained from your European trips, you want to be an anonymous sales girl?'

'Being an anonymous waiter at the Plaza didn't do you any harm when the time came to set up one of the most successful hotel groups in the world,' replied Florentyna.

Abel knew when he was beaten. He had only to look into the steel grey eyes of his beautiful daughter to realize she had made up her mind, and that no amount of persuasion, gentle or otherwise, was going to change her views.

After Florentyna had graduated from Radcliffe, she spent a month in Europe with her father, watching the progress of the latest Baron hotels. She officially opened the Brussels Baron where she made a conquest of the handsome young French-speaking managing director, whom Abel accused of smelling of garlic. She had to give him up three days later when it reached the kissing stage, but she never admitted to her father that garlic had been the reason.

Florentyna returned to New York with her father and immediately applied for the vacant position (the words used in the classified advertisement) of 'junior sales assistant' at Bloomingdale's. When she filled in the application form, she gave her name as Jessie Kovats, well aware that no one would leave her in peace if they ever thought she was the daughter of the Chicago Baron.

Despite protests from her father, she also left her suite in the Baron Hotel and started looking for her own place to live. Once again Abel gave in and presented Florentyna with a small but elegant cooperative flat on Fifty-seventh Street near the East River as a twenty-second birthday present.

Florentyna already knew her way around New York and enjoyed a full social life, but she had long ago resolved not to let her friends know that she was going to work at Bloomingdale's. She feared that they would want to come and visit her and, in days, her cleverly constructed cover would be blown, making it impossible to be treated as a normal trainee.

When her friends did inquire, she merely told them that she was helping to run the shops in her father's hotels. None of them gave her reply a second thought.

Jessie Kovats – it took her some time to get used to the name – started in cosmetics. After six months, she was ready to run her own beauty shop. The girls in Bloomingdale's worked in pairs, which Florentyna immediately turned to her advantage by choosing to work with the laziest girl in the department. This arrangement suited both girls as Florentyna's choice was a gorgeous, unenlightened blonde called Maisie who had only two interests in life: the clock pointing to the hour of six p.m. and men. The former happened once a day, the latter all the time.

The two girls soon became comrades without exactly being friends. Florentyna learned a lot from her partner about how to avoid work without being spotted by the floor manager, and also how to get picked up by a man.

The cosmetic counter's profits were well up after their first six months together, despite the fact that Maisie spent most of her time trying out the products rather than selling them. She could take two hours repainting her finger nails alone. Florentyna, in contrast, had a natural gift for selling that could not have been picked up at night school. That combined with an ability to learn quickly made it seem to her employers, after only a few weeks, as if she had been around for years.

The partnership with Maisie suited Florentyna ideally, and when they moved her to Better Dresses, by mutual agreement Maisie went along and passed her time by trying on new dresses all day while Florentyna sold them. Maisie could attract men – in tow with their wives or sweethearts – irrespective of the merchandise, simply by looking at them. Once they were ensnared, Florentyna could move in and sell something to them. It seemed hardly possible that the combination could work in Better Dresses, but Florentyna made Maisie's victims buy something, few escaping with untouched wallets.

The profits for that six months were up again, and the floor supervisor decided that the two girls obviously worked well together. Florentyna said nothing to contradict that impression. While other assistants in the shop were always complaining about how little work their partners did, Florentyna continually praised Maisie as the ideal workmate, who had taught her so much about how a big store operated. She didn't mention the useful advice that Maisie also imparted on how to deal with over-amorous men.

The greatest compliment an assistant can receive at Bloomingdale's is to be put on one of the counters facing the Lexington Avenue entrance, the first person to be seen by customers coming in through the main doors. To work on that counter was considered as a small promotion and it was rare for a girl to be invited to sell there until she had been with the store at least five years. Maisie had been with Bloomingdale's since she was seventeen, a full five years, while Florentyna had only just completed her first twelve months. But as their results had been so impressive, the manager decided to try the two girls out on the ground floor in the stationery department. Maisie was unable to derive any personal advantage from the stationery department, as she didn't care too much for reading and even less for writing. Florentyna wasn't sure after a year with her that she could read or write. Nevertheless, her new position pleased Maisie greatly because she adored being the centre of attention. So the girls continued their perfect partnership.

Abel admitted to George that he had once sneaked into Bloomingdale's to watch Florentyna at work, and he had to confess that she was damned good. He assured his vice-president that he was looking forward to her finishing the two-years training, so that he could employ the girl himself. They had both agreed that when Florentyna left Bloomingdale's, she would be made vice-president of the group, with special responsibility for the hotel stores. As Bloomingdale's was finding out, she was a chip off a formidable old block, and Abel had no doubt that Florentyna would have few problems taking on the responsibilities he was planning for her.

. . . .

Florentyna spent her last six months at Bloomingdale's on the ground floor in charge of six counters with the new title of junior supervisor. Her duties now included stock checking, the cash desks and overall supervision of eighteen sales clerks. Bloomingdale's had already decided that Jessie Kovats was the ideal candidate to be a future buyer.

Florentyna had not yet informed her employers that she would be leaving shortly to join her father as a vice-president of the Baron Group. As the six months was drawing to its conclusion, she began to wonder what would happen to poor Maisie after she had left, Maisie assumed Jessie was at Bloomingdale's for life – wasn't everybody? – and never gave the question a second thought. Florentyna thought she might even offer her a job in one of the shops in the New York Baron. As long as it was behind a counter at which men spent money, Maisie was a valuable asset.

One afternoon when Maisie was waiting on a customer – she was now in gloves, scarves and woolly hats – she pulled Florentyna aside and pointed to a young man who was loitering over the mittens.

'What do you think of him?' she asked, giggling.

Florentyna glanced up at Maisie's latest desire with her customary dis-interest, but on this occasion she had to admit to herself that he was rather attractive, and for once she was almost envious of Maisie.

'They only want one thing, Maisie.'

'I know,' said Maisie, 'and he can have it.'

'I'm sure he'll be pleased to hear that,' said Florentyna, laughing as she turned to wait on a customer who was becoming impatient at Maisie's indifference to her presence. Maisie took advantage of Florentyna's move and rushed off to serve the gloveless young man. Florentyna watched them both out of the corner of her eye. She was amused that he kept glancing nervously towards her, checking that Maisie wasn't being spied on by her supervisor. Maisie giggled away and the young man departed with a pair of dark blue leather gloves.

'Well, how did he measure up to your hopes?' asked Florentyna, conscious she felt a little jealous of Maisie's new conquest.

'He didn't,' replied Maisie. 'But I'm sure he'll be back again,' she added, grinning.

Maisie's prediction turned out to be correct, for the next day there he was, thumbing among the gloves and looking even more embarrassed.

'I suppose you had better go and wait on him,' said Florentyna.

Maisie hurried obediently away. Florentyna nearly laughed out loud when, a few minutes later, the young man departed with another pair of dark blue gloves.

'Two pairs,' declared Florentyna. 'I think I can say on behalf of Bloomingdale's, he deserves you.'

'But he still didn't ask me out,' said Maisie.

'What?' said Florentyna in mock disbelief. 'He must have a glove fetish.'

'It's very disappointing,' said Maisie, 'because I think he's neat.'

'Yes, he's not bad,' said Florentyna.

The next day when the young man arrived in the shop Maisie leapt forward, leaving an old lady in mid-sentence. Florentyna quickly took her place, once again watching Maisie out of the corner of her eye. This time the two of them appeared to be in deep conversation and the young man finally departed with yet another pair of dark blue leather gloves.

'It must be the real thing,' ventured Florentyna.

'Yes, I think it is,' replied Maisie, 'but he still hasn't suggested a date.'

Florentyna was flabbergasted.

'Listen,' said Maisie desperately, 'if he comes in tomorrow could you serve him? I think he is scared to ask me directly. He might find it easier to make a date through you.'

Florentyna laughed. 'A Viola to your Orsino.'

'What?' said Maisie.

'It doesn't matter,' said Florentyna. 'I wonder if I will be able to sell him a pair of gloves?'

If the man was anything he was consistent, thought Florentyna, as he pushed his way through the doors at exactly the same time the next day and immediately headed towards the glove counter. Maisie dug Florentyna in the ribs, and Florentyna decided the time had come to enjoy herself.

'Good afternoon, sir.'

'Oh, good afternoon,' said the young man looking surprised – or was it disappointment?

'Can I help you?' offered Florentyna.

'No – I mean, yes, I would like a pair of gloves,' he added unconvincingly.

'Yes, sir. Have you considered a dark blue pair? In leather? I'm sure we have your size – unless we're all sold out.'

The young man looked at her suspiciously as she handed him the gloves. He tried them on. They were a little too big. Florentyna offered him another pair but they were slightly too tight. He looked towards Maisie for inspiration but she was surrounded by a sea of male customers but she wasn't sinking because she even found the time to glance towards the young man

and grin. He grinned back nervously. Florentyna handed him another pair
of gloves. They fitted perfectly.

'I think that's what you're looking for,' said Florentyna.

'No, it's not really,' replied the embarrassed customer.

Florentyna decided the time had come to let the poor man off the hook
and lowering her voice, she said, 'I'll go and rescue Maisie. Why don't you
ask her out? I'm sure she will say yes.'

'Oh no,' said the young man. 'You don't understand. It's not her I want
to take out – it's you.'

Florentyna was speechless. The young man seemed to muster courage.

'Will you have dinner with me tonight?'

She heard herself saying, 'Yes.'

'Shall I pick you up at your home?'

'No,' said Florentyna a little too firmly. The last thing she wanted was
to be met at her apartment where it would be obvious to anyone that she
was not a salesgirl. 'Let's meet at a restaurant,' she added quickly.

'Where would you like to go . . .?'

Florentyna tried to think quickly of a place that would not be too
ostentatious.

'Allen's at Seventy-third and Third?' he ventured.

'Yes, fine,' said Florentyna, thinking how much better Maisie would have
been at handling the whole situation.

'Around eight o'clock suit you?'

'Around eight,' replied Florentyna.

The young man left with a smile on his face. Florentyna watched him
disappear onto the street, and suddenly realized that he had left without
buying a pair of gloves.

. . .

Florentyna took a long time choosing which dress she should wear for her
evening out. She wanted to be certain that the outfit didn't scream of
Bergdorf Goodman. She had acquired a small wardrobe especially for
Bloomingdale's, but the clothes were strictly for daytime use, and she had
never worn anything from that selection in the evening. If her date –
heavens, she didn't even know his name – thought she was a salesgirl she
mustn't disillusion him. She couldn't help feeling that she was actually
looking forward to the evening more than she ought to be.

She left her flat on East Fifty-seventh Street a little before eight and had
to wait for several minutes before she managed to hail an empty taxi.

'Allen's, please,' she said to the taxi driver.

'On Third Avenue.'

'Yes.'

'Sure thing, miss,' he replied.

When Florentyna arrived at the restaurant, she was a few minutes late.
Her eyes began to search for the young man. He was standing at the bar,
waving. He had changed into a pair of grey flannel slacks and a blue blazer.
Very Ivy League, thought Florentyna, but very good looking.

'I'm sorry to be late,' she began.

'It's not important. What's important is that you came.'

'You thought I wouldn't?' said Florentyna.

'I wasn't sure.' He smiled. 'I'm sorry, I don't know your name.'

'Jessie Kovats,' said Florentyna, determined not to give away her alias. 'And yours?'

'Richard Kane,' said the young man, thrusting out his hand.

She took it and he held onto her a little longer than she had expected.

'And what do you do when you're not buying gloves at Bloomingdale's?' she teased.

'I'm at Harvard Business School.'

'I'm surprised they didn't teach you that most people only have two hands.'

He laughed and smiled in such a relaxed and friendly way that she wished she could start again and tell him they might have met in Cambridge when she was at Radcliffe.

'Shall we order?' he said, taking her arm and leading her to a table.

Florentyna looked up at the menu on the blackboard.

'Salisbury steak?' she queried.

'A hamburger by any other name,' said Richard.

They both laughed, in the way two people do when they don't know each other, but want to. She could see he was surprised that she might have known his out-of-context quotation.

Florentyna had rarely enjoyed anyone's company more. Richard chatted about New York, the theatre and music – so obviously his first love – with such grace and charm that she was fully at ease. He may have thought she was a salesgirl but he was treating her as if she'd come from one of the oldest Brahmin families. He hoped he wasn't too surprised by her passion for the same things because, when he inquired, she told him nothing more than that she was Polish and lived in New York with her parents. As the evening progressed the deception became increasingly intolerable. Still, she thought, we may never see each other again after tonight, and then it will all be irrelevant.

When the evening did come to an end and neither of them could drink any more coffee, they left Allen's and Richard looked for a taxi, the only ones they saw were all full.

'Where do you live?' he asked.

'Fifty-seventh Street,' she said, not thinking about her reply.

'Then let's walk,' said Richard, taking Florentyna's hand.

She smiled her agreement. They started walking, stopping and looking at shop windows, laughing and smiling. Neither of them noticed the empty taxis that now rushed past them. It took them almost an hour to cover the sixteen blocks and Florentyna nearly told him the truth. When they reached Fifty-seventh Street she stopped outside a small old apartment house, some hundred yards from her own home.

'This is where my parents live,' she said.

He seemed to hesitate and then let go of her hand.

'I hope you will see me again,' said Richard.

'I'd like that,' replied Florentyna in a polite, dismissive way.

'Tomorrow?' asked Richard diffidently.

'Tomorrow?'

'Yes, why don't we go to the Blue Angel and see Bobby Short?' He took her hand again. 'It's a little more romantic than Allen's.'

Florentyna was momentarily taken aback. Her plans for Richard had not included any provisions for tomorrows.

'Not if you don't want to,' he added before she could recover.

'I'd love to,' she said quietly.

'I'm having dinner with my father, so why don't I pick you up at ten o'clock?'

'No, no,' said Florentyna, 'I'll meet you there. It's only two blocks away.'

'Ten o'clock then,' he bent forward and kissed her gently on the cheek. 'Goodnight, Jessie,' he said, and disappeared into the night.

Florentyna walked slowly back to her apartment, wishing she hadn't told so many lies about herself. Still, it might be over in a few days. She couldn't help feeling that she hoped it wouldn't.

.   .   .

Maisie, who hadn't yet forgiven her, spent a considerable part of the next day asking all about Richard. Florentyna kept trying unsuccessfully to change the subject.

Florentyna left Bloomingdale's the moment the store closed, the first time in nearly two years that she had left before Maisie. She had a long bath, put on the prettiest dress she thought she could get away with, and walked to the Blue Angel. When she arrived Richard was already waiting for her outside the cloakroom. He held her hand as they walked into the lounge where the words of Bobby Short came floating through the air.

Are you telling me the truth, or am I just another lie?

As Florentyna walked in, Short raised his arm in acknowledgement. Florentyna pretended not to notice. Mr Short had been a guest performer at The Baron on two or three occasions and it never occurred to Florentyna that he would remember her. Richard looked puzzled and then assumed he had been greeting someone else. When they took a table in the dimly-lit room, Florentyna sat with her back to the piano to be certain it wouldn't happen again.

Richard ordered a bottle of wine without letting go of her hand and then asked about her day. She didn't want to tell him; she wanted to tell him the truth – 'Richard, there is something I must ...'

'Hi, Richard.' A tall, handsome man stood at Richard's side.

'Hi, Steve. Can I introduce Jessie Kovats – Steve Mellon. Steven and I were at Harvard together.'

Florentyna listened to them chat about the New York Yankees, Eisenhower's handicap – his golf, and why Yale was going from bad to worse. Steve eventually left with a gracious, 'Nice to have met you, Jessie.'

The moment had passed.

Richard began to tell her of his plans once he had left business school, how he hoped to come to New York and join his father's bank, Lester's. She had heard the name before but couldn't remember in what connection. For some reason it worried her. They spent a long evening together, laughing, eating, talking, and just sitting, holding hands, listening to Bobby Short. When they walked home, Richard stopped on the corner of Fifty-seventh and kissed her for the first time. She couldn't recall any other occasion when she was so aware of a kiss. When he returned her to the shadows of Fifty-seventh Street, she left him and her white lies, aware that this time he had not mentioned tomorrow. She felt slightly wistful about the whole non-affair.

She was taken aback by how pleased she felt when Richard phoned her at Bloomingdale's on Monday, asking if she would go out with him on Friday evening.

.   .   .

They wound up spending most of that weekend together: a concert, a film – even the New York Knicks did not escape them. When the weekend was over Florentyna found she had told so many innocent lies about her background that she became inconsistent in her fabrication and puzzled Richard more than once by contradicting herself. It seemed to make it all the more impossible to tell him another entirely different, albeit true, story. When Richard returned to Harvard on the Sunday night, she persuaded herself that the deception would seem unimportant once the relationship had ended. But Richard phoned every day during the week and spent the next few weekends in her company: she began to realize it wasn't going to end that easily. She was falling in love with him. Once she had admitted that to herself, she realized that she had to tell him the truth the following weekend.

33

Richard sat through his morning lecture, daydreaming. He was so much in love with that girl, he could not even concentrate on the 'Twenty-nine crash'. He wished he could work out how to tell his father that he intended to marry a Polish girl who worked behind the scarf, glove and woolly hats counter at Bloomingdale's. Richard was unable to fathom why she was so unambitious for herself when she was obviously very bright: he was certain that if she had had the chances he had been given, she would not have ended up in Bloomingdale's. Richard decided that his parents would have to learn to live with his choice, because that weekend he was going to ask Jessie to be his wife.

Whenever Richard returned to his parent's home in New York on a Friday evening, he would always leave the house on East Sixty-eighth Street to go and pick up something from Bloomingdale's, normally a useless and unwanted item, simply so that he could let Jessie know that he was back in town; he had already given a pair of gloves to every relation he possessed. That Friday, he told his mother that he was going out to buy some razor blades.

'Don't bother, darling, you can use your father's,' she said.

'No, no, it's all right,' he said. 'I'll go and get some of my own. We don't use the same brand in any case,' he added feebly. 'I'll only be a few minutes.'

He almost ran the eight blocks to Bloomingdale's and managed to rush in just as they were closing the doors. He knew he would be seeing Jessie at seven thirty, but he could never resist a chance to chat with her. Steve had told him once that love was for suckers. He had written on his steamed-up shaving mirror that morning 'I am a sucker'. But when he reached Jessie's counter, she was nowhere to be seen. Maisie was standing in a corner filing her finger nails, and he asked her if Jessie was still around. Maisie looked up as if she had been interrupted from her one important task of the day.

'No, she's already gone home, Richard. Left a few seconds ago. She can't have gone far. I thought you were meeting her later.'

Richard ran out onto Lexington Avenue without replying. He searched for Jessie among the faces hurrying home, then spotted her on the other side of the street, heading towards Fifth Avenue. Since she obviously wasn't going home, he somewhat guiltily decided to follow her. As she reached Scribner's at Forty-eighth Street, he stopped and watched her go into the bookshop. If she wanted something to read, surely she could find what she wanted from Bloomingdale's. He was puzzled. He peered through the window as Jessie talked to a sales clerk who left her for a few moments and then returned with two books. He could just make out their titles: *The Affluent Society* by John Kenneth Galbraith and *Inside Russia Today* by John Gunther. Jessie signed for them – that surprised Richard – and left as he ducked around the corner.

'Who *is* she?' said Richard out loud as he watched her enter Bendel's. The doorman saluted respectfully, leaving a distinct impression of recognition. Once again Richard peered through the window as assistants fluttered around Florentyna with more than casual respect. An older lady appeared with a package which she had obviously been expecting. She opened it to reveal a simple, stunning, evening dress. Florentyna smiled and nodded as the assistant placed the dress in a brown and white box. Florentyna mouthed the words 'Thank you' and turned towards the door without even signing for her purchase. Richard was mesmerized by the scene and barely managed to avoid colliding with her as she ran out of the shop and jumped into a cab. He grabbed one himself, telling the driver to follow her. When the cab passed the small building outside of which they normally parted, he began to feel queasy. No wonder she had never asked him in. The cab in front continued for another hundred yards and stopped outside a spanking new block of flats complete with a uniformed hall porter who opened the door for her. With mingled anger and astonishment, he jumped out of the cab and started to march up to the door through which she had disappeared.

'That'll be ninety-five cents, fella,' said a voice behind him.

'Oh, sorry,' said Richard and thrust five dollars at him, showing no interest in his change.

'Thank you,' said the driver. 'Someone sure is happy today.'

Richard ran to the door of the building and managed to catch Florentyna at the lift. Florentyna watched the door slide open and stared at him speechlessly.

'Who are you?' demanded Richard.

'Richard,' she stammered. 'I was going to tell you everything this evening. I never seemed to find the right opportunity.'

'Like hell you were going to tell me,' he said, following Florentyna into her apartment. 'Stringing me along with a pack of lies for nearly three months. Now the time has come for the truth.'

Florentyna had never seen Richard angry before and suspected that it was very rare. He pushed his way past her brusquely and inspected the flat. At the end of the entrance hall, there was a large living room with a fine oriental rug. A superb grandfather clock stood opposite a side table on which there was a bowl of fresh flowers. The room was beautiful, even by the standards of Richard's own home.

'Nice place you've got yourself for a sales girl,' said Richard. 'I wonder which of your lovers pays for this.'

Florentyna slapped him so hard that her own palm stung. 'How dare you?' she said. 'Get out of my home.'

As she heard herself saying the words, she started to cry. She didn't want him to leave – ever. Richard took her in his arms.

'Oh, God, I'm sorry,' he said. 'That was a terrible thing to say. Please forgive me. It's just that I love you so much and thought I knew you so well; and now I find I don't know anything about you.'

'Richard, I love you too, and I'm sorry I slapped you. I didn't want to deceive you, but there's no one else – I promise you that.' Her voice cracked.

'I deserved it,' he said as he kissed her.

Clasped tightly in one another's arms, they sank onto the couch and remained almost motionless for some moments. Gently, he stroked her hair until her tears subsided. Help me to take my clothes off, she wanted to say, but remained silent, slipping her fingers through the gap between his two top shirt buttons. Richard seemed unwilling to make the next move.

'Do you want to sleep with me?' she asked quietly.

'No,' he replied. 'I want to stay awake with you all night.'

Without speaking, they undressed and made love, gently and shyly, frightened to hurt each other, desperately trying to please. Finally, with her head on his shoulder, they talked.

'I love you,' said Richard. 'I have since the first moment we met. Will you marry me? Because I don't give a damn who you are, Jessie, or what you do, but I know I must spend the rest of my life with you.'

'I want to marry you too, Richard, but first I have to tell you the truth.'

Florentyna pulled Richard's jacket over their naked bodies and told him all about herself, ending by explaining how she had come to be working at Bloomingdale's. When she had completed her story, Richard did not speak.

'Have you stopped loving me already?' she said. 'Now you know who I really am?'

'Darling,' said Richard, very quietly, 'my father hates your father.'

'What do you mean?'

'Just that, the only time I ever heard your father's name mentioned in his presence, he flew completely off the handle saying your father's sole purpose in life seemed to be a desire to ruin the Kane family.'

'What? Why?' said Florentyna, shocked. 'I've never heard of your father. How do they even know each other?'

It was Richard's turn to tell Florentyna everything his mother had told him about the quarrel with her father.

'Oh, my God,' she said. 'That must have been the "disloyalty" my father referred to when he changed banks after twenty-five years. What shall we do?'

'Tell them the truth,' said Richard, 'that we met innocently, fell in love and now we're going to be married, and nothing they can do will stop us.'

'Let's wait a few weeks,' said Florentyna.

'Why?' asked Richard. 'Do you think your father can talk you out of marrying me?'

'No, Richard,' she said, touching him gently as she placed her head back on his shoulder. 'Never, my darling, but let's find out if we can do anything to break it gently, before we present them both with a *fait accompli*. Anyway, maybe they won't feel as strongly as you imagine. After all, you said the affair with the airlines company was nearly five years ago.'

'They still feel stongly, I promise you that. My father would be outraged if he saw us together, let alone thought we were considering marriage.'

'All the more reason to leave it for a little before we break the news to them. That will give us time to think about the best way to go about it.'

He kissed her again. 'I love you, Jessie.'

'Florentyna.'

'That's something else I'm going to have to get used to,' he said. 'I love you, Florentyna.'

.   .   .

During the next four weeks, Florentyna and Richard found out as much as they could about their parents' feud, Florentyna by asking her mother and George Novak a set of carefully worded questions, Richard from his father's filing cabinet. The extent of the mutual hatred appalled them. It became more obvious with each discovery that there was no gentle way to break the news of their love. During the next four weeks they spent every free moment they could find together. Richard was always attentive and kind, and nothing was too much trouble. He went to extremes to take her mind off the problem that they knew they would eventually have to face. They went to the theatre, skating, and on Sundays took long walks through Central Park, always ending up in bed long before it was dark. Florentyna even accompanied Richard to watch the New York Yankees which she 'couldn't understand' and the New York Philharmonic which she 'adored'. She refused to believe Richard could play the cello until he gave her a private recital. She applauded enthusiastically when he had finished his favourite Brahms sonata without noticing that he was staring into her grey eyes.

'We have got to tell them,' he said, placing his bow on the stand and taking her into his arms.

'I know we must. I just don't want to hurt my father.'

It was his turn to say, 'I know.'

She avoided his eyes. 'Next Friday Daddy will be back from Washington.'

'Then it's next Friday,' said Richard, holding her so close she could hardly breathe.

Richard returned to Harvard on Monday morning and they spoke to each other on the phone every night, never weakening, determined that nothing would stop them.

On Friday Richard arrived in New York earlier than usual and spent an hour alone with Florentyna who had asked for a half-day off. As they walked to the corner of Fifty-seventh and Park, they stopped at the flashing red 'Don't Walk' sign, and Richard turned to Florentyna and asked her once again to marry him. He took a small red leather box out of his pocket, opened it and placed a ring on the third finger of her left hand, a sapphire set in diamonds, so beautiful that tears came to Florentyna's eyes; it was a perfect fit. Passers-by looked at them strangely as they stood on the corner, clinging to each other, ignoring the green light flashing 'Walk'. When eventually they did obey its command, they kissed before parting and walked in opposite directions to confront their parents. They had agreed to meet again at Florentyna's flat as soon as the ordeal was over. She tried to smile through her tears.

Florentyna walked towards the Baron Hotel, occasionally looking at her ring. It felt new and strange on her finger and she imagined that the eyes of all who passed by would be drawn to the magnificent sapphire and to her, it looked so beautiful next to the antique ring, her favourite of the past. She had been astonished when Richard had placed it on her finger. The problem of their parents' rivalry had made her forget rings or any of the other trappings that attend a happy engagement. She touched the diamond-encircled sapphire and found that it gave her courage, although she was aware that she was walking more and more slowly as the hotel drew nearer and nearer.

When she reached the reception desk, the clerk told her that her father was in the penthouse with George Novak. He called to say that Florentyna was on her way up. The lift reached the forty-second floor far too quickly for Florentyna, and she hesitated before leaving its safety. She stepped out onto the green carpet and heard the lift door slide closed behind her. She stood alone in the corridor for a moment before knocking quietly at her father's door. Abel opened it immediately.

'Florentyna, what a pleasant surprise. Come on in, my darling. I wasn't expecting to see you today.'

George Novak was standing by the window, looking down at Park Avenue. He turned to greet his goddaughter. Florentyna's eyes pleaded with him to leave. If he stayed, she knew she would lose her nerve. Go, go, go, she said inside her brain. George sensed her anxiety immediately.

'I must get back to work, Abel. There's a goddamn maharajah checking in tonight.'

'Tell him to park his elephants at the Plaza,' said Abel genially. 'Now Florentyna's here, stay and have another drink.'

George looked at Florentyna. 'No, Abel, I have to go. The man's taken the whole of the thirty-third floor. The least he'll expect is the vice-president to greet him. Goodnight, Florentyna,' he said, kissing her on the cheek and briefly clasping her arm, almost as though he knew that she needed strength. He left them alone and suddenly Florentyna wished he had not gone.

'How's Bloomingdale's?' said Abel, ruffling his daughter's hair affectionately. 'Have you told them yet they're going to lose the best floor manager they've had in years? They're sure going to be surprised when they hear that Jessie Kovats' next job will be to open the Cannes Baron.' He laughed out loud.

'I'm going to be married,' said Florentyna, shyly extending her left hand.

She could think of nothing to add so she simply waited for his reaction.

'This is a bit sudden, isn't it?' said Abel, more than a little taken aback.

'Not really, Daddy. I've known him for some time.'

'Do I know the boy? Have I ever met him?'

'No, Daddy, you haven't.'

'Where does he come from? What's his background? Is he Polish? Why have you been so secretive about him, Florentyna?'

'He's not Polish, Daddy. He's the son of a banker.'

Abel went white and picked up his drink, swallowing the liquor in one gulp. Florentyna knew exactly what must be going through his mind as he poured himself another drink, so she got the truth out quickly.

'His name is Richard Kane, Daddy.'

Abel swung round to face her. 'Is he William Kane's son?' he demanded.

'Yes, he is,' said Florentyna.

'You could consider marrying William Kane's son? Do you know what that man did to me? He's the man who was responsible for the death of my closest friend. Yes, he's the man who made Davis Leroy commit suicide and, not satisfied with that, he tried to bankrupt me. If David Maxton hadn't rescued me in time, Kane would have taken away my hotels and sold them without a second thought. And where would I be now if William Kane had had his way? You'd have been lucky to have ended up as a shop girl at Bloomingdale's. Have you thought about that, Florentyna?'

'Yes, Daddy, I've thought of little else these past few weeks. Richard and I are horrified about the hatred that exists between you and his father. He's facing him now.'

'Well, I can tell you how he'll react,' said Abel. 'He'll go berserk. That man would never allow that precious wasp son of his to marry you so you might as well forget the whole crazy idea, young lady.'

His voice had risen to a shout.

'I can't forget it, Father,' she said evenly, 'We love each other and we both need your blessing, not your anger.'

'Now you listen to me, Florentyna,' said Abel, his face now red with fury. 'I forbid you to see the Kane boy ever again. Do you hear me?'

'Yes, I hear you. But I will see him. I'll not be parted from Richard because you hate his father.'

She found herself clutching her ring finger and trembling slightly.

'It will not happen,' said Abel. 'I will never allow the marriage. My own daughter deserting me for the son of that bastard Kane. I say you will not marry him.'

'I am not deserting you. I would have run away with him if that was true, but I couldn't do that behind your back. I'm over twenty-one, and I will marry Richard. I intend to spend the rest of my life with him. Please help us, Daddy. Won't you meet him, and then you'll begin to understand why I feel the way I do about him?'

'He will never be allowed to enter my home. I do not want to meet any child of William Kane. Never, do you hear me?'

'Then I must leave you.'

'Florentyna, if you leave me, to marry the Kane boy, I'll cut you off without a penny. Without a penny, do you hear me?' Abel's voice softened.

'Now use your common sense, girl, you'll get over him. You're still young, and there are lots of other men who'd give their right arms to marry you.'

'I don't want lots of other men,' said Florentyna. 'I've met the man I'm going to marry, and it's not his fault that he is his father's son. Neither of us chose our fathers.'

'If my family isn't good enough for you, then get out,' said Abel. 'And I swear I won't have your name mentioned in my presence again.' He turned away and stared out of the window. 'For the last time, I warn you, Florentyna – do not marry that boy.'

'Daddy, we are going to be married. Although we're both past the stage of needing your consent, we do ask for your approval.'

Abel looked away from the window and walked towards her. 'Are you pregnant? Is that the reason? Do you have to get married?'

'No, Father.'

'Have you ever slept with him?' Abel demanded.

The question shook Florentyna but she didn't hesitate. 'Yes,' she replied. 'Many times.'

Abel raised his arm and hit her full across the face. The silver band caught the corner of her lip and she nearly fell. Blood started to trickle down her chin. She turned, ran out of the room crying, and leaned on the lift button, holding her bloody face. The door slid open and George stepped out. She had a fleeting glimpse of his shocked expression as she stepped quickly in to the car and jabbed at the button continuously. As George stood and watched her crying, the lift doors closed slowly.

Once Florentyna had reached the street, she took a cab straight to her own apartment. On the way, she dabbed at her cut lip with a Kleenex. Richard was already there, standing under the marquee, head bowed and looking miserable.

She jumped out of the cab and ran to him. Once they were upstairs, she opened the door and quickly closed it behind them, feeling blessedly safe.

'I love you, Richard.'

'I love you, too,' said Richard, as he threw his arms around her.

'I don't have to ask how your father reacted,' said Florentyna, clinging to him desperately.

'I've never seen him so angry,' said Richard. 'Called your father a liar and a crook, nothing more than a jumped-up Polish immigrant. He asked me why I didn't marry somebody from my own background.'

'What did you say to that?'

'I told him someone as wonderful as you couldn't be replaced by a suitably Brahmin family friend, and he completely lost his temper.'

Florentyna didn't let go of Richard as he spoke.

'Then he threatened to cut me off without a penny if I married you,' he continued. 'When will they understand we don't care a damn about their money? I tried appealing to my mother for support, but even she could not control his temper. He insisted that she leave the room. I have never seen him treat my mother that way before. She was weeping, which only made my resolve stronger. I left him in mid-sentence. God knows, I hope he doesn't take it out on Virginia and Lucy. What happened when you left?'

'My father hit me,' said Florentyna very quietly. 'For the first time in my life. I think he'll kill you if he finds us together. Richard darling, we must get out of here, before he finds out where you are, and he's bound to try here first. I'm so frightened.'

'No need for you to be frightened, Florentyna. We'll leave tonight and go as far away as possible and to hell with them both.'

'How quickly can you pack?' asked Florentyna.

'I can't,' said Richard. 'I can never return home now. You pack your things and then we'll go. I've got about a hundred dollars on me. How do you feel about marrying a hundred-dollar man?'

'As much as a shop girl can hope for, I suppose – and to think I'd dreamed of being a kept woman. Next you'll be wanting a dowry,' Florentyna added while rummaging in her bag. 'Well, I've got two hundred and twelve dollars and an American Express card, so you owe me fifty-six dollars, Richard Kane, but I'll consider repayment at a dollar a year.'

In thirty minutes Florentyna was packed. Then she sat down at her desk, scrawled a note and left the envelope on the table by the side of her bed.

Richard hailed a cab. Florentyna was delighted to find how capable Richard was in a crisis and it made her feel more relaxed. 'Idlewild,' he said, placing Florentyna's three cases in the boot.

At the airport he booked a flight to San Francisco; they chose the Golden Gate City simply because it seemed the more distant point on the map of America.

At seven thirty, the American Airlines Super Constellation 1049 taxied out onto the runway to start its seven-hour flight.

Richard helped Florentyna with her seat belt. She smiled at him.

'Do you know how much I love you, Mr Kane?'

'Yes, I think so – Mrs Kane,' he replied.

34

Abel and George arrived at Florentyna's flat on East Fifty-seventh Street a few minutes after she and Richard had left for the airport. Abel was already remorseful and regretting the blow he had struck his daughter. He did not care to conjecture about what his life would be like without his only child. He thought if he could only reach her before it was too late, he might, with gentle persuasion, still talk her out of marrying the Kane boy. He was willing to offer her anything to stop the marriage.

George rang the door bell as he and Abel stood outside her door. No one answered. George pressed the bell again, and they waited for some time before Abel used the key Florentyna had always left with him for emergencies. They searched the place, neither really expecting to find her.

'She must have left already,' said George, as he joined Abel in the bedroom.

'Yes, but where?' said Abel, and then he saw an envelope addressed to him on the table. He remembered the last letter left for him by the side of a bed that had not been slept in. He ripped it open.

Dear Daddy,
  Please forgive me for running away but I do love Richard and will not give him up because of your hatred for his father. We will be married right away and nothing you can do will prevent it. If you ever try to harm him in any way, you will be harming me. Neither of us intend to return to New York until you have ended the senseless feud between our family and the Kane's. I love you more than you will ever realize and I shall always be thankful for everything you have done for me. I pray that this is not the end of our relationship but until you can change your mind, 'Never seek the wind in the field – it is useless to try and find what is gone.'

Your loving daughter,
Florentyna

Abel collapsed onto the bed, and passed the letter to George, who read the handwritten note and asked helplessly, 'Is there anything I can do?'
  'Yes, George. I want my daughter back, even if it means dealing direct with that bastard Kane. There's only one thing I feel certain of: he will want this marriage stopped whatever sacrifice he has to make. Get him on the phone.'
  It took George some time to locate William Kane's unlisted number. The night security officer at Lester's Bank finally gave it to him when George insisted that it was a family emergency. Abel sat silently on the bed, Florentyna's letter in his hand, remembering how when she was a little girl, he had taught her the old Polish proverb that she had now quoted back to him. When George was put through to the Kane residence, a male voice answered the phone.
  'May I speak to Mr William Kane?' asked George.
  'Whom shall I say is calling?' asked the imperturbable voice.
  'Mr Abel Rosnovski,' said George.
  'I'll see if he is in, sir.'
  'I think that was Kane's butler. He's gone to look for him,' said George, as he passed the receiver over to Abel. Abel waited, his fingers tapping on the bedside table.
  'William Kane speaking.'
  'This is Abel Rosnovski.'
  'Indeed?' William's tone was icy. 'And when exactly did you think of setting up your daughter with my son? At the time, no doubt, when you failed so conspicuously to cause the downfall of my bank?'
  'Don't be such a damn . . .' Abel checked himself. 'I want this marriage stopped every bit as much as you do. I never tried to take away your son. I only learned of his existence today. I love my daughter even more than I hate you, and I don't want to lose her. Can't we get together and work something out between us?'
  'No,' said William. 'I asked that same question once in the past, Mr Rosnovski, and you made it very clear when and where you would meet me.

I can wait until then, because I am confident you will find it is you who are there, not I.'

'What's the good of raking over the past now, Kane? If you know where they are, perhaps we can stop them. That's what you want, too. Or are you so goddamn proud that you'll stand by and watch your son marry my girl rather than help ...?'

The telephone clicked as he spoke the word 'help'. Abel buried his face in his hands and wept. George took him back to the Baron.

Through that night and the following day, Abel tried every way he could think of to find Florentyna. He even rang her mother, who admitted that their daughter had told her all about Richard Kane.

'He sounded rather nice,' she added spitefully.

'Do you know where they are right now?' asked Abel impatiently.

'Yes.'

'Where?'

'Find out for yourself.' Another telephone click.

Abel placed advertisements in newspapers and even bought radio time. He tried to get the police involved, but they could only put out a general call since she was over twenty-one. No word came from her. Finally, he had to admit to himself that by the time he found her she would undoubtedly be married to the Kane boy.

He re-read her letter many times, and resolved that he would never attempt to harm the boy in any way. But the father, that was a different matter. He, Abel Rosnovski, had gone down on his knees and pleaded, and the bastard hadn't even listened. Abel vowed that when the chance presented itself, he would finish William Kane off once and for all. George became fearful at the intensity of his old friend's passion.

'Shall I cancel your European trip?' he asked.

Abel had completely forgotten that he was meant to accompany Florentyna to Europe after she had finished her two years with Bloomingdale's at the end of the month. She was going to open the Edinburgh Baron and the Cannes Baron. Now he didn't care who opened what, or whether the hotels were opened at all.

'I can't cancel,' replied Abel. 'I'll have to go and open the hotels myself, but while I'm away, George, you find out exactly where Florentyna is without letting her know. She mustn't think I'm spying on her; she would never forgive me if she found out. Your best bet may well be Zaphia, but be careful because you can be sure she will want to take every advantage of what has happened. It was obvious she had already briefed Florentyna on everything she knew about Kane.'

'Do you want Osborne to do anything about the Kane shares?'

'No, nothing for the moment. Now is not the appropriate time for finishing Kane off. When I do, I want to be certain that it's once and for all. Leave Kane alone for the time being. I can always come back to him. For now, concentrate on finding Florentyna.'

George promised that he would have found her by the time Abel returned.

* * *

Abel opened the Edinburgh Baron three weeks later. The hotel looked quite magnificent as it stood on the hill dominating the Athens of the north.

It was always little things that annoyed Abel most when he opened a new hotel and he would always check them on arrival. A small electric shock when you touched a light switch caused by nylon carpets. Room service that took forty minutes to materialize or a bed that was too small for anyone who was either fat or tall. The press was quick to point out that it had been expected that Florentyna Rosnovski, daughter of the Chicago Baron, would perform the opening ceremony. One of the gossip columnists, from the *Sunday Express*, hinted at a family rift and reported that Abel had not been his usual exuberant, bouncy self. Abel denied the suggestion unconvincingly, retorting that he was over fifty – not an age for bouncing, his public relations man had told him to say. The press remained unconvinced and the following day the *Daily Mail* printed a photograph of a discarded engraved bronze plaque, discovered on a rubbish heap, which read:

The Edinburgh Baron
opened by
Florentyna Rosnovski
October 17, 1957

Abel flew to Cannes. Another splendid hotel, this time overlooking the Mediterranean but it didn't help him to get Florentyna out of his mind. Another discarded plaque, this one in French. The openings were ashes without her.

Abel was beginning to dread that he might spend the rest of his life without seeing his daughter again. To kill the loneliness, he slept with some very expensive and some rather cheap women. None of them helped. William Kane's son now possessed the one person he truly loved. France no longer held any excitement for him, and once he had finished his business there, Abel flew onto Bonn where he completed negotiations for the site on which he would build the first Baron in Germany. He kept in constant touch with George by phone, but Florentyna had not been found, and there was some very disturbing news concerning Henry Osborne.

'He's got himself in heavy debt with the bookmakers again,' said George.

'I warned him last time that I was through bailing him out,' said Abel. 'He's been no damn use to anyone since he lost his seat in Congress. I suppose I'll have to deal with the problem when I get back.'

'He's making threats,' said George.

'There's nothing new about that. I've never let them worry me in the past,' said Abel. 'Tell him whatever it is he wants, it will have to wait until my return.'

'When do you expect to be back?' asked George.

'Three weeks, four at the most. I want to look at some sites in Turkey and Egypt. Hilton's already started building there, so I'm going to find out why. Which reminds me, George, the experts tell me you'll never be able to reach me once the plane has landed in the Middle East. Those damned Arabs haven't worked out how to find each other, let alone visitors from foreign countries, so I'll leave you to run everything as usual until you hear from me.'

Abel spent over three weeks looking at sites for new hotels all over the Arab states. His advisors were legion, most of them claiming the title of Prince,

each assuring Abel that they had the real influence as a very close personal
friend of the key minister, a distant cousin in fact. However, it always turned
out to be the wrong minister or too distant a cousin. The only solid conclusion
Abel reached, after twenty-three days in the dust, sand, and heat with soda
but no whisky, was that if his advisors' forecasts on the Middle East oil
reserves were accurate, the Gulf States were going to need a lot of hotels in
the long term and the Baron Group had to start planning carefully if they
were not to be left behind.

Abel managed to find several sites on which to build hotels, through his
several princes, but he did not have the time to discover which of them had
the real power to fix the officials. He objected to bribery only when the
money reached the wrong hands. At least in America, Henry Osborne had
always known which officials needed to be taken care of. Abel set up a small
office in Bahrain, leaving his local representative in no doubt that the Baron
Group was looking for sites throughout the Arab world, but not for princes
or the cousins of ministers.

He flew onto Istanbul, whre he almost immediately found the perfect
place to build a hotel, overlooking the Bosphorus, only a hundred yards from
the old British embassy. He mused as he stood on the barren ground of his
latest acquisition, recalling when he had last been here. He clenched his fist
and held the wrist of his right hand. He could hear again the cries of the
mob – it still made him feel frightened and sick although more than thirty
years had passed.

Exhausted from his travels, Abel flew home to New York. During the
interminable journey he thought of little but Florentyna, and whether
George had found her. As always, George was standing, waiting outside the
customs gate to meet him. His expression indicated nothing.

'What news?' asked Abel as he climbed into the back of the Cadillac while
the chauffeur put his bags in the trunk.

'Some good, some bad,' said George, as he pressed a button by the side
window. A sheet of glass glided up between the front and rear sections of
the car. 'Florentyna has been in touch with her mother. She's living in a
small apartment in San Francisco.'

'Married?' said Abel.

'Yes,' said George.

Neither spoke for some moments.

'And the Kane boy?' asked Abel.

'He's found a job in a bank. It seems a lot of people turned him down
because word got around that he didn't finish at the Harvard Business
School, and his father wouldn't supply a reference. Not many people will
consider employing him if as a consequence they might lose his father's
business. He finally was hired as a teller with the Bank of America. Way
below what he might have expected with his qualifications.'

'And Florentyna?'

'She's working as the assistant manager in a fashion shop called "Wayout
Columbus" near Golden Gate Park. She's also been trying to borrow money
from several banks.'

'Why? Is she in any sort of trouble?' asked Abel anxiously.

'No, she's looking for capital to open her own shop.'

'How much is she looking for?'

'Only thirty-four thousand dollars which she needs for the lease on a small building on Nob Hill.'

Abel sat back thinking about what George had said, his short fingers tapping on the car window. 'See that she gets the money, George. Make it look as if the transaction is an ordinary bank loan and and be sure that it's not traceable back to me.' He continued tapping. 'This must always remain simply between the two of us, George.'

'Anything you say, Abel.'

'And keep me informed of every move she makes, however trivial.'

'What about him?'

'I'm not interested in him,' said Abel. 'Now what's the bad news?'

'Trouble with Henry Osborne again. It seems he owes money everywhere. I'm also fairly certain his only source of income is now you. He's started making veiled threats about you condoning bribes in the early days when we were setting up the group. Says he's kept all the papers from the first day he met you when he claims he fixed an extra payment after the fire at the old Richmond in Chicago, and he now has a file three inches thick.'

'I'll deal with Henry in the morning,' said Abel.

George spent the remainder of the drive into Manhattan bringing Abel up to date on the rest of the group's affairs which were all satisfactory, except for a takeover of the Baron in Lagos after yet another coup. That never worried Abel. The next morning Abel saw Henry Osborne. He looked old and tired, and the once smooth handsome face was now heavily lined. He made no mention of the three-inch thick file.

'I need a little money to get me through a tricky period,' said Henry. 'I've been a bit unlucky.'

'Again, Henry? You should know better at your age. You're a born loser with horses and women. How much do you need this time?'

'Ten thousand would see me through,' said Henry.

'Ten thousand,' said Abel, spitting out the words. 'What do you think I am, a gold mine? It was only five thousand last time.'

'Inflation,' said Henry, trying to laugh.

'This is the last time, do you understand me?' said Abel as he took out his cheque book. 'Come begging once more, Henry, and I'll remove you from the board as a director and turn you out without a penny.'

'You're a real friend, Abel. I swear I'll never come back again, I promise you that, never again.' Henry plucked a Romeo y Julliyta from the humidor on the table in front of Abel and lit it. 'Thanks, Abel, you'll never regret your decision.'

Henry left, puffing away at the cigar, as George came in. George waited for the door to be closed.

'What happened with Henry?'

'I gave in for the last time,' said Abel. 'I don't know why – it cost me ten thousand.'

'Jesus, I feel like the brother of the prodigal son,' said George. 'Because he'll be back again. I'd be willing to put money on that.'

'He'd better not,' said Abel, 'because I'm through with him. Whatever he has done for me in the past, it's now quits. What's the latest news on Florentyna?'

'Florentyna's fine, but you were right about Zaphia: she's been making regular monthly trips to the coast to see them both.'

'Bloody woman,' said Abel.

'Mrs Kane has been out a couple of times as well,' added George.

'And Kane?'

'No sign of him relenting.'

'That's one thing we have in common,' said Abel.

'I've set up a facility for her with Crocker National Bank of San Francisco,' continued George. 'She made an approach to the loan officer there less than a week ago. The agreement will appear to her as if it's one of the bank's ordinary loan transactions, with no special favours. In fact, they're charging her half a per cent more than usual so there can be no reason for her to be suspicious. What she will never know is the the loan is covered by your guarantee.'

'Thanks, George, that's perfect. I'll bet you ten dollars she pays off the loan within two years and never needs to go back for another.'

'I'd want odds of five to one on that,' said George. 'Why don't you try Henry; he's more of a sucker.'

Abel laughed. 'Keep me briefed, George, on everything she's up to, everything.'

35

William felt he had been briefed on everything as he studied Thaddeus Cohen's quarterly report, and only one thing now worried him. Why was Abel Rosnovski still doing nothing with his vast shareholding in Lester's? William couldn't help remembering that he still owned six per cent of the bank and with two more per cent he could invoke Article Seven of Lester's by-laws. It was hard to believe that Rosnovksi still feared SEC regulations, especially as the Eisenhower administration was settled into its second term in the White House and had never shown any interest in pursuing the original inquiry.

William was fascinated to read that Henry Osborne was once again in financial trouble, and that Rosnovski still kept bailing him out. William wondered for how much longer that would go on, and what Henry had on Rosnovski. Was it possible that Rosnovski had enough problems of his own without adding William Kane to them? Cohen's report reviewed progress on the eight new hotels Rosnovski was building across the world. The London Baron was losing money and the Lagos Baron was out of commission; otherwise he continued to grow in strength. William re-read the attached clipping from the *Sunday Express*, reporting that Florentyna Rosnovski had not opened the Edinburgh Baron, and he thought about his son.

Then he closed the report and locked the file in his safe, convinced there was nothing in it of importance to concern himself with. His chauffeur drove him home.

William regretted his early loss of temper with Richard. Although he did not want the Rosnovski girl in his life, he wished he had not turned his back so irrevocably on his only son. Kate had pleaded on Richard's behalf, and she and William had had a long and bitter argument – so rare in their married life – which they had been unable to resolve. Kate tried every tactic from gentle persuasion to tears, but nothing seemed to move William. Virginia and Lucy also missed their brother. 'There's no one who will be critical of my paintings,' said Virginia.

'Don't you mean rude?' asked Kate.

Virginia tried to smile.

Lucy used to lock herself in the bathroom, turn on the water, and write secret letters to Richard, who could never figure out why they always seemed damp. No one dared to mention Richard's name in the house in front of William, but it was causing a sad rift within the family.

He had tried spending more time at the bank, even working round the clock in the hope that it might help. It didn't. The bank was once again making heavy demands on his energy at the very time when he most felt like a rest. He had appointed six new vice-presidents over the previous two years, hoping they would take some of the load off his shoulders. The reverse had turned out to be the case. They had created more work and more decisions from him to make and the brightest of them, Jake Thomas, already looked the most likely candidate to take William's place as chairman if Richard did not give up the Rosnovski girl. Although the profits of the bank continued to rise each year, William found he was no longer interested in making money for money's sake. Perhaps he now faced the same problem that Charles Lester had encountered: he had no son to leave his fortune and the chairmanship to now that he had cut Richard out of his life, rewritten his will and dismantled his trust.

. . .

In the year of their silver wedding anniversary, William decided to take Kate and the girls for a long holiday to Europe in the hope that it might help to put Richard out of their minds. They flew to London on a Boeing 707 and stayed at the Ritz. The hotel brought back many happy memories of William's first trip to Europe with Kate. They made a sentimental journey to Oxford and showed Virginia and Lucy the university city, and then went onto Stratford-on-Avon to see some Shakespeare: *Richard the Third* with Laurence Olivier. They could have wished for a king with another name.

On the return journey from Stratford they stopped at the church in Henley-on-Thames where William and Kate had been married. They would have stayed at the Bell Inn again, but they still had only one vacant room. An argument started between William and Kate in the car on the way back to London as to whether it had been the Reverend Tukesbury or the Reverend Dukesbury who had married them. They came to no satisfactory conclusion before reaching the Ritz. On one thing they were able to agree; the new roof on the parish church had worn well.

William kissed Kate gently when he climbed into bed that night. 'Best five hundred pounds I ever invested,' he said.

They flew on to Italy a week later, having seen every English sight any self-respecting American tourist is meant to visit and many they usually miss. In Rome, the girls drank too much bad Italian wine and made themelves ill on the night of Virginia's birthday, while William ate too much good pasta and put on seven pounds. All of them would have been so much happier if they could have talked of the forbidden topic of Richard. Virginia cried that night and Kate tried to comfort her.

'Why doesn't someone tell Daddy that some things are more important than pride?' Virginia kept asking.

Kate had no reply.

When they returned to New York, William was refreshed and eager once again to plunge back into his work at the bank. He lost the seven pounds in seven days.

As the months passed by, he felt things were becoming quite routine again. Routine disappeared from his mind when Virginia, just out of Sweetbriar, announced she was going to marry a student from the University of Virginia Law School. The news shook William.

'She's not old enough,' he said.

'Virginia's twenty-two,' said Kate. 'She's not a child any longer, William. How do you feel about becoming a grandfather?' she added, regretting the sequence of her words immediately she had spoken them.

'What do you mean?' said William, horrified. 'Virginia isn't pregnant, is she?'

'Good gracious, no,' said Kate, and then she spoke more softly as if she had been found out. 'Richard and Florentyna have had a baby.'

'How do you know?'

'Richard wrote to tell me the good news,' replied Kate. 'Hasn't the time come for you to forgive him, William?'

'Never,' said William and marched out of the room in anger.

Kate sighed wearily: he had not even asked if his grandchild was a boy or a girl.

. . .

Virginia's wedding took place in Trinity Church, Boston, on a beautiful spring afternoon in late March of the following year. William thoroughly approved of David Telford, the young lawyer with whom Virginia had chosen to spend the rest of her life.

Virginia had wanted Richard to be an usher and Kate had begged William to invite him to the wedding, but he had steadfastly refused. He had wanted to say yes, but he knew that Richard would never agree to coming without the Rosnovski girl. On the day of the wedding Richard sent a present and a telegram to his sister. William would not allow the telegram to be read at the reception afterwards.

BOOK SIX

36

Abel was sitting alone in his office on the forty-second floor of the New York Baron waiting to see a fund raiser from the Kennedy campaign. The man was already twenty minutes late. Abel was tapping his fingers impatiently on his desk when his secretary came in.

'Mr Vincent Hogan to see you, sir.'

Abel sprang out of his chair. 'Come in, Mr Hogan,' he said, slapping the good-looking young man on the back. 'How are you?'

'I'm fine, Mr Rosnovski I'm sorry I'm a little late,' said the unmistakably Bostonian voice.

'I didn't notice,' said Abel. 'Would you care for a drink, Mr Hogan?'

'No, thank you, Mr Rosnovski. I try not to drink when I have to see so many people in one day.'

'Absolutely right. I hope you won't mind if I have one,' said Abel. 'I'm not planning on seeing many people today.'

Hogan laughed like a man who knew he was in for a day of other people's jokes. Abel poured a whisky.

'Now, what can I do for you, Mr Hogan?'

'Well, Mr Rosnovski, we were hoping the party could once again count on your support.'

'I've always been a Democrat, as you know, Mr Hogan. I supported Franklin D. Roosevelt, Harry Truman, and Adlai Stevenson, although I couldn't understand what Adlai was talking about half the time.'

Both men laughed falsely.

'I also helped my old friend, Dick Daley, in Chicago and I've been backing young Ed Muskie – the son of a Polish immigrant, you know – since his campaign for governor of Maine back in '54.'

'You've been a loyal supporter of the party in the past, there's no denying that, Mr Rosnovski,' said Vincent Hogan, in a tone that indicated that the statutory time for small talk had run out. 'We also know the Democrats, not least of all former Congressman Osborne, have done the odd favour for you in return. I don't think it's necessary for me to go into any details of that unpleasant little incident.'

'That's long since past,' said Abel, 'and well behind me.'

'I agree,' said Mr Hogan, 'and although most self-made multi-millionaires couldn't face having their affairs looked into too closely, you will be the first to appreciate that we have to be especially careful. The candidate, as you will understand, cannot afford to take any personal risks so near the election. Nixon would love a scandal at this stage of the race.'

'We understand each other clearly, Mr Hogan. Now that's out of the way, how much were you expecting from me for the election campaign?'

'I need every penny I can lay my hands on.' Hogan's words came across clipped and slow. 'Nixon is gathering a lot of support across the country, and it's going to be a very close thing getting our man into the White House.'

'Well, I'll support Kennedy,' said Abel, 'if he supports me. It's as simple as that.'

'He's delighted to support you, Mr Rosnovski. We all realize that you're now a pillar of the Polish community, and Senator Kennedy is personally aware of the brave stand you took on behalf of your countrymen who are still in slave labour camps behind the Iron Curtain, not to mention the service you gave in the war. I have been authorized to let you know that the candidate has already agreed to open your new hotel in Los Angeles during his campaign trip.'

'That's good news,' said Abel.

'The candidate is also fully aware of your desire to grant Poland most favoured nation status in foreign trade with the United States.'

'No more than we deserve after our service in the last war,' said Abel, and paused briefly. 'What about the other little matter?' he asked.

'Senator Kennedy is canvassing Polish-American opinion at the moment, and we haven't met with any objections. He naturally cannot come to a final decision until after he is elected.'

'Naturally. Would two hundred and fifty thousand dollars help him make that decision?' asked Abel.

Vincent Hogan didn't speak.

'Two hundred and fifty thousand dollars it is then,' said Abel. 'The money will be in your campaign fund headquarters by the end of the week, Mr Hogan. You have my word on it.'

The business was over, the bargain struck. Abel rose. 'Please give Senator Kennedy my best wishes, and add that of course I hope he'll be the next President of the United States. I always loathed Richard Nixon after his despicable treatment of Helen Gahagan Douglas, and in any case, there are personal reasons why I don't want Henry Cabot Lodge as Vice-President.'

'I shall be delighted to pass on your message,' said Mr Hogan, 'and thank you for your continued support of the Democratic party, and in particular, of the candidate.' The Bostonian thrust out his hand. Abel grasped it.

'Keep in touch, Mr Hogan. I don't part with that sort of money without expecting a return on my investment.'

'I fully understand,' replied Vincent Hogan.

Abel showed his guest to the lift and returned smiling to his office. His fingers started to tap on the desk again. His secretary reappeared.

'Ask Mr Novak to come in,' said Abel.

George came through from his office a few moments later.

'I think I've pulled it off, George.'

'Congratulations, Abel, I'm delighted. If Kennedy becomes the next President, then one of your biggest dreams will be fulfilled. How proud Florentyna will be of you.'

Abel smiled when he heard her name. 'Do you know what that little minx has been up to?' he said, laughing. 'Did you see the *Los Angeles Times* last week, George?'

George shook his head, and Abel passed him a copy of the paper. One of the items was circled in red ink. George read the article aloud: 'Florentyna

Kane opens her third shop in Los Angeles. She already owns two in San Francisco and is hoping to open another in San Diego before the end of the year. "Florentyna's", as they are known, are fast becoming to California what Balenciaga is to Paris.'

George laughed as he put the paper down.

'She must have written the piece herself,' said Abel. 'I can't wait for her to open a Florentyna's in New York. I'll bet she achieves that within five years, ten at the most. Do you want to take another bet on that, George?'

'I didn't take the first one, if you remember, Abel, otherwise I would already have been out ten dollars.'

Abel looked up, his voice quieter. 'Do you think she'd come and see Senator Kennedy open the new Baron in Los Angeles, George? Do you think she might?'

'No unless the Kane boy is invited along as well.'

'Never,' said Abel. 'That Kane boy is nothing. I read all the facts in your last report, George. He's left the Bank of America to work with Florentyna; couldn't even hold down a good job, had to fall back on her success.'

'You're becoming a selective reader, Abel. You know very well that's not the way it was. I made the circumstances very clear. The Kane boy is in charge of the finances while Florentyna runs the shops, and it's proving to be an ideal partnership. Don't ever forget that a major bank offered Kane the chance to head up its European department but Florentyna begged him to join her when she no longer found it possible to control the finances herself. Abel, you'll have to face the fact that their marriage is a success. I know it's hard for you to stomach, but why don't you climb down off your high horse and meet the boy?'

'You're my closest friend, George. No one else in the world would dare to speak to me like that. So no one knows better than you why I can't climb down, not until that bastard Kane shows he is willing to meet me half way, but until then, I won't crawl again while he's still alive to watch me.'

'What if you were to die first, Abel? You're exactly the same age.'

'Then I'd lose and Florentyna inherits everything.'

'You told me she wouldn't get a thing. You were going to change your will in favour of your grandson.'

'I couldn't do it, George. When the time came to sign the documents, I just couldn't do it. What the hell, that damned grandson is going to end up with both our fortunes in the end.'

Abel removed a wallet from his inside pocket, shuffled through several old pictures of Florentyna and took out a new one of his grandson, which he proffered to George.

'Good-looking little boy.' said George.

'Sure is,' said Abel. 'The spitting image of his mother.'

George laughed. 'You never give up, do you, Abel?'

'What do you think they call him?'

'What do you mean?' said George. 'You know very well what his name is.'

'I mean what do you think they actually call him?'

'How should I know?' said George.

'Find out,' said Abel. 'I care.'

'How am I meant to do that?' said George. 'Have someone follow them while they're pushing the pram around Golden Gate Park? You left clear instructions that Florentyna must never find out that you're still taking an interest in her or the Kane boy.'

'That reminds me, I still have a little matter to settle with his father,' said Abel.

'What are you going to do about the Lester shares?' asked George. 'Because Peter Parfitt has been showing more interest in selling his two per cent lately, and I wouldn't trust Henry with the negotiations. With those two working on the sale, everybody will be in on the deal except you.'

'I'm doing nothing. Much as I hate Kane, I don't want any trouble with him until we know if Kennedy has won the election. So I'm leaving the whole situation dormant for the moment. If Kennedy fails, I'll buy Parfitt's two per cent and go ahead with the plan that we've already discussed. And don't worry yourself about Henry; I've already taken him off the Kane file. From now on I'm handling that myself.'

'I do worry, Abel. I know he's in debt again to half the bookmakers in Chicago, and I wouldn't be surprised if he arrived in New York on the scrounge any minute now.'

'Henry won't be coming here. I made the situation very clear last time I saw him that he wouldn't get another dime out of me. If he does come begging, he'll only lose his seat on the board and with it his only source of income.'

'That worries me even more,' said George. 'Let's say he took it on himself to go to Kane direct for the money.'

'Not possible, George. Henry is the one man alive who hates Kane even more than I do, and not without reason.'

'How can you be so sure of that?'

'William Kane's mother was Henry's second wife,' said Abel, 'and young William, aged only sixteen, threw him out of his own home.'

'Good God, how did you come across that piece of information?'

'There's nothing I don't know about William Kane,' said Abel. 'Or Henry for that matter. Absolutely nothing – from the fact that we started life on the same day, and I'd be willing to bet my good leg there's nothing he doesn't know about me so we have to be circumspect for the time being, but you need have no fear of Henry turning stool pigeon. He'd die before he had to admit his real name was Vittorio Tosna and he once served a jail sentence.'

'Good God – does Henry realize you know all this?'

'No, he doesn't. I've kept it to myself for years always believing, George, that if you think a man might threaten you at some time then you should keep a little more up your sleeve than your arm. I've never trusted Henry since the days he suggested swindling Great Western Casualty while he was still actually working for them, although I'd be the first to admit he's been very useful to me in the past and I am confident he isn't going to cause me any trouble in the future, because without his director's salary, he becomes penniless overnight. So forget Henry and let's be a little more positive. What's the latest date for the completion of the Los Angeles Baron?'

'Middle of September,' replied George.

'Perfect. That will be six weeks before the election. When Kennedy opens that hotel, the news will hit every front page in America.'

37

When William returned to New York, after a bankers' conference in Washington, he found a message awaiting him, requesting that he contact Thaddeus Cohen immediately. He hadn't spoken to Cohen for a considerable time, as Abel Rosnovski had caused no direct trouble since the abortive telephone conversation on the eve of Richard and Florentyna's marriage, nearly three years before. The successive quarterly reports had merely confirmed that Rosnovski was neither trying to buy or sell any of the bank's shares. Nevertheless, William called Thaddeus Cohen immediately and somewhat apprehensively. The lawyer told William that he had stumbled across some information which he did not wish to divulge over the phone. William asked him to come over to the bank as soon as it was convenient.

Thaddeus Cohen arrived forty minutes later. William heard him out in attentive silence.

When Cohen had finished his revelation, William said, 'Your father would never have approved of such underhand methods.'

'Neither would yours,' replied Thaddeus Cohen, 'but they didn't have to deal with the likes of Abel Rosnovski.'

'What makes you think your plan will work?'

'Look at the Bernard Goldfine and Sherman Adams case, only one thousand six hundred and forty-two dollars involved in hotel bills and a vicuna coat, but it sure embarrassed the hell out of the President when Adams was accused of preferred treatment because he was a Presidential assistant. We know Mr Rosnovski is aiming a lot higher than that. It should, therefore, be easier to bring him down.

'Game, set and match. How much is it going to cost me?'

'Twenty-five thousand at the outside, but I may be able to pull the whole deal off for less.'

'How can you be sure that Rosnovski doesn't realize that I am personally involved?'

'I'd use a third person who won't even know your name to act as an intermediary.'

'And if you pull it off, what you recommend we do then?'

'You send all the details to Senator John Kennedy's office, and I guarantee that will finish of Abel Rosnovski's ambitious plans once and for all because the moment his credibility has been shattered he will be a spent force and find it quite impossible to invoke Article Seven of the bank's by-laws – even if he did get hold of eight per cent of Lester's.'

'Maybe – if Kennedy becomes the President,' said William. 'But what happens if Nixon wins the election? He's way ahead in the opinion polls and I'd certainly back his chances against Kennedy. Can you really imagine that America would ever send a Roman Catholic to the White House? I can't, but then on the other hand I admit that an investment of twenty-five thousand is small enough if there's better than an outside chance the move will finish Abel Rosnovski off once and for all and leave me secure at the bank.'

'If Kennedy becomes President . . .'

William opened the drawer of his desk, took out a large cheque book marked 'private account' and wrote out the figures. Two, five, zero, zero, zero.

38

Abel's prediction that Kennedy's opening of the Baron would hit every front page did not turn out to be wholly accurate. Although the candidate did indeed open the hotel, he had to appear at dozens of other events in Los Angeles that day and face Nixon for a televised debate the following evening. Nevertheless, the opening of the newest Baron gained fairly wide coverage in the national press, and Vincent Hogan assured Abel privately that Kennedy had not forgotten the other little matter. Florentyna's shop was only a few hundred yards away, but father and daughter never did meet.

    .   .   .

After the Illinois returns came in, and John F. Kennedy looked certain to be the thirty-fifth President of the United States, Abel drank Mayor Daley's health and celebrated at the Democratic National Headquarters on Times Square. He did not return home to his bed until nearly five the next morning.

'Hell, I have a lot to celebrate,' he told George. 'I'm going to be the next . . .' He fell asleep before he finished the sentence. George smile and put him to bed.

    .   .   .

William watched the results of the election in the peace of his study on East Sixty-eighth Street. After the Illinois returns which were not confirmed until ten o'clock the next morning (William never had trusted Mayor Daley), Walter Cronkite declared it was all over bar the shouting, and William picked up his phone and dialled Thaddeus Cohen's home number.

All he said was, 'The twenty-five thousand dollars has turned out to be a wise investment, Thaddeus. Now let us be sure that there is no honeymoon period for Mr Rosnovski. But don't do anything until he makes his trip to Turkey.'

William placed the phone back on the hook and went to bed. He was disappointed that Richard Nixon had failed to beat Kennedy and that his distant cousin Henry Cabot Lodge would not be the Vice-President but it is an ill wind . . .

    .   .   .

When Abel received his invitation to be a guest at one of President

Kennedy's inauguration balls in Washington, DC, there was only one person he wanted to share the honour with. He talked the idea over with George and had to agree that Florentyna would never be willing to accompany him unless she was convinced that the feud with Richard's father could be finally resolved. So he knew he would have to go alone.

In order to be in Washington to attend the celebrations, Abel had had to postpone his latest trip to Europe and the Middle East for a few days. He could not afford to miss the inauguration, whereas he could always put back the date for the opening of the Istanbul Baron.

Abel had a new, rather conservative dark blue suit made specially for the occasion, and took over the Presidential Suite at the Washington Baron for the day of the inauguration. He enjoyed watching the vital young President deliver his inaugural speech, full of hope and promise for the future.

'A new generation of Americans, born in this country' – Abel only just qualified – 'tempered by war' – Abel certainly qualified – 'disciplined by a hard and bitter peace' – Abel made it again. 'Ask not what your country can do for you. Ask what you can do for your country.'

The crowd rose to a man and everyone ignored the snow that had failed to dampen the impact of John F. Kennedy's brilliant oratory.

Abel returned to the Washington Baron exhilarated. He showered before changing for dinner into white tie and tails, also made especially for the occasion. When he studied his ample frame in the mirror, Abel had to admit to himself that he was not the last word in sartorial elelgance. His tailor had done the best he could in the circumstances and did not complain that he had had to make three new and ever larger evening suits for Abel in the past three years. Florentyna would have chastised him for those unnecessary inches, as she used to call them, and for her he would have done something about it. Why did his thoughts always return to Florentyna? He checked his medals. First The Polish Veterans' Medal, next the decorations for his service in the desert and in Europe, and then his cutlery medals, as Abel called them, for distinguished service with knives and forks.

In all, seven inaugural balls were held in Washington that evening, and Abel's invitation directed him to the DC Armoury. He was placed at a table of Polish Democrats from New York and Chicago. They had a lot to celebrate. Edmund Muskie was in the Senate and ten more Polish Democrats had been elected to Congress. No one mentioned the two newly elected Polish Republicans. Abel spent a happy evening with two old friends, who along with him were founding members of the Polish-American Congress. They both asked after Florentyna.

The dinner was interrupted by the entrance of John F. Kennedy and his beautiful wife, Jacqueline. They stayed about fifteen minutes, chatted with a few carefully selected people and then moved on. Although Abel didn't actually speak to the President, despite leaving his table and placing himself strategically in his path, he did manage to have a word with Vincent Hogan as he was leaving with the Kennedy entourage.

'Mr Rosnovski, what a fortuitous meeting.'

Abel would like to have explained to the boy that with him nothing was fortuitous, but now was neither the time nor the place. Hogan took Abel's arm and guided him quickly behind a large marble pillar.

'I can't say too much at the moment, Mr Rosnovski, as I must stick with the President, but I think you can expect a call from us in the near future. Naturally, the President has rather a lot of appointments to deal with at the moment.'

'Naturally,' said Abel.

'But I am hoping,' continued Vincent Hogan, 'that in your case everything will be confirmed by late March or early April. May I be the first to offer my congratulaltions, Mr Rosnovski? I am confident you will serve the President well.'

Abel watched Vincent Hogan literally run off to be sure he caught up with the Kennedy party, who were already climbing into a fleet of open-door limousines.

'You look pleased with yourself,' said one of the Polish friends as Abel returned to his table and sat down to attack a tough steak, which would not have been allowed inside a Baron. 'Did Kennedy invite you to be his new Secretary of State?'

They all laughed.

'Not yet,' said Abel. 'But he did tell me the accommodation in the White House was not in the same class as the Baron.'

Abel flew back to New York the next morning after first visiting the Polish Chapel of Our Lady of Czestochowa in the National Shrine. It made him think of both Florentynas. Washington National airport was chaos and Abel eventually arrived at the New York Baron three hours later than planned. George joined him for dinner, and knew that all had gone well when Abel ordered a magnum of Dom Perignon.

'Tonight we celebrate,' said Abel. 'I saw Hogan at the ball and my appointment will be confirmed in the next few weeks. The official announcement will be made soon after I return from the Middle East.'

'Congratulations, Abel. I know of no one who deserves the honour more.'

'Thank you, George. I can assure you that your reward will not be in heaven, because when it's all official, I'm going to appoint you acting president of the Baron Group in my absence.'

Geroge drank another glass of champagne. They were already halfway through the bottle.

'How long do you think you'll be away this time, Abel?'

'Only three weeks. I want to check that those Arabs aren't robbing me blind and then go on to Turkey to open the Istanbul Baron. I think I'll take in London and Paris on the way.'

George poured some more champagne.

.   .   .

Abel had to spend three more days in London than he had originally anticipated, trying to sort out the hotel's problems, with a manager who kept blaming everything on the British unions. The London Baron had turned out to be one of Abel's few failures, although he never could put his finger on why the hotel continually lost money. He would have considered closing it, but the Baron Group had to have a presence in England's capital city, so once again he fired the manager and made a new appointment.

Paris presented a striking contrast. The hotel was one of his most successful in Europe, and he'd once admitted to Florentyna, as reluctantly as a parent admits to having a favourite child, that the Paris Baron was his favourite hotel. Abel found everything on the Boulevard Raspail well organized and spent only two days in Paris before flying on to the Middle East.

Abel now had sites in five of the Persian Gulf States, but only the Riyadh Baron had actually started construction. If he'd been a younger man, Abel would have stayed in the Middle East for a couple of years himself and sorted the Arabs out. But he couldn't abide the sand, the head, and never being certain when he could order a whisky. He thought he must be getting older, because he couldn't stand the natives either. He left them to one of his young assistant vice-presidents, who had been told that he would only be allowed to return and manage the infidels in America once Abel was sure he had proved a success with the holy and blessed ones from the Middle East.

He left the poor assistant vice-president in the richest private hell in the world and flew on to Turkey.

·   ·   ·

Abel had visited Turkey several times during the past few years to watch the progress of the Istanbul Baron. For Abel, there would always be something special about Constantinople, as he remembered the city. He was looking forward to opening a Baron in the country he had left to start a new life in America.

While he was unpacking his suitcase in yet another Presidential Suite, Abel found fifteen invitations awaiting his reply. There were always several invitations about the time of a hotel opening; a galaxy of freeloaders who wanted to be invited to any opening night party appeared on the scene as if by magic. On this occasion, however, two of the dinner invitations came as an agreeable surprise to Abel from men who certainly could not be classified as freeloaders: namely the ambassadors of America and Britain. The invitation to the old British embassy was particularly irresistible as he had not been inside the building for nearly forty years.

·   ·   ·

That evening, Abel dined as the guest of Sir Bernard Burrows, Her Majesty's Ambassador to Turkey. To his surprise he found that he had been placed at the right of the ambassador's wife, a privilege Abel had never been afforded in any other embassy in the past. When the dinner was over, he observed the quaint English tradition of the ladies leaving the room while the gentlemen sat alone to smoke cigars and drink port or brandy. Abel was invited to join the American ambassador, Fletcher Warren, for port in Sir Bernard's study. Sir Bernard was taking the American ambassador to task for allowing him to have the Chicago Baron to dinner before he had.

'The British have always been a presumptuous race,' said the American ambassador, lighting a large Cuban cigar.

'I'll say one thing for the Americans,' said Sir Bernard. 'They don't know when they're fairly beaten.'

Abel listened to the two diplomats' banter, wondering why he had been included in such a private gathering. Sir Bernard offered Abel some vintage port, and the American ambassador raised his glass.

'To Abel Rosnovski,' he said.

Sir Bernard also raised his glass. 'I understand that congratulations are in order,' he said.

Abel reddened and looked hastily towards Fletcher Warren, hoping he would help him out.

'Oh, have I let the cat out of the bag, Fletcher?' said Sir Bernard, turning to the American ambassador. 'You told me the appointment was common knowledge, old chap.'

'Fairly common,' said Fletcher Warren. 'Not that the British could ever keep a secret for very long.'

'Is that why your lot took such a devil of a time to discover we were at war with Germany?' replied Sir Bernard.

'And then moved in to make sure of the victory?'

'And the glory,' said Sir Bernard.

The American ambassador laughed. 'I'm told the official announcement will be made in the next few days.'

Both men looked at Abel, who remained silent.

'Well, then may I be the first to congratulate you, Your Excellency,' said Sir Bernard. 'I wish you every happiness in your new appointment.'

Abel flushed to hear aloud the appellation he had whispered so often to his shaving mirror during the past few months. 'You'll have to get used to being called Your Excellency, you know,' continued the British ambassador, 'and a whole lot of worse things than that, particularly all these damned functions you'll be made to attend one after another. If you have a weight problem now, it will be nothing compared to the one you'll have when you finish your term of office. You may yet live to be grateful for the Cold War. It's the one thing that might keep your social life within bounds.'

The American ambassador smiled. 'Well done, Abel, and may I add my best wishes for your continued success. When were you last in Poland?' he inquired.

'I've only been back home once for a short visit a few years ago,' said Abel. 'I've wanted to return ever since.'

'Well, you will be returning in triumph,' said Fletcher Warren. 'Are you familiar with our embassy in Warsaw?'

'No, I'm not,' admitted Abel.

'Not a bad building,' said Sir Bernard. 'Remembering you colonials couldn't get a foothold in Europe until after the Second World War. But the food is appalling. I shall expect you to do something about that, Mr Rosnovski. I'm afraid the only thing for it is that you'll have to build a Baron Hotel in Warsaw. As ambassador, that's the least they'll expect from an old Pole.'

Abel sat in a state of euphoria, laughing and enjoying Sir Bernard's feeble jokes. He found he was drinking a little more port than usual and felt at ease with himself and the world. He couldn't wait to return to America and tell Florentyna his news, now that the appointment seemed to be official. She would be so proud of him. He decided then and there that the moment he arrived back in New York he would go straight to San Francisco and make everything up with her. It was what he had wanted to do all along and now he had an excuse. Somehow he'd force himself to like the Kane boy. He must stop referring to him as 'the Kane boy'. What was his name – Richard? Yes, Richard. Abel felt a sudden rush of relief at having made the decision.

After the three men had returned to the main reception room and the ladies, Abel reached up and touched the British ambassador on the shoulder. 'I should be getting back, Your Excellency.'

'Back to the Baron,' said Sir Bernard. 'Allow me to accompany you to your car, my dear fellow.'

The ambassador's wife bade him goodnight at the door.

'Goodnight, Lady Burrows, and thank you for a memorable evening.'

She smiled. 'I know I'm not meant to know, Mr Rosnovski, but many congratulations on your appointment. You must be so proud to be returning to the land of your birth as your country's senior representative.'

'I am,' replied Abel simply.

Sir Bernard accompanied him down the marble steps of the British embassy to the waiting car. The chauffeur opened the door.

'Goodnight, Rosnovski,' said Sir Bernard, 'and good luck in Warsaw. By the way, I hope you enjoyed your first meal in the British embassy.'

'My second actually, Sir Bernard.'

'You've been before, old boy? When we checked through the guest book we couldn't find your name.'

'No,' said Abel. 'Last time I had dinner in the British embassy, I ate in the kitchen. I don't think they keep a guest book down there, but the meal was the best I'd had in years.'

Abel smiled as he climbed into the back of the car. He could see that Sir Bernard wasn't sure whether to believe him or not. As Abel was driven back to the Baron, his fingers tapped on the side windows, and he hummed to himself. He would have liked to have returned to America the next morning, but he couldn't cancel the invitation to dine with Fletcher Warren at the American embassy the following evening. Hardly the sort of thing a future ambassador does, old fellow, he could hear Sir Bernard saying.

Dinner with the American ambassador turned out to be another pleasant occasion. Abel was made to explain to the assembled guests how he had come to eat in the kitchens of the British embassy. When he told them the truth, they looked on in surprised admiration. He wasn't sure if many of them believed the story of how he nearly lost his hand, but they all admired the silver band, and that night, everyone called him 'Your Excellency'.

. . .

The next day, Abel was up early, ready for his flight to America. The DC8 flew into Belgrade, where he was grounded for sixteen hours, waiting for the plane to be serviced. Something wrong with the landing gear, they told him. He sat in the airport lounge, sipping undrinkable Yugoslavian coffee. The contrast between the British embassy and the snack bar in a communist-controlled country was not entirely lost on Abel. At last the plane took off, only to be delayed again in Amsterdam. This time they made him change planes.

When he finally arrived at Idlewild, Abel had been travelling for nearly thirty-six hours. He was so tired he could hardly walk. As he left the customs area, he suddenly found himself surrounded by newsmen, and the cameras started flashing and clicking. Immediately he smiled. The announcement must have been made, he thought. Now it's official. He stood as straight as he could and walked slowly and with dignity, disguising his limp. There was no sign of George, as the cameramen jostled each other unceremoniously to be sure of a picture.

Then he saw George standing at the edge of the crowd, looking like death.
Abel's heart lurched as he passed the barrier and a journalist, far from asking
him what it felt like to be the first Polish-American to be appointed ambassador to Warsaw, shouted: 'Do you have any answers to the charges?'

The cameras went on flashing and so did the questions.

'Are the accusations true, Mr Rosnovski?'

'How much did you actually pay Congressman Osborne?'

'Do you deny the charges?'

'Have you returned to America to face trial?'

They wrote down Abel's replies although he never spoke.

'Get me out of here,' shouted Abel above the crowd.

George squeezed forward and managed to reach Abel and then pushed
his way back through the crowd and bundled him into the waiting Cadillac.
Abel bent down and hid his head in his hands, as the cameras' flashbulbs
kept popping, and George shouted at the chauffeur to get moving.

'To the Baron, sir?' he asked.

'No, to Miss Rosnovski's flat on Fifty-seventh Street.'

'Why?' said Abel.

'Because the press is crawling all over the Baron.'

'I don't understand,' said Abel. 'In Istanbul they treat me as if I was the
ambassador's elect, and I return home to find I'm a criminal. What the hell
is going on, George?'

'Do you want to hear it all from me, or wait until you've seen your lawyer?'
asked George.

'Who have you got to represent me?' asked Abel.

'H. Trafford Jilks, the best defence attorney in America.'

'And the most expensive.'

'I didn't think you would be worrying about money at a time like this,
Abel.'

'You're right, George. I'm sorry. Where is he now?'

'I left him at the courthouse, but he said he'd come to the flat as soon as
he was through.'

'I can't wait that long, George. For God's sake put me in the picture. Tell
me the worst.'

George drew a deep breath. 'There's a warrant out for your arrest,' he
said.

'What the hell's the charge?'

'Bribery of government officials.'

'I've never been directly involved with a government official in my whole
life,' protested Abel.

'I know, but it turns out that Henry Osborne has been all along, and
everything he did seems to have been in your name or on your behalf.'

'Oh my God,' said Abel. 'I should never have employed the man. I let
the fact that we both hated Kane cloud my judgement. But I still find it hard
to believe Henry has given anyone the dirt, because he would only end up
implicating himself.'

'But Henry has disappeared,' said George, 'and suddenly, mysteriously,
all his debts have been cleared up.'

'William Kane,' said Abel, hissing the words out.

'We've found nothing that points in that direction,' said George. 'There's no proof he's involved in this at all.'

'Who needs proof? You tell me how the authorities got hold of all the details.'

'We do know that much,' said George. 'It seems an anonymous package containing a file was sent direct to the Justice Department in Washington.'

'Postmarked New York, no doubt,' said Abel.

'No. Chicago.'

Abel was silent for a few moments. 'It couldn't have been Henry who sent the evidence to them,' he said finally. 'That doesn't make any sense.'

'How can you be so sure?' asked George.

'because you said all his debts have been cleared up, and the Justice Department wouldn't pay out that sort of money unless they thought they were going to catch Al Capone. Henry must have sold his file to someone else. But who? The one thing we can be certain of is that he would never have released any information directly to Kane.'

'Directly?' said George.

'Directly,' repeated Abel. 'Perhaps he didn't sell it directly. Kane could have arranged for an intermediary to deal with the whole thing if he already knew that Henry was heavily in debt, and the bookmakers were threatening him.'

'That might be right, Abel, and it certainly wouldn't have taken an ace detective to discover the extent of Henry's financial problems. They were common knowledge to anyone sitting on a bar stool in Chicago, but don't jump to hasty conclusions just yet. Let's find out what your lawyer has to say.'

The Cadillac came to a halt outside Florentyna's former home, which Abel had retained and kept spotless in the hope that his daughter would one day return. George opened the door, and they walked through to join H. Trafford Jilks. Once they had settled down, George poured Abel a large whisky. He drank the malt in one gulp, and gave the empty glass back to George who re-filled it.

'Tell me the worst, Mr Jilks. Let's get it over with.'

'I am sorry, Mr Rosnovski,' he began. 'Mr Novak told me about Warsaw.'

'That's all over now, so we may as well forget "Your Excellency". You can be sure if Vincent Hogan were asked, he wouldn't even remember my name. Come on, Mr Jilks, what am I facing?'

'You've been indicted on seventeen charges of bribery and corruption of officials in fourteen different states. I've made provisional arrangements with the Justice Department for you to be arrested here at the flat tomorrow morning, and they will make no objection to bail being granted.'

'Very cosy,' said Abel, 'but what if they can prove the charges?'

'Oh, they should be able to prove some of the charges,' said H. Trafford Jilks matter of factly, 'but as long as Henry Osborne stays tucked away, they're going to find it very difficult to nail you on most of them. But you're going to have to live with the fact, Mr Rosnovski, that most of the real damage has already been done whether you're convicted or not.'

'I can see that only too well,' said Abel, glancing across at a picture of himself on the front page of the *Daily News*. 'So you find out, Mr Jilks, who

the hell bought that file from Henry Osborne. Put as many people to work
on the case as you need. I don't care about the cost. But you find out and
find out quickly, because if it turns out to be William Kane, I'm going to
finish that man off once and for all.'

'Don't get yourself into any more trouble than you are already,' said H.
Trafford Jilks. 'You're knee deep in as it is.'

'Don't worry,' said Abel. 'When I finish Kane, it'll be legal and way above
board.'

'Now listen carefully, Mr Rosnovski. You forget about William Kane for
the time being and start worrying about your impending trial, because it
will be the most important event ever to take place in your life unless you
don't mind spending the next ten years in jail. Now there's not much more
we can do tonight, so go to bed and catch some sleep. In the meantime, I'll
issue a short press statement denying the charges and saying that we have
a full explanation which will exonerate you completely.'

'Do we?' asked George hopefully.

'No,' said Jilks, 'but it will give me some much needed time to think. When
Mr Rosnovski has had a chance to check through that file of names, it
wouldn't surprise me to discover that he's never had direct contact with any
of them. It's possible that Henry Osborne always acted as an intermediary
without ever putting Mr Rosnovski fully in the picture. Then my job will
be to prove that Osborne exceeded his authority as a director of the group.
Mind you, Mr Rosnovski, if you did meet any of the people mentioned in
that file, for God's sake let me know, because you can be sure the Justice
Department will put them on the stand as witnesses to testify against us. But
we'll start worrying about that tomorrow. You go to bed and get some sleep.
You must be exhausted after your trip. I will see you first thing in the
morning.'

.   .   .

Abel was arrested quietly in his daughter's apartment at eight thirty a.m.
and driven away by a US marshal to the Federal District Court for the
Southern District of New York. The brightly coloured St Valentine's Day
decorations in store windows heightened Abel's sense of loneliness. Jilks had
hoped that his arrangements had been so discreet that the press would not
have picked them up, but when Abel reached the courthouse, he was once
again surrounded by photographers and reporters. He ran the gauntlet into
the courtroom with George in front of him and Mr Jilks behind. They sat
silently in an anteroom waiting for their case to be called.

When they were called, the indictment hearing lasted only a few minutes
and was a strange anti-climax. The clerk read the charges, H. Trafford Jilks
answered 'Not Guilty' to each one on behalf of his client and requested bail.
The government, as agreed, made no objection. Jilks asked Judge Prescott
for at least three months to prepare his defence. The judge set a trial date
of 17 May and, seemingly uninterested, moved on to the next case.

Abel was free again, free to face the press and more flashing bulbs of their
cameras. George had the car waiting for him at the bottom of the steps with
the door open. The engine was already running and Abel's chauffeur had
to do some very skilful driving to free himself from the determined reporters
who were still pursuing their story. He did not head back to the flat on East

Fifty-seventh Street until he was certain he had shaken them all off. Abel said nothing during the entire chase. When they reached their destination, he turned to George and put his arm on his shoulder.

'Now listen, George, you're going to have to run the group for at least three months while I get my defence sorted out with Mr Jilks. Let's hope you don't have to run it alone after that,' said Abel, trying to laugh.

'Of course I won't have to, Abel. Mr Jilks will get you off, you'll see.' George picked up his briefcase and touched Abel on the arm. 'Keep smiling,' he said and left.

'I don't know what I'd do without George,' Abel told his lawyer as they settled down in the front room. 'We came over on the boat together nearly forty years ago, and we've been through a hell of a lot since then. Now it looks as if there's a whole lot more ahead of us, so let's get on with it, Mr Jilks. Any sign of Henry Osborne yet?'

'No, but I have six men working on it, and I understand the Justice Department have at least another six so we can be pretty sure he'll turn up, not that we want them to find him first.'

'What about the man Osborne sold the file to?' asked Abel.

'I have some people I trust in Chicago detailed to run that down.'

'Good,' said Abel. 'Now the time has come to go over that file of names you left with me last night.'

Trafford Jilks began by reading the indictment and then he went over each of the charges in detail with Abel.

After nearly three weeks of constant meetings, when Jilks was finally convinced there was nothing else Abel could tell him, he left his client to rest. The three weeks had failed to turn up any leads as to the whereabouts of Henry Osborne, either from Traffort Jilks' men or the Justice Department. Jilks' men had also had no breakthrough on finding the person to whom Henry had sold his information and were beginning to wonder if Abel had guessed right.

As the trial date drew nearer, Abel started to face the possibility of actually going to jail. He was now fifty-five and afraid and ashamed at the prospect of spending the last few years of his life the same way as he had spent the first few. As H. Trafford Jilks had pointed out, if the government could prove they had a case, there was enough in Osborne's file to send him to the pen for a very long time. The injustice – as it seemed to him – of his predicament angered Abel. The malfeasances that Henry Osborne had committed in his name had been substantial but not exceptional; Abel doubted that any new business could have grown or any new money made without the sort of handouts and bribes documented with sickening accuracy in Trafford Jilks' file. He thought bitterly of the smooth, impassive face of the young William Kane, sitting in his Boston office all those years' ago on a pile of inherited money whose probably disreputable origins were safely buried under generations of respectability. Then Florentyna wrote, a touching letter enclosing some photographs of her son, saying that she still loved and respected Abel, and believed in his innocence.

Three days before the trial was due to open, the Justice Department found Henry Osborne in New Orleans. They undoubtedly would have missed him completely if he hadn't ended up in the local hospital with two broken legs.

A zealous policeman discovered Henry had received his injuries for welching on gambling debts. They don't like that in New Orleans. The policeman put two and two together and later that night, after the hospital had put plaster casts on both Osborne's legs, the Justice Department wheeled him on an Eastern Airlines flight to New York.

Henry Osborne was charged the next day with conspiracy to defraud, and he was denied bail. H. Trafford Jilks asked the court's permission to be allowed to question him. The court granted his request, but Jilks gained very little satisfaction from the interview. It became obvious that Osborne had already made his deal with the government, promising to turn state's evidence against Abel in return for lesser charges against him.

'No doubt Mr Osborne will find the charges against him are surprisingly minor,' commented the lawyer drily.

'So that's his game,' said Abel. 'I take the rap while he escapes. Now we'll never find out who he sold that goddamn file to.'

'No, there you are wrong, Mr Rosnovski. That was the one thing he was willing to talk about,' said Jilks. 'He said it wasn't William Kane. He would never have sold the file to Kane under any circumstances. A man from Chicago called Harry Smith paid Mr Osborne cash for the evidence, and, would you believe it, Harry Smith turns out to be an alias because there are dozens of Harry Smiths in the Chicago area and not a single one of them fits the description.'

'Find him,' said Abel. 'And find him before the trial starts.'

'We're already working on that,' said Jilks. 'If the man is still in Chicago we'll pin him down within the week. Osborne also added that this so-called Smith assured him he only wanted the file for private purposes. He had no intention of revealing the contents to anyone in authority.'

'Then why did "Smith" want the details in the first place?' asked Abel.

'The inference was blackmail. That's why Henry Osborne disappeared, to avoid you. If you think about that, Mr Rosnovski, he could be telling the truth. After all, the disclosures are extremely damaging to him, and he must have been as distressed as you when he heard the file was in the hands of the Justice Department. It's no wonder he decided to stay out of sight and turned state's evidence when he was eventually caught.'

'Do you know,' said Abel, 'the only reason I ever employed that man was because he hated William Kane as much as I did, and now Kane has done us both.'

'There's no proof that Mr Kane was in any way involved,' said Jilks.

'I don't need proof.'

The trial was delayed at the request of the government. They claimed they needed more time to question Henry Osborne before presenting their case, as he was now their principal witness. Trafford Jilks objected strongly and informed the court that the health of his client, who was no longer a young man, was failing under the strain of false accusations. The plea did not move Judge Prescott, who agreed to the government's request and postponed the trial for a further four weeks.

The month dragged on for Abel and two days before the trial was due to open, he resigned himself to being found guilty and facing a long jail sentence. Then H. Trafford Jilks' investigator in Chicago found the man called Harry Smith, who turned out to be a local private detective, who had used an alias under strict instructions from his client, a firm of lawyers in New York. It cost Jilks one thousand dollars and another twenty-four hours before Harry Smith revealed that the firm concerned had been Cohen, Cohen and Yablons.

'Kane's lawyer,' said Abel immediately on being told.

'Are you sure?' asked Jilks. 'I would have thought from all we know about William Kane that he would be the last person to use a Jewish firm.'

'Way back, when I bought the hotels from Kane's bank, some of the paperwork was covered by a man called Thomas Cohen. For some reason, the bank used two lawyers for the transaction.'

'What do you want me to do about it?' George asked Abel.

'Nothing,' said Trafford Jilks. 'I don't want any more trouble before the trial. Do you understand me, Mr Rosnovski?'

'Yes, sir,' said Abel. 'I'll deal with Kane when the trial's over. Now, Mr Jilks, listen and listen carefully. You must go back to Osborne immediately and tell him the file was sold by Harry Smith to William Kane, and that Kane used the contents to gain revenge on both of us, and stress the "both of us". I promise you when Osborne hears that, he's not going to open his mouth in the witness box, no matter what promises he's made to the Justice Department. Henry Osborne's the one man alive who may hate Kane more than I do.'

'Anything you say,' said Jilks, who clearly wasn't convinced, 'but I feel I must warn you, Mr Rosnovski, he's still putting the blame firmly on your shoulders, and to date he's been no help to our side at all.'

'You take my word for this, Mr Jilks. His attitude will change the moment he knows about Kane's involvement.'

H. Trafford Jilks obtained permission to spend ten minutes that night with Henry Osborne in his cell before going on home. Osborne listened but said nothing. Jilks was sure that his news had made no impression on the government's star witness and he decided he would wait until the next morning before telling Abel Rosnovski. He preferred that his client try to get a good night's sleep before the trial opened the next morning.

. . .

Four hours before the trail was due to start, Henry Osborne was found hanging in his cell by the guard bringing in his breakfast. He'd used a Harvard tie.

. . .

The trial opened for the government without their star witness and they appealed for a further extension. After hearing another impassioned plea by H. Trafford Jilks on the state of his client's health, Judge Prescott refused their request. The public followed every word of the 'Chicago Baron Trial' on television and in the newspapers and to Abel's horror, Zaphia sat in the public gallery seeming to enjoy every moment of his discomfort. After nine days in court, the prosecution knew that their case was not standing up too well and offered to make a deal with H. Trafford Jilks. During an adjournment, Jilks briefed Abel on their offer.

'They will drop all the main indictments of bribery if you will plead guilty

to the misdemeanours on two of the minor counts of attempting to improperly influence a public official.'

'What do you estimate are my chances of getting off completely if I turn
them down?'

'Fifty-fifty, I would say,' said Jilks.

'And if I don't get off?'

'Judge Prescott is tough. The sentence wouldn't be a day under six years.'

'And if I agree to the deal and plead guilty to the two minor charges, what
then?'

'A heavy fine. I would be surprised if it came to anything more than that,'
said Jilks.

Abel sat and considered the alternatives for a few moments.

'I'll plead guilty. Let's get the damn thing over with.'

The government lawyers informed the judge that they were dropping
fifteen of the charges against Abel Rosnovski. H. Trafford Jilks rose from his
place and told the court that his client wished to change his plea to guilty
on the two remaining misdemeanour charges. The jury was dismissed and
Judge Prescott was very hard on Abel in his summing-up, reminding him
that the right to do business did not include the right to suborn public
officials. Bribery was a crime and a worse crime when condoned by an
intelligent and competent man, who should not need to stoop to such levels.
In other countries, the judge added pointedly, making Abel feel like a raw
immigrant once again, bribery might be an accepted way of going about
one's daily life, but that was not the case in the United States of America.
Judge Prescott gave Abel a six months' suspended sentence and a twenty-
five thousand dollar fine plus costs.

George took Abel back to the Baron and the sat in the penthouse drinking
whisky for over an hour before Abel spoke.

'George, I want you to contact Peter Parfitt and pay him the one million
dollars he asked for his two per cent of Lester's, because once I have my
hands on eight per cent of the bank I am going to invoke Article Seven of
their by-laws and kill William Kane in his own board room.'

George nodded sadly in agreement.

. . .

A few days later the State Department announced that Poland had been
granted most favoured nation status in foreign trade with the United States,
and that the next American ambassador to Warsaw would be John Moors
Cabot.

39

On a bitter February evening, William sat back and re-read Thaddeus
Cohen's report. Henry Osborne had released all the information he had
needed to finish Abel Rosnovski and had taken his twenty-five thousand

dollars and disappeared. Very much in character, thought William as he replaced the well-worn copy of the Rosnovski file back in his safe. The original had been sent to the Justice Department in Washington DC some days before by Thaddeus Cohen.

When Abel Rosnovski had returned from Turkey and was subsequently arrested, William had waited for him to retaliate, expecting him to dump all his Interstate stock on the market immediately. This time, William was prepared. He had already warned his broker that Interstate might come onto the open market in large amounts with little warning. His instructions were clear. They were to be bought immediately so that the price did not drop. He was prepared to put up the money from his trust as a short-term measure, to avoid any unpleasantness at the bank. William had also circulated a memo among all the stockholders of Lester's asking them not to sell any Interstate stock without consulting him.

As the weeks passed and Abel Rosnovski made no move, William began to believe that Thaddeus Cohen had been correct in assuming that nothing had been traceable back to him. Rosnovski must surely be placing the blame firmly on Henry Osborne's shoulders.

Thaddeus Cohen was certain that with Osborne's evidence, Abel Rosnovski would end up behind bars for a very long time, which would prevent him from ever finding it possible to invoke Article Seven and be a threat to the bank or William Kane. William hoped that the verdict might also make Richard come to his senses and return home. Surely these latest revelations about that family could only make him detest the Rosnovski girl and realize that his father had been right all along.

William would have welcomed Richard back. There was now a gap on the board of Lester's created by the retirement of Tony Simmons and the death of Ted Leach. Richard would have to return to New York before William's sixty-fifth birthday in ten years, or it would be the first time in over a century that a Kane had not sat in a bank's board room. Cohen had reported that Richard had made a series of brilliant takeover bids for shops that Florentyna needed: but surely the opportunity to become the next chairman of Lester's Bank would mean more to Richard than living with that Rosnovski girl.

Another factor that worried William was that he did not care too much for the new breed of directors now working at the bank. Jake Thomas, the new vice-chairman was the firm favourite to succeed him as chairman. He might have been educated to Princeton and graduated Phi Beta Kappa, but he was flashy – too flashy – thought William and far too ambitious, not at all the right sort to be the next chairman of Lester's. He would have to hang on until his sixty-fifth birthday and try to convince Richard that he should join Lester's before then. William was only too aware that Kate would have had Richard back on any terms, but as the years passed, he had found it harder to give way to his better judgement. Thank heaven Virginia's marriage was going well, and now she was pregnant. If Richard refused to return home and give up that Rosnovski girl, he could still leave everything to Virginia – if only she produced a grandson.

William was at his desk in the bank when he had his first heart attack. Not a very serious one. The doctors told him he should rest a little and he would still live another twenty years. He told his doctor, another bright young man – how he missed Andrew MacKenzie – that he only wanted to survive for ten years to see out his term of office as chairman of the bank.

For the few weeks that he had to convalesce at home, William reluctantly allowed Jake Thomas the overall responsibility for the bank's decisions, but as soon as he returned, he quickly re-established his position as chairman for fear that Thomas might have taken on too much authority in his absence. From time to time, Kate plucked up the courage to beg him to let her make some direct approach to Richard, but William remained obstinate, saying, 'The boy knows he can come home whenever he wants to. All he has to do is end his relationship with that scheming girl.'

The day Henry Osborne killed himself, William had a second heart attack. Kate sat by his bedside all through the night, fearing he would die, but Abel Rosnovski's trial kept him alive. William followed the trial devoutly every day, and he knew Osborne's suicide could only put Rosnovski in a far stronger position. When Rosnovski was finally released with nothing more than a six month's suspended sentence and a twenty-five thousand dollar fine, the lightness of the penalty did not come as a surprise to William. It wasn't hard to figure out that the government must have agreed to a deal with Rosnovski's brilliant lawyer.

William was, however, surprised to find himself feeling slightly guilty and somewhat relieved that Abel Rosnovski had not been sent to prison.

Once the trial was over William didn't care if Rosnovski dumped his Interstate Airways stock or not. He was still ready for him. But nothing happened, and as the weeks passed, William began to lose interest in the Chicago Baron and could only think of Richard, whom he now desperately wanted to see again. 'Old age and fear of death allows for sudden changes of the heart,' he had once read. One morning in September, he informed Kate of his wish. She didn't ask why he had changed his mind; it was enough for her that William wanted to see his only son.

'I'll call Richard in San Francisco immediately and invite them both,' she told him, and was pleasantly surprised that the word 'both' didn't seem to shock her husband.

'That will be fine,' said William quietly. 'Please tell Richard that I want to see him again before I die.'

'Don't be silly, darling. The doctor said that if you take it easy you'll live for another twenty years.'

'I only want to complete my term as chairman at the bank and see Richard take my place on the board. That will be enough. Why don't you fly to the coast again and tell Richard of my request, Kate?'

'What do you mean, again?' asked Kate nervously.

William smiled. 'I know you've been to San Francisco several times already, my darling. For the last few years whenever I go away on a business trip, you've always used the excuse to visit your mother, but when she died last year, your excuses became increasingly improbably. We've been married for twenty-eight years and by now I think I'm aware of all your habits. You're still as lovely as the day I met you, my darling, but I do believe that at fifty-four you're unlikely to have a lover. So it wasn't all that hard for me to work out that you had been visiting Richard.'

'Yes, I have been seeing him,' said Kate. 'Why didn't you mention that you knew before?'

'In my heart I was glad,' said William. 'I hated the thought of his losing contact with us both. How is he?'

'Both of them are well, and you have a granddaughter now as well as a grandson.'

'A granddaughter as well as a grandson,' William repeated.

'Yes, she's called Annabel,' said Kate.

'And my grandson?' said William, inquiring for the first time.

When Kate told him his name he had to smile. It was only half a lie.

'Good,' said William. 'Well, you fly to San Francisco and see what can be done. Tell him I love him.' He had once heard another old man say that who was going to lose his son.

Kate was more content that night than she had been in years. She called Richard to say she would be flying out to stay with them the following week, bringing good news with her.

When Kate returned to New York three weeks later, William was pleased to learn that Richard and Florentyna could visit them at the end of November, which was the first opportunity for them to get away from San Francisco together. Kate was full of stories of how successful they both were, how young William Kane was the image of his grandfather and how they were all so much looking forward to coming back to New York for a visit.

William listened intently and found he was happy too, and at peace with himself. He had begun to fear that if Richard did not return home soon, he never would, and then the chairmanship of the bank would fall into Jake Thomas's lap. William did not care to think about that.

· · ·

William returned to work the following Monday in high spirits after his lengthy absence, having made a good recovery from his second heart attack and now feeling he had something worth living for.

'You must pace yourself a little more carefully,' the clever young doctor had told him, but he was determined to reestablish himself as chairman and president of the bank so he could make way for his only son. On his arrival at the bank he was greeted by the doorman, who told him that Jake Thomas was looking for him and had tried to reach him at home earlier. William thanked the senior member of the bank, the only person who had served Lester's more years than the chairman himself.

'Nothing's so important that it can't wait,' he said.

'No, sir.'

William walked slowly to the chairman's office. When he opened his door, he found three of his directors already in conference and Jake Thomas sitting firmly in William's chair.

'Have I been away that long,' said William, laughing. 'Am I no longer chairman of the board?'

'Yes, of course you are. Welcome back, William,' said Jake Thomas, moving quickly out of the Chairman's seat.

William had found it impossible to get used to Jake Thomas calling him by his first name. The new generation were all too familiar. They had only known each other a few years, and the man couldn't have been a day over forty.

'What's the problem?' he asked.

'Abel Rosnovski,' said Jake Thomas without expression.

William felt a sick feeling in the pit of his stomach and sat down in the nearest leather seat.

'What does he want this time?' he said wearily. 'Won't he let me finish my days in peace?'

Jake Thomas stood up and walked towards William.

'He intends to invoke Article Seven and hold a proxy meeting with the sole purpose of removing you from the chair.'

'He can't. He doesn't have the necessary eight per cent and the bank's by-laws state clearly that the chairman must be informed immediately if any outside person comes into possession of eight per cent of the stock.'

'He says he'll have the eight per cent by tomorrow morning.'

'No, no,' said William. 'I've kept a careful check on all the stock. No one would sell to Rosnovski. No one.'

'Peter Parfitt,' said Jake Thomas.

'No,' said William smiling triumphantly. 'I bought his shares a year ago through a third party.'

Jake Thomas looked shocked, and no one spoke for some time. William realized for the first time just how much Thomas wanted to be the next chairman of Lester's.

'Well,' said Jake Thomas. 'We must face the fact he claims he'll have eight per cent by tomorrow which would entitle him to elect three directors to the board and hold up any major policy decision for three months. The very provisions you put into the articles of incorporation to protect your long term position. He also intends to announce his decision in advertisements placed all across the country. For good measure, he's threatening to make a reverse takeover bid for Lester's using the Baron Group as the vehicle if he receives any opposition to his plans. He has made it clear that there is only one way he will drop the whole plan.'

'What that?' said William.

'If you submit your resignation as chairman of the bank,' replied Jake Thomas.

'That's blackmail,' said William, nearly shouting.

'Maybe, but if you do not resign by noon next Monday, he intends to make his announcement to all shareholders. He has already booked space in forty newspapers and magazines.'

'The man's gone mad,' said William. He took his handkerchief from his breast pocket and mopped his brow.

'That's not all he said,' Jake Thomas added. 'He has also demanded that no Kane replace you on the board during the next ten years and that your resignation should not give ill health or, indeed, any reason for your sudden departure.'

He held out a lengthy document bearing 'The Baron Group's' letterhead.

'Mad,' repeated William, when he had scanned the letter rapidly.

'Nevertheless, I've called a board meeting for tomorrow,' said Jake Thomas. 'At ten o'clock. I think we should discuss his demands in detail then, William.'

The three directors left William alone in his office and no one visited him during the day. He sat at his desk trying to contact some of the other directors, but he only managed to have a word with one or two of them and couldn't feel certain of their support. He realized the meeting was going to be a close run thing but as long as no one else had eight per cent he was safe, and he began to prepare his strategy to retain control of his own board room. He checked the list of stockholders: as far as he could tell, not one of them intended to release his stock. He laughed to himself. Abel Rosnovski had failed with his coup. He went home early that night, only telling Kate to cancel Richard's proposed visit, and then retired to his study to consider his tactics for defeating Abel Rosnovski for the last time. He didn't go to bed until three a.m., but by then he had decided what had to be done. Jake Thomas must be removed from the board so that Richard could take his place.

William arrived early for the board meeting the next morning and sat waiting in his office looking over his notes, confident of victory. He felt his plan had taken everything into account. At five to ten his secretary buzzed. 'A Mr Rosnovski is on the phone for you,' she said.

'What?' said William.

'Mr Rosnovski.'

'Mr Rosnovski.' William repeated the name in disbelief. 'Put him through,' he said, his voice quavering.

'Yes, sir.'

'Mr Kane?'

The slight accent that William could never forget. 'Yes, what do you want this time?'

'Under the by-laws of the bank I have to inform you that I now own eight per cent of Lester's shares and intend to invoke Article Seven unless my earlier demands are met by noon on Monday.'

'How did you get the final two per cent?' stammered William. The phone clicked. He quickly studied the list of shareholders trying to work out who had betrayed him. William was still trembling when it rang again.

'The board meeting is just about to begin, sir.'

As ten o'clock struck William entered the board room. Looking round the table, he suddenly realized how few of the younger directors he knew well. Last time he'd had a fight in this same room, he hadn't known any of the directors and he'd won. He smiled to himself, resonably confident he could still beat Abel Rosnovski, and rose to address the board.

'Gentlemen, this meeting, has been called because the bank has received a demand from Mr Abel Rosnovski of the Baron Group; a convicted criminal who has had the effrontery to issue a direct threat to me, namely that he will use his eight per cent holding in my bank to embarrass us and if this tactic fails he will attempt a reverse takeover bid, unless I resign from the presidency and chairmanship of this board without explanation. You all know that I have only nine years left to serve this bank until my retirement and, if I were to leave before then, my resignation would be totally misinterpreted in the financial world.'

William looked down at his notes, deciding to lead with his ace.

'I am willing, gentlemen, to pledge my entire shareholding and a further ten million dollars from my private trust to be placed at the disposal of the bank in order that you can counter any move Mr Rosnovski makes while still insuring Lester's against any financial loss. I hope, gentlemen, in those circumstances, I can expect your full support in my battle against Abel Rosnovski. I am sure you are not mean to give in to vulgar blackmail.'

The room was silent. William felt certain he had won, but then Jake Thomas asked if the board might question him about his relationship with Abel Rosnovski. The request took William by surprise, but he agreed without hesitation. Jake Thomas didn't frighten him.

'This vendetta between you and Abel Rosnovski,' said Jake Thomas, 'has been going on for over thirty years. Do you believe if we followed your plan that would be the end of the matter?'

'What else can the man do? What else can he do?' stuttered William, looking around the room for support.

'We can't be sure until he does it, but with an eight per cent holding in the bank he has powers every bit as great as yours,' said the new company secretary – not William's choice, he talked too much. 'And all we know is that neither of you seems able to give up this personal feud. Although you have offered ten million to protect our financial position, if Rosnovski were continually to hold up policy decisions, call proxy meetings, arrange take-over bids with no interest in the goodwill of the bank, it would undoubtedly cause panic. The bank and its subsidiary companies, to whom we have a duty as directors, would at best, be highly embarrassed and at worst, might eventually collapse.'

'No, no,' said William. 'With my personal backing we could meet him head on.'

'The decision we have to make today,' continued the company secretary, 'is whether there are any circumstances in which this board wants to meet Mr Rosnovski head on. Perhaps we are bound to be the losers in the long run.'

'Not if I cover the cost from my private trust,' said William.

'That you could do,' said Jake Thomas, 'but it's not just money we're discussing; much bigger problems arise for the bank. Now that Rosnovski can invoke Article Seven, he can play with us when and as he pleases. The bank could be spending its entire time doing nothing but trying to anticipate Abel Rosnovski's every move.'

Jake Thomas waited for the effect of what he had said to sink in. William remained silent. Then Thomas looked at William and continued: 'Now I must ask you a very serious personal question, Mr Chairman, which worries every one of us around this table, and I hope you'll be nothing less than frank with us when answering it, however unpleasant that may be for you.'

William looked up, wondering what the question could be. What had they been discussing behind his back? Who the hell did Jake Thomas think he was? William felt he was losing the initiative.

'I will answer anything that the board requires,' said William. 'I have nothing and no one to fear,' he said, looking pointedly at Jake Thomas.

'Thank you,' said Jake Thomas. 'Mr Chairman, were you in any way involved with sending a file to the Justice Department in Washington which caused Abel Rosnovski to be arrested and charged with fraud when at the same time you knew he was a major shareholder of the bank's?'

Did he tell you that?' demanded William.

'Yes, he claims you were the sole reason for his arrest.'

William stayed silent for a few moments, considering his reply, while he looked down at his notes. They didn't help. He had not thought that question would arise but he had never lied to the board in over twenty-three years. He couldn't start now.

'Yes, I did,' he said, breaking the silence. 'The information came into my hands, and I considered that it was nothing less than my duty to pass it on to the Justice Department.'

'How did the information come into your hands?'

William did not reply.

'I think we all know the answer to that question, Mr Chairman,' said Jake Thomas. 'Moreover, you let the authorities know without briefing the board of your action and by so doing you put all of us in jeopardy. Our reputations, our careers, everything this bank stands for over a personal vendetta.'

'But Rosnovski was trying to ruin me,' said William, aware he was now shouting.

'So in order to ruin him you risked the bank's stability and reputation.'

'It is my bank,' said William.

'It is not,' said Jake Thomas. 'You own eight per cent of the stock, as does Mr Rosnovski, and at the moment you are president and chairman of Lester's, but the bank is not yours to use for your own personal whim without consulting the other directors.'

'Then I will have to ask the board for a vote of confidence,' said William. 'I'll ask you to support me against Abel Rosnovski.'

'That is not what a vote of confidence would be about,' said the company secretary. 'The vote would be about whether you are the right man to run this bank in the present circumstances. Can't you see that, Mr Chairman?'

'So be it,' said William, turning his eyes away. 'This board must decide whether it wishes to end my career in disgrace now, after nearly a quarter of a century's service, or to yield to the threats of a convicted criminal.'

Jake Thomas nodded to the company secretary and voting slips were passed around to every board member. It looked to William as if everything had been decided before the meeting. He glanced around the crowded table at the twenty-nine men. Many of them he had chosen himself, but some of them he didn't know at all well. He had once heard that a small group of young directors openly supported the Democratic Party and John Kennedy. Some of them were looking at him; some were not. Surely they'd back him; they wouldn't let Rosnovski beat him. Not now. Please let me finish my term as chairman, he said to himself, then I'll go quietly and without any fuss – but not this way.

He watched the members of the board as they passed their voting slips back to the secretary. He was opening them slowly. The room was silent and all eyes were turned towards the secretary as he began opening the last few slips, noting down each aye and nay meticulously on a piece of paper placed in front of him that revealed two columns. William could see that one list of names was considerably longer than the other, but his failing eyesight did not permit him to decipher which was which. He could not accept that the day could have come when there would be a vote in his own board room between himself and Abel Rosnovski.

The secretary was saying something. William couldn't believe what he heard. By seventeen votes to twelve he had lost the confidence of the board. He managed to stand up. Abel Rosnovski had beaten him in the final battle. No one spoke as William left the board room. He returned to the Chairman's office and picked up his coat, stopping only to look at the portrait of Charles Lester for the last time, and then walked slowly down the long corridor and out of the front entrance.

The doorman said, 'Nice to have you back again, Mr Chairman. See you tomorrow, sir.'

William realized he would never see him again. He turned around and shook hands with the man who had directed him to the board room twenty-three years before.

The rather surprised doorman said, 'Goodnight, sir,' as he watched William climb into the back of his car for the last time.

His chauffeur took him home and when he reached East Sixty-eighth Street, William collapsed on his front door step. The chauffeur and Kate helped him into the house. Kate could see he was crying, and she put her arms round him.

'What is it, William? What's happened?'

'I've been thrown out of my own bank,' he wept. 'My own board no longer have confidence in me. When it mattered, they supported Abel Rosnovski.'

Kate managed to get him up to bed and sat with him through the night. He never spoke. Nor did he sleep.

.　　.　　.　　　　　　.

The announcement in the *Wall Street Journal* the following Monday morning said simply: 'William Lowell Kane, the president and chairman of Lester's Bank resigned after yesterday's board meeting.'

No mention of illness or any explanation was given for his sudden departure, and there was no suggestion that his son would take his place on the board. William knew that rumour would sweep through Wall Street and that the worst would be assumed. He sat in bed alone, caring no longer for this world.

.　　.　　.

Abel read the announcement of William Kane's resignation in the *Wall Street Journal* the same day. He picked up the phone, dialled Lester's Bank and asked to speak to the new chairman. A few seconds later Jake Thomas came on the line. 'Good morning, Mr Rosnovski.'

'Good morning, Mr Thomas. I'm just phoning to confirm that I shall release all my Interstate Airways shares to the bank at the market price this morning and my eight per cent holding in Lester's to you personally for two million dollars.'

'Thank you, Mr Rosnovski, that's most generous of you.'

'No need to thank me, Mr Chairman, it's no more than we agreed on when you sold me your two per cent of Lester's,' said Abel Rosnovski.

BOOK SEVEN

40

Abel was surprised to find how little satisfaction his final triumph had given him.

George tried to persuade him that he should go to Warsaw to look over sites for the new Baron but Abel didn't want to. As he grew older he became fearful of dying abroad and never seeing Florentyna again, and for months Abel showed no interest in the group's activities. When John F. Kennedy was assassinated on 22 November 1963, Abel became even more depressed and feared for America. Eventually George did convince him that a trip abroad could do no harm, and that things would perhaps seem a little easier for him when he returned.

Abel travelled to Warsaw where he obtained a highly confidential agreement to build the first Baron in the communist world. His command of the language impressed Warsawians, and he was proud to beat Holiday Inns and Intercontinental behind the Iron Curtain. He couldn't help thinking ... and it didn't help when Lyndon Johnson appointed John Gronowski to be the first Polish-American ambassador to Warsaw. But now nothing seemed to give any satisfaction. He had defeated Kane and lost his own daughter, and he wondered if the man felt the same way about his son. After Warsaw, he roamed the world, staying in his hotels, watching the construction of new ones. He opened the first Baron in Cape Town, South Africa, and flew back to Germany to open one in Düsseldorf.

Abel then spent six months in his favourite Baron in Paris, roaming the streets by day, and attending the opera at night, hoping it might revive happy memories by Florentyna.

He eventually left Paris and returned to America, after his long exile. As he descended the metal steps of an Air France 707 at Kennedy International Airport, his back hunched and his bald head covered with a black hat, nobody recognized him. George, as always, brought him up to date on group news. The profits, it seemed, were even higher as his keen young executives thrust forward in every major country in the world. Seventy-two hotels run by twenty-two thousand staff. Abel didn't seem to be listening. He only wanted news of Florentyna.

'She's well,' said George, 'and coming to New York early next year.'

'Why?' said Abel, suddenly excited.

'She's opening one of her shops on Fifth Avenue.'

'Fifth Avenue?'

'The eleventh Florentyna,' said George.

'Have you seen her?'

'Yes,' he admitted.

'Is she well, is she happy?'

'Both of them are very well and happy, and so successful. Abel, you should be very proud of them. Your grandson is quite a boy, and your grand-daughter's beautiful. The image of Florentyna when she was that age.'

'Will she see me?' said Abel.

'Will you see her husband?'

'No, George. I can never meet that boy, not while his father is still alive.'

'What if you die first?'

'You mustn't believe everything you read in the Bible.'

Abel and George drove in silence back to the hotel, and Abel dined alone in his room that night.

For the next six months, he never left the penthouse.

41

When Florentyna Kane opened her new boutique on Fifth Avenue in March 1967, everyone in New York seemed to be there, except William Kane and Abel Rosnovski.

Kate and Lucy had left William in bed muttering to himself while they went off to the opening of 'Florentyna's'.

George left Abel alone in his suite so that he could attend the celebrations. He had tried to talk Abel into going along with him. Abel grunted that his daughter had opened ten shops without him, and one more wouldn't make any difference. George told him he was a stubborn old fool and left for Fifth Avenue on his own. When he arrived at the shop, a magnificent modern boutique with thick carpets and the latest Swedish furniture – it reminded him of the way Abel used to do things – he found Florentyna, wearing a long blue gown with the now famous F on the high collar. She gave George a glass of champagne and introduced him to Kate and Lucy Kane who were chatting with Zaphia. Kate and Lucy were clearly happy and they surprised George by inquiring after Abel Rosnovski.

'I told him he was a stubborn old fool to miss such a good party. Is Mr Kane here?' he asked.

George was delighted by Kate Kane's happy reply.

. . .

William was still muttering angrily at the *New York Times*, something about Johnson's pulling his punches in Vietnam, when he folded the newspaper and got himself out of bed. He started to dress slowly, staring at himself in the mirror when he had finished. He looked like a banker. He scowled. How else should he look? He put on a heavy black overcoat and his old Homburg hat, picked up his black walking stick with the silver handle, the one Rupert Cork-Smith had left him, and somehow got himself out onto the street. The first time he had been out on his own, he thought, for the best part of three years, since that last serious heart attack. The maid was surprised to see him leaving the house unaccompanied.

It was an unusually warm spring evening, but William felt the cold after being in the house so long. It took him a considerable time to reach Fifth Avenue and Fifty-sixth Street, and when he eventually did arrive, the crowd was so large outside Florentyna's that he felt he didn't have the strength to fight his way through it. He stood at the kerb, watching the people enjoying themselves. Young people, happy and excited, thrusting their way into Florentyna's beautiful shop. Some of the girls were wearing the new mini skirts from London. What next? thought William, and then he saw his son talking to Kate. He had grown into such a fine looking man – tall, confident, and relaxed, he had an air of authority about him that reminded William of his own father. But in the bustle and continual movement, he couldn't quite work out which one was Florentyna. He stood there for nearly an hour enjoying the comings and goings, regretting the stubborn years he had thrown away.

The wind was beginning to race down Fifth Avenue. He'd forgotten how cold that March wind could be. He turned his collar up. He must get home, because they were all coming to dinner that night, and he was going to meet Florentyna and the grandchildren for the first time. His grandson and little Annabel and their father, his beloved son. He had told Kate what a fool he'd been and begged her forgiveness. All he remembered her saying was 'I'll always love you.' Florentyna had written to him. Such a generous letter. She had been so understanding and kind about the past. She had ended with 'I can't wait to meet you.'

He must get home. Kate would be cross with him if she ever discovered he'd been out on his own in that cold wind. But he had to see the opening of the shop and in any case tonight he would be with them all. He must leave now and let them enjoy their celebrations. They could tell him all about the opening over dinner. He wouldn't tell them he'd been there, that would always be his secret.

He turned to go home and saw an old man standing a few yards away in a black coat, with a hat pulled away down on his head, and a scarf around his neck. He, too, was cold. Not a night for old men, thought William, as he walked towards him. And then he saw the silver band on his wrist, just below his sleeve. In a flash it all came back to him, fitting into place for the first time. First the Plaza, then Boston, then Germany, and now Fifth Avenue. The man turned and started to walk towards him. He must have been standing there for a long time because his face was red from the wind. He stared at William out of those unmistakable blue eyes. They were now only a few yards apart. As they passed, William raised his hat to the old man. He returned the compliment, and they continued on their separate ways without a word.

I must get home, thought William, before they do. The joy of seeing Richard and his two grandchildren would make everything worthwhile again. He must come to know Florentyna, ask for her forgiveness, and trust that she would understand what he could scarcely understand himself now. Such a fine girl, they all told him.

When he reached East Sixty eighth Street, he fumbled for his key and opened the front door. Must turn on all the lights, he told the maid, and build the fire up to make them feel welcome. He was very contented and very, very tired.

'Draw the curtains,' he said, 'and light the candles on the dining room table. There's so much to celebrate.'

William couldn't wait for them all to return. He sat in the old crimson leather chair by a blazing fire and thought happily of the evening that lay ahead of him. Grandchildren around him, the years he had missed. When had his little grandson first said three? A chance to bury the past and earn forgiveness in the future. The room was so nice and warm after that cold wind, but the journey had been well worthwhile.

A few minutes later there was an excited bustle downstairs and the maid came in to tell William that his son had arrived. He was in the hall with his mother, and his wife and two of the loveliest children the maid had ever seen. And then she ran off to be sure that dinner would be ready for Mr Kane on time. He would want everything to be perfect for them that night.

When Richard came into the room, Florentyna was by his side. She looked quite radiant.

'Father,' he said. 'I would like you to meet my wife.'

William Lowell Kane would have turned to greet them but he could not. He was dead.

42

Abel placed the envelope on the table by the side of his bed. He hadn't dressed yet. Nowadays he rarely rose before noon. He tried to remove his breakfast tray from his knees onto the floor. A bending movement that demanded too much dexterity for his stiff body to accomplish. He inevitably ended by dropping the tray with a bang. It was no different today. He no longer cared. He picked up the envelope once more, and read the covering note for second time.

'We were instructed by the late Mr Curtis Fenton, sometime manager of the Continental Trust Bank, La Salle Street, Chicago, to send you the enclosed letter, when certain circumstances have come about. Please acknowledge receipt of this letter by signing the enclosed copy, returning it to us in the stamped addressed envelope supplied herewith.'

'Goddamn lawyers,' said Abel, and tore open the letter.

Dear, Mr Rosnovski:

This letter has been in the keeping of my lawyers until today for reasons which will become apparent to you as you read on.

When in 1951 you closed your accounts at the Continental Trust after over twenty years with the bank, I was naturally very unhappy and very concerned. My concern was engendered not by losing one of the bank's most valued customers, sad though that was, but because I know you felt that I had acted in a dishonourable fashion. What you were not aware of at the time was that I had specific instructions from your backer not to reveal certain facts to you.

When you first visited me at the bank in 1929, you requested financial help to clear the debt incurred by Mr Davis Leroy, in order that you might take possession of the hotels which then formed the Richmond Group. I was unable to find a backer, despite approaching several leading financiers myself. I took a personal interest, as I believed that you had an exceptional flair for your chosen career. It has given me a great deal of satisfaction to observe in old age that my confidence was not misplaced. I might add at this point that I also felt some responsibility, having advised you to buy twenty-five per cent of the Richmond Group from my client, Miss Amy Leroy, when I did not know the financial predicament that was facing Mr Leroy at that time. I digress.

I did not succeed in finding a backer for you and had given up all hope when you came to visit me on that Monday morning. I wonder if you remember that day. Only thirty minutes before your appointment I had a call from a financier who was willing to put up the necessary money, who, like me, had a great confidence in you personally. His only stipulation was, as I advised you at the time, that he insisted on remaining anonymous because of a potential conflict between his professional and private interests. The terms he offered, allowing you to gain eventual control of the Richmond Group, I considered at the time to be extremely generous and you rightly took full advantage of them. Indeed your backer was delighted when you found it possible, through your own diligence, to repay his original investment.

I lost contact with you both after 1951, but after I retired from the bank, I read a distressing story in the newspapers concerning your backer, which prompted me to write this letter, in case I died before either of you.

I write not to prove my good intentions in this whole affair, but so that you should not continue to live under the illusion that your backer and benefactor was Mr David Maxton of the Stevens Hotel. Mr Maxton was a great admirer of yours, but he never approached the bank in that capacity. The gentleman who made made the Baron Group possible, by his foresight and personal generosity was William Lowell Kane, the chairman of Lester's Bank, New York.

I begged Mr Kane to inform you of his personal involvement, but he refused to break the clause in his trust deed that stipulated that no benefactor should be privy to the investments of the family trust. After you had paid off the loan and he later learned of Henry Osborne's personal involvement with the Baron Group he became even more adamant that you should never be informed.

I have left instructions that this letter is to be destroyed if you die before Mr Kane. In those circumstances, he will receive a letter, explaining your total lack of knowledge of his personal generosity.

Whichever one of you receives a letter from me, it was a privilege to have served you both.

As ever,
your faithful servant,
Curtis Fenton.

Abel picked up the phone by the side of his bed. 'Find George for me,' he said. 'I need to get dresed.'

43

William Lowell Kane's funeral was well attended. Richard and Florentyna stood on one side of Kate; Virginia and Lucy were on the other. Grandmother Kane would have approved of the turn-out. Three senators, five congressmen, two bishops, most of the leading banks' chairman, and the publisher of the *Wall Street Journal* were all there. Jake Thomas and every director of the Lester's board was also present, their heads bowed in prayer to the God in whom William had never really believed.

No one noticed two old men, standing at the back of the gathering, their heads also bowed, looking as if they were not attached to the main party. They had arrived a few minutes late and left quickly at the end of the service. Florentyna thought she recognized the limp as the shorter old man hurried away. She told Richard. They didn't mention their suspicion to Kate Kane.

A few days later, the taller of the two old men went to see Florentyna in her shop on Fifth Avenue. He had heard she was returning to San Francisco and needed to seek her help before she left. She listened carefully to what he had to say and agreed to his request with joy.

Richard and Florentyna Kane arrived at the Baron Hotel the next afternoon. George Novak was there to meet and escort them to the forty-second floor. After ten years, Florentyna hardly recognized her father, now propped up in bed, half-moon glasses on the end of his nose, still no pillows, but smiling defiantly. They talked of happier days and both laughed a little and cried a lot.

'You must forgive us, Richard,' said Abel. 'The Polish are a sentimental race.'

'I know, my children are half Polish,' said Richard.

Later that evening they dined together, magnificent roast veal, appropriate for the return of the prodigal daughter, said Abel.

He talked of the future and how he saw the progress of his group.

'We ought to have a Florentyna's in every hotel,' he said.

She laughed and agreed.

He told Richard of his sadness concerning his father, revealing in detail the mistakes he had made for so many years, and how it had never crossed his mind even for a moment that he could have been his benefactor, and how he would have liked one chance to thank him personally.

'He would have understood,' said Richard.

'We met, you know, the day he died,' said Abel.

Florentyna and Richard stared at him in surprise.

'Oh yes,' said Abel. 'We passed each other on Fifth Avenue, he had come to watch the opening of your shop. He raised his hat to me. It was enough, quite enough.'

Abel had only one request of Florentyna. That she and Richard would accompany him on his journey to Warsaw in nine months' time for the opening of the latest Baron.

'Can you imagine,' he said, again excited, his fingers tapping the side table. 'The Warsaw Baron. Now there is a hotel that could only be opened by the president of the Baron Group.'

. . .

During the following months the Kanes visited Abel regularly and Florentyna grew very close to her father agan. Abel came to admire Richard and the common sense that tempered all his daughter's ambitions. He adored his grandson. And little Annabel was – what was that awful modern expression? – she was something else. Abel had rarely been happier in his life and began elaborate plans for his triumphant return to Poland to open the Warsaw Baron.

. . .

The president of the Baron Group opened the Warsaw Baron six months later than had been originally scheduled. Building contracts run late in Warsaw just as they do in every other part of the world.

In her first speech, as president of the group, she told her guests that her pride in the magnificent hotel was mingled with a feeling of sadness that her late father could not have been present to open the Warsaw Baron himself.

In his will, Abel left everything to Florentyna, with the single exception of a small bequest. The testament described the gift as a heavy engraved silver bracelet, rare, but of unknown value, and bearing the legend 'Baron Abel Rosnovski'.

The beneficiary was his grandson, William Abel Kane.

THE
PRODIGAL
DAUGHTER

To Peter, Joy, Alison, Clare and Simon

Prologue

'President of the United States,' she replied.

'I can think of more rewarding ways of bankrupting myself,' said her father, as he removed the half-moon spectacles from the end of his nose and peered at his daughter over the top of his newspaper.

'Don't be frivolous, Papa. President Roosevelt proved to us that there can be no greater calling than public service.'

'The only thing Roosevelt proved . . .' began her father. Then he stopped and returned to his paper, realizing that his daughter would consider the remark flippant.

The girl continued as if she were only too aware of what was going through her father's mind. 'I realize it would be pointless for me to pursue such an ambition without your support. My sex will be enough of a liability without adding the disadvantage of a Polish background.'

The newspaper barrier between father and daughter was abruptly removed. 'Don't ever speak disloyally of the Poles,' he said. 'History has proved us to be an honourable race who never go back on our word. My father was a baron . . .'

'Yes, I know, so was my grandfather, but he's not around now to help me become President.'

'More's the pity,' he said, sighing, 'as he would undoubtedly have made a great leader of our people.'

'Then why shouldn't his granddaughter?'

'No reason at all,' he said, as he stared into the steel grey eyes of his only child.

'Well then, Papa, will you help me? I can't hope to succeed without your financial backing.'

Her father hesitated before replying, placing the glasses back on the end of his nose and slowly folding his copy of the Chicago *Tribune*.

'I'll make a deal with you, my dear; after all that's what politics is about. If the result of the New Hampshire Primary turns out to be satisfactory, I'll back you to the hilt. If not, you must drop the whole idea.'

'What's your definition of satisfactory?' came back the immediate reply.

Again the man hesitated, weighing his words. 'If you win the Primary or capture over thirty per cent of the vote, I'll go all the way to the convention floor with you, even if it means I end up destitute.'

The girl relaxed for the first time during the conversation. 'Thank you, Papa. I couldn't have asked for more.'

'No, you certainly couldn't,' he replied. 'Now can I get back to finding out just how the Cubs could possibly have lost the seventh game of the series to the Tigers?'

'They were undoubtedly the weaker team, as the 9–3 score indicates.'

'Young lady, you may imagine you know a thing or two about politics but I can assure you that you know absolutely nothing about baseball,' the man said, as his wife entered the room. He turned his heavy frame towards her. 'Our daughter wants to run for President of the United States. What do you think about that?'

The girl looked up at her eagerly, waiting for a reply.

'I'll tell you what I think,' said the mother. 'I think it's well past her bedtime and I blame you for keeping her up so late.'

'Yes, I suppose you're right,' the husband said. 'Off you go to bed, little one.'

She came to her father's side, kissed him on the cheek and whispered, 'Thank you, Papa.'

The man's eyes followed his eleven-year-old daughter as she left the room and he noticed that the fingers on her right hand were clenched, making a small tight fist, something she always did when she was angry or determined. He suspected she was both on this occasion, but he realized that it would be pointless to try and explain to his wife that their only child was no ordinary mortal. He had long ago abandoned any attempt to involve his wife in his own ambitions, and was at least thankful that she was incapable of dampening their daughter's.

He returned to the Chicago Cubs and had to admit that his daughter's judgement might even be right on that subject.

Florentyna Rosnovski never referred to the conversation again for twenty-two years, but when she did she assumed her father would keep his end of the bargain. After all, the Polish are an honourable race who never go back on their word.

THE PAST
1934–1968

1

It had not been an easy birth, but then for Abel and Zaphia Rosnovski nothing had ever been easy, and in their own ways they had both become philosophical about that. Abel had wanted a son, an heir who would one day be chairman of the Baron Group. By the time the boy was ready to take over, Abel was confident that his own name would stand alongside those of Ritz and Statler and by then the Baron would be the largest hotel group in the world. Abel had paced up and down the colourless corridor of St Luke's Hospital waiting for the first cry, his slight limp becoming more pronounced as each hour passed. Occasionally he twisted the silver band that encircled his wrist and stared at the name so neatly engraved on it. He turned and retraced his steps once again, to see Doctor Dodek heading towards him.

'Congratulations, Mr Rosnovski,' he called.

'Thank you,' said Abel eagerly.

'You have a beautiful girl,' the doctor said as he reached him.

'Thank you,' repeated Abel, quietly, trying not to show his disappointment. He then followed the obstetrician into a little room at the other end of the corridor. Through an observation window Abel was confronted with a row of wrinkled faces. The doctor pointed to the father's first-born. Unlike the others her little fingers were curled into a tight fist. Abel had read somewhere that a child was not expected to do that for at least three weeks. He smiled, proudly.

Mother and daughter remained at St Luke's for another six days and Abel visited them every morning, leaving his hotel only when the last breakfast had been served, and every afternoon after the last lunch guest had left the dining room. Telegrams, flowers and the recent fashion of greeting cards surrounded Zaphia's iron-framed bed, reassuring evidence that other people too rejoiced in the birth. On the seventh day mother and unnamed child – Abel had considered six boys' names – returned home.

On the anniversary of the second week of their daughter's birth they named her Florentyna, after Abel's sister. Once the infant had been installed in the newly decorated nursery at the top of the house, Abel would spend hours simply staring down at his daughter, watching her sleep and wake, knowing that he must work even harder than he had in the past to ensure the child's future. He was determined that Florentyna would be given a better start in life than he had been. Not for her the dirt and deprivation of his childhood or the humiliation of arriving on the eastern seaboard of America as an immigrant with little more than a few valueless Russian rubles sewn into the jacket of an only suit.

He would ensure that Florentyna was given the formal education he had lacked, not that he had a lot to complain about. Franklin D. Roosevelt lived in the White House and Abel's little group of hotels looked as if they were going to survive the Depression. America had been good to this immigrant.

Whenever he sat alone with his daughter in the upstairs nursery he would reflect on his past, and dream of her future.

When he had first arrived in the United States he had found a job in a little butcher's shop on the lower East Side of New York, where he worked for two long years before filling a vacancy at the Plaza Hotel as a junior waiter. From Abel's first day, Sammy, the old Maître d', had treated him as though he was the lowest form of life. After four years, a slave trader would have been impressed by the work and unheard-of overtime that the lowest form of life did in order to reach the exalted position as Sammy's assistant head waiter in the Oak Room. During those early years Abel spent five afternoons a week poring over books at Columbia University, and after dinner had been cleared away read on late into the night.

His rivals wondered when he slept.

Abel was not sure how his newly-acquired degree could advance him while he still only waited on tables in the Oak Room of the Plaza Hotel. The question was answered for him by a well-fed Texan called Mr Davis Leroy, who had watched Abel serving guests solicitously for a week. Mr Leroy, the owner of eleven hotels, then offered Abel the position of assistant manager at his flagship, the Richmond Continental in Chicago, with the sole responsibility of running the restaurants.

Abel was brought back to the present when Florentyna turned over and started to thump the side of her crib. He extended a finger which his daughter grabbed like a lifeline thrown from a sinking ship. She started to bite the finger with what she imagined were teeth ...

When Abel first arrived in Chicago he found the Richmond Continental badly run down. It didn't take him long to discover why. The manager, Desmond Pacey, was cooking the books and as far as Abel could tell probably had been for the past thirty years. The new assistant manager spent his first six months gathering together the proof he needed to nail Pacey and then presented to his employer a dossier containing all the facts. When Davis Leroy realized what had been going on behind his back he immediately sacked Pacey, replacing him with his new protégé. This spurred Abel on to work even harder and he became so convinced that he could turn the fortunes of the Richmond Group around that when Leroy's ageing sister put up for sale her twenty-five per cent of the company's stock Abel cashed everything he owned to purchase them. Davis Leroy was touched by his young manager's personal commitment to the company and proved it by appointing him managing director of the group.

From that moment they became partners, a professional bond that developed into a close friendship. Abel would have been the first to appreciate how hard it was for a Texan to acknowledge a Pole as an equal. For the first time since he had settled in America, he felt secure – until he found out that the Texans were every bit as proud a clan as the Poles.

Abel still couldn't accept what had happened. If only Davis had confided in him, told him the truth about the extent of the group's financial trouble – who wasn't having problems during the Depression? – between them they could have sorted something out. At the age of sixty-two Davis Leroy had been informed by his bank that his overdraft was no longer covered by the value of the hotels and that they required further security before they would agree to pay next month's wages. In response to the bank's ultimatum, Davis Leroy had had a quiet dinner with his daughter and retired to the Presidential Suite on the twelfth floor with two bottles of bourbon. Then he had opened the window and jumped. Abel would never forget standing on the corner of Michigan Avenue at four in the morning having to identify a body he could recognize only by the jacket his mentor had worn the previous night. The lieutenant investigating the death had remarked that it had been the seventh suicide in Chicago that day. It didn't help. How could the policeman possibly know how much Davis Leroy had done for him, or how much more he had intended to return that friendship in the future? In a hastily composed will Davis had bequeathed the remaining seventy-five per cent of the Richmond Group stock to his managing director, writing to Abel that although the stock was worthless one hundred per cent ownership of the group might give him a better chance to negotiate new terms with the bank.

Florentyna's eyes opened, and she started to howl. Abel picked her up lovingly, immediately regretting the decision as he felt the damp clammy bottom. He changed her nappy quickly, drying the child carefully, before making a triangle of the cloth, not allowing the big pins anywhere near her body: any midwife would have nodded her approval at his deftness. Florentyna closed her eyes and nodded back to sleep on her father's shoulder. 'Ungrateful brat,' he murmured fondly as he kissed her on the cheek.

After Davis Leroy's funeral Abel had visited Kane and Cabot, the Richmond Group's bankers in Boston, and pleaded with one of the directors not to put the eleven hotels up for sale on the open market. He tried to convince the bank that if only they would back him, he could – given time – turn the balance sheet from red into black. The smooth, cold man behind the expensive partner's desk had proved intractable. 'I must act in the bank's best interests,' he had used as an excuse. Abel would never forget the humiliation of having to call a man of his own age 'sir' and still leave empty-handed. The man must have had the soul of a cash register not to realize how many people were affected by his decision. Abel promised himself, for the hundredth time, that one day he would get even with Mr William 'Ivy League' Kane.

Abel had travelled back to Chicago that night thinking that nothing else could go wrong in his life, only to find the Richmond Continental burned to the ground and the police accusing him of arson. Arson it proved to be, but at the hands of Desmond Pacey, bent on revenge. When arrested, he admitted readily to the crime as his only interest was the downfall of Abel. Pacey would have succeeded if the insurance company had not come to Abel's rescue. Until that moment, he had wondered if he would not have been better off in the Russian prisoner-of-war camp he had escaped from before fleeing to America. But then his luck turned when an anonymous backer who, Abel concluded, must have been Mr David Maxton of the Stevens Hotel, purchased the Richmond Group and offered Abel his old position as managing director and a chance to prove he could run the company at a profit.

Abel recalled how he had been reunited with Zaphia, the self-assured girl he had first met on board the ship that had brought them to America. How immature she had made him feel then, but not when they re-met and he discovered she was a waitress at the Stevens.

Two years had passed since then and, although the newly named Baron Group had failed to make a profit in 1933, they lost only twenty-three thousand dollars, greatly helped by Chicago's celebration of its centenary when over a million tourists had visited the city to enjoy the World's Fair.

Once Pacey had been convicted of arson, Abel had only to wait for the insurance money to be paid before he could set about rebuilding the hotel in Chicago. He had used the interim period to visit the other ten hotels in the group, sacking staff who showed the same pecuniary tendencies as Desmond Pacey and replacing them from the long lines of unemployed that stretched across America.

Zaphia began to resent Abel's journeys from Charleston to Mobile, from Houston to Memphis, continually checking over his hotels in the south. But Abel realized that if he was to keep his side of the bargain with the anonymous backer there would be little time to sit around at home, however much he adored his daughter. He had been given ten years to repay the bank loan; if he succeeded, a clause in the contract stipulated he would be allowed to purchase the remaining sixty per cent of the company's stock for a further three million dollars. Zaphia thanked God each night for what they already had and pleaded with him to slow down, but nothing was going to stop Abel from trying to fulfil that aim.

'Your dinner's ready,' shouted Zaphia at the top of her voice.

Abel pretended he hadn't heard and continued to stare down at his sleeping daughter.

'Didn't you hear me? Dinner is ready.'

'What? No, dear. Sorry. Just coming.' Florentyna's rejected red eiderdown lay on the floor beside her cot. Abel picked up the fluffy quilt and placed it carefully on top of the blanket that covered his daughter. He never wanted her to feel the cold. She smiled in her sleep. Was she having her first dream? Abel wondered, as he switched out the light.

2

Florentyna's christening was something everyone present was to remember – except Florentyna, who slept through the entire proceedings. After the ceremony at the Holy Name Cathedral on North Wabash, the guests made their way to the Stevens Hotel. Abel took a private room in the hotel and invited over a hundred guests to celebrate the occasion. His closest friend, George Novak, a fellow Pole who had occupied the bunk above him on the boat coming over from Europe, was to be one Kum while one of Zaphia's cousins, Janina, was to be the other.

The guests devoured a traditional ten-course dinner including pierogi and bigos while Abel sat at the head of the table accepting gifts on behalf of his daughter which included a silver rattle, US savings bonds, a copy of *Huckleberry Finn* and, finest of all, a beautiful antique emerald ring from Abel's unnamed benefactor. He only hoped that the man gained as much pleasure in the giving as his daughter later showed in the receiving. To mark the occasion, Abel presented his daughter with a large brown teddy bear with red eyes.

'It looks like Franklin D. Roosevelt,' said George, holding the bear up for all to see. 'This calls for a second christening – FDR.'

Abel raised his glass. 'Mr President,' he toasted – a name the bear never relinquished.

The party finally came to an end around three o'clock in the morning, when Abel had to requisition a laundry trolley from the hotel to transport all the gifts home. George waved to Abel as he headed up North Michigan Avenue pushing the trolley before him.

The happy father began whistling to himself as he recalled every moment of the wonderful evening. Only when Mr President fell off the trolley for a third time did he realize how crooked his path down Lake Shore Drive must have been. He picked up the bear and wedged it in the centre of the gifts and was about to attempt a straighter path when a hand touched his shoulder. Abel jumped round, ready to defend with his life anyone who wanted to steal Florentyna's first possessions. He stared up into the face of a young policeman.

'Maybe you can explain why you are pushing a Stevens Hotel laundry trolley down Michigan Avenue at three in the morning?'

'Yes, officer,' replied Abel.

'Well, let's start with what's in the packages.'

'Other than Franklin D. Roosevelt, I can't be certain.'

The policeman immediately arrested Abel on suspicion of theft. While the recipient of the gifts slept soundly under her red eiderdown in the little nursery at the top of their house on Rigg Street, her father spent a sleepless night on an old horsehair mattress in a cell at the local jail. George appeared at the court house first thing in the morning to verify Abel's story.

The next day Abel purchased a four-door maroon Buick from Peter Sosnkowski who ran a secondhand car lot in the Polish neighbourhood.

Abel began to resent having to leave Chicago and his beloved Florentyna even for a few days, fearing he might miss her first step, her first word or her first anything. From her birth, he had supervised her daily routine, never allowing Polish to be spoken in the house: he was determined there would be no trace of a Polish accent that would make her feel ill at ease in society.

Abel had intently waited for her first word, hoping it would be 'Papa', while Zaphia feared it might be some Polish word that would reveal that she had not been speaking English to her first-born when they were alone.

'My daughter is an American,' Abel had explained to Zaphia, 'and she must therefore speak English. Too many Poles continue to converse in their own language, thus ensuring that their children spend their entire lives in the north-west corner of Chicago being described as "Stupid Polacks" and ridiculed by everyone else they come across.'

'Except our countrymen who still feel some loyalty to the Polish empire,' said Zaphia defensively.

'The Polish empire? What century are you living in, Zaphia?'

'The twentieth century,' she said, her voice rising.

'Along with Dick Tracy and Famous Funnies, no doubt?'

'Hardly the attitude of someone whose ultimate ambition is to return to Warsaw as the first Polish ambassador.'

'I've told you never to mention that, Zaphia. Never.'

Zaphia, whose English remained irredeemably shaky, didn't reply but later grumbled to her cousins on the subject and continued to speak Polish only when Abel was out of the house. She was not impressed by the fact, so often trotted out by Abel, that General Motors's turnover was greater than Poland's budget.

By 1935, Abel was convinced that America had turned the corner and that the Depression was a thing of the past, so he decided the time had come to build the new Chicago Baron on the site of the old Richmond Continental. He appointed an architect and began spending more time in the Windy City and less on the road, as he was determined the hotel would turn out to be the finest in the Mid-West.

The Chicago Baron was completed in May 1936 and opened by the Democratic mayor, Edward J. Kelly. Both Illinois Senators were dancing attendance, only too aware of Abel's burgeoning power.

'Looks like a million dollars,' said J. Hamilton Lewis, the senior Senator.

'You wouldn't be far wrong,' said Abel, as he admired the thickly carpeted public rooms, the high stucco ceilings and the decorations in pastel shades of green. The final touch had been the dark green embossed B that adorned everything from the towels in the bathrooms to the flag that fluttered on the top of the forty-two storey building.

'This hotel already bears the hallmark of success,' said J. Hamilton Lewis, addressing the two thousand assembled guests, 'because, my friends, it is the man and not the building who will always be known as the Chicago Baron.' Abel was delighted by the roar that went up and smiled to himself. His public relations adviser had supplied that line to the Senator's speech writer earlier in the week.

Abel was beginning to feel at ease among big businessmen and senior politicians. Zaphia, however, had not adapted to her husband's change in fortunes and hovered uncertainly in the background, drinking a little too much champagne, and finally crept away before the dinner was served with a lame excuse about wanting to see that Florentyna was safely asleep. Abel accompanied his flushed wife towards the revolving door in silent irritation. Zaphia neither cared for nor understood success on Abel's scale and preferred to ignore his new world. She was only too aware how much this annoyed Abel and couldn't resist saying, 'Don't hurry home', as he bundled her into a cab.

'I won't,' he told the revolving door as he returned, pushing it so hard that it went around three more times after he had left it.

He returned to the hotel foyer to find Alderman Henry Osborne waiting for him.

'This must be the high point in your life,' the alderman remarked.

'High point? I've just turned thirty,' said Abel.

A camera flashed as he placed an arm around the tall, darkly handsome politician. Abel smiled towards the cameraman, enjoying the treatment he was receiving as a celebrity, and said, just loud enough for eavesdroppers to hear, 'I'm going to put Baron hotels right across the globe. I intend to be to America what César Ritz was to Europe. Stick with me, Henry, and you'll enjoy the ride.' The city alderman and Abel walked together into the dining room and once they were out of earshot Abel added: 'Join me for lunch tomorrow, Henry, if you can spare the time. There's something I need to discuss with you.'

'Delighted, Abel. A mere city alderman is always available for the Chicago Baron.'

They both laughed heartily, though neither thought the remark particularly funny.

It turned out to be another late night for Abel. When he returned home he went straight to the spare room, to be sure he didn't wake Zaphia – or that's what he told her the next morning

.   .   .

When Abel came into the kitchen to join Zaphia for breakfast Florentyna was sitting in her high chair smearing a bowlful of cereal enthusiastically round her mouth and biting at most things that remained within arms' reach – even if they weren't food. He kissed her on the forehead, the only place that seemed to have missed the cereal, and sat down to a plate of waffles and maple syrup. When he had finished, Abel rose from his chair and told Zaphia that he would be having lunch with Henry Osborne.

'I don't like that man,' said Zaphia, with feeling.

'I'm not crazy about him myself,' replied Abel. 'But never forget he's well placed in City Hall to be able to do us a lot of favours.'

'And a lot of harm.'

'Don't lose any sleep over that. You can leave the handling of Alderman Osborne to me,' said Abel as he brushed his wife's cheek and turned to leave.

'Presidunk,' said a voice, and both parents turned to stare at Florentyna, who was gesticulating at the floor where the eight-month-old Franklin D. Roosevelt lay on his furry face.

Abel laughed, picked up the much-loved teddy bear and placed him in the space Florentyna had left for him on the high chair.

'Pres-i-dent,' said Abel slowly and firmly.

'Presidunk,' insisted Florentyna.

Abel laughed again and patted Franklin D. Roosevelt on the head. So FDR was responsible not only for the New Deal but also for Florentyna's first political utterance.

Abel left the house to find his chauffeur waiting for him beside the new Cadillac. Abel's driving had become worse as the car he could afford improved. When he bought a Cadillac, George had advised a driver to go with it. That morning he asked the chauffeur to drive slowly as they approached the Gold Coast. Abel stared up at the gleaming glass of the Chicago Baron and marvelled that there was no other place on earth where a man could achieve so much so quickly. What the Chinese would have been happy to strive for in ten generations, he had achieved in less than fifteen years.

He leaped out of the car before his chauffeur could run around to open the door, walked briskly into the hotel and took the private express elevator to the forty-second floor where he spent the morning checking over every problem with which the new hotel was faced: one of the passenger elevators wasn't functioning properly; two waiters had been involved in a knife fight in the kitchen and had been sacked by George even before Abel had arrived; and the list of damages after the opening looked suspiciously high – Abel would have to check into possible theft by waiters being recorded in the books as breakage. He left nothing to chance in any of his hotels from who was staying in the Presidential Suite to the price of the eight thousand fresh bread rolls the catering department needed every week. He spent the morning dealing with queries, problems and decisions, stopping only when Alderman Osborne was ushered into Abel's office by his secretary.

'Good morning, Baron,' said Henry, patronizingly referring to the Rosnovski family title.

In Abel's younger days as a junior waiter at the Plaza in New York the title had been scornfully mimicked to his face. At the Richmond Continental when he was assistant manager it had figured in whispered jokes behind his back. Lately everyone mouthed the prefix with respect.

'Good morning, Alderman,' said Abel, glancing at the clock on his desk. It was five past one. 'Shall we have lunch?'

Abel guided Henry into the adjoining private dining room. To a casual observer Henry Osborne would hardly have seemed a natural soul-mate for Abel. Educated at Choate and then Harvard, as he continually reminded Abel, he had later served as a young lieutenant with the Marines in the World War. At six feet, with a full head of black hair lightly sprinkled with grey, he looked younger than his history insisted he had to bui

The two men had first met us a result of the fire at the old Richmond Continental. Henry was then working for the Great Western Casualty Insurance Company, which had, for as long as anyone could remember, insured the Richmond Group. Abel had been taken aback when Henry had suggested that a small cash payment would ensure a swifter flow of the claim papers through the head office. Abel did not possess a 'small cash payment' in those days; although the claim eventually found its way through, as Henry also believed in Abel's future.

Abel had learned for the first time about men who could be bought.

By the time Henry Osborne was elected to the Chicago City Council as an alderman, Abel *could* afford a small cash payment, and the building permit for the new Baron proceeded through City Hall as though on roller skates. When Henry later announced that he would be running for the United States House of Representatives for the Ninth District of Illinois, Abel was among the first to send a sizeable cheque for his campaign fund. While Abel remained wary of his new ally personally, he recognized that a tame politician could be of great help to the Baron Group. Abel took care to ensure that none of the small cash payments – he did not think of them as bribes, even to himself – was on the record, and felt confident that he could terminate the arrangement as and when it suited him.

The dining room was decorated in the same delicate shades of green as the rest of the hotel, but there was no sign of the embossed B anywhere in the room. The furniture was nineteenth century, and entirely in oak. Around the walls hung oil portraits from the same period, almost all imported. With the door closed, it was possible to imagine that one was in another world far away from the hectic pace of a modern hotel.

Abel took his place at the head of an ornate table that could have comfortably seated eight guests but that day was laid for only two.

'It's like being in a bit of old England,' said Henry, taking in the room.

'Not to mention Poland,' replied Abel, as a uniformed waiter served smoked salmon, while another poured them both a glass of Bouchard Chablis.

Henry stared down at the full plate in front of him. 'Now I can see why you're putting on so much weight, Baron.'

Abel frowned, and quickly changed the subject. 'Are you going to the Cubs' game tomorrow?'

'What's the point? They have a worse home record than the Republicans. Not that my absence will discourage the *Tribune* from describing the match as a close-fought battle bearing no relation to the score and but for a different set of circumstances, the Cubs would have pulled off a famous victory.'

Abel laughed.

'One thing's for sure,' continued Henry, 'you'll never see a night game at Wrigley Field. That ghastly innovation of playing under floodlights won't catch on in Chicago.'

'That's what you said about beer cans last year.'

It was Henry's turn to frown. 'You didn't ask me to lunch to hear my views on baseball or beer cans, Abel, so what little plan can I assist you with this time?'

'Simple. I want to ask your advice on what I should do about William Kane.'

Henry seemed to choke. I must speak to the chef: there shouldn't be any bones in smoked salmon, thought Abel before he continued.

'You once told me, Henry, in graphic detail what had happened when your path crossed Mr Kane's and how he ended up defrauding you of money. Well, Kane did far worse than that to me. During the Depression he put the squeeze on Davis Leroy, my partner and closest friend, and was the direct cause of Leroy's suicide. To make the matters worse Kane refused to support me when I wanted to take over the management of the hotels and try to put the group on a sound financial footing.'

'Who did back you in the end?' asked Henry.

'A private investor with the Continental Trust. The manager has never told me in so many words, but I've always suspected it was David Maxton.'

'The owner of the Stevens Hotel?'

'The same.'

'What makes you think it was him?'

'When I had the reception for my wedding and again for Florentyna's christening at the Stevens, the bill was covered by my backer.'

'That's hardly conclusive.'

'Agreed, but I'm certain it's Maxton, because he once offered me the chance to run the Stevens. I told him I was more interested in finding a backer for the Richmond Group, and within a week his bank in Chicago came up with the money from someone who could not reveal their identity because it would clash with their day to day business interests.'

'That's a little more convincing. But tell me what you have in mind for William Kane,' said Henry as he toyed with his wine glass and waited for Abel to continue.

'Something that shouldn't take up a lot of your time, Henry, but might well prove to be rewarding for you both financially and, as you hold Kane in the same high regard as I do, personally.'

'I'm listening,' said Henry, still not looking up from his glass.

'I want to lay my hands on a substantial shareholding in Kane's Boston bank.'

'You won't find that easy,' said Henry. 'Most of the stock is held in a family trust that cannot be sold without his personal concurrence.'

'You seem very well informed,' said Abel.

'Common knowledge,' said Henry.

Abel didn't believe him. 'So let's start by finding out the name of every shareholder in Kane and Cabot and see if any of them are interested in parting with their stock at a price considerably above par.'

Abel watched Henry's eyes light up as he began to work out how much might be in this transaction for him if he could make a deal with both sides.

'If he ever found out he'd play very rough,' said Henry.

'He's not going to find out,' said Abel. 'And even if he did we'd be at least two moves ahead of him. Do you think you are capable of doing the job?'

'I can try. What did you have in mind?'

Abel realized Henry was trying to find out what payment he might expect, but he hadn't finished yet. 'I want a written report the first day of every month showing Kane's shareholdings in any company, his business commitments and all details you can obtain of his private life. I want everything you come up with, however trivial it may seem.'

'I repeat, that won't be easy,' said Henry.

'Will a thousand dollars a month make the task easier?'

'Fifteen hundred certainly would,' replied Henry.

'A thousand dollars a month for the first six months. If you prove yourself, I'll raise the figure to fifteen hundred.'

'It's a deal,' said Henry.

'Good,' said Abel as he took his wallet from his inside pocket and extracted a cheque already made out to cash for one thousand dollars.

Henry studied the cheque. 'You were pretty confident I would fall into line, weren't you?'

'No, not altogether,' said Abel, as he removed a second cheque from his wallet and showed it to Henry. It was made out for fifteen hundred dollars. 'If you come up with some winners in the first six months, you'll only have lost three thousand dollars.'

Both men laughed.

'Now to a more pleasant subject,' said Abel. 'Are we going to win?'

'The Cubs?'

'No, the election.'

'Sure, Landon is in for a whipping. The Kansas Sunflower can't hope to beat FDR,' said Henry. 'As the President reminded us, that particular flower is yellow, has a black heart, is useful as parrot food and always dies before November.'

Abel laughed again. 'And how about you personally?'

'No worries. The seat has always been safe for the Democrats. The difficult thing was winning the nomination, not the election.'

'I look forward to your being a Congressman, Henry.'

'I'm sure you do, Abel, and I shall look forward to serving you as well as my other constituents.'

Abel looked at him quizzically. 'Considerably better, I should hope,' he commented as a sirloin steak that almost covered the plate was placed in front of him while another glass was filled with a Côte de Beaune 1929. The rest of the lunch was spent discussing Gabby Harnett's injury problems, Jesse Owens's four gold medals at the Berlin Olympics, and the possibility that Hitler would invade Poland.

'Never,' said Henry, and started to reminisce about the courage of the Poles at Mons in the Great War.

Abel didn't comment on the fact that no Polish regiment had seen action at Mons.

At two thirty-seven Abel was back at his desk, considering the problems of the Presidential Suite and the eight thousand fresh bread rolls.

He did not arrive home from the Baron that night until nine o'clock, only to find Florentyna already asleep. But she woke immediately as her father entered the nursery and smiled up at him.

'Presidunk, Presidunk, Presidunk.'

Abel smiled. 'Not me. You perhaps, but not me.' He picked his daughter up and kissed her on the cheek and sat with her while she repeated her one-word vocabulary over and over again.

3

In November 1936, Henry Osborne was elected to the United States House of Representatives for the Ninth District of Illinois. His majority was slightly smaller than his predecessor's, a fact which could be attributed only to his indolence as Roosevelt had carried every state except Vermont and Maine, and in Congress the Republicans were down to seventeen Senators and one hundred and three Representatives. But all that Abel cared about was that his man had a seat in the House, and he immediately offered him the chairmanship of the Planning Committee of the Baron Group. Henry gratefully accepted.

Abel channelled all his energy into building more and more hotels – with the help of Congressman Osborne, who seemed able to fix building permits wherever the Baron next desired. Abel always paid Henry for these favours with used notes. He had no idea what Henry did with the money, but it was evident that some of it had to be falling into the right hands, and he had no wish to know the details.

Despite his deteriorating relationship with Zaphia, Abel still wanted a son and began to despair when his wife failed to conceive. He initially blamed Zaphia, who longed for a second child, but eventually she nagged him into seeing a doctor. Abel was humiliated to learn that he had a low sperm count: the doctor attributed this to early malnutrition and told him that it was most unlikely he would ever be a father again. From that moment the subject was closed, and Abel lavished all his affections and hopes on Florentyna, who grew like a weed. The only thing in Abel's life that grew faster was the Baron Group. He built a new hotel in the north, and another in the south, while modernizing and streamlining the older hotels already in the group.

At the age of four, Florentyna attended her first nursery school. She insisted that Abel and Franklin D. Roosevelt accompany her on the opening day. Most of the other girls were chaperoned by women whom Abel was surprised to discover were not always their mothers but often nannies and, in one case, as he was gently corrected, a governess. That night he told Zaphia that he wanted someone similarly qualified to take charge of Florentyna.

'What for?' asked Zaphia sharply.

'So that no one in that school starts life with an advantage over our daughter.'

'I think it's a stupid waste of money. What would such a person be able to do for her that I can't?'

Abel didn't reply, but the next morning, he placed advertisements in the Chicago *Tribune*, the *New York Times* and the London *Times*, seeking applicants for the post of governess, stating clearly the terms offered. Hundreds of replies came in from all over the country from highly qualified women who wanted to work for the chairman of the Baron Group. Letters arrived from Radcliffe, Vassar and Smith; there was even one from the Federal Reformatory for Women in Alderson, West Virginia. But it was the reply from a lady who had obviously never heard of the Chicago Baron that intrigued him most.

> The Old Rectory
> Much Hadham
> Hertfordshire
> 12 September 1938

Dear Sir,

In reply to your advertisement in the personal column on the front page of today's issue of *The Times*, I should like to be considered for the post of governess to your daughter.

I am thirty-two years of age, and I am the sixth daughter of The Very Rev. L. H. Tredgold, and a spinster of the parish of Much Hadham in Hertfordshire. I am at present teaching in the local grammar school and assisting my father in his work as Rural Dean.

I was educated at Cheltenham Ladies' College where I studied Latin, Greek, French and English for my higher matriculation, before taking up a closed scholarship to Newnham College, Cambridge. At the university, I sat my finals gaining first-class awards in all three parts of the Modern Language tripos. I do not hold a Bachelor of Arts degree from the university, as their statutes preclude such awards to women.

I am available for interview at any time and I would welcome the opportunity to work in the New World.

I have the honour to remain, Sir,
Your obedient servant,
W. Tredgold

Abel found it hard to accept that there was such an institution as Cheltenham Ladies' College or indeed such a place as Much Hadham, and he was certainly suspicious of claims of first-class awards without degrees.

He asked his secretary to place a call to Washington. When he was finally put through to the person he wished to speak to he read the letter aloud.

The voice from Washington confirmed that every claim in the letter could be accurate; there was no reason to doubt its credibility.

'Are you sure there really is an establishment called Cheltenham Ladies' College?' Abel insisted.

'Most certainly I am, Mr Rosnovski. I was educated there myself,' replied the British ambassador's secretary.

That night Abel read the letter over again, this time to Zaphia.

'What do you think?' he asked, although he had already made up his mind.

'I don't like the sound of her,' said Zaphia, not looking up from the magazine she was reading. 'If we must have someone, why can't she be an American?'

'Think of the advantages Florentyna would have if she were tutored by an English governess.' Abel paused. 'She'd even be company for you.'

This time Zaphia did look up from her magazine. 'Why? Are you hoping she'll educate me as well?'

Abel made no reply.

The following morning he sent a cable to Much Hadham offering Miss Tredgold the position of governess.

Three weeks later when Abel went to pick up the lady from the Twentieth Century Limited at the La Salle Street Station, he knew immediately he had made the right decision. As she stood alone on the platform, three suitcases of differing sizes and vintages by her side, she could not have been anyone but Miss Tredgold. She was tall, thin and slightly imperious, and the bun that crowned her head gave her fully two inches in height over her employer.

Zaphia, however, treated Miss Tredgold as an intruder who had come to undermine her maternal position, and when she accompanied her to her daughter's room, Florentyna was nowhere to be seen. Two eyes peered suspiciously from under the bed. Miss Tredgold spotted the girl first and fell on her knees.

'I am afraid I won't be able to help you very much if you remain there, child. I'm far too big to live under a bed.'

Florentyna burst out laughing and crawled out.

'What a funny voice you have,' she said. 'Where do you come from?'

'England,' said Miss Tredgold, taking a seat beside her on the bed.
'Where's that?'
'About a week away.'
'Yes, but how far?'
'That would depend on how you travelled during the week. How many ways could I have travelled such a long distance? Can you think of three?'
Florentyna concentrated. 'From my house I'd take a bicycle and when I'd reached the end of America I'd take a ...'
Neither of them noticed that Zaphia had left the room.
It was only a few days before Florentyna turned Miss Tredgold into the brother and sister she could never have.
Florentyna would spend hours just listening to her new companion, and Ael watched with pride as the middle-aged spinster – he could never think of her as thirty-two, his own age – taught his four-year-old daughter a range of subjects he would have liked to know more about himself.
Abel asked George one morning if he could name Henry VIII's six wives; if he couldn't it might be wise for them to acquire two more governesses from Cheltenham Ladies' College before Florentyna ended up knowing more than they did. Zaphia did not want to know about Henry VIII or his wives, as she still felt Florentyna should be brought up according to simple Polish traditions, but she had long since given up trying to convince Abel on that subject. Zaphia carried out a routine that made it possible for her to avoid the new governess most of the day.
Miss Tredgold's daily routine on the other hand owed as much to the discipline of a Grenadier Guard's officer as to the teachings of Maria Montessori. Florentyna rose at seven o'clock and with a straight spine that never touched the back of the chair received instruction in table manners and posture until she had left the breakfast room. Between seven thirty and seven forty-five Miss Tredgold would pick out two or three items from the Chicago *Tribune*, read and discuss them with her and then question her on them an hour later. Florentyna took an immediate interest in what the President was doing, perhaps because he seemed to be named after her bear. Miss Tredgold found she had to use a considerable amount of her spare time diligently learning the strange American system of government to be certain no question that her ward might ask would go unanswered.
From nine to twelve, Florentyna and FDR attended nursery school where they indulged in the more normal pursuits of her contemporaries. When Miss Tredgold came to pick her up each afternoon it was easy to discern whether Florentyna had selected the clay, the scissors and paste or the finger painting that day. At the end of every play-school session she was taken straight home for a bath and change of clothes with a 'Tut, tut,' and the occasional 'I just don't know'.
In the afternoon, Miss Tredgold and Florentyna would set off on some expedition which Miss Tredgold had carefully planned that morning without Florentyna's knowledge – although this didn't stop Florentyna always trying to find out in advance what her governess had arranged.
'What are we going to do today?' or 'Where are we going?' Florentyna would demand.
'Be patient, child.'

'Can we still do it if it rains?'

'Only time will tell. But if we can't, be assured I shall have a contingency plan.'

'What's a 'tingency plan?' asked Florentyna, puzzled.

'Something you need when everything else you have planned is no longer possible,' Miss Tredgold explained.

Among such afternoon expeditions were walks around the park, visits to the zoo, even the occasional ride on the top of a trolley car, which Florentyna considered a great treat. Miss Tredgold also used the time to give her charge the first introduction to a few words of French, and she was pleasantly surprised to find that her ward showed a natural aptitude for languages. Once they had returned home, there would be half an hour with Mama before tea, followed by another bath before Florentyna was tucked up in bed by seven o'clock. Miss Tredgold would then read a few lines from the Bible or Mark Twain – not that the Americans seemed to know the difference, Miss Tredgold said in a moment of what she imagined was frivolity – and having turned the nursery light out she sat with her charge and FDR until they had both fallen asleep.

This routine was slavishly adhered to and broken only on such rare occasions as birthdays or national holidays when Miss Tredgold allowed Florentyna to accompany her to the United Artists theatre on West Randolph Street to see films such as *Snow White and the Seven Dwarfs* but not before Miss Tredgold had been to the show the previous week in order to ascertain that it was suitable for her ward. Walt Disney met with Miss Tredgold's approval, as did Laurence Olivier playing Heathcliff pursued by Merle Oberon, a film she went to watch three Thursdays running on her afternoon off at a cost of twenty cents a showing. She was able to convince herself it was worth sixty cents; after all, *Wuthering Heights* was a classic.

Miss Tredgold never stopped Florentyna asking questions about the Nazis, the New Deal and even a 'home run', although sometimes she obviously didn't understand the answers. The young girl soon discovered that her mother was not always able to satisfy her curiosity, and on several occasions Miss Tredgold, in order not to render an inaccurate answer, had to disappear into her room and consult the *Encyclopaedia Britannica*.

At the age of five Florentyna attended kindergarten at the Girls Latin School of Chicago where within a week she was moved up a grade because she was so far ahead of her contemporaries. In her world everything looked wonderful. She had Mama and Papa, Miss Tredgold and Franklin D. Roosevelt, and as far as her horizon could reach nothing seemed to be unobtainable.

Only the 'best families', as Abel described them, sent their children to the Latin School, and it came as something of a shock to Miss Tredgold that when she asked some of Florentyna's friends back for tea the invitations were politely declined. Florentyna's best friends, Mary Gill and Susie Jacobson, came regularly; but some of the parents of the other girls would make lame excuses for not accepting and Miss Tredgold soon came to realize that although the Chicago Baron might well have broken the chains of poverty he was still unable to break into some of the better drawing rooms in Chicago. Zaphia did not help, making little effort to get to know the other parents, let alone join any of their charity committees, hospital boards or the clubs to which so many of them seemed to belong.

Miss Tredgold did the best she could to help, but as she was only a servant in the eyes of most of the parents it was not easy for her. She prayed that Florentyna would never learn of these prejudices – but it was not to be.

Florentyna sailed through the first grade, more than holding her own academically with the group, and only her size reminded everyone that she was a year younger.

Abel was too busy building up his own empire to give much thought to his social standing or any problems Miss Tredgold might be facing. The group was showing steady progress with Abel looking well set by 1938 to be on target to repay the loan to his backer. In fact Abel was predicting profits of two hundred and fifty thousand dollars for the year, despite his heavy building programme.

His real worries were not in the nursery or the hotels, but almost five thousand miles away in his beloved homeland. His worst fears were realized when on 1 September 1939, Hitler marched into Poland, and Britain declared war on Germany two days later. With the outbreak of another war Abel seriously considered leaving control of the Baron Group to George – who was turning out to be a trusty lieutenant – while he sailed off to London to join the Polish army in exile. George and Zaphia managed to talk him out of the idea, so he concentrated instead on raising cash and sending the money to the British Red Cross, while lobbying Democratic politicians to join the war alongside the British.

'FDR needs all the friends he can get,' Florentyna heard her father declare one morning.

.   .   .

By the last quarter of 1939, Abel, with the help of a small loan from the First City Bank of Chicago, became the one hundred per cent owner of the Baron Group. He predicted in the annual report that profits for 1940 would be over half a million dollars.

Franklin D. Roosevelt – the one with the red eyes and the fluffy brown fur – rarely left Florentyna's side even when she progressed to second garade. Miss Tredgold considered that perhaps the time had come to leave FDR at home. In normal circumstances she would have insisted, there might have been a few tears and the matter would have been resolved; but against her better judgement she let the child have her own way. It was a decision that turned out to be one of Miss Tredgold's rare mistakes.

Every Monday, the boys of the Latin School joined the girls to be tutored in French by the modern languages teacher, Mademoiselle Mettinet. For everyone except Florentyna, this was a first, painful introduction to the language. As the class chanted *boucher, boulanger*, and *épicier* after Mademoiselle, Florentyna, more out of boredom than bravado, began holding a conversation with FDR in French. Her neighbour, a tall, rather lazy boy named Edward Winchester, who seemed unable to grasp the difference between *le* and *la*, leaned over and told Florentyna to stop showing off. Florentyna reddened. 'I was only trying to explain to FDR the difference between the masculine and the feminine.'

'Were you?' said Edward. 'Well, I'll show you *le différence*, Mademoiselle Know-All,' and in a fit of fury he grabbed FDR and with all the strength he could muster tore one of the bear's arms from its body. Florentyna remained rooted to her seat in shock as Edward then took the inkwell out of his desk and poured the contents over the bear's head.

Mademoiselle Mettinet, who had never approved of having boys in the same class as girls, rushed to the back of the room, but it was too late. FDR was already royal blue from head to toe and sat on the floor in the middle of a circle of stuffing from his severed arm. Florentyna grabbed her favourite friend, tears diluting the puddled ink. Mademoiselle Mettinet marched Edward to the headmaster's office and instructed the other children to sit in silence until she returned.

Florentyna crawled around the floor, trying hopelessly to put the stuffing back into FDR, when a fair-haired girl Florentyna had never liked leaned over and hissed, 'Serves you right, stupid Polack.' The class giggled at the girl's remark and some of them started to chant, 'Stupid Polack, stupid Polack, stupid Polack.' Florentyna clung on to FDR and prayed for Mademoiselle Mettinet's return.

It seemed like hours although it was only a few minutes before the French mistress reappeared, with Edward looking suitably crestfallen following in her wake. The chanting stopped the moment Mademoiselle Mettinet entered the room, but Florentyna couldn't even make herself look up. In the unnatural silence, Edward walked up to Florentyna and apologized in a voice that was as loud as it was unconvincing. He returned to his seat and grinned at his classmates.

When Miss Tredgold picked her charge up from school that afternoon she could hardly miss noticing that the child's face was red from crying and that she walked with a bowed head clinging on to a blue-faced FDR by his remaining arm. Miss Tredgold coaxed the whole story out of Florentyna before they reached home. She then gave the child her favourite supper of hamburger and ice cream, two dishes of which she normally disapproved, and put her to bed early, hoping she would quickly fall asleep. After a futile hour with nail brush and soap spent trying to clean up the indelibly stained bear, Miss Tredgold was forced to concede defeat. As she laid the damp animal by Florentyna's side, a small voice from under the bedcovers said, 'Thank you, Miss Tredgold. FDR needs all the friends he can get.'

When Abel returned a little after ten o'clock – he had taken to arriving home late almost every night – Miss Tredgold sought a private meeting with him. Abel was surprised by the request and led her at once through to his study. During the eighteen months she had been in his employ Miss Tredgold had always reported the week's progress to Mr Rosnovski on Sunday mornings between ten and ten thirty while Florentyna was attending Mass with her mother at the Holy Name Cathedral. Miss Tredgold's reports were always clear and accurate; if anything she had a tendency to underestimate the child's achievements.

'What's the problem, Miss Tredgold?' asked Abel, trying to sound unworried. With such a break in routine he dreaded the thought that she might want to give in her notice. Miss Tredgold repeated the story of what had happened at school that day.

Abel became redder and redder in the face as the story progressed and was scarlet before Miss Tredgold came to the end.

'Intolerable,' was his first word. 'Florentyna must be removed immediately. I shall personally see Miss Allen tomorrow and tell her exactly what I think of her and her school. I am sure that you will approve of my decision, Miss Tredgold.'

'No, sir, I do not,' came back an unusually sharp reply.

'I beg your pardon?' said Abel in disbelief.

'I believe you are as much to blame as the parents of Edward Winchester.'

'I?' said Abel. 'Why?'

'You should have told your daughter a long time ago the significance of being Polish and how to deal with any problems that might arise because of it. You should have explained the Americans' deep-seated prejudice against the Poles, a prejudice that is in my own opinion every bit as reprehensible as the English attitude towards the Irish, and only a few steps away from the Nazis' barbaric behaviour towards the Jews.'

Abel remained silent. It was a long time since anyone had told him he was wrong about anything.

'Do you have anything else to say?' he asked when he had recovered.

'Yes, Mr Rosnovski. If you remove Florentyna from Girls Latin, I shall give in my notice immediately. If on the first occasion the child encounters some problem you choose to run away from it, how can I hope to teach her to cope with life? Watching my own country at war because we wanted to go on believing Hitler was a reasonable man, if slightly misguided, I can hardly be expected to pass on the same misconstruction of events to Florentyna. It will be heartbreaking for me to have to leave her, because I could not love Florentyna more if she were my own child, but I cannot approve of disguising the real world because you have enough money to keep the truth conveniently hidden for a few more years, I must apologise for my frankness, Mr Rosnovski, as I feel I have gone too far, but I cannot condemn other people's prejudices while at the same time condoning yours.'

Abel sank back into his seat before replying. 'Miss Tredgold, you should have been an ambassador, not a governess. Of course you're right. What would you advise me to do?'

Miss Tredgold, who was still standing – she would never have dreamed of sitting in her employer's presence unless she was with Florentyna – hesitated.

'The child should rise thirty minutes earlier each day for the next month and be taught Polish history. She must learn why Poland is a great nation, and why the Poles were willing to challenge the might of Germany when alone they could never have hoped for victory. Then she will be able to face those who goad her about her ancestry with knowledge not ignorance.'

Abel looked her squarely in the eyes. 'I see now what George Bernard Shaw meant when he said that you have to meet the English governess to discover why Britain is great.'

They both laughed.

'I'm surprised you don't want to make more of your life, Miss Tredgold,' said Abel, suddenly aware that what he had said might have sounded offensive. If it had, Miss Tredgold gave no sign of being offended.

'My father had six daughters. He had hoped for a boy, but it was not to be.'

'And what of the other five?'

'They are all married,' she replied without bitterness.

'And you?'

'He once said to me that I was born to be a teacher and that the Lord's plan took us all in its compass so perhaps I might teach someone who does have a destiny.'

'Let us hope so, Miss Tredgold.' Abel would have called her by her first name but he did not know what it was. All he knew was she signed herself 'W. Tredgold' in a way that did not invite further inquiry. He smiled up at her.

'Will you join me in a drink, Miss Tredgold?'

'Thank you, Mr Rosnovski. A little sherry would be most pleasant.'

Abel poured her a dry sherry and himself a large whisky.

'How bad is FDR?'

'Maimed for life, I fear, which will only make the child love him the more. In the future I have decided that FDR must reside at home and will only travel when accompanied by me.'

'You're beginning to sound like Eleanor Roosevelt talking about the President.'

Miss Tredgold laughed once more and sipped her sherry. 'May I offer one more suggestion concerning Florentyna?'

'Certainly,' said Abel, who proceeded to listen intently to Miss Tredgold's recommendation. By the time they had finished their second drink, Abel had nodded his approval.

'Good,' said Miss Tredgold, 'then, with your permission, I will deal with that at the first possible opportunity.'

'Certainly,' repeated Abel. 'Of course, when it comes to these morning sessions, it may not be practical for me to do a whole month without a break.' Miss Tredgold was about to speak when Abel added, 'There may be appointments that I cannot re-schedule at such short notice, as I am sure you will understand.'

'You must, Mr Rosnovski, do what you think best, and if you find there is something more important than your daughter's future I am sure it is she who will understand.'

Abel knew when he was beaten. He cancelled all appointments outside Chicago for a full month and rose each morning thirty minutes early. Even Zaphia approved of Miss Tredgold's idea.

The first day Abel started by telling Florentyna how he had been born in a forest in Poland and adopted by a trapper's family, and how later he had been befriended by a great Baron who took him into his castle in Slonim, on the Polish–Russian border. 'He treated me like his own son,' Abel told her.

As the days went by, Abel revealed to his daughter how his sister Florentyna, after whom she had been named, joined him in the castle and the way he discovered the Baron was his real father.

'I know, I know how you found out,' cried Florentyna.

'How can you know, little one?'

'He only had one nipple,' said Florentyna. 'It must be, it must be. I've seen you in the bath. You only have one nipple, so you had to be his son. All the boys at school have two ...' Abel and Miss Tredgold stared at the child in disbelief as she continued, '... but if I'm your daughter, why have I got two?'

'Because it's only passed from father to son and is almost unknown in daughters.'

'It's not fair. I want only one.'

Abel began laughing. 'Well, perhaps if you have a son, he'll have only one.

'Time for you to braid your hair and get ready for school,' said Miss Tredgold.

'But it's just getting exciting.'

'Do as you are told, child.'

Florentyna reluctantly left her father and went to the bathroom.

'What do you think is going to happen tomorrow, Miss Tredgold?' she asked, on the way to school.

'I have no idea, child, but as Mr Asquith once advised, wait and see.'

'Was Mr Asquith in the castle with Papa?'

. . .

In the days that followed Abel explained what life was like in a Russian prison camp and what had caused him to limp. He went on to teach his daughter the stories the Baron had told him in the dungeons over twenty years before. Florentyna followed the stories of the legendary Polish hero Tadeusz Kosciuszko and all the other great figures through to the present day, while Miss Tredgold pointed to a map of Europe she had pinned on the bedroom wall.

He finally explained to his daughter how he had come into possession of the silver band that he wore on his wrist.

'What does it say?' demanded Florentyna, staring at the tiny engraved letters.

'Try to read the words, little one,' said Abel.

'Bar-on Ab-el Ros-nov-ski,' she stuttered out. 'But that's your name,' she insisted.

'And it was my father's.'

After a few more days Florentyna could answer all her father's questions, even if Abel couldn't always answer all of hers.

At school, Florentyna daily expected Edward Winchester to pick on her again, but he seemed to have forgotten the incident, and on one occasion even offered to share an apple with her.

Not everyone in the class, however, had forgotten, and one girl in particular, a fat, rather dull classmate, took special pleasure in whispering the words 'Stupid Polack' within her hearing.

Florentyna did not retaliate immediately, but waited until some weeks later when the girl, having come at the bottom of the class in a history test while Florentyna came top, announced, 'At least I'm not a Polack.' Edward Winchester frowned, but some of the class giggled.

Florentyna waited for total silence before she spoke. 'True. You're not a Polack, you're a third generation American, with a history that goes back about a hundred years. Mine can be traced for a thousand, which is why you are bottom in history and I am top.'

No one in the class ever referred to the subject again. When Miss Tredgold heard the story on the way home she smiled.

'Shall we tell Papa this evening?' asked Florentyna.

'No, my dear. Pride has never been a virtue. There are some occasions on which it is wise to remain silent.'

The six-year-old girl nodded thoughtfully before asking. 'Do you ever think a Pole could be President of the United States?'

'Certainly, if the American people can overcome their own prejudice.'

'And how about a Catholic?'

'That will become irrelevant, even in my lifetime.'

'And a woman?' added Florentyna.

'That might take a little longer, child.'

.   .   .

That night Miss Tredgold reported to Mr Rosnovski that his lessons had proved worthwhile.

'And when will you carry out the second part of your plan, Miss Tredgold?' Abel asked.

'Tomorrow,' she replied, smiling.

At three thirty the following afternoon Miss Tredgold was standing on the corner of the street, waiting for her ward to finish school. Florentyna came chattering out through the gates and they had walked for several blocks before she noticed that they were not taking their usual route home.

'Where are we going, Miss Tredgold?'

'Patience, child, and all will be revealed.'

Miss Tredgold smiled while Florentyna seemed more concerned with telling her how well she had done in an English test that morning, a monologue which she kept up all the way to Menomonee Street, where Miss Tredgold began to take more interest in the numbers on the doors than in Florentyna's real and imagined achievements.

At last they came to a halt outside a newly painted red door which displayed the number two hundred and eighteen. Miss Tredgold rapped on the door twice with her gloved knuckle. Florentyna stood by her side, silent for the first time since leaving school. A few moments passed before the door opened to reveal a man dressed in a grey sweater and blue jeans.

'I've come in response to your advertisement in the *Sun-Times*,' Miss Tredgold said before the man had a chance to speak.

'Ah, yes,' he replied. 'Will you come in?'

Miss Tredgold entered the house followed by a puzzled Florentyna. They were conducted through a narrow hall covered in photographs and multi-coloured rosettes before reaching the back door which led out to a yard.

Florentyna saw them immediately. They were in a basket on the far side of the yard and she ran towards them. Six yellow labrador puppies snuggled up close to their mother. One of them left the warmth of the clan and limped out of the basket towards Florentyna.

'This one's lame,' said Florentyna, immediately picking up the puppy and studying the animal's leg.

'Yes, I'm afraid so,' admitted the breeder. 'But there are still five others in perfect condition for you to choose from.'

'What will happen if nobody takes her?'

'I suppose . . .' – the breeder hesitated – 'she will have to be put to sleep.'

Florentyna stared desperately at Miss Tredgold as she clung to the dog, who was busily licking her face.

'I want this one,' said Florentyna without hesitation, fearful of Miss Tredgold's reaction.

'How much will that be?' asked Miss Tredgold, as she opened her purse.

'No change, ma'am. I'm happy to see that one go to a good home.'

'Thank you,' said Florentyna. 'Thank you.'

The puppy's tail never stopped wagging all the way to its new home while to Miss Tredgold's surprise Florentyna's tongue never wagged once. In fact, she didn't let go of her new pet until she was safely back inside the kitchen. Zaphia and Miss Tredgold watched as the young labrador limped across the kitchen floor towards a bowl of warm milk.

'She reminds me of Papa,' said Florentyna.

'Don't be impertinent, child,' said Miss Tredgold.

Zaphia stifled a smile. 'Well, Florentyna, what are you going to call her?'

'Eleanor.'

4

The first time Florentyna ran for President was in 1940 at the age of nine. Miss Evans, her teacher in second grade, decided to hold a mock election. The boys from the Latin School were invited to join the contest, and Edward Winchester, whom Florentyna had never quite forgiven for pouring blue ink over her bear, was chosen to run as the surrogate Wendell Willkie. Florentyna naturally ran as FDR.

It was agreed that each candidate would give a five-minute talk to the remaining twenty-seven members of the two classes. Miss Tredgold, without wishing to influence Florentyna, listened to her deliver her oration thirty-one times – or was it thirty-two? – as she remarked to Mr Rosnovski the Sunday morning before the great election.

Florentyna read the political columns of the Chicago *Tribune* out loud each day to Miss Tredgold searching for any scrap of information she could add to her speech. Kate Smith seemed to be singing 'God Bless America' everywhere and the Dow Jones Index had passed 150 for the first time: whatever that was, it seemed to favour the sitting candidate. Florentyna also read about the progress of the war in Europe, and the launching of a 36,600-ton battleship USS *Washington*, the first fighting vessel America had built in nineteen years.

'Why are we building a battleship if the President has promised that the American people will never have to go to war?'

'I presume it's in the best interest of our own defence,' suggested Miss Tredgold, who was furiously knitting socks for the boys back home. 'Just in case the Germans decided to attack us.'

'They wouldn't dare,' said Florentyna.

The day that Trotsky was slain with an ice pick in Mexico, Miss Tredgold kept the paper away from her charge, while on another morning she was quite unable to explain what nylons were and why the first 72,000 pairs were sold out in eight hours, the shops limiting the sale to two per customer.

Miss Tredgold, whose legs were habitually clad in beige lisle stockings of a shade optimistically entitled 'Allure', studied the item frowningly. 'I'm sure I shall never wear nylons,' she declared, and indeed she never did.

When election day came, Florentyna's head was crammed with facts and figures, some of which she did not understand but they gave her the confidence to feel she would win. The only problem that still concerned her was that Edward was bigger than her. Florentyna imagined that this was a definite advantage as she had read that twenty-seven of the thirty-two Presidents of the United States had been taller than their rivals.

The two contestants tossed a newly-minted Jefferson nickel to decide the order of speaking. Florentyna won and chose to speak first, a mistake she never made again in her life. She walked to the front of the class, a frail figure, and mindful of Miss Tredgold's final words of advice – 'Stand up straight, child. Remember you're not a question mark' – she stood bolt upright in the centre of the raised wooden platform in front of Miss Evans's desk and waited to be told she could begin. Her first few sentences came choking out. She explained her policies for ensuring the nation's finances remained stable while at the same time promising to keep the United States out of the war. 'There is no need for one American to die because the nations of Europe cannot stay at peace,' she declared – a sentence from one of Mr Roosevelt's speeches that she had learned by heart. Mary Gill started to applaud, but Florentyna took no notice and went on talking while, at the same time, pushing her dress down nervously with damp hands. Her last few sentences came out in a great rush, and she sat down to a lot of clapping and smiles.

Edward Winchester rose to follow her and a few of the boys from his class cheered him as he walked up to the blackboard. It was the first time Florentyna realized that some of the votes had been decided even before the speeches began. She only hoped that was true for her side as well. Edward told his classmates that winning at kickball was the same as winning for your country, and in any case Willkie stood for all the things that their parents believed in. Did they want to vote against the wishes of their fathers and mothers, because if they did support FDR they would lose everything? This line was greeted with a splutter of applause, so he repeated it. At the end of his speech, Edward was also rewarded with claps and smiles, but Florentyna convinced herself they were no louder or more widespread than hers had been.

After Edward had sat down, Miss Evans congratulated both candidates and asked the twenty-seven voters to take a blank page from their notebooks and write down the name of Edward or Florentyna, according to whom they felt should be President. Pens dipped furiously into inkwells, scratched across paper. Voting slips were blotted, folded, and then passed forward to Miss

Evans. When the teacher had received the last one, she began to unfold the little squares and place them in front of her in separate piles, a process that seemed to take hours. The whole classroom remained silent throughout the count which in itself was an unusual event. Once Miss Evans had completed the unfolding she counted the twenty-seven slips of paper slowly and carefully, and then double-checked them.

'The result of the mock election' – Florentyna held her breath – 'for President of the United States is thirteen votes for Edward Winchester' – Florentyna nearly cheered, she had won – '. . . and twelve votes for Florentyna Rosnovski. Two people left their papers blank, which is called abstaining.' Florentyna couldn't believe it. 'I therefore declare Edward Winchester, representing Wendell Willkie, to be the new President.'

It was the only election FDR lost that year, but Florentyna was unable to disguise her disappointment and ran to hide in the girls' locker room to be sure no one could see her crying. When she came out she found Mary Gill and Susie Jacobson waiting for her.

'It doesn't matter,' said Florentyna, trying to put a brave face on the result. 'At least I know both of you supported me.'

'We couldn't.'

'Why couldn't you?' asked Florentyna in disbelief.

'We didn't want Miss Evans to know that we weren't sure how to spell your name,' said Mary.

On the way home, after Miss Tredgold had heard the story seven times, she made so bold as to ask if the child had learned anything from the exercise.

'Oh, yes,' replied Florentyna emphatically. 'I'm going to marry a man with a very simple name.'

Abel laughed when he heard the story that night and repeated it to Henry Osborne over dinner. 'Better keep your eye on her, Henry, because it won't be long before she's after your seat.'

'I've got at least fifteen years before she can vote and by then I'll be ready to hand the constituency over to her.'

'What are you doing about convincing the International Relations Committee that we ought to be in this war?'

'FDR will do nothing until the result of the election is known. Everybody is aware of that, including Hitler.'

'If that's so, I only pray that Britain won't lose before we join in, because America will have to wait until November to confirm FDR as President.'

. . .

During the year Abel appointed architects for two more hotels in Washington and San Francisco and had begun his first project in Canada, the Montreal Baron. Although his thoughts were rarely far from the success of the group, something else still remained on his mind.

He wanted to be in Europe, and it wasn't to build hotels.

. . .

At the end of the autumn term, Florentyna got her first spanking. In later life she always associated this with snow. Her classmates decided to build a massive snowman and each member of the class had to bring something with which to decorate him. The snowman ended up with raisin eyes, a carrot nose, potato ears, an old pair of garden gloves, a cigar and a hat supplied by Florentyna. On the last day of the term all the parents were invited to view the snowman and many of them remarked on its hat. Florentyna beamed with pride until her father and mother arrived. Zaphia burst out laughing but Abel was not amused at the sight of his fine silk topper on the head of a grinning snowman. When they arrived home Florentyna was taken to her father's study and given a long lecture on the irresponsibility of taking things that did not belong to her. Abel bent her over his knee and gave her three hard slaps with a hairbrush.

That Saturday night was one she would never forget.

That Sunday morning was one America would always remember.

The Rising Sun appeared over Pearl Harbor on the wings of hostile aircraft and crippled the US battle fleet, vitually wiping out the base and killing 2,403 Americans. The United States declared war on Japan the following day and Germany three days later.

Abel immediately summoned George to inform him that he was going to join the American forces before they sailed for Europe. George protested, Zaphia pleaded and Florentyna cried. Miss Tredgold did not venture an opinion.

. . .

Abel knew he only had to settle one final thing before leaving America. He called for Henry.

'Did you spot the announcement in the *Wall Street Journal*, Henry? I nearly missed the item myself because of all the news about Pearl Harbor.'

'You mean the merger of Lester's with Kane and Cabot, which I predicted in last month's report? Yes, I already have the full details.' Henry passed over a file to Abel. 'I guessed that's what you wanted to see me about.'

Abel flipped through the file until he found the relevant article, underlined in red by Henry. He read the paragraph twice and then started to tap his fingers on the table. 'The first mistake Kane has made.'

'I think you might be right,' said Henry.

'You're earning your fifteen hundred dollars a month, Henry.'

'Perhaps it's time to make it two thousand.'

'Why?'

'Because of Article Seven of the new bank's rules.'

'What made him allow the new clause to be inserted in the first place?' said Abel.

'To protect himself. It has obviously never occurred to Mr Kane that someone might be trying to destroy him, but by exchanging all his shares in Kane and Cabot for the equivalent Lester shares he's lost control of one bank and not gained control of the new one because of Lester's being so much larger. While he only holds eight per cent of the shares in the new venture he has insisted on that clause to be sure that he can stop any transaction for three months, including the appointment of a new chairman.'

'So all we have to do is get hold of eight per cent of Lester's stock and use his own specially inserted clause against him as and when it suits us.' Abel paused. 'I don't imagine that will be easy.'

'That's why I've asked you for a raise.'

. . .

Abel found the task of being accepted for service in the armed forces considerably more difficult than he had at first imagined. The army was none too polite about his sight, his weight, his heart or his general physical condition. Only after some string-pulling did he manage to secure a job as a quartermaster with the Fifth Army under General Mark Clark who was waiting to sail to Africa. Abel jumped at the one chance to be involved in the war and disappeared to officers' training school. Miss Tredgold did not realize until he had left Rigg Street how much Florentyna was going to miss her father. She tried to convince the child that the war would not last long but she did not believe her own words. Miss Tredgold had read too much history.

Abel returned from training school as a major, slimmer and younger looking, but Florentyna hated seeing her father in uniform, because everyone else she knew in uniform was going away to somewhere beyond Chicago and they never seemed to come back. In February, Abel waved goodbye and left New York on the SS *Borinquen*. Florentyna, who was still only seven, was convinced goodbye meant for ever. Mother assured daughter that Papa would return home very quickly.

Like Miss Tredgold, Zaphia did not believe that – and this time neither did Florentyna.

. . .

Florentyna progressed to fourth grade, where she was appointed secretary of her class – which meant she kept weekly minutes of class meetings. When she read her report aloud to the rest of the class each week, no one in the fourth grade showed much interest, but in the heat and dust of Algiers, Abel, torn between laughter and tears, read each line of his daughter's earnest work as if it were the latest bestseller. Florentyna's most recent fad, much approved of by Miss Tredgold, was the Brownies, which allowed her to wear a uniform like her father. Not only did she enjoy dressing up in the smart brown outfit but she soon discovered that she could cover the sleeves with different coloured badges for such enterprises as varied as helping in the kitchen to collecting used stamps. Florentyna was awarded so many badges so quickly that Miss Tredgold was kept busy sewing them on and trying to find a new space for each one. Knots, cooking, gymnastics, animal care, handicrafts, stamps, hiking, followed quickly one after the other. 'It would have been easier if you had been an octopus,' said Miss Tredgold. But final victory was to be hers when her charge won a badge for needlework and had to sew the little yellow triangle on for herself.

. . .

When Florentyna progressed to the fifth grade, where the two schools joined together for most classes, Edward Winchester was appointed President of his class, mainly because of his feats on the sports field, while Florentyna held the post of secretary despite having better grades than anyone else including Edward. Her only disasters were in geometry, where she came second, and in the art room. Miss Tredgold always enjoyed rereading Florentyna's reports and positively relished the remarks of the art teacher. 'Perhaps if Florentyna splashed more paint on the paper than on everything that surrounded it, she might hope to become an artist rather than a plasterer and decorator.'

But the line Miss Tredgold quoted whenever she was asked about Florentyna's academic achievements came from her home-room teacher. 'This
pupil mustn't cry when she is second.'

. . .

As the months passed Florentyna became aware that many of the children
in her class had fathers involved in the war. She soon discovered that hers
was not the only home that had to face separation. Miss Tredgold enrolled
Florentyna in ballet and piano lessons to keep every moment of her spare
time occupied. She even allowed her to take Eleanor to the K-9 Corps as
a useful pet, but the labrador was sent home because she limped. Florentyna
wished they would do the same to her father. When the summer holidays
came Miss Tredgold, with the approval of Zaphia, extended their horizons
to New York and Washington, despite the travel restrictions imposed by the
war. Zaphia took advantage of her daughter's absence to attend charity
meetings in aid of Polish soldiers returning from the front.

Florentyna was thrilled by her first trip to New York even though she had
to leave Eleanor behind. There were skyscrapers, big department stores,
Central Park and more people than she had ever seen before; but despite
all the excitement, it was Washington she most wanted to visit. The journey
was Florentyna's first in an airplane, and Miss Tredgold's as well, and as
the plane followed the line of the Potomac River into Washington's National
Airport, Florentyna stared down in awe at the White House, the Washington Monument, the Lincoln Memorial, and the as yet unfinished Jefferson
Building. She wondered if it would be a memorial or a monument and asked
Miss Tredgold to explain the difference. Miss Tredgold hesitated and said
they would have to look the two words up in Webster's Dictionary when they
returned to Chicago, as she couldn't be certain there was a difference. It was
the first time that Florentyna realized Miss Tredgold didn't know everything.

'It's just like in the pictures,' she said as she stared down out of the tiny
airplane window at the Capitol.

'What did you expect?' said Miss Tredgold.

Henry Osborne had organized a special visit to the White House and a
chance to watch the Senate and House in session. Once she entered the
gallery of the Senate Chamber Florentyna was mesmerized, as each speaker
rose at his desk to speak. Miss Tredgold had to drag her away as one might
a boy from a football game, but it didn't stop her continually asking Henry
Osborne more and more questions. He was surprised by the knowledge the
nine-year-old girl already possessed even if she was the daughter of the
Chicago Baron.

Florentyna and Miss Tredgold spent the night at the Willard Hotel. Her
father had not yet built a Baron in Washington although Congressman
Osborne assured them that one was in the pipeline; in fact, he added, the
site had already been fixed.

'What does "fixed" mean, Mr Osborne?'

Florentyna received no satisfactory reply either from Henry Osborne or
from Miss Tredgold, and decided to look that up in Webster's Dictionary
as well.

That night Miss Tredgold tucked the child up in a large hotel bed and left the room, assuming that after such a long day her charge would quickly fall asleep. Florentyna waited for a few minutes before switching the light back on. She then retrieved her guide to the White House from under the pillow. FDR in a black cloak stared up at her. 'There can be no greater calling than public service' was printed boldly on the line underneath his name. She read the booklet twice through, but it was the final page that fascinated her most. She started to memorize it and fell asleep a few minutes after one, the light still on.

During the return flight home Florentyna studied the back page again carefully while Miss Tredgold read of the progress of the war in the Washington *Times Herald*. Italy had virtually surrendered, although it was clear that the Germans still believed they could win. Florentyna didn't interrupt Miss Tredgold's reading once between Washington and Chicago, and she wondered as the child was so quiet if she was exhausted from the travel. On returning home she allowed Florentyna to go to bed early, but not before she had written a thank-you letter to Congressman Osborne. When Miss Tredgold came to put the light out, Florentyna was still studying the guide to the White House.

It was exactly ten thirty when Miss Tredgold went down to the kitchen to make her nightly cup of cocoa before retiring to bed. On returning she heard what sounded like a chant. She tiptoed slowly to Florentyna's bedroom door, and stood alert, listening to the firmly whispered words. 'One, Washington; two, Adams; three, Jefferson; four, Madison.' She went through every President without a mistake. 'Thirty-one, Hoover; thirty-two FDR; thirty-three, Unknown; thirty-four, Unknown; thirty-five, thirty-six, thirty-seven, thirty-eight, thirty-nine, forty, forty-one, Unknown; forty-two ...' There was a moment's silence then: 'One, Washington; two, Adams; three, Jefferson ...' Miss Tredgold tiptoed back to her room and lay awake for some time staring at the ceiling, her untouched cocoa going cold beside her as she recalled her father's words: 'You were born to be a teacher and the Lord's plan takes us all in its compass: perhaps you will teach someone of destiny.' The President of the United States, Florentyna Rosnovski? No, thought Miss Tredgold, Florentyna was right. She would have to marry someone with a simple name.

.   .   .

Florentyna rose the next morning, bade Miss Tredgold *bonjour* and disappeared into the bathroom. After feeding Eleanor, who now seemed to eat more than she did, Florentyna read in the Chicago *Tribune* that FDR and Churchill had conferred on the unconditional surrender of Italy and told her mother joyfully that meant Papa would be home soon.

Zaphia said she hoped she was right and commented to Miss Tredgold how well she thought Florentyna was looking. 'And how did you enjoy Washington, my dear?'

'Very much, Mama. I think I'll live there one day.'

'Why, Florentyna, what would you do in Washington?'

Florentyna looked up and met Miss Tredgold's eye. She hesitated for a few seconds and then turned back to her mother. 'I don't know. I just thought Washington was a nice city. Would you please pass the marmalade, Miss Tredgold?'

5

Florentyna couldn't be sure how many of her weekly letters were reaching her father because they had to be mailed to a depot in New York for checking before they were sent on to wherever Major Rosnovski was stationed at the time.

The replies came back spasmodically, and sometimes Florentyna would receive as many as three letters in one week and then no word for three months. If a whole month passed without a letter, she began to believe her father had been killed in action. Miss Tredgold explained that that was not possible since the army always sent a telegram to inform a family if a relative was killed or missing. Each morning, Florentyna would be the first to go downstairs to search through the mail for her father's handwriting or the dreaded telegram. When she did receive a letter from her father she often found some of the words were blocked out with black ink. She tried holding them up to the light over the breakfast table but still she couldn't decipher them. Miss Tredgold told her that this was for her father's own safety, as he might have inadvertently written something that could be useful to the enemy if the letter had fallen into the wrong hands.

'Why would the Germans be interested in the fact that I am second in geometry?' asked Florentyna.

Miss Tredgold ignored the question and asked if she had enough to eat.

'I'd like another bit of toast.'

'A piece, child, a piece. A bit is something you put in a horse's mouth.'

.   .   .

Every six months Miss Tredgold would take her charge, accompanied by Eleanor, to Monroe Street to sit on a high stool with the dog on a box by her side, to smile at a flash bulb so that Major Rosnovski could watch his daughter and the labrador grow up by photograph.

'We can't have him not recognizing his only child when he returns home, can we?' she declared.

Florentyna would print her age and Eleanor's age in dog years firmly on the back of each photo and in a letter add the details of her progress at school, how she enjoyed tennis and swimming in the summer and football and basketball in the winter, also how her bookshelves were stacked with his old cigar boxes full of butterflies caught in a wonderful net that Mama had given her for Christmas. She added that Miss Tredgold had carefully chloroformed the butterflies before she pinned them and identified each one with its Latin name; how her mother had joined some charity committee and started taking an interest in the Polish League for Women; how she was growing vegetables in her victory garden, how she and Eleanor didn't like the meat shortage but that she liked bread and butter pudding while Eleanor preferred crunchy biscuits. She always ended each letter in the same way: 'Please come home tomorrow'.

The war stretched into 1944, and Florentyna followed the progress of the Allies in the Chicago *Tribune* and by listening to Edward R. Murrow's reports from London on the radio. Eisenhower became her idol and she nursed a secret admiration for General George Patton because he seemed to be a little bit like her father. On 6 June, the invasion of Western Europe was launched. Florentyna imagined that her father was on the beachhead and she was unable to understand how he could possibly hope to survive. She followed the Allies in their drive towards Paris on the map of Europe that Miss Tredgold had pinned to her playroom wall during the day of her lessons in Polish history. She began to believe that the war was at last coming to an end and that her father would soon return home.

She took to sitting hour after hour on the doorstep of their house on Rigg Street with Eleanor by her side watching the corner of the block. But the hours turned into days, the days into weeks, and Florentyna only became distracted from her vigil by the fact that both Presidential conventions were to be held in Chicago during the summer vacation, which gave her the opportunity to see her political hero in person.

The Republicans chose Thomas E. Dewey as their candidate in June, and later in July the Democrats again selected Roosevelt. Congressman Osborne took Florentyna along to the Amphitheatre to hear the President make his acceptance speech to the Convention. She was puzzled by the fact that whenever she saw Congressman Osborne, he was accompanied by a different woman. She must ask Miss Tredgold about that; she would be sure to have an explanation. After the candidate's speech, Florentyna stood in a long line waiting to shake hands with the President, but she was so nervous that she didn't look up as he was wheeled by.

It was the most exciting day of her life, and on the walk home she confided her interest in politics to Congressman Osborne. He did not point out to her that despite the war there wasn't a woman sitting in the Senate, and there were only two women in Congress.

In November Florentyna wrote to her father to tell him something she imagined he hadn't heard. FDR had won a fourth term. She waited months for his reply.

And then the telegram came.

Miss Tredgold could not extract the missive from the mail before the child spotted the small buff envelope. Her governess immediately carried the telegram to Mrs Rosnovski in the drawing room with a trembling Florentyna following in her wake, holding on to her skirt, with Eleanor a pace behind them. Zaphia tore the envelope open with nervous fingers, read the contents and burst into hysterical tears. 'No, no,' Florentyna cried. 'It can't be true, Mama. Tell me he's only missing,' and snatched the telegram from her speechless mother to read the contents. It read: MY WAR IS OVER, AM RETURNING HOME SOONEST, LOVE ABEL. Florentyna let out a whoop of joy and jumped on the back of Miss Tredgold, who fell into a chair that normally she would never have sat in. Eleanor, as if aware the usual codes could be broken, also jumped on the chair and started licking both of them while Zaphia burst out laughing.

Miss Tredgold could not convince Florentyna that 'soonest' might turn out to take some time since the army conducted a rigid system in deciding who should come home first, awarding points to those who had served the longest or had been wounded in battle. Florentyna remained optimistic but the weeks passed slowly.

One evening when she was returning home clutching yet another Brownie badge, this time for life-saving, she spotted a light shining through a small window that had not been lit for over three years. She forgot her life-saving achievement immediately, ran all the way down the street and had nearly beaten the door down before Miss Tredgold came to answer it. She dashed upstairs to her father's study, where she found him deep in conversation with her mother. She threw her arms around him and would not let go until finally he pushed her back to take a careful look at his eleven-year-old daughter.

'You're so much more beautiful than your photographs.'

'And you're in one piece, Papa.'

'Yes, and I won't be going away again.'

'Not without me, you won't,' said Florentyna, and clung on to him once more.

For the next few days, she pestered her father to tell her stories of the war. Had he met General Eisenhower? No. General Patton? Yes, for about ten minutes. General Bradley? Yes. Had he seen any Germans? No, but on one occasion he had helped to rescue a platoon that had been ambushed by the enemy at Remagen.

'And what happened –?'

'Enough, enough, young lady. You're worse than a staff sergeant on drill parade.'

Florentyna was so excited by her father's homecoming that she was an hour late for bed that night and still didn't sleep. Miss Tredgold reminded her how lucky she was that her Papa had returned without injury or disfigurement, unlike so many fathers of the children in her class.

When Florentyna heard that Edward Winchester's father had lost an arm at somewhere called Bastogne, she tried to tell him how sorry she was.

. . . . .

Abel quickly returned to the routine of his work. No one had recognized him when he first strode into the Baron: he had lost so much weight and looked so thin that the duty manager asled him who he was. The first decision Abel had to make was to order five new suits from Brooks Brothers because none of his pre-war clothes fitted him.

George Novak, as far as Abel could deduce from the annual reports he had been through, had kept the group on an even keel in his absence, even if he had taken no great strides forward. It was also from George that he learned that Henry Osborne had been re-elected to Congress for a fifth term. He asked his secretary to call Washington.

'Congratulations, Henry. Consider yourself elected to the board.'

'Thank you, Abel. You'll be glad to learn,' said Henry, 'that I have acquired six per cent of Lester's stock while you've been away rustling up gourmet dinners on Primus stoves for our top military brass.'

'Well done, Henry. What hope is there of getting our hands on the magic eight per cent?'

'A very good chance,' replied Henry. 'Peter Parfitt, who expected to be chairman of Lester's before Kane arrived on the scene, has been removed from the board and has about as much affection for Kane as a mongoose has for a cobra. Parfitt has made it very clear that he is willing to part with his two per cent.'

'Then what's stopping us?'

'He's demanding a million dollars for his holding, because I'm sure he's worked out that his shares are all you need to topple Kane, and there are not many stockholders left for me to buy from. But a million is way above the ten per cent over current stock value that you authorized me to proceed at.'

Abel studied the figures that Henry had left on his desk for him. 'Offer him seven hundred and fifty thousand,' he said.

⋅   ⋅   ⋅

George was thinking about far smaller sums when he next spoke to Abel. 'I allowed Henry a loan in your absence and he still hasn't paid the money back,' he admitted.

'A loan?'

'Henry's description, not mine,' said George.

'Who's kidding who? How much?' said Abel.

'Five thousand dollars. I'm sorry, Abel.'

'Forget it. If that's the only mistake you've made in the last three years, I'm a lucky man. What do you imagine Henry spends the money on?'

'Wine, women and song. There's nothing particularly original about our Congressman. There's also a rumour around the Chicago bars that he's started gambling quite heavily.'

'That's all I need from the latest member of the board. Keep an eye on him and let me know if the situation gets any worse.'

George nodded.

'And now I want to talk about expansion. With Washington pumping three hundred million dollars a day into the economy we must be prepared for a boom the like of which America has never experienced before. We must also start building Barons in Europe while land is cheap and most people are only thinking about survival. Let's begin with London.'

'For God's sake, Abel, the place is as flat as a pancake.'

'All the better to build on, my dear.'

⋅   ⋅   ⋅

'Miss Tredgold,' said Zaphia, 'I'm going to a fashion show this afternoon in aid of the Chicago Symphony Orchestra and I might not be back before Florentyna's bedtime.'

'Very good, Mrs Rosnovski,' said Miss Tredgold.

'I'd like to go,' said Florentyna.

Both women stared at the child in surprise.

'But it's only two days before your exams,' said Zaphia, anticipating that Miss Tredgold would thoroughly disapprove of Florentyna attending something as frivolous as a fashion show. 'What are you meant to be doing this afternoon?'

'Medieval history,' replied Miss Tredgold without hesitation. 'Charlemagne through to the Council of Trent.'

Zaphia was sad that her daughter was not being allowed to take an interest in feminine pursuits but rather was expected to act as a surrogate son, filling the gap for her husband's dissappointment at not having a boy.

'Then perhaps we'd better leave it for another time,' she said. Zaphia would have liked to put her foot down but realized that if Abel found out both she and Florentyna would suffer for it later.

However, for once Miss Tredgold surprised her.

'I am not sure I agree with you, Mrs Rosnovski,' she said. 'The occasion might well be the ideal one to introduce the child to the world of fashion and indeed of society.' Turning to Florentyna, she added, 'And a break from your studies a few days before exams can do you no harm.'

Zaphia looked at Miss Tredgold with new respect. 'Perhaps you would like to come yourself?' she added. It was the first time Zaphia had seen Miss Tredgold blush.

'No, thank you, no, I couldn't possibly.' She hesitated. 'I have letters, yes, letters to attend to, and I've set aside this afternoon to pen them.'

That afternoon, Zaphia was waiting by the main school gate dressed in a pink suit in place of Miss Tredgold in her usual sensible navy. Florentyna thought her mother looked extremely smart.

She wanted to run all the way to the fashion show and when she actually arrived she found it hard to remain still even though her seat was in the front row. She could have touched the haughty models as they picked their way gracefully down the brilliantly lit catwalk. As the pleated skirts swirled and dipped, tight-waisted jackets were taken off to reveal elegantly bare shoulders, and sophisticated ladies in floating yards of pale organza topped with silk hats drifted silently to unknown assignations behind a red velvet curtain. Florentyna sat entranced. When the last model had turned a full circle, signalling the show had ended, a press photographer asked Zaphia if he could take her picture. 'Mama,' said Florentyna urgently as he was setting up his tripod, 'you must wear your hat further forward if you want to be thought chic.'

Mother obeyed child for the first time.

When Miss Tredgold tucked Florentyna into bed that night she asked if she had enjoyed the experience.

'Oh, yes,' said Florentyna. 'I had no idea clothes could make you look so good.'

Miss Tredgold smiled, a little wistfully.

'And did you realize that they raised over eight thousand dollars for the Chicago Symphony Orchestra? Even Papa would have been impressed by that.'

'Indeed he would,' said Miss Tredgold, 'and one day you will have to decide how to use your wealth for the benefit of other people. It is not always easy being born with money.'

. . .

The next day, Miss Tredgold pointed out to Florentyna a picture of her mother in *Women's Wear Daily* under the caption, 'Baroness Rosnovski, who enters the fashion scene in Chicago'.

'When can I go to a fashion show again?' asked Florentyna.

'Not until you have been through Charlemagne and the Council of Trent,' said Miss Tredgold.

'I wonder what Charlemagne wore when he was crowned Holy Roman Emperor,' said Florentyna.

That night, locked into her room, with only the light of a torch to go by, she let down the hem of her school skirt and took two inches in at the waist.

. . .

Florentyna was now in her last term of middle school and Abel hoped she might win the coveted Upper School Scholarship. Florentyna was aware that her father could afford to send her to Upper School if she failed to win a scholarship, but she had plans for the money her father would save each year, but she had no way of knowing how well she had done when the final examination came to an end, as one hundred and twenty-two Illinois children had entered for the examination but only four scholarships were to be awarded. Florentyna had been warned by Miss Tredgold that she would not learn the result for at least a month. 'Patience is a virtue,' Miss Tredgold reminded her, and added with mock horror that she would return to England on the next boat if Florentyna did not come in the first three places.

'Don't be silly, Miss Tredgold, I shall be first,' Florentyna replied confidently, but as the days of the month went by she began to regret her bragging and confided to Eleanor during a long walk that she might have written cosine when she had meant sine in one of the geometry questions, and created an impossible triangle. 'Perhaps I shall come in second,' she ventured over breakfast one morning.

'Then I shall move to the employ of the parents of the child who comes first,' said Miss Tredgold imperturbably.

Abel smiled as he looked up from his copy of the morning paper. 'If you win a scholarship,' he said, 'you will have saved me one thousand dollars a year. If you come top, two thousand dollars.'

'Yes, Papa, and I have plans for that.'

'Oh do you, young lady? And may I inquire what you have in mind?'

'If I win a scholarship, I want you to invest the money in Baron Group shares until I'm twenty-one, and if I'm first I want you to do the same for Miss Tredgold.'

'Good gracious, no,' said Miss Tredgold, stretching to her full height, 'that would be most improper. I do apologize, Mr Rosnovski, for Florentyna's impudence.'

'It's not impudence, Papa. If I finish top, half the credit must go to Miss Tredgold.'

'If not more,' said Abel, 'and I'll agree to your demands. But on one condition.' He folded his paper carefully.

'What's that?' said Florentyna.

'How much do you have in your savings account, young lady'

'Three hundred and twelve dollars,' came back the immediate reply.

'Very well, if you fail to finish in the first four you must sacrifice the three hundred and twelve dollars to help me pay the tuition you haven't saved.'

Florentyna hesitated. Abel waited and Miss Tredgold did not comment.

'I agree,' said Florentyna at last.

'I have never bet in my life,' said Miss Tredgold, 'and I can only hope my dear father does not live to learn of this.'

'It should not concern you, Miss Tredgold.'

'It certainly does, Mr Rosnovski. If the child is willing to gamble her only three hundred and twelve dollars on the strength of what I have managed to do for her then I must repay in kind and also offer three hundred and twelve dollars towards her education if she fails to win a scholarship.'

'Bravo,' said Florentyna, and threw her arms around her governess.

'A fool and his money are soon parted,' declared Miss Tredgold.

'Agreed,' said Abel, 'for I have lost.'

'What do you mean, Papa?' asked Florentyna. Abel turned over the newspaper to reveal a small headline that read "The Chicago Baron's Daughter Wins Top Scholarship'.

'Mr Rosnovski, you knew all the time.'

'True, Miss Tredgold, but it is you who have turned out to be the better poker player.'

Florentyna was overjoyed and spent the last few days of her life at Middle School as the class heroine. Even Edward Winchester congratulated her.

'Let's go and have a drink to celebrate,' he suggested.

'What?' said Florentyna. 'I've never had a drink before.'

'No time like the present,' said Edward, and led her to a small classroom in the boys' end of the school. Once they were inside, he locked the door. 'Don't want to be caught,' he explained. Florentyna stood in admiring disbelief as Edward lifted the lid of his desk and took out a bottle of beer, which he prised open with a nickel. He poured the fat brown liquid into two dirty glasses, also extracted from the desk, and passed one over to Florentyna.

'Bottoms up,' said Edward.

'What does that mean?' asked Florentyna.

'Just drink the stuff,' he said, but Florentyna watched him take a gulp before she plucked up the courage to try a sip. Edward rummaged around in his jacket pocket and took out a crumpled packet of Lucky Strikes. Florentyna couldn't believe her eyes. The nearest she had been to a cigarette was the advertisement she had heard on the radio which said: 'Lucky Strike means fine tobacco. Yes, Lucky Strike means fine tobacco,' a theme that had driven Miss Tredgold mad. Without speaking, Edward removed one of the cigarettes from the packet, placed it between his lips, lit it and started puffing away. He blew some smoke recklessly into the middle of the room. Florentyna was mesmerized as he extracted a second cigarette and placed it between her lips. She did not dare to move as he struck another match and held the flame to the end of the cigarette. She stood quite still for fear it would catch her hair on fire.

'Inhale, you silly girl,' he said, so she puffed three or four times very quickly and then started coughing.

'You can take the thing out of your mouth, you know,' he said.

'Of course I know,' she said quickly, removing the cigarette the way she remembered Jean Harlow did in *Saratoga*.

'Good,' said Edward, and drank a large draught of his beer.

'Good,' said Florentyna, and did the same. For the next few minutes, she kept in time with Edward as he puffed his cigarette and gulped the beer.

'Great, isn't it?' said Edward.

'Great,' replied Florentyna.

'Like another?'

'No, thank you.' Florentyna coughed. 'But it was great.'

'I've been smoking and drinking for several weeks,' announced Edward.

'Yes, I can tell,' said Florentyna.

A bell sounded in the hall, and Edward quickly returned the beer, cigarettes and two butts to his desk before unlocking the door. Florentyna walked slowly back to her classroom. She felt dizzy and sick when she reached her desk and worse when she returned home an hour later, unaware that the smell of Lucky Strikes was still on her breath. Miss Tredgold did not comment and put her to bed immediately.

The next morning Florentyna woke in terrible discomfort, scabious eruptions on her chest and face. She looked at herself in the mirror and burst into tears.

'Chicken pox,' declared Miss Tredgold to Zaphia.

Chicken pox, the doctor confirmed later, and Miss Tredgold brought Abel to visit Florentyna in her room after the doctor had completed his examination.

'What's wrong with me?' asked Florentyna anxiously.

'I can't imagine,' said her father mendaciously. 'Looks like one of the plagues of Egypt to me. What do you think, Miss Tredgold?'

'I have only seen the like of it once before, and that was with a man in my father's parish who smoked, but of course that doesn't apply in this case.'

Abel kissed his daughter on the cheek, and he and Miss Tredgold both left the room.

'Did we pull it off?' asked Abel when they had reached his study.

'I cannot be certain, Mr Rosnovski, but I would be willing to wager one dollar that Florentyna never smokes again.'

Abel took out his wallet from an inside pocket, removed a dollar bill and then replaced it.

'No, I think not, Miss Tredgold. I am too aware what happens when I bet with you.'

. . . .

Florentyna once heard her headmistress remark that some incidents in history are so powerful in their impact that everyone can tell you exactly where they were when they first heard the news.

On 12 April 1945, at four forty-seven Abel was talking to a man representing a product called Pepsi-Cola who was pressing him to try out the drink in all the Baron hotels. Zaphia was shopping in Marshall Field's and Miss Tredgold had just come out of the United Artists Theatre where she had seen Humphrey Bogart in *Casablanca* for the third time. Florentyna was in her room looking up the word 'teen-ager' in Webster's Dictionary. The word was not yet acknowledged by Webster's when Franklin D. Roosevelt died in Warm Springs, Georgia.

Of all the tributes to the late President Florentyna read during the next few days, the one she kept for the rest of her life was from the New York *Post*. It read simply:

Washington, April 19th – Following are the latest casualties in the military services including next of kin.

ARMY – NAVY DEAD

ROOSEVELT, Franklin D., Commander-in-Chief, wife Mrs Anna Eleanor Roosevelt, The White House.

6

Entering upper school at Girls Latin prompted Florentyna's second trip to New York, as the only establishments that stocked the official school uniform were Marshall Field's in Chicago and, for shoes, Abercrombie & Fitch in New York. Abel snorted and declared it was inverted snobbery of the worst kind. Nevertheless as he had to travel to New York to check on the newly opened Baron, he agreed as a special treat to accompany Miss Tredgold and his eleven-year-old daughter on their journey to Madison Avenue.

Abel had long considered New York to be the only major city in the world not to boast a first-class hotel. He admired the Plaza, the Pierre and the Carlyle but did not think that any of the three held a candle to Claridge's in London, the George V in Paris or the Danieli in Venice, and only those achieved the standards he was trying to reproduce for the New York Baron.

Florentyna was aware that Papa was spending more and more time in New York, and it saddened her that the affection between her father and mother now seemed to be a thing of the past. The rows were becoming so frequent that she wondered if she was in any way to blame.

Once Miss Tredgold had purchased everything on the list that was available at Marshall Field's – three blue sweaters (navy), three blue skirts (navy), four shirts (white), six blue bloomers (dark), six pairs of grey socks (light), one navy-blue silk dress with white collar and cuffs – she planned the trip to New York.

Florentyna and Miss Tredgold took the train to Grand Central Station and on arrival in New York went straight to Abercrombie & Fitch where they selected two pairs of brown Oxfords.

'Such sensible shoes,' proclaimed Miss Tredgold. 'Nobody who wears Abercrombies needs fear going through life with flat feet.' They then proceeded on to Fifth Avenue. Miss Tredgold had walked several yards before she realized she was on her own. Turning around, she observed Florentyna's nose pressed against the pane of Elizabeth Arden's. She walked quickly back to join her. 'Ten shades of lipstick for the sophisticated woman,' read the sign in the window.

'Rose red is my favourite,' said Florentyna hopefully.

'The school rules are very clear,' said Miss Tredgold authoritatively. 'No lipstick, no nail polish, and no jewelry except a ring and a watch.'

Florentyna reluctantly left the rose-red lipstick and joined her governess on her march up Fifth Avenue towards the Plaza Hotel where her father was expecting them at the Palm Court for tea. Abel could not resist returning to the hotel where he had served his apprenticeship as a junior waiter, and although he recognized no one except Old Sammy, the head waiter in the Oak Room, everyone knew exactly who he was.

After macaroons and ice cream for Florentyna, a cup of coffee for Abel, and lemon tea and a watercress sandwich for Miss Tredgold, Abel returned to work. Miss Tredgold checked her New York itinerary and took Florentyna to the top of the Empire State Building. As the elevator reached the one hundred and second floor Florentyna felt quite giddy and they both burst out laughing when they discovered fog had come in from the East River and they couldn't even see as far as the Chrysler Building. Miss Tredgold checked her list again and decided that their time would be better spent visiting the Metropolitan Museum. Mr Francis Henry Taylor, the director, had just acquired a large canvas by Pablo Picasso. The oil painting turned out to be a woman with two heads and one breast coming out of her shoulder.

'What do you think of that?' asked Florentyna.

'Not a lot,' said Miss Tredgold. 'I rather suspect that when he was at school he received the same sort of art reports as you do now.'

Florentyna always enjoyed staying in one of her father's hotels when she was on a trip. She would happily spend hours walking around trying to pick up mistakes the hotel was making. After all, she pointed out to Miss Tredgold, they had their investment to consider. Over dinner that night in the Grill Room of the New York Baron, Florentyna told her father that she didn't think much of the hotel shops.

'What's wrong with them?' asked Abel, mouthing questions without paying much attention to the answers.

'Nothing you can point to easily,' said Florentyna, 'except that they are all dreadfully dull compared with real shops like the ones on Fifth Avenue.'

Abel scribbled a note on the back of his menus, 'shops dreadfully dull', and doodled around it carefully before he said: 'I shall not be returning to Chicago with you tomorrow, Florentyna.'

For once Florentyna was silent.

'Some problems have arisen with the hotel at this end and I must stay behind to see they don't get out of hand,' he said, sounding a little too well rehearsed.

Florentyna gripped her father's hand. 'Try and come back tomorrow. Eleanor and I always miss you.'

.   .   .

Once Florentyna had returned to Chicago Miss Tredgold set about preparing her for Upper School. Each day they would spend two hours studying a different subject but Florentyna was allowed to choose whether they should work in the mornings or the afternoons. The only exception to this rule was on Thursdays, when their sessions took place in the morning as it was Miss Tredgold's afternoon off.

At two o'clock promptly every Thursday she would leave the house and not return until seven that night. She never explained where she was going, and Florentyna never summoned up the courage to ask. But as the holiday progressed Florentyna became more and more curious about where Miss

Tredgold spent her time, until finally she resolved to discover for herself.

After a Thursday morning of Latin and a light lunch together in the kitchen, Miss Tredgold said goodbye to Florentyna and retired to her room. As two o'clock struck she opened the front door of the house and headed off down the street carrying a large canvas bag. Florentyna watched her carefully through her bedroom window. Once Miss Tredgold had turned the corner of Rigg Street, Florentyna dashed out and ran all the way to the end of the block. She peered around to see her mentor waiting at a bus stop just ten yards away. She could feel her heart beating at the thought of not being able to follow Miss Tredgold any farther. Within minutes she watched a bus draw up and come to a halt. She was about to turn back for home when she noticed Miss Tredgold disappear up the circular staircase of the doubledecker. Without hesitation, Florentyna ran and jumped on to the moving platform, then quickly made her way to the front of the bus.

When the ticket collector asked her where she was going Florentyna suddenly realized she had no idea of her destination.

'How far do you go?' she asked.

The collector looked at her suspiciously. 'The Loop,' he replied.

'One single for the Loop then,' said Florentyna confidently.

'That'll be fifteen cents,' said the conductor.

Florentyna fumbled in her jacket pocket to discover she had only ten cents.

'How far can I go for ten cents?'

'Rylands School,' came back the reply.

Florentyna passed over the money, praying that Miss Tredgold would reach her destination before she would have to get off, while not giving any thought to how she would make the return journey.

She sat low in her seat and watched carefully each time the bus came to a halt, but even after she had counted twelve stops Miss Tredgold still did not appear as the bus travelled along Lake Front, passing the University of Chicago.

'Your stop is next,' the conductor said firmly.

When the bus next came to a halt at Seventy-first Street, Florentyna knew she was beaten. She stepped down reluctantly on to the pavement thinking about the long walk home and determined that the following week she would have enough money to cover the journey both ways.

She stood unhappily watching the bus as it travelled a few hundred yards farther down the street before coming to a stop once more. A figure stepped out into the road which could only have been Miss Tredgold. She disappeared down a side street, looking as if she knew exactly where she was going.

Florentyna ran as hard as she could, but when she reached the corner, breathless, there was no sign of Miss Tredgold. Florentyna walked slowly down the street wondering where her governess could have gone. Perhaps into one of the houses, or might she have taken another side street? Florentyna decided she would walk to the end of the road and if she failed to spot her quarry then she would have to make her way home.

Just at the point when she was considering turning back she came into an opening that faced a large wrought-iron archway which had embossed on it in gold: South Shore Country Club.

Florentyna didn't consider for a moment that Miss Tredgold could be inside, but out of curiosity she peered through the gates.

'What do you want?' said a uniformed guard standing on the other side.

'I was looking for my governess,' said Florentyna lamely.

'What's her name?'

'Miss Tredgold,' Florentyna said unflinchingly.

'She's already gone into the club house,' said the guard, pointing towards a Victorian building surrounded by trees about a quarter of a mile up a steep rise.

Florentyna marched boldly through, without another word, staying on the path because 'Keep off the grass' signs were displayed every few yards. She kept her eye on the club house and had ample time to leap behind a tree when she saw Miss Tredgold emerge. She hardly recognized the lady dressed in red and yellow check tweed trousers, a heavy Fair Isle sweater and heavy brown brogues. A bag of golf clubs was slung comfortably over one shoulder.

Florentyna stared at her governess, mesmerized.

Miss Tredgold walked towards the first tee where she put down her bag and took out a ball. She placed it on a tee at her feet and selected a club from her bag. After a few practice swings she steadied herself, addressed the ball and hit it firmly down the middle of the fairway. Florentyna couldn't believe her eyes. She wanted to applaud but instead ran forward to hide behind another tree as Miss Tredgold marched off down the fairway.

Miss Tredgold's second shot landed only twenty yards from the edge of the green. Florentyna ran forward to a clump of trees at the side of the fairway and watched Miss Tredgold chip her ball up on to the green and hole it with two putts. Florentyna was left in no doubt that Miss Tredgold had been playing the game for some considerable time.

Miss Tredgold then removed a small white card from her jacket pocket and wrote on it, before heading towards the second tee. As she did so she gazed towards the second green, which was to the left of where Florentyna was hidden. Once again Miss Tredgold steadied herself, addressed the ball and swung, but this time she sliced her shot and the ball ended up only fifteen yards away from Florentyna's hiding place.

Florentyna looked up at the trees but they had not been made for climbing other than by a cat. She held her breath and crouched behind the widest but could not resist watching Miss Tredgold as she studied the lay of her ball. Miss Tredgold muttered something inaudible and then selected a club. Florentyna let out her breath as Miss Tredgold swung. The ball climbed high and straight before landing in the middle of the fairway again.

Florentyna watched Miss Tredgold replace her club in the bag.

'I should have kept a straighter arm on the first shot and then we would never have met.'

Florentyna assumed Miss Tredgold was admonishing herself yet again, and remained behind the tree.

'Come here, child.' Florentyna obediently ran out but said nothing.

Miss Tredgold took another ball from the side pocket of her bag and placed it on the ground in front of her. She selected a club and handed it to her charge.

'Try to hit the ball in that direction,' she said, pointing towards a flag about a hundred yards away.

Florentyna held the club awkwardly before taking several swings at the ball, on each occasion removing what Miss Tredgold called 'divots'. At last she managed to push it twenty yards towards the fairway. She beamed with pleasure.

'I see we are in for a long afternoon,' declared Miss Tredgold resignedly.

'I am sorry,' said Florentyna. 'Can you ever forgive me?'

'For following me, yes. But for the state of your golf, no. We shall have to start with the basics, as it seems in the future I am no longer to have Thursday afternoons to myself, now you have discovered my father's only sin.'

Miss Tredgold taught Florentyna how to play golf with the same energy and application as if it were Latin or Greek. By the end of the summer Florentyna's favourite afternoon was Thursday.

.   .   .

Upper School was very different from Middle School. There was a new teacher for every subject rather than one teacher for everything except gum. The pupils had to move from room to room for their classes, and for many of the activities the girls joined forces with the boys' school. Florentyna's favourite subjects were current affairs, Latin, French and English, although she couldn't wait for her twice-weekly biology classes because they gave her the chance to admire the school's collection of bugs under the microscope.

'Insects, dear child. You must refer to the little creatures as insects,' Miss Tredgold insisted.

'Actually, Miss Tredgold, they're nematodes.'

Florentyna also continued to take an interest in clothes and noticed that the mode for short dresses caused by the enforced economies of war was fast becoming outdated and that once again skirts were nearly reaching the ground. She was unable to do much about experimenting with fashion, as the school uniform was the same year in and year out; the children's department of Marshall Field's, it seemed, was not a great contributor to *Vogue*. However, she studied all the relevant magazines in the library and pestered her mother to take her to more shows. For Miss Tredgold, on the other hand, who had never allowed any man to see her knees, even in the self-denying days of Lend-Lease, the new fashion only proved she had been right all along.

At the end of Florentyna's first year in Upper School the modern languages mistress decided to put on a performance of *Saint Joan* in French. As Florentyna was the only pupil who could think in the language, she was chosen to play the Maid of Orleans and rehearsed for hours in the old nursery with Miss Tredgold playing every other part as well as being prompter and cue reader. Even when Florentyna was word-perfect, Miss Tredgold sat loyally through the daily one-woman shows.

'Only the Pope and I give audiences for one,' she told Florentyna as the phone rang.

'It's for you,' said Miss Tredgold.

Florentyna always enjoyed receiving phone calls, although it was not a practice that Miss Tredgold encouraged.

'Hello, it's Edward. I need your help.'

'Why? Don't tell me you've learnt to read?'

'No hope of that, silly. But I've been given the part of the Dauphin and I can't pronounce all the words.'

Florentyna tried not to laugh. 'Come around at five thirty and you can join the daily rehearsals. Although I must warn you, Miss Tredgold has been making a very good Dauphin up to now.'

Edward came around every night at five thirty and although Miss Tredgold occasionally frowned when 'the boy' lapsed back into an American accent he was 'just about ready' by the day of the dress rehearsal.

When the night of the performance itself came, Miss Tredgold instructed Florentyna and Edward that under no circumstances must they look out into the audience hoping to spot their parents, otherwise those watching the performance would not believe in the characters they were portraying. Most unprofessional, Miss Tredgold considered, and reminded Florentyna that Mr Noël Coward once left a performance of *Romeo and Juliet* because Mr John Gielgud looked straight at him during a soliloquy. Florentyna was convinced, though in truth she had no idea who Mr John Gielgud or Mr Noël Coward were.

When the curtain went up, Florentyna did not once look beyond the footlights. Miss Tredgold considered her efforts 'most commendable', and during the intermission particularly commented to Florentyna's mother on the scene in which the Maid is alone in the centre of the stage and talks to her voices. 'Moving', was Miss Tredgold's description. 'Unquestionably moving'. When the curtain finally fell, Florentyna received a rapturous ovation, even from those who had not been able to follow every word in French. Edward stood a pace behind her, relieved to have come through the ordeal without too many mistakes. Glowing with excitement, Florentyna removed her make-up, her first experience of lipstick and powder, changed back into her school uniform and joined her mother and Miss Tredgold with the other parents who were having coffee in the dining hall. Several people came over to congratulate her on her performance including the headmaster of the Boys Latin School.

'A remarkable achievement for a girl of her age,' he told Mrs Rosnovski. 'Though when you think about it she is only a couple of years younger than Saint Joan was when she challenged the entire might of the French establishment.'

'Saint Joan didn't have to learn someone else's lines in a foreign language,' said Zaphia, feeling pleased with herself.

Florentyna did not take in her mother's words as her eyes were searching the crowded hall for her father.

'Where's Papa?' she asked.

'He couldn't make it tonight.'

'But he promised,' said Florentyna. 'He *promised*.' Tears welled up in her eyes as she suddenly realized why Miss Tredgold had told her not to look beyond the footlights.

'You must remember, child, that your father is a very busy man. He has a small empire to run.'

'So did Saint Joan,' said Florentyna.

When Florentyna went to bed that night, Miss Tredgold came to turn out her light.

'Papa doesn't love Mama any more, does he?'

The bluntness of the question took Miss Tredgold by surprise and it was a few moments before she recovered.

'Of only one thing I am certain, child, and that is that they both love you.'

'Then why has Papa stopped coming home?'

'That I cannot explain but whatever his reasons we must be very understanding and grown-up,' said Miss Tredgold, brushing back a lock of hair that had fallen over Florentyna's forehead.

Florentyna felt very ungrown-up and wondered if Saint Joan had been so unhappy when she lost her beloved France. When Miss Tredgold closed the door quietly Florentyna put her hand under the bed to feel the reassuring wet nose of Eleanor. 'At least I'll always have you,' she whispered. Eleanor clambered up from her hiding place on to the bed and settled down next to Florentyna, facing the door: a quick retreat to her basket in the kitchen might prove necessary if Miss Tredgold reappeared.

Florentyna did not see her father during that summer vacation and had long stopped believing the stories that the growing hotel empire was keeping him away from Chicago. Whenever she mentioned him to her mother, Zaphia's replies were often bitter. Florentyna also found out from overheard telephone conversations that she was consulting lawyers.

Each day Florentyna would take Eleanor for a walk down Michigan Avenue in the hope that she might see her father's car drive by. One Wednesday, she decided to make a break in her routine and walk on the west side of the Avenue to study the stores that set the fashions for the Windy City. Eleanor was delighted to be reunited with the magnificent lampposts that had recently been placed for her at twenty-yard intervals. Florentyna had already purchased a wedding dress and a ball gown with her five dollars a week pocket money and was coveting an elegant five-hundred-dollar evening dress in the window of Martha Weathereds' on the corner of Oak Street when she saw her father's reflection in the glass. She turned, overjoyed, to see him coming out of Spaulding's on the opposite side of the street. Without a thought she dashed out into the road not looking either way as she called her father's name. A yellow cab jammed on its brakes and swerved violently, the driver aware of a flash of blue skirt then the heavy thud as the cab made contact. The rest of the traffic came to a screeching halt as the cab driver saw a stout, well-dressed man, followed by a policeman, run out into the middle of the road. A moment later Abel and the taxi driver stood in a state of shock staring down at the lifeless body. 'She's dead,' said the policeman, shaking his head, as he took out his notebook from his top pocket.

Abel fell on his knees, trembling. He looked up at the policeman. 'And the worst thing about it is I am to blame.'

'No, Papa, it was my fault,' wept Florentyna. 'I should never have rushed out into the road. I killed Eleanor by not thinking.'

The driver of the taxi that had hit the labrador explained that he had had no choice, he had to hit the dog to avoid colliding with the girl.

Abel nodded, picked up his daughter and carried her to the side of the road, not letting her look back at Eleanor's mangled body. He placed Florentyna in the back of his car and returned to the policeman.

'My name is Abel Rosno –'

'I know who you are, sir.'

'Can I leave everything to you, officer?'

'Yes, sir,' said the policeman, not looking up from his notebook.

Abel returned to his chauffeur and told him to drive them to the Baron. Abel held his daughter's hand as they walked through the crowded hotel corridor to the private elevator that whisked them to the forty-second floor. George met them when the gates sprang open. He was about to greet his goddaughter with a Polish quip when he saw the look on her face.

'Ask Miss Tredgold to come over immediately, George.'

'Of course,' said George, and disappeared into his own office.

Abel sat and listened to several stories about Eleanor without interrupting before tea and sandwiches arrived but Florentyna managed only a sip of milk. Then without any warning she changed the subject.

'Why don't you ever come home, Papa?' she asked.

Abel poured himself another cup of tea, a little spilling into the saucer. 'I've wanted to come home many times, and I hated missing *Saint Joan*, but your mother and I are going to be divorced.'

'Oh no, it can't be true. Papa ...'

'It's my fault, little one. I have not been a good husband and ...'

Florentyna threw her arms around her father. 'Does that mean I will never see you again?'

'No. I have made an agreement with your mother that you shall remain in Chicago while you are at school, but you will spend the rest of the time with me in New York. Of course you can always talk to me on the telephone whenever you want to.'

Florentyna remained silent as Abel gently stroked her hair.

Some time passed before there was a knock on the door and Miss Tredgold entered, her long dress swishing across the carpet as she came quickly to Florentyna's side.

'Can you take her home please, Miss Tredgold?'

'Of course, Mr Rosnovski.' Florentyna was still tearful. 'Come with me, child,' she said. Bending down, she whispered, 'Try not to show your feelings.'

The twelve-year-old girl kissed her father on the forehead, took Miss Tredgold's hand and left.

When the door closed, Abel, not having been brought up by Miss Tredgold, sat alone and wept.

7

It was at the beginning of her second year in Upper School that Florentyna first became aware of Pete Welling. He was sitting in a corner of the music room, playing the latest Broadway hit, 'Almost Like Being in Love' on the piano. He was slightly out of tune but Florentyna assumed it must be the piano. Pete didn't seem to notice her as she passed him, so she turned around and walked back again, but to no avail. He put a hand nonchalantly through his fair wavy hair and continued playing the piano, so she marched off pretending she hadn't seen him. By lunchtime the next day she knew that he was two grades above her, where he lived, that he was vice-captain of the football team, president of his class, and nearly seventeen. Her friend Susie Jacobson warned her that others had trod the same path without a great deal of success.

'But I assure you,' replied Florentyna, 'I have something to offer that will prove irresistible.'

That afternoon she sat down and composed what she imagined to be her first love letter. After much deliberation she chose purple ink and wrote in a bold slanting hand:

My dear Pete,

   I knew you were something special the first time I saw you. I think you play the piano beautifully. Would you like to come and listen to some records at my place?

Very sincerely,
Florentyna (Rosnovski)

Florentyna waited for the break before she crept down the corridor, imagining every eye to be on her as she searched for Pete Welling's hall locker. When she found it, she checked his name against the number on the top of the locker. Forty-two – she felt that was a good omen – and opened his locker door, left her letter on top of a maths book, where he couldn't miss it and returned to her classroom, palms sweating. She checked her own locker, on the hour every hour, expecting his reply, but none was forthcoming. After a week had passed, she began to despair until she saw Pete sitting on the steps of the chapel combing his hair. How daring to break two school rules at once, she thought. Florentyna decided this was her chance to find out if he had ever received her invitation.

She walked boldly towards him, but with only a yard to go she wished he would disappear in a cloud of dust because she couldn't think of anything to say. She stood still like a lamb in the gaze of a python but he saved her by saying, 'Hi.'

'Hi,' she managed. 'Did you ever find my letter?'

'Your letter?'

'Yes, I wrote to you last Monday about coming over to play some records at my place. I've got "Silent Night", and most of Bing Crosby's latest hits. Have you heard him singing "White Christmas"?' she asked, playing her trump card.

'Oh, it was you who wrote that letter,' he said.

'Yes, I saw you play against Francis Parker last week. You were fantastic. Who are you playing next?'

'It's in the school calendar,' he said, putting his comb into an inside pocket and looking over her shoulder.

'I'll be in the stands.'

'I'm sure you will,' he said as a tall blonde from the senior class wearing little white socks that Florentyna felt sure were not official school uniform ran over to Pete and asked if he had been waiting long.

'No, only a couple of minutes,' said Pete, and put his arm around her waist before turning back to Florentyna. 'I'm afraid you'll just have to get in line. But perhaps your time will come,' he said, laughing. 'In any case, I think Crosby's a square. Bix Beiderbecke is my man.'

As they walked away, Florentyna could hear him telling the blonde, 'That was the girl who sent me the note.' The blonde looked back over her shoulder and started laughing. 'She's probably still a virgin,' Pete added.

Florentyna went to the girls' locker room and hid until everyone else had gone home, dreading that they would all laugh at her once the story had gone the rounds. She didn't sleep that night, and the next morning she studied the other girls' faces but couldn't see any signs of sniggers or stares and decided to confide in Susie Jacobson to discover if the news was out. When Florentyna had finished her story, Susie burst out laughing.

'Not you as well,' Susie said.

Florentyna felt a lot better after Susie told her how far down the line she actually was. It gave her the courage to ask Susie if she knew what a virgin was.

'I'm not certain,' said Susie. 'Why do you ask?'

'Because Pete said I was probably one.'

'Then I think I must be one as well. I once overheard Mary Alice Beckman saying it was when a boy made love to you and nine months later you had a baby. Like Miss Horton told us about elephants, but they take two years.'

'I wonder what it feels like?'

'According to all the magazines Mary Alice keeps in her locker, it's dreamy.'

'Do you know anyone who's tried?'

'Margie McCormick claims she has.'

'She would claim anything, and if she has, why hasn't she had a baby?'

'She said she took "precautions", whatever they are.'

'If it's anything like having a period, I can't believe it's worth all the trouble,' said Florentyna.

'Agreed,' said Susie. 'I got mine again yesterday. Do you think men have the same problem?'

'Not a chance,' said Florentyna. 'They always end up with the best of every deal. Obviously we get the periods and the babies and they get shaving and the draft, but I shall have to ask Miss Tredgold about that.'

'I'm not sure she'll know,' said Susie.

'Miss Tredgold,' said Florentyna sounding confident, 'knows everything.'

That evening when Miss Tredgold was approached by a puzzled Florentyna, she did not hesitate to sit the child down and explain the birth process to her in the fullest details, warning her of the consequences of a rash desire to experiment. Florentyna sat and listened to Miss Tredgold in silence. When she had finished Florentyna asked, 'Then why is so much fuss made about the whole thing?'

'Modern society and loose morals make a lot of demands on girls, but always remember that each of us makes our own decision as to what others think of us and, more importantly, what we think of ourselves.'

'She *did* know all about becoming pregnant and having babies,' Florentyna said to Susie the next day with great authority.

'Does that mean you're going to remain a virgin?' asked Susie.

'Oh, yes,' said Florentyna. 'Miss Tredgold is still one.'

'But what about "precautions"?' demanded Susie.

'You don't need them if you remain a virgin,' Florentyna said, passing on her newly acquired knowledge.

The only other event of importance that year for Florentyna was her confirmation. Although Father O'Reilly, a young priest from the Holy Name Cathedral, officially instructed her, Miss Tredgold, resolutely suppressing the Church of England tenets of her youth, studied the Roman Catholic 'Orders in Confirmation' and took Florentyna painstakingly through her preparation, leaving her in no doubt of the obligations that her promises to our dear Lord brought upon her. The Roman Catholic Archbishop of Chicago, assisted by Father O'Reilly, administered the confirmation, and both Abel and Zaphia attended the service. Their divorce having been completed, they sat in separate pews.

Florentyna wore a simple white dress with a high neck, the hem falling a few inches below the knee. She had made the dress herself, with – when she was asleep – a little help from Miss Tredgold. The original design had come from a photograph in *Paris Match* of a dress worn by Princess Elizabeth. Miss Tredgold had brushed Florentyna's long dark hair for over an hour until it shone. She even allowed it to fall to her shoulders. Although she was only thirteen, the young confirmand looked stunning.

'My goddaughter is beautiful,' said George as he stood next to Abel in the front pew of the church.

'I know,' said Abel.

'No, I'm serious,' said George. 'Very soon there is going to be a line of men banging on the Baron's castle door demanding the hand of his only daughter.'

'As long as she's happy, I don't mind who she marries.'

After the service was over the family had a celebration dinner in Abel's private rooms at the Baron. Florentyna received gifts from her family and friends, including a beautiful leather-bound version of the Douai Bible from Miss Tredgold, but the present she treasured most was the one her father had kept safely until he felt she was old enough to appreciate it, the antique ring that had been given to Florentyna on her christening by the man who had put his faith in Papa and backed the Baron Group.

'I must write and thank him,' said Florentyna.

'You can't, my dear, as I am not certain who he is. I honoured my part of the bargain long ago, so now I will probably never discover his true identity.'

She slipped the antique ring on to the third finger of her left hand and throughout the rest of the day her eyes returned again and again to the sparkling little emeralds.

8

'How will you be voting in the Presidential election, madam?' asked the smartly dressed young man.

'I shall not be voting,' said Miss Tredgold, continuing down the street.

'Shall I put you down as "Don't know"?' said the man, running to keep up with her.

'Most certainly not,' said Miss Tredgold. 'I made no such suggestion.'

'Am I to understand you don't wish to state your preference?'

'I am quite happy to state my preference, young man, but as I come from Much Hadham in England it is unlikely to influence either Mr Truman or Mr Dewey.'

The man conducting the Gallup Poll retreated, but Florentyna watched him carefully because she had read somewhere that the results of such polls were now being taken seriously by all leading politicians.

It was 1948, and America was in the middle of another election campaign. Unlike the Olympics, the race for the White House was re-run every four years, war or peace. Florentyna remained loyal to the democrats but did not see how President Truman could possibly hold on to the White House after two such unpopular years as President. The Republican candidate, Thomas E. Dewey, had a lead of over eight per cent in the latest Gallup Poll and looked certain of victory.

Florentyna followed both campaigns closely and was delighted when Margaret Chase Smith beat three men to be chosen as the Republican Senatorial candidate for Maine. For the first time, the American people were able to follow the election on television. Abel had installed an RCA set at Rigg Street only months before he departed, but during term time Miss Tredgold would not allow Florentyna to watch 'that new-fangled machine' for more than one hour a day. 'It can never be a substitute for the written word,' she declared. 'I agree with Professor Chester L. Dawes of Harvard,' she added. 'Too many instant decisions will be made in front of the cameras that will later be regretted.'

Although she did not fully agree with Miss Tredgold's sentiments at the time, Florentyna selected her hour carefully, always choosing the CBS evening news, during which Douglas Edwards would give the campaign round-up, over Ed Sullivan's more popular 'Toast of the Town'. However, she still found time to listen to Ed Murrow on the radio. After all his broadcasts from London during the war, she, like so many other millions of Americans, remained loyal to his every word. She felt it was the least she could do.

During the summer vacation Florentyna parked herself in Congressman Osborne's campaign headquarters and, along with scores of other volunteers of assorted ages and ability, filled envelopes with 'A Message from your Congressman' and a bumper sticker that said in bold print 'Re-elect Osborne'. She and a pale, angular youth who never proffered any opinions would then lick the flap of each envelope and place it on a pile according to district, for hand delivery by another helper. By the end of each day her mouth and lips were covered in gum and she would return home feeling thirsty and sick.

One Thursday the receptionist in charge of the telephone inquiries asked if Florentyna could take her place while she took a break for lunch.

'Of course,' said Florentyna with tremendous excitement, and jumped into the vacated seat before the pale youth could volunteer.

'There shouldn't be any problems,' the receptionist said. 'Just say Congressman Osborne's office, and if you're not sure of anything, look it up in the campaign handbook. Everything you need to know is in there,' she added, pointing to the thick booklet by the side of the phone.

'I'll be just fine,' said Florentyna.

She sat in the exalted chair, staring at the phone, willing it to ring. She didn't have to wait long. The first caller was a man who wanted to know where he voted. That's a strange question, thought Florentyna.

'At the polls,' she said, a little pertly.

'Sure, I know that, you stupid bitch,' came back the reply. 'But where is my polling place?'

Florentyna was speechless for a moment, and then asked, very politely, where he lived.

'In the Seventh Precinct.'

Florentyna flicked through her guide. 'You should vote at Saint Chrysostom's Church on Dearborn Steeet.'

'Where's that?'

Florentyna studied the map. 'The church is located five blocks from the lake shore and fifteen blocks north of the Loop.' The phone clicked and immediately rang again.

'Is that Osborne's headquarters?'

'Yes, sir,' said Florentyna.

'Well, you can tell that lazy bastard I wouldn't vote for him if he was the only candidate alive.' The phone clicked again and Florentyna felt queasier than she had been when she was licking envelopes. She let the bell ring three times before she could summon up the courage to lift the receiver to answer.

'Hello,' she said nervously. 'This is Congressman Osborne's headquarters. Miss Rosnovski speaking.'

'Hello, my dear, my name is Daisy Bishop, and I will need a car to take my husband to the polls on election day because he lost both his legs in the last war.'

'Oh, I'm so sorry,' said Florentyna.

'Don't worry yourself, young lady. We wouldn't let wonderful Mr Roosevelt down.'

'But Mr Roosevelt is . . . Yes, of course you wouldn't. Can I please take down your telephone number and address?'

'Mr and Mrs Bishop, 653 West Buena Street, MA4–4816.'

'We will phone you on election morning to let you know what time the car will pick you up. Thank you for supporting the Democratic ticket, Mrs Bishop,' said Florentyna.

'We always do, my dear. Goodbye and good luck.'

'Goodbye,' said Florentyna, who took a deep breath and felt a little better. She wrote down a '2' in brackets – after the Bishops' name and placed the note in the file marked 'Transportation for Election Day'. Then she waited for the next call.

It was some minutes before the phone sounded again and by then Florentyna had fully regained her confidence.

'Good morning, is this the Osborne office?'

'Yes, sir,' said Florentyna.

'My name is Melvin Crudick and I want to know Congressman Osborne's views on the Marshall Plan.'

'The what plan?' said Florentyna.

'The Marshall Plan,' enunciated the voice authoritatively.

Florentyna frantically flipped the pages of the campaign handbook that she had been promised would reveal everything.

'Are you still there?' barked the voice.

'Yes, sir,' said Florentyna. 'I just wanted to be sure you were given a full and detailed answer on the Congressman's views. If you would be kind enough to wait one moment.'

At last Florentyna found the Marshall Plan and read through Henry Osborne's words on the subject.

'Hello, sir.'

'Yes,' said the voice, and Florentyna started to read it out loud.

'"Congressman Osborne approves of the Marshall Plan."' There was a long silence.

'Yes, I know he does,' said the voice from the other end.

Florentyna felt weak. 'Yes, he does support the plan,' she repeated.

'*Why* does he?' said the voice.

'Because it will benefit everyone in his district,' said Florentyna firmly, feeling rather pleased with herself.

'Pray tell me, how can giving six billion American dollars to Europe help the Ninth District of Illinois?' Florentyna could feel the perspiration on her forehead. 'Miss, you may inform your Congressman that because of your personal incompetence I shall be voting Republican on this occasion.'

Florentyna put the phone down and was considering running out of the door when the receptionist returned from her lunch. Florentyna did not know what to tell her.

'Anything interesting?' the girl asked as she resumed her place. 'Or was it the usual mixture of weirdos, perverts and cranks who have got nothing better to do with their lunch break?'

'Nothing special,' said Florentyna, nervously, 'except I think I've lost the vote of a Mr Crudick.'

'Not Mad Mel again? What was it this time, the House Un-American Activities Committee, the Marshall Plan or the slums of Chicago?'

Florentyna returned happily to licking envelopes.

.   .   .

On election day, Florentyna arrived at campaign headquarters at eight o'clock in the morning and spent the day telephoning registered Democrats to be sure they had voted. 'Never forget,' said Henry Osborne in his final pep talk to his voluntary helpers, 'no man has ever lived in the White House who hasn't carried Illinois.'

Florentyna felt very proud to think she was helping to elect a President and didn't take a break all day. At eight o'clock that evening, Miss Tredgold came to collect her. She had worked twelve hours without a rest, but never once did she stop talking all the way home.

'Do you think Mr Truman will win?' she asked finally.

'Only if he gets more than fifty per cent of the votes cast,' said Miss Tredgold.

'Wrong,' said Florentyna. 'It is possible to win a Presidential election in the United States by winning more electoral college votes than your opponent while failing to secure a majority of the plebiscite.' She then proceeded to give Miss Tredgold a brief lesson on how the American political system worked.

'Such a thing would never have happened if only dear George III had known where America was,' said Miss Tredgold. 'And I daily become aware that it will not be long before you have no further need of me, child.'

It was the first time Florentyna had ever considered that Miss Tredgold would not spend the rest of her life with her.

When they reached home, Florentyna sat down in her father's old chair to watch the early returns, but she was so tired that she dozed off in front of the fire. She, like most of America, went to sleep believing that Thomas Dewey had won the election. When Florentyna woke the next morning, she dashed downstairs to fetch the *Tribune*. Her fears were confirmed: 'Dewey Defeats Truman' ran the headline, and it took half an hour of radio bulletins and confirmation by her mother before Florentyna believed that Truman had been returned to the White House. An eleven o'clock decision had been made by the night editor of the *Tribune* to run a headline that he would not live down for the rest of his life. At least he had been right about Henry Osborne being returned to Congress for a sixth term.

.   .   .

When Florentyna went back to Girls Latin the next day, her home-room teacher called for her and made it quite clear that the election was now over and that the time had come to settle down and do some serious studying. Miss Tredgold agreed, and Florentyna worked with the same enthusiasm for her school exams as she had for President Truman.

During the year, she made the junior varsity hockey team, in which she played right wing without distinction and even managed to squeeze into the school's third tennis VI on one occasion. When the summer term was drawing to a close all the pupils received a note reminding them that if they wished to run for the Student Council their names must be sent to the headmaster of Boys Latin by the first Monday of the new school year. There were six representatives on the Council elected from both schools, and no one could remember a year when they had not all come from the twelfth grade. Nevertheless many of Florentyna's classmates suggested that she should allow her name to be put forward. Edward Winchester, who had years before given up trying to beat Florentyna at anything except arm wrestling, volunteered to help her.

'But anyone who helps me would have to be talented, good looking, popular and charismatic,' she teased.

'For once I agree with you,' said Edward. 'Any fool taking on such a cause will need every advantage possible to overcome the problem of their candidate being stupid, ugly, unapproachable and dull.'

'In which case it might be wise for me to wait another year.'

'Never,' said Edward. 'I can see no hope of improvement in such a short time. In any case, I want you on the council this year.'

'Why?'

'Because if you're the only eleventh grade student elected you'll be a near cert for President next year.'

'Really thought the whole thing through, haven't you?'

'And I would be willing to bet everything in my piggy bank that you have too.'

'Perhaps . . .' said Florentyna quietly.

'Perhaps?'

'Perhaps I'll consider running for the Student Council a year earlier.'

·   ·   ·

During the summer vacation, which Florentyna spent with her father at the New York Baron, she noticed that many of the big department stores now had millinery departments and wondered why there were not more shops specializing only in clothes. She spent hours in Best's, Saks and in Bonwit Teller's where she bought herself her first strapless evening dress – observing the different customers and comparing their individual preferences with those of shoppers who frequented Bloomingdale's, Altman's and Macy's. In the evening over dinner she would regale her father with all the knowledge she had acquired that day. Abel was so impressed by the speed with which Florentyna assimilated new facts that he began to explain to her in some detail how the Baron Group worked. By the end of her holiday, he was delighted with how much she had picked up about stock control, cash flow, advance reservations, the Employment Act of 1940, and even the cost of eight thousand fresh bread rolls. He warned George that his job as managing director of the group might be in jeopardy in the not-too-distant future.

'I don't think it's my job she's after, Abel.'

'No?' said Abel.

'No,' said George. 'It's yours.'

Abel took Florentyna to the airport on the final day of her holiday and presented her with a black-and-white Polaroid camera.

'Papa, what a fantastic present. Won't I be the neatest thing at school?'

'It's a bribe,' said Abel.

'A bribe?'

'Yes. George tells me you want to be Chairman of the Baron Group.'

'I think I'll start with the Student Council,' said Florentyna.

Abel laughed. 'Make sure you win a *place* on the Council first,' he said, then kissed his daughter on the cheek and waved goodbye as she disappeared up the steps of the waiting plane.

.   .   .

'I've decided to run.'

'Good,' said Edward. 'I have already compiled a list of every student in both schools. You must put a tick by all those who you feel are certain to support you and a cross by those who won't, so that I can work on the don't knows and firm up the backing of your supporters.'

'Very professional. How many people are running?'

'So far fifteen candidates for six places. There are four candidates you can't hope to beat, but it will be a close contest after that. I thought you'd be interested to know that Pete Welling is running.'

'That creep,' said Florentyna.

'Oh, I was led to believe that you were hopelessly in love with him.'

'Don't be so ridiculous, Edward, he's a sap. Let's go through the school lists.'

The election was due to take place at the end of the second week of the new school year, so the candidates had only ten days to gather votes. Many of Florentyna's friends dropped in at Rigg Street to assure her of their support. She was surprised to find some support where she least expected it, while other classmates whom she imagined were friends told Edward they would never back her. Florentyna discussed this problem with Miss Tredgold who warned her that if you ever run for any office which might bring you privilege or profit, it will always be your contemporaries who do not want to see you succeed in your ambitions. You need have no fear of those who are older or younger than yourself; they know you will never be their rival.

All the candidates had to write a mini-election address setting out the reason they wanted to be on the Student Council. Florentyna's was checked over by Abel, who refused to add or subtract anything, and by Miss Tredgold, who only commented on the grammar.

Voting was all day Friday at the end of the second week and the result was always announced by the headmaster after assembly the following Monday morning. It was a terrible weekend for Florentyna, and Miss Tredgold spent the entire time saying, 'Settle down, child.' Even Edward, who played tennis with her on Sunday afternoon, hardly raised a sweat, winning 6–0, 6–0.

'It wouldn't take Jack Kramer to tell you that you're not concentrating – "child".'

'Oh, do be quiet, Edward. I don't care whether I'm elected to the Student Council or not.'

Florentyna woke up at five o'clock on Monday morning and was dressed and ready for breakfast by six. She read the paper through three times from cover to cover and Miss Tredgold did not utter a word to her until it was time to leave for school.

'Remember, my dear, that Lincoln lost more elections than he won but still became President.'

'Yes, but I'd like to start out with a win,' said Florentyna.

The assembly hall was packed by nine o'clock. Morning prayers and the headmaster's announcements seemed to take for ever; Florentyna's eyes stared at the floor.

'And now I shall read the results of the Student Council election,' said the headmaster. 'There were fifteen candidates and six have been elected to the Council:

1st	Jason Morton (President)	109
2nd	Cathy Long	87
3rd	Roger Dingle	85
4th	Eddie Bell	81
5th	Jonathan Lloyd	79

The headmaster coughed and the room remained silent. 'Sixth Florentyna Rosnovski with seventy-six votes. The runner-up was Pete Welling with seventy-five votes. The first Council meeting will be in my office at ten thirty this morning. Assembly dismissed.'

Florentyna was overwhelmed and threw her arms around Edward.

'Don't forget – President next year.'

At the first Council meeting that morning, Florentyna, as junior member, was appointed Secretary.

'That will teach you to come in last,' laughed the new President, Jason Morton.

Back to writing notes that nobody else reads, thought Florentyna. But at least this time I can type them and perhaps next year I will be President. She looked up at the boy whose thin, sensitive face and seemingly shy manner had won him so many votes.

'Now privileges,' said Jason briskly, unaware of her gaze. 'The President is allowed to drive a car, while on one day a week the girls can wear pastel-coloured shirts and the boys can wear loafers instead of Oxfords. Council members are allowed to sign out of study hall when involved in school responsibilities and they can award demerits to any pupil who breaks a school rule.'

So that's what I fought so hard for, thought Florentyna, the chance to wear a pastel-coloured shirt and award demerits.

When she returned home that night Florentyna told Miss Tredgold every detail of what had happened, and she glowed with pride as she repeated the full result along with her new responsibilities.

'Who is poor Peter Welling,' inquired Miss Tredgold, 'who failed to be elected by only one vote?'

'Serves him right,' said Florentyna. 'Do you know what I said to that creep when I passed him in the corridor?'

'No, I'm sure I don't,' said Miss Tredgold apprehensively.

'"Now *you'll* have to get in line, but perhaps your time will come,"' she said, and burst out laughing.

'That was unworthy of you, Florentyna, and indeed of me. Be sure you never in your life express such an opinion again. The hour of triumph is not a time to belittle your rivals, rather it is a time to be magnanimous.'

Miss Tredgold rose from her seat and retired to her room.

. . .

When Florentyna went to lunch the next day, Jason Morton took the seat next to her. 'We're going to see a lot of each other now that you've been elected to the Student Council,' he said and smiled. Florentyna didn't smile back because Jason had the same reputation among the pupils of Girls Latin as Pete Welling, and she was determined not to make a fool of herself a second time.

Over lunch, they discussed the problem of the school orchestra's trip to Boston and what to do about the number of boys who had been caught smoking. Student councillors were limited in the punishments they were allowed to impose, and study hall detention on Saturday morning was about the most extreme terror they could evoke. Jason told Florentyna that if they went so far as to report the smokers to the headmaster, it would undoubtedly mean expulsion for the students involved. A dilemma had arisen among the councillors because no one feared Saturday's detention and equally no one believed they ever would be reported to the headmaster.

'If we allow the smoking to go on,' said Jason, 'very soon we will have no authority at all, unless we're determined to make a positive stand in full Council right from the beginning.'

Florentyna agreed with him and was surprised by his next question.

'Would you be up to a game of tennis on Saturday afternoon?'

Florentyna remained silent for a moment. 'Yes,' she said, trying to sound casual as she remembered that he was captain of the tennis team and her backhand was awful.

'Good, I'll pick you up at three o'clock. Will that be okay?'

'Fine,' said Florentyna, hoping she still sounded uninterested.

. . .

'That tennis dress is far too short,' said Miss Tredgold.

'I know,' said Florentyna, 'but it's last year's, and I've grown since then.'

'With whom are you playing?'

'Jason Morton.'

'You really cannot play tennis in a dress like that with a young man.'

'It's either this or the nude,' said Florentyna.

'Don't be cheeky with me, child. I shall allow you to wear the garment on this occasion, but be assured I shall have acquired a new dress for you by Monday afternoon.'

The front doorbell rang. 'He seems to have arrived,' said Miss Tredgold.

Florentyna picked up her racket and ran to the door.

'Don't run, child. Let the young man wait a little. We can't have him knowing how you feel about him, can we?'

Florentyna blushed, tied back her long dark hair with a ribbon and walked slowly to the front door.

'Hi, Jason,' she said, her voice casual again. 'Won't you come in?'

Jason, who was dressed in a smart tennis outfit that looked as if it had been purchased that morning, couldn't take his eyes off Florentyna. 'What a dress,' he ventured, and was about to say more when he saw Miss Tredgold leaving the room. He hadn't realized until that moment what a good figure Florentyna had. The moment he set eyes on Miss Tredgold he knew why he had never been allowed to find out.

'It's last year's, I'm afraid,' continued Florentyna, looking down at her slim legs. 'It's awful, isn't it?'

'No, I think it's swell. Come on, I've reserved a court for three thirty and someone else will grab it if we're a minute late.'

'Good heavens,' said Florentyna as she closed the front door. 'Is that yours?'

'Yes. Don't you think it's fantastic?'

'I would say, if asked to venture an opinion, that it had seen better days.'

'Oh, really,' said Jason. 'I thought it was rather snazzy.'

'If I knew what the word meant I might be able to agree with you. Pray, sir,' she said mockingly, 'am I expected to ride in that machine or help push it?'

'That is a genuine pre-war Packard.'

'Then it deserves an early burial,' said Florentyna as she took her seat in the front, suddenly realizing how much of her legs were showing.

'Has anyone taught you how to propel this lump of metal in a forward direction?' she inquired sweetly.

'No, not exactly,' said Jason.

'What?' said Florentyna in disbelief.

'I'm told driving is mostly common sense.'

Florentyna pushed down the handle of her door, opening it slightly, as if to get out. Jason put his hand on her thigh.

'Don't be silly, Tyna. I was taught by my father and I've been driving for nearly a year.'

Florentyna blushed, closed the door again and had to admit to herself that he drove rather well all the way to the tennis club even if the car did rattle and bump a little as it went over the holes in the road.

The tennis match was a desperate affair for Florentyna trying hard to win a point while Jason tried hard to lose one. Somehow Jason managed to win by only 6–2, 6–1.

'What I need is a Coke,' he said at the end of the match.

'What I need is a coach,' said Florentyna.

He laughed and took her hand as they left the court, and even though she felt sweaty and hot, he did not let her hand go until they reached the bar at the back of the club house. He bought one Coke and they sat drinking it from two straws in the corner of the room. When they had finished, Jason drove her home. On reaching Rigg Street, he leaned over and kissed her on the lips. Florentyna did not respond, more out of shock than for any other reason.

'Why don't you come to the movies with me tonight?' he said. '*On the Town* is showing at the United Artists Theatre.'

'Well, I normally ... Yes, I'd like that,' said Florentyna.

'Good, then I'll pick you up at seven.'

Florentyna watched the car as it chugged away, and tried to think of some reason that would persuade her mother she had to be out that evening. She found Miss Tredgold preparing tea in the kitchen.

'A good game, child?' asked Miss Tredgold.

'Not for him, I'm afraid. By the way he wants to take me to' – she hesitated – 'to Orchestra Hall for a concert this evening so I won't need any dinner.'

'How nice,' said Miss Tredgold. 'Be sure you're back before eleven or your mother will worry.'

Florentyna ran upstairs, sat on the end of the bed and started to think about what she could possibly wear that evening, how awful her hair looked and whether she could steal some of her mother's make-up. She stood in front of the mirror wondering how she could make her breasts look bigger without holding her breath all night.

At seven o'clock Jason returned dressed in a red sloppy Joe sweater and khakis and was met at the door by Miss Tredgold.

'How do you do, young man.'

'How do you do, ma'am,' said Jason.

'Would you like to come into the drawing room?'

'Thank you,' said Jason.

'And what is the concert you're taking Florentyna to?'

'The concert?'

'Yes, I wondered who was playing,' said Miss Tredgold. 'I read a good review of Beethoven's Third in the morning paper.'

'Oh, yeah, Beethoven's Third,' said Jason, as Florentyna appeared on the stairs. Both Miss Tredgold and Jason were stunned. One approved while the other didn't. Florentyna was wearing a green dress that fell just below the knee and revealed the sheerest nylon stockings with dark seams down the back. She walked slowly down the stairs, her long legs unsteady in high-heeled shoes, her small breasts looking larger than usual, her dark shining hair hanging down on her shoulders, reminiscent of Jennifer Jones and making Florentyna appear a lot older than her fifteen years. The only item she wore to which Miss Tredgold could take no exception was the watch she herself had given to Florentyna on her thirteenth birthday.

'Come on, Jason, or we'll be late,' said Florentyna, wanting to avoid any conversation with Miss Tredgold.

'Sure thing,' said Jason. Florentyna did not look back once for fear of being turned into a pillar of salt.

'Be sure she's home before eleven, young man,' commanded Miss Tredgold.

'Sure thing,' repeated Jason as he closed the front door. 'Where did you find her?'

'Miss Tredgold?'

'Yes, she's straight out of a Victorian novel. "Be sure she's home before eleven, young man,"' he mimicked as he opened the car door for her.

'Don't be rude,' said Florentyna, and smiled at him coquettishly.

There was a long line outside the theatre and Florentyna spent most of the time standing beside Jason facing the wall, fearing someone might recognize her. Once inside Jason quickly guided her to the back row with an air of having been there before.

She took her seat and when the lights went down she began to relax for the first time – but not for long. Jason leaned over, put his hand around her shoulder and started kissing her. She began to enjoy the sensation as he forced her lips open and their tongues touched for the first time. Then he broke away and they watched the titles go up on the screen. Florentyna liked Gene Kelly. Jason leaned over again and pressed his mouth against hers. Her lips parted. Almost immediately she felt a hand on her breast. She tried to remove his fingers but once again his backhand was too strong for her. After a few seconds she came up for air and took a quick look at the Statue of Liberty before Jason returned with his other hand and fondled her other breast. This time she managed to push him away but for only a few moments. Annoyed, he took out a packet of Camels and lit one. Florentyna couldn't believe what was happening. After a few puffs he stubbed the cigarette out and placed a hand between her legs. In near panic she stopped any further advance by squeezing her thighs closely together.

'Oh, come on,' said Jason. 'Don't be such a prude or you'll end up like Miss Tredgold,' and he bent over to kiss her once again.

'For heaven's sake, Jason, let's watch the movie.'

'Don't be silly. No one goes to a movie house to watch a film.' He put his hand back on her leg. 'Don't tell me you haven't done it before. Hell, you're nearly sixteen. What are you hoping to be? The oldest virgin in Chicago?'

Florentyna jumped up and pushed her way out, stumbling over several pairs of feet before she reached the aisle. Without straightening her dress she ran out of the theatre as fast as she could. Once outside, she attempted to run, but couldn't manage much more than walking pace in her mother's high heels, so she took the shoes off and ran in her stockinged feet. When she reached the front door of her house she tried to compose herself, hoping she could get up to her room without bumping into Miss Tredgold, but she failed. Miss Tredgold's bedroom door was ajar and as Florentyna tiptoed past, she said, 'Concert over early, my dear?'

'Yes ... no ... I mean I didn't feel very well,' said Florentyna, and she ran into her own room before Miss Tredgold could ask any more questions. She went to bed that night still trembling.

She woke early the next morning and although still angry with Jason she found herself laughing at what had taken place and even determined to go and see the film again, on her own this time. She liked Gene Kelly, but it was the first time she had seen her *real* idol on the screen, and she couldn't get over how skinny and vulnerable he looked.

At Student Council the next day, Florentyna could not make herself look at Jason while he was stating in a quiet firm voice that some senior boys who were not members of Council were becoming casual about their dress. He also added that the next person caught smoking would have to be reported to the headmaster or his own reputation as President would be undermined. Everyone except Florentyna nodded their agreement.

'Good, then I'll put a notice on the bulletin board to that effect.'

As soon as the meeting was over, Florentyna slipped off to class before anyone could speak to her. She finished her homework late that evening and did not set off for Rigg Street until a few minutes after six o'clock. As she reached the main school door, it started to rain and she remained under the archway hoping the storm would blow over quickly. As she stood there, Jason walked straight past her with a girl from twelfth grade. She watched them climb into his car and she bit her lip. The rain came down harder, so she decided to return to her classroom and type up the minutes of the Student Council meeting. On her way back into school she passed a small crowd studying a notice on the board confirming the Council's attitude to sloppy dress and smoking.

Florentyna took about an hour to complete the minutes of the Council meeting, partly because her mind wandered continually back to Jason's double standards. The rain had stopped by the time she had finished her typing and she closed her typewriter case and placed the minutes in the top drawer. As she walked back down the corridor, she thought she heard a noise coming from the boys' locker room. No one except members of Student Council was allowed to remain in school after seven o'clock without special permission so she turned back to see who it was. When she was a few yards away from the locker room the light under the door went off. She walked over and opened the door and switched the light back on. It was some time before Florentyna focused on the figure standing in the corner, trying to hide a cigarette behind his back, but he knew she had seen it.

'Pete,' she said in surprise.

'Well, Miss Student Councillor, you've caught me once and for all. Two major offences in one day. In school after hours, and smoking. Bang goes my chance of making Harvard,' Pete Welling said as he ground out the cigarette on the stone floor. The vision returned of the Student Council President stubbing out his cigarette the night before in the back of an unlit cinema.

'Jason Morton is hoping to go to Harvard, isn't he?'

'Yes. What's that got to do with it?' said Pete. 'Nothing will stop him making the Ivy League.'

'I just remembered. No girl is allowed in the boys' locker room at any time.'

'Yes, but you're a member of ...'

'Goodnight, Pete.'

.   .   .

Florentyna began to enjoy her new authority and took her duties and responsibilities on the Student Council very seriously, so much so that as the year passed Miss Tredgold feared Florentyna's studies were suffering because of it. She did not comment on the matter to Mrs Rosnovski, rather she considered it her duty to find a solution. She hoped that Florentyna's attitude might be nothing more than an adolescent phase of misplaced enthusiasm. Even Miss Tredgold, despite past experience of these problems, was surprised by how quickly Florentyna had changed since being entrusted with a little power.

By the middle of the second term Miss Tredgold realized the problem was past that stage and fast becoming out of control. Florentyna was beginning to take herself, and not her work, far too seriously. Her end-of-term report was far from good by her normal high standards, and Florentyna's home-room teacher more than hinted that she was becoming high-handed with some of the other students and giving out demerits a little too freely.

Miss Tredgold could not help noticing that Florentyna had not been receiving as many invitations to parties as she had in the past and her old friends did not seem to visit Rigg Street quite so frequently, except for the loyal Edward Winchester ... Miss Tredgold liked that boy.

Matters did not improve during the summer term and Florentyna began to be evasive when Miss Tredgold broached the subject of uncompleted homework. Zaphia, who had compensated for the loss of a husband by gaining ten pounds, was uncooperative. 'I haven't noticed anything unusual,' was her only comment when Miss Tredgold tried to discuss the problem.

Miss Tredgold pursed her lips and began to despair when one morning at breakfast Florentyna was downright rude when asked what she had planned to do for the weekend.

'I'll let you know if it concerns you,' she said without looking up from *Vogue*. Mrs Rosnovski showed no sign of noticing, so Miss Tredgold maintained a stony silence, judging that sooner or later the child was bound to come a cropper.

It came sooner.

9

'There's no reason for you to be that confident,' said Edward.

'Why? Who's going to beat me? I've been on the Council for nearly a year and everyone else on it is graduating,' said Florentyna, lounging back in one of the horsehair chairs reserved for members of the Student Council.

Edward remained standing. 'Yes, I realize that, but not everyone likes you.'

'What do you mean?'

'A lot of people think that since you've been on the Council you've become a bit too big for your boots.'

'I hope you're not among them, Edward.'

'No, I'm not. But I am worried that if you don't bother to mix a little more with the students in the lower grades you might be beaten.'

'Don't be silly. Why should I bother to get to know them when they already know me?' she asked, fiddling with some papers on the arm of her chair.

'What's come over you, Florentyna? You didn't act like this a year ago,' said Edward, looking down.

'If you don't like the way I carry out my duties, go and support someone else.'

'It has nothing to do with the way you carry out your duties – everyone acknowledges you've been the best Secretary anyone can remember – but different qualities are needed for President.'

'Thank you for the advice, Edward, but you will discover that I can survive without it.'

'Then you won't want me to help you this year?'

'Edward, you still haven't got the message. It's not a case of not wanting you but simply not needing you.'

'I wish you luck, Florentyna, and I only hope I'm proved wrong.'

'I don't need your luck either. Some things in this life depend on ability.'

Florentyna did not repeat this conversation to Miss Tredgold.

.   .   .

At the end of the academic year, Florentyna was surprised to find that she had finished first in only Latin and French, and overall had fallen to third in the class. Miss Tredgold read her school report carefully and it confirmed her worst fears, but she concluded there was no point in making any adverse comment to the child as she had stopped taking anyone's advice unless it confirmed her own opinions. Once again, Florentyna spent the summer vacation in New York with her father, who allowed her to work as an assistant in one of the hotel shops.

Florentyna rose early each morning and dressed in the pastel green uniform of a junior member of the hotel staff. She threw all her energy into learning how the little fashion shop was run and was soon putting forward new ideas to Miss Parker, the manageress, who was impressed – and not just because she was the Baron's daughter. As the days passed, Florentyna gained more confidence and, conscious of the power of her privileged position, she stopped wearing the shop uniform and even started to order some of the junior sales staff around. She was, however, sufficiently cautious never to do this in front of Miss Parker.

One Friday, when Miss Parker was in her office checking the morning's petty cash, Jessie Kovats, a junior sales assistant, arrived ten minutes late. Florentyna was standing at the door waiting for her.

'You're late again,' said Florentyna, but Jessie didn't bother to reply.

'Did you hear me, Miss Kovats?' demanded Florentyna.

'Sure did,' said Jessie, hanging up her raincoat.

'Then what is your excuse this time?'

'For you, I don't have to have an excuse.'

'We'll see about that,' said Florentyna, starting off towards Miss Parker's office.

'Don't bother yourself, bossy boots, I've had enough of you in any case,' said Jessie, who walked into Miss Parker's office and closed the door behind her. Florentyna pretended to tidy the counter while she waited for Jessie to return. A few minutes later the young assistant came out of the office, put her coat back on and left the shop without another word. Florentyna felt pleased with the result of her admonition. A few minutes later Miss Parker came out of her office.

'Jessie tells me she's leaving the shop because of you.'

'Miss Kovats is hardly a great loss,' volunteered Florentyna. 'She didn't exactly pull her weight.'

'That is not the point, Florentyna. I have to continue to run this shop after you return to school.'

'Perhaps by then we shall have weeded out the Jessie Kovats of this world who shouldn't, after all, be wasting my father's time and money.'

'Miss Rosnovski, this is a team. Not everyone can be clever and bright, or even hard-working, but within their limited abilities they do the best they can, and there have been no complaints in the past.'

'Could that possibly be because my father is too busy to keep a watchful eye on you, Miss Parker?'

Miss Parker visibly flushed and steadied herself on the counter. 'I think the time has come for you to work in another of your father's shops. I have served him for nearly twenty years and he has never once spoken to me in such a discourteous way.'

'Perhaps the time has come for *you* to work in another shop,' said Florentyna, 'and preferably not my father's.' Walking out of the front door, she made straight for the hotel's private elevator and pressed the button marked forty-two. On arrival, Florentyna informed her father's secretary that she needed to speak to him immediately.

'He's chairing a board meeting at the moment, Miss Rosnovski.'

'Then interrupt him and tell him that I wish to see him.'

The secretary hesitated, then buzzed through to Mr Rosnovski.

'I thought I told you not to disturb me, Miss Deneroff.'

'I apologize, sir, but your daughter is here and insists on seeing you.'

There was a pause. 'All right, send her in.'

'I am sorry, Papa, but this is something that can't wait,' Florentyna said as she entered the room, feeling suddenly less sure of herself as the eight men around the board-room table rose. Abel guided her through to his own office.

'Well, what is it that can't wait, my darling?'

'It's Miss Parker. She's stuffy, incompetent and stupid,' said Florentyna, and she poured out to her father her version of what had happened that morning with Jessie Kovats.

Abel's fingers never stopped tapping on the desk top as he listened to her tale. When she came to the end he flicked a switch on his intercom. 'Please ask Miss Parker in the fashion shop to come up immediately.'

'Thank you, Papa.'

'Florentyna, would you be kind enough to wait next door while I deal with Miss Parker.'

'Of course, Papa.'

A few minutes later, Miss Parker appeared, still looking flushed. Abel asked her what had happened. She gave an accurate account of the altercation, confining her view of Florentyna to the fact that she was a competent assistant but had been the sole reason that Miss Kovats, a long-serving member of her staff, had left. Others, Miss Parker pointed out, might leave too if Florentyna persisted with her attitude. Abel listened, barely controlling his anger. He gave Miss Parker his opinion and told her she would receive a letter by hand confirming his decision.

'If that is what you wish, sir,' said Miss Parker, and left.

Abel buzzed his secretary. 'Would you please ask my daughter to come back in, Miss Deneroff.'

Florentyna strode in. 'Did you tell Miss Parker what you thought, Papa?'

'Yes, I did.'

'She'll find it hard to get another job.'

'She won't need to.'

'Won't need to?'

'No, I gave her a raise and extended her contract,' he said, leaning forward and placing both hands firmly on his desk. 'If you ever treat a member of my staff that way again, I'll put you over my knee and thrash you, and it won't be a gentle tap with a hairbrush. Jessie Kovats has already left because of your insufferable behaviour and it is obvious no one in that shop likes you.'

Florentyna stared at her father in disbelief, then burst into tears.

'And you can save your tears for someone else,' continued Abel remorselessly. 'They don't impress me. I shouldn't have to remind you that I have a company to run. Another week of you and I would have had a crisis on my hands. You will now go down to Miss Parker and apologize for your disgraceful behaviour. You will also stay away from my shops until I decide you are ready to work in them again. And that is the last time you interrupt one of my board meetings. Do you understand?'

'But, Papa –'

'No buts. You will apologize to Miss Parker immediately.'

Florentyna ran out of her father's office and returned to her room in tears, packed her bags, left her green pastel dress on the bedroom floor and took a cab to the airport. Thirty-minutes later she was back in Chicago.

On learning of her departure, Abel phoned Miss Tredgold, who listened to what had taken place with dismay but not with surprise.

.   .   .

When Florentyna arrived home, her mother was still away at a health spa trying to shed a few unwanted pounds. Only Miss Tredgold was there to greet her.

'You're back a week early, I observe.'

'Yes, I got bored with New York.'

'Don't lie, child.'

'Must you pick on me as well?' said Florentyna, and ran upstairs to her room. That weekend she locked herself in and only crept down to the kitchen at odd times for meals. Miss Tredgold made no attempt to see her.

On the first day of school Florentyna put on one of the smart pastel shirts with the new style button-down collar she had bought at Bergdorf Goodman. She knew it would make every other girl at Girls Latin jealous. She was going to show them all how a future President of the Student Council should behave. As no member of Council could be elected for two weeks, she wore a different coloured shirt every day and took upon herself the responsibilities of President. She even started to think about what type of car she would talk her father into buying for her when she had won the election. At all times she avoided Edward Winchester, who had also put his own name forward for the Council, and she laughed openly at any comments made about his popularity. On the Monday of the third week, Florentyna went to morning assembly to hear herself confirmed as the new student President.

When Miss Allen, the headmistress, had read out the full list Florentyna could not believe her ears. She had not even finished in the first six. In fact, she was only barely the runner-up, and of all people Edward Winchester had been elected President. As she left the hall, no one commiserated with her and she spent the day in a silent daze at the back of the classroom. When she returned home that night, she crept up to Miss Tredgold's room and knocked gently on the door.

'Come.'

Florentyna opened the door slowly and looked towards Miss Tredgold who was reading at her desk.

'They didn't make me President,' she said quietly. 'In fact, they didn't even elect me to the Council.'

'I know,' Miss Tredgold replied, closing her Bible.

'How can you have known?' asked Florentyna.

'Because I wouldn't have voted for you myself.' The governess paused. 'But that's an end of the matter, child.'

Florentyna ran across the room and threw her arms around Miss Tredgold, who held her tightly.

'Good, now we shall have to start rebuilding bridges. Dry your tears, my dear, and we shall begin immediately. There is no time to be lost. Pad and pencil are needed.'

Florentyna wrote down the list dictated by Miss Tredgold and did not argue with any of her instructions. That night she wrote long letters to her father, Miss Parker (enclosing another letter for Jessie Kovats), Edward Winchester, and finally, although the name was not on her list, to Miss Tredgold. The next day she went to confession with Father O'Reilly. On returning to school Florentyna helped the newly-appointed Secretary with her first minutes, showing her the system she had found worked most satisfactorily. She wished the new President luck and promised that she would help him and his Council if she was ever needed. She spent the next week answering any queries that came up from the student councillors, but never volunteered advice. When Edward met her in the corridor a few days later he told her that the Council had voted to allow her to keep all her privileges. Miss Tredgold advised her to accept the offer with courtesy but at no time to take advantage of it. Florentyna put all her New York shirts in the bottom drawer and locked them away.

A few days later the headmistress called for her. Florentyna feared it would take longer to regain her respect, however determined she was to do so. When Florentyna arrived at her study the tiny, immaculately dressed woman gave her a friendly smile and motioned to a comfortable seat by her side.

'You must have been very disappointed by the election results.'

'Yes, Miss Allen,' said Florentyna, assuming she was to receive further chastisement.

'But by all accounts you have learned greatly from the experience, and I suspect you will be wanting to make amends.'

'It's too late, Miss Allen, I leave at the end of the year and can now never be President.'

'True, true. So we must look for other mountains to climb. I retire at the end of this year having been headmistress for twenty-five years, and I confess there is little left that I wish to achieve. The boys and girls of Latin have excellent admission records to Harvard, Yale, Radcliffe and Smith and we have always been better than every school in Illinois and as good as any on the east coast. However, there is one achievement that has eluded me.'

'What's that, Miss Allen?'

'The boys have won every major scholarship to the Ivy League universities at least once, Princeton three times, but one scholarship has eluded the girls for a quarter of a century. That is the James Adams Woolson Prize Scholarship in Classics at Radcliffe. I wish to enter your name for that scholarship. Should you win the prize my cup will be full.'

'I would like to try,' said Florentyna, 'but my record lately ...'

'Indeed,' said the headmistress, 'but as Mrs Churchill pointed out to Winston when he was surprisingly beaten in an election, "that may yet turn out to be a blessing in disguise".'

'"Some disguise."' They both smiled.

That night Florentyna studied the entry form for the James Adams Woolson Prize. The scholarship was open to every girl in America between the ages of sixteen and eighteen on 1 July of that year. There were three papers, one for Latin, one for Greek and a general paper on current affairs.

During the ensuing weeks, Florentyna spoke only Latin and Greek to Miss Tredgold before breakfast, and every weekend Miss Allen assigned her three general questions to be completed by the following Monday morning. As the examination day drew nearer, Florentyna became aware that the hopes of the whole school were with her. She sat awake at night with Cicero, Virgil, Plato and Aristotle, and every morning after breakfast she would write five hundred words on such varied subjects as the Twenty-Second Amendment or the significance of President Truman's power over Congress during the Korean War – even on the impact that television would have by going nationwide.

At the end of each day, Miss Tredgold checked through Florentyna's work, adding footnotes and comments before they would both collapse into bed, only to be up at six thirty the next morning to work their way through further old scholarship examination papers. Far from gaining confidence, Florentyna confided to Miss Tredgold that she became more frightened as each day passed.

The prize exam was set for early March at Radcliffe, and on the eve of the fateful day Florentyna unlocked her bottom drawer and took out her favourite shirt. Miss Tredgold accompanied her to the station and the few words they spoke on the way were in Greek. Her final words were: 'Don't spend the longest time on the easiest question.'

When they reached the platform, Florentyna felt an arm encircle her waist and a rose appeared in front of her.

'Edward, you nut.'

'That is not the way to address the President of the Student Council. Don't bother to come back if you fail to win the Woolson prize,' he said, and kissed her on the cheek.

Neither of them noticed the smile on Miss Tredgold's face.

Florentyna found an empty carriage and remembered very little of the journey, as she rarely looked up from her copy of the *Oresteia*.

When she arrived in Boston, she was met by a Ford 'Woody' station wagon which took her and four other girls who must have been on the same train to the Radcliffe Yard. During the journey spasmodic exchanges of

polite conversation punctuated long, tense silences. Florentyna was relieved
to find that she had been put in a residential house at 55 Garden Street in
a room of her own: she hoped she would be able to conceal how nervous she
was.

At six o'clock, the girls all met in Longfellow Hall where the Dean of
Instruction, Mrs Wilma Kirby-Miller, went over the details of the examination.

'Tomorrow, ladies, between nine and twelve, you will write the Latin
paper and in the afternoon between three and six the Greek paper. The
following morning you will complete the examination with a general paper.
It would be foolish to wish everyone success as you cannot all expect to win
the Woolson Prize, so I will only express the hope that when you have
completed the three papers, each and every one of you will feel that you
could not have done better.'

Florentyna returned to her room in Garden Street conscious of how little
she knew and feeling very lonely. She went down to the ground floor and
called her mother and Miss Tredgold on the pay phone. The next morning
she woke at three and read a few pages of Aristotle's *Politics* but nothing
would stick. When she came down at seven, she walked around the Radcliffe
Yard several times before going to Agassiz House for breakfast. She found
two telegrams awaiting her, one from her father, wishing her luck and
inviting her to join him for a trip to Europe during the summer holiday, and
the second from Miss Tredgold which read: 'The only thing we have to fear
is fear itself.'

After breakfast, she walked once again around the yard, this time with
several other silent girls, before taking her place in Longfellow Hall. Two
hundred and forty-three girls waited for the clock to chime nine, when the
proctors allowed them to open the little brown envelopes placed on the desk
in front of them. Florentyna read through the Latin paper once quickly and
then again carefully, before selecting those questions that she felt best
capable of answering. At twelve, the clock struck again and her blue books
were taken away from her. She returned to her room and read Greek for
two hours, eating a solitary Hershey bar for lunch. In the afternoon she
attempted three more questions in Greek. At six she was still writing amendments when the paper had to be handed in. She walked back to her little
room in Garden Street exhausted, fell on to the narrow bed and didn't stir
until it was time to eat. Over a late dinner, she listened to the same
conversations with different accents from Philadelphia to Houston, and from
Detroit to Atlanta: it was comforting to discover that everyone was as
nervous about the outcome of the examination as she was. Florentyna knew
that almost everyone who took the scholarship examination would be offered
a place at Radcliffe, and twenty-two could be awarded scholarships; but
only one could win the James Adams Woolson Prize.

On the second day she opened the brown envelope containing the general
paper, fearing the worst but relaxed a little when she read the first question:
'What changes do you imagine would have taken place in America if the
Twenty-Second Amendment had been passed before Roosevelt became
President?' She began to write furiously.

On Florentyna's return to Chicago, Miss Tredgold was standing on the platform waiting for her.

'I shall not ask if you consider you have won the prize, my dear, only if you did as well as you had hoped.'

'Yes,' said Florentyna, after some thought. 'If I don't win a scholarship, it will be because I am not good enough.'

'You can ask for no more, child, and neither can I, so the time has come to tell you that I shall be returning to England in July.'

'Why?' said Florentyna, stunned.

'What do you imagine there is left for me to do for you, now that you're off to university? I have been offered the post of head of the classics department at a girls' school in the West Country, starting in September, and I have accepted.'

'"You could not leave me if you knew how much I loved you."'

Miss Tredgold smiled at the quotation and produced the next line. '"It is because of how much I love you that I must now leave you, Perdano."'

Florentyna took her hand and Miss Tredgold smiled at the beautiful young woman who could already make men's heads turn as they passed by.

The last three weeks at school were not easy for Florentyna as she waited for the exam results. She tried to assure Edward that at least he was certain to gain a place at Harvard.

'They have more sports fields than lecture halls,' she teased, 'so you can't fail.'

He could fail and she knew it, and as each day passed, the hopes of both turned to fears. Florentyna had been told that the results of the examination would be known on 14 April. On that morning the headmistress called Florentyna to her study and sat her in a corner of the room while she called the registrar at Radcliffe. The registrar already had several people holding to speak to her. At last she took Miss Allen's call.

'Would you be kind enough to let me know if a Miss Florentyna Rosnovski has won a scholarship to Radcliffe?' asked the headmistress.

There was a long pause. 'How do you spell that name?'

'R-O-S-N-O-V-S-K-I.'

Another pause. Florentyna clenched her fist. Then the registrar's voice, audible to them both, came over the line: 'No, I am sorry to tell you that Miss Rosnovski's name is not among the list of scholars but over seventy per cent of those who took the scholarship examination will be offered a place at Radcliffe and will be hearing from us in the next few days.'

Neither Miss Allen nor Florentyna could mask their disappointment. As Florentyna came out of the study she found Edward waiting for her. He threw his arms around her and almost shouted, 'I'm going to Harvard. And how about you? Did you win the Woolson?' But he could see the answer in her face. 'I'm sorry,' he said. 'How thoughtless of me,' and held her in his arms as the tears came. Some younger girls who passed them giggled. Edward took her home and she, Miss Tredgold and her mother ate dinner together in silence.

Two weeks later, on Parents' Day, Miss Allen presented Florentyna with the school Classics Prize, but it was no consolation. Her mother and Miss

Tredgold applauded politely but Florentyna had told her father not to come to Chicago as there was nothing particular to celebrate.

After the presentation, Miss Allen tapped the lectern in front of her before she started to speak. 'In all my years at Girls Latin,' said the headmistress in clear, resonant tones, 'it was no secret that I wanted a pupil to win the James Adams Woolson Prize Scholarship to Radcliffe.' Florentyna stared down at the wooden floorboard between her feet. 'And this year,' continued Miss Allen, 'I was convinced that we had produced our finest scholar in twenty-five years and that my dream would be realized. Some weeks ago, I phoned Radcliffe to discover our entrant had not won a scholarship. But today I received a telegram which is nevertheless worth reading to you.'

Florentyna sat back, hoping her father was not responsible for some embarrassing message of congratulation.

Miss Allen put on her reading spectacles. ' "Name of Florentyna Rosnovski not announced among general scholars because happy to inform you she is winner of James Adams Woolson Prize. Please telegraph acceptance." ' The room erupted as pupils and parents cheered. Miss Allen raised a hand, and the hall fell silent. 'After twenty-five years I should have remembered that the Woolson is always announced separately at a later date. You must put it down to old age.' There was a polite ripple of laughter before Miss Allen continued: 'There are those of us here who believe that Florentyna will go on to serve her college and country in a manner that can only reflect well upon this school. I now have only one wish left: that I live long enough to witness it.'

Florentyna stood and looked towards her mother. Large tears were coursing down her cheeks.

No one present would have realized that the lady seated bolt upright next to Zaphia, staring straight in front of her, was revelling in the applause.

So much happiness and sadness now surrounded Florentyna, but nothing was to compare with her farewell to Miss Tredgold. On the train journey from Chicago to New York, during which Florentyna tried to express her love and gratitude, she handed the older woman an envelope.

'What'sthis, child?' asked Miss Tredgold.

'The four thousand shares of the Baron Group which we have earned over the past four years.'

'But that includes your shares as well as mine, my dear.'

'No,' said Florentyna, 'it doesn't take into account my saving on the Woolson Prize Scholarship.'

Miss Tredgold made no reply.

An hour later, Miss Tredgold stood on the dock in New York harbour waiting to board a ship, finally to release her charge to adult life.

'I shall think of you from time to time, my dear,' she said, 'and hope that my father was right about destiny.' Florentyna kissed Miss Tredgold on both cheeks and watched her mount the gangplank. When she reached the deck, Miss Tredgold turned, waved a gloved hand once and then hailed a porter, who picked up her bags and followed the stern-looking lady towards the private cabins. She did not look back at Florentyna, who stood like a statue on the quayside holding back the tears because she knew Miss Tredgold would not approve.

When Miss Tredgold reached her berth, she tipped the boy fifty cents and locked the door.

Winifred Tredgold sat on the end of the bunk and wept unashamedly.

10

Florentyna had not been so unsure about anything since her first day at the Girls Latin School. When she returned from her summer holiday in Europe with her father, a thick manila envelope from Radcliffe was awaiting her. It contained all the details of when and where she should report, what to wear, a course catalogue and the 'red book' outlining Radcliffe rules. Florentyna sat in bed studiously taking in page after page of information until she came to Rule 11a: 'If you entertain a man in your room for tea, at all times the door must be kept ajar, and all four feet must always be touching the floor.' Florentyna burst out laughing at the thought that the first time she made love it might be standing up, behind an open door, holding a cup of tea.

As the time drew nearer for her to leave Chicago, she began to realize just how much she had depended on Miss Tredgold. She packed three large suitcases which included all the new clothes she had bought on her European trip. Her mother, looking elegant in the latest Chanel suit, drove Florentyna to the station. When she boarded the train she was suddenly aware it was the first time she had travelled anywhere for any period of time without knowing somebody at the other end.

She arrived in Boston to find New England a beautiful contrast of September greens and browns. An old yellow school bus was waiting to transport students to the campus. As the ancient vehicle crossed the Charles, Florentyna looked through the back window to see the sun glinting off the dome of the State House. A few sails dotted the water and eight enthusiastic students were pulling their oars through the wash while an older man on a bicycle shouted orders through a megaphone as he rode along the towpath. When the bus came to a halt at Radcliffe, a middle-aged woman in academic dress herded the freshmen into Longfellow Hall, where Florentyna had taken the Woolson exam. There they were briefed on which hall they would live in during their first year, and their rooms were allocated to them. Florentyna drew room seven in Whitman Hall. A sophomore helped her carry her bags across to Whitman and then left her to unpack.

The room smelled as if the painters had moved out only the day before. It was clear that she was to share with two other girls: there were three beds, three chests of drawers, three desks, three desk chairs, three desk lamps, three pillows, three bedspreads and three sets of blankets, according to the check list that was left on the inside of the door. As there was no sign of her roommates she chose the bed nearest the window and started to unpack. She was just about to unlock the last suitcase when the door was flung open and a large trunk landed in the middle of the room.

'Hi,' said a voice that sounded to Florentyna more like a foghorn than a freshman from Radcliffe. 'My name is Bella Hellaman. I'm from San Francisco.'

Bella shook hands with Florentyna, who immediately regretted the act as she smiled up at the six-foot giant who must have weighed well over two hundred pounds. Bella looked like a double bass and sounded like a tuba. She began to size up the room.

'I knew they wouldn't have a bed large enough for me,' was her next pronouncement. 'My headmistress did warn me that I should have applied to a man's college.'

Florentyna burst out laughing.

'You won't laugh so loud when I keep you awake all night. I toss and turn so much you'll think you're on board a ship,' Bella warned as she pushed open the window above Florentyna's bed to let in the cold Boston air. 'What time do they serve dinner at this place? I haven't had a decent meal since I left California.'

'I've no idea, but it's all in the red book,' said Florentyna, picking her copy up from the side of her bed. She started flicking through the pages until she reached 'Meals, times of'. 'Dinner, six thirty to seven thirty.'

'Then at the stroke of six thirty,' Bella said, 'I shall be under starter's orders at the dining-room door. Have you found out where the gymnasium is?'

'To be honest, I haven't,' said Florentyna, grinning. 'It wasn't high on my list of priorities for the first day.'

There was a knock on the door, and Bella shouted, 'Come in.' Florentyna later learned that it had not been a shout, just her normal speaking voice. Into the room stepped a Dresden china blonde, dressed in a neat dark blue suit and with not a hair out of place. She smiled, revealing a set of small, even teeth. Bella smiled back at her as though her dinner had arrived early.

'My name is Wendy Brinklow. I think I'm sharing a room with you.' Florentyna wanted to warn her about Bella's handshake but it was too late. She stood and watched Wendy cringe.

'You'll have to sleep over there,' Bella said, pointing to the remaining bed. 'You don't by any chance know where the gymnasium is, do you?'

'Why should Radcliffe need a gymnasium?' said Wendy as Bella helped her in with her suitcases. Bella and Wendy started to unpack and Florentyna fiddled with her books, trying not to make it too obvious that she was fascinated by what came out of Bella's suitcases. First there were goalie pads, a breast pad, and two pairs of cleats, then a face mask which Florentyna tried on, two hockey sticks and finally a pair of hockey gloves. Wendy had all her clothes in neat little piles packed away in her drawer before Bella had even worked out where to put her hockey sticks. Eventually she just threw them under the bed.

When they had finished unpacking, the three girls set off for the dining hall. Bella was the first to reach the cafeteria line and loaded her plate so full with meat and vegetables that she had to balance it on the palm of her hand. Florentyna helped herself to what she considered a normal amount and Wendy managed a couple of spoonfuls of salad. Florentyna was beginning to feel they resembled Goldilocks's three bears.

Two of them had the sleepless night Bella had promised Florentyna, and it was several weeks before either she or Wendy managed eight hours of uninterrupted sleep. Years later Florentyna discovered that she could sleep anywhere, even in a crowded airport lounge, thanks to spending her freshman year with Bella.

Bella was the first freshman to play goalie for the Radcliffe varsity and she spent the year happily terrifying anyone who dared to try to score against her. She always shook hands with the few who did. Wendy spent a lot of the time being chased by men who visited the campus and some of the time being caught. She also passed more hours reading the Kinsey Report than her class notes.

'Darlings,' she said, eyes saucer wide, 'its a serious piece of academic work written by a distinguished professor.'

'The first academic work to sell over a million copies,' commented Bella, as she picked up her hockey sticks and left the room.

Wendy, seated in front of the one mirror in the room, started checking her lipstick.

'Who's it this time?' asked Florentyna.

'No one in particular,' she replied. 'But Dartmouth has sent their tennis team over to play Harvard and I couldn't think of a more pleasant way to spend the afternoon. Do you want to come along?'

'No thanks, but I would like to know the secret of how you find them,' said Florentyna, looking at herself appraisingly in the mirror. 'I can't remember when anyone other than Edward last asked me out.'

'It doesn't take a lot of research,' said Wendy. 'Perhaps you put them off.'

'How?' asked Florentyna, turning towards her.

Wendy put down her lipstick and picked up a comb. 'You're too obviously bright and intelligent, and not many men can handle that. You frighten them and that's not good for their egos.'

Florentyna laughed.

'I'm serious. How many men would have dared to approach your beloved Miss Tredgold, let alone make a pass at her?'

'So what do you suggest I do about it?' asked Florentyna.

'You're good-looking enough, and I don't know anyone with a better dress sense, so just act dumb and massage their ego; then they feel they have to take care of you. It always works for me.'

'But how do you stop them thinking they have the right to jump into bed with you after one hamburger?'

'Oh, I usually get three or four steaks before I let them try anything. And just occasionally I say yes.'

'That's all very well, but how did you handle it the first time?'

'God knows,' said Wendy. 'I can't remember that far back.'

Florentyna laughed again.

'If you come to the tennis with me you might get lucky. After all, there'll be five other men from Dartmouth, not to mention the six on the Harvard team.'

'No, I can't,' Florentyna said regretfully. 'I still have an essay on Oedipus to complete by six o'clock.'

'And we all know what happened to him,' said Wendy, grinning.

. . .

Despite their different interests, the three girls became inseparable, and Florentyna and Wendy would always spend Saturday afternoons watching Bella play hockey. Wendy even learned to scream 'Kill 'em,' from the sidelines, although it didn't sound very convincing. It was a hectic first year and Florentyna enjoyed regaling her father with stories of Radcliffe, Bella and Wendy.

She had to study hard as her adviser, Miss Rose, was quick to point out that the Woolson Scholarship came up for renewal every year and that it would do neither of their reputations any good if the prize were withdrawn. At the end of the year her grades were more than satisfactory, and she had also found time to join the Debating Society and was made freshman representative for the Radcliffe Democratic Club. But she felt her greatest achievement was trouncing Bella on the Fresh Pond golf course by seven shots.

. . .

In the summer vacation of 1952, Florentyna only spent two weeks in New York with her father because she had applied to be a page at the Chicago convention.

Once Florentyna had returned to her mother in Chicago she threw herself back into politics. The Republican Party convention had been held in the city two weeks earlier and the GOP had chosen Dwight D. Eisenhower and Richard Nixon as their candidates. Florentyna couldn't see how the Democrats would come up with anyone to challenge Eisenhower, the biggest national hero since Teddy Roosevelt. 'I like Ike' buttons were everywhere.

When on 21 July the Democratic convention opened, Florentyna was given the job of showing VIPs to their seats on the speakers' platform. During those four days she learned two things of value. The first was the importance of contacts and the second the vanity of politicians. Twice during the four days she placed Senators in the wrong seats, and they could not have made more fuss if she had ushered them into the electric chair. The brightest moment of her week came when a good-looking young Congressman from Massachusetts asked her where she was at college.

'When I was at Harvard,' he said, 'I spent far too much of my time at Radcliffe. They tell me it's the other way around.'

Florentyna wanted to say something witty and bright that he would remember but nothing came out, and it was many years before she saw John Kennedy again.

The climax of the convention came when she watched the delegates select Adlai Stevenson as their standard-bearer. She had greatly admired him when he was Governor of Illinois, but Florentyna did not believe that such an academic man could hope to defeat Eisenhower on election day. Despite the shouting, cheering and singing of 'Happy Days Are Here Again', few other people in that hall seemed to believe it either.

Once the convention was over, Florentyna went back to Henry Osborne's headquarters to try to help him retain his seat in Congress. This time she was put in charge of the switchboard inquiries but the responsibility gave her little pleasure as she had known for some time that the Congressman was not respected by his party workers let alone by his constituents. His reputation as a drinker and his second divorce were not helping him with the middle-class voters in his district.

Florentyna found him all too casual and glib about the trust the voters had placed in him, and she began to see why people had so little faith in their elected representatives. That faith took another blow when Eisenhower's Vice-Presidential candidate, Richard Nixon, addressed the nation on 23 September to explain away an eighteen thousand dollar slush fund which he claimed had been set up for him by a group of millionaire backers as 'necessary political expenses' and for 'exposing Communists'.

On the day of the election, Florentyna and her fellow workers were half-hearted about both of their candidates and those feelings were reflected at the polls. Eisenhower won the election by the largest popular vote in American history, 33,936,234 to 27,314,992. Among the casualties removed in the landslide was Representative Osborne.

. . . .

Disenchanted with politics, Florentyna returned to Radcliffe for her sophomore year, and put all her energy into her studies. Bella had been elected captain of hockey, the first sophomore to be so honoured. Wendy claimed to have fallen in love with a Dartmouth tennis player named Roger and, taking fashion advice from Florentyna, started studying bridal gowns in *Vogue*. Although they now all had single rooms in Whitman, the three girls still saw each other regularly. Florentyna never missed a hockey game, come rain or snow, both of which Cambridge frequently endured, while Wendy introduced her to several men who never quite seemed worthy of a third or fourth steak.

It was halfway through the spring semester that Florentyna returned to her room to find Wendy sitting on the floor in tears.

'What's the matter?' asked Florentyna. 'Your mid-terms? You haven't flunked them?'

'No, it's much worse than that.'

'What could be worse than that?'

'I'm pregnant.'

'What?' said Florentyna, kneeling down and putting an arm around her. 'How can you be so sure?'

'This is the second month I've missed my period.'

'Well, that's not conclusive, and if the worse comes to the worst, we know Roger wants to marry you.'

'He may not be the father.'

'Oh, my God,' said Florentyna. 'Who is?'

'I think it must have been Bob, the football player from Princeton. You met him, remember?'

Florentyna didn't. There had been quite a few during the year and she wasn't sure what to do next when Wendy couldn't even be certain of the father's name. All three girls sat up late into the night with Bella displaying a gentleness and understanding Florentyna would never have thought possible. It was decided that if Wendy missed her next period she would have to make an appointment to see the university gynaecologist, Doctor MacLeod.

Wendy did miss her next period, and asked Bella and Florentyna to accompany her when she went to Doctor MacLeod's office on Brattle Street. The doctor informed Wendy's class Dean of her pregnancy that night and no one was surprised by her decision. Wendy's father arrived the next day and thanked them both for all they had done before taking his daughter back to Nashville. It all happened so suddenly that neither of them could believe they wouldn't see Wendy again. Florentyna felt helpless and wondered if she could have done more.

At the end of her sophomore year, Florentyna began to believe she could win a coveted Phi Beta Kappa key. She was fast losing her interest in university politics; a combination of McCarthy and Nixon was not inspiring, and she became even more disillusioned by an incident that occurred at the end of the summer holidays.

Florentyna had returned to work for her father in New York. She had learned a lot since the 'Jessie Kovats' incident. In fact Abel was now happy to leave her in charge of various Baron shops when their managers were on vacation.

During one lunch break she tried to avoid a smartly dressed middle-aged man who was passing through the hotel lobby at the same time, but he spotted her, and shouted:

'Hi, Florentyna.'

'Hello, Henry,' she said with little enthusiasm.

He leaned forward and gripped her on both arms before kissing her on the cheek.

'It's your lucky day, my dear,' he said.

'Why?' asked Florentyna, genuinely puzzled.

'I have been stood up by my date tonight and I'm going to give you the chance to take her place.'

Get lost, is what she would have said if Henry Osborne had not been a director of the Baron Group, and she was about to make some suitable excuse when he added, 'I've got tickets for *Can-Can.*'

Since her arrival in New York Florentyna had been trying to get seats for Broadway's latest smash hit and had been told they were sold out for eight weeks, by which time she would have returned to Radcliffe. She hesitated for a moment and then said, 'Thank you, Henry.'

They agreed to meet at Sardi's, where they had a drink before walking over to the Shubert Theatre. The show lived up to Florentyna's expectation and she realized it would have been churlish of her not to accept Henry's invitation to supper afterwards. He took her to the Rainbow Room and it was there that the trouble started. He had three double scotches before the first course arrived and although he was not the first person to put a hand on her knee he was the first of her father's friends to do so. By the time they came to the end of the meal Henry had drunk so much he was barely coherent.

In the cab on the way back to the Baron, he stubbed out his cigarette and tried to kiss her. She squeezed herself into the corner of the cab, but it didn't deter him. She had no idea how to handle a drunk and didn't know until then how persistent they could be. When they reached the Baron, he insisted on accompanying Florentyna to her room, and she felt unable to refuse his overtures for fear any public row would reflect badly on her father. Once they were in the private elevator he tried to kiss her again and when they reached her small apartment on the forty-first floor Henry forced his way into her room as she opened the door. He immediately went over to the small bar and poured himself another large scotch. Florentyna regretted that her father was in France and that George would have left the hotel to go home long ago. She wasn't quite sure what to do next.

'Don't you think you should leave now, Henry?'

'What?' slurred Henry. 'Before the fun has begun?' he lurched towards her. 'A girl ought to show how grateful she is when a fellow has taken her to the best show in town and given her a first-class meal.'

'I am grateful, Henry, but I am also tired, and I would like to go to bed.'

'Exactly what I had in mind.'

Florentyna felt quite sick as he almost fell on her and ran his hands down her back, stopping only when he reached her buttocks.

'Henry, you had better leave before you do something you'll regret,' Florentyna said, feeling she sounded a little absurd.

'I'm not gonna regret anything,' he said as he tried to force down the zip on the back of her dress. 'And neither will you.'

Florentyna tried to push him away, but he was far too strong for her, so she began hitting him on the side of the arms.

'Don't put up too much of a fight, my dear,' he panted. 'I know you really want it, and I'll show you a thing or two those college boys won't know about.'

Florentyna's knees gave way and she collapsed on to the carpet with Henry on top of her, knocking the phone from a table on to the floor.

'That's better,' he said, 'I like a bit of spirit.'

He grabbed at her again, pinioning her arms above her head with one hand. He started moving his other hand up her thigh. With all the force she could muster she freed an arm and slapped Henry across the face but it only made him grab her hair tightly and push her dress up above her waist. There was a rip and Henry laughed drunkenly.

'It would have been easier ... if you had taken the damned thing off ... in the first place,' he said in breathless grunts as he extended the tear.

Florentyna stared helplessly backwards and saw a heavy crystal vase holding some roses next to where the phone had stood. With her free arm she pulled Henry towards her and started kissing him passionately on the face and neck.

'That's more like it,' he said, releasing her other arm.

Slowly she reached backwards for the vase. When she had it firmly in her hand, she broke away and brought the vase crashing down on the back of his skull. His head slumped forward and it took all her strength to push him off her. Florentyna's first reaction when she saw the blood pouring from his scalp was to fear that she had killed him. There was a loud knock on the door.

Startled, Florentyna tried to stand up, but she felt too weak in the knees. The knock came again, even louder, but this time accompanied by a voice that could belong to only one person. Florentyna staggered to the door and opened it to find Bella taking up the whole space between the jambs.

'You look awful.'

'I feel awful.' Florentyna stared down at her tattered Balenciaga evening dress.

'Who did that to you?'

Florentyna took a pace backwards and pointed to the motionless body of Henry Osborne.

'Now I see why your phone was off the hook,' said Bella as she strode over to the prostrate body. 'Got less than he deserved, I see.'

'Is he still alive?' asked Florentyna weakly.

Bella, knelt over him and checked his pulse, replying, 'Unfortunately, yes. It's only a flesh wound. He wouldn't have lived if I'd hit him. Now all he'll have to show for his trouble is a large bump on his head in the morning, which is not enough for a jerk like that. I think I'll throw him out of the window,' she added, picking Henry up and chucking him over her shoulder as if he were a sack of potatoes.

'No, Bella. We're on the forty-first floor.'

'He won't notice the first forty,' said Bella, and started walking towards the window.

'No, no,' said Florentyna.

Bella grinned before turning back. 'I'll be generous this time and put him in the freight elevator. The management can deal with him as they see fit.' Florentyna did not argue as Bella strode past her with Henry still over her shoulder. She returned a few moments later looking as if she had saved a penalty against Vassar.

'I've sent him to the basement,' she said with glee.

Florentyna was sitting on the floor sipping a Rémy Martin.

'Bella, am I ever going to be wooed romantically?'

'I'm the wrong person to ask. No one has ever tried to rape me, let alone be romantic.'

Florentyna fell into her arms laughing. 'Thank God you came when you did. Why are you here, not that I'm complaining?'

'Little Miss Efficiency has forgotten that I'm being put up in the hotel tonight because I'm playing hockey in New York tomorrow. The Devils against the Angels.'

'But they're both men's teams.'

'That's what they think, and don't interrupt. When I arrived at the desk they had no reservation in my name and the receptionist told me the hotel was packed, so I thought I would come up and complain to the management. Give me a pillow and I'll be happy to sleep in the bath.'

Florentyna held her head in her hands.

'Why are you crying?'

'I'm not, I'm laughing. Bella, you deserve a king-size bed and you shall have one.' Florentyna put the phone back on the hook and then picked up the receiver.

'Yes, Miss Rosnovski?'

'Is the Presidential Suite free tonight?'

'Yes, miss.'

'Please register it in the name of Miss Bella Hellaman and charge it to me. She'll be down to confirm in a minute.'

'Certainly, miss. How will I recognize Miss Hellaman?'

. . .

The next morning Henry Osborne called and begged Florentyna not to tell her father what had taken place the night before, pleading with her that it wouldn't have happened if he had not drunk so much and adding plaintively that he could not afford to lose his place on the board. Florentyna stared down at the red bloodstain on the carpet and reluctantly agreed.

11

When Abel returned from Paris he was appalled to learn that one of his directors had been found drunk in a freight elevator, and had needed seventeen stitches in his scalp.

'No doubt Henry is claiming he tripped over a dumb-waiter,' said Abel, before he unlocked his private drawer, took out an unmarked file and added another note to it.

'More likely a dumb blonde,' laughed George.

Abel nodded.

'Are you going to do anything about Henry?' George asked.

'Not at the moment. He's still useful as long as he has contacts in Washington. In any case, I'm up to my eyes with buildings in London and Paris and now I see the board wants me to look at possibilities in Amsterdam, Geneva, Cannes and Edinburgh. Not to mention the fact that Zaphia is threatening to take me to court if I don't increase her alimony.'

'Perhaps the easy way out would be to pension Henry off?' suggested George.

'Not quite yet,' replied Abel. 'There is still a reason why I need him.'

George couldn't think of even one.

. . .

'We'll kill 'em,' said Bella. Bella's decision to challenge Harvard's ice hockey team to a field hockey match came as no surprise to anyone except the Harvard team who politely declined the invitation without comment. Bella immediately took out a half-page advertisement in the Harvard *Crimson* which read:

'Harvard Jocks Flunk Radcliffe Challenge.'

The enterprising editor of the *Crimson*, who had seen the advertisement before it went to press, decided to interview Bella so she ended up on the front page as well. A photograph of Bella wearing her mask and pads, and brandishing a hockey stick, ran with the caption: 'She's more frightening when she takes the mask off.' Bella was delighted with the picture and with the caption.

Within a week Harvard had offered to send its third XI team to Radcliffe.

Bella refused, demanding varsity players only. A compromise was reached, with Harvard making up a team of four varsity players, four junior varsity players and three third XI players. A date was chosen and the necessary preparations were made. The undergraduates at Radcliffe began to get quite chauvinistic about the challenge, and Bella became a cult figure on campus.

'More figure than cult,' she told Florentyna.

Bella's tactics for trying to win the match were later described by the Harvard *Crimson* as nothing short of diabolical. When the Harvard team arrived in their bus they were met by eleven amazons with hockey sticks slung over their shoulders. The fit young men were immediately whisked off for lunch. Members of the Harvard squad never normally drink a drop before a match but as the girls, without exception, ordered beers, they felt honour-bound to join them. Most of the men managed three cans before lunch and also enjoyed the excellent wine served throughout the meal. None of the Harvard men thought to comment on Radcliffe's generosity or to ask if they were breaking any college rules. All twenty-two ended the lunch with a glass of champagne to toast the fortunes of both colleges.

The eleven Harvard men were then escorted to their locker room, where they found another magnum of champagne awaiting them. The eleven happy ladies left them to change. When the Harvard captain led his team out on to the hockey field he was met by a crowd of over five hundred spectators and eleven strapping girls whom he had never seen before in his life. Eleven other ladies, not unknown to the captain, were finding it hard to remain awake in the stand. Harvard was 3–0 down by half-time and was lucky to lose only 7–0. The Harvard *Crimson* might well have described Bella as a cheat, but the Boston *Globe* declared her to be a woman of great enterprise.

The captain of the Harvard team immediately challenged Bella to a replay against the full varsity squad. 'Exactly what I wanted in the first place,' she told Florentyna. Bella accepted by sending a telegram from one side of Cambridge Common to the other. It read: 'Your place or mine?' Radcliffe had to arrange for several cars to transport their supporters, their ranks swelled by Harvard's decision to put on a dance that evening after the game. Florentyna drove Bella and three other members of the team to the field across the river in her newly acquired 1952 Oldsmobile, with hockey sticks, shin pads and goalie pads piled high in the trunk. When they arrived, they did not meet up with any of the Harvard team before they reached the playing field. This time they were greeted by a crowd of three thousand, which included President Conant of Harvard and President Jordan of Radcliffe.

Bella's tactics again bordered on the dubious: each of her girls had clearly been instructed to play the man and not to concentrate too much on the ball. Ruthless hacking at vulnerable shins enabled them to hold Harvard to a scoreless first half.

The Radcliffe team nearly scored in the first minute of the second half which inspired them to rise above their normal game and it began to look as if the match might end in a draw when the Harvard centre forward, a man only slightly smaller than Bella, broke through and looked poised to score. He had reached the edge of the circle when Bella came charging out of her cage and hit him flat out with a shoulder charge. That was the last he remembered of the match and he departed a few seconds later on a stretcher. Both referees blew their whistles at once and a penalty was awarded to Harvard with only a minute to go. Their left wing was selected to take the shot. The five-foot-nine, slimly built man waited for the two teams to line up. He cracked the ball sharply to the right inner who lofted a shot straight into Bella's chest-pad. It dropped at her feet, and she kicked it to the right, where it landed back in front of the diminutive left winger. Bella charged at the slight figure, and gentle people in the crowd covered their eyes, but this time she had met her match. The left wing sidestepped deftly leaving the Radcliffe captain spread-eagled on the ground and himself ample time to flick the ball into the back of the net. The whistle blew and Radcliffe had lost 1–0.

It was the only occasion on which Florentyna had seen Bella cry, despite the crowd giving her a standing ovation as she led her team off the field. Although defeated Bella ended up with two compensations: the US Women's Hockey Team selected her to play for her country, and she had met her future husband.

Florentyna was introduced to Claude Lamont at the reception after the match. He looked even smaller in his neat blue blazer and grey flannel trousers than he had on the field.

'Little sweetheart, isn't he?' said Bella, patting him on the head. 'Amazing goal.' Florentyna was surprised that Claude did not seem to object. All he said was, 'Didn't she play a first-class game?'

Bella and Florentyna returned to their rooms in Radcliffe and changed for the dance. Claude accompanied both girls to the hall, which Bella compared with a cattle show as the men swarmed around her old roommate. They all wanted to dance the jitterbug with her, so Claude was dispatched to fetch enough food and drink to feed an army, which Bella disposed of while she watched her friend in a whirl of Trigère silk on the dance floor.

Florentyna first saw him sitting talking to a girl in the corner of the room while she was dancing. He must have been about six feet in height with wavy fair hair and a tan that only proved he did not spend his winter vacations in Cambridge. As she looked he turned towards the dance floor and their eyes met. Florentyna turned quickly away and tried to concentrate on what her partner was saying – something about America moving into the computer age and how he was going to climb on the bandwagon. When the dance ended, the talkative partner took her back to Bella. Florentyna turned to find him by her side.

'Have you had something to eat?' he asked.

'No,' she lied.

'Would you like to join my table?'

'Thank you,' she said, and left Bella and Claude discussing the relative merits of the value of wing to wing passing, comparing field hockey with ice hockey.

For the first few minutes neither of them spoke. He brought some food over from the buffet and then they both tried to speak at once. His name was Scott Forbes and he was majoring in history at Harvard. Florentyna had read about him in Boston's society columns, as the heir to the Forbes family business and one of the most sought-after young men in America. She wished it was otherwise. What's in a name, she said to herself, and she told him hers. It didn't seem to register.

'A pretty name for a beautiful woman,' he said. 'I'm sorry we haven't met before.' Florentyna smiled. He added, 'Actually I was at Radcliffe a few weeks ago, playing in the infamous hockey game when we lost 7–0.'

'You played in that match? I didn't notice you.'

'I'm not surprised. I spent most of the time on the ground feeling sick. I had never drunk so much in my life. Bella Hellaman may look big to you when you're sober, but she looks like a Sherman tank when you're drunk.'

Florentyna laughed and sat happily listening to Scott tell stories of Harvard, his family and his life in Boston. For the rest of the evening she danced only with one man and when the night came to an end he accompanied her back to Radcliffe.

'Can I see you tomorrow?' Scott asked.

'Yes, of course.'

'Why don't we drive out to the country and have lunch together?'

'I'd like that.'

. . .

Florentyna and Bella spent most of that night telling each other about their respective partners.

'Do you think it matters that he's straight out of the Social Register?'

'Not if he's a man worth taking seriously,' replied Bella, aware of just how real Florentyna's fears were. 'I have no idea if Claude is on any social register,' she added.

The next morning, Scott Forbes drove Florentyna out into the countryside in his old MG. She had never been happier in her life. They went to lunch in a little restaurant in Dedham that was full of people whom Scott seemed to know. Florentyna was introduced to a Lowell, a Winthrop, a Cabot and another Forbes. She was relieved to see Edward Winchester coming towards her from a corner table, leading an attractive dark-haired girl by the hand – at least, Florentyna thought, I know someone. She was astonished at how handsome and happy Edward looked and soon found out why, when he introduced his fiancée, Danielle.

'You two ought to get on famously,' said Edward.

'Why?' asked Florentyna, smiling at the girl.

'Danielle is French, and I've been telling her for a long time that I might have been the Dauphin but even when I declared you were a witch, you had to teach me how to pronounce *sorcière*.'

As Florentyna watched them depart hand in hand, Scott said quietly, '*Je n'aurais jamais pensé que je tomberais amoureux d'une sorcière.*'

Florentyna chose a simple meal of sole and agreed with his selection of Muscadet, grateful for her knowledge of food and wine, and was surprised to find at four o'clock that they were the only two left in the restaurant, with a head waiter hinting that the time might have come to prepare for the evening meal. When they returned to Radcliffe Scott kissed her gently on the cheek and said he would call her tomorrow.

He phoned during lunch the next day to ask if she could bear to watch him play ice hockey for the junior varsity against Penn on Saturday and suggested dinner together afterwards.

Florentyna accepted, masking her delight, for she couldn't wait to see him again. It seemed the longest week in her life.

On Saturday morning she made one important decision about her weekend with Scott. She packed a small suitcase and put it in the boot of the car before driving to the rink long before the face-off. She sat in the bleachers, waiting for Scott to arrive. For a moment she feared he might not feel the same way about her when they met for a third time but he dispelled that fear in a moment when he waved and skated across the ice towards her.

'Bella said I can't come home if you lose.'

'Perhaps I don't want you to,' he said, as he glided slantingly away.

She watched the game, becoming colder and colder. Scott hardly seemed to touch the puck all afternoon, but he still managed to get slammed repeatedly into the boards. She decided that it was a stupid sport but that she would not tell him so. After the match was over, she sat in her car waiting for him to change; then another reception and at last they were on their own. He took her to Locke-Ober's where again he seemed to know everyone, but this time she did not recognize anybody other than those she had seen in the fashionable magazines. He didn't notice, as he could not have been more attentive, which helped Florentyna relax. Once more, they were the last to leave and he drove her back to her car. He kissed her gently on the lips.

'Would you like to come to lunch at Radcliffe tomorrow?'

'I can't,' he said. 'I have a paper to finish in the morning, and I'm not sure I can complete it before two o'clock. You couldn't bear joining me for tea?'

'Of course I will, silly.'

'What a pity. If I had known I would have booked you a room in the guest quarters.'

'What a pity,' echoed Florentyna, thinking of the unopened suitcase lying in the trunk of her car.

.   .   .

The next day, Scott picked her up shortly after three and took her back to his rooms for tea. She smiled as he closed the door, remembering that it was still not allowed at Radcliffe. His room was considerably larger than hers and on his desk was a picture of an aristocratic, slightly severe-looking lady who could only have been his mother. As Florentyna took in the room she realized that none of the furniture belonged to Harvard.

After he had given her tea they listened to America's new singing idol, Elvis Presley, before Scott put on the no longer skinny Sinatra singing 'South of the Border' and they danced, each wondering what was in the other's mind. When they sat down on the sofa, he kissed her at first gently, then with passion. He seemed reluctant to go any further and Florentyna was both too shy and too ignorant to help him. Suddenly he placed a hand over her breast as if waiting for Florentyna's reaction. At last his hand moved to the top of her dress and fumbled with the first button. Florentyna made no attempt to stop him as he continued with the second. Soon he was kissing her, first on the shoulder, then on her breast. Florentyna wanted him so badly that she almost made the next move herself, but quite suddenly he stood up and took off his shirt. In response she quickly slipped out of her dress and let her shoes fall to the floor. They made their way to the bed, clumsily trying to remove what was left of each other's clothing. For a moment they stared at each other before climbing on to the bed. To her surprise the pleasure of making love seemed to be over in seconds.

'I'm sorry, I was awful,' said Florentyna.

'No, no, it was me.' He paused. 'I might as well admit it, that was my first time.'

'Not you as well?' she said, and they both burst out laughing.

They lay in each other's arms for the rest of the evening and made love twice more, each time with greater pleasure and confidence. When Florentyna woke in the morning, cramped and rather tired but exultantly happy, she felt instinctively they would spend the rest of their lives together. For the remainder of that term they saw one another every weekend, and sometimes during the week as well.

In the spring vacation, they met secretly in New York and Florentyna spent the happiest three days she could remember. *On the Waterfront, Limelight* and, on Broadway, *South Pacific* preceded the '21' club, Sardi's and even the Oak Room at the Plaza. In the morning they shopped, visited the Frick and walked through the park. When she returned home at night her arms were laden with presents that ended up by the side of her bed.

The spring term was idyllic and they were rarely out of each other's company. As it drew to a close, Scott invited Florentyna to spend a week in Marblehead during the spring vacation to meet his parents.

'I know they'll love you,' he said, as he put her on the train to Chicago.

'I hope so,' she replied.

Florentyna spent hours telling her mother how wonderful Scott was and how much she was bound to love him. Zaphia was delighted to see her daughter so happy, and genuinely looked forward to meeting Scott's parents. She prayed Florentyna had found someone with whom she could spend the rest of her life and not make an impulsive decision that she would later regret. Florentyna selected yards of different coloured silks from Marshall Field's and passed the evenings designing a dress she felt certain would capture the heart of Scott's mother.

The letter came on a Monday, and Florentyna immediately recognized Scott's handwriting. She tore the envelope open in happy anticipation but it contained only a short note saying that because of a change in his family plans he would have to postpone her trip to Marblehead. Florentyna read the letter again and again, looking for some hidden message. Remembering only how happily they had parted she decided to call his home.

'The Forbes residence,' said a voice that sounded like the butler's.

'May I speak to Mr Scott Forbes?' Florentyna could hear her voice quiver as she said his name.

'Who is calling him, ma'am?'

'Florentyna Rosnovski.'

'I'll see if he's in, ma'am.'

Florentyna clutched the phone and waited impatiently for Scott's reassuring voice.

'He's not at home at the moment, ma'am, but I will leave a message saying that you called.'

Florentyna didn't believe him and an hour later called again.

The voice said, 'He is still not back ma'am,' so she waited until eight that evening, when the same voice announced that he was at dinner.

'Then please tell him I'm calling.'

'Yes, ma'am.'

The voice returned a few moments later and said perceptibly less politely, 'He cannot be disturbed.'

'I don't believe it. I don't believe you've told him who it is.'

'Madam, I can assure you –'

Another voice came on the line, a lady's, with the ring of habitual authority.

'Who is this calling?'

'My name is Florentyna Rosnovski. I was hoping to speak to Scott as . . .'

'Miss Rosenovski, Scott is having dinner with his fiancée at the moment and cannot be disturbed.'

'His fiancée?' whispered Florentyna, her nails drawing blood from the palm of her hand.

'Yes, Miss Rosenovski.' The phone went dead. It took several seconds for the news to sink in, then Florentyna said out loud, 'Oh, my God, I think I'll die,' and fainted.

She woke to find her mother by the side of her bed.

'Why?' was Florentyna's first word.

'Because he wasn't good enough for you. The right man won't allow his mother to select the person he spends the rest of his life with.'

. . .

Once Florentyna returned to Cambridge matters did not improve. She was unable to concentrate on any serious work and often spent hours on her bed in tears. Nothing Bella could do or say seemed to help and she could devise no better tactic than belittlement, 'Not the sort of man I would want on my team.' Other men asked Florentyna for dates but she didn't accept any of them. Her father and mother became so worried for her that they even spoke to each other about the problem.

Finally when Florentyna was near to failing a course, Miss Rose warned her that she had a lot of work to do if she still hoped to win her Phi Beta Kappa key. Florentyna remained indifferent. During the summer vacation she stayed at home in Chicago, accepting no invitations to parties or dinners. She helped her mother choose some new clothes but bought none for herself. She read all the details of the 'society wedding of the year' as the Boston *Globe* referred to the marriage of Scott Forbes to Cynthia Knowles, but it only made her cry again. The arrival of a wedding invitation from Edward Winchester did not help. Later she tried to remove Scott from her thoughts by going to New York and working unheard-of hours for her father at the New York Baron. As the holiday drew to a close she dreaded returning to Radcliffe for her final year. No amount of advice from her father or sympathy from her mother seemed to improve matters. They both began to despair when she showed no interest in the preparations for her twenty-first birthday.

It was a few days before Florentyna was due to return to Radcliffe that she saw Edward across Lake Shore Drive. He looked as unhappy as she felt. Florentyna waved and smiled. He waved back but didn't smile. They stood and stared at each other until Edward crossed the road.

'How's Danielle?' she asked.

He stared at her. 'Haven't you heard?'

'Heard what?' said Florentyna.

He continued to stare at her as if he couldn't get out the words. 'She's dead.'

Florentyna gazed back at him in disbelief.

'She was driving too fast, showing off in my new Austin-Healey, and she turned the car over. I lived, she died.'

'Oh, my God,' Florentyna said, putting her arms around him. 'How selfish I've been.'

'No, I knew you had your own troubles.'

'Nothing compared with yours. Are you going back to Harvard?'

'I have to. Danielle's father insisted, said he would never forgive me if I didn't. So now I have something to work for. Don't cry, Florentyna, because once I start I can't stop.'

Florentyna shuddered. 'Oh, my God, how selfish I've been,' she repeated.

'Come over to Harvard some time. We'll play tennis and you can help me with my French verbs. It will be like old times.'

'Will it?' she said, wistfully. 'I wonder.'

12

When Florentyna returned to Radcliffe, she was greeted by a two-hundred-page course catalogue that took her three evenings to digest. From the catalogue she could choose one elective course outside her major area of study. Miss Rose suggested she ought to take up something new, something she might never have another chance to study in depth.

Florentyna had heard, as every other member of the university had, that Professor Luigi Ferpozzi would be spending a year as guest lecturer at Harvard, and conducting a seminar once a week. Since winning his Nobel Peace Prize he had roamed the world receiving accolades, and when he was awarded an honorary degree from Oxford the citation described him as the only man with whom the Pope and the President were in total agreement, other than God. The world's leading authority on Italian architecture had chosen Baroque Rome for his overall subject. 'City of the Eye and the Mind' was to be the title of his first lecture. The synopsis in the course catalogue was tempting: Gianlorenzo Bernini, the artist aristocrat, and Francesco Borromini, the stone cutter's son, transformed the Eternal City of the Caesars and the Popes into the most recognizable capital in the world. Prerequisites: knowledge of Latin and Italian, with German and French highly recommended. Limited to thirty students.

Miss Rose was not optimistic about Florentyna's chances of being among the chosen few. 'They tell me there is already a line from the Widener Library to Boston Common just to see him, not to mention the fact that he is a well known misogynist.'

'So was Julius Caesar.'

'When I was in the common room last night he didn't treat me like Cleopatra,' said Miss Rose. 'But I do admire the fact that he flew with Bomber Command during the Second World War. He was personally responsible for saving half the churches in Italy by seeing that the planes did not fly over important buildings.'

'Well, I want to be one of his chosen disciples,' said Florentyna.

'Do you?' said Miss Rose, drily. 'Well, if you fail,' she added laughing – as she scribbled a note for Professor Ferpozzi – 'you can always sign up for one of those science survey courses. They seem to have no limit on numbers.'

'Rocks for Jocks,' said Florentyna disparagingly. 'Not me. I'm off to ensnare Professor Ferpozzi.'

The next morning at eight thirty, a full hour before the professor was officially available to see anyone that day, Florentyna climbed the marble steps of the Widener Library. Once in the building, she took the elevator – large enough to hold herself and one book – to the top floor where the senior professors had offices under the eaves. An earlier generation had obviously decided that being far removed from zealous students more than made up for the long climb or the inconvenience of an always occupied elevator.

Once Florentyna had reached the top of the building she found herself standing in front of a frosted door. The name 'Professor Ferpozzi' was newly stencilled in black paint on the glass. She recalled that in 1945 it was this man who had sat with President Conant in Munich and between them they had decided the fate of German architecture: what should be preserved and what should be razed. She was only too aware that she shouldn't bother him for at least another hour. She half turned, intent on retreat, but the elevator was already disappearing to a lower floor. Turning again, she knocked boldly on the door. Then she heard the crash.

'Madonna! Whoever that is, go away. You have caused me to break my favourite teapot,' said an angry voice whose mother tongue could only have been Italian.

Florentyna stifled the impulse to run and instead slowly turned the door knob. She put her head round the door and looked into a room that must have had walls, but there was no way of knowing because books and periodicals were stacked from floor to ceiling as if they had taken the place of bricks and mortar.

In the middle of the clutter stood a professorial figure who could have been anywhere between forty and seventy. A tall man, he wore an old Harris tweed jacket and grey flannel trousers that looked as though they had been acquired from a secondhand shop or inherited from his grandfather. He was holding a brown china handle that moments before had been attached to a teapot. At his feet lay a teabag surrounded by fragments of brown china.

'I have been in possession of that teapot for over thirty years. I loved it second only to the *Pietà*, young woman. How do you intend to replace it?'

'As Michelangelo is not available to sculpt you another, I will have to go to Woolworth's and buy one.'

The professor smiled despite himself. 'What do you want?' he asked, picking up the teabag but leaving the remains of his teapot on the floor.

'To enroll in your course,' Florentyna replied.

'I do not care for women at the best of times,' he said, not facing her. 'And certainly not for one who causes me to break my teapot before breakfast. Do you possess a name?'

'Rosnovski.'

He stared at her for a moment before sitting at his desk and dropping the teabag into an ashtray. He scribbled briefly. 'Rosnovski, you have the thirtieth place.'

'But you don't know my grades or qualifications.'

'I am quite aware of your qualifications,' he said ominously. 'For next week's group discussion you will prepare a paper on' – he hesitated for a moment – 'on one of Borromini's earlier works, San Carlo alle Quattro Fontane. Good day,' he added, as Florentyna scribbled furiously on her notepad. He returned to the remains of his teapot, without giving her another thought.

Florentyna left, closing the door quietly behind her. She walked slowly down the marble steps trying to compose her thoughts. Why had he accepted her so quickly? How could he have known anything about her?

During the following week she spent long days in the crypts of the Fogg Museum poring over learned journals, making slides of the reproductions of Borromini's plans for San Carlo, even checking his lengthy expense list to see how much the remarkable building had cost. She also found time to visit the china department of Shreve, Crump & Lowe.

When Florentyna had completed the paper, she rehearsed it the night before and felt confident about the outcome, a confidence that evaporated the moment she arrived at Professor Ferpozzi's seminar. The room was already packed with expectant students and when she checked the list pinned to the wall she was horrified to discover that she was the only non-graduate present, the only non-Fine Arts student and the only woman on the course. A projector was placed on his desk facing a large white screen.

'Ah, the home wrecker returns,' the professor said, as Florentyna took the one remaining seat at the front. 'For those of you who have not come across Miss Rosnovski before, do not invite her home for tea.' He smiled at his own remark and tapped his pipe on the corner of the desk, a sign that he wished the class to commence.

'Miss Rosnovski,' he said with confidence, 'is going to give us a talk on Borromini's Oratorio de San Filippo Neri.' Florentyna's heart sank. 'No, no.' He smiled a second time. 'I am mistaken, it was, if I remember correctly, the Church of San Carlo.'

For twenty minutes Florentyna delivered her paper, showing slides and answering questions. Ferpozzi hardly stirred from behind his pipe, other than to correct her occasional mispronunciation of seventeenth-century Roman coins.

When Florentyna finally sat down, he nodded thoughtfully and declared, 'A fine presentation of the work of a genius.' She relaxed for the first time that day as Ferpozzi rose briskly to his feet. 'Now it is my painful duty to show you the contrast, and I want everyone to make notes in preparation for a full discussion next week.' Ferpozzi shuffled over to the projector and flicked his first slide into place. A building shone up on the screen behind the professor's desk.

Florentyna stared in dismay at a ten-year-old picture of the Chicago Baron towering above a cluster of elegant small-scale apartment buildings on Michigan Avenue. There was an eerie silence in the room, and one or two students were staring at her to see how she reacted.

'Barbaric, isn't it?' Ferpozzi's smile returned. 'I am not referring only to the building, which is a worthless piece of plutocratic self-congratulation, but to the overall effect that this edifice has on the city around it. Note the way the tower breaks the eye's sense of symmetry and balance in order to make certain that it's the only building we shall look at.' He flicked a second slide up on to the screen. This time it revealed the San Francisco Baron. 'A slight improvement,' he declared, staring into the darkness at his attentive audience, 'but only because since the earthquake of 1906 the city ordinances in San Francisco do not allow buildings to be more than twenty storeys in height. Now let's travel abroad,' he continued, turning to face the screen again. Up on the screen came the Cairo Baron, its gleaming windows reflecting the chaos and poverty of the slums huddled on top of each other in the distance.

'Who can blame the natives for backing the occasional revolution when such a monument to Mammon is placed in their midst while they try to survive in mud hovels that don't even stretch to electricity?' Inexorably, the professor produced slides of the Barons in London, Johannesburg and Paris, before saying, 'I want your critical opinion on all of these monstrosities by next week. Do they have any architectural value, can they be justified on financial grounds and will they ever be seen by your grandchildren? If so, why? Good day.'

Everyone filed out of the professor's room except Florentyna who unwrapped the brown paper parcel by her side.

'I have brought you a farewell present,' she said, and stood up, holding out an earthenware teapot. Just at the moment Ferpozzi opened his hands, she let go and the teapot fell to the ground at his feet and shattered into several pieces.

He stared at the fragments on the floor. 'I deserved no less,' he said, and smiled at her.

'That,' she rejoined, determined to say her piece, 'was unworthy of a man of your reputation.'

'Absolutely right,' he said, 'but I had to discover if you had backbone. So many women don't, you know.'

'Do you imagine your position allows you ...'

He waved a dismissive hand. 'Next week I shall read your defence of your father's empire with interest, young woman, and I shall be only too happy to be found wanting.'

'Did you imagine I would be returning?' she said.

'Oh yes, Miss Rosnovski. If you are half the woman my colleagues claim you are, I shall have a battle on my hands next week.'

Florentyna left, just stopping herself from slamming the door behind her.

For seven days she talked with architecture professors, Boston's city planners and international urban conservationists. She telephoned her father, mother and George Novak before coming to the reluctant conclusion that, although they all had different excuses, Professor Ferpozzi had not exaggerated. She returned to the top of the library a week later and sat at the back of the room, dreading what her fellow students would have come up with.

Professor Ferpozzi stared at her as she sank into her seat. He then tapped his pipe into an ashtray and addressed the class. 'You will leave your essays on the corner of my desk at the end of this session, but today I want to discuss the influence of Borromini's work on European churches during the century after his death.' Ferpozzi then delivered a lecture of such colour and authority that his thirty students hung on every word. When he had finished he selected a sandy-haired young man in the front row to prepare next week's paper on Borromini's first meeting with Bernini.

Once again, Florentyna remained seated while all the other students filed out, leaving their essays on the corner of Ferpozzi's desk. When they were alone, she handed him a brown paper parcel. He unwrapped it to find a Royal Worcester 'Viceroy' teapot in bone china, dated 1912. 'Magnificent,' he said. 'And it will remain so as long as no one drops it.' They both laughed. 'Thank you, young lady.'

'Thank you,' Florentyna replied, 'for not putting me through any further humiliation.'

'Your admirable restraint, unusual in a woman, made it clear that it was unnecessary. I hope you will forgive me, but it would have been equally reprehensible not to try and influence someone who will one day control the largest hotel empire in the world.' Such a thought had never crossed Florentyna's mind until that moment. 'Please assure your father that I always stay in a Baron whenever I have to travel. The rooms, the food and the service are quite the most acceptable of any of the major groups, and there is never anything to complain about once you are *inside* the hotel looking out. Be sure you learn as much about the stonecutter's son as I know about the empire-builder from Slonim. Being an immigrant is something your father and I will always be proud to have in common. Good day, young lady.'

Florentyna left the office below the eaves of Widener sadly aware of how little she knew of the workings of her father's empire.

During that year she concentrated hard on her modern language studies, but she could always be found on Tuesday afternoons sitting on a pile of books listening intently to Professor Ferpozzi's lectures. It was President Conant who remarked at dinner one night that it was sad that his learned colleague was having the kind of friendship with Florentyna that he really should have had thirty years before.

·   ·   ·

Graduation day at Radcliffe was a colourful affair. Proud, smartly dressed parents mingled with professors swathed in the scarlet, purple and multi-coloured hoods appropriate to their degrees. The academics glided about, resembling a convocation of bishops, informing the visitors how well their offspring had done, sometimes with a little considerate licence. In the case of Florentyna there was no need for exaggeration, for she had graduated summa cum laude and had been elected to Phi Beta Kappa earlier in the year.

It was a day of celebration and sadness for Florentyna and Bella, who were to live on opposite sides of America, one in New York and the other in San Francisco. Bella had proposed to Claude on 28 February of their junior year – 'Couldn't wait for Leap Year,' she explained – and they had been married in the Houghton chapel at Harvard during the spring vacation. Claude had insisted on, and Bella had agreed to, 'Love, honour and obey'. Florentyna had realized then how lucky they both were when Claude said to her at the reception, 'Isn't Bella beautiful?'

Florentyna smiled and turned to Bella who was saying that it was sad Wendy was not with them. 'Not that she ever did a day's work,' added Bella, grinning.

'Florentyna could not have worked harder in her final year, and frankly no one will be surprised by her achievements,' said Miss Rose.

'I am sure she owes a great deal to you, Miss Rose,' Abel replied.

'No, no, but I was hoping to convince Florentyna to return to Cambridge and carry out some research work for a PhD and then join the faculty, but she seems to have other ideas.'

'We certainly do,' said Abel. 'Florentyna will be joining the Baron Group as a director, with special resonsibilities for the leasing of the shops in the hotels. They have grown out of control in the last few years and I fear I have been neglecting them.'

'You didn't tell me that was what you had in mind, Florentyna,' boomed Bella. 'I thought you said ...'

'Shhhhh, Bella,' said Florentyna, putting a finger to her lips.

'Now what's this, young lady? Have you been keeping a secret from me?'

'Now's not the time or place, Papa.'

'Oh, come on, don't keep us in suspense,' said Edward. 'Is it the United Nations or General Motors who feel they cannot survive without you?'

'I must confess,' said Miss Rose, 'now that you have gained the highest qualifications this university can award I should be fascinated to know how you intend to use them.'

'Hoping to be a Rockette, perhaps,' said Claude.

'That's the nearest anyone has been yet,' said Florentyna.

Everyone laughed except Florentyna's mother.

'Well, if you can't find a job in New York, you can always come and work in San Francisco,' said Bella.

'I'll bear the offer in mind,' said Florentyna lightly.

To her relief, further discussion of her future was impossible because the graduation ceremony was about to begin. George Kennan, the former US ambassador to Russia, delivered the address. His speech was received enthusiastically. Florentyna particularly enjoyed the quotation from Bismarck which ended his peroration: 'Let us leave just a few tasks for our children to perform.'

'You'll deliver that address one day,' said Edward, as they passed Tricentennial Hall.

'And pray, sir, what will be my chosen subject?'

'The problems of being the first woman President.'

Florentyna laughed. 'You still believe it, don't you?'

'And so do you, even if it will always fall upon me to remind you.'

Edward had been seen regularly with Florentyna during the year, and friends hoped they might soon announce their engagement, but Edward knew that would never be. This was one woman who would always be unattainable, he thought. They were destined to be close friends, never lovers.

After Florentyna had packed her last few belongings and said goodbye to her mother, she checked that she had left nothing in her room and sat on the end of her bed reflecting on her time at Radcliffe. All she had to show for it was that she had arrived with three suitcases and was leaving with six and a Bachelor of Arts degree. A crimson ice hockey pennant once given to her by Scott was all that remained on the wall. Florentyna unpinned the pennant, held it for a moment, then dropped it into a waste-paper basket.

She sat in the back of the car with her father as the chauffeur drove out of the campus for the last time.

'Could you drive a little slower?' she asked.

'Certainly, ma'am.'

Florentyna turned and stared out of the rear window until the spires of Cambridge were no longer visible above the trees, and there was nothing left of her past to see.

13

The chauffeur brought the Rolls-Royce to a halt at the traffic lights on Arlington Street on the west side of the Public Garden. He waited for the lights to turn green while Florentyna chatted with her father about their forthcoming trip to Europe.

Just as the lights changed, another Rolls passed in front of them, turning off Commonwealth Avenue. Another graduate and parent were deep in conversation in the back.

'I sometimes think it would have been better for you to have gone to Yale, Richard,' she said.

Richard's mother looked at him approvingly. He already had the fine aristocratic looks that had attracted her to his father over twenty years before, and now he had made it five generations of the family who had graduated from Harvard.

'Why Yale?' he asked gently, pulling his mother back from her reminiscences.

'Well, it might have been more healthy for you to get away from the introverted air of Boston.'

'Don't let father hear you say that. He would consider such a suggestion nothing less than treason.'

'But do you have to return to Harvard Business School, Richard? Surely there must be other business schools?'

'Like father, I want to be a banker. If I'm going to follow in his footsteps, Yale isn't equipped to tie Harvard's laces,' he said mockingly.

A few minutes later the Rolls came to a halt outside a large house on Beacon Hill. The front door opened and a butler stood in the doorway.

'We have about an hour before the guests arrive,' said Richard, checking his watch. 'I'll go and change immediately. Mother, perhaps we could meet up a little before seven thirty in the West Room?' He even sounded like his father, she thought.

Richard bounded up the stairs two at a time; in most houses he could have managed three. His mother followed behind at a more leisurely pace, her hand never once touching the banister rail.

The butler watched them disappear before returning to the pantry. Mrs Kane's cousin, Henry Cabot Lodge, would be joining them for dinner, so he needed to double-check that everything below stairs was perfect.

Richard stood in the shower smiling at the thought of his mother's concern. He had always wanted to graduate from Harvard and improve on his father's achievements. He couldn't wait to enroll at the business school next fall, although he had to admit he was looking forward to taking Mary Bigelow to Barbados that summer. He had met Mary in the rehearsal rooms of the music society and later they were both invited to play in the university string quartet. The pert little lady from Vassar played the violin far better than he performed on the cello. When he eventually serenaded the reluctant Mary into bed he found she was again the better tuned, despite her pretence at inexperience. Since those days he had also discovered she was highly-strung.

Richard turned the dial to 'cold' for a brief moment before leaping out, drying and changing into evening dress. He checked himself in the mirror: double-breasted. Richard suspected he would be the only person that night wearing the latest fashion – not that it mattered when you were a little over six feet, slim and dark. Mary had once said that he looked good in everything from jock strap to morning coat.

He went downstairs and waited in the West Room for his mother to join him. When she appeared the butler served them both with a drink.

'Good heavens, are double-breasted suits back in fashion?' she inquired.

'You had better believe it. The very latest thing, Mother.'

'I can't believe it,' she said. 'I remember ...'

The butler coughed. They both looked around. 'The Honourable Henry Cabot Lodge,' he announced.

'Henry,' said Richard's mother.

'Kate, my dear,' he replied, before kissing her on the cheek. Kate smiled; her cousin was wearing a double-breasted jacket.

Richard smiled, because it looked twenty years old

.   .   .

Richard and Mary Bigelow returned from Barbados almost as brown as the natives. They stopped off in New York to have dinner with Richard's parents, who thoroughly approved of his choice. After all, she was the great-niece of Alan Lloyd, who had succeeded Richard's grandfather as chairman of the family bank.

As soon as Richard had returned to the Red House, their Boston residence on Beacon Hill, he quickly settled down and prepared himself for the business school. Everyone had warned him it was the most demanding course at the university with the largest drop-out rate, but once the term had started even he was surprised by how little free time he had to enjoy other pursuits. Mary began to despair when he had to relinquish his place in the string quartet and could manage to see her only at weekends.

At the end of his first year she suggested they take another vacation in Barbados and was disappointed to find he intended to stay put in Boston and continue studying.

When Richard returned for his final year he was determined to finish at or near the top of his class, and his father warned him not to relax until after the last exam paper had been completed. His father had added that if he did not make the top ten per cent he needn't apply for a position at the bank. He would not be accused of nepotism.

At Christmas, Richard joined his parents in New York, but remained for only three days before returning to Boston. His mother became quite anxious about the pressure he was putting himself under, but Richard's father pointed out that it was only for another six months. Then he could relax for the rest of his life. Kate reserved her opinion; she hadn't seen her husband relax in twenty-five years.

At Easter, Richard called his mother to say he ought to remain in Boston during the brief spring vacation, but she managed to convince him he should come down for his father's birthday. He agreed but added that he would have to return to Harvard the next morning.

Richard arrived at the family home on East Sixty-eighth Street just after four o'clock on the afternoon of his father's birthday. His mother was there to greet him as were his sisters, Virginia and Lucy. His mother thought he looked drawn and tired, and she longed for his exams to be over. Richard knew that his father would not break his routine at the bank for anyone's birthday. He would arrive home a few minutes after seven.

'What have you bought for Daddy's birthday?' inquired Virginia.

'I was waiting to seek your advice,' said Richard flatteringly, having quite forgotten about a present.

'That's what I call leaving it until the last moment,' said Lucy. 'I bought my present for him three weeks ago.'

'I know the very thing he needs,' said his mother. 'A pair of gloves. His old ones are nearly worn out.'

'Dark blue, leather, with no pattern,' said Richard laughing. 'I'll go to Bloomingdale's and choose a pair right now.'

He strode down Lexington Avenue, falling in with the pace of the city. He was already looking forward to joining his father in the fall, and felt confident that if there were no distractions in the last few months he would come out in that top ten per cent. He would emulate his father and one day be chairman of the bank. He smiled at the thought. He pushed open the doors of Bloomingdale's, strode up the steps and asked an assistant where he could buy some gloves. As he began making his way through the crowded store, he glanced at his watch. There would be plenty of time to change for dinner before his father returned. He looked up at the two girls behind the glove counter. He smiled; the wrong one smiled back.

The smiling girl came quickly forward. She was a honey blonde with a little too much lipstick and one more button undone than Bloomingdale's could possibly have approved of. Richard couldn't help but admire such confidence. A small name tag pinned over her left breast read 'Maisie Bates'.

'Can I help you, sir?' she asked.

'Yes,' said Richard. He glanced towards the dark-haired girl. 'I need a pair of gloves, dark blue, leather and no pattern,' he said without letting his eyes return to the blonde.

Maisie selected a pair and put them on Richard's hands, pushing the leather slowly down each finger and then holding them up for him to admire.

'If they don't suit you, you could try another pair.'

'No, that's just fine,' he said. 'Do I pay you or the other girl?'

'I can take care of you.'

'Damn,' said Richard under his breath. He left reluctantly, determined he would return the next day. Until that afternoon he had considered love at first sight the most ridiculous cliché, fit only for readers of women's magazines.

His father was delighted with the 'sensible' present, as he referred to the gloves over dinner that night, and even more delighted with Richard's progress at business school.

'If you are in the top ten per cent I shall be happy to consider offering you a position of trainee at the bank,' he said for the thousandth time.

Virginia and Lucy grinned. 'What if Richard comes out number one, Daddy? Will you make him chairman?' asked Lucy.

'Don't be frivolous, my girl. If Richard ever becomes chairman it will be because he will have earned the position after years of dedicated, hard work.' He turned to his son. 'Now, when are you returning to Harvard?'

Richard was about to say tomorrow, when he said, 'I think tomorrow.'

'Quite right,' was all his father commented.

The next day Richard returned not to Harvard, but to Bloomingdale's where he headed straight for the glove counter. Before he had any chance of letting the other girl serve him, Maisie pounced; he could do nothing about it, except purchase another pair of gloves and return home.

The following morning, Richard returned to Bloomingdale's for a third time and studied ties on the next counter until Maisie was busy serving a customer and the other girl was free. He then marched confidently up to the counter and waited for her to serve him. To Richard's horror, Maisie disengaged herself in mid-sentence from her customer and rushed over while the other girl took her place.

'Another pair of gloves?' giggled the blonde.

'Yes ... Yes,' he said lamely.

Richard left Bloomingdale's with yet another pair of gloves – dark blue, leather with no pattern.

The following day, he told his father he was still in New York because he had to gather some data from Wall Street to complete a paper. As soon as his father had left for the bank, he headed off to Bloomingdale's. This time he had a plan for ensuring he spoke to the other girl. He marched up to the glove counter fully expecting Maisie to rush up, when the other assistant came forward to serve him.

'Good morning, sir,' she said.

'Oh, good morning,' said Richard, suddenly at a loss for words.

'Can I help you?'

'No – I mean yes. I would like a pair of gloves,' he added unconvincingly.

'Yes, sir. Have you considered dark blue? In leather? I'm sure we have your size – unless we're sold out.'

Richard looked at the name on her lapel badge: Jessie Kovats. She passed him the gloves. He tried them on. They didn't fit. He tried another pair and looked towards Maisie. She grinned at him encouragingly. He grinned nervously back. Miss Kovats handed him another pair of gloves. This time they fitted perfectly.

'I think that's what you're looking for,' said Jessie.

'No, not really,' said Richard.

Jessie lowered her voice and said, 'I'll go and rescue Maisie. Why don't you ask her out? I'm sure she'll say yes.'

'Oh, no,' said Richard. 'You don't understand. It's not her I want to take out – it's you.'

Jessie looked totally surprised.

'Will you have dinner with me tonight?'

'Yes,' she said shyly.

'Shall I pick you up at your home?'

'No. Let's meet at the restaurant.'

'Where would you like to go?'

Jessie didn't reply.

'Allen's at Seventy-third and Third?' Richard suggested.

'Yes, fine,' was all Jessie said.

'Around eight suit you?'

'Around eight,' said Jessie.

Richard left Bloomingdale's with what he wanted – and it wasn't a pair of gloves.

.   .   .

Richard couldn't remember a time when he had spent all day thinking about a girl, but from the moment Jessie had said 'Yes', he had thought of nothing else.

Richard's mother was delighted that he had decided to spend another day in New York and wondered if Mary Bigelow was in town. Yes, she decided, when she passed the bathroom and heard Richard singing 'Once I had a secret love'.

Richard gave an unusual amount of thought to what he should wear that evening. He decided against a suit, finally selecting a dark blue blazer and a pair of grey flannel slacks. He also spent a little longer looking at himself in the mirror. Too Ivy League, he feared, but there wasn't much he could do about that at short notice.

He left the house on Sixty-eighth Street just before seven to avoid having to explain to his father why he was still in town. It was a crisp, clear evening and he arrived at Allen's a few minutes after seven thirty and ordered himself a Budweiser. Every few moments he checked his watch as the minute hand climbed up towards eight, and then every few seconds once it had passed the agreed hour, wondering if he would be disappointed when he saw her again.

He wasn't.

She stood in the doorway looking radiant in a simple blue dress that he assumed had come from Bloomingdale's, though any woman would have known it was a Ben Zuckerman. Her eyes searched the room. At last she saw Richard walking towards her.

'I am sorry to be late ...' she began.

'It's not important. What's important is that you came.'

'You thought I wouldn't?'

'I wasn't sure,' Richard said, smiling. They stood staring at each other. 'I'm sorry, I don't know your name,' he said, not wanting to admit he had seen it every day at Bloomingdale's.

She hesitated. 'Jessie Kovats. And yours?'

'Richard Kane,' he said, offering her his hand. She took it, and he found himself not wanting to let go.

'And what do you do when you're not buying gloves at Bloomingdale's?' asked Jessie.

'I'm at Harvard Business School.'

'I'm surprised they didn't teach you that most people only have two hands.'

He laughed, already delighted that it wasn't going to be her looks alone that would make the evening memorable.

'Shall we sit down?' suggested Richard, taking her arm and leading her to his table.

Jessie began to study the menu on the blackboard.

'Salisbury steak?' she inquired.

'A hamburger by any other name,' said Richard.

She laughed and he was surprised that she had picked up his out of context quotation so quickly, and then felt guilty, because as the evening progressed it became obvious that she had seen more plays, read more novels and even attended more concerts than he had. It was the first time in his life he regretted his single-minded dedication to studying.

'Do you live in New York?' he asked.

'Yes,' she said, as she sipped the third coffee Richard had allowed the waiter to pour. 'With my parents.'

'Which part of town?' he asked.

'East Fifty-seventh Street,' Jessie replied.

'Then let's walk,' he said, taking her hand.

Jessie smiled her agreement and they zigzagged back across the city together. To make the journey take longer Richard stopped to gaze at shop windows which he would normally have passed on the trot. Jessie's knowledge of fashion and shop management was daunting. Richard felt sorry that she had left school at sixteen to work in the Baron Hotel before going to Bloomingdale's.

It took them nearly an hour to cover the sixteen blocks. When they reached Fifty-seventh Street, Jessie stopped outside a small old apartment house.

'This is where my parents live,' she said. He held on to her hand.

'I hope you will see me again,' said Richard.

'I'd like that,' said Jessie, not sounding very enthusiastic.

'Tomorrow?' asked Richard diffidently.

'Tomorrow?' queried Jessie.

'Yes. Why don't we go to the Blue Angel and see Bobby Short?' He took her hand again. 'It's a little more romantic than Allen's.'

Jessie seemed uncertain, as if the request was causing her a problem.

'Not if you don't want to,' he added.

'I'd love to,' she said in a whisper.

'I'm having dinner with my father, so why don't I pick you up around ten o'clock?'

'No, no,' said Jessie. 'I'll meet you there. It's only two blocks away.'

'Ten o'clock then.' He leaned forward and kissed her on the cheek. It was the first time he was aware of a delicate perfume. 'Goodnight, Jessie,' he said, and walked away.

Richard began to whistle Dvorak's *Cello Concerto* and by the time he arrived home, had reached the end of the first movement. He couldn't recall an evening he had enjoyed more. He fell asleep thinking about Jessie instead of Galbraith or Freedman. The next morning he accompanied his father down to Wall Street and spent a day in the *Journal*'s library, taking only a short break for lunch. In the evening, over dinner, he told his father about the research he had been doing on reverse take-over bids and feared he might have sounded a little too enthusiastic.

After dinner, he went off to his room. He made sure that no one noticed him slip out of the front door a few minutes before ten. Once he had reached the Blue Angel he checked his table and returned to the foyer to wait for Jessie.

He could feel his heart beating and wondered why that had never happened with Mary Bigelow. When Jessie arrived, he kissed her on the cheek and led her into the lounge. Bobby Short's voice came floating through the air: 'Are you telling me the truth or am I just another lie?'

As Richard and Jessie walked in, Short raised his arm. Richard found himself acknowledging the wave although he had seen the artist only once before and had never been introduced to him.

They were guided to a table in the centre of the room where to Richard's surprise Jessie chose the seat with her back to the piano.

Richard ordered a bottle of Chablis and asked Jessie about her day.

'Richard, there is something I must –'

'Hi, Richard.' He looked away.

Standing by the table was another man dressed in dark blue blazer and grey flannel slacks.

'Hi, Steve. May I introduce Jessie Kovats – Steve Mellon. Steve and I were at Harvard together.'

'Seen the Yankees lately?' asked Steve.

'No,' said Richard. 'I only follow winners.'

'Like Eisenhower. With his handicap you would have thought he had been to Yale.' They chatted on for a few minutes. Jessie made no effort to interrupt them. 'Ah, she's arrived at last,' said Steve, looking towards the door. 'See you, Richard. Nice to have met you, Jessie.'

During the evening Richard told Jessie about his plans to come to New York and work at Lester's, his father's bank. She was such an intent listener he only hoped he hadn't been boring her. He enjoyed himself even more than the previous night and when they left he waved to Bobby Short as if they had grown up together. When they reached Jessie's home he kissed her on the lips for the first time. For a moment she responded, but then she said, 'Goodnight' and disappeared into the old apartment building.

The next morning he returned to Boston. As soon as he arrived back at the Red House he phoned Jessie: was she free to go to a concert on Friday? She said she was and for the first time in his life he crossed days off a calendar. Mary phoned him later in the week and he tried to explain to her as gently as possible why he was no longer available.

When the weekend came it was memorable. The New York Philharmonic, *Dial M for Murder* – Jessie even seemed to enjoy the New York Knicks. Richard reluctantly returned to Harvard on Sunday night. The next four months were going to be long weeks and short weekends. He phoned Jessie every day and they were rarely apart at weekends.

He began to dread Mondays.

. . .

During one Monday morning lecture, on the '29 crash, Richard found he couldn't concentrate. How was he going to explain to his father that he had fallen in love with a girl who worked behind the gloves, scarves and woollen hats counter at Bloomingdale's? Even to himself, Richard couldn't understand why such a bright, attractive girl could be so unambitious. If only Jessie had been given the opportunities he had had ... He scribbled her name on the top of his class notes. His father was going to have to learn to live with it. He stared at what he had written: Jessie Kane.

When Richard arrived back in New York that weekend, he made an excuse to his mother about running out of razor blades. His mother suggested that he use his father's.

'No, no, it's all right,' said Richard. 'I need some of my own. In any case, we don't use the same brand.'

Kate Kane thought this was strange because she knew they did.

Richard had to run the eight blocks to Bloomingdale's to be sure he would make the store before it closed. When he reached the glove counter, Jessie was nowhere to be seen. Maisie was standing in a corner filing her fingernails.

'Is Jessie around?' he asked her breathlessly.

'No, she's already gone home – she left a few minutes ago. She can't have gone far. Aren't you ... ?'

Richard ran out on to Lexington Avenue. He searched for Jessie's face among the figures hurrying home. He would have given up if he hadn't recognized the flash of red, a scarf he had given her. She was on the other side of the street, walking towards Fifth Avenue. Her apartment was in the opposite direction; somewhat guiltily he decided to follow her. When she reached Scribner's on Forty-eighth Street, he stopped and watched her go into the bookshop. If she wanted something to read, surely she could have picked it up at Bloomingdale's? He was puzzled. He peered through the window as Jessie talked to a sales clerk, who left her for a few moments and then returned with two books. He could just make out their titles: *The Affluent Society* by John Kenneth Galbraith and *Inside Russia Today* by John Gunther. Jessie signed for them – which surprised Richard – and left as he ducked around the corner.

'Who *is* she?' said Richard out loud as he watched her double back and enter Bendle's. The doorman saluted respectfully, leaving a distinct impression of recognition. Once again Richard peered through the window to see sales ladies fluttering around Jessie with more than casual respect. An older lady appeared with a package, which Jessie had obviously been expecting. She opened it to reveal a full-length evening dress in red. Jessie smiled and nodded as the sales lady placed the dress in a brown and white box. Then, mouthing the words 'Thank you', Jessie turned towards the door without even signing for her purchase. Richard barely managed to avoid colliding with her as she hastened out of the store to jump into a cab.

He grabbed a taxi that an old lady had originally thought was hers, and told the driver to follow Jessie's cab. 'Like the movies, isn't it?' said the cab driver. Richard didn't reply. When the cab passed the small apartment house outside of which they normally parted, he began to feel queasy. The taxi in front continued for another hundred yards and came to a halt outside a dazzling new apartment house complete with a uniformed doorman, who was quick to open the door for Jessie. With astonishment and anger, Richard jumped out of his cab and started to make his way up to the door through which she had disappeared.

'That'll be ninety-five cents, fella,' said a voice behind him.

'Oh, sorry,' said Richard. He thrust his hand into his pocket and took out a note, hurriedly pushing it at the cab driver, not thinking about the change.

'Thanks, buddy,' said the driver, clutching on to the five-dollar bill. 'Someone sure is happy today.'

Richard hurried through the door of the building and managed to catch Jessie as she stepped into the elevator. She stared at him but didn't speak.

'Who are you?' demanded Richard as the elevator door closed. The other two occupants stared in front of them with a look of studied indifference as the elevator glided up to the second floor.

'Richard,' she stammered. 'I was going to tell you everything this evening. I never seemed to find the right opportunity.'

'Like hell you were going to tell me,' he said, following her out of the elevator and into an apartment. 'Stringing me along with a pack of lies for nearly three months. Well, now the time has come for the truth.'

He pushed his way past her brusquely as she opened the door. He looked beyond her into the apartment while she stood helplessly in the passageway. At the end of the entrance hall there was a large living room with a fine oriental rug and a magnificent Georgian bureau. A handsome grandfather clock stood opposite a side table on which there was a bowl of fresh anemones. The room was impressive even by the standards of Richard's own home.

'Nice place you've got yourself for a salesgirl,' he said sharply. 'I wonder which of your lovers pays for this?'

Jessie took a pace towards him and slapped him so hard that her own palm stung. 'How dare you?' she said. 'Get out of my home.'

As she said the words, she started to cry. Richard took her in his arms. 'Oh, God, I'm sorry,' he said. 'That was a terrible thing to suggest. Please forgive me. It's just that I love you so much and imagined I knew you so well, and now I find I don't know a thing about you.'

'Richard, I love you too and I'm sorry I hit you. I didn't want to deceive you, but there's no one else – I promise you that.' She touched his cheek.

'It was the least I deserved,' he said as he kissed her.

Clasped tightly in one another's arms, they sank on to the sofa and for some moments remained almost motionless. Gently he stroked her hair until her tears subsided. Jessie slipped her fingers through the gap between his top two shirt buttons.

'Do you want to sleep with me?' she asked quietly.

'No,' he replied. 'I want to stay awake with you all night.'

Without speaking further, they undressed and made love, gently and shyly at first, afraid to hurt each other, desperately trying to please. Finally, with her head on his shoulder, they talked.

'I love you,' said Richard. 'I have since the first moment I saw you. Will you marry me? Because I don't give a damn who you are, Jessie, or what you do, but I know I must spend the rest of my life with you.'

'I want to marry you too, Richard, but first I have to tell you the truth.'

She pulled Richard's jacket over her naked body as he lay silent waiting for her to speak.

'My name is Florentyna Rosnovski,' she began, and then told Richard everything about herself. Florentyna explained why she had taken the name of Jessie Kovats – so that she would be treated like any other sales girl while she learned the trade, and not like the daughter of the Chicago Baron. Richard never spoke once during her revelation and remained silent when she came to the end.

'Have you stopped loving me already?' she asked. 'Now that you know who I really am?'

'Darling,' said Richard very quietly. 'My father hates your father.'

'What do you mean?'

'Just that the only time I ever heard your father's name mentioned in his presence, he flew completely off the handle, saying your father's sole purpose in life seemed to be a desire to ruin the Kane family.'

'What? Why?' said Florentyna, shocked. 'I've never heard of your father. How do they even know each other? You must be mistaken.'

'I wish I were,' said Richard, and repeated the little his mother had once told him about the quarrel with her father.

'Oh, my God. That must have been the "Judas" my father referred to when he changed banks after twenty-five years,' she said. 'What shall we do?'

'Tell them the truth,' said Richard. 'That we met innocently, fell in love and now we're going to be married. And that nothing they can do will stop us.'

'Let's wait for a few weeks,' said Florentyna.

'Why?' asked Richard. 'Do you think your father can talk you out of marrying me?'

'No, Richard,' she said, touching him gently as she placed her head back on his shoulder. 'Never, my darling. But let's find out if we can do anything to break the news gently before we present them both with a *fait accompli*. Anyway, maybe they won't feel as strongly as you imagine. After all, you said the problem with the Richmond Group was over twenty years ago.'

'They still feel every bit as strongly, I promise you that. My father would be outraged if he saw us together, let alone thought we were considering marriage.'

'All the more reason to leave it for a little before we break the news to them. That will give us time to consider the best way to go about it.'

He kissed her again. 'I love you, Jessie.'

'Florentyna.'

'That's something else I'm going to have to get used to,' he said.

·   ·   ·

To begin, Richard allocated one afternoon a week to researching the feud between the two fathers, but after a time it became an obsession, biting heavily into his attendance at lectures. The Chicago Baron's attempt to get Richard's father removed from his own board would have made a good case study for the Harvard Business School. The more he discovered the more Richard realized that his father and Florentyna's were formidable rivals. Richard's mother spoke of the feud as if she had needed to discuss it with someone for years.

'Why are you taking such an interest in Mr Rosnovski?' she asked.

'I came across his name when I was going through some back copies of the *Wall Street Journal*.' The truth, he thought, but a lie.

Florentyna took a day off from Bloomingdale's and flew to Chicago to tell her mother what had happened. When Florentyna pressed her as to what she knew of the row she spoke for almost an hour without interruption. Florentyna hoped her mother was exaggerating but a few carefully worded questions over dinner with George Novak made it painfully obvious that she hadn't been.

Every weekend the two lovers exchanged their knowledge, which only added to the catalogue of hate.

'It all seems so petty,' said Florentyna. 'Why don't they just meet and talk it over? I think they would get on rather well together.'

'I agree,' said Richard. 'But which one of us is going to try telling them that?'

'Both of us are going to have to, sooner or later.'

As the weeks passed Richard could not have been more attentive and kind. Although he tried to take Florentyna's mind off 'sooner or later' with regular visits to the theatre, the New York Philharmonic and long walks through the park, their conversation always drifted back to their parents.

Even during a cello recital which Richard gave her in her flat, Florentyna's mind was occupied by her father – how could he be so obdurate? As the Brahms sonata came to an end Richard put down his bow and stared into her grey eyes.

'We have got to tell them soon,' he said, taking her in his arms.

'I know we must. I just don't want to hurt my father.'

'I know.'

She looked down at the floor. 'Next Friday, Papa will be back from Washington.'

'Then it's next Friday,' said Richard quietly, not letting her go.

As Florentyna watched Richard drive away that night she wondered if she would be strong enough to keep her resolve.

On Friday, Richard ducked his morning lecture and travelled down to New York in time to spend the rest of the day with Florentyna.

They spent that afternoon going over what they would say when they respectively faced their parents. At seven o'clock the two left Florentyna's apartment on Fifty-seventh Street. They walked without talking. When they reached Park Avenue they stopped at the light.

'Will you marry me?'

It was the last question on Florentyna's mind as she braced herself to meet her father. A tear trickled down her cheek, a tear that she felt had no right to be there on the happiest moment of her life. Richard took a ring out of a little red box – a sapphire set in diamonds. He placed it on the third finger of her left hand. He tried to stop the tears by kissing her. They broke and stared at each other for a moment, then he turned and strode away.

They had agreed to meet again at the apartment as soon as their ordeal was over. She stared at the ring on her finger, next to the antique one, her favourite of the past.

As Richard walked up Park Avenue he went over the sentences he had so carefully composed in his mind and found himself on Sixty-eighth Street long before he felt he had completed the rehearsal.

He found his father in the drawing room drinking the usual Teacher's and soda before changing for dinner. His mother was complaining that his sister didn't eat enough. 'I think Virginia plans to be the thinnest thing in New York.' Richard wanted to laugh.

'Hello, Richard, I was expecting you earlier.'

'Yes,' said Richard. 'I had to see someone before I came home.'

'Who?' said his mother, not sounding particularly interested.

'The woman I am going to marry.'

They both looked at him astonished; it certainly wasn't the opening sentence Richard had planned so carefully.

His father was the first to recover. 'Don't you think you're a bit young? I feel sure you and Mary can afford to wait a little longer.'

'It's not Mary I intend to marry.'

'Not Mary?' said his mother.

'No,' said Richard. 'Her name is Florentyna Rosnovski.'

Kate Kane turned white.

'The daughter of Abel Rosnovski?' William Kane said without expression.

'Yes, Father,' said Richard firmly.

'Is this some sort of joke, Richard?'

'No, Father. We met in unusual circumstances and fell in love without either of us realizing there was a misunderstanding between our parents.'

'Misunderstanding? Misunderstanding?' he repeated. 'Don't you realize that jumped-up Polish immigrant spends most of his life trying to get me thrown off my own board – and once nearly succeeded? And you describe that as a "misunderstanding"? Richard, you will never see the daughter of

that crook again if you hope to sit on the board of Lester's Bank. Have you
thought about that?'

'Yes, Father, I have, and it will make no difference to my decision. I have
met the woman with whom I intend to spend the rest of my life and I am
proud that she would even consider being my wife.'

'She has tricked and ensnared you so that she and her father can finally
take the bank away from me. Can't you see through their plan?'

'Even you can't believe something as preposterous as that, Father.'

'Preposterous? He once accused me of being responsible for killing his
partner, Davis Leroy, when I ...'

'Father, Florentyna knew nothing of the circumstances surrounding your
quarrel until she met me. How can you be so irrational?'

'She has told you she's pregnant, so you will have to marry her.'

'Father, that was unworthy of you. Florentyna has never put the slightest
pressure on me from the moment we met. On the contrary.' Richard turned
to his mother. 'Won't you both meet her and then you'll understand how
it came about?'

Kate was going to reply when Richard's father shouted, 'No. Never,' and
turning to his wife, he asked her to leave them alone. As she left, Richard
could see that his mother was weeping.

'Now listen to me, Richard. If you marry the Rosnovski girl I will cut you
off without a penny.'

'You suffer like generations of our family, Father, from imagining money
can buy everything. Your son is not for sale.'

'But you could marry Mary Bigelow – such a respectable girl, and from
our own background.'

Richard laughed. 'Someone as wonderful as Florentyna couldn't be replaced by a suitable Brahmin family friend.'

'Don't you mention our heritage in the same breath as that stupid Polack.'

'Father, I never thought I would have to listen to such pathetic prejudice
from a normally sober person.'

William Kane took a pace towards his son. Richard never flinched. His
father stopped in his tracks. 'Get out,' he said. 'You're no longer a member
of my family. Never ...'

Richard left the room. As he walked across the hall he became aware that
his mother was leaning hunched against the banister. He went to her and
took her in his arms. She whispered, 'I'll always love you,' and released him
when she heard her husband come into the corridor.

Richard closed the front door gently behind him. He was back on Sixty-
eighth Street. His only thought was how Florentyna had managed to face
her own encounter. He hailed a cab and without looking back directed it
to Florentyna's apartment.

He had never felt so free in his life.

When he reached Fifty-seventh Street he asked the doorman if Florentyna
had returned. She hadn't, so he waited under the canopy, beginning to fear
she might not have been able to get away. He was deep in thought and didn't
notice when another cab came to a halt at the kerb and the frail figure of
Florentyna stepped out. She was holding a tissue to a bleeding lip. She rushed
towards him and they quickly went upstairs to the privacy of the apartment.

'I love you, Richard,' were her first words.

'I love you, too,' said Richard, and took her in his arms, holding her tightly as if it would solve their problems.

Florentyna didn't let go of Richard as he spoke.

'He threatened to cut me off without a penny if I married you,' he told her. 'When will they understand we don't care a damn about their money? I tried appealing to my mother for support, but even she couldn't control my father's temper. He insisted that she leave the room. I've never seen him treat my mother that way before. She was weeping, which only made my resolve stronger. I left him in mid-sentence. God knows, I hope he doesn't take it out on Virginia or Lucy. What happened when you told your father?'

'He hit me,' said Florentyna very quietly. 'For the first time in my life. I think he'll kill you if he finds us together. Richard darling, we must get out of here before he discovers where we are, and he's bound to try the apartment first. I'm so frightened.'

'No need for you to be frightened. We'll leave tonight and go as far away as possible and to hell with them both.'

'How quickly can you pack?' asked Florentyna.

'I can't,' said Richard. 'I can never return home now. You pack your things and then we'll go. I've got about a hundred dollars with me and my cello which is still in the bedroom. How do you feel about marrying a hundred-dollar man?'

'As much as a sales girl can hope for, I suppose – and to think I dreamed of being a kept woman. Next you'll be wanting a dowry.' Florentyna rummaged in her bag. 'Well, I've got two hundred and twelve dollars and an American Express card. You owe me fifty-six dollars, Richard Kane, but I'll consider repayment at a dollar a year.'

'I think I like the idea of a dowry better,' said Richard.

In thirty minutes Florentyna was packed. Then she sat down at her desk, scrawled a note to her father explaining she would never be willing to see him again unless he would accept Richard. She left the envelope on the table by the side of her bed.

Richard hailed a cab. 'Idlewild,' he said after placing Florentyna's three suitcases and his cello in the boot.

Once they had reached the airport Florentyna made a phone call. She was relieved when it was answered. When she told Richard the news he booked a flight.

At seven thirty the American Airlines Super Constellation 1049 taxied out on to the runway to start its seven-hour flight

Richard helped Florentyna with her seatbelt. She smiled at him.

'Do you know how much I love you, Mr Kane?'

'Yes, I think so – Mrs Kane,' he replied.

.   .   .

'You'll live to regret your actions tonight.'

He didn't reply immediately, but just sat motionless, staring in front of him. Then all he said was, 'You will never contact him again.'

She left the room without replying.

He sat alone in the crimson leather chair; time was suspended. He didn't hear the phone ring several times. The butler knocked quietly on the door and entered the room.

'A Mr Abel Rosnovski on the line, sir. Are you in?'

Willian Kane felt a sharp pain in the pit of his stomach. He knew he had to take the call. He rose from his chair and only by a supreme effort stopped himself from collapsing back into it. He walked over to the phone and picked it up.

'William Kane speaking.'

'This is Abel Rosnovski.'

'Indeed, and when exactly did you think of setting up your daughter with my son? At the time, no doubt, when you failed so conspicuously to cause the downfall of my bank.'

'Don't be such a damn ...' Abel checked himself before continuing. 'I want this marriage stopped every bit as much as you do. I never tried to take away your son. I only learned of his existence today. I love my daughter even more than I hate you and I don't want to lose her. Can't we get together and work something out between us?'

'No,' said William Kane.

'What's the good of raking over the past now Kane? If you know where they are, perhaps we can stop them. That's what you want too. Or are you so goddam proud that you'll stand by and watch your son marry my girl rather than help?'

William Kane hung up the phone and walked back to the leather chair. The butler returned. 'Dinner is served, sir.'

'No dinner, and I'm not at home.'

'Yes, sir,' said the butler and left the room.

William Kane sat alone. No one disturbed him until eight o'clock the next morning.

14

When Flight 1049 landed at San Francisco's International Airport, Florentyna hoped it hadn't been too short notice. Richard had hardly placed a foot on the tarmac when he saw a massive woman charge towards them and throw her arms around Florentyna. Florentyna still couldn't get her arms around Bella.

'You don't give a girl much time, do you? Calling just as you're boarding the plane.'

'I'm sorry, Bella, I didn't know until ...'

'Don't be silly. Claude and I had been grumbling that we didn't have anything to do this evening.'

Florentyna laughed and introduced the two of them to Richard.

'Is that all the luggage you have?' queried Bella, staring down at the three suitcases and the cello.

'We had to leave in rather a hurry,' explained Florentyna.

'Well, there's always been a home for you here,' said Bella, immmediately picking up two of the suitcases.

'Thank God for you, Bella. You haven't changed a bit,' said Florentyna.

'I have in one respect. I'm six months pregnant. It's just that I'm like a giant panda – nobody's noticed.'

The two girls dodged in and out of the airport traffic to the parking lot with Richard carrying the cello and Claude following in their wake. During the journey into San Francisco, Bella revealed that Claude had become an associate in the law firm of Pillsbury, Madison and Sutro.

'Hasn't he done well?' she said.

'And Bella's the senior physical education teacher at the local high school, and they haven't lost a hockey game since she joined them,' said Claude with equal pride.

'And what do you do?' said Bella, prodding a finger into Richard's chest. 'From your luggage I can only assume that you're an out-of-work musician.'

'Not exactly,' said Richard, laughing. 'I'm a would-be-banker, and I shall be looking for a job tomorrow.'

'When are you getting married?'

'Not for three weeks at least,' said Florentyna. 'I want to be married in a church, and they'll have to read the banns first.'

'So you'll be living in sin,' declared Claude as he drove past the 'San Francisco Welcomes Careful Drivers' sign. 'Quite the modern couple. I always wanted to, but Bella wouldn't hear of it.'

'And why did you leave New York so suddenly?' asked Bella, ignoring Claude's comment.

Florentyna explained how she had met Richard and the historic feud that existed between their fathers. Bella and Claude listened incredulously to the story, both remaining unusually silent, until the car came to a halt.

'This is our home,' said Claude, putting on the brakes firmly and leaving the car in first gear.

Florentyna got out on the side of a steep hill not quite overlooking the bay.

'We go higher up the hill when Claude becomes a partner,' said Bella. 'But this will have to do for now.'

'It's fantastic,' said Florentyna as they entered the little house. She smiled when she saw hockey sticks in the umbrella stand.

'I'll take you straight to your room so you can unpack.' Bella led the two guests up a small winding staircase to the spare room on the top floor. 'It may not be the Presidential Suite at the Baron, but it's better than joining the communes on the streets.'

It was some weeks before Florentyna discovered that Bella and Claude had spent the afternoon lugging their double bed up the stairs to the spare room and carrying the two singles back down so that Richard and Florentyna could spend their first night together.

It was four a.m. in New York when they finally climbed into bed.

'Well, now that Grace Kelly is no longer available, I suppose I'm stuck with you. Although I think Claude may be right. Perhaps we should live in sin.'

'If you and Claude lived together in sin, no one in San Francisco would even notice.'

'Any regrets so far?'

'Yes. I always hoped I'd end up with a man who slept on the left-hand side of the bed.'

. . .

In the morning, after a Bella-type breakfast, Florentyna and Richard scoured the papers for jobs.

'We must try and find something quickly. I don't think our money will last for more than a month,' said Florentyna.

'It may be easier for you. I can't believe that many banks will offer me a job without a degree or at least a reference from my father.'

'Don't worry,' said Florentyna, ruffling his hair. 'We can beat both our fathers.'

Richard turned out to be right. It took Florentyna only three days and her prospective employers one phone call to the personnel director at Bloomingdale's before she was offered a position at a young fashion shop called 'Wayout Columbus' which had advertised for a 'bright sales assistant' in the *Chronicle*. It was only another week before the manager realized what a bargain they had picked up.

Richard, on the other hand, plodded around San Francisco from bank to bank. The personnel director always asked him to call back and when he did there suddenly 'wasn't a position available at the present time' for someone with his qualifications. As the day of the wedding drew nearer Richard became increasingly anxious.

'You can't blame them,' he told Florentyna. 'They all do a lot of business with my father and they don't want to upset him.'

'Bunch of cowards. Can you think of anyone who has had a row with Lester's Bank and therefore refuses to deal with them?'

Richard buried his head in his hands and considered the question for a few moments. 'Only the Bank of America. My father had a quarrel with them once over a stop-loss guarantee which they took rather a long time to honour and it resulted in a considerable loss in interest. He swore he would never do business with them again. It's worth a try – I'll give them a call tomorrow.'

When the manager interviewed him the next day he asked if the reason Richard had applied to work at the Bank of America was the well known disagreement with his father.

'Yes, sir,' replied Richard.

'Good, then we both have something in common. You will start on Monday as a junior teller, and if you are indeed the son of William Kane I don't imagine you will stay in that position for long.'

. . .

On the Saturday of their third week in San Francisco, Richard and Florentyna were married in a simple ceremony at St Edward's Church on California Street. Father O'Reilly – accompanied by Florentyna's mother – flew in from Chicago to conduct the service. Claude gave the bride away and then ran round to Richard's side to be best man while Bella was the matron of honour, gargantuan in a pink maternity smock. The six celebrated that night with a dinner at DiMaggio's on Fisherman's Wharf. Richard and Florentyna's combined weekly salaries didn't cover the final bill, so Zaphia came to the rescue.

'If you four want to eat out again,' added Zaphia, 'just give me a call and I'll be out on the next plane.'

Bride and groom crept into bed at one o'clock in the morning.

'I never thought I would end up married to a bank teller.'

'I never thought I would end up married to a shop assistant, but sociologically it ought to make an ideal partnership.'

'Let's hope it doesn't end with sociology,' said Florentyna, turning off the light.

·   ·   ·

Abel tried every means at his disposal to discover where Florentyna had disappeared. After days of phone calls, telegrams, and even efforts to involve the police, he realized there was only one lead left open. He dialled a number in Chicago.

'Hello,' said a voice every bit as cold as William Kane's.

'You must know why I'm ringing.'

'I can guess.'

'How long have you known about Florentyna and Richard Kane?'

'About three months. Florentyna flew up to Chicago and told me all about him. Later I met Richard at the wedding. She didn't exaggerate. He's a rare man.'

'Do you know where they are right now?' demanded Abel.

'Yes.'

'Where?'

'Find out for yourself.' The line went dead. Someone else who didn't want to help.

On the desk in front of him lay an unopened file containing details of his forthcoming trip to Europe. He flicked over the pages. Two airplane tickets, two reservations in London, Edinburgh and Cannes. Two opera tickets, two theatre tickets, but now only one person was going. Florentyna would not be opening the Edinburgh Baron or the Cannes Baron.

He sank into a fitful sleep from which he didn't want to be woken. George found him slumped at his desk at eight o'clock the next morning.

He promised Abel by the time he had returned from Europe he would have located Florentyna, but Abel now realized after reading Florentyna's letter again and again that even if he did she wouldn't agree to see him.

15

'I would like to borrow thirty-four thousand dollars,' said Florentyna.

'What do you need the money for?' said Richard coldly.

'I want to take over the lease for a building on Nob Hill to open a fashion shop.'

'What are the terms of the lease?'

'Ten years, with an option to renew.'

'What security can you offer against the loan?'

'I own three thousand shares in the Baron Group.'

'But that's a private company,' said Richard, 'and the shares are in effect worthless as they can't be traded over the counter.'

'But the Baron Group is worth fifty million of anybody's money and my shares represent one per cent of the company.'

'How did you come into possession of these shares?'

'My father is the chairman of the company and he gave them to me on my twenty-first birthday.'

'Then why don't you borrow the money direct from him?'

'Oh, hell,' said Florentyna. 'Will they be that demanding?'

'I'm afraid so, Jessie.'

'Are all bank managers going to be as tough as you? They never treated me like this in Chicago.'

'That's because they had the security of your father's account. Anyone who doesn't know you is not going to be as accommodating. A loan manager has to consider that every new transaction will *not* be repaid, so unless his risk is covered twice over it's his job that will be on the line. When you borrow money you must always look across the table and consider the other person's point of view. Everyone who wants to borrow money is sure they are on to a winner, but the manager knows that over fifty percent of deals put up to him will eventually fail, or at best break even. So the manager has to pick and choose carefully to be certain he can always see a way of retrieving his money. My father used to say that most financial deals saw a return of one per cent for the bank, which didn't allow you the opportunity to make a one hundred per cent loss more than once every five years.'

'That all makes sense, so how do I answer, "Why don't you go to your father"?'

'Tell the truth. Remember, banking is based on trust, and if they know you're always being straight with them, they'll stand by you when you are going through hard times.'

'You still haven't answered the question.'

'You simply say: my father and I quarrelled over a family matter and now I wish to succeed in my own right.'

'Do you think that will work?'

'I don't know, but if it does, at least you'll have started with all your cards on the table. Right, let's go back over it again.'

'Must we?'

'Yes. No one owes you money, Jessie.'

'I would like to borrow thirty-four thousand dollars.'

'What do you need the money for?'

'I would like to take over –'

'Supper's ready,' roared Bella.

'Rescued,' said Florentyna.

'Only until after we've eaten. How many banks are you seeing on Monday?'

'Three. Bank of California, Wells Fargo and Crocker. Why don't I pop along to the Bank of America and you can simply pass the thirty-four thousand over the counter?'

'Because there are no mixed prisons in America.'

Claude put his head around the door. 'Hurry up, you two, or there won't be any left.'

. . .

George spent as much of his time following up leads on Florentyna as he did being managing director of the Baron Group. He was determined to come up with some concrete results before Abel returned from Europe.

George had a little more success in one quarter than Abel. Zaphia was pleased to inform him that she was making regular trips to the coast to see the happily married couple. It took George only one phone call to a travel agent in Chicago to discover that these trips had been to San Francisco. Within twenty-four hours he had Florentyna's address and phone number. On one occasion, George even managed a brief conversation with his goddaughter, but she was fairly reticent with him.

Henry Osborne made a pretext at wanting to help, but it soon became obvious that he only wished to know what was going on in Abel's life. He even tried to press George into lending him some more money.

'You'll have to wait until Abel returns,' George told him sharply.

'I am not sure I can last that long.'

'I'm sorry, Henry, but I don't have the authority to sanction personal loans.'

'Not even to a board member? You may live to regret that decision, George. After all, I know a lot more about how the group got started than you do, and I am sure there are others who would be willing to pay me for such information.'

. . .

George always arrived at Idlewild Airport thirty minutes early whenever Abel was returning from Europe. He knew the Baron, like a newly appointed director, would be impatient to learn of any developments within the group. But this time he felt certain Abel's opening question would be on a different subject.

As always Abel was one of the first through Customs and once he and George were seated in the back of the company Cadillac, he wasted no time on small talk.

'What news?' demanded Abel, only too aware that George would know to what he was referring.

'Some good, some bad,' said George as he pressed a button by the side window. Abel watched a sheet of glass glide up between the driver and the passenger section of the car. He tapped his finger on the side panel impatiently as he waited. 'Florentyna continues to be in touch with her mother. She's living in a small apartment in San Francisco with some old friends from Radcliffe days.'

'Married?'

'Yes.'

Abel didn't speak for some moments as if taking in the finality of the statement.

'And the Kane boy?' he asked.

'He's found a job in a bank. It seems a lot of people turned him down because word got around that he didn't complete Harvard Business School and his father wouldn't supply a reference. Not many people were willing to employ him if as a consequence they antagonized William Kane. He was finally hired as a junior teller with the Bank of America, at a salary way below what he might have expected with his qualifications.'

'And Florentyna?'

'She's working as the assistant manager in a fashion shop called "Wayout Columbus" near Golden Gate Park. She's also been trying to borrow money from several banks.'

'Why?' said Abel, sounding worried. 'Is she in any sort of trouble?'

'No, she's looking for capital to open her own shop.'

'How much is she hoping to raise?'

'She needs thirty-four thousand dollars for the lease on a small building that's become vacant on Nob Hill.'

Abel considered the information for a moment. 'See that she gets the money. Make it look as if the transaction is an ordinary bank loan and be sure that it's not traceable back to me.' He started tapping on the window again. 'This must always remain between the two of us, George.'

'Anything you say, Abel.'

'And keep me informed of every move she makes, however trivial.'

'What about Richard Kane?'

'I'm not interested in him,' said Abel. 'Now, what's the bad news?'

'Trouble with Henry Osborne again. It seems he owes money everywhere, and I'm fairly certain his only source of income is you. He's still making threats – about revealing that you condoned bribes in the early days when you had taken over the group. Says he's kept all the papers from the first day he met you, when he claims he fixed an extra payment after the fire at the old Richmond in Chicago. He's telling everyone that he now has a file on you three inches thick.'

'I'll deal with Henry in the morning,' said Abel.

. . .

Abel was fully up to date on the group's activities when Henry arrived for his private meeting. Abel looked up at him: the heavy drinking and the debts were beginning to take their toll. For the first time, Abel thought Henry looked older than his years.

'I need a little money to get me through a tricky period,' said Henry even before they had shaken hands. 'I've been a bit unlucky.'

'Again, Henry? You should know better at your age. How much do you need this time?'

'Ten thousand would see me through,' said Henry.

'Ten thousand,' said Abel, spitting out the words. 'What do you think I am, a gold mine? It was only five thousand last time.'

'Inflation,' said Henry, trying to laugh.

'This is the last time, do you understand me?' said Abel as he took out his cheque book. 'Come begging once more and I'll remove you from the board and turn you out without a penny.'

'You're a real friend, Abel. I swear I'll never come back again – I promise you that. Never again.' Abel watched Henry take a cigar from the humidor on the table in front of him and light it. George hadn't done that in twenty years. 'Thanks, Abel. You'll never regret your decision.'

Henry sauntered out of the office drawing on the cigar Abel waited for the door to be closed, then buzzed for George. He appeared moments later.

'What happened?'

'I gave in for the last time,' said Abel. 'I don't know why – it cost me ten thousand.'

'Ten thousand?' said George, sighing. 'You can be sure he'll be back again. I'd be willing to put money on that.'

'He'd better not,' said Abel, 'because I'm through with him. Whatever he's done for me in the past it's now quits. Anything new about my girl?'

'I've set up a facility for Florentyna with the Crocker National Bank of San Francisco,' said George. 'She has an appointment next Monday with the loan officer. The agreement will appear to her as one of the bank's ordinary loan transactions, with no special favours. In fact, they're charging her half a per cent more than usual so there can be no reason for her to be suspicious. What she doesn't know is that the money is covered by your guarantee.'

'Thanks, George, that's perfect. I'll bet you ten dollars she pays off the loan within two years and never needs to go back for another. Keep me briefed on everything she's up to. Everything.'

.   .   .

Florentyna visited three banks the following Monday. The Bank of California showed some interest, Wells Fargo none and Crocker asked her to call back. Richard was surprised and delighted.

'What terms did they discuss?'

'The Bank of California say they would want eight per cent and require to hold the deeds of the lease. Crocker wants eight and a half per cent, the deeds *and* my shares in the Baron Group.'

'Fair terms considering you have no banking history with them, but it will mean you must make a twenty-five per cent profit before taxes, just to break even.'

'I've worked it all out on paper, Richard, and I think I'll make thirty-two per cent in the first year.'

'I studied those figures last night, Jessie, and you're being overly optimistic. You have no hope of achieving that. In fact, I think the company will lose between seven and ten thousand dollars in the first year – so you'll just have to hope they believe in your long-term future.'

'That's exactly what the loan officer said.'

'When are they going to let you know their decision?'

'By the end of the week. It's worse than waiting for exam results.'

.   .   .

'You've done well, Kane,' said the manager. 'And I am advising head office to promote you. What I have in mind ...'

The phone buzzed on the manager's desk. He picked it up and listened.

'It's for you,' he said, surprised, before passing it to Richard.

'The Bank of California said their loans committee had turned me down, but Crocker said yes. Oh, Richard, isn't that wonderful?'

'Yes, ma'am, it's good news indeed,' said Richard avoiding the manager' eye.

'Well, that's very kind of you to say so, Mr Kane. Now I also have this sociological problem and I was wondering if you could help in some way.'

'Perhaps if you were to come around to the bank, ma'am, we could discuss it in greater detail.'

'What a great idea. I've always had this fantasy of making love in a bank vault surrounded by money. Lots and lots of Benjamin Franklins staring at me.'

'I agree with your proposition, ma'am, and I'll call you and confirm at the first possible opportunity.'

'Don't leave it too long or I may decide to move my account.'

'We always try to be of service at the Bank of America, ma'am.'

'If you look at my account, there's not much sign of it.'

The phone clicked.

.   .   .

'Where are we having the celebration?' asked Richard.

'I told you over the phone – in the bank vaults.'

'Darling, when you called I was in private conference with the manager, and he was offering me the number three post in the overseas department.'

'That's fantastic. Then it's a double celebration. Let's go to Chinatown and have five takeaways and five giant Cokes.'

'Why five, Jessie?'

'Because Bella will be joining us. Incidentally, Mr Kane, I prefer it when you call me "ma'am".'

'No, I think I'll stick with Jessie. It reminds me how far you've come since we met.'

Claude arrived that evening carrying a bottle of champagne under each arm. 'Let's open one immediately and celebrate,' said Bella.

'Agreed,' said Florentyna. 'But what about the other one?'

'It's to be saved for some special occasion that none of us could have anticipated,' Claude said firmly.

Richard opened the first bottle and poured out four glasses while Florentyna put the second in the corner of the fridge.

.   .   .

She signed the lease on the tiny building on Nob Hill the next day and the Kanes moved into the small apartment above the shop. Florentyna, Bella and Richard spent their weekends painting and cleaning while Claude, the most artistic of the four, printed the name 'Florentyna's' in royal blue above the shop window. A month later they were ready to open.

During her first week as owner, manageress and clerk, Florentyna contacted all the main wholesalers who had dealt with her father in New York. In no time she had a shop full of goods and ninety days' credit.

Florentyna opened the little shop on 1 August 1958. She always remembered the date because just after midnight Bella produced a twelve-pound baby.

Florentyna had sent out a large mailing announcing the opening of the store, choosing the day before the government raised postage stamps from three cents to four. She had also stolen an assistant named Nancy Ching –

who had Maisie's charm but fortunately not Maisie's I.Q. – from her old employers, 'Wayout Columbus'. On the morning of the opening, the two girls stood by the door in hopeful anticipation but only one person came into the shop the whole day and all he wanted to know was the way to the Mark Hopkins. The next morning, a young woman came in and spent an hour looking at all the shirts they had in from New York. She tried on several but left without purchasing anything. In the afternoon a middle-aged lady fussed about for a long time and finally bought a pair of gloves.

'How much will that be?' she asked.

'Nothing,' said Florentyna.

'Nothing?' queried the lady.

'That's correct. You are the first customer to make a purchase at Florentyna's and there will be no charge.'

'How kind of you,' said the lady. 'I shall tell all my friends.'

. . .

'You never gave me any gloves when I shopped at Bloomingdale's, Miss Kovats,' said Richard that evening. 'You'll be bankrupt by the end of the month if you go on like that.'

But this time his judgement proved wrong. The lady turned out to be President of the Junior League in San Francisco and one word from her was worth more than a full-page advertisement in the San Francisco *Chronicle*.

For the first few weeks Florentyna seemed to be working an eighteen-hour day, for as soon as the doors closed she would check the inventory while Richard went over the books. As the months passed she began to wonder how the little shop could ever hope to make a profit.

At the end of her first year they invited Bella and Claude to join in celebrating the loss of seven thousand three hundred and eighty dollars.

'We've got to achieve better results next year,' said Florentyna firmly.

'Why?' said Richard.

'Because our grocery bills are going to be larger.'

'Is Bella coming to live with us?'

'No. I'm pregnant.'

Richard was overjoyed and his only anxiety was that he couldn't stop Florentyna from working right up until the day she went into hospital. They celebrated the end of their second year with a small profit of two thousand dollars and a large son of nine pounds three ounces. He only had one nipple.

The decision on what they would call their first born, if it was a boy, had been decided weeks before.

. . .

George Novak was both shocked and delighted to be chosen as a godfather for Florentyna's son. Although he didn't admit as much, Abel was also pleased, for he welcomed any opportunity to find out what was happening in his daughter's life.

The day before the christening, George flew out to Los Angeles to check on the progress of the new Baron. Abel was determined to have the building complete by the middle of September in order that John Kennedy could open it while he was on the campaign trail. George then flew on to San Francisco confident that Abel's deadline would be met.

By nature, George took a long time to like people and even longer to trust them. It was not so with Richard Kane. George took to him immediately, and once he was able to see for himself what Florentyna had achieved in such a short time it became obvious that she could not have done it without her husband's common sense and cautious approach. George intended to leave Abel in no doubt how he felt about the boy when he returned to New York.

After a quiet dinner the two men played backgammon at a dollar a point, and discussed the christening. 'Not at all like Florentyna's,' George confided to Richard, who laughed at the thought of his reluctant father-in-law spending a night in jail.

'You seem to throw doubles all the time,' said George, sipping the Rémy Martin Richard had poured for him.

'My father . . .' said Richard, and then hesitated for a moment, 'always accused me of being a bad loser if I made any mention of doubles.'

George laughed. 'And how is your father?'

'I've no idea. There's been no contact with him since Jessie and I were married.' George still couldn't get used to hearing his goddaughter being referred to as Jessie. When he was told the reason why, he knew it would amuse Abel.

'I'm sorry your father seems to be reacting the same way as Abel,' said George.

'I remain in touch with my mother,' continued Richard sipping his brandy, 'but I can see no end to my father's attitude, especially while Abel continues to try and increase his holding in Lester's.'

'Are you sure of that?' asked George, sounding surprised.

'Two years ago every banker on Wall Street knew what he was up to.'

'Abel is now so set in his ways,' said George, 'I can't make him listen to reason. But I don't believe he will cause any more trouble at the moment,' he added, before returning to his brandy. Richard didn't inquire why: he realized that if George wanted to explain he would.

'You may, if Kennedy wins the election,' George continued, once he had put the glass down, 'Abel has an outside chance of a minor appointment in the new administration. I put it no higher than that.'

'Our ambassador to Poland, no doubt,' said Florentyna as she came into the room carrying a tray laden with coffee cups. 'He would be the first Polish immigrant to be so honoured. I've known about that ambition ever since our trip to Europe.'

George didn't reply.

'Is Henry Osborne behind this?' asked Florentyna.

'No, he doesn't even know about it,' said George, relaxing back in his chair. 'Your father no longer places any trust in him. Since Henry lost his seat in Congress he has proved unreliable, to say the least, and your father is even considering removing him from the board.'

'At last Papa has woken up to what a nasty piece of work Henry really is.'

'I think he has always known, but there's no denying Henry was useful to your father when he was in Washington. Personally I think he is still dangerous despite being removed from Congress.'

'Why?' asked Florentyna from her seat in the corner of the room.

'Because I suspect he knows too much about the enmity between Abel and

Richard's father, and if he gets into any more debt I fear he may trade that information with Mr Kane direct.'

'Never,' said Richard.

'How can you be so sure?' asked George.

'You mean after all these years you don't know?' Richard asked.

George stared from one to the other. 'Know what?'

'Obviously not,' said Florentyna.

'You'll need a double,' said Richard, and poured George another large brandy before continuing.

'Henry Osborne hates my father even more than Abel does.'

'What? Why?' said George, leaning forward.

'Henry was married to my grandmother, after my grandfather died.' Richard poured himself another coffee before continuing. 'Many years ago when he was a young man, he tried to part my grandmother from a small family fortune. Osborne didn't succeed because *my* father, aged only seventeen, discovered that his Harvard military background was nothing more than a front and proceeded to throw him out of his own home.'

'Omój Jezu!' said George. 'I wonder if Abel knows any of this.' He hadn't noticed it was his turn to throw the dice.

'Of course he does,' said Florentyna. 'It must have been the deciding factor for employing Henry in the first place. He needed someone on his side who he could be certain would never open his mouth to Kane.'

'How did you find out?'

'Pieced it together when Richard discovered I wasn't Jessie Kovats. Most of the stuff on Henry is in a file locked in the bottom of Papa's desk.'

'I thought I was too old to learn so much in one day,' said George.

'Your day's learning hasn't begun,' said Richard. 'Henry Osborne never went to Harvard, never served in the war, and his real name is Vittorio Togna.'

George didn't speak, just opened his mouth.

'We also know that Papa has six per cent of Lester's Bank. Just imagine the problems he would cause if he could lay his hands on another two per cent,' said Florentyna.

'We think he's trying to buy that two per cent from Peter Parfitt, the deposed chairman of Lester's, with the final aim of removing my father from his own board,' Richard added.

'That may have been right in the past.'

'Why not now?' queried Florentyna.

'Abel won't become involved with anything as silly as removing your father from the bank while Kennedy has him in mind for Warsaw. So you need have no fear in that direction. And perhaps that might make you consider coming as my guest to see the candidate open the new Baron in Los Angeles?'

'Is there any hope of Richard being invited as well?'

'You know the answer to that, Florentyna.'

'Another game, George?' said Richard, changing the subject.

'No, thank you. I know a winner when I see one.' He removed his wallet from an inside pocket and handed over eleven dollars. 'Mind you, I still blame the doubles.'

16

Nancy Ching had run the shop well while Florentyna was away in the hospital, but with Kane junior safely parked in a crib in the back room Florentyna was only too happy to return to work. She explained to Miss Tredgold when she sent the first photos of them together that she was hoping to be a responsible mother until it became impossible not to employ someone. 'Not that I'll find anyone like you outside of Much Hadham,' she added.

During the first two years of their marriage, both she and Richard had concentrated on building their careers. When Florentyna acquired her second shop, Richard also advanced another rung on the bank ladder.

Florentyna would have liked to spend more time concentrating on fashion trends rather than the day-to-day finances but she felt unable to ask Richard to spend every night on her books after he had returned from the bank. She discussed her bold ideas for the future with Nancy, who was a little sceptical about placing so many orders for small sizes.

'It may suit me' – the petite Chinese girl grinned – 'but not most American women.'

'I don't agree. Small is going to be beautiful and we must be the first to anticipate it. If American women think it's the trend, we are going to witness a skinny revolution the like of which will even make you look fat.'

Nancy laughed. 'Looking at your future orders for 4s and 6s, you'd better be right.'

Neither Richard nor Florentyna brought up the vexed subject of their families after George's visit since they both despaired of any reconciliation. They both spoke to their mothers on the phone from time to time, and although Richard received letters from his two sisters, he was particularly sad that he was not invited to attend Virginia's wedding. This unhappy state of affairs might have drifted on indefinitely had it not been for two events. The first was hard to avoid, while the second was caused by the wrong person picking up the phone.

The first occurred because it was Los Angeles's turn to open a Baron. Florentyna followed its progress with great interest while she was preparing to open her third shop. The new hotel was completed in September 1960 and Florentyna took the afternoon off to watch Senator John Kennedy perform the opening ceremony. She stood at the back of a large crowd that had come to see the candidate while she kept an eye on her father. He seemed to her a lot older and had certainly put on weight. From those who were surrounding him it was obvious that he was now well connected in Democratic circles. She wondered if Kennedy were elected would her father be offered 'the chance to serve under him'. Florentyna was impressed by the competent speech of welcome Abel made, but she was mesmerized by the young Presidential candidate who seemed to her to embody the new America. After she had heard him she passionately wanted John Kennedy to be the next President. As soon as the speech in San Francisco was over, she left the newly opened Baron resolved to give time and send money to the Ninth District of Illinois for the Kennedy campaign, although she suspected her father had already contributed a sum that would make her own efforts appear minuscule. Richard remained unshakeably Republican and a supporter of Nixon.

'No doubt you remember what Eisenhower said when he was asked about your standard-bearer?' Florentyna teased.

'Something unflattering, I'm sure.'

'A journalist asked him "What major decisions has the Vice-President participated in?"'

'And what was Ike's reply?'

'If you give me a week, I might think of one.'

. . .

During the remaining weeks of the campaign, Florentyna spent what free time she had addressing envelopes and answering phone calls at the Party's headquarters in San Francisco. Unlike the past two elections, she was convinced the Democrats had found a man in whom she could place unreserved support. The final television debate between the candidates reawakened in her the political ambitions so nearly buried by Henry Osborne. Kennedy's charisma and political insight were dazzling, while Florentyna was left to wonder how anyone who had followed the campaign could possibly vote Republican. Richard pointed out to her that charisma and good looks were not to be traded for a future policy and a proven record, even if it had to include a five o'clock shadow.

All through the election night Richard and Florentyna sat up watching the results. The twists, the turns and the upsets lasted all the way to California, where by the smallest margin in American electoral history Kennedy became President. Florentyna was ecstatic about the final outcome, while Richard maintained that Kennedy would never have made it without Mayor Daley and the Cook County ballot boxes – or lack of them.

'Would you vote the Democratic ticket if I were running for office?'

'It would depend on your policies. I'm a banker, not a sentimentalist.'

'Well, unsentimental banker, I want to open a fourth shop.'

'What?' said Richard.

'There's a bargain going in San Diego, a building with a lease of only two years to run but it could be renewable.'

'How much?'

'Thirty thousand dollars.'

'You're mad, Jessie. That's your projected profits for this year gone in expansion.'

'And while you're on the subject of expansion, I'm pregnant again.'

. . .

When the thirty-fifth President delivered his Inaugural Address Florentyna and Richard watched the ceremony on television in the apartment above the main shop.

'*Let the word go forth, from this time and place, to friend and foe alike, that the torch has been passed to a new generation of Americans, born in this century, tempered by war, disciplined by a hard and bitter peace'* – Florentyna's eyes never once left the man in whom so many people had placed their trust. When President Kennedy concluded his speech with the words, '*Ask not what your country can do for you. Ask what you can do for your country,*' Florentyna watched the crowd rise and found herself joining in the applause. She wondered how many people were clapping in other homes throughout America. She turned to Richard.

'Not bad for a Democrat,' he said, aware he was also clapping.

Florentyna smiled. 'Do you think my father is there?'

'Undoubtedly.'

'So now we sit and wait for the appointment.'

George wrote the next day to confirm that Abel had been in Washington for the celebrations. He ended on the words: 'Your father seems confident about going to Warsaw, and I am equally sure that if he is offered the position, it will be easier to get him to meet Richard.'

'What a friend George has turned out to be,' said Florentyna.

'To Abel as well as to us,' said Richard thoughtfully.

Each day Florentyna checked the new appointments as they were released by Press Secretary Pierre Salinger. But no announcement concerning the Polish ambassador was forthcoming.

17

When Florentyna did see her father's name in the paper, she could hardly miss it: the banner headline was all across the front page:

THE CHICAGO BARON ARRESTED

Florentyna read the story in disbelief.

NEW YORK–Abel Rosnovski, the international hotelier, known as the Chicago Baron, was arrested at eight thirty this morning at an apartment on East Fifty-seventh Street by agents of the FBI. The arrest took place after his return the previous night from a business trip to Turkey where he had opened the Istanbul Baron, the latest in his chain of hotels. Rosnovski was charged by the FBI with bribery and corruption of government officials in fourteen different states. The FBI also wants to question ex-Congressman Henry Osborne who has not been seen in Chicago for the past fortnight.

Rosnovski's defence attorney, H. Trafford Jilks, made a statement denying the charges and added that his client had a full explanation which would exonerate him completely. Rosnovski was granted bail in his own recognisance of ten thousand dollars.

The news story went on to report that rumours had been circulating in Washington for some time that the White House had been considering Mr Rosnovski as America's next ambassador to Poland.

That night Florentyna lay awake wondering how it could have all happened, and what her father must be going through. She assumed Henry was involved in some way, and decided to follow every scrap of information that was reported in the papers. Richard tried to comfort her by saying there were very few businessmen alive who had not at some stage in their careers been involved in a little bribery.

Three days before the trial was due to begin the Justice Department found Henry Osborne in New Orleans. He was arrested, charged and immediately turned State's evidence. The FBI asked Judge Prescott for a postponement to discuss with ex-Congressman Osborne the contents of a dossier on Rosnovski that had recently come into their possession. Judge Prescott granted the FBI a further four weeks to prepare their case.

The press soon discovered that Osborne, in order to clear his considerable debts, had sold the file that he had compiled over ten years while serving as a director of the Baron Group, to a firm of private investigators in Chicago. How the file had then come into the hands of the FBI remained a mystery.

Florentyna was fearful that with Henry Osborne as star witness for the prosecution her father might have to serve a long jail sentence. After another sleepless night, Richard suggested she ought to contact her father. She agreed, and wrote him a long letter assuring him of her support and her belief in his innocence. She was about to lick the envelope when she walked over to her desk, took out her favourite picture of her son and sent it to his grandfather.

Four hours before the trial was due to begin Henry Osborne was found hanging in his cell by a guard bringing in his breakfast. He had used a Harvard tie.

'Why did Henry commit suicide?' Florentyna asked her mother on the phone later that morning.

'Oh, that's easy to explain,' replied Zaphia. 'Henry thought the private investigator who cleared his debts wanted the file for the sole purpose of blackmailing your father.'

'And what was the real reason?' asked Florentyna.

'The file had been purchased anonymously in Chicago on behalf of William Kane, who then passed it on to the FBI.'

.   .   .

Florentyna could only feel hatred whenever she thought about William Kane; she couldn't stop herself from taking it out on Richard. But it was obvious that Richard was every bit as angry about his father's behaviour, which Florentyna discovered when she overheard a phone conversation between him and his mother.

'That was pretty tough,' said Florentyna when he finally put the phone down.

'Yes it was. My poor mother's getting it from both sides.'

'We haven't reached the last act of this tragedy,' said Florentyna. 'Papa has wanted to return to Warsaw for as long as I can remember. Now he will never forgive your father.'

.   .   .

Once the trial began, Florentyna followed the proceedings each day by phoning her mother in the evening after Zaphia had returned from the courtroom. When she listened to her mother's view on the day's happenings she wasn't always convinced they both wanted the same outcome.

'The trial is beginning to go in your father's favour,' she said in the middle of the week.

'How can you be so sure?' asked Florentyna.

'Since the FBI has lost its star witness their case hasn't stood up to much cross-examination. H. Trafford Jilks is making Henry Osborne sound like Pinocchio with a nose that is just about touching the ground.'

'Does that mean Papa will be proved innocent?'

'I wouldn't have thought so, but the courtroom officials are predicting that the FBI will end up having to make a deal.'

'What sort of deal?'

'Well, if your father pleads guilty to some minor offences, they will drop the main charges.'

'Will he get away with a fine?' asked Florentyna anxiously.

'If he's lucky. But Judge Prescott is tough, so he may still end up in jail.'

'Let's hope it's just a fine.'

Zaphia made no comment.

.　　.　　.

'Six months' suspended sentence for the Chicago Baron,' Florentyna heard the newscaster say on her car radio as she was driving to pick up Richard from the bank. She nearly collided with the Buick in front of her and pulled over into a 'no parking' zone so that she could concentrate on what the newscaster had to say.

'The FBI has dropped all the main indictments of bribery against Abel Rosnovski – known as the Chicago Baron – and the defendant pleaded guilty to misdemeanours on two minor counts of attempting to improperly influence a public official. The jury was dismissed. In his summing up Judge Prescott said. "The right to do business does not include the right to suborn public officials. Bribery is a crime and a worse crime when condoned by an intelligent and competent man, who should not need to stoop to such levels.

'"In other countries," the Judge added, "bribery might be an accepted way of life, but that is not the case in the United States." Judge Prescott gave Rosnovski a six months' suspended sentence and a twenty-five thousand dollar fine.

'In other news, President Kennedy has agreed to accompany the Vice-President to Dallas this fall ...' Florentyna turned off the radio to find someone tapping on the side window. She wound it down.

'Do you know that you're in a restricted area, ma'am?'

'Yes,' replied Florentyna.

'I'm afraid it's going to cost you ten dollars.'

.　　.　　.

'Twenty-five thousand dollars and a six months' suspended sentence. It could have been worse,' said George in the car on the way back to the Baron.

'Don't forget that I lost Poland,' said Abel, 'but that's all history now. Purchase the two per cent of the Lester's shares we need from Parfitt, even if it costs a million. That will make up the eight per cent of Lester's that I need to invoke Article Seven of their by-laws and then I can slaughter William Kane in his own board room.'

George nodded sadly.

.   .   .

A few days later the State Department announced that the next American ambassador to Warsaw would be John Moors Cabot.

18

The morning after Judge Prescott's verdict the second event occurred. The extension of the apartment phone rang in the shop and because Nancy was removing the light summer clothes from the window, replacing them with the new autumn collection, Florentyna answered it.

'Oh, I wondered if Mr Kane was in,' said a lady's voice. She sounded a long way off.

'No, I'm sorry, he has already left for the bank. Would you like to leave a message? It's Florentyna Kane speaking.'

There was no immediate reply and then a voice said: 'It's Katherine Kane – please don't hang up.'

'Why should I do that, Mrs Kane?' said Florentyna, her knees feeling so weak that she sank into a chair beside the phone.

'Because you must hate me, my dear, and I can't blame you,' Richard's mother said quickly.

'No, of course I don't hate you. Would you like Richard to call you back when he comes home?'

'Oh, no. My husband doesn't realize that I'm in touch with him. He would be very angry if he ever found out. No, what I was really hoping for will finally depend on you.'

'On me?'

'Yes. I desperately want to visit you and Richard and see my grandson – if you'll allow me.'

'I'd like that very much, Mrs Kane,' said Florentyna, not sure how she could sound more welcoming.

'Oh, how understanding of you. My husband is going to a conference in Mexico in three weeks' time and I could fly out on the Friday. Only I would have to be back first thing on Monday morning.'

When Richard heard the news he went straight to the refrigerator. Florentyna followed, bewildered. She smiled as he stripped the gold foil from Claude's bottle of Krug and began pouring.

Three weeks later Florentyna accompanied Richard to the airport to welcome his mother.

'But you're beautiful,' were Florentyna's first words as she greeted the elegant, slim lady who showed not the slightest sign of having spent the last six hours on a plane. 'And you make me feel terribly pregnant.'

'What were you expecting, my dear? An ogre with red horns and a long black tail?'

Florentyna laughed as Katherine Kane put an arm through hers and they walked off together, temporarily forgetting her son.

Richard was relieved to see how quickly the two of them became friends. When they arrived back at the flat Katherine reacted in the time-honoured way when she set eyes on her first grandchild.

'I do wish your father could see his grandson,' she said. 'But I fear it's now reached a stage where he won't even allow the subject to be discussed.'

'Do you know any more than we do about what is happening between the two men?' asked Richard.

'I wouldn't have thought so. Your father refused to let the bank support Davis Leroy when his hotel group collapsed, and Florentyna's father therefore blames my husband for the subsequent suicide of Mr Leroy. The whole unfortunate episode might have ended there if Henry Osborne hadn't come on to the scene.' She sighed. 'I pray to God the problem will be sorted out in my lifetime.'

'I fear one of them will have to die before the other comes to his senses,' said Richard. 'They are both so confoundedly obstinate.'

The four of them had a wonderful weekend together even if Kate's grandson did spend most of his time throwing his toys on to the floor. When they drove Katherine back to the airport on Sunday night she agreed to come and see them the next time her husband was away on business. Katherine's last words to Florentyna were, 'If only you and my husband could meet, he would be in no doubt why Richard fell in love with you.'

As she turned to wave goodbye, her grandson repeated his one-word vocabulary: 'Dada'. Katherine Kane laughed, 'What chauvinists men are. That was also Richard's first word. Has anyone ever told you what yours was, Florentyna?'

Annabel came screaming into this world a few weeks later, and Richard and Florentyna had a double celebration at the end of the year when Florentyna delivered a nineteen thousand one hundred and seventy-four dollar profit. Richard decided to mark the occasion by spending a small part of those profits on a golf membership of the Olympic Club.

Richard was given more responsibility in the overseas department of the bank, and started coming home an hour later. Florentyna decided the time had come to employ a full-time nanny so that she could concentrate on her work in the shops. She realized that she would never find a Miss Tredgold but Bella recommended a black girl called Carol who had graduated from high school the year before and was finding it hard to secure employment. Their son threw his arms around Carol the moment he met her. It brought home to Florentyna that prejudice was something children learn from their elders.

19

'I can't believe it,' said Florentyna. 'I never thought it would happen. What wonderful news. But what made him change his mind?'

'He's not getting any younger,' said Katherine Kane, her voice crackling down the phone, 'and he's frightened that if he and Richard don't patch up their differences soon he will retire from Lester's without a son on the board. He also believes that the man most likely to succeed him in the chair is Jake Thomas, and as Mr Thomas is only two years older than Richard, he certainly won't want a younger Kane in the board room.'

'I wish Richard was at home so I could tell him the news, but since he's been promoted to head of the overseas department he rarely gets back before seven. He'll be so pleased. I'll try not to show how nervous I am about meeting your husband,' said Florentyna.

'Not half as nervous as he is about meeting you. But have no fears, my dear, he's preparing the fatted calf for his prodigal son. Have you heard anything from your father since I last spoke to you?'

'No, nothing. I fear there's never going to be a fatted calf for the prodigal daughter.'

'Don't give up. Something may yet arise that makes him see the light. We'll all put our heads together when you come to New York.'

'I would love to believe it was still possible for Papa to be reconciled, but I've almost given up hope.'

'Well, let's be thankful that one father has at least come to his senses,' said Katherine. 'I'll fly out to see you and fix up all the details.'

'How soon can you come?'

'I could get away this weekend.'

When Richard came home that evening he was overjoyed by the news, and once he had finished reading the next chapter of *Winnie the Pooh* to his son, he settled down to listen to the details of his mother's news.

'We could go to New York around November,' said Richard.

'I'm not sure I can wait that long.'

'You've waited for over three years.'

'Yes, but that's different.'

'You always want everything to have happened yesterday, Jessie. That reminds me, I read your proposal for the new shop in San Diego.'

'And?'

'Basically the idea makes a lot of sense and I approve.'

'Good heavens. What next? I never thought I would hear such words from you, Mr Kane.'

'Now hold on, Jessie, it doesn't get my whole-hearted support because the one part of your expansion programme I don't understand is the necessity to employ your own designer.'

'That's easy enough to explain,' said Florentyna. 'Although we now have five shops my expenditure on buying clothes remains as high as forty per cent of turnover. If my own garments were designed for me, I would have two obvious advantages. First, I could cut down my immediate expenditure, and second we would be continually advertising our own product.'

'It also has a major disadvantage,' suggested Richard.

'What's that?'

'There can be no rebate on clothes returned within ninety days if we already own them.'

'Agreed,' said Florentyna. 'But the more we expand the more that problem will diminish. And if I choose the right designer we'll end up with our trade-mark clothes also being sold by our rivals.'

'Has that proved worthwhile for other designers?'

'In the case of Pierre Cardin, the designer became more famous than the shops.'

'Finding such a man won't be easy.'

'Didn't I find you, Mr Kane?'

'No, Jessie, I found you.'

Florentyna smiled. 'Two children, a sixth shop, and you're going to be invited to join the board of Lester's. Most important of all I have a chance to meet your father. What more could we want?'

'It hasn't happened yet.'

'Typical banker. Whatever the forecast, you expect it to rain by mid-afternoon.'

Annabel started to cry.

'See what I mean?' said Richard. 'Your daughter's at it again.'

'Why is it always my daughter who is bad and your son who is good?'

Despite Florentyna's desire to travel to New York immediately after Kate had returned to the east coast, she was more than fully occupied with opening the new shop in San Diego, keeping an eye on the other five shops, and somehow looking for the right designer, while still trying to be a mother. As the day for their journey to New York grew nearer she became more and more nervous. She selected her own wardrobe carefully and bought several new outfits for the children. She even purchased a new shirt with a thin red stripe running through it for Richard, but she doubted that he would wear it except at weekends. Florentyna lay awake each night anxious that Richard's father might not approve of her, but Richard kept reminding her of Katherine's words: 'Not half as nervous as he is.'

.   .   .

To celebrate the opening of the sixth shop and the imminent reconciliation with his father, Richard took Florentyna to a performance of *The Nutcracker* by the Italian State Ballet Company at the War Memorial Opera House. Richard didn't care much for the ballet himself but he was surprised to find Florentyna equally as restless during the performance. As soon as the house lights went up for the intermission he asked if anything was wrong.

'Yes. I've been waiting over an hour to find out who designed those fabulous costumes.' Florentyna started to thumb through her programme.

'I would have described them as outrageous,' said Richard.

'That's because you're colour-blind,' said Florentyna. Having found what she was looking for she started reading the programme notes to Richard. 'His name is Gianni di Ferranti. His biography says he was born in Milan in 1931 and that this is his first tour with the Italian State Ballet Company since leaving the Institute of Modern Art in Florence. I wonder if he would consider resigning from the company and working for me?'

'I wouldn't, with the inside information I have on the company,' said Richard, helpfully.

'Perhaps he's more adventurous than you, darling.'

'Or just mad. After all, he is Italian.'

'Well, there's only one way to find out,' said Florentyna, standing up.

'And how do you propose doing that?'

'By going backstage.'

'But you'll miss the second half of the performance.'

'The second half might not change my whole life,' said Florentyna, stepping into the aisle.

Richard followed her out of the building and they made their way around the outside to the stage door. A young security guard pushed open his window.

'Can I help you?' he asked, sounding as if it were the last thing he wanted to do.

'Yes,' Florentyna said confidently. 'I have an appointment with Gianni di Ferranti.'

Richard looked at his wife disapprovingly.

'Your name, please,' said the guard, picking up a phone.

'Florentyna Kane.'

The guard repeated the name into the mouthpiece, listened for a moment, then replaced the receiver.

'He says he's never heard of you.'

Florentyna was taken aback for a moment but Richard took out his wallet and placed a twenty-dollar bill on the ledge in front of the guard.

'Perhaps he has heard of me,' said Richard.

'You better go and find out,' said the guard, casually removing the note. 'Through the door, take the corridor to your right, second door on the left,' he added before slamming down the window.

Richard led Florentyna through the entrance.

'Most businessmen are involved in a little bribery at some stage in their careers,' she teased.

'Now don't get annoyed just because your lie failed,' said Richard, grinning.

When they reached the room, Florentyna knocked firmly and peered around the door.

A tall, dark-haired Italian was seated in one corner of the room eating spaghetti with a fork. Florentyna's first reaction was one of admiration. He was wearing a pair of tailored jeans and blue blazer over a casual open-necked shirt. But the thing that struck her most was the young man's long, artistic fingers. The moment he saw Florentyna he rose gracefully to his feet.

'Gianni,' she began expansively. 'What a privilege –'

'No,' said the man in a soft Italian accent. 'He's in the washroom.'

Richard smirked and received a sharp kick on the ankle. Florentyna was

about to speak again when the door opened and in walked a man no more
than five feet five, nearly bald, and from the programme notes she knew he
was not yet thirty. His clothes were beautifully cut, but the pasta had had
a greater effect on his waistline than it had had on his friend.

'Who are these people, Valerio?'

'Mrs Florentyna Kane,' said Florentyna before the young man could
speak. 'And this is my husband, Richard.'

'What do you want?' he asked, not looking at her while taking the seat
opposite his companion.

'To offer you a job as my designer.'

'Not another one,' he said, throwing his hands in the air.

Florentyna took a deep breath. 'Who else has spoken to you?'

'In New York, Yves Saint Laurent. In Los Angeles, Pierre Cardin. In
Chicago, Balmain. Need I go on?'

'But did they offer you a percentage of the profits?'

'What profits?' Richard wanted to ask, but remembered the kick on the
ankle.

'I already have six shops and we have plans for another six in the pipeline,'
Florentyna continued impulsively. She hoped that Gianni di Ferranti hadn't
noticed her husband's eyebrows rise dramatically at her words.

'The turnover could be millions within a few years,' she continued.

'Saint Laurent's turnover already is,' said di Ferranti, still not turning to
face her.

'Yes, but what did they offer you?'

'Twenty-five thousand dollars a year, and one per cent of the profits.'

'I'll offer you twenty thousand and five per cent.'

The Italian waved a dismissive hand.

'Twenty-five thousand dollars and ten per cent?' she said.

The Italian laughed, rose from his chair and opened the door for Florentyna and Richard to leave. She stood firm.

'You are the sort of person who would expect Zeffirelli to be available to
design your next shop while still hoping to retain Luigi Ferpozzi as honorary
adviser. Not that I could expect you to understand what I'm talking about,'
he added.

'Luigi,' said Florentyna, haughtily, 'is a dear friend of mine.'

The Italian placed his hands on his hips and roared with laughter. 'You
Americans are all the same. Next you'll be saying you designed the Pope's
vestments.'

Richard had some sympathy with him.

'Your bluff is called, signora. Ferpozzi came to see the show in Los Angeles
only last week and spoke to me at length about my work. Now at least I have
found a way to be rid of you.' Di Ferranti left the door open and picked up
the phone on his dressing table and without another word dialled a 213
number.

No one spoke while they waited for the call to be answered. Eventually
Florentyna heard a voice which she thought she recognized.

'Luigi?' said di Ferranti. 'It's Gianni. I have an American lady with me
called Mrs Kane who claims she is a friend of yours.'

He listened for a few moments, his smile becoming broader.

He turned to Florentyna. 'He says he doesn't know anyone called Mrs Kane, and perhaps you would feel more at home on Alcatraz?'

'No, I wouldn't care for Alcatraz,' said Florentyna. 'But tell him he thinks my father built it.'

Gianni di Ferranti repeated Florentyna's sentiments over the phone. As he listened to the reply his face became puzzled. He finally looked back at her. 'Luigi says to offer you a cup of tea. But only if you've brought your own pot.'

It took Florentyna two lunches, one dinner with Richard, one with her bankers, and an advance big enough to move Gianni and his friend Valerio from Milan to a new home in San Francisco to persuade the little Italian to join her as the company's new in-house designer. Florentyna was confident that this was the breakthrough she had been looking for. In the excitement of convincing Gianni she quite forgot they were only six days away from going to New York to meet Richard's father.

.   .   .

Florentyna and Richard were having breakfast that Monday morning when his face turned so white that she thought he was going to faint.

'What's the matter, darling?'

He pointed to the front page of the *Wall Street Journal* as if unable to speak. Florentyna read the bald announcement and silently handed the paper back to her husband. He read the statement slowly for a second time to be certain he understood the full implications. The brevity and force of the words were stunning. 'William Lowell Kane, the President and Chairman of Lester's Bank, resigned after Friday's board meeting.'

Richard knew that the city would put the worst interpretation possible on such a sudden departure, made without explanation or any suggestion of illness, especially as his only son, a banker, had not been invited to take his place on the board. He put his arms around Florentyna and held her close to his chest.

'Does it mean our trip to New York will be cancelled?'

'Not unless your father was the cause.'

'It can't happen – I won't *let* it happen. Not after waiting so long.'

The phone rang and Richard leaned over to answer it, not letting go of Florentyna.

'Hello?'

'Richard, it's mother. I've been trying to get away from the house. Have you heard the news?'

'Yes, I've just read it in the *Wall Street Journal*. What in heaven's name made father resign?'

'I'm not certain of all the details myself, but as far as I can gather, Mr Rosnovski has held six per cent of the bank's shares for the past ten years, and for some reason he only needed eight per cent to be able to remove your father from the chair.'

'To invoke Article Seven,' said Richard.

'Yes, that's right. But I'm still not sure what that means.'

'Well, father had the clause put into the bank's by-laws to protect himself from ever being taken over. He considered the clause was foolproof because only someone in possession of eight per cent or more could challenge his authority. He never imagined anyone other than the family could ever get their hands on such a large stake in the company. Father would never have given up his fifty-one per cent of Kane and Cabot to become chairman of Lester's if he had felt an outsider could remove him.'

'But that still doesn't explain why he had to resign.'

'I suppose Florentyna's father somehow got hold of another two per cent. That would have given him the same powers as father and made life at the bank impossible for him as chairman.'

'But how could he make life impossible?' It was now obvious to Richard that his father had not even confided in Kate about what was happening at the bank.

'Among the safeguards that Article Seven stipulates, if I remember correctly,' Richard continued, 'is that anyone in possession of eight per cent of the shares can hold up any transaction the bank is involved in for three months. I know from the bank's audit that Mr Rosnovski held six per cent. I suppose he obtained the other two per cent from Peter Parfitt.'

'No, he didn't get the shares from Parfitt,' said Kate. 'I know your father managed to secure those shares by getting an old friend to purchase them for considerably more than they were worth, which is why he has felt so relaxed and confident about the future lately.'

'Then the real mystery is how Mr Rosnovski got hold of the other two per cent. I know no one on the board who would have parted with their own shares unless . . .'

'Your three minutes are up, ma'am.'

'Where are you, Mother?'

'I'm in a pay phone. Your father has forbidden any of us to contact you ever again, and he never wants to set eyes on Florentyna.'

'But this has nothing to do with her, she's . . .'

'I'm sorry, ma'am, but your three minutes are up.'

'I'll pay for the call, operator.'

'I'm sorry, sir, but the call has been disconnected.'

Richard replaced the phone reluctantly.

Florentyna looked up. 'Can you forgive me, darling, for having a father who was involved in such a terrible thing? I know I will never forgive him.'

'Never prejudge anyone, Jessie,' said Richard, as he stroked her hair. 'I suspect that if we ever discover the whole truth we shall find that the blame is fairly evenly distributed on both sides. Now, young lady, you have two children and six stores to worry about and I, no doubt, have irate customers waiting for me at the bank. Put this whole incident behind you because I am convinced that the worst is now over.'

Florentyna continued to cling to her husband, thankful for the strength of his words, even if she did not believe them.

.   .   .

Abel read the announcement of William Kane's resignation in the *Wall Street Journal* the same day. He picked up the phone, dialled Lester's Bank and asked to speak to the new chairman. A few seconds later Jake Thomas came on the line. 'Good morning, Mr Rosnovski.'

'Good morning, Mr Thomas. I'm just phoning to confirm that I shall release this morning my eight per cent holding in Lester's to you personally for two million dollars.'

'Thank you, Mr Rosnovski, that's most generous of you.'

'No need to thank me, Mr Chairman. It's no more than we agreed on when you sold me your two per cent.'

Florentyna realized that it would take a considerable time to recover from the blow inflicted by her father. She wondered how it was still possible to love him and to hate him at the same time. She tried to concentrate on her fast-growing empire and to put the thought of never seeing her father again out of her mind.

Another blow, not as personal, but every bit as tragic for Florentyna was delivered on 22 November 1963. Richard called her from the bank, something he had never done before, to tell her that President Kennedy had been shot in Dallas, and early reports feared he might die.

20

Florentyna's newly acquired Italian designer Gianni di Ferranti, had come up with the idea of putting a small entwined double F on the collar or hem of all his garments. It looked most impressive and only added to the company's reputation. Although Gianni was the first to admit that it was nothing more than a copy of an idea that Yves Saint Laurent had used, nevertheless it worked.

Florentyna found time to fly to Los Angeles to check on a property that was up for sale on Rodeo Drive in Beverly Hills. Once she had seen it, she told Richard she had plans for a seventh Florentyna's. He said he would need to study the figures carefully before he could advise her if she should take up the offer, but he was under such pressure at the bank that it might have to wait a few days.

Not for the first time Florentyna felt the need of a partner or at least a financial director, now that Richard was so overworked. She would have liked to ask him to join her but she felt diffident about suggesting it.

'You'll have to put an advertisement in the *Chronicle* and see how many replies you get,' said Richard. 'I'll help you screen them and we can interview the short list together.'

Florentyna followed Richard's instructions, and within days the letters had flooded in from bankers, lawyers and accountants, all of whom showed considerable interest in the appointment. Richard helped Florentyna sift through the replies. Halfway through the evening he paused over a particular letter and said: 'I'm crazy.'

'I know, my darling, that's why I married you.'

'We've wasted four hundred dollars.'

'Why? You felt sure the advertisement would turn out to be a worthwhile investment.'

Richard handed her the letter he had been reading.

'Seems well qualified,' said Florentyna, after she had read it through. 'Since he's at the Bank of America, you must have your own opinion as to whether he's a suitable man to be my financial director.'

'He's eminently suitable. But who do you imagine will fill his position if he leaves the bank to join you?'

'I've no idea.'

'Well, since he's my boss, it might be me,' said Richard.

Florentyna burst out laughing. 'And to think I didn't have the courage to ask you. Still, I consider it four hundred dollars well spent – partner.'

Richard Kane left the Bank of America four weeks later and joined his wife as a fifty per cent partner and the Financial Director of Florentyna Inc. of San Francisco, Los Angeles and San Diego.

.   .   .

Another election went by. Florentyna didn't become involved because she was so overworked with her expanding empire. She admitted to Richard that she couldn't trust Johnson while she despised Goldwater. Richard put a bumper sticker on their car which Florentyna immediately tore off:

$$Au + H^2O = 1964$$

They agreed not to discuss the subject again, although Florentyna did gloat over the Democratic landslide that followed in November.

During the next year, their two children grew more quickly than the company, and on their son's fifth birthday they opened two more Florentyna's: in Chicago and Boston. Richard remained cautious about the speed at which the shops were springing up but Florentyna's pace never faltered. With so many new customers wanting to wear Gianni di Ferranti's clothes, she spent most of her spare time combing cities for prime sites.

By 1966 there was only one important city that did not boast a Florentyna's. She realised it might be years before a site fell vacant on the only avenue fit for the Florentyna's of New York.

21

'You're a stubborn old fool, Abel.'

'I know, but I can't turn the clock back now.'

'Well, I can tell you, nothing's going to stop me accepting the invitation.'

Abel looked up from his bed. He had hardly left the penthouse since that severe bout of 'flu six months before. After he had returned from an extensive trip to Poland, George was almost his only contact with the outside world. He knew his oldest friend was right, and he had to admit that it was tempting. He wondered if Kane would be going. He found himself hoping so, but he doubted it. The man was every bit as stubborn as he was ...

George voiced Abel's thoughts. 'I bet William Kane will be there.'

Abel made no comment. 'Have you the final run-down on Warsaw?'

'Yes,' said George sharply, angry that Abel had changed the subject. 'All the agreements are signed and John Gronowski couldn't have been more cooperative.'

John Gronowski, the first Polish ambassador to Warsaw, reflected Abel. *He would never recover from* . . .

'Your trip to Poland last year has achieved everything you could have hoped for. You will live to open the Warsaw Baron.'

'I always wanted Florentyna to open it,' said Abel quietly.

'Then invite her, but don't expect any sympathy from me. All you have to do is acknowledge Richard's existence. And even you must have woken up to the fact that their marriage is a success, otherwise *that* wouldn't be on the mantelpiece.' George stared across the room. There, propped up in front of a vase, stood an unanswered invitation.

.   .   .

Everyone in New York seemed to be there when Florentyna Kane opened her new boutique on Fifth Avenue. Florentyna, wearing a green dress that had been specially designed for her with the now famous double F on the high collar, stood near the entrance of the shop, greeting each of her guests and offering them a glass of champagne. Katherine Kane, accompanied by her daughter Lucy, was among the first to arrive and very quickly the floor was crowded with people whom Florentyna either knew very well or had never seen before. George Novak arrived a little later and delighted Florentyna by his first request – to be introduced to the Kanes.

'Will Mr Rosnovski be coming later?' Lucy asked innocently.

'I'm afraid not,' said George. 'I told him that he was a stubborn old fool to miss such a good party. Is Mr Kane here?'

'No, he's not been well lately and rarely leaves the house nowadays,' said Kate, and she then confided to George a piece of news that delighted him.

'How is my father?' Florentyna whispered into George's ear.

'Not well. I left him in bed in the penthouse. Perhaps when he hears that tonight you're going to . . .'

'Perhaps,' said Florentyna. She took Kate by the arm and introduced her to Zaphia. For a moment, neither of the old ladies spoke. Then Zaphia said, 'It's wonderful to meet you at last. Is your husband with you?'

The room became so crowded that it was almost impossible to move, and the ringing laughter and chatter left Florentyna in no doubt how well the opening was going, but now she had only one thing on her mind: dinner that evening.

.   .   .

Outside, a large crowd had gathered on the corner of Fifty-sixth Street to stare at what was going on and the traffic on Fifth Avenue had nearly come to a standstill as men and women, young and old, peered through the large plate glass windows.

A man stood in a doorway on the far side of the road. He wore a black coat, a scarf around his neck and a hat pulled well down on his head. It was a cold evening and the wind was whistling down Fifth Avenue. Not a day for old men, he thought, and wondered if after all it had been wise to leave the warmth of his bed. But he was determined that nothing would prevent his witnessing the opening of this shop. He fiddled with the silver band around his wrist and remembered the new will he had made, not leaving the heirloom to his daughter as he had originally promised.

He smiled as he watched young people surge in and out of the splendid shop, Through the window he could just make out his ex-wife talking to George, and then he saw Florentyna and a tear trickled down his lined cheek. She was even more beautiful than he remembered her. He wanted to cross the road that divided them and say, 'George was right, I've been a stubborn old fool for far too long. Can you possibly forgive me?' but instead he just stood and stared, his feet remaining fixed to the ground. He saw a young man by his daughter's side, tall, self-assured and aristocratic; he could only be the son of William Kane. A fine man, George had told him. How had he described him? Florentyna's strength. Abel wondered if Richard hated him and feared that he must. The old man turned up his collar, took one last look at his beloved daughter and turned to retrace his steps back to the Baron.

As he walked away from the shop he saw another man heading slowly along the pavement. He was taller than Abel, but his walk was just as unsteady. Their eyes met, but only for a moment, and as they passed each other the taller of the old men raised his hat. Abel returned the compliment and they continued on their separate ways without a word.

. . .

'Thank heavens, the last one has gone,' said Florentyna. 'And only just enough time for a bath before changing for dinner.'

Katherine Kane kissed her and said, 'See you in an hour.'

Florentyna locked the front door of the shop and, holding her children's hands tightly, she walked with them towards the Pierre. It would be the first time since her childhood she had stayed in a hotel in New York other than the Baron.

'Another day of triumph for you, my darling,' said Richard.

'To be followed by a night?'

'Oh, stop fussing, Jessie. Father will adore you.'

'It's been such a long time, Richard.'

Richard followed her through the front door of the Pierre, then caught up with his wife and put his arm around her. 'Ten wasted years, but now we have the chance to make up for the past.' Richard guided his family towards the elevator. 'I'll make sure that the children are washed and dressed while you have your bath.'

Florentyna lay in the bath, wondering how the evening would turn out. From the moment Kate Kane had told her of Richard's father's desire to see them all, she had feared he would change his mind once again; but now the meeting was only an hour away. She wondered if Richard was having the same misgivings. She stepped out of the bath, dried herself before putting on a hint of Joy, her favourite perfume, and a long blue dress especially chosen for the occasion: Kate had told her that her husband's favourite colour was blue. She hunted through her jewelry for something simple and slipped on the antique ring given to her so long ago by her father's backer. When she was fully dressed she stared at herself critically in the mirror:

thirty-three, no longer young enough to wear mini skirts, nor old enough to be elegant.

Richard came in from the adjoining room. 'You look stunning,' he said. 'The old man will fall in love with you on sight.' Florentyna smiled and brushed the children's hair while Richard changed. Their son, now seven, was wearing his first suit and looked quite grown-up; Annabel had on a red dress with a white ribbon around the hem: she had no problem with the latest mini fashion.

'I think we're all ready,' said Florentyna when Richard reappeared. She couldn't believe her eyes: he was wearing a shirt with a thin red stripe running through it.

The chauffeur opened the door of their hired Lincoln and Florentyna followed her children into the back. Richard sat in front. As the car drove slowly through the crowded New York streets Florentyna sat in silence. Richard leaned over and touched her hand. The chauffeur brought the car to a stop outside a small elegant brownstone apartment on Sixty-eighth Street.

'Now, children, remember you must be on your best behaviour,' said Florentyna.

'Yes, Mummy,' they said in unison, unawed by the thought of at last meeting one of their grandfathers.

Before they had even stepped out of the car the front door of the house was opened by an elderly man in a morning coat who bowed slightly.

'Good evening, ma'am,' he said. 'And how nice to see you again, Mr Richard.'

Kate was waiting in the hall to greet them. Florentyna's eyes were immediately drawn to an oil painting of a beautiful woman who sat in a crimson leather chair, hands resting in her lap.

'Richard's grandmother,' said Kate. 'I never knew her, but it's easy to see why she was considered one of the beauties of her day.'

Florentyna continued to stare.

'Is something wrong, my dear?' Kate asked.

'The ring,' she said, barely in a whisper.

'Yes, it's beautiful, isn't it?' said Kate, holding up her hand to display a diamond and sapphire ring. 'William gave it to me when he asked me to be his wife.'

'No, the other one in the portrait,' said Florentyna.

'The antique one, yes, quite magnificent. It had been in the family for generations but I fear it's been lost for some years. When I remarked on its disappearance to William he said he knew nothing of it.'

Florentyna raised her right hand and Kate stared down at the antique ring in disbelief. They all looked at the oil painting – there was absolutely no doubt.

'It was a christening present,' said Florentyna. 'Only I never knew who gave it to me.'

'Oh, my God,' said Richard. 'It never crossed my mind ...'

'And my father still doesn't know,' said Florentyna.

A maid bustled into the hall. 'Excuse me, ma'am, I've told Mr Kane that everybody has arrived. He asked if Richard and his wife would be kind enough to go up on their own.'

'You go on up,' said Kate. 'I'll join you in a few minutes with the children.'

Florentyna took her husband's arm and climbed the stairs, nervously fingering the antique ring. They entered the room to find William Lowell Kane sitting in the crimson leather chair by the fire. Such a fine-looking man, thought Florentyna, realizing for the first time what her husband would look like when he was old.

'Father,' said Richard, 'I would like you to meet my wife.'

Florentyna stepped forward, to be greeted by a warm and gentle smile on William Kane's face.

Richard waited for his father's response but Florentyna knew that the old man would never speak to her now.

22

Abel picked up the phone by the side of his bed. 'Find George for me. I need to get dressed.' Abel read the letter again. He couldn't believe William Kane had been his backer.

When George arrived, Abel didn't speak. He just handed over the letter. George read it slowly. 'Oh, my God,' he said.

'I must attend the funeral.'

George and Abel arrived at Trinity Church in Boston a few minutes after the service had begun. They stood behind the last row of respectful mourners. Richard and Florentyna stood on each side of Kate. Three senators, five congressmen, two bishops, most of the chairmen of the leading banks and the publisher of the *Wall Street Journal* were all there. The chairman and every director of the Lester's board were also present.

'Do you think they can forgive me?' asked Abel.

George did not reply.

'Will you go and see them?'

'Yes, of course.'

'Thank you, George. I hope William Kane had a friend as good as you.'

     .   .   .

Abel sat up in bed looking towards the door every few moments. When it eventually opened he hardly recognized the beautiful lady who had once been his 'little one'. He smiled defiantly as he stared over the top of his half-moon spectacles. George remained by the door as Florentyna ran to the side of the bed and threw her arms around her father – a long hug that couldn't make up for ten wasted years, he told her.

'So much to talk about,' he continued. 'Chicago, Poland, politics, the shops ... But first, Richard. Can he ever believe I didn't know until yesterday that his father was my backer?'

'Yes, Papa, because he only discovered it himself a day before you, and we are still not sure how you found out.'

'A letter from the lawyers of the First National Bank of Chicago who had been instructed not to inform me until after his death. What a fool I've been,' Abel added. 'Will Richard see me?' he asked, his voice sounding very frail.

'He wants to meet you so much, he and the children are waiting downstairs.'

'Send for them, send for them,' Abel said, his voice rising. George smiled and disappeared.

'And do you still want to be President?' Abel asked.

'Of the Baron Group?'

'No, of the United States. Because if you do, I well remember my end of the bargain. All the way to the convention floor even if it means I end up destitute.'

Florentyna smiled, but made no comment.

A few moments later there was a knock at the door. Abel tried to push himself up as Richard came into the room, followed by the children. The head of the Kane family walked forward and shook hands warmly with his father-in-law.

'Good morning, sir,' he said. 'It's an honour to meet you.'

Abel couldn't get any words out so Florentyna introduced him to Annabel and his grandson.

'And what is your name?' demanded the old man.

'William Abel Kane.'

Abel gripped the boy's hand. 'I am proud to have my name linked with that of your other grandfather.'

'You will never begin to know how sad I am about your father,' he said turning to Richard. 'I never realized. So many mistakes over so many years. It didn't cross my mind, even for a moment, that your father could have been my benefactor. God knows, I wish I could be given one chance to thank him personally.'

'He would have understood,' said Richard. 'But there was a clause in the deeds of the family trust which didn't allow him to reveal his identity because of the potential conflict between his professional and private interests. He would never have considered making an exception to any rule. That's why his customers trusted him with their life savings.'

'Even if it resulted in his own death?' asked Florentyna.

'I've been just as obdurate,' said Abel.

'That's hindsight,' said Richard. 'None of us could have known that Henry Osborne would cross our paths.'

'Your father and I met, you know, the day he died,' said Abel.

Florentyna and Richard stared at him in disbelief.

'Oh, yes,' said Abel. 'We passed each other on Fifth Avenue – he had come to watch the opening of your new shop. He raised his hat to me. It was enough, quite enough.'

Soon they were talking of happier days; both laughed a little and cried a lot.

'You must forgive us, Richard,' said Abel. 'The Polish are a sentimental race.'

'I know,' he replied. 'My children are half Polish.'

'Can you join me for dinner tonight?'

'Of course,' said Richard.

'Have you ever experienced a real Polish feast, my boy?'

'Every Christmas for the past ten years,' Richard replied.

Abel laughed, then talked of the future and how he saw the progress of his group. 'We ought to have one of your shops in every hotel,' he told Florentyna.

She agreed.

Abel had only one other request of Florentyna: that she and Richard would accompany him on his journey to Warsaw in nine months' time for the opening of the latest Baron. Richard assured him both of them would be there.

·   ·   ·

During the following months Abel was reunited with his daughter and quickly grew to respect his son-in-law. George had been right about the boy all along – why *had* he been so stubborn?

He confided in Richard that he wanted their return to Poland to be one Florentyna would never forget. Abel had asked his daughter to open the Baron Warsaw but she had insisted that only the President of the group could perform such a task, although she was anxious about her father's health.

Every week Florentyna and her father would follow the progress of the new hotel. As the time drew nearer for the opening the old man even practised his speech in front of her.

·   ·   ·

The whole family travelled to Warsaw together. They inspected the first Western hotel to be built behind the Iron Curtain, to be reassured that it was everything Abel had promised.

The opening ceremony took place in the massive gardens in front of the hotel. The Polish Minister of Tourism made the opening speech welcoming the guests. He then called upon the President of the Baron Group to say a few words before performing the opening ceremony.

Abel's speech was delivered exactly as he had written it and at its conclusion the thousand guests on the lawn rose and cheered.

The Minister of Tourism then handed a large pair of scissors to the President of the Baron Group. Florentyna cut the ribbon that ran across the entrance of the hotel and said, 'I declare the Baron Warsaw open.'

·   ·   ·

Florentyna had travelled to Slonim to scatter the ashes of her father in his birthplace. As she stood on the land where her father had been born she vowed never to forget her family's origins.

Richard tried to comfort her, but in the short time he had come to know his father-in-law he had recognized the many qualities he had passed on to his daughter.

Florentyna realized that she could never come to terms with their short reconciliation. She still had so much to tell her father and even more to learn from him. She continually thanked George for the time they had been allowed to share as a family, knowing the loss was every bit as deep for him. The last Baron Rosnovski was left on his native soil while his only child and oldest friend returned to America.

THE PRESENT
1968–1982

23

Florentyna Kane's appointment as chairman of the Baron Group was confirmed at the board meeting the day she returned from Warsaw. Richard's first piece of advice was that they should transfer the head office of Florentyna's from San Francisco to New York. A few days later the two of them flew back to stay in their little home on Nob Hill for the last time. They spent the next four weeks in California, making the necessary arrangements for their move, which included leaving the west coast operation in the competent hands of their senior manager and putting Nancy Ching in overall charge of the two shops in San Francisco. When it came to saying goodbye to Bella and Claude, Florentyna assured her closest friends that she would be flying back to the coast on a regular basis.

'Going as suddenly as you came,' said Bella.

It was only the second time she had seen Bella cry.

Once they had settled down in New York, Richard recommended that Florentyna should make the shops a subsidiary of the Baron Group so that the companies could be consolidated for tax purposes. Florentyna agreed and made George Novak President for life on his sixty-fifth birthday, giving him a salary that even Abel would have considered generous. Florentyna became chairman of the group and Richard its chief executive.

Richard found them a magnificent new home on East Sixty-fourth Street. They continued to live on the forty-second floor of the New York Baron while their new home was being decorated. William was enrolled at the fashionable Buckley school like his father before him, while Annabel went to Spence. Carol thought perhaps the time had come to look for another job, but at the mere mention of the subject, Annabel would burst into tears.

Florentyna spent every waking hour learning from George how the Baron Group was run. At the end of her first year as chairman, George Novak's private qualms as to whether his goddaughter would have the toughness necessary to run such a huge empire were entirely allayed, especially after her stand in the south on equal pay for Baron Group employees whatever their colour.

'She has inherited her father's genius,' George told Richard. 'All she lacks now is experience.'

'Time will take care of that,' Richard predicted.

.   .   .

Richard made a full report to the board on the state of the company after Florentyna's first year as chairman. The group declared a profit of over twenty-seven million dollars despite a heavy worldwide building schedule and the drop in the value of the dollar caused by the escalating war in Vietnam. Richard then presented his ideas to the board for a comprehensive investment programme for the seventies. He ended his report by recommending that this sort of exercise should be taken over by a bank.

'Agreed,' said Florentyna, 'but I still look upon you as a banker.'

'Don't remind me,' said Richard. 'Only with the turnover we now generate in more than fifty currencies and the fees we pay to the many financial institutions we employ, perhaps the time has come for us to control our own bank.'

'Isn't it nearly impossible nowadays to buy a bank outright?' asked Florentyna. 'And almost as hard to fulfil the government requirements for a licence to run one?'

'Yes it is, but we already own eight per cent of Lester's and we know what problems that created for my father. This time let's turn it to our advantage. What I should like to recommend to the board is . . .'

The following day Richard wrote to Jake Thomas, the chairman of Lester's, seeking a private interview. The letter he received in reply was guarded to the point of hostility. Their secretaries agreed on a time and place for the meeting.

.   .   .

When Richard entered the chairman's office Jake Thomas rose from behind his desk and ushered him into a seat before returning to the leather chair that had been occupied by Richard's father for more than twenty years. The bookcases were not as full or the flowers as fresh as Richard remembered. The chairman's greeting was formal and short but Richard was not cowed by Thomas's approach as he knew that he was bargaining from strength. There was no small talk.

'Mr Thomas, I feel that as I hold eight per cent of Lester's stock and have now moved to New York, the time has come for me to take my rightful place on the board of the bank.'

It was obvious from Jake Thomas's first words that he had anticipated what was on Richard's mind. 'I think in normal circumstances that might have been a good idea, Mr Kane, but as the board has quite recently filled its last place perhaps the alternative would be for you to sell your stock in the bank.'

It was exactly the answer Richard had expected. 'Under no circumstances would I part with my family shares, Mr Thomas. My father built this bank up to be one of the most respected financial institutions in America, and I intend to be closely involved in its future.'

'That's a pity, Mr Kane, because I am sure you are aware that your father did not leave the bank in the happiest of circumstances and I feel certain we could have offered you a reasonable price for your shares.'

'Better than the price my father-in-law offered you for yours?' said Richard.

Jake Thomas's cheeks flushed brick-red. 'I see you have only come here to be destructive,' he said.

'I have often found in the past that construction must be preceded by a little destruction, Mr Thomas.'

'I don't think you hold enough cards to make this house tumble,' the chairman retorted.

'No one knows better than you that two per cent may suffice,' said Richard.

'I can see no point in prolonging this conversation, Mr Kane.'

'For the time being, I agree with you, but you can be sure that it will be continued in the not too distant future,' said Richard.

He rose to leave. Jake Thomas did not accept his outstretched hand.

. . .

'If that's his attitude, we must declare war,' said Florentyna.

'Brave words,' said Richard, 'but before we make our next move I want to consult my father's old lawyer, Thaddeus Cohen. There's nothing he doesn't know about Lester's bank. Perhaps if we combine our knowledge we can come up with something.'

Florentyna agreed. 'George once told me something my father thought of doing if he failed to remove your father even when he had eight per cent.'

Richard listened intently as Florentyna outlined the plan.

'Do you think that might work in this case?' she asked her husband.

'We just might pull it off, but it would be one hell of a risk.'

'The only thing we have to fear is fear itself,' said Florentyna.

'Jessie, when will you learn that FDR was a politician, not a banker?'

. . .

Richard spent most of the next four days locked in consultation with Thaddeus Cohen at the city office of Cohen, Cohen, Yablons and Cohen.

'The only person who now holds eight per cent of Lester's stock is you,' he assured Richard from behind his desk. 'Even Jake Thomas has only two per cent. If your father had known that Thomas could only afford to hold on to Abel Rosnovski's stock for a few days, he might well have called his bluff and held on to the chair.'

The old family lawyer leaned back, placing both hands on top of his bald head.

'That piece of information will make victory even sweeter,' said Richard. 'Do you have the names of all the shareholders?'

'I'm still in possession of the names of the registered stockholders at the time that your father was the bank's chief executive. But by now it may be so out-of-date as to be rendered virtually useless. I don't have to remind someone with your training that you are entitled under state law to demand a formal inspection of the shareholders' list.'

'And I can imagine how long Thomas would take to release that.'

'Around Christmas would be my guess,' said Thaddeus Cohen, allowing himself a thin smile.

'What do you imagine would happen if I called an extraordinary meeting and gave a full account of how Jake Thomas sold his own stock in order to remove my father from the board?'

'You wouldn't gain a great deal from such an exercise, apart from embarrassing a few people. Jake Thomas would see that the meeting was held on an inconvenient day and badly attended. He would also undoubtedly obtain a fifty-one per cent proxy vote against any resolution you put forward. Into the bargain I suspect Mr Thomas would use such a move by you to re-wash dirty linen in public which would only add a further stain to your father's reputation. No, I think Mrs Kane has come up with the best idea so far and, if I may be permitted to say so, it is typical of her father's boldness in such matters.'

'But if we should fail?'

'I am not a betting man, but I'd back a Kane and Rosnovski against Jake Thomas any day.'

'If I agree, when should we launch the bid?' asked Richard.

'1 April,' Thaddeus Cohen said unhesitatingly.

'Why that date in particular?'

'Because it's the right length of time before everyone has to file their tax returns to be fairly certain that quite a number of people will be in need of some spare cash.'

Richard went over the detailed plan with Thaddeus Cohen again, and that night he explained it in full to Florentyna.

'How much do we stand to lose if we fail?' was her first question.

'Roughly?'

'Roughly.'

'Thirty-seven million dollars.'

'That's pretty rough,' said Florentyna.

'We don't exactly lose the money, but all our capital will be locked up in Lester's stock and that would put a severe restriction on the cash flow for the rest of the group, if we didn't control the bank.'

'What does Mr Cohen think of our chances of pulling that off?'

'Better than fifty-fifty. My father would never have considered going ahead with such odds,' added Richard.

'But my father would have,' said Florentyna. 'He always considered a glass to be half full, never half empty.'

'Thaddeus Cohen was right.'

'About what?'

'About you. He warned me that if you were anything like your father, prepare for battle.'

     .   .   .

During the next three months Richard spent most of his time with accountants, lawyers and tax consultants, who had all the paperwork completed for him by 15 March. That afternoon, he booked space on every major financial page in America for 1 April and informed the advertising departments that the copy would arrive by hand twenty-four hours prior to publication. He couldn't help reflecting on the date, and wondered if it would be he or Jake Thomas who would end up the fool. During the final two weeks Richard and Thaddeus Cohen checked over the plan again and again to be certain they hadn't overlooked anything and could be confident that the details of 'Operation Bust a Gut' remained known to only three people.

On the morning of 1 April, Richard sat in his office and studied the full-page advertisement in the *Wall Street Journal*:

The Baron Group announces that it will offer fourteen dollars for every Lester's Bank share. The current market value of Lester's shares is eleven dollars and a quarter. Any persons wishing to take advantage of this offer should contact their broker or write direct for details to Mr

Robin Oakley, Chase Manhattan Bank, One Chase Manhattan Plaza, New York, N.Y. 10005. This offer remains open until 15 July.

In his article on the facing page, Vermont Royster pointed out that this bold bid to take over Lester's must have had the support of Chase Manhattan, which would be holding the stock of the Baron Group as security. The columnist went on to predict that if the bid succeeded Richard Kane would undoubtedly be appointed the new chairman, a position his father had held for more than twenty years. If, on the other hand, the move failed, the Baron Gruop might find themselves with severe cash restrictions placed on their reserves for several years as the group would be encumbered with a large minority shareholding without actually controlling the bank. Richard could not have summed up the situation more accurately himself.

Florentyna called Richard's office to congratulate her husband on the way he had carried out 'Operation Bust a Gut'. 'Like Napoleon, you have remembered that the first rule of war is surprise.'

'Well, let's hope Jake Thomas is not my Waterloo.'

'You're such a pessimist, Mr Kane. Just remember, Mr Thomas is probably sitting in the nearest men's room at this moment, and he doesn't have a secret weapon and you do.'

'I do?' said Richard.

'Yes. Me.' The phone clicked and rang again immediately.

'Mr Thomas of Lester's Bank on the line for you, Mr Kane.'

I wonder if he has a phone in the men's room, thought Richard. 'Put him through,' he said, understanding for the first time a little of what the confrontation between his father and Abel Rosnovski must have been like.

'Mr Kane, I thought we ought to see if we can sort out our differences. Perhaps I was a little over-cautious in not offering you a place on the board immediately.'

'I'm no longer interested in a place on the board, Mr Thomas.'

'No? But I thought that –'

'No. I am now interested only in the chair.'

'You do realize that if you fail to secure fifty-one per cent of Lester's stock by 15 July, we could institute immediate changes in the allocation of bearers' stock and voting shares that will diminish the value of the stock you already hold? And I feel I should add that the members of the board already control between them forty per cent of Lester's stock, and I intend to contact all the other shareholders by telegram today with a recommendation not to take up your offer. Once I am in possession of another eleven per cent, you will have lost a small fortune.'

'That's a risk I'm willing to take,' said Richard.

'Well, if that's your attitude, Kane, I shall call a full shareholders' meeting for 23 July. If you haven't obtained your fifty-one per cent by then I shall personally see to it that you are kept out of any dealing with this bank for as long as I am chairman.' Without warning Thomas's tone changed from bullying to ingratiating. 'Now perhaps you might like to reconsider your position.'

'When I left your office, Mr Thomas, I made it clear what I had in mind. Nothing has changed.' Richard put the phone down, opened his diary to

23 July and put a line through the page, writing across it: *Stockholders meeting, Lester's Bank*, with a large question mark. He received Jake Thomas's telegram to all stockholders that afternoon.

Every morning Richard followed the response to his advertisement with calls to Thaddeus Cohen and Chase Manhattan. By the end of the first week they had picked up thirty-one per cent of the shares, which with Richard's own eight per cent meant that they held thirty-nine per cent in all. If Thomas had in fact started with forty per cent, it was going to be a tight finish.

Two days later Richard received a detailed letter sent by Jake Thomas to all shareholders in which he advised strongly against consideration of the offer from the Baron Group. 'Your interests would be transferred into the hands of a company which until recently was controlled by a man convicted of bribery and corruption,' stated the final paragraph. Richard was disgusted by Jake Thomas's personal attack on Abel and he had never seen anything make Florentyna so angry.

'We are going to beat him, aren't we?' she asked, her fingers clenched into a tight fist.

'It will be close. I know they have over forty per cent among the directors and their friends. As of four o'clock this afternoon we have forty-one per cent, so it's a battle for the last nineteen per cent that will decide who wins on 23 July.'

By the end of the month Richard heard nothing from Jake Thomas, which made him wonder if he had already captured fifty-one per cent, but with only eight weeks left until the stockholders' meeting it was Richard's turn to read over breakfast a full-page advertisement that made his heartbeat hit one hundred and twenty. On page thirty-seven of the *Wall Street Journal* Jake Thomas had made an announcement on behalf of Lester's. They were offering stock to be sold for a newly set-up pension fund on behalf of the bank's employees.

In an interview with the *Journal*'s chief reporter, Thomas explained that this was a major step in profit sharing and that the funding of retirement income would be a model to the nation both inside and outside the banking community.

Richard swore uncharacteristically as he left the table and walked towards the phone, leaving his coffee to go cold.

'What did you say?' asked Florentyna.

'Balls,' he repeated, and passed over the paper. She read the news while Richard was dialling.

'What does it mean?'

'It means that, even if we do acquire fifty-one per cent of the present stock, with Thomas's authorized issue of a further two million new shares – which you can be sure would be sold only to the institutions – it'll be impossible to defeat the bastard on 23 July.'

'Is it legal?' inquired Florentyna.

'That's what I'm about to find out,' said Richard.

Thaddeus Cohen gave him an immediate reply. 'It's legal, unless you succeed in getting a judge to stop them. I'm having the necessary papers drawn up now, but I warn you, if we are not granted a preliminary injunction you will never be chairman of Lester's.'

During the next twenty-four hours Richard found himself rushing in and out of lawyers' offices and courtrooms. He signed three affidavits and a judge in chambers heard the case for an injunction. This was followed by a special expedited appeal in front of a three-judge panel which, after a day of deliberation, decided by two to one in favour of holding up the share offering until the day after the extraordinary general meeting. Richard had won the battle but not the war; when he returned to his office the next morning he found he still had only forty-six per cent of the stock needed to defeat Jake Thomas.

'He must have the rest,' said Florentyna forlornly.

'I don't think so,' replied Richard.

'Why not?' she asked.

'Because he would not have bothered with that smoke screen exercise of the pension fund shares if he already had fifty-one per cent.'

'Good thinking, Mr Kane.'

'The truth is,' said Richard, 'that he believes *we* have fifty-one per cent. So where is the missing five per cent?'

During the last few days of June, Richard had to be stopped from phoning Chase Manhattan every hour to discover if they had received any more shares. When 15 July came he had forty-nine per cent, and was acutely aware that in exactly eight days Thomas would be able to issue new voting shares that would make it virtually impossible for him ever to gain control of Lester's. Because of the cash flow requirements of the Baron Group, he would have to dump some of his Lester's shares immediately – no doubt, as Jake Thomas had predicted, at a considerable loss. He found himself mumbling 'two per cent, only two per cent', several times during the day.

With only a week to go Richard found it hard to concentrate on the new hotel fire regulations pending before Congress when Mary Preston rang.

'I don't know a Mary Preston,' Richard told his secretary.

'She says you would remember her as Mary Bigelow.'

Richard smiled, wondering what she could possibly want. He hadn't seen her since leaving Harvard. He picked up his phone. 'Mary, what a surprise. Or are you only phoning to complain about bad service at one of the Baron hotels?'

'No, no complaints, although we once spent a night at a Baron if you can remember that far back.'

'How could I forget?' he said, not remembering.

'No, I was only calling to seek your advice. Some years ago my great-uncle, Alan Lloyd, left me three per cent of Lester's. I received a letter from a Mr Jake Thomas last week asking me to pledge those shares to the board and not to deal with you.'

Richard held his breath and could hear his heart beat.

'Are you still there, Richard?'

'Yes, Mary. I was just thinking. Well, the truth is ...'

'Now don't start a long speech, Richard. Why don't you and your wife come and spend a night in Florida with my husband and me and then you can advise us.'

'Florentyna doesn't return from San Francisco until Sunday ...'

'Then come on your own. I know Max would love to meet you.'

'Let me see if I can re-arrange a couple of things and then I will call you back within the hour.'

Richard phoned Florentyna who told him to drop everything and go on his own. 'On Monday morning we will be able to wave goodbye to Jake Thomas once and for all.'

Richard then informed Thaddeus Cohen of the news, who was delighted. 'On my list the stock is still under the name of Alan Lloyd.'

'Well, it's now in the name of Mrs Max Preston.'

'I don't give a damn what her name is, just go and get it.'

Richard flew down on Saturday afternoon and was met at the West Palm beach airport by Mary's chauffeur who drove him out to the Prestons. When Richard first saw the house Mary was living in he wondered how they could fill it without about twenty children. The vast mansion stood on the far side of a golf course on the Inter-coastal Waterway. It took six minutes to drive from the Lion Lodge gates to the imposing forty steps in front of the house. Mary was standing on the top step waiting to greet him. She was dressed in a well-cut riding outfit. Her fair hair still touched her shoulders. As Richard looked up at her he recalled what had first attracted him nearly fifteen years before.

The butler whisked away Richard's overnight bag and ushered him into a bedroom large enough to hold a small convention. On the end of the bed was a riding outfit.

Mary and Richard rode around the grounds before dinner, and although there was no sign of Max she said he was expected about seven. Richard was thankful that Mary never went beyond a canter. It had been a long time since he had ridden with her and he knew he was going to be stiff in the morning. When they returned to the house Richard had a bath and changed into a dark suit before going down to the drawing room a little after seven. The butler poured him a sherry. When Mary floated into the room in a delicate off-the-shoulder evening dress the butler handed her a large whisky without waiting to be asked.

'I am sorry, Richard, but Max has just phoned to say he has been held up in Dallas and won't be back until late tomorrow afternoon. He will be very disappointed not to meet you.' Before Richard could comment, she added: 'Now let's go and have dinner and you can explain to me why the Baron Group needs my three per cent.'

Richard took her slowly through the story of what had happened since his father had taken over from her great-uncle. He hardly noticed the first two courses of dinner, he became so intent.

'So with my three per cent,' said Mary, 'the bank can return safely into the hands of the Kanes?'

'Yes,' said Richard. 'Five per cent is still missing, but as we already have forty-nine per cent, you can put us over the top.'

'That's simple enough,' said Mary, as the soufflé dish was whisked away. 'I shall speak to my broker on Monday and arrange everything. Let's go and have a celebration brandy in the library.'

'You don't know what a relief that will be,' said Richard, rising from his chair and following his hostess down a long corridor.

The library turned out to be the size of a basketball court with almost as many seats. Mary poured Richard a coffee while the butler offered him a Hine. She told the butler that that was all she needed for the rest of the evening and sat down next to Richard on the sofa.

'Quite like old times,' said Mary, edging towards him.

Richard agreed as he came back from his daydream of being chairman of Lester's. He was enjoying the brandy and hardly noticed Mary rest her head on his shoulder. After she had poured him a second brandy he couldn't miss that her hand had shifted on to his leg. He took another sip of cognac. Suddenly and without warning she threw her arms around Richard and kissed him on the lips. When she eventually released him, he laughed and said, 'Just like old times.' He stood up and poured himself a large black coffee. 'What's keeping Max in Dallas?'

'Gas piping,' said Mary, without much enthusiasm. Richard remained standing by the mantelpiece.

During the next hour he learned all about gas piping and a little about Max. When the clock struck twelve he suggested it might be time to turn in. She made no comment, just rose from her seat and accompanied him up the vast staircase to his room. She walked away before he could kiss her goodnight.

Richard found it hard to sleep as his mind was a mixture of elation at having secured Mary's three per cent of Lester's coupled with his plans for how the take-over of the bank would be carried out with a minimum of disruption. He realized that, even as ex-chairman, Jake Thomas could still be a nuisance and was considering ways of controlling Thomas's anger at losing the take-over battle when he heard a slight click from the bedroom door. He glanced towards it to see the handle turning, and then the door itself pushed slowly open. Mary stood silhouetted, wearing a see-through pink negligee.

'Are you still awake?'

Richard lay motionless, wondering if he could get away with pretending to be asleep. But he was aware she might have seen him move, so he said, sleepily, 'Yes.' He was amused by the thought that this was not a time for thinking on his feet.

Mary padded over to the edge of the bed and sat down. 'Would you like anything?'

'A good night's sleep,' said Richard.

'I can think of two ways of helping you achieve that,' said Mary, leaning forward and stroking the back of his head. 'You could take a sleeping pill, or we could make love.'

'That's a nice idea, but I've already taken the sleeping pill,' said Richard, drowsily.

'It doesn't seem to have had the desired effect, so perhaps we should try the second remedy,' said Mary. She lifted the negligee over her head, allowing it to fall to the floor. Then without another word she slipped under the covers, drawing herself close to Richard. Richard could feel that her firm figure was that of a woman who did a lot of exercise and had had no children.

'Hell, I wish I hadn't taken that pill,' said Richard, 'or at least I could stay another night.'

Mary started kissing Richard's neck while running a hand down his back until she reached between his legs.

Christ, thought Richard, I'm only human. And then a door slammed. Mary threw back the covers, grabbed her negligee, ran across the room, and disappeared faster than a thief when a hall light is turned on. Richard pulled the sheets back over his body and listened to a murmur of conversation which he couldn't make out. He spent the rest of the night in a fitful sleep.

When he came down to breakfast the next morning, he found Mary chatting to an elderly man who must once have been very handsome.

The man rose and shook Richard by the hand. 'Allow me to introduce myself. I'm Max Preston,' he said. 'Although I hadn't planned to be with you this weekend, my business finished early and I managed to catch the last flight out of Dallas. I certainly wouldn't have wanted you to leave my home without having experienced true southern hospitality.' Max and Richard chatted over breakfast about the problems they were both facing on Wall Street. They were deep into the effects of Nixon's new tax regulations when the butler announced that the chauffeur was waiting to take Mr Kane to the airport.

The Prestons accompanied Richard down the forty steps to the waiting car, where Richard turned and kissed Mary on the cheek, thanked her for all she had done and shook Max warmly by the hand.

'I hope we shall meet again,' said Max.

'That's a nice idea. Why don't you give me a call when you're next in New York?' Mary smiled at him gently.

Mary and Max Preston waved as the Rolls-Royce glided down the long drive. Once his plane had taken off, Richard felt a tremendous sense of relief. The stewardess served him a cocktail and he began to think about his plans for Monday. To his delight Florentyna was waiting for him on his return to Sixty-fourth Street.

'The shares are ours,' he told her triumphantly and went over the full details during dinner. They fell asleep on the sofa by the fire a little before midnight, Florentyna's hand resting on his leg.

The next morning Richard placed a call through to Jake Thomas to inform him he was now in possession of fifty-one per cent.

Richard could hear an intake of breath.

'As soon as the certificates are in my lawyer's hands, I shall come over to the bank and let you know how I expect the transition to be carried out.'

'Of course,' said Thomas resignedly. 'May I ask from whom you obtained the last two per cent?'

'Yes, from an old friend of mine, Mary Preston.'

There was a pause at the other end. 'Not Mrs Max Preston of Florida?' asked Jake Thomas.

'Yes,' said Richard triumphantly.

'Then you needn't bother to come over, Mr Kane, because Mrs Preston lodged her three per cent of Lester's with us four weeks ago and we have been in possession of the stock certificates for some time.' The phone clicked. It was Richard's turn to gasp.

When Richard told Florentyna about the new development all she could say was: 'You should have slept with the damned woman. I bet Jake Thomas would have.'

'Would you have slept with Scott Forbes in the same circumstances?'

'Good God, no, Mr Kane.'

'Precisely, Jessie.'

Richard spent another sleepless night thinking of how that final two per cent might still be acquired. It was obvious that both sides now had forty-nine per cent of the stock. Thaddeus Cohen had already warned him that he must face reality and start thinking of ways to recoup the maximum amount of cash for the shares he already had. Perhaps he should take a leaf out of Abel's book and sell heavily the day before the meeting. Richard continued to toss and turn as useless ideas rushed through his mind. He turned over once again and tried to catch some sleep precisely when Florentyna woke with a start.

'Are you awake?' she asked quietly.

'Yes, chasing two per cent.'

'So am I. Do you remember your mother telling us that someone had purchased two per cent from a Mr Peter Parfitt on behalf of your father to stop my father getting his hands on it?'

'Yes, I do,' said Richard.

'Well, perhaps they haven't heard about our offer.'

'My darling, it's been in every paper in the United States.'

'So have the Beatles, but not everyone has heard of them.'

'I suppose it's worth a try,' said Richard, picking up the phone by the side of his bed.

'Who are you calling? The Beatles?'

'No, my mother.'

'At four o'clock in the morning? You can't ring your mother in the middle of the night.'

'I can and I must.'

'I wouldn't have told you if I'd known you might do that.'

'Darling, there are only two and a half days to go before I lose you thirty-seven million dollars, and the owner of the shares we need so badly might live in Australia.'

'Good point, Mr Kane.'

Richard dialled the number and waited. A sleepy voice answered the phone.

'Mother?'

'Yes, Richard. What time is it?'

'Four o'clock in the morning. I'm sorry to bother you, but there is no one else I can turn to. Now please listen carefully. You once said that a friend of father's bought two per cent of Lester's shares from Peter Parfitt to keep the stock from falling into the hands of Florentyna's father. Can you remember who it was?'

There was a pause. 'Yes, I think so. It will come back to me if you hold on a minute. Yes, it was an old friend from England, a banker who had been at Harvard with your father. The name will come in a moment.' Richard held his breath. Florentyna sat up in bed.

'Dudley, Colin Dudley, the chairman of ... oh dear, I can't remember.'

'Don't worry, Mother, that's enough to be getting on with. You go back to sleep.'

'What a thoughtful and considerate son you are,' said Kate Kane as she put the phone down.

'Now what, Richard?'

'Just make breakfast.'

Florentyna kissed him on the forehead and disappeared.

Richard picked up the phone. 'International operator, please. What time is it in London?'

'Seven minutes past nine.'

Richard flicked through his personal phone book and said, 'Please connect me to 01-735-7227.'

He waited impatiently. A voice came on the line.

'Bank of America.'

'Put me through to Jonathan Coleman, please.'

Another wait.

'Jonathan Coleman.'

'Good morning, Jonathan, it's Richard Kane.'

'Nice to hear from you, Richard. What are you up to?'

'I need some information urgently. Which bank is Colin Dudley chairman of?'

'Hold on a minute, Richard, and I'll look him up in the *Bankers' Year Book*.' Richard could hear the pages turning. 'Robert Fraser and Company,' came back the reply. 'Only now he's Sir Colin Dudley.'

'What's his number?'

'493-3211.'

'Thank you, Jonathan. I'll give you a call when I'm next in London.'

Richard wrote the number on the corner of an envelope and dialled the international operator again as Florentyna came into the bedroom.

'Getting anywhere?'

'I'm about to find out. Operator, can you please get me a number in London, 493-3211.' Florentyna sat on the end of the bed while Richard waited.

'Robert Fraser and Company.'

'May I speak to Sir Colin Dudley, please.'

'Who shall I say is calling, sir?'

'Richard Kane of the Baron Group, New York.'

'Hold on please, sir.'

Richard waited again.

'Good morning. Dudley here.'

'Good morning, Sir Colin. My name is Richard Kane. I think you knew my father?'

'Of course. We were at Harvard together. Good chap, your old man. I was very sad to read about his death. Wrote to your mother at the time. Where are you calling from?'

'New York.'

'Get up early, you Americans, don't you? So what can I do for you?'

'Do you still own two per cent of Lester's Bank shares?' Richard held his breath again.

'Yes, I do. Paid a bloody king's ransom for them. Still, can't complain. Your father did me a few favours in his time.'

'Would you consider selling them, Sir Colin?'

'If you're willing to offer me a sensible price.'

'How much would you consider sensible?'

There was a long pause. 'Eight hundred thousand dollars.'

'I accept,' said Richard, without hesitation, 'but I must be able to pick them up tomorrow, and I'm not risking a courier service. If I bank-transfer the money, can you have all the paperwork done by the time I arrive?'

'Simple, dear boy,' Dudley said without demur. 'I'll also have a car meet you at the airport and put at your disposal while you're in London.'

'Thank you, Sir Colin.'

'Go easy with the "Sir", young fellow. I've reached that age when I prefer to be called by my Christian name. Just let me know when you expect to arrive and everything will be ready for you.'

'Thank you ... Colin.'

Richard put the phone down.

'You're not getting dressed, are you?'

'I certainly am. I won't get any more sleep tonight. Now where's my breakfast?'

By six o'clock, Richard was booked on the nine fifteen flight from Kennedy Airport. He had also booked himself on a return flight the following morning at eleven arriving back in New York by one thirty-five the following afternoon, giving him twenty-four hours to spare before the stockholders' meeting at two o'clock on Wednesday.

'Running things a bit close, aren't we?' said Florentyna, 'but, fear not, I believe in you. By the way, William is expecting you to bring him back a model of a red London bus.'

'You're always making these major commitments on my behalf. It's a heavy load I carry as the chief executive of your group.'

'I know, dear, and to think it's only because you sleep with the chairman.'

.   .   .

By seven Richard was seated at his office desk writing explicit instructions for the transfer of the eight hundred thousand dollars by telex to Robert Fraser and Company, Albemarle Street, London W.1. Richard knew the money would be in Sir Colin Dudley's bank long before he was. At seven thirty he was driven to the airport and he checked in. The 747 took off on time and he arrived at London's Heathrow at ten o'clock that night. Sir Colin Dudley had been as good as his word. A driver was waiting to pick him up and whisk him off to the Baron. The manager had put him in the Davis Leroy Suite. The Presidential Suite, he explained, was already occupied by Mr Jagger. The rest of his group had taken over the ninth floor.

'I don't think I know the group,' said Richard. 'What area do they specialize in?'

'Singing,' said the manager.

When Richard checked at the reception desk, there was a message waiting for him from Sir Colin suggesting they meet at the bank at nine the following morning.

Richard dined quietly in his rooms and called Florentyna to bring her up to date before going to bed.

'Hang in there, Mr Kane. We're all depending on you.'

Richard woke at seven and packed before going down to breakfast. His father had always gone on about the kippers in London, so he ordered them with some anticipation. When he had finished the last morsel, he realized that they were so good that he would undoubtedly bore his own son with the same story for many years to come. After breakfast, he walked round Hyde Park to kill the hour before the bank opened. The park was green and the flowerbeds a mass of untouched roses. He couldn't help but compare its beauty to Central Park, and recalled that London still had five royal parks of a similar size.

As nine o'clock struck, Richard walked in the front door of Robert Fraser and Company in Albemarle Street only a few hundred yards from the Baron. A secretary ushered him through to Sir Colin Dudley's office.

'Had a feeling you'd be on time, old fellow, so I have everything prepared for you. I once remember finding your father sitting on the doorstep with the milk bottles. Everybody drank black coffee that day.'

Richard laughed.

'Your eight hundred thousand dollars arrived before close of business yesterday so all I have to do is sign the share certificates over to you in the presence of a witness.' Sir Colin flicked a switch. 'Can you come in, Margaret?' Sir Colin's private secretary watched the chairman of one bank sign the transfer certificates so that the recipient could become the chairman of another bank.

Richard checked over the documents, carefully signed his part of the agreement and was handed a receipt for eight hundred thousand dollars.

'Well, I hope that all the trouble you've taken in coming yourself will ensure that you become the chairman of Lester's, old chap.'

Richard stared at the elderly man with the white walrus moustache, bald head and military bearing. 'I had no idea you realized ...'

'Wouldn't want you Americans to think we're altogether asleep over here. Now you bustle off and catch the eleven o'clock from Heathrow and you'll make your meeting easily: not many of my customers pay as promptly as you do. By the way, congratulations on that moon chappie.'

'What?' said Richard.

'You've put a man on the moon.'

'Good heavens,' said Richard.

'No, not quite,' said Sir Colin, 'but I'm sure that's what NASA has planned next.'

Richard laughed and thanked Sir Colin again. He walked quickly back to the Baron, literally humming. He knew exactly what it felt like to be the man on the moon. He had left his overnight bag with the porter so he was able to check out quickly, and Sir Colin's chauffeur drove him back to Heathrow. Richard entered Terminal Three well in time to check in for the eleven o'clock flight. He was going to be back in New York with twenty-four hours to spare: if his father had had to make the same transaction before he became chairman the process would have taken at least two weeks.

Richard sat in the Clipper Club lounge toying with a Martini while reading in *The Times* about Rod Laver's fourth Wimbledon triumph, unable to see the fog descending outside. It wasn't until thirty minutes later that an announcement warned passengers that there would be a short delay on all flights. An hour later, they called Richard's flight, but as he walked across the tarmac he could see the fog growing denser by the minute. He sat in his seat, belt fastened, reading a copy of the previous week's *Time* magazine, willing himself not to look outside, waiting to feel the plane move. Nixon, he read, had named the first women generals, Colonel Elizabeth Hoisington and Colonel Anne Mae Hays; no doubt the first Nixon initiative that Florentyna would approve of, he thought.

'We are sorry to announce that this flight has been delayed until further notice because of fog.' A groan went up inside the first-class cabin. 'Passengers should return to the terminal where they will be issued with luncheon vouchers and advised when to reboard the aircraft. Pan American apologizes for the delay and hopes it will not cause any great inconvenience.' Richard had to smile, despite himself. Back inside the terminal, he went around to every ticket counter to discover who had the first plane out. It turned out to be an Air Canada flight to Montreal. He reserved a seat, after being told that his Pan Am flight to New York was now the twenty-seventh in line for departure. He then checked the flights out of Montreal to New York. There was one every two hours and the flying time was just over an hour. He pestered Pan American and Air Canada every thirty minutes but the polite bland reply remained unvaried: 'I'm sorry, sir, we can do nothing until the fog lifts.'

At two in the afternoon, he called Florentyna to warn her about the delay.

'Not impressive, Mr Kane. While you're on the phone, did you manage to pick up a red London bus for William?'

'Damn. I completely forgot.'

'Not doing very well today, Mr Kane. Better try the duty-free gift shop, hadn't we?'

Richard found an airport shop that sold several sizes of London buses. He selected a large plastic one and paid for it with the last of his English money. With the bus safely under his arm he decided to use his luncheon voucher. He sat down to the worst airport lunch he had ever had: one thin piece of beef about an inch square that had been misleadingly described as a minute steak on the menu, along with three tired lettuce leaves posing as a side salad. He checked his watch. It was already three o'clock. For two hours, he tried to read a copy of *The French Lieutenant's Woman* but he was so anxious listening to every radio announcement that he never got past page four.

At seven o'clock, after Richard had walked around Terminal Three several times, he began to think it would soon be too late for planes to take off whatever the weather. The loudspeaker forbodingly warned of an important announcement to follow shortly. He stood like a statue as the words came out. 'We are sorry to announce that all flights out of Heathrow have been cancelled until tomorrow morning with the exception of Iran Air Flight 006 to Jeddah and Air Canada flight 009 to Montreal.' Richard had been saved by his foresight: he knew the Air Canada flight would be completely sold out within minutes. Once again he sat in a first-class lounge. Although the flight was further delayed it was eventually called a few minutes after eight. Richard almost cheered when the 747 took off a little after nine o'clock. Thereafter he found himself checking his watch every few minutes. The flight was uneventful except for more appalling food and the plane eventually landed at Montreal airport shortly before eleven.

Richard sprinted to the American Airlines counter to discover that he had missed the last flight to New York by a few minutes. He swore out loud.

'Don't worry, sir, there is a flight at ten twenty-five tomorrow morning.'

'What time does it arrive in New York?'

'Eleven thirty.'

'Two hours and thirty minutes to spare,' he said out loud. 'It's a bit tight. Can I hire a private plane?' The clerk looked at his watch, 'Not at this time of night, sir.'

Richard thumped the desk and reserved a seat and took a room in the Airport Baron and phoned Florentyna.

'Where are you now?' she asked.

'The Airport Baron, Montreal.'

'Curiouser and curiouser.'

Richard explained what had happened.

'Poor darling. Did you remember the red London bus?'

'Yes, I'm clinging on to it, but my overnight bag is still on the Pan Am flight to New York.'

'And the stock certificates?'

'They are in my briefcase and have never left my side.'

'Well done, Mr Kane. I'll have a car waiting for you at the airport and Mr Cohen and I will be at the stockholders' meeting at Lester's clutching on to our forty-nine per cent. So if you're in possession of your two per cent, Jake Thomas will be on the dole by this time tomorrow.'

'How can you be so cool about it?'

'You've never let me down yet. Sleep well.'

Richard did not sleep well, and was back at the American Airlines terminal hours before the plane was due for boarding. There was a slight delay but the captain was still anticipating that he could land at Kennedy by eleven thirty. Richard had no baggage and felt confident he could now make the meeting with at least half an hour to spare. For the first time in over twenty-four hours he began to relax, and even made some notes for his first speech as Lester's chairman.

When the 707 arrived at Kennedy it began to circle the airport. Richard looked out of his little window and could clearly see the building in Wall Street that he had to be at within two hours. He thumped his knee in anger. At last the plane descended a few hundred feet, only to start circling again.

'This is Captain James McEwen speaking. I am sorry for this delay, but we have been put into a holding pattern because of traffic congestion. It seems there are some delayed flights from London now arriving into New York.' Richard wondered if the Pan American flight from Heathrow would land before he did.

Five minutes, ten minutes, fifteen minutes. Richard checked the agenda. Item number one – a motion to reject the take-over bid by the Baron Group. Item number two – the issue of new voting shares. If they couldn't prove they had fifty-one per cent, Jake Thomas would close the proceedings within minutes of the meeting starting. The plane began to descend and the wheels touched the ground at twelve twenty-seven. Richard sprinted through the terminal. He passed his chauffeur on the run, who quickly followed him to the car park, where Richard once again checked his watch. An hour and twenty minutes to spare. He was going to make the meeting comfortably.

'Step on it,' said Richard.

'Yes, sir,' said the chauffeur as he moved into the left-hand lane of the Van Wyck Expressway. Richard heard the siren a few minutes later and a policeman on a motorcycle overtook the car and waved them on to the hard shoulder. The policeman parked and walked slowly towards Richard who had already leaped out of the car. Richard tried to explain it was a matter of life and death.

'It always is,' said the officer. 'Either that or "My wife is having a baby".' Richard left his chauffeur to deal with the policeman while he tried to hail a passing cab: but they were all full. Sixteen minutes later the policeman let them go. It was one twenty-nine as they crossed the Brooklyn Bridge and turned on to FDR Drive. Richard could see the giant skyscrapers of Wall Street in the distance but the cars were bumper to bumper all the way. It was six minutes to two before they reached Wall Street when Richard could bear it no longer and jumped out of the car, briefcase under one arm, a red London bus under the other, and sprinted the last three blocks, dodging slow pedestrians and fast honking cab drivers. He heard the clock at Trinity Church chime two as he reached Bowling Green and prayed that it was fast as he raced up the steps of the Lester's building, suddenly realizing he didn't know where the meeting was being held.

'Fifty-first floor, sir,' the doorman informed him.

The 30 to 60 elevator was full with the post-lunch hour crowd and it stopped at 31 – 33 – 34 – 42 – 44 – 47 – 50 – 51. Richard jumped out of the elevator and ran down the corridor following the red arrow that indicated where the meeting was taking place. As he arrived in the crowded room, one or two faces turned to look at him. There must have been over five hundred people seated listening to the chairman, but he was the only shareholder sweating from head to toe. He was greeted by the sight of a cool Jake Thomas, who gave him a knowing smile from the platform. Richard realized he was too late. Florentyna was sitting in the front row, her head bowed. He took a seat at the back of the room and listened to the chairman of Lester's.

'All of us believe that the decision that has been made today is in the best interests of the bank. In the circumstances that your board of directors faced, no one will have been surprised by my request, and Lester's will now continue its traditional role as one of America's great financial institutions. Item number two,' said Jake Thomas. Richard felt sick. 'My final task as chairman of Lester's is to propose that the new chairman be Mr Richard Kane.'

Richard could not believe his ears. A little old lady rose from her seat in the front row and said that she would like to second the motion because she felt that Mr Kane's father had been one of the finest chairmen the bank had ever had. There was a round of applause as the old lady sat down.

'Thank you,' said Jake Thomas. 'Those in favour of the resolution?' Richard stared into the body of the hall as hands shot into the air.

'Those against.' Jake Thomas looked down from the platform. 'Good, the resolution is carried unanimously. I am now happy to invite your new chairman to address you. Ladies and gentlemen, Mr Richard Kane.' Richard walked forward and everyone stood up and applauded. As he passed Florentyna he handed her the red bus.

'Glad you accomplished *something* on your trip to London,' she whispered.

Richard walked, dazed, on to the platform. Jake Thomas shook his hand warmly and then took a seat on the end of the row.

'I have little to say on this occasion,' began Richard, 'other than to assure you that I wish Lester's to carry on in the same tradition as it did under my father and that I will dedicate myself to that end.' Unable to think of anything else to add, he smiled and said, 'I thank you for your attendance today and look forward to seeing you all at the annual meeting.' There followed another round of applause and the shareholders began to disperse chattering.

As soon as they could escape from those who wished to talk to Richard, either to congratulate him or tell him how they felt Lester's should be run, Florentyna led him away to the chairman's office. He stood and stared at the portrait of his father that hung over the fireplace and turned to his wife.

'How did you manage it, Jessie?'

'Well, I remembered a piece of advice my governess taught me when I was younger. Contingency, Miss Tredgold used to say. Always have a contingency plan ready in case it rains. When you called from Montreal I was afraid there might be an outside chance it would pour, and you wouldn't make the meeting. So I rang Thaddeus Cohen and explained what my contingency plan was, and he spent the morning drawing up the necessary documents.'

'What documents?' said Richard.

'Patience, Mr Kane. I do feel after my triumph that I have the right to spin out this tale a little longer.'

Richard remained impatiently silent.

'When I had the vital document in my hand, I phoned Jake Thomas and asked if he could see me twenty minutes before the stockholders' meeting was due to start. Had you arrived in time, I would have cancelled the confrontation with Mr Thomas, but you didn't.'

'But your plan ...'

'My father – no fool – told me once a skunk, always a skunk, and he turned out to be right. At the meeting with Thomas I informed him that we were in possession of fifty-one per cent of Lester's stock. He was disbelieving until I mentioned the name of Sir Colin Dudley and then he turned quite pale. I placed the whole bundle of certificates on the table in front of him and, before he could check them, told him that if he sold me his two per cent before two o'clock I would still pay him the full fourteen dollars per share. I added that he must also sign a document saying he would resign as chairman and make no attempt to interfere in any future dealings involving Lester's Bank. For good measure, although it was not in the contract, he must propose you for chairman.'

'My God, Jessie, you have the nerve of ten men.'

'No. One woman.'

Richard laughed. 'What was Thomas's response?'

'Asked what I would do if he refused. If you refuse, I told him, we'll sack you publicly without compensation for loss of office. Then I pointed out to him that he would have to sell his stock for the best price he could get on the open market because as long as we had fifty-one per cent of Lester's he would play no part in the future of the bank.'

'And then?'

'He signed there and then without even consulting his fellow directors.'

'Brilliant, Jessie, both in conception and execution.'

'Thank you, Mr Kane. I do hope that now you are chairman of a bank you won't be running all over the world getting yourself delayed, missing meetings and having nothing to show for your troubles other than a model of a red London bus. By the way, did you remember to bring a present for Annabel?'

Richard looked embarrassed. Florentyna bent down and handed him an FAO Schwarz shopping bag. He lifted out a package that showed a picture of a toy typewriter on the outside with 'Made in England' printed all along the bottom of the box.

'Just not your day is it, Mr Kane? By the way, Neil Armstrong got back quicker than you did. Perhaps we should invite him to join the board?'

.   .   .

Richard read Vermont Royster's article in the *Wall Street Journal* the next morning:

Mr Richard Kane seems to have won a bloodless coup in his bid to become chairman of Lester's. There was no vote taken by shareholders at the extraordinary meeting, and his succession to the chair was proposed by the retiring incumbent, Jake Thomas, and carried unanimously.

Many stockholders present at the meeting referred to the traditions and standards set by the late William Lowell Kane, the present chairman's father. Lester's stock ended the day up two points on the New York Exchange.

'That's the last we'll hear of Jake Thomas,' said Florentyna.

24

Richard had never heard of Major Abanjo before that morning. Neither had anyone else in America other than those who took an over-zealous interest in the affairs of Nambawe, Central Africa's smallest state. Nevertheless, it was Major Abanjo who caused Richard to run late for his most important appointment that day, the eleventh birthday party of his only son.

When Richard arrived back at the apartment on Sixty-fourth Street, Major Abanjo was driven from his mind by Annabel, who had a few minutes earlier poured a pot of tea over William's hand because she wasn't receiving enough attention. She hadn't realized that it was boiling hot. It seemed that Carol had been in the kitchen fussing over the birthday cake at the time. Annabel was getting even less attention now that William was screaming at the top of his voice and all the other children had to be sent home. A few minutes later Annabel was also screaming, after Richard had placed her across his knee and administered six hard whacks with his slipper before both children were put to bed – William with two aspirins and an ice pack to help him sleep and Annabel as a further punishment. Eleven candles – and one to grow on – had burned themselves down to the icing on the large cake that remained untouched on the dining-room table.

'I'm afraid William will have a scar on his right hand for the rest of his life,' said Florentyna after she had checked to see that her son was at last asleep.

'Still, he took it like a man.'

'I don't agree,' said Florentyna. 'He never once grumbled.'

'It probably wouldn't have happened if I had been on time,' said Richard, ignoring her comment. 'Damn Major Abanjo.'

'Who is Major Abanjo?' asked Florentyna.

'A young army officer who was behind the coup in Nambawe today.'

'Why should a little African state stop you being on time for William's birthday party?'

'That little African state has an outstanding five-year loan agreement of three hundred million dollars that Lester's led on in 1966 and the repayment date is due in three months' time.'

'We are in for three hundred million dollars?' said Florentyna, flabbergasted.

'No, no,' said Richard. 'We covered the first fifteen per cent of the loan, and the remaining eighty-five million was divided among thirty-seven other financial institutions.'

'Can we survive a loss of forty-five million dollars?'

'Yes we can, as long as the Baron Group remains our friend,' said Richard, smiling at his wife. 'It's three years' profits down the drain, not to mention a severe blow to our reputation with the other thirty-seven banks involved and the inevitable drop in our stock price tomorrow.'

Lester's stock price dropped the next day by more than Richard had anticipated, for two reasons. The newly self-appointed President of Nambawe, General Abanjo, announced that he had no intention of honouring previous government commitments made with any 'fascist regime' including America, Britain, France, Germany and Japan. Richard wondered how many Russian bankers were boarding planes to Central Africa at that moment.

The second reason became apparent when a reporter from the *Wall Street Journal* called Richard and asked him if he had any statement to make about the coup.

'I really have nothing to say,' said Richard, trying to sound as if the whole episode were about as troublesome to him as brushing a fly off his sleeve. 'I feel sure the problem will sort itself out during the next few days. After all, the loan is only one of many that Lester's is involved with at the present time.'

'Mr Jake Thomas might not agree with that opinion,' said the journalist.

'You have spoken to Mr Thomas?' said Richard in disbelief.

'Yes, he called the *Journal* earlier today and had an off-the-record conversation with our publisher, leaving us in no doubt that he would be surprised if Lester's could survive such a demand on cash flow.'

'No comment,' said Richard curtly, and put the phone down.

At Richard's request, Florentyna called a board meeting of the Baron Group to ensure enough financial backing to see that Lester's could survive a run on its stock. To their surprise, George was not at all convinced that the Baron Group should enmesh itself in Lester's problems. He told them that he had never approved of using the Baron shares as security for the takeover of the bank in the first place.

'I remained silent at the time but I'm not willing to do so on a second occasion,' he said, his hands resting on the board-room table. 'Abel never liked throwing good money after bad whatever his personal involvement. He used to say that anyone could *talk* about future profits and start spending money they hadn't yet earned. Have you considered that we might both end up going bankrupt?'

'The sum involved is not that large to the Baron Group,' said Richard.

'Abel always considered any loss caused ten times the problem of any profit,' George told him. 'And what outstanding loans do you have to other countries around the world which could be taken over while we are asleep in bed?'

'Only one outside the EEC, and that's a loan of two hundred million to the Shah of Iran. Again we are the lead bank with a commitment of thirty million, but Iran has never missed an interest payment by so much as an hour.'

'When is their final payment due?' asked George.

Richard flicked through a bulky file that lay on the table in front of him and ran his forefinger down a column of figures. Although nettled by George's attitude, he was pleased to be well-prepared for any query that might arise.

'19 June 1978.'

'Then I want an assurance you won't involve the bank again when the loan comes up for renewal,' said George firmly.

'What?' said Richard. 'The Shah is as safe as the Bank of England –'

'Which hasn't proved to be so solid lately.'

Richard was beginning to look angry and was about to respond when Florentyna interrupted.

'Hold on, Richard. If Lester's agrees not to renew its loan with the Shah in 1978, or involve itself in any further Third World commitments, George, will you in turn agree to the Baron Group's underwriting the forty-five million loss on the African contract?'

'No, I'd still need some more convincing.'

'Like what?' said Richard.

'Richard, you don't have to raise your voice. I am still the President of the Baron Group and have given thirty years of my life to building the company up to its present position. I don't intend at this late stage to watch that achievement demolished in thirty minutes.'

'I'm sorry,' said Richard. 'I haven't had much sleep for the last four days. What would you like to know, George?'

'Other than the agreement with the Shah, is Lester's committed to any other loans over ten million?'

'No,' said Richard. 'Most major country to country loans are serviced by the prime banks like Chase or Chemical and we end up with only a tiny percentage of the capital sum. Obviously Jake Thomas felt that Nambawe, which is rich in copper and manganite, was as sure a bet as he could hope to find.'

'We already know, to our cost, that Mr Thomas is fallible,' said George. 'So, what other loans above five million remain outstanding to the bank?'

'Two,' replied Richard. 'One with General Electricity in Australia for seven million, which is secured by the government, and one with ICI in London. Both are five-year loans with set payment dates and so far repayments have been met on schedule.'

'So if the group wrote off the forty-five million, how long would it take Lester's to recoup the loss?'

'That would depend on the percentage any lender required and over what period of time the money was loaned.'

'Fifteen per cent over five years.'

'Fifteen per cent?' repeated Richard, shocked.

'The Baron Group is not a charity, Richard, and as long as I am President it is not in business to prop up ailing banks. We are hoteliers by trade and have shown a seventeen per cent return on our money over the past thirty years. If we loaned you forty-five million, could you pay it back in five years at fifteen per cent?'

Richard hesitated, scribbled some figures on the pad in front of him and checked his file before he spoke. 'Yes, I am confident we could repay every penny in five years, even assuming the African contract is a total write-off,' he said quietly.

'I think we must treat the contract precisely that way,' said George. 'My informants tell me that the former head of state, King Erobo, has escaped to London, taken up residence at Claridge's and is looking at a house which is for sale in Chelsea Square. It appears he has more money stashed away in Switzerland than anyone other than the Shah, so I feel he is unlikely to return to Africa in a hurry – and I can't say I blame him.' Richard tried to smile as George continued. 'Subject to all you have told us being confirmed by the Baron's auditors, I agree to covering the African loan on the terms stated, and I wish you luck. Richard. I'll also let you in on a little secret: Abel didn't like Jake Thomas any more than you do, which is what tipped the balance for me.' George closed his file. 'I hope you will both excuse me now as I have a lunch appointment with Conrad Hilton and he has never once been late in thirty years.'

When George had closed the door behind him, Richard turned to Florentyna. 'Jesus, whose side does he think he's on?'

'Ours,' replied Florentyna. 'Now I know why my father happily trusted him to run the group while he went off to fight the Germans.'

A statement in the *Wall Street Journal* the following day, confirming that the Baron Group had underwritten Lester's loans, caused the bank's stocks to rise again and Richard settled down to what he called 'my five years of drudgery.'

'What are you going to do about Jake Thomas?'

'Ignore him,' said Richard. 'Time is on my side. No bank in New York will employ him once it's known that he is willing to run to the press whenever he has a disagreement with his past employers.'

'But how will anyone find out?'

'Darling, if the *Wall Street Journal* knows, everybody knows.'

Richard turned out to be right; the whole story was repeated back to him over a lunch he had with a director of Bankers Trust only a week later. The director went on to remark, 'That man's broken the golden rule of banking. From now on, he'll even find it hard to open a current account.'

William recovered from his burns far more quickly than Florentyna had expected and returned to school a few days later with a scar on his hand too small even to impress his friends. For the first few days after the accident Annabel looked away every time she saw the scar and seemed genuinely contrite.

'Do you think he's forgiven me?' she asked her mother.

'Of course, my darling. William is just like his father – forgets any quarrel by the next morning.'

.   .   .

Florentyna considered that the time had come for her to make a tour of the Baron hotels in Europe. Her staff worked out a detailed itinerary which took in Rome, Paris, Madrid, Lisbon, Berlin, Amsterdam, Stockholm, London and even Warsaw. She felt a new confidence in leaving George in control, she told Richard as they were driven to the airport. He agreed and then reminded her that they had never been apart for as long as three weeks since the day they had met.

'You'll survive, darling.'

'I'll miss you, Jessie.'

'Now, don't you get all sentimental. You know that I have to work for the rest of my life to make sure that my husband can continue posing as chairman of a New York bank.'

'I love you,' said Richard.

'I love you too,' said Florentyna. 'But you still owe me fifteen million and fifty-six dollars.'

'Where does the fifty-six come from?' said Richard.

'From our days in San Francisco. You've never repaid me that fifty-six dollars I lent you before we were married.'

'*You* said it was a dowry.'

'No, you said it was a dowry. I said it was a loan. I think I shall have to take George's advice about how it should be repaid as soon as I return. Perhaps fifteen per cent over five years would seem reasonable, Mr Kane, which means you must now owe me around four hundred dollars.' She leaned up and kissed him goodbye.

Richard was driven back to New York by the chauffeur and on arrival at his office he immediately phoned Cartier's in London. He gave clear instructions what he required and said it had to be ready in eighteen days.

The time had come for Richard to prepare his annual general report for the bank. The red African figure maddened him. Without it, Lester's would have shown a healthy profit: so much for hoping he would beat Jake Thomas's figures in his first year. All that the stockholders would remember was a thumping loss compared with 1970.

Richard followed Florentyna's detailed schedule with interest every day and made sure that he caught up with her by phone at least once in every capital. She seemed pleased by most of what she had seen, and although she had a few ideas for changes she had to admit that the hotels on the Continent were well run by the group's European directors. Any excess expenditure had been caused by her own demands for higher standards of architecture. When she phoned from Paris Richard passed on the news that William had won the class mathematics prize and that he was now confident that his son would be accepted by St Paul's. And since the hot water incident Annabel had tried a little harder at school and had even scraped herself off the bottom of the class. She considered it the best news Richard had given her.

'Where's your next stop?' Richard asked.

'London,' she replied.

'Great. I've got a feeling I know someone you'll want to call when you're there,' he said with a chuckle, and went to bed feeling better than he had for some days.

He heard from Florentyna a lot earlier than he had expected. Around six o'clock the next morning Richard was in a deep sleep, dreaming that he and General Abanjo were having a shoot-out; Richard pulled the trigger, the bullet fired. Then the phone rang. He woke up and lifted the receiver, expecting to hear General Abanjo's last words.

'I love you.'

'What?' he said.

'I love you.'

'Jessie, do you know what time it is?'

'A few minutes after twelve.'

'It's eight minutes past six in New York.'

'I only wanted to tell you how much I love my diamond brooch.'

Richard smiled.

'I'm going to wear it to lunch with Sir Colin and Lady Dudley. They are due to arrive any minute to take me to the Mirabelle, so I must say goodbye. Talk to you tomorrow – my today.'

'You're a nut.'

'By the way, I don't know if it's of any interest to you, but there's a reporter on the midday news here in England saying something about a certain General Abanjo being killed in a counter-coup in some Central African state and the old king will be returning home tomorrow to a hero's welcome.'

'*What?*'

'The king is just being interviewed now so I'll repeat what he's saying. "My government intends to honour all the debts it has incurred with our friends in the western world."'

'What?' repeated Richard, once again.

'He looks such a nice fellow now that he's got the crown back on his head. Goodnight, Mr Kane. Sleep well.'

.   .   .

As Richard was leaping up and down on his bed, there was a knock on Florentyna's door, and Sir Colin and Lady Dudley came into her suite.

'Are you ready, young lady?' asked Sir Colin.

'I certainly am,' said Florentyna.

'You look very pleased with yourself. No doubt the reinstatement of King Erobo has brought the roses back to your cheeks.'

'Well informed as you are, Sir Colin, that is not the reason,' said Florentyna as she glanced down at the card that lay on the table in front of her and read the words again.

I hope that this will be acceptable security until I can return the fifty-six dollars, plus interest.

Mr Kane

'What a lovely brooch you're wearing,' said Lady Dudley. It's a donkey, isn't it? Does that signify anything in particular?'

'It certainly does, Lady Dudley. It means the giver intends to vote for Nixon again.'

'Then you have to give him elephant cuff-links in return,' said Sir Colin.

'You know, Richard was right: it doesn't pay to underestimate the British, said Florentyna.

.   .   .

After lunch Florentyna phoned Miss Tredgold at her school. The school secretary put her through to the staff room. Miss Tredgold, it turned out, did not need to be informed about the late General Abanjo, but seemed more interested in all the news about William and Annabel. Florentyna's second call was to Sotheby's – this time in person. On arrival she asked to see one of the heads of department.

'It may be many years before such a collector's item comes under the hammer, Mrs Kane,' the expert told her.

'I understand,' said Florentyna. 'But please let me know the moment it does.'

'Certainly, madam,' said the expert as he wrote down Florentyna's name and address.

.   .   .

When Florentyna returned to New York three weeks later she settled down to institute the changes she had been considering on her European tour. By the end of 1972, with her energy, George's wisdom and Gianni di Ferranti's genius, she was able to show an increased profit. Thanks to King Erobo being as good as his word, Richard also declared a handsome profit.

On the night of the annual stockholders' meeting, Richard, Florentyna and George went out for a celebration dinner. Even though George had officially retired on his sixty-fifth birthday, he still came into his office every morning at eight o'clock. It had taken only twenty-four hours for everyone at the Baron to realize his retirement party had been a misnomer. Florentyna began to appreciate how lonely George must be now that he had lost most of his contemporaries and how close he had been to her father. She never once suggested that he should slow down, because she knew it was pointless, and it gave her particular happiness whenever George took Annabel and William on outings. Both the children called him 'Grandpapa' which brought tears to his eyes and always guaranteed them a large ice cream.

Florentyna thought she knew how much George did for the group but the truth only came home to her after his retirement could no longer be postponed. George died peacefully in his sleep in October 1972. In his will, he left everything to the Polish Red Cross. A short note addressed to Richard asked him to act as his executor.

Richard carried out George's every wish to the letter and even travelled to Warsaw accompanied by Florentyna to meet the President of the Polish Red Cross to discuss how George's donation could best be put to use. When they returned to New York Florentyna sent a directive to all managers in the group that the finest suite in each hotel was no longer to be the Presidential Suite but was to be renamed the 'George Novak Suite'.

.   .   .

When Richard woke the morning after they had returned from Warsaw, Florentyna, who had been waiting impatiently for him to open his eyes, told her husband that although George had taught her so much in life, he had now added to her learning even in death.

'What are you talking about?'

'George left everything he possessed to charity, but never once referred to the fact that my father rarely made charitable contributions other than the occasional gift to Polish or political causes. I'm every bit as remiss myself, and if you hadn't added a footnote to the group's annual general report concerning tax relief for charitable donations, I would never have given the matter a second thought.'

'As I'm sure you're not planning for something after your death, what do you have in mind?'

'Why don't we set up a foundation in memory of both our fathers? Let's bring the two families together. What they failed to do in their lifetime, let us do in ours.'

Richard sat up and stared at his wife as she got out of bed and continued to talk as she walked towards the bathroom.

'The Baron Group should donate one million dollars a year to the foundation,' she said.

'Spending only the income, never the capital,' he interjected.

Florentyna closed the bathroom door, which gave Richard a few moments to consider her proposal. He could still be surprised by her bold, sweeping approach to any new venture, even if, as he suspected, she had not thought through who would run the day-to-day administration of such an enterprise once it had taken off. He smiled to himself when the bathroom door reopened.

'We could spend the income derived from such a trust on first-generation immigrants who are not getting the chance of a decent education.'

'And also create scholarships for exceptionally gifted children whatever their background,' said Richard, getting out of bed.

'Brilliant, Mr Kane, and let us hope that occasionally the same person will qualify for both.'

'Your father would have,' said Richard as he disappeared into the bathroom.

Thaddeus Cohen insisted on coming out of retirement to draw up the deeds of the foundation to cover the wishes of both Kanes. It took him over a month. When the trust fund was launched, the national press welcomed the financial commitment as another example of how Richard and Florentyna Kane were able to combine bold originality with common sense.

A reporter from the Chicago *Sun-Times* phoned Thaddeus Cohen to inquire why the foundation was so named. Cohen explained that 'Remagen' had been chosen because it was the battlefield on which Colonel Rosnovski had unknowingly saved the life of Captain Kane.

'I had no idea they had met on a battlefield,' said a young voice.

'Neither did they,' replied Thaddeus Cohen. 'It was only discovered after their deaths.'

'Fascinating. Tell me, Mr Cohen, who is going to be the first trustee of the Remagen Foundation?'

'Professor Luigi Ferpozzi.'

. . .

Both Lester's Bank and the Baron Group set new records for the following year as Richard established himself as a force on Wall Street and Florentyna visited her hotels in the Middle East and Africa. King Erobo held a banquet in Florentyna's honour when she arrived in Nambawe, and although she promised to build a hotel in the capital city she wouldn't be drawn into an explanation why Lester's had not been among the banks involved with the king's latest international loan.

William had a good first year at St Paul's, showing the same flair for maths which his father had before him. As they had been taught by the same master, both father and son avoided asking for any comparison. Annabel did not progress as quickly as William, although her teacher had to admit she had improved, even if she had fallen in love with Bob Dylan.

'Who's he?' asked Florentyna.

'I don't know,' said Richard, 'but I'm told he's doing for Annabel what Sinatra did for you twenty-five years ago.'

. . .

When Florentyna started her sixth year as chairman of the group she found she was beginning to repeat herself. Richard seemed to find new challenges all the time, while Gianni di Ferranti appeared to be well in control of the chain of shops without bothering to ask her anything other than where to send the cheques. The Baron Group was now so efficient, and her management team so competent, that no one showed a great deal of concern one morning when Florentyna didn't come into the office.

That evening, when Richard was sitting in the crimson leather chair by the fire reading *The Billion Dollar Killing*, she expressed her thoughts out loud.

'I'm bored.'

Richard made no comment.

'It's time I did something with my life other than build on my father's achievements,' she added.

Richard smiled but didn't look up from his book.

25

'You're allowed three guesses as to who this is.'

'Am I given any clues?' asked Florentyna, annoyed that she knew the voice but couldn't quite place it.

'Good-looking, intelligent and a national idol.'

'Paul Newman.'

'Feeble. Try again.'

'Robert Redford.'

'Worse still. One more chance.'

'I need another clue.'

'Appalling at French, not much better at English and still in love with you.'

'Edward. Edward Winchester. A voice from the past – only you don't sound as if you've changed a bit.'

'Wishful thinking. I'm over forty, and by the way so will you be next year.'

'How can I be when I'm only twenty-four this year?'

'What, again?'

'No, I have been on ice for the last fifteen years.'

'Not from what I've read about you. You go from strength to strength.'

'And how about you?'

'I'm a partner in a law firm in Chicago: Winston and Strawn.'

'Married?'

'No, I've decided to wait for you.'

Florentyna laughed. 'If you've taken this long to phone and propose, I should warn you that I've been married for over fifteen years and I have a son of fourteen and a daughter of twelve.'

'All right then, I won't propose, but I would like to see you. It's a private matter.'

'A private matter? Sounds intriguing.'

'If I were to fly to New York one day next week, would you have lunch with me?'

'I'd enjoy that.' Florentyna flicked over the pages of her calendar. 'How about next Tuesday?'

'Suits me. Shall we say the Four Seasons, one o'clock?'

'I'll be there.'

Florentyna put down the phone and sat back in her chair. Other than Christmas cards and the odd letter, she had had very little contact with Edward for sixteen years. She walked across to the mirror and studied herself. A few small lines were beginning to appear around the eyes and mouth. She turned sideways to confirm that she had kept her slim figure. She didn't feel old. There was no denying that she had a daughter who could already make young men stop in the street for a second glance, and a teenage son she now had to look up to. It wasn't fair. Richard didn't look forty: a few white tufts appearing at the sides of the temples and the hair perhaps a shade thinner than it had been, but he was every bit as slim and vigorous as the day they had met. She admired the fact that he still found time to play squash at the Harvard Club twice a week and practise the cello most weekends. Edward's phone call made her think of middle age for the first time; how morbid. She would be thinking of death next. Thaddeus Cohen had died the previous year; only her mother and Kate Kane remained of that generation.

Florentyna tried to touch her toes and couldn't, so she returned to the monthly statements of the Baron Group for reassurance. London was still not paying its way, even though the hotel occupied one of the finest sites in Mayfair. Somehow the English seemed to combine impossible wage demands with high unemployment and staff shortages all at the same time. In Riyadh they had had to clear out almost the entire management because of theft, and in Poland the government would still not allow the group to take any exchangeable currency out of the country. But despite these minor problems, all of which could be sorted out by her management team, the company was in good shape.

Florentyna had confidently assured Richard that the Baron Group profits would be over forty-one million for 1974, whereas Lester's would be lucky to touch eighteen million. Richard, however, had predicted that Lester's profits would pass the Baron Group's by 1974. She feigned disdain but knew when it came to financial forecasts he was rarely wrong.

Her thoughts floated back to Edward when the phone rang. Gianni di Ferranti wondered if she would like to see his new collection for the Paris show, which put her old classmate out of her mind until one o'clock the following Tuesday.

. . .

Florentyna arrived at the Four Seasons a few minutes after one, wearing one of Gianni's new dresses in midi-length bottle-green silk with a sleeveless jacket over it. She wondered if she would still recognize Edward. She walked up the wide staircase to find him waiting for her on the top step. She privately hoped she had aged as well as he had.

'Edward,' she cried, 'you haven't changed a bit.' He laughed. 'No, no,' mocked Florentyna, 'I've always liked grey hair and the extra weight suits you. I wouldn't expect anything less of a distinguished lawyer from my home town.'

He kissed her on both cheeks like a French general and then she put her arm through his as they followed the maître d' through to their table. A bottle of champagne awaited them.

'Champagne. How lovely. What are we celebrating?'

'Just being with you again, my dear.' Edward noticed that Florentyna seemed to be lost in thought. 'Is something wrong?' he inquired.

'No. I was just remembering myself sitting on the floor at Girls Latin, crying, while you tore the arm off Franklin D. Roosevelt and then poured royal-blue ink over his head.'

'You deserved it, you were a dreadful little show-off. FDR didn't. Poor little bear. Is he still around?'

'Oh, yes. He's taken up residence in my daughter's bedroom and as she has managed to keep his remaining arm and both legs I can only reluctantly conclude that Annabel handles young men better than I did.'

Edward laughed. 'Shall we order? I have so much to talk to you about. It's been fun following your career on the television and in the papers but I want to see if you've changed.'

Florentyna ordered salmon and a side salad while Edward chose the prime rib with asparagus.

'I'm intrigued.'

'By what?' asked Edward.

'Why a Chicago lawyer would fly all the way to New York just to see an hotelier.'

'I do not come as a Chicago lawyer and I have no interest in talking to an hotelier. I come as treasurer of the Cook County Democratic Party.'

'I gave one hundred thousand dollars to the Chicago Democrats last year,' said Florentyna. 'Mind you, Richard donated one hundred thousand to the New York Republicans.'

'I don't want your money, Florentyna, although I know you have supported the Ninth District financially at every election. It's you I want.'

'That's a new line,' she said, grinning. 'Men have stopped saying that to me lately. You know, Edward,' she continued, her tone changing, 'I've been so overworked during the last few years, I barely have had the time to vote, let alone become personally involved. What's more, since Watergate I found Nixon detestable, Agnew worse, and with Muskie a non-runner I was only left with George McGovern, who didn't exactly inspire me.'

'But surely ...'

'I also have a husband, two young children, and a two hundred milion dollar company to run.'

'And what are you going to do for the next twenty years?'

She smiled to herself. 'Turn it into a billion dollar company.'

'In other words, just repeat yourself. Now I agree with you about McGovern and Nixon – one was too good and the other too bad – and I don't see anyone on the horizon who excites me.'

'So now you want me to run for President in '76?'

'No, I want you to run for Congress as the representative of the Ninth District of Illinois.'

Florentyna dropped her fork. 'If I remember the job specification correctly, it's an eighteen-hour day, forty-two thousand five hundred dollars a year, no family life, and your constituents are allowed to be as rude to you as they like. Worst of all, you are required to live in the Ninth District of Illinois.'

'That wouldn't be so bad. The Baron is in the Ninth District, and besides, it's just a stepping-stone.'

'To what?'

'To the Senate.'

'When the whole state can be rude to you.'

'And then the Presidency.'

'When the rest of the world can join in. Edward, this is not Girls Latin and I don't have two lives, one which can run my hotels and one ...'

'And one in which you can give back some of what you have taken from others.'

'That's a bit rough, Edward.'

'Yes, it certainly was. I apologize. But I have always believed you could play a role in national politics, as you did once yourself, and I feel the time is right, especially as I am now convinced you haven't changed.'

'But I haven't been involved in politics at a grass-roots level, let alone a national level, for years.'

'Florentyna, you know as well as I do that most people in Congress have neither your experience nor your intelligence. That goes for most Presidents, come to think of it.'

'I'm flattered, Edward, but not convinced.'

'Well, I can tell you that a group of us in Chicago are convinced you should come home and run for the Ninth District.'

'Henry Osborne's old seat?'

'Yes. The Democrat who won back Osborne's seat in '54 is retiring this session and Mayor Daley wants a strong candidate to ward off any Republican challenger.'

'A Polish woman?'

'With the woman *Time* said ran behind only Jackie Kennedy and Margaret Mead in the nation's esteem.'

'You're mad, Edward. Who needs it?'

'I suspect you do, Florentyna. Just give me one day in your life, come to Chicago and meet the people who want you. Express in your own words how you feel about the future of our country. Won't you at least do that for me?'

'All right, I'll think about it and call you in a few days. But I warn you, Richard will think I'm nuts.'

. . .

On that count Florentyna turned out to be wrong. Richard had arrived home late that night after a trip to Boston, and told her over breakfast that she had been talking in her sleep.

'What did I say?'

Richard stared at her. 'Something I have always suspected,' he replied.

'And what was that?'

'Can I afford to run?'

Florentyna made no reply.

'Why did Edward want to see you for lunch so urgently?'

'He wants me to return to Chicago and stand for Congress.'

'So that's what brought it on. Well, I think you should consider the offer seriously, Jessie. For a long time you have been critical of the fact that competent women don't go into politics. And you have always been outspoken about the abilities of those who do enter public life. Now you can stop complaining and do something about it.'

'But what about the Baron Group?'

'The Rockefeller family managed to survive when Nelson became Governor; no doubt the Kane family will survive somehow. In any case, the group now employs twenty-seven thousand people, so I imagine we can find ten men to take your place.'

'Thank you, Mr Kane. But how do I live in Illinois while you're in New York?'

'That's easily solved. I'll fly to Chicago every weekend. Wednesday nights you can fly to New York and now that Carol has agreed to stay it shouldn't be too unsettling for the children. When you're elected, I'll take the shuttle down to Washington Wednesday nights.'

'You sound as though you've been thinking about this for some time, Mr Kane.'

.   .   .

Florentyna flew out to Chicago a week later and was met at O'Hare airport by Edward. It was pouring, and the wind was blowing so hard that even Edward, tightly clutching a large umbrella with both hands, could only just protect her from the rain.

'Now I know why I wanted to come back to Chicago,' she said as she scampered into the car, cold and wet. They were driven into the city while Edward briefed her on the people she would meet.

'They're all party workers and faithful stalwarts who have only read about you or have seen you on television. They'll be surprised to find that you only have two arms, two legs, and a head like any one of them.'

'How many do you expect to be at the meeting?'

'Around sixty. Seventy would be exceptional.'

'And all you want me to do is meet them, and then say a few words about my feelings on national affairs?'

'Yes.'

'Then I can return home?'

'If that's what you want to do.'

The car came to a halt outside the Cook County Democratic headquarters on Randolph Street where Florentyna was greeted by a Mrs Kalamich, a fat homely woman who led her through to the main hall. Florentyna was shocked to find it was packed with people, some standing at the back. As she walked in, they began to applaud.

'You told me there would only be a few people, Edward,' she whispered.

'I am as surprised as you are. I expected about seventy, not over three hundred.'

Florentyna suddenly felt nervous as she was introduced to the members of the selection committee, and then led on to the stage. She sat next to Edward, aware of how cold the room was and how the hall was full of people with hope in their eyes, people who enjoyed so few of the privileges she took for granted. How different this room was from her own board room, full of men in Brooks Brothers suits who ordered Martinis before dinner. For the first time in her life she felt embarrassed by her wealth and hoped it didn't show.

Edward rose from his chair in the centre of the platform.

'Ladies and gentlemen, it is my privilege tonight to introduce a woman who has gained the respect and admiration of the American people. She has built up one of the largest financial empires in the world, and I believe she could now build a political career of the same dimensions. I hope she will launch that career in this room tonight. Ladies and gentlemen, Mrs Florentyna Kane.'

Florentyna rose nervously to her feet. She wished she had spent more time preparing her speech.

'Thank you, Mr Winchester, for your kind words. It's wonderful to be back in Chicago, my home town, and I appreciate so many of you turning out for me on this cold, wet night.

'I, like you, feel let down by the political leaders of the day I believe in a strong America, and if I were to enter the political arena I would dedicate myself to those words Franklin D. Roosevelt said in this city over thirty years ago. "There can be no greater calling than Public service."

'My father came to Chicago as an immigrant from Poland and only in America could he have achieved the success he did. Each of us must play our role in the destiny of the country we love, and I shall always remember your kindness in inviting me to be considered as your candidate. Be assured that I shall not make my final decision lightly. I have not come with a long prepared speech as I would prefer to answer the questions you consider important.'

She sat down and three hundred people applauded enthusiastically. When the noise had died down, Florentyna answered questions on subjects ranging from the US bombing of Cambodia to legalized abortion, from Watergate to the energy crisis. It was the first time she had attended any meeting without all the facts and figures at her fingertips, and she was surprised to find how strongly she felt on so many issues. After she had answered the final question, over an hour later, the crowd rose and started chanting 'Kane for Congress', refusing to stop until she left the platform. It was one of those rare moments in her life when she wasn't sure what to do next. Edward came to her rescue.

'I knew they would love you,' said Edward, obviously delighted.

'But I was awful,' she shouted back, above the noise.

'Then I can't wait to find out what you're like when you're good.'

Edward led her off the platform as the crowd surged forward. A pale man in a wheelchair managed to touch her arm. She turned.

'This is Sam,' said Edward. 'Sam Hendrick. He lost both his legs in Vietnam.'

'Mrs Kane,' he said. 'You won't remember me; we once licked envelopes together in this hall for Stevenson. If you decide to run for Congress, my wife and I will work night and day to see you are elected. Many of us in Chicago have always believed you would come home and represent us.' His wife, who stood behind the chair, nodded and smiled.

'Thank you,' said Florentyna. She turned and tried to walk to the exit, but it was blocked by outstretched hands and well wishers. She was stopped again at the door, this time by a girl of about twenty-five who told her, 'I lived in your old room in Whitman and Radcliffe and, like you, once stood in Soldier Field and listened to President Kennedy. America needs another Kennedy. Why shouldn't it be a woman?'

Florentyna stared at the eager, intense young face. 'I've graduated and work in Chicago now,' the girl continued, 'but the day you run, a thousand students from Illinois will be on the streets to see that you are elected.'

Florentyna tried to catch her name but was pushed on by the crowd. At last Edward managed to bustle her through the throng and into a waiting car which drove them back to the airport. She didn't speak during the journey. When they arrived at O'Hare, the black chauffeur jumped out and opened the door for her. She thanked him.

'It's a pleasure, Mrs Kane. I want to thank you for the stand you took for my people in the south. We won't forget that you led our struggle for equal pay and all the hotels in the country had to follow. I hope I'll have a chance to vote for you.'

'Thank you again,' said Florentyna, smiling.

Edward took her to the terminal and guided her to the departure gate.

'Made your flight in good time. Thank you for coming, Florentyna. Please let me know when you have made up your mind.' He paused. 'If you feel you can't go ahead with the nomination, I shall always understand.' He kissed her lightly on the cheek and left.

On the flight back, Florentyna sat alone thinking about what had happened that night and how unprepared she had been for such a demonstration. She wished her father could have been in the hall to witness it.

A stewardess asked for her drink order.

'Nothing, thank you.'

'Is there anything else I can do for you, Mrs Kane?'

Florentyna looked up, surprised that the young girl knew her name.

'I used to work in one of your hotels.'

'Which one?' asked Florentyna.

'The Detroit Baron. Barons would always be the first choice for stewardesses for a stop-over. If only America was governed the way you run your hotels, we wouldn't be in the trouble we're in now,' she said before moving on down the aisle.

Florentyna flicked through a copy of *Newsweek*. Under the headline 'How far does Watergate reach?' she studied the faces of Ehrlichman, Haldeman and Dean before closing the magazine. On the cover was a picture of Richard Nixon and the caption: 'When was the President told?'

A little after midnight, she arrived back at East Sixty-fourth Street. Richard was sitting up in the crimson chair by the fire. He rose to greet her.

'Well, did they ask you to run for President of the United States?'

'No. But how do you feel about Congresswoman Kane?'

.   .   .

Florentyna phoned Edward the next day. 'I am willing to put my name forward as the Democratic candidate for Congress,' she said.

'Thank you. I ought to try and express my thoughts more fully, but for now – thank you.'

'Edward, may I know who would have been the candidate if I had said no?'

'They were pressing me to run myself. But I told them I had a better candidate in mind. As I'm certain this time round you'll take advice, even if you became President.'

'I never did become Class President.'

'I did, and I've still ended up serving you.'

'Where do I start, coach?'

'The Primary will be in March, so you'd better reserve every weekend between now and the fall.'

'I already have, starting this weekend – and can you tell me who was the young woman from Radcliffe who stopped me at the door and talked about Kennedy?'

'Janet Brown. In spite of her age, she's already one of the most respected case workers in the city's Human Services department.'

'Do you have her phone number?'

During the week Florentyna informed the Baron board of directors of her decision. They appointed Richard co-chairman of the group and elected two new directors.

Florentyna called Janet Brown and offered her a job as her full-time political assistant and was delighted by Janet's immediate acceptance. She then added two new secretaries to her staff for political work only. Finally she called the Chicago Baron and instructed them to leave the thirty-eighth floor free, warning them she would need the entire floor left at her disposal for at least a year.

'Taking it seriously, aren't we?' said Richard later that evening.

'Indeed I am, because I'm going to have to work very hard if you're ever going to be the First Gentleman.'

26

'Are you expecting much opposition?'

'Nothing of real consequence,' said Edward. 'There may be a protest candidate or two, but as the committee is fully behind you, the real fight should be with the Republicans.'

'Do we know who their candidate is likely to be?'

'Not yet. My spies tell me it's between two men, Ray Buck, who seems to be the choice of the retiring member, and Stewart Lyle, who's served on the City Council for the past eight years. They'll both run a good campaign, but that's not our immediate problem. With so little time left, we must concentrate on the Democratic Primary.'

'How many people do you think will vote in the Primary?' asked Florentyna.

'Can't be certain. All we do know is that there are roughly one hundred and fifty thousand registered Democrats and that the turnout is usually between forty-five and fifty per cent. So that would point to around seventy or eighty thousand.'

Edward unfolded a large map of Chicago and placed it in front of Florentyna.

'The boundaries of the constituency are marked in red and run from

Chicago Avenue in the south to the Evanston border in the north, from Ravenswood and Western Highway in the west to the lake in the east.'

'The district hasn't changed since the days of Henry Osborne,' said Florentyna, 'so it should all come back to me very quickly.'

'Let's hope so, because our main task is to see that as many Democrats in that area are aware of who you are through the press, advertising, television and public appearances. Whenever they open their newspaper, turn on the radio or watch TV Florentyna Kane must be with them. The voters must feel you are everywhere and they must believe your only interest is in them. In fact, there can be no major function in Chicago between now and 19 March at which you are not present.'

'Suits me,' said Florentyna. 'I've already set up my campaign headquarters in the Chicago Baron, which my father had foresight to build in the heart of the district. I propose to spend weekends here and any free days during the week at home with my family, so where do you want me to start?'

'I've called a press conference for next Monday, to be held at Democratic headquarters. A short speech followed by a question-and-answer session, and then we'll serve them coffee so you can meet all the key people individually. As you enjoy thinking fast on your feet, you should relish meeting the press.'

'Any particular advice?'

'No, just be yourself.'

'You may live to regret that.'

.   .   .

Edward's judgement turned out to be right. After Florentyna had made a short opening statement the questions came thick and fast. Under his breath, Edward whispered the names of the various journalists as each rose to his feet.

The first was Mike Royko, of the Chicago *Daily News*.

'Why do you think it appropriate that a New York millionairess should run for the Ninth District of Illinois?'

'In this context,' said Florentyna standing to take the questions, 'I am not a New York millionairess. I was born in St Luke's Hospital and brought up on Rigg Street. My father, who came to this country with nothing but the clothes he stood in, founded the Baron Group right here in the Ninth District. I believe we must always fight to ensure that any immigrant arriving on our shores today, whether he be from Vietnam or Poland, has the opportunity to achieve the same goals as my father did.'

Edward pointed to another journalist for the next question.

'Do you consider it a disadvantage to be a woman when seeking public office?'

'Perhaps to a limited or ill-informed person I would have to answer yes, but not with any intelligent voter who puts the issues before outdated prejudices. Which of you if involved in a traffic accident on the way home today would think twice if the first doctor on the scene turned out to be a woman? I hope the issue of sex will soon be as irrelevant as that of religion. It seems a century ago that people asked John F. Kennedy if he thought the Presidency might change because he was a Roman Catholic. I notice nowadays the question never arises with Teddy Kennedy. Women are already playing leading roles in other nations. Golda Meir in Israel and Indira Gandhi in India are just two examples. I consider it sad that in a nation of two hundred and thirty million people women number not one of the hundred Senators and only sixteen out of the four hundred and thirty-four members of Congress.'

'What does your husband feel about you wearing the trousers in your family?' demanded an unsolicited questioner. Laughter broke out in certain parts of the room and Florentyna waited for complete silence.

'He's far too intelligent and successful for such a pathetic question to occur to him.'

'What is your attitude on Watergate?'

'A sad episode in American political history which I hope will be behind us before too long, but not forgotten.'

'Do you feel President Nixon should resign?'

'That's a moral decision and one for the President to make himself.'

'Would you resign if you were President?'

'I wouldn't have to break into any hotels. I already own one hundred and forty-three.' A burst of laughter followed by applause gave Florentyna a little more confidence.

'Do you think the President should be impeached?'

'That's a question Congress will have to decide based on the evidence the Judiciary Committee is considering, including the White House tapes, if and when President Nixon releases them. But the resignation of the Attorney-General, Elliot Richardson, a man whose integrity has never been in question, should ring warning bells for the general public.'

'Where do you stand on abortion?'

'I shall not fall into the trap that Senator Mason did only last week when asked the same question, to which he replied, "Gentlemen, that one's below the belt".' Florentyna waited for the laughter to die down before saying in a more serious tone. 'I am a Roman Catholic by birth and upbringing, so I feel strongly about the protection of the unborn child. However, I also believe there are situations in which it is both necessary and indeed morally correct for a qualified doctor to carry out an abortion.'

'Can you give an example?'

'Rape would be an obvious one, and also in a case where the mother's health is in danger.'

'Isn't that against the teachings of your church?'

'That is correct, but I have always believed in the separation of church and state. Any person who runs for public office must be willing to take stands on certain issues that will not please all of the people all of the time. I think Edmund Burke summed it up better than I could hope to do when he said, "Your representative owes you, not his industry only, but his judgement, and he betrays instead of serving you, if he sacrifices it to your opinion."'

Edward sensed the effect of the last statement and promptly rose from his chair. 'Well, ladies and gentlemen of the press, I think the time has come to adjourn for coffee, which will give you the opportunity to meet Florentyna Kane personally – although I am sure by now you know why we feel she is the right person to represent the Ninth District in Congress.'

For the next hour, Florentyna faced a further barrage of personal and political questions, some of which, had they been put to her in the privacy of her own home, she would have found objectionable, but she was quickly learning that one cannot be a public figure and hope to maintain a private stance on anything. When the last journalist had left, she collapsed into a chair, not even having had the time to drink one cup of coffee.

'You were great,' said Janet Brown. 'Didn't you think so, Mr Winchester?'

Edward smiled. 'Good, not great, but I blame myself for not warning you about the difference between being chairman of a private company and running for public office.'

'What are you getting at?' asked Florentyna, surprised.

'Some of those journalists are very powerful and they talk to hundreds of thousands of people every day through their columns. They want to tell their readers that they know you personally and once or twice you were a little too aloof, and with the man from the *Tribune* you were just plain rude.'

'Was that the man who asked about who wore the trousers?'

'Yes.'

'What was I supposed to say?'

'Turn it into a joke.'

'It wasn't funny, Edward, and it was he who was rude.'

'Possibly, but he's not the one who's running for public office and you are, so he can say what he likes. And don't ever forget his column is read by more than five hundred thousand people in Chicago every day including most of your constituents.'

'So you want me to compromise myself?'

'No, I want you to get elected. When you're in the House, you can prove to everyone that they were right in voting for you. But just now you're an unknown commodity with a lot going against you. You're a woman, you're Polish and you're a millionairess. That combination is going to arouse just about every form of prejudice or jealousy in most ordinary people. The way to counter those feelings is always to appear humorous, kind and interested in people who do not share the privileges you have.'

'Edward, it's not me who should be running for public office, it's you.'

Edward shook his head. 'I know you're the right person, Florentyna, but I realize now that it will take a little time for you to adjust to your new environment. Thank God you've always been a quick learner. By the way, I don't disagree with the sentiments you voiced so vociferously, but as you seem to like quoting statesmen of the past, don't forget Jefferson's comment to Adams. "You can't lose votes with a speech you didn't make."'

Again Edward turned out to be right: the press the next day gave Florentyna a mixed reception, and the *Tribune* reporter called her the worst sort of opportunistic carpetbagger he had ever had the misfortune to come across on the political trail – surely Chicago could find a local person? Otherwise he would have to recommend for the first time that his readers vote Republican. Florentyna was horrified and adjusted quickly to the fact that a journalist's ego was sometimes even more sensitive than a politician's. She settled down to working five days a week in Chicago, meeting people, talking to the press, appearing on television, fund raising and then going over it all again whenever she saw Richard. Even Edward was beginning to feel confident that the tide was turning her way, when the first blow came.

'Ralph Brooks? Who on earth is Ralph Brooks?' asked Florentyna.

'A local lawyer, very bright and very ambitious. I'd always thought his sights were set on the State's Attorney's office en route to the federal bench, but it seems I'm wrong. I wonder who put him up to this?'

'Is he a serious candidate?' Florentyna asked.

'He certainly is. A local boy, educated at the University of Chicago before going on to Yale Law School.'

'Age?' asked Florentyna.

'Late thirties.'

'And of course he's good-looking?'

'Very,' said Edward. 'When he rises in court every woman on the jury wants him to win. I always avoid opposing him if I can.'

'Does this Olympian have any disadvantages?'

'Naturally. Any man who has been a lawyer in this city is bound to have made a few enemies, and I know for certain Mayor Daley won't be overjoyed about his entry into the race, since Ralph Brooks is an obvious rival for his son.'

'What am I expected to do about him?'

'Nothing,' said Edward. 'When asked, you simply give the standard answer: say it's democracy at work and may the best man – or woman – win.'

'He's left himself with only five weeks before the Primary.'

'Sometimes that's a clever tactic; he'll hope you've run out of steam. The one good thing to come out of this is that Mr Brooks will have killed any complacency among our workers. Everyone will now know they have a fight on their hands, which will be good training for when we face the Republicans.'

Florentyna was reassured that Edward still sounded confident, although he confided in Janet Brown later that it was going to be one hell of a fight. During the next five weeks Florentyna learned just how much of a fight. Everywhere she went, Ralph Brooks seemed to have been there just before her. Every time she made a press statement on a major issue. Brooks had given his opinion the night before. But as the day of the Primary drew nearer, she learned to play Brooks at his own game, and beat him at it. However, just at the point when the opinion polls showed she was holding her head he played an ace that Florentyna hadn't foreseen. She read the details on the front page of the Chicago *Tribune*.

'Brooks Challenges Kane to Debate' ran the headline. She knew that with all his court experience and practice at cross-examination he was bound to be a formidable opponent. Within minutes of the paper hitting the streets, the phone in her headquarters was besieged with queries from the press. Would she accept the challenge? Was she avoiding him? Didn't the people of Chicago have the right to see both candidates debate the issues? Janet held them off while Florentyna held a hasty conference with Edward. It lasted for three minutes, during which Florentyna wrote out a statement for Janet to read to all inquirers.

'Florentyna Kane is delighted to accept the invitation to debate Ralph Brooks and looks forward to the encounter.'

During the week Edward appointed a representative to consult with

Brooks's campaign manager in determining the time and place for the debate.

The Thursday before the Primary was the date agreed by both sides; the venue was to be the Bernard Horwich Jewish Community Centre on West Touhy. Once the local CBS-TV affiliate had agreed to cover the debate, both candidates knew that the outcome of the election might well depend on the confrontation. Florentyna spent days preparing her speech and answering questions shot at her by Edward, Janet and Richard. It brought back memories of Miss Tredgold and their preparation for the Woolson Prize Scholarship.

On the night of the debate every seat in the Community Centre was taken. People were standing at the back while others sat on window sills. Richard had flown in from New York for the occasion, and he and Florentyna arrived a half hour before the debate was due to begin. She went through the usual ordeal of television make-up while Richard found himself a seat in the front row.

She was greeted by warm applause as she entered the hall and took her seat on the stage. Ralph Brooks arrived moments later to an equally tumultous applause. He pushed back his hair rather self-consciously as he strode across the floor. No woman in the room took her eyes from him, including Florentyna. The chairman of the Ninth District Democratic Congressional Committee welcomed them both before taking them to one side to remind them that they would each make an opening speech, which would be followed by a question-and-answer session, and then they would be invited to make a closing statement. They both nodded; the chairman was only repeating what had been agreed to by their representatives days before. He then took a new half-dollar from his pocket and Florentyna stared at the head of John Kennedy. The chairman spun the coin, and she called heads. Kennedy looked up at her again.

'I'll speak second,' she said, not even hesitating.

Without another word, they walked back on to the stage. Florentyna took a seat on the right of Edward while Ralph Brooks sat on his left. At eight o'clock, the moderator banged the gavel and called the meeting to order. 'Mr Brooks will address you first and then Mrs Kane will speak. The speeches will be followed by a question-and-answer session.'

Ralph Brooks rose and Florentyna stared up at the tall, handsome man. She had to admit it: if a film director had been casting for the role of President, Ralph Brooks would be given the part. From the moment he started to speak, Florentyna was in no doubt that she would not have to travel beyond Chicago to face a more formidable rival. Brooks was relaxed and assured, his delivery was professional without sounding glib.

'Ladies and gentlemen, fellow Democrats,' he began. 'I stand before you tonight, a local man who has made his way in life right here in Chicago. My great-grandfather was born in this city and for four generations the Brooks family has practiced law from our offices on La Salle Street, always serving this community to the best of our ability. I offer myself today as your candidate for Congress in the belief that representatives of the people should always come from the grass-roots of their community. I do not have the vast wealth that is at the disposal of my opponent, but I bring a dedication to and care for this district that I hope you will feel surpasses wealth.' There was an outburst of applause, but Florentyna could see several people who were not joining in. 'On the issues of crime prevention, housing, public transportation and health, I have for several years sought to promote public good in the courts of Chicago. I now seek the opportunity to promote your interests in the United States House of Representatives.'

Florentyna listened intently to each well delivered phrase and was not surprised when Brooks sat down to applause that was loud and sustained. Edward rose to make Florentyna's introduction. When he had finished, she stood up – and wanted to run out of the hall. Richard smiled up at her from the front row and she regained her confidence.

'My father came to America over fifty years ago,' she began, 'having escaped first from the Germans and then from the Russians. After educating himself in New York he came to Chicago where he founded the hotel group of which I have the privilege of being chairman, right here in the Ninth District. A group that now employs twenty-seven thousand people in every state of America. When my father's career was at its zenith, he left this country to fight the Germans again and he returned to America with a Bronze Star. I was born in this city and went to high school not a mile from this hall, a Chicago education that made it possible for me to go to college. Now I have returned home wishing to represent the people who made my American dream possible.'

Loud applause greeted Florentyna's words, but she noticed once again that several people did not join in. 'I hope I will not be prevented from holding office because I was born with wealth. If that were to be a disqualification, Jefferson, Roosevelt and Kennedy would never have held office. I hope I will not be prevented because my father was an immigrant. If that were the case, then one of the greatest mayors this community has ever known, Anton Cermak, would never have worked in City Hall, and if I am to be prevented because I am a woman, then half the population of America must be disqualified along with me.' This was greeted with loud applause from all parts of the hall. Florentyna drew a deep breath.

'I do not apologize for being the daughter of an immigrant. I do not apologize for being wealthy. I do not apologize for being a woman, and I will never be apologetic about wanting to represent the people of Chicago in the United States Congress.' The applause was deafening. 'If it is not my destiny to represent you, I shall support Mr Brooks. If, on the other hand, I have the honour of being selected to be your candidate, you can be assured that I shall tackle the problems that Chicago faces with the same dedication and energy I put into making my company one of the most successful hotel groups in the world.'

Florentyna sat down to continuing applause and looked towards her husband, who was smiling. She relaxed for the first time and stared into the hall where some people even stood to applaud although she was only too aware most of them were on her staff. She checked her watch: eight twenty-eight. She had timed it perfectly. 'Laugh-In' was almost due on TV and the Chicago Black Hawks would be warming up on channel nine. There would be a lot of changing of channels in the next few minutes. Judging by the frown on Ralph Brooks's face he was equally aware of the scheduling.

After questions – which brought no surprises – and the closing statements, Florentyna and Richard left the hall surrounded by well-wishers and returned to their room at the Baron. They waited nervously for a bellboy to deliver the first edition of the papers. The overall verdict was in favour of Florentyna. Even the *Tribune* said it had been a very close-run affair.

During the last three days of the campaign before the Primary, Florentyna pounded pavement, pressed flesh and walked the entire route of the St Patrick's Day Parade before literally collapsing into a hot bath every night. She was woken by Richard each morning with a cup of hot coffee, after which she started the whole mad process again.

·　　·　　·

'The great day has at last arrived,' said Richard.

'Not a moment too soon,' said Florentyna. 'I am not sure my legs can go through anything like this ever again.'

'Have no fear. All will be revealed tonight,' said Richard from behind a copy of *Fortune*.

Florentyna rose and dressed in a simple blue suit of a crease-resistant fabric: although she still felt crumpled at the end of each day. She put on what Miss Tredgold would have called sensible shoes, having already worn out two pairs on the campaign trail. After breakfast, she and Richard walked down to the local school. She cast her vote for Florentyna Kane. It felt strange. Richard as a registered New York Republican remained outside.

In a heavier turnout than Edward had predicted, 49,312 other people voted for Florentyna that day, while 42,972 voted for Ralph Brooks.

Florentyna Kane had won her first election.

·　　·　　·

The Grand Old Party candidate turned out to be Stewart Lyle, who was an easier opponent than Ralph Brooks. He was an old-fashioned Republican who was always charming and courteous and who did not believe in personal confrontation. Florentyna liked him from the day they met and had no doubt that, if elected, he would have represented the district with compassion, but after Nixon had resigned on 9 August and Ford had pardoned the ex-President, the Democrats looked set for a landslide win.

Florentyna was among those elected on the bandwagon. She captured the Ninth District of Illinois with a majority over the Republican candidate of more than 27,000. Richard was the first to congratulate her.

'I am so proud of you, my darling,' he smiled mischievously. 'Mind you, I'm sure Mark Twain would have been as well.'

'Why Mark Twain?' asked Florentyna, puzzled.

'Because it was he who said: "Suppose you were an idiot and suppose you were a member of Congress. But I repeat myself."'

27

William and Annabel joined their father and mother for Christmas at the Kane family house on Cape Cod. Florentyna enjoyed having the children around her for the festivities, and they soon recharged all her human batteries.

William, nearly fifteen, was already talking about going to Harvard and spent every afternoon poring over maths books that even Richard didn't understand. Annabel spent most of her holiday on the phone talking long distance about boys to different school friends until Richard finally had to explain to her how the Bell Telephone Company made its money. Florentyna read Michener's *Centennial* and under pressure from her daughter listened to Roberta Flack singing 'Killing Me Softly With His Song' loudly, again and again. Richard got so sick of the record he begged Annabel to turn the damn thing over. She did, and for the first time Richard listened to a popular record he knew he would enjoy for the rest of his life. Annabel was puzzled when she saw her mother smile at the lyrics her father seemed entranced by:

Jessie come home, there's a hole in the bed
where you slept, and now it's getting cold.
Jessie, the blues ...

When the Christmas vacation came to an end Florentyna flew back to New York with Richard. It took her a week of going over reports on the Baron Group and being briefed by the heads of each department before she felt she had covered everything that had happened in her absence.

During the year they had completed hotels in Brisbane and Johannesburg, and were refurbishing old Barons in Nashville and Cleveland. In Florentyna's absence, Richard had slowed the forward planning programme down a little but had still managed to increase the profits to a record forty-five million dollars for the year ending 1974. Florentyna was in no position to complain, as Lester's was on target to show a massive increase in the credit column that year.

Florentyna's only anxiety was that Richard, for the first time in his life, was beginning to look his age: lines were appearing on his forehead and around his eyes that could only have resulted from continual and considerable stress. When she taxed him with working uncivilized hours (even his cello practice seemed less frequent) he chided her that it was a hard road to toil when one wanted to be First Gentleman.

Congresswoman Kane flew into Washington in early January. She had sent Janet Brown on to the capital in December to head up her Congressional staff and work out the transition with her predecessor's office. When Florentyna joined her, everything seemed to be organized, down to the George Novak Suite at the Washington Baron. Janet had made herself indispensable during the previous six months, and Florentyna was well prepared when the first session of the 94th Congress was ready to open. Janet had allocated the $227,270 a year each House member is permitted to staff the office. She did this with stringent care, placing the emphasis on competence in her selection whatever the age of any applicant. She had appointed a personal secretary to Florentyna named Louise Drummond, a legislative assistant, a press secretary, four legislative correspondents to research issues as well as to handle mail, two further secretaries and a receptionist. In addition, Florentyna had left three case workers in her district office under a capable Polish field representative.

Florentyna had been assigned rooms on the seventh floor of the Longworth Building, the oldest and middle of the three House buildings. Janet told her that her office had been occupied in the past by Lyndon Johnson, John Lindsay and Pete McCloskey. '"Hear no evil, see no evil, speak no evil,"' she commented. Florentyna's new office suite was only two hundred yards from the Capitol, and she could always go directly to the chamber on the little subway if the weather was inclement or if she wished to avoid the ubiquitous herded groups of Washington sightseers.

Florentyna's personal office was a modest-sized room already cluttered with massive brown congressional furniture, a wooden desk, a large brown leather sofa, several dark, uncomfortable chairs and two glass-fronted cabinets. From the way the office had been left, it was easy to believe that the previous occupant had been male.

Florentyna quickly filled the bookcases with a copy of the US Code, the Rules of the House, the Hurd Annotated Illinois Revised Statutes, and Carl Sandburg's six-volume biography of Lincoln, one of her favourite works despite his party. She then hung some water colours of her own choice on the drab cream walls in an effort to cover the nail holes left by the previous tenant. On her desk she placed a family photograph taken outside their first shop in San Francisco and when she discovered that each member of Congress was entitled to plants from the botanical gardens, she instructed Janet to claim their maximum allocation as well as arranging for fresh flowers on her desk every Monday.

She also asked Janet to decorate the front office in a way that was both welcoming and dignified; under no circumstances were there to be any portraits of her on view. Florentyna disliked the way most of her colleagues filled their reception areas with self-lauding memorabilia.

She reluctantly agreed to place the flag of Illinois and the United States flag behind her desk.

On the afternoon before Congress convened she held a reception for her family and campaign workers. Richard and Kate flew down with the children, and Edward accompanied Florentyna's mother and Father O'Reilly from Chicago. Florentyna had sent out nearly one hundred invitations to friends and supporters all across the country, and to her surprise over seventy people turned up.

During the celebrations she took Edward aside and invited him to join the board of the Baron Group; full of champagne, he accepted and then forgot about the offer until he received a letter from Richard confirming the appointment and adding that it would be valuable for Florentyna to have two boardroom views to consider while she concentrated on her political career.

When Richard and Florentyna climbed into yet another Baron king-size bed that night, he told her once more how proud he was of her achievement.

'I couldn't have done it without your support, Mr Kane.'

'There was no suggestion that I supported you, Jessie, though I reluctantly admit to considerable pleasure at your victory. Now I must catch up with the group's European forecasts before I switch off the light on my side of the bed.'

'I do wish you would slow down a bit, Richard.'

'I can't, my darling. Neither of us can. That's why we're so good for each other.'

'Am I good for you?' asked Florentyna.

'In a word, no. If I could have it all back, I would have married Maisie and saved the money on several pairs of gloves.'

'Good God, I wonder what Maisie is up to nowadays.'

'Still in Bloomingdale's. Having given up any hope of me, she's married a travelling salesman, so I suppose I am stuck with you. Now can I get down to reading this report?'

She took the report out of his hand and dropped it on the floor.

'No, darling.'

.   .   .

When the first session of the 94th Congress opened Speaker Carl Albert, dressed sombrely in a dark suit, took his place on the podium and banged his gavel as he gazed down into the semi-circle of members seated in their green leather chairs. Florentyna turned in her place and smiled up at Richard and her family, who had been allocated places in the gallery above. When she looked around the chamber at her colleagues, she couldn't help thinking that they were the worst-dressed group of people she had ever seen in her life. Her bright-red wool suit, in the latest midi fashion, made her conspicuous by exception.

The Speaker asked the House chaplain, the Reverend Edward Latch, to pronounce the benediction. This was followed by an opening speech by the leaders of both parties and an address by the Speaker. Mr Albert reminded Congressmen that they should keep their speeches brief and to refrain from making too much noise in the chamber while others were at the podium. He then adjourned the session and everyone left the chamber to attend some of the dozens of receptions given on the opening day.

'Is that all you have to do, Mummy?' asked Annabel.

Florentyna laughed. 'No, darling, that's just the opening session; the real work starts tomorrow.'

Even Florentyna was surprised the next morning. Her mail contained one hundred and sixty-one items, including two out-of-date Chicago papers, six 'Dear Colleague' letters, from Congressmen she had yet to meet, fourteen invitations to trade association receptions, seven letters from special interest groups; several invitations to address meetings – some out of Chicago and Washington – three dozen letters from constituents, two requests to be placed on her mailing list, fifteen résumés from hopeful job-seekers, and a note from Carl Albert to say that she had been placed on the Appropriations and Small Businesses committees.

The mail looked manageable compared with the ceaseless telephone demands for everything from Florentyna's official photograph to press interviews. The Washington reporters from the Chicago papers called regularly, but Florentyna was also contacted by the local Washington press, who were always intrigued by new female additions to Congress, especially those who did not resemble all-in wrestlers. Florentyna quickly learned the names she should know, including those of Maxine Cheshire and Betty Beale, as well as David Broder and Joe Alsop. Before the end of March, she had been the subject of a front-page 'Style' interview in the *Post* and had appeared in Washingtonian Magazine's 'New Stars on the Hill'. She turned down the continual invitations to appear on 'Panorama', and began to question where the proper balance lay between gaining visibility, which would be of use in influencing issues, and losing all her free time to the media.

During those first few weeks, Florentyna seemed to do nothing except run very fast trying to remain on the same spot. She considered herself fortunate to be the Illinois delegation's choice for a vacancy on the powerful Appropriations Committee, the first freshman in years to be so honoured, but discovered nothing had been left to chance when she opened a scrawled note from Mayor Daley which simply read, 'You owe me one'.

Florentyna found her new world fascinating but it felt rather like being back at school as she searched the corridors for committee rooms, sprinted through the underground to the Capitol to record her vote, met with lobbyists, studied briefing books and signed hundreds of letters. The idea of getting a signature machine grew increasingly appealing.

An elderly Democratic colleague from Chicago advised her on the wisdom of sending out a constituent newsletter to her one hundred and eighty thousand households every two months. 'Remember, my dear,' he added, 'it may appear as though you are doing nothing more than papering the Ninth District, but there are only three ways of assuring your re-election: the frank, the frank and the frank.'

He also advised Florentyna to assign two of her district staffers to clip every article from the local newspapers that referred to a constituent. Voters began receiving congratulations on their weddings, births, community achievements – and even basketball victories now that eighteen-year-olds had the vote. Florentyna always added a personal word or two in Polish where appropriate, quietly thanking her mother for disobeying her father's orders over the teaching of Polish.

With the help of Janet, who was always in the office before her and still there when she left, Florentyna slowly got on top of the paperwork, and by the 4 July recess she was almost in control. She had not yet spoken on the floor and had said very little in any committee hearings. Sandra Read, a House colleague from New York, had advised her to spend the first six months listening, the second six months thinking and the third six months speaking occasionally.

'What about the fourth six months?' asked Florentyna.

'You'll be campaigning for re-election,' came the reply.

On weekends she would regale Richard with stories of the bureaucratic waste of the taxpayers' money and the lunacy with which America's democratic system was conducted.

'I thought you had been elected to change all that?' he said, looking down at his wife, who was sitting cross-legged on the floor in front of him, clutching her knees.

'It will take twenty years to change anything. Are you aware that committees make decisions involving millions of dollars, but half the members haven't the slightest idea what they're voting on and the other half don't even attend but vote by proxy.'

'Then you will have to become chairman of a committee, and see to it that your members do their homework and attend hearings.'

'I can't.'

'What do you mean, you can't?' asked Richard, finally folding his morning newspaper.

'You can only become the chairman of a committee by seniority, so it's irrelevant when you reach the peak of your mental prowess. If there is someone who had been on the committee longer than you, he automatically gets the job. At this moment, of twenty-two standing committees there are three committee chairmen in their seventies, and thirteen in their sixties, which leaves only six under sixty. I've worked out that I will become chairman of the Appropriations Committee on my sixty-eighth birthday, having served twenty-eight years in the House. That is if I win the thirteen elections in between, because if you lose one, you start again. It's taken me only a few weeks to work out why so many southern states elect freshmen to Congress who are under thirty. If we ran the Baron Group the way Congress is run we'd have been bankrupt long ago.'

Florentyna was slowly coming to accept the fact that it would take years to reach the top of the political tree, and the truth was that the climb consisted of a long hard grind, known as 'serving your time'. 'Go along and get along', was the way her committee chairman put it. She decided that if it was going to be any different for her, she would have to turn the disadvantage of being a freshman into the advantage of being a woman.

It happened in a way she could never have planned. She did not speak on the House floor for the first six months, although she had sat in her seat for hours watching how the debates were conducted and learning from those who used their limited speaking time with skill. When a distinguished Republican, Robert C. L. Buchanan, announced he would be proposing an anti-abortion amendment to the Defence Appropriations Bill, Florentyna felt the time had come to deliver her maiden speech.

She wrote to the chairman and asked for permission to speak against the motion. He sent back a courteous reply, reminding her she would only be allowed five minutes and wishing her luck.

Buchanan spoke with great emotion to a silent chamber and used his five minutes with the skill of a professional House man. Florentyna thought him the worst sort of backwoodsman, and as he spoke, added some notes to her carefully prepared speech. When Buchanan sat down, Sandra Read was recognized, and she made a powerful case against the amendment although she was regularly interrupted by noisy comments from the floor. A third speaker added nothing to the debate, simply reiterating the words of Robert Buchanan, to be sure his views were on the record and would be in his local newspaper. Speaker Albert then recognized 'the distinguished gentle lady from Illinois'. Florentyna rose with some trepidation and made her way to the speaking rostrum in the well of the House, trying to keep her hands from trembling too noticeably.

'Mr Speaker, I must apologize to the House for rising for the first time to address members on a note of controversy, but I cannot support the amendment for several reasons.' Florentyna started by talking about the role of a mother who wanted to continue a professional career. She then proceeded to outline the reasons why Congress should not adopt the amendment. She was aware of being nervous and unusually inarticulate, and after a minute or so noticed that Buchanan and the other Republican who had spoken before her were now holding a heated discussion which only encouraged some of the members in the chamber to talk among themselves while others left their seats to chat to colleagues. Soon the noise reached such a pitch that Florentyna could hardly hear the sound of her own voice. Suddenly in the middle of a sentence, she stopped speaking and stood in silence.

The Speaker banged his gavel and asked if she had yielded her time to anyone.

She turned to Carl Albert and said, 'No, Mr Speaker, I do not intend to continue.'

'But the distinguished member was in the middle of a sentence.'

'Indeed I was, Mr Speaker, but it has become obvious to me that there are some in this august chamber who are more interested in the sound of their own voices than in anyone else's views.' Buchanan rose to object, but was gavelled down as out of order by the Speaker. Uproar broke out, and members who had never noticed her before stared at Florentyna.

She remained at the rostrum as the Speaker went on to bang his gavel continually. When the noise died down, Florentyna continued. 'I am aware, Mr Speaker, that it takes several years in this place before one can hope to get anything done, but I had not realized that it might take as many years before anyone would have the good manners to listen to what one had to say.'

Once again pandemonium broke out while Florentyna remained silently clutching on to the rostrum. She was now trembling from head to toe. Eventually the Speaker brought the chamber to order.

'The Honourable Member's point is well taken,' he said, staring down at the two offenders, who looked more than a little embarrassed. 'I have mentioned this habit to the House on several occasions in the past. It has taken a new member to remind us how discourteous we have become. Perhaps the distinguished gentle lady from Illinois would now like to resume.' Florentyna checked the point she had reached in her notes. The House waited in expectant silence.

She was about to continue when a hand rested firmly on her shoulder. She turned to see a smiling Sandra Read by her side. 'Sit down. You've beaten them all. If you speak now it can only spoil the effect you've created. As soon as the next speaker rises, leave the chamber immediately.' Florentyna nodded, yielded the remainder of her time, before returning to her seat.

Speaker Albert recognized the next speaker and Florentyna walked towards the Speaker's gallery exit with Sandra Read. When they reached the doors Sandra left her with the words, 'Well done. Now you're on your own.'

Florentyna did not understand what Sandra had meant until she walked into the lobby and found herself surrounded by reporters.

'Can you step outside?' asked an interviewer from CBS. Florentyna followed him where she was met by television cameras, reporters and flash bulbs.

'Do you think that Congress is a disgrace?'

'Will your stand help the pro-choice advocates?'

'How would you change the procedure?'

'Did you plan the whole exercise?'

Question after question came flying at Florentyna, and before the evening was out Senator Mike Mansfield, the Democratic Majority Leader in the Senate, had called to congratulate her and she had been asked by Barbara Walters to appear on the 'Today' show.

The following morning the *Washington Post*'s version of events in the chamber made it sound as though Florentyna had single-handedly caused a declaration of war. Richard called to read the caption underneath her photograph on the front page of the *New York Times*: 'Woman of courage arrives in Congress', and as the morning wore on it became obvious that Congresswoman Kane had become famous overnight because she *hadn't* made a speech. Phyllis Mills, a Representative from Pennsylvania, warned her the following day that she had better choose her next subject carefully because the Republicans would be lying in wait for her with sharpened knives.

'Perhaps I should quit while I'm ahead,' said Florentyna.

When the initial furore had subsided and her mail had dropped from one thousand letters per week back to the usual three hundred, Florentyna began to settle down to building a serious reputation. In Chicago that reputation was already growing as she found from her twice-monthly visits. Her constituents were coming to believe that she could actually influence the course of events. This worried Florentyna because she was quickly discovering how little room a politician has for manoeuvre outside the established guidelines. At a local level, however, she felt that she could help people who were often simply overwhelmed by the bureaucratic system. She decided to add another staff member to the Chicago office to handle the extra case work.

Richard was delighted to see how rewarding Florentyna found her new career, and tried to take as much pressure off her as possible when it came to the day-to-day business of the Baron Group. Edward Winchester helped considerably by taking on some of the responsibilities, both in New York and Chicago. In Chicago, Edward had gained considerable sway in the smoke-filled rooms as Mayor Daley recognized the need for a new breed of political operative in the wake of the 1972 Presidential election. It seemed Daley's old supporters were coming to terms with Florentyna's future. Richard was full of praise for Edward's contribution as a member of the board and was already considering inviting him to join Lester's as well.

· · ·

No sooner had Florentyna completed her first year in Congress than she complained to Richard that she would soon have to start campaigning again.

'What a crazy system that sends you to the House for only two years; no sooner have you settled into the place than you have to recycle the campaign bumper stickers.'

'How would you change it?' asked Richard.

'Well, senators are in a far better position, coming up for election only every six years, so I think I would make Congressional terms at least four years in length.'

When she repeated her grouse to Edward in Chicago he was sympathetic but pointed out that in her case she didn't look as if she would have any real opposition from the Democrats or the Republicans.

'What about Ralph Brooks?'

'He seems to have his eye firmly set on the State's Attorney's office since his recent marriage. Perhaps with his wife's social background she doesn't want to see him in Washington politics.'

'Don't believe it,' said Florentyna. 'He'll be back.'

· · ·

In September, Florentyna flew to New York and, together with Richard, drove William up to Concord, New Hampshire, to start his fifth-form year at St Paul's. The car was packed with more stereo equipment, Rolling Stones records and athletic gear than books. Annabel was now in her first year at the Madeira so she could be near her mother, but she still showed no signs of wanting to follow Florentyna to Radcliffe.

Florentyna was disappointed that Annabel's sole interests always seemed to centre on boys and parties. Not once during the holidays did she discuss her progress at school or even open a book. She avoided her brother's company and would even change the subject whenever William's name came up in conversation. It became more obvious every day that she was jealous of her brother's achievements.

Carol did the best she could to keep her occupied but on two occasions Annabel disobeyed her father and once returned home from a date hours after she had agreed.

Florentyna was relieved when the time came for Annabel to return to school as she had decided not to overreact to her daughter's holiday escapades. She hoped it was nothing more than an adolescent stage she was passing through.

· · ·

Struggling to survive in a man's world was nothing new for Florentyna and she began her second year in Congress with considerably more confidence. Life at the Baron had been a little sheltered in comparison with politics. After all, she had been the chairman of the group and Richard had always been there by her side. Edward was quick to point out that perhaps having to fight a little harder than any man was no bad preparation for the time when she would have to face new rivals. When Richard asked her how many of her colleagues she considered capable of holding down a place on the board of the Baron Group, she had to admit that there were very few.

Florentyna enjoyed her second year far more than her first, and there were many highlights: in February she successfully sponsored an amendment to a Bill which exempted from any taxation scientific publications selling under ten thousand copies per issue. In April she fought several provisions in Reagan's budget proposal. In May, she and Richard received an invitation to a reception at the White House for Queen Elizabeth II. But the most pleasing aspect of the whole year was the feeling that for the first time she was actually influencing issues that affected her constituents' lives.

The invitation that gave her the most pleasure that year came from Transportation Secretary William Coleman to view the tall ships enter New York Harbour in honour of the Bicentennial. It reminded her that America also had a history she could be proud of.

In all, it was a memorable year for Florentyna, and the only sad event that occurred was the death of her mother who had been afflicted with respiratory trouble for many months. For over a year Zaphia had dropped out of Chicago life at the very moment when she had been dominating the society columns. She had told Florentyna as far back as 1968, when she had brought the revolutionary Saint Laurent show to the Windy City, 'These new fashions simply don't compliment a woman of my age.' After that she was rarely seen at any of the major charity events and her name soon began to disappear from the embossed notepaper used for such occasions. She was happy to spend hours listening to stories about her grandchildren, and she often offered a word of motherly advice that her daughter had grown to respect.

Florentyna had wanted a quiet funeral. As she stood by the grave – with her son and daughter on each side of her – listening to the words of Father O'Reilly, she realized that she could no longer hope for privacy, even in death. As the coffin was lowered into the grave the flash bulbs continued to pop until the earth had completely covered the wooden casket and the last of the Rosnovskis was buried.

.   .   .

During the final few weeks before the Presidential election, Florentyna spent more of her time in Chicago, leaving Janet in Washington to run the office. After Representative Wayne Hayes admitted paying a member of his staff fourteen thousand dollars a year salary even though she could not type a word or answer the phone, Janet and Louise put in for a rise.

'Yes, but Miss Ray is supplying a service for Mr Hayes that I have not yet found necessary in my office,' said Florentyna.

'But the problem in this office is the other way around,' said Louise.

'What do you mean?' asked Florentyna.

'We spend our life being propositioned by members who think we're a Capitol Hill perk.'

'How many members have propositioned you, Louise?' said Florentyna, laughing.

'Over a couple of dozen,' said Louise.

'And how many have you accepted?'

'Three,' said Louise, grinning.

'And how many have propositioned you?' said Florentyna, turning to Janet.

'Three,' said Janet.

'And how many did you accept?'

'Three,' said Janet.

When they had stopped laughing, Florentyna said, 'Well, perhaps Joan Mondale was right. What the Democrats do to their secretaries, the Republicans do to the country. You both get a rise.'

.   .   .

Edward turned out to be accurate about her selection. She was unopposed as the Democratic candidate, and the Primary for the Ninth District was virtually a walkover. Stewart Lyle, who ran again as the Republican candidate, admitted privately to her that he now had little chance. 'Re-elect Kane' stickers seemed to be everywhere.

Florentyna looked forward to a new session of Congress with a Democratic President in the White House. The Republicans had selected Jerry Ford after a tough battle with Governor Reagan, while the Democrats had chosen Jimmy Carter, a man she had barely heard of until the New Hampshire Primary.

Ford's Primary battle against Ronald Reagan did not enhance the President's cause and the American people had still not forgiven him for pardoning Nixon. On the personal front, Ford seemed incapable of avoiding naïve mistakes such as bumping his head on helicopter doors and falling down airplane steps. And during a television debate with Carter, Florentyna sat horrified when he suggested that there was no Soviet domination of Eastern Europe. 'Tell the Polish people that,' she said indignantly to the small screen.

The Democratic candidate committed his share of mistakes as well, but in the end it seemed to Richard that Carter's image as an anti-Washington, evangelical Christian, when viewed against the problems Ford had inherited from his links with Nixon, would be enough to give Carter the election by a small margin.

'Then why was I returned with an increased majority?' Florentyna demanded.

'Because many Republicans voted for you but not for Carter.'

'Were you among them?'

'I plead the Fifth Amendment.'

28

Richard wore a smart dark suit on the day of the Inauguration but was sorry the President had insisted that no one wear morning dress. The Kane family watched the new President deliver a speech that lacked the charisma of Kennedy or the wisdom of Roosevelt but its simple message of Christian honesty above all else captured the mood of the moment. America wanted a decent, homespun man in the White House and everyone was willing him to succeed. President Ford sat on his immediate left; President Nixon was conspicuously absent. Florentyna felt the tone for Carter's Administration was set with the words:

'I have no dream to set forth today, but rather urge a fresh faith in the old dream. We have learned that "more" is not necessarily "better"; that even our great nation has recognized limits, and that we can neither answer all questions nor solve all problems.'

The Washington crowds were delighted when the new President, the First Lady and their daughter Amy walked down Pennsylvania Avenue hand in hand to the White House, and it was obvious that the Secret Service were quite unprepared for such a break with tradition.

'Dancer is on the move,' said one of them over his two-way radio. 'God help us if we are going to have four years of spontaneous gestures.'

That evening the Kanes attended one of the seven 'People's Parties', as Carter had named them, to commemorate the Inauguration. Florentyna was dressed in a new Gianni di Ferranti gown of white with a faint trace of gold thread which kept the camera bulbs flashing all night. During the evening they were both introduced to the President, who seemed to Florentyna to be as shy in person as he was in public.

When Florentyna took her seat on the floor of the chamber for the start of the 95th Congress it felt like returning to school, with all the back-slapping, hand shaking, hugging and noisy discussion about what members had been up to during the recess.

'Glad to see you won again.'

'Was it a hard campaign?'

'Don't imagine you'll be able to select your own committee now that Mayor Daley is dead.'

'What did you think of Jimmy's address?'

The new Speaker, Tip O'Neill, took his place in the centre of the podium, banged his gavel, called everyone to order and the whole process began again.

Florentyna had moved up two places on the Appropriations Committee, following one retirement and one defeat since the last election. She now understood how the committee system worked but still feared it would be many years and several elections before she made any real headway for the causes she espoused. Richard had suggested she concentrate on a field in which she could gain more public recognition and she had wavered between abortion and tax reform. Richard counselled against too close an association with abortion and reminded her of how her colleagues referred to Elizabeth Holtzman as 'Congressperson Holzperson'. Florentyna agreed in principle but was no nearer deciding what her special subject should be when the subject chose itself.

A debate of the Defence Appropriations Bill was taking place on the floor of the House, and Florentyna sat listening as members casually discussed the allocation of billions of dollars on defence spending. She did not sit on the Defence Sub-Committee on which Robert C. L. Buchanan was the ranking Republican, but she was deeply interested in his opinions. Buchanan was reminding the House that Defence Secretary Brown had recently asserted that the Russians now had the capability to destroy American satellites in space. Buchanan went on to demand that the new President spend more money on defence and less in other areas. Florentyna still considered Buchanan the worst sort of conservative fool and in a moment of anger rose to challenge him. Everyone in the chamber remembered their last confrontation and knew that Buchanan would have to allow her to state her case.

'Would the Congressman yield for a question?'

'I yield to the gentle lady from Illinois.'

'I am grateful to the distinguished gentleman and would like to inquire where the extra money for these grandiose military schemes will come from?'

Buchanan rose slowly to his feet. He wore a three-piece tweed suit and his silver hair was parted neatly to the right. He rocked from leg to leg like a cavalry officer on a cold parade ground. 'These "grandiose schemes" are no more and no less than those requested by the committee on which I serve and, if I remember correctly, that committee still has a majority from the party which the distinguished member from Illinois represents.' Loud laughter greeted Buchanan's remarks. Florentyna stood up a second time; Buchanan immediately gave way again.

'I am still bound to inquire of the distinguished gentleman from Tennessee where he intends to get this money. From education, hospitals, welfare perhaps?' The chamber was silent.

'I would not take it from anyone, ma'am, but I would warn the gentle lady from Illinois that if there is not enough money for defence we may not need any money for education, hospitals or welfare.'

Buchanan picked up a document from his table and informed the House of the exact figures spent in the previous year's budget in all the departments Florentyna had mentioned. They showed that in real terms defence spending had dropped more than all the others. 'It's members like the gentle lady who come to the chamber without facts, equipped with nothing more than a vague feeling that defence spending is too high, that make the Kremlin leaders rub their hands with glee while the reputation of the House is at the same time diminished. It is the type of ill-informed attitude that tied the hands of President Roosevelt and left us so little time to come to terms with the menace of Hitler.'

Florentyna wished she had never entered the chamber that afternoon as members from both sides echoed their agreement. As soon as Buchanan had finished his remarks she left the floor and returned quickly to her office.

'Janet, I want all the committee reports from the Appropriations Sub-Committee on Defence for the last ten years, and ask my legislative researchers to join us immediately,' she said even before she reached her desk.

'Yes, ma'am,' said Janet, somewhat surprised, as Florentyna had never mentioned defence in the three years she had known her. The staffers filed in and sank on to Florentyna's old sofa.

'For the next few months I plan to concentrate on defence matters. I need you to go over the reports of the sub-committee during the last ten years and mark up any relevant passages. I am trying to get a realistic appraisal of America's military strength, if we were called upon to defend ourselves against an attack from the Soviets.' The four assistants were writing

furiously. 'I want all the major works on the subject including the CIA
Team A and Team B evaluations, and I want to be briefed when lectures
or seminars on defence or related matters take place in Washington. I want
all press comments from the *Washington Post*, the *New York Times*, *Newsweek*
and *Time* put in a file for me every Friday night. No one must be able to
quote something I haven't had a chance to consider.'

The assistants were as surprised as Janet because they had been concentrating their efforts on small business and tax reform for over two years. They
were not going to have many free weekends during the coming months.
Once they had departed Florentyna picked up the phone and dialled five
digits. When a secretary answered, she requested an appointment with the
Majority Leader.

'Of course, Mrs Kane. I will ask Mr Chadwick to call you later today.'

Florentyna was ushered into the Majority Leader's office at ten o'clock
the next morning.

'Mark, I want to be put on the Appropriations Sub-Committee on
Defence.'

'I wish it were that easy, Florentyna.'

'I know, Mark. But this is the first favour I've asked for in three years.'

'There is only one slot open on that sub-committee and so many members
are twisting my arm it's amazing that I'm not permanently in splints.
Nevertheless, I'll give your request my serious consideration.' He made a
note on the pad in front of him. 'By the way, Florentyna, the League of
Women Voters is holding its annual meeting in my district, and they've
invited me to make the key speech on the opening day. Now I know how
popular you are with the League and I was hoping you might find it possible
to fly up and do the speech of introduction.'

'I'll give your request my serious consideration,' said Florentyna smiling.

She received a note from the Speaker's office two days later informing her
of her appointment as the junior member of the Appropriations Sub-
Committee on Defence. Three weeks later she flew to Texas and told the
League of Women Voters that as long as there were men like Mark Chadwick in Congress they need have no fears for America's well-being. The
women applauded loudly while Florentyna turned to find Mark grinning
– with one arm behind his back.

. . .

During the summer vacation the whole family went to California. They
spent the first ten days in San Francisco with Bella and her family in their
new home, high up on the hill, now overlooking the bay.

Claude had become a partner in the law firm, and Bella had been
appointed an assistant headmistress. If anything, Richard decided, Claude
was a little thinner and Bella a little larger than when they had last seen
them.

The holiday would have been enjoyed by everyone if Annabel hadn't
frequently disappeared off on her own. Bella gripping a hockey stick firmly in
her hand left Florentyna in no doubt how she would have dealt with the girl.

Florentyna tried to keep harmony between the two families, but a confrontation was unavoidable when Bella found Annabel in the attic smoking
pot and asked what she thought she was doing.

'Mind your own business,' she said, as she inhaled once more.

When Florentyna lost her temper with Annabel she informed her mother that if she took more interest in *her* welfare and less in that of her constituents perhaps she could have expected a little more from her.

When Richard heard the story he immediately ordered Annabel to pack and accompanied her back to the east coast while Florentyna and William travelled on to Los Angeles for the rest of their holiday.

Florentyna spent an unhappy time phoning Richard twice a day to find out how Annabel was. She and William returned home a week early.

In September, William entered his freshman year at Harvard, taking up residence in the Yard, on the top floor of Gray's Hall, making the fifth generation of Kanes that had been educated at Cambridge. Annabel returned to the Madeira School, where she seemed to make little progress despite the fact that she started spending most weekends under her parents' watchful eyes in Washington.

.   .   .

During the next session of Congress Florentyna allocated all her spare time to reading the defence papers and books her staffers put in front of her. She became engrossed in the problems the nation faced if it wished to remain strategically safe. She read papers by experts, spoke to Assistant Secretaries at the Defence Department, and studied the major US treaties with her NATO allies. She visited the Air Force SAC headquarters, toured US bases in Europe and the Far East, observed army manoeuvres in North Carolina and California, even spent a weekend submerged in a nuclear submarine. She sought meetings with admirals and generals, as well as having discussions with privates and non-commissioned officers, but she never once raised her voice in the House chamber and only asked questions in committee hearings, where she was often struck by the fact that the most expensive weapons were not always the most effective. She began to realize that the military had a long way to go in improving its readiness which had not been fully tested since the Cuba confrontation. After a year of listening and studying she came to the conclusion that Buchanan had been right and it was she who had been the fool. America had no choice but to increase defence spending while Russia remained so openly aggressive. She was surprised to find how much she enjoyed her new discipline and realized much how her views had been changed when a colleague openly referred to her as a hawk.

She studied all the papers on the M-X missile system, when it came under the jurisdiction of the House Armed Services Committee. As soon as the so-called Simon Amendment to hold up the authorization of the system appeared on the calendar she asked Chairman Galloway to be recognized during the debate.

Florentyna listened intently as other members gave their views for and against the amendment. Robert Buchanan gave a considered speech against it. When he took his seat Florentyna was surprised the Speaker called on her next. She rose to a packed house. Representative Buchanan said in a voice loud enough to carry, 'We are now about to hear the views of an expert.' One or two Republicans seated near him laughed as Florentyna walked to the front of the podium. She placed her notes on the lectern in front of her.

'Mr Speaker, I address the House as a convinced supporter of the M-X missile. America cannot afford to delay any further the defence of this country because a group of Congressmen claim they want more time to read the relevant documents. Those papers have been available to every member of the House for over a year. It hardly needs a course in speed reading for members to have done their homework before today. The truth is that this amendment is nothing more than a delaying tactic for members who are opposed to the M-X missile system. I condemn those members as men with their heads in the sand, heads that will remain in the sand until the Russians have made their first pre-emptive strike. Don't they realize America must also have a first-strike capability?

'I approve of the Polaris submarine system but we cannot hope to push all our nuclear problems out to sea, especially now that navy intelligence informs us that the Russians have a submarine that can travel at a speed of forty knots and remain below the ocean for four years – four years, Mr Speaker – without returning to base. The argument that the citizens of Nevada and Utah are in more danger from the M-X system than anyone else is spurious. The land where the missiles would be deployed is already owned by the government and is at present occupied by one thousand nine hundred and eighty sheep and three hundred and seventy cows. I do not believe the American people need to be mollycoddled on the subject of the nation's safety. They have elected us to carry out long-term decisions, not go on talking while we become weaker by the minute. Some members of Congress would make Nero appear to the American people as a man who was giving a violin concert in aid of the Rome fire brigade.'

When the laughter had diminished, Florentyna became very grave. 'Have members so quickly forgotten that in 1935 more people worked for the Ford Motor Company then served in the United States armed forces? Have we also forgotten that in the same year we had a smaller army than Czechoslovakia, a country since trampled on by Germany and Russia in turn? We had a navy half the size of that of France, a country humiliated by the Germans while we sat and watched, and an air force that even Hollywood didn't bother to hire for war movies. When the threat of Hitler first arose we could not have rattled a sabre at him. We must be certain such a situation can never arise again.

'The American people have never seen the enemy on the beaches of California or on the docksides of New York, but that does not mean that the enemy does not exist. As late as 1950, Russia had as many combat planes as the United States, four times as many troops and thirty tank divisions to America's one. We must never allow ourselves to be at such a disadvantage again. Equally I pray that our great nation will never be involved in another débâcle such as Vietnam, and that none of us will live to see another American die in combat. But our enemies must always be aware that we will meet aggression head on. Like the eagle that bestrides our standard, we will hover always alert to the defence of our friends and the protection of our citizens.'

Some members on the floor of the House started to applaud.

'To each American who says our defence expenditure is too costly, I reply let them look to the countries behind the Iron Curtain and see that no price is too high to pay for the democratic freedom we take for granted in this country. The Iron Curtain is drawn across East Germany, Czechoslovakia, Hungary and Poland, with Afghanistan and Yugoslavia guarding their borders in daily expectation of that curtain being drawn still further, perhaps even reaching the Middle East. After that the Soviets will not be satisfied until it encircles the entire globe.' The House was so silent that Florentyna dropped her voice before she continued. 'Many nations have through history played their role in the protection of the free world. That responsibility has now been passed to the leaders of this commonwealth. Let our grandchildren never say we shirked that responsibility in a cheap exchange for popularity. Let us assure America's freedom by being willing to make a sacrifice now. Let us be able to say to every American that we did not shirk our duty in the face of danger. Let there be in this House no Nero, no fiddler, no fire and no victory for our enemies.'

Members in the chamber cheered while Florentyna remained standing. The Speaker repeated his attempts to gavel the meeting to order. When the last cheer had died she spoke almost in a whisper.

'Let that sacrifice never again be the lives of America's youth, or replaced by the dangerous illusion that we can keep peace in the world without providing for its defence against aggression. Adequately protected, America can exert her influence without fear, govern without terror and still remain the bastion of the free world. Mr Speaker, I oppose the Simon Amendment as irrelevant, and worse, irresponsible.'

Florentyna took her seat and she was quickly surrounded by colleagues from both sides who praised her speech. The press heaped further praise on her the next day and all the networks included passages from her speech in their evening bulletins. Florentyna was shocked at how glibly they described her as an expert on defence. Two papers even talked of her as a future Vice-President.

Once again Florentyna's mail rose to over a thousand letters a week, but there were three letters that particularly moved her. The first was a dinner invitation from an ailing Hubert Humphrey. She accepted but, like the other guests, did not attend. The second came from Robert Buchanan, simply written in a bold hand:

'I salute you, madam.'

The third was an anonymous scrawled note from Ohio:

'You are a commie traitor bent on destroying America with impossible defence commitments. The gas chamber is too good a place for people like you. You should be strung up with that dummy Ford and that pimp Carter. Why don't you get back to the kitchen where you belong, bitch?'

'How would one reply?' asked Janet, stunned by the letter.

'You can't, Janet. Repudiating that sort of mindless prejudice is beyond even your skilful hand. Let's be thankful that ninety-nine per cent of the letters are from fair-minded people who wish to express their views honestly. Though I confess if I knew his address I'd be tempted to reply for the first time in my life, "Up Yours".'

After a hectic week during which she seemed to be perpetually pursued by phone messages, Florentyna spent a quiet weekend with Richard. William was home from Harvard and was quick to show his mother a cartoon from the *Boston Globe* depicting her as a heroine with the head of an eagle, punching a bear on the nose. Annabel phoned from school to tell her mother that she wouldn't be home that weekend.

Florentyna played tennis with her son that Saturday and it took her only a few minutes to realize how fit he was and what a dreadful state she was in. She couldn't pretend walking around golf courses kept her in any real shape. With each shot it became more obvious that William wasn't trying very hard. She was relieved to be told that he couldn't play another set because he had a date that evening. She scribbled a note to Janet to order an exercycle from Hammacher Schlemmer.

Over dinner that night Richard told Florentyna that he wanted to build a Baron in Madrid and that he was thinking of sending Edward to check the building sites.

'Why Edward?'

'He's asked to go. He's working almost full-time for the group now and has even rented an apartment in New York.'

'What can have happened to his law practice?'

'He's become counsel to the firm and says that if you can change your whole career at forty, why shouldn't he? Since Daley's death he hasn't found it a full-time job proving you're worth a place in Congress. I must say he's like a schoolboy who's found himself locked up in a candy store. It's taken a great load off my shoulders. He's the only man I know who works as hard as you.'

'What a good friend he has turned out to be.'

'Yes, I agree. You do realize he's in love with you, don't you?'

'What?' said Florentyna.

'Oh, I don't mean he wants to leap into bed with you, not that I could blame him if he did. No, he simply adores you, but he would never admit it to anyone, although it wouldn't take a blind man to see that.'

'But I never –'

'No, of course you haven't, my darling. Do you think I would have been considering putting him on the board of Lester's if I thought I might lose my wife to him?'

'I wish he would find himself a wife.'

'He'll never marry anyone as long as you are around, Jessie. Just be thankful that you have two men who adore you.'

· · ·

When Florentyna returned to Washington after the weekend she was greeted with another pile of the invitations that had been coming in with increasing frequency. She sought Edward's advice as to what she should do about them.

'Select about half a dozen of the major invitations to places where your views can be expected to reach the maximum number of people, and explain to the others that your work load does not permit you to accept at the moment. But remember to end each letter of refusal with a personal handwritten line. One day when you are seeking a bigger audience than the Ninth District of Illinois there will be people whose only contact with you will be that letter, and on that alone they will decide whether they are for or against you.'

'You're wise old thing, Edward.'

'Ah, but you mustn't forget I'm a year older than you, my dear.'

. . .

Florentyna took Edward's advice and spent two hours every night dealing with the letters prompted by her speech on defence. At the end of five weeks she had answered every one, by which time her mail had almost returned to normal proportions. She accepted invitations to speak at Princeton and the University of California at Berkeley. She also addressed the cadets of West Point and the midshipmen at Annapolis and was to be the guest of Max Cleveland at a Washington lunch to honour Vietnam veterans. Everywhere she went Florentyna was introduced as one of America's leading authorities on defence. She became so involved and fascinated by the subject that it terrified her how little she really knew and only made her study the subject even more intensively. Somehow she kept up with her work in Chicago, but the more she became a public figure the more she had to assign tasks to her staff. She appointed two more assistants to her Washington office and another in Chicago at her own expense. She was now spending over one hundred thousand dollars a year out of her own pocket. Richard described it as reinvesting in America.

29

'Anything that can't wait?' asked Florentyna, glancing down at a desk full of correspondence that had arrived that morning. The 95th Congress was winding down and most members were once again more concerned about being re-elected than about sitting in Washington working on legislation. At this stage of the session assistants were spending almost all their time dealing with constituency problems rather than concentrating on national affairs. Florentyna disliked a system that made hypocrites of normally honest people as soon as another election loomed.

'There are three matters that I ought to draw to your attention,' said Janet in her habitually efficient manner. 'The first is that your voting record can hardly be described as exemplary. It has fallen from eighty-nine percent during the last session to seventy-one per cent this session and your opponents are bound to jump on that fact, claiming that you are losing interest in your job and should be replaced.'

'But the reason I've been missing votes is that I've been visiting defence bases and accepting so many out-of-state engagements. I can't help it if half my colleagues want me to speak in their districts.'

'*I* am aware of that,' said Janet, 'but you can't expect the voters of Chicago to be pleased that you're in California and Princeton when they expect you to be in Washington. It might be wise for you to accept no more invitations from other members or well-wishers until the next session and if you make most of the votes during the last few weeks we may push you back above eighty per cent.'

'Keep reminding me, Janet. What's second?'

'Ralph Brooks has been elected State's Attorney of Chicago, so he should be out of your hair for a while.'

'I wonder,' said Florentyna, scribbling a note on her pad to remind herself to write and congratulate him. Janet placed a copy of the Chicago *Tribune* in front of her. Mr and Mrs Brooks stared up at her. The caption read: 'The new State's Attorney attends charity concert in aid of the Chicago Symphony Orchestra.'

'Doesn't miss a trick, does he?' commented Florentyna. 'I bet his voting record would always be over eighty per cent. And the third thing?'

'You have a meeting with Don Short at ten a.m.'

'Don Short?'

'He's a director of Aerospace Plan, Research and Development Inc. (APRD),' said Janet. 'You agreed to see him because his company has a contract with the government to build radar stations for tracking enemy missiles. They are now bidding for the new navy contract to put their equipment into American warships.'

'Now I remember,' said Florentyna. 'Somebody produced an excellent paper on the subject. Dig it out for me, will you?'

Janet passed over a brown manila file. 'I think you'll find everything is in there.'

Florentyna smiled and flicked quickly through the papers. 'Ah, yes, it all comes back. I shall have one or two pointed questions for Mr Short.'

For the next hour she dictated letters before reading through the briefing file. She found time to jot down several questions before Mr Short arrived.

'Congresswoman, this is a great honour,' said Don Short, thrusting out his hand as Janet accompanied him into Florentyna's room as ten o'clock struck. 'We at Aerospace Plan look upon you as one of the last bastions of hope for the free world.'

It was very rare for Florentyna to dislike someone on sight, but it was clear that Don Short was going to fall firmly into that category. Around five foot seven and twenty pounds overweight, he was a man in his early fifties and nearly bald except for a few strands of black hair which had been carefully combed over the dome of his head. He wore a check suit and carried a brown leather Gucci briefcase. Before Florentyna had acquired her present hawkish reputation she had never been visited by the Don Shorts of this world, as no one thought it worthwhile to lobby her. However, since she had been on the Defence Sub-Committee Florentyna had received endless invitations to dinners, travel-free junkets, and had even been sent gifts ranging from bronze model F-15s to manganese nodules encased in lucite.

Florentyna only accepted those invitations that were relevant to the issues she was working on at the time, and with the exception of a model of Concorde she returned every gift she had been sent with a polite note. She kept the statue of Concorde on her desk to remind everyone that she believed in excellence whichever country was responsible. She had been told that Margaret Thatcher had a replica of Apollo 11 on her desk in the House of Commons and she assumed it was there for the same reason.

Janet left the two of them alone and Florentyna ushered Don Short into a comfortable chair. He crossed his legs, giving Florentyna a glimpse of hairless skin where his trousers failed to meet his sock.

'A nice office you have here. Are those your children?' he asked, jabbing a pudgy finger at the photos on Florentyna's desk.

'Yes,' said Florentyna.

'Such good-looking kids – take after their mother. He laughed nervously.

'I think you wanted to talk to me about the XR-108, Mr Short?'

'That's right; but do call me Don. We believe it's the one piece of equipment the US Navy cannot afford to be without. The XR-108 can track and pinpoint an enemy missile at a distance of over ten thousand miles. Once the XR-108 is installed in every American carrier, the Russians will never dare attack America, because America will always be sailing the high seas, guarding her people while they sleep.' Mr Short stopped almost as if he were expecting applause. 'What is more, my company's equipment can photograph every missile site in Russia,' he continued, 'and beam the picture straight on to a television screen in the White House Situation Room. The Russians can't even go to the john without us taking a photo of them.' Mr Short laughed again.

'I have studied the capabilities of the XR-108 in depth, Mr Short, and I wonder why Boeing claims it can produce essentially the same piece of equipment at only seventy-two per cent of your price.'

'Our equipment is far more sophisticated, Mrs Kane, and we have a proven record in the field, having already supplied the US Army.'

'Your company did not complete the tracking stations for the Army by the date specified in your contract, and handed the government a cost overrun of seventeen per cent on the original estimate – or, to be more precise – twenty-three million dollars.' Florentyna had not once looked at her notes.

Don Short started to lick his lips. 'Well, I'm afraid inflation has taken its toll on everyone, not least the aerospace industry. Perhaps if you could spare a little time to meet our board members, the problem would become clearer to you. We might even arrange a dinner.'

'I rarely attend dinners, Mr Short. I have long believed that the only person who makes any profit over dinner is the maître d'.'

Don Short laughed again. 'No, no, I meant a testimonial dinner in your honour. We would invite, say, five hundred people at fifty dollars a head which you could add to your campaign fund, or to whatever you need the cash for,' he added, almost in a whisper.

Florentyna was about to throw the man out when her secretary arrived with some coffee. By the time Louise left, Florentyna had controlled her temper and made a decision.

'How does that work, Mr Short?'

'Well, my company likes to give a helping hand to its friends. We understand some of your bills for re-election can be pretty steep, so we hold a dinner to raise a little cash and if all the guests don't turn up but still send their fifty dollars – well, who's to know?'

'As you say, Mr Short, who's to know?'

'Shall I set that up then?'

'Why don't you, Mr Short?'

'I knew we could work together.'

Florentyna just managed a tight-lipped smile as Don Short offered a moist hand before Janet showed him out.

'I'll be in touch, Florentyna,' he said, turning back.

'Thank you.'

As soon as the door closed the voting bells started to ring. Florentyna glanced up at the clock on which tiny white bulbs were flashing to show that she still had five minutes to reach the chamber. 'Well, there's one I can pick up,' she said, and left to run to the elevator reserved for members of Congress. When she reached the basement she jumped on the subway that went between Longworth and the Capitol and took a seat next to Bob Buchanan.

'How are you going to vote?' he asked.

'Good heavens,' said Florentyna, 'I don't even know what we are voting for or against yet.'

Her thoughts were still focused on Don Short and what she was going to do about his dinner.

'You're okay this time. It's lifting the retirement age cap from sixty-five to seventy, and on that one I am sure we can both vote the same way.'

'It's only a plot to keep old men like you in Congress, and see that I never get to chair any committees.'

'Wait until you're sixty-five, Florentyna. Then you might feel differently.'

The subway reached the basement of the Capital and the two representatives took the elevator up to the chamber together. It pleased Florentyna that this diehard Republican now looked upon her as a fully fledged member of the club. When they reached the chamber they rested on the brass rail at the back, waiting for their names to be called.

'I never enjoy standing on your side of the chamber,' he said. 'After all these years, it still feels strange.'

'Some of us are quite human, you know, and I'll let you in on a secret: my husband voted for Jerry Ford.'

'Wise man, your husband,' chuckled Buchanan.

'Perhaps your wife voted for Jimmy Carter?'

The old man suddenly looked sad. 'She died last year,' he said.

'I *am* sorry,' said Florentyna. 'I had no idea.'

'No, no, my dear. I realized that, but rejoice in your family because they are not always with you, and the one thing I have discovered is that this place can only be a poor substitute for a real family, whatever you imagine you achieve. They've started calling the Bs so I will leave you to your thoughts ... I shall find standing on this side of the aisle more pleasant in the future.'

Florentyna smiled and reflected how their mutual respect had been conceived in mutual mistrust. She was thankful that the party differences so crudely displayed on election platforms disappeared in the privacy of everyday work. A few moments later, they called the Ks and once she had punched her card into the voting pocket she went back to her office and phoned Bill Pearson, the Majority whip, to ask for an immediate interview.

'Must it be this minute?'

'This minute, Bill.'

'I suppose you want me to put you on the Foreign Affairs Committee.'

'No, it's far more serious than that.'

'Then you had better come around right away.'

Bill Pearson puffed away at his pipe as he listened to Florentyna recount what had happened in her office that morning. 'We know a lot of this sort of thing goes on, but we're rarely able to prove it. Your Mr Short seems to have provided an ideal chance to catch someone with their radar scanner in the pie. You go through with the whole charade, Florentyna, and keep me briefed. The moment they hand over any money we'll jump on Aerospace Plan like a ton of bricks, and if in the end we can't prove anything, at least the exercise might make other members of Congress think twice before getting themselves involved in these sorts of shenanigans.'

Over the weekend Florentyna told Richard about Don Short, but he showed no surprise. 'The problem's a simple one. Some Congressmen have only their salaries to live on, so the temptation to pick up cash must sometimes be overwhelming, especially if they are fighting for a seat they could lose and have no assured job to fall back on.'

'If that's the case, why did Mr Short bother with me?'

'That's also easy to explain. I receive half a dozen personal approaches a year at the bank. The sort of people who offer bribes imagine no one can resist the chance to make a quick buck without Uncle Sam finding out, because that's the way they would react themselves. You would be surprised how many millionaires would sell their mothers for ten thousand dollars in cash.'

Don Short phoned during the week and confirmed that a testimonial dinner had been arranged in Florentyna's honour at the Mayflower Hotel. He expected about five hundred people to be present. Florentyna thanked him, then buzzed Louise on the intercom and asked her to write the date in the appointment book.

.   .   .

Because of the pressure Florentyna was under with Congressional business and out-of-state trips over the next few weeks, she nearly missed Don Short's testimonial dinner altogether. She was on the floor of the House supporting a colleague's amendment to a Small Businesses Bill, when Janet hurried into the chamber.

'Have you forgotten the Aerospace Plan dinner?'

'No, but it's not for another week,' said Florentyna.

'If you check your card, you'll find it's tonight and you're due there in twenty minutes,' said Janet. 'And don't forget there are five hundred people waiting for you.'

Florentyna apologized to her colleague and quickly left the chamber and ran to the Longworth garage. She drove out into the Washington night well above the speed limit. She turned off Connecticut Avenue at De Sales Street and left her car in a lot before walking through the side entrance of the

Mayflower. She was a few minutes late, her thoughts far from collected, and arrived to find Don Short, dressed in a tight-fitting dinner jacket, standing in the lobby waiting to greet her. Florentyna suddenly realized that she had not had time to change and hoped that the dress she was wearing did not look too casual.

'We've taken a private room,' he said as he led her towards the lift.

'I didn't realize the Mayflower had a banquet room that could seat five hundred,' she said as the elevator doors closed.

Don Short laughed. 'That's a good one,' he said and led his guest into a room that – had it been packed – would have held twenty people. He introduced her to everyone present, which took a few moments; there were only fourteen guests.

Over dinner, Florentyna listened to Don Short's blue stories and tales of Aerospace Plan's triumphs. She wasn't sure that she could get through the whole evening without exploding. At the end of the dinner Don rose from his seat, tapped a spoon on his empty glass and made a fulsome speech about his close friend Florentyna Kane. The applause when he sat down was as loud as one could hope for from fourteen people. Florentyna made a short reply of thanks and managed to escape a few minutes after eleven, at least grateful that the Mayflower had provided an excellent meal.

Don Short escorted her back to the parking lot and as she climbed into her car, he handed her an envelope. 'I'm sorry so few people turned up, but at least all the absentees sent in their fifty dollars.' He grinned as he closed the car door.

After Florentyna had driven back to the Baron, she tore open the envelope and studied the contents: a cheque for twenty-four thousand three hundred dollars made out to cash.

She told Bill Pearson the whole story the following morning and handed over the envelope. 'This,' he said, waving the cheque, 'is going to open a whole can of worms.' He smiled and locked the twenty-four thousand three hundred dollars away in his desk.

Florentyna left for the weekend, feeling she had carried out her part of the exercise rather well. Even Richard congratulated her. 'Although we could have done with the cash ourselves,' he said.

'What do you mean?' asked Florentyna.

'I think the Baron's profits are going to take a big drop this year.'

'Good heavens, why?'

'A series of financial decisions implemented by President Carter which are harming the hotels while ironically helping the bank – we have inflation running at fifteen per cent while prime rate is sixteen. I fear the expense account business trip is the first cutback for most companies who have discovered the telephone is cheaper. So we are not filling all our rooms and we end up having to raise the prices – which only gives the business community even more reason to cut back on business travel. Into the bargain, food prices have rocketed while wages are trying to keep up with inflation.'

'Every other hotel group must be faced with the same problem.'

'Yes, but the decision to move the corporate offices out of the New York Baron last year turned out to be far more expensive than I budgeted for. 450

Park Avenue may be a good address but we could have built two hotels in the south in exchange for having that on our letterhead.'

'But that decision released three floors in the New York hotel which allowed us to operate the new banquet rooms.'

'And still the hotel only made a profit of two million while sitting on real estate worth forty million.'

'But there has to be a Baron in the centre of New York. You couldn't think of selling our most prestigious hotel.'

'Until it loses money.'

'But our reputation ...'

'Your father was never sentimental about reputation when measured against profits.'

'So what are we doing about it?'

'I'm going to commission McKinsey and Company to carry out a detailed assessment of the whole group. They will give us an interim report in three months, and complete the study in twelve months. I've already spoken to a Mr Michael Hogan at McKinsey – he's drawing up a proposal.'

'Surely moving in the top consultants in New York will cost us even more money?'

'Yes, it'll be expensive, but I wouldn't be surprised to discover that it will save us a considerable amount in the long run. We must remember that modern hotels all around the world are serving different customers from those your father built Barons for. I want to be sure we're not missing something that's staring us in the face.'

'But can't our senior executives give us that sort of advice?'

'When McKinsey moved into Bloomingdale's,' said Richard, 'they recommended that the store should change the location of seventeen of its counters from their traditional positions. Simple, you might say, but the profits were up twenty-one per cent in the following year when none of the executive staff had considered any changes were necessary, Perhaps we face the same problem without realizing it.'

'Hell, I feel so out of touch.'

'Don't worry, Jessie darling, nothing is going to be acted on that doesn't meet with your full approval.'

'And how is the bank surviving?'

'Ironically, Lester's is making more money on loans and overdrafts than at any time since the Depression. My decision to move into gold when Carter won the election has paid off handsomely. If Carter is re-elected, I shall buy more gold. If Reagan captures the White House I shall sell the same day. But don't you worry. As long as you keep earning your fifty-seven thousand five hundred a hear as a Congresswoman, I'll sleep easy knowing we have something to fall back on in bad times. By the way, have you told Edward about Don Short and the twenty-four thousand dollars?'

'Twenty-four thousand three hundred. No, I haven't spoken to him in days, and when I do all he wants to talk about is how to run a hotel group.'

'I'm inviting him to join the Lester's board at the annual meetings. It will be the bank next.'

'He'll be running the whole show soon,' said Florentyna.

'That's exactly what I'm planning for when I become the First Gentleman.'

. . .

When Florentyna arrived back in Washington, she was surprised to find there was no message awaiting her from Bill Pearson. His secretary told her that he was in California campaigning, which reminded her how close the election was. Janet was quick to point out that the legislature was sleeping on its feet again, waiting for the new session, and that perhaps it might be wise for Florentyna to spend more time in Chicago.

On Thursday, Bill Pearson phoned from California to tell Florentyna that he had spoken with the ranking Republican and the chairman of the Defence Sub-Committee, and they both felt it would cause more trouble than it was worth to raise the issue before the election. He asked her not to declare the donation, because his investigation would be hampered.

Florentyna strongly disagreed with his advice and even considered raising the whole issue with the ranking committee members herself, but when she phoned Edward he counselled against such a move on the grounds that the whip's office undoubtedly possessed more information about bribery than she did, and it might look as if she were working behind their backs. Florentyna reluctantly agreed to wait until after the election.

Somehow Florentyna – with continual reminders from Janet – managed to push her voting record up to over eighty per cent by the end of the session, but only at the cost of turning down every invitation outside Washington that appeared in front of her, and she suspected there had been a whole lot more that Janet had prevented from landing on her desk. When Congress adjourned, Florentyna returned to Chicago to prepare for another election.

She was surprised to find, during the campaign, that she spent a considerable part of her time sitting in the Cook County Democratic headquarters on Randolph Street. Although Carter's first year had not lived up to the expectations of the American voters, it was well known that the local Republicans were finding it hard to convince anyone to run against Florentyna. To keep her occupied, her staff sent her off to speak on behalf of other Democratic candidates in the state as often as possible.

In the end, Stewart Lyle agreed to run again but only after he had made it clear to his committee that he was not going to stomp around the district night and day or waste any more of his money. The GOP was not pleased with Lyle when he said in a private conversation – forgetting that nothing was private during an election campaign – 'There is only one difference between Kane and the late Mayor Daley – Kane is honest.'

. . .

The Ninth District of Illinois agreed with Stewart Lyle and sent Florentyna back to Congress with a slightly increased majority, but she noted the loss of fifteen of her colleagues from the House and three from the Senate. Among the casualties was Bill Pearson.

Florentyna called Bill at his home in California several times to commiserate, but he was always out. Each time she left a message on the answering machine, but he did not return her calls. She discussed the problem with Richard and Edward, who both advised her to see the Majority Leader immediately.

When Mark Chadwick heard the story he was horrified and said he would be in touch with Bill Pearson at once and speak to her later that day. Mark was as good as his word and phoned back to report something that chilled Florentyna: Bill Pearson had denied any knowledge of the twenty-four thousand three hundred dollars and was claiming that he had never discussed a bribe case with Florentyna. Pearson had reminded Chadwick that if Florentyna had received twenty-four thousand three hundred dollars from any source she was bound by law to report it either as a campaign contribution or as income. No mention of the money had been made on her campaign forms and, under House rules, she was not entitled to receive an honorarium of over seven hundred and fifty dollars from anyone. Florentyna explained to the Majority Leader that Bill Pearson had asked her not to declare the money. Mark assured Florentyna that he believed her but was not quite clear how she was going to prove that Pearson was lying. It was common knowledge, he added, that Pearson had been in financial trouble since his second divorce. 'Two alimonies when you're out of work would flatten most good men,' he pointed out.

Florentyna agreed to let Mark make a full investigation while she remained silent on the matter. Don Short rang during the week to congratulate her on her victory and to remind her that the contract with the Navy for the missile programme was up for discussion in the sub-committee that Thursday. Florentyna bit her lip after Don Short's next statement: 'I'm glad you cashed the cheque because I'm sure the money came in useful at election time.'

Florentyna immediately asked the Majority Leader to postpone the vote on the missile programme until he had completed his inquiry on Bill Pearson. Mark Chadwick explained that he couldn't comply with her request because the allocated funds would go elsewhere if the decision were held up. Although Defence Secretary Brown didn't care which company was awarded the contract, he had warned them that all hell would break loose if a decision were postponed any longer. Finally, Chadwick reminded Florentyna of her own speech about members who held up defence contracts. She didn't waste any time arguing.

'Are you getting anywhere with your inquiries, Mark?'

'Yes. We know the cheque was cashed at the Riggs National Bank on Pennsylvania Avenue.'

'My bank, and my branch,' said Florentyna in disbelief.

'By a lady of about forty-five who wore dark glasses.'

'Is there any good news?' she asked.

'Yes,' replied Mark. 'The manager considered the sum large enough to make a note of the bill numbers in case some query arose later. How about that for irony?' She tried to smile. 'Florentyna, in my opinion, you have two choices. You can blast the entire thing open at Thursday's meeting or you can keep quiet until I have the whole messy business sorted out. One thing you can't do is talk publicly about Bill Pearson's involvement until I get to the bottom of it.'

'What do you want me to do?'

'The party would probably prefer you to keep quiet, but I know what I would do if the decision was left to me.'

'Thank you, Mark.'

'No one's going to love you for it. But that's never stopped you in the past.'

.   .   .

When Defence Sub-Committee chairman Thomas Lee gavelled the hearing to order, Florentyna had already been in her seat for several minutes making notes. The radar satellite contract was the sixth item on the agenda and she did not speak on the first five items. When she looked towards the press table and the seats occupied by the public she could not avoid the smiling Don Short.

'Item number six,' said the chairman, stifling a slight yawn at the length each subject on the agenda was taking. 'We must discuss today the three companies that have bid on the Navy's missile project. The Defence Department Office of Procurement will make the final decision, but they are still waiting our considered opinion. Who would like to open the discussion?'

Florentyna raised her hand.

'Congresswoman Kane.'

'I have no particular preference, Mr Chairman, between Boeing and Grumman but under no circumstances could I support the Aerospace Plan bid.' Don Short's face turned ashen with disbelief.

'Can you tell the committee why you feel so strongly against Aerospace Plan, Mrs Kane?'

'Certainly, Mr Chairman. My reasons arise from a personal experience. Some weeks ago an employee of Aerospace Plan came to visit me in my offices in order to go over the reasons why his company should be awarded this contract. Later he attempted to bribe me with a cheque for twenty-four thousand three hundred dollars in exchange for my vote today. That man is now in this room and will no doubt have to answer to the courts for his actions later.'

When the chairman of the committee had finally brought the meeting back to order, Florentyna explained how the testimonial dinner had worked and she named Don Short as the man who had given her the money. She turned to look at him, but he had vanished. Florentyna continued her statement but avoided making any reference to Bill Pearson. She still considered that to be a party matter, but when she finished her story she couldn't help noticing that two other members of the committee were as white as Don Short had been.

'In view of this serious allegation made by my colleague, I intend to delay any decision on this item until a full inquiry has been carried out,' Chairman Lee announced.

Florentyna thanked him and left for her office immediately. She walked down the corridor, surrounded by reporters, but made no reply to any of their insistent questions.

She talked to Richard on the phone that night, and he warned her that the next few days were not going to be pleasant.

'Why, Richard? I've only told the truth.'

'I know. But now there are a group of people fighting for their lives on that committee and they only see you as the enemy, so you can forget the Marquis of Queensberry rules.'

When she read the papers the next morning, she found out exactly what Richard had meant.

'Congresswoman Kane Accuses Aerospace Plan of Bribery', ran one headline while another read, 'Company Lobbyist Claims Member of Congress Took Money as Campaign Contribution'. Once Florentyna had seen that most of the papers were running roughly the same story she jumped out of bed, dressed quickly, went without breakfast and drove straight to the Capitol. When she reached her office she studied all the papers in detail, and without exception they all wanted to know where the twenty-four thousand three hundred dollars had disappeared. 'And so do I,' said Florentyna out loud. The headline in the Chicago *Sun-Times* was the most unfortunate: 'Representative Kane Accuses Space Company of Bribery After Cheque Cashed'. True, but misleading.

Richard called to say that Edward was already on his way down from New York and not to talk to the press until she had spoken with him. She would not have been able to in any case because the FBI sent two senior agents to interview her at ten o'clock that morning.

In the presence of Edward and the Majority Leader, Florentyna made a complete statement, the FBI men asked her not to inform the press of Bill Pearson's involvement until they had completed their own investigation. Once again, she reluctantly agreed.

During the day some members of the House went out of their way to congratulate her. Others conspicuously avoided her.

In a lead story in the Chicago *Tribune* that afternoon the paper wanted to know where the twenty-four thousand three hundred dollars had disappeared. They said it was their unfortunate duty to remind the public that Congresswoman Kane's father had been tried and found guilty of bribery of a public official in the Chicago courts in 1962. Florentyna could almost hear Ralph Brooks calling from the State Attorney's office to let them have all the salient details.

Edward helped Florentyna to keep her temper and Richard flew down from New York every night to be with her. Three days and three nights passed, while the papers kept the story running and Ralph Brooks made a statement from the State Attorney's office saying: 'Much as I admire Mrs Kane and believe in her innocence I feel it might be wise in the circumstances for her to step down from Congress until the FBI investigation is completed.' It made Florentyna even more determined to stay put, especially when Mark Chadwick phoned to tell her not to give up. It could only be a matter of time before the guilty man was brought to justice.

On the fourth day, with no more news from the FBI, Florentyna was at her lowest point when a reporter from the *Washington Post* phoned.

'Mrs Kane, may I ask how you feel about Congressman Buchanan's statement on Aerogate?'

'Has he turned against me as well?' she asked quietly.

'Hardly,' said the voice from the other end of the line. 'I'll read what he said. I quote: "I have known Representative Kane for nearly five years as a bitter adversary and she is many things that drive me to despair but, as we say in Tennessee, you'll have to swim to the end of the river to find anyone more honest. If Mrs Kane is not to be trusted, then I do not know one honest person in either chamber of Congress." '

Florentyna phoned Bob Buchanan a few minutes later.

'Now don't you go thinking I'm getting soft in my old age,' he barked. 'You put a foot wrong in that chamber and I'll cut it off.' Florentyna laughed for the first time in days.

It was a cold December wind that whistled across the east front of the Capitol as Florentyna walked back alone to the Longworth Building after the last vote that day. The newsboy on the corner was shouting out the evening headlines. She couldn't catch what he was saying - something, someone, arrested. She ran towards the boy, fumbling in her pocket for a coin, but all she could find was a twenty-dollar bill.

'I can't change that,' the boy said.

'Don't bother,' said Florentyna as she grabbed the paper and read the lead story first quickly and then slowly. 'Former Congressman Bill Pearson,' she read aloud as if she wanted to be sure the newsboy could hear, 'has been arrested by the FBI in Fresno, California, in connection with the Aerogate scandal. Over seventeen thousand dollars in cash was found hidden in the rear bumper of his new Ford. He was taken to the nearest police station, questioned and later charged with grand larceny and three other misdemeanours. The young woman who was with him at the time was also charged, as an accomplice.'

Florentyna leaped up and down in the snow as the newsboy quickly pocketed the twenty dollars and ran to sell his papers on another corner. He had always been warned about those Hill types.

. . .

'My congratulations on the news, Mrs Kane.' The maître d'hôtel of the Jockey Club was the first of several to comment that evening. Richard had flown down from New York to take Florentyna to a celebration dinner. On her way into the oak-panelled room, other politicians and members of Washington society came over to say how pleased they were that the truth was at last out. Florentyna smiled at each one of them, a Washington smile that she had learned to develop after nearly five years in politics.

The next day the Chicago *Tribune* and the *Sun-Times* came out with glowing tributes to their representative's ability to stay calm in a crisis. Florentyna gave a wry smile, determined to back her own judgement in the future. Any comment from Ralph Brooks's office was conspicuously absent. Edward sent a large bunch of freesias, while William sent a telegram from Harvard: SEE YOU TONIGHT IF YOU'RE NOT THE WOMAN IN FRESNO STILL BEING HELD FOR FURTHER QUESTIONING. Annabel arrived home seemingly unaware of her mother's recent problems to announce she had been accepted at Radcliffe. Her headmistress at the Madeira School later confided to Florentyna that her daughter's acceptance had turned out to be a very close thing, although it couldn't have hurt that Mr Kane had been at Harvard and that she herself had attended Radcliffe. Florentyna was surprised that her reputation was such that she could influence her daughter's future without lifting a finger and confessed to Richard later what a relief it was that Annabel's life was more settled.

Richard asked his daughter in what subject she planned to major.

'Psychology and social relations,' Annabel replied without hesitation.

'Psychology and social relations are not real subjects but merely an excuse to talk about yourself for three years,' Richard declared.

William, now a sophomore at Harvard, nodded in sage agreement with his father, and later asked the old man if he could up his allowance to five hundred dollars a term.

When an amendment to the Health Bill, prohibiting abortions after ten weeks, came up on the calendar, Florentyna spoke for the first time since the Aerogate scandal. As she rose from her place, she was greeted with friendly smiles and a ripple of applause from both sides of the aisle. Florentyna made a powerful plea for the life of the mother over that of the unborn child, reminding Congress that there were only eighteen other members who could even experience pregnancy. Bob Buchanan rose from his place and referred to the distinguished lady from Chicago as the worst sort of simpleton who would be claiming next that you could not discuss a future space programme unless one had circled the moon and he pointed out that there was only one member in either house who had managed that.

.   .   .   .

Within a few days Don Short and his twenty-four thousand three hundred dollars seemed to be a thing of the past as Florentyna returned to her normal hectic Congressional schedule. She had moved up two more notches on the Appropriations Committee, and when she looked around the table she began to feel like an old-timer.

30

When Florentyna returned to Chicago she found Democrats were voicing aloud their fears that having Jimmy Carter in the White House might not necessarily help their chances. Gone were the days when an incumbent could take it for granted that he would be returned to the Oval Office and take with him those of his party who were fighting marginal seats. Richard reminded Florentyna that Eisenhower was the last President to complete two terms.

The Republicans were also beginning to flex their muscles and after the announcement that Jerry Ford would not seek the Presidency, George Bush and Ronald Reagan appeared to be the front runners. In the corridors of Congress it was being openly suggested the Edward Kennedy should run against Carter.

Florentyna continued her daily work in the House and avoided being associated with either camp, although she received overtures from both campaign managers and more than her usual allocation of White House invitations. She remained non-committal, as she wasn't convinced that either candidate was right to lead the party in 1980.

While others spent their time campaigning, Florentyna put pressure on the President to take a stronger line when dealing with heads of state from the Warsaw Pact and pressed for a firmer commitment to NATO; but she appeared to make little headway. When Jimmy Carter told an astonished audience that he was surprised the Russians could go back on their word, Florentyna said despairingly to Janet that any Pole in Chicago could have told him that.

But her final split with the President came when the so-called students took over the American Embassy in Tehran on 4 November 1979, and held fifty-three Americans hostage. The President appeared to do little except make 'Born Again' speeches and say his hands were tied. Florentyna proceeded to bombard the White House by every means at her disposal, demanding that the President should stand up for America. When eventually he did attempt a rescue mission, it aborted, resulting in a sad loss of reputation for the United States in the eyes of the rest of the world.

During a defence debate on the floor of the House soon after this humiliating exercise, Florentyna departed from her notes to deliver an off-the-cuff remark. 'How can a nation that possesses the energy, genius and originality to put a man on the moon fail to land three helicopters safely in a desert?' She had momentarily forgotten that the proceedings of the House were now televised and all three networks showed that part of her speech on their evening news bulletins.

She didn't need to remind Richard of George Novak's wisdom in insisting on not renewing Lester's loan to the Shah and when the Russians marched over the Afghanistan border, Richard cancelled their holiday to watch the Olympics in Moscow.

The Republicans went to Detroit in July and chose Ronald Reagan with George Bush as his running mate. A few weeks later the Democrats came to New York and the Party confirmed Jimmy Carter with even less enthusiasm than they had showed for Adlai Stevenson. When the victorious Carter entered Madison Square Garden, even the balloons refused to come down from the ceiling.

Florentyna tried to continue her work in a Congress that was uncertain which would be the majority party in a few months' time. She pushed through amendments on the Defence Appropriations Bill and the Paperwork Reduction Act. As the election drew nearer, she began to fear that the fight for her own seat might be close when the Republicans replaced Stewart Lyle with an enthusiastic young advertising executive, Ted Simmons.

With Janet prodding her, she once again pushed her voting record up to around eighty per cent by only accepting invitations to speak in Washington or Illinois during the last six months prior to the election.

Carter and Reagan seemed to be living in Chicago, flying in and out of Illinois like two cuckoos in one clock. The polls were declaring it was too close to call, but Florentyna was not convinced after she had seen the candidates debate in Cleveland in front of a television audience estimated at one hundred million Americans. The next day Bob Buchanan told her that Reagan might not have won the debate, but he sure as hell hadn't lost it, and for someone trying to remove the White House incumbent that was all important.

As election day drew nearer, the issue of the hostages became more and more a focal point in the minds of the American people, who began to doubt that Carter could ever resolve the problem. On the streets of Chicago, supporters told Florentyna that they would return her to Congress, but they could not back Carter for a second term. Richard said he knew exactly how they felt and predicted that Reagan would win easily. Florentyna took his view seriously and spent the last few weeks of the campaign working as if she were an unknown candidate fighting her first election. Her efforts were not helped by a torrential rainstorm in Chicago that pounded the streets right up until election day.

When the last vote had been counted even she was surprised by the size of the Reagan victory, which took the Senate with him on his coat tails and only just failed to capture the House for the Republicans.

Florentyna was returned to Congress with her majority cut to twenty-five thousand. She flew into Washington, battered but not beaten a few hours before the hostages returned.

.   .   .

The new President lifted the spirit of the nation with his Inaugural Address. Richard, sitting in a morning coat, smiled all the way through the speech and applauded loudly at the section he quoted to Florentyna for several years after.

We hear much of special interest groups, but our concern must be for a special interest group that has been too long neglected. It knows no sectional boundaries, crosses ethnic and racial divisions and political party lines. It is made up of men and women who raise our food, patrol our streets, man our mines and factories, teach our children, keep our homes and heal us when we're sick. Professionals, industrialists, shopkeepers, clerks, cabbies and truck drivers. They are, in short, we the people, this breed called Americans.

After the speech had been enthusiastically received the President gave a final wave to the crowd in front of the main stand and turned to leave the podium.

Two Secret Service men guided him through a human aisle created by the guard of honour.

Once the Presidential party had reached the bottom of the steps, Mr Reagan and the First Lady climbed into the back of a large limousine obviously unwilling to follow the example of the Carters and walk down Constitution Avenue to their new home. As the car moved slowly off, one of the Secret Service men flicked a switch on his two-way radio. 'Rawhide returns to Crown' was all he said, and then, staring through a pair of binoculars, followed the limousine all the way to the White House gates.

.   .   .

When Florentyna returned to Congress in January 1981, it was a different Washington. Republicans no longer needed to beg support for every measure they espoused, because elected representatives knew the country was demanding change. Florentyna enjoyed the new challenge of studying the programme Reagan sent up to the Hill and was only too happy to support great sections of it.

She had become so preoccupied with amendments to the Reagan budget and defence programme that Janet had to point out to her an item in the Chicago *Tribune* which might eventually remove her from the House.

Senator Nichols of Illinois announced this morning that he would not be seeking re-election to the Senate in 1982.

Florentyna was sitting at her desk, taking in the significance of this statement when the editor of the Chicago *Sun-Times* called to ask her if she would be entering the race for the Senate in 1982. Florentyna realized that it was only natural for the press to speculate on her candidacy after three and a half terms as a representative.

'It doesn't seem that long ago,' she teased, 'that your distinguished journal was suggesting I should resign.'

'There was an English Prime Minister who once said that a week was a long time in politics! So where do you stand, Florentyna?'

'It's never crossed my mind,' she said, laughing.

'That's one statement no one is going to believe, and I am certainly not going to print. Try again.'

'Why are you pushing me so hard when I still have over a year to decide?'

'You haven't heard?'

'Heard what?' she asked.

'At a press conference held this morning at City Hall the State's Attorney announced that he's a candidate.'

. . .

'Ralph Brooks To Run For Senate,' ran the banner headline across the afternoon editions of the state's papers. Many reporters mentioned in their columns that Florentyna had not yet made a decision on whether she would challenge the State's Attorney. Once again pictures of Mr and Mrs Brooks stared up at Florentyna. The damn man seems to get better looking all the time, she grumbled. Edward called from New York to say he thought she should run but advised her to hold back until the Brooks publicity machine ran out of steam. 'You might even be able to orchestrate your announcement so that it looks as if you are bowing to public pressure.'

'Who are the party faithful backing?'

'My estimate is 60–40 in your favour, but since I'm no longer even a committeeman it's hard to predict. Don't forget it's over a year to the Primary so there's no need to rush in especially now that Brooks has made his move. You can sit and wait until the tie suits you.'

'Why do you think he announced so early?'

'To try and frighten you off, I suppose. Maybe he figures you might hold back until 1984.'

'Perhaps that's a good idea.'

'No, I don't agree. Never forget what happened to John Culver in Iowa. He decided to wait because he felt it would be easier later when weaker opposition was around so his personal assistant ran instead of him and won the seat.'

'I'll think about it and let you know.'

The truth was that Florentyna thought of little else during the next few weeks, because she knew that if she could beat Brooks this time, he would be finished once and for all. She was in no doubt that Ralph Brooks still had ambitions that stretched about sixteen blocks beyond the Senate. On Janet's advice, she now accepted every major invitation to speak in the state and turned down almost all other outside commitments. 'That will give you a chance to find out how the land lies,' said Janet.

'Keep nagging me, Janet.'

'Don't worry, I will. That's what you pay me for.'

Florentyna found herself flying to Chicago twice a week for nearly six months and her voting record in Congress was barely above sixty per cent. Ralph Brooks had the advantage of not living in Washington four days a week or having his record in court expressed in percentage terms. Added to that, Chicago's Mayor Jane Byrne was only halfway through her first term. There were those who said one woman in Illinois politics was quite enough. Nevertheless Florentyna felt confident after she had covered most of the state that Edward had been right, she did have a 60–40 chance of defeating Ralph Brooks. In truth she believed that defeating Brooks might be harder than getting elected to the Senate, as the mid-term election traditionally ran against the White House incumbent.

One day Florentyna did leave clear in her diary was for the annual meeting of the Vietnam Veterans of America. They had chosen Chicago for the celebrations and invited Senator John Tower of Texas and Florentyna to be the key speakers. The Illinois press was quick to point out the respect with which outsiders treated their favourite daughter. The paper went on to say that the very fact that the vets could couple her with the chairman of the Senate's Armed Services Committee was high praise indeed.

. . .

Florentyna was carrying a full load in the House. She successfully sponsored the 'good Samaritan' amendment to the Superfund Act, making its implementation more flexible for companies that made genuine efforts to dispose of toxic wastes. Even Bob Buchanan supported her Good Samaritan amendment.

While she was leaning on the rail at the back of the chamber waiting for the vote on the final passage of her amendment, he told her that he hoped she would run for the Senate seat.

'You're only saying that because you want to see me out of this place.'

He chuckled. 'That would have been one compensation, I must admit, but I don't think you can stay here much longer if you're destined to live in the White House.'

Florentyna looked at him in astonishment. He didn't even glance towards her but continued to gaze into the packed chamber.

'I have no doubt you'll get there. I just thank God I won't be alive to witness your inauguration,' he continued before going off to vote for Florentyna's amendment.

. . .

Whenever Florentyna went to Chicago she avoided the question of her candidacy for the Senate, although it was obviously on everyone else's mind. Edward pointed out to her that if she did not run this time it might be her last chance for twenty years as Ralph Brooks was still only forty-four and it would be virtually impossible to defeat him once he was the incumbent.

'Especially when he has "the Brooks charisma",' mocked Florentyna in reply. 'In any case,' she continued, 'who would be willing to wait twenty years?'

'Harold Stassen,' Edward replied.

Florentyna laughed. 'And everyone knows how well he did. I'll have to make up my mind one way or the other before I speak to the Vietnam Vets.'

.   .   .

Florentyna and Richard spent the weekend at Cape Cod and were joined by Edward on the Saturday evening.

Late into the night they discussed every alternative facing Florentyna as well as the effect it would have on Edward's work at the Baron if he were to be in charge of the campaign. When they retired to bed in the early hours of Sunday morning they had come to one conclusion.

.   .   .

The International Room of the Conrad Hilton Hotel was packed with two thousand men and the only other women in sight were waitresses. Richard had accompanied Florentyna to Chicago and was seated next to Senator Tower. When Florentyna rose to address the gathering she was trembling. She began by assuring the vets of her commitment to a strong America and then went on to tell them of her pride in her father when he had been awarded the Bronze Star by President Truman, and of her greater pride in them for having served their country in America's first unpopular war. The veterans whistled and banged their tables in delight. She reminded them of her commitment to the M-X missile system and her determination that Americans would live in fear of no one, especially the Soviets.

'I want Moscow to know,' she said, 'that there may be some men in Congress who would be happy to compromise America's position but not this woman.' The vets cheered again. 'The present isolationist policy President Reagan seems determined to pursue will not help Poland in its present crisis or whichever nation the Russians decide to attack next. At some point we must stand firm, and we cannot afford to wait until the Soviets have camped along the Canadian border.' Even Senator Tower showed his approval of that sentiment.

Florentyna waited for complete silence before saying, 'I have chosen tonight, while I am assembled with a group of people whom everyone in America admires, to say that as long as there are men and women who are willing to serve their country as you have done, I hope to continue to serve in the public life of this great nation, and to that end I intend to submit my name as a candidate for the United States Senate.'

Few people in the room heard the word 'Senate' because pandemonium broke out. Everyone in the gathering who could stand, stood and those who couldn't banged their tables. Florentyna ended her address with the words, 'I pledge myself to an America that does not fear war from any aggressor. At the same time, I pray that you are the last group of veterans this country ever needs.'

When she sat down, the cheering lasted for several minutes and Senator Tower went on to praise Florentyna for one of the finest speeches he had ever heard.

.   .   .

Edward flew in from New York to mastermind the campaign while Janet kept in daily touch from Washington. Money flowed in from every quarter; the work that Florentyna had put in for her constituents was now beginning to pay off. With twelve weeks to go to the Primary, the polls consistently showed a 58–42 lead for candidate Kane across the state.

All through the campaign, Florentyna's assistants were willing to work late into the night, but even they could not arrange for her to be in two places at once. Ralph Brooks criticized her voting record along with the lack of real results she had achieved as a representative in Congress. Some of his attacks began to hit home while Brooks continued to show the energy of a ten year old. Despite this, he didn't seem to make much headway as the polls settled around 55–45 in her favour. Word reached Florentyna that Ralph Brooks's camp was feeling despondent and his campaign contributions were drying up.

Richard flew into Chicago every weekend and the two of them lived out of suitcases, often sleeping in the homes of downstate volunteers. One of Florentyna's younger campaign workers drove them tirelessly around the state in a small blue Chevette. Florentyna was shaking hands outside factory gates on the outskirts of cities before breakfast, attending grange meetings in the rural towns of Illinois before lunch, but somehow she still found time to fit in occasional banking associations and editorial boards in Chicago during the afternoon before the inevitable evening speech and a welcome night at the Baron. During the same period somehow she never missed the monthly meetings of the Remagen Trust.

When she did eat, it was endless Dutch-treat breakfasts and pot-luck dinners. At night before falling into bed she would jot down some more facts and figures – picked up in that day's travels – into a dog-eared black briefing book that was never far from her side. She fell asleep trying to remember names, countless names of people who would be insulted if she ever forgot the role they had played in her campaign. Richard would return to New York on Sunday night every bit as tired as Florentyna. Never once did he complain or bother his wife with any problems facing the bank or the Baron Group. She smiled up at him as they said goodbye at yet another cold February airport: she noticed he was wearing a pair of the blue leather gloves he had bought for his father in Bloomingdale's over twenty years before.

'I still have one more pair to go through Jessie, before I can start looking for another woman,' he said, and left her smiling.

Each morning Florentyna rose more determined. If she was sad about anything, it was how little she saw of William and Annabel. William, now sporting a Fidel Castro moustache, looked set for a summa cum laude while Annabel brought a different young man home each vacation.

From past experience, Florentyna had learned to expect a thunderbolt to land some time during an election campaign, but she had not imagined that a meteorite would accompany it. During the past year, Chicago had been shaken by a series of brutal local murders committed by a man the press had dubbed 'the Chicago Cut-throat'. After the killer had slashed the throat of each of his victims, he carved a heart on their foreheads to leave the police in no doubt who had struck again. More and more in public gatherings Florentyna and Ralph Brooks found that they were being tackled on the question of law and order. At night the streets of Chicago were almost deserted because of the reputation of the killer whom the police were unable to apprehend. To Florentyna's relief, the murderer was caught one night on the Northwestern University campus after he had been taken by surprise while in the act of attacking a college girl.

Florentyna made a statement the next morning in praise of the Chicago police force and wrote a personal note to the officer who made the arrest. She supposed that was the end of the matter until she read the morning paper. Ralph Brooks had announced that he was personally going to prosecute the case against the Chicago Cut-throat even if it resulted in his sacrificing the Senate seat. It was a brilliant stroke that even Florentyna had to admire. Papers all across the nation ran pictures of the handsome State's Attorney next to that of the vicious killer.

The trial began five weeks before the Primary and proceedings had obviously been speeded up because of the State's Attorney's influence. It meant Ralph Brooks was on the front page every day, demanding the death penalty so that the people of Chicago could once again walk the streets safely at night. Florentyna made press statement after press statement on the energy crisis, airport noise regulations, grain price supports, even Russia's troops movements on the Polish border after martial law was instituted and the Solidarity leaders were locked up, but she couldn't knock the State's Attorney off the front page. At a meeting with the editorial board of the *Tribune*, Florentyna complained good-naturedly to the editor, who was apologetic but pointed out that Ralph Brooks was selling newspapers. Florentyna sat in her Washington office, impotently aware that she had no effective way of countering her opponent.

In the hope that the clash might give her a chance to shine for a change, she challenged Ralph Brooks to a public debate. But the State's Attorney informed the press that he could not consider any such confrontation while so grave a public responsibility rested on his shoulders. 'If I lose my chance to represent the good people of Illinois because of this decision, so be it,' he repeated again and again. Florentyna watched another percentage point slip away.

On the day that the Chicago Cut-throat was convicted, the polls showed that Florentyna's lead had fallen to 52–48. There were two weeks to go.

.   .   .

Florentyna was planning to spend those last fourteen days stumping through the state when the meteorite landed.

Richard phoned the Tuesday after the trial had ended to tell her that Annabel's roommate had called to say Annabel had not returned to Radcliffe on Sunday night, and she hadn't heard from her since. Florentyna flew to New York immediately. Richard informed the police and hired a private detective to find his daughter, and then sent Florentyna back to Chicago after the police had assured her that they would do whatever they could.

When Florentyna arrived back in Chicago she walked around in a daze, phoning Richard every hour, but he had no news for her. With a week to go, the polls showed Florentyna leading only 51–49 and Edward tried to make her concentrate on the campaign but the words of Bob Buchanan kept coming back to her. '*This place can only be a poor substitute for a real family.*' She began to wonder if only ... After a bad weekend during which Florentyna felt she had lost more votes than she had gained, Richard called in excitement to say that Annabel had been found and that she had been in New York the whole time.

'Thank God,' said Florentyna, tears of relief welling up in her eyes. 'Is she all right?'

'She's okay, and resting in Mount Sinai hospital.'

'What happened?' asked Florentyna anxiously.

'She's had an abortion.'

Florentyna flew back to New York that morning to be with her daughter. On the return flight she thought she recognized a Party worker sitting a few rows back. There was something about his smile. Once she had arrived at the hospital she discovered that Annabel had not even realized she had been reported missing. Edward begged Florentyna to return to Chicago as the media were continually asking where she was. Although they had managed to keep Annabel's private life out of the newspapers, they were becoming highly suspicious of why Florentyna was in New York rather than Illinois. For the first time, she ignored Edward's advice.

Ralph Brooks was quick to leap in and suggest that she had returned to New York because there was a crisis at the Baron Group and that that had always been her first priority. With Edward pulling and Annabel pushing, Florentyna returned to Chicago on Monday night to find every paper in Illinois saying the election was too close to call.

On the Tuesday morning Florentyna read the headline that she most dreaded: 'Candidate's Daughter Has Abortion'. The article that followed revealed every detail, even down to the bed Annabel was in. 'Keep your head down and pray,' was all Edward said as he dragged her through a nerve-racking day.

Florentyna rose at six o'clock on election day and Edward drove her to as many polling places as she could reach in fourteen hours. At every stop, campaign workers waved blue and white 'Kane for Senate' placards and handed out leaflets on Florentyna's positions on the major issues. At one stop a voter asked Florentyna for her views on abortion. Florentyna looked at the woman indignantly and said, 'I can assure you that my views haven't changed,' before realizing that the question was totally innocent.

Her workers were tireless in their efforts to get out every Kane supporter, and Florentyna didn't stop working until the polls closed. She prayed that she had held on in the way Carter had against Ford in 1976. Richard flew in that night with news that Annabel had returned to Radcliffe and was feeling fine.

When Florentyna returned to the Baron, husband and wife sat alone in their suite. Three televisions were tuned into the networks as the returns came in from all over the state deciding which one of them would be chosen to oppose the Republican candidate in November. At eleven o'clock, Florentyna had a two per cent lead. At twelve o'clock Brooks was one per cent ahead. At two o'clock, Florentyna had edged back into the lead by less than one per cent. At three o'clock she fell asleep in Richard's arms. He did not wake her when he knew the outcome because he wanted her to sleep.

A little later he nodded off himself and woke with a start to find her looking out of the window, her fist clenched. The television kept flashing up the result: Ralph Brooks selected as Democratic candidate for the Seante by seven thousand one hundred and eighteen votes, a margin of less than half a percent. On the screen was a picture of Brooks waving and smiling to his supporters.

Florentyna turned around and stared at the screen once more. Her eyes did not rest on the triumphant State's Attorney but on a man standing directly behind him. Now she knew where she had seen that smile before.

.   .   .

Florentyna's political career had come to a halt. She was now out of Congress and would have to wait another two years before she could even hope to re-enter public life. After Annabel's problems, she wondered if the time had come to return to the Baron Group and a more private existence. Richard didn't agree.

'I would be sorry if you gave up politics after all the time you have put into it.'

'Perhaps that's the point. If I hadn't become so involved with my own life and taken a little more interest in Annabel, she might not be facing an identity crisis.'

'An identity crisis. That's the sort of garbage I'd expect to hear from one of her sociology professors, not from you. I haven't noticed William collapsing under the strain of an "identity crisis". Darling, Annabel has had an affair and was careless; it's as simple as that. If everyone who took a lover was considered abnormal, there would only be a few of us strange ones left. What she most needs at this moment is to be treated as a friend by you.'

.   .   .

Florentyna dropped everything and took Annabel to Barbados that summer. During long walks along the beach, she learned of the affair her daughter had had with someone at Vassar; Florentyna still couldn't get used to the idea of men going to women's colleges. Annabel wouldn't name the man and tried to explain that although she still liked him, she didn't want to spend the rest of her life with him. 'Did you marry the first man you went to bed with?' she asked. Florentyna didn't reply immediately, and then told her about Scott Forbes.

'What a creep,' said Annabel after she had heard the story. 'How lucky you were to find Dad in Bloomingdale's.'

'No, Annabel, as your father continually reminds me, he did the finding.'

Mother and daughter grew closer together in those few days than they had been for years. Richard and William joined them in the second week of the holiday, and they spent fourteen days together getting plump and brown.

Richard was delighted to find Annabel and Richard so relaxed in each other's company and touched when his daughter started referring to William as 'my big brother'. Richard and Annabel regularly beat William and Florentyna at golf in the afternoons before spending long evenings chatting over dinner.

When the holiday came to an end they were all sad to be returning home. Florentyna confessed that she did not feel like throwing herself back into the political fray, until Annabel insisted that the last thing she wanted was a mother who sat home and cooked.

It felt strange to Florentyna that she would not be fighting a campaign herself that year. During her battle with Brooks for the Senate, the Democrats had selected Noel Silverman, a capable young Chicago attorney, to run for her seat in Congress. Some members of the committee admitted that they would have held up the decision if they thought Brooks had had the slightest chance of winning the party's nomination for the Senate.

Many voters asked Florentyna to run as an independent candidate but she knew the party would not approve, especially as they would be looking for another Senatorial representative in two years' time: the other United States Senator, David Rodgers, had repeatedly made it clear that he would not be running for re-election in 1984.

Florentyna flew into Chicago to speak on behalf of Noel Silverman on several occasions and was delighted when he won the seat, even if only by three thousand two hundred and twenty-three votes.

Florentyna faced the fact that she would now have to spend two years in the political wilderness and it didn't ease the pain when she read the Chicago *Tribune*'s headline the day after the election:

BROOKS ROMPS HOME IN SENATE RACE

THE FUTURE
1982–1995

31

William first brought Joanna Cabot home at Christmas. Florentyna knew instinctively that they would be married, and not just because her father turned out to be a distant relation of Richard's. Joanna was dark-haired, slim and graceful – and shyly expressive of her obvious feelings for William. For his part William was attentive and conspicuously proud of the young woman who stood quietly by his side. 'I suppose I might have expected you to produce a son who has been educated in New York, lived in Washington and Chicago but ends up returning to Boston to choose his wife,' Florentyna teased.

'William is your son as well,' Richard reminded her. 'And what makes you think he'll marry Joanna, anyway?'

Florentyna just laughed. 'I predict Boston in the spring.' She turned out to be wrong: they had to wait until the summer.

William was in his final year as an undergraduate, and had taken his business boards and was waiting anxiously to be accepted at the Harvard Business School.

'In my day,' said Richard, 'you waited until you had finished school and had made a little money before you thought about marriage.'

'That just isn't true, Richard. You left Harvard early to marry me and for several weeks afterwards I kept you.'

'You never told me that, Dad,' said William.

'Your father has what in politics is called a selective memory.'

William left laughing.

'I still think . . .'

'They're in love, Richard. Have you grown so old you can't see what's staring you in the face?'

'No, but . . .'

'You're not yet fifty and you're already acting like an old fuddy-duddy. William is almost the same age as you when you married me. Well, haven't you anything to say?'

'No. You're just like all politicians: you keep interrupting.'

The Kanes went to stay with the Cabots early in the new year, and Richard immediately liked John Cabot, Joanna's father, and was surprised that, with so many friends in common, they had not met before. Joanna had two younger sisters, who spent the weekend running around Richard.

'I've changed my mind,' Richard said that Saturday night in bed. 'I think Joanna is just what William needs.'

Florentyna put on an extreme mid-European accent and asked: 'What if Joanna had been a little Polish immigrant who sold gloves in Bloomingdale's?'

Richard took Florentyna in his arms and said, 'I would have told him not to buy three pairs of gloves because it would work out cheaper just to marry the girl.'

Preparations for the forthcoming wedding seemed complicated and demanding to Florentyna, who remembered vividly how simply she and Richard had been marrried and how Bella and Claude had lugged the double bed up the stairs in San Francisco. Luckily Mrs Cabot wanted to handle all the arrangements herself, and whenever something was expected of the Kanes, Annabel was only too happy to leap forward as the family representative.

·   ·   ·

In early January, Florentyna returned to Washington to clear out her office. Colleagues in Washington stopped and chatted with her as if she hadn't left the House. Janet was waiting for her with a pile of letters, most of them from people saying how sorry they were that Florentyna would not be returning to Congress but hoping that she would run for the Senate again in two years' time.

Florentyna answered every one of them but couldn't help wondering if something might go wrong in 1984 as well. If it did that would finish her political career completely.

Florentyna left the Capitol for New York only to find herself getting in everyone's way. The Baron Group and Lester's were being competently run by Richard and Edward. The group had changed considerably since Richard had implemented the many improvements suggested by McKinsey and Company. She was continually surprised by the new Baron of Beef restaurants that could now be found on every ground floor and thought she would never get used to the computer banks alongside the hairdresser's in the hotel lobby. When Florentyna went to see Gianni to check on the progress of the shops, he assumed she had only come in for a new dress.

·   ·   ·

During those first few months away from Washington, Florentyna became more restless than she could remember. She travelled to Poland twice and could only feel despair for her countrymen as she looked around at the devastation. She wondered where the Russians would strike next. Florentyna took advantage of these journeys to meet European leaders who continually referred to their fear that America was becoming more and more isolationist with each succeeding President.

When she returned to America once again the question of whether she should run for the Senate loomed in front of her. Janet, who had remained on Florentyna's staff, began to discuss tactics with Edward Winchester which included regular trips to Chicago for Florentyna who accepted any speaking engagements in Illinois that came her way. Florentyna felt relieved when Senator Rodgers called her over the Easter recess to say that he hoped she would run for his seat the following year and added that she could rely on his backing.

As Florentyna checked over the Chicago newspapers each week she could not help noticing that Ralph Brooks was already making a name for himself in the Senate. He had somehow managed to get on the prestigious Foreign Relations Committee as well as the Agriculture Committee – so important to Illinois farmers. He was also the only freshman Senator to be appointed to the Democratic Task Force on Regulatory Reform.

It made her more determined, not less.

. . .

William and Joanna's wedding turned out to be one of the happiest days of Florentyna's life. Her twenty-two-year-old son standing in tails next to his bride brought back to her memories of his father in San Francisco. The silver band hung loosely on his left wrist, and Florentyna smiled as she noticed the little scar on his right hand. Joanna, although she looked shy and demure, had already rid her future husband of some of his more eccentric habits, among them several gaudy ties and the Fidel Castro moustache William had been so proud of before he had met her. Grandmother Kane, as everyone now referred to Kate, was looking more and more like a pale-blue battleship in full steam as she ploughed through the guests, kissing some while allowing others – those few older than herself – to kiss her. At seventy-five she was still elegant without a suggestion of a failing faculty. She was able also the one member of the family who could remonstrate with Annabel and get away with it.

After a memorable reception laid on by Joanna's parents at their Beacon Hill home – it included four hours of dancing to the ageless music of the Lester Lanin orchestra, William and his bride flew off to Europe for their honeymoon while Richard and Florentyna returned to New York. Florentyna knew that the time was fast approaching when she would have to make an announcement about the Senate seat, and she decided to phone the retiring Senator and seek his advice on how he would like her to word any statement.

She called David Rodgers at his office in the Dirksen Building. As she dialled the number, it struck her how odd it was that they now saw so little of each other when only a few months previously, they had spent half of their lives within a two hundred yard radius. The Senator wasn't in, so she left a message to say that she had called. He did not return her call for several days and finally his secretary rang to explain that his schedule had been impossibly tight. Florentyna reflected on the fact that this wasn't David Rodgers's style. She hoped that she was just imagining the rebuff until she discussed what was going on with Edward.

'There's a rumour going around that he wants his wife to take over the seat,' he told her.

'Betty Rodgers? But she's always claimed she couldn't abide public life. I can't believe she'd choose to continue his now that David's retiring.'

'Well, don't forget that since her children left home three years ago she's been on the Chicago City Council. Perhaps that's given her the taste for higher things.'

'How serious do you think she is?'

'I don't know, but a couple of phone calls and I can find out.'

Florentyna found out even before Edward because she had a call from one of her ex-assistants in Chicago, who said the Cook County party machine was talking about Mrs Rodgers as if she were already the candidate.

Edward called back later the same day to say that he had discovered that the state committee was holding a caucus to consider putting Betty Rodgers's name up as the candidate, although the polls indicated that over eighty per cent of registered Democrats supported Florentyna as David Rodgers's successor. 'It doesn't help,' added Edward, 'that Senator Brooks is openly backing Betty Rodgers.'

'Surprise, surprise,' said Florentyna. 'What do you think my next move ought to be?'

'I don't think you can do anything at the moment. I know you have strong support on the committee and it's very much in the balance, so perhaps it might be wise not to become too closely involved. Just go on working in Chicago and appear to remain above it all.'

'But what if she is chosen?'

'Then you will have to run as an independent candidate and beat her.'

'It's almost impossible to overcome the party machine, as you reminded me a few months back, Edward.'

'Truman did.'

. . .

Florentyna heard a few minutes after the meeting was over that the committee had voted by a majority of 6–5 to place Betty Rodgers's name forward as the official Democratic candidate for the Senate at a full caucus meeting later in the month. David Rodgers and Ralph Brooks had both voted against Florentyna.

She couldn't believe that only six people could make such an important decision and during the following week she had two unpleasant phone conversations, one with Rodgers, the other with Brooks, who both pleaded with her to put party unity before personal ambition. 'The sort of hypocrisy you'd expect from a Democrat,' commented Richard.

Many of Florentyna's supporters begged her to fight but she was not convinced, especially when the state chairman called and asked her to announce formally, for the unity of the party, that she would not be a candidate on this occasion. After all, he pointed out, Betty will probably only do one six-year term.

Which will be long enough for Ralph Brooks, Florentyna thought.

She listened to much advice over the next few days, but on a trip to Washington it was Bob Buchanan who told her to read *Julius Caesar* more carefully.

'The whole play?' asked Florentyna.

'No, I should concentrate on Mark Antony if I were you, my dear.'

Florentyna called the Democratic Party chairman and told him she was willing to come to the caucus and state that she was not a candidate, but she was unwilling to endorse Betty Rodgers.

The chairman readily accepted the compromise.

The meeting was held ten days later at the Democratic State Central Committee in the Bismarck Hotel on West Randolph Street, and when Florentyna arrived the hall was already packed. She could sense from the loud applause she received as she entered the room that the meeting might not go as smoothly as the committee had planned.

Florentyna took her assigned seat on the platform at the end of the second row. The chairman sat in the middle of the front row behind a long table with two Senators, Rodgers and Brooks, on his right and left. Betty Rodgers

sat next to her husband and didn't once look at Florentyna. The secretary
and treasurer completed the front row. The chairman gave Florentyna a
polite nod when she appeared. The other committee members sat in the
second row with Florentyna. One of them whispered, 'You were crazy not
to put up a fight.'

At eight o'clock the chairman invited David Rodgers to address the
meeting. The Senator had always been respected as a diligent worker for his
constituents, but even his closest aides would not have described him as an
orator. He started by thanking everyone for their support in the past and
expressed the hope that they would now pass that loyalty on to his wife. He
gave a rambling talk on his work during the last twenty-four years as a
Senator and sat down to what might at best, have been described as polite
applause.

The chairman spoke next, outlining his reasons for proposing Betty Rodgers as the next candidate. 'At least it will be easy for the voters to remember
her name.' He laughed as did one or two people on the platform but
surprisingly few in the body of the hall. He then went on to spend the next
ten minutes expounding the virtues of Betty Rodgers and the work she had
done as a city councillor. He spoke to a silent hall. And sat down to a
smattering of applause. He waited a moment, then, in a perfunctory fashion,
introduced Florentyna.

She had made no notes because she wanted what she had to say to sound
off the cuff, even though she had been rehearsing every word for the past
ten days. Richard had wanted to accompany her but she told him not to
bother as everything had been virtually decided before the first word was
spoken. The truth was that she did not want him there because his support
might cast doubt on her apparent innocence.

When the chairman sat down, Florentyna came forward to the centre of
the stage and stood right in front of Ralph Brooks.

'Mr Chairman, I have come to Chicago today to announce that I am not
a candidate for the United States Senate.'

She paused and there were cries of 'Why not?' and 'Who stopped you?'

She went on as though she had heard nothing. 'I have had the privilege
of serving my district in Chicago for six years in the United States House
of Representatives and I look forward to working for the best interests of the
people in the future. I have always believed in party unity –'

'But not party fixing,' someone shouted.

Once again, Florentyna ignored the interruption. 'So I shall be happy to
back the candidate you select to be on the Democratic ticket,' she said, trying
to sound convincing.

An uproar started, amid which cries of 'Senator Kane, Senator Kane,'
were clearly audible.

David Rodgers looked pointedly at Florentyna as she continued. 'To my
supporters, I say that there may come another time and another place, but
it will not be tonight, so let us remember in this key state that it is the
Republicans we have to defeat, not ourselves. If Betty Rodgers becomes the
next Senator, I feel certain that she will serve the party with the same ability
we have grown to expect from her husband. Should the Republicans capture
the seat, you can be assured that I shall devote myself to seeing we win it

back in six years' time. Whatever the outcome, the committee can depend on my support in this crucial state during election year.'

Florentyna quickly resumed her seat in the second row as her supporters cheered and cheered.

When the chairman had brought everybody to order, which he tried to do as quickly as possible, he called upon the next United States Senator from Illinois, Mrs Betty Rodgers, to address the meeting. Until then, Florentyna had kept her head bowed but she could not resist glancing up at her adversary. Betty Rodgers clearly had not been prepared for any opposition and looked in an agitated state as she fidgeted with her notes. She read a prepared speech, sometimes almost in a whisper, and although it was well researched the delivery made her husband sound like Cicero. Florentyna felt sad and embarrassed for her and almost started to feel guilty about her own tactics but she still despised the committee for putting Betty Rodgers through such an ordeal. She began to wonder to what extremes Ralph Brooks would go to keep her out of the Senate. When Betty Rodgers sat down she was shaking like jelly, and Florentyna quietly left the platform and stepped out of a side door so that she would no longer embarrass them. She hailed a cab and asked the driver to take her to O'Hare airport.

'Sure thing, Mrs Kane,' came back the reply. 'I do hope you're going to run for the Senate again. You'll win the seat easy this time.'

'No, I shall not be running,' Florentyna said flatly. 'The Democratic candidate will be Betty Rodgers.'

'Who's she?' asked the taxi driver.

'Senator Rodgers's wife.'

'What's she know about the job? Her husband wasn't that hot,' he said testily, and drove the rest of the way in silence. It gave Florentyna the opportunity to reflect that she would *have* to run as an independent candidate if she were ever going to have any chance of winning a seat in the Senate. Her biggest anxiety was splitting the vote with Betty Rodgers and letting a Republican take the seat. The party would never forgive her if that was the eventual outcome. It would spell the end of her political career. Brooks now looked as if he were going to win either way. She cursed herself for not beating him when she had the chance.

The cab came to a halt outside the terminal building. As she paid the driver he said, 'It still doesn't make sense to me. I'll tell you, lady, my wife thinks you're going to be President. I can't see it myself because I could never vote for a woman.'

Florentyna laughed.

'No offence meant, lady.'

'No offence taken,' she said, and doubled his tip.

She checked her watch and made her way to the boarding gate: another thirty minutes before take-off. She bought copies of *Time* and *Newsweek* from the news-stand. Bush on both covers: the first shots of the Presidential campaign were being fired. She looked up at the telemonitor to check the New York gate number: '12C'. It amused her to think of the extremes the officials at O'Hare would go to in order to avoid 'Gate 13'. She sat down in a red plastic swivel chair and began to read the profile on George Bush. She became so engrossed in the article that she did not hear the loudspeaker.

The message was repeated. 'Mrs Florentyna Kane, please go to the nearest white courtesy telephone.'

Florentyna continued reading about the Zapata Oil company executive who had gone through the House, the Republican National Committee, the CIA and the US Mission in China to become Vice-President. A TWA passenger representative came over and touched her lightly on the shoulder. She looked up.

'Mrs Kane, isn't that for you?' the young man said, pointing at a loud-speaker.

Florentyna listened. 'Yes, it is, thank you.' She walked across the lounge to the nearest phone. At times like this, she always imagined one of the children had been involved in an accident and even now she had to remind herself that Annabel was over twenty-one and William was married. She picked up the phone.

Senator Rodgers's voice came over loud and clear. 'Florentyna, is that you?'

'Yes it is,' she replied.

'Thank God I caught you. Betty has decided she doesn't want to run after all. She feels the campaign would be too great a strain on her. Can you come back before this place is torn apart?'

'What for?' asked Florentyna, her mind in a whirl.

'Can't you hear what's going on here?' said Rodgers. Florentyna listened to cries of 'Kane, Kane, Kane', as clear as Rodgers's own voice.

'They want to endorse you as the official candidate and no one is going to leave until you return.'

Florentyna's fingers clenched into a fist. 'I am not interested, David.'

'But Florentyna, I thought ...'

'Not unless I have the backing of the committee and you personally propose my name in nomination.'

'Florentyna, anything you say. Betty always thought you were the right person for the job. It was just that Ralph Brooks pushed her into it.'

'Ralph Brooks?'

'Yes, but Betty now realizes that was nothing more than a self-serving exercise. So for God's sake come back.'

'I'm on my way.' Florentyna almost ran down the corridor to the taxi stand. A cab shot up to her side.

'Where to this time, Mrs Kane?'

She smiled. 'Back to where we started.'

'I suppose you know where you're going, but I can't understand how an ordinary guy like me is meant to put any faith in politicians I just don't know.'

Florentyna prayed that the driver would be silent on the return journey so that she could compose her thoughts, but this time he treated her to a diatribe: on his wife, whom he ought to leave; his mother-in-law, who wouldn't leave him; his son, who was on drugs and didn't work, and his daughter, who was living in a California commune run by a religious cult. 'What a bloody country – beg your pardon, Mrs Kane,' he said as they drew up beside the hall. God, how she'd wanted to tell him to shut up. She paid him for the second time that evening.

'Maybe I will vote for you after all when you run for President,' he said. She smiled. 'And I could work on the people who ride this cab – there must be at least three hundred each week.'

Florentyna shuddered – another lesson learned.

She tried to collect her thoughts as she entered the building. The audience had risen from their seats and were cheering wildly. Some clapped their hands above their heads while others stood on chairs. The first person to greet her on the platform was Senator Rodgers and then his wife, who gave Florentyna a smile of relief. The chairman shook her hand heartily. Senator Brooks was nowhere to be seen: sometimes she really hated politics. She turned to face her supporters in the hall and they cheered even louder: sometimes she really loved politics.

Florentyna stood in the centre of the stage, but it was five minutes before the chairman could bring the meeting to order. When there was complete silence, she simply said: 'Thomas Jefferson once remarked: "I have returned sooner than I expected." I am happy to accept your nomination for the United States Senate.'

She was not allowed to deliver a further word that night as they thronged around her. A little after twelve thirty she crept into her room at the Chicago Baron. Immediately she picked up the phone and started dialling 212, forgetting that it was one thirty in New York.

'Who is it?' said a drowsy voice.

'Mark Antony.'

'Who?'

'I come to bury Betty, not to praise her.'

'Jessie, have you gone mad?'

'No, but I have been endorsed as the Democratic candidate for the United States Seante.' Florentyna explained how it had come about.

'George Orwell said a lot of terrible things were going to happen round about now, but he made no mention of you waking me up in the middle of the night just to announce you are going to be a Senator.'

'I just thought you would like to be the first to know.'

'Perhaps you'd better call Edward.'

'Do you think I ought to? You've already reminded me that it's one thirty in New York.'

'I know it is, but why should I be the only person you wake up in the middle of the night to misquote *Julius Caesar* to?'

· · ·

Senator Rodgers kept his word and backed Florentyna throughout her whole campaign. For the first time in years she was free of pressures from Washington and could devote all her energies to an election. This time there were no thunderbolts or meteors that could not be contained, although Ralph Brooks's lukewarm support on one occasion and implied praise of her Republican opponent on another did not help her cause.

The main interest in the country that year was the Presidential campaign. The major surprise was the choice of the Democratic Presidential candidate, a man who had come from nowhere to beat Walter Mondale and Edward Kennedy in the Primaries with his programme dubbed the 'Fresh Approach'. The candidate visited Illinois on no less than six occasions during the campaign, appearing with Florentyna every time.

On the day of the election, the Chicago papers said once again that the Senate race was too close to call. The pollsters were wrong and the loquacious cab driver was right because at eight thirty Central time, the Republican candidate conceded an overwhelming victory for Florentyna. Later the pollsters tried to explain away their statistical errors by speculating that many men would not admit they were going to vote for a woman. Either way it didn't matter, because the new President-elect's telegram said it all:

WELCOME BACK TO WASHINGTON, SENATOR KANE.

32

Nineteen eighty-five was to be a year for funerals, which made Florentyna feel every day of her fifty-one years.

She returned to Washington to find she had been allocated a suite in the Russell Building, a mere six hundred yards from her old Congressional office in the Longworth Building. For several days while she was settling in, she found herself still driving into the Longworth garage rather than the Russell courtyard. She also couldn't get used to being addressed as Senator, especially by Richard, who could mouth the title in such a way as to make it sound like a term of abuse. 'You may imagine your status has increased but they still haven't given you a raise in salary. I can't wait for you to be President,' he added. 'Then at least you will earn as much as one of the bank's Vice-Presidents.'

Florentyna's salary might not have risen, but her expenses had, as once again she surrounded herself with a team many Senators would envy. She would have been the first to acknowledge the advantage of a strong financial base outside the world of politics. Most of her old team returned and were supplemented by new assistants who were in no doubt about Florentyna's future. Her office in the Russell Building was in suite four hundred and forty. The other four rooms were now occupied by the fourteen assistants, led by the intrepid Janet Brown, whom Florentyna had decided long ago was married to her job. In addition, Florentyna now had four offices throughout Illinois with three assistants working in each of them.

Her new office overlooked the courtyard, with its fountain and cobblestoned parking area. The green lawn would be a popular lunch place for Senate assistants during the warm weather, and for an army of squirrels in the winter.

Florentyna told Richard that she estimated she would be paying out of her own pocket over two hundred thousand dollars a year more than her Senatorial allowance, an amount which varies from Senator to Senator depending on the size of their state and its population, she explained to her husband. Richard smiled and made a mental note to donate exactly the same sum to the Republican Party.

No sooner had the Illinois State Seal been affixed to her office door than Florentyna received the telegram. It was simple and stark: WINIFRED TREDGOLD PASSED AWAY ON THURSDAY AT ELEVEN O'CLOCK.

It was the first time Florentyna was aware of Miss Tredgold's Christian name. She checked her watch, made two overseas calls and then buzzed for Janet to explain where she would be for the next forty-eight hours. By one o'clock that afternoon she was on board Concorde, and she arrived in London three hours and twenty-five minutes later at nine twenty-five. The chauffeur-driven car she had ordered was waiting for her as she emerged from Customs and drove her down the M4 motorway to Wiltshire. She checked into the Landsdowne Arms Hotel and read Saul Bellow's *The Dean's December* until three o'clock in the morning to counter the jet-lag. Before turning the light out she called Richard.

'Where are you?' were his first words.

'I'm booked into a small hotel at Calne in Wiltshire, England.'

'Why, pray? Is the Senate doing a fact-finding mission on English pubs?'

'No, my darling. Miss Tredgold has died, and I'm attending the funeral tomorrow.'

'I'm sorry,' said Richard. 'If you had let me know I would have come with you. We both have a lot to thank that lady for.' Florentyna smiled. 'When will you be coming home?'

'Tomorrow evening's Concorde.'

'Sleep well, Jessie. I'll be thinking of you – and Miss Tredgold.'

At nine thirty the next morning a maid brought in a breakfast tray of kippers, toast with Cooper's Oxford marmalade, coffee and a copy of the London *Times*. She sat in bed savouring every moment, an indulgence she would never have allowed herself in Washington. By ten thirty she had absorbed *The Times* and was not surprised to discover the British were having the same problems with inflation and unemployment as those that prevailed in America. Florentyna got up and dressed in a simple black knitted suit. The only jewelry she wore was the little watch that Miss Tredgold had given her on her thirteenth birthday.

The hotel porter told her that the church was about a mile away and as the morning was so clear and crisp she decided to walk. What the local had failed to point out to her was that the journey was uphill the whole way and his 'about' was a 'guesstimate'. As she strode along, she reflected on how little exercise she had taken lately, despite the pristine exercycle now lodged at Cape Cod. She had also allowed the jogging mania to pass her by.

The tiny Norman church, surrounded by oaks and elms, was perched on the side of the hill. On the noticeboard was an appeal for twenty-five thousand pounds to save the church roof; according to a little blob of red on a thermometer over one thousand pounds had already been collected. To Florentyna's surprise, she was met in the vestry by a waiting verger and led to a place in the front pew next to an imperious lady who could only have been the headmistress.

The church was far fuller than Florentyna had expected, and the school had supplied the choir. The service was simple and the address given by the parish priest left Florentyna in no doubt that Miss Tredgold had continued to teach others with the same dedication and common sense that had influenced the whole of Florentyna's life. She tried not to cry during the address as she knew Miss Tredgold would not have approved, but she nearly succumbed when they sang her governess's favourite hymn, 'Rock of Ages'.

When the service was over, Florentyna filed back with the rest of the congregation through the Norman porch and stood in the little churchyard to watch the mortal remains of Winifred Tredgold disappear into the ground. The headmistress, a carbon copy of Miss Tredgold – Florentyna found it hard to believe that such women still existed – said she would like to show Florentyna something of the school before she left. On their way back through the grounds, she learned that Miss Tredgold had never talked about Florentyna except to her two or three closest friends, but when the headmistress opened the door of a small bedroom in a cottage on the school estate, Florentyna could no longer hold back the tears. By the bed was a photograph of a vicar whom Florentyna recognized as Miss Tredgold's father and by its side, in a small silver Victorian frame, stood a picture of Florentyna graduating from Girls Latin next to an old Bible. In the bedside drawer, they discovered every one of Florentyna's letters written over the past thirty years; the last one remained unopened by her bed.

'Did she know I had been elected to the Senate?' Florentyna asked diffidently.

'Oh, yes, the whole school prayed for you that day. It was the last occasion on which Miss Tredgold read the lesson in chapel, and before she died she asked me to write to tell you that she felt her father had been right, and she had indeed taught a woman of destiny. My dear, you must not cry, her belief in God was so unshakeable that she died in total peace with this world. Miss Tredgold also asked me to give you her Bible and this envelope, which you must not open until you have returned home. It's something she bequeathed you in her will.'

As Florentyna left, she thanked the headmistress for all her kindness and added that she had been touched and surprised at being met by the verger when no one knew she was coming.

'Oh, you should not have been surprised, child,' said the headmistress. 'I never doubted for a moment that you would come.'

. . .

Florentyna travelled back to London clutching the envelope. She longed to open it, like a child who has seen a package in the hall but knows it is for his birthday the following day. She caught Concorde at six thirty that evening, arriving back at Dulles by five thirty p.m. She was seated at her desk in the Russell Building by six thirty the same evening. She stared at the envelope marked 'Florentyna Kane' and then slowly tore it open. She pulled out the contents, four thousand Baron Group stock. Miss Tredgold had died presumably unaware that she was worth over a half a million dollars. Florentyna took out her pen and wrote out a cheque for twenty-five thousand pounds for a new church roof in memory of Miss Winifred Tredgold and sent the shares to Professor Ferpozzi to be placed at the disposal of the Remagen Trust. When Richard heard the story he told Florentyna that his father had once acted in the same way, but the sum required had been only five hundred pounds. 'It seems even God is affected by inflation,' he added.

· · ·

Washington was preparing for another inauguration. On this occasion Senator Kane was placed in the VIP stand from which the new incumbent was to make his speech. She listened intently to the blueprint for American policy over the next four years, now referred to by everyone as the 'Fresh Approach'.

'You're getting nearer the podium every time,' Richard had told her at breakfast.

Florentyna glanced around among her colleagues and friends in a Washington where she now felt at ease. Senator Ralph Brooks, a row in front of her, was even nearer the President. His eyes never left the podium.

Florentyna found herself on the Defence Sub-Committee of the Appropriations Committee and on the Environment and Public Works Committee. She was also asked to chair the Committee on Small Business. Her days once again resembled a never-ending chase for more hours. Janet and her assistants would brief her in lifts, cars, planes, en route to vote on the floor, and even on the run between committee rooms. Florentyna was tireless in her efforts to complete her daily schedule and all fourteen staffers wondered how much they could pile on her before she cracked under the strain. In the Senate, Florentyna quickly enhanced the reputation she had made for herself in the House of Representatives by speaking only on matters on which she was well briefed, and then with compassion and common sense. She still remained silent on issues on which she did not consider herself well informed. She voted against her party on several defence matters and twice over the new energy policy provoked by the latest war in the Middle East.

As the only Democratic woman Senator, she received invitations to speak all over the nation and other Senators soon learned that Florentyna Kane was not the token Democratic woman in the Senate but someone whom they could never afford to underestimate.

Florentyna was pleased to find how often she was invited to the inner sanctum of the Majority Leader's office to discuss matters of policy as well as party problems.

During her first session as a Senator, Florentyna sponsored an amendment on the Small Business Bill, giving generous tax concessions to companies who exported over thirty-five per cent of their products. For a long time she had believed that companies who did not seek to sell their goods in an overseas market were suffering from the same delusions of grandeur as the English in the mid-century, and that if they were not careful, Americans would enter the twenty-first century with the same problems that the British had failed to come to terms with in the 1980s.

In her first three months she had answered five thousand four hundred and sixteen letters, voted seventy-nine times, spoken on eight occasions in the chamber, fourteen times outside and missed lunch on forty-three of the last ninety days.

'I don't need to diet,' she told Janet, 'I weigh less than when I was twenty-four and opened my first shop in San Francisco.'

· · ·

The second death was every bit as much of a shock because the whole family has spent the previous weekend together in Cape Cod.

The maid reported to the butler that Mrs Kate Kane had not come down to breakfast as the grandfather clock chimed eight. 'Then she must be dead,' said the butler.

Kate Kane was seventy-nine when she failed to come down for breakfast and the family gathered for a Brahmin funeral. The service was held at Trinity Church, Copley Square and could not have been in greater contrast to the service for Miss Tredgold, for this time the bishop addressed a congregation who between them could have walked from Boston to San Francisco on their own land. All the Kanes and Cabots were present along with two other Senators and a Congressman. Almost everyone who had ever known Grandmother Kane, and a good many of those who had not, filled the pews behind Richard and Florentyna.

Florentyna glanced across at William and Joanna. Joanna looked as though she would be giving birth in about a month, and it made Florentyna feel sad that Kate had not lived long enough to become Great-Grandmother Kane.

After the funeral, they spent a sombre family weekend in the Red House on Beacon Hill. Florentyna would never forget Kate's tireless efforts to bring her husband and son together. Richard was now the sole head of the Kane family, which Florentyna realized would add further responsibility to his already impossible work load. She also knew that he would not complain and it made her feel guilty that she was unable to do much about making his life any easier.

Like a typical Kane, Kate's will was sensible and prudent; the bulk of the estate was left to Richard and his sisters, Lucy and Virginia, and large settlements were made on William and Annabel. William was to receive two million dollars on his thirtieth birthday. Annabel, on the other hand, was to live off the interest of a further two million until she was forty-five or had two legitimate children. Grandmother Kane hadn't missed much.

. . .

In Washington, the battle for the mid-term election had already begun and Florentyna was glad to have a six-year term before she faced the voters again, giving her a chance for the first time to do some real work without the biennial break for party squabbles. Nevertheless, so many of her colleagues invited her to speak in their states that she seemed to be working just as hard, and the only request she politely refused was in Tennessee: she explained she could not speak against Bob Buchanan, who was seeking re-election for the last time.

The little white card which Louise gave her each night was always filled with appointments from dawn to dusk indicating the routine for the following day:

'7.45: breakfast with a visiting foreign minister of defence. 9.00: staff meeting. 9.30: Defence Sub-Committee hearing. 11.30: interview with Chicago *Tribune*. 12.30: lunch with six Senate colleagues to discuss defence budget. 2.00: weekly radio broadcast. 2.30: photo on Capitol steps with Illinois 4-H'ers. 3.15: staff briefing on Small Business Bill. 5.30: drop by reception of Associated General Contractors. 7.00: cocktail party at French

Embassy. 8.00: dinner with Donald Graham of the *Washington Post*. 11.00: phone Richard at the Denver Baron.'

As a Senator, Florentyna was able to reduce her trips to Illinois to every other weekend. On every other Friday, she would catch the US Air flight to Providence, where she would be met by Richard on his way up from New York. They would then drive out on Route Six to the Cape, which gave them a chance to catch up with each other's week.

Richard and Florentyna spent their free weekends in Cape Cod, which had become their family home since Kate's death, Richard having given the Red House to William and Joanna.

On Saturday mornings, they would lounge around reading newspapers and magazines. Richard might play the cello while Florentyna would look over the paperwork she had brought with her from Washington. When weather permitted, they played golf in the afternoon and whatever the weather, backgammon in the evening. Florentyna always ended up owing Richard a couple of hundred dollars which he said he would donate to the Republican Party if she ever honoured her gambling debts. Florentyna always queried the value of giving to the Massachusetts Republican Party, but Richard pointed out that he also supported a Republican Governor and Senator in New York.

Patriotically, Joanna gave birth to a son on Washington's birthday, and they christened him Richard. Suddenly Florentyna was a grandmother.

People magazine stopped describing her as the most elegant lady in Washington and started calling her the best-looking grandmother in America. This caused a flurry of letters of protest including hundreds of photographs of other glamorous grannies for the editor to consider, which only made Florentyna even more popular.

·   ·   ·

The rumours that she would be a strong contender for the Vice-Presidency in 1988 started in July when the Small Business Association made her Illinoisan of the Year and a *Newsweek* poll voted her Woman of the Year. Whenever she was questioned on the subject, she reminded her inquirers that she had been in the Senate for less than a year and that her first priority was to represent her state in Congress, although she couldn't help noticing that she was being invited to the White House more and more often for sessions with the President. It was the first time that being the one woman in the majority party was turning out to be an advantage.

·   ·   ·

Florentyna learned of Bob Buchanan's death when she asked why the flag on the Russell Building was at half-mast. The funeral was on the Wednesday when she was due to offer an amendment to the Public Health Service Act in the Senate and address a seminar on defence at the Woodrow Wilson International Centre for Scholars. She cancelled one, postponed the other and flew to Nashville, Tennessee.

Both of the state's Senators and its seven remaining Congressmen were present. Florentyna stood next to her House colleagues in silent tribute. As they waited to go into the Lutheran chapel, one of them told her that Bob had five sons and one daughter. Gerald, the youngest had been killed in

Vietnam. She thanked God that Richard had been too old and William too young to be sent to that pointless war.

Steven, the eldest boy, led the Buchanan family into the chapel. Tall and thin, with a warm open face, he could only have been the son of Bob and when Florentyna spoke to him after the service he revealed the same southern charm and straight approach that had endeared his father to her. Florentyna was delighted when she learned that Steven was going to run for his father's seat in the coming special election.

'It will give me someone new to quarrel with,' she said, smiling.

'He greatly admired you,' said Steven.

Florentyna was not prepared to see her photograph all over the major newspapers the next morning being described as a gallant lady. Janet placed a *New York Times* editorial on top of her press clippings for her to read:

Representative Buchanan had not been well known to the citizens of New York, but it was a comment on his service in Congress that Senator Kane flew to Tennessee to attend his funeral. It is the sort of gesture that is rarely seen in politics today and is just another reason why Senator Kane is one of the most respected legislators in either House.

Florentyna was rapidly becoming the most sought-after politician in Washington. Even the President admitted that the demands on her time weren't running far short of his. But among the invitations that came that year there was one she accepted with considerable pride. Harvard invited her to run for election to the Board of Overseers in the spring and to address the Graduation Day ceremony that June. Even Richard put a note in his diary to keep the day free.

Florentyna looked up the list of those who had preceded her in this honour – from George Marshall outlining the plan to reconstruct post-war Europe to Alexander Solzhenitsyn describing the West as decadent and lacking in spiritual values.

Florentyna spent many hours preparing her Harvard address, aware that the media traditionally gave the speech considerable coverage. She practised paragraphs daily in front of a mirror, in the bath, even on the golf course with Richard. She wrote the complete text herself – in longhand, but accepted numerous amendments from Janet, Richard and Edward on its content.

The day before she was due to deliver the speech, Florentyna received a telephone call from Sotheby's. She listened to the head of the department and agreed to his suggestion. When they had settled on a maximum price, he said he would let her know the outcome immediatly after the auction. Florentyna felt the timing could not have been better. She flew up to Boston that night, to be met at Logan airport by an enthusiastic young undergraduate who drove her into Cambridge and dropped her off at the Faculty Club. President Bok greeted her in the foyer and congratulated her on her election to the board, and then took her through to be introduced to the other overseers, who numbered among the thirty, two Nobel Prize winners, one for literature and one for science; two ex-cabinet secretaries, an Army general, a judge, an oil tycoon and two other university Presidents. Florentyna sat through the meeting amused by how courteous the overseers all were to one another and she could not help but contrast their approach with that of a House committee.

The guest room they put at her disposal brought back memories of Florentyna's student days and she even had to phone Richard from the corridor. He was in Albany dealing with some tax problems caused by Jack Kemp, the new Republican Governor of New York State.

'I'll be with you for the lunch,' he promised. 'By the way, I see tomorrow's speech was worthy of a mention by Dan Rather on CBS "News" tonight. It had better be good if you hope to keep me from watching the Yankees on channel eleven.'

'Just see you are in your place on time, Mr Kane.'

'Just you make sure it's as good as your speech to the Vietnam Veterans of America, because I'm travelling a long way to hear you, Senator.'

'How could I have fallen in love with you, Mr Kane?'

'It was, if I remember rightly, "Adopt an Immigrant Year", and we Bostonians were exhibiting our usual social conscience.'

'Why did it continue after the end of the year?'

'I decided it was my duty to spend the rest of my life with you.'

'Good decision, Mr Kane.'

'I wish I were with you now, Jessie.'

'You wouldn't if you could see the room they've given me. I've only a single bed, so you would be spending the night on the floor. Be on time tomorrow, because I want you to hear this speech.'

'I will. But I must say it's taking you a long time to convert me to a Democrat.'

'I'll try again tomorrow. Goodnight, Mr Kane.'

Richard was woken the next morning by the telephone at the Albany Baron. He assumed it would be Florentyna on the line with some Senatorial comment, but it turned out to be New York Air to say there would be no flights out of Albany that day because of a one-day action by maintenance workers that was affecting every airline.

'Christ,' said Richard, uncharacteristically, then jumped into a cold shower where he added some other new words to his vocabulary. Once he was dry, he tried to get dressed while dialling the front desk. He dropped the phone and had to start again.

'I want a rental car at the front entrance immediately,' he said, dropped the phone again and finished dressing. He then called Harvard, but they had no idea where Senator Kane was at that particular moment. He left a message explaining what had happened, ran downstairs, skipped breakfast and picked up the keys to a Ford Executive. Richard was held up in the rush-hour traffic and it took him another thirty minutes to find Route 90 East. He checked his watch: he would only have to do a steady sixty to be in Cambridge in time for the speech at two o'clock. He knew how much this one meant to Florentyna, and he was determined not to be late.

The last few days had been a nightmare, so much so he hadn't bothered Florentyna with the theft in Cleveland, the kitchen walk-out in San Francisco, the seizing of the hotel in Cape Town, tax problems over his mother's estate – all happening while the price of gold was collapsing because of the civil war in South Africa. Richard tried to put all these problems out of his mind. Florentyna could always tell when he was tired or over-anxious, and he did not want her to be worrying about situations he knew he could sort out eventually. Richard wound the car window down to let in some fresh air.

The rest of the weekend he was going to do nothing but sleep and play the cello; it would be the first break they had both had for over a month. No children, as William would be in Boston with his own family and Annabel in Mexico – leaving nothing more strenuous to consider than a round of golf for two whole days. He wished he didn't feel so tired. 'Damn,' he said out loud. He'd forgotten the roses – had planned to send them to Florentyna from the airport as usual.

Florentyna was given two messages just before lunch. The man from Sotheby's phoned to say that she had been successful in her bid, and a college porter delivered Richard's news. She was delighted by the first and disappointed by the second, although she smiled at the thought that Richard would be worrying about the roses. Thanks to Sotheby's, she now had something for him he had wanted all his life.

Florentyna had spent the morning in the formal graduation proceedings at the Tercentenary Theatre. The sight of all three networks setting up their cameras on the lawn for the afternoon ceremony made her feel even more nervous, and she hoped no one noticed that she had eaten almost nothing at lunch.

At one forty-five, the overseers left for the yard where alumni reunion classes had already gathered. She thought back to her own class . . . Bella . . . Wendy . . . Scott . . . Edward . . . and now she had returned, as Edward had predicted, as Senator Kane. She took her seat on the platform outside the Tercentenary Theatre next to President Horner of Radcliffe and looked down at the card on the other chair beside her. It read, 'Mr Richard Kane – husband of Senator Kane'. She smiled at how much that would have annoyed him, and scribbled underneath, 'What took you so long?' She must remember to leave the card on the mantelpiece. Florentyna knew that if Richard arrived after the ceremony had begun he would have to find a seat on the lawn. The announcement of elections, conferring of honorary degrees, and reports of gifts received by the university, was followed by an address from President Bok. Florentyna sat and listened as he introduced her. She scanned the rows in front of her, as far as her eye could see, but was still unable to spot Richard.

'President Horner, distinguished visitors, ladies and gentlemen. It is a great honour for me today to present one of Radcliffe's most distinguished alumnae, a woman who has captured the imagination of the American people. Indeed, I know many of us believe that Radcliffe will one day have *two* Presidents.' Seventeen thousand guests burst into spontaneous applause. 'Ladies and gentlemen, Senator Florentyna Kane.'

Florentyna was shaking when she rose from her seat. She checked her notes as the great television lights were switched on, momentarily blinding her so that she could see nothing but a blur of faces. She prayed Richard's was among them.

'President Bok, President Horner. I stand before you more nervous now than I was when I first came to Radcliffe thirty-three years ago and I couldn't find the dining room for two days because I was too frightened to ask anyone.' The laughter eased Florentyna's tension. 'Now I see seated in front of me men and women, and if I recall correctly from my Radcliffe rule book, men may only enter the bedrooms "between the hours of three and five p.m." and "must at all times keep both feet on the ground". If the rule still exists today, I am bound to ask how the poor things ever get any sleep.'

The laughter continued for several seconds before Florentyna was able to start again. 'Over thirty years ago I was educated at this great university and it has set the standard for everything I have tried to achieve in my life. The pursuit of excellence has always been to Harvard of paramount importance and it is a relief to find in this changing world that the standards attained today by your graduates are even higher than they were in my generation. There is a tendency among the old to say that the youth of today do not compare with their forefathers. I am reminded of a carving on the side of one of the tombs of the Pharaohs which translated reads: "The young are lazy and preoccupied with themselves and will surely cause the downfall of the world as we know it."'

The graduates cheered while the parents laughed. 'Winston Churchill once said: "When I was sixteen, I thought my parents knew nothing. When I was twenty-one, I was shocked to discover how much they had picked up in the last five years."' The parents applauded and the students smiled. 'America is often looked upon as a great monolithic land mass, with a vast centralized economy. It is neither of these things. It is two hundred and twenty-five million people who make up something more diverse, more complicated, more exciting, than any other nation on earth and I envy all of you who wish to play a role in the future of our country and feel sorry for those who do not. Harvard University is famous for its tradition of service in medicine, teaching, the law, religion and the arts. It must be thought a modern tragedy that more young people do not consider politics an honourable and worthwhile profession. We must change the atmosphere in the corridors of power so that the very brightest of our youth does not dismiss, virtually without consideration, a career in public life.

'None of us has ever doubted for a moment the integrity of Washington, Adams, Jefferson or Lincoln. Why shouldn't we today produce another generation of statesmen who will bring back to our vocabulary the words duty, pride and honour without such a suggestion being greeted with sarcasm or scorn?

'This great university produced John Kennedy, who once said when receiving an honorary degree from Yale, "And now I have the best of both worlds, a Harvard education and a Yale degree."'

When the laughter had died down, Florentyna continued: 'I, Mr President, have the best of every world, a Radcliffe education and a Radcliffe degree.'

Seventeen thousand people rose to their feet and it was a considerable time before Florentyna could continue. She smiled as she thought how proud Richard would be, because he had suggested that line to her when she was rehearsing in the bath, and she had not been sure that it would work.

'As young Americans, take pride in your country's past achievements, but strive to make them nothing more than history. Defy old myths, break new barriers, challenge the future, so that at the end of this century, people will say of us that our achievements rank alongside those of the Greeks, the Romans and the British in advancing freedom and a just society for all people on this planet. Let no barriers be unassailable and no aims too high and when the crazy whirligig of time is over, let it be possible for you to say as Franklin D. Roosevelt did, "There is a mysterious cycle in human events. To some generations much is given, of other generations much is expected, but this generation of Americans has a rendezvous with destiny."'

Once again, everyone on the lawn broke into spontaneous applause. When it subsided, Florentyna lowered her voice almost to a whisper. 'My fellow alumni, I say to you, I am bored by cynics, I despise belittlers, I loathe those who think there is something sophisticated and erudite in running our nation down, because I am convinced that this generation of our youth, who will take the United States into the twenty-first century, has another rendezvous with destiny. I pray that many of them are present today.'

When Florentyna sat down she was the only person who remained seated. Journalists were to remark the next day that even the cameramen whistled. Florentyna looked down aware that she had made a favourable impression on the crowd, but she still needed Richard for final confirmation. Mark Twain's words came back to her: 'Sorrow can take care of itself, but to get the true benefit of joy, you must share it.' As Florentyna was led off the stage, the students cheered and waved, but her eyes searched only for Richard. Making her way out of the Tercentenary Yard, she was stopped by dozens of people, but her thoughts remained elsewhere.

Florentyna heard the words, 'Who will tell her?' while she was trying to listen to a student who was going to Zimbabwe to teach English. She swung around to stare at the troubled face of Matina Horner, the Radcliffe President

'It's Richard, isn't it?' said Florentyna quickly.

'Yes, I'm afraid so. He has been involved in a car accident.'

'Where is he?'

'In Newton-Wellesley Hospital, about ten miles away. You must leave immediately.'

'How bad is it?'

'Not good, I'm afraid.'

A police escort rushed Florentyna down the Massachusetts Turnpike to the Route 16 exit as she prayed, Let him live. Let him live.

As soon as the police car arrived outside the main entrance of the hospital she ran up the steps. A doctor was waiting for her.

'Senator Kane, I'm Nicholas Eyre, chief of surgery. We need your permission to operate.'

'Why? Why do you need to operate?'

'Your husband has severe head injuries. And it's our only chance to save him.'

'Can I see him?'

'Yes, of course.' He led her quickly to the emergency room where Richard lay unconscious beneath a plastic sheet, a tube coming out of his mouth, his skull encased in stained white gauze. Florentyna collapsed on to the bedside chair and stared down at the floor, unable to bear the sight of her mutilated husband. Would the brain damage be permanent or could he recover?

'What happened?' she asked the surgeon.

'The police can't be certain, but a witness said your husband veered across the divider on the turnpike for no apparent reason and collided with a tractor-trailer. There seems to have been no mechanical fault with the car he was driving, so they can only conclude he fell asleep at the wheel.'

Florentyna steeled herself to raise her eyes and look again at the man she loved.

'Can we operate, Mrs Kane?'

'Yes,' said a faint voice that only an hour before had brought thousands of people to their feet. She was led into a corridor and sat alone. A nurse came up. They needed a signature; she scribbled her name. How many times had she done that today?

She sat alone in the corridor, a strange hunched up figure in an elegant dress, on the little wooden chair. She remembered how she had met Richard in Bloomingdale's when she thought he had fallen for Maisie; how they made love only moments after their first row and how they had run away and with the help of Bella and Claude she had become Mrs Kane; the births of William and Annabel; that twenty-dollar bill that fixed the meeting in San Francisco with Gianni; returning to New York as partners to run the Baron Group and Lester's; how he had then made Washington possible; how she had smiled when he played the cello for her; how he had laughed when she beat him at golf. She had always wanted to achieve so much for him, and he had always been selfless in his love for her. He must live so that she could devote herself to making him well again.

In times of helplessness one suddenly believes in God. Florentyna fell on her knees and begged for her husband's life.

Hours passed before Dr Eyre returned to her side. Florentyna looked up hopefully.

'Your husband died a few minutes ago,' was all the surgeon said.

'Did he say anything to you before he died?' Florentyna asked.

The chief of surgery looked embarrassed.

'Whatever it was my husband said, I should like to know, Dr Eyre.'

The surgeon hesitated. 'All he said, Mrs Kane, was, "Tell Jessie I love her".'

Florentyna bowed her head.

The widow knelt alone and prayed.

· · ·

It was the second funeral of a Kane in Trinity Church in as many months. William stood between two Mrs Kanes dressed in black, as the bishop reminded them that in death there is life.

Florentyna sat alone in her room that night and cared no longer for this life. In the hall lay a package marked: 'Fragile, Sotheby Parke Bernet, contents one cello, Stradivarius.'

· · ·

William accompanied his mother back to Washington on Monday; the news-stand at Logan airport was ablaze with headlines from her speech. Florentyna didn't even notice.

William remained at the Baron with his mother for three days until she sent him back to his wife. For hours Florentyna would sit alone in a room full of Richard's past. His cello, his photographs, even the last unfinished game of backgammon.

Florentyna began to arrive at the Senate by mid-morning. Janet couldn't get her to answer her mail except for the hundreds of letters and telegrams expressing sorrow at Richard's death. She failed to show up at committee meetings and forgot appointments with people who had travelled great distances to see her. On one occasion, she even missed presiding over the Senate, a chore Senators took in turn when the Vice-President was absent – for a defence debate. Even her most ardent admirers doubted if she would ever fully regain her impetuous enthusiasm for politics.

As the weeks turned into months, Florentyna began to lose her best assistants who feared she no longer had the ambition for herself that they had once had for her. Complaints from her constituents, low key for the first six months after Richard's death, now turned to an angry rumble, but still Florentyna went aimlessly about her daily routine. Senator Brooks quite openly suggested an early retirement for the good of the party, and continued to voice this opinion in the smoke-filled rooms of Illinois's political headquarters. Florentyna's name began to disappear from the White House guest lists and she was no longer seen at the cocktail parties held by Mrs John Sherman Cooper, Mrs Lloyd Dreegar or Mrs George Renchard.

Both William and Edward travelled regularly to Washington in an effort to try to stop her from thinking about Richard, and to bring her back to taking an interest in her work. Neither of them succeeded.

Florentyna spent a quiet Christmas at the Red House in Boston. William and Joanna found it difficult to adapt to the change that had taken place in so short a time. The once elegant and incisive lady had become listless and dull. It was an unhappy Christmas for everyone except the ten-month-old Richard who was learning to hoist himself up by pulling on anything he could get hold of. When Florentyna returned to Washington in the New Year, matters did not improve, and even Edward began to despair.

Janet Brown waited nearly a year before she told Florentyna that she had been offered the job of administrative assistant in Senator Hart's office.

'You must accept the offer, my dear. There is nothing left for you here. I shall serve out my term and then retire.'

Janet too pleaded with Florentyna but it had no effect.

Florentyna glanced through her mail, barely noticing a letter from Bella chiding her about not turning up for their daughter's wedding, and signed some more letters that she hadn't written or even bothered to read. When she checked her watch, it was six o'clock. An invitation from Senator Pryor to a small reception lay on the desk in front of her. Florentyna dropped the smartly embossed card into the waste-paper basket, picked up a copy of the *Washington Post* and decided to walk home alone. She had never once felt alone when Richard had been alive.

She came out of the Russell Building, crossed Delaware Avenue and cut over the grass of Union Station Plaza. Soon Washington would be a blaze of colours. The fountain splashed as she came to the paved walkway. She reached the steps leading down to New Jersey Avenue and decided to rest for a moment on the park bench. There was nothing to rush home for. She began to recall the look on Richard's face as Jake Thomas welcomed him as chairman of Lester's. He did look a fool standing there with a large red London bus under his arm. Reminiscing about such incidents in their life together brought her as near to happiness now as she ever expected to achieve.

'You're on my bench.'

Florentyna blinked and looked to her side. A man wearing dirty jeans and an open brown shirt with holes in the sleeves sat on the other end of the bench, staring at her suspiciously. He had not shaved for several days, which made it hard for Florentyna to determine his age.

'I'm sorry, I didn't realize it was your bench.'

'Been my bench, Danny's bench, these last thirteen years,' said the grimy face. 'Before that it was Ted's and when I go Matt gets it.'

'Matt?' repeated Florentyna uncomprehendingly.

'Yeah, Matt the Grain. He's asleep behind parking lot sixteen waiting for me to die.' The tramp chuckled. 'But I tell you the way he goes through that grain alcohol, Matt will never take over this bench. You not thinking of staying long, are you lady?'

'No, I hadn't planned to,' said Florentyna.

'Good,' said Danny.

'What do you do during the day?'

'Oh, this and that. Always know where we can get soup from church kitchens, and some of that stuff they throw out from the swanky restaurants can keep me going for days. I had the best part of a steak at the Monocle yesterday. I think I'll try the Baron tonight.'

Florentyna tried not to show her feelings. 'You don't work?'

'Who'd give Danny work? I haven't had a job in fifteen years – since I left the Army back in '70. Nobody wanted this old vet, should have died for my country in Nam – would have made things easier for everyone.'

'How many vets are there like you?'

'In Washington?'

'Yes, in Washington.'

'Hundreds.'

'Hundreds?' repeated Florentyna.

'Not as bad as some cities. New York they throw you in jail as quick as look at you. When are you thinking of going, lady?' he said eyeing her suspiciously.

'Soon. May I ask ...?'

'You ask too many questions, so it's my turn. Okay if I have the paper when you leave?'

'The *Washington Post?*'

'Good quality, that,' said Danny.

'You read it?'

'No.' He laughed. 'I wrap myself up in it, keeps me warm as a hamburger if I stay very still.'

She passed him the paper. She stood up and smiled at Danny, noticing for the first time that he had only one leg.

'Wouldn't have a quarter to spare an old soldier?'

Florentyna rummaged through her bag. She had only a ten-dollar bill and thirty-seven cents in change. She handed the money to Danny.

He stared at her offering in disbelief. 'There's enough here for both Matt and me to have some real food,' he exclaimed. The tramp paused and looked at her more closely. 'I know you, lady,' Danny said suspiciously. 'You're that Senator lady. Matt always says he's going to get an appointment with you and explain a thing or two about how you spend government money. But I told him what those little receptionists do when they see the likes of us walk in – they call the capital cops and grab the disinfectant. Don't even ask us to sign the guest book. I told Matt not to waste his valuable time.'

Florentyna watched Danny as he began to make himself comfortable on his bench by covering himself very professionally with the *Washington Post*. 'Any case, I told him you would be much too busy to bother with him, and so would the other ninety-nine.' He turned his back on the distinguished Senator from Illinois and lay very still. Florentyna said goodnight before walking down the steps to the street where she was met by a policeman outside the entrance to the underground parking lot.

'The man on that bench?'

'Yes, Senator,' said the officer. 'Danny, Danny One-Leg; he didn't cause you any trouble, I hope?'

'No, not at all,' said Florentyna. 'Does he sleep there every night?'

'Has for the past ten years, which is how long I've been on the force. Cold nights, he moves to a grate behind the Capital. He's harmless enough, not like some of those at the back of lot sixteen.'

Florentyna lay awake the rest of the night only nodding off occasionally as she thought about Danny One-Leg and the hundreds suffering from the same plight as his. At seven thirty the next morning she was back in her office on Capital Hill. The first person to arrive was Janet at eight thirty, and she was shocked to find Florentyna's head buried in *The Modern Welfare Society* by Arthur Quern. Florentyna looked up.

'Janet, I want all the current unemployment figures, broken down into states, and then into ethnic groups. I also need to know, with the same breakdowns, how many people are on social security and what percentage have not worked for over two years. Then I want you to find out how many of them have served in the armed forces. Compile a list of every leading authority ... You're crying, Janet.'

'Yes, I am,' she said.

Florentyna came from behind her desk and put her arms round her. 'It's over, my dear, let's forget the past and get this show back on the road.'

33

It took everyone in Congress only a month to discover that Senator Kane was back with a vengeance. And when the President phoned her personally, she knew that her attacks on his Fresh Approach were coming home to the one house where things could be changed.

'Florentyna, I'm eighteen months away from election day and you are taking my Fresh Approach campaign apart. Do you want the Republicans to win the next election?'

'No, of course not, but with your Fresh Approach we only spent in one year on welfare what we spent on defence in six weeks. Do you realize how many people in this country don't even eat one square meal a day?'

'Yes, Florentyna, I do ...'

'Do you also know what the figures are for people who sleep on the streets each night in America? Not India, not Africa, not Asia; I'm talking about America. And how many of those people haven't had a job in ten years; not ten weeks or ten months but ten years, Mr President?'

'Florentyna, whenever you call me Mr President I know I'm in trouble. What do you of all people expect me to do? You have always been among those Democrats who advocate a strong defence programme.'

'And I still do, but there are millions of people across America who wouldn't give a damn if the Russians came marching down Pennsylvania Avenue right now, because they don't believe they could be any worse off.'

'I hear what you're saying, but you've become a hawk in dove's clothing, and those sort of statements may make wonderful headlines for you, but what do you expect me to do about it?'

'Set up a Presidential commission to look into how our welfare money is spent. I already have three of my staff working on the problem at the moment and I intend to present some of the facts they are unearthing about misuse of funds at the earliest date. I can promise you, Mr President, the figures will make your hair curl.'

'Have you forgotten I'm nearly bald, Florentyna?' She laughed. 'I like the idea of a commission.' The President paused. 'I could even float the concept at my next press conference.'

'Why don't you do that, Mr President? And tell them about the man who has been sleeping on a bench for thirteen years little more than a stone's throw away from the White House while you slumbered in the Lincoln bedroom. A man who lost a leg in Vietnam and doesn't even know he is entitled to sixty-three dollars a week compensation from the Veterans Administration. And if he did, he wouldn't know how to collect it, because his local VA office is in Texas, and if in an inspired moment they decided to send a cheque to him where would they address it? A park bench, near the Capital?'

'Danny One-Leg,' said the President.

'So you know about Danny?'

'Who doesn't? He's had more good publicity in two weeks than I've had in two years. I'm even considering an amputation. I fought for my country in Korea, you know.'

'And you've managed to take care of yourself ever since.'

'Florentyna, if I set up a Presidential commission on welfare, will you give it your support?'

'I certainly will, Mr President.'

'And will you stop attacking Texas?'

'That was unfortunate. A junior researcher of mine discovered Danny had come from Texas. But do you realize that in spite of the illegal immigrant problem, over twenty per cent of the people of Texas have an annual income of less than ... ?'

'I know, I know, Florentyna, but *you* seem to forget that my Vice-President comes from Houston and he hasn't had a day's rest since Danny One-Leg hit the front pages.'

'Poor old Pete,' said Florentyna. 'He will be the first Vice-President who has had something to worry about, other than where his next meal is coming from.'

'And you mustn't be hard on Pete, he plays his role.'

'You mean balances the ticket so that you can stay in the White House.'

'Florentyna, you're a wicked lady, and I warn you that I intend to open my press conference next Thursday by saying I have come up with a brilliant idea.'

'*You*'ve come up with the idea?'

'Yes,' said the President. 'There must be some compensation for taking the heat all the time. I repeat that I have come up with this brilliant idea of a Presidential commission on "Waste in Welfare" and ...' the President hesitated for a minute '... That Senator Kane has agreed to be the chairman. Now will that keep you quiet for a few days?'

'Yes,' said Florentyna, 'and I'll try to report within one year so that you have time before the election to describe to the voters your bold new plans to sweep away the cobwebs of the past and usher in the Fresh Approach.'

'Florentyna.'

'I'm sorry, Mr President. I couldn't resist that.'

.   .   .

Janet didn't know where Florentyna was going to find the time to chair such an important commission. Her appointment books already needed the assistant with the smallest handwriting to complete each page.

'I need three hours clear every day for the next six months,' said Florentyna.

'Sure thing,' said Janet. 'How do you feel about two o'clock to five o'clock every morning?'

'Suits me,' said Florentyna, 'but I'm not sure we could get anyone else to sit on a commission under those conditions.' Florentyna smiled. 'And we're going to need more assistants.'

Janet had already filled all the vacancies that had been created from resignations during the past few months. She had appointed a new press secretary, a new speech writer, and four more legislative researchers from some of the outstanding young college graduates who were now banging on Florentyna's door. 'Let's be thankful that the Baron Group can afford the extra cost,' Janet added.

Once the President had made his announcement, Florentyna set to work. Her commission consisted of twenty members, plus a professional support staff of eleven. She divided the commission itself, so that half were professional people who had never needed welfare in their lives nor given the subject much thought until asked to do so by Florentyna, while the other half were currently on welfare, or unemployed. A clean-shaven Danny, wearing his first suit, joined Florentyna's staff as a full-time adviser. The originality of the idea took Washington by surprise. Article after article was written on Senator Kane's 'Park Bench Commissioners' Danny One-Leg told stories that made the other half of the committee realize how deep-seated the problem was and how many abuses still needed to be corrected, so that those in genuine need received fair recompense.

Among those who were questioned by the committee were Matt the Grain, who now slept on the bench Danny had vacated, and 'Charlie Wendon', an ingenious convict from Leavenworth who, for a parole deal arranged by Florentyna, told the committee how he had been able to milk a thousand dollars a week out of welfare before the police caught up with him. The man had so many aliases he was no longer sure of his own name; at one point he had supported seventeen wives, forty-one dependent children and nineteen dependent parents, all of whom were non-existent except on the national welfare computer. Florentyna thought he might be exaggerating until he showed the commission how to get the President of the United States on to the computer as unemployed, with two dependent children, living with his ageing mother at 1600 Pennsylvania Avenue, Washington, D.C. Wendon also went on to confirm something she had already feared, that he was small fry compared with the professional crime syndicates who thought nothing of raking in fifty thousand dollars a week through phony welfare recipients.

She later discovered that Danny One-Leg's real name was on the computer and that someone else had been collecting his money for the past thirteen years. It didn't take a lot longer to discover that Matt the Grain and several of his friends from parking lot sixteen were also on the computer although they had never received a penny themselves.

Florentyna went on to prove that there were over a million people entitled to aid who were not receiving it, while, at the same time, the money was disappearing elsewhere. She became convinced that there was no need to ask Congress for more money, just for safeguards designed to ensure that the annual pay-out of over ten billion dollars was reaching the right people. Many of those who needed help simply couldn't read or write, and so never returned to the government office once they had been presented with long forms to complete. Their names became an easy source of income for even a small-time crook. When Florentyna presented her report to the President ten months later, he sent a series of new safeguards to Congress for their immediate consideration. He also announced that he would be drawing up a new Welfare Reform Programme before the election. The press was fascinated by the way Florentyna had got the President's name and address on the unemployment computer; from MacNelly to Peters, the cartoonists had a field day, while the FBI made a series of welfare fraud arrests right across the country.

The press praised the President for his initiative, and the *Washington Post* declared that Senator Kane had done more in one year for those in genuine need than the New Deal and the Great Society put together. This was indeed a 'fresh approach'; Florentyna had to smile. Rumours began to circulate that she would replace Pete Parkin as Vice-President when the election came round. On Monday she was on the cover of *Newsweek* for the first time and across the bottom ran the words: 'America's First Woman Vice-President?' Florentyna was far too shrewd a politician to be fooled by press speculation. She knew that when the time came, the President would stick with Parkin, balance the ticket and be sure of the south. Much as he admired Florentyna, the President wanted another four years in the White House.

. . .

Once again, Florentyna biggest problem in life was in determining priorities among the many issues and people that competed for her attention. Among the requests from Senators to help them with their campaigns was one from Ralph Brooks. Brooks, who never lost the opportunity to describe himself as the state's senior Senator, had recently been appointed chairman of the Senate Energy Committee, which kept him in the public eye. He had received considerable praise for his handling of the oil tycoons and leaders of big business. Florentyna was aware that he never spoke well of her in private, but when proof of this came back to her she dismissed it as unimportant. She was surprised, however, when he asked her to share a TV commercial spot with him, saying how well they worked together and the importance of both Illinois Senators being Democratic. After she'd been urged to cooperate by the party chairman in Chicago, Florentyna agreed, although she had not spoken to her Senate colleague more than a couple of times a month during her entire term in Congress. She hoped her endorsement might patch up their differences. It didn't. Two years later when she came up for re-election, his support for her was rarely above a whisper.

As the Presidential election drew nearer, more and more Senators seeking re-election asked Florentyna to speak on their behalf. During the last six months of 1988 she rarely spent a weekend at home; even the President invited her to join him in several campaign appearances. He had been delighted by the public reaction to the Kane Commission report on welfare, and he agreed to the one request Florentyna made of him, although he knew Pete Parkin and Ralph Brooks would be furious when they heard.

Florentyna had had little or no social life since Richard's death, although she had managed to spend an occasional weekend with William, Joanna and her two-year-old grandson Richard at the Red House on Beacon Hill. Whenever she found a weekend free to be back at the Cape, Annabel would join her.

Edward, who was now chairman of the Baron Group and vice-chairman of Lester's Bank, reported to her at least once a week, producing results even Richard would have been proud of. On Cape Cod he would join her for golf, but unlike the results of her battles with Richard, Florentyna always won. Each time she did she would donate her winnings to the local Republican club in Richard's memory. The local GOP man obligingly recorded the gifts as coming from an anonymous donor as Florentyna's constituents would have been hard put to understand her reasons for supporting both sides.

Edward left Florentyna in no doubt of his feelings for her and once hesitantly went so far as to propose. Florentyna kissed her closest friend gently on the cheek. 'I will never marry again,' she said, 'but if you ever beat me at a round of golf, I'll consider your offer.' Edward immediately started taking golf lessons, but Florentyna was always too good for him.

. . .

When the press got hold of the news that Senator Kane had been chosen to deliver the key speech at the Democratic convention in Detroit, they again started writing about her as a possible Presidential candidate in 1992. Edward became excited about these suggestions, but she reminded him that they had also considered forty-three other candidates in the last six months. As the President had predicted, Pete Parkin was livid when the suggestion was voiced that the Vice-Presidency would be handed to Florentyna but eventually calmed down when he realized that the President had no intention of dropping him from the ticket. It only convinced Florentyna that the Vice-President was going to be her biggest rival if she did decide to run in four years' time.

The President and Pete Parkin were re-nominated at a dull party convention, with only a handful of dissenters and favourite sons to keep the delegates awake. Florentyna wistfully recalled livelier conventions, such as the GOP's 1976 mêlée, during which Nelson Rockefeller had pulled a phone socket out of the floor in the Kansas City convention hall.

Florentyna's key speech was received by the delegates in decibels second only to those accorded to the President's speech of acceptance, and it caused posters and campaign buttons to appear on the final day with the words: 'Kane for '92'. Only in America could ten thousand campaign buttons appear overnight, thought Florentyna, and she took one home for young Richard. Her Presidential campaign was beginning without her even lifting a finger.

During the final weeks before the election, Florentyna travelled to almost as many marginal states as the President himself and the press suggested that her unstinting loyalty might well have been a factor in the Democrats' slim victory. Ralph Brooks was retuned to the Senate with a slightly increased majority. It reminded Florentyna that her own re-election to the Senate was now only two years away.

When the first session of the 101st Congress opened, Florentyna found that many of her colleagues in both houses were openly letting her know of their support should she decide to put her name forward for the Presidency. She realized that some of them would be saying exactly the same thing to Pete Parkin, but she made a note of each one and always sent a handwritten letter of thanks the same day.

Her hardest task before facing re-election for the Senate was to steer the new Welfare Bill through both houses, and the job took up most of her time. She personally sponsored seven amendments to the bill which included the federal government being responsible for all costs, setting a nationwide minimum income, and a major overhaul of social security. She spent hours badgering, cajoling, coaxing and almost bribing her colleagues until the bill became law. She stood behind the President when he signed the new Act in the Rose Garden. Cameras rolled and shutters clicked from the ring of press photographers standing behind a cordoned-off area. It was the greatest single achievement of Florentyna's political career. The President delivered a self-serving statement and then rose to shake Florentyna's hand. 'This is the lady whom we can thank for "The Kane Act",' he said and whispered in her ear, 'Good thing the VP's in South America or I would never hear the end of it.'

Press and public alike praised the skill and determination with which Senator Kane had guided the bill through Congress and the *New York Times* said that if she achieved nothing more in her political career, she would have placed on the books a piece of legislation that would stand the test of time. Under the new law, no one in genuine need would forfeit his rights, while at the other end of the scale, those who played the 'Welfare Charade' would now end up behind bars.

As soon as the fuss had blown over, Florentyna tried to return to the normal daily life of a Senator. Janet warned her that she must spend more time in the state now that the election was less than nine months away. Nearly all the senior members of the party offered their services to Florentyna when she came up for re-election, but it was the President who broke into a heavy schedule to support her and drew the biggest crowd when he spoke at the convention hall in Chicago. As they walked up the steps together to the strains of 'Happy Days Are Here Again' he whispered, 'Now, I am going to get my revenge for all the flak you've given me over the past five years.'

The President described Florentyna as the woman who had given him more problems than his wife and now he heard she wanted to sleep in his bed at the White House. When the laughter died down, he added, 'And if she does aspire to that great office, America could not be better served.'

The next day the press suggested that the statement was a direct snub to Pete Parkin and that Florentyna would have the backing of the President if she decided to run. The President denied this interpretation of what he had said, but from that moment on Florentyna was placed in the unfortunate position of being the front-runner for 1992. When the results of her Senate race came in even Florentyna was surprised by the size of her victory, as most Democratic Senators had lost ground in the usual mid-term election swing against the White House. Florentyna's overwhelming victory confirmed the party's view that it had found not only a standard-bearer but something far more important: a winner.

The week of the first session of the 102nd Congress opened with Florentyna's picture on the cover of *Time*. Full profiles of her life, giving the details of her playing St Joan at Girls Latin and winning the Woolson Scholarship to Radcliffe, were meticulously chronicled. They even explained why her late husband had called her Jessie. She had become the best known woman in America. 'This charming fifty-six-year-old woman,' said *Time* in its summation, 'is both intelligent and witty. Only beware when you see her hand clench into a tight fist because it's then she becomes a heavyweight.'

During the new session, Florentyna tried to carry out the normal duties of a Senator but she was daily being asked by colleagues, friends and the press when she would be making a statement about her intentions to run or not for the White House. She tried to sidetrack them by taking more interest in the major issues of the day. At the time Quebec elected a left-wing government, she flew to Canada to participate in exploratory talks with British Columbia, Alberta, Saskatchewan and Manitoba about federation with America. The press followed her and after she returned to Washington, the media stopped describing her as a politician but America's first stateswoman.

Pete Parkin was already informing anyone and everyone who wanted to listen that he intended to run, and an official announcement was considered imminent. The Vice-President was five years older than Florentyna and she knew this would be his last opportunity to hear 'Hail to the Chief' played for him. Florentyna felt it might be her only chance. She remembered Margaret Thatcher telling her when she stood for Prime Minister, 'The only difference between the leader of a party being a man or a woman is, if a woman loses, the men won't give you a second chance.'

Florentyna had no doubt what Bob Buchanan would have advised had he still been alive. Read *Julius Caesar*, my dear, but this time Brutus and not Mark Antony.

She and Edward spent a quiet weekend together at Cape Cod, and while he lost yet another golf match they discussed the tide in the affairs of one woman, the flood and the possible fortune.

By the time that Edward returned to New York and Florentyna to Washington, the decision had finally been made.

34

'. . . and to that end I declare my candidacy for the office of President of the United States.'

Florentyna gazed into the Senate Caucus Room at the three hundred and fifty applauding members of the audience who occupied a space that the sergeant-at-arms insisted should only hold three hundred. Television camera crews and press photographers lobbed and dodged to prevent their frames from being filled with the backs of anonymous heads. Florentyna remained standing during the prolonged applause that followed her announcement. When the noise had finally ebbed Edward stepped up to face the battery of microphones at the podium.

'Ladies and gentlemen,' he said. 'I know the candidate will be delighted to answer your questions.'

Half the people in the room started to speak at once and Edward nodded to a man in the third row to indicate that he could ask the first question.

'Albert Hunt of the *Wall Street Journal*,' he said. 'Senator Kane, who do you think will be your toughest opponent?'

'The Republican candidate,' she said without hesitation. There was a ripple of laughter and some applause. Edward smiled and called for the next question.

'Senator Kane, is this really a bid to be Pete Parkin's running mate?'

'No, I am not interested in the office of Vice-President,' replied Florentyna. 'At best it's a period of stagnation while you wait around in the hope of doing the real job. At worst I am reminded of Nelson Rockefeller's words: "Don't take the number two spot unless you're up for a four-year advanced seminar in political science and a lot of state funerals." I'm not in the mood for either.'

'Do you feel America is ready for a woman President?'

'Yes, I do, otherwise I would not be willing to run for the office, but I will be in a better position to answer that question on 3 November.'

'So you think the Republicans might select a woman?'

'No, they don't have the courage for such a bold move. They will watch the Democrats make a success of the idea and copy it when the next election comes around.'

'Do you feel you have enough experience to hold this office?'

'I have been a wife, a mother, the chairman of a multi-million dollar corporation, a member of the House for eight years and a Senator for seven. In the public career I've chosen, the Presidency is the number one spot. So, yes, I believe I am now qualified for that job.'

'Do you expect the success of your Welfare Act to help you with the votes of the poor and black communities?'

'I hope the Act will bring me support from every sector. My main intent with that piece of legislation was to ensure that both those who contribute to welfare through taxation and those who benefit from the legislation will feel that the provisions made are both just and humane in a modern society.'

'After the Russian invasion of Yugoslavia, would your administration take a harder line with the Kremlin?'

'After Hungary, Czechoslovakia, Afghanistan, Poland and now Yugoslavia, the latest Soviet offensive on the Pakistan border reinforces my long-standing conviction that we must remain vigilant in the defence of our people. We must always remember that the fact that the two biggest oceans on earth have protected us in the past is no guarantee of our safety in the future.'

'The President has described you as a hawk in dove's clothing.'

'I'm not sure if that's a comment on my dress or my looks, but I suspect that the combination of those two birds looks not unlike the American eagle.'

'Do you feel we can keep a special relationship with Europe after the election results in France and Britain?'

'The decision of the French to return to a Gaullist government while the British voted for a new Labour Administration does not greatly concern me. Jacques Chirac and Roy Hattersley have both proved to be good friends of America in the past, and I see no reason why that should change in the future.'

'Do you expect Ralph Brooks's support for your campaign?'

It was the first question that had taken Florentyna by surprise. 'Perhaps you should ask him, but naturally I hope that Senator Brooks will feel pleased by my decision.' She could think of nothing else to add.

'Senator Kane, do you approve of the current Primary system?'

'No. Although I am not a supporter of a national Primary, the present system is by any standards archaic. America seems to have developed a process for the selection of a President that is more responsive to the demands of the network news programmes than it is to the needs of modern government. It also encourages dilettante candidates. Today, you have a better chance of becoming President if you are temporarily out of work, having been left several million by your grandmother. You then have four years off to devote to running around the country collecting delegates, while the people best qualified for the job are probably doing a full day's work elsewhere. If I became President, I would seek to send a bill to the Congress which would not handicap anyone from running for the Presidency through lack of time or money. We must reinstate the age-old precept that anyone born in this country, with both the desire to serve and the ability to do the job, will not find themselves disqualified before the first voter goes to the polls.'

The questions continued to come at Florentyna from all parts of the room and she took the last one over an hour later.

'Senator Kane, if you become President, will you be like Washington and never tell a lie or like Nixon and have your own definition of the truth?'

'I cannot promise I will never lie. We all lie, sometimes to protect a friend or a member of our family, and if I was President perhaps to protect one's country. Sometimes we lie just because we don't want to be found out. The one thing I can assure you of is that I am the only woman in America who has never been able to lie about her age.' When the laughter died down Florentyna remained standing. 'I would like to end this press conference by saying that whatever the outcome of my decision today, I wish to express my thanks as an American for the fact that the daughter of an immigrant has found it possible to run for the highest office in the land. I do not believe such an ambition would be attainable in any other country in the world.'

* * *

Florentyna's life began to change the moment she left the room; four Secret Service agents formed a circle around the candidate, the lead one skilfully creating a passage for her through the mass of people.

Florentyna smiled when Brad Staimes introduced himself and explained that for the duration of her candidacy, there would always be four agents with her night and day, working in eight-hour shifts. Florentyna couldn't help noticing that two of the agents were women whose build and physical appearance closely resembled her own. She thanked Mr Staimes but never quite became used to seeing one of the agents whenever she turned her head. The agents' tiny earphones distinguished them from well-wishers and Florentyna recalled the story about an elderly lady who attended a Nixon rally in 1972. She approached a Nixon aide at the end of the candidate's speech and said she would definitely vote for his re-election because he obviously sympathized with those who, like herself, were hard of hearing.

Following the press conference, Edward chaired a strategy meeting in Florentyna's office to work out a rough schedule for the coming campaign. The Vice-President had announced some time before that he was a candidate and several other contestants had thrown their hats into the ring, but the press had already decided that the real battle was going to be between Kane and Parkin.

Edward had lined up a formidable team of pollsters, finance chairmen and policy advisers who were well supplemented by Florentyna's seasoned staff in Washington led by Janet Brown.

First Edward outlined his day-by-day plan leading up to the first Primary in New Hampshire, and from there to California, all the way to the convention floor in Detroit. Florentyna had tried to arrange for the convention to be held in Chicago, but the Vice-President vetoed the idea; he wasn't challenging Florentyna on her home ground. He reminded the Democratic committee that the choice of Chicago and the riots that followed might have been the single reason that Humphrey lost to Nixon in 1968.

Florentyna had already faced the fact that it would be almost impossible for her to beat the Vice-President in the southern states so it was vital that she should get off to a strong start in New England and the Mid-West. She agreed that during the next three months she would devote seventy-five per cent of her energies to the campaign, and for several hours her team threw around ideas for the best use of that time. It was also agreed that she would make regular trips to the major cities that voted in the first three Primaries and, if she made a strong showing in New Hampshire, a traditionally conservative area, they would plan their forward strategy accordingly.

Florentyna dealt with as much of her Senate work as possible between making frequent trips to New Hampshire, Vermont and Massachusetts. Edward had chartered a six-seater Lear jet for her with two pilots available around the clock so that she could leave Washington at a moment's notice. All three Primary states had set up strong campaign headquarters, and everywhere Florentyna went she spotted as many 'Kane for President' posters and bumper stickers as she did for Pete Parkin.

With only seven weeks left until the first Primary Florentyna began to spend more and more of her time chasing the one hundred and forty-seven thousand registered Democrats in the state. Edward did not expect her to capture more than thirty per cent of the votes, but he felt that might well be enough to win the Primary and persuade doubters that she was an electoral asset. Florentyna needed every delegate she could secure before they arrived in the south, even if possible to pass the magic one thousand six hundred and sixty-six by the time she reached the convention hall in Detroit.

The early signs were good. Florentyna's private pollster, Kevin Palumbo, assured her that the race with the Vice-President was running neck and neck, and Gallup and Harris seemed to confirm that view. Only seven per cent of the voters said they would not under any circumstances vote for a woman, but Florentyna knew just how important seven per cent could be if the final outcome was close.

Florentyna's schedule included brief stops at over one hundred and fifty of New Hampshire's two hundred and fifty small towns. Despite the hectic nature of each day, she grew to love the classical New England milltowns, the crustiness of the Granite State's farmers and the stark beauty of its winter landscape.

She served as a starter for a dogsled race in Franconia and visited the most northerly settlement near the Canadian border. She learned to respect the penetrating insights of local newspaper editors, many of whom had retired from high-level jobs with national magazines and news services. She avoided discussions of one particular issue after discovering that New Hampshire residents stoutly defended their right to oppose a state income tax, thus attracting a host of high-income professionals from across the Massachusetts border.

More than once she had occasion to be thankful for the death of William Loeb, the newspaper publisher, whose outrageous misuse of the Manchester *Union Leader* had single-handedly destroyed the candidacies of Edmund Muskie and George Bush before her. It was no secret that Loeb had had no time for women in politics.

Edward was able to report that money was flowing into their head-quarters in Chicago and 'Kane for President' offices were springing up in every state. Some of them had more volunteers than they could physically accommodate; the overspill turned dozens of living rooms and garages throughout America into makeshift campaign headquarters.

In the final seven days before the first Primary, Florentyna was interviewed by Barbara Walters, Dan Rather and Frank Reynolds, as well as appearing on all three morning news programmes. As Andy Miller, her press secretary, pointed out, fifty-two million people watched her interview with Barbara Walters and it would have taken over five hundred years to shake the hands of that number of voters in White River Junction. Nevertheless her local managers still saw to it that she visited nearly every old people's home in the state.

Despite this, Florentyna had to pound the streets of New Hampshire towns, shaking hands with papermill workers in Berlin, as well as with the somewhat inebriated denizens of the VFW and American Legion posts, which seemed to exist in every town. She learned to work the ski-lift lines in the smaller hills rather than the famous resorts which were often peopled by a majority of non-voting visitors from New York or Massachusetts.

If she failed with this tiny electorate of the northern tip of America, Florentyna knew it would raise major doubts about her credibility as a candidate.

Whenever she arrived in a city, Edward was always there to meet her and he never let her stop until the moment she stepped back on to her plane.

Edward told her that they could thank heaven for the curiosity value of a woman candidate. His advance team never had to worry about filling any hall where Florentyna was to speak with potted plants rather than with Granite State voters.

Pete Parkin, who had a good luck streak with funeral duty, proved that the Vice-President had little else to do; he spent even more time in the state than Florentyna could. When the day of the Primary came, Edward was able to show that someone in the Kane team had contacted by phone, letter or personal visit one hundred and forty-seven thousand registered Democrats but, he added, obviously so had Pete Parkin because many of them had remained non-committal and some even hostile.

On the final evening, Florentyna held a rally in Manchester which over three thousand people attended. When Janet told her that tomorrow she would be about one-fiftieth of the way through the campaign, Florentyna replied, 'Or already finished.' She went to her motel room a little after midnight followed by the camera crews of CBS, NBC, ABC, Cable News and four agents from the Secret Service, all of whom were convinced she was going to win.

The voters of New Hampshire woke up to drifting snow and icy winds. Florentyna spent the day driving from polling place to polling place thanking the party faithful until the last poll closed. At eleven minutes past nine, CBS was the first to tell the national audience that the turnout was estimated at forty-seven per cent, which Dan Rather considered high in view of the weather conditions. The early voting pattern showed that the pollsters had proved right: Florentyna and Pete Parkin were running neck and neck, each taking over the lead during the night but never by more than a couple of percentage points. Florentyna sat in her motel room with Edward, Janet, her closest assistants and two Secret Service agents, watching the final results come in.

'The outcome couldn't have been closer if they had planned it,' said Jessica Savitch, who announced the result first for NBC. 'Senator Kane thirty-one per cent, Vice-President Parkin thirty, Senator Bill Bradley sixteen per cent and the rest of the voters scattered among five others who in my opinion,' added Savitch, 'needn't bother to book a hotel room for the next Primary.'

Florentyna recalled her father's words: *If the result of the New Hampshire Primary turns out to be satisfactory ...*

She left for Massachusetts with six delegates committed to her; Pete Parkin had five. The national press declared no winner but five losers. Only three candidates were seen in Massachusetts, and Florentyna seemed to have buried the bogey that as a woman she couldn't be a serious contender.

. . .

In Massachusetts she had fourteen days to capture as many of the one hundred and eleven delegates as possible, and here her work pattern hardly varied. Each day she would carry out the schedule that Edward had organized for her, a programme that ensured that the candidate met as many voters as possible and found some way to get on the morning or evening news.

Florentyna posed with babies, union leaders and Italian restauranteurs; she ate scallops, linguine, Portuguese sweetbread and cranberries; she rode the MTA, the Nantucket ferry and the Alameda bus line the length of the Massachusetts Turnpike; she jogged on beaches, hiked in the Berkshires and shopped in Boston's Quincy Market, all in an effort to prove she had the stamina of any man. Nursing her aching body in a hot bath, she came to the conclusion that had her father remained in Russia, her route to the Presidency of the USSR couldn't have been any harder.

In Massachusetts, Florentyna held off Pete Parkin for a second time, taking forty-seven delegates to the Vice-President's thirty-nine. The same day in Vermont, she captured eight of the state's twelve delegates. Because of the upsets already achieved by Florentyna, the political pollsters were saying that more people were answering 'Yes' when asked 'Could a woman win the Presidential election?' But even she was amused when she read that six per cent of the voters had not realized that Senator Kane was a woman. The press was quick to point out that her next big test would be in the south, where the Florida, Georgia and Alabama Primaries all fell on the same day. If she could hold on there she had a real chance, because the Democratic race had become a private battle between herself and the Vice-President. Bill Bradley, having secured only eleven per cent of the votes in Massachusetts, had dropped out because of lack of funds although his name remained on the ballot in several states and no one doubted he would be a serious candidate sometime in the future. Bradley had been Florentyna's first choice as running mate, and she already had the New Jersey Senator on her short list for consideration for Vice-President.

When the Florida ballots were counted, it came as no surprise that the Vice-President had taken sixty-two of the one hundred delegates and he repeated the trend in Georgia by winning 40–23, followed by Alabama where he captured twenty-eight of the forty-five voters. But Pete Parkin was not, as he had promised the press, 'trouncing the little lady when she puts her elegant toes in the south'. Parkin was increasingly trying to outdo Florentyna as a champion of the military, but his choice of legislation setting up the so-called 'Fort Gringo Line' along the Mexican–American border was beginning to rebound on him in the south-west, where he had imagined he was unbeatable.

Edward and his team were now working several Primaries ahead as they criss-crossed back and forth across the country; Florentyna thanked heaven for her ample campaign funds as the Lear jet touched down in state after state. Her energy remained boundless and if anything it was the Vice-President who began to stammer and sound tired and hoarse at the end of each day. Both candidates had to fit in trips to San Juan, and when Puerto Rico held its Primary in mid-March, twenty-five of the forty-one delegates favoured Florentyna. Two days later, she arrived back in her home state for the Illinois Primary, trailing Parkin 164–194.

The Windy City came to a standstill as its inhabitants welcomed their favourite daughter, giving her every one of the one hundred and seventy-nine Illinois delegates so that she went back into the lead with three hundred and forty-three delegates. However, when they moved on to New York, Connecticut, Wisconsin and Pennsylvania, the Vice-President eroded the lead until he arrived in Texas trailing only five hundred and ninety-one to Florentyna's six hundred and fifty-five.

No one was surprised when Pete Parkin took one hundred per cent of the delegates in his home state; they hadn't had a President since Lyndon Baines Johnson and the male half of Texas believed that while J. R. Ewing might have had his faults, he had been right about a woman's place being in the home. The Vice-President left his ranch outside Houston with a lead of seven hundred and forty-three to Florentyna's six hundred and fifty-five.

Travelling round the country under such tremendous daily pressure, both candidates found an off-the-cuff remark or an unwary comment could easily turn out to be tomorrow's headline. Pete Parkin was the first to make a gaffe when he got Peru mixed up with Paraguay and the photographers went wild when he rode in a chauffeured Mercedes through Flint on one of his motorcades. Nor was Florentyna without her mishaps. In Alabama, when asked if she would consider a black running mate as Vice-President, she replied, 'Of course, I've already considered the idea.' It took repeated statements to persuade the press that she had not already invited one of America's black leaders to join her ticket.

Her biggest mistake, however, was in Virginia. She addressed the University of Virginia Law School on the parole system and the changes she would like to make if she became President. The speech had been written and researched for her by one of the assistants in Washington who had been with Florentyna since her days as a Congresswoman. She read the text through carefully the night before, making only a few minor changes, admiring the way the piece had been put together, and delivered the speech to a crowded hall of law students who received it enthusiastically. When she left for an evening meeting of the Charlottesville Rotary Club to talk on the problems facing cattle farmers, she dismissed all thought of the earlier speech until she read the local paper the next morning during breakfast at the Boar's Head Inn.

The Richmond *News-Leader* came out with a story that all the national papers picked up immediately. A local journalist covering the biggest scoop of his life suggested that Florentyna's speech was outstanding because it had been written by one of Senator Kane's most trusted staff members, Allen Clarence, who was an ex-convict himself, having been given a six-month jail sentence with a year's probation before going to work for Florentyna. Few of the papers pointed out that the offence had been drunken driving without a licence, and that Clarence had been released on appeal after three months. When questioned by the press on what she intended to do about Mr Clarence, she said, 'Nothing.'

Edward told her that she must fire him immediately, however unfair it might seem, because those sections of the press who were against her – not to mention Pete Parkin – were having a field day repeating that one of her most trusted members of staff was an ex-con. 'Can you imagine who will be running the jails in this country if that woman is elected?' became Parkin's hourly off-the-cuff remark. Eventually Allen Clarence voluntarily resigned, but by then the damage had been done. By the time they reached California, Pete Parkin had increased his lead, with nine hundred and ninety-one delegates to Florentyna's eight hundred and eighty-three.

When Florentyna arrived in San Francisco, Bella was there to meet her at the airport. She might have put on thirty years, but she still hadn't lost any pounds. By her side stood Claude, one enormous son and one skinny daughter. Bella ran towards Florentyna the moment she saw her, only to be blocked by burly Secret Service agents. She was rescued by a hug from the candidate. 'I've never seen anything like her,' muttered one of the Secret Service men. 'She could kick start a Jumbo.' Hundreds of people stood at the perimeter of the tarmac chanting 'President Kane', and Florentyna, accompanied by Bella, walked straight over to them. Hands flew in Florentyna's direction, a reaction that never failed to lift her spirits. The Placards read 'California for Kane' and for the first time the majority of the crowd was made up of men. When she turned to leave them and go into the terminal she saw scrawled all over the side of a wall in red, 'Do you want a Polack bitch for President?' and underneath in white, 'Yes'.

Bella, now the headmistress of one of the largest schools in California, had also, after Florentyna had won a seat in the Senate, become the city's Democratic committee chairwoman.

'I always knew you would run for President, so I thought I had better make certain of San Francisco.'

Bella did make certain, with her one thousand so-called volunteers banging on every door. California's split personality – conservative in the south, liberal in the north – made it hard to be the kind of centrist candidate Florentyna wanted to be. But her efficiency, compassion and intelligence converted even some of the most hardened Marin County left-wingers and Orange County Birchers. San Francisco's turnout was second only to Chicago's. Florentyna wished she had fifty-one Bellas because the vote in San Francisco was enough to give her sixty-nine per cent of the state. It had been Bella who had made it possible for Florentyna to arrive in Detroit for the convention with one hundred and twenty-eight more delegates than Parkin.

Over a celebration dinner, Bella warned Florentyna that the biggest problem she was facing was not 'I'll never vote for a woman' but that 'She has too much money'.

'Not that old chestnut. I can't do any more about that,' said Florentyna. 'I've already put my own Baron stock into the foundation.'

'That's the point – no one knows what the foundation does. I realize it helps children in some way, but how many children, and how much money is involved?'

'The trust last year spent over three million dollars on 3,112 immigrants from under-privileged backgrounds. Added to that, four hundred and two gifted children won Remagen Scholarships to American universities and one went on to be our first Rhodes Scholar to Oxford.'

'I wasn't aware of that,' said Bella, 'but I'm continually reminded that Pete Parkin built a feeble little library for the University of Texas at Austin. He's made sure that the building is as well known as the Widener Library at Harvard.'

'So what do you feel Florentyna should be doing?' asked Edward.

'Why don't you let Professor Ferpozzi hold his own press conference? He's a man the public will take notice of. After that everyone will know that Florentyna Kane cares about other people and spends her own money on them to prove it.'

The next day, Edward worked on placing articles in selected magazines and organized a press conference. They ended up with a small piece in most journals and newspapers, but *People* magazine did a cover picture of Florentyna with Albert Schmidt, the Remagen Rhodes Scholar. When it was discovered that Albert was a German immigrant whose grandparents had fled from Europe after escaping from a prisoner-of-war camp, David Hartman interviewed the young man the next day on 'Good Morning, America'. After that he seemed to be getting more publicity than Florentyna.

On her way back to Washington that weekend, Florentyna heard that the Governor of Colorado, whom she had never particularly considered a friend or political ally, had endorsed her without advance warning at a solar energy symposium in Boulder. Her approach to industry and conservation, he told the convention, offered the resource-rich western states their best hope for the future.

That day ended on an even higher note when Reuters tapped out the news right across America that the Welfare Department had delivered their first major report since the implementation of the Kane Act. For the first time since Florentyna's overhaul of the social service system, the number of welfare recipients leaving the register in a given year had surpassed the number of new applicants coming on.

Florentyna's financial backing was always a problem as even the most ardent supporters assumed she could foot her own campaign bills. Parkin, with the backing of the oil tycoons led by Marvin Snyder of Blade Oil, had never had to face the same problem. But during the next few days campaign contributions flowed in to Florentyna's office, along with telegrams of support and good wishes.

Influential journalists in London, Paris, Bonn and Tokyo began to tell their readers that if America wanted a President of international status and credibility there was no contest between Florentyna Kane and the cattle farmer from Texas.

Florentyna was delighted whenever she read these articles, but Edward reminded her that neither the readers nor the writers could pull any levers on any voting machines in America, although he felt for the first time they had Parkin on the run. He was also quick to point out that there were still more than four hundred of the three thousand three hundred and thirty-one delegates who after the Primaries and caucuses remained undecided. The political pundits estimated that two hundred of them were leaning towards the Vice-President while about a hundred would come out in favour of Florentyna. It looked as if it was going to be the closest convention roll call since Reagan ran against Ford.

. . .

After California, Florentyna returned to Washington with another suit-case full of dirty clothes. She knew she would have to cajole, coax and twist the arms of those four hundred delegates who still remained undecided. During the next four weeks, she spoke personally to three hundred and eighty-eight of them, some of them three or four times. It was always the women she found the least helpful, although it was obvious they were all enjoying the attention that was being showered on them, especially as in a month's time no one would ever phone them again.

Edward ordered a computer terminal for Florentyna's suite at the convention which had on-line access to the records at campaign headquarters. Information on all four hundred and twelve delegates who remained uncommitted, along with a short life history of each, right down to their hotel rooms in Detroit, was available. When he reached the convention city, he intended to be ready to put his final plan into operation.

. . .

For five days during the next week, Florentyna made certain she was never far from a television set. The Republicans were at the Cow Palace, San Francisco, haggling over whom they wanted to lead them, no one having excited the voters during the Primaries.

The choice of Russell Warner came as no surprise to Florentyna. He had been campaigning for the Presidency ever since he had become Governor of Ohio. The press's description of Warner as a good Governor in a bad year reminded Florentyna that her main task would be to defeat Parkin. Once again, Florentyna felt it was going to be easier to defeat the Republican standard-bearer than the opposition within her own party.

. . .

The weekend before the convention, Florentyna and Edward joined the family on Cape Cod. Exhausted, Florentyna still managed to beat Edward in a round of golf, and she thought he looked even more tired than she felt. She was thankful that the Baron was run so well by its new, young directors, who now included William.

Florentyna and Edward were both due to fly into Detroit on Monday morning where they had taken over yet another Baron. The hotel would be filled with Florentyna's staff, supporters, the press and one hundred and twenty-four of those uncommitted delegates.

As she said goodnight to Edward and then to the Secret Service men and women – whom she was beginning to treat as her adopted family – on Sunday night, Florentyna knew the next four days were going to be the most important in her political career.

35

When Jack Germond of the *Baltimore Sun* asked Florentyna on the plane when she had started working on her acceptance speech, she replied, 'Since my eleventh birthday.'

On the flight from New York to Detroit Metro Airport, Florentyna had read through her acceptance speech, already drafted in case she was nominated on the first ballot. Edward had predicted that she would not secure victory on the first roll call, but Florentyna felt she had to be prepared for any eventuality.

Her advisers considered the result was much more likely to be known after the second or even the third ballot by which time Senator Bradley would have released his one hundred and eighty-nine delegates.

During the previous week, she had drawn up a short list of four people whom she thought worthy of consideration to join her on the ticket as Vice-President. Bill Bradley still led the field and Florentyna felt he was her natural successor to the White House, but she was also considering Sam Nunn, Gary Hart and David Pryor.

Florentyna's thoughts were interrupted when the plane landed and she looked out of the windows to see a large, excited crowd awaiting her. She couldn't help wondering how many of them would also be there tomorrow when Pete Parkin arrived. She checked her hair in her compact mirror; a few white strands were showing in the dark hair but she made no attempt to disguise them, and she smiled at the thought that Pete Parkin's hair had remained the same implausible colour for the past thirty years. Florentyna wore a simple linen suit and her only piece of jewelry was a diamond-studded donkey.

Florentyna unbuckled her seat belt, rose and ducked her head under the overhead compartment. She stepped into the aisle and as she turned to leave, everyone in the plane began applauding. She suddenly realized that if she lost the nomination, this would be the last time that she would see them all together. Florentyna shook hands with all the members of the press corps, some of whom had been on the trail with her for five months. A crew member opened the cabin door and Florentyna stepped out on to the staircase, squinting into the July sun. The crowd let up a yell of 'There she is', and Florentyna walked down the steps and straight towards the waving banners because she always found that direct contact with the voters recharged her. As she touched the tarmac, she was once again surrounded by the Secret Service who dreaded crowds they could never control. She might sometimes think of being assassinated when she was alone, but never when she was in a crowd. Florentyna clasped outstretched hands and greeted as many people as possible before Edward guided her away to the waiting motorcade.

A line of ten small new Fords reminded her that Detroit had finally come to terms with the energy crisis. If Pete Parkin were to make the mistake of being driven in a Mercedes in this city, she would be the Democratic choice before Alabama cast its first vote. Secret Service men filled the first two cars while Florentyna was in the third, with Edward in front by the driver. Florentyna's personal doctor rode in the fourth and her staff filled the remaining six 'mighty midgets', as the new small Ford had been dubbed. A press corps bus followed at the rear with police outriders dotted up and down the motorcade.

The front car moved off at a snail's pace so that Florentyna could wave to the crowds, but as soon as they reached Interstate 94, the cars travelled into Detroit at a steady fifty miles an hour.

For twenty minutes Florentyna relaxed in the back seat during the drive into the mid-town New Centre area, where the motorcade exited at Woodward Avenue, turned south towards the river, and slowed down to about five miles an hour as the crowds filled the street to catch a glimpse of Senator Kane. Florentyna's organizing committee in Detroit had distributed one hundred thousand handbills showing the exact route she would take when she arrived in the city, and her supporters cheered her all the way to the Baron Hotel east of the Renaissance Centre on the Detroit River. The Secret Service begged her to change the route but she wouldn't hear of it.

Dozens of photographers and television crews were poised awaiting her arrival as Florentyna stepped out of her car and climbed the steps of the Detroit Baron; the whole area was lit up by flashbulbs and arc lights. Once she was inside the hotel lobby, the Secret Service men whisked her away to the twenty-fourth floor, which had been reserved for her personal use. She quickly checked over the George Novak Suite to see that everything she required was there because she knew that this was going to be her prison for the next four days. The only reason she would leave that room would be either to accept the nomination as the Democratic Party candidate or to declare her support for Pete Parkin.

A bank of telephones had been installed so that Florentyna could keep in touch with the four hundred and twelve wavering delegates. She spoke to thirty-eight of them before dinner that night and then sat up until two o'clock the next morning, going over the names and backgrounds of those whom her team genuinely felt had not made up their minds.

Next morning, the Detroit *Free Press* was filled with pictures of her arrival in Detroit, though in truth she knew Pete Parkin would receive the same enthusiastic coverage tomorrow. At least she was relieved that the President had decided to remain on the sidelines when it came to supporting either candidate. The press had already treated that as a moral victory for Florentyna.

She put the newspaper down and began to watch the closed circuit television to see what was going on in the convention hall during the first morning. She also kept an eye on all three channels at lunchtime in case any one network came up with some exclusive piece of news that the other two had missed and on which the press would demand her instant reaction.

During the day, thirty-one of the wavering delegates were brought to meet her on the twenty-fourth floor. As the hour progressed, they were served coffee, iced tea, hot tea and cocktails. Florentyna stuck to iced tea or she would have been drunk by eleven o'clock.

She watched in silence as Pete Parkin arrived in *Air Force II* at the Detroit airport. One assistant told her that his crowd was smaller than the one that had turned out for her yesterday, while another said it was larger. She made a mental note of the assistant who said that Parkin's crowd was larger today and decided to listen to his opinions more carefully in the future.

Pete Parkin made a short speech at a specially set-up podium on the tarmac, his Vice-President seal of office glistening in the sun. He said how delighted he was to be in the city that could rightly describe itself as the car capital of the world. 'I should know,' he added, 'I've owned Fords all my life. Florentyna smiled.

By the end of two days under 'house arrest', Florentyna had complained so much about being cooped up all day that on Tuesday morning the Secret Service took her down in a freight lift so that she could stroll along the river front and enjoy the fresh air and the low skyline of Windsor, Canada, on the opposite bank. She had gone only a few paces before she was surrounded by well-wishers who wanted to shake her hand.

When she returned, Edward had some good news: five uncommitted delegates had decided to vote for her on the first ballot. He estimated that they only needed another seventy-three to be over the magic one thousand six hundred and sixty-six. On the monitor she followed the programme on the floor of the convention hall. A black school superintendent from Delaware expounded Florentyna's virtues and when she mentioned her name the blue placards filled the hall with 'Kane for President'. During the speech that followed red placards demanding 'Parkin for President' were in equal abundance. She paced around the suite until one thirty by which time she had seen forty-three more delegates and spoken on the phone to another fifty-eight.

The second day of the convention was devoted to the major platform speeches on policy, finance, welfare, defence and the key speech by Senator

Pryor. Time and time again, delegates would declare that whichever of the two great candidates was selected, they would go on to beat the Republicans in November; but most of the delegates on the floor kept up a steady hum of conversation, all but oblivious to the men and women on the platform who might well make up a Democratic cabinet.

Florentyna broke away from the welfare debate to have a drink with two delegates from Nevada who were still undecided. She realized their next stop would probably be Parkin, who would also promise them their new highway, hospital, university or whatever excuse they came up with to visit both candidates. At least tomorrow night they would have to come down finally in someone's favour. She told Edward she wanted a fence put up in the middle of the room.

'Why?' asked Edward.

'So that wavering delegates have somewhere to sit when they come to meet me.'

Reports flowed in during the day about what Pete Parkin was up to, which seemed to be much the same as Florentyna except that he was booked into the Westin Hotel at the Renaissance Centre. As neither of them could go into the convention arena, their daily routines continued: delegates, phone calls, press statements, meetings with party officials, and finally bed without much sleep.

On Wednesday, Florentyna was dressed by six o'clock in the morning and was driven quickly to the convention hall. Once they had arrived at the Joe Louis Arena, she was shown the passage she would walk down to deliver her acceptance speech if she were the chosen candidate. She walked out on to the platform and stood in front of the banked microphones, staring out at the twenty-one thousand empty seats. The tall, thin placards that rose from the floor high into the air proudly proclaimed the name of every state from Alabama to Wyoming. She made a special note of where the Illinois delegation would be seated so that she could wave to them the moment she entered the hall.

An enterprising photographer who had slept under a seat in the convention hall all night began taking photographs of her before he was smartly ushered out of the hall by the Secret Service. Florentyna smiled as she looked towards the ceiling where two hundred thousand red, white and blue balloons waited to cascade down on the victor. She had read somewhere that it would have taken fifty college students, using bicycle pumps, one week to fill them with air.

'Okay for testing, Senator Kane?' said an impersonal voice from she could not tell where.

'My fellow Americans, this is the greatest moment in my life, and I intend to ...'

'That's fine, Senator. Loud and clear,' said the chief electrician as he walked up through the empty seats. Pete Parkin was scheduled to go through the same routine at seven o'clock.

Florentyna was driven back to her hotel where she had breakfast with her closest staff, who were all nervous and laughed at each other's jokes, however feeble, but fell silent whenever she spoke. They watched Pete Parkin doing his usual morning jog for the television crews; it made them all hysterical when someone in an NCB windcheater holding a mini-camera accelerated past a breathless Vice-President three times to get a better picture.

The roll call vote was due to start at nine that evening. Edward had set up fifty phone lines direct to every state chairman on the convention floor so that he could be in constant touch if something unexpected happened. Florentyna was seated behind a desk with only two phones, but at the single touch of a button she had access to any of the fifty lines. While the hall was beginning to fill they tested each line and Edward pronounced that they were ready for anything, and now all they could do was use every minute left to contact more delegates. By five-thirty that evening, Florentyna had spoken to three hundred and ninety-two of them in three days.

By seven o'clock the Joe Louis Arena was almost packed, although there was still a full hour to go until the names were placed in nomination. No one who had travelled to Detroit wanted to miss one minute of the unfolding drama.

At seven-thirty, Florentyna watched the party officials begin to take their seats on the stage and she remembered her days as a page at the Chicago Convention when she had first met John Kennedy. She knew then that they had all been told to arrive at certain times; the later you were asked the more senior you were. Forty years on, and she was hoping to be asked last.

The biggest cheer of the evening was reserved for Senator Bill Bradley, who had already announced he would address the convention if there was a deadlock after the first ballot. At seven forty-five, the Speaker of the House of Representatives, Marty Lynch, rose and tried to bring the convention to order but he could scarcely make himself heard above the klaxons, whistles, drums, bugles and cries of 'Kane' and 'Parkin' from supporters trying to outscream each other. Florentyna sat watching the scene but showed no sign of emotion. When finally there was a semblance of order, the chairman introduced Mrs Bess Gardner, who had been chosen to record the votes, although everyone in the hall knew that the results would flash up on to the vast video screen above her head before she even had a chance to confirm them.

At eight o'clock the chairman brought his gavel down; some saw the little wooden hammer hit the base but no one heard it. For another twenty minutes the noise continued as the chairman still made no impression on the delegates. Eventually at eight twenty-three Marty Lynch could be heard asking Rich Daley, the mayor of Chicago, to place the name of Senator Kane in nomination; ten more minutes of noise before the mayor was able to deliver his nominating speech. Florentyna and her staff sat in silence through a speech that described her public record in the most glowing terms. She also listened attentively when Senator Ralph Brooks nominated Pete Parkin. The reception of both proposals by the delegates would have made a full symphony orchestra sound like a tin whistle. Nominations for Bill Bradley and the usual handful of predictable favourite sons followed in quick succession.

.   .   .

At nine o'clock, the chairman looked down into the body of the hall and called upon Alabama to cast its vote. Florentyna sat staring at the screen like a prisoner about to face trial by jury – wanting to know the verdict even before she had heard the evidence. The perspiring chairman of the Alabama delegation picked up his microphone and shouted, 'The great state of Alabama, the heart of the south, casts twenty-eight votes for Vice-President Parkin and seventeen votes for Senator Kane.' Although everyone had known how Alabama was going to vote since 11 March, over four months before, this didn't stop Parkin posters from being waved frantically, and it was another twelve minutes before the chairman was able to call on Alaska.

'Alaska, the forty-ninth state to join the Union, casts seven of its votes for Senator Kane, the forty-second President of the United States, three for Pete Parkin and one for Senator Bradley.' It was the turn of Florentyna's followers to unleash a prolonged uproar in support of their candidate, but Parkin led the field for the first half hour until California declared two hundred and fourteen for Senator Kane, ninety-two for Parkin.

'God bless Bella,' said Florentyna, but had to watch the Vice-President go back into the lead with the help of Florida, Georgia and Idaho. When they reached the state of Illinois the convention nearly came to a halt, Mrs Kalamich, who had welcomed Florentyna the first night in Chicago nearly twenty years before, had been chosen as vice-chairman of the Illinois Democratic Party in convention year to deliver the verdict of her delegates.

'Mr Chairman, this is the greatest moment of my life' – Florentyna smiled as Mrs Kalamich continued – 'to say to you that the great state of Illinois is proud to cast every one of its one hundred and seventy-nine votes for its favourite daughter and the first woman President of the United States, Senator Florentyna Kane.' The Kane supporters went berserk as she took the lead for the second time, but Florentyna knew her rival would create the same effect when the moment came for Texas to declare their allegiance, and in fact Parkin went ahead for a second time with one thousand four hundred and forty delegates to Florentyna's one thousand three hundred and seventy-one after his home state had given their verdict. Bill Bradley had picked up ninety-seven delegates along the way and now looked certain to end up with enough votes to prevent there being an outright winner on the first round.

As the chairman pressed forward with each state – Utah, Vermont, Virginia – the network computers were already flashing up on the screen that there would be no winner on the first ballot, but it was ten forty-seven before Tom Brokaw announced the first round verdict: one thousand five hundred and twenty-two for Senator Kane, one thousand four hundred and eighty for Vice-President Parkin, one hundred and eighty-nine for Senator Bradley and one hundred and forty for favourite sons.

The chairman told the delegates that Senator Bradley would now address them. Another eleven minutes passed before he could speak. Florentyna had talked to him on the phone every day of the convention and steadfastly avoided asking him to join her ticket as Vice-President, because she felt such an offer would smack of bribery rather than of choosing him because she felt he was the right man to succeed her. Although Ralph Brooks was the favourite for the post in the Parkin camp, Florentyna couldn't help wondering if Pete Parkin had already offered Bradley the chance to join him.

At last the senior Senator from New Jersey was able to address the convention. 'My fellow members of the Democratic Party,' he began. 'I thank you for the support you have given me during this election year, but the time has come for me to withdraw from this Presidential race and release my delegates to vote the way their conscience guides them.' The hall fell almost silent. Bradley spoke for several minutes about the sort of person he wanted to see in the White House but did not openly support either candidate. He closed with the words: 'I pray you will select the right person to lead our country,' and was cheered for several minutes after he had returned to his seat.

By this time, most people in suite 2400 of the Baron had no nails left; only Florentyna remained outwardly calm, although Edward noticed that her fist was clenched. He quickly returned to work on the green section of his master printout, which showed only the Bradley delegates, but there wasn't much he could do while they were all on the floor except phone the chairman of each state committee and keep them working. The phones came ringing back; it seemed that the Bradley delegates were also split down the middle. Some of them would even continue to vote for Bradley in the second round in case the convention became deadlocked and had to turn to him in the end.

The second roll call vote started at eleven twenty-one with Alabama, Alaska and Arizona showing no changes. The balloting dragged on from state to state until they recorded the Wyoming decision at twelve twenty-three. At the end of the second round, the convention was still undecided, with the only important change being that Pete Parkin had taken a slight lead – 1,629–1,604 – while ninety-eight delegates had remained uncommitted or faithful to Senator Bradley.

At twelve thirty-seven the chairman said, 'Enough is enough, we'll start the roll call again tomorrow evening at seven o'clock.'

'Why not first thing tomorrow morning?' asked one of Florentyna's sleepless, young aides as he was leaving the arena.

'As the hour pointed out,' said Janet, 'elections are run for the benefit of the networks, and ten o'clock tomorrow morning just isn't prime time.'

'Are the networks going to be responsible for which candidate we choose?' he asked.

They both laughed. The sleepless aide repeated the same comment twenty-four hours later – when neither of them laughed.

The exhausted delegates slumped off to their rooms, aware that on a third ballot most states freed their delegates from their original pledges, which meant that they could now vote any way they pleased. Edward and his team didn't know where to start, but they picked up the printout and went through each delegate from Alabama to Wyoming for a third time that night, hoping they would have a plan for every state by eight o'clock the next morning.

Florentyna hardly slept that night and at ten past six she walked back into the living room of her suite in a dressing gown to find Edward still poring over the lists.

'I'll need you at eight,' he said, not looking up at her.

'Good morning,' she said, and kissed him on the forehead.

'Good morning.'

Florentyna stretched and yawned. 'What happens at eight?'

'We speak to thirty Bradley and undeclared delegates an hour all through the day. I want you to have spoken to at least two hundred and fifty by five this afternoon. We'll have all six phones manned every minute of that time so that there will never be less than two people waiting to speak to you.'

'Won't eight be a little early?' asked Florentyna.

'No,' said Edward. 'But I won't bother the west coast delegates until after lunch.'

Florentyna returned to her room realizing yet again how much thought Edward had put into her whole campaign, and she remembered Richard saying how lucky she was to have two men who adored her.

At eight o'clock, she started work with a large glass of orange juice by her side. As the morning proceeded, the team became more convinced that the first roll call that evening would give the majority to their candidate. The feeling in that room was turning to one of victory.

At ten forty Bill Bradley rang to say that if his delegates caused another deadlock he was going to recommend they vote for Florentyna. Florentyna thanked him.

. . .

At eleven thirty-seven Edward passed Florentyna the phone. This time it wasn't a well-wisher.

'It's Pete Parkin here. I think we ought to get together. Can I come and see you immediately?'

Florentyna wanted to say 'I'm far too busy' but only said 'Yes'.

'I'll be right over.'

'Whatever can he want?' said Edward as Florentyna handed him back the phone.

'I have no idea, but we don't have long to wait before we find out.'

Pete Parkin arrived via the freight lift with two Secret Service agents and his campaign manager.

After unnatural pleasantries had been exchanged – the two candidates hadn't spoken to each other for the past six months – and coffee poured, the contenders were left alone. They sat in comfortable chairs facing each other. They might as well have been discussing the weather, not which one of them should rule the Western world. The Texan got straight down to business.

'I am prepared to make a deal with you, Florentyna.'

'I'm listening.'

'If you withdraw I'll offer you the Vice-Presidency.'

'You must be –'

'Hear me out, Florentyna,' said Parkin, putting up his massive hand like a traffic cop. 'If you accept my offer, I will only serve one term if elected, and then I'll support you for the job in 1996 with full White House backing. You're five years younger than I am and there is no reason why you shouldn't complete two full terms.'

Over the previous thirty minutes Florentyna had thought of many reasons why her rival might want to see her, but she had not been prepared for this.

'If you don't accept my offer and I win tonight, I'll be giving the number two spot to Ralph Brooks, who has already confirmed that he is willing to run.'

'I'll call you by two this afternoon,' was all that Florentyna said.

Once Pete Parkin had left with his aides, Florentyna discussed the offer with Edward and Janet, who both felt that they had come too far to give in now. 'Who knows what the situation might be in four years' time?' Edward pointed out. 'You might be like Humphrey trying to recover from Johnson. In any case, we only need a deadlock this time and Bradley's delegates will push us comfortably over the top on the fourth ballot.'

'And I bet Parkin knows that,' added Janet.

Florentyna sat motionless listening to her different advisers and then asked to be left alone.

Florentyna phoned Pete Parkin at one forty-three and politely declined his offer, explaining she was confident that she was going to win on the first ballot that night. He made no reply.

By two o'clock the press had got hold of the news of the secret meeting and the phones in suite 2400 never stopped as they tried to find out what had happened. Edward kept Florentyna concentrating on the delegates and with each call she was becoming more and more assured that Pete Parkin's move had been made more out of desperation than confidence. 'He's played his final card,' said Janet, smirking.

At six o'clock everyone in suite 2400 was back in front of the television: there were no longer any delegates left to speak to; they were all on the convention floor. Edward still had his phone bank linked up to all the state chairmen and the early reports back from them indicated that the feeling they had picked up votes all through the day was accurate.

Exactly at the point when Florentyna relaxed and felt confident for the first time, the bombshell fell. Edward had just handed her yet another iced tea when CBS flashed up on the screen 'Newsbreak' and a camera went over to Dan Rather, who told a stunned audience only fifteen minutes before the roll call was due to start that he was about to interview Vice-President Parkin on the reason for his secret meeting with Senator Kane. The CBS camera panned down on the florid face of the big Texan and to Florentyna's horror, the whole thing was going out live on the vast screen in the convention hall. She remembered that the Rules Committee had decided to allow anything to go up on the screen that might affect the delegates; this was meant to stop rumours spreading around the convention hall about what was really going on outside, to be sure that what had happened between Ford and Reagan in the 1980 convention over the picking of a running mate could never happen again. It was the first time that the delegates in the hall had been unanimously silent for four days.

The camera switched back to the CBS interviewer.

'Mr Vice-President, we know you had a meeting with Senator Kane today. Can you tell me the reason you asked to see her?'

'Certainly, Dan. It was first and foremost because I am interested in the unity of my party and above all, Dan, in beating the Republicans.'

Florentyna and her staff were mesmerized. She could see the delegates on the floor hanging on every word and she was helpless to do anything but listen.

'Can I ask what took place at that meeting?'

'I asked Senator Kane if she would be willing to serve as my Vice-President and make up a Democratic team that would be unbeatable.'

'How did she reply to your suggestion?'

'She said she wanted to think the offer over. You see, Dan, I believe together we can lick the Republicans.'

'Ask him what my final answer was,' said Florentyna, but it was no use; the cameras were already switching to a half-crazed convention hall ready for the first vote. Edward phoned the CBS and demanded equal time for Florentyna. Dan Rather agreed to interview Senator Kane immediately, but Florentyna knew that they were already too late. Once the voting had started the committee had agreed that nothing would go on that screen except the ballot tally. No doubt they would have to revise the rule by the next convention, but all Florentyna could think of was Miss Tredgold's views on television: '*Too many instant decisions will be made that will later be regretted.*'

The chairman banged his gavel and called upon Alabama to begin the roll call and the Camellia State showed a two-vote switch to Parkin. When Florentyna lost one delegate from Alaska and two from Arizona she knew her only hope was another deadlock so that she could put her version of the meeting with Parkin on television before the next vote. She sat and watched herself lose one vote here and a couple there but when Illinois held firm she hoped the tide might turn. Edward and the team had been working the phones non stop.

Then the next blow came.

Edward received a call from one of his campaign managers on the floor to say that Parkin assistants had started a rumour in the hall that Florentyna had accepted his offer. A rumour he knew Florentyna would never be able to trace back directly to Parkin or have time to rebut. Although as each state's turn came to vote, Edward fought to stem the tide. When they reached West Virginia, Parkin only needed twenty-five more delegates to go over the top. They gave him twenty-one, so he needed four from the penultimate state, Wisconsin. Florentyna was confident that all three delegates from Wyoming, the final state to vote, would remain loyal to her.

'The great state of Wisconsin, mindful of its responsibility tonight' – once again the hall was totally silent – 'and believing in the unity of the party above all personal considerations gives all its eleven votes to the next President of the United States, Pete Parkin.'

The delegates went berserk. In suite 2400 the result was met with stunned silence.

Florentyna had been beaten by a cheap but brilliant trick. And its true genius was that if she denied everything and gave her version of Parkin's behaviour, the Democrats might well lose the White House to the Republicans and she would be made the scapegoat.

Thirty minutes later, Pete Parkin arrived at the Joe Louis Arena amid cheers and the strains of 'Happy Days Are Here Again'. He spent another twelve minutes waving to the delegates and when at last he managed to bring the hall to silence he said: 'I hope to stand on this platform tomorrow night with the greatest lady in America and place before the nation a team that will whip the Republicans so that those elephants will never forget it.'

Once again the delegates roared their approval. During the next hour

Florentyna's staff crept back to their rooms until Edward was left alone with her.

'Do I accept?'

'You have no choice. If you don't, and the Democrats lose, the blame will be placed at your door.'

'And if I tell the truth?'

'It will be misunderstood; they will say you're a bad loser after your opponent had held out the olive branch of reconciliation. And don't forget President Ford predicted ten years ago that the first woman President would have to have been Vice-President before the American people would find the idea acceptable.'

'That might be true, but if Richard Nixon were alive today,' said Florentyna bitterly, 'he would be on the phone to Pete Parkin congratulating him on a trick far superior to any he pulled off against Muskie or Humphrey.' Florentyna yawned. 'I'm going to bed, Edward, I will have made a decision by the morning.'

At eight thirty Pete Parkin sent an emissary to ask if Florentyna had made up her mind. She replied that she wanted to see him again in private.

This time, Parkin arrived with three television companies in tow and as many reporters who could get hold of red press passes. When they were alone, Florentyna found it hard to control her temper even though she had decided not to remonstrate with Parkin but simply asked if he would confirm that he intended to serve one term.

'Yes,' he said, looking Florentyna straight in the eye.

'And at the next election you'll give me your full backing?'

'You have my word on that,' he said.

'On those terms I'm willing to serve as Vice-President.'

When he had left the room, Edward listened to what had taken place and said, 'We know exactly what his word is worth.'

.   .   .

As she entered the convention hall later that night, Florentyna was greeted by a cascade of noise. Pete Parkin held her hand up high, and the delegates once more roared their approval. Only Ralph Brooks looked sour.

Florentyna felt her acceptance speech as Vice-Presidential candidate was below her best, but they cheered her just the same. However, the biggest cheer of the evening was raised for Pete Parkin when he addressed the delegates; after all, he had been introduced as their new hero, the man who had brought honest unity to the party.

Florentyna flew to Boston and retreated to Cape Cod the next morning after a nauseating press conference with the Democratic candidate, who kept referring to her as 'that great little lady from Illinois'.

When they parted, in full view of the press, he kissed her on the cheek. She felt like a prostitute who had accepted his money and found it was too late to change her mind about going to bed.

36

Taking advantage of the fact that the campaign did not start until after Labour Day, Florentyna returned to Washington to catch up on her neglected Senatorial duties. She even found time to visit Chicago.

She spoke to Pete Parkin on the phone every day and certainly he could not have been more friendly and cooperative about fitting in with her arrangements. They agreed to meet at his White House office to discuss the final plan for the campaign. Florentyna tried to fulfil all her other commitments before the meeting so she could devote herself entirely to electioneering during the last nine weeks.

On 2 September, accompanied by Edward and Janet, Florentyna arrived at the west wing of the White House to be greeted by Ralph Brooks, who clearly remained a trusted lieutenant of the candidate. She was determined not to be the cause of any friction between herself and Brooks so near the election, especially as she knew that Brooks had expected to be the Vice-Presidential candidate himself. Senator Brooks took them from the reception area through to Pete Parkin's office. It was the first time Florentyna had seen the room she might occupy in a few weeks, and she was surprised by the warmth, with its yellow walls and ivory moulding. Fresh flowers sat on Parkin's mahogany desk, and the walls were hung with Remington oil paintings. Parkin's love of the west, Florentyna thought. The late summer sun flooded in through the south-facing windows.

Pete Parkin jumped up from behind his desk and came over to greet her, just a little too effusively. Then they all sat around a table in the centre of the room.

'I think you all know Ralph,' said Pete Parkin with a slightly uncomfortable laugh. 'He's worked out a campaign strategy which I am sure you'll find most impressive.'

Ralph Brooks unfolded a large map of the United States on the table in front of them. 'I feel the main consideration to keep uppermost in our minds is that to capture the White House we must have two hundred and seventy electoral college votes. Although it is obviously important and satisfying to win the popular vote, as we all know it's still the electoral college which selects the next President. For this reason, I have coloured the states black that I feel we have least chance of winning, and white those that are traditionally safe in the Democrat column. That leaves the key marginal states which I've marked in red, which between them make up one hundred and seventy-one electoral college votes.

'I believe both Pete and Florentyna should visit all the red states at least once, but Pete should concentrate his energies in the south while Florentyna spends most of her time in the north. Only California, with its massive forty-five electoral votes, will have to be visited by both of you regularly. During the sixty-two days left before the election, we must use every spare minute on states where we have a genuine chance and make only token visits to those fringe areas we captured in the 1964 landslide. As for our own white states, we must be prepared to visit them all once so that we cannot be accused of taking them for granted. I consider Ohio a no-hoper as it's Russell Warner's home state, but we mustn't let the Republicans assume Florida is theirs just because Warner's running mate was once the state's senior Senator. Now I've also worked out a daily routine for you both, starting next Monday,' he continued, handing the candidate and Florentyna separate sheaves of paper, 'and I think you should be in contact with each other at least twice a day, at eight o'clock in the morning and eleven o'clock at night, always Central Time.'

Florentyna found herself impressed by the work Ralph Brooks had put in before the briefing and could appreciate why Parkin had become so reliant on him. For the next hour Brooks answered queries that arose from his plan, and agreement was reached on their basic strategy for the campaign. At twelve thirty, the Vice-President and Florentyna walked on to the north portico of the White House to speak to the press. Ralph Brooks seemed to have statistics for everything: The press, he warned them, were divided like everyone else. One hundred and fifty papers with twenty-two million readers were already supporting the Democrats, while one hundred and forty-two with twenty-one point seven million readers were backing the Republicans. If they needed to know, he added, he could supply the relevant facts for any paper in the country.

Florentyna looked out across the lawn at Lafayette Square, dotted with lunchtime strollers and picnickers. If elected, she would rarely again be able to visit Washington's parks and memorials. Not unaccompanied, anyway. Parkin escorted her back to the Vice-President's office when the press had asked all the usual questions and received the usual answers. When they returned to the office they found that Parkin's Filipino stewards had set up lunch on the conference table. Florentyna came away from the meeting feeling a lot better about how matters were working out, especially since the Vice-President had twice in Brooks's hearing referred to their earlier agreement concerning 1996. Still Florentyna considered that it would be a long time before she could totally trust Parkin.

On 7 September she flew into Chicago to start her part of the election campaign but found that even though the press was still hard put to keep up with the daily routine she put herself through, she lacked the drive that had been a trademark of her earlier campaigning.

The Brooks plan ran smoothly for the first few days as Florentyna travelled through Illinois, Massachusetts and New Hampshire. She met with no surprises until she arrived in New York where the press was waiting in large numbers at the Albany airport. They wanted to know her views about Pete Parkin's treatment of Mexican Chicanos. Florentyna confessed that she didn't know what they were talking about, so they told her that the candidate had said that he had never had any trouble with Chicanos on his ranch; they were like his own children. Civil rights leaders were up in arms all over the country and all Florentyna could think of to say was, 'I am sure he has been misunderstood or else his words have been taken out of context.'

Russell Warner, the Republican candidate, said there could be no misunderstanding. Pete Parkin was simply a racist. Florentyna kept repudiating these statements although she suspected they were rooted in truth. Both Florentyna and Pete Parkin had to break off from their scheduled plans to fly to Alabama and attend the funeral of Ralph Abernathy. Ralph Brooks described the death of an aide as timely. When Florentyna heard what he had said she nearly swore at him in front of the press.

Florentyna continued her travels through Pennsylvania, West Virginia and Virginia, before going on to California, where she was joined by Edward. Bella and Claude took them out to a restaurant in Chinatown. The manager gave them a corner alcove where no one could see them, or more important, hear them, but the relaxed break only lasted for a few hours before Florentyna had to fly on to Los Angeles.

The press was becoming bored with the petty squabbles between Parkin and Warner over everything except real issues, and when the two candidates appeared together on a television debate in Pittsburgh, the universal opinion was that they had both lost, and that the only person of Presidential stature in the whole campaign was turning out to be Senator Kane. Many journalists expressed the view that it was a tragedy that Senator Kane had ever let it be known she was willing to be Pete Parkin's running mate.

'I'll write what really happened in my memoirs,' she told Edward. 'Only by then who will care?'

'In truth, no one,' replied Edward. 'How many Americans could tell you the name of Harry Truman's Vice-President?'

The next day, Pete Parkin flew into Los Angeles to join Florentyna for one of their few joint appearances. She met him at the airport. He walked off *Air Force II* holding up Missouri's *Unterrified Democrat*, the only paper which had run as its headline 'Parkin Wins Debate'. Florentyna had to admire the way he could make a rhinoceros look thin-skinned. California was to be the last stop before returning to their own states, and they held a final rally in the Rose Bowl. Parkin and Florentyna were surrounded by stars, half of whom were on stage for the free publicity they were guaranteed whichever candidate was in town. Along with Dustin Hoffman, Al Pacino and Jane Fonda, Florentyna spent most of her time signing autographs. She didn't know what to say to the girl who, puzzled by her signature, asked: 'Which was your last movie?'

The following morning, Florentyna flew back to Chicago while Pete Parkin left for Texas. As soon as Florentyna's 707 touched down in the Windy City, she was greeted by a crowd of over thirty thousand people, the biggest any candidate had had on the campaign trail.

.   .   .

On the morning of the election she voted at the elementary school in the Ninth District, in the presence of the usual group of reporters from the networks and the press. She smiled for them, knowing she would be forgotten news within a week if the Democrats lost. She spent the day going from committee room to polling places to television studio, and ended up back at her suite in the Chicago Baron a few minutes after the polls had closed.

Florentyna indulged herself with her first really long hot bath in over five months and a change of clothes that was not affected by whom she was spending the evening with. Then she was joined by William, Joanna, Annabel and Richard who, at the age of six, was being allowed to watch his first election. Edward arrived just after ten thirty and for the first time in his life saw Florentyna with her shoes off and her feet propped up on a table.

'Miss Tredgold wouldn't have approved.

'Miss Tredgold never had to do seven months of campaigning without a break,' she replied.

In a room full of food, drink, family and friends, Florentyna watched the results come in from the east coast. It was obvious from the moment that New Hampshire went to the Democrats and Massachusetts to the Republicans that they were all in for a long night. Florentyna was delighted that the weather had been dry right across the nation that day. She had never forgotten Theodore H. White telling her that America always voted Republican until five on election day. From that time on, working men and women on their way home decide whether to stop at the polls; if they do and *only* if they do, the country will go Democratic. It looked as though a lot of them had stopped by, but she wondered if it would turn out to be enough. By midnight, the Democrats had taken Illinois and Texas but lost Ohio and Pennsylvania and when the voting machines closed down in California, three hours after New York, America still hadn't elected a President. The private polls conducted outside the voting stations proved only that the nation's largest state wasn't wild about either candidate.

At the George Novak Suite in the Chicago Baron, some ate, some drank, some slept. But Florentyna remained wide awake throughout the whole proceedings and at two thirty-three, CBS announced the result she had been waiting for: California had been won by the Democrats, the returns showing 50.0 to 49.9, a margin of a mere three hundred and thirty-two thousand votes, giving the election to Parkin. Florentyna picked up the phone by her side.

'Are you calling the President-elect to congratulate him?' asked Edward.

'No,' said Florentyna. 'I'm calling Bella to thank her for putting him there.'

37

Florentyna spent the next few days in Cape Cod having a total rest, only to find she kept waking at six each morning with nothing to do except wait for the morning papers. She was delighted when Edward joined her on Wednesday, but couldn't get used to him affectionately addressing her as 'VP.'

Pete Parkin had already called a press conference at his Texas ranch to say he would not be naming his cabinet until the New Year. Florentyna returned to Washington on 14 November, for the lame-duck session of Congress, and prepared for her move from the Russell Building to the White House. Although her time was fully occupied in the Senate and Illinois, it came as a surprise to her that she spoke to the President-elect only two or three times a week and then on the phone. Congress adjourned two weeks after Thanksgiving, and Florentyna returned to Cape Cod for a family Christmas with a grandson who kept calling her Grannie President.

'Not yet,' she replied.

.   .   .

On 9 January the President arrived in Washington and held a press conference to announce his cabinet. Although Florentyna had not been consulted on his new appointments no one was expecting any real surprises: Charles Selover was made Secretary of Defence and would have been everyone's choice. Paul Rowe retained his position as Director of the CIA, Pierre Levale became Attorney-General and Michael Brewer, National Security Adviser. Florentyna didn't raise an eyebrow until he came to his choice for Secretary of State. She sat in disbelief when the President declared: 'Chicago can rightly be proud of having produced the Vice-President as well as the Secretary of State.'

.   .   .

By Inauguration Day, Florentyna's personal belongings in the Baron had been packed up and were all ready for delivery to the Vice-President's official residence on Observatory Circle. The huge Victorian house seemed grotesquely large for a family of one. For this Inauguration, Florentyna's whole family sat in seats one row behind Pete Parkin's wife and daughters, while Florentyna sat on one side of the President, Ralph Brooks sat immediately behind him. When she stepped forward to take the oath of office, her only thought was to wish that Richard were there by her side to remind her she was getting closer and closer. Glancing sideways at Pete Parkin, she concluded that Richard would still have voted Republican.

The Chief Justice, William Rehnquist, gave her a warm smile as she repeated after him the oath of office for the Vice-President.

'"I do solemnly swear that I will support and defend the Constitution of the United States against all enemies, foreign and domestic...."'

Florentyna's words sounded clear and confident, perhaps because she had learned the oath by heart. Annabel winked at her as she returned to her seat amid deafening applause.

After the Chief Justice administered the Presidential oath to Parkin, Florentyna listened intently as America's new chief executive delivered his Inaugural Address about which she had not been consulted and hadn't even seen in final draft until the night before. Once again he referred to her as the greatest little lady in the land.

After the Inauguration ceremony was over, Parkin, Brooks and Florentyna joined Congressional leaders for lunch in the Capitol. Her Senate colleagues gave Florentyna a warm welcome when she took her place on the dais. After lunch they climbed into limousines for the drive down Pennsylvania Avenue that would lead the Inaugural parade. Sitting in the enclosed viewing stand in front of the White House Florentyna watched the floats, marching bands and assorted governors roll by representing every one of the fifty states. She stood and applauded when the farmers of Illinois saluted her, and then after making a token visit to every one of the Inaugural balls she spent her first night in the Vice-President's house and realized the closer she got to the top, the more alone she became.

. . .

The next morning, the President held his first cabinet meeting. This time Ralph Brooks sat on his right-hand side. The group, visibly tired from the seven Inaugural balls the night before, assembled in the Cabinet Room. Florentyna sat at the far end of the long oval table, surrounded by men with whose views she had rarely been in accord in the past, aware that she was going to have to spend four years battling against them before she could hope to form her own cabinet. She wondered how many of them knew about her deal with Parkin.

. . .

As soon as Florentyna had settled into her wing of the White House, she appointed Janet as head of her personal office. Many of the positions left vacant by Parkin's staff she also filled with her old team from the campaign and Senate days.

Of the remaining staff she inherited, she quickly learned how valuable their skills and special qualifications would have been had they not disappeared one by one as the President offered them executive branch jobs. Within three months, Parkin had denuded her office of all the most competent staff, even reaching into her inner circle of advisers.

Florentyna tried not to show her anger when the President offered Janet the position of Under Secretary of the Department of Health and Human Service.

Janet didn't hesitate over the new opportunity: and in a handwritten letter to the President she accepted the great compliment he had paid her but explained in detail why she felt unable to consider any government position other than to serve the Vice-President.

'If you can wait four years, so can I,' she explained.

. . .

Florentyna had often read that the life of the Vice-President was, to quote John Nance Garner, 'not worth a bucketful of warm spit', but even she was surprised to find how little real work she had to do compared with her days in Congress. She had received more letters when she had been a Senator. Everyone seemed to write to the President or their Congressman. Even the people had worked out that the Vice-President had no power. Florentyna enjoyed presiding over the Senate for important debates, because it kep her in contact with colleagues who would be helping her again in four years' time. They made sure she was aware of what was being said covertly in the halls of Congress, as well as on the House and Senate floor. Many Senators used her to get messages through to the President, but as time went by she began to wonder whom she should use for the same purpose, as the days turned into weeks in which Pete Parkin did not bother to consult her on any major issue.

During her first year as Vice-President, Florentyna made goodwill tours to Brazil and Japan, attended the funerals of Willy Brandt in Berlin and

Edward Heath in London, carried out on-site inspections of three natural disasters and chaired so many special task forces that she felt qualified to publish her own guide to how the government works.

The first year went slowly, the second even slower. The only highlight was being sent to represent the government at the crowning of King Charles III in Westminster Abbey after Queen Elizabeth II's abdication in 1994. Florentyna stayed with Ambassador John Sawyer at Winfield House, conscious of how similar their respective roles were in the matter of form over substance. She seemed to spend hours chatting about how the world was run and what the President was doing on subjects such as the building up of Russian troops on the Pakistan border. She gained most of her information from the *Washington Post* and envied Ralph Brooks's real involvement as Secretary of State. Although she kept herself well informed as to what was going on in the world at large, for only the second time in her life she was bored. She longed for 1996, fearing her years as Vice-President would yield very few positive results.

. . .

Once *Air Force II* had landed back at Andrews, Florentyna returned to her work and spent the rest of the week checking through the State and CIA traffic that had piled up in her absence abroad. She rested over the weekend despite CBS informing the public that the dollar had suffered as a result of the international crisis. The Russians were massing more forces on the Pakistan border, a fact which the President had dismissed in his weekly press conference as 'not of great importance'. The Russians, he assured the assembled journalists, were not interested in crossing any borders into countries that had treaties with the United States.

During the following week the panic seemed to subside and the dollar recovered. 'It's a cosmetic recovery' — Florentyna pointed out to Janet — 'caused by the Russians. The international brokers are reporting that the Bank of Moscow is selling gold which is exactly what they did before invading Afghanistan. I do wish bankers would not treat history on a week-to-week basis.'

Although several politicians and journalists contacted Florentyna to stress their fears, she could only placate them as she watched proceedings from the wings. She even considered making an appointment to see the President but by Friday evening most Americans were on their way home for a peaceful weekend convinced the immediate danger had passed. Florentyna remained in her office in the West Wing that Friday evening and read through the cables from ambassadors and agents on the Indian sub-continent. The more she read the more she felt unable to share the President's relaxed stance. As there was very little she could do about it, she neatly stacked up the papers, put them into a special red folder and prepared to go home. She checked her watch. Six thirty-two. Edward had flown down from New York, and she was due to join him for dinner at seven thirty. She was laughing about the thought of filing her own papers when Janet rushed into the office.

'There's an intelligence report that the Russians are mobilizing,' she said.

'Where's the President?' was Florentyna's immediate reaction.

'I've no idea. I saw him leaving the White House by helicopter about three hours ago.'

Florentyna reopened her file and stared back down at the cables while Janet remained standing in front of her desk.

'Well, who *will* know where he is?'

'You can be sure Ralph Brooks does,' said Janet.

'Get me the Secretary of State on the line.'

Janet left for her own office while Florentyna checked through the reports again. She quickly went over the salient points raised by the American ambassador in Islamabad before rereading the assessments of General Pierce Dixon, the chairman of the joint chiefs of staff.

The Russians, it was reliably documented, now had ten divisions of troops on the Afghanistan-Pakistan border and their forces had been multiplying over the past few days. It was known that half their Pacific fleet was sailing towards Karachi, while two battlegroups were carrying out 'exercises' in the Indian Ocean. General Dixon directed an increased intelligence watch when it was confirmed that fifty MIG 25s and SU 7s had landed at Kabul military airport at six that evening. Florentyna checked her watch: nine minutes past seven.

'Where is the bloody man?' she said out loud. Her phone buzzed.

'The Secretary of State on the line for you,' said Janet. Florentyna waited for several seconds.

'What can I do for you?' asked Ralph Brooks, sounding as if Florentyna had interrupted him.

'Where is the President?' she asked for a third time.

'At this moment he's on *Air Force I*,' said Brooks quickly.

'Stop lying, Ralph. It's transparent, even on the phone. Now tell me where the President is.'

'Halfway to California.'

'If we have the Soviets on the move and an increased intelligence watch, why hasn't he been advised to return?'

'We have advised him, but he has to land to refuel.'

'As you well know, *Air Force I* doesn't need to refuel for that length of journey.'

'He isn't on *Air Force I*.'

'Why the hell not?'

No reply came.

'I suggest you level with me, Ralph, even if it's only to save your own skin.'

There was a further pause.

'He was on his way to see a friend in California when the crisis broke.'

'I don't believe it,' said Florentyna. 'Who does he think he is? The President of France?'

'I have everything under control,' said Brooks, ignoring her comment. 'His plane will touch down at Colorado airport in a few minutes' time. The President will immediately transfer to an Air Force F15 and be back in Washington within two hours.'

'What type of aircraft is he on at the moment?' asked Florentyna.

'A private 737 owned by Marvin Snyder of Blade Oil.'

'Can the President enter the secure National Command System network from the plane?' asked Florentyna. No reply was forthcoming. 'Did you hear what I said?' she rapped out.

'Yes,' said Ralph. 'The truth is that the plane doesn't have complete security.'

'Are you telling me that over the next two hours any ham radio enthusiast could tune into a conversation between the President and the chairman of the joint chiefs of staff?'

'Yes,' admitted Ralph.

'I'll see you in the Situation Room,' said Florentyna, and slammed down the phone.

She came out of her office almost on the run. Two surprised Secret Service officers quickly followed her as she headed down the narrow staircase past small portraits of former Presidents. Washington faced her on the bottom of the stairs before she turned into the wide corridor that led to the Situation Room. The security guard already had the door open that led into the secretarial section. She passed through a room of buzzing telexes and noisy typewriters while yet another security man opened the oak-panelled door of the Situation Room for her. Her Secret Service men remained outside as she marched in.

Ralph Brooks was seated in the President's chair giving orders to a bevy of military personnel. Four of the remaining nine seats were already occupied – around a table that almost took up the whole room. Immediately to the right of Brooks sat the Secretary of Defence, Charles Selover, and on his right the Director of the CIA, Paul Rowe. Opposite them sat the chairman of the joint chiefs of staff, General Dixon, and the National Security Adviser, Michael Brewer. The door at the end of the room that led into the Communications area was wide open.

Brooks swung around to face her. Florentyna had never seen him with his coat off and a shirt button undone.

'No panic,' he said. 'I'm on top of everything. I'm confident the Russians won't make any move before the President returns.'

'I don't expect that's what the Russians have in mind,' said Florentyna. 'While the President is unexplainably absent, we must be prepared for them to make any move that suits them.'

'Well, it's not your problem, Florentyna. The President has left me in control.'

'On the contrary, it *is* my problem,' said Florentyna firmly refusing to take a seat. 'In the absence of the President the responsibility for all military matters passes to me.'

'Now listen, Florentyna, I'm running the shop, and I don't want you interfering.' The gentle buzz of conversation between personnel around the room came to an abrupt halt as Brooks stared angrily at Florentyna. She picked up the nearest phone. 'Put the Attorney-General on the screen.'

'Yes, ma'am,' said the operator.

A few seconds later Pierre Levale's face appeared on one of the six televisions encased in the oak panelling along the side of the wall.

'Good evening, Pierre, it's Florentyna Kane. We have an increased intelligence watch on our hands and for reasons I am not willing to discuss the President is indisposed. Will you make it clear to the Secretary of State who holds executive responsibility in such a situation?'

Everyone in the room stood still and stared up at the worried face on the screen. The lines on Pierre Levale's face had never been more pronounced. They all knew he had been a Parkin appointment, but he had shown on past occasions that he thought more highly of the rule of law than of the President.

'The Constitution is not always clear on these matters,' he began, 'especially after the Bush-Haig showdown, following the attempt on Ronald Reagan's life. But, in my judgement, in the President's absence all power is vested in the Vice-President, and that is how I would advise the Senate.'

'Thank you, Pierre,' said Florentyna still looking at the screen. 'Please put that in writing and see that a copy is on the President's desk immediately on completion.' The Attorney-General disappeared from the screen.

'Now that that's settled, Ralph, brief me quickly.'

Brooks reluctantly vacated the President's chair, while a staff officer opened a small panel below the light switch by the door. He pressed a button and the beige curtain that stretched along the wall behind the President's chair opened. A large screen came down from the ceiling with a map of the world on it.

Charles Selover, the Secretary of Defence, rose from his chair as different coloured lights shone all over the map. 'The lights indicate the position of all known hostile forces,' he said as Florentyna swung around to face the map. 'The red ones are submarines, the green ones aircraft, and the blue ones full army divisions.'

'A West Point plebe looking at that map could tell you exactly what the Russians have in mind,' said Florentyna, as she stared at the mass of red lights in the Indian Ocean, green lights at Kabul airport and blue lights stretched along Afghanistan's border with Pakistan.

Paul Rowe then confirmed that the Russians had been massing armies on the Pakistan border for several days and within the last hour a coded message from a CIA agent behind the lines suggested that the Soviets intended to cross the border of Pakistan at ten o'clock Eastern Standard Time. He handed her a set of decoded cables and answered each of her questions as they arose.

'The President told me,' said Brooks pointedly when Florentyna had read the final message, 'that he feels Pakistan is not another Poland and that the Russians wouldn't dare to go beyond the Afghanistan border.'

'I think we are about to find out if his judgement is sound,' she said.

'The President,' he added, 'has been in touch with Moscow during the week, as well as the Prime Minister of England, the President of France and the West German Chancellor. They all seem to agree with his assessment.'

'Since then the situation has changed radically,' said Florentyna sharply. 'It's obvious that I shall have to speak to the Soviet President myself.'

Once again Brooks hesitated. 'Immediately,' Florentyna added. Brooks picked up the phone. Everyone in the room waited while the circuit was linked. Florentyna had never spoken to President Andropov before and she could feel her heart beating. She knew her phone would be monitored to pick up the slightest reaction she unwittingly displayed, as it would be for the Soviet leader. It was always said that it was this device that had enabled the Russians to run roughshod over Jimmy Carter.

A few minutes later Andropov came on the line. 'Good evening, Mrs Kane,' he said, not acknowledging her title, his voice as clear as if he were in the next room. After four years at the Court of St James the Russian President's accent was minimal and his command of the language impressive. 'May I ask where President Parkin is?'

Florentyna could feel her mouth go dry. The Soviet President continued before she could reply.

'In California with his mistress, no doubt.' It didn't surprise Florentyna that the Russian President knew more about Parkin's movements than she did. It was now obvious why the Russians had chosen ten o'clock to cross the Pakistan border.

'You're right,' said Florentyna. 'And as he will be indisposed for at least another two hours you will have to deal with me. I therefore wish you to be left in no doubt that I am taking full Presidential responsibility in his absence.' She could feel small beads of sweat but didn't dare to touch her forehead.

'I see,' said the former head of the KGB. 'Then may I ask what is the purpose of this call?'

'Don't be naïve, Mr President. I want you to understand that if you put one member of your armed forces over the border with Pakistan, America will retaliate immediately.'

'That would be very brave of you, Mrs Kane,' he said.

'You obviously don't understand the American political system, Mr President. It requires no "bravery" at all. As Vice-President I am the one person in America who has nothing to lose and everything to gain.' This time the silence was not of her making. Florentyna felt her confidence growing. He had given her the chance to continue before he could reply. 'If you do not turn your battle fleet south, withdraw all ten army divisions from the border with Pakistan and fly your MIG 25s and SU 7s back to Moscow, I shall not hesitate to attack you on land, sea and air. Do you understand?'

The phone went dead.

Florentyna swivelled around.

By now the room was a buzz again with professionals who had previously only played 'games' in this situation and now waited like Florentyna to see if all their training, experience and knowledge was about to be tested.

Ralph Brooks held a hand over the mouthpiece of his phone and reported that the President had landed in Colorado and wanted to speak to Florentyna. She picked up the red security phone by her side.

'Florentyna? Is that you?' came down the phone in a broad Texas accent.

'Yes, Mr President.'

'Now hear me, lady. Ralph has briefed me and I am on my way back immediately. I'll be with you in under two hours. So don't do anything rash – and be sure the press don't get to hear of my absence.'

'Yes, Mr President.' The phone went dead.

'General Dixon?' she said, not bothering to look at Brooks.

'Yes, ma'am,' said the four-star general who had not spoken until then.

'How quickly can we mobilize a retaliatory force into the battle area?' she asked the chief of staff.

'Within the hour, I could have ten squadrons of F 111's in the air from our bases in Europe, directed towards targets in the USSR. The Mediterranean Fleet is in almost constant contact with the Russians, but perhaps we should move it closer to the Indian Ocean.'

'How long would it take to reach the Indian Ocean?'

'Two to four days, ma'am.'

'Then issue the order, General. And, if possible, make it two.'

Florentyna didn't have to wait long for the next report to come up on the screen. It was the one she feared most. The Russian fleet still ploughed on relentlessly towards Karachi while more and more Soviet divisions were massing at Salabad and Asadabadon on the Afghanistan border.

'Get me the President of Pakistan,' said Florentyna.

He was on the line in moments.

'Where is President Parkin?' was his first question.

'Not you as well?' Florentyna wanted to say, but in fact replied. 'On his way back from Camp David. He will be with us shortly.' She briefed him on the actions she had taken to date and made it clear how far she was willing to go.

'Thank God for one brave man,' said Murbaze Bhutto.

'Just stay on the open line and we will keep you briefed if anything changes,' said Florentyna, ignoring the compliment

'Shall I get the Russian President back?' asked Ralph Brooks.

'No,' said Florentyna. 'Get me the Prime Minister of Britain, the President of France and the Chancellor of West Germany.'

She checked her watch: seven thirty-five. Within twenty minutes Florentyna had spoken to all three leaders. The British agreed to her plan, the French were sceptical but would cooperate, while the Germans were unhelpful.

The next piece of information Florentyna received was that Russian MIG 25s at Kabul Military Airport were being prepared for take-off.

Immediately she ordered General Dixon to place all forces on standby. Brooks leaned forward to protest but by then everyone present had placed their careers in the hands of one woman. Many of them watched her closely and noted she showed no emotion.

General Dixon came back into the Situation Room. 'Ma'am, the F 111's are now ready for take-off, the Sixth Fleet is steaming full speed towards the Indian Ocean and a brigade of paratroopers can be dropped at Landi Kotal on to the borders of Pakistan within six hours.'

'Good,' said Florentyna quietly. The telex continued to rap out the message that the Russians were still advancing on every front.

'Don't you think we should renew contact with Andropov before it's too late?' asked Brooks. Florentyna noticed his hands were shaking.

'Why should we contact him? I have nothing to add. If we turn back now it will always be too late,' said Florentyna quietly.

'But we must try to negotiate a compromise, or by this time tomorrow the President will look like a jackass,' said Brooks standing over her.

'Why?' asked Florentyna.

'Because in the end you will have to give in.'

Florentyna made no reply but swivelled back in her chair to face General Dixon who was standing by her side.

'In one hour, ma'am, we will be over Soviet airspace.'

'Understood,' said Florentyna.

Ralph Brooks picked up the ringing phone by his side. General Dixon returned to the Operations Room.

'The President is preparing to land at Andrews Air Force Base. He'll be with us in twenty minutes,' Brooks told Florentyna. 'talk to the Russians and tell them to back off until he returns.'

'No,' said Florentyna. 'If the Russians don't turn back now you can be certain they will let the whole world know exactly where the President was at the moment they crossed the Afghanistan border. In any case I am still convinced they will turn back.'

'You've gone mad, Florentyna,' he shouted, rising from his chair.

'I don't think I have ever been saner,' she replied.

'Do you imagine the American people will thank you for involving them in a war over Pakistan?' asked Brooks.

'It's not Pakistan we're discussing,' said Florentyna. 'India will be next, followed by West Germany, France, Britain and finally Canada. And you, Ralph, would still be looking for excuses to avoid any confrontation even when the Soviets were marching down Constitution Avenue.'

'If that's your attitude I wash my hands of the whole affair,' said Brooks.

'And no doubt you will receive the same footnote in history as the last person who carried out that ignominious act.'

'Then I shall tell the President you overruled me and countermanded my orders,' said Brooks, his voice rising with every word.

Florentyna looked up at the handsome man who was now red in the face. 'Ralph, if you're going to wet your pants, can you please go and do it in the little boys' room and not the Situation Room?'

Brooks stormed out.

'Twenty-seven minutes to go, and still no sign of the Russians turning back,' whispered Dixon in her ear. A message came through on the telex that the fifty MIG 25s and Su 7s were taking off and would be over Pakistan air space within thirty-four minutes.

General Dixon was back by her side. 'Twenty-three minutes, ma'am.'

'How do you feel, General?' Florentyna tried to sound relaxed.

'Better than the day I marched into Berlin as a lieutenant, ma'am.'

Florentyna asked a staff major to check all three networks. She began to realize what Kennedy had been through over Cuba. The major pressed some buttons in front of him. CBS was showing a Popeye cartoon, NBC a basketball game and ABC an old Ronald Reagan movie. She checked through everything on the little TV screen once again but there was no change. Now she could only pray she would be given enough time to be proved right. She sipped at a cup of coffee that had been left at her elbow. It tasted bitter. She pushed it to one side as President Parkin stormed into the room, followed by Brooks. The President was wearing an open-necked shirt, a sports jacket and check trousers.

'What the hell is going on?' were his first words. Florentyna had stepped out of the President's chair, when General Dixon came forward.

'Twenty minutes to go ma'am.'

'Now brief me quickly, Florentyna,' demanded Parkin, taking his place in the President's chair. She sat down on the President's right and told him what she had done right up to the moment he walked in.

'You fool,' he shouted when she had finished. 'Why didn't you listen to Ralph? He would never have got us into this trouble.'

'I am aware of exactly what the Secretary of State would have done presented with the same set of circumstances,' said Florentyna coldly.

'General Dixon,' said the President, turning his back on Florentyna. 'What is the exact position of your forces?' the general briefed President Parkin. Maps continually flashing up on the screen behind him showed the latest Russian position.

'In sixteen minutes' time the F 111 bombers will be over enemy territory.'

'Get me the President of Pakistan,' said Parkin, banging the table in front of him.

'He's holding on an open line,' said Florentyna quietly.

The President grabbed the phone, hunched his shoulders over the table and started speaking in a confidential tone.

'I'm sorry it's worked out this way, but I have no choice but to reverse the Vice-President's decision. She didn't understand the full implication of her actions. Now I don't want you to feel that we are deserting you. Be assured we will negotiate a peaceful withdrawal from your territory at the first possible opportunity,' said Parkin.

'For God's sake you can't desert us now,' said Bhutto.

'I must do what is best for all of us,' replied Parkin.

'Like you did in Afghanistan.'

Parkin ignored the comment and slammed down the phone.

'General?'

'Yes, sir,' said Dixon stepping forward.

'How much time have I got?'

He looked up at the small digital clock, suspended from the ceiling in front of him. 'Eleven minutes and eighteen seconds,' he said.

'Now listen and listen carefully. The Vice-President took on too much responsibility in my absence and I must now find a way out of this mess without egg landing on all our faces. I'm sure you agree, General.'

'Anything you say, Mr President, but in the circumstances I'd stick with it.'

'There are wider considerations that go beyond the military. So I want you to –'

A yell went up from the far side of the room from a hitherto unknown colonel. For a moment he stopped even the President speaking.

'What is it?' shouted Parkin.

The colonel now stood to attention. 'The Russian fleet has turned back and is now heading south,' he said, reading a cable.

The President was speechless. The colonel continued, 'The MIG 25s and Su 7s are flying north-west to Moscow.' A cheer went up drowning the rest of the colonel's pronouncement. Telexes buzzed out confirmation all over the room.

'General,' said Parkin, turning to the chairman of the joint chiefs, 'we've won. It's a triumphant day for you and America.' He hesitated for a moment before adding, 'And I want to know that I'm proud to have led my country through this hour of peril.'

No one in the Situation Room laughed, and Brooks quickly added, 'Congratulations, Mr President.' Everyone started cheering again, while several personnel walked over to congratulate Florentyna.

'General, bring your boys home. They've carried out a fantastic operation. Congratulations, you too did a great job.'

'Thank you, Mr President,' said General Dixon. 'But I feel the praise should go to –'

The President turned to Ralph Brooks and said, 'This calls for a celebration, Ralph. All of you will remember this day for the rest of your lives. The day we showed the world America couldn't be pushed around.'

Florentyna was now standing in the corner as if she had had nothing to do with what had happened in that room. She left a few minutes later as the President continually ignored her. She returned to her office on the first floor and put away the red file, slamming the cabinet closed, before returning home. No wonder Richard had never voted Democrat.

.   .   .

'A gentleman's been waiting for you since seven thirty,' were the first words the butler said when she returned to her home on Observatory Circle.

'Good God,' said Florentyna out loud and rushed through to the drawing room where she found Edward, eyes closed, slumped on the sofa in front of the fire. She kissed him on the forehead and he woke immediately.

'Ah, my dear, been rescuing the world from a fate worse than death, no doubt?'

'Something like that,' said Florentyna pacing up and down as she told Edward everything that had happened at the White House that evening. Edward had never seen her so angry.

'Well, I'll say one thing for Pete Parkin,' Edward said, when she had reached the end of her story, 'he's consistent.'

'He won't be after tomorrow.'

'What do you mean?'

'Precisely that. Because I'm going to hold a press conference in the morning to let everybody know exactly what happened. I'm sick and tired of his devious and irresponsible behaviour, and I know that most people who were in the Situation Room tonight will confirm everything I've told you.'

'That would be both rash and irresponsible,' said Edward, staring into the fire in front of him.

'Why?' asked Florentyna, surprised.

'Because America would be left with a lame-duck President. You might be the hero of the hour, but within days you would be despised.'

'But –' began Florentyna.

'No buts. On this occasion you will have to swallow your pride and be satisfied with using what happened tonight as a weapon to remind Parkin of his agreement over the one-term presidency.'

'And let him get away with it?'

'And let *America* get away with it,' said Edward, firmly.

Florentyna continued pacing and didn't speak for several minutes. 'You're right,' she said finally. 'I was being short-sighted. Thank you.'

'So might I have been if I had experienced what you went through at first hand.'

Florentyna laughed. 'Come on,' she said and stopped pacing for the first time. 'Let's have something to eat. You must be starving.'

'No, no,' said Edward, looking at his watch. 'Although I must confess, VP, that you're the first girl who's kept me waiting three and a half hours for a dinner date.'

. . .

Early the next morning the President phoned her.

'That was a great job you did yesterday, Florentyna, and I appreciate the way you carried out the earlier part of the operation.'

'You hardly showed it at the time, Mr President,' she said, barely controlling her anger.

'I intend to address the nation today,' said Parkin, ignoring Florentyna's comment, 'and although this isn't the time to tell them I shall not be seeking re-election, when the time does come I shall remember your loyalty.'

'Thank you, Mr President,' was all Florentyna could manage to say.

The President addressed the nation at eight o'clock that night on all three networks. Other than a passing mention of Florentyna he left the distinct impression that he had been in complete control of operations when the Russians turned back.

One or two national newspapers suggested that the Vice-President had been involved in the negotiations with the Russian leader, but as Florentyna was not available to confirm this Parkin's version went almost unchallenged.

Two days later Florentyna was sent to Paris for the funeral of Giscard d'Estaing. By the time she returned to Washington the public was worked up about the final game of the World Series and Parkin was a national hero.

. . .

With the first Primary little more than eight months away, she told Edward that the time had come to start planning for the 1996 Presidential campaign. To that end, Florentyna accepted invitations to speak all over America, and during the year she addressed voters in thirty-three states. She was delighted to find that wherever she went the public took it for granted she was going to be the next President. Her relationship with Pete Parkin remained cordial, but she had had to remind the President that the time was drawing near for him to make the announcement about his intentions to serve only one term in office, so that she could officially launch her campaign.

One Monday in July, when she had returned to Washington from a speaking engagement in Nebraska, she found a note from the President saying that he would be making those intentions clear in a statement to the nation that Thursday. Edward had already started work on a strategic outline for a '96 campaign so that, as soon as the President had announced that he would not be running again, the Kane effort would be ready to move into top gear.

'His timing is perfect, VP,' he said. 'We have fourteen months before the election campaign, and you needn't even declare you're the candidate before October.'

Florentyna sat alone in the Vice-President's office that Thursday evening waiting for the President to deliver his statement. The three networks were carrying his speech and all of them had talked of the rumour that, at sixty-five Parkin was not considering a second term. Florentyna waited impatiently as a camera panned down from the façade of the White House and into the Oval Office, where President Parkin sat behind his desk.

'My fellow Americans,' he began, 'I have always believed in keeping you informed of my plans as I do not want any speculation about my personal future, as to whether I shall be running again for this onerous office in fourteen months' time' – Florentyna smiled – 'I therefore wish to take this opportunity to make my intentions clear so that I can complete this session without involving myself in party politics.' Florentyna nearly leaped out of her seat in delight as Parkin now leaned forward in what the press referred to as 'his sincere stance' before continuing. 'The President's job is here in the Oval Office serving the people and to that end I announce that although I shall be a candidate for President at the next election, I will leave the electioneering to my Republican opponents while I continue to work for your best interests in the White House. I hope you will allow me the privilege of serving you for another four years. God bless you all.'

Florentyna was speechless for some moments. Finally she picked up the phone by her side and dialled the Oval Office. A woman's voice answered.

'I'm on my way to see the President immediately.' Florentyna slammed down the phone and walked out of her room towards the Oval Office.

The President's private secretary met her at the door. 'The President is in conference right now, but I expect him to be free at any moment.'

Florentyna paced up and down the corridor for thirty-seven minutes before she was finally shown in.

Her first words were, 'Pete Parkin. You're a liar and a cheat,' spitting out the words even before the door had closed.

'Now just a minute, Florentyna, I feel for the good of the nation ...'

'For the good of Pete Parkin, who can't keep his end of any bargain, God help this country. Well, I can tell you one thing, I am not willing to run as your Vice-President for a second term.'

'I'm sorry to hear that,' said the President, sitting down in his chair and making a note on the pad in front of him, 'but I naturally accept your decision with regret. Not that it would have made a lot of difference.'

'What do you mean?' said Florentyna.

'I wasn't intending to ask you to join me on the ticket for a second time, but you have made the whole problem a lot easier for me by refusing to be considered. The party will now understand why I had to look to someone else for the coming election.'

'You would lose the election if I ran against you.'

'No, Florentyna, we would both lose and the Republicans might even win the Senate and the House. That wouldn't make you the most popular little lady in town.'

'You won't get my backing in Chicago. No President has ever won the election without Illinois and they will never forgive you.'

'They might if I replaced one Senator from the state with another.'

Florentyna turned cold. 'You wouldn't dare,' she said.

'If I pick Ralph Brooks, I think you will find he's a popular enough choice. So will the people of Illinois when I say that I see him as my natural successor in five years' time.'

Florentyna left without another word. She must have been the only person who had ever slammed the Oval Office door.

38

When Florentyna went over the details of the Parkin meeting for Edward the following Saturday on the golf course at Cape Cod, he confessed that the news came as no great surprise.

'He may not be much of a President, but he knows more about Machiavellian politics than Nixon and Johnson put together.'

'I should have listened to you in Detroit when you warned me this would happen.'

'What did your father always say about Henry Osborne? Once a skunk, always a skunk.'

There was a slight breeze and Florentyna threw a few blades of grass into the air to determine its direction. Satisfied, she took a ball from her golf bag, set it up and hit a long drive. To her surprise the wind took the ball slightly to the right and into some brush.

'Didn't properly anticipate the wind, VP, did you?' volunteered Edward. 'I can only believe this must be my day to beat you, Florentyna.' He hit his ball right down the centre of the fairway, but twenty yards shorter than Florentyna's.

'Things are bad, Edward, but not yet that bad,' she said, smiling, and proceeded to take the first hole with a chip out of the rough and a long putt.

'Early days,' said Edward, as they were about to tee off on the second hole. He asked Florentyna about her future plans.

'Parkin is right: I can't make a fuss as such an outburst would only play into the hands of the Republicans; so I have decided to be realistic about my future.'

'And what does that mean?'

'I'll see this fourteen months out as Vice-President and then I'd like to return to New York as chairman of the Baron Group. I've had an almost unique view of the company since my continual travelling around the globe, and I think I shall be able to institute some new ideas that could put us far ahead of any of our competitors.'

'Then it sounds as though we have an interesting time ahead of us,'

Edward said, smiling as he joined her to walk to the second green. He tried to concentrate on his game while Florentyna went on talking.

'I would also like to join the board of Lester's. Richard always wanted me to find out how a bank worked from the inside. He never stopped telling me he paid his directors a higher salary than the President of the United States.'

'You'll have to consult William on that, not me.'

'Why?' asked Florentyna.

'Because he's taking over as chairman on 1 January next year. He knows more about banking than I ever will. He's inherited all Richard's natural instincts for high finance. I'll stay on as a director for a few more years, but I'm confident that the bank couldn't be in better hands.'

'Is he old enough for such a responsibility?'

'Same age as you were when you first became chairman of the Baron Group,' said Edward.

'Well, at least we'll have one President in the family,' Florentyna said as she missed a two-foot putt.

'One hole each, VP.' Edward marked his card and studied the two hundred and ten yard dog-leg that lay in front of him. 'Now I know how you intend to occupy half of your time. So do you have anything planned for the other half?'

'Yes,' said Florentyna. 'The Remagen Trust has lacked direction since the death of Professor Ferpozzi. I have decided to head it up myself. Do you know how much the trust has on deposit nowadays?'

'No, but it would only take one phone call to find out,' said Edward, trying to concentrate on his swing.

'I'll save you a quarter,' said Florentyna. 'Twenty-nine million dollars, bringing in an annual income of nearly four million dollars. Edward, the time has come to build the first Remagen University with major scholarships for the children of first-generation immigrants.'

'And remember, VP, gifted children, whatever their background,' said Edward, teeing up.

'You're sounding more and more like Richard every day,' she laughed.

Edward swung. 'I wish my golf was as good as his,' he added as he watched his little white ball head high and far before hitting a tree.

Florentyna didn't seem to notice. And after she had hit her ball firmly down the middle of the fairway, hey both walked off in different directions. They could not continue their conversation until they had reached the green where Florentyna went on talking about where the new university would be built, how many students it should admit in its first year, who should be the first President. She ended up losing the third and fourth holes. Florentyna began to concentrate on her game but still had to scramble to square the match by the ninth.

'I shall be particularly pleased to give your hundred dollars to the Republican party today,' Florentyna said. 'Nothing would give me more pleasure than seeing Parkin and Brooks bite the dust.'

Florentyna sighed as she hit a bad short iron from the tee towards the tenth green.

'I'm far from beaten yet,' said Edward.

Florentyna ignored him. 'What a waste my years in government have been,' she said.

'No, I can't agree with that,' said Edward, still practising his swings. 'Six years in Congress, a further eight in the Senate and ending up the first woman Vice-President. And I suspect history will ultimately record your role over the invasion of Pakistan far more accurately than Parkin has felt necessary. Even if you have achieved less than you'd hoped, you've made the task a lot easier for the next woman who wants to go the whole way. Ironically I believe if you were the Democratic candidate at the next election, you would win easily.'

'The public opinion polls certainly agree with you.' Florentyna tried to concentrate, but sliced her tee shot. 'Damn,' she said as her ball disappeared into the woods.

'You're not at the top of your game today, VP,' said Edward. He proceeded to win the tenth and eleventh holes but then threw away the twelfth and thirteenth with over-anxious putts.

'I think we should build a Baron in Moscow,' said Florentyna when they had reached the fourteenth green. 'That was always my father's ultimate ambition. Did I ever tell you that the Minister for Tourism, Mikhail Zokovlov, had long tried to interest me in the idea? I have to go on that frightful culture trip to Moscow next month which will be a wonderful opportunity to discuss the idea with him in greater detail. Thank God for the Bolshoi Ballet, borsch and caviar. At least they've never tried to get me in bed with some handsome young man.'

'Not while they know about our golf deal,' chuckled Edward.

They split the fourteenth and fifteenth and Edward won the sixteenth hole. 'We are about to discover what you are like under pressure,' said Florentyna.

Edward proceeded to lose the seventeenth by missing a putt of only three feet so that the match rested on the last hole. Florentyna drove well, but Edward, thanks to a lucky bounce off the edge of a small rise, came within a few feet of her. He put his second shot only twenty yards from the green and found it hard to suppress a smile as they walked down the centre of the fairway together.

'You have a long way to go yet, Edward,' said Florentyna, as she sent her ball flying into a sand trap.

Edward laughed.

'I would remind you how good I am with a sand wedge and putter,' said Florentyna, and proved her point by pitching the ball only four feet from the hole.

Edward chipped up from twenty yards to within six feet.

'This may be the last chance you'll ever have,' she said.

Edward held his putter firmly and jabbed at the ball and watched it teeter on the edge of the hole before disappearing into the cup. He threw his club high into the air and cheered.

'You haven't won yet,' said Florentyna, 'but no doubt it will be the nearest you'll ever get.' She steadied herself as she checked the line between ball and hole. If she sank her putt, the match was halved and she was off the hook.

'Don't let the helicopters distract you,' Edward said.

'The only thing that is distracting me, Edward, is you. Be warned, you will not succeed. Since the rest of my life depends on this shot, you can be assured that I shall not make a mistake. In fact,' she said, taking a step back, 'I shall wait until the helicopters have passed over.'

Florentyna stared up into the sky and waited for the four helicopters to fly past. Their chopping noise grew louder and louder.

'Did you have to go to quite such lengths to win, Edward?' she asked as one of the helicopters began to descend.

'What the hell is going on?' said Edward anxiously.

'I have no idea,' said Florentyna. 'But I suspect we are about to find out.'

Her skirt whipped around her legs as the first helicopter landed a few yards off the green of the eighteenth hole. Even as the blades continued to rotate an army colonel leaped out and rushed over to Florentyna. A second officer jumped out and stood by the helicopter, carrying a small black briefcase. Florentyna and Edward stared at the colonel as he stood to attention and saluted.

'Madam President,' he said. 'The President is dead.'

Florentyna clenched her hand into a tight fist as the eighteenth hole was surrounded by agents from the Secret Service. She glanced again at the black nuclear command briefcase which was now her sole responsibility, the trigger she hoped she would never have to pull. It was only the second time in her life she felt what real responsibility meant.

'How did it happen?' she asked calmly.

The colonel continued in clipped tones. 'The President returned from his morning jog and retired to his room to shower and change for breakfast. It was over twenty minutes before any of us felt that something might be wrong so I was sent to check, but it was already too late. The doctor said he must have had a massive coronary. He has had two minor heart attacks during the last year, but on both occasions we managed to keep them out of the press.'

'How many people know of his death?'

'Three members of his personal staff, his doctor, Mrs Parkin and the Attorney-General, whom I informed immediately. On his instructions, I was detailed to find you and see that the oath of office is administered as quickly as is convenient. I am then to accompany you to the White House where the Attorney-General is waiting to announce the details of the President's death. The Attorney-General hopes that these arrangements meet with your approval.'

'Thank you, Colonel. We had better return to my home immediately.'

Florentyna, accompanied by Edward, the colonel, the officer with the black box and four Secret Service agents, climbed aboard the Army aircraft. As the chopper whirled up into the air, Florentyna gazed down at the eighteenth green where her ball, a diminishing white speck, remained four feet from the hole. A few minutes later, the helicopter landed on the grass in front of Florentyna's Cape Cod house while the other three remained hovering overhead.

Florentyna led them all into the living room, where young Richard was playing with his father and Bishop O'Reilly, who had flown in for a quiet weekend.

'Why are there helicopters flying over the house, Grandma?' Richard asked.

Florentyna explained to her grandson what had happened. William and Joanna rose from their chairs, not sure what to say.

'What do we do next, Colonel?' asked Florentyna.

'We'll need a Bible,' said the colonel, 'and the oath of office.'

Florentyna went to her study table in the corner of the room and from the top drawer took out Miss Tredgold's Bible. A copy of the Presidential oath was not as easy to find. Edward thought it might be in Theodore White's *The Making of the President: 1972*, which he remembered was in the library. He was right.

The colonel phoned the Attorney-General, and checked that the wording was correct. Pierre Levale then spoke to Bishop O'Reilly and explained how he should administer the oath.

In the living room of her Cape Cod home, Florentyna Kane stood beside her family, with Colonel Max Perkins and Edward Winchester acting as witnesses. She took the Bible in her right hand and repeated the words after Bishop O'Reilly.

'I, Florentyna Kane, do solemnly swear that I will faithfully execute the office of President of the United States and will to the best of my ability, preserve, protect and defend the Constitution of the United States, so help me God.'

Thus Florentyna Kane became the forty-third President of the United States.

William was the first to congratulate his mother and then they all tried to join in at once.

'I think we should leave for Washington, Madam President,' the colonel suggested a few minutes later.

'Of course.' Florentyna turned to the old family priest. 'Thank you, Monsignor,' she said. But the bishop did not reply; for the first time in his life, the little Irishman was lost for words. 'I shall need you to perform another ceremony for me in the near future.'

'And what might that be, my dear?'

'As soon as we have a free weekend Edward and I are going to be married.' Edward looked even more surprised and delighted than the moment he heard Florentyna had become President. 'I remembered a little too late,' she continued, 'that if you fail to complete a hole in match-play competition, it is automatically awarded to your opponent.'

Edward took her in his arms as Florentyna said, 'My darling, I will need your wisdom and your strength, but most of all your love.'

'You've had them for nearly forty years already, VP. I mean ...'

Everyone laughed.

'I think we should leave now, Madam President,' the colonel prompted. Florentyna nodded in agreement as the phone rang. Edward walked over to the desk and picked it up. 'It's Ralph Brooks. Says he needs to speak to you urgently.'

'Would you apologize to the Secretary of State, Edward, and explain I am not available at the moment.' Edward was about to convey the message when she added, 'And ask him if he would be kind enough to join me at the White House.'

Edward smiled as the forty-third President of the United States walked towards the door. The colonel accompanying her pressed a switch on his two-way radio and spoke softly into it: 'Baroness returning to Crown. The contract has been signed.'

NOT A PENNY MORE, NOT A PENNY LESS

To Mary and the fat men

Acknowledgments

I acknowledge all the help I received from so many people in writing this book and wish to thank them: David Niven, Jr., who made me do it, Sir Noel and Lady Hall who made it possible, Adrian Metcalfe, Anthony Rentoul, Colin Emson, Ted Francis, Godfrey Barker, Willy West, Madame Tellegen, David Stein, Christian Neffe, Dr John Vance, Dr David Weeden, the Rev. Leslie Styler, Robert Gasser, Professor Jim Bolton, and Jamie Clark; Gail and Jo for putting it together; and my wife, Mary, for the hours spent correcting and editing.

Prologue

'Jörg, expect $7 million from Crédit Parisien in the No. 2 account by 6 p.m. tonight, Central European time, and place it with first-class banks and triple "A" commercial names. Otherwise, invest it in the overnight Euro-dollar market. Understood?'

'Yes, Harvey.'

'Place $1 million in the Banco do Minas Gerais, Rio de Janeiro, in the names of Silverman and Elliott and cancel the call loan at Barclays Bank, Lombard Street. Understood?'

'Yes, Harvey.'

'Buy gold on my commodity account until it reaches $10 million and then hold until you receive further instructions. Try and buy in the troughs and don't rush – be patient. Understood?'

'Yes, Harvey.'

Harvey Metcalfe realized that the last instruction was unnecessary. Jörg Birrer was one of the most conservative bankers in Zürich and, more important to Harvey, had over the past twenty-five years proved to be one of the shrewdest.

'Can you join me at Wimbledon on Tuesday, June 25th at 2 p.m., Centre Court, my usual debenture seat?'

'Yes, Harvey.'

The telephone clicked into place. Harvey never said goodbye. He had never understood the niceties of life and it was too late to start learning now. He picked up the phone, dialled the seven digits which would give him the Lincoln Trust in Boston, and asked for his secretary.

'Miss Fish?'

'Yes, sir.'

'Remove the file on Prospecta Oil and destroy it. Destroy any correspondence connected with it and leave absolutely no trace. Understood?'

'Yes, sir.'

The telephone clicked again. Harvey Metcalfe had given similar orders three times in the last twenty-five years and by now Miss Fish had learnt not to question him.

Harvey breathed deeply, almost a sigh, a quiet exhalation of triumph. He was now worth at least $25 million, and nothing could stop him. He opened a bottle of Krug champagne 1964, imported from Hedges & Butler of London. He sipped it slowly and lit a Romeo y Julieta Churchill, which an Italian immigrant smuggled in for him in boxes of two hundred and fifty once a month from Cuba. He settled back for a mild celebration. In Boston, Massachusetts, it was 12.20 p.m. – nearly time for lunch.

. . .

In Harley Street, Bond Street, the King's Road and Magdalen College, Oxford, it was 6.20 p.m. Four men, unknown to each other, checked the market price of Prospecta Oil in the final edition of the London *Evening Standard*. It was £3.70. All four of them were rich men, looking forward to consolidating their already successful careers.

Tomorrow they would be penniless.

1

Making a million legally has always been difficult. Making a million illegally has always been a little easier. Keeping a million when you have made it is perhaps the most difficult of all. Henryk Metelski was one of those rare men who had managed all three. Even if the million he had made legally came after the million he had made illegally, Metelski was still a yard ahead of the others: he had managed to keep it all.

Henryk Metelski was born on the Lower East Side of New York on 17 May 1909, in a small room that already slept four children. He grew up through the Depression, believing in God and one meal a day. His parents were from Warsaw and had emigrated from Poland at the turn of the century. Henryk's father was a baker by trade and had soon found a job in New York, where immigrant Poles specialized in baking black rye bread and running small restaurants for their countrymen. Both parents would have liked Henryk to be an academic success, but he was never destined to become an outstanding pupil at his high school. His natural gifts lay elsewhere. A cunning, smart little boy, he was far more interested in the control of the underground school market in cigarettes and liquor than in stirring tales of the American Revolution and the Liberty Bell. Little Henryk never believed for one moment that the best things in life were free, and the pursuit of money and power came as naturally to him as the pursuit of a mouse to a cat.

When Henryk was a pimply and flourishing fourteen-year-old, his father died of what we now know to be cancer. His mother outlived her husband by no more than a few months, leaving the five children to fend for themselves. Henryk, like the other four, should have gone into the district orphanage for destitute children, but in the mid-1920s it was not hard for a boy to disappear in New York – though it was harder to survive. Henryk became a master of survival, a schooling which was to prove very useful to him in later life.

He knocked around the Lower East Side with his belt tightened and his eyes open, shining shoes here, washing dishes there, always looking for an entrance to the maze at the heart of which lay wealth and prestige. His first chance came when his room-mate Jan Pelnik, a messenger boy on the New York Stock Exchange, put himself temporarily out of action with a sausage garnished with salmonella. Henryk, deputed to report his friend's mishap to the Chief Messenger, upgraded food-poisoning to tuberculosis, and talked himself into the ensuing vacancy. He then changed his room, donned a new uniform, lost a friend, and gained a job.

Most of the messages Henryk delivered during the early 'twenties read 'Buy'. Many of them were quickly acted upon, for this was a boom era. He watched men of little ability make fortunes while he remained nothing more than an observer. His instincts directed him towards those individuals who made more money in a week on the Stock Exchange than he could hope to make in a lifetime on his salary.

He set about learning how to master the way the Stock Exchange operated, he listened to private conversations, opened sealed messages and found out which closed company reports to study. By the age of eighteen he had four years' experience of Wall Street: four years which most messenger boys would have spent simply walking across crowded floors, delivering little pink pieces of paper; four years which to Henryk Metelski were the equivalent of a Master's Degree from the Harvard Business School. He was not to know that one day he would lecture to that august body.

One morning in July 1927 he was delivering a message from Halgarten & Co., a well-established brokerage house, making his usual detour via the washroom. He had perfected a system whereby he could lock himself into a cubicle, study the message he was carrying, decide whether the information was of any value to him and if it was, immediately telephone Witold Gronowich, an old Pole who managed a small insurance firm for his fellow countrymen. Henryk reckoned to pick up an extra $20 to $25 a week for the inside knowledge he supplied. Gronowich, in no position to place large sums on the market, never let any of the leaks lead back to his young informant.

Sitting on the lavatory seat, Henryk began to realize that this time he was reading a message of considerable importance. The Governor of Texas was about to grant the Standard Oil Company permission to complete a pipeline from Chicago to Mexico, all other public bodies involved having already agreed to the proposal. The market was aware that the company had been trying to obtain this final permission for nearly a year, but the general view was that the Governor would turn it down. The message was to be passed direct to John D. Rockefeller's broker, Tucker Anthony, immediately. The granting of this permission to build a pipeline would open up the entire North to a ready supply of oil, and that could only mean increased profits. It was obvious to Henryk that Standard Oil stock must rise steadily on the market once the news had broken, especially as Standard Oil already controlled 90 per cent of the oil refineries in America.

In normal circumstances Henryk would have sent on this information direct to Mr Gronowich, and was about to do so when he noticed a rather overweight man who was also leaving the washroom, drop a piece of paper. As there was no one else about at the time, Henryk picked it up and retreated back into his private cubicle, thinking that at best it would reveal another piece of information. In fact, it was a cheque for $50,000 made out to cash from a Mrs Rose Rennick.

Henryk thought quickly, and not on his feet. He left the washroom at speed and was soon standing outside on Wall Street itself. He made his way to a small coffee-shop on Rector Street and sat there pretending to drink a Coca-Cola while he carefully worked out his plan. He then proceeded to act on it.

First, he cashed the cheque at a branch of the Morgan Bank on the south-west side of Wall Street, knowing that in his smart uniform as a messenger at the Exchange he would easily pass as a carrier for some distinguished firm. He then returned to the Exchange and acquired from a floor broker 2,500 Standard Oil shares at $19\frac{7}{8}$, leaving himself $126.61 change after brokerage charges. He placed the $126.61 in a Checking Account with the Morgan Bank. Then, waiting in tense anticipation for an announcement from the Governor's office, he put himself through the motions of a normal day's work, too preoccupied with Standard Oil even to make a detour via the washroom with the messages he carried.

No announcement came. Henryk could not know that the news was being held up until the Exchange had officially closed at 3 p.m. in order to allow the Governor himself to buy shares anywhere and everywhere he could lay his grubby hands on them. Henryk went home that night petrified that he had made a disastrous mistake. He had visions of losing his job and everything he had built up over the past four years. Perhaps he would even end up in jail.

He was unable to sleep that night and became steadily more restless in his small open-windowed but airless room. At 1 a.m. he could stand the uncertainty no longer, so he jumped out of bed, shaved, dressed and took a subway to Grand Central Station. From there he walked to Times Square where with trembling hands he bought the first edition of the Wall Street Journal. For a moment he couldn't take in the news, although it was shrieking at him in banner headlines:

GOVERNOR GRANTS OIL PIPE RIGHTS TO ROCKEFELLER

and a secondary headline:

HEAVY TRADING EXPECTED IN STANDARD OIL SHARES

Dazed, Henryk walked to the nearest all-night café, on West 42nd Street, and ordered a large hamburger and French fries, which he covered in ketchup and nibbled at like a man eating his last breakfast before facing the electric chair, rather than his first on the way to fortune. He read the full details of Rockefeller's coup on page one, which spread over to page fourteen, and by 4 a.m. he had bought the first three editions of the *New York Times* and the first two editions of the *Herald Tribune*. The lead story was the same in each. Henryk hurried home, giddy and elated, and changed into his uniform. He arrived at the Stock Exchange at 8 a.m. and went through the motions of a day's work, thinking only of how to carry out the second part of his plan.

When the Stock Exchange opened officially, Henryk went over to the Morgan Bank and requested a loan of $50,000 against the security of his 2,500 Standard Oil shares, which had opened that morning at $21\frac{1}{4}$. He placed the loan in his Checking Account and instructed the bank to issue him a draft for the $50,000 to be made out to Mrs Rose Rennick. He left the bank and looked up the address and telephone number of his un-witting benefactor.

Mrs Rennick, a widow who lived off the investments left by her late husband, lived in a small apartment on 62nd Street, which Henryk knew to be one of the most fashionable parts of New York. The call from a Henryk Metelski, asking to see her on an urgent private matter, came as something of a surprise to her, but a final mention of Halgarten & Co. gave her a little more confidence and she agreed to see him at the Waldorf-Astoria at 4 p.m. that afternoon.

Henryk had never been inside the Waldorf-Astoria, but after four years on the Stock Exchange there were few prominent hotels or restaurants he had not heard mentioned in other people's conversations. He realized that Mrs Rennick was more likely to have tea with him there than to see a man with a name like Henryk Metelski in her own apartment, especially as his Polish accent was more pronounced over the telephone than it was face to face.

As Henryk stood in the thickly carpeted lobby of the Waldorf, he blushed at his sartorial naïveté. Imagining that everybody was staring at him, he buried his short, amply-covered frame in an elegant chair in the Jefferson Room. Some of the other patrons of the Waldorf were amply covered too, but Henryk felt that *Pommes de Terre Maître d'Hôtel* were more likely to have caused their obesity than French fries. Vainly wishing he had put a little less grease on his black wavy hair and a little more on his down-at-heel shoes, he scratched nervously at an irritating pustule on the side of his mouth and waited. His suit, in which he felt so assured and prosperous among his friends, was shiny, skimpy, cheap and loud. He did not blend in with the décor, still less with the patrons of the hotel, and, feeling inadequate for the first time in his life, he picked up a copy of the *New Yorker*, hid behind it, and prayed for his guest to arrive quickly. Waiters fluttered deferentially around the well-provendered tables, ignoring Henryk with instinctive superciliousness. One, he noticed, did nothing more than circle the tearoom delicately proffering lump sugar from silver tongs in a white-gloved hand: Henryk was enormously impressed.

Rose Rennick arrived a few minutes after four, accompanied by two small dogs and wearing an outrageously large hat. Henryk thought she looked over sixty, overweight, overmade-up and overdressed, but she had a warm smile and appeared to know everyone, as she moved from table to table, chatting to the regular Waldorf-Astoria set. Eventually reaching what she had rightly assumed to be Henryk's table, she was rather taken aback, not only to find him so strangely dressed, but also looking even younger than his eighteen years.

Mrs Rennick ordered tea while Henryk recited his well-rehearsed story: there had been an unfortunate mistake with her cheque, which had been wrongly credited to his firm at the Stock Exchange on the previous day; his boss had instructed him to return the cheque immediately and to say how much they regretted the unfortunate error. Henryk then passed over the draft for $50,000 and added that he would lose his job if she insisted on taking the matter any further, as he had been entirely responsible for the mistake. Mrs Rennick had, in fact, only been informed of the missing cheque that morning and did not realize that it had been cashed, as it would have taken a few days to clear her account. Henryk's perfectly genuine anxiety as he stumbled through his tale would have convinced a far more critical observer of human nature than Mrs Rennick. Readily she agreed to let the matter drop, only too pleased to have her money returned; as it was in the form of a draft from the Morgan Bank, she had lost nothing. Henryk breathed a sigh of relief and for the first time that day began to relax and enjoy himself. He even called for the waiter with the sugar and silver tongs.

After a respectable period of time had passed, Henryk explained that he must return to work, thanked Mrs Rennick for her co-operation, paid the bill and left. Outside on the street he whistled with relief. His new shirt was soaked in sweat (Mrs Rennick would have called it perspiration), but he was out in the open and could breathe freely again. His first major operation had been a success.

He stood on Park Avenue, amused that the venue for his confrontation with Mrs Rennick had been the Waldorf, the very hotel where John D. Rockefeller, the President of Standard Oil, had a suite. Henryk had arrived on foot and used the main entrance, while Mr Rockefeller had earlier arrived by subway and taken his private lift to the Waldorf Towers. Although few New Yorkers were aware of it, Rockefeller had had his own private station built fifty feet below the Waldorf-Astoria to save him travelling the eight blocks to Grand Central Station, there being no stop between there and 125th Street. (The station remains to this day, but as no Rockefellers live at the Waldorf-Astoria, the train never stops there.) While Henryk had been discussing his $50,000 with Mrs Rennick, Rockefeller had been considering an investment of $5,000,000 with Andrew W. Mellon, President Coolidge's Secretary of the Treasury, fifty-seven floors above him.

The next morning Henryk returned to work as usual. He knew he had only five days' grace to sell the shares and clear his debt with the Morgan Bank and the stockbroker, as an account on the New York Stock Exchange runs for five business days or seven calendar days. On the last day of the account the shares were standing at $23\frac{1}{4}$. He sold at $23\frac{1}{8}$, and cleared his overdraft of $49,625 and, after expenses, realized a profit of $7,490 which he left deposited with the Morgan Bank.

Over the next three years, Henryk stopped ringing Mr Gronowich, and started dealing for himself, in small amounts to begin with, but growing larger as he gained in experience and confidence. Times were still good, and while he didn't always make a profit, he had learnt to master the occasional bear market as well as the more common bull. His system in the bear market was to sell short – not a practice considered to be entirely ethical in business. He soon mastered the art of selling shares he didn't own in expectation of a subsequent fall in their price. His instinct for market trends refined as rapidly as did his taste for clothes, and the guile learnt in the backstreets of the Lower East Side always stood him in good stead. Henryk soon discovered that the whole world was a jungle – sometimes the lions and tigers wore suits.

When the stock market collapsed in 1929 Henryk had turned his $7,490 into $51,000 of liquid assets, having sold on every share he possessed the day after the Chairman of Halgarten & Co. jumped out of one of the Stock Exchange windows. Henryk had got the message. With his newly acquired income he had moved into a smart apartment in Brooklyn and started driving a rather ostentatious red Stutz. Henryk realized at an early age that he had come into the world with three main disadvantages – his name, background and impecunity. The money problem was solving itself, and now the time had come to expunge the other two. To that end, he had made an application to change his name by court order to Harvey David Metcalfe. When the application was granted, he ceased all further contact with his friends from the Polish community, and in May 1930 he came of age with a new name, new background, and very new money.

It was later that year at a football game that he first met Roger Sharpley and discovered that the rich have their problems too. Sharpley, a young man from Boston, had inherited his father's company, which specialized in the import of whisky and the export of furs. Educated at Choate and later in Dartmouth College, Sharpley had all the assurance and charm of the Boston set, so often envied by his fellow countrymen. He was tall and fair, looked as if he came from Viking stock, and with his air of the gifted amateur, found most things came easily to him – especially women. He was in every way a total contrast to Harvey. Although they were poles apart, the contrast acted like a magnet and attracted the one to the other.

Roger's only ambition in life was to become an officer in the Navy, but after graduating from Dartmouth he had had to return to the family business because of his father's ill-health. He had only been with the firm a few months when his father died. Roger would have liked to have sold Sharpley & Son to the first bidder, but his father had made a codicil to his will to the effect that if the firm were sold before Roger's fortieth birthday (that being the last day one can enlist for the U.S. Navy), the money gained from the sale would be divided equally among his other relatives.

Harvey gave Roger's problem considerable thought, and after two lengthy sessions with a skilful New York laywer, suggested a course of action to Roger: Harvey would purchase 49 per cent of Sharpley & Son for $100,000 and the first $20,000 profit each year. At the age of forty, Roger could relinquish the remaining 51 per cent for a further $100,000. The Board would consist of three voting members – Harvey, Roger and one nominated by Harvey, giving him overall control. As far as Harvey was concerned, Roger could join the Navy and need only attend the annual shareholders meeting.

Roger could not believe his luck. He did not even consult anyone at Sharpley & Son, knowing only too well that they would try to talk him out of it. Harvey had counted on this and had assessed his quarry accurately. Roger gave the proposition only a few days' consideration before allowing the legal papers to be drawn up in New York, far enough away from Boston to be sure the firm did not learn what was going on. Meanwhile, Harvey returned to the Morgan Bank, where he was now looked upon as a man with a future. Since banks deal in futures, the manager agreed to help him in his new enterprise with a loan of $50,000 to add to his own $50,000, enabling Harvey to acquire 49 per cent of Sharpley & Son, and become its fifth President. The legal documents were signed in New York on October 28th, 1930.

Roger left speedily for Newport, Rhode Island, to commence his Officers Training programme in the US Navy. Harvey left for Grand Central Station to catch the train for Boston. His days as a messenger boy on the New

York Stock Exchange were over. He was twenty-one years of age and the President of his own company.

What looked like disaster to most, Harvey could always turn into triumph. The American people were still suffering under Prohibition, and although Harvey could export furs, he could no longer import whisky. This had been the main reason for the fall in the company profits over the past decade. But Harvey soon found that with a little bribery, involving the Mayor of Boston, the Chief of Police and the Customs officials on the Canadian border, plus a payment to the Mafia to ensure that his products reached the restaurants and speak-easies, somehow the whisky imports went up rather than down. Sharpley & Son lost its more respectable and long-serving staff, and replaced them with animals better-suited to Harvey Metcalfe's particular jungle.

From 1930 to 1933 Harvey went from strength to strength, but when Prohibition was finally lifted by President Roosevelt after overwhelming public demand, the excitement went with it, Harvey allowed the company to continue to deal in whisky and furs while he branched out into new fields. In 1933 Sharpley & Son celebrated a hundred years in business. In three years Harvey had lost 97 years of goodwill and doubled the profits. It took him five years to reach his first million and only another four to double the sum again, which was when he decided the time had come for Harvey Metcalfe and Sharpley & Son to part company. In twelve years from 1930 to 1942, he had built up the profits from $30,000 to $910,000. He sold the company in January 1944 for $7,000,000, paying $100,000 to the widow of Captain Roger Sharpley of the US Navy and keeping $6,900,000 for himself.

Harvey celebrated his thirty-fifth birthday by buying at a cost of $4 million a small, ailing bank in Boston called the Lincoln Trust. At the time it boasted a profit of approximately $500,000 a year, a prestigious building in the centre of Boston and an unblemished and somewhat boring reputation. Harvey intended to change both its reputation and its balance sheet. He enjoyed being the President of a bank – but it did nothing to improve his honesty. Every dubious deal in the Boston area seemed to emanate from the Lincoln Trust, and although Harvey increased the bank's profits to $2 million per annum during the next five years, his personal reputation was never in credit.

. . .

Harvey met Arlene Hunter in the winter of 1949. She was the only daughter of the President of the First City Bank of Boston. Until then Harvey had never taken any real interest in women. His driving force had always been making money, and although he considered the opposite sex a useful relaxation in his free time, on balance he found them an inconvenience. But having now reached what the glossy magazines referred to as middle age and having no heir to leave his fortune to, he calculated that it was time to find a wife who would present him with a son. As with everything else that he had wanted in his life, he considered the problem very carefully.

Harvey had first run into Arlene when she was thirty-one; quite literally, when she had backed her car into his new Lincoln. She could not have been a greater contrast to the short, uneducated, overweight Pole. She was nearly six feet tall, slim and although not unattractive, she lacked confidence and was beginning to think that marriage had passed her by. Most of her school friends were already on their second divorces and felt rather sorry for her. Harvey's extravagant ways came as a welcome change after her parents' prudish discipline, which she often felt was to blame for her awkwardness with men of her own age. She had only had one affair – a disastrous failure, thanks to her total innocence – and until Harvey arrived, no one had seemed to be willing to give her a second chance. Arlene's father did not approve of Harvey, and showed it, which only made him more attractive to her. Her father had not approved of any of the men she had associated with, but on this occasion he was right. Harvey on the other hand realized that to marry the First City Bank of Boston with the Lincoln Trust could only be of long-term benefit to him, and with that in mind he set out, as he always did, to conquer. Arlene didn't put up much of a battle.

Arlene and Harvey were married in 1951 at a wedding more memorable for those who were absent than those who attended. They settled into Harvey's Lincoln home outside of Boston and very shortly afterwards Arlene announced she was pregnant. She gave Harvey a daughter almost a year to the day after their marriage.

They christened her Rosalie, and she became the centre of Harvey's attention; his own disappointment came when a prolapse closely followed by a hysterectomy prevented Arlene from bearing him any more children. He sent Rosalie to Bennetts, the most expensive girls' school in Washington, and from there she was accepted at Vassar to major in English. This even pleased old man Hunter, who had grown to tolerate Harvey and adore his grand-daughter. On gaining her degree, Rosalie continued her education at the Sorbonne, after a fierce disagreement with her father concerning the type of friends she was keeping, particularly the ones with long hair who didn't want to go to Vietnam – not that Harvey had done much during the Second World War, except to cash in on every shortage. The final crunch came when Rosalie dared to suggest that morals were not to be decided only by length of hair or political views. Harvey missed her, but refused to admit the fact to Arlene.

Harvey had three loves in his life: the first was still Rosalie, the second was his paintings, and the third his orchids. The first had started the moment his daughter was born. The second was a love that had developed over many years and had been kindled in the strangest way. A client of Sharpley & Son was about to go bankrupt while still owing a fairly large sum of money to the company. Harvey got wind of it and went round to confront him, but the rot had already set in and there was no longer any hope of securing cash. Determined not to leave empty-handed, Harvey took with him the man's only tangible asset – a Renoir valued at $10,000.

Harvey's intention was to sell the picture quickly before it could be proved that he was a preferred creditor, but he became so entranced with the fine brushwork and the delicate pastel shades that his only desire was to own more. When he realized that pictures were not only a good investment, but that he actually liked them as well, his collection and his love grew hand in hand. By the early 1970s, Harvey had a Manet, two Monets, a Renoir, two Picassos, a Pissarro, a Utrillo, a Cézanne, as well as most of the recognized lesser names, and he had become quite a connoisseur of the Impressionist period. His one remaining desire was to possess a Van Gogh, and only recently he had failed to acquire *L'Hôpital de St Paul à St Rémy* at the Sotheby-Parke Bernet Gallery in New York, when Dr Armand Hammer of Occidental Petroleum had outbid him – $1,200,000 had been just a little too much for Harvey.

Earlier, in 1966, he had failed to acquire Lot 49, *Mademoiselle Ravoux*, from Christie, Manson & Woods, the London art dealers; although the Rev. Theodore Pitcairn, representing the Lord's New Church in Bryn Athyn, Pennsylvania, had pushed him over the top, he had only whetted his appetite further. The Lord giveth, and on that occasion the Lord had taken away. Although it was not fully appreciated in Boston, it was already recognized in the art world that Harvey had one of the finest Impressionist collections in the world, almost as widely admired as that of Walter Annenberg, President Nixon's Ambassador to London who, like Harvey, had been one of the few people to build up a major collection since the Second World War.

Harvey's third love was his prize collection of orchids, and he had three times been a winner at the New England Spring Flower Show in Boston, twice beating old man Hunter into second place.

. . .

Harvey now travelled to Europe once a year. He had established a successful stud in Kentucky and liked to see his horses run at Longchamp and Ascot. He also enjoyed watching Wimbledon, which he considered was still the greatest tennis tournament in the world. It amused him to do a little business in Europe at the same time, giving him the opportunity to make some more money for his Swiss bank account in Zürich. He did not need a Swiss account, but somehow he got a kick out of doing Uncle Sam.

. . .

Although Harvey had mellowed over the years and cut down on his more dubious deals, he could never resist the chance to take a risk if he thought the reward was likely to be big enough. One such golden opportunity presented itself in 1964 when Her Majesty's Government invited applications for exploration and production licences in the North Sea. At that time neither the British Government nor the civil servants involved had any idea of the future significance of North Sea oil, or the role it would eventually play in British politics. If the Government had known that in 1978 the Arabs would be holding a pistol to the heads of the rest of the world, and the British House of Commons would have eleven Scottish Nationalist Members of Parliament, it would surely have reacted in a totally different way.

On 13 May 1964, the Secretary of State for Power laid before Parliament 'Statutory Instrument – No. 708 – Continental Shelf – Petroleum'. Harvey read this particular document with great interest, thinking that it might well be a means of making an exceptional killing. He was particularly fascinated by Paragraph 4 of the document, which read:

Persons who are citizens of the United Kingdom and Colonies and are resident in the United Kingdom or who are bodies corporate incorporated in the United Kingdom may apply in accordance with these Regulations for:

(a) a production licence; or,
(b) an exploration licence.

When he had studied the Regulations in their entirety, he had to sit back and think hard. Only a small amount of money was required to secure a production and exploration licence. As Paragraph 6 went on to point out:

'(1) with every application for a production licence there shall be paid a fee of two hundred pounds with an additional fee of five pounds for every block after the first ten in respect whereof that application is made.

(2) With every application for an exploration licence there shall be paid a fee of twenty pounds.'

Harvey couldn't believe it. How easy it would be to use such a licence to create the impression of a vast enterprise! For a few hundred dollars he could be alongside such names as Shell, BP, Total, Gulf and Occidental.

Harvey went over the Regulations again and again, hardly believing that the British Government could release such potential for so small an investment. Only the application form, an elaborate and exacting document, now stood in his way. Harvey was not a British subject, none of his companies was British and he realized he would have problems of presentation. He decided that his application must therefore be backed by a British bank and that he would set up a company whose directors would win the confidence of the British Government.

With this in mind, early in 1964, he registered at Companies House in England a firm called Prospecta Oil, using Malcolm, Bottnick and Davis as his solicitors and Barclays Bank, who were already the Lincoln Trust's representatives in Europe, as his bankers. Lord Hunnisett became Chairman of the company and several distinguished public figures joined the Board, including two ex-Members of Parliament who had lost their seats when the Labour Party won the 1964 Election. Prospecta Oil issued 2,000,000 10-pence shares at one pound, which were all taken up for Harvey by nominees. He also deposited $500,000 in the Lombard Street branch of Barclays Bank.

Having thus created the front, Harvey then used Lord Hunnisett to apply for the licence from the British Government. The new Labour Government elected in October 1964 was no more aware of the significance of North Sea oil than the earlier Conservative administration. The Government's requirements for a licence were a rent of £12,000 a year for the first six years, 12½ per cent revenue tax, and a further Capital Gains tax on profits; but as Harvey's plan was to reap profits for himself rather than the company that presented no problems.

On 22 May 1965, the Minister of Power published in the *London Gazette* the name of Prospecta Oil among the fifty-two companies granted production licences. On 3 August 1965, Statutory Instrument No. 1531 allocated the actual areas. Prospecta Oil's was 51° 50′ 00″ N: 2° 30′ 20″ E, a site adjacent to one of BP's holdings.

Then Harvey sat back, waiting for one of the companies which had acquired North Sea sites to strike oil. It was a longish wait but Harvey was in no hurry, and not until June 1970 did BP make a big commercial strike in their Forties Field. BP had already spent over $1 billion in the North Sea and Harvey was determined to be one of the main beneficiaries. He was now on to another winner, and immediately set the second part of his plan in motion.

Early in 1972 he hired an oil rig which, with much flourish and advance publicity, he had towed out to the Prospecta Oil site. Having hired the rig on the basis of being able to renew the contract if he made a successful strike, he engaged the minimum number of workers allowed by the Government Regulations, and then proceeded to drill to 6,000 feet. After this drilling had been completed he released from the company's employment all those involved, but told Reading & Bates, from whom he had rented the rig, that he would be requiring it again in the near feature and therefore would continue to pay the rental.

Harvey then released Prospecta Oil shares on to the market at the rate of a few thousand a day for the next two months, all from his own stock, and whenever the financial journalists of the British Press rang to ask why these shares were steadily rising, the young public relations officer at Prospecta Oil's city office would say, as briefed, that he had no comment to make at present but there would be a press statement in the near future; some newspapers put two and two together and made about fifteen. The shares climbed steadily from 10 pence to nearly £2 under the guidance of Harvey's chief executive in Britain, Bernie Silverman, who, with his long experience of this kind of operation, was only too aware of what his boss was up to. Silverman's main task was to ensure that nobody could show a direct connection between Metcalfe and Prospecta Oil.

In January 1974 the shares stood at £3. It was then that Harvey was ready to move on to the third part of his plan, using Prospecta Oil's enthusiastic new recruit, a young Harvard graduate called David Kesler, as the fall-guy.

2

David pushed his glasses back on to the bridge of his nose and read the advertisement in the Business Section of the *Boston Globe* again, to make sure he was not dreaming. It could have been tailor-made for him:

> Oil Company based in Great Britain, carrying out extensive work in the North Sea off Scotland, requires a young executive with experience in the stock market and/or financial marketing. Salary $25,000 a year. Accommodation supplied. Based in London. Apply Box No. 217A.

Knowing it could lead to other openings in an expanding industry, David thought it sounded like a challenge and wondered if they would consider him experienced enough. He recalled what his tutor in European affairs used to say: 'If you must work in Great Britain, better make it the North Sea. With their union problems, there's nothing else great about the country.'

David Kesler was a lean, clean-shaven young American, with a crew cut which would have been better suited to a lieutenant in the Marines, a fresh complexion and an unquenchable earnestness. David wanted to succeed in business with all the fervour of the new Harvard Business School graduate. He had spent six years in all at Harvard, the first four studying mathematics for his Bachelor degree, and the last two across the Charles River at the Business School. Recently graduated and armed with a BA and an MBA, he was looking for a job that would reward him for the exceptional capacity for hard work he knew he possessed. Never a brilliant scholar, he envied those natural academics among his classmates who mastered post-Keynesian economic theories like children learning their multiplication tables. David had worked ferociously for six years, only lifting his nose far enough from the grindstone to fit in a daily workout at the gymnasium and the occasional weekend watching Harvard Jocks defending the honour of the university on the football field or on the basketball court. He would have enjoyed playing himself, but that would have meant less time for study.

He read the advertisement again, and then typed a carefully prepared letter to the box number. A few days passed before a reply came, summoning him for an interview at a local hotel on the following Wednesday at 3.00.

David arrived at 2.45 p.m. at the Copley Hotel on Huntingdon Avenue, the adrenalin pumping through his body. He repeated the Harvard Business School motto to himself as he was ushered into a small private room: look British, think Yiddish.

Three men, who introduced themselves as Silverman, Cooper and Eliot, interviewed him. Bernie Silverman, a short, grey haired, check-tied New Yorker with a solid aura of success, was in charge. Cooper and Elliott sat and watched David silently.

Silverman spent a considerable time giving David an enticing description of the company's background and its future aims. Harvey had trained Silverman carefully and he had at his well-manicured fingertips all the glib expertise needed by the right-hand man in a Metcalfe coup.

'So there you have it, Mr Kesler. We're involved in one of the biggest commercial opportunities in the world, drilling for oil in the North Sea off Scotland. Our company, Prospecta Oil, has the backing of a group of banks in America. We have been granted licences from the British Government and we have the financing. But companies are made not by money, Mr Kesler, but by people – it's as simple as that. We're looking for a man who will work night and day to help put Prospecta Oil on the map, and we'll pay the right man a top salary to do just that. If we offer you the position, you'll be working in our London office under the immediate direction of our Managing Director, Mr Elliott.'

'Where are the company headquarters?'

'New York, but we have offices in Montreal, San Francisco, London, Aberdeen, Paris and Brussels.'

'Is the company looking for oil anywhere else?'

'Not at the moment,' answered Silverman. 'We're sinking millions into the North Sea after BP's successful strike, and the fields around us have so far had a one-in-five success ratio, which is very high in our business.'

'When would you want the successful applicant to start?'

'Some time in January, when he's completed a government training course on management in oil,' said Richard Elliott. The slim, sallow No. 2 sounded as if he was from Georgia. The government course was a typical Harvey Metcalfe touch – maximum credibility for minimum expense.

'And the company apartment,' said David, 'where's that?'

Cooper spoke:

'You'll have one of the company flats in the Barbican, a few hundred yards away from our London City office.'

David had no more questions – Silverman had covered everything and seemed to know exactly what he wanted.

Ten days later David received a telegram inviting him to join Silverman for lunch at the 21 Club in New York. When David arrived at the restaurant, he recognized a host of well-known faces at nearby tables and felt new confidence: his host obviously knew what he was about. Their table was in one of the small alcoves selected by businessmen who prefer their conversations to remain confidential.

Silverman was genial and relaxed. He stretched the conversation out a little, discussing irrelevancies, but finally, over a brandy, offered David the position in London. David was delighted: $25,000 a year, and the chance to be involved with a company which obviously had such an exciting future. He did not hesitate in agreeing to start his new appointment in London on 1 January.

. . .

David Kesler had never been to England before: how green the grass was, how narrow the roads, how closed in by hedges and fences were the houses! It felt like Toy Town after the vast highways and large automobiles of New York. The small flat in the Barbican was clean and impersonal and, as Mr Cooper had said, convenient for the office a few hundred yards away in Threadneedle Street.

Prospecta's office consisted of seven rooms on one floor of a large Victorian building; Silverman's was the only office with a prestigious air about it. There was a tiny reception area, a telex room, two rooms for secretaries, a larger room for Mr Elliott and another small one for himself. It seemed very poky to David, but as Silverman was quick to point out, office rent in the City of London was $30 a square foot compared with $10 in New York.

Bernie Silverman's secretary, Judith Lampson, ushered David through to the well appointed office of the Chief Executive. Silverman sat in a large black swivel chair behind a massive desk, which made him look like a midget. By his side were postioned four telephones, three white and one red. David was later to learn that the important-looking red telephone was directly connected to a number in the States, but he never actually discovered to whom.

'Good morning, Mr Silverman. Where would you like me to start?'

'Bernie, please call me Bernie. Take a seat. Notice the change in the price of the company's shares in the last few days?'

'Oh, yes,' enthused David, 'Up a half to nearly $6. I suppose it's because of our new bank backing and the other companies' successful strikes?'

'No,' said Silverman in a low tone designed to give the impression that no one else must hear this part of the conversation, 'the truth is that we've made a big strike ourselves, but we haven't yet decided when to announce it. It's all in this geologist's report.' He threw a smart, colourful document over his desk.

David whistled under his breath. 'What are the company's plans at the moment?'

'We'll announce the strike,' said Silverman quietly, picking at his india rubber as he talked, 'in about three weeks' time, when we're certain of the full extent and capacity of the hole. We want to make some plans for coping with the publicity and the sudden inflow of money. The shares will go through the roof, of course.'

'The shares have already climbed steadily. Perhaps some people already know?'

'I guess that's right,' said Silverman. 'The trouble with that black stuff is once it comes out of the ground you can't hide it.' Silverman laughed.

'Is there any harm in getting in on the act?' asked David.

'No, as long as it doesn't harm the company in any way. Just let me know if anyone wants to invest. We don't have the problems of inside information in England – none of the restrictive laws we have in America.'

'How high do you think the shares will go?'

Silverman looked him straight in the eye and then said casually, '$20.'

Back in his own office, David carefully read the geologist's report that Silverman had given him: it certainly looked as if Prospecta Oil had made a successful strike, but the extent of the find was not, as yet, entirely certain. When he had completed the report, he glanced at his watch and cursed. The geologist's file had totally absorbed him. He threw the report into his briefcase and took a taxi to Paddington Station, only just making the 6.15 train. He was due in Oxford for dinner with an old classmate from Harvard.

On the train down to the university city he thought about Stephen Bradley, who had been a friend in his Harvard days and had generously helped David and other students in mathematics classes that year. Stephen, now a visiting Fellow at Magdalen College, was undoubtedly one of the most brilliant scholars of David's generation. He had won the Kennedy Memorial Scholarship to Harvard and later in 1970 the Wister Prize for Mathematics, the most sought-after award in the mathematical faculty. Although in monetary terms this award was a derisory $80 and a medal, it was the reputation and job offers it brought with it that made the competition so keen. Stephen had won it with consummate ease and nobody was surprised when he was successful in his application for a Fellowship at Oxford. He was now in his third year of research at Magdalen. His papers on Boolean algebra appeared at short intervals in the *Proceedings of the London Mathematical Society*, and it had just been announced that he had been elected to a Chair in Mathematics back at his alma mater, Harvard, to commence in the fall.

The 6.15 train from Paddington arrived in Oxford an hour later and the short taxi ride from the station down New College Lane brought him to Magdalen at 7.30. One of the College porters escorted David to Stephen's rooms, which were spacious, ancient, and comfortably cluttered with books, cushions and prints. How unlike the antiseptic walls of Harvard, thought David. Stephen was there to greet him. He didn't seem to have changed one iota. His suit seemed to hang off his tall, thin, ungainly body; no tailor would ever have employed him as a dummy. His heavy eyebrows protruded over his out-of-date round-rimmed spectacles, which he almost seemed to hide behind in his shyness. He ambled over to David and welcomed him, one minute an old man, the next younger than his thirty years. Stephen poured David a Jack Daniels and they settled down to chat. Although Stephen never looked upon David as a close friend at Harvard, he had enjoyed coaching him and always found him eager to learn; besides, he always welcomed an excuse to entertain Americans at Oxford.

'It's been a memorable three years, David,' said Stephen, pouring him a second drink. 'The only sad event was the death of my father last winter. He took such an interest in my life at Oxford and gave my academic work so much support. He's left me rather well off, actually ... Bath plugs were obviously more in demand than I realized. You might be kind enough to advise me on how to invest some of the money, because at the moment it's just sitting on deposit in the bank. I never seem to have the time to do anything about it, and when it comes to investments I haven't a clue.'

That started David off about his demanding new job with Prospecta Oil.

'Why don't you invest your money in my company, Stephen. We've had a fantastic strike in the North Sea, and when they announce it the shares are going to go through the roof. The whole operation would only take a month or so and you could make the killing of a lifetime. I only wish I had some of my own money to put into it.'

'Have you had the full details of the strike?'

'No, but I've seen the geologist's report, and that makes pretty good reading. The shares are already going up fast and I'm convinced they'll reach $20. The problem is that time is already running out.'

Stephen glanced at the geologist's report, thinking he would study it carefully later.

'How does one go about an investment of this sort?' he asked.

'Well, you find a respectable stockbroker, buy as many shares as you can afford and then wait for the strike to be announced. I'll keep you informed on how things are going and advise you when I feel is the best time to sell.'

'That would be extremely thoughtful of you, David.'

'It's the least I can do after all the help you gave me with maths at Harvard.'

'Oh, that was nothing. Let's go and have some dinner.'

Stephen led David to the college dining hall, an oblong oak-panelled room covered in pictures of past Presidents of Magdalen, bishops and academics. The long wooden tables at which the undergraduates were eating filled the body of the hall, but Stephen shuffled up to the High Table and offered David a more comfortable seat. The students were a noisy, enthusiastic bunch – Stephen didn't notice them, but David was enjoying the whole experience.

The seven-course meal was formidable and David wondered how Stephen kept so thin with such daily temptations. When they reached the port, Stephen suggested they return to his rooms rather than join the crusty old dons in the Senior Common Room.

Late into the night, over the rubicund Magdalen port, they talked about North Sea oil and Boolean algebra, each admiring the other for his mastery of his subject. Stephen, like most academics, was fairly credulous outside the bounds of his own discipline. He began to think that an investment in Prospecta Oil would be a very astute move on his part.

In the morning, they strolled down Addison's Walk near Magdalen Bridge, where the grass grows green and lush by the Cherwell. Reluctantly, David caught a taxi at 9.45 leaving Magdalen behind him and passing New College, Trinity, Balliol and finally Worcester, where he saw scrawled across the college wall, '*c'est magnifique mais ce n'est pas la gare*'. He caught the 10.00 a.m. train back to London. He had enjoyed his stay at Oxford and hoped he had been able to help his old Harvard friend, who had done so much for him in the past.

.   .   .

'Good morning, David.'

'Good morning, Bernie. I thought I ought to let you know I spent the evening with a friend at Oxford, and he may invest some money in the company. It might be as much as $250,000.'

'That's fine, David, keep up the good work. You're doing a great job.'

Silverman showed no surprise at David's news, but once back in his own office he picked up the red telephone.

'Harvey?'

'Yes.'

'Kesler seems to have been the right choice. He may have talked a friend of his into investing $250,000 in the company.'

'Good. Now listen carefully. Brief my broker to put 40,000 shares on the market at just over $6 a share. If Kesler's friend does decide to invest in the company, mine will be the only large block of shares immediately available.'

.   .   .

After a further day's consideration, Stephen noticed that the shares of Prospecta Oil moved from £2.75 to £3.05 and decided the time had come to invest in what he was now convinced must be a winner. He trusted David, and had been impressed by the glossy geologist's report. He rang Kitcat & Aitken, a firm of stockbrokers in the City, and instructed them to buy $250,000-worth of shares in Prospecta Oil. Harvey Metcalfe's broker released 40,000 shares when Stephen's request came on to the floor of the stock exchange and the transaction was quickly completed. Stephen's purchase price was £3.10.

After investing his father's inheritance, Stephen spent the next few days happily watching the shares climb to £3.50, even before the expected announcement. Though Stephen didn't realize it, it was his own investment that had caused the shares to rise. He began to wonder what he would spend the profit on even before he had realized it. He decided not to cash in immediately, but hold on; David thought the shares would reach $20, and in any case he had promised to tell him when to sell.

Meanwhile, Harvey Metcalfe began to release a few more shares on to the market, because of the interest created by Stephen's investment. He was beginning to agree with Silverman that David Kesler, young, honest, and with all the enthusiasm of a man in his first appointment, had been an excellent choice. It was not the first time that Harvey had used this ploy, keeping himself well away from the action while placing the responsibility on inexperienced, innocent shoulders.

At the same time, Richard Elliott, acting as the company spokesman, leaked stories to the press about large buyers coming into the market, which in itself occasioned a flood of small investors and kept the price steady.

. . .

One lesson a man learns in the Harvard Business School is that an executive is only as good as his health. David never felt happy without a regular medical check-up; he rather enjoyed being told he was in good shape, but perhaps should take things a little easier. His secretary, Miss Rentoul, had therefore made an appointment for him with a Harley Street doctor.

Dr Robin Oakley was by anyone's standards a successful man. At thirty-seven he was tall and handsome, with a head of dark hair that looked as if it would never recede. He had a classic strong face and the self-assurance that came from proven success. He still played squash twice a week, which helped him look enviably younger than his contemporaries. Robin had remained fit since his Cambridge days, which he left with a Rugby Blue and an upper-second-class degree. He had gone on to complete his medical training at St Thomas's, where once again his Rugby football rather than his medical skill brought him into prominence with those who decide the future careers of young men. When he qualified, he went to work as an assistant to a highly successful Harley Street practitioner, Dr Eugene Moffat. Dr Moffat was successful not so much in curing the stick as in charming the rich, especially middle-aged women, who came to see him again and again however little seemed to be wrong with them. At fifty guineas a visit that had to be regarded as success.

Moffat had chosen Robin Oakley as his assistant for exactly those qualities which he himself displayed, and which had made him so sought-after. Robin Oakley was unquestionably good-looking, personable, well-educated – and just clever enough. Robin settled very well into Harley Street and the Moffat system, and when the older man died suddenly in his early sixties, he took over his mantle with the ease with which a crown prince would take over a throne. Robin continued to build up the practice, losing none of Moffat's ladies other than by natural causes, and did remarkably well for himself. He had a wife and two sons, a comfortable country house a few miles outside Newbury in Berkshire, and a considerable saving in blue chip securities. He never complained at his good fortune and enjoyed life, at the same time being, he had to confess, a little bored with it all. He was beginning to find that the bland role of sympathetic doctor was almost intolerably cloying. Would the world come to an end if he admitted that he neither knew nor cared just what was causing the minute patches of dermatitis on Lady Fiona Fisher's diamond-studded hands? Would the Heavens descend if he told the dreaded Mrs Page-Stanley that she was a malodorous old woman in need of nothing more medically taxing than a new set of dentures? And would he be struck off it he personally administered to the nubile Miss Lydia de Villiers a good dose of what she so clearly indicated she desired?

David Kesler arrived on time for his appointment. He had been warned by Miss Rentoul that in England doctors and dentists cancel if you are late and still charge you.

He stripped and lay on Robin Oakley's couch. The doctor took his blood pressure, listened to his heart, and made him put out his tongue, an organ that seldom stands up well to public scrutiny. As he tapped and poked his way over David's body, they chatted.

'What brings you to work in London, Mr Kesler?'

'I'm with an oil company in the City. I expect you've heard of us – Prospecta Oil?'

'No,' said Robin. 'Can't say I have. Bend your legs up please.' He hit David's knee-caps smartly, one after the other, with a patella hammer. The legs jumped wildly.

'Nothing wrong with those reflexes.'

'You will, Dr Oakley, you will. Things are going very well for us. Watch out for our progress in the papers.'

'Why?' said Robin, smiling, 'Struck oil, have you?'

'Yes,' said David quietly, pleased with the impression he was creating, 'As a matter of fact, we've done just that.'

Robin prodded David's abdomen for a few seconds. 'Good muscular wall, not fat, no sign of an enlarged liver. Young man, you're in good physical shape.'

Robin left him in the examination room to get dressed and thoughtfully wrote out a brief report on Kesler for his records, while his mind dwelt on deeper things. An oil strike.

Harley Street doctors, although they routinely keep private patients waiting for three-quarters of an hour in a gas-fired waiting-room equipped with one out-of-date copy of *Punch*, never let them feel rushed once they are in the consulting-room. Robin had no intention of rushing Mr Kesler.

'There's very little wrong with you, Mr Kesler. Some signs of anaemia, which I suspect are caused by nothing more than overwork and your recent rushing about. I'm going to give you some iron tablets which should quickly take care of that. Take two a day, morning and night.' He scribbled an illegible prescription for the tablets and handed it to David.

'Many thanks. It's kind of you to give me so much of your time.'

'Not at all. How are you finding London?' asked Robin. 'Very different from America, I expect.'

'Sure – the pace is much slower. Once I've mastered how long it takes to get something done here I'll be halfway to victory.'

'Do you have many friends in London?'

'No,' replied David, 'I have one or two buddies at Oxford from my Harvard days, but I haven't yet made contact with many people in London.'

Good, thought Robin, here is a chance for me to find out a little more about the oil game, and spend some time with a man who makes most of patients look as if they had both feet in the grave. It might even shake me out of my lethargy. He continued 'Would you care to join me for lunch later in the week? You might like to see one of our antique London clubs.'

'How very kind of you.'

'Excellent. Will Friday suit you?'

'It certainly will.'

'Then let's say one o'clock at the Athenaeum Club in Pall Mall.'

David returned to his City desk, picking up his tablets on the way. He took one immediately. He was beginning to enjoy his stay in London. Silverman seemed pleased with him, Prospecta Oil was doing well and he was already meeting some interesting people. Yes, he felt this was going to be a very happy period in his life.

. . .

On Friday at 12.45 p.m., David arrived at the Athenaeum, a massive white building on the corner of Pall Mall, overlooked by a statue of the Duke of York. David was amazed by the size of the rooms and his commercial mind could not help wondering what price they would fetch as office space. The place appeared to be full of moving waxworks who, Robin later assured him, were in fact distinguished generals and diplomats.

They lunched in the Coffee Room, dominated by a Rubens of Charles II, and talked about Boston, London, squash, and their shared passion for Katherine Hepburn. Over coffee, David readily told Robin the details of the geologist's findings on the Prospecta Oil site. The shares had now climbed to £3.60 on the London Stock Exchange, and were still going up.

'Sounds like a good investment,' said Robin, 'and as it's your own company, it might be worth the risk.'

'I don't think there's much of a risk,' said David, 'as long as the oil is actually there.'

'Well, I'll certainly consider it most seriously over the weekend.'

They parted on the steps of the Athenaeum, David to a conference on the Energy Crisis organized by the *Financial Times*, Robin to his home in Berkshire. His two young sons were back from prep school for the weekend and he was looking forward to seeing them again. How quickly they had passed from babies to toddlers, to boys; soon they would be young men, he thought. And how reassuring to know their future was secure. Perhaps he should make that future a little more secure by investing in David Kesler's company. He could always put the money back into blue chip shares once the strike had been announced.

Bernie Silverman was also pleased to hear the possibility of a further investment.

'Congratulations, my boy. 'We're going to need a lot of capital to finance the pipe-laying operations, you know. Pipe-laying can cost $2 million per mile. Still, you're playing your part. I've just had word from head office that we are to give you a $5,000 bonus for your efforts. Keep up the good work.'

David smiled. This was business in the proper Harvard tradition. If you bring home the results, you get the rewards.

'When will the strike be officially announced?' he asked.

'Some time in the next few days.'

David left Silverman's office with a glow of pride.

Silverman immediately contacted Harvey Metcalfe on the red phone, and he set the routine in motion once again. Metcalfe's brokers released on to the market 35,000 shares at £3.73 and approximately 5,000 each day on to the open market, always being able to feel when the market had taken enough and thus keeping the price steady. Once again, the shares climbed when Dr Oakley invested heavily in the market, this time to £3.90, keeping David, Robin and Stephen all happy. They were not to know that Harvey was releasing more shares each day because of the interest they had caused, and that this was now creating a market of its own.

David decided to spend some of his bonus on a painting for his little flat in the Barbican, which he felt was rather grey. About $2,000, he thought, something that was going to appreciate in value. David quite enjoyed art for art's sake, but he liked it even more for business's sake. He spent Friday afternoon tramping around Bond Street, Cork Street and Bruton Street, the home of the London art galleries. The Wildenstein was too expensive for his pocket and the Marlborough too modern for his taste. The painting he finally picked out was at the Lamanns Gallery in Bond Street.

The gallery, just three doors away from Sotheby's, consisted of one vast room with a worn grey carpet and red faded wallpaper. As David was later to learn, the more worn the carpet, the more faded the walls, the greater the success and reputation of the gallery. There was a staircase at the far end of the room, against which some unregarded paintings were stacked, backs to the world. David sorted through them on a whim and found, to his delight, something that appealed to him.

It was an oil by Leon Underwood called *Venus in the Park*. The large, rather sombre canvas contained about six men and women sitting on metal chairs at circular tea-tables. Among them, in the foreground, was a comely naked woman with generous breasts and long hair. Nobody was paying her the slightest attention and she sat gazing out of the picture, inscrutable, a symbol of warmth and love in indifferent surroundings. David found her utterly compelling.

The gallery proprietor, Jean-Pierre Lamanns, advanced on him, adorned in an elegantly tailored suit, as befitted a man who rarely received cheques for less than a thousand pounds. At thirty-five, he could afford the little extravagances of life, and his Gucci shoes, Yves St Laurent tie, Turnbull & Asser shirt and Piaget watch left no one, especially women, in any doubt that he knew what he was about. He was an Englishman's vision of a Frenchman, slim and neat with longish, dark wavy hair and deep brown eyes that hinted at being a little sharp. He was capable of being pernickety and demanding, with a wit that was often as cruel as it was amusing, which may have been one of the reasons why he had not married. There certainly had been no shortage of applicants. Customers, however, saw only his charming side. As David wrote out his cheque, Jean-Pierre rubbed his forefinger backwards and forwards over his fashionable moustache, only too happy to discuss the picture.

'Underwood is one of the greatest sculptors and artists in England today.

He even tutored Henry Moore, you know. I believe he is underestimated because of his dislike of journalists and the press, whom he describes as nothing more than drunken scribblers.'

'Hardly the way to endear oneself to the media,' murmured David, as he handed over the cheque for £850, feeling agreeably prosperous. Although it was the most expensive purchase he had ever made, he felt the picture was a good investment and, more important, he liked it.

Jean-Pierre took David downstairs to show him the Impressionist and Modern collection he had built up over many years, continuing to enthuse about Underwood. They celebrated David's first acquisition over a whisky in Jean-Pierre's office.

'What line of business are you in, Mr Kesler?'

'I work with a small oil company called Prospecta Oil, who are exploring prospects in the North Sea.'

'Had any success?' enquired Jean-Pierre, a little too innocently.

'Well, between the two of us, we're rather excited about the future. It's no secret that the company shares have gone from £2 to nearly £4 in the last few weeks, but no one knows the real reason.'

'Would it be a good investment for a poor little art dealer like myself?' asked Jean-Pierre.

'I'll tell you how good an investment I think it is,' said David. 'I am putting $3,000 in the company on Monday, which is all I have left in the world – now that I've captured Venus, that is. We'll shortly be making a rather important announcement.'

A twinkle came into Jean-Pierre's eye. To one of his Gallic subtlety, a nod was as good as a wink. He did not pursue the line of conversation any further.

.   .   .

'When's the strike going to be announced, Bernie?'

'I'm expecting it early next week. We've had a few problems. Nothing we can't lick, though.'

That gave David some relief, as he had taken up 500 shares himself that morning, investing the remaining $3,000 from his bonus. Like the others, he was hoping for a quick profit.

.   .   .

'Rowe Rudd.'

'Frank Watts, please. Jean-Pierre Lamanns.'

'Good morning, Jean-Pierre. What can we do for you?'

'I want to buy 25,000 Prospecta Oil.'

'Never heard of them. Hold on a minute ... New company, very low capital. A bit risky, J.-P. I wouldn't recommend it.'

'It's all right, Frank, I only want them for two or three weeks, then you can sell. I've no intention of holding onto them. When did the account start?'

'Yesterday.'

'Right. Buy this morning and sell them before the end of the account, or earlier. I'm expecting an announcement next week, so once they go over £5 you can get rid of them. No need to be greedy, but buy them in my company name, I don't want the deal traced back to me – it might embarrass the informant.'

'Right, sir. Buy 25,000 Prospecta Oil at market price and sell before the last day of the account, or sooner if instructed.'

'Correct, I'll be in Paris all next week looking at pictures, so don't hesitate to sell once they go over £5.'

'Right, J.-P. Have a good trip.'

.   .   .

The red telephone rang.

'Rowe Rudd are looking for a substantial block of shares. Do you know anything about it?'

'No idea, Harvey. It must be David Kesler again. Do you want me to speak to him?'

'No, say nothing. I've released another 25,000 shares at £3.90 Kesler's only got to do one more big one and I'll be out. Prepare our plan for seven days before the end of this Stock Exchange account.'

'Right, boss. You know quite a few people are also buying in small amounts.'

'Yes, just as before, they all have to tell their friends they're onto a good thing. Say nothing to Kesler.'

.   .   .

'You know, David,' said Richard Elliott, 'you work too hard. Relax. We're going to have enough work on our hands when the announcement's made.'

'I guess so,' said David. 'Work's just a habit with me now.'

'Well, why don't you take tonight off and join me for a spot of something at Annabel's?'

David was flattered by the invitation to London's most exclusive nightclub and accepted enthusiastically.

David's hired Ford Cortina looked somewhat out of place that evening in Berkeley Square among the double-parked Rolls-Royces and Mercedes. He made his way down the little iron staircase into the basement, which at one time must have been more than the servants' quarters for the elegant town house above. Now it was a splendid club, with a restaurant, discothèque and a small elegant bar, the walls covered in old prints and pictures. The main dining-room was dimly lit and crowded with small tables, most of them already occupied. The décor was Regency and extravagant. Mark Birley, the owner, had in the short period of ten years made Annabel's the most sought-after club in London, with a waiting list for membership of well over a thousand. The discothèque was playing in the far corner of a crowded dance floor, on which you couldn't have parked two Cadillacs. Most of the couples were dancing very close to each other – they had little choice. David was somewhat surprised to observe that nearly all of the men on the floor were about twenty years older than the girls they held in their arms. The head waiter, Louis, showed David to Richard Elliott's table, realizing it was David's first visit to the club by the way he stared at all the personalities of the day. Oh well, thought David, perhaps one day they'll be staring at me.

After an exceptionally good dinner Richard Elliott and his wife joined the crowd on the dance floor, while David returned to the little bar surrounded by comfortable red settees and struck up a conversation with someone who introduced himself as James Brigsley. Even if he did not treat the whole world as such, Mr Brigsley certainly treated Annabel's as a stage. Tall, blond and aristocratic, his eyes alight with good humour, he seemed at ease with everyone around him. David admired his assured manner, something he had never acquired and feared he never would. His accent, even to David's untutored ears, was resonantly upper-class.

David's new acquaintance talked of his visits to the States, flattering him by remarking how much he had always liked the Americans. After some time, David was able quietly to ask the head waiter who the Englishman was.

'He's Lord Brigsley, the eldest son of the Earl of Louth, sir.'

What do you know, thought David, lords look like anyone else, especially when they've had a few drinks. Lord Brigsley was tapping David's glass.

'Would you care for another?'

'Thank you very much, my lord,' said David.

'Don't bother with all that nonsense. The name's James. What are you doing in London?'

'I work for an oil company. You probably know my Chairman, Lord Hunnisett. I've never met him myself, to tell you the truth.'

'Sweet old buffer,' said James. 'His son and I were at Harrow together. If you're in oil, perhaps you can tell me what to do with my Shell and BP shares.'

'Hold on to them,' said David. 'It's sensible to remain in any commodities, especially oil, as long as the British Government doesn't get greedy and try to take control of the assets themselves.'

Another double whisky arrived. David was beginning to feel just slightly tipsy.

'What about your own company?' enquired James.

'We're rather small,' said David, 'But our shares have gone up more than any other oil company in the last three months. Even so, I suspect they've nowhere near reached their zenith.'

'Why?' demanded James.

David glanced round and lowered his voice to a confidential whisper.

'Well, I expect you realize that if you make an oil strike in a big company it can only put the percentage of your profits up by a tiny amount. but if you make a strike in a small company, naturally that profit will be reflected as a considerably larger percentage of the whole.'

'Are you telling me you've made a strike?'

'Perhaps I shouldn't have said that,' said David. 'I'd be obliged if you'd treat that remark in confidence.'

.   .   .

David could not remember how he arrived home or who put him to bed, and he appeared rather late in the office the next morning.

'I am sorry, Bernie, I overslept after a very good evening with Richard at Annabel's.'

'Doesn't matter a bit. Glad you enjoyed yourself.'

'I hope I wasn't indiscreet, but I told some lord, whose name I can't even remember, that he ought to invest in the company. I may have been a little too enthusiastic.'

'Don't worry, David, we're not going to let anyone down and you need the rest. You've been working your ass off.'

· · ·

James Brigsley left his London flat in Chelsea and took a taxi to his bank, Williams & Glyn's. James was an extrovert by nature and at Harrow his only real love had been acting; but when he had left school, his father had refused to allow him to go on the stage and insisted that he complete his education at Christ Church, Oxford, where again he took a greater interest in the Dramatic Society than in gaining a degree in his chosen subject of Politics, Philosophy and Economics. James had never mentioned to anyone since leaving Oxford the class of degree he managed to secure, but for better or worse the fourth-class Honours degree was later abolished. After Oxford he joined the Grenadier Guards, which gave him considerable scope for his histrionic talents. This was indeed to be James's introduction to society life in London, and he succeeded as well as a personable, rich young viscount might be expected to do in the circumstances.

When he had completed his two years in the Guards, the earl gave him a 250-acre farm in Hampshire to occupy his time, but James did not care for the coarser country life. He left the running of the farm to a manager and once again concentrated on his social life in London. He would dearly have liked to go on the stage, but he knew the old man still considered Mrs Worthington's daughter's ambition an improper one for a future peer of the realm. The fifth earl didn't think a great deal of his eldest son one way and another, and James did not find it easy to persuade his father that he was shrewder than he was given credit for. Perhaps the inside information David Kesler had let slip after a few drinks would give him the opportunity to prove his old dad wrong.

In Williams & Glyn's fine old building in Birchin Lane, James was ushered into the manager's office.

'I should like to borrow some money against my farm in Hampshire,' said Lord Brigsley.

Philip Izard, the manager, knew Lord Brigsley well and was also acquainted with his father. Although he had respect for the earl's judgement, he did not have a great deal of time for the young lord. Nevertheless, it was not for him to query a customer's request, especially when the customer's family was one of the longest-standing in the bank's history.

'Yes, my lord, what sum do you have in mind?'

'Well, it seems that farmland in Hampshire is worth about £1,000 an acre and is still climbing. Why don't we say £150,000? I should then like to invest the money in shares.'

'Will you agree to leave the deeds with the bank as security?' enquired Izard.

'Yes, of course. What difference does it make to me where they are?'

'Then I am sure we will find it acceptable to advance you a loan of £150,000 at 2 per cent above base rate.'

James was not at all sure what base rate was, but he knew that Williams & Glyn's were as competitive as everyone else in such matters and that their reputation was beyond dispute.

'Thank you,' said James. 'Please acquire for me 35,000 shares in a company called Prospecta Oil.'

'Have you checked carefully into this company, my lord?' inquired Izard.

'Yes, of course I have,' said Lord Brigsley, very sharply. He was not in awe of the bank-managerial class.

. . .

In Boston, Harvey Metcalfe was briefed over the telephone by Silverman of the meeting in Annabel's between David Kesler and a nameless peer who seemed to have more money than sense. Harvey released 40,000 shares on to the market at £4.80. Williams & Glyn's acquired 35,000 of them and, once again, the remainder was taken up by small investors. The shares rose a little, Harvey Metcalfe was now left with only 30,000 shares of his own, and over the next four days he was able to dispose of them all. It had taken him fourteen weeks to off-load his entire stock in Prospecta Oil at a profit of just over $6 million.

On the Friday morning, the shares stood at £4.90 and Kesler had, in all innocence, occasioned four large investments: Harvey Metcalfe studied them in detail before putting through a call to Jörg Birrer.

. . .

Stephen Bradley had bought 40,000 shares at $6.10
Dr Robin Oakley had bought 35,000 shares at $7.23
Jean-Pierre Lamanns had bought 25,000 shares at $7.80
James Brigsley had bought 35,000 shares at $8.80
David Kesler himself had bought 500 shares at $7.25.

Among them they had purchased 135,000 shares at a cost of just over $1 million. They had also kept the price rising, giving Harvey the chance to off-load all his own stock on to a natural market.

Harvey Metcalfe had done it again. His name was not on the letterhead and now he possessed no shares. Nobody would be able to place any blame on him. He had done nothing illegal; even the geologist's report contained enough ifs and buts to pass in a court of law. As for David Kesler, Harvey could not be blamed for his youthful over-enthusiasm. He had never even met the man. Harvey Metcalfe opened a bottle of Krug Privée Cuvée 1964, imported from Hedges and Butler of London. He sipped it slowly, then lit a Romeo y Julieta Churchill, and settled back for a mild celebration.

. . .

David, Stephen, Robin, Jean-Pierre and James celebrated at the weekend as well. Why not? Their shares were at £4.90 and David had assured them all that they would reach £10. On Saturday morning David ordered his first bespoke suit from Aquascutum, Stephen tut-tutted his way through the end-of-vacation examination papers he had set his freshmen students, Robin attended his sons' prep school Sports Day, Jean-Pierre re-framed a Renoir, and James Brigsley went shooting, convinced that at last he had one in the eye for his father.

3

David arrived at the office at 9 a.m. on Monday to find that the front door was locked. He could not understand it. The secretaries were supposed to be in by 8.45.

After waiting around for over an hour, he walked to the nearest telephone box and dialled Bernie Silverman's home number. There was no reply. He then rang Richard Elliott at home: the ringing tone continued. He rang the Aberdeen office with the same result. He decided to return to the office. There must be a simple explanation, he thought. Was he day-dreaming? Or was it Sunday? No – the streets were jammed with people and cars.

When he arrived back at the office a young man was nailing up a board. '2,500 sq ft to let. Apply Conrad Ritblat.'

'What do you think you are doing?' David demanded.

'The old tenants have given notice and left. We're looking for new ones. Are you interested in looking over the property?'

'No,' said David, backing away in panic. 'No, thank you.'

He raced down the street, sweat beginning to show on his forehead, praying that the telephone box would still be empty.

He flicked quickly through the L–R directory and looked up Bernie Silverman's secretary, Judith Lampson. This time there was a reply.

'Judith, in God's name, what's going on?' His voice could have left her in no doubt how anxious he was.

'No idea,' replied Judith. 'I was given my notice on Friday night with a month's pay in advance and no explanation.'

David dropped the telephone. The truth was slowly beginning to dawn on him although he still wanted to believe there was some simple explanation. Whom could he turn to? What should he do?

He returned in a daze to his flat in the Barbican. The morning post had arrived in his absence. It included a letter from the landlords of his flat:

Corporation of London,
Barbican Estate Office,
London EC2
01–628–4341

Dear Sir,

We are sorry to learn you will be leaving at the end of the month, and would like to take this opportunity of thanking you for the payment of rent in advance.

We should be pleased if you would kindly deposit the keys to this office at your earliest convenience.

Yours faithfully,

C. J. Caselton
Estate Manager.

David stood frozen in the middle of the room, gazing at his new Underwood with sudden loathing.

Finally, fearfully, he dialled his stockbrokers.

'What price are Prospecta Oil this morning?'

'They've dipped to £3.80,' replied the broker.

'Why have they fallen?'

'I've no idea, but I'll make some enquiries and ring you back.'

'Please put my 500 shares on the market immediately.'

'500 Prospecta Oil at market price. Yes, sir.'

David put the phone down. It rang a few minutes later. It was his broker.

'They've only made £3.50 – exactly what you paid for them.'

'Would you credit the sum to my account at Lloyd's Bank, Moorgate Branch?'

'Of course, sir.'

David did not leave the flat for the rest of the day or night. He lay on his bed chain-smoking, wondering what he ought to do next, sometimes looking out of his little window over a rain-drenched City of banks, insurance companies, stockbrokers and public companies – his own world, but for how much longer? In the morning, as soon as the market opened, he rang his broker again, in the hope that they would have some new information.

'Can you give me any more news on Prospecta Oil?' His voice was tense and weary now.

'The news is bad, sir. There's been a spate of heavy selling and the shares have dropped to £2.80 on the opening of business this morning.'

'Why? What the hell's going on?' His voice rose with every word.

'I've no idea, sir,' replied a calm voice that always made one per cent, win or lose.

David replaced the receiver. All those years at Harvard were about to be blown away in a puff of smoke. An hour passed, but he did not notice it.

He ate lunch in an inconspicuous restaurant and read a disturbing report in the London *Evening Standard* by its City Editor, David Malbert, headlined 'The Mystery of Prospecta Oil'. By the close of the Stock Exchange at 4 p.m. the shares had fallen to £1.60.

David spent another restless night. He thought with pain and humiliation of how easily two months of good salary, a quick bonus and a good deal of smooth talk had bought his unquestioning belief in an enterprise that should have excited all business suspicion. He felt sick as he recalled his man-to-man tips on Prospecta Oil, whispered confidentially into willing ears.

On Wednesday morning, dreading what he knew he was bound to hear, David once again rang the broker. The shares had collapsed to £1 and there was no longer a market for them. He left the flat and walked over to Lloyd's bank where he closed his account and drew out the remaining £1,345. The cashier smiled at him as she passed over the notes, thinking what a successful young man he must be.

David picked up the final edition of the *Evening Standard* (the one marked '7RR' in the right-hand corner). Prospecta Oil had dropped again, this time to 25 pence. Numbed, he returned to his flat. The housekeeper was on the stairs.

'The police have been round enquiring after you, young man,' she said haughtily.

David climbed the stairs, trying to look unperturbed.

'Thank you, Mrs Pearson. I guess it's another parking fine I forgot to pay.'

Panic had now taken over completely: David never felt so small, so lonely and so sick in his life. He packed everything he owned into a suitcase, except the painting, which he left hanging on the wall, and booked a one-way ticket to New York.

4

Stephen Bradley was delivering a lecture on group theory at the Mathematics Institute in Oxford to a class of third-year undergraduates the morning David left. Over breakfast he had read with horror in the *Daily Telegraph* of the collapse of Prospecta Oil. He had immediately rung his broker, who was still trying to find out the full facts for him. He then phoned David Kesler, who seemed to have vanished without trace.

The lecture Stephen was delivering was not going well. He was pre-occupied, to say the least. He could only hope that the undergraduates would misconstrue his absent-mindedness as brilliance, rather than recognize it for what it was – total despair. He was at least thankful that it was his final lecture of the Hilary term.

Stephen looked at the clock at the back of the lecture theatre every few minutes, until at last it pointed to the hour and he was able to return to his rooms in Magdalen College. He sat in his old leather chair wondering where to start. Why the hell had he put everything into one basket? How could he, normally so logical, so calculating, have been so recklessly stupid and greedy? He had trusted David, and still found it hard to believe that his friend was in any way involved with the collapse. Perhaps he shouldn't have taken for granted that someone he had befriended at Harvard must automatically be right. There had to be a simple explanation. Surely he must be able to get all his money back. The telephone rang. Perhaps it was his broker with more concrete news.

As he picked up the phone, he realized for the first time that the palms of his hands were slippery with sweat.

'Stephen Bradley.'

'Good morning, sir. I am sorry to bother you. My name is Detective Inspector Clifford Smith of the Fraud Squad, Scotland Yard. I was wondering if you would be kind enough to see me this afternoon?'

Stephen hesitated, thinking wildly for a minute that he might have done something criminal by investing in Prospecta Oil.

'Certainly, Inspector,' he replied uncertainly, 'would you like me to travel to London?'

'No, sir,' replied the Inspector, 'we'll come to you. We can be in Oxford by 4 p.m., if that's convenient.'

'I'll expect you then. Goodbye, Inspector.'

Stephen replaced the receiver. What could they want? He knew little of English law and hoped he was not going to be involved with the police as well. All this just six months before he was due to return to Harvard as a professor. Stephen was even beginning to wonder if that would materialize.

. . .

The Detective Inspector was about 5 ft 11 in in height, and somehwere between forty-five and fifty. His hair was turning grey at the sides, but brilliantine toned it in with the original black. His shabby suit, Stephen suspected, was more indicative of a policeman's pay than of the Inspector's personal taste. His heavy frame would have fooled most people into thinking he was rather slow. In fact, Stephen was in the presence of one of the few men in England who fully understood the criminal mind. Time and time again he had been the man behind the arrest of international defrauders. He had a tired look that came from years of putting men behind bars for major crimes, only to see them freed again shortly after and living comfortably off the spoils of their shady transactions. In his opinion, crime did pay. The department was so understaffed that some of the smaller fry even got away scot-free; often the office of the Director of Public Prosecutions would decide it would be too expensive to follow the case through to a proper conclusion. On other occasions, the Fraud Squad simply did not have the back-up staff to finish the job properly.

The Detective Inspector was accompanied by Detective Sergeant Ryder, a considerably younger man – 6 ft 1 in, thin in body and face. His large brown eyes had a more innocent look against his sallow skin. He was at least a little better dressed than the Inspector, but then, thought Stephen, he probably wasn't married.

'I'm sorry about this intrusion, sir,' began the Inspector, after he had settled himself comfortably in the large armchair usually occupied by Stephen, 'but I'm making inquiries into a company called Prospecta Oil. Now before you say anything, sir, we realize that you had no personal involvement in the running of this company or indeed its subsequent collapse. But we do need your help, and I would prefer to ask you a series of questions which will bring out the points I need answered, rather than have you just give me a general assessment. I must tell you, sir, you don't have to answer any of my questions if you don't want to.'

Stephen nodded.

'First, sir, what made you invest such a large amount in Prospecta Oil?'

The Inspector had in front of him a sheet of paper with a list of all the investments made in the company over the past four months.

'The advice of a friend,' replied Stephen.

'Mr David Kesler, no doubt?'

'Yes.'

'How do you know Mr Kesler?'

'We were students at Harvard together and when he took up his appointment in England to work for an oil company, I invited him down to Oxford for old times' sake.'

Stephen went on to detail the full background of his association with

David, and the reason he had been willing to invest such a large amount. He ended his explanation by asking if the Inspector thought that David was criminally involved in the rise and fall of Prospecta Oil.

'No, sir. My own view is that Kesler, who incidentally has made a run for it and left the country, is no more than the dupe of bigger men. But we would still like to question him, so if he contacts you, please let me know immediately. Now, sir,' the Inspector continued, 'I'm going to read you a list of names and I would be obliged if you could tell me whether you have ever met, spoken to or heard of any of them . . . Harvey Metcalfe?'

'No,' said Stephen.

'Bernie Silverman?'

'I've never met or spoken to him, but David did mention his name in conversation when he dined with me here in college.'

The Detective Sergeant was writing down everything Stephen said, slowly and methodically.

'Richard Elliott?'

'The same applies to him as Silverman.'

'Alvin Cooper?'

'No,' said Stephen.

'Have you had any contact with anyone else who was involved in the company?'

'No.'

For well over an hour the Inspector quizzed Stephen on minor points, but he was unable to give him very much help, although he had kept a copy of the geologist's report.

'Yes, we are in possession of one of those documents, sir,' said the Inspector, 'but it's cleverly worded. I doubt if we'll be able to rely much on that for evidence.'

Stephen sighed and offered the two men some whisky and poured himself a dimmish dry sherry.

'Evidence against whom or for what, Inspector?' he said as he returned to his chair. 'It's clear to me that I've been taken for a sucker. I probably don't need to tell you what a fool I've made of myself. I put my shirt on Prospecta Oil because it sounded like a sure-fire winner, and ended up losing everything I had without having a clue what to do about it. What in heaven's name has been going on in Prospecta Oil?'

'Well, sir,' said the Inspector, 'you'll appreciate there are aspects of the case I'm not at liberty to discuss with you. Indeed, there are some things that aren't very clear to us yet. But the game isn't a new one, and this time it's been played by an old pro, a very cunning old pro. It works something like this: a company is set up or taken over by a bunch of villains who acquire the majority of the shares. They invent a plausible story about a new discovery or super product that will send the shares up, whisper it in a few willing ears, release their own shares onto the market and let them be snapped up by the likes of you, sir, at a higher price. Then they clear off with the profit they have made, after which the shares collapse because the company has no real substance. As often as not, it ends with dealings in the shares being suspended on the stock market, and finally in the compulsory liquidation of the company. That hasn't happened yet in this case, and it may not. The London Stock Exchange is only just recovering from the Caplan fiasco and they don't want another scandal on their hands. I'm sorry to say that we can hardly ever recover the money, even if we produce enough evidence to nail the villains. They have it all stashed away all over the world before you can say Dow-Jones Index.'

Stephen groaned. 'My God, you make it all sound so appallingly simple, Inspector. The geologist's report was a fake, then?'

'Not exactly, sir. Very impressively worded and well presented, but with plenty of ifs and buts; and one thing is for certain; the DPP's office is hardly likely to spend millions finding out if there *is* any oil in that part of the North Sea.'

Stephen buried his head in his hands and mentally cursed the day he met David Kesler.

'Tell me, Inspector, who put Kesler up to this? Who was the real brains behind it all?'

The Inspector realized only too well the terrible agony Stephen was going through. During his career he had faced many men in the same position, and he was grateful for Stephen's co-operation.

'I'll answer any questions I feel cannot harm my own inquiry,' said the Inspector. 'But it's no secret that the man we'd like to nail is Harvey Metcalfe.'

'Who's Harvey Metcalfe, for God's sake?'

'He's a first-generation American who's had his fingers in more dubious deals in Boston than you've had hot dinners. Made himself a multi-millionaire and a lot of other people bankrupt on the way. His style is so professional and predictable now we can smell the man a mile off. It will not amuse you to learn that he is a great benefactor of Harvard – does it to ease his conscience, no doubt. We've never been able to pin anything on him in the past, and I doubt if we'll be able to this time either. He was never a director of Prospecta Oil, and he only bought and sold shares on the open market. He never, as far as we know, even met David Kesler. He hired Silverman, Cooper and Elliott to do the dirty work, and they found a bright enthusiastic young man all freshly washed behind the ears to sell their story for them. I'm afraid it was a bit unlucky for you, sir, that the young man in question was your friend, David Kesler.'

'Never mind him, poor sod,' said Stephen. 'What about Harvey Metcalfe? Is he going to get away with it again?'

'I fear so,' said the Inspector. 'We have warrants out for the arrest of Silverman, Elliott and Cooper. They all beat it off to South America. After the Ronald Biggs fiasco I doubt if we'll ever get an extradition order to bring them back, even though the American and Canadian police also have warrants out for them. They were fairly cunning too. They closed the London office of Prospecta Oil, surrendered the lease and returned it to Conrad Ritblat, the estate agents, and gave notice to both secretaries with one month's pay in advance. They cleared the bill on the oil rig with Reading & Bates. They paid off their hired hand, Mark Stewart in Aberdeen, and took the Sunday morning flight to Rio de Janeiro, where there was $1 million in a private account waiting for them. Another two or three years, after they've spent all the money, and they'll undoubtedly turn up again with different names and a different company. Harvey Metcalfe rewarded them well and left David Kesler holding the baby.'

'Clever boys,' said Stephen.

'Oh, yes,' said the Inspector, 'it was a neat little operation. Worthy of the talents of Harvey Metcalfe.'

'Are you trying to arrest David Kesler?'

'No, but as I said we would like to question him. He bought and sold 500 shares, but we think that was only because he believed in the oil strike story himself. In fact, if he was wise, he would return to England and help the police with their inquiries, but I fear the poor man has panicked under pressure and made a bolt for it. The American police are keeping an eye out for him.'

'One last question,' said Stephen. 'Are there any other people who made such fools of themselves as I did?'

The Inspector gave this question long consideration. He had not had as much success with the other big investors as he had had with Stephen. They had all been evasive about their involvement with Kesler and Prospecta Oil. Perhaps if he released their names it might bring them out in some way.

'Yes, sir, but ... you must understand that you never heard about them from me.'

Stephen nodded.

'For your own interest you could find out what you need to know by making some discreet inquiries through the Stock Exchange. There were four main punters, of whom you were one. Between the four of you you lost approximately $1 million. The others were a Harley Street doctor, Robin Oakley, a London art dealer called Jean-Pierre Lamanns, and a farmer, the unluckiest of all, really. As far as I can gather, he mortgaged his farm to put up the money. Titled young gentleman: Viscount Brigsley. Metcalfe's snatched the silver spoon out of his mouth, all right.'

'No other big investors?'

'Two or three banks burnt their fingers badly, but there were no other private investors above £10,000. What you, the banks and the other big investors did was to keep the market buoyant long enough for Metcalfe to off-load his entire holding.'

'I know, and worse, I foolishly advised some of my friends to invest in the company as well.'

'Er ... there are two or three small investors from Oxford, yes sir,' said the Inspector, looking down at the sheet of paper in front of him, 'but don't worry – we won't be approaching them. Well, that seems to be all. It only leaves me to thank you for your cooperation and say we may be in touch again some time in the future. In any case, we'll keep you informed of developments, and I hope you'll do the same for us.'

'Of course, Inspector. I do hope you have a safe journey back to town.' The two policemen downed their drinks and left.

Stephen could never recall if it was while sitting in his armchair looking out at the Cloisters, or later in bed that night, that he decided to employ his academic mind to carry out a little research on Harvey Metcalfe and his fellow dupers. His grandfather's advice to him, when as a small child he failed to win their nightly game of chess, floated across his mind: Stevie, don't get cross, get even. He was pleased he had given his final lecture and finished work for the term, and as he fell asleep at 3 a.m. only one name was on his lips: Harvey Metcalfe.

5

Stephen awoke at about 5.30 a.m. He seemed to have been heavily, dreamlessly asleep, but as soon as he came to, the nightmare started again. He forced himself to use his mind constructively, to put the past firmly behind him and see what could be done about the future. He washed, shaved, dressed and missed college breakfast, occasionally murmuring to himself 'Harvey Metcalfe'. He then pedalled to Oxford station on an ancient bicycle, his preferred mode of transport in a city blocked solid with juggernaut lorries and full of unintelligible one-way systems. He left Ethelred the Unsteady padlocked to the station railings. There were as many bicycles standing in the ranks as there are cars in other railway stations.

He caught the 8.17 train so favoured by those who commute from Oxford to London every day. All the people at breakfast seemed to know each other and Stephen felt like an uninvited guest at someone else's party. The ticket collector bustled through the buffet car and clipped Stephen's first-class ticket. The man opposite Stephen produced a second-class ticket from behind his copy of the *Financial Times*. The collector clipped it grudgingly.

'You'll have to return to a second-class compartment when you've finished your breakfast, sir. The restaurant car is first class, you know.'

Stephen considered the implication of these remarks as he watched the flat Berkshire countryside jolt past, and his coffee cup lurched unsampled in its saucer before he turned his mind to the morning papers. *The Times* carried no news of Prospecta Oil that morning. It was, he supposed, an insignificant story, even a dull one. Not kidnap, not arson, not even rage; just another shady business enterprise collapsing – nothing there to hold the attention of the front page for more than one day. Not a story he would have given a second thought to himself but for his own involvement, which gave it all the making of a personal tragedy.

At Paddington he pushed through the ants rushing round the forecourt, glad that he had chosen the closeted life of a university or, more accurately, that it had chosen him. Stephen had never come to terms with London – he found the city large and impersonal, and he always took a taxi everywhere for fear of getting lost on the buses or the underground. Why didn't the English number their streets so Americans would know where they were?

'*The Times* office, Printing House Square.'

The cabby nodded and moved his black Austin deftly down the Bayswater Road, alongside a rain-sodden Hyde Park. The crocuses at Marble Arch looked sullen and battered, splayed wetly on the close grass. Stephen was impressed by London cabs: they never had a scrape or mark on them.

He had once been told that cab-drivers are not allowed to pick up fares unless their vehicles are in perfect condition. How different from New York's battered yellow monsters, he thought. The cabby proceeded to swing down Park Lane to Hyde Park Corner, past the House of Commons and along the Embankment. The flags were out in Parliament Square. Stephen frowned. What was the lead story he had read over so inattentively in the train? Ah yes, a meeting of Commonwealth leaders. He supposed he must allow the world to go about its daily business as usual.

Stephen was unsure how to tackle the problem of checking Harvey Metcalfe out. Back at Harvard he would have had no trouble, first making a bee-line for his father's old friend Hank Swaltz, the business correspondent of the *Herald American*. Hank would be sure to have supplied him with the inside dope. The diary correspondent of *The Times*, Richard Compton-Miller, was by no means as appropriate a contact, but he was the only British press man Stephen had ever met. Compton-Miller had been visiting Magdalen the previous spring to write a feature on the time-honoured observance of May Day in Oxford. The choristers on the top of the College tower had sung the Miltonian salute as the sun peeped over the horizon on May 1st:

> Hail, bounteous May, that doth inspire
> Mirth and youth and warm desire.

On the banks of the river beneath Magdalen bridge where Compton-Miller and Stephen had stood, several couples had clearly been inspired.

Later, Stephen had been more embarrassed than flattered by his appearance in the resulting piece written by Compton-Miller for *The Times* diary: academics are sparing with the word brilliant, but journalists are not. The more self-important of Stephen's Senior Common Room colleagues had not been amused to see him described as the brightest star in a firmament of moderate luminescence.

The taxi pulled into the forecourt and came to a stop by the side of a massive hunk of sculpture by Henry Moore. *The Times* and the *Observer* shared a building with separate entrances, *The Times*'s by far the more prestigious. Stephen asked the sergeant behind the desk for Richard Compton-Miller, and was directed to the fifth floor and then to his little private cubicle at the end of the corridor.

It was only a little after 10 a.m. when Stephen arrived, and the building was practically deserted. Compton-Miller later explained that a national newspaper does not begin to wake up until 11 a.m. and generally indulges in a long lunch hour until about 3. Between then and putting the paper to bed, about 8.30 p.m. for all but the front page, the real work is done. There is usually a complete change of staff, staggered from 5 p.m. onwards, whose job it is to watch for major news stories breaking during the night. They always have to keep a wary eye on what is happening in America, because if the President makes an important statement in the afternoon in Washington they are already going to press in London. Sometimes the front page can change as often as five times during the night; in the case of the assassination of President Kennedy, news of which first reached England about 7 p.m. on the evening of 22 November 1963, the entire front page had to be scrapped to make way for the tragedy.

'Richard, it was kind of you to come in early for me. I didn't realize that you started work so late. I rather take my daily paper for granted.'

Richard laughed. 'That's OK. We must seem a lazy bunch to you, but this place will be buzzing at midnight when you're tucked up in bed and sound asleep. Now, how can I help you?'

'I'm trying to do a little research on a fellow countryman of mine called Harvey Metcalfe. He's a substantial benefactor of Harvard, and I want to flatter the old boy by knowing all about him when I return.' Stephen didn't care very much for the lie, but these were strange circumstances he now found himself in.

'Hang on here and I'll go and see if we have anything in the cutting room on him.'

Stephen amused himself by reading the headlines pinned up on Compton-Miller's board – obviously stories he had taken some pride in: 'Prime Minister to Conduct Orchestra at Royal Festival Hall', 'Miss World loves Tom Jones', 'Muhammad Ali says "I will be Champion Again"'.

Richard returned fifteen minutes later, carrying a thickish file.

'Have a go at that, Descartes. I'll be back in an hour and we can have some coffee.'

Stephen nodded and smiled gratefully. Descartes never had to solve the problems he was facing.

Everything Harvey Metcalfe wanted the world to know was in that file, and a little bit he didn't want the world to know. Stephen learned of his yearly trips to Europe to visit Wimbledon, of the success of his horses at Ascot and of his pursuit of Impressionist pictures for his private art collection. William Hickey of the *Daily Express* had on one occasion titillated his readers with a plump Harvey clad in Bermuda shorts and a report that he spent two or three weeks a year on his private yacht at Monte Carlo, gambling at the Casino. Hickey's tone was something less than fulsome. The Metcalfe fortune was in his opinion too new to be respectable. Stephen wrote down meticulously all the facts he thought relevant and was studying the photographs when Richard returned.

He took Stephen off to have some coffee in the canteen on the same floor. Cigarette smoke swirled mistily round the girl at the cashier's desk at the end of the self-service counter.

'Richard, I don't quite have all the information I might need. Harvard want to touch this man for quite a large sum: I believe they are thinking in terms of about $1 million. Where could I find out some more about him?'

'*New York Times*, I should imagine,' said Compton-Miller. 'Come on, we'll give Terry Robards a visit.'

The *New York Times* office in London was also on the fifth floor of *The Times* building in Printing House Square. Stephen thought of the vast *New York Times* building on 43rd Street and wondered if the London *Times* had a reciprocal arrangement, and was secreted away in their basement. Terry Robards turned out to be a wiry American wearing a perpetual smile. Terry immediately made Stephen feel at ease, a knack he had developed almost subconsciously over the years and which was a great asset when digging a little deeper for stories.

Stephen repeated his piece about Metcalfe. Terry laughed.

'Harvard aren't too fussy where they get their money from, are they? That guy has discovered more legal ways of stealing money than the Internal Revenue Service.'

'You don't say,' said Stephen innocently.

The *New York Times* file on Harvey was voluminous. 'Metcalfe's rise from Messenger Boy to Millionaire', as one headline put it, was documented admirably. Stephen took further careful notes. The details of Sharpley & Son fascinated him, as did the facts on some war-time arms dealing and the background of his wife Arlene and their daughter Rosalie. There was a picture of both of them, but the daughter was only fifteen at the time. There were also long reports of two court cases some twenty-five years past, in which Harvey had been charged with fraud but never convicted, and a more recent case in 1956 concerning a share transfer scheme in Boston. Again Harvey had escaped the law, but the District Attorney had left the jury in little doubt of his views on Mr Metcalfe. The most recent press stories were all in the gossip columns: Metcalfe's paintings, his horses, his orchids, his daughter's success at Vassar and his trips to Europe. Of Prospecta Oil there was not a word. Stephen had to admire Harvey's ability to conceal his more dubious activities from the press.

Terry invited his fellow expatriate to lunch. Newsmen always like new contacts and Stephen looked like a promising one. He asked the cabby to go to Whitfield Street. As they inched their way out of the City into the West End, Stephen hoped that the meal would be worth the journey. He was not disappointed.

Lacy's restaurant was airy and bedecked with clean linen and young daffodils. Terry said it was greatly favoured by press men. Margaret Costa, the cookery writer and her chef husband, Bill Lacy, certainly knew their onions. Over delicious watercress soup followed by *Médaillons de veau à la crème au calvados* and a bottle of *Château de Péronne 1972*, Terry became quite expansive on the subject of Harvey Metcalfe. He had interviewed him once at Harvard on the occasion of the opening of Metcalfe Hall, which included a gymnasium and four indoor tennis courts.

'Hoping to get himself an honorary degree one day,' said Terry cynically, 'but not much hope, even if he gives a billion.'

Stephen noted the words thoughtfully.

'I guess you could get some more facts on the guy at the American Embassy,' said Terry. He glanced at his watch. 'No, hell, the library closes at 4 p.m. Too late today. Time I got back to the office now America's awake.'

Stephen wondered if press men ate and drank like that every day. They made University dons look positively celibate – and however did they manage to get a paper out?

Stephen fought his way on to the 5.15 train to return with the Oxford-bound commuters, and only when he was alone in his room did he begin to study the results of his day's work. Though exhausted, he forced himself to sit at his desk until he had prepared the first neat draft of a dossier on Harvey Metcalfe.

Next day Stephen again caught the 8.17 to London, this time buying a second-class ticket. The ticket collector repeated his piece about leaving the restaurant car after he had finished his meal.

'Sure,' said Stephen, as he toyed with the remains of his coffee for the rest of the hour-long journey, never shifting from first class. He was pleased with himself: he had saved £2, and that was exactly how Harvey Metcalfe would have behaved.

At Paddington he followed Terry Robards' advice and took a taxi to the American Embassy, a vast monolithic building which sprawls over 250,000 square feet and is nine storeys high, stretching the entire length of one side of Grosvenor Square. It was not, however, as elegant as the American Ambassador's magnificent official residence, Winfield House in Regents Park, where Stephen had been summoned to drinks last year, which was once the private home of Barbara Hutton before it was sold to the American government in 1946. Certainly, either of them was large enough for seven husbands, thought Stephen.

The entrance to the Embassy Reference Library on the ground floor was firmly shut. Stephen was reduced to a close study of the plaques on the wall in the corridor outside, honouring recent Ambassadors to the Court of St James. Reading backwards from Walter Annenberg, he had reached Joseph Kennedy when the doors of the library swung open, not unlike a bank. The prim girl behind a sign marked 'Enquiries' was not immediately forthcoming on the subject of Harvey Metcalfe.

'Why do you require this information?' she asked sharply.

This threw Stephen for a moment, but he quickly recovered. 'I'm returning to Harvard in the fall as a professor and I feel I should know more about his involvement with the university. I'm at present a Visiting Fellow at Magdalen College, Oxford.'

Stephen's answer motivated the girl to immediate action and she produced a file within a few minutes. Though by no means as racy as the *New York Times*'s, it did put figures on the amounts Harvey Metcalfe had donated to charity and gave precise details of his gifts to the Democratic Party. Most people do not divulge the exact amount they give to political parties, but Harvey only knew about lights – no one seemed to have told him about bushels.

Having finished his research at the Embassy, Stephen took a taxi to the Cunard offices in St James's Square and spoke to a booking clerk and from there on to Claridge's in Brook Street, where he spent a few minutes with the duty manager. A telephone call to Monte Carlo completed his research. He travelled back to Oxford on the 5.15.

Stephen returned to his college rooms. He felt he now knew as much about Harvey Metcalfe as anyone, except perhaps for Arlene and Detective Inspector Clifford Smith of the Fraud Squad. Once again he stayed up into the early hours completing his dossier, which now ran to over forty typewritten pages.

When the dossier was finally completed he went to bed and fell into a deep sleep. He rose again early in the morning, strolled across the Cloisters to a Common Room breakfast and helped himself to eggs, bacon, coffee and toast. He then took his dossier to the Bursar's office where he made four copies of every document, ending up with five dossiers in all. He strolled back across Magdalen Bridge, admiring as always the trim flower beds of the University Botanic Gardens beneath him on his right, and called in at Maxwell's Bookshop on the other side of the bridge.

Stephen returned to his rooms with five smart files all of different colours. He then placed the five dossiers in the separate files and put them in a drawer of his desk which he kept locked. Stephen had a tidy and methodical mind, as a mathematician must: a mind the like of which Harvey Metcalfe had never yet come up against.

Stephen then referred to the notes he had written after his interview with Detective Inspector Smith and rang Directory Enquiries, asking for the London addresses and telephone numbers of Dr Robin Oakley, Jean-Pierre Lamanns and Lord Brigsley. Directory Enquiries refused to give him more than two numbers at any one time. Stephen wondered how the GPO expected to make a profit. In the States the Bell Telephone Company would happily have given him a dozen telephone numbers and still ended with the inevitable 'You're welcome'.

The two he managed to wheedle out of his reluctant informant were Dr Robin Oakley at 122 Harley Street, London W1, and Jean-Pierre Lamanns at the Lamanns Gallery, 40 New Bond Street, W1. Stephen then dialled Directory Enquiries a second time and requested the number and address of Lord Brigsley.

'No one under Brigsley in Central London,' said the operator. 'Maybe he's ex-Directory. That is, if he really is a lord,' she sniffed.

Stephen left his study for the Senior Common Room, where he thumbed through the latest copy of *Who's Who* and found the noble lord:

BRIGSLEY, Viscount; James Clarence Spencer; b. 11 Oct. 1942; Farmer; *s* and *heir* of 5th Earl of Louth, *cr* 1764, *qv. Educ*: Harrow; Christ Church, Oxford (BA). Pres. Oxford University Dramatic Society. Lt Grenadier Guards 1966–68. *Recreations*: polo (not water), shooting. *Address*: Tathwell Hall, Louth, Lincs. *Clubs*: Garrick, Guards.

Stephen then strolled over to Christ Church and asked the secretary in the Treasurer's office if she had in her records a London address for James Brigsley, matriculated 1963. It was duly supplied as 119 King's Road, London SW3.

Stephen was beginning to warm to the challenge of Harvey Metcalfe. He left Christ Church by Peckwater and the Canterbury Gate, out into the High and back to Magdalen, hands in pockets, composing a brief letter in his mind. Oxford's nocturnal slogan-writers had been at work on a college wall again: 'Deanz meanz feinz' said one neatly painted graffito. Stephen, the reluctant Junior Dean of Magdalen, responsible for undergraduate discipline, smiled. If they were funny enough he would allow them to remain for one term, if not, he would have the porter scrub them out immediately. Back at his desk, he wrote down what had been in his mind.

Magdalen College,
Oxford.
April 15th

Dear Dr Oakley,
    I am holding a small dinner party in my rooms next Thursday evening for a few carefully selected people.

I would be delighted if you could spare the time to join me, and I think you would find it worth your while to be present.

Yours sincerely,
Stephen Bradley

ps: I am sorry David Kesler is unable to join us.
Black Tie. 7.30 for 8 p.m.

Stephen changed the sheet of letter paper in his old Remington typewriter and addressed similar letters to Jean-Pierre Lamanns and Lord Brigsley. Then he sat thinking for a little while before picking up the internal telephone.

'Harry?' he said to the head porter. 'If anyone rings the lodge to ask if the college has a fellow called Stephen Bradley, I want you to say, "Yes, sir, a new Mathematics Fellow from Harvard, already famous for his dinner parties." Is that clear, Harry?'

'Yes, sir,' said Harry Woodley, the head porter. He had never understood Americans – Dr Bradley was no exception.

All three men did ring and inquire, as Stephen had anticipated they might. He himself would have done the same in the circumstances. Harry remembered his message and repeated it carefully, although the callers still seemed a little baffled.

'No more than me, or is it I?' muttered the head porter.

Stephen received acceptances from all three during the next week, James Brigsley's arriving last, on the Friday. The crest on his letter paper announced a promising motto: *ex nihilo omnia.*

The butler to the Senior Common Room and the college chef were consulted, and a meal to loosen the tongues of the most taciturn was planned:

Coquilles St Jacques	Pouilly Fuissé 1969
Carrée d'agneau en croûte	Feux St Jean 1970
Casserôle d'artichauds et champignons	
Pommes de terre boulangère	
Griestorte with raspberries	Barsac Ch. d'Yquem 1927
Camembert frappé	Port Taylor 1947
Café	

Everything was ready; all Stephen could do now was wait for the appointed hour.

. . .

On the stroke of 7.30 p.m. on the appointed Thursday Jean-Pierre arrived. Stephen admired the elegant dinner-jacket and large floppy bow-tie that his guest wore, while he fingered his own little clip-on, surprised that Jean-Pierre Lamanns, who had such obvious savoir-faire, could also have fallen victim to Prospecta Oil. Stephen plunged into a monologue on the significance of the isosceles triangle in modern art while Jean-Pierre stroked his moustache. It was not a subject Stephen would normally have chosen to speak on without a break for five minutes, and he was only saved from the inevitability of more direct questions from Jean-Pierre by the arrival of Dr Robin Oakley. Robin had lost a few pounds in the past month, but Stephen could see why his practice in Harley Street was a success. He was, in the words of H. H. Munro, a man whose looks made it possible for women to forgive any other trifling inadequacies. Robin studied his shambling host, wondering whether he dared to ask immediately if they had ever met before. No, he decided; he would leave it a little and hope perhaps some clue as to why he had been invited would materialize during dinner. The David Kesler PS worried him.

Stephen introduced him to Jean-Pierre and they chatted while their host checked the dinner-table. Once again the door opened, and with a little more respect than previously displayed, the porter announced, 'Lord Brigsley'. Stephen walked forward to greet him, suddenly unsure whether he should bow or shake hands. Although James did not know anyone present at the strange gathering, he showed no signs of discomfort and entered easily into the conversation. Even Stephen was impressed by James's relaxed line of small talk, although he couldn't help recalling his academic results when at Christ Church and wondered whether the noble lord would in fact be an asset to his plans.

The culinary efforts of the chef worked their intended magic. No guest could possibly have asked his host why the dinner party was taking place while such delicately garlic-flavoured lamb, such tender almond pastry, such excellent wine, were still to hand.

Finally, when the servants had cleared the table and port was on its way round for the second time, Robin could stand it no longer:

'If it's not a rude question, Dr Bradley.'

'Do call me Stephen.'

'Stephen, may I ask what is the purpose of this select little gathering?'

Six eyes bored into him demanding an answer to the same question.

Stephen rose and surveyed his guests. He walked around the table twice before speaking and then started his discourse by recalling the entire history of the past few weeks. He told them of his meeting in that very room with David Kesler, his investment in Prospecta Oil, followed soon afterwards by the visit of the Fraud Squad, and their disclosure about Harvey Metcalfe. He ended his carefully prepared speech with the words, 'Gentlemen, the truth is that the four of us are in the same bloody mess.' He felt that sounded suitably British.

Jean-Pierre reacted even before Stephen could finish what he was saying.

'Count me out. I couldn't be involved in anything quite so ridiculous as that. I am a humble art dealer, not a speculator.'

Robin Oakley also jumped in before Stephen was given the chance to reply:

'I've never heard anything so preposterous. You must have contacted the wrong man. I'm a Harley Street doctor – I don't know the first thing about oil.'

Stephen could see why the Fraud Squad had had trouble with these two and why they had been so thankful for his cooperation. They all looked at Lord Brigsley, who raised his eyes and said very quietly:

'Absolutely right on every detail, Dr Bradley, and I'm in more of a pickle than you. I borrowed £150,000 to buy the shares against the security of my small farm in Hampshire and I don't think it will be long before the bank insists that I dispose of it. When they do and my dear old pa, the fifth earl, finds out, it's curtains for me unless I become the sixth earl overnight.'

'Thank you,' said Stephen. As he sat down, he turned to Robin and raised his eyebrows interrogatively.

'What the hell,' said Robin, 'You're right – I was involved. David Kesler was a patient of mine and in a rash moment I invested £100,000 in Prospecta Oil as a temporary advance against my securities. God only knows what made me do it. As the shares are only worth 50 pence I'm stuck with them. I have a shortfall at my bank which they're beginning to fuss about. I also have a large mortgage on my country home in Berkshire and a heavy rent on my Harley Street consulting-room, a wife with expensive tastes and two boys at the best private prep school in England. I've hardly slept a wink since Detective Inspector Smith visited me two weeks ago.' He looked up. His face had drained of colour and the suave self-confidence of Harley Street had gone. Slowly, they all turned and stared at Jean-Pierre.

'All right, all right,' he admitted, 'me too. I was in Paris when the damned thing folded under me, so now, I'm stuck with the useless shares. £80,000 borrowed against my stock at the gallery. And what's worse, I advised some of my friends to invest in the bloody company too.'

Silence enveloped the room. It was Jean-Pierre who broke it again:

'So what do you suggest, Professor,' he said sarcastically. 'Do we hold an annual dinner to remind us what fools we've been?'

'No, that was not what I had in mind.' Stephen hesitated, realizing that what he was about to suggest was bound to cause even more commotion. Once again he rose to his feet, and said quietly and deliberately:

'We have had our money stolen by a very clever man who has proved to be an expert in share fraud. None of us is knowledgeable about stocks and shares, but we are all experts in our own fields. Gentlemen I therefore suggest we steal it back.

– NOT A PENNY MORE AND NOT A PENNY LESS.'

A few seconds' silence was followed by uproar.

'Just walk up and take it I suppose?' said Robin.

'Kidnap him,' mused James.

'Why don't we just kill him and claim the life insurance?' said Jean-Pierre.

Several moments passed. Stephen waited until he had complete silence again, and then he handed round the four dossiers marked 'Harvey Metcalfe' with each of their names below. A green dossier for Robin, a blue one for James and a yellow for Jean-Pierre. The red master copy Stephen kept for himself. They were all impressed. While they had been wringing their hands in unproductive dismay, it was obvious that Stephen Bradley had been hard at work.

Stephen continued:

'Please read your dossier carefully. It will brief you on everything that is known about Harvey Metcalfe. Each of you must take the document away and study the information, and then return with a plan of how we are, between us, to extract $1,000,000 from him without his ever being aware of it. All four of us must come up with a separate plan. Each may involve the other three in his own operation. We will return here in fourteen days' time and present our conclusions. Each member of the team will put $10,000 into the kitty as a float and I, as the mathematician, will keep a running account. All expenses incurred in retrieving our money will be added to Mr Metcalfe's bill, starting with your journey down here this evening and the cost of the dinner tonight.'

Jean-Pierre and Robin began to protest again, but it was James who stopped the proceedings, by simply saying:

'I agree. What have we got to lose? On our own we've no chance at all: together we might just tweak the bastard.'

Robin and Jean-Pierre looked at each other, shrugged and nodded.

The four of them settled down to discuss in detail the material Stephen had acquired over the past few days. They left the college a little after midnight, each agreeing to have a plan ready for the Team's consideration in fourteen days' time. None of them was quite sure where it all might end, but each was relieved to know he was no longer on his own.

Stephen decided that the first part of the Team versus Harvey Metcalfe had gone as well as he could have wished. He only hoped his conspirators would now get down to work. He sat in his armchair, stared at the ceiling and continued thinking.

6

Robin retrieved his car from the High Street, not for the first time in his life being thankful for the 'Doctor on Call' sticker which always gave him an extra degree of freedom when parking. He headed back towards his home in Berkshire. There was no doubt about it, Stephen Bradley was a very impressive man; Robin was determined to come up with something that would ensure that he played his full part.

Robin let his mind linger a little on the delightful prospect of recovering the money he had so ill-advisedly entrusted to Prospecta Oil and Harvey Metcalfe. It must be worth a try: after all, he might as well be struck off the register of the General Medical Council for attempted robbery as for bankruptcy. He wound the window of the car down a little way to dispel the last delicious effects of the claret and considered Stephen's challenge more carefully.

The journey between Oxford and his country house passed very quickly. His mind was so preoccupied with Harvey Metcalfe that when he arrived home to his wife there were large sections of the journey that he could not even remember. Robin had only one talent to offer, apart from his natural charm, and he hoped that he was right in thinking that particular talent was the strength in his armour and a weakness in Harvey Metcalfe's. He began to repeat aloud something that was written on page 16 of Stephen's dossier, 'One of Harvey Metcalfe's recurrent worries is ...'

'What was it all about, darling?'

His wife's voice brought Robin quickly to his senses and he locked the briefcase containing the green Metcalfe dossier.

'You still awake, Mary?'

'Well, I'm not not talking in my sleep, love.'

Robin had to think quickly. He had not yet steeled himself to tell Mary the details of his foolish investment, but he had let her know about the dinner in Oxford, not at that time realizing it was in any way connected with Prospecta Oil.

'It was a tease, sweetheart. An old friend of mine from Cambridge has been appointed a lecturer at Oxford, so he dragged a few of his contemporaries down for dinner and we had a damn good evening. Jim and Fred from my old college were there, but I don't expect you remember them.'

A bit weak, thought Robin, but the best he could do at 1.15 in the morning.

'Sure it wasn't some beautiful girl?' said Mary.

'I'm afraid Jim and Fred could hardly be described as beautiful, even by their loving wives.'

'Do lower your voice, Robin, or you'll wake the children.'

'I'm going down again in two weeks time to ...'

'Oh, come to bed and tell me about it at breakfast.'

Robin was relieved to be let off the hook until the morning. He clambered in beside his fragrant silk-clad wife and ran his finger hopefully down her vertebral column to her coccyx.

'You'll be lucky, at this time of night,' she mumbled.

They both slept.

· · ·

Jean-Pierre had booked himself in at the Eastgate Hotel in the High. There was to be an undergraduate exhibition the next day at the Christ Church Art Gallery. Jean-Pierre was always on the look-out for new young talent which he could contract to the Lamanns Gallery. It was the Marlborough Gallery, a few doors away from him in Bond Street, that had taught the London art world the astuteness of buying up young artists and being closely identified with their careers. But for the moment, the artistic future of his gallery was not uppermost in Jean-Pierre's mind: its very survival was threatened, and the quiet American don from Magdalen had offered him the chance of redress. He settled down in his comfortable hotel bedroom, oblivious of the late hour, reading his dossier and working out where he could fit into the jig-saw. He was not going to allow two Englishmen and a Yank to beat him. His father had been relieved at Rochefort by the British in 1918 and released from a prisoner-of-war camp near Frankfurt by the Americans in 1945. Nothing was going to stop him being a full participant in this operation. He read his yellow dossier late into the night: the germ of an idea was beginning to form in his mind.

· · ·

James made the last train from Oxford and looked for an empty carriage where he could settle down to study the blue dossier. He was a worried man: he was sure the other three would each come up with a brilliant plan and, as had always seemed to be the case in the past, he would be found lacking. He had never been under any real pressure before – everything had come to him so easily; now it had all gone just as easily. A foolproof scheme for relieving Harvey Metcalfe of some of his excess profits was not James' idea of an amusing pastime. Still, the awful vision of his father discovering that the Hampshire farm was mortgaged up to the hilt was always there to keep his mind on the job. But fourteen days was such a short time: where on earth should he begin? He was not a professional man like the other three and had no particular skills to offer. He could only hope that his stage experience might come in useful at some point.

He bumped into the ticket collector, who was not surprised to find James was the holder of a first-class ticket. The quest for an empty compartment was in vain. James concluded that Richard Marsh must be trying to run the railways at a profit. Whatever next? Still more aggravating, they would probably give him a knighthood for his pains.

The next best thing to an empty compartment, James always thought, was one containing a beautiful girl – and this time his luck was in. One of the compartments was occupied by a truly stunning creature who looked as if she was alone. The only other person in the carriage was a middle-aged lady reading *Vogue*, who showed no signs of knowing her travelling companion. James settled down in the corner with his back to the engine. They had all been sworn to total secrecy, and Stephen had cautioned them against reading the dossiers in anyone else's company. James feared that of the four of them he was going to find it the most difficult to remain silent: a companionable man, he found secrets rather burdensome. He touched his overcoat pocket, the one holding the dossier in the envelope supplied by Stephen Bradley. What an efficient man he was, thought James. Alarmingly brainy, too. He was bound to have a dozen clever plans ready for consideration by the next meeting. James frowned and stared out of the window hoping some serendipitous idea would strike him. Instead he found himself studying the reflection of the profile of the girl sitting opposite him.

She had a shiny nob of dark brown hair, a slim straught nose and her large hazel eyes seemed fixed on the book she held in her lap. James wondered if she was as entirely oblivious of his presence as she appeared to be, and reluctantly decided that she was. His eyes slipped down to the gentle curve of her breast, softly encased in angora. He craned his neck slightly to see what sort of legs the reflection had. Damn it, she was wearing boots. He looked back at the face again. It was now looking back at him, faintly amused. Embarrassed, he switched his attention to the third occupant of the carriage, the unofficial chaperone in front of whom James lacked the courage even to strike up a conversation with the beautiful profile.

In desperation he stared at the cover of the middle-aged lady's *Vogue*. Another beautiful girl. And then he looked more carefully. It wasn't another girl, it was the same girl. To begin with, he could hardly believe his eyes, but a quick check against the genuine article left him in no doubt. As soon as *Vogue* was relinquished in favour of *Queen*, James leant across and asked the chaperone if he might be allowed to read it.

'Station bookstalls are closing earlier and earlier,' he said idiotically. 'I couldn't get anything to read.'

The chaperone agreed reluctantly.

He turned to the second page. 'Cover: Picture yourself like this ... black silk georgette dress with chiffon handkerchief points. Ostrich-feather boa. turban with flower, matching dress. Made to measure by Zandra Rhodes. Anne's hair by Jason at Vidal Sassoon. Photograph by Lichfield. Camera: Hasselblad.'

James was quite unable to picture himself like that. But at least he now knew the girl's name, Anne. The next time the real-life version looked up, he showed her by sign language that he had spotted the photograph. She smiled briefly at James and then returned to her book.

At Reading station the middle-aged lady left, taking *Vogue* with her. Couldn't be better, mused James. Anne looked up, faintly embarrassed, and smiled hopefully at the few passers-by walking up and down the corridor looking for a seat. James glared at them as they passed. No one entered the carriage. James had won the first round. As the train gathered speed he tried his opening gambit, which was quite good by his normal standards:

'What a super picture on the front of *Vogue* taken by my old friend Patrick Lichfield.'

Anne Summerton looked up. She was even more beautiful than the picture James had referred to. Her dark hair, cut softly in the latest Vidal Sassoon style, her big hazel eyes and faultless skin gave her a gentle look that James found irresistible. She had that slim, graceful body that all leading models need to earn their living, but Anne also had a presence that most of them would never have. James was quite stunned and wished she would say something.

Anne was used to men trying to pick her up but she was rather taken aback by the remark about Lord Lichfield. If he was a friend, it would be offhand not to be at least polite. On a second glance she found James's diffidence rather charming. He had used the self-deprecating approach many times with great success, but this time it was perfectly genuine. He tried again.

'It must be a hell of a job being a model.'

What a bloody silly line, he thought. Why couldn't he just say to her, I think you're absolutely fantastic? Can we talk a little and if I still think you're fantastic perhaps we can take it from there? But it never worked that way. He knew he would have to go through the usual routine.

'It's bearable if the contracts are good,' she replied, 'but today's been particularly tiring.' Her voice was gentle, and the faint translatlantic accent appealed to James. 'I've been smiling my head off all day, modelling an advertisement for Close-Up toothpaste: the photographer never seemed to be satisfied. The only good thing about it was that it ended a day earlier than expected. How do you know Patrick?'

'We were fags together at Harrow in our first year. He was rather better than me at getting out of work.'

Anne laughed – a gentle, warm laugh. It was obvious he knew Lord Lichfield.

'Do you see much of him now?'

'Occasionally at dinner parties, but not regularly. Does he photograph you a lot?'

'No,' said Anne, 'the cover picture for *Vogue* was the only time.'

As they chatted on, the thirty-five minute journey between Reading and

London seemed to pass in a flash. Walking down the platform of Paddington Station with Anne, James ventured:

'Can I give you a lift home? My car is parked round the corner in Craven Street.'

Anne accepted, relieved not to have to search for a taxi at that late hour.

James drove her home in his Alfa Romeo. He had already decided that he could not hold on to that particular luxury for much longer with petrol going up and cash flow going down. He chattered merrily all the way to her destination, which turned out to be a block of flats in Cheyne Row overlooking the Thames; much to Anne's surprise he just dropped her off at the front door and said goodnight. He did not even ask for her telephone number and he only knew her Christian name. In fact, she did not have any idea what his name was. Pity, she thought as she closed the front door; he had been a rather pleasant change from the men who worked on the fringe of the advertising media, who imagined they had an automatic right to a girl's compliance just because she posed in a bra.

James knew exactly what he was doing. He had always found a girl was more flattered if he called her when she least expected it. His tactics were to leave the impression that she had seen the last of him, especially when the first meeting had gone well. He returned to his home in the King's Road and considered the situation. Unlike Stephen, Robin and Jean-Pierre, with thirteen days to go, he still had no ideas for defeating Harvey Metcalfe. But he was hatching plans for Anne.

.   .   .

On walking in the morning, Stephen began to do a little more research. He started with a close study of the way the university was administered. He visited the Vice-Chancellor's office in the Clarendon Building, where he spent some time asking strange questions of his personal secretary, Miss Smallwood. She was most intrigued. He then left for the office of the University Registrar, where he was equally inquisitive. He ended the day by visiting the Bodleian Library, and copying out some of the University Statutes. Among other outings during the next fourteen days was a trip to the Oxford tailors, Shepherd and Woodward, and a full day at the Sheldonian Theatre to watch the brief ceremony as a batch of students took their Bachelor of Arts degrees. Stephen also studied the layout of the Randolph, the largest hotel in Oxford. This he took some considerable time over, so much so that the manager became inquisitive and Stephen had to leave before he became suspicious. His final trip was a return journey to the Clarendon to meet the Secretary of the University Chest, and to be taken on a guided tour of the building by the porter. Stephen warned him that he anticipated showing an American around the building on the day of Encaenia, but remained vague.

'Well, that won't be easy ...' began the porter. Stephen carefully and deliberately folded a pound note and passed it to the porter '... though I'm sure we'll be able to work something out, sir.'

In between his trips all over the university city, Stephen did a lot of thinking in the big leather chair and a lot more writing at his desk. By the fourteenth day his plan was perfected and ready for presentation to the other three. He had put the show on the road, as Harvey Metcalfe might have said, and he intended to see it had a long run.

.   .   .

Robin rose early on the morning after the Oxford dinner, and avoided awkward questions from his wife at breakfast about his experience the night before. He travelled up to London as soon as he could get away, and on arrival in Harley Street was greeted by his efficient secretary-cum receptionist, Miss Meikle.

Elspeth Meikle was a dedicated, dour Scot who looked upon her work as nothing less than a vocation. Her devotion to Robin, not that she ever called him that even in her own mind, was obvious for all to see.

'I want as few appointments as possible over the next fourteen days, Miss Meikle.'

'I understand, Dr Oakley,' she said.

'I have some research to carry out and I don't want to be interrupted when I'm alone in my study.'

Miss Meikle was somewhat surprised. She had always thought of Dr Oakley as a good physician, but had never known him in the past to over-indulge in research work. She padded off noiselessly in her white-shod feet to admit the first of a bunch of admirably healthy ladies to Dr Oakley's clinic.

Robin disposed of his patients with less than dignified speed. He went without lunch and began the afternoon by making several telephone calls to the Boston Infirmary and several to a leading gastroenterologist for whom he had been a houseman at Cambridge. Then he pressed the buzzer to summon Miss Meikle.

'Could you pop round to H. K. Lewis for me, Miss Meikle, and put two books on my account. I want the latest edition of Polson and Tattersall's *Clinical Toxicology* and Harding Rain's book on the bladder and abdomen.'

'Yes, sir,' she said, quite unperturbed at the thought of interrupting her lunchtime sandwich to fetch them.

They were on his desk before he had completed his calls, and he immediately started reading long sections of them carefully. The following day he cancelled his morning clinic and went to St Thomas's Hospital to watch two of his old colleagues at work. His confidence in the plan he had formulated was growing. He returned to Harley Street and wrote some notes on the techniques he had observed that morning, much as he had done in his student days. He paused to remember the words Stephen had used:

'Think as Harvey Metcalfe would. Think for the first time in your life, not as a cautious professional man, but as a risk-taker, as an entrepreneur.'

Robin was tuning in to Harvey Metcalfe's wavelength, and when the time came he would be ready for the American, the Frenchman and the lord. But would they be willing to fall in with his plan? He looked forward to their meeting.

.   .   .

Jean-Pierre returned from Oxford the next day. None of the youthful artists had greatly impressed him, though he had felt that Brian Davis's still life showed considerable promise and had made a mental note to keep an eye on his future work. When he arrived back in London he started, like Robin and Stephen, on his research. A tentative idea that had come to him in the Eastgate Hotel was beginning to germinate. Through his numerous contacts in the art world he checked all the buying and selling of major Impressionist paintings over the previous twenty years and made a list of the pictures which were currently thought to be on the market. He then contacted the one person who held it in his power to set his plan in motion. Fortunately the man whose help he most needed, David Stein, was in England and free to visit him: but would he fall in with the plan?

Stein arrived late the following afternoon and spent two hours with Jean-Pierre privately in his little room in the basement of the Lamanns Gallery. When he left Jean-Pierre was smiling to himself. A final afternoon spent at the German Embassy in Belgrave Square, followed by a call to Dr Wormit of the Preussischer Kulturbesitz in Berlin and a further one to Mme Tellegen at the Rijksbureau in The Hague, gave him all the information he required. Even Metcalfe would have praised him for the final touch. There would be no relieving the French this time. The American and the Englishman had better be up to scratch when he presented his plan.

.   .   .

On waking in the morning the last thing James had on his mind was an idea for outwitting Harvey Metcalfe. His thoughts were fully occupied with more important things. He telephoned Patrick Lichfield at home.

'Patrick?'

'Yes,' mumbled a voice.

'James Brigsley.'

'Oh, hello James. Haven't seen you for some time. What are you doing waking a fellow up at this filthy hour?'

'It's 10 a.m. Patrick.'

'Is it? It was the Berkeley Square Ball last night and I didn't get to bed until four. What can I do for you?'

'You took a picture for *Vogue* of a girl whose first name was Anne.'

'Summerton,' said Patrick without hesitation. 'Got her from the Stacpoole Agency.'

'What's she like?'

'No idea,' said Patrick. 'I thought she was awfully nice. She just thought I wasn't her type.'

'Obviously a woman of taste, Patrick. Now go back to sleep.' James put the phone down.

Anne Summerton was not listed in the telephone directory – so that ploy had failed. James remained in bed, scratching the stubble on his chin, when a triumphant look came into his eye. A quick flip through the S–Z directory revealed the number he required. He dialled it.

'The Stacpoole Agency.'

'Can I speak to the manager?'

'Who's calling?'

'Lord Brigsley.'

'I'll put you through, my lord.'

James heard the phone click and the voice of the manager.

'Good morning, my lord. Michael Stacpoole speaking. Can I help you?'

'I hope so, Mr Stacpoole. I have been let down at the last moment and I'm looking for a model for the opening of an antique shop and I'll need a classy sort of a bird. You know the kind of girl.'

James then described Anne as if he had never met her.

'We have two models on our books who I think would suit you, my lord,' offered Stacpoole. 'Pauline Stone and Anne Summerton. Unfortunately, Pauline is in Birmingham today for the launching of the new Allegro car and Anne is completing a toothpaste session in Oxford.'

'I need a girl today,' James said. How he would have liked to have informed Stacpoole that Anne was back in town. 'If you find either of them are free for any reason, perhaps you would ring me at 735–7227.'

James rang off, a little disappointed. At least, he thought, if nothing comes of it today he could start planning his part in the Team versus Harvey Metcalfe. He was just resigning himself to that when the phone rang. A shrill, high-pitched voice announced:

'This is the Stacpoole Agency. Mr Stacpoole would like to speak to Lord Brigsley.'

'Speaking,' said James.

'I'll put you through, my lord.'

'Lord Brigsley?'

'Yes.'

'Stacpoole here, my lord. It seems Anne Summerton is free today. When would you like her to come to your shop?'

'Oh,' said James, taken aback for a second. 'The shop is in Berkeley Street, next to the Empress Restaurant. It's called Albemarle Antiques. Perhaps we could meet outside at 12.45?'

'I'm sure that will be acceptable, my lord. If I don't ring you back in the next ten minutes, you can assume the meeting is on. Perhaps you'd be kind enough to let us know if she's suitable. We normally prefer you to come to the office, but I'm sure we can make an exception in your case.'

'Thank you,' said James and put the phone down, pleased with himself.

James stood on the west side of Berkeley Street in the doorway of the Mayfair Hotel so that he could watch Anne arriving. When it came to work, Anne was always on time, and at 12.40 p.m. she appeared from the Piccadilly end of the street. Her skirt was of the latest elegant length, but this time James could see that her legs were as slim and shapely as the rest of her. She stopped outside the Empress Restaurant and looked in bewilderment at the Brazilian Trade Centre on her right and the Rolls-Royce showrooms of H. R. Owen on her left.

James strode across the road, a large grin on his face.

'Good morning,' he said casually.

'Oh hello,' said Anne, 'what a coincidence.'

'What are you doing here all alone and looking lost?' said James.

'I'm trying to find a shop called Albemarle Antiques. You don't know it by any chance? I must have the wrong street. As you go in for knowing lords, you might know the owner, Lord Brigsley?'

James smiled:

'I am Lord Brigsley.'

Anne looked surprised and then burst out laughing. She realized what James had done and was flattered by the compliment.

They lunched together at the Empress, James's favourite eating place in town. He explained to Anne why it had been Lord Clarendon's favourite restaurant as well – 'Ah,' he had once declared, 'the millionaires are just a little fatter, and the mistresses are just a little thinner, than in any other restaurant in town.'

The meal was a triumph and James had to admit that Anne was the best thing that had happened to him for a long time. After lunch she asked where the agency should send their account.

'With what I have in mind for the future,' replied James, 'they'd better be prepared for a large bad debt.'

7

Stephen wrung James warmly by the hand the way the Americans will and presented him with a large whisky on the rocks. Impressive memory, thought James, as he took a gulp to give himself a little Dutch courage, and then joined Robin and Jean-Pierre. By unspoken mutual consent, the name of Harvey Metcalfe was not mentioned. They chattered inconsequentially of nothing in particular, each clutching his own dossier, until Stephen summoned them to the table. Stephen had not, on this occasion, exercised the talents of the college chef and the butler to the Senior Common Room. Instead, sandwiches, beer and coffee were stacked neatly on the table, and the college servants were not in evidence.

'This is a working supper,' said Stephen firmly, 'and as Harvey Metcalfe will eventually be footing the bill, I've cut down considerably on the hospitality. We don't want to make our task unnecessarily harder by eating our way through hundreds of dollars per meeting.'

The other three sat down quietly as Stephen took out some closely-typed sheets of paper.

'I'll begin,' he said, 'with a general comment. I've been doing some further research into Harvey Metcalfe's movements over the next few months. He seems to spend every summer doing the same round of social and sporting events. Most of the details are already well documented in your files. My latest findings are summarized on this separate sheet which should be added as page 38A of your dossiers. It reads:

Harvey Metcalfe will arrive in England on the morning of 21 June on board the QE2, docking at Southampton. He has already reserved the Trafalgar Suite for his crossing and booked a Rolls-Royce from Guy Salmon to take him to Claridge's. He will stay there for two weeks in the Royal Suite and he has his own debenture tickets for every day of the Wimbledon Championships. When they are over he flies to Monte Carlo to stay on his yacht *Messenger Boy* for another two weeks. He then returns to London and Claridge's to see his filly,

Rosalie, run in the King George VI and Queen Elizabeth Stakes. He has a private box at Ascot for all five days of Ascot Week. He returns to America on a Pan American jumbo jet from London Heathrow on 29 July, flight no. 009 at 11.15 to Logan International Airport, Boston.'

The others attached page 38A to their dossiers, aware once again how much detailed research Stephen had undertaken. James was beginning to feel ill, and it certainly was not the excellent sandwiches that were causing his discomfort.

'The next decision to be taken,' said Stephen, 'is to allocate the times during Metcalfe's trip to Europe when each plan will be put into operation. Robin, which section would you prefer?'

'Monte Carlo,' said Robin without hesitation. 'I need to catch the bastard off his home ground.'

'Anyone else want Monte Carlo?'

Nobody spoke.

'Which would you prefer, Jean-Pierre?'

'I'd like Wimbledon fortnight.'

'Any other takers?'

Again, nobody spoke. Stephen continued:

'I'm keen to have the Ascot slot myself and the short time before he returns to America. What about you, James?'

'It won't make any difference what period I have,' said James rather sheepishly.

'Right,' said Stephen.

Everybody, except James, seemed to be warming to the exercise.

'Now expenses. Have all of you brought your cheques for $10,000? I think it's wise to think in dollars as that was the currency Harvey Metcalfe worked in.'

Each member of the Team passed over a cheque to Stephen. At least, thought James, this is something I can do as well as the others.

'Expenses to date?'

Each passed a chit to Stephen again and he began to work out figures on his stylish little HP 65 calculator, the digits glowing red in the dimly-lit room.

'The shares cost us $1 million. Expenses to date are $142, so Mr Metcalfe is in debt to us to the tune of $1,000,142. Not a penny more and not a penny less,' he repeated. 'Now to our individual plans. We will take them in the order of execution.' Stephen was pleased with that word. 'Jean-Pierre, Robin, myself and finally James. The floor is yours, Jean-Pierre.'

Jean-Pierre opened a large envelope and took out four sets of documents. He was determined to show that he had the measure of Stephen as well as of Harvey Metcalfe. He handed round photographs and road maps of the West End and Mayfair. Each street was marked with a number, indicating how many minutes it took to walk. Jean-Pierre explained his plan in great detail, starting with the crucial meeting he had had with David Stein, and ending with the roles the others would have to carry out.

'All of you will be needed on the day. Robin will be the journalist, James the representative from Sotheby's, and Stephen, you will act as the purchaser.

You must practise speaking English with a German accent. I shall also require two tickets for the whole of Wimbledon fortnight on the Centre Court opposite Harvey Metcalfe's debenture box.'

Jean-Pierre consulted his notes.

'That is to say, opposite box No. 17. Can you arrange that, James?'

'No problem. I'll have a word with Mike Gibson, the Club referee, in the morning.'

'Good. Finally, then you must all learn to operate these little boxes of tricks. They are called Pye Pocketfones and don't forget that the use and ownership of them are illegal.'

Jean-Pierre produced four miniature sets and handed three to Stephen.

'Any questions?'

There was a general murmur of approval. There were going to be no loose ends in Jean-Pierre's plan.

'My congratulations,' said Stephen. 'That should get us off to a good start. Now, how about you, Robin?'

Robin relayed the story of his fourteen days. He reported on his meeting with the specialist, and explained the toxic effects of anticholinesterase drugs.

'This one will be hard to pull off; we'll have to be patient and wait for the right opportunity. But, we must stay prepared every moment Metcalfe is in Monte Carlo.'

'Where will we be staying in Monte Carlo?' asked James. 'I usually go to the Metropole. Better not make it there.'

'No, it's all right, James, I have provisional reservations at the Hôtel de Paris from June 29th to July 4th. However, before that you are all to attend several working sessions at St Thomas's Hospital.'

Diaries were consulted, and a series of meetings agreed upon.

'Here is a copy of Houston's *Short Textbook of Medicine* for each of you. You must all read the chapter on severe cuts and bruises. I don't want any of you to stick out like sore thumbs when we're all dressed in white. You, Stephen, will come to Harley Street the week after next for an intensive medical course, as you must be totally convincing as a doctor.'

Robin had chosen Stephen because he felt that with his academic mind he would pick up the most in the short time available.

'Jean-Pierre, you must attend a gaming club every evening for the next month and learn exactly how baccarat and blackjack are played, and how to continue playing for several hours at a time without losing money. It'll help if you get hold of Peter Arnold's *The Encyclopedia of Gambling* from Hatchards. James, you will learn to drive a small van through the rush hour traffic, and you are also to report to Harley Street next week so that we can try a dry run together.'

All eyes were wide open. If they pulled that one off they could do anything. Robin could see the anxiety in their faces.

'Don't worry,' he said, 'my profession has been carried on by witch-doctors for a thousand years. People never argue when they're confronted with a trained man, and you, Stephen, are going to be a trained man.'

Stephen nodded. Academics could be equally naïve. Hadn't that been exactly what had happened to all of them with Prospecta Oil?

'Remember,' said Robin, 'Stephen's comment at the bottom of page

33 of the dossier ... "At all times we must think like Harvey Metcalfe".'

Robin gave a few more details of how certain procedures were to be carried out. He then answered demanding questions for twenty-eight minutes. Finally, Jean-Pierre softened:

'I thought none of you would beat me, but Robin's plan is brilliant. If we get the timing right we'll only need an ounce of luck.'

James was beginning to feel distinctly uneasy as his time drew nearer. He rather wished he had never accepted the invitation to dinner in the first place and regretted being the one to urge the others to take up Stephen's challenge. At least the duties he had been given in the first two operations were well within his scope.

'Well, gentlemen,' said Stephen, 'you've both risen admirably to the occasion, but my proposals will make more demands on you.'

Stephen began to reveal the fruits of his research during the past two weeks and the substance of his plan. They all felt rather like students in the presence of a professor. Stephen's lecturing tone was not intention; it was a manner he had developed, and like so many academics, he was unable to switch it off in private company. He produced a calendar for Trinity Term and outlined how the university weeks worked, the role of its Chancellor, Vice-Chancellor, the Registrar and the Secretary of the University Chest. Like Jean-Pierre, he supplied maps to each member of the Team, this time of Oxford. He had carefully marked a route from the Sheldonian Theatre to Lincoln College, and from Lincoln to the Randolph Hotel, and had drawn up a contingency plan if Harvey Metcalfe insisted on using his car, despite the one-way system.

'Robin, you must study what the Vice-Chancellor does at Encaenia. It won't be like Cambridge; the two universities do everything the same but not identically. You must know the routes he's likely to take on that day and his habits backwards. I've arranged for a room at Lincoln to be at your disposal on the final day. Jean-Pierre, you will study and master the duties of the Registrar at Oxford and know the alternative route marked on your map so that you never come face to face with Robin. James, you must know how the Secretary of the University Chest goes about his work – the location of his office, which banks he deals with and how the cheques are cashed. You must also know the routes he's likely to take on the day of Encaenia as if they were part of your father's estate. I have the easiest role on the day, because I will be myself in everything but name. You must all learn how to address each other correctly and we'll have a dress rehearsal in the ninth week of term, on a Tuesday when the university is fairly quiet. Any questions?'

Silence reigned, but it was a silence of respect. All could see that Stephen's operation would demand split-second timing and that they would have to run through it several times to cover all contingencies. But if they were convincing they could hardly fail.

'Now, the ascot part of my plan is simple. I will only want Jean-Pierre and James inside the Members' Enclosure. I shall need two Enclosure tickets which I'm hoping you can acquire, James.'

'You mean badges, Stephen,' corrected James.

'Oh, do I?' said Stephen. 'I also require someone in London to send the necessary telegram. That'll have to be you, Robin.'

'Agreed,' said Robin.

For nearly an hour the others asked several questions of detail in order to be as familiar with the plan as Stephen was.

James asked no questions and his mind began to drift, hoping the earth would swallow him up. He even began to wish that he had never met Anne, although she was hardly to blame. In fact, he could not wait to see here again. What was he going to say when they . . .

'James, wake up,' said Stephen sharply. 'We're all waiting.'

Six eyes were now fixed on him. They had produced the ace of hearts, diamonds and spades. But had he the ace of trumps? James was flustered and poured himself another drink.

'You bloody upper-class twit,' said Jean-Pierre, 'you haven't got an idea, have you?'

'Well, actually, I've given the problem a lot of thought, but nothing seemed to come.'

'Useless – worse than useless,' said Robin.

James was stammering helplessly. Stephen cut him short.

'Now listen, James, and listen carefully. We meet here again in twenty-one days' time. By then we must know each others' plans backwards. One error could blow the whole thing. Do you understand?'

James nodded – he was determined not to let them down in that.

'And what's more,' said Stephen firmly, 'you must have your own plan ready for scrutiny. Is that also clear?'

'Yes,' mumbled James unhappily.

'Any other questions?' said Stephen.

There were none.

'Right. We go through the three individual operations again in full.'

Stephen ignored the muttered protests.

'Remember, we're up against a man who isn't used to being beaten. We won't get a second chance.'

For an hour and a half they went through the details of each operation in the order of action. First, Jean-Pierre during Wimbledon fortnight: second, Robin in Monte Carlo: third, Stephen during and after Ascot.

It was late and they were all weary when they finally rose from the table. They departed sleepily, each with several tasks to carry out before their next meeting. Each went his separate way, but all were due to meet again the following Friday in the Jericho Theatre of St Thomas's Hospital.

8

The next twenty days turned out to be an exacting time for all four of them. Each had to master the other plans as well as organizing his own. Friday brought them all together for the first of many sessions at St Thomas's

Hospital, which would have been entirely successful if James had managed to stay on his feet. It was not the sight of blood that daunted him – the sight of the knife was enough. The only virtue from James's standpoint was that he once again avoided having to explain why he had not come up with any ideas of his own.

The next week was almost full time, with Stephen in Harley Street taking a potted course in one particular field of medicine at a fairly high level.

James spent several hours driving an old van through the heavy traffic from St Thomas's to Harley Street, preparing for his final test in Monte Carlo, which he felt could only be considerably easier. He also returned to Oxford for a week, learning how the Secretary of the University Chest's office operated, and also studying the movements of the Secretary himself, Mr Caston.

Jean-Pierre, at a cost to Mr Metcalfe of $25 and a 48-hour wait, became an overseas member of The Claremont, London's most distinguished gaming club, and passed his evenings watching the wealthy and lazy play baccarat and blackjack, their stakes often reaching £1,000. After three weeks of watching he ventured to join the Golden Nugget casino in Soho, where the stakes rarely exceeded £5. By the end of the month he had played for 56 hours, but so conservatively that he was only showing a small loss.

James's overriding worry was still his personal contribution. The more he grappled with the problem, the less he came to grips with it. He turned it over and over in his mind, even when he was travelling through London at high speed. One night after returning the van to Carnie's in Lots Road, Chelsea, he drove his Alfa Romeo over to Anne's flat by the river, wondering if he dared confide in her.

Anne was preparing a special meal for James. She was aware that he not only appreciated good food, but had taken it for granted all his life. The homemade gazpacho was smelling good and the *Coq au vin* was all but ready. Lately she had found herself avoiding modelling assignments out of London as she did not care to be away from James for any length of time. She was also conscious that he was the first man for some time that she would have been willing to go to bed with – and to date he had made no efforts to leave the dining-room.

James arrived carrying a bottle of Beaune Montée Rouge 1971 – even his wine cellar was fast diminishing. He only hoped it would last long enough for the plans to come to fruition. Not that he felt an automatic right to a part of the bounty while he failed to contribute his own plan.

Anne looked stunning. She was wearing a long black dress of some soft material that tantalized James with the reticence with which it outlined her shape. She wore no makeup or jewellery, and her heavy nob of hair gleamed in the candlelight. The meal was a triumph for Anne, and James started wanting her badly. She seemed nervous, spilling a little ground coffee as she filtered two strong tiny cups. What was in her mind? He did not want to blunder with unwanted attentions. James had had much more practice at being loved than at being in love. He was used to adulation, to ending up in bed with girls who made him shudder in the cold clear light of morning. Anne affected him in an entirely different way. He wanted to be close to her, to hold her and to love her. Above all, he wanted her to be there in the morning.

Anne cleared away the supper, avoiding James's eye, and they settled down to brandy and Lena Horne singing 'I Get Along Without You Very Well'. She sat, hands clasped round her knees on the floor at James's feet, staring into the fire. Tentatively, he put out a hand and stroked her hair. She sat unresponsive for a moment and then bent her head back and stretched out her arm to bring his face down to hers. He responded, leaning forward and stroking her cheek and nose with his mouth, holding her head in his hands, his fingers gently exploring her ears and neck. Her skin smelled faintly of jasmine and her open mouth glinted in the firelight as she smiled up at him. He kissed her and slid his hands down on to her body. She felt soft and slight under his hands. He caressed her breasts gently, and moved down beside her, his body pressing against hers. Wordlessly, he reached behind her and unzipped her dress and watched it fall to the ground. He stood up, his eyes never leaving hers, and undressed quickly. She glanced at his body and smiled shyly.

'Darling James,' she said softly.

.   .   .

After they had made love, like two people in love and not as lovers, Anne settled her head on James's shoulder and stroked the hair on his chest with a fingertip.

'What's the matter, James? I know I'm rather shy. But it will ...'

'You were beautiful. God knows, you were perfect. That's not the problem ... Anne, I have to tell you something, so just lie back and listen.'

'You're married.'

'No, it's far worse than that.' James lay silent for a moment, lit a cigarette and inhaled deeply. There are occasions in life when revelation is made easier by circumstance; it all came out in an uncoordinated jumble. 'Anne darling, I've made a bloody fool of myself by investing a vast sum of money with a bunch of crooks who've stolen it. I haven't even told my family – they'd be terribly distressed if they ever found out. To make matters better or worse, I've got myself involved with three other chaps who found themselves in the same predicament, and now we're all trying to get our money back. They're nice fellows, full of bright ideas, but I haven't a clue how to begin to keep my part of the bargain. What with the worry of being £150,000 down the drain and having to keep racking my brain for a good idea, I'm half frantic. You're the only thing that's kept me sane the last month.'

'James, start again, but slower this time,' said Anne.

Thus James revealed the entire history of Prospecta Oil, from his meeting with David Kesler at Annabel's to his invitation to dine with Stephen Bradley at Magdalen, finally explaining why he had been driving a hired van like a maniac through the rush hour. The only detail James left out was the name of their intended victim, as he felt that by withholding that he was not completely violating his bond of secrecy with the rest of the Team.

Anne inhaled very deeply.

'I hardly know what to say. It's incredible. It's so unbelievable that I believe every word.'

'I feel better just for telling someone, but it would be terrible if the others ever found out.'

'James, you know I won't say a word to anyone. I'm just so very sorry you're in such a mess. You must let me see if I can come up with an idea. Why don't we work together without letting the others know?'

James felt better already.

She began stroking the inside of his leg. Twenty minutes later, they sank into a blissful sleep, dreaming up plans to defeat Harvey Metcalfe.

9

In Lincoln, Massachusetts, Harvey Metcalfe began to prepare for his annual trip to England. He intended to enjoy himself thoroughly and expensively. He had plans for transferring some more money from his numbered accounts in Zürich to Barclays Bank, Lombard Street, ready to buy yet another stallion from one of the Irish stables to join his stud in Kentucky. Arlene had decided not to accompany him on this trip: she did not care too much for Ascot and even less for Monte Carlo. In any case, it gave her the chance to spend some time with her ailing mother in Vermont, who still had little respect for her prosperous son-in-law.

Harvey checked with his secretary that all the arrangements for the holiday had been completed. There was never any need to check up on Miss Fish, it was simply habit on Harvey's part. Miss Fish had been with him for twenty-five years, from the days when he had first taken over the Lincoln Trust. Most of the respectable staff had walked out on Harvey's arrival, or shortly afterwards, but Miss Fish had remained, nursing in her unalluring bosom ever fainter hopes of eventual marriage to Harvey. By the time Arlene appeared on the scene, Miss Fish was an able and completely discreet accomplice without whom Harvey could hardly have operated. He paid her accordingly, so she swallowed her chagrin at the thought of another Mrs Metcalfe, and stayed put.

Miss Fish had already booked the short flight to New York and the Trafalgar Suite on the QE2. The trip across the Atlantic was almost the only total break Harvey ever had from the telephone or telex. The bank staff were instructed to contact the great liner only in dire emergency. On arrival at Southampton it would be the usual Rolls-Royce to London and the private suite at Claridge's, which Harvey judged to be one of the last English hotels, along with the Connaught and Browns, where his money allowed him to mix with what he called 'class'.

Harvey flew to New York in high good humour, relaxing and drinking a couple of Manhattans on the way. The arrangements on board ship were as impeccable as ever. The Captain, Peter Jackson, always invited the occupant of the Trafalgar Suite or the Queen Anne Suite to join him on the first night out at the Captain's table. At $1,250 a day for the suites it could hardly be described as an extravagant gesture on Cunard's part. On such occasions, Harvey was always on his best behaviour, although even that struck most onlookers as somewhat brash.

One of the Italian stewards was detailed to arrange a little diversion for Harvey, preferably in the shape of a tall blonde with a large bosom. The going rate for the night was $200, but the Italian could charge Harvey $250 and still get away with it. At 5 ft 7 in and 227 lb, Harvey's chances of picking up a young thing in the discothèque were slender, and by the time he had lashed out on drinks and dinner, he could have spent almost as much money and achieved absolutely nothing. Men in Harvey's position do not have time for that sort of failure and expect everything in life to have its price. As the voyage was only five nights, the steward was able to keep Harvey fully occupied, although he felt it was just as well that Harvey had not booked a three-week Mediterranean cruise.

Harvey spent his days catching up with the latest novels he had been told he must read and also taking a little exercise, a swim in the morning and a painful session in the gymnasium during the afternoon. He reckoned to lose 10 lb during the crossing, which was pleasing, but somehow Claridge's always managed to put it back on again before he returned to the States. Fortunately, his suits were tailored by Bernard Weatherill of Dover Street, Mayfair, who by dint of near-genius and impeccable skill made him look well-built rather than distinctly fat. At £300 per suit it was the least he could expect.

When the five days were drawing to a close, Harvey was more than ready for land again. The women, the exercise and the fresh air had quite revived him and he had lost all of 11 lb on the crossing. He felt a good deal of this must have come off the night before, which he had spent with a young Indian girl who had made the *Kama Sutra* look like a Boy Scouts' handbook.

One of the advantages of real wealth is that menial tasks can always be left to someone else. Harvey could no longer remember when he last packed or unpacked a suitcase, and when the ship docked at the Ocean Terminal it came as no surprise to him to discover everything packed and ready for Customs — a $100 bill for the head steward seemed to bring men in little white coats from every direction.

Harvey always enjoyed disembarking at Southampton. The English were a race he liked, though he feared he would never understand them. He found them always so willing to be trodden on by the rest of the world. Since the Second World War, they had relinquished their colonial power in a way no American business man would have ever considered for an exit from his own boardroom. Harvey had finally given up trying to understand the British way of business during the 1967 devaluation of the pound. Every jumped-up speculator on the face of the globe had taken advantage of the inside knowledge. Harvey knew on the Tuesday morning that Harold Wilson was going to devalue any time after Friday, 5 p.m. Greenwich Mean Time, when the Bank of England closed for the weekend. On the Thursday even the junior clerk at the Lincoln Trust knew. It was no wonder that the Old Lady of Threadneedle Street was raped and despoiled of an estimated £1½ billion over the next few days. Harvey had often thought that if only the British could liven up their boardrooms and get their tax structure right, they might end up being the richest nation in the world, instead of a nation which, as *The Economist* had stated, could now be taken over by the Arabs with ninety days of oil revenue. While the British flirted with socialism and still retained a *folie de grandeur*, they seemed doomed to sink into insignificance. But still Harvey adored them.

He strode down the gangplank like a man with a purpose. Harvey had never learnt to relax completely, even when he was on vacation. He could spend just about four days away from the world, but if he had been left on the QE2 any longer he would have been negotiating to buy the Cunard Steamship Company. Harvey had once met the Chairman of Cunard, Vic Matthews, at Ascot and had been baffled to hear him harking on the prestige and reputation of the company. Harvey had expected him to brag about the balance sheet. Prestige interested Harvey, of course, but he always let people know how much he was worth first.

Customs clearance was given with the usual speed. Harvey never had anything of consequence to declare on his European trips, and after they had checked two of his Gucci suitcases, the other seven were allowed through without inspection. The chauffeur opened the door of the white Rolls-Royce Corniche. The vehicle sped through Hampshire and into London in a little over two hours, which gave Harvey time for a rest before dinner.

Albert, the head doorman at Claridge's, stood smartly to attention and saluted as the car drew up. He knew Harvey of old and was aware that he had come, as usual, for Wimbledon and Ascot. Albert would undoubtedly receive a 50 pence tip every time he opened the white Rolls door. Harvey didn't know the difference between a 50 pence and 10 pence piece – a difference which Albert had welcomed since the introduction of decimalization in Britain. Moreover, Harvey always gave Albert £5 at the end of Wimbledon fortnight if an American won the singles title. An American invariably reached the finals, so Albert always placed a bet with Ladbrokes on the other finalist and won either way. Gambling appealed to both Harvey and Albert; only the sums involved were different.

Albert arranged for the luggage to be sent up to the Royal Suite, which during the year had already been occupied by King Constantine of Greece, Princess Grace of Monaco and Emperor Hailé Selassié of Ethiopia, all with considerably more conviction than Harvey. But Harvey still considered that his annual holiday at Claridge's was more assured than theirs.

The Royal Suite is on the first floor at Claridge's and can be reached by an elegant sweeping staircase from the ground floor, or by a commodious lift with its own seat. Harvey always took the lift up and walked down. At least that way he convinced himself he was taking some exercise. The suite itself consists of four rooms: a small dressing-room, a bedroom, a bathroom, and an elegant drawing-room overlooking Brook Street. The furniture and pictures make it possible for you to believe that you are still in Victorian England. Only the telephone and television dispel the illusion. The room is large enough to be used for cocktail parties or by visiting heads of state to entertain large parties. Henry Kissinger had received Harold Wilson there only the week before. Harvey enjoyed the thought of that. It was about as close as he was going to get to either man.

After a shower and change of clothes, Harvey glanced through his waiting mail and telexes from the bank, which were all routine. He took a short nap before going down to dine in the main restaurant.

There in the large foyer was the usual string quartet, looking like out-of-work refugees from Hungary. Harvey even recognized the four musicians. He had reached that time in life when he did not like change; the management of Claridge's, aware that the average age of their customers was over fifty, catered accordingly. François, the head waiter, showed Harvey to his usual table.

Harvey managed a little shrimp cocktail and a medium fillet steak with a bottle of Mouton Cadet. As he leaned forward to study the sweets trolley, he did not notice the four young men eating in the alcove on the far side of the room.

. . .

Stephen, Robin, Jean-Pierre and James all had an excellent view of Harvey Metcalfe. He would have had to bend double and move slightly backwards to have any sight of them.

'Not exactly what I expected,' commented Stephen.

'Put on a bit of weight since those photographs you supplied,' said Jean-Pierre.

'Hard to believe he's real after all this preparation,' remarked Robin.

'The bastard's real enough,' said Jean-Pierre, 'and a million dollars richer because of our stupidity.'

James said nothing. He was still in disgrace after his futile efforts and excuses at the last full briefing, although the other three had to admit that they did receive good service wherever they went with him. Claridge's was proving to be no exception.

'Wimbledon tomorrow,' said Jean-Pierre. 'I wonder who'll win the first round?'

'You will of course,' chipped in James, hoping to soften Jean-Pierre's acid comments about his own feeble efforts.

'We can only win your round, James, if we ever fill in an entry form.'

James sank back into silence.

'I must say, looking at the size of Metcalfe, we ought to get away with your plan, Robin,' said Stephen.

'If he doesn't die of cirrhosis of the liver before we're given the chance,' replied Robin. 'How do you feel about Oxford now you've seen him, Stephen?'

'I don't know yet. I'll feel better when I've belled the cat at Ascot. I want to hear him speak, watch him in his normal environment, get the feel of the man. You can't do all that from the other side of the dining-room.'

'You may not have to wait too long. This time tomorrow we may know everything we need to know – or all be in West End Central Police Station,' said Robin. 'Maybe we won't even pass Go, let alone collect £200.'

'We have to – I can't afford bail,' said Jean-Pierre.

. . .

When Harvey had downed a large snifter of Rémy Martin VSOP he left his table, slipping the head waiter a crisp new pound note.

'The bastard,' said Jean-Pierre with great feeling. 'It's bad enough knowing he's stolen our money, but it's humiliating having to watch him spend it.'

The four of them prepared to leave, the object of their outing achieved. Stephen paid the bill and carefully added the sum to the list of expenses against Harvey Metcalfe. Then they left the hotel separately and as inconspicuously as possible. Only James found this difficult as all the waiters and porters insisted on saying 'Goodnight, my lord.'

Harvey took a stroll round Berkeley Square and did not even notice the tall young man slip into the doorway of Moyses Stevens, the florists, for fear of being spotted by him. Harvey could never resist asking a policeman the way to Buckingham Palace, just to compare his reaction with that of a New York cop, leaning on a lamp post, chewing gum, holster on hip. As Lenny Bruce had said on being deported from England, 'Your pigs is so much better than our pigs'. Yes, Harvey liked England.

He arrived back at Claridge's at about 11.15 p.m., showered and went to bed – a large double bed with that glorious feel of clean linen sheets. There would be no women for him at Claridge's or, if there were, it would be the last time he would find the Royal Suite available to him during Wimbledon or Ascot. The room moved just a little, but then after five days on an ocean liner it was unlikely to be still for a couple of nights. He slept well in spite of it, without a worry on his mind.

10

Harvey rose at 7.30 a.m., a habit he could not break, but he did allow himself the holiday luxury of breakfast in bed. Ten minutes after he had called room service, the waiter arrived with a trolley laden with half a grapefruit, bacon and eggs, toast, steaming black coffee, a copy of the previous day's *Wall Street Journal*, and the morning edition of *The Times*, *Financial Times* and *International Herald Tribune*.

Harvey was not sure how he would have survived on a European trip without the *International Herald Tribune*, known in the trade as the 'Trib'. This unique paper, published in Paris, is jointly owned by the *New York Times* and the *Washington Post*. Although only one edition of 120,000 copies is printed, it does not go to press until the New York Stock Exchange is closed. Therefore, no American need wake up in Europe out of touch. When the *New York Herald Tribune* folded in 1966, Harvey had been among those who advised John H. Whitney to keep the *International Herald Tribune* going in Europe. Once again, Harvey's judgement had been proved sound. The *International Herald Tribune* went on to absorb its faltering rival, the *New York Times*, which had never been a success in Europe. From then on the paper went from strength to strength.

Harvey ran an experienced eye down the Stock Exchange lists in the *Wall Street Journal* and the *Financial Times*. His bank now held very few shares as he, like Jim Slater in England, had suspected that the Dow-Jones Index would collapse and had therefore gone almost entirely liquid, holding only some South African gold shares and a few well-chosen stocks about which he had inside information. The only monetary transaction he cared to undertake with the market so shaky was to sell the dollar short and buy gold, so that he caught the dollar on the way down and gold on the way up. There were already rumours in Washington that the President of the United States had been advised by his Secretary of the Treasury, George Schultz, to allow the American people to buy gold on the open market later that year or early the following year. Harvey had been buying gold for the past fifteen years: all the President was going to do was to stop him from breaking the law. Harvey was of the opinion that the moment the Americans were able to buy gold, the bubble would burst and the price of gold would recede – the real money would be made while the speculators anticipated the rise, and Harvey intended to be out of gold well before it came onto the American market. Once the President made it legal, Harvey couldn't see a profit in it.

Harvey checked the commodity market in Chicago. He had made a killing in copper a year before. Inside information from an African ambassador had made this possible – information the ambassador had imparted to too many people. Harvey had not been surprised to read that he had later been recalled to his homeland and shot.

He could never resist checking the price of Prospecta Oil, now at an all-time low of $\frac{1}{8}$: there could be no trading in the stock, simply because there would only be sellers and no buyers. The shares were virtually worthless. He smiled sardonically and turned to the sports page of *The Times*.

Rex Bellamy's article on the forthcoming Wimbledon Championships tipped John Newcombe as favourite and Jimmy Connors, the new American star who had just won the Italian Open, as the best outside bet. The British press wanted the 39-year-old Ken Rosewall to win. Harvey could well remember the epic final between Rosewall and Drobny in 1954, which had run to 58 games. Like most of the crowd, he had supported the 33-year-old Drobney, who had finally won after three hours of play, 13–11, 4–6, 6–2, 9–7. This time, Harvey wanted history to repeat itself and Rosewall to win, though he felt the popular Australian's chance had slipped by during the ten years which the professionals were barred from Wimbledon. Still, he saw no reason why the fortnight should not be a pleasant break, and perhaps there might be an American victor even if Rosewall couldn't manage it.

Harvey had time for a quick glance at the art reviews before finishing his breakfast, leaving the papers strewn over the floor. The quiet Regency furniture, the elegant service and the Royal Suite did nothing for Harvey's habits. He padded into the bathroom for a shave and shower. Arlene told him that most people did it the other way round – showered and then ate breakfast. But, as Harvey pointed out to her, most people did things the other way round from him, and look where it got them.

Harvey habitually spent the first morning of Wimbledon fortnight visiting the Summer Exhibition at the Royal Academy in Piccadilly. He would then follow this with visits to most of the West End's major galleries – Agnew's, Tooths, the Marlborough, Wildenstein – all within easy walking distance of Claridge's. This morning would be no exception. If Harvey was anything, he was a creature of habit, which was something the Team were quickly learning.

After he had dressed and bawled out room service for not leaving enough whisky in his cabinet, he headed down the staircase, emerged through the swing door on to Davies Street and strode off towards Berkeley Square.

Harvey did not observe a studious young man with a two-way radio on the other side of the road.

'He's left the hotel by the Davies Street entrance,' said Stephen quietly to his little Pye Pocketfone, 'and he's heading towards you, James.'

'I'll pick him up as he comes into Berkeley Square, Stephen. Robin can you hear me?'

'Yes.'

'I'll let you know as soon as I spot him. You stay put at the Royal Academy.'

'Right you are,' said Robin.

.   .   .

Harvey strolled round Berkeley Square, down into Piccadilly and through the Palladian arches of Burlington House. With a bad grace, he stood and queued with the assorted humanity in the forecourt, shuffling past the Astronomical Society and the Society of Antiquaries. He did not see another young man opposite standing in the entrance of the Chemical Society, deep in a copy of *Chemistry in Britain*. Finally, Harvey made it up the red-carpeted ramp into the Royal Academy itself. He handed the cashier £5.00 for a season ticket, realizing that he would probably want to return at least three or four times. He spent the rest of the morning studying the 1,182 pictures, none of which had been exhibited anywhere else in the world before the opening day, in accordance with the stringent rules of the Academy. Despite that ruling, the Hanging Committee had still had over 5,000 pictures to choose from.

On the opening day of the exhibition the month before, Harvey had acquired, through his agent, a watercolour by Alfred Daniels of the House of Commons for £350 and two oils by Bernard Dunstan of English provincial scenes for £125 each. The Summer Exhibition was still, in Harvey's estimation, the best value in the world. Even if he did not want to keep all the pictures himself, they made wonderful presents when he returned to the States. The Daniels reminded him of a Lowry he had bought some twenty years before at the Academy for £80: that had turned out to be another shrewd investment.

Harvey made a special point of looking at the Bernard Dunstans in the Exhibition. Of course, they were all sold. Dunstan was one of the artists whose pictures always sold in the first minutes of the opening day. Although Harvey had not been in London on that day, he had had no difficulty in buying what he wanted. He had planted a man at the front of the queue, who had obtained a catalogue and marked those artists he knew Harvey could resell easily if he made a mistake and keep if his judgement were right. When the exhibition opened on the dot of 10 a.m., the agent had gone straight to the purchasing desk and acquired the five or six pictures he had marked in the catalogue before he or anyone other than the Academicians had seen them. Harvey studied his vicarious purchases with care. On this occasion he was happy to keep them all. If there had been one that did not quite fit in with his collection, he would have returned the picture for resale, undertaking to purchase it if nobody else showed any interest. In twenty years he had acquired over a hundred pictures by this method and returned a mere dozen, never once failing to secure a resale. Harvey had a system for everything.

At 1 p.m., after a thoroughly satisfactory morning, he left the Royal Academy. The white Rolls-Royce was waiting for him in the forecourt.

'Wimbledon.'

'Shit.'

'What did you say?' queried Stephen.

'S.H.I.T. He's gone to Wimbledon, so today's down the drain,' said Robin.

That meant Harvey would not return to Claridge's until at least seven or eight that evening. A rota had been fixed for watching him, and Robin accordingly picked up his Rover 3500 V8 from a parking meter in St James's Square and headed off to Wimbledon. James had obtained two tickets for every day of the Championships opposite Harvey Metcalfe's debenture box.

Robin arrived at Wimbledon a few minutes after Harvey and took his seat in the Centre Court, far enough back in the sea of faces to remain inconspicuous. The atmosphere was already building up for the opening match. Wimbledon seemed to be getting more popular every year and the Centre Court was packed to capacity. Princess Alexandra and the Prime Minister were in the Royal Box awaiting the entrance of the gladiators. The little green scoreboards at the southern end of the court were flashing up the names of Kodeš and Stewart as the umpire took his seat on the high chair in the middle of the court directly overlooking the net. The crowd began to applaud as the two athletes, both dressed in white, entered the court carrying four rackets each. Wimbledon does not allow its competitors to dress in any colour other than white, although they had relaxed a little by permitting the trimming of the ladies' dresses to be coloured.

Robin enjoyed the opening match between Kodeš and an unseeded player from the United States, who gave the champion a hard time before losing to the Czech 6–3, 6–4, 9–7. Robin was sorry when Harvey decided to leave in the middle of an exciting doubles match. Back to duty, he told himself, and followed the white Rolls at a safe distance to Claridge's. On arriving, he telephoned James's flat, which was being used as the Team's headquarters in London, and briefed Stephen.

'May as well call it a day,' said Stephen. 'We'll try again tomorrow. Poor old Jean-Pierre's heart-beat reached 150 this morning. He may not last many days of false alarms.'

.   .   .

When Harvey left Claridge's the following morning he went through Berkeley Square into Bruton Street and then on into Bond Street, stopping only 50 yards from Jean-Pierre's gallery. But he turned east instead of west and slipped into Agnew's, where he had an appointment with Sir Geoffrey Agnew, the head of the family firm, for news of Impressionist pictures on the market. Sir Geoffrey was anxious to get away to another meeting and could only spend a few minutes with Harvey. He had nothing worthwhile to offer him.

Harvey left Agnew's soon afterwards clutching a small consolation prize of a maquette by Rodin, a mere bagatelle at £800.

'He's coming out,' said Robin, 'and heading in the right direction.' Jean-Pierre held his breath, but Harvey stopped once again, this time at the

Marlborough Gallery to study their latest exhibition of Barbara Hepworth. He spent over an hour appreciating her beautiful work, but decided the prices were now outrageous. He had bought two Hepworths only ten years before for £800. The Marlborough was now asking between £7,000 and £10,000 for her work. So he left and continued up Bond Street.

'Jean-Pierre?'

'Yes,' replied a nervous voice.

'He's reached the corner of Conduit Street and he's about 50 yards away from your front door.'

Jean-Pierre prepared his window, removing the Graham Sutherland watercolour of the Thames and the Boatman.

'He's turned left, the bastard,' said James, who was stationed opposite the gallery. 'He's walking down Bruton Street on the right-hand side.'

Jean-Pierre put the Sutherland back on the easel in the window and retired to the lavatory, muttering to himself:

'I can't cope with two shits at once.'

Harvey meanwhile stepped into an inconspicuous entrance on Bruton Street and climbed the stairs to Tooths, more hopeful of finding something in a gallery which had become famous for its Impressionists. A Klee, a Picasso and two Salvador Dalis – not what Harvey was looking for. Though very well executed, the Klee was not as good as the one in his dining-room in Lincoln, Massachusetts. Besides, it might not fit in with any of Arlene's decorative schemes. Nicholas Tooth, the managing director, promised to keep his eyes open and ring Harvey at Claridge's should anything of interest turn up.

'He's on the move again, but I think he's heading back to Claridge's.'

James willed him to turn round and return in the direction of Jean-Pierre's gallery, but Harvey strode purposefully towards Berkeley Square, only making a detour to the O'Hana Gallery. Albert, the head doorman, had told him there was a Renoir in the window, and indeed there was. But it was only a half-finished canvas which Renoir had obviously used for a practice run or had disliked enough to leave unfinished. Harvey was curious as to the price and entered the gallery.

'£30,000,' said the assistant, as if it was $10 and a snip at that.

Harvey whistled through the gap between his front teeth. It never ceased to amaze him that an inferior picture by a first-rank name could fetch £30,000 and an outstanding picture by an artist with no established reputation could only bring a few hundred dollars. He thanked the assistant and left.

'A pleasure, Mr Metcalfe.'

Harvey was always flattered by people who remembered his name. But hell, they ought to remember – he had purchased a Monet from them last year for £62,000.

'He's definitely on his way back to the hotel,' said James.

Harvey spent only a few minutes in Claridge's, picking up one of their famous specially prepared luncheon hampers of caviar, beef, ham and cheese sandwiches and chocolate cake for later consumption at Wimbledon.

James was next on the rota for the Championships and decided to take Anne with him. Why not – she knew the truth. It was Ladies' Day and the turn of Billie Jean King, the vivacious American champion, to take the court. She was up against the unseeded American, Kathy May, who looked as if she was in for a rough time. The applause Billie Jean received was unworthy of her abilities, but for some reason she had never become a Wimbledon favourite. Harvey was accompanied by a guest who James thought had faintly Mid-European look.

'Which one is your victim?' asked Anne.

'He's almost exactly opposite us talking to the man in a light grey suit who looks like a government official from the EEC.'

'The short fat one?' asked Anne.

'Yes,' said James.

Whatever comments Anne made were interrupted by the umpire's call of 'Play' and everyone's attention focused on Billie Jean. It was exactly 2 p.m.

.   .   .

'Kind of you to invite me to Wimbledon, Harvey,' said Jörg Birrer. 'I never seem to get the chance for much relaxation nowadays. You can't leave the market for more than a few hours without some panic breaking out somewhere in the world.'

'If you feel that way it's time for you to retire,' said Harvey.

'No one to take my place,' said Birrer. 'I've been chairman of the bank for ten years now and finding a successor is turning out to be my hardest task.'

'First game to Mrs King. Mrs King leads by one game to love in the first set.'

'Now, Harvey, I know you too well to expect this invitation to have been just for pleasure.'

'What an evil mind you have, Jörg.'

'In my profession I need it.'

'I just wanted to check how my three accounts stand and brief you on my plans for the next few months.

'Game to Mrs King. Mrs King leads by two games to love in the first set.'

'Your No. 1 official account is a few thousand dollars in credit. Your numbered commodity account,' – at this point Birrer unfolded a small piece of unidentifiable paper with a set of neat figures printed on it – 'is short by $3,726,000, but you are holding 37,000 ounces of gold at today's selling price of $135 an ounce.'

'What's your advice on that?'

'Hold on, Harvey. I still think your President is either going to announce a new gold standard or allow your fellow-countrymen to buy gold on the open market some time next year.'

'That's my view too, but I'm still convinced we want to sell a few weeks before the masses come in. I have a theory about that.'

'I expect you're right, as usual Harvey.'

'Game to Mrs King. Mrs King leads by three games to love in the first set.'

'What are your charges on my overdraft?'

'1½ per cent above inter-bank rate, which at present is 13.25, and therefore we're charging you 14.75 per cent per annum, while gold is rising in price at nearly 70 per cent per annum. It can't go on that way; but there are still a few months left in it.'

'OK,' said Harvey, 'hold on until November 1st and we'll review the position again then. Coded telex as usual. I don't know what the world would do without the Swiss.'

'Just take care, Harvey. Do you know there are more specialists in our police force on fraud than there are for homicide?'

'You worry about your end, Jörg, and I'll worry about mine. The day I get uptight about a few underpaid bureaucrats from Zürich who haven't got any balls, I'll let you know. Now, enjoy your lunch and watch the game. We'll have a talk about the other account later.'

'Game to Mrs King. Mrs King leads by four games to love in the first set.'

'They're very deep in conversation,' said Anne, 'I can't believe they're enjoying the match.'

'He's probably trying to buy Wimbledon at cost price,' laughed James. 'The trouble with seeing the man every day is that one begins to have a certain respect for him. He's the most organized man I've ever come across. If he's like this on holiday, what the hell is he like at work?'

'I can't imagine,' said Anne.

'Game to Miss May. Mrs King leads by four games to one in the first set.'

'No wonder he's so overweight. Just look at him stuffing the cake down.' James lifted his Zeiss binoculars. 'Which reminds me to ask, darling, what have you brought for lunch?'

Anne dug into her hamper and unpacked a crisp salad in French bread for James. She contented herself with nibbling a stick of celery.

'Getting far too fat,' she explained. 'I'll never get into those winter clothes I'm supposed to be modelling next week.' She touched James's knee and smiled. 'It must be because I'm so happy.'

'Well, don't get too happy. I prefer you thin.'

'Game to Mrs King. Mrs King leads by five games to one in the first set.'

'This is going to be a walkover,' said James. 'It so often is in the opening match. People only come to see if the champion's in good form, and I think she'll be very hard to beat this year now she's after Helen Moody's record of eight Wimbledon championships.'

'Game and first set to Mrs King by six games to one. Mrs King leads one set to love. New balls, please. Miss May to serve.'

'Do we have to watch him all day?' asked Anne.

'No, we must make sure he returns to the hotel and doesn't change his plans suddenly or anything silly like that. If we miss our chance when he walks past Jean-Pierre's gallery, we may not get another one.'

'What do you do if he does decide to change his plans?'

'God knows, or to be more accurate, Stephen knows – he's the master-mind.'

'Game to Mrs King. Mrs King leads by one game to love in the second set.'

'Poor Miss May, she's about as successful as you are James. How is the Jean-Pierre operation looking?'

'Awful. Metcalfe hasn't been anywhere near the gallery. He was within 30 yards of the window today and marched off in the opposite direction. Poor Jean-Pierre nearly had heart failure. But we're more hopeful of tomorrow. So far he seems to have covered Piccadilly and the top end of Bond Street, and the one thing we can be sure of with Harvey Metcalfe is that he's thorough. So he's almost bound to cover our bit of territory at one time or another.'

'You should all have taken out life insurance for $1 million, naming the other three as beneficiaries,' said Anne, 'and then if one of you have a heart attack, the others would all get their money back.'

'It's no laughing matter, Anne. It's bloody nerve-racking while you're hanging around, especially when you have to wait for him to make all the moves.'

'Game to Mrs King. Mrs King leads by two games to love in the second set and by one set to love.'

'How about your own plan?'

'Nothing. Useless. And now we've started on the others I seem to have less time to concentrate on my own.'

'Why don't I seduce him?'

'Not a bad idea, but you'd have to be pretty special to get £100,000 out of him, when he can hang around outside the Hilton or in Shepherd Market and get it for £30. If there's one thing we've learnt about that gentleman it's that he expects value for money. At £30 a night it would take you just under fifteen years to repay my share, and I'm not sure the other three would be willing to wait that long. In fact, I'm not sure they'll wait another fifteen days.'

'We'll think of something, don't worry,' said Anne.

'Game to Miss May, Mrs King leads by two games to one and by one set to love.'

'Well, well. Miss May has managed another game. Excellent lunch, Harvey.'

'A Claridge's special,' said Harvey, 'so much better than getting caught up with the crowds in the restaurant where you can't even watch the tennis.'

'Billie Jean is making mincemeat of the poor girl.'

'No more than I expected,' said Harvey. 'Now, Jörg, to my second numbered account.'

Once again the unidentifiable piece of paper that bore a few numbers appeared. It is this discretion of the Swiss that leads half the world, from heads of state to Arab sheiks, to trust them with their money. In return the Swiss maintain one of the healthiest economies in the world. The system works, so why go elsewhere? Birrer spent a few seconds studying the figures.

'On April 1st – only you could have chosen that day, Harvey – you transferred $7,486,000 to your No. 2 account, which was already in credit $2,791,428. On April 2nd, on your instructions, we placed $1 million in the Banco do Minas Gerais in the names of Mr Silverman and Mr Elliott. We covered the bill with Reading & Bates for the hire of the rig for

$420,000 and several other bills amounting to $104,112, leaving your present No. 2 account standing at $8,753,316.'

'Game to Mrs King. Mrs King leads three games to one in the second set and by one set to love.'

'Very good,' said Harvey.

'The tennis or the money?' said Birrer.

'Both. Now, Jörg, I anticipated needing about $2 million over the next six weeks. I want to purchase one or two pictures in London. I have seen a Klee that I quite like and there are still a few galleries I want to visit. If I'd known the Prospecta Oil venture was going to be such a success, I'd have outbid Armand Hammer at the Sotheby-Parke Bernet for that Van Gogh last year. I shall also need some ready cash for some new horses at the Ascot Blood Stock Auctions. My stud's running down and it's still one of my greatest ambitions to win the King George and Elizabeth Stakes.' (James would have winced if he could have heard Harvey describe the race so inaccurately.) 'My best result so far, as you know, was third place, and that's not good enough. This year I've entered Rosalie, my best filly for years. If I lose I'll have to build up the stud again, but I'm damn well going to win this year.'

'Game to Mrs King. Mrs King leads four games to one and by one set to love.'

'So is Mrs King, it seems,' said Birrer. 'I'll brief my senior cashier that you're likely to be drawing large amounts over the next few weeks.'

'Now I don't wish the remainder to lie idle, so I want you to purchase more gold carefully over the next few months, with a view to off-loading it in the New Year. If the market does take a downward turn, I'll phone you in Zürich. At the close of business each day you are to loan the out-standing balance on an overnight basis to first-class banks and triple "A" commercial names.'

'What are you going to do with it all, Harvey, if those cigars don't get you first?'

'Oh, lay off, Jörg, you sound like my doctor. I've told you a hundred times, next year I retire, I quit, finito.'

'I can't see you dropping out of the rat race voluntarily, Harvey. It pains me to think how much you're worth now.'

Harvey laughed.

'I can't tell you that, Jörg. It's like Aristotle Onassis said – if you can count it, you haven't got any.'

'Game to Mrs King. Mrs King leads by five games to one and by one set to love.'

'How's Rosalie? We still have your instructions to pass the accounts on to her in Boston if anything should happen to you.'

'She's well. Phoned me this morning to tell me she won't be able to join me at Wimbledon because she's tied up with her work. I expect she'll end up marrying some rich American and won't need it. Enough of them have asked her. Can't be easy for her to decide if they like her or my money. I'm afraid we had a row about that a couple of years back and she still hasn't forgiven me.'

'Game, set and match to Mrs King: 6–1, 6–1.'

Harvey, Jörg, James and Anne joined in the applause while the two women left the court, curtseying in front of the Royal Box to the President of the All England Club, His Royal Highness The Duke of Kent. Harvey and Jörg Birrer stayed for the next match, a doubles, and then returned to Claridge's together for dinner.

James and Anne had enjoyed their afternoon at Wimbledon and when they had seen Harvey safely back to Claridge's, accompanied by his mid-European friend, they returned to James's flat.

. . .

'Stephen, I'm back. Metcalfe is settled in for the night. On parade at 8.30 tomorrow morning.'

'Well done James. Maybe he'll bite then.'

'Let's hope so.'

The sound of running water led James to the kitchen in search of Anne. She was elbow-deep in suds, attacking a soufflé dish with a scourer. She turned and brandished it at him.

'Darling, I don't want to be offensive about your daily, but this is the only kitchen I've ever been in where you have to do the washing up before you make the dinner.'

'I know. She only ever cleans the clean bits of the flat. Her work load's getting lighter by the week.'

He sat on the kitchen table, admiring her slim body.

'Will you scrub my back like that if I go and have a bath before dinner?'

'Yes, with a scourer.'

. . .

The water was deep and comfortably hot. James lay back in it luxuriously, letting Anne wash him. Then he stepped dripping out of the bath.

'You're a bit overdressed for a bathroom attendant, darling,' he said. 'Why don't you do something about it?'

Anne slipped out of her clothes while James dried himself. When he went into the bedroom, Anne was already huddled under the sheets.

'I'm cold,' she said.

'Fear not,' said James. 'You're about to be presented with your very own six-foot water bottle.'

She took him in her arms.

'Liar, you're freezing.'

'And you're lovely,' said James, trying to hold on to every part of her at once.

'How's your plan going, James?'

'I don't know yet, I'll tell you in about twenty minutes.'

She didn't speak again for nearly half an hour, when she said:

'Out you get. The baked cheese will be ready by now and in any case I want to remake the bed.'

'No need to bother about that, you silly woman.'

'Yes, there is. Last night I didn't sleep at all. You pulled all the blankets over to your side and I just watched you huddled up like a self-satisfied cat while I froze to death. Making love to you isn't at all what Harold Robbins promised it would be.'

'When you've finished chattering, woman, set the alarm for 7 a.m.'

'7 a.m.? You don't have to be at Claridge's until 8.30.'

'I know, but I want to go to work on an egg.'

'James, you really must give up your undergraduate sense of humour.'

'Oh, I thought it was rather funny.'

'Yes, darling. Why don't you get dressed before the dinner is burnt to a cinder?'

.   .   .

James arrived at Claridge's at 8.29 a.m. Whatever his own inadequacies, he was determined not to fail the others in their plans. He tuned in to check that Stephen was in Berkeley Square and Robin in Bond Street.

'Morning,' said Stephen. 'Had a good night?'

'Bloody good,' said James.

'Sleep well, did you?' asked Stephen.

'Hardly a wink.'

'Stop making us jealous,' said Robin, 'and concentrate on Harvey Metcalfe.'

James stood in the doorway of Slater's, the furriers, watching the early morning cleaners leave for home and the first of the office staff arriving.

Harvey Metcalfe was going through his normal routine of breakfast and the papers. Just before he had gone to bed he had a telephone call from his wife in Boston and another from his daughter during breakfast the next morning, which started his day well. He decided to continue his pursuit of an Impressionist picture in some of the other galleries in Cork Street and Bond Street. Perhaps Sotheby's would be able to help him.

He left the hotel at 9.47 a.m. at his usual brisk pace.

'Action stations.'

Stephen and Robin snapped out of their day-dreaming.

'He's just entered Bruton Street. Now he's heading for Bond Street.'

Harvey walked briskly down Bond Street, past the territory he had already covered.

'Only 50 yards off now, Jean-Pierre,' said James. '40 yards, 30 yards, 20 yards ... Oh no, damn it, he's gone into Sotheby's. There's only a sale of medieval painted panels on there today. Hell, I didn't know he was interested in them.'

He glanced up the road at Stephen, padded out and aged to the condition of a wealthy, middle-aged business man for the third day in a row. The cut of the collar and the rimless glasses proclaimed him as West German. Stephen's voice came over the speaker:

'I am going into Jean-Pierre's gallery. James, you stay north of Sotheby's on the far side of the street and report in every fifteen minutes. Robin, you go inside and dangle the bait under Harvey's nose.'

'But that's not in the plan, Stephen,' stammered Robin.

'Use your initiative and get on with it otherwise all you'll be doing is taking care of Jean-Pierre's heart condition and receiving no fees. Right?'

'Right,' said Robin nervously.

Robin walked into Sotheby's and made a surreptitious bee-line for the nearest mirror. Yes, he was still unrecognizable. Upstairs, he spotted Harvey near the back of the sale room, and planted himself on a nearby seat in the row behind him.

The sale of medieval painted panels was well under way. Harvey knew he ought to like them, but could not bring himself to condone the Gothic partiality for jewellery and bright, gilded colours. Behind him, Robin hesitated but then struck up a quiet-voiced conversation with his neighbour.

'Looks all very fine to me, but I've no knowledge of the period. I'm so much happier with the modern era. Still, I must think of something appropriate to say for my readers.'

Robin's neighbour smiled politely.

'Do you have to cover all the auctions?'

'Almost all – especially when there may be surprises. In any case, at Sotheby's you can always find out what's going on everywhere else. Only this morning one of the assistants gave me a tip that the Lamanns Gallery may have something special in the Impressionist field.'

Robin beamed the whispered information carefully at Harvey's right ear and then sat back and waited to see if it had created any effect. Shortly afterwards, he was rewarded by the sight of Harvey squeezing out of his row to leave. Robin waited for three more lots to be auctioned, then followed him, fingers crossed.

Outside, James had been keeping a patient vigil.

'10.30 – no sign of him.'

'Roger.'

'10.45 – still no sign of him.'

'Roger.'

'11.00 – he's still inside.'

'Roger.'

'11.12 action stations, action stations.'

James slipped quickly into the Lamanns Gallery as Jean-Pierre once again removed from his window the Sutherland watercolour of the Thames and the Boatman, and replaced it with an oil by Van Gogh, as magnificent an example of the master's work as a London gallery had ever seen. Now came the acid test: the litmus paper was walking purposefully down Bond Street towards it.

The picture had been painted by David Stein, who had achieved notoriety in the art world for faking 300 paintings and drawings by well-known Impressionists, for which he had received a total of $864,000 and, later, four years. He was only exposed when he put on a Chagall exhibition at the Niveaie Gallery in Madison Avenue in 1969. Unknown to Stein, Chagall himself was in New York at the time for an exhibition at the museum in Lincoln Center where two of his most famous works were on display. On being informed of the Niveaie exhibition, Chagall furiously reported the pictures to the District Attorney's office as fakes. Stein had already sold one of the imitation Chagalls to Louis D. Cohen at a price of nearly $100,000, and to this day there is a Stein Chagall and a Stein Picasso at the Galleria d'Arte Moderna in Milan. Jean-Pierre was confident that what Stein had achieved in the past in New York and Milan he could now repeat in London.

Stein had continued to paint Impressionist pictures, but now signed them with his own name; thanks to his indubitable talent he was still making a handsome living. He had known and admired Jean-Pierre for several years and when he heard the story of Metcalfe and Prospecta Oil, he agreed to produce a Van Gogh for $10,000 and to sign the painting with the master's famous 'Vincent'.

Jean-Pierre had gone to considerable lengths to identify a Van Gogh that had vanished in mysterious circumstances, so that Stein could resurrect it to tempt Harvey. He had started with la Faille's comprehensive *oeuvres* catalogue, *The Works of Vincent Van Gogh,* and selected from it three pictures that had hung in the National Gallery in Berlin prior to the Second World War. In la Faille, they were entered under Nos. 485, *Les Amoureux* (*The Lovers*), 628, *La Moisson* (*The Harvest*), and 766, *Le Jardin de Daubigny* (*The Garden of Daubigny*). The last two were known to have been bought in 1929 by the Berlin Gallery, and *Les Amoureux* probably was bought around the same time. At the start of the war, all three had disappeared.

Jean-Pierre then contacted Professor Wormit of the Preussischer Kulturbesitz. The Professor, a world authority on missing works of art, was able to rule out one of the possibilities, *Le Jardin de Daubigny*; soon after the war it apparently had reappeared in the collection of Siegfried Kramarksy in New York, though how it got there remains a mystery. Kramarsky had subsequently sold the painting to the Nichido Gallery in Tokyo, where it now hangs. The Professor confirmed that the fate of the other two Van Goghs remained unknown.

Next Jean-Pierre turned to Madame Tellegen-Hoogendoorm of the Dutch Rijksbureau voor Kunsthistorische Documentatie. Madame Tellegen was the acknowledged authority on Van Gogh and gradually, with her expert help, Jean-Pierre pieced together the story of the missing paintings. They had been removed, along with many others, from the Berlin National Gallery in 1937 by the Nazis, despite vigorous protests from the Director, Dr Hanfstaengl, and the Keeper of Paintings, Dr Hentzen. The paintings, stigmatized by the philistinism of the National Socialists as degenerate art, were stored in a depot in the Kopenickerstrasse in Berlin. Hitler himself visited the depot in January 1938, and legalized the proceedings as an official confiscation.

What happened to the two Van Goghs after that, nobody knows. Many of the Nazi-confiscated works were quietly sold abroad by Joseph Angerer, an agent of Hermann Goering, to obtain much-needed foreign currency for the Führer. Some were disposed of in a sale organized by the Fischer Art Gallery in Lucerne on June 30, 1939. But many of the works in the depot in the Kopenickerstrasse were simply burned, stolen, or are still missing.

Jean-Pierre managed to obtain black-and-white reproductions of *Les Amoureux* and *La Moisson*: no colour positives survive, if they were ever made. It seemed to Jean-Pierre unlikely that any colour reproductions of two paintings last seen in 1938 would exist anywhere. He therefore settled down to choose between the two.

Les Amoureux was the larger of the two, at 76 × 91 cm. However, Van Gogh did not seem to have been satisfied with it. In October 1889 (letter No. 556) he referred to 'a very poor sketch of my last canvas'. Moreover, it was impossible to guess the colour of the background. *La Moisson*, in contrast, had pleased Van Gogh. He had painted the oil in September 1889 and written of it, 'I feel very much inclined to do the reaper once more for my mother' (letter No. 604). He had in fact already painted three other very similar pictures of a reaper at harvest time. Jean-Pierre was able to obtain colour transparencies of two of them, one from the Louvre and the other from the Rijksmuseum, where they now hang. He studied the sequence. The position of the sun, and the play of light on the scene, were practically the only points of difference. Jean-Pierre was therefore able to see in his mind's eye what *La Moisson* must have looked like in colour.

Stein agreed with Jean-Pierre's final choice and he studied the black-and-white reproduction of *La Moisson* and the colour transparencies of its sister paintings long and minutely before he set to work. He then found an insignificant late-nineteenth-century French work, and skilfully removed the paint from it, leaving a clean canvas except for a vital stamp on the back which even Stein could not have reproduced. He marked on the canvas the exact size of the picture, 48.5 × 53 cm and selected a palette knife and brush of the type that Van Gogh had favoured. Six weeks later *La Moisson* was finished. Stein varnished it, and baked it for four days in an oven at a gentle 85°F to age it. Jean-Pierre provided a heavy gilt Impressionist frame and it was well ready for Harvey Metcalfe's scrutiny.

. . .

Harvey, acting on his overheard tip, could see no harm in dropping into the Lamanns Gallery. He was about five paces away when he first caught sight of the picture being taken out of the window. He could not believe his eyes. A Van Gogh, without a doubt, and a superlative one at that. *La Moisson* had actually been on display for only two minutes.

Harvey almost ran into the gallery, only to discover Jean-Pierre deep in conversation with Stephen and James. None of them took any notice of him. Stephen was addressing Jean Pierre in a guttural accent.

'170,000 guineas seems high, but it is a fine example. Can you be sure it is the picture that disappeared from Berlin in 1937?'

'You can never be sure of anything, but you can see on the back of the canvas the stamp of the Berlin National Gallery, and the Bernheim Jeune have confirmed they sold it to the Germans in 1927. The rest of its history is well chronicled back to 1890. It seems certain that it was looted from the museum in the upheaval of the war.'

'How did you come into possession of the painting?'

'From the private collection of a member of the British aristocracy who wishes to remain anonymous.'

'Excellent,' said Stephen. 'I would like to reserve it until 4 p.m. when I will bring round a cheque for 170,000 guineas from the Dresdner Bank AG. Will that be acceptable?'

'Of course, sir,' replied Jean-Pierre. 'I will place a red dot on it.'

James, in the sharpest of suits and a dashing trilby, hovered knowledgeably behind Stephen.

'It certainly is a marvellous example of the master's work,' he remarked ingratiatingly.

'Yes. I took it round to Julian Barron at Sotheby's and he seemed to like it.'

James retreated mincingly to the end of the gallery, relishing his role as a connoisseur. At that moment Robin walked in, a copy of the *Guardian* sticking out of his pocket.

'Good morning, Mr Lamanns. I heard a rumour at Sotheby's about a Van Gogh which I'd always thought must be in Russia. I'd like to write a few paragraphs about the history of the painting and how you came into possession of it for tomorrow's paper. Is that OK by you?'

'I should be delighted,' said Jean-Pierre, 'although actually I have just reserved the picture for Herr Drosser, the distinguished German dealer, at 170,000 guineas.'

'Very reasonable,' said James knowingly from the end of the gallery. 'I think it's the best Van Gogh I have seen in London since *Mademoiselle Revoux* and I'm only sorry my house won't be auctioning it. You're a lucky man, Mr Drosser. If you ever decide to sell it, don't hesitate to contact me.' James handed Stephen a card and smiled at Jean-Pierre.

Jean-Pierre watched James. It was a fine performance. Robin began to take notes in what he hoped looked like shorthand and again addressed Jean-Pierre.

'Do you have a photograph of the picture?'

'Of course.'

Jean-Pierre opened a drawer and took out a colour photograph of the picture with a typewritten description attached. He handed it to Robin.

'Do watch the spelling of Lamanns, won't you? I get so bored with being confused with a French motor car race.'

He turned to Stephen.

'So sorry to keep you waiting, Herr Drosser. How would you like us to despatch the picture?'

'You can send it to me at the Dorchester tomorrow morning, room 120.'

'Certainly, sir.'

Stephen started to leave.

'Excuse me, sir,' said Robin, 'can I take the spelling of your name?'

'D.R.O.S.S.E.R.'

'And may I have permission to quote you in my article?'

'You may. I am with my purchase very pleased. Good day, gentlemen.'

Stephen bowed his head smartly, and departed. He stepped out into Bond Street and to the horror of Jean-Pierre, Robin and James, Harvey, without a moment's hesitation also walked out.

Jean-Pierre collapsed heavily on his Georgian mahogany desk and looked despairingly at Robin and James.

'God Almighty, the whole thing's a fiasco. Six weeks of preparation, three days of agony, and then he walks out on us.' Jean-Pierre looked at *La Moisson* angrily.

'I thought Stephen assured us that Harvey would stay and bargain with Jean-Pierre. It's in his character,' mimicked James plaintively. 'He'd never let the picture out of his sight.'

'Who the hell thought up this bloody silly enterprise?' muttered Robin.

'Stephen,' they all cried together, and rushed to the window.

'What an interesting maquette by Henry Moore,' said an impeccably corsetted middle-aged lady, her hand firmly placed on the bronze loin of a naked acrobat. She had slipped unnoticed into the gallery while the three had been grumbling. 'How much are you asking for it?'

'I will be with you in a minute, madam,' said Jean-Pierre. 'Oh hell, I think Metcalfe's following Stephen. Get him on the pocket radio, Robin.'

'Stephen, can you hear me? Whatever you do, don't look back. We think Harvey's only a few yards behind you.'

'What the hell do you mean he's only a few yards behind me? He's meant to be in the gallery with you buying the Van Gogh. What are you all playing at?'

'Harvey didn't give us a chance. He walked straight out after you before any of us could continue as planned.'

'Very clever. Now what am I meant to do?'

Jean-Pierre took over:

'You'd better go to the Dorchester just in case he is actually following you.'

'I don't even know where the Dorchester is,' yelped Stephen.

Robin came to his rescue:

'Take the first right, Stephen, and that'll bring you into Bruton Street, keep walking as straight as you can until you reach Berkeley Square. Stay on the line, but don't look back or you may turn into a pillar of salt.'

'James,' said Jean-Pierre, thinking on his feet not for the first time in his life. 'You take a taxi immediately to the Dorchester and book room 120 in the name of Drosser. Have the key ready for Stephen the moment he walks through the door, then make yourself scarce. Stephen, are you still there?'

'Yes.'

'Did you hear all that?'

'Yes. Tell James to book 110 or 191 if 120 is not available.'

'Roger,' replied Jean-Pierre. 'Get going, James.'

James bolted out of the gallery and barged in front of a woman who had just hailed a taxi, a thing he had never done before.

'The Dorchester,' he hollered, 'as fast as you can go.'

The taxi shot off.

'Stephen, James has gone and I'm sending Robin to follow Harvey so he can keep you briefed and guide you to the Dorchester. I'm staying put. Everything else OK?'

'No,' said Stephen, 'start praying. I've reached Berkeley Square. Where now?'

'Across the garden then continue down Hill Street.'

Robin left the gallery and ran all the way to Bruton Street until he was only 50 yards behind Harvey.

'Now about the Henry Moore,' said the well-corsetted lady.

'Screw Henry Moore,' said Jean-Pierre, not even looking around.

The steel-reinforced bosom heaved.

'Young man, I have never been spoken to in . . .'

But Jean-Pierre had already reached the lavatory, and closed the door.

. . . .

'You're crossing South Audley Street now, then continue into Deanery Street. Keep going, don't turn right or left and don't whatever you do look back. Harvey is still about 50 yards behind you. I'm a little more than 50 yards behind him,' said Robin. Passers-by stared at the man talking into his little instrument.

. . .

'Is Room 120 free?'

'Yes, sir, they checked out this morning, but I'm not sure if it's ready for occupancy yet. I think the maid may still be clearing the room. I'll have to check, sir,' said the tall receptionist in the morning suit, which indicated that he was a senior member of the floor staff.

'Oh, don't worry about that,' said James, his German accent far better than Stephen's. 'I always have that room. Can you book me in for one night? Name's Drosser, Herr – um – Helmut Drosser.'

He slipped a pound over the counter.

'Certainly, sir.'

. . .

'That's Park Lane, Stephen. Look right – the big hotel on the corner straight in front of you is the Dorchester. The semi-circle facing you is the main entrance. Go up the steps, past the big man in the green overcoat, and through the revolving door and you'll find reception on your right. James ought to be there waiting for you.'

Robin was grateful that the annual dinner of the Royal Society for Medicine had been held at the Dorchester last year.

'Where's Harvey?' bleated Stephen.

'Only 40 yards behind you.'

Stephen quickened his pace, ran up the steps of the Dorchester and pushed through the revolving door so hard that the other residents coming out found themselves on the street faster than they had planned. Thank God, James was standing there holding a key.

'The lift's over there,' said James, pointing. 'You've only chosen one of the most expensive suites in the hotel.'

Stephen glanced in the direction James had indicated and turned back to thank him. But James was already heading off to the American Bar to be sure he was well out of sight when Harvey arrived.

Stephen left the lift at the first floor and found that the Dorchester, which he had never entered before, was as traditional as Claridge's, its thick royal blue and golden carpets leading to a magnificently appointed corner suite which overlooked Hyde Park. He collapsed into an easy chair, not quite sure what to expect next. Nothing had gone as planned.

. . .

Jean-Pierre waited at the gallery, James sat in the American Bar and Robin loitered by the side of Barclays Bank, Park Lane, a mock-tudor building 50 yards from the entrance of the Dorchester.

. . .

'Have you a Mr Drosser staying at this hotel? I think it's room 120,' barked Harvey.

The receptionist looked through the card index.

'Yes, sir. Is he expecting you?'

'No, but I'll have a word with him on the house phone.'

'Of course, sir. If you'd be kind enough to go through the small archway on your left you will find five telephones. One of them is a house phone.'

Harvey marched through the archway as directed.

'Room 120,' he instructed the operator, who sat in his own little section, wearing the green Dorchester uniform with golden castles on the lapels.

'Cubicle No. 1, please, sir.'

'Mr Drosser?'

'Speaking,' said Stephen, summoning up his German accent for a sustained effort.

'My name is Harvey Metcalfe. I wonder if I could come up and have a word with you? It's about the Van Gogh you bought this morning.'

'Well, it's a little inconvenient at the moment. I am about to take a shower and I do have a lunch appointment.'

'I won't keep you more than a few minutes.'

Before Stephen could reply, the telephone had clicked. A few moments later there was a knock on the door. Stephen's legs wobbled. He answered it nervously. He had changed into a white Dorchester dressing-gown and his brown hair was somewhat dishevelled and darker than normal. It was the only disguise he could think of at such short notice as the original plan had not allowed for a face-to-face meeting with Harvey.

'Sorry to intrude, Mr Drosser, but I had to see you immediately. I know you have just purchased a Van Gogh from the Lamanns Gallery and I was hoping that, as you are a dealer, you might be willing to sell it on for a quick profit.'

'No, thank you,' said Stephen, relaxing for the first time. 'I've wanted a Van Gogh for my gallery in Munich for many years. I'm sorry, Mr Metcalfe, it's not for sale.'

'Listen, you paid 170,000 guineas for it. What's that in dollars?'

Stephen paused.

'Oh, about $435,000.'

'I'll give you $15,000 if you release the picture to me. All you have to do is ring the gallery and tell them that the picture is now mine and that I will cover the bill.'

Stephen sat silent, not sure how to handle the situation without blowing it. Think like Harvey Metcalfe, he told himself.

'$20,000 in cash and you've got a deal.'

Harvey hesitated. Stephen's legs wobbled again.

'Done,' said Harvey, 'Ring the gallery immediately.'

Stephen picked up the telephone.

'Can you get me the Lamanns Gallery in Bond Street as quickly as possible please – I have a lunch appointment.'

A few seconds later the call came through.

'Lamanns Gallery.'

'I would like to speak to Mr Lamanns.'

'At last, Stephen. What the hell is happening your end?'

'Ah, Mr Lamanns, this is Herr Drosser. You remember, I was in your gallery earlier this morning.'

'Of course I remember, you fool. What are you going on about Stephen? It's me – Jean-Pierre.'

'I have a Mr Metcalfe with me.'

'Christ, I'm sorry, Stephen. I didn't . . .'

'And you can expect him in the next few minutes.'

Stephen looked towards Harvey who nodded his assent.

'You are to release the Van Gogh I purchased this morning to Mr Metcalfe and he will give you a cheque for the full amount, 170,000 guineas.'

'Out of disaster, triumph,' said Jean-Pierre quietly.

'I'm very sorry I shall not be the owner of the picture myself, but I have, as the Americans would say, had an offer I can't refuse. Thank you for the part you played,' said Stephen and put the telephone down.

Harvey was writing out a cheque to cash for $20,000.

'Thank you, Mr Drosser. You have made me a happy man.'

'I am not complaining myself,' said Stephen honestly. He escorted Harvey to the door and they shook hands.

'Goodbye, sir.'

'Good day, Mr Metcalfe.'

Stephen closed the door and tottered to the chair, almost too weak to move.

.   .   .

Robin and James saw Harvey leave the Dorchester. Robin followed him in the direction of the gallery, his hopes rising with each stride. James took the lift to the first floor and nearly ran to Room 120. He banged on the door. Stephen jumped at the noise. He didn't feel he could face Harvey again. He opened the door.

'James, it's you. Cancel the room, pay for one night and then join me in the cocktail bar.'

'Why? What for?'

'A bottle of Krug 1964 Privée Cuvée.'

.   .   .

One down and three to go.

11

Jean-Pierre was the last to arrive at Lord Brigsley's King's Road flat. He felt he had earned the right to make an entrance. Harvey's cheques had been cleared and the Lamanns Gallery account was for the moment $447,560 in credit. The painting was in Harvey's possession and the heavens had not yet fallen in. Jean-Pierre had cleared more money in two months of crime than he had in ten years of legitimate trading.

The other three greeted him with the acclaim normally reserved for a sporting hero, and a glass of James's last bottle of Veuve Clicquot 1959.

'We were lucky to pull it off,' said Robin.

'We weren't lucky,' said Stephen. 'We kept our nerve under pressure, and the one thing we've learned from the exercise is that Harvey can change the rules in the middle of the game.'

'He almost changed the game, Stephen.'

'Agreed. So we must always remember that we shall fail unless we can be as successful, not once, but four times. We must not underestimate our opponent just because we've won the first round.'

'Relax, Professor,' said James. 'We can get down to business again after dinner. Anne came in this afternoon especially to make the salmon mousse, and it won't go down well with Harvey Metcalfe.'

'When am I going to meet this fabulous creature?' asked Jean-Pierre.

'When this is all over and behind us.'

'Don't marry her, James. She's only after our money.'

They all laughed. James hoped the day would come when he could tell them she had known all along. He produced the *boeuf en croûte* and two bottles of Echezeaux 1970. Jean-Pierre sniffed the sauce appreciatively.

'On second thoughts she ought to be seriously considered if her touch in bed is half as deft as it is in the kitchen.'

'You're not going to get the chance to be the judge of that, Jean-Pierre. Content yourself with admiring her French dressing.'

'You were quite outstanding this morning, James,' said Stephen, steering the conversation away from Jean-Pierre's pet subject. 'You should go on the stage. As a member of the British aristocracy, your talent's simply wasted.'

'I've always wanted to, but my old pa is against it. Those who live in expectation of a large inheritance must expect to have to toe the filial line.'

'Why don't we let him play all four parts in Monte Carlo?' suggested Robin.

The mention of Monte Carlo sobered them up.

'Down to work,' said Stephen. 'We have so far received $447,560. Expenses with the picture and an unexpected night at the Dorchester were $11,142 so Metcalfe still owes us $563,582. Think of what we've still lost, not of what we've gained. Now for the Monte Carlo operation, which depends upon split-second timing and our ability to sustain our roles for several hours. Robin will bring us up to date.'

Robin retrieved the green dossier from the briefcase by his side and studied his notes for a few moments.

'Jean-Pierre, you must grow a beard, starting today, so that in three weeks' time you'll be unrecognizable. You must also cut your hair very short.' Robin grinned unsympathetically at Jean-Pierre's grimace. 'Yes, you'll look absolutely revolting.'

'That,' said Jean-Pierre, 'will not be possible.'

'How are the baccarat and blackjack coming on?' continued Robin.

'I have lost $37 in five weeks, which includes my member's fee at the Claremont and the Golden Nugget.'

'It all goes on expenses,' said Stephen. 'That puts the bill up to $563,619.'

The others laughed. Only Stephen's lips did not move. He was in sober earnest.

'James, how is your handling of the van going?'

'I can reach Harley Street from St Thomas's in 14 minutes. I should be able to do the actual run in Monte Carlo in about 11 minutes, though naturally I shall want to do some practice runs the day before. To start with I'll have to master driving on the wrong side of the road.'

'Strange how everybody except the British drives on the wrong side of the road,' observed Jean-Pierre.

James ignored him.

'I'm not sure of all the continental road signs either.'

'They are detailed in the Michelin guide that I gave you as part of my dossier.'

'I know, but I'll still feel easier when I've experienced the actual run and not just studied maps. There are quite a few one-way streets in Monaco and I don't want to be stopped going down the wrong one with Harvey Metcalfe unconscious in the back.'

'Don't worry. You'll have ample time when we're there. So, that only leaves Stephen, who's about the most competent medical student I've ever had. You're confident of your newly acquired knowledge, I hope?'

'About as confident as I am with your American accent, Robin. Anyway, I trust that Harvey Metcalfe will be in no state of mind to worry about such trivialities by the time we meet up.'

'Don't worry, Stephen. Believe me, he wouldn't even register who you were if you introduced yourself as Herr Drosser with a Van Gogh under both arms.'

Robin handed round the final schedule of rehearsals for Harley Street and St Thomas's, and once again consulted the green file.

'I've booked four single rooms on different floors at the Hôtel de Paris and confirmed all the arrangements with the Centre Hospitalier Princesse Grace. The hotel is reputed to be one of the best in the world – it's certainly expensive enough – but it's convenient for the Casino. We fly to Nice on Monday, the day after Harvey is due to arrive on his yacht.'

'What do we do for the rest of the week?' inquired James innocently.

Stephen resumed control:

'We master the green dossier backwards, frontwards and sideways for a full dress rehearsal on Friday. The most important thing for you, James, is to get a grip of yourself and let us know what you intend to do.'

James sunk back into gloom.

Stephen closed his file briskly.

'That seems to be all we can cover tonight.'

'Hang on, Stephen,' said Robin. 'Let's strip you off once more. I'd like to see if we can do it in 90 seconds.'

Stephen lay down slightly reluctantly in the middle of the room, and James and Jean-Pierre swiftly and carefully removed all his clothes.

'87 seconds. Excellent,' said Robin, looking down at Stephen, naked except for his watch. 'Hell, look at the time. I must get back to Newbury. My wife will think I have a mistress and I don't fancy any of you.'

Stephen dressed himself quickly while the others prepared to leave. A few minutes later, James stood by the front door, watching them depart one by one. As soon as Stephen was out of sight, he bounded downstairs into the kitchen.

'Did you listen?'

'Yes, darling. They're all rather nice and I don't blame them for being cross with you. They're being very professional about the whole venture, while you sounded like the only amateur. We'll have to think up something good for you to match them. We're over a week before Mr Metcalfe goes to Monte Carlo and we must use the time constructively.'

James sighed: 'Well, let's enjoy tonight. At least this morning was a triumph.'

'Yes, but not yours. Tomorrow we work.'

12

'Passengers for flight 017 to Nice are now requested to board the aircraft at gate No. 7,' boomed the loudspeaker at Heathrow's No. 1 terminal.

'That's us,' said Stephen.

The four of them took the escalator to the first floor, and walked down the long corridor. After being searched for guns, bombs, and whatever else terrorists are searched for, they proceeded down the ramp.

They sat separately, never speaking or even looking at each other. Stephen had warned them that the flight could well be sprinkled with Harvey's friends, and each imagined himself to be sitting next to the closest of them.

James gazed moodily at the cloudless sky and brooded. He and Anne had read every book they could lay their hands on that even hinted at stolen money or successful duplicity, but they had found nothing they could plagiarize. Even Stephen, in between being undressed and practised upon at St Thomas's, was becoming daunted by the task of finding a winning plan for James.

The Trident touched down at Nice at 13.40, and the train journey from Nice to Monte Carlo took them a further twenty minutes. Each member of the team made his own way to the elegant Hôtel de Paris in the Place du Casino. At 7 p.m. they were all present in room 217.

'All settled into your rooms?'

The other three nodded. 'So far, so good,' said Robin. 'Right, let's go over the timing. Jean-Pierre, you will go to the Casino tonight and play a few hands of baccarat and blackjack. Try to acclimatize to the place and learn your way around. In particular, master any variations in the rules there might be from the Claremont, and be sure you never speak in English. Do you foresee any problems?'

'No, can't say I do, Robin. In fact I may as well go now and start rehearsing.'

'Don't lose too much of our money,' said Stephen.

Jean-Pierre, resplendent in beard and dinner-jacket, grinned and slipped out of room 217 and down the staircase, avoiding the lift. He walked the short distance from the hotel to the famous Casino.

Robin continued:

'James, you take a taxi from the Casino to the hospital. On arrival you will leave the meter running for a few minutes and then return to the Casino. You can normally rely on a taxi to take the shortest route, but to be sure, tell the driver it's an emergency. That'll give you the opportunity of seeing which traffic lanes he uses under pressure. When he's returned you to the Casino, walk the route from there to the hospital and back. Then you can assimilate it in your own time. After you've mastered that, repeat the same procedure for the route between the hospital and Harvey's yacht. Never enter the Casino or even get close enough to the boat to be seen. Being seen now means being recognized later.'

'What about my knowledge of the Casino on the night of the operation?'

'Jean-Pierre will take care of that. He'll meet you at the door because Stephen won't be able to leave Harvey. I don't think they will charge you the 12 franc entrance fee if you're wearing a white coat and carrying a stretcher, but have it ready to be sure. When you've completed the walk, go to your room and stay there until our meeting at 11 a.m. tomorrow. Stephen and I will also be going to the hospital to check that all the arrangements have been carried out as cabled from London. If at any time you see us, ignore us.'

As James left room 217, Jean-Pierre arrived at the Casino.

The Casino stands in the heart of Monte Carlo overlooking the sea, surrounded by the most beautiful gardens. The present building has several wings, the oldest of which was designed by Charles Garnier, the architect of the Paris Opera House. The gambling rooms, which were added in 1910, are linked by an atrium to the Salle Garnier in which operas and ballets are performed.

Jean-Pierre marched up the marble staircase to the entrance and paid his 12 francs. The gambling rooms are vast, full of the decadence and grandeur of Europe at the turn of the century. Massive red carpets, statues, paintings and tapestries give the building an almost regal appearance and the portraits lend an air of a country home still lived in. Jean-Pierre found the clientèle were of all nationalities: Arabs and Jews played next to each other at the roulette wheel and chatted away with an ease that would have been unthinkable at the United Nations. Jean-Pierre felt totally relaxed in the unreal world of the wealthy. Robin had assessed his character accurately and given him a role he could master with aplomb.

Jean-Pierre spent over three hours studying the layout of the Casino – its gambling rooms, bars and restaurants, the telephones, the entrances and exits. Then he turned his attention to the gambling itself. He discovered that two shoes of baccarat were played in the Salons Privés at 3 p.m. and 11 p.m., and learned from Pierre Cattalano, the head of the public relations department of the Casino, which of the private rooms Harvey Metcalfe preferred to play in.

Blackjack is played in the Salon des Amériques from 11 a.m. daily. There are three tables, and Jean-Pierre's informant told him that Harvey always played on table No. 2, seat No. 3. Jean-Pierre played a little blackjack and baccarat, to discover any slight variations in rules there might be from the Claremont. In fact there were none, as the Claremont still adheres to French rules.

Harvey Metcalfe arrived noisily at the Casino just after 11 p.m., leaving a trail of cigar ash leading to his baccarat table. Jean-Pierre, inconspicuous at the bar, watched as the head croupier first showed Harvey politely to a reserved seat, and then walked through to the Salon des Amériques to the No. 2 blackjack table and placed a discreet white card marked 'Réservé' on one of the chairs. Harvey was clearly a favoured client. The management knew as well as Jean-Pierre which games Harvey Metcalfe played. At 11.27 p.m. Jean-Pierre left quietly and returned to the solitude of his hotel room where he remained until 11 a.m. the next day. He phoned no one and did not use room service.

James's evening also went well. The taxi-driver was superb. The word 'emergency' brought out the Walter Mitty in him: he travelled through Monte Carlo as if it were nothing less than the Rally itself. When James arrived at the hospital in 8 minutes 44 seconds, he genuinely felt a little sick and had to rest for a few minutes in the Entrée des Patients before returning to the taxi.

'Back to the Casino, but much slower, please.'

The journey back along the Rue Grimaldi took just over eleven minutes and James decided he would settle for trying to cover it in about ten. He paid off the taxi-driver and carried out the second part of his instructions.

Walking to the hospital and back took just over an hour. The night air was gentle on his face, and the streets crowded with lively chattering people. Tourism is the chief source of income for the Principality, and the Monégasques take the welfare of their visitors very seriously. James passed innumerable little pavement restaurants and souvenir shops stocked with expensive trinkets of no significance that once bought would be forgotten or lost within a week. Noisy groups of holiday-makers strolled along the pavements, their multilingual babel forming a meaningless chorus to James's thoughts of Anne. On arrival back at the Casino, James then took a taxi to the harbour to locate *Messenger Boy*, Harvey's yacht, and from there once more to the hospital. He then walked the same route and, like Jean-Pierre, he was safely in his room before midnight, having completed his first task.

Robin and Stephen found the walk to the hospital from their hotel took a little over 40 minutes. On arrival Robin asked the receptionist if he could see the superintendent.

'The night superintendent is now on duty,' said a freshly starched French nurse. 'Who shall I say is asking him for?'

Her English pronunciation was excellent and they both avoided a smile at her slight mistake.

'Doctor Wiley Barker of the University of California.'

Robin began to pray that the French superintendent would not happen to know that Wiley Barker, President Nixon's physician and one of the most respected surgeons in the world, was actually touring Australia at the time lecturing to the major universities.

'Bonsoir, Docteur Barker. Monsieur Bartise à votre service. Votre visite fait grand honneur à notre hôpital humble.'

Robin's newly acquired American accent stopped any further conversation in French.

'I would like to check the layout of the theatre,' said Robin, 'and confirm that we have it provisionally booked for tomorrow from 11 p.m. to 4 a.m. for the next five days.'

'That is quite correct, Docteur Barker,' said the superintendent, looking down at a clip-board. 'The theatre is off the next corridor. Will you follow me, please?'

The theatre was not dissimilar to the one the four of them had been practising in at St Thomas's – two rooms with a rubber swing door dividing them. The main theatre was well equipped and a nod from Robin showed Stephen that it had all the instruments he required. Robin was impressed. Although the hospital had only some 200 beds, the theatre itself was of the highest standard. Rich men had obviously been ill there before.

'Will you be requiring an anaesthetist or any nurses to assist you, Docteur Barker?'

'No,' said Robin. 'I have my own anaesthetist and staff, but I will require a tray of laparotomy instruments to be laid out every night. However, I will be able to give you at least an hour's warning before you need make any final preparations.'

'That's plenty of time. Will there be anything else, sir?'

'Yes, the special vehicle I ordered. Can it be ready for my driver at 12 p.m. tomorrow?'

'Yes, Docteur Barker. It will be in the small car park behind the hospital and your driver can pick up the keys from the reception.'

'Can you recommend an agency from which I can hire an experienced nurse for post-operative care?'

'Bien sûr, the Auxiliaire Médical of Nice will be only too happy to oblige – at a certain price, of course.'

'Of course,' said Robin. 'And that reminds me to ask, have all your expenses been dealt with?'

'Yes, Docteur. We received a cheque from California last Thursday for $7,000.'

Robin had been very pleased with that touch. It had been so simple. Stephen had contacted his bank at Harvard and asked them to send a draft from the First National City Bank in San Francisco to the hospital secretary at Monte Carlo.

'Thank you for all your help, Monsieur Bartise. You have been most obliging. Now you do understand that I am not quite sure which night I shall be bringing my patient in. He's a sick man, although he doesn't know it, and I have to prepare him for the operation.'

'Of course, mon cher Docteur.'

'Finally, I would appreciate it if you would tell as few people as possible that I am in Monte Carlo. I am trying to snatch a holiday at the same time as working.'

'I understand, Docteur Barker. You can be assured of my discretion.'

Robin and Stephen bade forewell to Monsieur Bartise and took a taxi back to the hotel.

'I'm always slightly humiliated by how well the French speak our language compared with our grasp of theirs,' said Stephen.

'It's all the fault of you bloody Americans,' said Robin.

'No, it isn't. If France had conquered America, your French would be
excellent. Blame it on the Pilgrim Fathers.'

Robin laughed. Neither of them spoke again until they reached room
217 for fear of being overheard. Stephen had no doubts about the responsibility and risk they were taking with Robin's plan.

· · ·

Harvey Metcalfe was on the deck of his yacht, sunbathing and reading
the morning papers. *Nice-Matin,* irritatingly enough, was in French. He
read it laboriously, with the aid of a dictionary, to see if there were any
social events to which he ought to get himself invited. He had gambled
late into the night, and was enjoying the sun's rays on his fleshy back.
If money could have obtained it, he would have been 6 ft and 170 lb
with a handsome head of hair, but no amount of suntan oil would stop
his balding dome from burning, so he covered it with a cap inscribed with
the words 'I'm sexy'. If Miss Fish could see him now ...

At 11 a.m., as Harvey turned over and allowed the sun to see his massive
stomach, James strolled into room 217 where the rest of the Team were
waiting for him.

Jean-Pierre reported on the layout of the Casino and Harvey Metcalfe's
habits. James brought them up to date on the result of his race through
the city the night before and confirmed that he thought he could cover
the distance in just under eleven minutes.

'Perfect,' said Robin. 'Stephen and I took 15 minutes by taxi from the
hospital to the hotel so if Jean-Pierre warns me immediately the balloon
goes up in the Casino, I should have enough time to see that everything
is ready before you all arrive.'

'I do hope the balloon will be going down, not up, in the casino,' remarked Jean-Pierre.

'I have booked an agency nurse to be on call from tomorrow night.
The hospital has all the facilities I require. It'll take about two minutes
to walk a stretcher from the front door to the theatre, so from the moment
James leaves the car park I should have at least 16 minutes to prepare
myself. James, you'll be able to pick up the vehicle from the hospital car
park at 12 p.m. The keys have been left in reception in the name of Dr
Barker. Do a couple of practice runs and no more. I don't want you causing
interest by looking conspicuous. And could you leave this parcel in the
back, please.'

'What is it?'

'Three long white laboratory coats and a stethoscope for Stephen. While
you're at it, better check that you can unfold the stretcher easily. When
you've finished the two runs, put the vehicle back in the car park and
return to your room until 11 p.m. From then through to 4 a.m. you'll
have to wait in the car park until you get the "action stations" or "all
clear" signal from Jean-Pierre. Everybody buy new batteries for your trans-
mitters. I don't want the whole plan to collapse for the sake of a tenpenny
battery. I'm afraid there's nothing much for you to do, Jean-Pierre, until
this evening, except relax. I hope you have some good books in your room.'

'Can't I go to the Princess Cinema and see François Truffaut's *La Nuit
Américaine*? I just adore Jacqueline Bisset. Vive la France.'

'My dear Jean-Pierre, Miss Bisset's from Reading,' said James.

'I don't care. I still want to see her.'

'A frog he would a-wooing go,' said James mockingly.

'But why not?' said Robin. 'The last thing Harvey will do is take in an intellectual French film with no sub-titles. Hope you enjoy it – and good luck tonight, Jean-Pierre.'

Jean-Pierre left for his room as quietly as he had come, leaving the rest of them together in room 217.

'Right, James. You can do your practice runs any time that suits you. Just make sure you're wide awake tonight.'

'Fine. I'll go and pick up the keys from the hospital reception. Let's just hope nobody stops me for a real emergency.'

'Now, Stephen, let's go over the details again. There's more than money to lose if we get this one wrong. We'll start from the top. What do you do if the nitrous oxide falls below five litres ...'

. . .

'Station check – station check – operation Metcalfe. This is Jean-Pierre. I am on the steps of the Casino. Can you hear me, James?'

'Yes. I am in the car park of the hospital. Out.'

'Robin here. I am on the balcony of room 217. Is Stephen with you, Jean-Pierre?'

'Yes. He's drinking on his own at the bar.'

'Good luck and out.'

Jean-Pierre carried out a station check every hour on the hour from 7 p.m. until 11 p.m., merely to inform Robin and James that Harvey had not arrived.

Eventually, at 11.16, he did show up, and took his reserved place at the baccarat table. Stephen stopped sipping his tomato juice and Jean-Pierre moved over and waited patiently by the table for one of the men seated on the left or right of Harvey to leave. An hour passed by. Harvey was losing a little, but continued to play. So did the tall thin American on his right and the Frenchman on his left. Another hour and still no movement. Then suddenly the Frenchman on the left of Metcalfe had a particularly bad run, gathered his few remaining chips and left the table. Jean-Pierre moved forward.

'I am afraid, Monsieur, that that seat is reserved for another gentleman,' said the banker. 'We do have an unreserved place on the other side of the table.'

'It's not important,' said Jean-Pierre, who backed away, not wanting to be remembered, cursing the deference with which the Monégasques treat the wealthy. Stephen could see from the bar what had happened and made furtive signs to leave. They were all back in room 217 just after 2 a.m.

. . .

'What a bloody silly mistake. Merde, merde, merde. I should have thought of reservations the moment I knew Harvey had one.'

'No, it was my fault. I don't know anything about how casinos work and I should have queried it during rehearsals,' said Robin, stroking his newly acquired moustache.

'No one is to blame,' chipped in Stephen. 'We still have three more nights, so no need to panic. We'll just have to work out how to overcome the seating problem, but for now we'll all get some sleep and meet again in this room at 10 a.m.'

They left, a little depressed. Robin had sat waiting in the hotel on edge for four hours. James was cold and bored in the hospital car park, Stephen was sick of tomato juice and Jean-Pierre had been on his feet by the baccarat table waiting for a seat that wasn't even available.

. . .

Once again Harvey lounged in the sun. He was now a light pink and was hoping to be a better colour towards the end of the week. According to his copy of the *New York Times*, gold was still climbing and the Deutschmark and the Swiss franc remained firm, while the dollar was on the retreat against every currency except sterling. Sterling stood at $2.42. Harvey thought a more realistic price was $1.80 and the sooner it reached that the better.

Nothing new, he thought, when the sharp ring of a French telephone roused him. He never could get used to the sound of foreign telephones. The attentive steward bustled out on deck with the instrument on an extension lead.

'Hi, Lloyd. Didn't know you were in Monte ... why don't we get together? ... 8 p.m.? ... Me too ... I'm even getting brown ... Must be getting old ... What? ... Great, I'll see you then.'

Harvey replaced the receiver and asked the steward for a large whisky on the rocks. He once again settled down happily to the morning's financial bad news.

. . .

'That seems to be the obvious solution,' said Stephen.

They all nodded their approval.

'Jean-Pierre will give up the baccarat table and book a place next to Harvey Metcalfe on his blackjack table in the Salon des Amériques and wait for him to change games. We know both the seat numbers Harvey plays at and we'll alter our own plans accordingly.'

Jean-Pierre dialled the number of the Casino and asked to speak to Pierre Cattalano:

'Réservez-moi la deuxième place à la table 2 pour le vingt-et-un soir et demain soir, s'il vous plaît.'

'Je pense que cette place est déjà réservée, Monsieur. Un instant, s'il vous plaît, je vais vérifier.'

'Peut-être que 100 francs la rendra libre,' replied Jean-Pierre.

'Mais certainement, Monsieur. Présentez-vous à moi dès votre arrivée, et le nécessaire sera fait.'

'Merçi,' said Jean-Pierre and replaced the receiver. 'That's under control.'

Jean-Pierre was visibly sweating, though had his call had no other outcome than to secure him a reserved seat, not a drop of perspiration would have appeared. They all returned to their rooms.

When the clock in the town square struck twelve, Robin was waiting quietly in room 217, James stood in the car park humming 'I Get Along Without You Very Well', Stephen was at the bar of the Salon des Amériques toying with yet another tomato juice and Jean-Pierre was at seat No. 2

on table No. 2, playing blackjack. Both Stephen and Jean-Pierre saw Harvey come through the door, chatting to a man in a loud-checked jacket which only a Texan could have worn outside his own back yard. Harvey and his friend sat down together at the baccarat table. Jean-Pierre beat a hasty retreat to the bar.

'Oh, no. I give up.'

'No, you don't,' whispered Stephen. 'Back to the hotel.'

. . .

Spirits were very low when they were all assembled in room 217, but it was agreed that Stephen had made the right decision. They could not risk the entire exercise being carefully observed by a friend of Harvey's.

'The first operation is beginning to look a bit too good to be true,' said Robin.

'Don't be silly,' said Stephen. 'We had two false alarms then, and the entire plan had to be changed at the last minute. We can't expect him just to walk in and hand over his money. Now snap out of it, all of you, and go and get some sleep.'

They returned to their separate rooms, but not to much sleep. The strain was beginning to tell.

. . .

'That's enough I think, Lloyd. A goodish evening.'

'For you, you mean, Harvey, not for me. You are one of nature's winners.'

Harvey patted the checked shoulder expansively. If anything pleased him more than his own success, it was other people's failure.

'Do you want to spend the night on my yacht, Lloyd?'

'No thanks. I must get back to Nice. I have a meeting in Paris, France, tomorrow lunch. See you soon, Harvey – take care of yourself.' He dug Harvey in the ribs jocularly. 'That's a fair-sized job.'

'Goodnight, Lloyd,' said Harvey, a little stiffly.

. . .

The next evening Jean-Pierre did not arrive at the Casino until 11 p.m. Harvey Metcalfe was already at the baccarat table minus Lloyd. Stephen was at the bar looking angry, and Jean-Pierre glanced at him apologetically as he took his seat at the blackjack table. He played a few hands to get the feel, trying to keep his losses fairly limited without drawing attention to the modesty of his stakes. Suddenly Harvey left the baccarat table and stalked into the Salon des Amériques, glancing at the roulette tables as he passed more out of curiosity than interest. He detested games of pure chance, and considered baccarat and blackjack games of skill. He headed to table No. 2 seat No. 3, on Jean-Pierre's left. Jean-Pierre felt his adrenalin start pumping round and his heart-beat rise up to 120 again. Stephen left the Casino for a few minutes to warn James and Robin that Harvey had moved to the blackjack table and was now sitting next to Jean-Pierre. He then returned to the bar and waited.

There were seven punters at the blackjack table. On Box No. 1, a middle-aged lady smothered in diamonds, who looked as if she might be passing time while her husband played roulette or perhaps baccarat. On Box No. 2, Jean-Pierre. On Box No. 3, Harvey. On Box No. 4, a dissipated young man with the world-weariness that usually goes with a large unearned income. On Box No. 5, an Arab in full robes. On Box No. 6, a not-unattractive actress who was clearly resting, Jean-Pierre suspected, with the occupant of Box No. 5; and on Box No. 7, an elderly, straight-backed aristocratic Frenchman in evening dress.

'A large black coffee,' Harvey drawled to the slim waiter in his smart brown jacket.

Monte Carlo does not allow hard liquor to be sold at the tables or girls to serve the customers. In direct contrast to Las Vegas, the Casino's business is gambling, not booze or women. Harvey had enjoyed Vegas when he was younger, but the older he became the more he appreciated the sophistication of the French. He had grown to prefer the formal atmosphere and decorum of this particular Casino. Although at the No. 3 table only he, the aristocratic Frenchman and Jean-Pierre wore dinner-jackets, it was frowned upon by the management to be dressed in any way that might be described as casual.

A moment later, piping hot coffee in a large golden cup arrived at Harvey's side. Jean-Pierre eyed it nervously while Harvey placed 100 francs on the table next to Jean-Pierre's 3-franc chip, the minimum and maximum stake allowed. The dealer, a tall young man of not more than thirty, who was proud of the fact that he could deal a hundred hands in an hour, slipped the cards deftly out of the shoe. A king for Jean-Pierre, a four for Harvey, a five for the young man on Harvey's left and a six for the dealer. Jean-Pierre's second card was a seven. He stuck. Harvey drew a ten and also stuck. The young man on Harvey's left also drew a ten and asked the dealer to twist again. It was an eight – bust.

Harvey despised amateurs in any field and even fools know you don't twist if you have twelve or more when the dealer's card face up is a three, four, five or six. He grimaced slightly. The dealer dealt himself a ten and a six. Harvey and Jean-Pierre were winners. Jean-Pierre ignored the fate of the other players.

The next round was unwinnable, Jean-Pierre stuck at eighteen, two nines which he chose not to split as the dealer had drawn Harvey stuck on eighteen, an eight and a jack, and the young man on the left bust again. The bank drew a queen – 'Black Jack' – and took the table.

The next hand gave Jean-Pierre a three, Harvey a seven and the young man a ten. The dealer drew himself a seven. Jean-Pierre drew an eight and doubled his stake to 6 francs and then drew a ten – vingt-et-un. Jean-Pierre did not blink. He realized he was playing well and that he must not draw attention to himself, but let Harvey take it for granted. In fact Harvey hadn't even noticed him: his attention was riveted on the young man on his left, who seemed anxious to make a gift to the management on every hand. The dealer continued, giving Harvey a ten and the young man an eight, leaving them both no choice but to stick. The dealer drew a ten, giving himself seventeen. He paid Jean-Pierre, left Harvey's stake and paid the young man. The management was happy to pay the young man occasionally, if only to keep him sitting there all night.

There were no more cards left in the shoe. The dealer made a great show of re-shuffling the four packs and invited Harvey to cut the cards before replacing them in the shoe. They slipped out again: a ten for Jean-

Pierre, a five for Harvey, a six for the young man and a four for the dealer. Jean-Pierre drew an eight. The cards were running well. Harvey drew a ten and stuck at fifteen. The young man drew a ten and asked for another card. Harvey could not believe his eyes and whistled through the gap in his front teeth. Sure enough, the next card was a king. The young man was bust. The dealer dealt himself a jack and then an eight, making twenty-two, but the young man had learned nothing from it. Harvey stared at him. When would he discover that, of the fifty-two cards in the pack, no less than sixteen have a face value of ten?

Harvey's distraction gave Jean-Pierre the opportunity he had been waiting for. He slipped his hand into his pocket and took the prostigmin tablet Robin had given him into the palm of his left hand. He sneezed, pulling his handkerchief from his breast pocket in a well-rehearsed gesture with his right hand. At the same time, he quickly and unobtrusively dropped the tablet into Harvey's coffee. It would, Robin had assured him, be an hour before it took effect. To begin with Harvey would only feel a little sick; then he would get rapidly worse until the pain was too much to bear, before finally collapsing in absolute agony.

Jean-Pierre turned to the bar, gripped his right-hand fist three times and then placed it in his pocket. Stephen left immediately and warned Robin and James from the steps of the Casino that the prostigmin tablet was in Metcalfe's drink. It was now Robin's turn to be tested under pressure. First he rang the hospital and asked the sister on duty to have the theatre in full preparation. Then he rang the nursing agency and asked for the nurse he had booked to be waiting in the hospital reception in exactly ninety minutes' time. He sat alone, nervously waiting for another call from the Casino.

Stephen returned to the bar. Harvey had started to feel a little sick, but was loath to leave. Despite the growing pain, his greed was forcing him to play on. He drank the rest of this coffee and ordered another one, hoping it would clear his head. The coffee did not help and Harvey began to feel steadily worse. An ace and a king followed by a seven, a four and a ten, and then two queens helped him to stay at the table. Jean-Pierre forced himself not to look at his watch. The dealer gave Jean-Pierre a seven, Harvey another ace and the young man a two. Quite suddenly, almost exactly on the hour, Harvey could bear the pain no longer. He tried to stand up and leave the table.

'Le jeu a commencé, Monsieur,' the dealer said formally.

'Go stuff yourself,' said Harvey and collapsed to the ground, gripping his stomach in agony. Jean-Pierre sat motionless while the croupiers and gamblers milled around helplessly. Stephen fought his way through the circle which had gathered round Harvey.

'Stand back, please. I am a doctor.'

The crowd moved back quickly, relieved to have a professional man on the scene.

'What is it, Doctor?' gasped Harvey, who felt the end of the world was about to come.

'I don't know yet,' replied Stephen. Robin had warned him that from collapse to passing out might be as short a time as ten minutes, so he set to work fast. He loosened Harvey's tie and took his pulse. He then undid his shirt and started feeling his abdomen.

'Have you a pain in the stomach?'

'Yes,' groaned Harvey.

'Did it come on suddenly?'

'Yes.'

'Can you try and describe the quality of the pain? Is it stabbing, burning or gripping?'

'Gripping.'

'Where is it most painful?'

Harvey touched the right side of his stomach. Stephen pressed down the tip of the ninth rib, making Harvey bellow with pain.

'Ah,' said Stephen, 'a positive Murphy's sign. You probably have an acutely inflamed gall-bladder. I'm afraid that may mean gallstones.' He continued to palpate the massive abdomen gently. 'It looks as if a stone has come out of your gall-bladder and is passing down the tube to your intestine – it's the squeezing of that tube that's giving you such dreadful pain. I'm afraid your gall-bladder and the stone must be removed at once. I can only hope there is someone at the hospital who can perform an emergency operation.'

Jean-Pierre came in bang on cue:

'Doctor Wiley Barker is staying at my hotel.'

'Wiley Barker, the American surgeon?'

'Yes, yes,' said Jean-Pierre. 'The chap who's been taking care of Nixon.'

'My God, what a piece of luck. We couldn't have anyone better, but he might turn out to be very expensive.'

'I don't give a damn about the expense,' wailed Harvey.

'Well, it might be as high as $50,000.'

'I don't care if it's $100,000,' screamed Harvey. At that moment he would have been willing to part with his entire fortune.

'Right,' said Stephen. 'You, sir,' looking at Jean-Pierre, 'ring for an ambulance and then contact Doctor Barker and ask if he can get to the hospital immediately. Tell him it's an emergency. This gentleman requires a surgeon of the highest qualifications.'

'You're damn right I do,' said Harvey, and passed out.

Jean-Pierre left the Casino and called over his transmitter:

'Action stations. Action stations.'

Robin left the Hôtel de Paris and took a taxi. He would have given $100,000 to change places with the driver, but the car was already moving relentlessly towards the hospital. It was too late to turn back now.

James smashed the ambulance into first gear and rushed to the Casino, siren blaring. He was luckier than Robin. With so much to concentrate on he didn't have time to consider the consequences of what he was doing.

Eleven minutes and forty-one seconds later he arrived, leapt out of the driver's seat, opened the back door, gathered the stretcher and rushed up the Casino steps in his long white coat. Jean-Pierre was standing expectantly on the top step waiting for him. No words passed between them as he guided James quickly through the Salon des Amériques where Stephen was bending over Harvey. The stretcher was placed on the floor. It took all three of them to lift Harvey Metcalfe's 227 lb on to the canvas. Stephen and James picked up the stretcher and took him quickly through to the waiting ambulance, followed by Jean-Pierre.

'Where are you going with my boss?' demanded a voice.

Startled, the three of them turned round. It was Harvey Metcalfe's chauffeur, standing by the white Rolls-Royce. After a moment's hesitation, Jean-Pierre took over.

'Mr Metcalfe has collapsed and has to go to hospital for an emergency operation. You must return to the yacht immediately, tell the staff to have his cabin ready and await further instructions.'

The chauffeur touched his cap and ran to the Rolls-Royce. James leapt behind the wheel, while Stephen and Jean-Pierre joined Harvey in the back of the vehicle.

'Hell, that was close. Well done, Jean-Pierre. I was speechless,' admitted Stephen.

'It was nothing,' said Jean-Pierre, sweat pouring down his face.

The ambulance shot off like a scalded cat. Stephen and Jean-Pierre both replaced their jackets with the long white laboratory coats left on the seat and Stephen put the stethoscope round his neck.

'It looks to me as if he's dead,' said Jean-Pierre.

'Robin says he isn't,' said Stephen.

'How can he tell from four miles away?'

'I don't know. We'll just have to take his word for it.'

James screeched to a halt outside the entrance to the hospital. Stephen and Jean-Pierre hurried their patient through to the operating theatre. James returned the ambulance to the car park and quickly joined the others in the theatre.

Robin, scrubbed up and gowned, was there to meet them at the door and while they were strapping Harvey Metcalfe to the operating table in the small room next to the theatre, he spoke for the first time:

'All of you, change your clothes. And Jean-Pierre, you scrub up as instructed.'

All three of them changed and Jean-Pierre started to wash immediately – a long, laborious process which Robin had firmly taught him must never be cut short. Post-operative septicaemia formed no part of his plan. Jean-Pierre appeared from the scrubbing-up room ready for action.

'Now, relax. We've done this nine times already. Just carry on exactly as if we were still in St Thomas's.'

Stephen moved behind the mobile Boyles machine. For four weeks he had been training as an anaesthetist: he had rendered James and a faintly protesting Jean-Pierre unconscious twice each in practice runs at St Thomas's. Now was his chance to exercise his new powers over Harvey Metcalfe.

Robin removed a syringe from a plastic packet and injected 250 mg of thiopentone into Harvey's arm. The patient sank back into a deep sleep. Quickly and efficiently Jean-Pierre and James undressed Harvey and then covered him in a sheet. Stephen placed the mask from the Boyles machine over Metcalfe's nose. The two flow-meters on the back of the machine showed 5 litres of nitrous oxide and 3 litres of oxygen.

'Take his pulse,' said Robin.

Stephen placed a finger in front of the ear just above the lobe to check the pre-auricular pulse. It was 70.

'Wheel him through into the theatre,' instructed Robin.

James pushed the trolley into the next room until it was just under the operating lights. Stephen trundled the Boyles machine along behind them.

The operating theatre was windowless and coldly sterile. Gleaming white tiles covered every wall from floor to ceiling, and it contained only the equipment needed for one operation. Jean-Pierre had covered Harvey with a sterile green sheet, leaving only his head and left arm exposed. One trolley of sterile instruments, drapes and towels had been carefully laid out by the theatre nurse, and stood covered with a sterile sheet. Robin hung the bottle of intravenous fluid from a standard near the head of the table and taped the end of the tubing to Harvey's left arm to complete the preparation. Stephen sat at the head of the table with the Boyles machine and adjusted the face-mask over Harvey's mouth and nose. Only one of the three massive operating lights hanging directly over Harvey had been turned on, causing a spotlight effect on the protruding bulge of his abdomen.

Eight eyes stared down on their victim. Robin continued:

'I shall give exactly the same instructions as I did in all our rehearsals, so just concentrate. First, I shall clean the abdomen with a skin preparation of iodine.'

Robin had all the instruments ready on the side of the table next to Harvey's feet. James lifted the sheet and folded it back over Harvey's legs, then he carefully removed the sterile sheet covering the trolley of instruments and poured iodine into one of the small basins. Robin picked up a swab in a pair of forceps and dipped it in the iodine solution. With a swift action up, down, and over the abdomen, he cleaned about 1 square foot of Harvey's massive body, throwing the swab into a bin and repeating the action with a fresh one. Next he placed a sterile towel below Harvey's chin, covering his chest, and another over his hips and thighs. A third one he placed lengthways along the left-hand side of his body and a final one along the right-hand side, leaving a 9 inch square of flabby belly exposed. He put a towel clip on each corner to secure them safely and then placed the laparotomy drapes over the prepared site. Robin was now ready.

'Scalpel.'

Jean-Pierre placed what he would have called a knife firmly in Robin's outstretched palm, as a runner might when passing a baton. James's apprehensive eyes met Jean-Pierre's across the operating table, while Stephen concentrated on Harvey's breathing. Robin hesitated only for a second and then made a 10 cm paramedian incision, reaching about 3 cm into the fat. Robin had rarely seen a larger stomach: he could probably have gone as far as 8 cm deep without reaching the muscle. Blood started flowing everywhere, which Robin stopped with diathermy. No sooner had he finished the incision and stanched the flow of blood than he began to stitch up the patient's wound with a 3/0 interrupted plain catgut for stitches.

'That will dissolve within a week,' he explained.

He then closed the skin with a 2/0 interrupted plain silk, using an atraumatic needle. Then he cleaned the wound, removing the patches of blood that still remained. Finally, he placed a medium self-adhesive wound dressing over his handiwork.

James took off the drapes and sterile towels and placed them in the bin while Robin and Jean-Pierre put Metcalfe into a hospital gown and carefully packed his clothes in a grey plastic bag.

'He's coming round,' said Stephen.

Robin took another syringe and injected 10 mg of diazepan.

'That will keep him asleep for at least 30 minutes,' he said, 'and in any case, he'll be ga-ga for about three hours and won't remember much of what has happened. James, fetch the ambulance immediately and bring it round to the front of the hospital.'

James left the theatre and changed back into his clothes, a procedure which he could now perform in 90 seconds. He disappeared to the car park.

'Now, you two, get changed and then place Harvey very carefully in the ambulance and Jean-Pierre, wait in the back with him. Stephen, you carry out your next assignment.'

Stephen and Jean-Pierre changed quickly, back into their long white coats and wheeled the slumbering Harvey Metcalfe gently towards the ambulance. Once safely in, Stephen ran to the public telephone by the hospital entrance, checked a piece of paper in his wallet and dialled.

'Hello, *Nice-Matin*? My name's Terry Robards of the *New York Times*. I'm here on holiday, and I have a great little story for you ...'

Robin returned to the operating theatre and wheeled the trolley of instruments he had used to the sterilizing room, and left them there to be dealt with by the hospital theatre staff in the morning. He picked up the plastic bag containing Harvey's clothes and, going through to the changing room, quickly removed his operating gown, cap and mask and put on his own clothes. He went in search of the theatre sister, and smiled charmingly at her.

'All finished, ma soeur. I have left the instruments by the sterilizer. Please thank Monsieur Bartise for me once again.'

'Oui, Monsieur. Notre plaisir. Je suis heureuse d'être à même de vous aider. Votre infirmière de l'Auxiliaire Médicale est arrivée.'

A few moments later, Robin walked to the ambulance, accompanied by the agency nurse. He helped her into the back.

'Drive very slowly and carefully to the harbour.'

James nodded and set off at funeral pace.

'Nurse Faubert.'

'Yes, Docteur Barker.' Her hands were tucked primly under her blue cape, and her French accent was enchanting. Robin thought Harvey would not find her ministrations unwelcome.

'My patient has just had an operation for the removal of a gall stone and will need plenty of rest.'

With that Robin took out of his pocket a gall stone the size of an orange with a hospital tag on it which read 'Harvey Metcalfe'. Robin had in fact acquired the huge stone from St Thomas's Hospital, the original owner being a 6 ft 6 in West Indian bus conductor on the No. 14 route. Stephen and Jean-Pierre stared at it in disbelief. The nurse checked her new charge's pulse and respiration.

'If I were your patient, Nurse Faubert,' said Jean-Pierre, 'I should take good care never to recover.'

By the time they arrived at the yacht, Robin had briefed the nurse on diet and rest, and told her that he would be round to see his patient at 11 a.m. the next day. They left Harvey sleeping soundly in his large cabin, stewards and staff clucking attentively.

James drove the other three back to the hospital, deposited the ambulance in the car park and left the keys with reception. The four of them then headed back to the hotel by separate routes. Robin was the last to arrive at room 217, just after 3.30 a.m. He collapsed into an armchair.

'Will you allow me a whisky, Stephen?'

'Yes, of course.'

'Good God, he meant it,' said Robin, and downed a large Johnny Walker before handing the bottle over to Jean-Pierre.

'He will be all right, won't he?' said James.

'You sound quite concerned for him. Yes, he can have his ten stitches out in a week's time and all he'll have is a nasty scar to brag about to his friends. I must get some sleep. I have to see our victim at 11 tomorrow morning and the confrontation may well be harder than the operation. You were all great tonight. My God, am I glad we had all those sessions at St Thomas's. If you're ever out of work and I need a croupier, a driver and an anaesthetist, I'll know who to ring.'

The others left and Robin collapsed on to his bed, exhausted. He fell into a deep sleep and woke just after 8 the next morning, to discover he was still fully dressed. That had not happened to him since his days as a young houseman, when he had been on night duty after a fourteen-hour day without a break. Robin had a long soothing bath in very hot water. He dressed and put on a clean shirt and suit, ready for his face-to-face meeting with Harvey Metcalfe. His newly acquired moustache and rimless glasses and the success of the operation made him feel a little like the famous surgeon he was impersonating.

The other three all appeared during the next hour to wish him luck and elected to wait in room 217 for his return. Stephen had checked them all out of the hotel and booked a flight to London for late that afternoon. Robin left, again taking the staircase rather than the lift. Once outside the hotel, he walked a little way before hailing a taxi to drive him to the harbour.

It was not hard to find the *Messenger Boy*. She was a gleaming, newly painted 100-footer lying at the east end of the harbour. She sported a massive Panamanian flag on her stern mast, which Robin assumed must be for tax purposes. He ascended the gangplank and was met by Nurse Faubert.

'Bonjour, Docteur Barker.'

'Good morning, Nurse. How is Mr Metcalfe?'

'He has had a very peaceful night and is having a light breakfast and making a few telephone calls. Would you like to see him now?'

'Yes, please.'

Robin entered the magnificent cabin and faced the man he had spent eight weeks plotting and planning against. He was talking into the telephone:

'Yes, I'm fine, dear. But it was an A-1 emergency at the time. Don't worry, I'll live,' and he put the telephone down. 'Doctor Barker, I have just spoken to my wife in Massachusetts and told her that I owe you my life. Even at 5 a.m. she seemed pleased. I understand that I had private surgery, a private ambulance and that you saved my life. Or that's what it says in *Nice-Matin*.'

There was the old picture of Harvey in Bermuda shorts on the deck of the *Messenger Boy*, familiar to Robin from his dossier. The headline read 'Millionaire s'évanouit au Casino' over 'La Vie d'un Millionnaire Américain a été sauvée par une Opération Urgente Dramatique!' Stephen would be pleased.

'Tell me, Doctor,' said Harvey with relish, 'was I really in danger?'

'Well, you were on the critical list, and the consequences might have been fairly serious if we hadn't removed this from your stomach.' Robin took out the inscribed gall stone from his pocket with a flourish.

Harvey's eyes grew large as saucers.

'Gee, have I really been walking round with that inside me all this time? Isn't that something? I can't thank you enough. If ever I can do anything for you, Doctor, don't hesitate to call on me.' He offered Robin a grape. 'Look, you're going to see me through this thing, aren't you? I don't think the nurse fully appreciates the gravity of my case.'

Robin thought fast.

'I'm afraid I'm not free to do that, Mr Metcalfe. My holiday finishes today and I have to return to California. Nothing urgent: just a few elective surgeries and a rather heavy lecture schedule.' He shrugged deprecatingly. 'Not exactly earth-shattering but it helps me keep up a way of life I have grown accustomed to.'

Harvey sat bolt upright, tenderly holding his stomach.

'Now you listen to me, Doctor Barker. I don't give a damn about a few students. I'm a sick man and I need you here until I've fully recovered. I'll make it worth your while to stay, don't you worry. I never grudge the money where my health is concerned, and what's more if it will persuade you, I'll make the cheque out to cash. The last thing I want Uncle Sam to know is how much I'm worth.'

Robin coughed delicately, wondering how American doctors approached the ticklish subject of fees with their patients.

'The cost could be rather high if I'm not to be out of pocket by staying. It might be as much as $80,000.' Robin drew a deep breath.

Harvey didn't blink.

'Sure. You're the best. That's not a lot of money to stay alive.'

'Very well. I'll get back to my hotel and see if it's possible to rearrange my schedule for you.'

Robin retreated from the sick-room and the white Rolls-Royce took him back to the hotel. In room 217 they all sat staring at Robin in disbelief as he completed his story.

'Stephen, for Christ's sake, the man's a raving hypochondriac. He wants me to stay on here while he convalesces. None of us planned for that.'

Stephen looked up coolly:

'You'll stay here and play ball. Why not give him value for money – at his own expense, of course. Go on, get on the blower and tell him you'll be round to hold his hand every day at 11 a.m. We'll just have to go back without you. And keep the hotel bill down, won't you?'

Robin picked up the telephone . . .

· · ·

Three young men left the Hôtel de Paris after a long lunch in room 217, allowing themselves another bottle of Krug '64, and then returned to Nice Airport in a taxi, catching BA flight 012 at 16.10 to London Heathrow. They were once again in separate seats. One sentence remained on Stephen's mind from Robin's reported conversation with Harvey Metcalfe.

'If ever I can do anything for you, don't hesitate to call me at any time.'

· · ·

Robin visited his patient once a day, borne in the white Corniche with white-walled tyres and a chauffeur in a white uniform. Only Harvey could be quite so brash, he thought. On the third, Nurse Faubert asked for a private word with him.

'My patient,' she said plaintively, 'is making improper advances when I change his dressing.'

Robin allowed Dr Wiley Barker the liberty of an unprofessional remark.

'Can't say I altogether blame him. Still, be firm, Nurse. I'm sure you must have encountered that sort of thing before.'

'*Naturellement*, but never from a patient only three days after major surgery. His constitution, it must be *formidable*.'

'I tell you what, let's catheterize him for a couple of days. That'll cramp his style.' She smiled. 'It must be pretty boring for you cooped up here all day,' Robin continued. 'Why don't you come and have a spot of supper with me after Mr Metcalfe has gone to sleep tonight?'

'I should love to, Docteur. Where shall I meet you?'

'Room 217, Hôtel de Paris,' said Robin unblushingly. 'Say 9 p.m.'

'I'll look forward to it, Docteur.'

· · ·

'A little more Chablis, Angeline?'

'No more, thank you, Wiley. That was a meal to remember. I think, maybe, you have not yet had everything you want?'

She got up, lit two cigarettes and put one in his mouth. Then she moved away, her long skirt swinging slightly from the hips. She wore no bra under her pink shirt. She exhaled smokily and watched him.

Robin thought of the blameless Doctor Barker in Australia, of his wife and children in Newbury, and the rest of the Team in London. Then he put them all out of his mind.

'Will you complain to Mr Metcalfe if I make improper advances to you?'

'From you, Wiley,' she smiled, 'they will not be improper.'

· · ·

Harvey made a talkative recovery, and Robin removed the stitches gravely on the sixth day.

'That seems to have healed very cleanly, Mr Metcalfe. Take it easy, and you should be back to normal by the middle of next week.'

'Great. I have to get over to England right away for Ascot week. You know, my horse Rosalie is favourite this year. I suppose you can't join me as my guest? What if I have a relapse?'

Robin suppressed a smile.

'Don't worry. You're getting along fine. Sorry I can't stay to see how Rosalie performs at Ascot.'

'So am I, Doc. Thanks again, anyway. I've never met a surgeon like you before.'

And you're not likely to again, thought Robin, his American accent beginning to fray at the edges. He bid his adieus to Harvey with relief and to Angeline with regret, and sent the chauffeur back from the hotel with a copper-plate bill:

Dr Wiley Franklin Barker
presents his Compliments to
Mr Harvey Metcalfe
and begs to inform him that the Bill for
Professional Services rendered is
$80,000
in respect of surgery and post-operative treatment.

The chauffeur was back within the hour with a cash cheque for $80,000. Robin bore it back to London in triumph.

·   ·   ·

Two down and two to go.

13

The following day, Friday, Stephen sat on Robin's examination couch in Harley Street and addressed the troops.

'The Monte Carlo operation was a total success in every way, thanks to Robin keeping his cool. The expenses were fairly high, though. The hospital and hotel bills totalled $11,351, while we received $80,000. Therefore, we've had $527,560 returned to us, and expenses so far have come to $22,530, which leaves Mr Metcalfe still in debt to the tune of $494,970. Does everyone agree with that?'

There was a general murmur of approval. Their confidence in Stephen's arithmetic was unbounded, although in fact, like all algebraists, he found working with figures somewhat tedious.

'Incidentally, Robin, however did you manage to spend $73.50 on dinner last Wednesday night? What did you have, caviar and champagne?'

'Something a little out of the ordinary,' admitted Robin. 'It seemed to be called for at the time.'

'I'd bet more than I laid out in Monte Carlo that I know who joined you for dinner, and I bet she shared more than a table with you too,' said Jean-Pierre, taking his wallet out of his pocket. 'Here you are Stephen, 219 francs – my winnings from the Casino on Wednesday night. If you'd left me alone in peace, we needn't have bothered with Robin's butchery.

I could have won the whole amount back on my own. I think the least I deserve is Nurse Faubert's telephone number.'

Jean-Pierre's remarks went straight over Stephen's head.

'Well done, Jean-Pierre, it'll all come off expenses. At today's exchange rate, your 219 francs,' he paused for a moment and tapped out on his calculator, 'is worth $46.76. That brings the expenses down to $22,483.24.

'Now, my plans for Ascot are simple. James has acquired two badges for the Members' Enclosure at a cost of $10. We know that Harvey Metcalfe also has a badge, as all owners do, so as long as we get our timing right and make it look natural, he should once again fall into our trap. James will keep us briefed on the walkie-talkie and will follow the movements of Metcalfe from his arrival to his leaving. Jean-Pierre will wait by the entrance of the Members' Enclosure and follow him in. Robin will send the telegram from Heathrow Airport at 1 p.m., so Harvey ought to receive it during lunch in his private box. That part of the plan is easy. It's if we manage to lure him to Oxford that we all have to be on our toes. I must confess, it'd make a pleasant change if Ascot were to work first time.'

Stephen grinned widely.

'That would give us much needed extra time to go over the Oxford plan again. Any questions?'

'You don't need us for part (*a*) of the Oxford plan, only (*b*)?' asked Robin, checking Stephen's notes.

'That's right. I can manage part (*a*) on my own. In fact, it will be better if you all remain in London on that night, well out of the way. Our next priority must be to think up some ideas for James or he might, heaven preserve us, even think up something for himself. I'm becoming very concerned about this,' continued Stephen, 'because once Harvey returns to America we'll have to deal with him on his own ground. To date he's always been at the venue of our choosing. James would stick out like a sore thumb in Boston, even though he's the best actor of the four of us. In Harvey's words, "It would be a whole different ball game.".

James sighed lugubriously and studied the Axminster carpet.

'Poor old James – don't worry, you drove that ambulance like a trooper,' said Robin.

'Perhaps you could learn to learn to fly a plane and then we could hijack him,' suggested Jean-Pierre.

· · ·

Stephen returned for a few days' recuperation to Magdalen College. He had started the entire exercise eight weeks before and two of the team had succeeded far beyond his expectations. He was conscious that he must crown their efforts with something that would live on in the legends of Oxford long after his departure.

· · ·

Jean-Pierre returned to work in his gallery in Bond Street. Since he only had to deliver one sentence at Ascot he was not going to be overtaxed, although part (*b*) of Stephen's Oxford plan kept him nightly in front of a mirror rehearsing his role.

James took Anne down to Stratford-upon-Avon for the weekend. The

Royal Shakespeare Company obliged with a sparkling performance of *Much Ado about Nothing* and afterwards, walking along the banks of the Avon, James proposed. Only the royal swans could have heard her reply. The diamond ring James had noticed in the window of Cartier while he had been waiting for Harvey Metcalfe to join Jean-Pierre in the gallery, looked even more beautiful on her slender finger. James's happiness seemed complete. If only he could come up with a plan and shock them all, he would want for nothing. He discussed it with Anne again that night, considering new ideas and old ones, still getting nowhere.

But an idea was beginning to formulate in her mind.

14

On Monday morning James dróve Anne back to London and changed into the most debonair of his suits. Anne had to return to work, despite James's suggestion that she should accompany him to Ascot. She felt the others would not approve of her presence and would suspect that James had confided in her.

Although James had not told her the details of the Monte Carlo exercise, Anne knew every step of the planned proceedings at Ascot and she could tell that James was nervous. Still, she would be seeing him that night and would know the worst by then. James looked lost. Anne was only thankful that Stephen, Robin and Jean-Pierre held the baton most of the time in this relay team – but the idea that was taking shape in her mind just might surprise them all.

Stephen rose early and admired his grey hair in the mirror. The result had been expensively achieved the previous day in the hairdressing salon of Debenhams. He dressed carefully, putting on his one respectable grey suit and blue checked tie. These were brought out for all special occasions, ranging from a talk to students at Sussex University to a dinner with the American Ambassador. No one had told him the colours clashed and the suit sagged unfashionably at the elbow and knees, because by Stephen's standards it was elegance itself. He travelled from Oxford to Ascot by train, while Jean-Pierre came from London by car. They met up with James at the Belvedere Arms at 11 a.m., almost a mile from the course.

Stephen immediately telephoned Robin to confirm that all three of them had arrived and asked for the telegram to be read over to him.

'That's perfect, Robin. Now travel to Heathrow and send it at exactly 1 p.m.'

'Good luck, Stephen. Grind the bastard into the dust.'

Stephen returned to the others and confirmed that Robin had the London end under control.

'Off you go, James, and let us know the minute Harvey arrives.'

James downed a bottle of Carlsberg and departed. The problem was that he kept bumping into friends and he could hardly explain why he was prevented from joining them.

Harvey arrived at the members' car park just after midday, his white Rolls-Royce shining like a Persil advertisement. The car was being stared at by all racegoers with an English disdain which Harvey mistook for admiration. He led his party to the private box. His newly tailored suit had taxed the ingenuity of Bernard Weatherill to the utmost. A red carnation in his buttonhole and a hat to cover his bald head left him nearly unrecognisable, and James might have missed him had it not been for the white Rolls-Royce. James followed the little group at a careful distance until he saw Harvey enter a door marked 'Mr Harvey Metcalfe and Guests'.

'He's in his private box,' said James.

'Where are you?' asked Jean-Pierre.

'Directly below him on the ground level by a course bookmaker called Sam O'Flaherty.'

'No need to be rude about the Irish, James,' said Jean-Pierre. 'We'll be with you in a few minutes.'

James stared up at the vast white stand, which accommodated 10,000 spectators in comfort and gave an excellent view of the racecourse. He was finding it hard to concentrate on the job in hand as once again he had to avoid relations and friends. First was the Earl of Halifax, and then that frightful girl he had so unwisely agreed to take to Queen Charlotte's Ball last spring. What was the creature's name? Ah yes. The Hon. Selina Wallop. How appropriate. She was wearing a mini-skirt that was a good four years out of fashion and a hat which looked as if it could never come into fashion. James jammed his trilby over his ears, looked the other way and passed the time by chatting to Sam O'Flaherty about the 3.20, the King George VI and Queen Elizabeth Stakes. O'Flaherty quoted the latest odds on the favourite at the top of his voice:

'Rosalie at 6:4, owned by that American, Harvey Metcalfe, and ridden by Pat Eddery.'

Eddery was on the way to becoming the youngest-ever champion jockey – and Harvey always backed winners.

Stephen and Jean-Pierre joined James at the side of Sam O'Flaherty's bag. His tick-tack man was standing on an upturned orange box beside him and swinging his arms like a semaphore sailor aboard a sinking ship.

'What's your fancy, gentlemen?' Sam asked the three of them.

James ignored Stephen's slight frown of disapproval.

'£5 each way on Rosalie,' he said, and handed over a crisp £10 note, receiving in return a little green card with the series number and 'Sam O'Flaherty' stamped right across the middle.

'I must presume, James, this is an integral part of your as yet undisclosed plan,' said Jean-Pierre. 'What I should like to know is, if it works, how much do we stand to make?'

'9.10 after tax if Rosalie wins,' chipped in Sam O'Flaherty, his stub cigar bobbing up and down in his mouth as he spoke.

'Hardly a great contribution towards $1 million, James. Well, we're off to the Members' Enclosure. Let us know the moment Harvey leaves his box. My guess is that around 1.45 he'll come and look at the runners and riders for the two o'clock, so that gives us a clear hour.'

. . .

The waiter opened another bottle of Krug 1964 and began pouring it for Harvey's guests; three bankers, two economists, a couple of ship-owners and a distinguished City journalist.

Preferring his guests to be famous and influential, Harvey always invited people who would find it almost impossible to refuse because of the business he might put their way. He was delighted with the company he had assembled for his big day. Senior among them was Sir Howard Dodd, the ageing chairman of the merchant bank that bore his name, but which actually referred to his great-grandfather. Sir Howard was 6 ft 2 in, as straight as a ramrod, and looked more like a Grenadier Guard than a respectable banker. The only thing he had in common with Harvey was the hair, or lack of hair, on his balding head. His young assistant, Jamie Clark, accompanied him. Just over thirty and extremely bright, he was there to be sure his chairman did not commit the bank to anything he might later regret. Although he had a sneaking admiration for Harvey, Clark did not think him the sort of customer the bank should do business with. Nevertheless, he was far from averse to a day at the races.

The two economists, Mr Colin Emson and Dr Michael Hogan from the Hudson Institute, were there to brief Harvey on the parlous state of the British economy. They could not have been more different. Emson was a totally self-made man who had left school at fifteen and educated himself. Using his social contacts, he had built up a company specializing in taxation, which had been remarkably successful thanks to the British Government's habit of putting through a new Finance Act every few weeks. Emson was 6 ft tall, solid and genial, game to help the party along whether Harvey lost or won. Hogan, in contrast, had been to all the right places – Winchester, Trinity College, Oxford, and the Wharton Business School in Pennsylvania. A spell with McKinsey, the management consultants, in London had made him one of the best-informed economists in Europe. Those who observed his slim, sinewy body would not have been surprised to learn that he had been an international squash player. Dark-haired, with brown eyes that rarely left Harvey, he found it hard not to show his contempt; this was his fifth invitation to Ascot – Harvey, it seemed was never going to take no for an answer.

The Kundas brothers, second-generation Greeks who loved racing almost as much as ships, could hardly be told apart, with their black hair, swarthy skins and heavy dark eyebrows. It was difficult to guess how old they were, and nobody knew how much they were worth. They probably did not know themselves. Harvey's final guest, Nick Lloyd of the *News of the World*, had come along to pick up any dirt he could about his host. He had come near to exposing Metcalfe in the mid-'sixties, but another scandal had kept less juicy stories off the front page for several weeks, and by then Harvey had escaped. Lloyd, hunched over the inevitable triple gin with a faint suggestion of tonic, watched the motley bunch with interest.

'Telegram for you, sir.'

Harvey ripped it open. He was never neat about anything.

'It's from my daughter Rosalie. It's cute of her to remember, but damn it all, I named the horse after her. Come on everybody, let's eat.'

They all took their seats for lunch – cold vichyssoise, pheasant and strawberries. Harvey was even more loquacious than usual, but his guests took no notice, aware he was nervous before the race and knowing that he would rather be a winner of this trophy than any he could be offered in America. Harvey himself could never understand why he felt that way. Perhaps it was the special atmosphere of Ascot which appealed to him so strongly – the combination of lush green grass and gracious surroundings, of elegant crowds and an efficiency of organization which made Ascot the envy of the racing world.

'You must have a better chance this year than ever before, Harvey,' said the senior banker.

'Well, you know, Sir Howard, Lester Piggott is riding the Duke of Devonshire's horse, Crown Princess, and the Queen's horse, Highclere, is the joint favourite, so I can't afford to over-estimate my chances. When you've been third twice before, and then favourite and not placed, you begin to wonder if one of your horses is going to make it.'

'Another telegram, sir.'

Once again Harvey's fat little finger ripped it open.

' "All best wishes and good luck for the King George VI and Queen Elizabeth Stakes". It's from the staff of your bank, Sir Howard. Jolly good show.'

Harvey's Polish-American accent made the English expression sound slightly ridiculous.

'More champagne, everybody.'

Another telegram arrived.

'At this rate, Harvey, you'll need a special room at the Post Office.' There was laughter all round at Sir Howard's feeble joke. Once again Harvey read it out aloud:

' "Regret unable to join you Ascot. Heading soonest California. Grateful look out for old friend Professor Rodney Porter, Oxford Nobel Prize Winner. Don't let English bookies stitch you up. Wiley B., Heathrow Airport". It's from Wiley Barker. He's the guy who did stitch me up in Monte Carlo. He saved my life. He took out a gall stone the size of that bread roll you're eating, Dr Hogan. Now how the hell am I supposed to find this Professor Porter?' Harvey turned to the head waiter. 'Find my chauffeur.'

A few seconds later the smartly-clad Guy Salmon flunkey appeared.

'There's a Professor Rodney Porter of Oxford here today. Go find him.'

'What does he look like, sir?'

'How the hell do I know,' said Harvey. 'Like a professor.'

The chauffeur regretfully abandoned his plans for an afternoon at the railings and departed, leaving Harvey and his guests to enjoy the strawberries, the champagne and the string of telegrams that were still arriving.

'You know if you win, the cup will be presented by the Queen,' said Nick Lloyd.

'You bet. It'll be the crowning moment of my life to win the King George and Elizabeth Stakes and meet Her Majesty The Queen. If Rosalie wins, I'll suggest my daughter marries Prince Charles – they're about the same age.'

'I don't think even you will be able to fix that, Harvey.'

'What'll you do with the odd £81,000 prize money, Mr Metcalfe?' asked Jamie Clark.

'Give it to some charity,' said Harvey, pleased with the impression the remark made on his guests.

'Very generous, Harvey. Typical of your reputation.' Nick Lloyd gave Michael Hogan a knowing look. Even if the others didn't, they both knew what was typical of his reputation.

The chauffeur returned to report that there was no trace of a solitary professor anywhere in the champagne bar, balcony luncheon room or the paddock buffet, and that he'd been unable to gain access to the Members' Enclosure.

'Naturally not,' said Harvey rather pompously. 'I shall have to find him myself. Drink up and enjoy yourselves.'

Harvey rose and walked to the door with the chauffeur. Once he was out of earshot of his guests, he said: 'Get your ass out of here and don't give me any crap about not being able to find him or you can find something for yourself – another job.'

The chauffeur bolted. Harvey turned to his guests and smiled.

'I'm going to look at the runners and riders for the 2 o'clock.'

'He's leaving the box now,' said James.

'What's that you're saying?' asked an authoritative voice he recognized. 'Talking to yourself, James?'

James stared at the noble Lord Somerset, 6 ft 1 in and still able to stand his full height, an MC and a DSO in the First World War. He still exuded enthusiastic energy although the lines on his face suggested that he had passed the age at which the Maker had fulfilled his contract.

'Oh hell. No, sir, I was just ... em ... coughing.'

'What do you fancy in the King George VI and Queen Elizabeth Stakes?' asked the peer of the realm.

'Well, I have put £5 each way on Rosalie, sir.'

⋅ ⋅ ⋅

'He seems to have cut himself off,' said Stephen.

'Well, buzz him again,' said Jean-Pierre.

⋅ ⋅ ⋅

'What's that noise, James? Have you taken to a hearing-aid or something?'

'No, sir. It's ... it's ... it's a transistor radio.'

'Those things ought to be banned. Bloody invasion of privacy.'

'Absolutely right, sir.'

⋅ ⋅ ⋅

'What's he playing at, Stephen?'

'I don't know – I think something must have happened.'

'Oh my god, it's Harvey heading straight for us. You go into the Members' Enclosure, Stephen, and I'll follow you. Take a deep breath and relax. He hasn't seen us.'

Harvey marched up to the official blocking the entrance to the Members' Enclosure.

'I'm Harvey Metcalfe, the owner of Rosalie, and this is my badge.'

The official let Harvey through. Thirty years ago, he thought, they would not have let him into the Members' Enclosure if he'd owned every horse in the race. Then racing at Ascot was only held on four days a year, jolly social occasions. Now it was twenty-four days a year and big business. Times had changed. Jean-Pierre followed closely, showing his pass without speaking to the official.

A photographer broke away from stalking the outrageous hats for which Ascot has such a reputation, and took a picture of Harvey just in case Rosalie won the King George VI Stakes. As soon as his bulb flashed he rushed over to the other entrace, where Linda Lovelace, the star of *Deep Throat*, the film running to packed houses in New York but banned in England, was trying to enter the Members' Enclosure. In spite of being introduced to a well-known London banker, Richard Szpiro, just as he was entering the Enclosure, she was not succeeding. She was wearing a top hat and morning suit with nothing under the top coat, and no one was going to bother with Harvey while she was around. When Miss Lovelace was quite certain that every photographer had taken a picture of her attempting to enter the Enclosure she left, swearing at the top of her voice, her publicity stunt completed.

Harvey returned to studying the horses as Stephen moved up to within a few feet of him.

'Here we go again,' said Jean-Pierre in French and went smartly over to Stephen and, standing directly between the two of them, shook Stephen's hand warmly, declaring in a voice that was intended to carry:

'How are you, Professor Porter? I didn't know you were interested in racing.'

'I'm not really, but I was on my way back from a seminar in London and thought it a good opportunity to see how ...'

'Professor Porter,' cried Harvey. 'I'm honoured to make your acquaintance, sir, my name is Harvey Metcalfe from Boston, Massachusetts. My good friend, Dr Wiley Barker, who saved my life, told me you'd be here today on your own, and I am going to make sure you have a wonderful afternoon.'

Jean-Pierre slipped away unnoticed. He could not believe how easy it had been. The telegram had worked like a charm.

.　　.　　.

'Her Majesty The Queen; His Royal Highness The Duke of Edinburgh; Her Royal Highness Queen Elizabeth The Queen Mother; and her Royal Highness The Princess Anne are now entering the Royal Box.'

The massed bands of the Brigade of Guards struck up the National Anthem:

'God Save the Queen.'

The crowd of 25,000 rose and sang loyally out of tune.

'We should have someone like that in America,' said Harvey to Stephen, 'to take the place of Richard Nixon. We wouldn't have any Watergate problems then.'

Stephen thought his fellow American was being just a little unfair. Richard Nixon was almost a saint by Harvey Metcalfe's standards.

'Come and join me in my box, Professor, and meet my other guests. The damned box cost me £750, we may as well fill it. Have you had some lunch?'

'Yes, I've had an excellent lunch, thank you,' Stephen lied – something else Harvey had taught him. He had stood by the Members' Enclosure for an hour, nervous and pensive, unable even to manage a sandwich, and now he was starving.

'Well, come and enjoy the champagne,' roared Harvey.

On an empty stomach, thought Stephen.

'Thank you, Mr Metcalfe. I am a little lost. This is my first Royal Ascot.'

'This isn't Royal Ascot, Professor. It's the last day of Ascot Week, but the Royal Family always comes to see the King George and Elizabeth Stakes, so everybody dresses up.'

'I see,' said Stephen timidly, pleased with his deliberate error.

Harvey collared his find and took him back to the box.

'Everybody, I want you to meet my distinguished friend, Rodney Porter. He's a Nobel Prize Winner, you know. By the way, what's your subject, Rod?'

'Biochemistry.'

Stephen was getting the measure of Harvey. As long as he played it straight, the bankers and shippers, and even the journalists, would never doubt that he was the cleverest thing since Einstein. He relaxed a little and even found time to fill himself with smoked salmon sandwiches when the others were not looking.

Lester Piggott won the 2 o'clock on Olympic Casino and the 2.30 on Roussalka, achieving his 3,000th win. Harvey was getting steadily more nervous. He talked incessantly without making much sense. He had sat through the 2.30 without showing any interest in the result and consumed more and more champagne. At 2.50 he called for them all to join him in the Members' Enclosure to look at his famous filly. Stephen, like the others, trailed behind him in a little pseudo-royal entourage.

Jean-Pierre and James watched the procession from a distance.

'He's too deep in to climb out now,' said Jean-Pierre.

'He looks relaxed enough to me,' replied James. 'Let's make ourselves scarce. We can only get under his feet.'

They headed into the champagne bar, which was filled with red-faced men who looked as if they spent more time drinking than they did watching the racing.

'Isn't she beautiful, Professor? Almost as beautiful as my daughter. If she doesn't win today I don't think I'm ever going to make it.'

Harvey left his little clique to have a word with the jockey, Pat Eddery, to wish him luck. Peter Walwyn, the trainer, was giving final instructions before the jockey mounted and left the Enclosure. The ten horses were then paraded in front of the stand before the race, a custom only carried out at Ascot for the King George VI and Queen Elizabeth Stakes. The gold, purple and scarlet colours of Her Majesty The Queen's horse Highclere led the procession, followed by Crown Princess, who was giving Lester Piggott a little trouble. Directly behind her came Rosalie, looking very relaxed, fresh and ready to go. Buoy and Dankaro trotted behind rosalie, with the outsiders Mesopotamia, ropey and Minnow bringing up the rear. The crowd rose to cheer the horses and Harvey beamed with pride, as if he owned every horse in the race.

'... and I have with me today the distinguished American owner, Harvey Metcalfe,' said Julian Wilson into the BBC TV outside-broadcast camera. 'I'm going to ask him if he'd be kind enough to give me his views on the King George VI and Queen Elizabeth Stakes, for which he has the joint favourite, Rosalie. Welcome to England, Mr Metcalfe. How do you feel about the big race?'

'It's a thrill to be here, just to participate in the race once again. Rosalie's got a great chance. Still, it's not winning that matters. It's taking part.'

Stephen flinched. Baron de Coubertin, who had first made that remark when opening the 1896 Olympics, must have turned in his grave.

'The latest betting shows Rosalie to be the joint favourite with Her Majesty The Queen's Horse, Highclere. How do you feel about that?'

'I'm just as worried about the Duke of Devonshire's Crown Princess. Lester Piggott is always hard to beat on a great occasion. He won the first two races and he'll be all set for this one – Crown Princess is a fine little filly.'

'Is a mile and a half a good distance for Rosalie?'

'Results this season show it's definitely her best distance.'

'What will you do with the £81,240 prize money?'

'The money is not important, it hasn't even entered my mind.'

It had certainly entered Stephen's mind.

'Thank you, Mr Metcalfe, and the best of luck. And now over for the latest news of the betting.'

Harvey moved back to his group of admirers and suggested that they return to watch the race from the balcony just outside his box.

Stephen was fascinated to observe Harvey at such close quarters. He had become nervous and even more mendacious than usual under pressure – not at all the icy, cool, operator they had all feared him to be. This man was human, susceptible and could be beaten.

They all leant over the rails watching the horses being put into the stalls. Crown Princess was still giving a little trouble while all the others waited. The tension was becoming unbearable.

'They're off,' boomed the loudspeaker.

As twenty-five thousand people raised glasses to their eyes, Harvey said, 'She's got a good start – she's well placed,' continuing to give everybody a running commentary until the last mile, when he became silent. The others also waited in silence, intent on the loudspeaker.

'They're into the straight mile – Minnow leads the field around the bend – with Buoy and Dankaro, looking relaxed, just tucked in behind him – followed by Crown Princess, Rosalie and Highclere ...

'As they approach the six-furlong marker – Rosalie and Crown Princess come up on the stand side with Highclere making a bid ...

'Five furlongs to go – Minnow still sets the pace, but is beginning to tire as Crown Princess and Buoy make up ground ...

'Half a mile to go – Minnow still just ahead of Buoy, who has moved up into second place, perhaps making her move too early ...

'Three furlongs from home – they're quickening up just a little – Minnow sets the pace on the rails – Buoy and Dankaro are now about a length behind – followed by Rosalie, Lester Piggott on Crown Princess and the Queen's filly Highclere all making ground ...

'Inside the two-furlong marker – Highclere and Rosalie move up to challenge Buoy – Crown Princess is right out of it now ...

'A furlong to go ...'

The commentator's voice rose in pitch and volume.

'It's Joe Mercer riding Highclere who hits the front, just ahead of Pat Eddery on Rosalie – two hundred yards to go – they're neck and neck – one hundred yards to go – it's anybody's race and on the line it's a photo finish between the gold, purple and scarlet colours of Her Majesty the Queen and the black-and-green check colours of the American owner, Harvey Metcalfe – M. Moussac's Dankaro was third.'

Harvey stood paralysed, waiting for the result. Even Stephen felt a little sympathy for him. None of Harvey's guests dared to speak for fear they might be wrong.

'The result of The King George VI and The Queen Elizabeth Stakes.' Once again the loudspeaker boomed out and silence fell over the whole course:

'The winner is No. 5, Rosalie.'

The rest of the result was lost in the roar of the crowd and the bellow of triumph from Harvey. Pursued by his guests, he raced to the nearest lift, pressed a pound note into the lift-girl's hand and shouted, 'Get this thing moving'. Only half of his guests managed to jump in with him. Stephen was among them. Once they reached the ground floor, the lift gates opened and Harvey came out like a thoroughbred, past the champagne bar, through the rear of the Members' Enclosure into the Winners' Enclosure, and flung his arms round the horse's neck, almost unseating the jockey. A few minutes later he triumphantly led Rosalie to the little white post marked 'FIRST'. The crowd thronged around him, offering their congratulations.

The Clerk of the Course, Captain Beaumont, stood by Harvey's side, briefing him on the procedure that would be followed when he was presented. Lord Abergavenny, the Queen's representative at Ascot, accompanied Her Majesty to the Winners' Enclosure.

'The winner of The King George VI and The Queen Elizabeth Stakes – Mr Harvey Metcalfe's Rosalie.'

Harvey was in a dream world. Flash-bulbs popped and film cameras followed him as he walked towards the Queen. He bowed and received his trophy. The Queen, resplendent in a turquoise silk suit and matching turban that could only have been designed by Norman Hartnell, said a few words, but for the first time in his life Harvey was speechless. Taking a pace backwards, he bowed again and returned to his place accompanied by loud applause.

Back in his box the champagne flowed and everybody was Harvey's friend. Stephen realized this was not the moment to try anything clever. He must bide his time and watch his quarry's reaction to these changed circumstances. He stayed quietly in a corner, letting the excitement subside, and observed Harvey carefully.

It took another race before Harvey was half back to normal and Stephen decided the time had now come to act. He made as if to leave.

'Are you going already, Professor?'

'Yes, Mr Metcalfe. I must return to Oxford and mark some scripts before tomorrow morning.'

'I always admire the work you boys put in. I hope you enjoyed yourself?' Stephen avoided Shaw's famous riposte, 'I had to, there was nothing else to enjoy'.

'Yes, thank you, Mr Metcalfe. An amazing achievement. You must be a very proud man.'

'Well, I guess so. It's been a long time coming, but it all seems worthwhile now ... Rod, it's too bad you have to leave us. Can't you stay on a little longer and join my party at Claridge's tonight?'

'I should have liked that, Mr Metcalfe, but you must visit me at my college at Oxford and allow me to show you the university.'

'That's swell. I have a couple of days after Ascot and I've always wanted to see Oxford, but I never seem to have found the time.'

'It's the university Garden Party next Wednesday. Why don't you join me for dinner at my college on Tuesday evening and then we can spend the following day looking at the university and go on to the Garden Party?' Stephen scribbled a few directions on a card.

'Fantastic. This is turning out to be the best vacation I've ever had in Europe. How are you getting back to Oxford, Professor?'

'By train.'

'No, no,' said Harvey. 'My Rolls-Royce will take you. It'll be back well in time for the last race.'

And before Stephen could protest, the chauffeur was called for.

'Take Professor Porter back to Oxford and then return here. Have a good trip, Professor. I'll look forward to seeing you next Tuesday at 8 p.m. Great meeting you.'

'Thank you for a wonderful day, Mr Metcalfe, and congratulations on your splendid victory.'

Seated in the back of the white Rolls-Royce on his way to Oxford, the car which Rolls had boasted he and he alone would travel in, Stephen relaxed and smiled to himself. Taking a small notebook from his pocket he made an entry:

'Deduct 98 pence from expenses, the price of a single second-class ticket from Ascot to Oxford.'

15

'Bradley,' said the Senior Tutor. 'you're going a bit grey at the edges, dear boy. Is the office of Junior Dean proving too much for you?'

Stephen had wondered whether any of the Senior Common Room would think the change in the colour of his hair worthy of comment. Dons are seldom surprised by anything their colleagues do.

'My father went grey at an early age, Senior Tutor, and there seems to be no way of defying heredity ...'

'Ah well, dear boy, you'll look all the more distinguished at next week's Garden Party.'

'Oh yes,' smiled Stephen, who had been thinking of nothing else. 'I'd quite forgotten about that.'

He returned to his rooms where the rest of the Team were assembled and waiting for their next briefing.

'Wednesday is the day of the Encaenia and the Garden Party,' began Stephen without as much as a 'Good morning, gentlemen'. His students made no protest. 'Now the one thing we've learnt about our millionaire friend is that when we take him away from his own environment he still continues to assume he knows everything. We've now shown that his bluff can be called, as long as we know what's going to happen next and he doesn't. It's only the same skill he used when promoting Prospecta Oil – always keeping one step ahead of us. Now, we're going to keep two steps ahead of him by having a rehearsal today and a full dress-rehearsal tomorrow.'

'Time spent on reconnaissance is seldom wasted,' muttered James. It was about the only sentiment he could recall from his Army Cadet days at Harrow.

'Haven't had to spend much time on reconnaissance for your plan, have we?' chipped in Jean-Pierre.

Stephen ignored the interruptions.

'Now, the whole process on the day will take about seven hours for me and four hours for you, which includes the time required for make-up; we'll need an extra session on that from James the day before.'

'How often will you need my two sons?' asked Robin.

'Only once, on the Wednesday. Too many runs at it will make them look stiff and awkward.'

'When do you imagine Harvey will want to return to London?' inquired Jean-Pierre.

'I rang Guy Salmon to check their timetable and they've been instructed to have him back at Claridge's by 7 p.m., so I've assumed we have only until 5.30.'

'Clever,' said Robin.

'It's awful,' said Stephen. 'I even think like the man now. Right, let's go over the whole plan once again. We'll take it from the red dossier, halfway down page 16. When I leave All Souls ...'

. . . . .

On Sunday and Monday they carried out full rehearsals. By the Tuesday they knew every route Harvey could take and where he would be at any given moment of the day from 9 a.m. to 5.30 p.m. Stephen hoped he had covered every eventuality. He had little choice. They were only going to be allowed one crack at this one. Any mistakes like Monte Carlo and there would be no second chance. The dress-rehearsal went to a second.

'I haven't worn clothes like this since I was six years old and attending a fancy-dress party,' said Jean-Pierre. 'We're going to be anything but inconspicuous.'

'There'll be red and blue and black all round you on the day,' said Stephen. 'It's like a circus for peacocks. No one will give us a second look, not even you, Jean-Pierre.'

They were all nervous again, waiting for the curtain to go up. Stephen was glad they were on edge: he had no doubt that the moment they relaxed with Harvey Metcalfe, they would be found out.

The Team spent a quiet weekend. Stephen watched the College Dramatic Society's annual effort in Magdalen gardens, Robin took his wife to Glyndebourne and was uncommonly attentive, Jean-Pierre read *Goodbye Picasso* by David Douglas Duncan, and James took Anne to Tathwell Hall in Lincolnshire, to meet his father, the fifth earl.

Even Anne was nervous that weekend.

· · ·

'Harry?'

'Doctor Bradley.'

'I have an American guest dining with me in my rooms tonight. His name is Harvey Metcalfe. When he arrives will you see he is brought over to my rooms, please.'

'Certainly, sir.'

'And one small thing. He seems to have mistaken me for Professor Porter of Trinity College. Don't correct the mistake, will you? Just humour him.'

'Certainly, sir.'

Harry retreated into the Porter's Lodge shaking his head sadly. Of course, all academics went dotty in the end, but Dr Bradley had been afflicted at an unusually tender age.

· · ·

Harvey arrived at eight. He was always on time in England. The head porter guided him through the cloisters and up the old stone staircase to Stephen's rooms.

'Mr Metcalfe, sir.'

'How are you, Professor?'

'I'm well, Mr Metcalfe. Good of you to be so punctual.'

'Punctuality is the politeness of princes.'

'I think you'll find it is the politeness of kings, and, in this particular instance, of Louis XVIII.' For a moment Stephen forgot that Harvey wasn't a pupil.

'I'm sure you're right, Professor.'

Stephen mixed him a large whisky. His guest's eyes took in the room and settled on the desk.

'Gee – what a wonderful set of photographs. You with the late President Kennedy, another with the Queen and even the Pope.'

That touch was due to Jean-Pierre, who had put Stephen in contact with a photographer who had been in jail with his artist friend David Stein. Stephen was already looking forward to burning the photographs and pretending they had never existed.

'Let me give you another to add to your collection.'

Harvey pulled out of his inside coat pocket a large photograph of himself receiving the trophy for the King George VI and Queen Elizabeth Stakes from the Queen.

'I'll sign it for you, if you like.'

Without waiting for a reply, he scribbled an exuberant signature diagonally across the Queen.

'Thank you,' said Stephen. 'I can assure you I will treasure it with the same affection as I do my other photographs. I certainly appreciate you sparing the time to visit me here, Mr Metcalfe.'

'It's an honour for me to come to Oxford, and this is such a lovely old college.'

Stephen really believed he meant it, and he suppressed the inclination to tell Harvey the story of the late Lord Nuffield's dinner at Magdalen. For all Nuffield's munificence to the university, the two were never on entirely easy terms. When a manservant assisted the guest's departure after a college feast, Nuffield took the proffered hat ungraciously. 'Is this mine?' he said, disdainfully. 'I wouldn't know, my lord,' was the rejoinder, 'but it's the one you came with.'

Harvey was gazing a little blankly at the books on Stephen's shelves. The disparity between their subject matter, pure mathematics, and the putative Professor Porter's discipline, biochemistry, happily failed to arrest him.

'Do brief me on tomorrow.'

'Surely,' said Stephen. Why not? He had briefed everyone else. 'Let me first call for dinner and I'll go through what I've planned for you and see if it meets with your approval.'

'I'm game for anything. I feel ten years younger since this trip to Europe – it must've been the operation – and I'm thrilled about being here at Oxford University.'

Stephen wondered if he really could stand seven hours of Harvey Metcalfe, but for another $250,000 and his reputation with the rest of the Team . . .

The college servants brought in shrimp cocktail.

'My favourite,' said Harvey. 'How did you know?'

Stephen would have liked to say, 'There's very little I don't know about you', but he satisfied himself with, 'A fortunate guess. Now, if we meet up at 10 tomorrow morning we can take part in what is thought to be the most interesting day in the university calendar. It's called Encaenia.'

'What's that?'

'Well, once a year at the end of Trinity Term, which is the equivalent of the summer term in an American university, we celebrate the ending of the university year. There are several ceremonies followed by a magnificent Garden Party, which will be attended by the Chancellor and Vice-Chancellor of the university. The Chancellor is the former British Prime Minister, Harold Macmillan, and the Vice-Chancellor is Mr Habakkuk. I'm hoping it will be possible for you to meet them both, and we should manage to cover everything in time for you to be back in London by 7 p.m.'

'How did you know I had to be back by 7?'

'You warned me at Ascot.' Stephen could lie very quickly now. He was afraid that if they did not get their million soon he would end up a hardened criminal.

Harvey enjoyed his meal, which Stephen had planned almost too cleverly, each course featuring one of Harvey's favourite dishes. After Harvey had drunk a good deal of after-dinner brandy (price £7.25 per bottle, thought Stephen) they strolled through the quiet Magdalen Cloisters past the Song School. The sound of the choristers rehearsing a Gabrieli mass hung gently in the air.

'Gee, I'm surprised you allow record players on that loud,' said Harvey.

Stephen escorted his guest to the Randolph Hotel, pointing out the iron cross set in Broad Street outside Balliol College, said to mark the spot on which Archbishop Cranmer was burnt at the stake for heresy in 1556. Harvey forbore to say that he had never even heard of the reverend gentleman.

Stephen and Harvey parted on the steps of the Randolph.

'See you in the morning, Professor. Thanks for a great evening.'

'My pleasure. I'll pick you up at 10 a.m. Sleep well – you have a full day ahead of you tomorrow.'

Stephen returned to Magdalen and immediately called Robin.

'All's well, but I nearly went too far. The meal was altogether too carefully chosen – I even had his favourite brandy. Still, it'll keep me on my toes tomorrow. We must remember to avoid overkill. See you then, Robin.'

Stephen reported the same message to Jean-Pierre and James before falling gratefully into bed. The same time tomorrow he would be a wiser man, but would he be a richer one?

16

At 5 a.m. the sun rose over the Cherwell, and those few Oxonians who were about that early would have been left in no doubt as to why the connoisseurs consider Magdalen to be the most beautiful college at either Oxford or Cambridge. Nestling on the banks of the river, its perpendicular architecture is easy on the eye. King Edward VII, Prince Henry, Cardinal Wolsey, Edward Gibbon and Oscar Wilde had all passed through its portals. But the only thing that was passing through Stephen's mind as he lay awake that morning was the education of Harvey Metcalfe.

He could hear his own heartbeat, and for the first time he knew what Robin and Jean-Pierre had been through. It seemed a lifetime since their first meeting only three months before. He smiled to himself at the thought of how close they had all become in their common aim of defeating Harvey Metcalfe. Although Stephen, like James, was beginning to have a sneaking admiration for the man, he was now even more convinced that Metcalfe could be outmanoeuvred when he was not on home ground. For over two hours Stephen lay motionless in bed, deep in thought, going over his plan again and again. When the sun had climbed over the tallest tree, he rose, showered, shaved and dressed slowly and deliberately, his mind still on the day ahead.

He made his face up carefully to age himself by fifteen years. It took him a considerable time, and he wondered whether women had to struggle as long in front of the mirror to achieve the opposite effect. He donned his gown, a magnificent scarlet, proclaiming him a Doctor of Philosophy of the University of Oxford. It amused him that Oxford had to be different.

Every other university abbreviated this universal award for research work, to Ph.D. In Oxford, it was D.Phil. He studied himself in the mirror.

'If that doesn't impress Harvey Metcalfe, nothing ever will.'

And what's more, he had the right to wear it. He sat down to study his red dossier for the last time. He had read the closely typewritten pages so often that he practically knew them by heart.

He avoided breakfast. Looking nearly fifty, he would undoubtedly have caused a stir amongst his colleagues, though probably the older dons would have failed to observe anything unusual in his appearance.

Stephen headed out of the college into the High, unnoticed among the thousand or so other graduates all dressed like fourteenth-century archbishops. Anonymity on that particular day was going to be easy. That, and the fact that Harvey would be bemused by the strange traditions of the ancient university, were the two reasons why Stephen had chosen Encaenia for his day of battle.

He arrived at the Randolph at 9.55 a.m. and informed one of the younger bell-boys that his name was Professor Porter and that he had come to pick up Mr Metcalfe. Stephen took a seat in the lounge. The young man scurried away and returned moments later with Harvey.

'Mr Metcalfe – Professor Porter.'

'Thank you,' said Stephen. He made a mental note to return and tip the bell-boy. That touch had been useful, even if it was only part of his job.

'Good morning, Professor,' said Harvey, taking a seat. 'So tell me, what have I let myself in for?'

'Well,' said Stephen, 'Encaenia begins officially when all the notables of the university take a breakfast of champagne, strawberries and cream at Jesus College, which is known as Lord Nathaniel Crewe's Benefaction.'

'Who's this Lord Crewe guy? Will he be at the breakfast?'

'Only in spirit; the great man died some three hundred years ago. Lord Nathaniel Crewe was a Doctor of the university and the Bishop of Durham, and he left £200 a year to the university as a Benefaction to provide the breakfast and an oration which we shall hear later. Of course, the money he willed no longer covers expenses nowadays, with rising prices and inflation, so the university has to dip into its own pocket to continue the tradition. When breakfast is over there is a procession and parade to the Sheldonian Theatre.'

'What happens then?'

'The parade is followed by the most exciting event of the day. The presentation of the Honorands for degrees.'

'The what?' said Harvey.

'The Honorands,' said Stephen. 'They are the distinguished men and women who have been chosen by the senior members of the university to be awarded Oxford honorary degrees.' Stephen looked at his watch. 'In fact, we must leave now to be sure of having a good position on the route from which to watch the procession.'

Stephen rose and guided his guest out of the Randolph Hotel. They strolled down the Broad and found an excellent spot just in front of the Sheldonian Theatre, where the police cleared a little space for Stephen because of his scarlet gown. A few minutes later the procession wound into sight round the corner from the Turl. The police held up all the traffic and kept the public on the pavement.

'Who are the guys in front carrying those clubs?' inquired Harvey.

'They are the University Marshal and the Bedels. They are carrying maces to safeguard the Chancellor's procession.'

'Jesus, of course it's safe. This isn't Central Park, New York.'

'I agree,' said Stephen, 'but it hasn't always been so over the past three hundred years, and tradition dies hard in England.'

'And who's that behind the Bedel fellows?'

'The one wearing the black gown with gold trimmings is the Chancellor of the university, accompanied by his page. The Chancellor is the Right Honourable Harold Macmillan, who was Prime Minister of Great Britain in the late '50s and early '60s.'

'Oh yes, I remember the guy. Tried to get the British into Europe but De Gaulle wouldn't have it.'

'Well, I suppose that's one way of remembering him. Now, he's followed by the Vice-Chancellor, Mr Habakkuk, who is also the Principal of Jesus College.'

'You're losing me, Professor.'

'Well, the Chancellor is always a distinguished Englishman who was educated at Oxford; but the Vice-Chancellor is a leading member of the university itself and is usually chosen from the heads of one of the colleges.'

'Got it, I think.'

'Now, after him, we have the University Registrar, Mr Caston, who is a fellow of Merton College. He is the senior administrator of the university, or you might look on him as the university's top civil servant. He's directly responsible to the Vice-Chancellor and Hebdomadal Council, who are the sort of cabinet for the university. Behind them we have the Senior Proctor, Mr Campbell of Worcester College, and the Junior Proctor, the Reverend Doctor Bennett of New College.'

'What's a Proctor?'

'For over 700 years the Proctors have been responsible for decency and discipline in the university.'

'What? Those two old men take care of 9,000 rowdy youths?'

'Well, they are helped by the bulldogs,' said Stephen.

'Ah, that's better, I suppose. A couple of bites from an old English bulldog would keep anyone in order.'

'No, no,' protested Stephen, trying desperately not to laugh. 'The name bulldog is given to the men who help the Proctors keep order. Now, finally in the procession you can observe that tiny crocodile of colour: it consists of heads of colleges who are Doctors of the university, Doctors of the university who are not heads of colleges and the heads of colleges who are not doctors of the university, in that order.'

'Listen, Rod, all doctors mean to me is pain and money.'

'They are not that sort of doctor,' replied Stephen.

'Forget it. I love everything but don't expect me to understand what it's all about.'

Stephen watched Harvey's face carefully. He was drinking the scene in and had already become quieter.

'The long line will now proceed into the Sheldonian Theatre and all the people in the procession will take their places in the hemicycle.'

'Excuse me, sir, what type of cycle is that?'

'The hemicycle is a round bank of seats inside the theatre, distinguished only by being the most uncomfortable in Europe. But don't you worry. Thanks to your well-known interest in education at Harvard I've managed to arrange special seats for us and there will just be time for us to secure them ahead of the procession.'

'Well, lead the way, Rod. Do they really know what goes on at Harvard here?'

'Why yes, Mr Metcalfe. You have a reputation in university circles as a generous man interested in financing the pursuit of academic excellence.'

'Well, what do you know.'

Very little, thought Stephen.

He guided Harvey to his reserved seat in the balcony, not wanting his guest to be able to see the individual men and women too clearly. The truth of the matter was that the senior members of the university in the hemicycle were so covered from head to toe in gowns and caps and bow-ties and bands, that even their mothers would not have recognized them. The organist played his final chord and the guests settled.

'The organist,' said Stephen, 'is from my own college. He's the Choragus, the leader of the chorus, and Deputy Professor of Music.'

Harvey could not take his eyes off the hemicycle and the scarlet-clad figures. He had never seen a sight like it in his life. The music stopped and the Chancellor rose to address the assembled company in vernacular Latin.

'Causa hujus convocationis est ut ...'

'What the hell's he saying?'

'He's telling us why we're here,' explained Stephen. 'I'll try and guide you through it.'

'Ite Bedelli,' declared the Chancellor, and the great doors opened for the Bedels to go and fetch the Honorands from the Divinity School. There was a hush as they were led in by the Public Orator, Mr J. G. Griffith, who presented them one by one to the Chancellor, enshrining the careers and achievements of each in polished and witty Latin prose.

Stephen's translation, however, followed a rather more liberal line and was embellished with suggestions that their doctorates were as much the result of financial generosity as of academic prowess.

'That's Lord Amory. They're praising him for all the work he has done in the field of education.'

'How much did he give?'

'Well, he *was* Chancellor of the Exchequer. And there's Lord Hailsham. He has held eight Cabinet positions, including Secretary of State for Education and finally Lord Chancellor. Both he and Lord Amory are receiving the degree of Doctor of Civil Law.'

Harvey recognized Dame Flora Robson, the actress, who was being honoured for a distinguished lifetime in the theatre; Stephen explained that she was receiving the degree of Doctor of Letters, as was the Poet Laureate, Sir John Betjeman. Each was presented with his scroll by the Chancellor, shaken by the hand and then shown to a seat in the front row of the hemicycle.

The final Honorand was Sir George Porter, Director of the Royal Institution and Nobel Laureate. He received his honorary degree of Doctor of Science.

'My namesake, but no relation. Oh well, nearly through,' said Stephen. 'Just a little prose from John Wain, the Professor of Poetry, about the benefactors of the university.'

Mr Wain delivered the Crewian Oration, which took him some twelve minutes, and Stephen was grateful for something so lively in a language they could both understand. He was only vaguely aware of the recitations of undergraduate prize winners which concluded the proceedings.

The Chancellor of the university rose and led the procession out of the hall.

'Where are they all off to now?' asked Harvey.

'They are going to have lunch at All Souls, where they will be joined by other distinguished guests.'

'God, what I would give to be able to attend that.'

'I have arranged it,' replied Stephen.

Harvey was quite overwhelmed.

'How did you fix that, Professor?'

'The Registrar was most impressed by the interest you have shown in Harvard and I think they hope you might find it possible to assist Oxford in some small way, especially after your wonderful win at Ascot.'

'What a great idea. Why didn't I think of that?'

Stephen tried to show little interest, hoping that by the end of the day he would have thought of it. He had learnt his lesson on overkill. The truth was that the Registrar had never heard of Harvey Metcalfe, but because it was Stephen's last term at Oxford he had been put on the list of invitations by a friend who was a Fellow of All Souls.

They walked over to All Souls, just across the road from the Sheldonian Theatre. Stephen attempted, without much success, to explain the nature of All Souls to Harvey. Indeed, many Oxonians themselves find the college something of an enigma.

'It's corporate name,' Stephen began, 'is the College of All Souls of the Faithful Departed of Oxford, and it resonantly commemorates the victors of Agincourt. It was intended that masses should forever be said there for the repose of their souls. Its modern role is unique in academic life. All Souls is a society of graduates distinguished either by promise or achievement, mostly academic, from home and abroad, with a sprinkling of men who have made their mark in other fields. The college has no undergraduates, and generally appears to the outside world to do much as it pleases with its massive financial and intellectual resources.'

Stephen and Harvey took their places among the hundred or more guests at the long table in the noble Codrington Library. Stephen spent the entire time ensuring that Harvey was kept fully occupied and was not too obvious. He was thankfully aware that on such occasions people never remember whom they meet or what they say, and happily introduced Harvey to everyone around as a distinguished American philanthropist. He was fortunately placed some way from the Vice-Chancellor, the Registrar and the Secretary of the University Chest.

Harvey was quite overcome by the new experience and was content just to listen to the distinguished men around him – which surprised Stephen, who had feared he would never stop talking. When the meal was over and the guests had risen, Stephen drew a deep breath and played one of his riskier cards. He deliberately marched Harvey up to the Chancellor.

'Chancellor,' he said to Harold Macmillan.

'Yes, young man.'

'May I introduce Mr Harvey Metcalfe from Boston. Mr Metcalfe, as you will know, Chancellor, is a great benefactor of Harvard.'

'Yes, of course. Capital, capital. What brings you to England, Mr Metcalfe?'

Harvey was nearly speechless.

'Well, sir, I mean Chancellor, I came to see my horse Rosalie run in the King George and Elizabeth Stakes.'

Stephen was now standing behind Harvey and made signs to the Chancellor that Harvey's horse had won the race. Harold Macmillan, as game as ever and never one to miss a trick, replied:

'Well, you must have been very pleased with the result, Mr Metcalfe.'

'Well, sir, I guess I was lucky.'

'You don't look to me the type of man who depends on luck.'

Stephen took his career firmly in both hands.

'I am trying to interest Mr Metcalfe in supporting some research we are doing at Oxford, Chancellor.'

'What a good idea.' No one knew better than Harold Macmillan, after seven years of leading a political party, how to use flattery on such occasions. 'Keep in touch, young man. Boston was it, Mr Metcalfe? Do give my regards to the Kennedys.'

Macmillan swept off, resplendent in his academic dress. Harvey stood dumbfounded.

'What a great man. What an occasion. I feel I'm part of history. I just wish I deserved to be here.'

Having completed his task, Stephen was determined to escape before any mistakes could be made. He knew Harold Macmillan would shake hands with and talk to over a thousand people that day and the chances of his remembering Harvey were minimal. In any case, it would not much matter if he did. Harvey was, after all, a genuine benefactor of Harvard.

'We ought to leave before the senior members, Mr Metcalfe.'

'Of course, Rod. You're the boss.'

'I think that would be courtesy.'

Once they were out on the street Harvey glanced at his large Jaeger le Coultre watch. It was 2.30 p.m.

'Excellent,' said Stephen, who was running three minutes late for the next rendezvous. 'We have just over an hour before the Garden Party. Why don't we take a look at one or two of the colleges.'

They walked slowly up past Brasenose College and Stephen explained that the name really meant 'brass nose' and that the famous original brass nose, a sanctuary knocker of the thirteenth century, was still mounted in the hall. A hundred yards further on, Stephen directed Harvey to the right.

'He's turned right, Robin, and he's heading towards Lincoln College,' said James, well hidden in the entrance of Jesus College.

'Fine,' said Robin and checked his two sons. Aged seven and nine, they stood awkwardly, in unfamiliar Eton suits, ready to play their part as pages, unable to understand what Daddy was up to.

'Are you both ready?'

'Yes, Daddy,' they replied in unison.

Stephen continued walking slowly towards Lincoln, and they were no more than a few paces away when Robin appeared from the main entrance of the college in the official dress of the Vice-Chancellor, bands, collar, white tie and all. He looked fifteen years older and as much like Mr Habakkuk as possible. Perhaps not quite so bald, thought Stephen.

'Would you like to be presented to the Vice-Chancellor?' asked Stephen.

'That would be something,' said Harvey.

'Good afternoon, Vice-Chancellor, may I introduce Mr Harvey Metcalfe.'

Robin doffed his academic cap and bowed. Stephen returned the compliment in like manner. Robin spoke before Stephen could continue:

'Not the benefactor of Harvard University?'

Harvey blushed and smiled at the two little boys who were holding the Vice-Chancellor's train. Robin continued:

'This is a pleasure, Mr Metcalfe. I do hope you are enjoying your visit to Oxford. Mind you, it's not everybody who's fortunate enough to be shown around by a Nobel Laureate.'

'I've enjoyed it immensely, Vice-Chancellor, and I'd like to feel I could help this university in some way.'

'Well, that is excellent news.'

'Look, gentlemen, I'm staying here at the Randolph Hotel. It would be my great pleasure if you could all have tea with me later this afternoon.'

Robin and Stephen were thrown for a moment. He'd done it again – the unexpected. Surely the man realized that on the day of Encaenia the Vice-Chancellor did not have a moment free to attend private tea parties.

Robin recovered first.

'I'm afraid that would be difficult. One has so many responsibilities on a day like this, you understand. Perhaps you could join me in my rooms at the Clarendon Building? That would give us a chance to have a more private discussion?'

Stephen immediately picked up the lead:

'How kind of you, Vice-Chancellor. Will 4.30 be convenient?'

'Yes, yes, that will be fine, Professor.'

Robin tried not to look as if he wanted to run a mile. Although they had only been standing there for about five minutes, to him it seemed a lifetime. He had not objected to being a journalist, or an American surgeon, but he genuinely hated being a Vice-Chancellor. Surely someone would appear at any moment and recognize him for the fraud he was. Thank

God most of the undergraduates had gone home the week before. He began to feel even worse when a tourist started taking photos of him.

Now Harvey had turned all their plans upside down. Stephen could only think of Jean-Pierre and of James, the finest string to their dramatic bow, loitering uselessly in fancy dress behind the tea tent at the Garden Party in the grounds of Trinity College, waiting for them.

'Perhaps it might be wise, Vice-Chancellor, if we were to invite the Registrar and the Secretary of the University Chest to join us?'

'First-class idea, Professor. I'll ask them to be there. It isn't every day we're visited by such a distinguished philanthropist. I must take my leave of you now, sir, and proceed to my Garden Party. An honour to have made your acquaintance, Mr Metcalfe, and I look forward to seeing you again at 4.30.'

They shook hands warmly, and Stephen guided Harvey towards Exeter College while Robin darted back into the little room in Lincoln that had been arranged for him. He sank heavily into a seat.

'Are you all right, Daddy?' asked his elder son, William.

'Yes, I'm fine.'

'Do we get the ice cream and Coca-Cola you promised us if we didn't say a word?'

'You certainly do,' said Robin.

Robin slipped off all the paraphernalia – the gown, hood, bow-tie and bands – and placed them back in a suitcase. He returned to the street just in time to watch the real Vice-Chancellor, Mr Habakkuk, leave Jesus College on the opposite side of the road, obviously making his way towards the Garden Party. Robin glanced at his watch. If they had run five minutes late the whole plan would have struck disaster.

Meanwhile, Stephen had done a full circle and was now heading towards Shepherd & Woodward, the tailor's shop which supplies academic dress for the university. He was, however, preoccupied with the thought of getting a message through to James. Stephen and Harvey came to a halt in front of the shop window.

'What magnificent robes.'

'That's the gown of a Doctor of Letters. Would you like to try it on and see how you look?'

'That would be great. But would they allow it?' said Harvey.

'I'm sure they won't object.'

They entered the shop, Stephen still in his full academic dress as a Doctor of Philosophy.

'My distinguished guest would like to see the gown of a Doctor of Letters.'

'Certainly, sir,' said the young assistant, who was not going to argue with a Fellow of the University.

He vanished to the back of the shop and returned with a magnificent red gown with grey facing and a black, floppy velvet cap. Stephen forged on, brazen-faced.

'Why don't you try them on, Mr Metcalfe? Let's see what you would look like as an academic.'

The assistant was somewhat surprised. He wished Mr Venables would return from his lunch break.

'Would you care to come through to the fitting-room, sir?'

Harvey disappeared. Stephen slipped out on to the road.

'James, can you hear me? Oh hell, for God's sake answer, James.'

'Cool down, old fellow. I'm having a deuce of a time putting on this ridiculous gown, and in any case, our rendezvous isn't for another seventeen minutes.'

'Cancel it.'

'Cancel it?'

'Yes, and tell Jean-Pierre as well. Both of you report to Robin and meet up as quickly as possible. He will fill you in on the new plans.'

'New plans. Is everything all right, Stephen?'

'Yes, better than I could have hoped for.'

Stephen clicked off his speaker and rushed back into the tailor's shop.

Harvey reappeared as a Doctor of Letters; a more unlikely sight Stephen had not seen for many years.

'You look magnificent.'

'What do they cost?'

'About £100, I think.'

'No, no. How much would I have to give ... ?'

'I have no idea. You would have to discuss that with the Vice-Chancellor after the Garden Party.'

Harvey took a long look at himself in the mirror, and then returned to the dressing-room while Stephen thanked the assistant, asked him to wrap up the gown and cap and send them to the Clarendon building to be left with the porter in the name of Sir John Betjeman. He paid cash. The assistant looked even more bewildered.

'Yes, sir.'

He was not sure what to do, except continue praying for Mr Venables' arrival. His prayers were answered some ten minutes later, but by then Stephen and Harvey were well on their way to Trinity College and the Garden Party.

'Mr Venables, I've just been asked to send the full D.Litt. dress to Sir John Betjeman at the Clarendon Building.'

'Strange. We kitted him out for this morning's ceremony weeks ago. I wonder why he wants a second outfit.'

'He paid cash.'

'Well, send it round to the Clarendon, but be sure it's in his name.'

.   .   .

When Stephen and Harvey arrived at Trinity College shortly after 3.30, the elegant green lawns, the croquet hoops having been removed, were already crowded with over a thousand people. The members of the university wore an odd hybrid dress: best lounge suits or silk dresses topped with gowns, hoods and caps. Cups of tea and crates of strawberries and cucumber sandwiches were disappearing rapidly.

'What a swell party this is,' said Harvey unintentionally mimicking Frank Sinatra. 'You certainly do things in style here, Professor.'

'Yes, the Garden Party is always rather fun. It's the main social event of the university year, which as I explained, is just ending. Half the senior members here will be snatching an afternoon off from reading examination scripts. Exams for the final-year undergraduates have only just ended.'

Stephen observed the Vice-Chancellor, the Registrar and the Secretary of the University Chest carefully, and steered Harvey well away from them, introducing him to as many of the older members of the university as possible, hoping they would not find the encounter too memorable. They spent just over three-quarters of an hour moving from person to person, Stephen feeling rather like an aide-de-camp to an incompetent dignitary whose mouth must be kept shut for fear of a diplomatic incident. Despite Stephen's anxious approach, Harvey was clearly having the time of his life.

· · ·

'Robin, Robin, can you hear me?'

'Yes, James.'

'Where are you?'

'I'm in the Eastgate Restaurant: come and join me here and bring Jean-Pierre.'

'Fine. We'll be there in five minutes. No, make it ten. With my disguise, I'd better go slowly.'

Robin paid his bill. The children had finished their reward, so he took them out of the Eastgate to a waiting car and instructed the driver, who had been hired especially for the day, to return them to Newbury. They had played their part and now could only get in the way.

'Aren't you coming home with us, Dad?' demanded Jamie.

'No, I'll be back later tonight. Tell your mother to expect me about seven.'

Robin returned to the Eastgate to find Jean-Pierre and James hobbling towards him.

'Why the change of plan?' asked Jean-Pierre. 'It's taken me over an hour to get dressed and ready.'

'Never mind. You're still in the right gear. We had a stroke of luck. I chatted up Harvey in the street and the cocky bastard invited me to tea with him at the Randolph Hotel. I said that would be impossible, but asked him to join me at the Clarendon. Stephen suggested that you two should be invited along as well.'

'Clever,' said James. 'No need for the deception at the Garden Party.'

'Let's hope it's not too clever,' said Jean-Pierre.

'Well, at least we can do the whole damn charade behind closed doors,' said Robin, 'which ought to make it easier. I never did like the idea of walking through the streets with him.'

'With Harvey Metcalfe nothing is ever going to be easy,' said Jean-Pierre.

'I'll get myself into the Clarendon Building by 4.15,' continued Robin. 'You will appear a few minutes after 4.20, Jean-Pierre, and then you, James, about 4.25 p.m. But keep exactly to the same routine, act as if the meeting had taken place, as originally planned, at the Garden Party and we had all walked over to the Clarendon together.'

· · ·

Stephen suggested to Harvey that they should return to the Clarendon Building, as it would be discourteous to be late for the Vice-Chancellor.

'Sure.' Harvey glanced at his watch. 'Jesus, it's 4.30 already.'

They left the Garden Party and walked quickly down towards the

Clarendon Building at the bottom of the Broad, Stephen explaining en route that the Clarendon was a sort of Oxford White House where all the officers and officials of the university had their rooms.

The Clarendon is a large, imposing eighteenth-century building which could be mistaken by a visitor for another college. A few steps lead up to an impressive hallway, and on entering you realize you are in a magnificent old building which has been converted for use as offices, with as few changes as possible.

When they arrived the porter greeted them.

'The Vice-Chancellor is expecting us,' said Stephen.

The porter had been somewhat surprised when Robin had arrived fifteen minutes earlier and told him that Mr Habakkuk had asked him to wait in his room; even though Robin was in full academic dress, the porter kept a beady eye on him, not expecting the Vice-Chancellor or any of his staff to return from the Garden Party for at least another hour. The arrival of Stephen gave him a little more confidence. He well remembered the pound he had received for his guided tour of the building.

The porter ushered Stephen and Harvey through to the Vice-Chancellor's rooms and left them alone, tucking another pound note into his pocket.

The Vice-Chancellor's room was in no way pretentious and its beige carpet and pale walls would have given it the look of any middle-ranking civil servant's office, had it not been for the magnificent picture of a village square in France by Wilson Steer which hung over the marble fireplace.

Robin was staring out of the vast windows overlooking the Bodleian Library.

'Good afternoon, Vice-Chancellor.'

Robin spun round. 'Oh, welcome, Professor.'

'You remember Mr Metcalfe?'

'Yes, indeed. How nice to see you again.' Robin shuddered. All he wanted to do was to go home. They chatted for a few minutes. Another knock and Jean-Pierre entered.

'Good afternoon, Registrar.'

'Good afternoon, Vice-Chancellor, Professor Porter.'

'May I introduce Mr Harvey Metcalfe.'

'Good afternoon, sir.'

'Registrar, would you like some ...'

'Where's this man Metcalfe.'

The three of them stood, stunned, as a man looking ninety entered the room on sticks. He hobbled over to Robin, winked, bowed and said:

'Good afternoon, Vice-Chancellor,' in a loud, crotchety voice.

'Good afternoon, Horsley.'

James went over to Harvey and prodded him with his sticks as if to make sure he was real.

'I have read about you, young man.'

Harvey had not been called young man for thirty years. The others stared at James in admiration. None of them knew that in his last year at university James had played *L'Avare* to great acclaim. His Secretary of the Chest was simply a repeat performance, and even Molière would have been pleased with it. James continued:

'You have been most generous to Harvard.'

'That's very kind of you to mention it, sir,' said Harvey respectfully.

'Don't call me sir, young man. I like the look of you – call me Horsley.'

'Yes, Horsely, sir,' blurted Harvey.

The others were only just able to keep a straight face.

'Well, Vice-Chancellor,' continued James. 'You can't have dragged me halfway across the city for my health. What's going on? Where's my sherry?'

Stephen wondered if James was overdoing it, but looking at Harvey saw that he was evidently captivated by the scene. How could a man so mature in one field be so immature in another, he thought. He was beginning to see how Westminster Bridge had been sold to at least four Americans in the past twenty years.

'Well, we were hoping to interest Mr Metcalfe in the work of the university and I felt that the Secretary of the University Chest should be present.'

'What's this chest?' asked Harvey.

'Sort of treasury for the university,' replied James, his voice loud, old and very convincing. 'Why don't you read this?' and he thrust into Harvey's hand an Oxford University Calendar, which Harvey could have obtained at Blackwell's bookshop for £2 as indeed James had.

Stephen was not sure what move to make next when, happily for him, Harvey took over.

'Gentlemen, I would like to say how proud I am to be here today. This has been a wonderful year for me. I was present when an American won Wimbledon, I finally obtained a Van Gogh. My life was saved by a wonderful, wonderful surgeon in Monte Carlo and now here I am in Oxford surrounded by all this history. Gentlemen, it would give me a great deal of pleasure to be associated with this famous university.'

James took the lead again:

'What have you in mind?' he shouted at Harvey, adjusting his hearing-aid.

'Well, sir, I achieved my life's ambition when I received the King George and Elizabeth trophy from your Queen, but the prize money, well, I would like to use that to make a benefaction to your university.'

'But that's over £80,000,' gasped Stephen.

'£81,240 to be exact, sir. But why don't I call it $250,000.'

Stephen, Robin and Jean-Pierre were speechless. James alone was left to command the day. This was the opportunity he had needed to show why his great-grandfather had been one of Wellington's most respected generals.

'We accept. But it would have to be anonymous,' said James. 'I think I can safely say in the circumstances that the Vice-Chancellor would inform Mr Harold Macmillan and Hebdomadal Council, but we would not want a fuss made of it. Of course, Vice-Chancellor, I would ask you to consider an honorary degree.'

Robin was so conscious of James's obvious control of the entire situation that he could only add:

'How would you recommend we go about it, Horsley?'

'Cash cheque, so nobody can trace the money back to Mr Metcalfe. We can't have those bloody men from Cambridge chasing him for the rest of his life. Same way as we did for Sir David – no fuss.'

'I agree,' said Jean-Pierre, not having the vaguest idea what James was talking about. Neither, for that matter, had Harvey.

James nodded to Stephen, who left the Vice-Chancellor's office and made his way to the porter's room to inquire if a parcel had been left for Sir John Betjeman.

'Yes, sir. I don't know why they left it here. I'm not expecting Sir John.'

'Don't worry,' said Stephen. 'He's asked me to pick it up for him.'

Stephen returned to find James holding forth to Harvey on the importance of keeping his donation as a bond between himself and the university.

Stephen undid the box and took out the magnificent gown of a Doctor of Letters. Harvey turned red with embarrassment and pride as Robin placed it on his shoulders, chanting *De mortuis nil nisi bonum. Dulce et decorum est pro patria mori. Per ardua ad astra. Nil desperandum.*'

'Many congratulations,' bellowed James. 'A pity we could not have organized this to be part of today's ceremony, but for such a munificent gesture as yours we could hardly wait another year.'

Brilliant, thought Stephen, Laurence Olivier could not have done better.

'That's fine by me,' said Harvey, as he sat down and made out a cheque to cash. 'You have my word that this matter will never be mentioned to anyone.'

None of them believed that.

They stood in silence as Harvey rose and passed the cheque to James.

'No, sir.' James transfixed him with a glare.

The others looked dumbfounded.

'The Vice-Chancellor.'

'Of course,' said Harvey. 'Excuse me, sir.'

'Thank you,' said Robin, his hand trembling as he received the cheque. 'A most gracious gift, and you may be sure we shall put it to good use.'

There was a loud knock on the door. They all looked round terrified except for James, who was now ready for anything. It was Harvey's chauffeur. James had always hated the pretentious white uniform with the white hat.

'Ah, the efficient Mr Mellor,' said Harvey. 'Gentlemen, I guarantee he's been watching every move we've made today.'

The four froze, but the chauffeur had clearly made no sinister deductions from his observations.

'Your car is ready, sir. You wanted to be back at Claridge's by 7 p.m. to be in good time for your dinner appointment.'

'Young man,' bellowed James.

'Yes, sir,' whimpered the chauffeur.

'Do you realize you are in the presence of the Vice-Chancellor of this university?'

'No, sir. I'm very sorry, sir.'

'Take your hat off immediately.'

'Yes, sir.'

The chauffeur removed his hat and retreated to the car, swearing under his breath.

'Vice-Chancellor, I sure hate to break up our party, but as you've heard I do have an appointment ...'

'Of course, of course, we understand you're a busy man. May I once again officially thank you for your most generous donation, which will be used to benefit many deserving people.'

'We all hope you have a safe journey back to the States and will remember us as warmly as we shall remember you,' added Jean-Pierre.

Harvey moved towards the door.

'I will take my leave of you now, sir,' shouted James. 'It will take me twenty minutes to get down those damned steps. You are a fine man and you have been most generous.'

'It was nothing,' said Harvey expansively.

True enough, thought James, nothing to you, but everything to us.

Stephen, Robin and Jean-Pierre accompanied Harvey from the Clarendon to the waiting Rolls.

'Professor,' said Harvey, 'I didn't quite understand everything the old guy was saying.' As he spoke he shifted the weight of his heavy robes on his shoulders self-consciously.

'Well, he's very deaf and very old, but his heart's in the right place. He wanted you to know that this has to be an anonymous donation as far as the university is concerned, though, of course, the Oxford hierarchy will be informed of the truth. If it were to be made public all sorts of undesirables who have never done anything for education in the past would come trooping along on the day of Encaenia wanting to buy an honorary degree.'

'Of course, of course. I understand. That's fine by me,' said Harvey. 'I want to thank you for a swell day, Rod, and I wish you all the luck for the future. What a shame our friend Wiley Barker wasn't here to share it all.'

Robin blushed.

Harvey climbed into the Rolls-Royce and waved enthusiastically to the three of them as they watched the car start effortlessly on its journey back to London.

.   .   .

Three down and one to go.

.   .   .

'James was brilliant,' said Jean-Pierre. 'When he first came in I didn't know who the hell it was.'

'I agree,' said Robin. 'Let's go and rescue him – he's truly the hero of the day.'

They all three ran up the steps, forgetting that they looked somewhere between the ages of fifty and sixty, and rushed back into the Vice-Chancellor's room to congratulate James, who lay silent in the middle of the floor. He had passed out.

.   .   .

In Magdalen an hour later, with the help of Robin and two large whiskies, James was back to his normal health.

'You were fantastic,' said Stephen, 'just at the point when I was beginning to lose my nerve.'

'You would have received an Academy Award if we could have put it on screen,' said Robin. 'Your father will have to let you go on the stage after that performance.'

James basked in his first moment of glory for three months. He could not wait to tell Anne.

'Anne.' He quickly looked at his watch. '6.30. Oh hell, I must leave at once. I'm meant to be meeting Anne at eight. See you all next Monday in Stephen's rooms for dinner. By then I'll try to have my plan ready.'

James rushed out of the room.

'James.'

His face reappeared round the door. They all said in chorus: 'Fantastic.'

He grinned, ran down the stairs and leapt into his Alfa Romeo, which he now felt they might allow him to keep, and headed towards London at top speed.

It took him 59 minutes from Oxford to the King's Road. The new motorway had made a considerable difference since his undergraduate days. Then the journey had taken anything from an hour and a half to two hours through High Wycombe or Henley.

The reason for his haste was that the meeting with Anne was most important and under no circumstances must he be late; tonight he was due to meet her father. All James knew about him was that he was a senior member of the Diplomatic Corps in Washington. Diplomats always expect you to be on time. He was determined to make a good impression on her father, particularly after Anne's successful weekend at Tathwell Hall. The old man had taken to her at once and never left her side. They had even managed to agree on a wedding date, subject, of course, to the approval of Anne's parents.

James had a quick cold shower and removed all his makeup, losing some dirty years in the process. He had arranged to meet Anne for a drink at Les Ambassadeurs in Mayfair before dinner, and as he put on his dinner-jacket he wondered if he could make it from the King's Road to Hyde Park Corner in 12 minutes: it would require another Monte Carlo. He leapt into his car, revving it quickly through the gears, shot along to Sloane Square, through Eaton Square, up past St George's Hospital, round Hyde Park Corner into Park Lane, and arrived at 7.58 p.m.

'Good evening, my lord,' said Mr Mills, the club owner.

'Good evening. I'm dining with Miss Summerton and I've had to leave my car double-parked. Can you take care of it?' said James, dropping the keys and a pound note into the doorman's white-gloved hand.

'Delighted, my lord. Show Lord Brigsley to the private rooms.'

James followed the head porter up the red staircase and into a small Regency room where dinner had been laid for three. He could hear Anne's voice in the next room. She came through, looking even more beautiful than usual in a floating mint-green dress.

'Hello, darling. Come on, I want you to meet Daddy.'

James followed Anne into the next room.

'Daddy, this is James. James, this is my father.'

James went red and then white, and then he felt green.

'How are you, my boy. I've heard so much about you from Rosalie that I can't wait to get acquainted.'

17

'Call me Harvey.'

James stood aghast and speechless. Anne jumped into the silence.

'Would you like a whisky, James?'

James found his voice with difficulty.

'Thank you.'

'I want to know all about you, young man,' continued Harvey, 'what you get up to and why I've seen so little of my daughter in the past few weeks, though I think I can guess the answer to that.'

James drank the whisky in one gulp and Anne quickly refilled his glass.

'You see so little of your daughter because I'm always modelling, which means that I'm very rarely in London.'

'I know, Rosalie ...'

'James knows me as Anne, Daddy.'

'We christened you Rosalie. It was a good enough name for your mother and me and it ought to be good enough for you.'

'Daddy, whoever heard of a top European model calling herself Rosalie Metcalfe? All my friend know me as Anne Summerton.'

'What do you think, James?'

'I was beginning to think I didn't know her at all,' replied James, recovering slowly. It was obvious that Harvey did not suspect a thing. He had not seen James face to face at the gallery, he had never seen him at Monte Carlo or Ascot, and James had looked ninety years of age at Oxford earlier in the day. He was beginning to believe he had got away with it. But how the hell could he tell the others at their Monday meeting that the final plan, his plan, would be to outwit not Harvey Metcalfe, but his future father-in-law?

'Shall we go through to dinner?'

Harvey did not wait for a reply. He marched on into the adjoining room.

'Rosalie Metcalfe,' whispered James fiercely. 'You've got some explaining to do.'

Anne kissed him gently on the cheek.

'You're the first person who's given me the chance to beat my father at anything. Can't you forgive me? ... I do love you ...'

'Come on, you two. Anyone would think you'd never met before.'

Anne and James joined Harvey for dinner. James was amused by the sight of the shrimp cocktail and remembered how Stephen had regretted that touch at Harvey's Magdalen dinner.

'Well, James, I understand you and Anne have fixed a date for the wedding.'

'Yes, sir, if it meets with your approval.'

'Of course I approve. I was hoping Anne would marry Prince Charles after I'd won the King George and Elizabeth Stakes, but an earl will have to do for my only daughter.'

They both laughed, neither of them thinking it was remotely funny.

'I wish you'd come to Wimbledon this year, Rosalie. Imagine, me there on Ladies' Day and the only company I had was a boring old Swiss banker.'

Anne looked at James and grinned.

The waiters cleared the table and wheeled in a trolley bearing a crown of lamb in immaculate cutlet frills, which Harvey studied with great interest.

'Still,' said Harvey, chattering on, 'it was thoughtful of you to ring me at Monte Carlo, my dear. I really thought I was going to die, you know. James, you wouldn't have believed it. They removed a gall stone the size of a baseball from my stomach. Thank God, the operation was performed by one of the greatest surgeons in the world, Wiley Barker, the President's surgeon. He saved my life.'

Harvey promptly undid his shirt and revealed a 4 inch scar across his vast stomach.

'What do you think of that, James?'

'Remarkable.'

'Daddy, really. We're having dinner.'

'Stop fussing, honey. It won't be the first time James has seen a man's stomach.'

It's not the first time I've seen that one, thought James.

Harvey pushed his shirt back into his trousers and continued:

'Anyway, it was really kind of you to phone me.' He leant over and patted her hand. 'I was a good boy too. I took your advice and kept that nice Doctor Barker on for another week in case any complications arose. Mind you, the price these doctors ...'

James dropped his wine glass. The claret covered the tablecloth with a red stain.

'I'm so sorry.'

'You all right, James?'

'Yes, sir.'

James looked at Anne in silent outrage. Harvey was quite unperturbed.

'Bring a fresh tablecloth and some more wine for Lord Brigsley.'

The waiter opened a fresh bottle of claret and James decided it was his turn to have a little fun. Anne had been laughing at him for three months. Why shouldn't he tease her a little, if Harvey gave him the chance? Harvey was still talking.

'You a racing man, James?'

'Yes, sir, and I was delighted by your victory in the King George VI and Queen Elizabeth Stakes – for more reasons than you realize.'

In the diversion caused by the waiters clearing the table, Anne whispered *sotto voce*:

'Don't try to be too clever, darling – he's not as stupid as he sounds.'

'Well, what do you think of her?'

'I beg your pardon, sir?'

'Rosalie.'

'Magnificent. I put £5 each way on her.'

'Yes, it was a great occasion for me and I was sorry you missed it, Rosalie, because you would have met the Queen and a nice guy from Oxford University called Professor Porter.

'Professor Porter?' inquired James, burying his face in his wine glass.

'Yes, Professor Porter, James. Do you know him?'

'No, sir, I can't say I do, but didn't he win a Nobel Prize?'

'He sure did and he gave me a wonderful time at Oxford. I enjoyed myself so much I ended up presenting the university with a cheque for $250,000 to be used for research of some kind, so he should be happy.'

'Daddy, you know you're not meant to tell anybody about that.'

'Sure, but James is family now.'

'Why can't you tell anyone else, sir?'

'Well, it's a long story, James, but it was quite an honour for me. You do understand this is highly confidential, but I was Professor Porter's guest at Encaenia. I lunched at All Souls with Mr Harry Macmillan, your dear old Prime Minister, and then I attended the Garden party, and afterwards I had a meeting with the Vice-Chancellor in his private rooms along with the Registrar and the Secretary of the University Chest. Were you at Oxford, James?'

'Yes, sir. The House.'

'The House?' queried Harvey.

'Christ Church, sir.'

'I'll never understand Oxford.'

'No, sir.'

'You must call me Harvey. Well, as I was saying, we all met at the Clarendon and they stammered and stuttered and they were totally lost for words, except for one funny old guy, who was ninety if he was a day. The truth is that those people just don't know how to approach millionaires for money, so I put them out of their embarrassment and took over. They'd have gone on all day about their beloved Oxford, so eventually I had to shut them up and simply wrote out a cheque for $250,000.'

'That was very generous, Harvey.'

'I'd have given them $500,000 if the old boy had asked. James, you've gone quite white. Do you feel all right?'

'I'm sorry. Yes, I'm fine. I was quite carried away with your description of Oxford.'

Ann joined in:

'Daddy, you made an agreement with the Vice-Chancellor that you would keep your gift as a bond between the university and yourself, and you must promise never to repeat that story again.'

'I think I shall wear the robes for the first time when I open the new Metcalfe library at Harvard in the fall.'

'Oh, no sir,' stammered James a little too quickly, 'that wouldn't be quite the thing. You should only wear full robes in Oxford on ceremonial occasions.'

'Gee, what a shame. Still, I know what sticklers you English are for etiquette. Which reminds me, we ought to discuss your wedding. I suppose you two will want to live in England?'

'Yes, Daddy, but we'll visit you every year and when you make your annual trip to Europe you can come and stay with us.'

The waiters cleared the table again and reappeared with Harvey's favourite strawberries. Anne tried to steer the conversation to domestic issues and stop her father returning to what he'd been up to during the past two months, while James did everything to get him back on the subject.

'Coffee or liqueur, sir?'

'No, thank you,' said Harvey. 'Just the check. I thought we'd have a drink in my suite at Claridge's, Rosalie. I have something to show you both. It's a bit of a surprise.'

'I can't wait, Daddy. I love surprises. Don't you, James?'

'Normally yes, but I think I've had enough for one day.'

.   .   .

James left them and drove the Alfa Romeo to Claridge's garage so that Anne could have a few moments alone with her father. They strolled along Curzon Street, arm in arm.

'Isn't he wonderful, Daddy?'

'Yeah, great guy. Didn't seem too bright to begin with, but he cheered up as the meal went on. And fancy my little girl turning out to be a genuine English lady. Your Momma's tickled pink and I'm pleased that we've patched up our silly quarrel.'

'Oh, you helped a lot, Daddy.'

'I did?' queried Harvey.

'Yes, I managed to get things back into perspective during the last few weeks. Now tell me, what is your little surprise?'

'Wait and see, honey. It's your wedding present.'

James rejoined them at the entrance to Claridge's. He could tell from Anne's look that Harvey had given him the seal of parental approval.

'Good evening, sir. Good evening, my lord.'

'Hi there Albert. Could you fix some coffee and a bottle of Rémy Martin to be sent up to my suite?'

'Right away, sir.'

James had never seen the Royal Suite before. Off the small entrance room, there is a master bedroom on the right and a sitting-room on the left. Harvey took them straight to the sitting-room.

'Children, you are about to see your wedding present.'

He threw the door open in dramatic style and there on the far wall, facing them, was the Van Gogh. They both stared, quite unable to speak.

'That's exactly how it left me,' said Harvey. 'Speechless.'

'Daddy.' Anne swallowed. 'A Van Gogh. But you've always wanted a Van Gogh. You've dreamed of possessing one for years. I couldn't possibly deprive you of it now, and anyway I couldn't think of having anything as valuable as that in my house. Think of the security risk – we don't have the protection you have.' Anne stammered on. 'We couldn't let you sacrifice the pride of your collection, could we, James?'

'Absolutely not,' said James with great feeling. 'I wouldn't have a moment's peace with that on the premises.'

'Keep the painting in Boston, Daddy, in a setting worthy of it.'

'But I thought you'd love the idea, Rosalie.'

'I do, I do, Daddy, I just don't want the responsibility, and in any case Mother must have the chance to enjoy it too. You can always leave it to James and me if you like.'

'What a great idea, Rosalie. That way we can both enjoy the painting. Now I shall have to think of another wedding present. She nearly got the better of me then, James, and she hasn't done that in twenty-four years.'

'Well, I've managed it two or three times lately, Daddy, and I'm still hoping I shall do it once more.'

Harvey ignored Anne's remark and went on talking.

'That's the King George and Elizabeth trophy,' he said, pointing to a magnificent bronze sculpture of a horse and jockey with his hoop and quartered cap studded with diamonds. The race is so important they present a new trophy every year – so it's mine for life.'

James was thankful that the trophy at least was genuine.

The coffee and brandy arrived and they settled down to discuss the wedding in detail.

'Now, Rosalie, you must fly over to Lincoln next week and help your mother with the arrangements, otherwise she'll panic and nothing will get done. And, James, you let me know how many people you'll have coming over and I'll put them up at the Ritz. The wedding will be in Trinity Church, Copley Square, and we'll have a real English-style reception afterwards back in my home in Lincoln. Does all that make sense, James?'

'Sounds wonderful. You're a very well organized man, Harvey.'

'Always have been, James. Find it pays in the long run. Now, you and Rosalie must get the details sewn up before she comes over next week; you may not have realized it, but I'm returning to America tomorrow.'

Page 38A of the blue dossier, thought James.

James and Anne spent another hour chatting about the wedding arrangements and left Harvey just before midnight.

'I'll see you first thing in the morning, Daddy.'

'Goodnight, sir.'

James shook hands and left.

'I told you he was super.'

'He's a fine young man and your mother will be very pleased.'

James said nothing to Anne in the lift on the way down because two other men stood beside them in silence, also intent on reaching the ground floor. But once they were in the Alfa Romeo he took Anne by the scruff of her neck, threw her across his legs, and spanked her so hard that she didn't know whether to laugh or cry.

'What's that for?'

'Just in case you ever forget after we're married who's the head of this household.'

'You male chauvinist pig, I was only trying to help.'

James drove at furious speed to Anne's flat.

'What about all your so-called background – "My parents live in Washington and Daddy's in the Diplomatic Corps",' James mimicked. 'Some diplomat.'

'I know, darling, but I had to think of something once I'd realized who it was you were up against.'

'What in hell's name am I going to tell the others?'

'Nothing. You invite them to the wedding, explain that my mother is American and that's why we're getting married in Boston. I'd give the earth to see their faces when they discover who your father-in-law is. In any case, you still have a plan to think of and you can't possibly let them down.'

'But the circumstances have changed.'

'No, they haven't. The truth of the matter is that they've all succeeded and you've failed, so you be sure you think of a plan by the time you reach America.'

'It's obvious now that we wouldn't have succeeded without your help.'

'Nonsense, darling. I had nothing to do with Jean-Pierre's scheme. I just added some background colour here and there – promise you'll never spank me again?'

'Certainly I will, every time I think of that picture, but now, darling . . .'

'James, you're a sex maniac.'

'I know, darling. How do you think we Brigsleys have reared tribes of little lords for generations?'

.   .   .

Anne left James early the next morning to spend some time with her father, and they both saw him off at the airport on the midday flight to Boston. Anne could not resist asking in the car on the way back what James had decided to tell the others. She could get no response other than:

'Wait and see. I'm not having it changed behind my back. I'm only too glad you're off to America on Monday.'

18

Monday was a double hell for James. First, he had to see Anne off on the morning TWA flight for Boston, and then he had to spend the rest of the day preparing for the Team meeting in the evening. The other three had now completed their operations and would be waiting to hear what he had come up with. It was twice as hard now he knew that the victim was to be his father-in-law, but he realized that Anne was right and he could not put that forward as an excuse. Nevertheless, he still had to relieve Harvey of $250,000. To think he could have done it with one sentence at Oxford. That was another thing he could not tell the rest of the Team.

As Oxford had been Stephen's victory, the Team dinner was at Magdalen College and James travelled out of London just after the rush hour, past the White City Stadium and on down the M40 to Oxford.

'You're always last, James,' said Stephen.

'Sorry, I've been up to my eyes . . .'

'Preparing a good plan, I hope,' said Jean-Pierre.

James didn't answer. How well they all knew each other now, he thought.

In twelve weeks James felt he had come to know more about these three men than any of the so-called friends he'd known for twenty years. For the first time he understood why his father continually referred back to friendships formed during the war with men he normally would never have met. He began to realize how much he was going to miss Stephen when he returned to America. Success was, in fact, going to split them up. James would have been the last to go through the agony of another Prospecta Oil, but it had certainly had its compensations.

Stephen could never treat any occasion as a celebration, and as soon as the servants had brought in the first course and left, he banged the table with a spoon and declared that the meeting was in progress.

'Make me a promise,' said Jean-Pierre.

'What's that?' asked Stephen.

'When we have every last penny back, I can sit at the top of the table and you won't speak until you're spoken to.'

'Agreed,' said Stephen, 'but not until we do have every last penny. The position at the moment is that we've received $777,560. Expenses on this operation have totalled $5,178, making a grand total of $27,661.24. Therefore, Metcalfe still owes us $250,101.24.'

Stephen handed round a copy of the current balance sheet.

'These sheets are to be added to your own folders as pages 63C. Any questions?'

'Yes, why were the expenses so high for this operation?' asked Robin.

'Well, over and above the obvious things,' said Stephen, 'the truth is that we've been hit by the floating exchange rate of sterling against the dollar. At the beginning of this operation you could get $2.44 to the pound. This morning I could only get $2.32. I'm spending in pounds but charging Metcalfe in dollars at the going rate.'

'Not going to let him off with one penny, are you?' said James.

'Not one penny. Now, before we go on I should like to place on record ...'

'This gets more like a meeting of the House of Commons every time,' said Jean-Pierre.

'Stop croaking, frog,' said Robin.

'Listen, you Harley Street pimp.'

Uproar broke out. The college scouts, who had seen some rowdy gatherings in their time, wondered if they would have to be called in to help before the evening was completed.

'Quiet,' the sharp, senatorial voice of Stephen brought them all back to order. 'I know you're in high spirits, but we still have to get $250,101.24.'

'We must on no account forget the 24 cents, Stephen.'

'You weren't as noisy the first time you had dinner here, Jean-Pierre:

> The man that once did sell the lion's skin
> While the beast liv'd, was killed with hunting him.'

The table was silent.

'Harvey still owes the Team money and it'll be just as hard to acquire the last quarter as it was with the first three-quarters. Before I hand over to James, I'd like to place on record that his performance at the Clarendon was nothing less than brilliant.'

Robin and Jean-Pierre banged the table in appreciation and agreement.
'Now, James, we're all ears.'

Once again the room fell into silence.

'My plan is nearly complete,' began James.

The others looked disbelieving.

'But I have something to tell you, which I hope will allow me a short respite before we carry it out.'

'You're going to get married.'

'Quite right, Jean-Pierre as usual.'

'I could tell the moment you walked in. When do we meet her, James?'

'Not until it's too late for her to change her mind, Jean-Pierre.'

Stephen consulted his diary.

'How much reprieve are you asking for?'

'Well, Anne and I are getting married on August 3rd, in Boston. Anne's mother is American,' explained James, 'and although Anne lives in England, it would please her mother if she was married at home. Then there'll be the honeymoon and after that we anticipate returning to England on August 25th. My plan for Mr Metcalfe ought to be carried out on September 15th, the closing day of the Stock Exchange account.'

'I'm sure that's acceptable, James. All agreed?'

Robin and Jean-Pierre nodded.

James launched into his plan.

'I shall require a telex and seven telephones. They'll need to be installed in my flat. Jean-Pierre will have to be in Paris at the Bourse, Stephen in Chicago on the commodity market and Robin in London at Lloyds. I will present a full blue dossier as soon as I return from my honeymoon.'

They were all struck dumb with admiration and James paused for dramatic effect.

'Very good, James,' said Stephen. 'We'll await the details with interest. What further instructions do you have?'

'First, Stephen, you must know the opening and closing price of gold in Johannesburg, Zürich, New York and London each day for the next month. Jean-Pierre, you must know the price of the Deutschmark, the French franc and the pound against the dollar every day during the same period, and Robin must master a telex machine and PBX 8-line switchboard by September 2nd. You must be as competent as an international operator.'

'Always get the easy jobs, Robin, don't you?' said Jean-Pierre.

'You can . . .'

'Shut up, both of you,' said James.

Their faces registered surprise and respect.

'I've made notes for all of you to work on.'

James handed two typewritten sheets to each member of the Team.

'You add these to your dossiers as pages 74 and 75 and they should keep you occupied for at least a month. Finally, you're all invited to the wedding of Miss Anne Summerton to James Brigsley. I shan't bother issuing you wish formal invitations at such short notice, but I've reserved seats for us on a 747 on the afternoon of August 2nd and we're all booked in at the Ritz in Boston for the night. I hope you'll honour me by being ushers.'

Even James was impressed by his own efficiency. The others received the plane tickets and instructions with astonishment.

'We'll meet at the airport at 3 p.m. and during the flight I shall test you on your dossier notes.'

'Yes, sir,' said Jean-Pierre.

'Your test, Jean-Pierre, will be in both French and English, as you'll be required to converse in two languages over a trans-Atlantic telephone, and appear expert on foreign currency exchange.'

There were no more jokes about James that evening, and as he travelled back up the motorway he felt a new man. Not only had he been the star of the Oxford plan; now he had the other three on the run. He would come out on top and do his old pa yet.

19

For a change James was the first to arrive at a meeting and the others joined him at Heathrow. He had gained the upper hand and was determined not to lose it. Robin arrived last, clutching an armful of newspapers.

'We're only going to be away for two days,' said Stephen.

'I know, but I always miss the English papers, so I've brought enough for tomorrow as well.'

Jean-Pierre threw his arms up in Gallic despair.

They checked their luggage through the No. 3 Terminal and boarded the British Airways 747 flight to Logan International Airport.

'It's more like a football ground,' said Robin, stepping for the first time inside a jumbo jet.

'It holds 350 people. About the size of the crowds most of your English clubs deserve,' said Jean-Pierre.

'Cut it out,' said James sternly, not realizing that they were both nervous passengers and were only trying to relieve the tension. Later, during take-off, they both pretended to read, but as soon as the plane reached 3,000 feet and the little white light that says 'fasten seat-belts' switched off, they were back in top form.

The Team chewed its way stolidly through a plastic dinner of cold chicken and Algerian red wine.

'I do hope, James,' said Jean-Pierre, 'that your father-in-law will feed us a little better.'

After the meal James allowed them to watch the film, but insisted that as soon as it was over they must prepare to be tested one by one. Robin and Jean-Pierre moved back fifteen rows to watch *The Sting*. Stephen stayed in his seat to be grilled by James.

James handed Stephen a typewritten sheet of forty questions on the price of gold all over the world and the market movements during the past four weeks. Stephen completed it in twenty-two minutes, and it came as no surprise to James to find that every answer was correct: Stephen had always been the backbone of the Team, and it was his logical brain that had really defeated Harvey Metcalfe.

Stephen and James dozed intermittently until Robin and Jean-Pierre returned, when they were given their forty questions. Robin took thirty minutes over his and scored 38 out of 40. Jean-Pierre took twenty-seven minutes and scored 37.

'Stephen got 40 out of 40,' said James.

'He would,' said Jean-Pierre.

Robin looked a little sheepish.

'And so will you by September 2nd. Understood?'

They both nodded.

'Have you seen *The Sting*?' asked Robin.

'No,' replied Stephen. 'I rarely go to the cinema.'

'They're not in our league. One big operation, and they don't even keep the money.'

'Go to sleep, Robin.'

The meal, the film and James's quizzes had taken up most of the six-hour flight and they all nodded off in the last hour, to be woken up suddenly by:

'This is your captain speaking. We are approaching Logan International Airport and our flight is running twenty minutes late. We expect to land at 7.15 in approximately ten minutes. We hope you have enjoyed your flight and will travel again with British Airways.'

Customs took a little longer than usual as they all three had brought presents for the wedding and did not want James to know what they were. They had considerable trouble in explaining to the customs officer why one of the two Piaget watches had inscribed on the back: 'Part of the illicit profits from Prospecta Oil – the three who had plans.'

When they finally escaped the customs official, they found Anne standing at the entrance by a large Cadillac waiting to chauffeur them to the hotel.

'Now we know why it took you so long to come up with something: you were genuinely distracted. Congratulations, James, you're entirely forgiven,' said Jean-Pierre, and threw his arms round Anne as only a Frenchman could. Robin introduced himself and kissed her gently on the cheek. Stephen shook hands with her rather formally. They bustled into the car, Jean-Pierre sitting next to Anne.

'Miss Summerton,' stuttered Stephen.

'Do call me Anne.'

'Will the reception be at the hotel?'

'No,' replied Anne, 'at my parents' house, but there'll be a car to pick you up and take you there after the wedding. Your only responsibility is to see that James gets to the church by 3.30. Other than that you have nothing to worry about. While I think of it, James, your father and mother arrived yesterday and they're staying with my parents. We thought it might not be a good idea for you to spend this evening at home because Mother's flapping about everything.'

'Anything you say, darling.'

'If you should change your mind between now and tomorrow,' said Jean-

Pierre, 'I find myself available. I may not be blessed with noble blood, but there are one or two compensations we French can always offer.'

Anne smiled to herself. 'You're a little late, Jean-Pierre. In any case, I don't like beards.'

'But I only ...' began Jean-Pierre.

The others glared at him.

. . .

At the hotel they left Anne and James alone while they went to unpack. 'Do they know, darling?'

'They haven't the slightest idea,' replied James. 'They're going to get the surprise of their life tomorrow.'

'Is your plan ready?'

'Wait and see.'

'Well, I have one,' said Anne. 'When's yours scheduled for?'

'September 13th.'

'I win then – mine's for tomorrow.'

'What, you weren't meant to ...'

'Don't worry. You just concentrate on getting married ... to me.'

'Can't we go somewhere?'

'No, you terrible man. You can wait until tomorrow.'

'I do love you.'

'Go to bed, you silly thing. I love you too, but I must go home, otherwise nothing'll be ready.'

James took the lift to the seventh floor and joined the others for coffee. 'Anyone for blackjack?'

'Not with you, you pirate,' said Robin. 'You've been tutored by the biggest crook alive.'

The Team were in top form and looking forward to the wedding. In spite of the transatlantic time dislocation they didn't depart for their separate rooms until well after midnight. Even then, James lay awake for some time, turning over the same question in his mind:

'I wonder what she's up to this time?'

20

Boston in August is as beautiful a city as any in America, and the Team enjoyed a large breakfast in James's room.

'I don't think he looks up to it,' said Jean-Pierre. 'You're the captain of the Team, Stephen. I volunteer to take his place.'

'It'll cost you $250,000.'

'Agreed,' said Jean-Pierre.

'You don't have $250,000,' said Stephen. 'You have $187,474.69, being one quarter of what's been raised so far, so my decision is that James must be the bridegroom.'

'It's an Anglo-Saxon plot,' said Jean-Pierre, 'and when James has successfully completed his plan and we have the full amount, I shall re-open negotiations.'

They sat talking and laughing for a long time over the toast and coffee. Stephen regarded them fondly, regretting, how rarely they would meet once, *if*, he corrected himself sternly, James's operation were accomplished successfully. If Harvey Metcalfe had ever had a team like this on his side instead of against him, he would have been the richest man in the world.

'You're dreaming, Stephen.'

'Yes, I'm sorry. I mustn't forget that Anne has put me in charge.'

'Here we go again,' said Jean-Pierre. 'What time shall we report, Professor?'

'One hour from now, fully dressed to inspect James and take him to the church. Jean-Pierre, you will go and buy four carnations – three red ones and one white. Robin, you will arrange for the taxi and I shall take care of James.'

Robin and Jean-Pierre left, singing the *Marseillaise* lustily in two different keys. James and Stephen watched them depart.

'How are you feeling, James?'

'Great. I'm only sorry that I didn't complete my plan before today.'

'Doesn't matter at all. September 13th will be quite early enough. In any case, the break will do us no harm.'

'We'd never have managed it without you. You know that, don't you, Stephen? We'd all be facing ruin and I wouldn't even have met Anne. We all owe you so much.'

Stephen stared fixedly out of the window, unable to reply.

.   .   .

'Three red and one white,' said Jean-Pierre, 'as instructed, and I presume the white one is for me.'

'Pin it on James. Not behind his ear, Jean-Pierre.'

'You look fantastic, but I still fail to see what the lady sees in you,' said Jean-Pierre, fixing the white carnation in James's buttonhole. Although the four of them were ready to leave, they still had half an hour to kill before the taxi was due. Jean-Pierre opened a bottle of champagne and they toasted James's health, the Team's health, Her Majesty The Queen, the President of the United States, and finally, with simulated reluctance, the President of France. Having finished the bottle, Stephen thought it wise for them to leave immediately and dragged the other three down to the waiting taxi.

'Keep smiling, James. We're with you.'

And they bundled him into the back.

The taxi took only a few minutes to reach Trinity Church, Copley Square, and the driver was not unhappy to be rid of the four of them.

'3.15 p.m. Anne will be very pleased with me,' said Stephen.

He escorted the bridegroom to the front pew on the right-hand side of the church, while Jean-Pierre made eyes at the prettiest of the girls. Robin helped hand out the wedding sheets while one thousand overdressed guests waited for the bride.

Stephen had just come to Robin's aid on the steps of the church and

Jean-Pierre had joined them, suggesting they took their seats, when the Rolls-Royce arrived. They were riveted to the steps by the beauty of Anne in her Balenciaga wedding gown. Her father stepped out behind her. She took his arm and proceeded to climb the steps.

The three stood motionless, like sheep in the stare of a python.

'The bastard.'

'Who's been conning who?'

'She must have known all along.'

Harvey beamed vaguely at them as he walked past with Anne on his arm. They proceeded down the aisle.

'Good God,' thought Stephen. 'He didn't recognize any of us.'

They took their places at the back of the church, out of earshot of the vast congregation. The organist stopped playing when Anne reached the altar.

'Harvey can't know,' said Stephen.

'How do you work that out?' asked Jean-Pierre.

'Because James would never have put us through this unless he'd passed the test himself at some earlier date.'

'Good thinking,' whispered Robin.

'I require and charge you both, as ye will answer at the dreadful day of judgement when the secrets of all hearts shall be disclosed ...'

'I'd like to know one or two secrets right now,' said Jean-Pierre. 'To start with, how long has she known?'

'James Clarence Spencer, wilt thou have this woman to thy wedded wife, to live together after God's ordinance in the Holy estate of Matrimony? Wilt thou love her, comfort her, honour and keep her in sickness and in health and, forsaking all other, keep thee only unto her, so long as ye both shall live?'

'I will.'

'Rosalie Arlene, wilt thou have this man to thy wedded husband, to live ...'

'I think,' said Stephen, 'we can be sure that she's a fully fledged member of the Team; otherwise we could never have succeeded at Monte Carlo or Oxford.'

'... so long as ye both shall live?'

'I will.'

'Who giveth this woman to be married to this man?'

Harvey bustled forward and took Anne's hand and gave it to the priest.

'I James Clarence Spencer, take thee, Rosalie Arlene, to my wedded wife ...'

'And what's more, why should he recognize us when he's only seen each of us once, and not as we really are,' continued Stephen.

'And thereto I plight thee my troth.'

'I, Rosalie Arlene, take thee, James Clarence Spencer, to my wedded husband ...'

'But he must have a chance of working it out if we hang around,' said Robin.

'Not necessarily,' said Stephen. 'No need to panic. Our secret has always been to catch him off home ground.'

'But now he's on home ground,' said Jean-Pierre.

'No, he isn't. It's his daughter's wedding day and it's totally strange to the man. Naturally, we avoid him at the reception, but we don't make it too obvious.'

'You'll have to hold my hand,' said Robin.

'I will,' volunteered Jean-Pierre.

'Just remember to act naturally.'

'... and thereto I give thee my troth.'

Anne was quiet and shy, her voice only just reaching the astonished three at the back. James's was clear and firm:

'With this ring I thee wed, with my body I thee worship, and with all my worldly goods I thee endow ...'

'And with some of ours too,' said Jean-Pierre.

'In the name of the Father, and of the Son and of the Holy Spirit. Amen.'

'Let us pray,' intoned the priest.

'I know what I'm going to pray,' said Robin. 'To be delivered out of the power of our enemy and from the hands of all that hate us.'

'O Eternal God, Creator and Preserver of all mankind ...'

'We're near the end now,' said Stephen.

'An unfortunate turn of phrase,' offered Robin.

'Silence,' said Jean-Pierre. 'I agree with Stephen. We've got the measure of Metcalfe, just relax.'

'Those whom God hath joined together let no man put asunder.'

Jean-Pierre continued mumbling to himself, but it didn't sound like a prayer.

The blast of Handel's Wedding March from the organ brought them all back to the occasion. The ceremony was over and Lord and Lady Brigsley walked down the aisle watched by two thousand smiling eyes. Stephen looked amused, Jean-Pierre envious, and Robin nervous. James smiled beatifically as he passed them.

After a ten-minute session for the photographers on the steps of the church, the Rolls-Royce carried the newly married couple back to the Metcalfes' house in Lincoln. Harvey and the Countess of Louth took the second car, and the Earl and Arlene, Anne's mother, took the third. Stephen, Robin and Jean-Pierre followed some twenty minutes later, still arguing the pros and cons of bearding the lion in his own den.

Harvey Metcalfe's Georgian house was magnificent, with an oriental garden leading down to a lake, great beds of roses and in the conservatory his pride and joy, his collection of rare orchids.

'I never thought I'd see this,' said Jean-Pierre.

'Nor me,' said Robin, 'and now that I have, I'm not too happy.'

'Let's run the gauntlet,' said Stephen. 'I suggest that we join the receiving line at well-separated intervals. I'll go first. Robin, you come second, at least twenty places behind, and Jean-Pierre, you come third, at least twenty places behind Robin, and *act naturally*. We're just friends of James's from England. Now, when you take your places in the queue, listen to the conversation. Try and find someone who's a close friend of Harvey's and jump immediately in front of them. When it comes to your turn to shake hands,

Harvey's eyes will already be on the next person because he won't know you and will want to talk to them. That way we should escape.'

'Brilliant, Professor,' said Jean-Pierre.

.   .   .

The queue seemed interminably long. A thousand people shuffled past the outstretched hands of Mr and Mrs Metcalfe, the Earl and Countess of Louth, and Anne and James. Stephen eventually made it and passed with flying colours.

'So glad you could come,' said Anne.

Stephen did not reply.

'Good to see you, Stephen.'

'We all admire your plan, James.'

Stephen slipped into the main ballroom and hid behind a pillar on the other side of the room, as far as he could be from the multi-storey wedding cake in the centre.

Robin was next and avoided looking Harvey in the eyes.

'How kind of you to come all this way,' said Anne.

Robin mumbled something under his breath.

'Hope you've enjoyed yourself today, Robin?'

James was obviously having the time of his life. After being put through it in the same way by Anne, he was relishing the Team's discomfiture.

'You're a bastard, James.'

'Not too loud, old fellow. My mother and father might hear you.'

Robin slipped through to the ballroom and, after a search behind all the pillars, found Stephen.

'Did you get through all right?'

'I think so, but I don't want to see him ever again. What time is the plane back?'

'8 p.m. Now don't panic. Keep your eye out for Jean-Pierre.'

'Bloody good thing he kept his beard,' said Robin.

Jean-Pierre shook hands with Harvey, who was already intent on the next guest as Jean-Pierre had, by shameless queue-barging, managed to secure a place in front of a Boston banker who was obviously a close friend of Harvey's.

'Good to see you, Marvin.'

Jean-Pierre had escaped. He kissed Anne on both cheeks, whispered in her ear, 'Game, set and match to James,' and went off in search of Stephen and Robin. He forgot his original instructions when he found himself face to face with the chief bridesmaid.

'Did you enjoy the wedding?' she asked.

'Of course. I always judge weddings by the bridesmaids, not the bride.'

She blushed with pleasure.

'This must have cost a fortune,' she continued.

'Yes, my dear, and I know whose,' said Jean-Pierre, slipping his arm around her waist.

Four hands grabbed a protesting Jean-Pierre and unceremoniously dragged him behind the pillar.

'For God's sake, Jean-Pierre. She's not a day over seventeen. We don't want to go to jail for rape of a juvenile as well as theft. Drink this and behave yourself.' Robin thrust a glass of champagne into his hand.

.   .   .

The champagne flowed and even Stephen had a little too much. They were all clinging to their pillar for support by the time the toast-master called for silence.

'My lords, ladies and gentlemen. Pray silence for the Viscount Brigsley, the bridegroom.'

James made an impressive speech. The actor in him took over and the Americans adored it. Even his father had a look of admiration on his face. The toast-master then introduced Harvey, who spoke long and loud. He cracked his favourite joke about marrying off his daughter to Prince Charles, at which the assembled guests roared heartily as they always do at weddings, even for the weakest joke. He ended by calling the toast for the bride and groom.

When the applause had died down, and the hubbub of chatter had struck up again, Harvey took an envelope from his pocket and kissed his daughter on the cheek.

'Rosalie, here's a little wedding present for you, to make up for letting me keep the Van Gogh. I know you'll put it to good use.'

Harvey passed her the white envelope. Inside there was a cheque for $250,000. Anne kissed her father with genuine affection.

'Thank you, Daddy, I promise you James and I will use it wisely.'

She hurried off in pursuit of James, whom she found besieged by a group of American matrons:

'Is it true you're related to the Queen ...?'

'I never met a real live lord ...'

'I do hope you'll invite us over to see your castle ...?'

'There are no castles in the King's Road,' said James, relieved to be rescued by Anne.

'Darling, can you spare me a minute?'

James excused himself and followed Anne, but they found it almost impossible to escape the crowd.

'Look,' she said. 'Quickly.'

James took the cheque.

'Good God – $250,000.'

'You know what I'm going to do with it, don't you?'

'Yes, darling.'

Anne hunted for Stephen, Robin and Jean-Pierre, which was not an easy task as they were still hidden behind a pillar in the far corner. She was eventually guided to the spot by the subdued but spirited rendering of 'Who Wants to be a Millionaire?' issuing from behind it.

'Can you lend me a pen, Stephen?'

Three pens shot out for her use.

She took the cheque from the middle of her bouquet and wrote on its back, 'Rosalie Brigsley – pay Stephen Bradley'. She handed it to him.

'Yours, I believe.'

The three of them stared at the cheque. She was gone before they could even comment.

'What a girl our James has gone and married,' said Jean-Pierre.

'You're drunk, you frog,' said Robin.

'How dare you, sir, suggest that a Frenchman could get drunk on champagne. I demand satisfaction. Choose your weapons.'

'Champagne corks.'

'Quiet,' said Stephen. 'You'll give yourselves away.'

'Well now, tell me, Professor, what's the latest financial position?'

'I'm just working it out now,' said Stephen.

'What?' said Robin and Jean-Pierre together, but they were too happy to argue.

'He still owes us $101 and 24 cents.'

'DISGRACEFUL,' said Jean-Pierre. 'Burn the place down.'

. . .

Anne and James left to change, while Stephen, Robin and Jean-Pierre forced down some more champagne. The toast-master announced that the bride and groom would be leaving in approximately fifteen minutes and requested the guests to gather in the main hall and courtyard.

'Come on, we must watch them go,' said Stephen. The drink had given them new confidence and they took their places near the car.

It was Stephen who heard Harvey say, 'God damn it. Do I have to think of everything?' and watched him look round his guests until his eyes fell on the trio. Stephen's legs turned to jelly as Harvey's finger beckoned him.

'Hey, you, weren't you an usher?'

'Yes, sir.'

'Rosalie is going to leave at any moment and there are no flowers for her. God knows what's happened to them, but there are no flowers. Grab a car. There's a florist half a mile down the road, but hurry.'

'Yes, sir.'

'Say, don't I know you from somewhere?'

'Yes, sir. I mean, no sir. I'll go and get the flowers.'

Stephen turned and fled. Robin and Jean-Pierre, who had been watching horrified, thinking that Harvey had at last rumbled them, ran after him. When he reached the back of the house, Stephen came to a halt and stared at the most beautiful bed of roses. Robin and Jean-Pierre shot straight past him, stopped, turned round and staggered back.

'What the hell are you up to – picking flowers for your own funeral?'

'It's only Metcalfe's wishes. Somebody forgot the flowers for Anne and I have five minutes to get them, so start picking.'

'Mes enfants, do you see what I see?'

The others looked up. Jean-Pierre was staring rapturously at the conservatory.

. . .

Stephen rushed back to the front of the house, the prize orchids in his arms, followed by Robin and Jean-Pierre. He was just in time to pass them over to Harvey before James and Anne came out of the house.

'Magnificent. They're my favourite flowers. How much were they?'

'$100,' replied Stephen, without thinking.

Harvey handed over two $50 bills. Stephen retreated, sweating, to join Robin and Jean-Pierre.

James and Anne fought their way through the crowd. No man in the gathering could take his eyes off her.

'Oh Daddy, orchids, how beautiful.' Anne kissed Harvey. 'You've made this the most wonderful day in my life ...'

The Rolls-Royce moved slowly down the drive away from the large crowd on its way to the airport, where James and Anne were to catch the flight to San Francisco, their first stop on the way to Hawaii. As the car glided round the house, Anne stared at the empty conservatory and then at the flowers in her arms. James did not notice. He was thinking of other things.

'Do you think they'll ever forgive me?' he said.

'I'm sure they'll find a way, darling. But do let me into a secret. Did you really have a plan?'

'I knew you wouldn't be able to resist asking me that, and the truth is ...'

The car purred effortlessly along the highway and only the chauffeur heard his reply.

.   .   .

Stephen, Robin and Jean-Pierre watched the guests dispersing, most of them saying their goodbyes to the Metcalfes.

'Don't let's risk it,' said Robin.

'Agreed,' said Stephen.

'Let's invite him out to dinner,' said Jean-Pierre.

The other two grabbed him and threw him into a taxi.

'What's that you have under your morning coat, Jean-Pierre?'

'Two bottles of Krug dix-neuf soixante-quatre. It seemed such a shame to leave them there on their own. I thought they might get lonely.'

Stephen instructed the driver to take them back to the hotel.

'What a wedding. Do you think James ever had a plan?' asked Robin.

'I don't know, but if he has it will only have to bring in $1.24.'

'We should have retrieved the money he made from his win on Rosalie at Ascot,' mused Jean-Pierre.

.   .   .

After packing and signing out of the hotel, they took another taxi to Logan International Airport and, with considerable help from the British Airways staff, managed to board the plane.

'Damn,' said Stephen. 'I wish we hadn't left without the $1.24.'

21

Once on board, they drank the champagne Jean-Pierre had captured at the wedding. Even Stephen seemed content, although he did occasionally revert to the theme of the missing $1.24.

'How much do you imagine this champagne cost?' teased Jean-Pierre.

'That's not the point. Not a penny more, not a penny less.'

Jean-Pierre decided he would never understand academics.

'Don't worry, Stephen. I've every confidence that James's plan will bring in $1.24.'

Stephen would have laughed, but it gave him a headache.

'To think that girl knew everything.'

.   .   .

On arrival at Heathrow, they had little trouble in clearing customs. The purpose of the trip had never been to bring back gifts. Robin made a detour to W. H. Smiths and picked up *The Times* and the *Evening Standard*. Jean-Pierre bargained with a taxi-driver about the fare to central London.

'We're not some bloody Americans who don't know the rate or the route and can be easily fleeced,' he was saying, still not yet sober.

The taxi-driver grumbled to himself as he nosed his black Austin towards the motorway. It was not going to be his day.

Robin read the papers happily, one of those rare people who could read in a moving car. Stephen and Jean-Pierre satisfied themselves with watching the passing traffic.

'Jesus Christ.'

Stephen and Jean-Pierre were startled. They had rarely heard Robin swear. It seemed out of character.

'God Almighty.'

This was too much for them, but before they could inquire, he began to read out loud:

'"BP announced a strike in the North Sea which is likely to produce 200,000 barrels of oil a day. The strike is described by their Chairman, Sir Eric Drake, as a major find. The British Petroleum Forties Field is one mile from the so far unexplored Prospecta Oil field and rumours of a bid by BP have sent Prospecta Oil shares to a record high of $12.25 at the close of business."'

'Nom de Dieu,' said Jean-Pierre. 'What do we do now?'

'Oh well,' said Stephen. 'I suppose we'll have to work out a plan for how to give it all back.'

A QUIVER FULL OF ARROWS

To Robin and Carolyn

Author's note

Of these twelve short stories, eleven are based on known incidents (some embellished with considerable licence).

Only one is totally the result of my own imagination

In the case of 'The Century' I took my theme from three different cricket matches. Lovers of Wisden will have to do some considerable delving to uncover them.

'The Luncheon' was inspired by W. Somerset Maugham.

J.A.

The Chinese Statue

The little Chinese statue was the next item to come under the auctioneer's hammer. Lot 103 caused those quiet murmurings that always precede the sale of a masterpiece. The auctioneer's assistant held up the delicate piece of ivory for the packed audience to admire while the auctioneer glanced around the room to be sure he knew where the serious bidders were seated. I studied my catalogue and read the detailed description of the piece, and what was known of its history.

The statue had been purchased in Ha Li Chuan in 1871 and was referred to as what Sotheby's quaintly described as 'the property of a gentleman', usually meaning that some member of the aristocracy did not wish to admit that he was having to sell off one of the family heirlooms. I wondered if that was the case on this occasion and decided to do some research to discover what had caused the little Chinese statue to find its way into the auction rooms on that Thursday morning over one hundred years later.

'Lot No. 103,' declared the auctioneer. 'What am I bid for this magnificent example of ... ?'

.   .   .

Sir Alexander Heathcote, as well as being a gentleman, was an exact man. He was exactly six-foot-three and a quarter inches tall, rose at seven o'clock every morning, joined his wife at breakfast to eat one boiled egg cooked for precisely four minutes, two pieces of toast with one spoonful of Cooper's marmalade, and drink one cup of China tea. He would then take a hackney carriage from his home in Cadogan Gardens at exactly eight-twenty and arrive at the Foreign Office at promptly eight-fifty-nine, returning home again on the stroke of six o'clock.

Sir Alexander had been exact from an early age, as became the only son of a general. But unlike his father, he chose to serve his Queen in the diplomatic service, another exacting calling. He progressed from a shared desk at the Foreign Office in Whitehall to third secretary in Calcutta, to second secretary in Vienna, to first secretary in Rome, to Deputy Ambassador in Washington, and finally to minister in Peking. He was delighted when Mr Gladstone invited him to represent the government in China as he had for some considerable time taken more than an amateur interest in the art of the Ming dynasty. This crowning appointment in his distinguished career would afford him what until then he would have considered impossible, an opportunity to observe in their natural habitat some of the great statues, paintings and drawings which he had previously been able to admire only in books.

When Sir Alexander arrived in Peking, after a journey by sea and land that took his party nearly two months, he presented his seals patent to the Empress Tzu-Hsi and a personal letter for her private reading from Queen

Victoria. The Empress, dressed from head to toe in white and gold, received her new Ambassador in the throne room of the Imperial Palace. She read the letter from the British monarch while Sir Alexander remained standing to attention. Her Imperial Highness revealed nothing of its contents to the new minister, only wishing him a successful term of office in his appointment. She then moved her lips slightly up at the corners which Sir Alexander judged correctly to mean that the audience had come to an end. As he was conducted back through the great halls of the Imperial Palace by a Mandarin in the long court dress of black and gold, Sir Alexander walked as slowly as possible, taking in the magnificent collection of ivory and jade statues which were scattered casually around the building much in the way Cellini and Michaelangelo today lie stacked against each other in Florence.

As his ministerial appointment was for only three years, Sir Alexander took no leave, but preferred to use his time to put the Embassy behind him and travel on horseback into the outlying districts to learn more about the country and its people. On these trips he was always accompanied by a Mandarin from the palace staff who acted as interpreter and guide.

On one such journey, passing through the muddy streets of a small village with but a few houses called Ha Li Chuan, a distance of some fifty miles from Peking, Sir Alexander chanced upon an old craftsman's working place. Leaving his servants, the minister dismounted from his horse and entered the ramshackled wooden workshop to admire the delicate pieces of ivory and jade that crammed the shelves from floor to ceiling. Although modern, the pieces were superbly executed by an experienced craftsman and the minister entered the little hut with the thought of acquiring a small memento of his journey. Once in the shop he could hardly move in any direction for fear of knocking something over. The building had not been designed for a six-foot-three and a quarter visitor. Sir Alexander stood still and enthralled, taking in the fine scented jasmine smell that hung in the air.

An old craftsman bustled forward in a long, blue coolie robe and flat black hat to greet him; a jet black plaited pigtail fell down his back. He bowed very low and then looked up at the giant from England. The minister returned the bow while the Mandarin explained who Sir Alexander was and his desire to be allowed to look at the work of the craftsman. The old man was nodding his agreement even before the Mandarin had come to the end of his request. For over an hour the minister sighed and chuckled as he studied many of the pieces with admiration and finally returned to the old man to praise his skill. The craftsman bowed once again, and his shy smile revealed no teeth but only genuine pleasure at Sir Alexander's compliments. Pointing a finger to the back of the shop, he beckoned the two important visitors to follow him. They did so and entered a veritable Aladdin's Cave, with row upon row of beautiful miniature emperors and classical figures. The minister could have happily settled down in the orgy of ivory for at least a week. Sir Alexander and the craftsman chatted away to each other through the interpreter, and the minister's love and knowledge of the Ming dynasty was soon revealed. The little craftsman's face lit up with this discovery and he turned to the mandarin and in a hushed voice made a request. The Mandarin nodded his agreement and translated.

'I have, Your Excellency, a piece of Ming myself that you might care to see. A statue that has been in my family for over seven generations.'

'I should be honoured,' said the minister.

'It is I who would be honoured, Your Excellency,' said the little man who thereupon scampered out of the back door, nearly falling over a stray dog, and on to an old peasant house a few yards behind the workshop. The minister and the Mandarin remained in the back room, for Sir Alexander knew the old man would never have considered inviting an honoured guest into his humble home until they had known each other for many years, and only then after he had been invited to Sir Alexander's home first. A few minutes passed before the little blue figure came trotting back, pigtail bouncing up and down on his shoulders. He was now clinging on to something that from the very way he held it close to his chest, had to be a treasure. The craftsman passed the piece over for the minister to study. Sir Alexander's mouth opened wide and he could not hide his excitement. The little statue, no more than six inches in height, was of the Emperor Kung and as fine an example of Ming as the minister had seen. Sir Alexander felt confident that the maker was the great Pen Q who had been patronized by the Emperor, so that the date must have been around the turn of the fifteenth century. The state's only blemish was that the ivory base on which such pieces usually rest was missing, and a small stick protruded from the bottom of the imperial robes; but in the eyes of Sir Alexander nothing could detract from its overall beauty. Although the craftsman's lips did not move, his eyes glowed with the pleasure his guest evinced as he studied the ivory Emperor.

'You think the statue is good?' asked the craftsman through the interpreter.

'It's magnificent,' the minister replied. 'Quite magnificent.'

'My own work is not worthy to stand by its side,' added the craftsman hunbly.

'No, no,' said the minister, though in truth the little craftsman knew the great man was only being kind, for Sir Alexander was holding the ivory statue in a way that already showed the same love as the old man had for the piece.

The minister smiled down at the craftsman as he handed back the Emperor Kung and then he uttered perhaps the only undiplomatic words he had ever spoken in thirty-five years of serving his Queen and country.

'How I wish the piece was mine.'

Sir Alexander regretted voicing his thoughts immediately he heard the Mandarin translate them, because he knew only too well the old Chinese tradition that if an honoured guest requests something the giver will grow in the eyes of his fellow men by parting with it.

A sad look came over the face of the little old craftsman as he handed back the figure to the minister.

'No, no. I was only joking,' said Sir Alexander, quickly trying to return the piece to its owner.

'You would dishonour my humble home if you did not take the Emperor, Your Excellency,' the old man said anxiously and the Mandarin gravely nodded his agreement.

The minister remained silent for some time. 'I have dishonoured my own home, sir,' he replied, and looked towards the Mandarin who remained inscrutable.

The little craftsman bowed. 'I must fix a base on the statue,' he said, 'or you will not be able to put the piece on view.'

He went to a corner of the room and opened a wooden packing chest that must have housed a hundred bases for his own statues. Rummaging around he picked out a base decorated with small, dark figures that the minister did not care for but which nevertheless made a perfect fit; the old man assured Sir Alexander that although he did not know the base's history, the piece bore the mark of a good craftsman.

The embarrassed minister took the gift and tried hopelessly to thank the little old man. The craftsman once again bowed low as Sir Alexander and the expressionless Mandarin left the little workshop.

As the party travelled back to Peking, the Mandarin observed the terrible state the minister was in, and uncharacteristically spoke first:

'Your Excellency is no doubt aware,' he said, 'of the old Chinese custom that when a stranger has been generous, you must return the kindness within the calendar year.'

Sir Alexander smiled his thanks and thought carefully about the Mandarin's words. Once back in his official residence, he went immediately to the Embassy's extensive library to see if he could discover a realistic value for the little masterpiece. After much diligent research, he came across a drawing of a Ming statue that was almost an exact copy of the one now in his possession and with the help of the Mandarin he was able to assess its true worth, a figure that came to almost three years' emolument for a servant of the Crown. The minister discussed the problem with Lady Heathcote and she left her husband in no doubt as to the course of action he must take.

The following week the minister despatched a letter by private messenger to his bankers, Coutts & Co. in the Strand, London, requesting that they send a large part of his savings to reach him in Peking as quickly as possible. When the funds arrived nine weeks later the minister again approached the Mandarin, who listened to his questions and gave him the details he had asked for seven days later.

The Mandarin had discovered that the little craftsman, Yung Lee, came from the old and trusted family of Yung Shau who had for some five hundred years been craftsmen. Sir Alexander also learned that many of Yung Lee's ancestors had examples of their work in the palaces of the Manchu princes. Yung Lee himself was growing old and wished to retire to the hills above the village where his ancestors had always died. His son was ready to take over the workshop from him and continue the family tradition. The minister thanked the mandarin for his diligence and had only one more request of him. The Mandarin listened sympathetically to the Ambassador from England and returned to the palace to seek advice.

A few days later the Empress granted Sir Alexander's request.

Almost a year to the day the minister, accompanied by the Mandarin, set out again from Peking for the village of Ha Li Chuan. When Sir Alexander arrived he immediately dismounted from his horse and entered the workshop that he remembered so well, the old man was seated at his bench, his flat hat slightly askew, a piece of uncarved ivory held lovingly between his fingers. He looked up from his work and shuffled towards the minister, not recognizing his guest immediately until he could almost touch the foreign giant. Then he bowed low. The minister spoke through the Mandarin:

'I have returned, sir, within the calendar year to repay my debt.'

'There was no need, Your Excellency. My family is honoured that the little statue lives in a great Embassy and may one day be admired by the people of your own land.'

The minister could think of no words to form an adequate reply and simply requested that the old man should accompany him on a short journey.

The craftsman agreed without question and the three men set out on donkeys towards the north. They travelled for over two hours up a thin winding path into the hills behind the craftsman's workshop, and when they reached the village of Ma Tien they were met by another Mandarin, who bowed low to the minister and requested Sir Alexander and the craftsman to continue their journey with him on foot. They walked in silence to the far side of the village and only stopped when they had reached a hollow in the hill from which there was a magnificent view of the valley all the way down to Ha Li Chuan. In the hollow stood a newly completed small white house of the most perfect proportions. Two stone lion dogs, tongues hanging over their lips, guarded the front entrance. The little old craftsman who had not spoken since he had left his workshop remained mystified by the purpose of the journey until the minister turned to him and offered:

'A small, inadequate gift and my feeble attempt to repay you in kind.'

The craftsman fell to his knees and begged forgiveness of the Mandarin as he knew it was forbidden for an artisan to accept gifts from a foreigner. The Mandarin raised the frightened blue figure from the ground, explaining to his countryman that the Empress herself had sanctioned the minister's request. A smile of joy came over the face of the craftsman and he slowly walked up to the doorway of the beautiful little house unable to resist running his hand over the carved lion dogs. The three travellers then spent over an hour admiring the little house before returning in silent mutual happiness back to the workshop in Ha Li Chuan. The two men thus parted, honour satisfied, and Sir Alexander rode to his Embassy that night content that his actions had met with the approval of the Mandarin as well as Lady Heathcote.

The minister completed his tour of duty in Peking, and the Empress awarded him the Silver Star of China and a grateful Queen added the KCVO to his already long list of decorations. After a few weeks back at the Foreign Office clearing the China desk, Sir Alexander retired to his native Yorkshire, the only English county whose inhabitants still hope to be born and die in the same place – not unlike the Chinese. Sir Alexander spent his final years in the home of his late father with his wife and the little Ming Emperor. The statue occupied the centre of the mantelpiece in the drawing room for all to see and admire.

Being an exact man, Sir Alexander wrote a long and detailed will in which he left precise instructions for the disposal of his estate, including what was to happen to the little statue after his death. He bequeathed the Emperor Kung to his first son requesting that he do the same, in order that the statue might always pass to the first son, or a daughter if the direct male line faltered. He also made a provision that the statue was never to be disposed of, unless the family's honour was at stake. Sir Alexander Heathcote died at the stroke of midnight on his seventieth year.

．　．　．

His first-born, Major James Heathcote, was serving his Queen in the Boer War at the time he came into possession of the Ming Emperor. The Major was a fighting man, commissioned with the Duke of Wellington's Regiment, and although he had little interest in culture even he could see the family heirloom was no ordinary treasure, so he loaned the statue to the regimental mess at Halifax in order that the Emperor could be displayed in the dining room for his brother officers to appreciate.

When James Heathcote became Colonel of the Dukes, the Emperor stood proudly on the table alongside the trophies won at Waterloo and Sebastopol in the Crimea and Madrid. And there the Ming Statue remained until the colonel's retirement to his father's house in Yorkshire, when the Emperor returned once again to the drawing room mantelpiece. The colonel was not a man to disobey his late father, even in death, and he left clear instructions that the heirloom must always be passed on to the first-born of the Heathcotes unless the family honour was in jeopardy. Colonel James Heathcote MC did not die a soldier's death; he simply fell asleep one night by the fire, the *Yorkshire Post* on his lap.

The colonel's first-born, the Reverend Alexander Heathcote, was at the time presiding over a small flock in the parish of Much Hadham in Hertfordshire. After burying his father with military honours, he placed the little Ming Emperor on the mantelpiece of the vicarage. Few members of the Mothers' Union appreciated the masterpiece but one or two old ladies were heard to remark on its delicate carving. And it was not until the Reverend became the Right Reverend, and the little statue found its way into the Bishop's palace that the Emperor attracted the admiration he deserved. Many of those who visited the palace and heard the story of how the Bishop's grandfather had acquired the Ming statue were fascinated to learn of the disparity between the magnificent statue and its base. It always made a good after-dinner story.

God takes even his own ambassadors, but He did not do so before allowing Bishop Heathcote to complete a will leaving the statue to his son, with his grandfather's exact instructions carefully repeated. The Bishop's son, Captain James Heathcote, was a serving officer in his grandfather's regiment, so the Ming statue returned to the mess table in Halifax. During the Emperor's absence, the regimental trophies had been augmented by those struck for Ypres, the Marne and Verdun. The regiment was once again at war with Germany, and young Captain James Heathcote was killed on the beaches of Dunkirk and died intestate. Thereafter English law, the known wishes of his great-grandfather and common sense prevailed, and the little Emperor came into the possession of the captain's two-year-old son.

Alex Heathcote was, alas, not of the mettle of his doughty ancestors and he grew up feeling no desire to serve anyone other than himself. When Captain James had been so tragically killed, Alexander's mother lavished everything on the boy that her meagre income would allow. It didn't help, and it was not entirely young Alex's fault that he grew up to be, in the words of his grandmother, a selfish, spoiled little brat.

When Alex left school, only a short time before he would have been expelled, he found he could never hold down a job for more than a few weeks. It always seemed necessary for him to spend a little more than he, and finally his mother, could cope with. The good lady, deciding she could take no more of this life, departed it, to join all the other Heathcotes, not in Yorkshire, but in heaven.

In the swinging sixties, when casinos opened in Britain, young Alex was convinced that he had found the ideal way of earning a living without actually having to do any work. He developed a system for playing roulette with which it was impossible to lose. He did lose, so he refined the system and promptly lost more; he refined the system once again which resulted in him having to borrow to cover his losses. Why not? If the worst came to the worst, he told himself, he could always dispose of the little Ming Emperor.

The worst did come to the worst, as each one of Alex's newly refined systems took him progressively into greater debt until the casinos began to press him for payment. When finally, one Monday morning, Alex received an unsolicited call from two gentlemen who seemed determined to collect some eight thousand pounds he owed their masters, and hinted at bodily harm if the matter was not dealt with within fourteen days, Alex caved in. After all, his great-great-grandfather's instructions had been exact: the Ming Statue was to be sold if the family honour was ever at stake.

Alex took the little Emperor off the mantelpiece in his Cadogan Gardens flat and stared down at its delicate handiwork, at least having the grace to feel a little sad at the loss of the family heirloom. He then drove to Bond Street and delivered the masterpiece to Sotheby's, giving instructions that the Emperor should be put up for auction.

The head of the Oriental department, a pale, thin man, appeared at the front desk to discuss the masterpiece with Alex, looking not unlike the Ming statue he was holding so lovingly in his hands.

'It will take a few days to estimate the true value of the piece,' he purred, 'but I feel confident on a cursory glance that the statue is as fine an example of Pen Q as we have ever had under the hammer.'

'That's no problem,' replied Alex, 'as long as you can let me know what it's worth within fourteen days.'

'Oh, certainly,' replied the expert. 'I feel sure I could give you a floor price by Friday.'

'Couldn't be better,' said Alex.

During that week he contacted all his creditors and without exception they were prepared to wait and learn the appraisal of the expert. Alex duly returned to Bond Street on the Friday with a large smile on his face. He knew what his great-great-grandfather had paid for the piece and felt sure that the statue must be worth more than ten thousand pounds. A sum that would not only yield him enough to cover all his debts but leave him a little over to try out his new refined, refined system on the roulette table. As he climbed the steps of Sotheby's, Alex silently thanked his great-great-grandfather. He asked the girl on reception if he could speak to the head of the Oriental department. She picked up an internal phone and the expert appeared a few moments later at the front desk with a sombre look on his face. Alex's heart sank as he listened to his words:

'A nice little piece, your Emperor, but unfortunately a fake, probably about two hundred, two hundred and fifty years old but only a copy of the original, I'm afraid. Copies were often made because ...'

'How much is it worth?' interrupted an anxious Alex.

'Seven hundred pounds, eight hundred at the most.'

Enough to buy a gun and some bullets, thought Alex sardonically as he turned and started to walk away.

'I wonder, sir ...' continued the expert.

'Yes, yes, sell the bloody thing,' said Alex, without bothering to look back.

'And what do you want me to do with the base?'

'The base?' repeated Alex, turning round to face the Orientalist.

'Yes, the base. It's quite magnificent, fifteenth century, undoubtedly a work of genius, I can't imagine how ...'

.   .   .   .

'Lot No. 103,' announced the auctioneer. 'What am I bid for this magnificent example of ... ?'

The expert turned out to be right in his assessment. At the auction at Sotheby's that Thursday morning I obtained the little Emperor for seven hundred and twenty guineas. And the base? That was acquired by an American gentleman of not unknown parentage for twenty-two thousand guineas.

The Luncheon

She waved at me across a crowded room of the St Regis Hotel in New York. I waved back realizing I knew the face but I was unable to place it. She squeezed past waiters and guests and had reached me before I had a chance to ask anyone who she was. I racked that section of my brain which is meant to store people, but it transmitted no reply. I realized I would have to resort to the old party trick of carefully worded questions until her answers jogged my memory.

'How *are* you, darling?' she cried, and threw her arms around me, an opening that didn't help as we were at a Literary Guild cocktail party, and anyone will throw their arms around you on such occasions, even the directors of the Book-of-the-Month Club. From her accent she was clearly American and looked to be approaching forty, but thanks to the genius of modern make-up might even have overtaken it. She wore a long white cocktail dress and her blonde hair was done up in one of those buns that looks like a cottage loaf. The overall effect made her appear somewhat like a chess queen. Not that the cottage loaf helped because she might have had dark hair flowing to her shoulders when we last met. I do wish women would realize that when they change their hair style they often achieve exactly what they set out to do: look completely different to any unsuspecting male.

'I'm well, thank you,' I said to the white queen. 'And you?' I inquired as my opening gambit.

'I'm just fine, darling,' she replied, taking a glass of champagne from a passing waiter.

'And how's the family?' I asked, not sure if she even had one.

'They're all well,' she replied. No help there. 'And how is Louise?' she inquired.

'Blooming,' I said. So she knew my wife. But then not necessarily, I thought. Most American women are experts at remembering the names of men's wives. They have to be, when on the New York circuit they change so often it becomes a greater challenge than *The Times* crossword.

'Have you been to London lately?' I roared above the babble. A brave question, as she might never have been to Europe.

'Only once since we had lunch together.' She looked at me quizzically. 'You don't remember who I am, do you?' she asked as she devoured a cocktail sausage.

I smiled.

'Don't be silly, Susan,' I said. 'How could I ever forget?'

She smiled.

I confess that I remembered the white queen's name in the nick of time. Although I still had only vague recollections of the lady, I certainly would never forget the lunch.

.   .   .

I had just had my first book published and the critics on both sides of the Atlantic had been complimentary, even if the cheques from my publishers were less so. My agent had told me on several occasions that I shouldn't write if I wanted to make money. This created a dilemma because I couldn't see how to make money if I didn't write.

It was around this time that the lady, who was now facing me and chattering on oblivious to my silence, telephoned from New York to heap lavish praise on my novel. There is no writer who does not enjoy receiving such calls, although I confess to having been less than captivated by an eleven-year-old girl who called me collect from California to say she had found a spelling mistake on page forty-seven and warned me she would ring again if she discovered another. However, this particular lady might have ended her transatlantic congratulations with nothing more than goodbye if she had not dropped her own name. It was one of those names that can, on the spur of the moment, always book a table at a chic restaurant or a seat at the opera which mere mortals like myself would have found impossible to achieve given a month's notice. To be fair, it was her husband's name that had achieved the reputation, as one of the world's most distinguished film producers.

'When I'm next in London you must have lunch with me,' came crackling down the phone.

'No,' said I gallantly, 'you must have lunch with *me*.'

'How perfectly charming you Engish always are,' she said.

I have often wondered how much American women get away with when they say those few words to an Englishman. Nevertheless, the wife of an Oscar-winning producer does not phone one every day.

'I promise to call you when I'm next in London,' she said.

And indeed she did, for almost six months to the day she telephoned again, this time from the Connaught Hotel to declare how much she was looking forward to our meeting.

'Where would you like to have lunch?' I said, realizing a second too late, when she replied with the name of one of the most exclusive restaurants in town, that I should have made sure it was I who chose the venue. I was glad she couldn't see my forlorn face as she added with unabashed liberation:

'Monday, one o'clock. Leave the booking to me – I'm known there.'

On the day in question I donned my one respectable suit, a new shirt which I had been saving for a special occasion since Christmas, and the only tie that looked as if it hadn't previously been used to hold up my trousers. I then strolled over to my bank and asked for a statement of my current account. The teller handed me a long piece of paper unworthy of its amount. I studied the figure as one who has to take a major financial decision. The bottom line stated in black lettering that I was in credit to the sum of thirty-seven pounds and sixty-three pence. I wrote out a cheque for thirty-seven pounds. I feel that a gentleman should always leave his account in credit, and I might add it was a belief that my bank manager shared with me. I then walked up to Mayfair for my luncheon date.

As I entered the restaurant I observed too many waiters and plush seats for my liking. You can't eat either, but you can be charged for them. At a corner table for two sat a woman who, although not young, was elegant. She wore a blouse of powder blue crêpe-de-chine, and her blonde hair was rolled away from her face in a style that reminded me of the war years, and had once again become fashionable. It was clearly my transatlantic admirer, and she greeted me in the same 'I've known you all my life' fashion as she was to do at the Literary Guild cocktail party years later. Although she had a drink in front of her I didn't order an apéritif, explaining that I never drank before lunch – and would like to have added, 'but as soon as your husband makes a film of my novel, I will.'

She launched immediately into the latest Hollywood gossip, not so much dropping names as reciting them, while I ate my way through the crisps from the bowl in front of me. A few minutes later a waiter materialized by the table and presented us with two large embossed leather menus, considerably better bound than my novel. The place positively reeked of unnecessary expense. I opened the menu and studied the first chapter with horror; it was eminently putdownable. I had no idea that simple food obtained from Covent Garden that morning could cost quite so much by merely being transported to Mayfair. I could have bought here the same dishes for a quarter of the price at my favourite bistro, a mere one hundred yards away, and to add to my discomfort I observed that it was one of those restaurants where the guest's menu made no mention of the prices. I settled down to study the long list of French dishes which only served to remind me that I hadn't eaten well for over a month, a state of affairs that was about to be prolonged by a further day. I remembered my bank balance and morosely reflected that I would probably have to wait until my agent sold the Icelandic rights of my novel before I could afford a square meal again.

'What would you like?' I said gallantly.

'I always enjoy a light lunch,' she volunteered. I sighed with premature relief, only to find that light did not necessarily mean 'inexpensive'.

She smiled sweetly up at the waiter, who looked as if *he* wouldn't be wondering where his next meal might be coming from, and ordered just a sliver of smoked salmon, followed by two tiny tender lamb cutlets. Then she hesitated, but only for a moment, before adding 'and a side salad'.

I studied the menu with some caution, running my finger down the prices, not the dishes.

'I also eat lightly at lunch,' I said mendaciously. 'The chef's salad will be quite enough for me.' The waiter was obviously affronted but left peaceably.

She chatted of Coppola and Preminger, of Al Pacino and Robert Redford, and of Greta Garbo as if she saw her all the time. She was kind enough to stop for a moment and ask what I was working on at present. I would have liked to have replied – on how I was going to explain to my wife that I only have sixty-three pence left in the bank; whereas I actually discussed my ideas for another novel. She seemed impressed, but still made no reference to her husband. Should I mention him? No. Mustn't sound pushy, or as though I needed the money.

The food arrived, or that is to say her smoked salmon did, and I sat silently watching her eat my bank account while I nibbled a roll. I looked up only to discover a wine waiter hovering by my side.

'Would you care for some wine?' said I, recklessly.

'No, I don't think so,' she said. I smiled a little too soon: 'Well, perhaps a little something white and dry.'

The wine waiter handed over a second leather-bound book, this time with golden grapes embossed on the cover. I searched down the pages for half bottles, explaining to my guest that I never drank at lunch. I chose the cheapest. The wine waiter reappeared a moment later with a large silver salver full of ice in which the half bottle looked drowned, and, like me, completely out of its depth. A junior waiter cleared away the empty plate while another wheeled a large trolley to the side of our table and served the lamb cutlets and the chef's salad. At the same time a third waiter made up an exquisite side salad for my guest which ended up bigger than my complete order. I didn't feel I could ask her to swap.

To be fair, the chef's salad was superb – although I confess it was hard to appreciate such food fully while trying to work out a plot that would be convincing if I found the bill came to over thirty-seven pounds.

'How silly of me to ask for white wine with lamb,' she said, having nearly finished the half bottle. I ordered a half bottle of the house red without calling for the wine list.

She finished the white wine and then launched into the theatre, music and other authors. All those who were still alive she seemed to know and those who were dead she hadn't read. I might have enjoyed the performance if it hadn't been for the fear of wondering if I would be able to afford it when the curtain came down. When the waiter cleared away the empty dishes he asked my guest if she would care for anything else.

'No, thank you,' she said – I nearly applauded. 'Unless you have one of your famous apple surprises.'

'I fear the last one may have gone, madam, but I'll go and see.'

Don't hurry, I wanted to say, but instead I just smiled as the rope tightened around my neck. A few moments later the waiter strode back in triumph weaving between the tables holding the apple surprise, in the palm of his hand, high above his head. I prayed to Newton that the apple would obey his law. It didn't.

'The last one, madam.'

'Oh, what luck,' she declared.

'Oh, what luck,' I repeated, unable to face the menu and discover the price. I was now attempting some mental arithmetic as I realized it was going to be a close run thing.

'Anything else, madam?' the ingratiating waiter inquired.

I took a deep breath.

'Just coffee,' she said.

'And for you, Sir?'

'No, no, not for me.' He left us. I couldn't think of an explanation for why I didn't drink coffee.

She then produced from the large Gucci bag by her side a copy of my novel, which I signed with a flourish, hoping the head waiter would see me and feel I was the sort of man who should be allowed to sign the bill as well, but he resolutely remained at the far end of the room while I wrote the words 'An unforgettable meeting' and appended my signature.

While the dear lady was drinking her coffee I picked at another roll and called for the bill, not because I was in any particular hurry, but like a guilty defendant at the Old Bailey I preferred to wait no longer for the judge's sentence. A man in a smart green uniform, whom I had never seen before appeared carrying a silver tray with a folded piece of paper on it looking not unlike my bank statement. I pushed back the edge of the check slowly and read the figure: thirty-six pounds and forty pence. I casually put my hand into my inside pocket and withdrew my life's possessions and then placed the crisp new notes on the silver tray. They were whisked away. The man in the green uniform returned a few moments later with my sixty pence change, which I pocketed as it was the only way I was going to get a bus home. The waiter gave me a look that would have undoubtedly won him a character part in any film produced by the lady's distinguished husband.

My guest rose and walked across the restaurant, waving at, and occasionally kissing people that I had previously only seen in glossy magazines. When she reached the door she stopped to retrieve her coat, a mink. I helped her on with the fur, again failing to leave a tip. As we stood on the Curzon Street pavement, a dark blue Rolls-Royce drew up beside us and a liveried chauffeur leaped out and opened the rear door. She climbed in.

'Goodbye, darling,' she said, as the electric window slid down. 'Thank you for such a lovely lunch.'

'Goodbye,' I said, and summoning up my courage added: 'I do hope when you are next in town I shall have the opportunity of meeting your distiguished husband.'

'Oh, darling, didn't you know?' she said as she looked out from the Rolls-Royce.

'Know what?'

'We were divorced ages ago.'

'Divorced?' said I.

'Oh, yes,' she said gaily, 'I haven't spoken to him for years.'

I just stood there looking helpless.

'Oh, don't worry yourself on my account,' she said. 'He's no loss. In any case I have recently married again' – another film producer, I prayed – 'In fact, I quite expected to bump into my husband today – you see, he owns the restaurant.'

Without another word the electric window purred up and the Rolls-Royce glided effortlessly out of sight leaving me to walk to the nearest bus stop.

        .   .   .

As I stood surrounded by Literary Guild guests, staring at the white queen with the cottage loaf bun, I could still see her drifting away in that blue Rolls-Royce. I tried to concentrate on her words.

'I knew you wouldn't forget me, darling,' she was saying. 'After all, I did take you to lunch, didn't I?'

The Coup

The blue and silver 707 jet, displaying a large 'P' on its tail plane, taxied to a halt at the north end of Lagos International Airport. A fleet of six black Mercedes drove up to the side of the aircraft and waited in a line resembling a land-bound crocodile. Six sweating, uniformed drivers leaped out and stood to attention. When the driver of the front car opened his rear door, Colonel Usman of the Federal Guard stepped out, and walked quickly to the bottom of the passenger steps which had been hurriedly pushed into place by four of the airport staff.

The front section cabin door swung back and the colonel stared up into the gap, to see, framed against the dark interior of the cabin, a slim, attractive hostess dressed in a blue suit with silver piping. On her jacket lapel was a large 'P'. She turned and nodded in the direction of the cabin. A few seconds later, an immaculately dressed tall man with thick black hair and deep brown eyes replaced her in the doorway. The man had an air of effortless style about him which self-made millionaires would have paid a considerable part of their fortune to possess. The colonel saluted as Senhor Eduardo Francisco de Silveira, head of the Prentino empire gave a curt nod.

De Silveira emerged from the coolness of his air-conditioned 707 into the burning Nigerian sun without showing the slightest sign of discomfort. The colonel guided the tall, elegant Brazilian, who was accompanied only by his private secretary, to the front Mercedes while the rest of the Prentino staff filed down the back stairway of the aircraft and filled the other five cars. The driver, a corporal who had been detailed to be available night and day for the honoured guest, opened the rear door of the front car and saluted. Eduardo de Silveira showed no sign of acknowledgement. The corporal smiled nervously, revealing the largest set of white teeth the Brazilian had ever seen.

'Welcome to Lagos,' the corporal volunteered. 'Hope you make very big deal while you are in Nigeria.'

Eduardo did not comment as he settled back into his seat and stared out of the tinted window to watch some passengers of a British Airways 707 that had landed just before him form a long queue on the hot tarmac as they waited patiently to clear customs. The driver put the car into first gear and the black crocodile proceeded on its journey. Colonel Usman who was now in the front seat beside the corporal, soon discovered that the Brazilian guest did not care for small talk, and the secretary who was seated by his employer's side never once opened his mouth. The colonel, used to doing things by example, remained silent, leaving de Silveira to consider his plan of campaign.

Eduardo Francisco de Silveira had been born in the small village of Rebeti, a hundred miles north of Rio de Janeiro, heir to one of the two most powerful family fortunes in Brazil. He had been educated privately in Switzerland before attending the University of California in Los Angeles. He went on to complete his education at the Harvard Business School. After Harvard he returned from America to work in Brazil where he started neither at the top or the bottom of the firm but in the middle, managing his family's mining interests in Minas Gerais. He quickly worked his way to the top, even faster than his father had planned, but then the boy turned out to be not so much a chip as a chunk off the old block. At twenty-nine he married Maria, eldest daughter of his father's closest friend, and when twelve years later his father died Eduardo succeeded to the Prentino throne. There were seven sons in all: the second son, Alfredo, was now in charge of banking; João ran shipping; Carlos organized construction; Manoel arranged food and supplies; Jaime managed the family newspapers, and little Antonio, the last – and certainly the least – ran the family farms. All the brothers reported to Eduardo before making any major decision, for he was still chairman of the largest private company in Brazil, despite the boastful claims of his old family enemy, Manuel Rodrigues.

When General Castelo Branco's military regime overthrew the civilian government in 1964 the generals agreed that they could not kill off all the de Silveiras or the Rodrigues so they had better learn to live with the two rival families. The de Silveiras for their part had always had enough sense never to involve themselves in politics other than by making payments to every government official, military or civilian, according to his rank. This ensured that the Prentino empire grew alongside whatever faction came to power. One of the reasons Eduardo de Silveira had allocated three days in his crowded schedule for a visit to Lagos was that the Nigerian system of government seemed to resemble so closely that of Brazil, and at least on this project he had cut the ground from under Manuel Rodrigues' feet which would more than make up for losing the Rio airport tender to him. Eduardo smiled at the thought of Rodrigues not realizing that he was in Nigeria to close a deal that could make him twice the size of his rival.

As the black Mercedes moved slowly through the teeming noisy streets paying no attention to traffic lights, red or green, Eduardo thought back to his first meeting with General Mohammed, the Nigerian Head of State, on the occasion of the President's official visit to Brazil. Speaking at the dinner given in General Mohammed's honour, President Ernesto Geisel declared a hope that the two countries would move towards closer cooperation in politics and commerce. Eduardo agreed with his unelected leader and was happy to leave the politics to the President if he allowed him to get on with the commerce. General Mohammed made his reply, on behalf of the guests, in an English accent that normally would only be associated with Oxford. The general talked at length of the project that was most dear to his heart, the building of a new Nigerian capital in Abuja, a city which he considered might even rival Brasilia. After the speeches were over, the general took de Silveira on one side and spoke in greater detail of the Abuja city project asking him if he might consider a private tender. Eduardo smiled and only wished that his enemy, Rodrigues, could hear the intimate conversation he was having with the Nigerian Head of State.

. . .

Eduardo studied carefully the outline proposal sent to him a week later, after the general had returned to Nigeria, and agreed to his first request by despatching a research team of seven men to fly to Lagos and complete a feasibility study on Abuja.

One month later, the team's detailed report was in de Silveira's hands. Eduardo came to the conclusion that the potential profitability of the project was worthy of a full proposal to the Nigerian government. He contacted General Mohammed personally to find that he was in full agreement and authorized the go-ahead. This time twenty-three men were despatched to Lagos and three months and one hundred and seventy pages later, Eduardo signed and sealed the proposal designated as, 'A New Capital for Nigeria'. He made only one alteration to the final document. The cover of the proposal was in blue and silver with the Prentino logo in the centre: Eduardo had that changed to green and white, the national colours of Nigeria, with the national emblem of an eagle astride two horses: he realized it was the little things that impressed generals and often tipped the scales. He sent ten copies of the feasibility study to Nigeria's Head of State with an invoice for one million dollars.

When General Mohammed had studied the proposal he invited Eduardo de Silveira to visit Nigeria as his guest, in order to discuss the next stage of the project. De Silveira telexed back, provisionally accepting the invitation, and pointing out politely but firmly that he had not yet received reimbursement for the one million dollars spent on the initial feasibility study. The money was telexed by return from the Central Bank of Nigeria and de Silveira managed to find four consecutive days in his diary for 'The New Federal Capital project': his schedule demanded that he arrived in Lagos on a Monday morning because he had to be in Paris at the latest by the Thursday night.

While these thoughts were going through Eduardo's mind, the Mercedes drew up outside Dodan Barracks. The iron gates swung open and a full armed guard gave the general salute, an honour normally afforded only to a visiting Head of State. The black Mercedes drove slowly through the gates and came to a halt outside the President's private residence. A brigadier waited on the steps to escort de Silveira through to the President.

The two men had lunch together in a small room that closely resembled a British officers' mess. The meal consisted of a steak, that would not have been acceptable to any South American cowhand surrounded by vegetables that reminded Eduardo of his schooldays. Still, Eduardo had never yet met a soldier who understood that a good chef was every bit as important as a good batman. During the lunch they talked in overall terms about the problems of building a whole new city in the middle of an equatorial jungle.

The provisional estimate of the cost of the project had been one thousand million dollars but de Silveira warned the President that the final outcome might well end up nearer three thousand million dollars the President's jaw dropped slightly. De Silveira had to admit that the project would be the most ambitious that Prentino International had ever tackled, but he was quick to point out to the President that the same would be true of any construction company in the world.

De Silveira, not a man to play his best card early, waited until the coffee to slip into the conversation that he had just been awarded, against heavy opposition (that had included Rodrigues), the contract to build an eight-lane highway through the Amazonian jungle, which would eventually link up with the Pan-American highway, a contract second in size only to the one they were now contemplating in Nigeria. The President was impressed and inquired if the venture would not prevent de Silveira involving himself in the new capital project.

'I'll know the answer to that question in three days' time,' replied the Brazilian, and undertook to have a further discussion with the Head of State at the end of his visit when he would let him know if he was prepared to continue with the scheme.

After lunch Eduardo was driven to the Federal Palace Hotel where the entire sixth floor had been placed at his disposal. Several complaining guests who had come to Nigeria to close deals involving mere millions had been asked to vacate their rooms at short notice to make way for de Silveira and his staff. Eduardo knew nothing of these goings on, as there was always a room available for him wherever he arrived in the world.

The six Mercedes drew up outside the hotel and the colonel guided his charge through the swing doors and past reception. Eduardo had not checked himself into a hotel for the past fourteen years except on those occasions when he chose to register under an assumed name, not wanting anyone to know the identity of the woman he was with.

The chairman of Prentino International walked down the centre of the hotel's main corridor and stepped into a waiting lift. His legs went weak and he suddenly felt sick. In the corner of the lift stood a stubby, balding, overweight man, who was dressed in a pair of old jeans and a tee-shirt, his mouth continually opening and closing as he chewed gum. The two men stood as far apart as possible, neither showing any sign of recognition. The lift stopped at the fifth floor and Manuel Rodrigues, chairman of Rodrigues International SA, stepped out leaving behind him the man who had been his bitter rival for thirty years.

Eduardo held on to the rail in the lift to steady himself as he still felt dizzy. How he despised that uneducated self-made upstart whose family of four half-brothers, all by different fathers, claimed they now ran the largest construction company in Brazil. Both men were as interested in the other's failure as they were in their own success.

Eduardo was somewhat puzzled to know what Rodrigues could possibly be doing in Lagos as he felt certain that his rival had not come into contact with the Nigerian President. After all, Eduardo had never collected the rent on a small house in Rio that was occupied by the mistress of a very senior official in the government's protocol department. And the man's only task was to be certain that Rodrigues was never invited to any function attended by a visiting dignitary when in Brazil. The continual absence of Rodrigues from these state occasions ensured the absent-mindedness of Eduardo's rent collector in Rio.

Eduardo would never have admitted to anyone that Rodrigues' presence worried him, but he nevertheless resolved to find out immediately what had brought his old enemy to Nigeria. Once he reached his suite de Silveira instructed his private secretary to check what Manuel Rodrigues was up to.

Eduardo was prepared to return to Brazil immediately if Rodrigues turned out to be involved in any way with the new capital project, while one young lady in Rio would suddenly find herself looking for alternative accommodation.

Within an hour, his private secretary returned with the information that his chairman had requested. Rodrigues, he had discovered, was in Nigeria to tender for the contract to construct a new port in Lagos and was apparently not involved in any way with the new capital, and in fact was still trying to arrange a meeting with the President.

'Which minister is in charge of the ports and when am I due to see him?' asked de Silveira.

The secretary delved into his appointments file. 'The Minister of Transport,' the secretary said. 'You have an appointment with him at nine o'clock on Thursday morning.' The Nigerian Civil Service had mapped out a four-day schedule of meetings for de Silveira that included every cabinet minister involved in the new city project. 'It's the last meeting before your final discussion with the President. You then fly on to Paris.'

'Excellent. Remind me of this conversation five minutes before I see the minister and again when I talk to the President.'

The secretary made a note in the file and left.

Eduardo sat alone in his suite, going over the reports on the new capital project submitted by his experts. Some of his team were already showing signs of nervousness. One particular anxiety that always came up with a large construction contract was the principal's ability to pay, and pay on time. Failure to do so was the quickest route to bankruptcy, but since the discovery of oil in Nigeria there seemed to be no shortage of income and certainly no shortage of people willing to spend that money on behalf of the government. These anxieties did not worry de Silveira as he always insisted on a substantial payment in advance; otherwise he wouldn't move himself or his vast staff one centimetre out of Brazil. However, the massive scope of this particular contract made the circumstances somewhat unusual. Eduardo realized that it would be most damaging to his international reputation if he started the assignment and then was seen not to complete it. He re-read the reports over a quiet dinner in his room and retired to bed early, having wasted an hour in vainly trying to place a call through to his wife.

De Silveira's first appointment the next morning was with the Governor of the Central Bank of Nigeria. Eduardo wore a newly-pressed suit, fresh shirt, and highly polished shoes: for four days no one would see him in the same clothes. At eight-forty-five there was a quiet knock on the door of his suite and the secretary opened it to find Colonel Usman standing to attention, waiting to escort Eduardo to the bank. As they were leaving the hotel Eduardo again saw Manuel Rodrigues, wearing the same pair of jeans, the same crumpled tee-shirt, and probably chewing the same gum as he stepped into a BMW in front of him. De Silveira only stopped scowling at the disappearing BMW when he remembered his Thursday morning appointment with the minister in charge of ports, followed by a meeting with the President.

The Governor of the Central Bank of Nigeria was in the habit of proposing how payment schedules would be met and completion orders would be guaranteed. He had never been told by anyone that if the payment was seven days overdue he could consider the contract null and void, and they could take it or leave it. The minister would have made some comment if Abuja had not been the President's pet project. That position established, de Silveira went on to check the bank's reserves, long-term deposits, overseas commitments, and estimated oil revenues for the next five years. He left the Governor in what could only be described as a jelly-like state. Glistening and wobbling. Eduardo's next appointment was an unavoidable courtesy call on the Brazilian Ambassador for lunch. He hated these functions as he believed embassies to be fit only for cocktail parties and discussion of out-of-date trivia, neither of which he cared for. The food in such establishments was invariably bad and the company worse. It turned out to be no different on this occasion and the only profit (Eduardo considered everything in terms of profit and loss) to be derived from the encounter was the information that Manuel Rodrigues was on a short list of three for the building of the new port in Lagos, and was expecting to have an audience with the President on Friday if he was awarded the contract. By Thursday morning that will be a short list of two and there will be no meeting with the President, de Silveira promised himself, and considered that was the most he was likely to gain from the lunch until the Ambassador added:

'Rodrigues seems most keen on you being awarded the new city contract at Abuja. He's singing your praises to every minister he meets. Funny,' the Ambassador continued, 'I always thought you two didn't see eye to eye.'

Eduardo made no reply as he tried to fathom out what trick Rodrigues could be up to by promoting his cause.

Eduardo spent the afternoon with the Minister of Finance and confirmed the provisional arrangements he had made with the Governor of the bank. The Minister of Finance had been forewarned by the Governor what he was to expect from an encounter with Eduardo de Silveira and that he was not to be taken aback by the Brazilian's curt demands. De Silveira, aware that this warning would have taken place, let the poor man bargain a little and even gave way on a few minor points that he would be able to tell the President about at the next meeting of the Supreme Military Council. Eduardo left the smiling minister believing that he had scored a point or two against the formidable South American.

That evening, Eduardo dined privately with his senior advisers who themselves were already dealing with the ministers' officials. Each was now coming up with daily reports about the problems that would have to be faced if they worked in Nigeria. His chief engineer was quick to emphasize that skilled labour could not be hired at any price as the Germans had already cornered the market for their extensive road projects. The financial advisers also presented a gloomy report, of international companies waiting six months or more for their cheques to be cleared by the central bank. Eduardo made notes on the views they expressed but never ventured an opinion himself. His staff left him a little after eleven and he decided to take a stroll around the hotel grounds before retiring to bed. On his walk through the luxuriant tropical gardens he only just avoided a face-to-face confrontation with Manuel Rodrigues by darting behind a large Iroko plant. The little man passed by champing away at his gum, oblivious to Eduardo's baleful glare. Eduardo informed a chattering grey parrot of his most secret thoughts: by Thursday afternoon, Rodrigues, you will be on your way back to Brazil with a suitcase full of plans that can be filed under 'abortive projects'. The parrot cocked his head and screeched at him as if he had been let in on his secret. Eduardo allowed himself a smile and returned to his room.

Colonel Usman arrived on the dot of eight-forty-five again the next day and Eduardo spent the morning with the Minister of Supplies and Cooperatives – or lack of them, as he commented to his private secretary afterwards. The afternoon was spent with the Minister of Labour checking over the availability of unskilled workers and the total lack of skilled operatives. Eduardo was fast reaching the conclusion that, despite the professed optimism of the ministers concerned, this was going to be the toughest contract he had ever tackled. There was more to be lost than money if the whole international business world stood watching him fall flat on his face. In the evening his staff reported to him once again, having solved a few old problems and unearthed some new ones. Tentatively, they had come to the conclusion that if the present regime stayed in power, there need be no serious concern over payment, as the President had earmarked the new city as a priority project. They had even heard a rumour that the army would be willing to lend-lease part of the Service Corps if there turned out to be a shortage of skilled labour. Eduardo made a note to have this point confirmed in writing by the Head of State during their final meeting the next day. But the labour problem was not what was occupying Eduardo's thoughts as he put on his silk pyjamas that night. He was chuckling at the idea of Manuel Rodrigues' imminent and sudden departure for Brazil. Eduardo slept well.

He rose with renewed vigour the next morning, showered and put on a fresh suit. The four days were turning out to be well worth while and a single stone might yet kill two birds. By eight-forty-five, he was waiting impatiently for the previously punctual colonel. The colonel did not show up at eight-forty-five and had still not appeared when the clock on his mantelpiece struck nine. De Silveira sent his private secretary off to find out where he was while he paced angrily backwards and forwards through the hotel suite. His secretary returned a few minutes later in a panic with the information that the hotel was surrounded by armed guards. Eduardo did not panic. He had been through eight coups in his life from which he had learnt one golden rule: the new regime never kills visiting foreigners as it needs their money every bit as much as the last government. Eduardo picked up the telephone but no one answered him so he switched on the radio. A tape recording was playing:

'This is Radio Nigeria, this is Radio Nigeria. There has been a coup. General Mohammed has been overthrown and Lieutenant Colonel Dimka has assumed leadership of the new revolutionary government. Do not be afraid; remain at home and everything will be back to normal in a few hours. This is Radio Nigeria, this is Radio Nigeria. There has been a ...'

Eduardo switched off the radio as two thoughts flashed through his mind. Coups always held up everything and caused chaos, so undoubtedly he had

wasted the four days. But worse, would it now be possible for him even to
get out of Nigeria and carry on his normal business with the rest of the
world?

By lunchtime, the radio was playing martial music interspersed with the
tape recorded message he now knew off by heart. Eduardo detailed all his
staff to find out anything they could and to report back to him direct. They
all returned with the same story; that it was impossible to get past the soldiers
surrounding the hotel so no new information could be unearthed. Eduardo
swore for the first time in months. To add to his inconvenience, the hotel
manager rang through to say that regretfully Mr de Silveira would have to
eat in the main dining room as there would be no room service until further
notice. Eduardo went down to the dining room somewhat reluctantly only
to discover that the head waiter showed no interest in who he was and placed
him unceremoniously at a small table already occupied by three Italians.
Manuel Rodrigues was seated only two tables away: Eduardo stiffened at
the thought of the other man enjoying his discomfiture and then remembered it was that morning he was supposed to have seen the Minister of Ports.
He ate his meal quickly despite being served slowly and when the Italians
tried to make conversation with him he waved them away with his hand,
feigning lack of understanding, despite the fact that he spoke their language
fluently. As soon as he had finished the second course he returned to his
room. His staff had only gossip to pass on and they had been unable to make
contact with the Brazilian Embassy to lodge an official protest. 'A lot of good
an official protest will do us,' said Eduardo, slumping down in his chair.
'Who do you send it to, the new regime or the old one?'

He sat alone in his room for the rest of the day, interrupted only by what
he thought was the sound of gunfire in the distance. He read the New Federal
Capital project proposal and his advisers' reports for a third time.

The next morning Eduardo, dressed in the same suit as he had worn on
the day of his arrival, was greeted by his secretary with the news that the
coup had been crushed; after fierce street fighting, he informed his unusually
attentive chairman, the old regime had regained power but not without
losses; among those killed in the uprising had been General Mohammed, the
Head of State. The secretary's news was officially confirmed on Radio
Nigeria later that morning. The ringleader of the abortive coup had been
one Lieutenant Colonel Dimka: Dimka, along with one or two junior
officers, had escaped, and the government had ordered a dusk to dawn
curfew until the evil criminals were apprehended.

Pull off a coup and you're a national hero, fail and you're an evil criminal;
in business it's the same difference between bankruptcy and making a
fortune, considered Eduardo as he listened to the news report. He was
beginning to form plans in his mind for an early departure from Nigeria
when the newscaster made an announcement that chilled him to the very
marrow.

'While Lieutenant Colonel Dimka and his accomplices remain on the run,
airports throughout the country will be closed until further notice.'

When the newscaster had finished his report, martial music was played
in memory of the late General Mohammed.

Eduardo went downstairs in a flaming temper. The hotel was still surrounded by armed guards. He stared at the fleet of six empty Mercedes which was parked only ten yards beyond the soldiers' rifles. He marched back into the foyer, irritated by the babble of different tongues coming at him from every direction. Eduardo looked around him: it was obvious that many people had been stranded in the hotel overnight and had ended up sleeping in the lounge or the bar. He checked the paperback rack in the lobby for something to read but there were only four copies left of a tourist guide to Lagos; everything had been sold. Authors who had not been read for years were now changing hands at a premium. Eduardo returned to his room which was fast assuming the character of a prison, and baulked at reading the New Federal Capital project for a fourth time. He tried again to make contact with the Brazilian Ambassador to discover if he could obtain special permission to leave the country as he had his own aircraft. No one answered the Embassy phone. He went down for an early lunch only to find the dining room was once again packed to capacity. Eduardo was placed at a table with some Germans who were worrying about a contract that had been signed by the government the previous week, before the abortive coup. They were wondering if it would still be honoured. Manuel Rodrigues entered the room a few minutes later and was placed at the next table.

During the afternoon, de Silveira ruefully examined his schedule for the next seven days. He had been due in Paris that morning to see the Minister of the Interior, and from there should have flown on to London to confer with the chairman of the Steel Board. His calendar was fully booked for the next ninety-two days until his family holiday in May. 'I'm having this year's holiday in Nigeria,' he commented wryly to an assistant.

What annoyed Eduardo most about the coup was the lack of communication it afforded with the outside world. He wondered what was going on in Brazil and he hated not being able to telephone or telex Paris or London to explain his absence personally. He listened addictively to Radio Nigeria on the hour every hour for any new scrap of information. At five o'clock, he learned that the Supreme Military Council had elected a new President who would address the nation on television and radio at nine o'clock that night.

Eduardo de Silveira switched on the television at eight-forty-five; normally an assistant would have put it on for him at one minute to nine. He sat watching a Nigerian lady giving a talk on dressmaking, followed by the weather forecast man who supplied Eduardo with the revealing information that the temperature would continue to be hot for the next month. Eduardo's knee was twitching up and down nervously as he waited for the address by the new President. At nine o'clock, after the national anthem had been played, the new Head of State, General Obasanjo, appeared on the screen in full dress uniform. He spoke first of the tragic death and sad loss for the nation of the late President, and went on to say that his government would continue to work in the best interest of Nigeria. He looked ill at ease as he apologized to all foreign visitors who were inconvenienced by the attempted coup but went on to make it clear that the dusk to dawn curfew would continue until the rebel leaders were tracked down and brought to justice. He confirmed that, all airports would remain closed until Lieutenant Colonel Dimka was in safe custody. The new President ended his statement by saying that all other forms of communication would be opened up again as soon as possible. The national anthem was played for a second time, while Eduardo thought of the millions of dollars that might be lost to him by his incarceration in that hotel room, while his private plane sat idly on the tarmac only a few miles away. One of his senior managers opened a book as to how long it would take for the authorities to capture Lieutenant Colonel Dimka; he did not tell de Silveira how short the odds were on a month.

Eduardo went down to the dining room in the suit he had worn the day before. A junior waiter placed him at a table with some Frenchmen who had been hoping to win a contract to drill bore holes in the Niger state. Again Eduardo waved a languid hand when they tried to include him in their conversation. At that very moment he was meant to be with the French Minister of the Interior, not with some French hole-borers. He tried to concentrate on his watered-down soup, wondering how much longer it would be before it would be just water. The head waiter appeared by his side, gesturing to the one remaining seat at the table, in which he placed Manuel Rodrigues. Still neither man gave any sign of recognizing the other. Eduardo debated with himself whether he should leave the table or carry on as if his oldest rival was still in Brazil. He decided the latter was more dignified. The Frenchman began an argument among themselves as to when they would be able to get out of Lagos. One of them declared emphatically that he had heard on the highest authority that the government intended to track down every last one of those involved in the coup before they opened the airports and that might take up to a month.

'What?' said the two Brazilians together, in English.

'I can't stay here for a month,' said Eduardo.

'Neither can I,' said Manuel Rodrigues.

'You'll have to, at least until Dimka is captured,' said one of the Frenchmen, breaking into English. 'So you must both relax yourselves, yes?'

The two Brazilians continued their meal in silence. When Eduardo had finished he rose from the table and without looking directly at Rodrigues said goodnight in Portuguese. The old rival inclined his head in reply to the salutation.

The next day brought forth no new information. The hotel remained surrounded with soldiers and by the evening Eduardo had lost his temper with every member of staff with whom he had come into contact. He went down to dinner on his own and as he entered the dining room he saw Manuel Rodrigues sitting alone at a table in the corner. Rodrigues looked up, seemed to hesitate for a moment, and then beckoned to Eduardo. Eduardo himself hesitated before walking slowly towards Rodrigues and taking the seat opposite him. Rodrigues poured him a glass of wine. Eduardo, who rarely drank, drank it. Their conversation was stilted to begin with, but as both men consumed more wine so they each began to relax in the other's company. By the time coffee had arrived, Manuel was telling Eduardo what he could do with this god-forsaken country.

'You will not stay on, if you are awarded the ports contract?' inquired Eduardo.

'Not a hope,' said Rodrigues, who showed no surprise that de Silveira knew of his interest in the ports contract. 'I withdrew from the short list the day before the coup. I had intended to fly back to Brazil that Thursday morning.'

'Can you say why you withdrew?'

'Labour problems mainly, and then the congestion of the ports.'

'I am not sure I understand,' said Eduardo, understanding full well but curious to learn if Rodrigues had picked up some tiny detail his own staff had missed.

Manuel Rodrigues paused to ingest the fact that the man he had viewed as his most dangerous enemy for over thirty years was now listening to his own inside information. He considered the situation for a moment while he sipped his coffee. Eduardo didn't speak.

'To begin with, there's a terrible shortage of skilled labour, and on top of that there's this mad quota system.'

'Quota system?' said Eduardo innocently.

'The percentage of people from the contractor's country which the government will allow to work in Nigeria.'

'Why should that be a problem?' said Eduardo, leaning forward.

'By law, you have to employ at a ratio of fifty nationals to one foreigner so I could only have brought over twenty-five of my top men to organize a fifty million dollar contract, and I'd have had to make do with Nigerians at every other level. The government are cutting their own throats with the wretched system; they can't expect unskilled men, black or white, to become experienced engineers overnight. It's all to do with their national pride. Someone must tell them they can't afford that sort of pride if they want to complete the job at a sensible price. That path is the surest route to bankruptcy. On top of that, the Germans have already rounded up all the best skilled labour for their road projects.'

'But surely,' said Eduardo, 'you charge according to the rules, however stupid, thus covering all eventualities, and as long as you're certain that payment is guaranteed ...'

Manuel raised his hand to stop Eduardo's flow: 'That's another problem. You can't be certain. The government reneged on a major steel contract only last month. In so doing,' he explained, 'they had bankrupted a distinguished international company. So they are perfectly capable of trying the same trick with me. And if they don't pay up, who do you sue? The Supreme Military Council?'

'And the ports problem?'

'The port is totally congested. There are one hundred and seventy ships desperate to unload their cargo with a waiting time of anything up to six months. On top of that, there is a demurrage charge of five thousand dollars a day and only perishable foods are given any priority.'

'But there's always a way round that sort of problem,' said Eduardo, rubbing a thumb twice across the top of his fingers.

'Bribery? It doesn't work, Eduardo. How can you possibly jump the queue when all one hundred and seventy ships have already bribed the harbour master? And don't imagine that fixing the rent on a flat for one of his mistresses would help either,' said Rodrigues grinning. 'With that man you will have to supply the mistress as well.'

Eduardo held his breath but said nothing.

'Come to think of it,' continued Rodrigues, 'if the situation becomes any worse, the harbour master will be the one man in the country who is richer than you.'

Eduardo laughed for the first time in three days.

'I tell you, Eduardo, we could make a bigger profit building a salt mine in Siberia.'

Eduardo laughed again and some of the Prentino and Rodrigues staff dining at other tables stared in disbelief at their masters.

'You were in for the big one, the new city of Abuja?' said Manuel.

'That's right,' admitted Eduardo.

'I have done everything in my power to make sure you were awarded that contract,' said the other quietly.

'What?' said Eduardo in disbelief. 'Why?'

'I thought Abuja would give the Prentino empire more headaches than even you could cope with, Eduardo, and that might possibly leave the field wide open for me at home. Think about it. Every time there's a cutback in Nigeria, what will be the first head to roll off the chopping block? "The unnecessary city" as the locals call it.'

'The unnecessary city?' repeated Eduardo.

'Yes, and it doesn't help when you say you won't move without advance payment. You know as well as I do, you will need one hundred of your best men here full time to organize such a massive enterprise. They'll need feeding, salaries, housing, perhaps even a school and a hospital. Once they were settled down here, you can't just pull them off the job every two weeks because the government is running late clearing the cheques. It's not practical and you know it.' Rodrigues poured Eduardo de Silveira another glass of wine.

'I had already taken that into consideration,' Eduardo said as he sipped the wine, 'but I thought that with the support of the Head of State.'

'The late Head of State –

'I take your point, Manuel.'

'Maybe the next Head of State will also back you, but what about the one after that? Nigeria has had three coups in the past three years.'

Eduardo remained silent for a moment.

'Do you play backgammon?'

'Yes. Why do you ask?'

'I must make *some* money while I'm here.' Manuel laughed.

'Why don't you come to my room,' continued de Silveira. 'Though I must warn you I always manage to beat my staff.'

'Perhaps they always manage to lose,' said Manuel, as he rose and grabbed the half empty bottle of wine by its neck. Both men were laughing as they left the dining room.

After that, the two chairmen had lunch and dinner together every day. Within a week, their staff were eating at the same tables. Eduardo could be seen in the dining room without a tie while Manuel wore a shirt for the first time in years. By the end of a fortnight, the two rivals had played each other at table tennis, backgammon and bridge with the stakes set at one hundred dollars a point. At the end of each day Eduardo always seemed to end up owing Manuel about a million dollars which Manuel happily traded for the best bottle of wine left in the hotel's cellar.

Although Lieutenant Colonel Dimka had been sighted by about forty thousand Nigerians in about as many different places, he still remained resolutely uncaptured. As the new President had insisted, airports remained closed but communications were opened which at least allowed Eduardo to telephone and telex Brazil. His brothers and wife were sending replies by the hour, imploring Eduardo to return home at any cost: decisions on major contracts throughout the world were being held up by his absence. But Eduardo's message back to Brazil was always the same: as long as Dimka is on the loose, the airports will remain closed.

It was on a Tuesday night during dinner that Eduardo took the trouble to explain to Manuel why Brazil had lost the World Cup. Manuel dismissed Eduardo's outrageous claims as ill-informed and prejudiced. It was the only subject on which they hadn't agreed in the past three weeks.

'I blame the whole fiasco on Zagalo,' said Eduardo.

'No, no, you cannot blame the manager,' said Manuel. 'The fault lies with our stupid selectors who know even less about football than you do. They should never have dropped Leao from goal and in any case we should have learned from the Argentinian defeat last year that our methods are now out of date. You must attack, attack, if you want to score goals.'

'Rubbish. We still have the surest defence in the world.'

'Which means the best result you can hope for is a 0–0 draw.'

'Never . . .' began Eduardo.

'Excuse me, sir.' Eduardo looked up to see his private secretary standing by his side looking anxiously down at him.

'Yes, what's the problem?'

'An urgent telex from Brazil, sir.'

Eduardo read the first paragraph and then asked Manuel if he would be kind enough to excuse him for a few minutes. The latter nodded politely. Eduardo left the table and as he marched through the dining room seventeen other guests left unfinished meals and followed him quickly to his suite on the top floor, where the rest of his staff were already assembled. He sat down in the corner of the room on his own. No one spoke as he read through the telex carefully, suddenly realizing how many days he had been imprisoned in Lagos.

The telex was from his brother Carlos and the contents concerned the Pan-American road project, an eight-lane highway that would stretch from Brazil to Mexico. Prentinos had tendered for the section that ran through the middle of the Amazon jungle and had to have the bank guarantees signed and certified by midday tomorrow; Tuesday. But Eduardo had quite forgotten which Tuesday it was and the document he was committed to sign by the following day's deadline.

'What's the problem?' Eduardo asked his private secretary. 'The Banco do Brasil have already agreed with Alfredo to act as guarantors. What's stopping Carlos signing the agreement in my absence?'

'The Mexicans are now demanding that responsibility for the contract be shared because of the insurance problems: Lloyd's of London will not cover the entire risk if only one company is involved. The details are all on page seven of the telex.'

Eduardo flicked quickly through the pages. He read that his brothers had already tried to put pressure on Lloyd's, but to no avail. That's like trying to bribe a maiden aunt into taking part in a public orgy, thought Eduardo, and he would have told them as much if he had been back in Brazil. The Mexican Government was therefore insisting that the contract be shared with an international construction company acceptable to Lloyd's if the legal documents were to be signed by the midday deadline the following day.

'Stay put,' said Eduardo to his staff, and he returned to the dining room alone, trailing the long telex behind him. Rodrigues watched him as he scurried back to their table.

'You look like a man with a problem.'

'I am,' said Eduardo. 'Read that.'

Manuel's experienced eye ran down the telex, picking out the salient points. He had tendered for the Amazon road project himself and could still recall the details. At Eduardo's insistence, he re-read page seven.

'Mexican bandits,' he said as he returned the telex to Eduardo. 'Who do they think they are, telling Eduardo de Silveira how he must conduct his business. Telex them back immediately and inform them you're chairman of the greatest construction company in the world and they can roast in hell before you will agree to their pathetic terms. You know it's far too late for them to go out to tender again with every other section of the highway ready to begin work. They would lose millions. Call their bluff, Eduardo.'

'I think you may be right, Manuel, but any hold-up now can only waste my time and money, so I intend to agree to their demand and look for a partner.'

'You'll never find one at such short notice.'

'I will.'

'Who?'

Eduardo de Silveira hesitated only for a second. 'You, Manuel. I want to offer Rodrigues International SA fifty per cent of the Amazon road contract.'

Manuel Rodrigues looked up at Eduardo. It was the first time that he had not anticipated his old rival's next move. 'I suppose it might help cover the millions you owe me in table tennis debts.'

The two men laughed, then Rodrigues stood up and they shook hands gravely. De Silveira left the dining room on the run and wrote out a telex for his manager to transmit.

'Sign, accept terms, fifty per cent partner will be Rodrigues International Construction SA, Brazil.'

'If I telex that message, sir, you do realize that it's legally binding?'

'Send it,' said Eduardo.

Eduardo returned once again to the dining room where Manuel had ordered the finest bottle of champagne in the hotel. Just as they were calling for a second bottle, and singing a spirited version of *Esta Cheganda a hora*, Eduardo's private secretary appeared by his side again, this time with two telexes, one from the President of the Banco do Brasil and a second from his brother Carlos. Both wanted confirmation of the agreed partner for the

Amazon road project. Eduardo uncorked the second bottle of champagne without looking up at his private secretary.

'Confirm Rodrigues International Construction to the President of the bank and my brother,' he said as he filled Manuel's empty glass. 'And don't bother me again tonight.'

'Yes, sir,' said the private secretary and left without another word.

Neither man could recall what time he climbed into bed that night but de Silveira was abruptly awakened from a deep sleep by his secretary early the next morning. Eduardo took a few minutes to digest the news. Lieutenant Colonel Dimka had been caught in Kano at three o'clock that morning, and all the airports were now open again. Eduardo picked up the phone and dialled three digits.

'Manuel, you've heard the news? ... Good ... Then you must fly back with me in my 707 or it may be days before you get out ... One hour's time in the lobby ... See you then.'

At eight-forty-five there was a quiet knock on the door and Eduardo's secretary opened it to find Colonel Usman standing to attention, just as he had done in the days before the coup. He held a note in his hand. Eduardo tore open the envelope to find an invitation to lunch that day with the new Head of State, General Obasanjo.

'Please convey my apologies to your President,' said Eduardo, 'and be kind enough to explain that I have pressing commitments to attend to in my own country.'

The colonel retired reluctantly. Eduardo dressed in the suit, shirt and tie he had worn on his first day in Nigeria and took the lift downstairs to the lobby where he joined Manuel who was once more wearing jeans and a tee-shirt. The two chairmen left the hotel and climbed into the back of the leading Mercedes and the motorcade of six began its journey to the airport. The colonel, who now sat in front with the driver, did not venture to speak to either of the distinguished Brazilians for the entire journey. The two men, he would be able to tell the new President later, seemed to be preoccupied with a discussion on an Amazon road project and how the responsibility should be divided between their two companies.

Customs were bypassed as neither man had anything they wanted to take out of the country other than themselves, and the fleet of cars came to a halt at the side of Eduardo's blue and silver 707. The staff of both companies climbed aboard the rear section of the aircraft, also engrossed in discussion on the Amazon road project.

A corporal jumped out of the lead car and opened the back door, to allow the two chairmen to walk straight up the steps and board the front section of the aircraft.

As Eduardo stepped out of the Mercedes, the Nigerian driver saluted smartly. 'Goodbye, sir,' he said, revealing the large set of white teeth once again.

Eduardo said nothing.

'I hope,' said the corporal politely, 'you made very big deal while you were in Nigeria.'

The First Miracle

Tomorrow it would be 1 AD, but nobody had told him.

If anyone had, he wouldn't have understood because he thought that it was the forty-third year in the reign of the Emperor, and in any case, he had other things on his mind. His mother was still cross with him and he had to admit that he'd been naughty that day, even by the standards of a normal thirteen-year-old. He hadn't meant to drop the pitcher when she had sent him to the well for water. He tried to explain to his mother that it wasn't his fault that he had tripped over a stone; and that at least was true. What he hadn't told her was that he was chasing a stray dog at the time. And then there was that pomegranate; how was he meant to know that it was the last one, and that his father had taken a liking to them? The boy was now dreading his father's return and the possibility that he might be given another thrashing. He could still remember the last one when he hadn't been able to sit down for two days without feeling the pain, and the thin red scars didn't completely disappear for over three weeks.

He sat on the window ledge in a shaded corner of his room trying to think of some way he could redeem himself in his mother's eyes, now that she had thrown him out of the kitchen. Go outside and play, she had insisted, after he had spilt some cooking oil on his tunic. But that wasn't much fun as he was only allowed to play by himself. His father had forbidden him to mix with the local boys. How he hated this country; if only he were back home with his friends, there would be so much to do. Still, only another three weeks and he could ... The door swung open and his mother came into the room. She was dressed in the thin black garments so favoured by locals: they kept her cool, she had explained to the boy's father. He had grunted his disapproval so she always changed back into imperial dress before he returned in the evening.

'Ah, there you are,' she said, addressing the crouched figure of her son.

'Yes, Mother.'

'Daydreaming as usual. Well, wake up because I need you to go into the village and fetch some food for me.'

'Yes, Mother, I'll go at once,' the boy said as he jumped off the window ledge.

'Well, at least wait until you've heard what I want.'

'Sorry, Mother.'

'Now listen, and listen carefully.' She started counting on her fingers as she spoke. 'I need a chicken, some raisins, figs, dates and ... ah yes, two pomegranates.'

The boy's face reddened at the mention of the pomegranates and he stared down at the stone floor, hoping she might have forgotten. His mother put her hand into the leather purse that hung from her waist and removed two small coins, but before she handed them over she made her son repeat the instructions.

'One chicken, raisins, figs, dates, and two pomegranates,' he recited, as he might the modern poet, Virgil.

'And be sure to see they give you the correct change,' she added. 'Never forget the locals are all thieves.'

'Yes, Mother ...' For a moment the boy hesitated.

'If you remember everything and bring back the right amount of money, I might forget to tell your father about the broken pitcher and the pomegranate.'

The boy smiled, pocketed the two small silver coins in his tunic, and ran out of the house into the compound. The guard who stood on duty at the gate removed the great wedge of wood which allowed the massive door to swing open. The boy jumped through the hole in the gate and grinned back at the guard.

'Been in more trouble again today?' the guard shouted after him.

'No, not this time,' the boy replied. 'I'm about to be saved.'

He waved farewell to the guard and started to walk briskly towards the village while humming a tune that reminded him of home. He kept to the centre of the dusty winding path that the locals had the nerve to call a road. He seemed to spend half his time removing little stones from his sandals. If his father had been posted here for any length of time he would have made some changes; then they would have had a real road, straight and wide enough to take a chariot. But not before his mother had sorted out the serving girls. Not one of them knew how to lay a table or even prepare food so that it was at least clean. For the first time in his life he had seen his mother in a kitchen, and he felt sure it would be the last, as they would all be returning home now that his father was coming to the end of his assignment.

The evening sun shone down on him as he walked; it was a very large red sun, the same red as his father's tunic. The heat it gave out made him sweat and long for something to drink. Perhaps there would be enough money left over to buy himself a pomegranate. He couldn't wait to take one home and show his friends how large they were in this barbaric land. Marcus, his best friend, would undoubtedly have seen one as big because his father had commanded a whole army in these parts, but the rest of the class would still be impressed.

The village to which his mother had sent him was only two miles from the compound and the dusty path ran alongside a hill overlooking a large valley. The road was already crowded with travellers who would be seeking shelter in the village. All of them had come down from the hills at the express orders of his father, whose authority had been vested in him by the Emperor himself. Once he was sixteen, he too would serve the Emperor. His friend Marcus wanted to be a soldier and conquer the rest of the world. But he was more interested in the law and teaching his country's customs to the heathens in strange lands.

Marcus had said, 'I'll conquer them and then you can govern them.'

A sensible division between brains and brawn he had told his friend, who didn't seem impressed and had ducked him in the nearest bath.

The boy quickened his pace as he knew he had to be back in the compound before the sun disappeared behind the hills. His father had told him many times that he must always be locked safely inside before sunset. He was aware that his father was not a popular man with the locals, and he had warned his son that he would always be safe while it was light as no one would dare to harm him while others could watch what was going on, but once it was dark anything could happen. One thing he knew for certain: when he grew up he wasn't going to be a tax collector or work in the census office.

When he reached the village he found the narrow twisting lanes that ran between the little white houses swarming with people who had come from all the neighbouring lands to obey his father's order and be registered for the census, in order that they might be taxed. The boy dismissed the plebs from his mind. (It was Marcus who had taught him to refer to all foreigners as plebs.) When he entered the market place he also dismissed Marcus from his mind and began to concentrate on the supplies his mother wanted. He mustn't make any mistakes this time or he would undoubtedly end up with that thrashing from his father. He ran nimbly between the stalls, checking the food carefully. Some of the local people stared at the fair-skinned boy with the curly brown hair and the straight, firm nose. He displayed no imperfections or disease like the majority of them. Others turned their eyes away from him; after all, he had come from the land of the natural rulers. These thoughts did not pass through his mind. All the boy noticed was that their native skins were parched and lined from too much sun. He knew that too much sun was bad for you: it made you old before your time, his tutor had warned him.

At the end stall, the boy watched an old woman haggling over an unusually plump live chicken and as he marched towards her she ran away in fright, leaving the fowl behind her. He stared at the stallkeeper and refused to bargain with the peasant. It was beneath his dignity. He pointed to the chicken and gave the man one denarius. The man bit the round silver coin and looked at the head of Augustus Caesar, ruler of half the world. (When his tutor had told him, during a history lesson, about the Emperor's achievements, he remembered thinking, I hope Caesar doesn't conquer the whole world before I have a chance to join in.) The stallkeeper was still staring at the silver coin.

'Come on, come on, I haven't got all day,' said the boy sounding like his father.

The local did not reply because he couldn't understand what the boy was saying. All he knew for certain was that it would be unwise for him to annoy the invader. The stallkeeper held the chicken firmly by the neck and taking a knife from his belt cut its head off in one movement and passed the dead fowl over to the boy. He then handed back some of his local coins, which had stamped on them the image of a man the boy's father described as 'that useless Herod'. The boy kept his hand held out, palm open, and the local placed bronze talents into it until he had no more. The boy left him talentless and moved to another stall, this time pointing to bags containing raisins, figs and dates. The new stallkeeper made a measure of each for which he received five of the useless Herod coins. The man was about to protest about the barter but the boy stared at him fixedly in the eyes, the way he had seen his father do so often. The stallkeeper backed away and only bowed his head.

Now, what else did his mother want? He racked his brains. A chicken, raisins, dates, figs and ... of course, two pomegranates. He searched among the fresh-fruit stalls and picked out three pomegranates, and breaking one open, began to eat it, spitting out the pips on the ground in front of him. He paid the stallkeeper with the two remaining bronze talents, feeling pleased that he had carried out his mother's wishes while still being able to return home with one of the silver denarii. Even his father would be impressed by that. He finished the pomegranate and, with his arms laden, headed slowly out of the market back towards the compound, trying to avoid the stray dogs that continually got under his feet. They barked and sometimes snapped at his ankles: they did not know who he was.

When the boy reached the edge of the village he noticed the sun was already disappearing behind the highest hill, so he quickened his pace, remembering his father's words about being home before dusk. As he walked down the stony path, those still on the way towards the village kept a respectful distance, leaving him a clear vision as far as the eye could see, which wasn't all that far as he was carrying so much in his arms. But one sight he did notice a little way ahead of him was a man with a beard – a dirty, lazy habit his father had told him – wearing the ragged dress that signified that he was of the tribe of Jacob, tugging a reluctant donkey which in turn was carrying a very fat woman. The woman was, as their custom demanded, covered from head to toe in black. The boy was about to order them out of his path when the man left the donkey on the side of the road and went into a house which from its sign, claimed to be an inn.

Such a building in his own land would never have passed the scrutiny of the local councillors as a place fit for paying travellers to dwell in. But the boy realized that this particular week to find even a mat to lay one's head on might be considered a luxury. He watched the bearded man reappear through the door with a forlorn look on his tired face. There was clearly no room at the inn.

The boy could have told him that before he went in, and wondered what the man would do next, as it was the last dwelling house on the road. Not that he was really interested; they could both sleep in the hills for all he cared. It was about all they looked fit for. The man with the beard was telling the woman something and pointing behind the inn, and without another word he led the donkey off in the direction he had been indicating. The boy wondered what could possibly be at the back of the inn and, his curiosity roused, followed them. As he came to the corner of the building, he saw the man was coaxing the donkey through an open door of what looked like a barn. The boy followed the strange trio and watched them through the crack left by the open door. The barn was covered in dirty straw and full of chickens, sheep and oxen, and smelled to the boy like the sewers they built in the side streets back home. He began to feel sick. The man was clearing away some of the worst of the straw from the centre of the barn, trying to make a clean patch for them to rest on – a near hopeless task, thought the boy. When the man had done as best he could he lifted the fat woman down from the donkey and placed her gently in the straw. Then he left her and went over to a trough on the other side of the barn where one of the oxen was drinking. He cupped his fingers together, put them in the trough and filling his hands with water, returned to the fat woman.

The boy was beginning to get bored and was about to leave when the woman leaned forward to drink from the man's hands. The shawl fell from her head and he saw her face for the first time.

He stood transfixed, staring at her. He had never seen anything more beautiful. Unlike the common members of her tribe, the woman's skin was translucent in quality, and her eyes shone, but what most struck the boy was her manner and presence. Never had he felt so much in awe, even remembering his one visit to the Senate House to hear a declamation from Augustus Caesar.

For a moment he remained mesmerized, but then he knew what he must do. He walked through the open door towards the woman, fell on his knees before her and offered the chicken. She smiled and he gave her the pomegranates and she smiled again. He then dropped the rest of the food in front of her, but she remained silent. The man with the beard was returning with more water, and when he saw the young foreigner he fell on his knees spilling the water onto the straw and then covered his face. The boy stayed on his knees for some time before he rose, and walked slowly towards the barn door. When he reached the opening, he turned back and stared once more into the face of the beautiful woman. She still did not speak.

The young Roman hesitated only for a second, and then bowed his head.

It was already dusk when he ran back out onto the winding path to resume his journey home, but he was not afraid. Rather he felt he had done something good and therefore no harm could come to him. He looked up into the sky and saw directly above him the first star, shining so brightly in the east that he wondered why he could see no others. His father had told him that different stars were visible in different lands, so he dismissed the puzzle from his mind, replacing it with the anxiety of not being home before dark. The road in front of him was now empty so he was able to walk quickly towards the compound, and was not all that far from safety when he first heard the singing and shouting. He turned quickly to see where the danger was coming from, staring up into the hills above him. To begin with, he couldn't make sense of what he saw. Then his eyes focused in disbelief on one particular field in which the shepherds were leaping up and down, singing, shouting and clapping their hands. The boy noticed that all the sheep were safely penned in a corner of the field for the night, so they had nothing to fear. He had been told by Marcus that sometimes the shepherds in this land would make a lot of noise at night because they believed it kept away the evil spirits. How could anyone be that stupid, the boy wondered, when there was a flash of lightning across the sky and the field was suddenly ablaze with light. The shepherds fell to their knees, silent, staring up into the sky for several minutes as though they were listening intently to something. Then all was darkness again.

The boy started running towards the compound as fast as his legs could carry him; he wanted to be inside and hear the safety of the great gate close behind him and watch the centurion put the wooden wedge firmly back in its place. He would have run all the way had he not seen something in front of him that brought him to a sudden halt. His father had taught him never to show any fear when facing danger. The boy caught his breath in case it would make them think that he was frightened. He was frightened, but he marched proudly on, determined he would never be forced off the road. When they did meet face to face, he was amazed.

Before him stood three camels and astride the beasts three men, who stared down at him. The first was clad in gold and with one arm proteted something hidden beneath his cloak. By his side hung a large sword, its sheath covered in all manner of rare stones, some of which the boy could not even name. The second was dressed in white and held a silver casket to his breast, while the third wore red and carried a large wooden box. The man robed in gold put up his hand and addressed the boy in a strange tongue which he had never heard uttered before, even by his tutor. The second man tried Hebrew but to no avail and the third yet another tongue without eliciting any response from the boy.

The boy folded his arms across his chest and told them who he was, where he was going, and asked where they might be bound. He hoped his piping voice did not reveal his fear. The one robed in gold replied first and questioned the boy in his own tongue.

'Where is he that is born King of the Jews? For we have seen his star in the east, and are come to worship him.'

'King Herod lives beyond the . . .'

'We speak not of King Herod,' said the second man, 'for he is but a king of men as we are.'

'We speak,' said the third, 'of the King of Kings and are come to offer him gifts of gold, frankincense and myrrh.'

'I know nothing of the King of Kings,' said the boy, now gaining in confidence. 'I recognize only Augustus Caesar, Emperor of the known world.'

The man robed in gold shook his head and, pointing to the sky, inquired of the boy: 'You observe that bright star in the east. What is the name of the village on which it shines?'

The boy looked up at the star, and indeed the village below was clearer to the eye than it had been in sunlight.

'But that's only Bethlehem,' said the boy, laughing. 'You will find no King of Kings there.'

'Even there we shall find him,' said the second king, 'for did not Herod's chief priest tell us:

And thou Bethlehem, in the land of Judah,
Art not least among the princes of Judah,
For out of thee shall come a Governor
That shall rule my people Israel.'

'It cannot be,' said the boy now almost shouting at them. 'Augustus Caesar rules Israel and all the known world.'

But the three robed men did not heed his words and left him to ride on towards Bethlehem.

Mystified the boy set out on the last part of his journey home. Although the sky had become pitch black, whenever he turned his eyes towards

Bethlehem the village was still clearly visible in the brilliant starlight. Once again he started running towards the compound, relieved to see its outline rising up in front of him. When he reached the great wooden gate, he banged loudly and repeatedly until a centurion, sword drawn, holding a flaming torch, came out to find out who it was that disturbed his watch. When he saw the boy, he frowned.

'Your father is very angry. He returned at sunset and is about to send out a search party for you.'

The boy darted past the centurion and ran all the way to his family's quarters, where he found his father addressing a sergeant of the guard. His mother was standing by his side, weeping.

The father turned when he saw his son and shouted: 'Where have you been?'

'To Bethlehem.'

'Yes, I know that, but whatever possessed you to return so late? Have I not told you countless times never to be out of the compound after dark? Come to my study at once.'

The boy looked helplessly towards his mother, who was still crying, but not out of relief, and turned to follow his father into the study. The guard sergeant winked at him as he passed by but the boy knew nothing could save him now. His father strode ahead of him into the study and sat on a leather stool by his table. His mother followed and stood silently by the door.

'Now tell me exactly where you have been and why you took so long to return, and be sure to tell me the truth.'

The boy stood in front of his father and told him everything that had come to pass. He started with how he had gone to the village and taken great care in choosing the food and in so doing had saved half the money his mother had given him. How on the way back he had seen a fat lady on a donkey unable to find a place at the inn and then he explained why he had given her the food. He went on to describe how the shepherds had shouted and beat their breasts until there was a great light in the sky at which they had all fallen silent on their knees, and then finally how he had met the three robed men who were searching for the King of Kings.

The father grew angry at his son's words.

'What a story you tell,' he shouted. 'Do tell me more. Did you find this King of Kings?'

'No, Sir. I did not,' he replied, as he watched his father rise and start pacing around the room.

'Perhaps there is a more simple explanation as to why your face and fingers are stained red with pomegranate juice,' he suggested.

'No, Father. I did buy an extra pomegranate but even after I had bought all the food, I still managed to save one silver denarius.'

The boy handed the coin over to his mother believing it would confirm his story. But the sight of the piece of silver only made his father more angry. He stopped pacing and stared down into the eyes of his son.

'You have spent the other denarius on yourself and now you have nothing to show for it?'

'That's not true, Father, I ...'

'Then I will allow you one more chance to tell me the truth,' said his father as he sat back down. 'Fail me, boy, and I shall give you a thrashing that you will never forget for the rest of your life.'

'I have already told you the truth, Father.'

'Listen to me carefully, my son. We were born Romans, born to rule the world because our laws and customs are tried and trusted and have always been based firmly on absolute honesty. Romans never lie; it remains our strength and the weakness of our enemies. That is why we rule while others are ruled and as long as that is so the Roman Empire will never fall. Do you understand what I am saying, my boy?'

'Yes, Father, I understand.'

'Then you'll also understand why it is imperative to tell the truth.'

'But I have not lied, Father.'

'Then there is no hope for you,' said the man angrily. 'And you leave me only one way to deal with this matter.'

The boy's mother wanted to come to her son's aid, but knew any protest would be useless. The father rose from his chair and removed the leather belt from around his waist and folded it double, leaving the heavy brass studs on the outside. He then ordred his son to touch his toes. The young boy obeyed without hesitation and the father raised the leather strap above his head and brought it down on the child with all his strength. The boy never flinched or murmured, while his mother turned away from the sight, and wept. After the father had administered the twelfth stroke he ordered his son to go to his room. The boy left without a word and his mother followed and watched him climb the stairs. She then hurried away to the kitchen and gathered together some olive oil and ointments which she hoped would soothe the pain of her son's wounds. She carried the little jars up to his room, where she found him already in bed. She went over to his side and pulled the sheet back. He turned on to his chest while she prepared the oils. Then she removed his night tunic gently for fear of adding to his pain. Having done so, she stared down at his body in disbelief.

The boy's skin was unmarked.

She ran her fingers gently over her son's unblemished body and found it to be as smooth as if he had just bathed. She turned him over, but there was not a mark on him anywhere. Quickly she covered him with the sheet.

'Say nothing of this to your father, and remove the memory of it from your mind forever, because the very telling of it will only make him more angry.'

'Yes, Mother.'

The mother leaned over and blew out the candle by the side of the bed, gathered up the unused oils and tiptoed to the door. At the threshold, she turned in the dim light to look back at her son and said:

'Now I know you were telling the truth, Pontius.'

The Perfect Gentleman

I would never have met Edward Shrimpton if he hadn't needed a towel. He stood naked by my side staring down at a bench in front of him, muttering, 'I could have sworn I left the damn thing there.'

I had just come out of the sauna, swathed in towels, so I took one off my shoulder and passed it to him. He thanked me and put out his hand.

'Edward Shrimpton,' he said smiling. I took his hand and wondered what we must have looked like standing there in the gymnasium locker room of the Metropolitan Club in the early evening, two grown men shaking hands in the nude.

'I don't remember seeing you in the club before,' he added.

'No, I'm an overseas member.'

'Ah, from England. What brings you to New York?'

'I'm pursuing an American novelist whom my company would like to publish in England.'

'And are you having any success?'

'Yes, I think I'll close the deal this week – as long as the agent stops trying to convince me that his author is a cross between Tolstoy and Dickens and should be paid accordingly.'

'Neither was paid particularly well, if I remember correctly,' offered Edward Shrimpton as he energetically rubbed the towel up and down his back.

'A fact I pointed out to the agent at the time who only countered by reminding me that it was my House who had published Dickens originally.'

'I suggest,' said Edward Shrimpton, 'that you *remind* him that the end result turned out to be successful for all concerned.'

'I did, but I fear this agent is more interested in "up front" than posterity.'

'As a banker that's a sentiment of which I could hardly disapprove as the one thing we have in common with publishers is that our clients are always trying to tell us a good tale.'

'Perhaps you should sit down and write one of them for me?' I said politely.

'Heaven forbid, you must be sick of being told that there's a book in every one of us so I hasten to assure you that there isn't one in me.'

I laughed, as I found it refreshing not to be informed by a new acquaintance that his memoirs, if only he could find the time to write them, would overnight, be one of the world's best sellers.

'Perhaps there's a story in you, but you're just not aware of it,' I suggested.

'If that's the case, I'm afraid it's passed me by.'

Mr Shrimpton re-emerged from behind the row of little tin cubicles and handed me back my towel. He was now fully dressed and stood, I would have guessed, a shade under six feet. He wore a Wall Street banker's pinstripe suit and, although he was nearly bald, he had a remarkable physique for a man who must have been well into his sixties. Only his thick white moustache gave away his true age, and would have been more in keeping with a retired English colonel than a New York banker.

'Are you going to be in New York long?' he inquired, as he took a small leather case from his inside pocket and removed a pair of half-moon spectacles and placed them on the end of his nose.

'Just for the week.'

'I don't suppose you're free for lunch tomorrow, by any chance?' he inquired, peering over the top of his glasses.

'Yes, I am. I certainly can't face another meal with that agent.'

'Good, good, then why don't you join me and I can follow the continuing drama of capturing the elusive American Author?'

'And perhaps I'll discover there is a story in you after all.'

'Not a hope,' he said, 'you would be backing a loser if you depend on that,' and once again he offered his hand. 'One o'clock, members' dining room suit you?'

'One o'clock, members' dining room,' I repeated.

As he left the locker room I walked over to the mirror and straightened my tie. I was dining that night with Eric McKenzie, a publishing friend, who had originally proposed me for membership of the club. To be accurate, Eric McKenzie was a friend of my father rather than myself. They had met just before the war while on holiday in Portugal and when I was elected to the club, soon after my father's retirement, Eric took it upon himself to have dinner with me whenever I was in New York. One's parents' generation never see one as anything but a child who will always be in need of constant care and attention. As he was a contemporary of my father, Eric must have been nearly seventy and, although hard of hearing and slightly bent, he was always amusing and good company, even if he did continually ask me if I was aware that his grandfather was Scottish.

As I strapped on my watch, I checked that he was due to arrive in a few minutes. I put on my jacket and strolled out into the hall to find that he was already there, waiting for me. Eric was killing time by reading the out-of-date club notices. Americans, I have observed, can always be relied upon to arrive early or late; never on time. I stood staring at the stooping man, whose hair but for a few strands had now turned silver. His three-piece suit had a button missing on the jacket which reminded me that his wife had died last year. After another thrust-out hand and exchange of welcomes, we took the lift to the second floor and walked to the dining room.

The members' dining room at the Metropolitan differs little from any other men's club. It has a fair sprinkling of old leather chairs, old carpets, old portraits and old members. A waiter guided us to a corner table which overlooked Central Park. We ordered, and then settled back to discuss all the subjects I found I usually cover with an acquaintance I only have the chance to catch up with a couple of times a year – our families, children, mutual friends, work; baseball and cricket. By the time we had reached cricket we had also reached coffee, so we strolled down to the far end of the room and made ourselves comfortable in two well-worn leather chairs. When the coffee arrived I ordered two brandies and watched Eric unwrap a large Cuban cigar. Although they displayed a West Indian band on the outside, I knew they were Cuban because I had picked them up for him from a tobacconist in St James's, Piccadilly, which specializes in changing the labels for its American customers. I have often thought that they must be the only shop in the world that changes labels with the sole purpose of making a superior product appear inferior. I am certain my wine merchant does it the other way round.

While Eric was attempting to light the cigar, my eyes wandered to a board on the wall. To be more accurate it was a highly polished wooden plaque with oblique golden lettering painted on it, honouring those men who over the years had won the club's Backgammon Championship. I glanced idly down the list, not expecting to see anybody with whom I would be familiar, when I was brought up by the name of Edward Shrimpton. Once in the late thirties he had been the runner-up.

'That's interesting,' I said.

'What is?' asked Eric, now wreathed in enough smoke to have puffed himself out of Grand Central Station.

'Edward Shrimpton was runner-up in the club's Backgammon Championship in the late thirties. I'm having lunch with him tomorrow.'

'I didn't realize you knew him.'

'I didn't until this afternoon,' I said, and then explained how we had met.

Eric laughed and turned to stare up at the board. Then he added, rather mysteriously: 'That's a night I'm never likely to forget.'

'Why?' I asked.

Eric hesitated, and looked uncertain of himself before continuing: 'Too much water has passed under the bridge for anyone to care now.' He paused again, as a hot piece of ash fell to the floor and added to the burn marks that made their own private pattern in the carpet. 'Just before the war Edward Shrimpton was among the best half dozen backgammon players in the world. In fact, it must have been around that time he won the unofficial world championship in Monte Carlo.'

'And he couldn't win the club championship?'

'Couldn't would be the wrong word, dear boy. "Didn't" might be more accurate.' Eric lapsed into another preoccupied silence.

'Are you going to explain?' I asked, hoping he would continue, 'or am I to be left like a child who wants to know who killed Cock Robin?'

'All in good time, but first allow me to get this damn cigar started.'

I remained silent and four matches later, he said 'Before I begin, take a look at the man sitting over there in the corner with the young blonde.'

I turned and glanced back towards the dining room area, and saw a man attacking a porterhouse steak. He looked about the same age as Eric and wore a smart new suit that was unable to disguise that he had a weight problem: only his tailor could have smiled at him with any pleasure. He was seated opposite a slight, not unattractive strawberry blonde of half his age who could have trodden on a beetle and failed to crush it.

'What an unlikely pair. Who are they?'

'Harry Newman and his fourth wife. They're always the same. The wives I mean – blonde hair, blue eyes, ninety pounds, and dumb. I can never understand why any man gets divorced only to marry a carbon copy of the original.'

'Where does Edward Shrimpton fit into the jigsaw?' I asked, trying to guide Eric back on to the subject.

'Patience, patience,' said my host, as he relit his cigar for the second time. 'At your age you've far more time to waste than I have.'

I laughed and picked up the cognac nearest to me and swirled the brandy around in my cupped hands.

'Harry Newman,' continued Eric, now almost hidden in smoke, 'was the fellow who beat Edward Shrimptom in the final of the club championship that year, although in truth he was never in the same class as Edward.'

'Do explain,' I said, as I looked up at the board to check that it was Newman's name that preceded Edward Shrimpton's.

'Well,' said Eric, 'after the semi-final, which Edward had won with consummate ease, we all assumed the final would only be a formality. Harry had always been a good player, but as I had been the one to lose to him in the semi-finals, I knew he couldn't hope to survive a contest with Edward Shrimpton. The club final is won by the first man to twenty-one points, and if I had been asked for an opinion at the time I would have reckoned the result would end up around 21–5 in Edward's favour. Damn cigar,' he said, and lit it for a fourth time. Once again I waited impatiently.

'The final is always held on a Saturday night, and poor Harry over there,' said Eric, pointing his cigar towards the far corner of the room while depositing some more ash on the floor, 'who all of us thought was doing rather well in the insurance business, had a bankruptcy notice served on him the Monday morning before the final – I might add through no fault of his own. His partner had cashed in his stock without Harry's knowledge, disappeared, and left him with all the bills to pick up. Everyone in the club was sympathetic.

'On the Thursday the press got hold of the story, and for good measure they added that Harry's wife had run off with the partner. Harry didn't show his head in the club all week, and some of us wondered if he would scratch from the final and let Edward win by default as the result was such a foregone conclusion anyway. But the Games Committee received no communication from Harry to suggest the contest was off so they proceeded as though nothing had happened. On the night of the final, I dined with Edward Shrimpton here in the club. He was in fine form. He ate very little and drank nothing but a glass of water. If you had asked me then I wouldn't have put a penny on Harry Newman even if the odds had been ten to one.

'We all dined upstairs on the third floor, as the Committee had cleared this room so that they could seat sixty in a square around the board. The final was due to start at nine o'clock. By twenty to nine there wasn't a seat left in the place, and members were already standing two deep behind the square: it wasn't every day we had the chance to see a world champion in action. By five to nine, Harry still hadn't turned up and some of the members were beginning to get a little restless. As nine o'clock chimed, the referee went over to Edward and had a word with him. I saw Edward shake his head in disagreement and walk away. Just at the point, when I thought the referee would have to be firm and award the match to Edward, Harry strolled in looking very dapper adorned in a dinner jacket several sizes smaller than the suit he is wearing tonight. Edward went straight up to him, shook him warmly by the hand and together they walked into the centre of the room. Even with the throw of the first dice there was a tension about that match. Members were waiting to see how Harry would fare in the opening game.'

The intermittent cigar went out again. I leaned over and struck a match for him.

'Thank you, dear boy. Now, where was I? Oh, yes, the first game. Well, Edward only just won the first game and I wondered if he wasn't concentrating or if perhaps he had become a little too relaxed while waiting for his opponent. In the second game the dice ran well for Harry and he won fairly easily. From that moment on it became a finely fought battle, and by the time the score had reached 11–9 in Edward's favour the tension in the room was quite electric. By the ninth game I began watching more carefully and noticed that Edward allowed himself to be drawn into a back game, a small error in judgement that only a seasoned player would have spotted. I wondered how many more subtle errors had already passed that I hadn't observed. Harry went on to win the ninth making the score 18–17 in his favour. I watched even more diligently as Edward did just enough to win the tenth game and, with a rash double, just enough to lose the eleventh, bring the score to 20 all, so that everything would depend on the final game. I swear that nobody had left the room that evening, and not one back remained against a chair; some members were even hanging on to the window ledges. The room was now full of drink and thick with cigar smoke, and yet when Harry picked up the dice cup for the last game you could hear the little squares of ivory rattle before they hit the board. The dice ran well for Harry in that final game and Edward only made one small error early on that I was able to pick up; but it was enough to give Harry game, match and championship. After the last throw of the dice everyone in that room, including Edward, gave the new champion a standing ovation.'

'Had many other members worked out what had really happened that night?'

'No, I don't think so,' said Eric. 'And certainly Harry Newman hadn't. The talk afterwards was that Harry had never played a better game in his life and what a worthy champion he was, all the more for the difficulties he laboured under.'

'Did Edward have anything to say?'

'Toughest match he'd been in since Monte Carlo and only hoped he would be given the chance to avenge the defeat next year.'

'But he wasn't,' I said, looking up again at the board. 'He never won the club championship.'

'That's right. After Roosevelt had insisted we help you guys out in England, the club didn't hold the competition again until 1946, and by then Edward had been to war and had lost all interest in the game.'

'And Harry?'

'Oh, Harry. Harry never looked back after that; must have made a dozen deals in the club that night. Within a year he was on top again and even found himself another cute little blonde.'

'What does Edward say about the result now, thirty years later?'

'Do you know that remains a mystery to this day. I have never heard him mention the game once in all that time.'

Eric's cigar had come to the end of its working life and he stubbed the remains out in an ashless ashtray. It obviously acted as a signal to remind him that it was time to go home. He rose a little unsteadily and I walked down with him to the front door.

'Goodbye my boy,' he said, 'do give Edward my best wishes when you have lunch with him tomorrow. And remember not to play him at backgammon. He'd still kill you.'

. . .

The next day I arrived in the front hall a few minutes before our appointed time, not sure if Edward Shrimpton would fall into the category of early or late Americans. As the clock stuck one, he walked through the door: there has to be an exception to every rule. We agreed to go straight up to lunch since he had to be back in Wall Street for a two-thirty appointment. We stepped into the packed lift, and I pressed the No. 3 button. The doors closed like a tired concertina and the slowest lift in America made its way towards the second floor.

As we entered the dining room, I was amused to see Harry Newman was already there, attacking another steak, while the little blonde lady was nibbling a salad. He waved expansively at Edward Shrimpton, who returned the gesture with a friendly nod. We sat down at a table in the centre of the room and studied the menu. Steak and kidney pie was the dish of the day, which was probably the case in half the mens' clubs in the world. Edward wrote down our orders in a neat and legible hand on the little white slip provided by the waiter.

Edward asked me about the author I was chasing and made some penetrating comments about her earlier work, to which I responded as best I could while trying to think of a plot to make him discuss the pre-war backgammon championship, which I considered would make a far better story than anything she had ever written. But he never talked about himself once during the meal, so I despaired. Finally, staring up at the plaque on the wall, I said clumsily:

'I see you were runner-up in the club backgammon championship just before the war. You must have been a fine player.'

'No, not really,' he replied. 'Not many people bothered about the game in those days. There is a different attitude today with all the youngsters taking it so seriously.'

'What about the champion?' I said, pushing my luck.

'Harry Newman? – He was an outstanding player, and particularly good under pressure. He's the gentleman who greeted us when we came in. That's him sitting over there in the corner with his wife.'

I looked obediently towards Mr Newman's table but my host added nothing more so I gave up. We ordered coffee and that would have been the end of Edward's story if Harry Newman and his wife had not headed straight for us after they had finished their lunch. Edward was on his feet long before I was, despite my twenty-year advantage. Harry Newman looked even bigger standing up, and his little blonde wife looked more like the dessert than his spouse.

'Ed,' he boomed, 'how are you?'

'I'm well, thank you, Harry,' Edward replied. 'May I introduce my guest?'

'Nice to know you,' he said. 'Rusty, I've always wanted you to meet Ed Shrimpton because I've talked to you about him so often in the past.'

'Have you, Harry?' she squeaked.

'Of course. You remember, honey. Ed is up there on the backgammon honours board,' he said, pointing a stubby finger towards the plaque. 'With only one name in front of him and that's mine. And Ed was the world champion at the time. Isn't that right, Ed?'

'That's right, Harry.'

'So I suppose I really should have been the world champion that year, wouldn't you say?'

'I couldn't quarrel with that conclusion,' replied Edward.

'On the big day, Rusty, when it really mattered, and the pressure was on, I beat him fair and square.'

I stood in silent disbelief as Edward Shrimpton still volunteered no disagreement.

'We must play again for old times' sake, Ed,' the fat man continued. 'It would be fun to see if you could beat me now. Mind you, I'm a bit rusty nowadays, Rusty.' He laughed loudly at his own joke but his spouse's face remained blank. I wondered how long it would be before there was a fifth Mrs Newman.

'It's been great to see you again, Ed. Take care of yourself.'

'Thank you, Harry,' said Edward.

We both sat down again as Newman and his wife left the dining room. Our coffee was now cold so we ordered a fresh pot. The room was almost empty and when I had poured two cups for us Edward leaned over to me conspiratorially and whispered:

'Now there's a hell of a story for a publisher like you,' he said. 'I mean the real truth about Harry Newman.'

My ears pricked up as I anticipated his version of the story of what had actually happened on the night of that pre-war backgammon championship over thirty years before.

'Really?' I said, innocently.

'Oh, yes,' said Edward. 'It was not as simple as you might think. Just before the war Harry was let down very badly by his business partner who not only stole his money, but for good measure his wife as well. The very week that he was at his lowest he won the club backgammon championship, put all his troubles behind him and, against the odds, made a brilliant comeback. You know, he's worth a fortune today. Now, wouldn't you agree that that would make one hell of a story?'

One-Night Stand

The two men had first met at the age of five when they were placed side by side at school, for no more compelling reason than that their names, Thompson and Townsend, came one after each other on the class register. They soon became best friends, a tie which at that age is more binding than any marriage. After passing their eleven-plus examination they proceeded to the local grammar school with no Timpsons, Tooleys or Tomlinsons to divide them and, having completed seven years in that academic institution, reached an age when one either has to go to work or to university. They opted for the latter on the grounds that work should be put off until the last possible moment. Happily, they both possessed enough brains and native wit to earn themselves places at Durham University to read English.

Undergraduate life turned out to be as sociable as primary school. They both enjoyed English, tennis, cricket, good food and girls. Luckily, in the last of these predilections they differed only on points of detail. Michael, who was six-foot-two, willowy with dark curly hair, preferred tall, bosomy blondes with blue eyes and long legs. Adrian, a stocky man of five-foot-ten, with straight, sandy hair always fell for small, slim, dark-haired, dark-eyed girls. So whenever Adrian came across a girl that Michael took an interest in or vice versa, whether she was an undergraduate or barmaid, the one would happily exaggerate their friend's virtues. Thus they spent three idyllic years in unison at Durham, gaining considerably more than a Bachelor of Arts degree. As neither of them had impressed the examiners enough to waste a further two years expounding their theories for a Ph.D. they could no longer avoid the real world.

Twin Dick Whittingtons, they set off for London, where Michael joined the BBC as a trainee while Adrian was signed up by Benton & Bowles, the international advertising agency, as an accounts assistant. They acquired a small flat in the Earl's Court Road which they painted orange and brown, and proceeded to live the life of two young blades, for that is undoubtedly how they saw themselves.

Both men spent a further five years in this blissful bachelor state until they each fell for a girl who fulfilled their particular requirements. They were married within weeks of each other; Michael to a tall, blue-eyed blonde whom he met while playing tennis at the Hurlingham Club: Adrian to a slim, dark-eyed, dark-haired executive in charge of the Kellogg's Cornflakes account. Both officiated as the other's best man and each proceeded to sire three children at yearly intervals, and in that again they differed, but as before only on points of detail, Michael having two sons and a daughter, Adrian two daughters and a son. Each became godfather to the other's first-born son.

Marriage hardly separated them in anything as they continued to follow much of their old routine, playing cricket together at weekends in the summer and football in the winter, not to mention regular luncheons during the week.

After the celebration of his tenth wedding anniversary, Michael, now a senior producer with Thames Television, admitted rather coyly to Adrian that he had had his first affair: he had been unable to resist a tall, well-built blonde from the typing pool who was offering more than shorthand at seventy words a minute. Only a few weeks later, Adrian, now a senior account manager with Pearl and Dean, also went under, selecting a journalist from Fleet Street who was seeking some inside information on one of the companies he represented. She became a tax-deductible item. After that, the two men quickly fell back into their old routine. Any help they could give each other was provided unstintingly, creating no conflict of interests because of their different tastes. Their married lives were not suffering – or so they convinced each other – and at thirty-five, having come through the swinging sixties unscathed, they began to make the most of the seventies.

Early in that decade, Thames Television decided to send Michael off to America to edit an ABC film about living in New York, for consumption by British viewers. Adrian, who had always wanted to see the eastern seaboard, did not find it hard to arrange a trip at the same time as he claimed it was necessary for him to carry out some more than usually spurious research for an Anglo-American tobacco company. The two men enjoyed a lively week together in New York, the highlight of which was a party held by ABC on the final evening to view the edited edition of Michael's film on New York, 'An Englishman's View of the Big Apple'.

When Michael and Adrian arrived at the ABC studios they found the party was already well under way, and both entered the room together, looking forward to a few drinks and an early night before their journey back to England the next day.

They spotted her at exactly the same moment.

She was of medium height and build with soft green eyes and auburn hair – a striking combination of both men's fantasies. Without another thought each knew exactly where he desired to end up that particular night and, in a minds with but a single idea, they advanced purposefully upon her.

'Hello, my name is Michael Thompson.'

'Hello,' she replied. 'I'm Debbie Kendall.'

'And I'm Adrian Townsend.'

She offered her hand and both tried to grab it. When the party had come to an end, they had, between them, discovered that Debbie Kendall was an ABC floor producer on the evening news spot. She was divorced and had two children who lived with her in New York. But neither of them was any nearer to impressing her, if only because each worked so hard to outdo the other; they both showed off abominably and even squabbled over fetching their new companion her food and drink. In the other's absence they found themselves running down their closest friend in a subtle but damning way.

'Adrian's a nice chap if it wasn't for his drinking,' said Michael.

'Super fellow Michael, such a lovely wife and you should see his three adorable children,' added Adrian.

They both escorted Debbie home and reluctantly left her on the doorstep of her 68th Street apartment. She kissed the two of them perfunctorily on the cheek, thanked them and said goodnight. They walked back to their hotel in silence.

When they reached their room on the nineteenth floor of the Plaza, it was Michael who spoke first.

'I'm sorry,' he said. 'I made a bloody fool of myself.'

'I was every bit as bad,' said Adrian, 'we shouldn't fight over a woman. We never have done in the past.'

'Agreed,' said Michael. 'So why not an honourable compromise?'

'What do you suggest?'

'As we both return to London tomorrow morning, let's agree whichever one of us comes back first . . .'

'Perfect,' said Adrian and they shook hands to seal the bargain, as if they were both back at school playing a cricket match, and had to decide on who should bat first. The deal made, they climbed into their respective beds, and slept soundly.

. . .

Once back in London both men did everything in their power to find an excuse for returning to New York. Neither contacted Debbie Kendall by phone or letter as it would have broken their gentleman's agreement, but when the weeks grew to be months both became despondent and it seemed that neither was going to be given the opportunity to return. Then Adrian was invited to Los Angeles to address a Media Conference. He remained unbearably smug about the whole trip, confident he would be able to drop into New York on the way to London. It was Michael who discovered that British Airways were offering cheap tickets for wives who accompanied their husbands on a business trip: Adrian was therefore unable to return via New York. Michael breathed a sigh of relief which turned to triumph when he was selected to go to Washington and cover the President's Address to Congress. He suggested to the head of Outside Broadcasts that it would be wise to drop into New York on the way home and strengthen the contacts he had previously made with ABC. The head of Outside Broadcasts agreed, but told Michael he must be back the following day to cover the opening of Parliament.

Adrian phoned up Michael's wife and briefed her on cheap trips to the States when accompanying your husband. 'How kind of you to be so thoughtful Adrian but alas my school never allows time off during term, and in any case,' she added, 'I have a dreadful fear of flying.'

Michael was very understanding about his wife's phobia and went off to book a single ticket.

. . .

Michael flew to Washington on the following Monday and called Debbie Kendall from his hotel room, wondering if she would even remember the two vainglorious Englishmen she had briefly met some months before, and if she did whether she would also recall which one he was. He dialled nervously and listened to the ringing tone. Was she in, was she even in New York? At last a click and a soft voice said hello.

'Hello, Debbie, it's Michael Thompson.'

'Hello, Michael. What a nice surprise. Are you in New York?'

'No, Washington, but I'm thinking of flying up. You wouldn't be free for dinner on Thursday by any chance?'

'Let me just check my diary.'

Michael held his breath as he waited. It seemed like hours.

'Yes, that seems to be fine.'

'Fantastic. Shall I pick you up around eight?'

'Yes, thank you, Michael. I'll look forward to seeing you then.'

Heartened by this early success Michael immediately penned a telegram of commiseration to Adrian on his sad loss. Adrian didn't reply.

Michael took the shuttle up to New York on the Thursday afternoon as soon as he had finished editing the President's speech for the London office. After settling into another hotel room – this time insisting on a double bed just in case Debbie's children were at home – he had a long bath and a slow shave, cutting himself twice and slapping on a little too much aftershave. He rummaged around for his most telling tie, shirt and suit, and after he had finished dressing he studied himself in the mirror, carefully combing his freshly washed hair to make the long thin strands appear casual as well as cover the parts where his hair was beginning to recede. After a final check, he was able to convince himself that he looked less than his thirty-eight years. Michael then took the lift down to the ground floor, and stepping out of the Plaza on to a neon-lit Fifth Avenue he headed jauntily towards 68th Street. En route, he acquired a dozen roses from a little shop at the corner of 65th Street and Madison Avenue and, humming to himself, proceeded confidently. He arrived at the front door of Debbie Kendall's little brownstone at eight-five.

When Debbie opened the door, Michael thought she looked even more beautiful than he had remembered. She was wearing a long blue dress with a frilly white silk collar and cuffs that covered every part of her body from neck to ankles and yet she could not have been more desirable. She wore almost no make-up except a touch of lipstick that Michael already had plans to remove. Her green eyes sparkled.

'Say something,' she said smiling.

'You look quite stunning, Debbie,' was all he could think of as he handed her the roses.

'How sweet of you,' she replied and invited him in.

Michael followed her into the kitchen where she hammered the long stems and arranged the flowers in a porcelain vase. She then led him into the living room, where she placed the roses on an oval table beside a photograph of two small boys.

'Have we time for a drink?'

'Sure. I've booked a table at Elaine's for eight-thirty.'

'My favourite restaurant,' she said, with a smile that revealed a small dimple on her cheek. Without asking, Debbie poured two whiskies and handed one of them to Michael.

What a good memory she has, he thought, as he nervously kept picking up and putting down his glass, like a teenager on his first date. When Michael had eventually finished his drink, Debbie suggested that they should leave.

'Elaine wouldn't keep a table free for one minute, even if you were Henry Kissinger.'

Michael laughed, and helped her on with her coat. As she unlatched the door, he realized there was no baby-sitter or sound of children. They must be staying with their father, he thought. Once on the street, he hailed a cab and directed the driver to 87th and 2nd. Michael had never been to Elaine's before. The restaurant had been recommended by a friend from ABC who had assured him: 'That joint will give you more than half a chance.'

As they entered the crowded room and waited by the bar for the Maître d', Michael could see it was the type of place that was frequented by the rich and famous and wondered if his pocket could stand the expense and, more importantly, whether such an outlay would turn out to be a worthwhile investment.

A waiter guided them to a small table at the back of the room, where they both had another whisky while they studied the menu. When the waiter returned to take their order, Debbie wanted no first course, just the veal piccate, so Michael ordered the same for himself. She refused the addition of garlic butter. Michael allowed his expectations to rise slightly.

'How's Adrian?' she asked.

'Oh, as well as can be expected,' Michael replied. 'He sends you his love, of course.' He emphasized the word love.

'How kind of him to remember me, and please return mine. What brings you to New York this time, Michael? Another film?'

'No. New York may well have become everybody's second city, but this time I only came to see you.'

'To see me?'

'Yes, I had a tape to edit while I was in Washington, but I always knew I could be through with that by lunch today so I hoped you would be free to spend an evening with me.'

'I'm flattered.'

'You shouldn't be.'

She smiled. The veal arrived.

'Looks good,' said Michael.

'Tastes good, too,' said Debbie. 'When do you fly home?'

'Tomorrow morning, eleven o'clock flight, I'm afraid.'

'Not left yourself time to do much in New York.'

'I only came up to see you,' Michael repeated. Debbie continued eating her veal. 'Why would any man want to divorce you, Debbie?'

'Oh, nothing very original, I'm afraid. He fell in love with a twenty-two year old blonde and left his thirty-two year old wife.'

'Silly man. He should have had an affair with the twenty-two year old blonde and remained faithful to his thirty-two year old wife.'

'Isn't that a contradiction in terms?'

'Oh, no, I don't think so. I've never thought it unnatural to desire someone else. After all, it's a long life to go through and be expected never to want another woman.'

'I'm not so sure I agree with you,' said Debbie thoughtfully. 'I would like to have remained faithful to one man.'

Oh hell, thought Michael, not a very auspicious philosophy.

'Do you miss him?' he tried again.

'Yes, sometimes. It's true what they say in the glossy menopause magazines, one can be very lonely when you suddenly find yourself on your own.'

That sounds more promising, thought Michael, and he heard himself saying: 'Yes, I can understand that, but someone like you shouldn't have to stay on your own for very long.'

Debbie made no reply.

Michael refilled her glass of wine nearly to the brim, hoping he could order a second bottle before she finished her veal.

'Are you trying to get me drunk, Michael?'

'If you think it will help,' he replied laughing.

Debbie didn't laugh. Michael tried again.

'Been to the theatre lately?'

'Yes, I went to *Evita* last week. I loved it' – wonder who took you, thought Michael – 'but my mother fell asleep in the middle of the second act. I think I shall have to go and see it on my own a second time.'

'I only wish I was staying long enough to take you.'

'That would be fun,' she said.

'Whereas I shall have to be satisfied with seeing the show in London.'

'With your wife.'

'Another bottle of wine please, waiter.'

'No more for me, Michael, really.'

'Well, you can help me out a little.' The waiter faded away. 'Do you get to England at all yourself?' asked Michael.

'No, I've only been once when Roger, my ex, took the whole family. I loved the country. It fulfilled every one of my hopes but I'm afraid we did what all Americans are expected to do. The Tower of London, Buckingham Palace, followed by Oxford and Stratford, before flying on to Paris.'

'A sad way to see England; there's so much more I could have shown you.'

'I suspect when the English come to America they don't see much outside of New York, Washington, Los Angeles, and perhaps San Francisco.'

'I agree,' said Michael, not wanting to disagree. The waiter cleared away their empty plates.

'Can I tempt you with a dessert, Debbie?'

'No, no, I'm trying to lose some weight.'

Michael slipped a hand gently around her waist. 'You don't need to,' he said. 'You feel just perfect.'

She laughed. He smiled.

'Nevertheless, I'll stick to coffee, please.'

'A little brandy?'

'No, thank you, just coffee.'

'Black?'

'Black.'

'Coffee for two, please,' Michael said to the hovering waiter.

'I wish I had taken you somewhere a little quieter and less ostentatious,' he said, turning back to Debbie.

'Why?'

Michael took her hand. It felt cold. 'I would like to have said things to you that shouldn't be listened to by people on the next table.'

'I don't think anyone would be shocked by what they overheard at Elaine's, Michael.'

'Very well then. Do you believe in love at first sight?'

'No, but I think it's possible to be physically attracted to a person on first meeting them.'

'Well I must confess, I was to you.'

Again she made no reply.

The coffee arrived and Debbie released her hand to take a sip. Michael followed suit.

'There were one hundred and fifty women in that room the night we met, Debbie, and my eyes never left you once.'

'Even during the film?'

'I'd seen the damn thing a hundred times. I feared I might never see you again.'

'I'm touched.'

'Why should you be? It must be happening to you all the time.'

'Now and then,' she said. 'But I haven't taken anyone too seriously since my husband left me.'

'I'm sorry.'

'No need. It's just not that easy to get over someone you've lived with for ten years. I doubt if many divorcees are quite that willing to jump into bed with the first man who comes along as all the latest films suggest.'

Michael took her hand again, hoping fervently he did not fall into that category.

'It's been such a lovely evening. Why don't we stroll down to the Carlyle and listen to Bobby Short?' Michael's ABC friend had recommended the move if he felt he was still in with a chance.

'Yes, I'd enjoy that,' said Debbie.

Michael called for the bill – eighty-seven dollars. Had it been his wife sitting on the other side of the table he would have checked each item carefully, but not on this occasion. He just left five twenty dollar bills on a side plate and didn't wait for the change. As they stepped out on to 2nd Avenue, he took Debbie's hand and together they started walking downtown. On Madison Avenue they stopped in front of shop windows and he bought her a fur coat, a Cartier watch and a Balenciaga dress. Debbie thought it was lucky that all the stores were closed.

They arrived at the Carlyle just in time for the eleven o'clock show. A waiter, flashing a pen torch, guided them through the little dark room on the ground floor to a table in the corner. Michael ordered a bottle of champagne as Bobby Short struck up a chord and drawled out the words: 'Georgia, Georgia, oh, my sweet ...' Michael, now unable to speak to Debbie above the noise of the band, satisfied himself with holding her hand and when the entertainer sang, 'This time we almost made the pieces fit, didn't we, gal?' he leaned over and kissed her on the cheek. She turned and smiled – was it faintly conspiratorial, or was he just wishful thinking? – and then she sipped her champagne. On the dot of twelve, Bobby Short shut the piano lid and said, 'Goodnight, my friends, the time has come for all you good people to go to bed – and some of you naughty ones too.' Michael laughed a little too loud but was pleased that Debbie laughed as well.

They strolled down Madison Avenue to 68th Street chatting about inconsequential affairs, while Michael's thoughts were of only one affair. When they arrived at her 68th Street apartment, she took out her latch key.

'Would you like a nightcap?' she asked without any suggestive intonation.

'No more drink, thank you, Debbie, but I would certainly appreciate a coffee.'

She led him into the living room.

'The flowers have lasted well,' she teased, and left him to make the coffee. Michael amused himself by flicking through an old copy of *Time* magazine, looking at the pictures, not taking in the words. She returned after a few minutes with a coffee pot and two small cups on a lacquered tray. She poured the coffee, black again, and then sat down next to Michael on the couch, drawing one leg underneath her while turning slightly towards him. Michael downed his coffee in two gulps, scalding his mouth slightly. Then, putting down his cup, he leaned over and kissed her on the mouth. She was still clutching onto her coffee cup. Her eyes opened briefly as she manoeuvred the cup onto a side table. After another long kiss she broke away from him.

'I ought to make an early start in the morning.'

'So should I,' said Michael, 'but I am more worried about not seeing you again for a long time.'

'What a nice thing to say,' Debbie replied.

'No, I just care,' he said, before kissing her again.

This time she responded; he slipped one hand on to her breast while the other one began to undo the row of little buttons down the back of her dress. She broke away again.

'Don't let's do anything we'll regret.'

'I know we won't regret it,' said Michael.

He then kissed her on the neck and shoulders, slipping her dress off as he moved deftly down her body to her breast, delighted to find she wasn't wearing a bra.

'Shall we go upstairs, Debbie? I'm too old to make love on the sofa.'

Without speaking, she rose and led him by the hand to her bedroom which smelled faintly and deliciously of the scent she herself was wearing.

She switched on a small bedside light and took off the rest of her clothes, letting them fall where she stood. Michael never once took his eyes off her body as he undressed clumsily on the other side of the bed. He slipped under the sheets and quickly joined her. When they had finished making love, an experience he hadn't enjoyed as much for a long time, he lay there pondering on the fact that she had succumbed at all, especially on their first date.

They lay silently in each other's arms before making love for a second time, which was every bit as delightful as the first. Michael then fell into a deep sleep.

He woke first the next morning and stared across at the beautiful woman who lay by his side. The digital clock on the bedside table showed seven-o-three. He touched her forehead lightly with his lips and began to stroke her hair. She woke lazily and smiled up at him. Then they made morning love, slowly, gently, but every bit as pleasing as the night before. He didn't speak as she slipped out of bed and ran a bath for him before going to the kitchen to prepare breakfast. Michael relaxed in the hot bath crooning a

Bobby Short number at the top of his voice. How he wished that Adrian could see him now. He dried himself and dressed before joining Debbie in the smart little kitchen where they shared breakfast together. Eggs, bacon, toast, English marmalade, and steaming black coffee. Debbie then had a bath and dressed while Michael read the *New York Times*. When she reappeared in the living room wearing a smart coral dress, he was sorry to be leaving so soon.

'We must leave now, or you'll miss your flight.'

Michael rose reluctantly and Debbie drove him back to his hotel, where he quickly threw his clothes into a suitcase, settled the bill for his unslept-in double bed and joined her back in the car. On the journey to the airport they chatted about the coming elections and pumpkin pie almost as if they had been married for years or were both avoiding admitting the previous night had ever happened.

Debbie dropped Michael in front of the Pan Am building and put the car in the parking lot before joining him at the check-in counter. They waited for his flight to be called.

'Pan American announces the departure of their Flight Number 006 to London Heathrow. Will all passengers please proceed with their boarding passes to Gate Number Nine?'

When they reached the 'passengers-only' barrier, Michael took Debbie briefly in his arms. 'Thank you for a memorable evening,' he said.

'No, it is I who must thank you, Michael,' she replied as she kissed him on the cheek.

'I must confess I hadn't thought it would end up quite like that,' he said.

'Why not?' she asked.

'Not easy to explain,' he replied, searching for words that would flatter and not embarrass. 'Let's say I was surprised that ...'

'You were surprised that we ended up in bed together on our first night? You shouldn't be.'

'I shouldn't?'

'No, there's a simple enough explanation. My friends all told me when I got divorced to find myself a man and have a one-night stand. The idea sounded fun but I didn't like the thought of the men in New York thinking I was easy.' She touched him gently on the side of his face. 'So when I met you and Adrian, both safely living over three thousand miles away, I thought to myself "whichever one of you comes back first" ...'

The Century

'Life is a game,' said A. T. Pierson, thus immortalizing himself without actually having to do any real work. Though E. M. Forster showed more insight when he wrote 'Fate is the Umpire, and Hope is the Ball, which is why I will never score a century at Lord's.'

. . .

When I was a freshman at University, my room mate invited me to have dinner in a sporting club to which he belonged called Vincent's. Such institutions do not differ greatly around the Western world. They are always brimful of outrageously fit, healthy young animals, whose sole purpose in life seems to be to challenge the opposition of some neighbouring institution to ridiculous feats of physical strength. My host's main rvials, he told me with undergraduate fervour, came from a high-thinking, plain-living establishment which had dozed the unworldly centuries away in the flat, dull, fen country of England, cartographically described on a map as Cambridge. Now the ultimate ambition of men such as my host was simple enough: in whichever sport they aspired to beat the 'Tabs' the select few were rewarded with a Blue. As there is no other way of gaining this distinction at either Oxford or Cambridge, every place in the team is contested for with considerable zeal. A man may be selected and indeed play in every other match of the season for the University, even go on to represent his country, but if he does not play in the Oxford and Cambridge match, he cannot describe himself as a Blue.

My story concerns a delightful character I met that evening when I dined as a guest at Vincent's. The undergraduate to whom I refer was in his final year. He came from that part of the world that we still dared to describe in those days (without a great deal of thought) as the colonies. He was an Indian by birth, and the son of a man whose name in England was a household word, if not a legend, for he had captained Oxford and India at cricket, which meant that outside of the British Commonwealth he was about as well known as Babe Ruth is to the English. The young man's father had added to his fame by scoring a century at Lord's when captaining the University cricket side against Cambridge. In fact, when he went on to captain India against England he used to take pride in wearing his cream sweater with the wide dark blue band around the neck and waist. The son, experts predicted, would carry on in the family tradition. He was in much the same mould as his father, tall and rangy with jet-black hair, and as a cricketer, a fine right-handed batsman and a useful left-arm spin bowler. (Those of you who have never been able to comprehend the English language let alone the game of cricket might well be tempted to ask why not a fine right-arm batsman and a useful left-handed spin bowler. The English, however, always cover such silly questions with the words: Tradition, dear boy, tradition.)

The young Indian undergraduate, like his father, had come up to Oxford with considerably more interest in defeating Cambridge than the examiners. As a freshman, he had played against most of the English county sides, notching up a century against three of them, and on one occasion taking five wickets in an innings. A week before the big match against Cambridge, the skipper informed him that he had won his Blue and that the names of the chosen eleven would be officially announced in *The Times* the following day. The young man telegraphed his father in Calcutta with the news, and then went off for a celebratory dinner at Vincent's. He entered the Club's dining room in high spirits to the traditional round of applause afforded to a new Blue, and as he was about to take a seat he observed the boat crew, all nine of them, around a circular table at the far end of the room. He walked across to the captain of boats and remarked: 'I thought you chaps sat one behind each other.'

Within seconds, four thirteen-stone men were sitting on the new Blue while the cox poured a jug of cold water over his head.

'If you fail to score a century', said one oar, 'we'll use hot water next time.' When the four oars had returned to their table, the cricketer rose slowly, straightened his tie in mock indignation, and as he passed the crews' table, patted the five-foot one inch, 102-pound cox on the head and said, 'Even losing teams should have a mascot.'

This time they only laughed but it was in the very act of patting the cox on the head that he first noticed his thumb felt a little bruised and he commented on the fact to the wicket-keeper who had joined him for dinner. A large entrecôte steak arrived and he found as he picked up his knife that he was unable to grip the handle properly. He tried to put the inconvenience out of his mind, assuming all would be well by the following morning. But the next day he woke in considerable pain and found to his dismay that the thumb was not only black but also badly swollen. After reporting the news to his captain he took the first available train to London for a consultation with a Harley Street specialist. As the carriage rattled through Berkshire, he read in *The Times* that he had been awarded his Blue.

The specialist studied the offending thumb for some considerable time and expressed his doubt that the young man would be able to hold a ball, let alone a bat, for at least a fortnight. The prognosis turned out to be accurate and our hero sat disconsolate in the stand at Lord's, watching Oxford lose the match and the twelfth man gain his Blue. His father, who had flown over from Calcutta especially for the encounter, offered his condolences, pointing out that he still had two years left in which to gain the honour.

As his second Trinity term approached, even the young man forgot his disappointment and in the opening match of the season against Somerset scored a memorable century, full of cuts and drives that reminded *aficionados* of his father. The son had been made Secretary of cricket in the closed season as it was universally acknowledged that only bad luck and the boat crew had stopped him from reaping his just reward as a freshman. Once again, he played in every fixture before the needle match, but in the last four games against county teams he failed to score more than a dozen runs and did not take a single wicket, while his immediate rivals excelled themselves. He was going through a lean patch, and was the first to agree with his captain that with so much talent around that year he should not be risked against Cambridge. Once again he watched Oxford lose the Blues match and his opposite number the Cambridge Secretary, Robin Oakley, score a faultless century. A man well into his sixties sporting an MCC tie came up to the young Indian during the game, patted him on the shoulder, and remarked that he would never forget the day his father had scored a hundred against Cambridge: it didn't help.

When the cricketer returned for his final year, he was surprised and delighted to be selected by his fellow teammates to be captain, an honour never previously afforded to a man who had not been awarded the coveted Blue. His peers recognized his outstanding work as Secretary and knew if he could reproduce the form of his freshman year he would undoubtedly not only win a Blue but go on to represent his country.

The tradition at Oxford is that in a man's final year he does not play cricket until he has sat Schools, which leaves him enough time to play in the last three county matches before the Varsity match. But as the new captain had no interest in graduating, he by-passed tradition and played cricket from the opening day of the summer season. His touch never failed him for he batted magnificently and on those rare occasions when he did have an off-day with the bat, he bowled superbly. During the term he led Oxford to victory over three county sides, and his team looked well set for their revenge in the Varsity match.

As the day of the match drew nearer, the cricket correspondent of *The Times* wrote that anyone who had seen him bat this season felt sure that the young Indian would follow his father into the record books by scoring a century against Cambridge: but the correspondent did add that he might be vulnerable against the early attack of Bill Potter, the Cambridge fast bowler.

Everyone wanted the Oxford captain to succeed, for he was one of those rare and gifted men whose charm creates no enemies.

When he announced his Blues team to the press, he did not send a telegram to his father for fear that the news might bring bad luck, and for good measure he did not speak to any member of the boat crew for the entire week leading up to the match. The night before the final encounter he retired to bed at seven although he did not sleep.

.   .   .

On the first morning of the three-day match, the sun shone brightly in an almost cloudless sky and by eleven o'clock a fair sized crowd were already in their seats. The two captains in open necked white shirts, spotless white pressed trousers and freshly creamed white boots came out to study the pitch before they tossed. Robin Oakley of Cambridge won and elected to bat.

By lunch on the first day Cambridge had scored seventy-nine for three and in the early afternoon, when his fast bowlers were tired from their second spell and had not managed an early breakthrough, the captain put himself on. When he was straight, the ball didn't reach a full length, and when he bowled a full length, he was never straight; he quickly took himself off. His less established bowlers managed the necessary breakthrough and Cambridge were all out an hour after tea for 208.

The Oxford openers took the crease at ten to six; forty minutes to see through before close of play on the first day. The captain sat padded up on the pavilion balcony, waiting to be called upon only if a wicket fell. His instructions had been clear: no heroics, bat out the forty minutes so that Oxford could start afresh the next morning with all ten wickets intact. With only one over left before the close of play, the young freshman opener had his middle stump removed by Bill Potter, the Cambridge fast bowler. Oxford were eleven for one. The captain came to the crease with only four balls left to face before the clock would show six-thirty. He took his usual guard, middle and leg, and prepared himself to face the fastest man in the Cambridge side. Potter's first delivery came rocketing down and was just short of a length, moving away outside the off stump. The ball nicked the corner of the bat – or was it pad? – and carried to first slip, who dived to his right and took the catch low down. Eleven Cambridge men screamed 'Howzat'. Was the captain going to be out – for a duck? Without waiting for the umpire's decision he turned and walked back to the pavilion, allowing no expression to appear on his face though he continually hit the side of his pad with his bat. As he climbed the steps he saw his father, sitting on his own in the members' enclosure. He walked on through the Long Room, to cries of 'Bad luck, old fellow' from men holding slopping pints of beer, and 'Better luck in the second innings' from large-bellied old Blues.

The next day, Oxford kept their heads down and put together a total of 181 runs, leaving themselves only a twenty-seven run deficit. When Cambridge batted for a second time they pressed home their slight advantage and the captain's bowling figures ended up as eleven overs, no maidens, no wickets, forty-two runs. He took his team off the field at the end of play on the second day with Cambridge standing at 167 for seven, Robin Oakley the Cambridge captain having notched up a respectable sixty-three not out, and he looked well set for a century.

On the morning of the third day, the Oxford quickies removed the last three Cambridge wickets for nineteen runs in forty minutes and Robin Oakley ran out of partners, and left the field with eighty-nine not out. The Oxford captain was the first to commiserate with him. 'At least you notched a hundred last year,' he added.

'True,' replied Oakley, 'so perhaps it's your turn this year. But not if I've got anything to do with it!'

The Oxford captain smiled at the thought of scoring a century when his team only needed 214 runs at a little under a run a minute to win the match.

The two Oxford opening batsmen began their innings just before midday and remained together until the last over before lunch when the freshman was once again clean bowled by Cambridge's ace fast bowler, Bill Potter. The captain sat on the balcony nervously, padded up and ready. He looked down on the bald head of his father, who was chatting to a former captain of England. Both men had scored centuries in the Varsity match. The captain pulled on his gloves and walked slowly down the pavilion steps, trying to look casual; he had never felt more nervous in his life. As he passed his father, the older man turned his sun-burned face towards his only child and smiled. The crowd warmly applauded the captain all the way to the crease. He took guard, middle and leg again, and prepared to face the attack. The eager Potter who had despatched the captain so brusquely in the first innings came thundering down towards him hoping to be the cause of a pair. He delivered a magnificent first ball that swung in from his legs and beat the captain all ends up, hitting him with a thud on the front pad.

'Howzat?' screamed Potter and the entire Cambridge side as they leaped in the air.

The captain looked up apprehensively at the umpire who took his hands out of his pockets and moved a pebble from one palm to the other to remind him that another ball had been bowled. But he affected no interest in the appeal. A sigh of relief went up from the members in the pavilion. The captain managed to see through the rest of the over and returned to lunch nought not out, with his side twenty-four for one.

After lunch Potter returned to the attack. He rubbed the leather ball on his red-stained flannels and hurled himself forward, looking even fiercer than he had at start of play. He released his missile with every ounce of venom he possessed, but in so doing he tried a little too hard and the delivery was badly short. The captain leaned back and hooked the ball to the Tavern boundary for four, and from that moment he never looked as if anyone would prise him from the crease. He reached his fifty in seventy-one minutes, and at ten past four the Oxford team came into tea with the score at 171 for five and the skipper on eighty-two not out. The young man did not look at his father as he climbed the steps of the pavilion. He needed another eighteen runs before he could do that and by then his team would be safe. He ate and drank nothing at tea, and spoke to no one.

After twenty minutes a bell rang and the eleven Cambridge men returned to the field. A minute later, the captain and his partner walked back out to the crease, their open white shirts flapping in the breeze. Two hours left for the century and victory. The captain's partner only lasted another five balls and the captain himself seemed to have lost that natural flow he had possessed before tea, struggling into the nineties with ones and twos. The light was getting bad and it took him a full thirty minutes to reach ninety-nine, by which time he had lost another partner: 194 for seven. He remained on ninety-nine for twelve minutes, when Robin Oakley the Cambridge captain took the new ball and brought his ace speed man back into the attack.

Then there occurred one of the most amazing incidents I have ever witnessed in a cricket match. Robin Oakley set an attacking field for the new ball – three slips, a gully, cover point, mid off, mid on, mid wicket and a short square leg, a truly vicious circle. He then tossed the ball to Potter who knew this would be his last chance to capture the Oxford captain's wicket and save the match; once he had scored the century he would surely knock off the rest of the runs in a matter of minutes. The sky was becoming bleak as a bank of dark clouds passed over the ground, but this was no time to leave the field for bad light. Potter shone the new ball once more on his white trousers and thundered up to hurl a delivery that the captain jabbed at and missed. One or two fielders raised their hands without appealing. Potter returned to his mark, shining the ball with even more relish and left a red blood-like stain down the side of his thigh. The second ball, a yorker, beat the captain completely and must have missed the off stump by about an inch; there was a general sigh around the ground. The third ball hit the captain on the middle of the pad and the eleven Cambridge men threw their arms in the air and screamed for leg before wicket but the umpire was not moved. The captain jabbed at the fourth ball and it carried tentatively to mid on, where Robin Oakley had placed himself a mere twenty yards in front of the bat, watching his adversary in disbelief as he set off for a run he could never hope to complete. His batting partner remained firmly in his crease, incredulous: one didn't run when the ball was hit to mid on unless it was the last delivery of the match.

The captain of Oxford, now stranded fifteen yards from safety, turned and looked at the captain of Cambridge, who held the ball in his hand. Robin Oakley was about to toss the ball to the wicket-keeper who in turn was waiting to remove the bails and send the Oxford captain back to the pavilion, run out for ninety-nine, but Oakley hesitated and, for several seconds the two gladiators stared at each other and then the Cambridge captain placed the ball in his pocket. The Oxford captain walked slowly back to his crease while the crowd remained silent in disbelief. Robin Oakley tossed the ball to Potter who thundered down to deliver the fifth ball, which was short, and the Oxford captain effortlessly placed it through the covers for four runs. The crowd rose as one and old friends in the pavilion thumped the father's back.

He smiled for a second time.

Potter was now advancing with his final effort and, exhausted, he delivered another short ball which should have been despatched to the boundary with ease but the Oxford captain took one pace backwards and hit his own stumps. He was out, hit wicket, bowled Potter for 103. The crowd rose for a second time as he walked back to the pavilion and grown men who had been decorated in two wars had tears in their eyes. Seven minutes later, everyone left the field, drenched by a thunderstorm.

The match ended in a draw.

Broken Routine

Septimus Horatio Cornwallis did not live up to his name. With such a name he should have been a cabinet minister, an admiral, or at least a rural dean. In fact, Septimus Horatio Cornwallis was a claims adjuster at the head office of the Prudential Assurance Company Limited, 172 Holborn Bars, London EC1.

Septimus's names could be blamed on his father, who had a small knowledge of Nelson, on his mother who was superstitious, and on his great-great-great-grandfather who was alleged to have been a second cousin of the illustrious Governor-General of India. On leaving school Septimus, a thin, anaemic young man prematurely balding, joined the Prudential Assurance Company; his careers master having told him that it was an ideal opening for a young man with his qualifications. Some time later, when Septimus reflected on the advice, it worried him, because even he realized that he had no qualifications. Despite this set-back, Septimus rose slowly over the years from office boy to claims adjuster (not so much climbing the ladder as resting upon each rung for some considerable time), which afforded him the grandiose title of assistant deputy manager (claims department).

Septimus spent his day in a glass cubicle on the sixth floor, adjusting claims and recommending payments of anything up to one million pounds. He felt if he kept his nose clean (one of Septimus's favourite expressions), he would, after another twenty years, become a manager (claims department) and have walls around him that you couldn't see through and a carpet that wasn't laid in small squares of slightly differing shades of green. He might even become one of those signatures on the million pound cheques.

Septimus resided in Sevenoaks with his wife, Norma, and his two children, Winston and Elizabeth, who attended the local comprehensive school. They would have gone to the grammar school, he regularly informed his colleagues, but the Labour government had stopped all that.

Septimus operated his daily life by means of a set of invariant sub-routines, like a primitive microprocessor, while he supposed himself to be a great follower of tradition and discipline. For if he was nothing, he was at least a creature of habit. Had, for some unexplicable reason, the KGB wanted to assassinate Septimus, all they would have had to do was put him under surveillance for seven days and they would have known his every movement throughout the working year.

Septimus rose every morning at seven-fifteen and donned one of his two pin-head patterned dark suits. He left his home at 47 Palmerston Drive at seven-fifty-five, having consumed his invariable breakfast of one soft-boiled egg, two pieces of toast, and two cups of tea. On arriving at Platform One of Sevenoaks station he would purchase a copy of the *Daily Express* before boarding the eight-twenty-seven to Cannon Street. During the journey

Septimus would read his newspaper and smoke two cigarettes, arriving at Cannon Street at nine-seven. He would then walk to the office, and be sitting at his desk in his glass cubicle on the sixth floor, confronting the first claim to be adjusted, by nine-thirty. He took his coffee break at eleven, allowing himself the luxury of two more cigarettes, when once again he would regale his colleagues with the imagined achievements of his children. At eleven-fifteen he returned to work.

At one o'clock he would leave the Great Gothic Cathedral (another of his expressions) for one hour, which he passed at a pub called The Havelock where he would drink a half-pint of Carlsberg lager with a dash of lime, and eat the dish of the day. After he finished his lunch, he would once again smoke two cigarettes. At one-fifty-five he returned to the insurance records until the fifteen minute tea break at four o'clock which was another ritual occasion for two more cigarettes. On the dot of five-thirty, Septimus would pick up his umbrella and reinforced steel briefcase with the initials SHC in silver on the side and leave, double locking his glass cubicle. As he walked through the typing pool, he would announce with a mechanical jauntiness 'See you same time tomorrow, girls', hum a few bars from *The Sound of Music* in the descending lift, and then walk out into the torrent of office workers surging down High Holborn. He would stride purposefully towards Cannon Street station, umbrella tapping away on the pavement while he rubbed shoulders with bankers, shippers, oil men, and brokers, not discontent to think himself part of the great City of London.

Once he reached the station, Septimus would purchase a copy of the *Evening Standard* and a packet of ten Benson & Hedges cigarettes from Smith's bookstall, placing both on the top of his Prudential documents already in the briefcase. He would board the fourth carriage of the train on Platform Five at five-fifty, and secure his favoured window seat in a closed compartment facing the engine, next to the balding gentleman with the inevitable *Financial Times*, and opposite the smartly dressed secretary who read long romantic novels to somewhere beyond Sevenoaks. Before sitting down he would extract the *Evening Standard* and the new packet of Benson & Hedges from his briefcase, put them both on the armrest of his seat, and place the briefcase and his rolled umbrella on the rack above him. Once settled, he would open the packet of cigarettes and smoke the first of the two which were allocated for the journey while reading the *Evening Standard*. This would leave him eight to be smoked before catching the five-fifty the following evening.

As the train pulled into Sevenoaks station, he would mumble goodnight to his fellow passengers (the only word he ever spoke during the entire journey) and leave, making his way straight to the semi-detached at 47 Palmerston Drive, arriving at the front door a little before six-forty-five. Between six-forty-five and seven-thirty he would finish reading his paper or check over his children's homework with a tut-tut when he spotted a mistake, or a sigh when he couldn't fathom the new maths. At seven-thirty his 'good lady' (another of his favoured expressions) would place on the kitchen table in front of him the *Woman's Own* dish of the day or his favourite dinner of three fish fingers, peas and chips. He would then say 'If God had meant fish to have fingers, he would have given them hands,' laugh, and

cover the oblong fish with tomato sauce, consuming the meal to the accom-
paniment of his wife's recital of the day's events. At nine, he watched the
real news on BBC 1 (he never watched ITV) and at ten-thirty he retired
to bed.

This routine was adhered to year in year out with breaks only for holidays,
for which Septimus naturally also had a routine. Alternate Christmases were
spent with Norma's parents in Watford and the ones in between with
Septimus's sister and brother-in-law in Epsom, while in the summer, their
high spot of the year, the family took a package holiday for two weeks in
the Olympic Hotel, Corfu.

Septimus not only liked his life-style, but was distressed if for any reason
his routine met with the slightest interference. This humdrum existence
seemed certain to last him from womb to tomb, for Septimus was not the
stuff on which authors base two hundred thousand word sagas. Nevertheless
there was one occasion when Septimus's routine was not merely interfered
with, but frankly, shattered.

One evening at five-twenty-seven, when Septimus was closing the file on
the last claim for the day, his immediate superior, the Deputy Manager,
called him in for a consultation. Owing to this gross lack of consideration,
Septimus did not manage to get away from the office until a few minutes
after six. Although everyone had left the typing pool, still he saluted the
empty desks and silent typewriters with the invariable 'See you same time
tomorrow, girls,' and hummed a few bars of *Edelweiss* to the descending lift.
As he stepped out of the Great Gothic Cathedral it started to rain. Septimus
reluctantly undid his neatly rolled umbrella, and putting it up dashed
through the puddles, hoping that he would be in time to catch the six-thirty-
two. On arrival at Cannon Street, he queued for his paper and cigarettes
and put them in his briefcase before rushing on to Platform Five. To add
to his annoyance, the loudspeaker was announcing with perfunctory apology
that three trains had already been taken off that evening because of a go
slow.

Septimus eventually fought his way through the dripping, bustling crowds
to the sixth carriage of a train that was not scheduled on any timetable. He
discovered that it was filled with people he had never seen before and, worse,
almost every seat was already occupied. In fact, the only place he could find
to sit was in the middle of the train with his back to the engine. He threw
his briefcase and creased umbrella onto the rack above him and reluctantly
squeezed himself into the seat, before looking around the carriage. There was
not a familiar face among the other six occupants. A woman with three
children more than filled the seat opposite him, while an elderly man was
sleeping soundly on his left. On the other side of him, leaning over and
looking out of the window, was a young man of about twenty.

When Septimus first laid eyes on the boy he couldn't believe what he saw.
The youth was clad in a black leather jacket and skin-tight jeans and was
whistling to himself. His dark, creamed hair was combed up at the front and
down at the sides, while the only two colours of the young man's outfit that
matched were his jacket and fingernails. But worst of all to one of Septimus's
sensitive nature was the slogan printed in boot studs on the back of his jacket.

'Heil Hitler' it declared unashamedly over a white-painted Nazi sign and, as if that were not enough, below the swastika in gold shone the words: 'Up yours'. What was the country coming to? thought Septimus. They ought to bring back National Service for delinquents like that. Septimus himself, had not been eligible for National Service on account of his flat feet.

Septimus decided to ignore the creature, and picking up the packet of Benson & Hedges on the armrest by his side, lit one and began to read the *Evening Standard*. He then replaced the packet of cigarettes on the armrest, as he always did, knowing he would smoke one more before reaching Sevenoaks. When the train eventually moved out of Cannon Street the darkly clad youth turned towards Septimus and, glaring at him, picked up the packet of cigarettes, took one, lit it, and started to puff away. Septimus could not believe what was happening. He was about to protest when he realized that none of his regulars was in the carriage to back him up. He considered the situation for a moment and decided that Discretion was the better part of Valour. (Yet another of the sayings of Septimus.)

When the train stopped at Petts Wood, Septimus put down the newspaper although he had scarcely read a word and as he nearly always did, took his second cigarette. He lit it, inhaled, and was about to retrieve the *Evening Standard* when the youth grabbed at the corner, and they ended up with half the paper each. This time Septimus did look around the carriage for support. The children opposite started giggling, while their mother consciously averted her eyes from what was taking place, obviously not wanting to become involved; the old man on Septimus's left was now snoring. Septimus was about to secure the packet of cigarettes by putting them in his pocket when the youth pounced on them, removed another and lit it, inhaled deeply, and then blew the smoke quite deliberately across Septimus's face before placing the cigarettes back on the armrest. Septimus's answering glare expressed as much malevolence as he was able to project through the grey haze. Grinding his teeth in fury, he returned to the *Evening Standard*, only to discover that he had ended up with situations vacant, used cars and sports sections, subjects in which he had absolutely no interest. His one compensation, however, was his certainty that sport was the only section the oik really wanted. Septimus was now, in any case, incapable of reading the paper, trembling as he was with the outrages perpetrated by his neighbour.

His thoughts were now turning to revenge and gradually a plan began to form in his mind with which he was confident the youth would be left in no doubt that virtue can sometimes be more than its own reward. (A variation on a saying of Septimus). He smiled thinly and, breaking his routine, he took a third cigarette and defiantly placed the packet back on the armrest. The youth stubbed out his own cigarette and, as if taking up the challenge, picked up the packet, removed another one and lit it. Septimus was by no means beaten; he puffed his way quickly through the weed, stubbed it out, a quarter unsmoked, took a forth and lit it immediately. The race was on for there were now only two cigarettes left. But Septimus, despite a great deal of puffing and coughing, managed to finish his fourth cigarette ahead of the youth. He leaned across the leather jacket and stubbed his cigarette out in the window ashtray. The carriage was now filled with smoke, but the youth was still puffing as fast as he could. The children opposite were coughing and the woman was waving her arms around like a windmill. Septimus ignored her and kept his eye on the packet of cigarettes while pretending to read about Arsenal's chances in the FA cup.

Septimus then recalled Montgomery's maxim that surprise and timing in the final analysis are the weapons of victory. As the youth finished his fourth cigarette and was stubbing it out the train pulled slowly into Sevenoaks station. The youth's hand was raised, but Septimus was quicker. He had anticipated the enemy's next move, and now seized the cigarette packet. He took out the ninth cigarette and, placing it between his lips, lit it slowly and luxuriously, inhaling as deeply as he could before blowing the smoke out straight into the face of the enemy. The youth stared up at him in dismay. Septimus then removed the last cigarette from the packet and crumpled the tobacco into shreds between his first finger and thumb, allowing the little flakes to fall back into the empty packet. Then he closed the packet neatly, and with a flourish replaced the little gold box on the armrest. In the same movement he picked up from his vacant seat the sports section of the *Evening Standard*, tore the paper in half, in quarters, in eighths and finally in sixteenths, placing the little squares in a neat pile on the youth's lap.

The train came to a halt at Sevenoaks. A triumphant Septimus, having struck his blow for the silent majority, retrieved his umbrella and briefcase from the rack above him and turned to leave.

As he picked up his briefcase it knocked the armrest in front of him and the lid sprang open. Everyone in the carriage stared at its contents. For there, on top of his Prudential documents, was a neatly folded copy of the *Evening Standard* and an unopened packet of ten Benson & Hedges cigarettes.

Henry's Hiccup

When the Grand Pasha's first son was born in 1900 (he had sired twelve daughters by six wives) he named the boy Henry after his favourite king of England. Henry entered this world with more money than even the most blasé tax collector could imagine and therefore seemed destined to live a life of idle ease.

The Grand Pasha who ruled over ten thousand families, was of the opinion that in time there would be only five kings left in the world – the kings of spades, hearts, diamonds, clubs, and England. With this conviction in mind, he decided that Henry should be educated by the British. The boy was therefore despatched from his native Cairo at the age of eight to embark upon a formal education, young enough to retain only vague recollections of the noise, the heat, and the dirt of his birthplace. Henry started his new life at the Dragon School, which the Grand Pasha's advisers assured him was the finest preparatory school in the land. The boy left this establishment four years later, having developed a passionate love for the polo field and a thorough distaste for the classroom. He proceeded, with the minimum academic qualifications, to Eton, which the Pasha's advisers assured him was the best school in Europe. He was gratified to learn the school had been founded by his favourite king. Henry spent five years at Eton, where he added squash, golf and tennis to his loves, and applied mathematics, jazz and cross-country running to his dislikes.

On leaving school, he once again failed to make more than a passing impression on the examiners. Nevertheless, he was found a place at Balliol College, Oxford, which the Pasha's advisers assured him was the greatest University in the world. Three years at Balliol added two more loves to his life: horses and women, and three more ineradicable aversions: politics, philosophy and economics.

At the end of his time in *statu pupillari*, he totally failed to impress the examiners and went down without a degree. His father, who considered young Henry's two goals against Cambridge in the Varsity polo match a wholly satisfactory result of his University career, despatched the boy on a journey round the world to complete his education. Henry enjoyed the experience, learning more on the race course at Longchamps and in the back streets of Benghazi than he ever had acquired from his formal upbringing in England.

The Grand Pasha would have been proud of the tall, sophisticated and handsome young man who returned to England a year later showing only the slightest trace of a foreign accent, if he hadn't died before his beloved son reached Southampton. Henry, although broken-hearted, was certainly not broke, as his father had left him some twenty million in known assets, including a racing stud at Suffolk, a 100-foot yacht in Nice, and a palace in Cairo. But by far the most important of his father's bequests was the finest manservant in London, one Godfrey Barker. Barker could arrange or re-arrange anything, at a moment's notice.

Henry, for the lack of something better to do, settled himself into his father's old suite at the Ritz, not troubling to read the situations vacant column in the *London Times*. Rather he embarked on a life of single-minded dedication to the pursuit of pleasure, the only career for which Eton, Oxford and inherited wealth had adequately equipped him. To do Henry justice, he had, despite a more than generous helping of charm and good looks, enough common sense to choose carefully those permitted to spend the unforgiving minute with him. He selected only old friends from school and University who, although they were without exception not as well breached as he, weren't the sort of fellows who came begging for the loan of a fiver to cover a gambling debt.

Whenever Henry was asked what was the first love of his life, he was always hard pressed to choose between horses and women, and as he found it possible to spend the day with the one and the night with the other without causing any jealousy or recrimination, he never overtaxed himself with resolving the problem. Most of his horses were fine stallions, fast, sleek, velvet-skinned, with dark eyes and firm limbs; this would have adequately described most of his women, except that they were fillies. Henry fell in and out of love with every girl in the chorus line of the London Palladium, and when the affairs had come to an end, Barker saw to it that they always received some suitable memento to ensure no scandal ensued. Henry also won every classic race on the English turf before he was thirty-five and Barker always seemed to know the right year to back his master.

Henry's life quickly fell into a routine, never dull. One month was spent in Cairo going through the motions of attending to his business, three months in the south of France with the occasional excursion to Biarritz, and for the remaining eight months he resided at the Ritz. For the four months he was out of London his magnificent suite overlooking St James's Park remained unoccupied. History does not record whether Henry left the rooms empty because he disliked the thought of unknown persons splashing in the sunken marble bath or because he simply couldn't be bothered with the fuss of signing in and out of the hotel twice a year. The Ritz management never commented on the matter to his father; why should they with the son? This programme fully accounted for Henry's year except for the odd trip to Paris when some home counties girl came a little too close to the altar. Although almost every girl who met Henry wanted to marry him, a good many would have done so even if he had been penniless. However, Henry saw absolutely no reason to be faithful to one woman. 'I have a hundred horses and a hundred male friends,' he would explain when asked. 'Why, should I confine myself to one female?' There seemed no immediate answer to Henry's logic.

The story of Henry would have ended there had he continued life as destiny seemed content to allow, but even the Henrys of this world have the occasional hiccup.

.   .   .

As the years passed Henry grew into the habit of never planning ahead as experience – and his able manservant, Barker – had always led him to believe that with vast wealth you could acquire anything you desired at the last minute, and cover any contingencies that arose later. However, even Barker couldn't formulate a contingency plan in response to Mr Chamberlain's statement of 3 September 1939, that the British people were at war with Germany. Henry felt it inconsiderate of Chamberlain to have declared war so soon after Wimbledon and the Oaks, and even more inconsiderate of the Home Office to advise him a few months later that Barker must stop serving the Grand Pasha and, until further notice, serve His Majesty the King instead.

What could poor Henry do? Now in his fortieth year he was not used to living anywhere other than the Ritz, and the Germans who had caused Wimbledon to be cancelled were also occupying the George V in Paris and the Negresco in Nice. As the weeks passed and daily an invasion seemed more certain Henry came to the distasteful conclusion that he would have to return to a neutral Cairo until the British had won the war. It never crossed Henry's mind, even for one moment, that the British might lose. After all, they had won the First World War and therefore they must win the Second. 'History repeats itself' was about the only piece of wisdom he recalled clearly from three years of tutorials at Oxford.

Henry summoned the manager of the Ritz and told him that his suite was to be left unoccupied until he returned. He paid one year in advance, which he felt was more than enough time to take care of upstarts like Herr Hitler, and set off for Cairo. The manager was heard to remark later that the Grand Pasha's departure for Egypt was most ironic; he was, after all, more British than the British.

Henry spent a year at his palace in Cairo and then found he could bear his fellow countrymen no longer, so he removed himself to New York only just before it would have been possible for him to come face to face with Rommel. Once in New York, Henry bivouacked in the Pierre Hotel on Fifth Avenue, selected an American manservant called Eugene, and waited for Mr Churchill to finish the war. As if to prove his continuing support for the British, on the first of January every year he forwarded a cheque to the Ritz to cover the cost of his rooms for the next twelve months.

Henry celebrated V-J Day in Times Square with a million Americans and immediately made plans for his return to Britain. He was surprised and disappointed when the British Embassy in Washington informed him that it might be some time before he was allowed to return to the land he loved, and despite continual pressure and all the influence he could bring to bear, he was unable to board a ship for Southampton until July 1946. From the first-class deck he waved goodbye to America and Eugene, and looked forward to England and Barker.

Once he had stepped off the ship onto English soil he headed straight for the Ritz to find his rooms exactly as he had left them. As far as Henry could see, nothing had changed except that his manservant (now the batman to a general) could not be released from the armed forces for at least another six months. Henry was determined to play his part in the war effort by surviving without him for the ensuing period, and remembering Barker's words: 'Everyone knows who you are. Nothing will change,' he felt confident all would be well. Indeed on the *Bonheur-du-jour* in his room at the Ritz was an invitation to dine with Lord and Lady Lympsham in their Chelsea Square home the following night. It looked as if Barker's prediction was turning out to be right: everything would be just the same. Henry penned an affirmative reply to the invitation, happy with the thought that he was going to pick up his life in England exactly where he had left off.

The following evening Henry arrived on the Chelsea Square doorstep a few minutes after eight o'clock. The Lympshams, an elderly couple who had not qualified for the war in any way, gave every appearance of not even realizing that it had taken place or that Henry had been absent from the London social scene. Their table, despite rationing, was as fine as Henry remembered and, more important one of the guests present was quite unlike anyone he could ever remember. Her name, Henry learned from his host, was Victoria Campbell, and she turned out to be the daughter of another guest, General Sir Ralph Colquhoun. Lady Lympsham confided to Henry over the quails' eggs that the sad young thing had lost her husband when the allies advanced on Berlin, only a few days before the Germans had surrendered. For the first time Henry felt guilty about not having played some part in the war.

All through dinner, he could not take his eyes from young Victoria whose classical beauty was only equalled by her well-informed and lively conversation. He feared he might be staring too obviously at the slim, dark-haired girl with the high cheek bones; it was like admiring a beautiful sculpture and wanting to touch it. Her bewitching smile elicited an answering smile from all who received it. Henry did everything in his power to be the receiver and was rewarded on several occasions, aware that, for the first time in his life, he was becoming totally infatuated – and was delighted to be.

The ensuing courtship was an unusual one for Henry, in that he made no attempt to persuade Victoria to compliance. He was sympathetic and attentive, and when she had come out of mourning he approached her father and asked if he might request his daughter's hand in marriage. Henry was overjoyed when first the General agreed and later Victoria accepted. After an announcement in *The Times* they celebrated the engagement with a small dinner party at the Ritz, attended by one hundred and twenty close friends who might have been forgiven for coming to a conclusion that Attlee was exaggerating about his austerity programme. After the last guest had left Henry walked Victoria back to her father's home in Belgrave Mews, while discussing the wedding arrangements and his plans for the honeymoon.

'Everything must be perfect for you, my angel,' he said, as once again he admired the way her long, dark hair curled at the shoulders. 'We shall be married in St Margaret's, Westminster, and after a reception at the Ritz we will be driven to Victoria Station where you will be met by Fred, the senior porter. Fred will allow no one else to carry my bags to the last carriage of the Golden Arrow. One should always have the last carriage, my darling,' explained Henry, 'so that one cannot be disturbed by other travellers.'

Victoria was impressed by Henry's mastery of the arrangements, especially remembering the absence of his manservant, Barker.

Henry warmed to his theme. 'Once we have boarded the Golden Arrow, you will be served with China tea and some wafer-thin smoked salmon sandwiches which we can enjoy while relaxing on our journey to Dover.

When we arrive at the Channel port, you will be met by Albert whom Fred will have alerted. Albert will remove the bags from our carriage, but not before everyone else has left the train. He will then escort us to the ship, where we will take sherry with the captain while our bags are being placed in cabin number three. Like my father, I always have cabin number three; it is not only the largest and most comfortable stateroom on board, but the cabin is situated in the centre of the ship, which makes it possible to enjoy a comfortable crossing even should one have the misfortune to encounter bad weather. And when we have docked in Calais you will find Pierre waiting for us. He will have organized everything for the front carriage of the Flèche d'Or.'

'Such a programme must take a considerable amount of detailed planning,' suggested Victoria, her hazel eyes sparkling as she listened to her future husband's description of the promised tour.

'More tradition than organization I would say, my dear,' replied Henry, smiling, as they strolled hand in hand across Hyde Park. 'Although, I confess, in the past Barker has kept his eye on things should any untoward emergency arise. In any case I have *always* had the front carriage of the Flèche d'Or because it assures one of being off the train and away before anyone realizes that you have actually arrived in the French capital. Other than Raymond, of course.'

'Raymond?'

'Yes, Raymond, a servant *par excellence*, who adored my father, he will have organized a bottle of Veuve Cliquot '37 and a little Russian caviar for the journey. He will also have ensured that there is a couch in the railway carriage should you need to rest, my dear.'

'You seem to have thought of everything, Henry darling,' she said, as they entered Belgrave Mews.

'I hope you will think so, Victoria; for when you arrive in Paris which I have not had the opportunity to visit for so many years, there will be a Rolls-Royce standing by the side of the carriage, door open, and you will step out of the Flèche d'Or into the car and Maurice will drive us to the George V, arguably the finest hotel in Europe. Louis, the manager, will be on the steps of the hotel to greet you and he will conduct us to the bridal suite with its stunning view of the city. A maid will unpack for you while you retire to bathe and rest from the tiresome journey. When you are fully recovered we shall dine at Maxim's, where you will be guided to the corner table furthest from the orchestra by Marcel, the finest head waiter in the world. As you are seated, the musicians will strike up "A Room with A View" my favourite tune, and we will then be served with the most magnificent langouste you have ever tasted, of that I can assure you.'

Henry and Victoria arrived at the front door of the general's small house in Belgrave Mews. He took her hand before continuing.

'After you have dined, my dear, we shall stroll into the Madeleine where I shall buy a dozen red roses from Paulette, the most beautiful flower girl in Paris. She is almost as lovely as you.' Henry sighed and concluded: 'Then we shall return to the George V and spend our first night together.'

Victoria's hazel eyes showed delighted anticipation. 'I only wish it could be tomorrow,' she said.

Henry kissed her gallantly on the cheek and said: 'It will be worth waiting for, my dear, I can assure you it will be a day neither of us will ever forget.'

'I'm sure of that,' Victoria replied as he released her hand.

· · ·

On the morning of his wedding Henry leaped out of bed and drew back the curtains with a flourish, only to be greeted by a steady drizzle.

'The rain will clear by eleven o'clock,' he said out loud with immense confidence, and hummed as he shaved slowly and with care.

The weather had not improved by mid-morning. On the contrary, heavy rain was falling by the time Victoria entered the church. Henry's disappointment evaporated the instant he saw his beautiful bride; all he could think of was taking her to Paris. The ceremony over, the Grand Pasha and his wife stood outside the church, a golden couple, smiling for the press photographers as the loyal guests scattered damp rice over them. As soon as they decently could, they set off for the reception at the Ritz. Between them they managed to chat to every guest present, and they would have been away in better time had Victoria been a little quicker changing and the general's toast to the happy couple been considerably shorter. The guests crowded onto the steps of the Ritz, overflowing on the pavements in Piccadilly to wave goodbye to the departing honeymooners, and were only sheltered from the downpour by a capacious red awning.

The general's Rolls took the Grand Pasha and his wife to the station, where the chauffeur unloaded the bags. Henry instructed him to return to the Ritz as he had everything under control. The chauffeur touched his cap and said: 'I hope you and madam have a wonderful trip, sir,' and left them. Henry stood on the station, looking for Fred. There was no sign of him, so he hailed a passing porter.

'Where is Fred?' inquired Henry.

'Fred who?' came the reply.

'How in heaven's name should I know?' said Henry.

'Then how in hell's name should I know?' retorted the porter.

Victoria shivered. English railway stations are not designed for the latest fashion in silk coats.

'Kindly take my bags to the end of the train,' said Henry.

The porter looked down at the fourteen bags. 'All right,' he said reluctantly.

Henry and Victoria stood patiently in the cold as the porter loaded the bags onto his trolley and trundled them off along the platform.

'Don't worry, my dear,' said Henry. 'A cup of Lapsang Souchong tea and some smoked salmon sandwiches and you'll feel a new girl.'

'I'm just fine,' said Victoria, smiling, though not quite as bewitchingly as normal, as she put her arm through her husband's. They strolled along together to the end carriage.

'Can I check your tickets, sir?' said the conductor, blocking the entrance to the last carriage.

'My what?' said Henry, his accent sounding unusually pronounced.

'Your tic ... kets,' said the conductor, conscious he was addressing a foreigner.

'In the past I have always made the arrangements on the train, my good man.'

'Not nowadays you don't, sir. You'll have to go to the booking office and buy your tickets like everyone else, and you'd better be quick about it because the train is due to leave in a few minutes.'

Henry stared at the conductor in disbelief. 'I assume my wife may rest on the train while I go and purchase the tickets?' he asked.

'No, I'm sorry, sir. No one is allowed to board the train unless they are in pssession of a valid ticket.'

'Remain here, my dear,' said Henry, 'and I will deal with this little problem immediately. Kindly direct me to the ticket office, porter.'

'End of Platform Four, governor,' said the conductor, slamming the train door annoyed at being described as a porter.

That wasn't quite what Henry had meant by 'direct me'. Nevertheless, he left his bride with the fourteen bags and somewhat reluctantly headed back towards the ticket office at the end of Platform Four, where he went to the front of a long line.

'There's a queue, you know, mate,' someone shouted.

Henry didn't know. 'I'm in a frightful hurry,' he said.

'And so am I,' came back the reply, 'so get to the back.'

Henry had been told that the British were good at standing in queues, but as he had never had to join one before that moment, he was quite unable to confirm or deny the rumour. He reluctantly walked to the back of a queue. It took some time before Henry reached the front.

'I would like to take the last carriage to Dover.'

'You would like what ... ?'

'The last carriage,' repeated Henry a little more loudly.

'I am sorry, sir, but every first-class seat is sold.'

'I don't want a seat,' said Henry. 'I require the carriage.'

'There are no carriages available nowadays, sir, and as I said, all the seats in first class are sold. I can still fix you up in third class.'

'I don't mind what it costs,' said Henry. 'I must travel first class.'

'I don't have a first-class seat, sir. It wouldn't matter if you could afford the whole train.'

'I can,' said Henry.

'I still don't have a seat left in first class,' said the clerk unhelpfully.

Henry would have persisted, but several people in the queue behind him were pointing out that there were only two minutes before the train was due to leave and that they wanted to catch it even if he didn't.

'Two seats then,' said Henry, unable to make himself utter the words 'third class'.

Two green tickets marked Dover were handed through the little grille. Henry took them and started to walk away.

'That will be seventeen and sixpence please, sir.'

'Oh, yes of course,' said Henry apologetically. He fumbled in his pocket and unfolded one of the three large white five-pound notes he always carried on him.

'Don't you have anything smaller?'

'No, I do not,' said Henry, who found the idea of carrying money vulgar enough without it having to be in small denominations.

The clerk handed back four pounds and a half-crown. Henry did not pick up the half-crown.

'Thank you, sir,' said the startled man. It was more than his Saturday bonus.

Henry put the tickets in his pocket and quickly returned to Victoria, who was smiling defiantly against the cold wind; it was not quite the smile that had originally captivated him. Their porter had long ago disappeared and Henry couldn't see another in sight. The conductor took his tickets and clipped them.

'All aboard,' he shouted, waved a green flag and blew his whistle.

Henry quickly threw all fourteen bags through the open door and pushed Victoria onto the moving train before leaping on himself. Once he had caught his breath he walked down the corridor, staring into the third class carriages. He had never seen one before. The seats were nothing more than thin worn-out cushions, and as he looked into one half-full carriage a young couple jumped in and took the last two adjacent seats. Henry searched frantically for a free carriage but he was unable even to find one with two seats together. Victoria took a single seat in a packed compartment without complaint, while Henry sat forlornly on one of the suitcases in the corridor.

'It will be different once we're in Dover,' he said, without his usual self-confidence.

'I am sure it will, Henry,' she replied, smiling kindly at him.

The two-hour journey seemed interminable. Passengers of all shapes and sizes squeezed past him in the corridor, treading on his Lobbs hand-made leather shoes, with the words:

'Sorry, sir.'

'Sorry, guv.'

'Sorry, mate.'

Henry put the blame firmly on the shoulders of Clement Attlee and his ridiculous campaign for social equality, and waited for the train to reach Dover Priory Station. The moment the engine pulled in Henry leaped out of the carriage first, not last, and called for Albert at the top of his voice. Nothing happened, except a stampede of people rushed past him on their way to the ship. Eventually Henry spotted a porter and rushed over to him only to find he was already loading up his trolley with someone else's luggage. Henry sprinted to a second man and then on to a third and waved a pound note at a fourth, who came immediately and unloaded the fourteen bags.

'Where to, guv?' asked the porter amicably.

'The ship,' said Henry, and returned to claim his bride. He helped Victoria down from the train and they both ran through the rain until, breathless, they reached the gangplank of the ship.

'Tickets sir,' said a young officer in a dark blue uniform at the bottom of the gangplank.

'I always have cabin number three,' said Henry between breaths.

'Of course, sir,' said the young man and looked at his clip board. Henry smiled confidently at Victoria.

'Mr and Mrs William West.'

'I beg your pardon?' said Henry.

'You must be Mr William West.'

'I am certainly not. I am the Grand Pasha of Cairo.'

'Well, I'm sorry, sir, cabin number three is booked in the name of a Mr William West and family.'

'I have never been treated by Captain Rogers in this cavalier fashion before,' said Henry, his accent now even more pronounced. 'Send for him immediately.'

'Captain Rogers was killed in the war, sir. Captain Jenkins is now in command of this ship and he never leaves the bridge thirty minutes before sailing.'

Henry's exasperation was turning to panic. 'Do you have a free cabin?'

The young officer looked down his list. 'No, sir, I'm afraid not. The last one was taken a few minutes ago.'

'May I have two tickets?' asked Henry.

'Yes, sir,' said the young officer. 'But you'll have to buy them from the booking office on the quayside.'

Henry decided that any further argument would be only time-consuming so he turned on his heel without another word, leaving his wife with the laden porter. He strode to the booking office.

'Two first-class tickets to Calais,' he said firmly.

The man behind the little glass pane gave Henry a tired look. 'It's all one class nowadays, sir, unless you have a cabin.'

He proferred two tickets. 'That will be one pound exactly.'

Henry handed over a pound note, took his tickets, and hurried back to the young officer.

The porter was off-loading their suitcases onto the quayside.

'Can't you take them on board,' cried Henry, 'and put them in the hold?'

'No, sir, not now. Only the passengers are allowed on board after the ten-minute signal.'

Victoria carried two of the smaller suitcases while Henry humped the twelve remaining ones in relays up the gangplank. He finally sat down on the deck exhausted. Every seat seemed already to be occupied. Henry couldn't make up his mind if he was cold from the rain or hot from his exertions. Victoria's smile was fixed firmly in place as she took Henry's hand.

'Don't worry about a thing, darling,' she said. 'Just relax and enjoy the crossing; it will be such fun being out on deck together.'

The ship moved sedately out of the calm of the bay into the Dover Straits. Later that night Captain Jenkins told his wife that the twenty-five mile journey had been among the most unpleasant crossings he had ever experienced. He added that he had nearly turned back when his second officer, a veteran of two wars, was violently sick. Henry and Victoria spent most of the trip hanging over the rails getting rid of everything they had consumed at their reception. Two people had never been more happy to see land in their life than Henry and Victoria were at the first sight of the Normandy coastline. They staggered off the ship, taking the suitcases one at a time.

'Perhaps France will be different,' Henry said lamely, and after a perfunctory search for Pierre he went straight to the booking office and obtained two third-class seats on the Flèche d'Or. They were at least able to sit next to each other this time, but in a carriage already occupied by six other passengers as well as a dog and a hen. The six of them left Henry in no doubt that they enjoyed the modern habit of smoking in public and the ancient custom of taking garlic in their food. He would have been sick again at any other time but there was nothing left in his stomach. Henry considered walking up and down the train searching for Raymond but feared it could only result in him losing his seat next to Victoria. He gave up trying to hold any conversation with her above the noise of the dog, the hen and the Gallic babble, and satisfied himself by looking out of the window, watching the French countryside and, for the first time in his life, noting the name of every station through which they passed.

Once they arrived at the Gare du Nord Henry made no attempt to look for Maurice and simply headed straight for the nearest taxi rank. By the time he had transferred all fourteen cases he was well down the queue. He and Victoria stood there for just over an hour, moving the cases forward inch by inch until it was their turn.

'*Monsieur?*'

'Do you speak English?'

'*Un peu, un peu.*'

'Hotel George V.'

'*Oui, mais je ne peux pas mettre toutes les valises dans le coffre.*'

So Henry and Victoria sat huddled in the back of the taxi, bruised, tired, soaked and starving, surrounded by leather suitcases, only to be bumped up and down over the cobbled stones all the way to the George V.

The hotel doorman rushed to help them as Henry offered the taxi driver a pound note.

'No take English money, monsieur.'

Henry couldn't believe his ears. The doorman happily paid the taxi driver in francs and quickly pocketed the pound note. Henry was too tired even to comment. He helped Victoria up the marble steps and went over to the reception desk.

'The Grand Pasha of Cairo and his wife. The bridal suite, please.'

'*Oui, monsieur.*'

Henry smiled at Victoria.

'You 'ave your booking confirmation with you?'

'No,' said Henry, 'I have never needed to confirm my booking with you in the past. Before the war I ...'

'I am sorry, sir, but the 'otel is fully booked at the moment. A conference.'

'Even the bridal suite,' asked Victoria.

'Yes, Madam, the chairman and his lady, you understand.' He nearly winked.

Henry certainly did not understand. There had always been a room for him at the George V whenever he had wanted one in the past. Desperate, he unfolded the second of his five-pound notes and slipped it across the counter.

'Ah,' said the booking clerk, 'I see we still have one room unoccupied, but I fear it is not very large.'

Henry waved a listless hand.

The booking clerk banged the bell on the counter in front of him with the palm of his hand, and a porter appeared immediately and escorted them to the promised room. The booking clerk had been telling the truth. Henry could only have described what they found themselves standing in as a box room. The reason that the curtains were perpetually drawn was that the view over the chimneys of Paris, was singularly unprepossessing, but that was not to be the final blow, as Henry realized, staring in disbelief at the sight of the two narrow single beds. Victoria started unpacking without a word while Henry sat despondently on the end of one of them. After Victoria had sat soaking in a bath that was the perfect size for a six-year-old, she lay down exhausted on the other bed. Neither spoke for nearly an hour.

'Come on, darling,' said Henry finally. 'Let's go and have dinner.'

Victoria rose loyally but reluctantly and dressed for dinner while Henry sat in the bath, knees on nose, trying to wash himself before changing into evening dress. This time he phoned the front desk and ordered a taxi as well as booking a table at Maxim's.

The taxi driver did accept his pound note on this occasion, but as Henry and his bride entered the great restaurant he recognized no one and no one recognized him. A waiter led them to a small table hemmed in between two other couples just below the band. As he walked into the dining room the musicians struck up 'Alexander's Rag Time Band'.

They both ordered from the extensive menu and the langouste turned out to be excellent, every bit as good as Henry had promised of Maxim's, but by then neither of them had the stomach to eat a full meal and the greater part of both their dishes was left on the plate.

Henry found it hard to convince the new head waiter that the lobster had been superb and that they had purposely come to Maxim's not to eat it. Over coffee, he took Victoria's hand and tried to apologize.

'Let us end this farce,' he said, 'by completing my plan and going to the Madeleine and presenting you with the promised flowers. Paulette will not be in the square to greet you but there will surely be someone who can sell us roses.'

Henry called for the bill and unfolded the third five-pound note (Maxim's are always happy to accept other people's currency and certainly didn't bother him with any change) and they left, walking hand in hand towards the Madeleine. For once Henry turned out to be right, for Paulette was nowhere to be seen. An old lady with a shawl over her head and a wart on the side of her nose stood in her place on the corner of the square, surrounded by the most beautiful flowers.

Henry selected a dozen of the longest stemmed red roses and then placed them in the arms of his bride. The old lady smiled at Victoria.

Victoria returned her smile.

'*Dix francs, monsieur,*' said the old lady to Henry.

Henry fumbled in his pocket, only to discover he had spent all his money. He looked despairingly at the old lady who raised her hands, smiled at him, and said:

'Don't worry, Henry, have them on me. For old time's sake.'

A Matter of Principle

Sir Hamish Graham had many of the qualities and most of the failings that result from being born to a middle-class Scottish family. He was well educated, hard working and honest, while at the same time being narrow-minded, uncompromising and proud. Never on any occasion had he allowed hard liquor to pass his lips and he mistrusted all men who had not been born north of Hadrian's Wall, and many of those who had.

After spending his formative years at Fettes School, to which he had won a minor scholarship, and at Edinburgh University, where he obtained a second-class honours degree in engineering, he was chosen from a field of twelve to be a trainee with the international construction company, TarMac (named after its founder, J. L. McAdam, who discovered that tar when mixed with stones was the best constituent for making roads). The new trainee, through diligent work and uncompromising tactics, became the firm's youngest and most disliked project manager. By the age of thirty Graham had been appointed deputy managing director of TarMac and was already beginning to realize that he could not hope to progress much farther while he was in someone else's employ. He therefore started to consider forming his own company. When two years later the chairman of TarMac, Sir Alfred Hickman, offered Graham the opportunity to replace the retiring managing director, he resigned immediately. After all, if Sir Alfred felt he had the ability to run TarMac he must also be competent enough to start his own company.

The next day, young Hamish Graham made an appointment to see the local manager of the Bank of Scotland who was responsible for the TarMac account, and with whom he had dealt for the past ten years. Graham explained to the manager his plans for the future, submitting a full written proposal, and requesting that his overdraft facility might be extended from fifty pounds to ten thousand. Three weeks later Graham learned that his application had been viewed favourably. He remained in his lodgings in Edinburgh, while renting an office in the north of the city (or, to be more accurate, a room at ten shillings a week). He purchased a typewriter, hired a secretary and ordered some unembossed headed letter-paper. After a further month of diligent interviewing, he employed two engineers, both graduates of Aberdeen University, and five out-of-work labourers from Glasgow.

During those first few weeks on his own Graham tendered for several small road contracts in the central lowlands of Scotland, the first seven of which he failed to secure. Preparing a tender is always tricky and often expensive, so by the end of his six months in business Graham was beginning to wonder if his sudden departure from TarMac had not been foolhardy. For the first time in his life he experienced self-doubt, but that was soon removed by the

Ayrshire County Council, who accepted his tender to construct a minor road which was to join a projected school with the main highway. The road was only five hundred yards in length but the assignment took Graham's little team seven months to complete and when all the bills had been paid and all expenses taken into account Graham Construction made a net loss of £143.10s.6d.

Still, in the profit column was a small reputation which had been invisibly earned, and caused the Ayrshire Council to invite him to build the school at the end of their new road. This contract made Graham Construction a profit of £420 and added still further to his reputation. From that moment Graham Construction went from strength to strength, and as early as his third year in business he was able to declare a small pre-tax profit, and this grew steadily over the next five years. When Graham Construction was floated on the London Stock Exchange the demand for the shares was oversubscribed ten times and the newly quoted company was soon considered a blue-chip institution, a considerable achievement for Graham to have pulled off in his own lifetime. But then the City likes men who grow slowly and can be relied on not to involve themselves in unnecessary risks.

In the sixties Graham Construction built motorways, hospitals, factories, and even a power station, but the achievement the chairman took most pride in was Edinburgh's newly completed art gallery, which was the only contract that showed a deficit in the annual general report. The invisible earnings column however recorded the award of knight bachelor for the chairman.

Sir Hamish decided that the time had come for Graham Construction to expand into new fields, and looked, as generations of Scots had before him, towards the natural market of the British Empire. He built in Australia and Canada with his own finances, and in India and Africa with a subsidy from the British government. In 1963 he was named 'Businessman of the Year' by *The Times* and three years later 'Chairman of the Year' by *The Economist*. Sir Hamish never once altered his methods to keep pace with the changing times, and if anything grew more stubborn in the belief that his ideas of doing business were correct whatever anyone else thought; and he had a long credit column to prove he was right.

In the early seventies, when the slump hit the construction business, Graham Construction suffered the same cut in budgets and lost contracts as any of its major competitors. Sir Hamish reacted in a predictable way, by tightening his belt and paring his estimates while at the same time refusing one jot to compromise his business principles. The company therefore grew leaner and many of his more enterprising young executives left Graham Construction for firms which still believed in taking on the occasional risky contract.

Only when the slope of the profits graph started taking on the look of a downhill slalom did Sir Hamish become worried. One night, while brooding over the company's profit-and-loss account for the previous three years, and realizing that he was losing contracts even in his native Scotland, Sir Hamish reluctantly came to the conclusion that he must tender for less established work, and perhaps even consider the odd gamble.

His brightest young executive, David Heath, a stocky, middle-aged bachelor, whom he did not entirely trust – after all, the man had been educated south of the border and worse, some extraordinary place in the United States called the Wharton Business School – wanted Sir Hamish to put a toe into Mexican waters. Mexico, as Heath was not slow to point out, had discovered vast reserves of oil off their eastern coast and had overnight become rich with American dollars. The construction business in Mexico was suddenly proving most lucrative and contracts were coming up for tender with figures as high as thirty to forty million dollars attached to them. Heath urged Sir Hamish to go after one such contract that had recently been announced in a full-page advertisement in *The Economist*. The Mexican Government were issuing tender documents for a proposed ring road around their capital, Mexico City. In an article in the business section of the *Observer*, detailed arguments were put forward as to why established British companies should try to fulfil the ring road tender. Heath had offered shrewd advice on overseas contracts in the past that Sir Hamish had subsequently let slip through his fingers.

The next morning, Sir Hamish sat at his desk listening attentively to David Heath, who felt that as Graham Construction had already built the Glasgow and Edinburgh ring roads any application they made to the Mexican Government had to be taken seriously. To Heath's surprise, Sir Hamish agreed with his project manager and allowed a team of six men to travel to Mexico to obtain the tender documents and research the project.

The research team was led by David Heath, and consisted of three other engineers, a geologist and an accountant. When the team arrived in Mexico they obtained the tender documents from the Minister of Works and settled down to study them minutely. Having pinpointed the major problems they walked around Mexico City with their ears open and their mouths shut and made a list of the problems they were clearly going to encounter: the impossibility of unloading anything at Vera Cruz and then transporting the cargo to Mexico City without half of the original assignment being stolen, the lack of communications between ministries, and worst of all the attitude of the Mexicans to work. But David Heath's most positive contribution to the list was the discovery that each minister had his own outside man, and that man had better be well disposed to Graham Construction if the firm were to be even considered for the short list. Heath immediately sought out the Minister of Works' man, one Victor Perez, and took him to an extravagant lunch at the *Fonda el Refugio* where both of them nearly ended up drunk, although Heath remained sober enough to agree all of the necessary terms, conditional upon Sir Hamish's approval. Having taken every possible precaution, Heath agreed on a tender figure with Perez which was to include the minister's percentage. Once he had completed the report for his chairman, he flew back to England with his team.

On the evening of David Heath's return, Sir Hamish retired to bed early to study his project manager's conclusions. He read the report through the night as others might read a spy story, and was left in no doubt that this was the opportunity he had been looking for to overcome the temporary setbacks Graham Construction was now suffering. Although Sir Hamish would be up against Costains, Sunleys, and John Brown, as well as many international companies, he still felt confident that any application he made must have a 'fair chance'. On arrival at his office the next morning Sir Hamish sent for David Heath, who was delighted by the chairman's initial response to his report.

Sir Hamish started speaking as soon as his burly project manager entered the room, not even inviting him to take a seat.

'You must contact our Embassy in Mexico City immediately and inform them of our intentions,' pronounced Sir Hamish. 'I may speak to the Ambassador myself,' he said, intending that to be the concluding remark of the interview.

'Useless,' said David Heath.

'I beg your pardon?'

'I don't wish to appear rude, sir, but it doesn't work like that any more. Britain is no longer a great power dispensing largesse to all far flung and grateful recipients.'

'More's the pity,' said Sir Hamish.

The project manager continued as though he had not heard the remark.

'The Mexicans now have vast wealth of their own and the United States, Japan, France and Germany keep massive embassies in Mexico City with highly professional trade delegations trying to influence every ministry.'

'But surely history counts for something,' said Sir Hamish. 'Wouldn't they rather deal with an established British company than some upstarts from – ?'

'Perhaps, sir, but in the end all that really matters is which minister is in charge of what contract and who is his outside representative.'

Sir Hamish looked puzzled. 'Your meaning is obscure to me, Mr Heath.'

'Allow me to explain, sir. Under the present system in Mexico, each ministry has an allocation of money to spend on projects agreed to by the government. Every Secretary of State is acutely aware that his tenure of office may be very short, so he picks out a major contract for himself from the many available. It's the one way to ensure a pension for life if the government is changed overnight or the minister simply loses his job.'

'Don't bandy words with me, Mr Heath. What you are suggesting is that I should bribe a government official, I have never been involved in that sort of thing in thirty years of business.'

'And I wouldn't want you to start now,' replied Heath. 'The Mexican is far too experienced in business etiquette for anything as clumsy as that to be suggested, but while the law requires that you appoint a Mexican agent, it must make sense to try and sign up the minister's man, who in the end is the one person who can ensure that you will be awarded the contract. The system seems to work well, and as long as a minister deals only with reputable international firms and doesn't become greedy, no one complains. Fail to observe either of those two golden rules and the whole house of cards collapses. The minister ends up in Le Cumberri for thirty years and the company concerned has all its assets expropriated and is banned from any future business dealings in Mexico.'

'I really cannot become involved in such shenanigans,' said Sir Hamish. 'I still have my shareholders to consider.'

'*You* don't have to become involved,' Heath rejoined. 'After we have tendered for the contract you wait and see if the company has been short-listed and then, if we have, you wait again to find out if the minister's man approaches us. I know the man, so if he does make contact we have a deal. After all, Graham Construction is a respectable international company.'

'Precisely, and that's why it's against my principles,' said Sir Hamish with hauteur.

'I do hope, Sir Hamish, it's also against your principles to allow the Germans and the Americans to steal the contract from under our noses.'

Sir Hamish glared back at his project manager but remained silent.

'And I feel I must add, sir,' said David Heath moving restlessly from foot to foot, 'that the pickings in Scotland haven't exactly yielded a harvest lately.'

'All right, all right, go ahead,' said Sir Hamish reluctantly. 'Put in a tender figure for the Mexico City ring road and be warned if I find bribery is involved, on your head be it,' he added, banging his closed fist on the table.

'What tender figure have you settled on, sir?' asked the project manager. 'I believe, as I stressed in my report that we should keep the amount under forty million dollars.'

'Agreed,' said Sir Hamish who paused for a moment and smiled to himself before saying: 'Make it $39,121,110.'

'Why that particular figure, sir?'

'Sentimental reasons,' said Sir Hamish, without further explanation.

David Heath left, pleased that he had convinced his boss to go ahead but he feared it might in the end prove harder to overcome Sir Hamish's principles than the entire Mexican government. Nevertheless he filled in the bottom line of the tender as instructed and then had the document signed by three directors including his chairman, as required by Mexican law. He sent the tender by special messenger to be delivered at the Ministry of Buildings in Paseo de la Reforma: when tendering for a contract for over thirty-nine million dollars, one does not send the document by first-class post.

Several weeks passed before the Mexican Embassy in London contacted Sir Hamish, requesting that he travel to Mexico City for a meeting with Manuel Unichurtu, the minister concerned with the city's ring road project. Sir Hamish remained sceptical, but David Heath was jubilant, because he had already learned through another source that Graham Construction was the only tender being seriously considered at that moment, although there were one or two outstanding items still to be agreed on. David Heath knew exactly what that meant.

A week later Sir Hamish, travelling first class, and David Heath, travelling economy, flew out of Heathrow bound for Mexico International airport. On arrival they took an hour to clear customs and another thirty minutes to find a taxi to take them to the city, and then only after the driver had bargained with them for an outrageous fare. They covered the fifteen-mile journey from the airport to their hotel in just over an hour and Sir Hamish was able to observe at first hand why the Mexicans were so desperate to build a ring road. Even with the windows down the ten-year-old car was like an oven that had been left on high all night, but during the journey Sir Hamish never once loosened his collar or tie. The two men checked into their rooms, phoned the minister's secretary to inform her of their arrival, and then waited.

For two days, nothing happened.

David Heath assured his chairman that such a hold up was not an unusual course of events in Mexico as the minister was undoubtedly in meetings most of the day, and after all wasn't '*mañana*' the one Spanish word every foreigner understood?

On the afternoon of the third day, only just before Sir Hamish was threatening to return home, David Heath received a call from the minister's man, who accepted an invitation to join them both for dinner in Sir Hamish's suite that evening.

Sir Hamish put on evening dress for the occasion, despite David Heath's counselling against the idea. He even had a bottle of *Fina La Ina* sherry sent up in case the minister's man required some refreshment. The dinner table was set and the hosts were ready for seven-thirty. The minister's man did not appear at seven-thirty, or seven-forty-five, or eight o'clock or eight-fifteen, or eight-thirty. At eight-forty-nine there was a loud rap on the door, and Sir Hamish muttered an inaudible reproach as David Heath went to open it and find his contact standing there.

'Good evening, Mr Heath, I'm sorry to be late. Held up with the minister, you understand.'

'Yes, of course,' said David Heath. 'How good of you to come, Señor Perez. May I introduce my chairman, Sir Hamish Graham?'

'How do you do, Sir Hamish? Victor Perez at your service.'

Sir Hamish was dumbfounded. He simply stood and stared at the little middle-aged Mexican who had arrived for dinner dressed in a grubby white tee-shirt and Western jeans. Perez looked as if he hadn't shaved for three days and reminded Sir Hamish of those bandits he had seen in B-Movies when he was a schoolboy. He wore a heavy gold bracelet around his wrist that could have come from Cartier's and a tiger's tooth on a platinum chain around his neck that looked as if it had come from Woolworth's. Perez grinned from ear to ear, pleased with the effect he was causing.

'Good evening,' replied Sir Hamish stiffly, taking a step backwards. 'Would you care for a sherry?'

'No, thank you, Sir Hamish. I've grown into the habit of liking your whisky, on the rocks with a little soda.'

'I'm sorry, I only have ...'

'Don't worry, sir, I have some in my room,' said David Heath, and rushed away to retrieve a bottle of Johnnie Walker he had hidden under the shirts in his top drawer. Despite this Scottish aid, the conversation before dinner among the three men was somewhat stilted, but David Heath had not come five thousand miles for an inferior hotel meal with Victor Perez, and Victor Perez in any other circumstances would not have crossed the road to meet Sir Hamish Graham even if he'd built it. Their conversation ranged from the recent visit to Mexico of Her Majesty The Queen – as Sir Hamish referred to her. – to the proposed return trip of President Portillo to Britain. Dinner might have gone more smoothly if Mr Perez hadn't eaten most of the food with his hands and then proceeded to clean his fingers on the side of his jeans. The more Sir Hamish stared at him in disbelief the more the little Mexican would grin from ear to ear. After dinner David Heath thought the time had come to steer the conversation towards the real purpose of the meeting, but not before Sir Hamish had reluctantly had to call for a bottle of brandy and a box of cigars.

'We are looking for an agent to represent the Graham Construction Company in Mexico, Mr Perez, and you have been highly recommended,' said Sir Hamish, sounding unconvinced by his own statement.

'Do call me Victor.'

Sir Hamish bowed silently and shuddered. There was no way this man was going to be allowed to call him Hamish.

'I'd be pleased to represent you, Hamish,' continued Perez, 'provided that you find my terms acceptable.'

'Perhaps you could enlighten us as to what those – hm, terms – might be,' said Sir Hamish stiffly.

'Certainly,' said the little Mexican cheerfully. 'I require ten per cent of the agreed tender figure, five per cent to be paid on the day you are awarded the contract and five per cent whenever you present your completion certificates. Not a penny to be paid until you have received your fee, all my payments deposited in an account at Credit Suisse in Geneva within seven days of the National Bank of Mexico clearing your cheque.'

David Heath drew in his breath sharply and stared down at the stone floor.

'But under those terms you would make nearly four million dollars,' protested Sir Hamish, now red in the face. 'That's over half our projected profit.'

'That, as I believe you say in England, Hamish, is your problem, you fixed the tender price,' said Perez, 'not me. In any case, there's still enough in the deal for both of us to make a handsome profit which is surely fair as we bring half the equation to the table.'

Sir Hamish was speechless as he fiddled with his bow tie. David Heath examined his fingernails attentively.

'Think the whole thing over, Hamish,' said Victor Perez, sounding unperturbed, 'and let me know your decision by midday tomorrow. The outcome makes little difference to me.' The Mexican rose, shook hands with Sir Hamish and left. David Heath, sweating slightly, accompanied him down in the lift. In the foyer he clasped hands damply with the Mexican.

'Goodnight, Victor. I'm sure everything will be all right – by midday tomorrow.'

'I hope so,' replied the Mexican, 'for your sake.' He strolled out of the foyer whistling.

Sir Hamish, a glass of water in his hand, was still seated at the dinner table when his project manager returned.

'I do not believe it is possible that that – that that man can represent the Secretary of State, represent a government minister.'

'I am assured that he does,' replied David Heath.

'But to part with nearly four million dollars to such an individual ...'

'I agree with you, sir, but that is the way business is conducted out here.'

'I can't believe it,' said Sir Hamish. 'I *won't* believe it. I want you to make an appointment for me to see the minister first thing tomorrow morning.'

'He won't like that, sir. It might expose his position, and put him right out in the open in a way that could only embarrass him.'

'I don't give a damn about embarrassing him. We are discussing a bribe, do I have to spell it out for you, Heath? A bribe of nearly four million dollars. Have you no principles, man?'

'Yes, sir, but I would still advise you against seeing the Secretary of State. He won't want any of your conversation with Mr Perez on the record.'

'I have run this company my way for nearly thirty years, Mr Heath, and I shall be the judge of what I want on the record.'

'Yes, of course, sir.'

'I will see the Secretary of State first thing in the morning. Kindly arrange a meeting.'

'If you insist, sir,' said David Heath resignedly.

'I insist.'

The project manager departed to his own room and a sleepless night. Early the next morning he delivered a handwritten, personal and private letter to the minister, who sent a car round immediately for the Scottish industrialist.

Sir Hamish was driven slowly through the noisy, exuberant, bustling crowds of the city in the minister's black Ford Galaxy with flag flying. People made way for the car respectfully. The chauffeur came to a halt outside the Ministry of Buildings and Public Works in Paseo de la Reforma and guided Sir Hamish through the long, white corridors to a waiting room. A few minutes later an assistant showed Sir Hamish through to the Secretary of State and took a seat by his side. The minister, a severe looking man who appeared to be well into his seventies, was dressed in an immaculate white suit, white shirt and blue tie. He rose, leaned over the vast expanse of green leather and offered his hand.

'Do have a seat, Sir Hamish.'

'Thank you,' the chairman said, feeling more at home as he took in the minister's office; on the ceiling a large propellor-like fan revolved slowly round making little difference to the stuffiness of the room, while hanging on the wall behind the minister was a signed picture of President José Lopez Portillo, in full morning dress and below the photo a plaque displaying a coat of arms.

'I see you were educated at Cambridge.'

'That is correct, Sir Hamish, I was up at Corpus Christi College for three years.'

'Then you know my country well, sir.'

'I do have many happy memories of my stays in England, Sir Hamish; in fact, I still visit London as often as my leave allows.'

'You must take a trip to Edinburgh some time.'

'I have already done so, Sir Hamish. I attended the Festival on two occasions and now know why your city is described as the Athens of the north.'

'You are well informed, Minister.'

'Thank you, Sir Hamish. Now I must ask how I can help you. Your assistant's note was rather vague.'

'First let me say, Minister, that my company is honoured to be considered for the city ring road project and I hope that our experience of thirty years in construction, twenty of them in the third world' – he nearly said the undeveloped countries, an expression his project manager had warned him against – 'is the reason you, as Minister in charge, found us the natural choice for this contract.'

'That, and your reputation for finishing a job on time at the stipulated price,' replied the Secrtary of State. 'Only twice in your history have you returned to the principal asking for changes in the payment schedule. Once in Uganda when you were held up by Amin's pathetic demands, and the other project, if I remember rightly, was in Bolivia, an airport, when you were unavoidably delayed for six months because of an earthquake. In both cases, you completed the contract at the new price stipulated and my principal advisers think you must have lost money on both occasions.' The Secretary of State mopped his brow with a silk handkerchief before continuing. 'I would not wish you to think my government takes these decisions of selection lightly.'

Sir Hamish was astounded by the Secretary of State's command of his brief, the more so as no prompting notes lay on the leather-topped desk in front of him. He suddenly felt guilty at the little he knew about the Secretary of State's background or history.

'Of course not, Minister. I am flattered by your personal concern, which makes me all the more determined to broach an embarrassing subject that has . . .'

'Before you say anything else, Sir Hamish, may I ask you some questions?'

'Of course, Minister.'

'Do you still find the tender price of $39,121,110 acceptable in *all* the circumstances?'

'Yes, Minister.'

'That amount still leaves you enough to do a worthwhile job while making a profit for your company?'

'Yes, Minister, but . . .'

'Excellent, then I think all you have to decide is whether you want to sign the contract by midday today.' The minister emphasized the word midday as clearly as he could.

Sir Hamish, who had never understood the expression 'a nod is as good as a wink', charged foolishly on.

'There is, nevertheless, one aspect of the contract I feel that I should discuss with you privately.'

'Are you sure that would be wise, Sir Hamish?'

Sir Hamish hesitated, but only for a moment, before proceeding. Had David Heath heard the conversation that had taken place so far, he would have stood up, shaken hands with the Secretary of State, removed the top of his fountain pen and headed towards the contract – but not his employer.

'Yes, Minister, I feel I must,' said Sir Hamish firmly.

'Will you kindly leave us, Miss Vieites?' said the Secretary of State.

The assistant closed her shorthand book, rose and left the room. Sir Hamish waited for the door to close before he began again.

'Yesterday I had a visit from a countryman of yours, a Mr Victor Perez, who resides here in Mexico City and claims –'

'An excellent man,' said the Minister very quietly.

Still Sir Hamish charged on. 'Yes, I daresay he is, Minister, but he asked to be allowed to represent Graham Construction as our agent and I wondered –'

'A common practice in Mexico, no more than is required by the law,' said the Minister, swinging his chair round and staring out of the window.

'Yes, I appreciate that is the custom,' said Sir Hamish now talking to the minister's back, 'but if I am to part with ten per cent of the government's money I must be convinced that such a decision meets with your personal approval.' Sir Hamish thought he had worded that rather well.

'Um,' said the Secretary of State, measuring his words, 'Victor Perez is a good man and has always been loyal to the Mexican cause. Perhaps he leaves an unfortunate impression sometimes, not out of what you would call the "top drawer", Sir Hamish, but then we have no class barriers in Mexico.' The Minister swung back to face Sir Hamish.

The Scottish industrialist flushed. 'Of course not, Minister, but that, if you will forgive me, is hardly the point. Mr Perez is asking me to hand over nearly four million dollars, which is over half of my estimated profit on the project without allowing for any contingencies or mishaps that might occur later.'

'You chose the tender figure, Sir Hamish. I confess I was amused by the fact you added your date of birth to the thirty-nine million.'

Sir Hamish's mouth opened wide.

'I would have thought,' continued the minister, 'given your record over the past three years and the present situation in Britain, you were not in a position to be fussy.'

The minister gazed impassively at Sir Hamish's startled face. Both started to speak at the same time. Sir Hamish swallowed his words.

'Allow me to tell you a little story about Victor Perez. When the war was at its fiercest' (the old Secretary of State was referring to the Mexican Revolution, in the same way that an American thinks of Vietnam or a Briton of Germany when they hear the word 'war'), 'Victor's father was one of the young men under my command who died on the battlefield at Celaya only a few days before victory was ours. He left a son born on the day of independence who never knew his father. I have the honour, Sir Hamish, to be godfather to that child. We christened him Victor.'

'I can understand that you have a responsibility to an old comrade but I still feel four million is –'

'Do you? Then let me continue. Just before Victor's father died I visited him in a field hospital and he asked only that I should take care of his wife. She died in childbirth. I therefore considered my responsibility passed on to their only child.'

Sir Hamish remained silent for a moment. 'I appreciate your attitude, Minister, but ten per cent of one of your largest contracts?'

'One day,' continued the Secretary of State, as if he had not heard Sir Hamish's comment, 'Victor's father was fighting in the front line at Zacatecas and looking out across a minefield he saw a young lieutenant, lying face down in the mud with his leg nearly blown off. With no thought for his own safety, he crawled through that minefield until he reached the lieutenant and then he dragged him yard by yard back to the camp. It took him over three hours. He then carried the lieutenant to a truck and drove him to the nearest field hospital, undoubtedly saving his leg, and probably his life. So you see the government have good cause to allow Perez's son the privilege of representing them from time to time.'

'I agree with you, Minister,' said Sir Hamish quietly. 'Quite admirable.' The Secretary of State smiled for the first time. 'But I still confess I cannot understand why you allow him such a large percentage.'

The minister frowned. 'I am afraid, Sir Hamish, if you cannot understand that, you can never hope to understand the principles we Mexicans live by.'

The Secretary of State rose from behind his desk, limped to the door and showed Sir Hamish out.

The Hungarian Professor

Coincidences, writers are told (usually by the critics) must be avoided, although in truth the real world is full of incidents that in themselves are unbelievable. Everyone has had an experience that if they wrote about it would appear to others as pure fiction.

The same week that the headlines in the world newspapers read 'Russia invades Afghanistan, America to withdraw from Moscow Olympics' there also appeared a short obituary in *The Times* for the distinguished Professor of English at the University of Budapest. 'A man who was born and died in his native Budapest and whose reputation remains assured by his brilliant translation of the works of Shakespeare into his native Hungarian. Although some linguists consider his *Coriolanus* immature they universally acknowledge his *Hamlet* to be a translation of genius.'

. . .

Nearly a decade after the Hungarian Revolution I had the chance to participate in a student athletics meeting in Budapest. The competition was scheduled to last for a full week so I felt there would be an opportunity to find out a little about the country. The team flew in to Ferihegy Airport on the Sunday night and we were taken immediately to the Hotel Ifushag. (I learned later that the word meant youth in Hungarian). Having settled in, most of the team went to bed early as their opening round heats were the following day.

Breakfast the next morning comprised of milk, toast and an egg, served in three acts with long intervals between each. Those of us who were running that afternoon skipped lunch for fear that a matinee performance might cause us to miss our events completely.

Two hours before the start of the meeting, we were taken by bus to the Nép stadium and unloaded outside the dressing rooms (I always feel they should be called undressing rooms). We changed into track suits and sat around on benches anxiously waiting to be called. After what seemed to be an interminable time but was in fact only a few minutes, an official appeared and led us out on to the track. As it was the opening day of competition, the stadium was packed. When I had finished my usual warm-up of jogging, sprinting and some light callisthenics, the loudspeaker announced the start of the 100m race in three languages. I stripped off my track suit and ran over to the start. When called, I pressed my spikes against the blocks and waited nervously for the starter's pistol. Felkészülni, Kész – bang. Ten seconds later the race was over and the only virtue of coming last was that it left me six free days to investigate the Hungarian capital.

Walking around Budapest reminded me of my childhood days in Bristol just after the war, but with one noticeable difference. As well as the bombed-out buildings, there was row upon row of bullet holes in some of the walls.

The revolution, although eight years past, was still much in evidence, perhaps because the nationals did not want anyone to forget. The people on the streets had lined faces, stripped of all emotion, and they shuffled rather than walked, leaving the impression of a nation of old men. If you inquired innocently why, they told you there was nothing to hurry for, or to be happy about, although they always seemed to be thoughtful with each other.

On the third day of the games, I returned to the Nép stadium to support a friend of mine who was competing in the semi-finals of the 400m hurdles which was the first event that afternoon. Having a competitor's pass, I could sit virtually anywhere in the half-empty arena. I chose to watch the race from just above the final bend, giving me a good view of the home straight. I sat down on the wooden bench without paying much attention to the people on either side of me. The race began and as my friend hit the bend crossing the seventh hurdle with only three hurdles to cover before the finishing line, I stood and cheered him heartily all the way down the home straight. He managed to come in third, ensuring himself a place in the final the next day. I sat down again and wrote out the detailed result in my programme. I was about to leave, as there were no British competitors in the hammer or the pole vault, when a voice behind me said:

'You are English?'

'Yes,' I replied, turning in the direction from which the question had been put.

An elderly gentleman looked up at me. He wore a three-piece suit that must have been out of date when his father owned it, and even lacked the possible virtue that some day the style might come back into fashion. The leather patches on the elbows left me in no doubt that my questioner was a bachelor for they could only have been sewn on by a man – either that or one had to conclude he had elbows in odd places. The length of his trousers revealed that his father had been two inches taller than he. As for the man himself, he had a few strands of white hair, a walrus moustache, and ruddy cheeks. His tired blue eyes were perpetually half-closed like the shutter of a camera that has just been released. His forehead was so lined that he might have been any age between fifty and seventy. The overall impression was of a cross between a tram inspector and an out-of-work violinist.

I sat down for a second time.

'I hope you didn't mind my asking?' he added.

'Of course not,' I said.

'It's just that I have so little opportunity to converse with an Englishman. So when I spot one I always grasp the nettle. Is that the right colloquial expression?'

'Yes,' I said, trying to think how many Hungarian words I knew. Yes, No, Good morning, Goodbye, I am lost, Help.

'You are in the student games?'

'Were, not are,' I said. 'I departed somewhat rapidly on Monday.'

'Because you were not rapid enough, perhaps?'

I laughed, again admiring his command of my first language.

'Why is your English so excellent?' I inquired.

'I'm afraid it's a little neglected,' the old man replied. 'But they still allow me to teach the subject at the University. I must confess to you that I have absolutely no interest in sport, but these occasions always afford me the opportunity to capture someone like yourself and oil the rusty machine, even if only for a few minutes.' He gave me a tired smile but his eyes were now alight.

'What part of England do you hail from?' For the first time his pronouncement faltered as 'hail' came out as 'heel'.

'Somerset,' I told him.

'Ah,' he said, 'perhaps the most beautiful county in England.' I smiled, as most foreigners never seem to travel much beyond Stratford-on-Avon or Oxford. 'To drive across the Mendips,' he continued, 'through perpetually green hilly countryside and to stop at Cheddar to see Gough's caves, at Wells to be amused by the black swans ringing the bell on the Cathedral wall, or at Bath to admire the lifestyle of classical Rome, and then perhaps to go over the county border and on to Devon ... Is Devon even more beautiful than Somerset, in your opinion?'

'Never,' said I.

'Perhaps you are a little prejudiced,' he laughed. 'Now let me see if I can recall:

Of the western counties there are seven
But the most glorious is surely that of Devon.

Perhaps Hardy, like you, was prejudiced and could think only of his beloved Exmoor, the village of Tiverton and Drake's Plymouth.'

'Which is *your* favourite county?' I asked.

'The North Riding of Yorkshire has always been underrated, in my opinion,' replied the old man. 'When people talk of Yorkshire, I suspect Leeds, Sheffield and Barnsley spring to mind. Coal mining and heavy industry. Visitors should travel and see the dales there; they will find them as different as chalk from cheese. Lincolnshire is too flat and so much of the Midlands must now be spoilt by sprawling towns. The Birminghams of this world hold no appeal for me. But in the end I come down in favour of Worcestershire and Warwickshire, quaint old English villages nestling in the Cotswolds and crowned by Stratford-upon-Avon. How I wish I could have been in England in 1959 while my countrymen were recovering from the scars of revolution. Olivier performing Coriolanus, another man who did not want to show his scars.'

'I saw the performance,' I said. 'I went with a school party.'

'Lucky boy. I translated the play into Hungarian at the age of nineteen. Reading over my work again last year made me aware I must repeat the exercise before I die.'

'You have translated other Shakespeare plays?'

'All but three, I have been leaving *Hamlet* to last, and then I shall return to *Coriolanus* and start again. As you are a student, am I permitted to ask which University you attend?'

'Oxford.'

'And your College?'

'Brasenose.'

'Ah. BNC. How wonderful to be a few yards away from the Bodleian, the greatest library in the world. If I had been born in England I should have wanted to spend my days at All Souls, that is just opposite BNC, is it not?'

'That's right.'

The professor stopped talking while we watched the next race, the first semi-final of the 1,500 metres. The winner was Anfras Patovich, a Hungarian, and the partisan crowd went wild with delight.

'That's what I call support,' I said.

'Like Manchester United when they have scored the winning goal in the Cup Final. But my fellow countrymen do not cheer because the Hungarian was first,' said the old man.

'No?' I said, somewhat surprised.

'Oh, no, they cheer because he beat the Russian.'

'I hadn't even noticed,' I said.

'There is no reason why you should, but their presence is always in the forefront of our minds and we are rarely given the opportunity to see them beaten in public.'

I tried to steer him back to a happier subject. 'And before you had been elected to All Souls, which college would you have wanted to attend?'

'As an undergraduate, you mean?'

'Yes.'

'Undoubtedly Magdalen is the most beautiful college. It has the distinct advantage of being situated on the River Cherwell; and in any case I confess a weakness for perpendicular architecture and a love of Oscar Wilde.' The conversation was interrupted by the sound of a pistol and we watched the second semi-final of the 1,500 metres which was won by Orentas of the USSR and the crowd showed its disapproval more obviously this time, clapping in such a way that left hands passed by right without coming into contact. I found myself joining in on the side of the Hungarians. The scene made the old man lapse into a sad silence. The last race of the day was won by Tim Johnston of England and I stood and cheered unashamedly. The Hungarian crowd clapped politely.

I turned to say goodbye to the professor, who had not spoken for some time.

'How long are you staying in Budapest?' he asked.

'The rest of the week. I return to England on Sunday.'

'Could you spare the time to join an old man for dinner one night?'

'I should be delighted.'

'How considerate of you,' he said, and he wrote out his full name and address in capital letters on the back of my programme and returned it to me. 'Why don't we say tomorrow at seven? And if you have any old newspapers or magazines do bring them with you,' he said looking a little sheepish. 'And I shall quite understand if you have to change your plans.'

· · ·

I spent the next morning looking over St Matthias Church and the ancient fortress, two of the buildings that showed no evidence of the revolution. I then took a short trip down the Danube before spending the afternoon supporting the swimmers at the Olympic pool. At six I left the pool and went back to my hotel. I changed into my team blazer and grey slacks, hoping I looked smart enough for my distinguished host. I locked my door, and started towards the lift and then remembered. I returned to my room to pick up the pile of newspapers and magazines I had collected from the rest of the team.

Finding the professor's home was not as easy as I had expected. After meandering around cobbled streets and waving the professor's address at several passers-by, I was finally directed to an old apartment block. I ran up the three flights of the wooden staircase in a few leaps and bounds, wondering how long the climb took the professor every day. I stopped at the door that displayed his number and knocked.

The old man answered immediately as if he had been standing there, waiting by the door. I noticed that he was wearing the same suit he had had on the previous day.

'I am sorry to be late,' I said.

'No matter, my own students also find me hard to find the first time,' he said, grasping my hand. He paused. 'Bad to use the same word twice in the same sentence. "Locate" would have been better, wouldn't it?'

He trotted on ahead of me, not waiting for my reply, a man obviously used to living on his own. He led me down a small, dark corridor into his drawing room. I was shocked by its size. Three sides were covered with indifferent prints and watercolours, depicting English scenes, while the fourth wall was dominated by a large bookcase. I could spot Shakespeare, Dickens, Austen, Trollope, Hardy, even Waugh and Graham Greene. On the table was a faded copy of the *New Statesman* and I looked round to see if we were on our own, but there seemed to be no sign of a wife or child either in person or picture, and indeed the table was only set for two.

The old man turned and stared with childish delight at my pile of newspapers and magazines.

'*Punch, Time* and the *Observer*, a veritable feast,' he declared gathering them into his arms before placing them lovingly on his bed in the corner of the room.

The professor then opened a bottle of Szürkebarát and left me to look at the pictures while he prepared the meal. He slipped away into an alcove which was so small that I had not realized the room contained a kitchenette. He continued to bombard me with questions about England, many of which I was quite unable to answer.

A few minutes later he stepped back into the room, requesting me to take a seat. 'Do be seated,' he said, on reflection. 'I do not wish you to remove the seat. I wish you to sit on it.' He put a plate in front of me which had on it a leg of something that might have been a chicken, a piece of salami and a tomato. I felt sad, not because the food was inadequate, but because he believed it to be plentiful.

After dinner, which despite my efforts to eat slowly and hold him in conversation, did not take up much time, the old man made some coffee which tasted bitter and then filled a pipe before we continued our discussion. We talked of Shakespeare and his views on A. L. Rowse and then he turned to politics.

'Is it true,' the professor asked, 'that England will soon have a Labour government?'

'The opinion polls seem to indicate as much,' I said.

'I suppose the British feel that Sir Alec Douglas-Home is not swinging enough for the sixties,' said the professor, now puffing vigorously away at his pipe. He paused and looked up at me through the smoke. 'I did not offer you a pipe as I assumed after your premature exit in the first round of the competition you would not be smoking.' I smiled. 'But Sir Alec,' he continued, 'is a man with long experience in politics and it's no bad thing for a country to be governed by an experienced gentleman.'

I would have laughed out loud had the same opinion been expressed by my own tutor.

'And what of the Labour leader?' I said, forbearing to mention his name.

'Moulded in the white heat of a technological revolution,' he replied. 'I am not so certain. I liked Gaitskell, an intelligent and shrewd man. An untimely death. Attlee, like Sir Alec, was a gentleman. But as for Mr Wilson, I suspect that history will test his mettle – a pun which I had not intended – in that white heat and only then will we discover the truth.'

I could think of no reply.

'I was considering last night after we parted,' the old man continued, 'the effect that Suez must have had on a nation which only ten years before had won a world war. The Americans should have backed you. Now we read in retrospect, always the historian's privilege, that at the time Prime Minister Eden was tired and ill. The truth was he didn't get the support from his closest allies when he most needed it.'

'Perhaps we should have supported you in 1956.'

'No, no, it was too late then for the West to shoulder Hungary's problems. Churchill understood that in 1945. He wanted to advance beyond Berlin and to free all the nations that bordered Russia. But the West had had a belly full of war by then and left Stalin to take advantage of that apathy. When Churchill coined the phrase "the Iron Curtain", he foresaw exactly what was going to happen in the East. Amazing to think that when that great man said, "if the British Empire should last a thousand years", it was in fact destined to survive for only twenty-five. How I wish he had still been around the corridors of power in 1956.'

'Did the revolution greatly affect your life?'

'I do not complain. It is a privilege to be the Professor of English in a great University. They do not interfere with me in my department and Shakespeare is not yet considered subversive literature.' He paused and took a luxuriant puff at his pipe. 'And what will you do, young man, when you leave the University – as you have shown us that you cannot hope to make a living as a runner?'

'I want to be a writer.'

'Then travel, travel, travel,' he said. 'You cannot hope to learn everything from books. You must see the world for yourself if you ever hope to paint a picture for others.'

I looked up at the old clock on his mantelpiece only to realize how quickly the time had passed.

'I must leave you, I'm afraid; they expect us all to be back in the hotel by ten.'

'Of course,' he said smiling at the English Public School mentality. 'I will accompany you to Kossuth Square and then you will be able to see your hotel on the hill.'

As we left the flat, I noticed that he didn't bother to lock the door. Life had left him little to lose. He led me quickly through the myriad of narrow roads that I had found so impossible to navigate earlier in the evening, chatting about this building and that, an endless fund of knowledge about his own country as well as mine. When we reached Kossuth Square he took my hand and held on to it, reluctant to let go, as lonely people often will.

'Thank you for allowing an old man to indulge himself by chattering on about his favourite subject.'

'Thank you for your hospitality,' I said, 'and when you are next in Somerset you must come to Lympsham and meet my family.'

'Lympsham? I cannot place it,' he said, looking worried.

'I'm not surprised. The village only has a population of twenty-two.'

'Enough for two cricket teams,' remarked the professor. 'A game, I confess, with which I have never come to grips.'

'Don't worry,' I said, 'neither have half the English.'

'Ah, but I should like to. What is a gully, a no-ball, a night watchman? The terms have always intrigued me.'

'Then remember to get in touch when you're next in England and I'll take you to Lord's and see if I can teach you something.'

'How kind,' he said, and then he hesitated before adding: 'But I don't think we shall meet again.'

'Why not?' I asked.

'Well, you see, I have never been outside Hungary in my whole life. When I was young I couldn't afford to and now I don't imagine that those in authority would allow me to see your beloved England.'

He released my hand, turned and shuffled back into the shadows of the side streets of Budapest.

I read his obituary in *The Times* once again as well as the headlines about Afghanistan and its effect on the Moscow Olympics.

He was right. We never met again.

Old Love

Some people, it is said, fall in love at first sight but that was not what happened to William Hatchard and Philippa Jameson. They hated each other from the moment they met. This mutual loathing commenced at the first tutorial of their freshmen terms. Both had come up in the early thirties with major scholarships to read English language and literature, William to Merton, Philippa to Somerville. Each had been reliably assured by their schoolteachers that they would be the star pupil of their year.

Their tutor, Simon Jakes of New College, was both bemused and amused by the ferocious competition that so quickly developed between his two brightest pupils, and he used their enmity skilfully to bring out the best in both of them without ever allowing either to indulge in outright abuse. Philippa, an attractive, slim red-head with a rather high-pitched voice, was the same height as William so she conducted as many of her arguments as possible standing in newly acquired high-heeled shoes, while William, whose deep voice had an air of authority, would always try to expound his opinions from a sitting position. The more intense their rivalry became the harder the one tried to outdo the other. By the end of their first year they were far ahead of their contemporaries while remaining neck and neck with each other. Simon Jakes told the Merton Professor of Anglo-Saxon Studies that he had never had a brighter pair up in the same year and that it wouldn't be long before they were holding their own with him.

During the long vacation both worked to a gruelling timetable, always imagining the other would be doing a little more. They stripped bare Blake, Wordsworth, Coleridge, Shelley, Byron, and only went to bed with Keats. When they returned for the second year, they found that absence had made the heart grow even more hostile; and when they were both awarded alpha plus for their essays on Beowulf, it didn't help. Simon Jakes remarked at New College high table one night that if Philippa Jameson had been born a boy some of his tutorials would undoubtedly have ended in blows.

'Why don't you separate them?' asked the Dean, sleepily.

'What, and double my work-load?' said Jakes. 'They teach each other most of the time: I merely act as referee.'

Occasionally the adversaries would seek his adjudication as to who was ahead of whom, and so confident was each of being the favoured pupil that one would always ask in the other's hearing. Jakes was far too canny to be drawn; instead he would remind them that the examiners would be the final arbiters. So they began their own subterfuge by referring to each other, just in earshot, as 'that silly woman', and 'that arrogant man'. By the end of their second year they were almost unable to remain in the same room together.

In the long vacation William took a passing interest in Al Jolson and a girl called Ruby while Philippa flirted with the Charleston and a young naval lieutenant from Dartmouth. But when term started in earnest these interludes were never admitted and soon forgotten.

At the beginning of their third year they both, on Simon Jakes' advice, entered for the Charles Oldham Shakespeare prize along with every other student in the year who was considered likely to gain a First. The Charles Oldham was awarded for an essay on a set aspect of Shakespeare's work, and Philippa and William both realized that this would be the only time in their academic lives that they would be tested against each other in closed competition. Surreptitiously, they worked their separate ways through the entire Shakespearian canon, from *Henry VI* to *Henry VIII*, and kept Jakes well over his appointed tutorial hours, demanding more and more refined discussion of more and more obscure points.

The chosen theme for the prize essay that year was 'Satire in Shakespeare'. *Troilus and Cressida* clearly called for the most attention but both found there were nuances in virtually every one of the bard's thirty-seven plays. 'Not to mention a gross of sonnets,' wrote Philippa home to her father in a rare moment of self-doubt. As the year drew to a close it became obvious to all concerned that either William or Philippa had to win the prize while the other would undoubtedly come second. Nevertheless no one was willing to venture an opinion as to who the victor would be. The New College porter, an expert in these matters, opening his usual book for the Charles Oldham, made them both evens, ten to one the rest of the field.

Before the prize essay submission date was due, they both had to sit their final degree examination. Philippa and William confronted the examination papers every morning and afternoon for two weeks with an appetite that bordered on the vulgar. It came as no surprise to anyone that they both achieved first class degrees in the final honours school. Rumour spread around the University that the two rivals had been awarded alphas in every one of their nine papers.

'I would be willing to believe that is the case,' Philippa told William. 'But I feel I must point out to you that there is a considerable difference between an alpha plus and an alpha minus.'

'I couldn't agree with you *more*,' said William. 'And when you discover who has won the Charles Oldham, you will know who was awarded *less*.'

With only three weeks left before the prize essay had to be handed in they both worked twelve hours a day, falling asleep over open text books, dreaming that the other was still beavering away. When the appointed hour came they met in the marble-floored entrance hall of the Examination Schools, sombre in subfusc.

'Good morning, William, I do hope your efforts will manage to secure a place in the first six.'

'Thank you, Philippa. If they don't I shall look for the names C. S. Lewis, Nichol Smith, Nevil Coghill, Edmund Blunden, R. W. Chambers and H. W. Garrard ahead of me. There's certainly no one else in the field to worry about.'

'I am only pleased,' said Philippa, as if she had not heard his reply, 'that you were not seated next to me when I wrote my essay, thus ensuring for the first time in three years that you weren't able to crib from my notes.'

'The only item I have ever cribbed from you, Philippa, was the Oxford to London timetable, and that I discovered later to be out-of-date, which was in keeping with the rest of your efforts.'

They both handed in their twenty-five thousand word essays to the collector's office in the Examination Schools and left without a further word, returning to their respective colleges impatiently to await the result.

William tried to relax the weekend after submitting his essay, and for the first time in three years he played some tennis, against a girl from St Anne's, failing to win a game, let alone a set. He nearly sank when he went swimming, and actually did so when punting. He was only relieved that Philippa had not been witness to any of his feeble physical efforts.

On Monday night after a resplendent dinner with the Master of Merton, he decided to take a walk along the banks of the Cherwell to clear his head before going to bed. The May evening was still light as he made his way down through the narrow confines of Merton Wall, across the meadows to the banks of the Cherwell. As he strolled along the winding path, he thought he spied his rival ahead of him under a tree reading. He considered turning back but decided she might already have spotted him, so he kept on walking.

He had not seen Philippa for three days although she had rarely been out of his thoughts: once he had won the Charles Oldham, the silly woman would have to climb down from that high horse of hers. He smiled at the thought and decided to walk nonchalantly past her. As he drew nearer, he lifted his eyes from the path in front of him to steal a quick glance in her direction, and could feel himself reddening in anticipation of her inevitable well-timed insult. Nothing happened so he looked more carefully, only to discover on closer inspection that she was not reading: her head was bowed in her hands and she appeared to be sobbing quietly. He slowed his progress to observe, not the formidable rival who had for three years dogged his every step, but a forlorn and lonely creature who looked somewhat helpless.

William's first reaction was to think that the winner of the prize essay competition had been leaked to her and that he had indeed achieved his victory. On reflection, he realized that could not be the case: the examiners would only have received the essays that morning and as all the assessors read each submission the results could not possibly be forthcoming until at least the end of the week. Philippa did not look up when he reached her side – he was even unsure whether she was aware of his presence. As he stopped to gaze at his adversary William could not help noticing how her long red hair curled just as it touched the shoulder. He sat down beside her but still did not stir.

'What's the matter?' he asked. 'Is there anything I can do?'

She raised her head, revealing a face flushed from crying.

'No, nothing William, except leave me alone. You deprive me of solitude without affording me company.'

William was pleased that he immediately recognized the little literary allusion. 'What's the matter, Madame de Sévigné?' he asked, more out of curiosity than concern, torn between sympathy and catching her with her guard down.

It seemed a long time before she replied.

'My father died this morning,' she said finally, as if speaking to herself.

It struck William as strange that after three years of seeing Philippa almost every day he knew nothing about her home life.

'And your mother?' he said.

'She died when I was three. I don't even remember her. My father is –' She paused. 'Was a parish priest and brought me up, sacrificing everything he had to get me to Oxford, even the family silver. I wanted so much to win the Charles Oldham for him.'

Willim put his arm tentatively on Philippa's shoulder.

'Don't be absurd. When you win the prize, they'll pronounce you the star pupil of the decade. After all, you will have had to beat me to achieve the distinction.'

She tried to laugh. 'Of course I wanted to beat you, William, but only for my father.'

'How did he die?'

'Cancer, only he never let me know. He asked me not to go home before the summer term as he felt the break might interfere with my finals and the Charles Oldham. While all the time he must have been keeping me away because he knew if I saw the state he was in that would have been the end of my completing any serious work.'

'Where do you live?' asked William, again surprised that he did not know.

'Brockenhurst. In Hampshire. I'm going back there tomorrow morning. The funeral's on Wednesday.'

'May I take you?' asked William.

Philippa looked up and was aware of a softness in her adversary's eyes that she had not seen before. 'That would be kind, William.'

'Come on then, you silly woman,' he said. 'I'll walk you back to your college.'

'Last time you called me "silly woman" you meant it.'

William found it natural that they should hold hands as they walked along the river bank. Neither spoke until they reached Somerville.

'What time shall I pick you up?' he asked, not letting go of her hand.

'I didn't know you had a car.'

'My father presented me with an old MG when I was awarded a first. I have been longing to find some excuse to show the damn thing off to you. It has a press button start, you know.'

'Obviously he didn't want to risk waiting to give you the car on the Charles Oldham results.' William laughed more heartily than the little dig merited.

'Sorry,' she said. 'Put it down to habit. I shall look forward to seeing if you drive as appallingly as you write, in which case the journey may never come to any conclusion. I'll be ready for you at ten.'

On the journey down to Hampshire, Philippa talked about her father's work as a parish priest and inquired after William's family. They stopped for lunch at a pub in Winchester. Rabbit stew and mashed potatoes.

'The first meal we've had together,' said William.

No sardonic reply came flying back; Philippa simply smiled.

After lunch they travelled on to the village of Brockenhurst. William brought his car to an uncertain halt on the gravel outside the vicarage. An elderly maid, dressed in black, answered the door, surprised to see Miss

Philippa with a man. Philippa introduced Annie to William and asked her to make up the spare room.

'I'm so glad you've found yourself such a nice young man,' remarked Annie later. 'Have you known him long?'

Philippa smiled. 'No, we met for the first time yesterday.'

Philippa cooked William dinner, which they ate by a fire he had made up in the front room. Although hardly a word passed between them for three hours, neither was bored. Philippa began to notice the way William's untidy fair hair fell over his forehead and thought how distinguished he would look in old age.

The next morning, she walked into the church on William's arm and stood bravely through the funeral. When the service was over William took her back to the vicarage, crowded with the many friends the parson had made.

'You mustn't think ill of us,' said Mr Crump, the vicar's warden, to Philippa. 'You were everything to your father and we were all under strict instructions not to let you know about his illness in case it should interfere with the Charles Oldham. That is the name of the prize, isn't it?'

'Yes,' said Philippa. 'But that all seems so unimportant now.'

'She will win the prize in her father's memory,' said William.

Philippa turned and looked at him, realizing for the first time that he actually wanted her to win the Charles Oldham.

They stayed that night at the vicarage and drove back to Oxford on the Thursday. On the Friday morning at ten o'clock William returned to Philippa's college and asked the porter if he could speak to Miss Jameson.

'Would you be kind enough to wait in the Horsebox, sir,' said the porter as he showed William into a little room at the back of the lodge and then scurried off to find Miss Jameson. They returned together a few minutes later.

'What on earth are you doing here?'

'Come to take you to Stratford.'

'But I haven't even had time to unpack the things I brought back from Brockenhurst.'

'Just do as you are told for once; I'll give you fifteen minutes.'

'Of course,' she said. 'Who am I to disobey the next winner of the Charles Oldham? I shall even allow you to come up to my room for one minute and help me unpack.'

The porter's eyebrows nudged the edge of his cap but he remained silent in deference to Miss Jameson's recent bereavement. Again it surprised William to think that he had never been to Philippa's room during their three years. He had climbed the walls of all the women's colleges to be with a variety of girls of varying stupidity but never with Philippa. He sat down on the end of the bed.

'Not there, you thoughtless creature. The maid has only just made it. Men are all the same, you never sit in chairs.'

'I shall one day,' said William. 'The chair of English Language and Literature.'

'Not as long as I'm at this University, you won't,' she said, as she disappeared into the bathroom.

'Good intentions are one thing but talent is quite another,' he shouted at her retreating back, privately pleased that her competitive streak seemed to be returning.

Fifteen minutes later she came out of the bathroom in a yellow flowered dress with a neat white collar and matching cuffs. William thought she might even be wearing a touch of make-up.

'It will do our reputations no good to be seen together,' she said.

'I've thought about that,' said William. 'If asked, I shall say you're my charity.'

'Your charity?'

'Yes, this year I'm supporting distressed orphans.'

Philippa signed out of college until midnight and the two scholars travelled down to Stratford, stopping off at Broadway for lunch. In the afternoon they rowed on the River Avon. William warned Philippa of his last disastrous outing in a punt. She admitted that she had already heard of the exhibition he had made of himself, but they arrived safely back at the shore: perhaps because Philippa took over the rowing. They went to see John Gielgud playing Romeo and dined at the Dirty Duck. Philippa was even quite rude to William during the meal.

They started their journey home just after eleven and Philippa fell into a half sleep as they could hardly hear each other above the noise of the car engine. It must have been about twenty-five miles outside of Oxford that the MG came to a halt.

'I thought,' said William, 'that when the petrol gauge showed empty there was at least another gallon left in the tank.'

'You're obviously wrong, and not for the first time, and because of such foresight you'll have to walk to the nearest garage all by yourself – you needn't imagine that I'm going to keep you company. I intend to stay put, right here in the warmth.'

'But there isn't a garage between here and Oxford,' protested William.

'Then you'll have to carry me. I am far too fragile to walk.'

'I wouldn't be able to manage fifty yards after that sumptuous dinner and all that wine.'

'It is no small mystery to me, William, how you could have managed a first class honours degree in English when you can't even read a petrol gauge.'

'There's only one thing for it,' said William. 'We'll have to wait for the first bus in the morning.'

Philippa clambered into the back seat and did not speak to him again before falling asleep. William donned his hat, scarf and gloves, crossed his arms for warmth, and touched the tangled red mane of Philippa's hair as she slept. He then took off his coat and placed it so that it covered her.

Philippa woke first, a little after six, and groaned as she tried to stretch her aching limbs. She then shook William awake to ask him why his father hadn't been considerate enough to buy him a car with a comfortable back seat.

'But this is the niftiest thing going,' said William, gingerly kneading his neck muscles before putting his coat back on.

'But it isn't going, and won't without petrol,' she replied getting out of the car to stretch her legs.

'But I only let it run out for one reason,' said William following her to the front of the car.

Philippa waited for a feeble punch line and was not disappointed.

'My father told me if I spent the night with a barmaid then I should simply order an extra pint of beer, but if I spent the night with the vicar's daughter, I would have to marry her.'

Philippa laughed. William, tired, unshaven, and encumbered by his heavy coat, struggled to get down on one knee.

'What are you doing, William?'

'What do you think I'm doing, you silly woman. I am going to ask you to marry me.'

'An invitation I am happy to decline, William. If I accepted such a proposal I might end up spending the rest of my life stranded on the road between Oxford and Stratford.'

'Will you marry me if I win the Charles Oldham?'

'As there is absolutely no fear of that happening I can safely say, yes. Now do get off your knee, William, before someone mistakes you for a straying stork.'

The first bus arrived at five-past-seven that Saturday morning and took Philippa and William back to Oxford. Philippa went to her rooms for a long hot bath while William filled a petrol can and returned to his deserted MG. Having completed the task, he drove straight to Somerville and once again asked if he could see Miss Jameson. She came down a few minutes later.

'What you again?' she said. 'Am I not in enough trouble already?'

'Why so?'

'Because I was out after midnight, unaccompanied.'

'You were accompanied.'

'Yes, and that's what's worrying them.'

'Did you tell them we spent the night together?'

'No, I did not. I don't mind our contemporaries thinking I'm promiscuous, but I have strong objections to their believing that I have no taste. Now kindly go away, as I am contemplating the horror of your winning the Charles Oldham and my having to spend the rest of my life with you.'

'You know I'm bound to win, so why don't you come live with me now?'

'I realize that it has become fashionable to sleep with just anyone nowadays, William, but if this is to be my last weekend of freedom I intend to savour it, especially as I may have to consider committing suicide.'

'I love you.'

'For the last time, William, go away. And if you haven't won the Charles Oldham don't ever show your face in Somerville again.'

William left, desperate to know the result of the prize essay competition. Had he realized how much Philippa wanted him to win he might have slept that night.

On Monday morning they both arrived early in the Examination Schools and stood waiting impatiently without speaking to each other, jostled by the other undergraduates of their year who had also been entered for the prize. On the stroke of ten the chairman of the examiners, in full academic dress, walking at tortoise-like pace, arrived in the great hall and with a considerable pretence at indifference pinned a notice to the board. All the undergraduates who had entered for the prize rushed forward except for William and Philippa who stood alone, aware that it was now too late to influence a result they were both dreading.

A girl shot out from the mêlée around the notice board and ran over to Philippa.

'Well done, Phil. You've won.'

Tears came to Philippa's eyes as she turned towards William.

'May I add my congratulations,' he said quickly, 'you obviously deserved the prize.'

'I wanted to say something to you on Saturday.'

'You did, you said if I lost I must never show my face in Somerville again.'

'No, I wanted to say: I do love nothing in the world so well as you; is not that strange?'

He looked at her silently for a long moment. It was impossible to improve upon Beatrice's reply.

'As strange as the thing I know not,' he said softly.

A college friend slapped him on the shoulder, took his hand and shook it vigorously. *Proxime accessit* was obviously impressive in some people's eyes, if not in William's.

'Well done, William.'

'Second place is not worthy of praise,' said William disdainfully.

'But you won, Billy boy.'

Philippa and William stared at each other.

'What do you mean?' said William.

'Exactly what I said. You've won the Charles Oldham.'

Philippa and William ran to the board and studied the notice.

Charles Oldham Memorial Prize
The examiners felt unable on this occasion to award
the prize to one person and have therefore decided
that it should be shared by

They gazed at the notice board in silence for some moments. Finally, Philippa bit her lip and said in a small voice.

'Well, you didn't do too badly, considering the competition. I am prepared to honour my undertaking but by this light I take thee for pity.'

William needed no prompting. 'I would not deny you, but by this good day I yield upon great persuasion, for I was told you were in a consumption.'

And to the delight of their peers and the amazement of the retreating don, they embraced under the notice board.

Rumour had it that from that moment on they were never apart for more than a few hours.

. . .

The marriage took place a month later in Philippa's family church at Brockenhurst. 'Well, when you think about it,' said William's room-mate, 'who else could she have married?' The contentious couple started their honeymoon in Athens arguing about the relative significance of Doric and Ionic architecture of which neither knew any more than they had covertly conned from a half-crown tourist guide. They sailed on to Istanbul, where William prostrated himself at the front of every mosque he could find while

Philippa stood on her own at the back fuming at the Turks' treatment of women.

'The Turks are a shrewd race,' declared William, 'so quick to appreciate real worth.'

'Then why don't you embrace the Moslim religion, William, and I need only be in your presence once a year.'

'The misfortune of birth, a misplaced loyalty and the signing of an unfortunate contract dictate that I spend the rest of my life with you.'

Back at Oxford, with junior research fellowships at their respective colleges, they settled down to serious creative work. William embarked upon a massive study of word usage in Marlowe and, in his spare moments, taught himself statistics to assist his findings. Philippa chose as her subject the influence of the Reformation on seventeenth-century English writers and was soon drawn beyond literature into art and music. She bought herself a spinet and took to playing Dowland and Gibbons in the evening.

'For Christ's sake,' said William, exasperated by the tinny sound, 'you won't deduce their religious convictions from their key signatures.'

'More informative than ifs and ands, my dear,' she said, imperturbably, 'and at night so much more relaxing than pots and pans.'

Three years later, with well-received D.Phils, they moved on, inexorably in tandem, to college teaching fellowships. As the long shadow of fascism fell across Europe, they read, wrote, criticized and coached by quiet firesides in unchanging quadrangles.

'A rather dull Schools year for me,' said William, 'but I still managed five firsts from a field of eleven.'

'An even duller one for me,' said Philippa, 'but somehow I squeezed three firsts out of six, and you won't have to invoke the binomial theorem, William, to work out that it's an arithmetical victory for me.'

'The chairman of the examiners tells me,' said William, 'that a greater part of what your pupils say is no more than a recitation from memory.'

'He told me,' she retorted, 'that yours have to make it up as they go along.'

When they dined together in college the guest list was always quickly filled, and as soon as grace had been said, the sharpness of their dialogue would flash across the candelabra.

'I hear a rumour, Philippa, that the college doesn't feel able to renew your fellowship at the end of the year?'

'I fear you speak the truth, William,' she replied. 'They decided they couldn't renew mine at the same time as offering me yours.'

'Do you think they will ever make you a Fellow of the British Academy, William?'

'I must say, with some considerable disappointment, never.'

'I am sorry to hear that; why not?'

'Because when they did invite me, I informed the President that I would prefer to wait to be elected at the same time as my wife.'

Some non-University guests sitting in high table for the first time took their verbal battles seriously; others could only be envious of such love.

One Fellow uncharitably suggested they rehearsed their lines before coming to dinner for fear it might be thought they were getting on well together. During their early years as young dons, they became acknowledged as the leaders in their respective fields. Like magnets, they attracted the brightest undergraduates while apparently remaining poles apart themselves.

'Dr Hatchard will be delivering half these lectures,' Philippa announced at the start of the Michaelmas Term of their joint lecture course on Arthurian legend. 'But I can assure you it will not be the better half. You would be wise always to check which Dr Hatchard is lecturing.'

When Philippa was invited to give a series of lectures at Yale, William took a sabbatical so that he could be with her.

On the ship crossing the Atlantic, Philippa said, 'Let's at least be thankful the journey is by sea, my dear, so we can't run out of petrol.'

'Rather let us thank God,' replied William, 'that the ship has an engine because you would even take the wind out of Cunard's sails.'

The only sadness in their lives was that Philippa could bear William no children, but if anything it drew the two closer together. Philippa lavished quasi-maternal affection on her tutorial pupils and allowed herself only the wry comment that she was spared the probability of producing a child with William's looks and William's brains.

At the outbreak of war William's expertise with handling words made a move into cipher-breaking inevitable. He was recruited by an anonymous gentleman who visited them at home with a briefcase chained to his wrist. Philippa listened shamelessly at the keyhole while they discussed the problems they had come up against and burst into the room and demanded to be recruited as well.

'Do you realize that I can complete *The Times* crossword puzzle in half the time my husband can?'

The anonymous man was only thankful that he wasn't chained to Philippa. He drafted them both to the Admiralty section to deal with enciphered wireless messages to and from German submarines.

The German signal manual was a four-letter code book and each message was reciphered, the substitution table changing daily. William taught Philippa how to evaluate letter frequencies and she applied her new knowledge to modern German texts, coming up with a frequency analysis that was soon used by every code-breaking department in the Commonwealth.

Even so breaking the ciphers and building up the master signal book was a colossal task which took them the best part of two years.

'I never knew your ifs and ands could be so informative,' she said admiringly of her own work.

When the allies invaded Europe husband and wife could together, often break ciphers with no more than half a dozen lines of encoded text to go on.

'They're an illiterate lot,' grumbled William. 'They don't encipher their umlauts. They deserve to be misunderstood.'

'How can you give an opinion when you never dot your i's William?'

'Because, I consider the dot is redundant and I hope to be responsible for removing it from the English language.'

'Is that to be your major contribution to the scholarship, William, if so I am bound to ask how anyone reading the work of most of our undergraduates' essays would be able to tell the difference between an l and an i.'

'A feeble argument my dear, that if it had any conviction would demand that you put a dot on top of an n so as to be sure it wasn't mistaken for an h.'

'Keep working away at your theories, William, because I intend to spend my energy removing more than the dot and the l from Hitler.'

In May 1945 they dined privately with the Prime Minister and Mrs Churchill at Number Ten Downing Street.

'What did the Prime Minister mean when he said to me he could never understand what you were up to?' asked Philippa in the taxi to Paddington Station.

'The same as when he said to me he knew exactly what you were capable of, I suppose,' said William.

.   .   .

When the Merton Professor of English retired in the early nineteen-fifties the whole University waited to see which Doctor Hatchard would be appointed to the chair.

'If Council invite you to take the chair,' said William, putting his hand through his greying hair, 'it will be because they are going to make me Vice-Chancellor.'

'The only way you could ever be invited to hold a position so far beyond your ability would be nepotism, which would mean I was already Vice-Chancellor.'

The General Board, after several hours' discussion of the problem, offered two chairs and appointed William and Philippa full professors on the same day.

When the Vice-Chancellor was asked why precedent had been broken he replied: 'Simple; if I hadn't given them both a chair, one of them would have been after my job.'

That night, after a celebration dinner when they were walking home together along the banks of the Isis across Christ Church Meadows, in the midst of a particularly heated argument about the quality of the last volume of Proust's monumental works, a policeman, noticing the affray, ran over to them and asked:

'Is everything all right, madam?'

'No, it is not,' William interjected, 'this woman has been attacking me for over thirty years and to date the police have done deplorably little to protect me.'

In the late fifties Harold Macmillan invited Philippa to join the board of the IBA.

'I suppose you'll become what's known as a telly don,' said William, 'and as the average mental age of those who watch the box is seven you should feel quite at home.'

'Agreed,' said Philippa. 'Twenty years of living with you has made me fully qualified to deal with infants.'

The chairman of the BBC wrote to William a few weeks later inviting him to joing the Board of Governors.

'Are you to replace "Hancock's Half Hour" or "Dick Barton, Special Agent"?' Philippa inquired.

'I am to give a series of twelve lectures.'

'On what subject, pray?'

'Genius.'

Philippa flicked through the *Radio Times*. 'I see that "Genius" is to be viewed at two o'clock on a Sunday morning, which is understandable, as it's when you are at your most brilliant.'

· · ·

When William was awarded an honorary doctorate at Princeton, Philippa attended the ceremony and sat proudly in the front row.

'I tried to secure a place at the back,' she explained, 'but it was filled with sleeping students who had obviously never heard of you.'

'If that's the case, Philippa, I am only surprised you didn't mistake them for one of your tutorial lectures.'

As the years passed many anecdotes, only some of which were apocryphal, passed into the Oxford fabric. Everyone in the English school knew the stories about the 'fighting Hatchards'. How they spent their first night together. How they jointly won the Charles Oldham. How Phil would complete *The Times* crossword before Bill had finished shaving. How they were both appointed to professional chairs on the same day, and worked longer hours than any of their contemporaries as if they still had something to prove, if only to each other. It seemed almost required by the laws of symmetry that they should always be judged equals. Until it was announced in the New Year's Honours that Philippa had been made a Dame of the British Empire.

'At least our dear Queen has worked out which one of us is truly worthy of recognition,' she said over the college dessert.

'Our dear Queen,' said William, selecting the Madeira, 'knows only too well how little competition there is in the women's colleges: sometimes one must encourage weaker candidates in the hope that it might inspire some real talent lower down.'

After that, whenever they attended a public function together, Philippa would have the MC announce them as Professor William and Dame Philippa Hatchard. She looked forward to many happy years of starting every official occasion one up on her husband, but her triumph lasted for only six months as William received a knighthood in the Queen's Birthday Honours. Philippa feigned surprise at the dear Queen's uncharacteristic lapse of judgement and forthwith insisted on their being introduced in public as Sir William and Dame Philippa Hatchard.

'Understandable,' said William. 'The Queen had to make you a Dame first in order that no one should mistake you for a lady. When I married you, Philippa, you were a young fellow, and now I find I'm living with an old Dame.'

'It's no wonder,' said Philippa, 'that your poor pupils can't make up their minds whether you're homosexual or you simply have a mother fixation. Be thankful that I did not accept Girton's invitation: then you would have been married to a mistress.'

'I always have been, you silly woman.'

· · ·

As the years passed, they never let up their pretended belief in the other's mental feebleness. Philippa's books, 'works of considerable distinction' she insisted, were published by Oxford University Press while William's 'works of monumental significance' he declared, were printed at the presses of Cambridge University.

The tally of newly appointed professors of English they had taught as undergraduates soon reached double figures.

'If you will count polytechnics, I shall have to throw in Maguire's readership in Kenya,' said William.

'You did not teach the Professor of English at Nairobi,' said Philippa. 'I did. You taught the Head of State, which may well account for why the University is so highly thought of while the country is in such disarray.'

In the early sixties they conducted a battle of letters in the TLS on the works of Philip Sidney without ever discussing the subject in each other's presence. In the end the editor said the correspondence must stop and adjudicated a draw.

They both declared him an idiot.

.   .   .

If there was one act that annoyed William in old age about Philippa, it was her continued determination each morning to complete *The Times* crossword before he arrived at the breakfast table. For a time, William ordered two copies of the paper until Philippa filled them both in while explaining to him it was a waste of money.

One particular morning in June at the end of their final academic year before retirement, William came down to breakfast to find only one space in the crossword left for him to complete. He studied the clue: 'Skelton reported that this landed in the soup.' He immediately filled in the eight little boxes.

Philippa looked over his shoulder. 'There's no such word, you arrogant man,' she said firmly. 'You made it up to annoy me.' She placed in front of him a very hard boiled egg.

'Of course there is, you silly woman; look whym-wham up in the dictionary.'

Philippa checked in the *Oxford Shorter* among the cookery books in the kitchen, and trumpeted her delight that it was nowhere to be found.

'My dear Dame Philippa,' said William, as if he were addressing a particularly stupid pupil, 'you surely cannot imagine because you are old and your hair has become very white that you are a sage. You must understand that the Shorter Oxford Dictionary was cobbled together for simpletons whose command of the English language stretches to no more than one hundred thousand words. When I go to college this morning I shall confirm the existence of the word in the OED on my desk. Need I remind you that the OED is a serious work which, with over five hundred thousand words, was designed for scholars like myself?'

'Rubbish,' said Philippa. 'When I am proved right, you will repeat this story word for word, including your offensive nonword, at Somerville's Gaudy Feast.'

'And you, my dear, will read the Collected Works of John Skelton and eat humble pie as your first course.'

'We'll ask old Onions along to adjudicate.'

'Agreed.'

'Agreed.'

With that, Sir William picked up his paper, kissed his wife on the cheek and said with an exaggerated sigh, 'It's at times like this that I wished I'd lost the Charles Oldham.'

'You did, my dear. It was in the days when it wasn't fashionable to admit a woman had won anything.'

'You won me.'

'Yes, you arrogant man, but I was led to believe you were one of those prizes one could return at the end of the year. And now I find I shall have to keep you, even in retirement.'

'Let us leave it to the Oxford English Dictionary, my dear, to decide the issue the Charles Oldham examiners were unable to determine,' and with that he departed for his college.

'There's no such word,' Philippa muttered as he closed the front door.

.   .   .

Heart attacks are known to be rarer among women than men. When Dame Philippa suffered hers in the kitchen that morning she collapsed on the floor calling hoarsely for William, but he was already out of earshot. It was the cleaning woman who found Dame Philippa on the kitchen floor and ran to fetch someone in authority. The Bursar's first reaction was that she was probably pretending that Sir William had hit her with a frying pan but nevertheless she hurried over to the Hatchards' house in Little Jericho just in case. The Bursar checked Dame Philippa's pulse and called for the college doctor and then the Principal. Both arrived within minutes.

The Principal and the Bursar stood waiting by the side of their illustrious academic colleague but they already knew what the doctor was going to say.

'She's dead,' he confirmed. 'It must have been very sudden and with the minimum of pain.' He checked his watch; the time was nine-forty-seven. He covered his patient with a blanket and called for an ambulance. He had taken care of Dame Philippa for over thirty years and he had told her so often to slow down that he might as well have made a gramophone record of it for all the notice she took.

'Who will tell Sir William?' asked the Principal. The three of them looked at each other.

'I will,' said the doctor.

It's a short walk from Little Jericho to Radcliffe Square. It was a long walk from Little Jericho to Radcliffe Square for the doctor that day. He never relished telling anyone of the death of a spouse but this one was going to be the unhappiest of his career.

When he knocked on the professor's door, Sir William bade him enter. The great man was sitting at his desk poring over the Oxford Dictionary, humming to himself.

'I told her, but she wouldn't listen, the silly woman,' he was saying to himself and then he turned and saw the doctor standing silently in the doorway. 'Doctor, you must be my guest at Somerville's Gaudy next Thursday week where Dame Philippa will be eating humble pie. It will be nothing less than game, set, match and championship for me. A vindication of thirty years' scholarship.'

The doctor did not smile, nor did he stir. Sir William walked over to him and gazed at his old friend intently. No words were necessary. The doctor said only, 'I'm more sorry than I am able to express,' and he left Sir William to his private grief.

Sir William's colleagues all knew within the hour. College lunch that day was spent in a silence broken only by the Senior Tutor inquiring of the Master if some food should be taken up to the Merton professor.

'I think not,' said the Master. Nothing more was said.

Professors, Fellows and students alike crossed the front quadrangle in silence and when they gathered for dinner that evening still no one felt like conversation. At the end of the meal the Senior Tutor suggested once again that something should be taken up to Sir William. This time the Master nodded his agreement and a light meal was prepared by the college chef. The Master and the Senior Tutor climbed the worn steps to Sir William's room and while one held the tray the other gently knocked on the door. There was no reply, so the Master, used to William's ways, pushed the door ajar and looked in.

The old man lay motionless on the wooden floor in a pool of blood, a small pistol by his side. The two men walked in and stared down. In his right hand, William was holding the Collected Works of John Skelton. The book was opened at *The Tunnyng of Elynour Rummyng*, and the word 'whymwham' was underlined.

a 1529, Skelton, *E. Rummyng* 75

After the Sarasyns gyse,
Woth a whym wham,
Knyt with a trym tram,
Upon her brayne pan.

Sir William, in his neat hand, had written a note in the margin: 'Forgive me, but I had to let her know.'

'Know what, I wonder?' said the Master softly to himself as he attempted to remove the book from Sir William's hand, but the fingers were already stiff and cold around it.

. . .

Legend has it that they were never apart for more than a few hours.